Penny Vincenzi is one of Brit
authors. Since her first novel,
she has written thirteen bestse

Her first 'proper' job was at t
after which she went to secretar.............
and later became a journalist, writing for *The Times*, the *Daily Mail* and *Cosmopolitan* amongst many others, before turning to fiction. Several years later, over four million copies of Penny's books have been sold worldwide and she is universally held to be the 'doyenne of the modern blockbuster' (*Glamour*).

Penny Vincenzi is married, with four daughters, and divides her time between London and Gower, South Wales.

Also by Penny Vincenzi

Novels

Old Sins
Wicked Pleasures
An Outrageous Affair
Another Woman
Forbidden Places
The Dilemma
The Glimpses
Windfall
Almost a Crime
Sheer Abandon
An Absolute Scandal
The Best of Times
The Decision

The Spoils of Time Series

No Angel
Something Dangerous
Into Temptation

Non-Fiction

There's One Born Every Minute
A Survival Guide for Parents
Taking Stock: Over 75 Years of the Oxo Cube

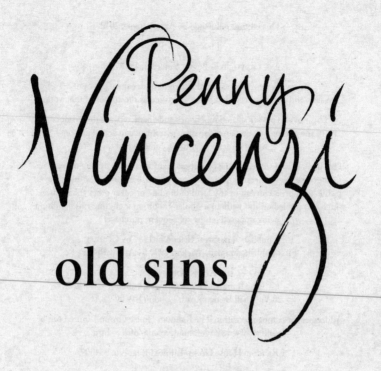

Penny Vincenzi

old sins

Old sins cast long shadows.
Irish proverb

arrow books

This edition published by Arrow Books 2012

4 6 8 10 9 7 5 3

Copyright © Penny Vincenzi, 1989

Penny Vincenzi has asserted her right under the Copyright,
Designs and Patents Act, 1988, to be identified as the author of this work.

First published in Great Britain in 1989 by Century
First published in paperback in 1990 by Arrow Books

Arrow Books
The Random House Group Limited
20 Vauxhall Bridge Road, London SW1V 2SA

Addresses for companies within The Random House Group Limited can be
found at: www.randomhouse.co.uk/offices.htm

The Random House Group Limited Reg. No. 954009

www.randomhouse.co.uk

A CIP catalogue record for this book is
available from the British Library

ISBN 9780099571582

The Random House Group Limited supports The Forest Stewardship
Council® (FSC®), the leading international forest certification organisation.
Our books carrying the FSC label are printed on FSC® certified paper.
FSC is the only forest certification scheme endorsed by the leading
environmental organisations, including Greenpeace. Our
paper procurement policy can be found at
www.randomhouse.co.uk/environment

Printed and bound in Great Britain by Clays Ltd, St Ives PLC

Acknowledgements

Books are never a solo performance; I would like to thank the small army of people who have given their time and expertise to help me get *Old Sins* on stage:

In England, Robin Vincent, Sarah Gilbert, Nicky Lyons-Maris and Stephen Sutton from Clarins Cosmetics, Janet Fitch, Lindy Woodhead, Sally O'Sullivan, Major Anthony Harvie MC, Minna and Peveril Bruce, Tim and Maxi Hudson, Geoff Hollows, Jo Foley, Sue Stapely, Peter Townsend, Fred Perry, Caroline Richards, Penny Rossi, Vicky Carrel, James Crocker; in New York, Brian Sharoff, Carol Schuler, Lewis Sterler, Ruth and Michael Harris; in Los Angeles, Clive and Elaine Dawson, Gabrielle Donnelly, Debra Ghali, John Hiscock, Cathy Hudson, Anita Alberts, Benjamin Urmston.

And crucially, Desmond Elliott for continuing faith and encouragement; Rosemary Cheetham for inspirational editing and knowing how the book should be; Susan Lamb for some dazzling communication; Patricia Taylor Chalmers, Julia Forrest and Charlotte Bell for administering much-needed nuts and bolts; and most importantly, my husband Paul, and our four daughters Polly, Sophie, Emily and Claudia for their unstinting, uncomplaining and loving support through a long year.

A New Introduction
from the Author

It hardly seems possible that it's been twenty-three years since *Old Sins* was first published. Little did I think, as I rather tremulously typed "Chapter One", that it would change my life and career in the way it did. *Old Sins* was my first book, and writing it was both incredibly exciting and the steepest learning curve I'd ever been on. I might have been writing all my life, but up to now I'd been a journalist; here I was, spinning a story, creating characters, working out plots and sub-plots. It was all a completely new world to me.

What I learnt almost straight away was that all that matters are the characters; that if they're right, if they're really living breathing people whom readers will get involved with and care about, the rest follows. I wasn't really prepared for the way those characters took on a life of their own and quite often refused to do what I had planned; or that the plot would take off in a completely different direction from what I had originally planned. But as I wrote *Old Sins*, I also learnt to trust this fact; and realised that what made writing fiction most fun was watching the story grow, day by day. I also discovered that research not only gave the story a background; it often helped to develop the plot.

Looking back, I would say I enjoyed writing *Old Sins* almost more than any of the other books because every day was such a discovery and a delight. It was also very scary, but I had a brilliant (and very patient) editor and an ability to meet a deadline, a skill learnt on all the magazines and newspapers I'd worked on.

I wrote The End at two in the morning, just about nine months after that Chapter One – quite a baby – and burst into tears of triumph!

It was the first of many books, of course. After *Old Sins* the characters and plots kept on coming. But this book will always have a special place in my heart, and it is wonderful to know that it's now being re-issued.

I hope you enjoy it now as much as I did then.

Penny Vincenzi
January 2012

Prologue

London, May 1985

Rosamund Emerson looked across the room at her stepmother and her father's mistress and decided he couldn't possibly have loved either of them.

Not to have subjected them to this; to have insisted that they met, under these circumstances. She found the thought comforting.

Just for a moment, just a brief moment, it was almost worth all her own pain, her sorrow that he had died, to witness theirs: and the added distress they were feeling by being forced to be in the same room, observing a degree of social nicety.

They were sitting, the two of them, on either side of the heavy marble fireplace, in the first-floor boardroom of the family solicitors' office in Lincoln's Inn, both formidably quiet and still, neither looking at the other; occasionally Camilla would shift in her chair, and turn another page of the magazine she was reading (*Ms*, Roz noted with a stab of vicious amusement, such inappropriate reading for a mistress, so deeply symptomatic of Camilla's earnest American feminism) but Phaedria stared fixedly into the fire, almost unblinking; she seemed barely conscious.

Roz felt an almost overpowering urge to go over and wave her hand in front of her face, to say 'boo'. This personification of grief, the latest of the many roles she had watched Phaedria play over the past two and a half years – ranging from child bride to wronged wife, via media cult figure – was probably, she thought, the most pathetic. She was doing it well though; as she had done all of them. God in heaven, why had her father not seen through her earlier? She sighed, her own unhappiness surfacing again, fiercer for the brief respite; the pain made her irritable, impatient. What the hell was going on? Why wasn't anything happening? Why did she bother being punctual, when half the family – well, a good third of it – still hadn't arrived?

And what was Henry Winterbourne doing? He was so hopelessly inefficient; just because Winterbourne and Winterbourne had looked after the family since 1847 (when old Sir Gerald Winterbourne had offered his services to his friend Marcus Morell in settlement of a gambling debt) nobody ever seemed to question his tendency to behave as if Queen Victoria was still on the throne and his inability to recognize the close association between time and money. Well, Roz was about to question it, and to find herself a lawyer of her own: someone young, hungry, and who appeared to be a little more au fait with the existence of such late twentieth-century aids to efficiency as the word processor, the motorbike messenger and the fax machine; Roz was always mildly surprised to find Henry using a telephone and not signing his letters with a quill pen.

She walked over to the large Georgian window, and looked down briefly on Lincoln's Inn in the late spring sunshine, trying to distract herself, take in what she saw, but it was all meaningless: barristers striding about in their court robes and wigs, pink ribbon-bound papers under their arms (why pink, she wondered idly – such a frivolous, unsuitable colour – why not black?) sober-suited solicitors making a business of hurrying, bustling along, some ordinary people – clients she supposed – walking more slowly, a pair of extremely elderly looking judges, heads together, in earnest discussion. All those people with happy straightforward lives, and here was hers a complex nightmare. And quite possibly about to become more complex, more of a nightmare. She turned and looked back into the room; her husband was hovering rather helplessly in the doorway, trying to look purposeful, as if he was actually doing something.

'C. J.,' she said, 'Would you get me a drink please, not coffee, something stronger. And while you're about it, could you ask Jane why we're being kept waiting like this. I have a meeting at two-thirty, I can't spend the entire day here. I do think it's too bad of Henry not to get things properly organized. And also is there any news of the others? Have they got the wrong day or something? I just don't understand why nobody in this family can get themselves together without being hours late for everything.'

C. J. Emerson, christened Christopher John, but nicknamed by his initials in the good old American tradition when he was

8

only two years old, turned obediently to go in search of Jane Gould, Henry Winterbourne's secretary, and almost collided with her as she walked in with an armful of files.

'Oh, Jane,' he said apologetically, 'I'm sorry to bother you when you're obviously very busy, but do you have anything stronger than coffee on the premises? My wife particularly is feeling the strain, and I think we could all do with something to lift our spirits.'

Jane Gould looked at him with immense sympathy. She had rarely seen a man more miserable: like a dog, she thought, who has been thoroughly whipped already, and is waiting in the certain knowledge of a second onslaught. She wondered, and was not alone in wondering, why C. J. stayed with Roz, how he had ever got mixed up with her in the first place; he was so gentle, and charming too, and so good-looking, with his brown eyes, his freckly face, his floppy hair.

'Well,' she said, her usual irritation at being treated like a waitress by clients eased by her sympathy for him, 'we've got some sherry. Would that do? Nothing stronger, I'm afraid.'

'No, no,' said C. J., anxious to be as little trouble as possible. 'I'm sure sherry will be just fine. Thank you so much. Oh, and Jane –'

'Yes, Mr Emerson?'

'Jane, do you have any idea what this delay is about? Is Henry going to be very much longer? Eleven, he said, and it's so unlike him to be unpunctual.'

Jane's face went instantly and loyally blank. 'I'm afraid I couldn't possibly tell you,' she said. 'I have no idea what can be delaying Mr Winterbourne. But I'm sure he'll be with us as soon as he possibly can.'

Roz appeared at C.J.'s side. 'Jane, dear, I'm afraid that isn't good enough,' she said. 'Just go and find Henry, will you, and tell him we need to get on. We are all – well, most of us,' she added with a ferocious glance at Phaedria, 'busy people. We can't afford to sit about for hours on end just because Henry hasn't prepared things properly. And is there any news of my mother and Lord Garrylaig, or Mrs Brookes? I suppose they're all held up in the traffic?'

'I'm sorry, Mrs Emerson,' said Jane calmly. 'It isn't quite hours, of course, only about twenty minutes. But I can see it's irritating for you. Mr Winterbourne is just on the phone to New York. He really won't be very long, I'm sure. And yes, I was just coming in to tell you, Mrs Brookes has just telephoned from her car. She is, indeed, in a dreadful hold-up on the Embankment. No news from your mother, I'm afraid, but I expect it's the same kind of problem. Anyway, I'll get you your drink. Would Lady Morell like some sherry do you think? And Miss North?'

'I really can't speak for them, I'm afraid,' said Roz smoothly. 'I suggest you ask them yourself. I daresay Lady Morell would like anything that's going. That's her usual style.'

C. J. looked at her nervously. She was wearing a black crepe Jean Muir dress, which skimmed over her tall slim body; her long, long legs were encased in black tights; she wore no jewellery at all, her dark hair was cut very short. She looked dramatic, almost severe. Roz was not beautiful and certainly not pretty, and the fact caused her much anguish; and yet she was striking-looking, she turned heads, with her white skin, her very green eyes, her strong mouth, her straight if rather large nose. And men liked Roz; they were drawn to her in preference to her prettier sisters, she was better fun, she was direct, she was sharp and clever. She was also extremely sexy.

'Roz,' said C. J., who spent much of his life wishing she was less direct and who did not benefit greatly from the fun, nor even the sexiness, 'please don't start saying things we could all regret.'

'C. J.,' said Roz, with quiet savagery, 'I shall say what I like and about whom I like, and I have no intention of regretting any of it. I am finding it very hard to endure the sight of Phaedria sitting there like a queen of tragedy when it's patently obvious she's got exactly what she's been after ever since she married my father. All I can hope is that she will get a few unpleasant shocks when his will is read. Clearly she isn't going to be homeless or penniless – unfortunately, in my opinion – but maybe she won't get quite as much as she has clearly been hoping for. As for Camilla North, well I really cannot – oh, Jane dear, how kind, but I really don't like sherry. Haven't you got anything else at all?'

'I'm afraid not,' said Jane, irritation breaking into her bland tones. 'We don't stock a full bar. I can get you some more coffee, of course.'

'Oh, forget it,' said Roz, turning back into the room.

'Here Jane, I'll have the sherry,' said C. J. hastily, stifling the thought of the bourbon he had been planning to ask for. 'That's very kind, very kind indeed. Would you like me to ask the others what they'd all like? Save you the trouble?'

'Yes, thank you Mr Emerson,' said Jane Gould, 'that would be kind. I'll see if I can hurry Mr Winterbourne along.'

C. J. went back into the main room, and across to the fireplace. 'Phaedria, can I get you anything to drink? A sherry, or maybe something stronger?'

Phaedria Morell looked up at him and smiled. 'That's sweet of you, C. J., but what I'd really like is something hot. Coffee or something. And C. J., could you possibly ask Jane if she could bring in a heater of some kind, it's so cold in here.'

C. J. looked at her in astonishment; the temperature in the room was a good seventy-five; he had already removed his jacket and was now glowing profusely in his Brooks Brothers shirt. Phaedria, who was huddled deep into the folds of her sable coat, her hands in the pockets, was clearly, he decided, suffering from shock.

'I will if you like,' he said, 'but the fire is doing its best for you. Try the coffee first.'

Phaedria looked at the flames leaping in the gas-fired fake coal in apparent surprise. 'Good heavens,' she said, 'do you know I hadn't noticed it was alight? Don't worry, C. J., I'm sure the coffee will do the trick. Oh, and do we have any idea why this is taking so long? We seem to have been here for ever. And where are the others?'

'Not really,' said C. J. carefully. 'Apparently Henry is on the phone to the States. And Susan, and presumably Eliza and Peveril as well, are stuck in traffic. Now be sure to shout if the coffee doesn't warm you up. Er, Camilla, would you like anything?'

Camilla North looked up slowly from her magazine, shaking back her heavy gold-red hair, brushing a speck of dust disdainfully from her cream silk dress; she looked immaculate, cool and in command, not in the least as if she had just made the flight from New York, and if she was fazed by being confronted by much of the Morell family, including her lover's widow, she certainly did not show it. She appeared to consider the question very carefully.

'I'd like a mineral water, C. J., if that's not too difficult. But still, not sparkling.'

'Fine,' said C. J. 'Ice?'

Camilla looked at him in apparent astonishment. 'Oh, no thank you,' she said, 'not ice. Not with water.' She made it sound as if ice was as unsuitable an addition to water as gravy or black treacle. 'In fact, C. J., unless it's room temperature I won't have it at all, thank you.'

'Why not?' said Phaedria curiously. They were the first words she had ever spoken to Camilla.

'Well,' said Camilla, seriously courteous, 'iced liquid of any kind is very bad for the digestion. It predisposes the system towards gall bladder disease. Or so my yoga instructor tells me.'

'Good heavens,' said Phaedria, 'I had no idea. I love it iced. Only the sparkling sort though.'

'Well really, you shouldn't drink that at all,' said Camilla, 'it is very seldom naturally sparkling, as of course you must know, and it often has a considerably higher content of salts.'

'Oh, dear,' said Phaedria, 'well that's a shame. I hate the still sort.'

C. J. held his breath. He had been watching them warily all morning, half expecting them suddenly to hurl a stream of abuse at one another, fearful at the way they had settled together, either side of the fire, and here they were, discussing the relative virtues of mineral waters. Deciding that room temperature in Henry Winterbourne's boardroom had to be practically boiling – why did the wretched man have to have that fire alight almost all the year round: tradition he supposed – he moved off in search of further orders.

'Letitia,' he said, crossing the room to another large wing-backed leather chair set at the end of the large mahogany table. 'Would you like a sherry?'

Letitia Morell, Roz's grandmother and one of the few people in the family C. J. felt properly at ease with, had also been reading a magazine; it was *Tatler*, as appropriate to her tastes as *Ms* was to Camilla's, and she was totally engrossed in the social section, her eyes moving swiftly from captions to pictures and back again. 'Look,' she said, 'Roz's school friend Rosie Howard Johnson. Did you ever know her, C. J.?'

'Er no,' said C. J., 'no, I don't think so.'

'Well she's just got married. To Lord Pulgrave. I always liked her so much. Such a lovely dress. Where *is* Roz? I'd like to show her.'

'Er, I think she's in the rest room,' said C. J.

'The what, darling? Oh, you mean the lavatory. Such a curious name they have for it in your country. Well anyway, never mind. Yes please, C. J., I'd love a drink. But not sherry; I do hate it, especially in the morning. I always think it's rather common. I don't suppose Henry has any champagne?'

'I shouldn't think so for a moment,' said C. J. 'Jane did say only sherry. I'm sorry, Letitia. Shall I go and see if I can find some for you?'

'Oh, good gracious, no. Sweet of you, but I wouldn't dream of it,' said Letitia. 'I'll have the sherry. It will be better than nothing. Oh dear, I seem to have been drinking much too much ever since Julian died. It's the only way I can get through a lot of the time.'

C. J. looked at her tenderly. She was very old, eighty-seven, but until the death of her son three weeks ago she had very rarely looked anything near that age. Suddenly now she seemed smaller, frailer than she had been, a little shaky. But she was beautifully dressed today in a vivid red suit (from Chanel, decided C. J., who was clever at such things), sheer black stockings on her still-shapely legs, black low-heeled shoes; her snowy hair was immaculate, her almost-mauve eyes surprisingly sparkly; she was courage incarnate, he thought, smiling at her in a mixture of affection and admiration.

'All right,' he said, 'I'll buy you some champagne at lunch time if you like. Will that do?'

'Of course. Thank you, darling. Oh, how nice, here's Eliza. And Peveril. Oh, thank goodness. C. J., go and tell Roz her mother is here, it will calm her down a bit.' C. J. thought this was very unlikely, but went off obediently in search of Roz; Letitia patted the chairs on either side of her and beamed at the new arrivals being propelled gently into the room by Jane Gould. 'Come in, you two, and sit here with me. I was just saying to C. J., Eliza, Rosie Howard Johnson has just got married. Did you go to the wedding?'

Eliza, Countess of Garrylaig, crossed the room and bent and kissed Letitia. 'Hallo, Letitia, darling, how are you? We've had the most dreadful journey from Claridge's, haven't we, Peveril? It took almost as long as the entire trip from Scotland. We hardly moved at all for about forty minutes. No, no we didn't go to Rosie's wedding. Peveril doesn't like weddings, do you, darling?'

Peveril, Ninth Earl of Garrylaig, half bowed to Letitia, and settled down thankfully in the seat beside her.

'Morning, Letitia my dear. God, I hate London. Dreadful morning . . . dreadful. No, I don't like weddings. The service always makes me cry, and the receptions bore me to tears. Saves on handkerchiefs to stay away.'

He beamed at her and patted her hand. He was tall, white-haired, charmingly courteous and acutely vague, and only came properly to life when he was pursuing some animal, fish or bird – and presumably, Letitia thought, his wife. He was dressed as always in extremely elderly tweeds; he looked, she thought, amongst the collection of people in the room, like a wise old buzzard settled briefly but very deliberately among a gathering of feckless birds of paradise. Quite why the dashing Eliza, then the Vicomtesse du Chene, formerly Mrs Peter Thetford and once Mrs Julian Morell, had married him only a few years earlier was something that probably only she herself and Letitia really understood. Even Letitia found it difficult entirely to accept; Peveril was nearer her own age than Eliza, and they seemed to have absolutely nothing in common. But then Eliza had always had a predilection for people considerably older than herself, and a talent for charming them; beginning with Julian Morell, so many years ago. And there was no doubt she was very fond of Peveril and was making him extremely happy. Letitia smiled at them both.

'I'm afraid the only thing on offer is sherry, but after being stuck in that traffic, perhaps even that would be welcome. Or would you rather have coffee?'

'Oh, I think coffee,' said Eliza. 'I do hate sherry. What about you, Peveril, darling?'

'What's that? Oh, no, not coffee, thank you. Dreadful stuff. I'll just have a glass of water if I may.'

'I'm sure you may,' said Letitia. 'I'll ask Jane.'

Peveril looked round the room and his eyes rested on Phaedria. He beamed happily and went over to her; he had always liked her.

'Morning, Phaedria my dear. How are you?'

Phaedria looked up at him and smiled back. 'I'm fine, Peveril, thank you. It's lovely to see you. And you, Eliza. I'm sorry you've had such an awful journey.'

Peveril studied her more closely.

'You don't look fine, my dear, if you don't mind my saying so. You look a bit peaky.'

'Oh, Peveril, don't be so tactless,' said Eliza. 'Of course she's looking peaky. Poor angel.'

She walked over to the fireplace and kissed Phaedria. 'It's lovely to see you, darling. I wish you'd come up and stay with us for a bit. It would do you so much good.'

'I will,' said Phaedria, clearly trying to sound enthusiastic. 'I will. But not just yet. Thank you,' she added dutifully.

Eliza patted her hand. 'Well, when you're ready. Ah,' she added, a thick ice freezing over her bright voice, 'Camilla. Good morning.'

'Good morning, Eliza,' said Camilla, smiling calmly back at her. 'How are you?'

'I'm extremely well, thank you. I don't think, Camilla, you have ever met my husband. Have you?'

'No, I don't think I have,' said Camilla. Her smile became more gracious still; in deference to Peveril's age she stood up.

'How do you do. I'm Camilla North.'

Only Peveril, Letitia thought, watching this cameo with a sort of pained pleasure, could fail to appreciate the fine irony of this tableau: the two wives of Julian Morell grouped with the mistress who had usurped them both.

He smiled, half bowed over Camilla's outstretched hand.

'Heard a lot about you, my dear. How do you do. Nice to meet you at last.'

'Peveril,' said Eliza briskly, 'come along, let's go and sit down with Letitia.'

'I'll sit down when I'm ready, Eliza,' said Peveril firmly. 'Been sitting much too long this morning as it is. Nice to stand up for a bit. Do sit down again, Miss North. You must be tired,

I believe you've only flown in this morning. I expect you've got that jet jag or whatever it calls itself.'

'Jet lag,' said Camilla, smiling at him again, 'but no, I don't suffer from that at all. I have discovered that providing I eat only raw food and drink nothing but water, I'm perfectly all right.'

'Good lord,' said Peveril, 'who'd have thought it? Raw food, eh? So do you ask them to serve you your lunch uncooked? What an idea; I expect they're pretty grateful to you, aren't they? Saves them a bit of trouble. Raw food. Good heavens.' He smiled at her benignly; Camilla, most unusually at a loss as to what to say, smiled back at him. Eliza turned rather irritably and looked out of the window.

Letitia smiled at Peveril and wondered if she dared make a joke about Camilla making off with Eliza's fourth husband, as well as her first; she decided it would be in too bad taste even by her standards, and that Eliza would certainly not appreciate it; for want of anything else to do, she returned to her *Tatler*.

'Eliza, can I get you a sherry? And you sir?'

C. J. had come back into the room, and witnessed the tableau also; he smiled rather nervously at Eliza as she blew him a kiss. He was always rather afraid of what she might say or do. She was phenomenally tactless. And still so beautiful, he thought. What a mother-in-law to have. Poor Roz, no wonder she had all those hang-ups about her looks with a beautiful mother and grandmother. Eliza was forty-nine years old, awesomely chic, (Jasper Conran, who adored dressing amusing middle-aged ladies, travelled up to Garrylaig Castle twice a year with his designs and to stay the weekend), beautifully, if a trifle heavily, made up, her silvery blonde hair cut in a perfectly sculptured bob, her body as slender and supple as it had been thirty-one years ago when she had married Julian Morell.

'No thank you, darling. Just some coffee,' said Eliza. 'And some water for Peveril, please. And C. J., what on earth is going on? I thought we were late. Nobody seems to be here. Where's Henry? And what's Roz doing?'

C. J. was beginning to feel like an air steward, nursing his passengers through an incipient disaster.

'Roz is on the phone to her office. She's worried about some meeting she has this afternoon. Susan is on her way. And I don't know what's happened to Henry, I'm afraid. I'm sure its nothing to worry about.'

'Well, let's hope not.' C. J. went off again with his orders. Eliza looked after him. 'Poor C. J.,' she said, apparently irrelevantly.

'I do wish Susan would arrive,' said Letitia fretfully. 'She always makes me feel so much better. And Roz too, which is probably more to the point.'

'Where is she?' said Eliza.

'She's looking at houses with Richard. He has this plan to move down to the country. Wiltshire. Such a mistake, I think, when you've lived in London all your life. Of course everyone in Wiltshire is terribly nice.'

'Everyone, Granny Letitia?'

It was Roz; she had come back into the room and heard her grandmother's words; she was smiling for the first time that day. Letitia smiled back up at her.

'Why don't you come and sit here with me, darling? Yes, everyone. So many of the very best people live there.'

'Granny Letitia, you're such a snob.'

'I know, darling. I'm not ashamed of it. In my young day it was a virtue. It was called having standards.'

'Ah. I see.'

'I was just saying,' said Letitia, 'that I wished Susan would arrive.'

'So do I. And I really don't want her to go and live in Wiltshire, with the best people.'

'Well,' said Letitia quietly, 'it will suit her. She is one of the very best. Oh, Susan darling, there you are. I was just saying you were one of the very best people.'

Susan Brookes had hurried into the room; she smiled at Letitia and bent and kissed her cheek. 'Not by your standards I'm not. I'm surprised at you, Letitia. Letting the side down like that. And me only an honorary member of this family. Sacrilege.'

'Oh, Susan, don't be difficult,' said Roz. 'And come and sit by Granny Letitia. She's in a naughty mood. She needs keeping in order. And if I can find C. J. I'll ask for a drink for you. What would you like?'

'Tea, please,' said Susan. 'I haven't missed anything

important, have I? And I don't suppose there's anything to eat, is there? I'm famished.'

Roz looked at her and smiled again, leant forward and kissed her gently on the cheek. Susan was a tall, thin woman with bright brown hair, heavily flecked with grey; she was not classically good-looking but with a strong humorous face, a clear beautiful skin and startlingly bright blue eyes. She was in her mid sixties now, and in some ways she looked older, as her face tended to gauntness. But she had a style of her own: she was beautifully and very simply dressed in a navy wool suit and cream silk shirt, her only jewellery a pearl necklace and earrings, which no one, with the exception of Letitia, could ever remember seeing her without.

'Oh Susan,' said Roz, feeling much better suddenly, restored to something near normality, 'can any of us think of an occasion when you didn't feel famished? I'll get C. J. to find something for you.'

She walked out of the door again; Susan and Letitia looked after her.

'How is she, do you think?' asked Susan quietly.

'I think she's in a terrible state,' said Letitia. 'Eaten up with hatred of Phaedria, who she seems to blame in some way for Julian's death, desperately unhappy, wretched that she didn't say goodbye to him – oh, I know it was her own fault –'

'Poor Roz,' said Susan. 'Poor, poor Roz. I've known her all her life, and I've never felt sorrier for her than I do now. What on earth can we do to help her?'

'God knows,' said Letitia with a sigh. 'God knows. She will persist in making things worse for herself. She always has, of course. And Phaedria too, I feel so sorry for her. She looks dreadful, poor child. So alone. Well, perhaps today will help in some way. Although I can't imagine how.'

Absolutely on cue, Henry Winterbourne suddenly appeared in the room, followed by Jane with yet more files (I bet they're just for show, thought Roz) and C. J. bearing a tray and looking like a particularly inept waiter as he hurried round trying to deliver his complex order.

Henry took up his place at the head of the table, his back to the window. 'Good morning,' he said. 'I am extremely sorry to have kept you waiting. A very tedious call from New York. Do forgive me.'

He opened the top file on the table, took a large envelope out of it and set it firmly in front of him. Everyone slowly, very slowly, as if in a badly directed play, took up new positions. Phaedria got up and sat with her back to the fire at the end of the table, pulling her coat more closely round her. Peveril sat next to her, assuming an oddly protective role. Eliza settled in the chair next to him. Camilla stood up and walked round to take up the chair nearest to Henry. Letitia and Susan stopped talking. Roz took up a challenging position, standing alone by the door, every ounce of her formidable energy focused on Henry's face.

Henry smiled faintly round the room, catching everyone's eye in turn with the right amount of sadness and sympathy, bestowing a smile here, a conspiratorial look there. Smooth bastard, thought C. J., finally divesting himself of the tray and moving over to sit next to Susan.

'Lady Morell, are you all right?' said Henry suddenly.

Everyone looked at Phaedria; she was resting her head on her hands on the table. She appeared to be about to faint.

'Phaedria, let me take you outside,' said C. J.

'I'll take her,' said Eliza, getting up and crossing over to Phaedria, putting her arm around her shoulders. 'She needs some air.'

'No, no really I'm all right,' said Phaedria, 'I'm sorry, just a bit dizzy, that's all. Perhaps I could have a glass of water.'

'I'll get it,' said C. J. quickly, grateful for something to do.

'C. J.,' said Roz from where she was standing, 'do settle down, you've been rushing round with drinks all morning. Jane will fetch Phaedria a glass of water, I'm sure. Jane dear,' she called through the doorway, at Jane's back, 'could you fetch Lady Morell a glass of water, please? The strain of the occasion is proving a little too much for her.'

She watched Phaedria carefully as she took the glass of water, sipped at it half-heartedly, put it down, leant back in her chair, shaking the dark waterfall of hair from her face. Looking at her, Roz did have to admit she looked ill. Her skin was starkly white, rather than its usual creamy pale, and she seemed thinner than ever, shrunk into herself. God, she hated her. So much, Phaedria had taken from her, so much that should have been hers, and what were they all to learn now, how much more was to go Phaedria's way, away from her, Julian Morell's daughter, his only child, his rightful heir? Roz swallowed, fixed her eyes on Henry's face. She must concentrate. The words she was to hear, had to hear, were what mattered just now, not her thoughts, her emotions. Time for them later.

'Very well,' said Henry. 'Perhaps I could begin. Now as you may appreciate, this is an out of the ordinary occasion. These days, public readings of wills are very unusual. Although, of course, perfectly legal. And it was at Sir Julian's request that it should be conducted in this way. In the presence of you all. He particularly specified that you should all –' His gaze fell briefly, unbidden, on Camilla, then shifted hastily again. 'All be here. There are of course minor beneficiaries, staff and so on, who were not required to attend. So – perhaps the best thing now is just for me to read the will. If any of you have any – comments, or questions, perhaps you could save them to the end.'

Christ, thought Roz, what on earth is the old woman going on about?

She shifted her weight slightly on to the other leg, took a sip of her drink, and fixed her eyes on Henry's face again.

Henry began to read: 'I, Julian Morell, of Hanover Terrace, London, N.W.1, Company Director, hereby revoke all previous wills and testamentary dispositions . . .'

It began slowly, with a trickle of small bequests; it was like the start of a party, Roz thought, with only one or two guests arrived, making stiff and stilted conversation. The atmosphere was cold, tense, uncomfortable.

There were five-thousand-pound legacies for minor staff: the housekeeper and the gardener at the house in Sussex, the part-time secretary Julian had employed in Paris for ten years, and elderly Mrs Bagnold who had directed the cleaners of the offices in Dover Street for longer than anyone could remember.

Mrs Bagnold was also bequeathed a set of 'Victorian watercolours she had once admired, to do exactly what she likes with, she may sell them tomorrow if she wishes, without fear of incurring my displeasure from wherever I may be.'

As Henry read out this part of the will, Phaedria looked up

and caught Letitia's eye, in a sudden flash of humour. He is still fun, that look said, he is still making life good.

'To Sarah Brownsmith, my patient and very loyal secretary, I bequeath £10,000, both early Hockneys, and the use of my house on Eleuthera in the Bahamas, for at least one month a year, at a time mutually agreeable to her and my wife. This is in the devout hope that as she lies in the sunshine, she will think kindly of me and forgive me the many years of exasperation and overwork I have inflicted upon her.

'To the head waiter at the Mirabelle Restaurant, the chief wine waiter at the Connaught Hotel and my good friend Peter Langan, the sum of £5,000 each for the great happiness and gastronomic good fortune they have brought me.

'To Martin Dodsworth, my trainer, £10,000, my three Stubbs, and my brood mare Prince's Flora, and to Michael O'Leary, my jockey, £5,000 and a yearling of his choice from my stable. To Tony Price, my groom, the same.

'To Jane Gould, secretary to my solicitor, Henry Winterbourne, I bequeath my Hispano Suiza because I know how much pleasure it will give her, and a £1,000 a year maintenance allowance with which to care for it.'

Jane, sitting quietly at the back of the room, beamed with pleasure; she and her husband belonged to the MG Club and were staunch followers of the London to Brighton rally, but the possession of such a car was quite beyond the dreams of her own personal avarice. Roz wondered briefly and rather irritably where the rest of the Morell vintage car stable would go; her father had known how much she loved them. It would be very sad if the collection was to be broken up and scattered piecemeal. If this was a taster of the rest of the will, she didn't like it at all.

'To my good friend Peveril, Earl of Garrylaig, my Holbein, and the two Rembrandts, which will hang so happily in the gallery at Garrylaig, and my grandfather's guns, which have always deserved better hands than mine to rest in.'

'I say, how kind,' murmured Peveril, flushed with pleasure (more at the contemplation of the guns than the Rembrandts). Eliza smiled at him fondly and patted his hand.

The party had begun now; the room was humming with tension and nervous energy.

'To my first wife, Eliza, Countess of Garrylaig, in appreciation for the gift of my daughter Rosamund, and for several interesting and entertaining years –' Henry at this point cleared his throat, reached for a glass of water and paused a moment '– I bequeath my collections of Lalique glass and Chiparus figures, and my apartment in Sutton Place, New York, all of which I know will give her immense pleasure and be put to excellent use.'

'That's true,' said Eliza.

There was a brief silence.

'To Camilla North, in recognition of many years of tolerance, companionship and wisdom, I bequeath the following: my apartment in Sydney, my hunter, Rose Red, and my collection of Sydney Nolans, as a memento of the expertise and pleasure she gave me in the course of their collection.'

That's a lot, thought Roz, illogically pleased. A lot for a mistress. Even a long-standing one. That's a smack in the eye for Phaedria. Without even realizing she was doing it she smiled at Camilla; Letitia reflected it was the first time she had probably ever voluntarily done such a thing, and shuddered mildly at what she could only assume was the reason.

Camilla's beautiful face was expressionless; she sat with her eyes fixed on Henry, her hands clasped loosely in her lap. No one was to know that she was concentrating with some fervour on her relaxation therapy, and that if she gave up for one moment, stopped breathing deeply, chanting her mantra silently to herself, she would be in grave danger of bursting into tears, hysterical laughter or both.

'To my very dear friend Susan Brookes, who has worked with me for so many years on this company, and without whom I would not be where I am today, I bequeath my house in Nice, and the sum of £5 million free of tax.'

Good God, thought Roz. He isn't leaving anyone else that sort of money. What on earth has he done that for?

Then she saw Susan looking at her: flushed, her eyes suspiciously bright. Watched her as she unmistakably winked at her and realized why: to give Susan pleasure to be sure, but also to burden her, discomfort her in her passionate, between-the-wars socialism, leave her wondering what on earth to do with it. They had been such good friends, such affectionately life-long opponents, Susan and her father, and she was the one person he had never quite been able to get the better of. Until now.

Oh well, thought Roz. No doubt the Labour Party and Mother Teresa will be benefiting considerably from that. She was wrong.

'This bequest is for the sole benefit of Mrs Brookes, and is not to be passed on to anyone with the exception of Mrs Brookes' two daughters; should the house in Nice be sold, the monies realized should pass to her daughters also.'

Oh God, thought Roz. Oh God, he was a clever awkward bastard. She looked at Susan and smiled, winked back. She felt briefly better.

'To my son-in-law Christopher John Emerson, I bequeath my two Monets, my collection of Cartier cufflinks, all the shares in my property company in the Caribbean, my hotels in the Seychelles, and the Bahamas, neither of which would have been so successfully built without his commercial and visual skills, and the 1950 Rolls Corniche which he has always so admired. Plus the entire contents of my wine cellar, in recognition of the knowledge and appreciation he will bring to it. I expect it to be added to with wines which will grace and indeed improve it.'

Suddenly, Roz felt, her father was back with them, in the room, charming, witty, civilized; she saw him looking at her, smiling, trying to win her over, make her do what he wanted, she could hear his voice, see his graceful, deceptively relaxed figure, feel herself being pulled into the wilful web he spun around everyone who was close to him. She swallowed hard, blinked away the rising tears; tried to concentrate on the present.

Phaedria was sitting very upright now, her dark eyes fixed on Henry's face; she had taken off her coat at last. She was wearing a dress of brilliant peacock blue, as bright, brighter than Letitia's red suit, but what on Letitia looked defiant, courageous, on Phaedria seemed odd, shocking, inappropriate.

And now it was Letitia's turn: 'To my mother, my best and dearest friend, I bequeath £3 million free of tax from my Guernsey bank account, the whole of which may be spent at Harrods should she so wish, my hotel in Paris, in recognition of

23

her great love for the city, and my entire collection of historic cars, with the exception of the Hispano Suiza and the Rolls Corniche already mentioned, knowing how much she will love and enjoy them. And what an adornment she will be on the occasions she drives any of them, which I trust will be frequently. Should she wish to dispose of them for any reason, I would only request that a Motor Museum should be established in my name and the entire collection should be placed within it. Also, my first edition prints of *Jungle Book*, and an oil painting of Edward Prince of Wales by Sir James Holbrooke, in acknowledgement of the important part she played in his life.'

There was a long silence; Susan reached out and took Letitia's hand; Letitia looked down into her lap. Then she smiled bravely at Henry.

'Do go on, Henry dear. Although,' she added, sparkling through her tears, 'as Queen of England *manqué*, I wonder if I might ask for another small glass of sherry.'

'Of course,' said Henry. 'Jane, would you . . .'

Jane did.

Henry waited until everyone was quiet again, and then cleared his throat, rather loudly.

'To my granddaughter, Miranda Emerson, I bequeath £2 million free of tax from my Guernsey bank account, to be held in trust for her by her mother, until Miranda reaches the age of twenty-one. The trust to be administered for her by my firm of solicitors, Winterbourne and Winterbourne. I also bequeath her the sum of £100,000 free of tax, to be spent entirely on horses, in recognition of her already apparent talent for horsemanship, and their upkeep, training, and any related activities she herself might wish to pursue.'

'How old is that child?' said Letitia quietly to Susan. 'Three? Well, that should buy her the odd pony.'

'Er – if I might continue. To my beloved daughter Rosamund –' again a pause. Roz tensed, closed her eyes briefly – 'I bequeath the following: £5 million free of tax, all of the horses in my stables at Marriotts Manor, with the exception of the aforementioned Rose Red (That was cruel, thought Letitia, Phaedria loved those horses) and' – Henry paused, looking at Roz carefully, for a brief second – 'forty-nine per cent of the shares in Morell Industries.'

There was a long, hurtful silence. Roz clenched her fists, folded her lips; whatever she did, she knew, she must not move or make a sound, otherwise everything would break out, she would scream, punch the air, Henry, Phaedria, anyone. She looked at the floor, at her feet; they suddenly looked very far away. Then she managed, with a supreme act of courage, to meet Phaedria's eyes.

The expression in them was thoughtful, concerned, almost kind; but still triumphant. I have won, that look said. I have won and you have not.

Henry paused again, then perceptibly straightened and continued reading.

'To my dear wife, Phaedria Morell' – only dear wife, thought Roz savagely, her rage and misery lifting just for a moment, I was his beloved daughter, she is only his dear wife – 'I bequeath the following: £10 million free of tax, my house in Hanover Terrace, Regent's Park, London; Lower Marriotts Manor, in the County of Sussex; Turtle Cove House on the Island of Eleuthera in the Bahamas, and my entire collection of paintings, with the exception of the two Stubbs, the Rembrandts, the Hockneys and the Sidney Nolans already mentioned.'

There was yet another silence. That's funny, thought Roz, who is getting his plane? He loved that plane.

Henry looked round the room again with an expression almost impossible to interpret; there was a challenge in that look and amusement, much apprehension, a sort of triumph even, and as it brushed over Phaedria, tenderness and concern. He took a long drink of water, cleared his throat, shifted in his chair – anything, thought Roz, anything rather than continue. Finally he looked back at the document on his desk.

'I also bequeath my wife Phaedria forty-nine per cent of the shares in Morell Industries.'

The mathematical implication of this bequest hit the room slowly; the silence grew heavier. Phaedria was no longer pale, she was flushed, she could feel sweat breaking out on her forehead. Roz was standing almost to attention now, her eyes very bright in her white face, her fists clenched. C. J. was looking with equal apprehension from Roz to Phaedria; Camilla was no longer relaxed but taut – tense, thought C. J., who had always rather admired her, like a race horse under starter's orders, hardly able to contain herself and her nervous energy. Eliza broke the stillness; she got up suddenly and walked over to the window, turned to face the room from behind Henry's chair, intense interest on her face.

'Do go on,' she said. 'I imagine there must be more.'

'Yes,' said Henry, and looked down again at his desk. 'Finally, I bequeath the remaining two per cent of shares in Morell Industries to Miles Wilburn, in the hope and indeed belief that he will use them wisely and well. I also bequeath my Lear jet to Miles Wilburn, as he may find a need for greater mobility in the future, together with the residue of the estate. There remains only for me to bid you all farewell and to say that I hope you will in time see the wisdom of what I have done.'

The first sound to break the silence again was of Eliza laughing; it began as a smothered chuckle and became a gorgeous, joyous peal. 'He did have style,' she said, to no one in particular, 'real style.'

Almost simultaneously Phaedria fainted, simply slid out of her chair and on to the floor.

Living the events of the next hour over and over again in her mind, Roz could only remember nightmarish oddly inconsequential fragments: of C.J. and Henry helping Phaedria into another room; of her own loud and inappropriate demand for a stiff drink; of Letitia suggesting to her that they should go outside together and get some fresh air, and her irritable wretched refusal; of her mother asking inane questions of Peveril, of Letitia, of Susan, of C.J., if any of them had ever met or heard of a Miles Wilburn, and even more inane suggestions that he might be the son, cousin, brother, uncle of various men she had known or that Julian had known; of Camilla, become suddenly part of the previously hostile gathering, offering to go through her old address books and diaries (all predictably stored and filed in date order) in search of some kind of clue; of Henry, fussily important, returning to the room and professing as much ignorance of Miles as the rest of them, while volunteering the strangely relevant and unexpected information that he had not drawn up the will, or even set eyes on it until Julian had died and Phaedria had found it in the safe and sent it over to him; of her own savagely swift personal revelation as to the cause of Phaedria's faintness; of Henry's insistence, largely she felt for her mother's benefit, that no whisper of the will must reach the outside world, and particularly that part of it centred in Fleet Street; of the departure of the family, in small, disparate groups, oddly subdued (with the exception of Phaedria, glassily pale, but possessed of a strange almost feverish excitement); and lastly the sound of her own voice, the panic and despair she was feeling disguised in a harsh brightness, declaring that she knew that whoever and wherever Mr Wilburn might be, she would personally hate him unreservedly for the whole of the rest of her life.

'Miles,' said the girl from the depths of the bed. 'Miles, you just have to get up. It's almost seven, and you have that meeting with your uncle this morning. And you know how important it is. Miles, please wake up.'

Miles put out his hand, his eyes still closed, and traced the outline of her breasts, moved down over her abdomen, rested tenderly for a moment on the mound of pubic hair; then moved on, gently, relentlessly probing her secret places, feeling her soft moistness, parting her; she could feel his penis hardening, rising against her, and her own juices obediently, delightfully, start to flow.

'Miles,' she said, in a last desperate effort to divert him. 'Miles, please.'

'You don't have to ask,' he said, smiling into her eyes, deliberately misunderstanding; and for a while everything was forgotten, the debts, the lawsuit, the trap closing in on him, all lost in a tangle of hair and skin and pleasure and desire.

Chapter One

Wiltshire, France, London, 1939–1948

Julian Morell's enemies often said he could never quite make up his mind who he loved more, his mother or himself.

This judgement, pronounced as frequently in company boardrooms as at dinner parties, might well have been considered just a little harsh; but there was certainly sufficient truth in it to ensure its frequent repetition. And certainly anyone observing the two of them dining together at the Ritz one evening in the autumn of 1952 would have been irresistibly reminded of it – watching Julian looking alternately fondly at his mother, and almost as fondly into the mirror behind her.

They looked alike to a degree; they were both dark-haired, both tall and slim, but Julian's eyes were brown and his face was long and already threatening to be gaunt. Letitia had deep, almost purple, blue eyes and the kind of bone structure that would look good for another fifty years: high cheekbones, and a very slight squarishness to the jaw. She had the sort of mouth possessed by all great beauties of the twenties and thirties: a perfect bow, neither full nor thin; and a nose of classical straightness. But the most remarkable thing about her (and this would not have seemed quite so remarkable to anybody who had not known she was fifty-four years old) was her skin. It was not only much admired, Letitia's skin, it was hugely commented upon; it not only inspired admiration, it defied science. It was soft and dewy, and extraordinarily unlined, and one of her more florid admirers had once said (rather unfortunately for him) that as he sat looking at it, it seemed to him to be more and more like looking into a rose petal.

Everything else about Letitia Morell's extraordinary beauty could be explained away by face lifts (she was rumoured to have had three already), expensive skin treatments, skilled *maquillage*, and the attentions of the best cosmetic chemists in the country placed permanently at her disposal, but the fact was that Miss Arden and Madame Rubinstein, with many of the same advantages, did not look nearly as young as she did.

Julian, on the other hand, could easily have been older than his thirty-two years; he had the kind of looks that settle on a face in their owner's mid twenties, and stay, relatively unchanged, for thirty years or more. He was conventionally good-looking; he had his mother's straight nose, and rather sharply defined mouth, but his eyes were very dark. They were remarkable eyes, curiously expressionless for much of the time, but with a capacity to light up and to dance when he was amused or setting out to charm (which was frequently) and to disturb, particularly women; they held an expression that was almost insolent, probing, amused, shrewd; they were hard eyes to meet, without feeling threatened, in some way or another, pleasurably or otherwise. His hair was a little longer than the current vogue; and his clothes bore the unmistakable mark of much attention and a strong sense of style. His dark grey suit, beautifully and clearly hand made, nevertheless had lapels just fractionally wider, the jacket a touch longer, flaring only a little more at the back, than the classic style his tailor would have offered him; his shirt was not white or cream, but very pale blue; his red silk tie was tied in a Windsor knot; and his shoes (hand made for him by Lobb) were softer, and lighter-looking, than those on most of the feet under most of the tables in the room. His watch was a classic gold Cartier, on a black leather strap; on the little finger of his left hand he wore a heavy gold signet ring; and although he did not smoke himself, he always had with him a slim gold cigarette case, permanently filled with the oval Passing Clouds cigarettes so beloved by the stylish of the fifties, and a gold Dunhill lighter. These lay between them on the table now; Letitia, who had been young in the twenties (and had once most famously danced the Charleston with the Prince of Wales in the Glass Slipper Nightclub, an event she was given to reliving in ever greater detail after a glass or two of champagne), and had seen the cigarette as a symbol of emancipation and sophistication, still occasionally smoked before or after a meal through a long black cigarette holder. She was using it now, as she studied the menu, reaching out to cover Julian's hand with her own as he lit it for her, smiling at him through the cloud of smoke; certainly they did not look, the two of them, like mother and son at all, but a wonderful-looking couple amusing and interesting one another intensely.

'Mother,' said Julian fondly, 'you do look particularly amazing. How long have you spent with Adam Sarsted this evening?'

'Oh, darling, *hours*,' said Letitia, smiling at him and stroking his cheek appreciatively, 'he takes longer and longer every single time. He's got a marvellous new foundation he wanted to demonstrate and I do have to say I think it's extremely good. But I had to listen to him extolling its virtues for at least twice as long as it took to put it on.'

'Well, he works on his own,' said Julian, 'he needs to talk about the things he's been doing from time to time. Listening to him is an investment. He was talking to me about that foundation. I'm glad it's good. He's a clever chap. Worth all that money I pay him. Or don't you think so?'

'Mmm,' said Letitia thoughtfully. 'Just. Yes, I suppose so. But I do keep telling you, darling, the very best cosmetic chemists are in New York. You really should think about finding some people over there. Next time you go I might come with you and talk to a few, if you won't.'

'Well, maybe I will – when I go,' said Julian, 'and I'd love to have you with me. But I honestly don't think you're going to find anyone better than Sarsted. The man's a genius.'

'No, he's not a genius,' said Letitia, 'he's a very good chemist and that's all. He hasn't got any creativity. He isn't inspired. He doesn't have any ideas.'

'Mother, darling, we have enough ideas between us to keep a dozen cosmetic companies afloat. Stop fussing. What do you want to drink?'

'Gin and french. And I'm hungry. Do let's order quickly. Last time we had dinner here I seem to remember eating so much melba toast I scrunched when I moved. So common, nibbling.'

'Mother,' said Julian, laughing and signalling at the waiter, 'you could never look common. However much you nibbled. Not in that dress, anyway.'

'Do you like it, darling? Good. Cavanagh. Such a clever man.' She glanced over her shoulder into the mirror behind her and smiled briefly at her reflection; white crepe dress, accordion pleated from the shoulders, swathed across the bosom and drawn into a tiny waist with a narrow, pale suede cummerbund; her dark hair was swept back, around her neck she wore the fabled treble-stranded Morell pearls given to her by her mother-in-law on her wedding day, and the overtly fake cluster of beads and diamante in her ears gave a style and wit to the discreet taste of the rest.

'Where on earth did you get those Christmas trees?' said Julian, touching one of the earrings. 'I've never seen anything like them in my life.'

'I'm very glad to hear it. I'd have thought it was a fearful waste of twenty pounds if you had. I got them at the Dior boutique in Paris. It's a heavenly place. Full of all sorts of wonderful things. Next time you want an amusing present for someone, I suggest you go there.'

'Ah,' said Julian, 'I'll remember. Thank you. It's no use looking at me in that hopeful way, Mother, you're not going to get any gossip out of me about anyone I might or might not want to find an amusing present for. Now just tell me what you want to eat.'

'I'm not looking hopeful,' said Letitia, 'quite the reverse. I find it much more restful when you aren't in love with anybody. I just thought it must be about time, that's all. Quails' eggs, I think. And the turbot. Lovely. Lots of potatoes and spinach. To give me strength for tomorrow.'

'What are you doing tomorrow?'

'Meeting the accountants.'

'There's nothing to worry about, is there?' said Julian sharply.

'No, of course not. Don't fuss. You're more of an old woman than I am, Julian, when it comes to money. It's just that I dislike the new man rather, and I know they're going to query the investment budget.'

'Are you sure it's the right way to go? Should we talk about it?'

'Absolutely, and no we shouldn't. We've talked about it quite enough already. We need the new factory and we need a complete new range of filling machinery. Don't worry about it, I'll deal with them. That's my department, you stick to cosmetic concepts.'

'Don't patronize me, Mother. I don't like it.' The lighthearted look left his face briefly; his eyes grew darker and he pushed his hair back from his forehead with a rough, impatient gesture. It was an act that his fellow directors and his mistresses came to know swiftly; it meant trouble and got him his way. 'Do you want another drink?'

'Yes, please. And I'm not patronizing you. The secret of success, as you're so fond of telling everybody else, is knowing what you're good at and doing it. I'm good at sums. You're good at concepts. Although . . .'

'What?'

'Well, that brings me back to the chemist. Julian, you really do need someone better than Sarsted. The truly great cosmetic chemists are artists as well as scientists. They think laterally. They don't just look at a formula and mix it; they look at a formula and dream or they dream and then look at formulas.'

'So where are we failing, Mother?' said Julian, pushing his hair back again, crumbling a bread roll to pieces and pushing it round his plate. 'Just tell me that. Everything seems fine to me. We're doing brilliantly. Snapping at Arden's heels, worrying Rubinstein. I had lunch with Norman Parkinson yesterday. He said that every model he's worked with for the past three months was using Juliana make-up. Audrey Withers told me only last week they keep permanent sets of it in the *Vogue* studios. We can't meet the demand for *Je*. I just can't see what basis you have for criticism.'

'Julian, do calm down,' said Letitia. 'I'm not criticizing you. I'm simply saying we could do even better with a truly inspired chemist.'

'And I'm saying we're quite inspired enough,' said Julian, 'I don't want any more creativity in the company.'

'No,' said Letitia tartly, 'you wouldn't like the competition. Now get on with your food. Perhaps it's time you did have a new girlfriend. It might improve your temper. Or even,' she added, looking at him thoughtfully, 'a wife. Thirty-two is far too old to be a bachelor.'

She looked at him with amusement as he tried not to show how ruffled he was; pushing his food around his plate just as he had when he was a small boy and she thwarted him taking huge gulps of milk – rather as the hugely expensive sancerre was going down now.

32

*

Letitia had always loved Julian in a curiously unmaternal way, and they had both of them known it; his elder brother James had been the perfect textbook little boy, exactly like his father, serious, quiet, blue-eyed, fair-haired, fascinated by farming as soon as he could walk, tramping round in his wellington boots after the cowman, up at dawn with his father every day, keeping logbooks of milk yields and stock prices as soon as he could write.

Julian, three years younger, was extraordinarily different; with his dark hair and eyes, his passion for reading, his sociable nature (at five he was already pinning party invitations on to the wall in his bedroom and counting the days to each one). He took a polite interest in the farm, but no more; he was more likely to be found reading in the drawing room, or listening to the radio, or best of all chatting to anybody at all who was prepared to listen to him, than outside or in the barns, or even the stables. He did have a considerable passion for his pony, and rode her extremely well, if rather showily: 'Like a girl,' James said more than once rather scornfully, and indeed he was far more likely to win the show classes than the children's gymkhana games like Walk, Trot and Gallop or an Obstacle Race. He was clever, quick and very funny, even as a small boy, full of amusing observations and quick sharp comment; he and his mother became very early friends, companions and confidants. His father, Edward, kind, good-natured and absolutely conventional, adored James, but found Julian hard to understand.

The difference between the two little boys was the subject of much gossip in Wiltshire; and nobody ever understood in any case why a nice, straightforward man like Edward Morell had married someone as patently unsuited to the life of farmer's wife as Letitia Farnworth, but there it was, he had brought her down to meet his parents, having met her at a party in London, quite literally blushing with pride, in 1915, and married her a year later.

The reason for that was perfectly simple and straightforward, of course: he had fallen deeply in love with her, and remained so until the day he died. The real puzzle, and one recognized by the more discerning, was why Letitia should have married Edward; beautiful, sparkling, witty as she was, and he so quiet, so shy, so modest. It was on Julian's twenty-first when, given that this was London in 1941, she still managed to orchestrate a very good birthday party for him (supper and dancing at the gallant Savoy, which like most of the great London hotels was resolutely refusing even to acknowledge that the war was much more than a minor inconvenience), that she told him: 'You're old enough to know now, my angel, and I don't want anyone giving you a garbled version.' She had been engaged to and much in love with a young officer in the Guards, Harry Whigham, who had gone to France, and been blown to pieces before even her first letter had reached him. Confronted by this and the almost equally appalling fact that virtually every other young man in England was facing the same fate, and terrified at seventeen by the prospect of spinsterhood, she had seen salvation in Edward Morell. He would not be going to France because he was a farmer; he was good-looking, he was kind, and he was modestly well off. Still in shock from Harry Whigham's death, she accepted Edward's proposal of marriage only three months later; they were married two months after that, this being wartime and the normal conventions set aside, and it was only after the birth of James that she properly realized what she had done.

'But Julian, darling,' she said, filling her champagne glass and raising it to him for at least the dozenth time that night, 'I don't want you to think it was a bad marriage. I made Edward, your father, very happy, he never knew for an instant that he wasn't the great love of my life, and to the day he died I was certainly his.'

She said this not with any kind of conceit, but a serene conviction; Julian looked at her and leant forward and kissed her on the cheek.

'Yes,' he said, 'but what about you? Were you happy? It sounds like hell.'

'Oh, not at all,' said Letitia lightly, 'I'm not the going-through-hell sort. You of all people ought to know that. Positive, that's what we are, my angel, both of us; I made the most of it, and I was perfectly happy. There was you, and there was James, and Edward was the sweetest man on God's earth. The only really sad thing was when your little sisters died. But you know all about that, and you were a great comfort to me at the time. Even though you were only two. Now let's dance, this is getting maudlin, and then we'd better – oh, hell, there's the siren. Shall we go to the shelter or dance?'

'I'd like to dance,' said Julian, slightly reluctantly, for he had often longed to talk to her about the death of his small twin sisters, and had always been briskly discouraged, 'with the bravest and most beautiful woman in the room.'

Edward Morell had died in 1939. For the duration of the war, James ran the farm, while Julian enlisted in the Signals (rejecting the infantry regiments as too predictable), and spent a frustrated two years in England, rising to the rank of captain; finally by a combination of shameless string-pulling on the part of Letitia's cousin, a colonel in Intelligence, and some sheer bloody-minded persistence on his own, he managed to gain an interview with the SOE, the Special Operations Executive directing the British leg of the Resistance movement.

Julian had a considerable talent for languages, he was a brilliant radio operator, and he was immensely self-confident; he was sent for the preliminary selection for F Section, and passed with distinction. He then went to Scotland where he learnt such assorted skills as living off the land, handling explosives, dropping off a train moving at 40 mph and killing competently in a wide spectrum of ways. His instructor in this was a venerable-looking, white-haired gentleman who looked like a particularly benevolent academic; he personally taught Julian a Chinese method of stifling a man to death, leaving no traces whatsoever of violence. A pamphlet was produced by the Germans in 1942 describing this and some of Syke's other methods, the ultimate tribute to their efficiency.

Finally Julian was sent to an establishment in the New Forest where he was trained in the more conventional skills of espionage, ciphers, secret inks and, perhaps most crucially, of withstanding interrogation.

He was one of the youngest men on the course; permanently under suspicion because of it, he never cracked, never did anything remotely to suggest that he would be unable to deal with any of the demands made of him; he was just twenty-two when he was finally sent to France after a personal interview with the famous commander of F Section, Maurice Buckmaster.

He was not required, to his inevitable disappointment, to set lines of explosives across the Normandy countryside, or personally scale the walls of German prison camps in order to free his comrades, but what he did have to do required in its own way as much courage, as much ice-cold determination and steadfastness, and it was certainly as essential.

His task was to gather information – perfectly basic, simple information in the area around Chartres – about such unremarkable things as bus and train routes, and timetables, stamp prices, curfew regulations, and relay these things, so crucial in the planning of covers and escape routes, to SOE in London by radio. His cover was as tutor to the small son of a French countess, herself an extraordinarily brave member of the Resistance; her husband had been a colonel in the French artillery and killed in the first three months of the war. Julian's code name was Philippe Renard, his age on his forged papers given as eighteen; the image he set out to project was of someone effete, a little fey, possibly homosexual, certainly timid. It was the first time in his life that he could give rein to his considerable talents as an actor, to display his ability to climb inside another person's skin, however briefly, and he played the part brilliantly; even Amelie Dessange was half inclined to believe in it, and regarded him with a mixture of tolerance and contempt. Her small son Maurice, on the other hand, adored him and was permanently tagging along behind him, a small devoted slave. This provided further useful cover; it was easy to stand unsuspected in shop queues, at bus stops and in post offices, chatting pleasantly to the locals and asking them how best to reach such and such a place on which bus or train, with a small boy clinging to his hand.

His radio transmitter, smuggled into the Comtesse's house in the gardener's wheelbarrow, was kept in an upper attic; the door to the tiny room, leading out from one of the servants' bedrooms, was covered by a huge trunk, filled with the dead Comte's uniforms, medals and sword. Every night Julian would read to Maurice until he fell asleep, dine alone in the kitchen and then climb the stairs for his appointment with London. Sometimes there was little information, sometimes a lot; in any case he had to make contact to let them know he was safe.

36

He lived with Amelie Dessange for over a year, in a curious mixture of closeness and detachment. She was to him a remote, unsmiling figure, who occasionally asked him if he had enough to eat, or how Maurice was getting along with his lessons, always hurrying about the house, leaving it for brief spells, supposedly to visit her mother in the next village, or to take some of her garden produce to the market. He did not like her particularly, but he knew how brave she was, and how clever, and he admired her; she was not exactly beautiful, she had rather strange, strong colouring, very dark red hair and white, immensely freckled skin; her eyes, which snapped at him impatiently while she talked, were brown, dark dark brown, without a fleck of green, and her mouth was narrow and tense. But she had a certain grace, and a tension which made him very aware of her sexually; in other circumstances he would have talked to her, made her laugh, flirted with her, as it was he kept quietly to himself and allowed her to think of him whatever she wished.

One night, the Germans had come to call, as they put it, a routine visit; he was passing along the upper landing on his way to his room, and he heard them come into the hall. They meant no great harm, and there were only two of them, they were simply obeying orders and making sure nothing overtly out of order was taking place at the chateau, but Amelie was exceptionally rude that night; she shouted at them to leave her house, and when one of them put his hand on her arm, she spat at him. The other grabbed her, shouting at the old man who had opened the door to fetch the boy; Julian, racing down the stairs, watched her, panting struggling in the soldier's arms while little Maurice was led down from his bedroom in his nightgown. For a long time they all stood there; nobody spoke, nobody moved. Then the soldier tipped his gun under Maurice's chin, his eyes on Amelie's face. 'You should learn some manners, Madame la Comtesse,' he said, 'otherwise we may have to teach some to the boy.'

He flung her aside, motioned the other soldier to release Maurice, and they left, clanging the door shut behind them. Julian moved towards Amelie as she stood weeping quietly, held out his arms; she moved into them. Maurice joined them, and they stood there, the three of them holding one another in the cold dark hall, for a long time.

'Come, Maurice,' she said in the end, 'you must go back to bed. The Germans have gone, they did us no harm, and you were very brave. Jean-Michel,' she added to the old man, who was sitting silent and shaking on the stairs, looking at her helplessly like a child himself, 'you too, are you all right?'

'Yes,' he said, getting wearily to his feet, 'I'm all right. Let me take you up to your room, Maurice.'

'Maman, you come with me, please.'

The boy was white-faced, sobbing quietly, shaking with fear and cold.

'It's all right, Jean-Michel,' said Amelie, 'I'll put him back to bed. Go and take a brandy for yourself and try to sleep.'

They started up the stairs together, and Maurice looked back, holding out his hand to Julian. 'Can Philippe come too, Maman, and read me a story?'

'Of course, and I will come and hear the story too.'

Julian was reading a translation of the *Just So Stories* to Maurice. He found the stories soothing, their humour refreshing, and when he was homesick comforting, and Maurice adored them all. Tonight he read the story of The Elephant's Child, for a long time, unwilling to relinquish the mood of closeness and tenderness that bound them together; finally Maurice fell asleep and Amelie led Julian out of the room and into her sitting room.

'Brandy?'

'Yes, please.'

'Thank you for all you did tonight. You are so good for Maurice. I should have said so before. I'm sorry. And I'm glad you are here.'

'I am too,' he said, smiling at her.

'Are you really only eighteen?'

'No. A little more.'

'I thought so.'

They drank the brandy. 'Come and sit here by me,' she said, and started suddenly to cry.

'Don't,' he said, 'don't. It's all right. You're so brave.'

'I'm lonely,' she said, 'so lonely. And so hopeless.'

'Don't be. You're not alone. And we can't afford to lose hope,' he said. And he took her in his arms, simply to comfort her, and suddenly there was another mood between them, urgent, almost shocking in its violence. He turned her face to kiss it.

'No,' she said, 'not here. Maurice might come. Upstairs.'

It was the first time he had slept with anyone so sexually accomplished. He was not totally inexperienced, but the things Amelie showed him that night, a blend of gentleness and almost brutal passion, stayed with him always. They made love over and over again, until the dawn had broken, and they were both exhausted, and the world for both of them had narrowed entirely to one room, one bed; to piercing desire, to tender exploration, and again and again, the surging roar of release. In the morning she looked at him as they lay there, unable to feel anything any more but a sweet weariness, and she kissed him, all of him, first his lips, then his shoulders, his chest, his stomach, buried her face in his pubic hair, tongued his penis gently, and then raised herself on her elbow and smiled at him.

'I haven't done much of this sort of thing,' he said, taking her fingers and kissing them tenderly, one by one, 'not with anyone who – well, who knew so much. I'm not very practised.'

'You did very beautifully,' she said, in English, 'you are a fine lover. Now,' briskly, getting up from the bed and pulling on her robe, 'get up. This is not a good idea. It would get out and they would be suspicious. It must not happen again.'

It never did.

In time Julian did more challenging and dangerous work. He became, amongst other things, quite a formidable forger, and spent a year in the house of a country postman, who produced a large percentage of the documents issued to escaping prisoners en route to the South or to England.

He developed a love of Northern France and its curiously English, lush countryside; he was captured, interrogated and escaped; he spent three months of the German occupation hiding, his cover finally blown, living rough, killing wild animals, catching fish; he made himself extremely ill eating poisonous fungi he mistook for mushrooms and lay for days in a cave, too weak and in too much pain even to crawl from his own vomit. But he recovered. And he escaped from all of it, returning home in 1945 hugely changed; the charming, flippant boy a complex man, his courage and his brilliance unquestionably established. He had learnt to live with solitude and with fear; he had learnt to fix his mind absolutely on the end and to disregard the means; he had learnt to be ruthless, cruel, devious and totally pragmatic; he had learnt to trust no one but himself; to set aside sentiment, personal loyalty, and perhaps most crucially self-doubt.

Letitia looked at him as he sat before the fire in the drawing room at Maltings the night he came home, his initial joy and pleasure lost in exhaustion and hurtful memories, and realized that he had aged not five years but a lifetime.

Before her sat an old man who had seen and faced the very worst and now had to remember and live with it for the rest of his life; and the fact that he was only twenty-five years old was absolutely irrelevant.

He had lost innocence, he had lost faith in human nature, he had lost trust and to a degree he had lost happiness. And what, she wondered, gazing into the fire with him, and trying to imagine what he saw there, had he found?

Julian turned to her and smiled suddenly; aware, as he always had been, of the drift of her thoughts. 'It's all right, Mother, I'm not going to crack up on you. You mustn't worry about me. It's not all been bad.'

'Hasn't it?'

'No. A lot of it has been good.'

'In what way?'

'Oh, the loyalty, the friendship. And seeing the sheer power of people's courage. People were so brave. They risked not just death, that was the easy option; they risked terrible things: prison, torture, the capture of their families. But they went on. It was extraordinary.'

'It's a powerful thing, hope,' said Letitia. Her eyes were bright with tears.

'Yes, it is. So powerful that it worked. In the end. But it was a long time. And we couldn't forget, any of us, ever.'

'Will you go back, will you see any of them again?'

'I don't know. I might. It's hard to know. Nothing would be the same. After being so close, knowing such trust, such – well, love I suppose. Could you go back just on an idle visit? I don't think so.'

'Maybe not.' She was silent. 'Where did you live? How did you live?'

'Oh, all kinds of places. All over Northern France. With Amelie Dessange, I told you about her, for a long time. I stayed on a farm for a while, labouring, towards the end. I lived rough for a while, as you know. Most recently I was further up the coast, quite near Deauville, lodging with a funny old chap. You'd have liked him. He was a chemist. Still is, of course. He escaped. God knows how. Only one in his family who did.' He was quiet suddenly, his jaw tightening; he took a gulp of whisky and then looked at her and tried to smile.

'Knowing him was very good for me. It's given me lots of ideas. In fact I know what I want to do now. With my life, I mean.'

'What, my darling?' said Letitia, turning the evening determinedly back into a positive occasion. 'Tell me. I've thought about it so much, I do hope it's not a career in the Foreign Office. Or the army.'

'God forbid,' said Julian, 'they both require a degree of self-abnegation, and I've had quite enough of that. No, I want to go into the pharmaceutical business. And possibly cosmetics.'

'Julian, darling,' said Letitia, half amused, half astonished, 'whatever gave you that idea?'

'Oh,' said Julian, his eyes dancing, enjoying her slight unease with the situation and this rather unmasculine notion. 'This old boy. I worked in his lab with him quite a lot. You know I loved chemistry at school. I'd have read it at Oxford if the war hadn't happened.'

'Do you think you'll ever want to go now?' said Letitia. 'They said they'd keep your place.'

'No. Fooling around with a lot of kids. Couldn't possibly.'

'It's a pity in a way.'

'So are lots of things.'

'I suppose so.'

'Well, anyway, you'd be surprised what I learnt. I can make all kinds of things. A jolly good cough mixture. A sleeping draught. Anti-inflammatory medicine. All sorts. And then I started fiddling around with creams and lotions and that sort of thing.'

'Do you mean skin creams?'

'Yes.'

'Darling,' said Letitia, patting his hand, 'I'd sell my soul for something like that. All you can buy now is Pond's Cold Cream. Too awful. You didn't bring any of your creams back with you, did you?'

'Fraid not. But I have got the formulas. And when I've settled down a bit I thought I'd fix up some sort of lab in one of the outhouses and play about a bit. It's fascinating stuff, Mother. I know it's an odd thing to bring back with you from the war, but there it is. I think I could make a business of it. It must be better than an addiction to pornography, or the burning desire to write a manual on fifty-five new ways to kill a man. So many of the chaps got bitter and defeated.'

'Weren't you afraid of that?' said Letitia.

'No, not at all. I knew I wouldn't, I wouldn't allow it.'

It was an extraordinarily revealing remark. Letitia took it in, put it temporarily aside, and then turned back to the future.

'I love the idea, Julian, but how are you going to get started? It's not a world that either of us knows a lot about.'

'No,' said Julian, accepting her involvement without question, 'but we can learn. Would you like to help?'

'Of course I would. I'd love to. But I haven't got any money. Not on the scale you'd need, anyway. And James certainly hasn't. It's no use looking here for backing. And I can't imagine there will be any about for quite a long while.'

'I didn't mean money. You can always find money if you've got ideas. And I've got lots. And anyway there's going to be a big boom in a year or two, you see. People will be spending money like there's no tomorrow. Or rather there was no yesterday. To annihilate. To forget.' Another silence. 'So I do think it's an excellent time. Both to raise money and to start new ventures. And I really would appreciate your help. I know you'd be very good at it all. Where are you going?'

'To get a bottle of wine. To toast your future.'

'Our future,' said Julian firmly. 'Our company.'

He was right: there was a boom. But it was a little longer coming than he had anticipated. The first two years after the war were almost as austere as the preceding five. Companies were manufacturing as fast as they could but the Attlee

Government was obsessed with economic recovery and everything worth having was being exported. One of the more enraging sights of 1946 was a windowful of desirable things bearing the message 'for export only'. Everything the heart and indeed the stomach could desire was still rationed; and without the patriotic fervour of war to ease the pangs, people were growing immensely irritable.

One night James Morell, who had become increasingly estranged from his brother, came in from the farm, sat down and ate his supper without a word, and then, taking a deep breath, announced that he would like Julian to move out of Maltings; he was planning on getting married, he said, and sharing a home with anyone, however agreeable, was not a good beginning to any marriage. The house was his, he ran the farm, Julian had been talking for months about how he was going to start his own business; it was time, James felt, that he went and got on with it. He had some money, after all; James was tired of supporting him.

Julian, first amused, became irritable; his outrage increased when Letitia took James' side and said she quite agreed, that he should go, and that she had no intention of encroaching on James' marital status either.

'We shall go to London together, and start a new life,' she said, somewhat dramatically, adding that James was perfectly right in his view, that Julian had been talking about his plans for quite long enough and that it was time he put them into practice.

'It's all very well,' said Julian, reeling slightly at this double onslaught, 'but I don't have any money, I can't get a house in London. Or start a business. There's no money to be had anywhere.'

'Oh, for heaven's sake,' said Letitia, 'have you not heard of the mortgage? And you have some money your father left you. You said yourself only the other day that it was melting away, as if that fact had nothing to do with you. Very silly. I've thought so for a long time. And anyway, I've got a little money. We'll manage.'

James, relieved that the interview with his mother and brother had been less embarrassing and painful than he had feared, said he thought he would go and visit Caroline Reever Smith, the noisily good-natured object of his affections, and hurriedly left; Julian looked at Letitia over the supper table a trifle darkly.

'Thanks for your support,' he said. 'I hope you realize you've just talked us out of a home.'

'Oh, Julian, don't be so ridiculous. You sound like a spoilt child. Of course I haven't. Where is your spirit of adventure? I've talked us into a new one. It'll be the greatest fun. I've been thinking about it for quite a long time, as a matter of fact. Now, I think we should live in Chelsea. In fact I don't want to contemplate living anywhere else. Goodness, I can't even begin to believe it after all these years. Just off Walton Street, I think: Harrods round the corner, Peter Jones down the road, Harvey Nichols, Woolland's.'

'You sound as if you're reciting a litany,' said Julian, laughing.

'I am. I feel exactly like someone who's been excommunicated, and just been allowed back into the fold.'

'All right, I don't care where we go. Lots of pretty girls in Chelsea anyway.'

'Lots. Now darling, you've also got to think about premises. For your business. Let's forget about starting big and waiting for the banks, and just start. All you need is something very modest, a big garage even would do for now, which you could fit out as a lab. I expect you could contract out any kind of bottling and labelling. The thing to do at this stage is get the biggest mortgage available on the house, and keep your capital for the business. You'll find that harder to raise money for, and you'll get a bigger tax concession on a personal mortgage than anything. Anyway, I'll put in any money I can rake up. I've been meaning to sell a few shares anyway, they're just beginning to recover nicely. Only I'll leave it as long as I can.'

'Mother, you really are full of surprises,' said Julian looking at her in genuine admiration, 'first cash-flow forecasting for the farm, then capital investment programme for Morell Pharmaceuticals, all in one evening. You will be financial director, won't you? And my factory manager as well?'

'Until I get a better offer,' said Letitia. 'Of course I will, Julian, I've always loved the idea of money and business and

44

making more. It excites me. Only it's something I've never had much of a chance to do anything about in the wilds of Wiltshire. I've often tried to suggest improvements and investment on the farm, but James and your father would never listen to me.'

'Well, I'll listen. Gratefully. And as often as I can. And now while we're in such communicative mood, Mother, and I've sat so politely while you put me just ever so gently in my place, will you tell me something? Something I've always wanted to know?'

'I can't imagine what,' said Letitia, just a trifle too lightly.

'Yes, you can. The twins.'

'What about the twins?'

'Well, I don't know, I just know there was more to that than you've ever admitted. Some mystery. Something strange.'

'Nonsense. Nothing of the sort. They were born ... prematurely. They died. Nothing more to tell than that.' But her eyes shadowed, and her jaw tightened; Julian watching her felt the emotion struggling in her.

'Mother, please tell me. If it's something that concerns me in some way, I have a right to know what it is. And I can find out anyway. I think James has some idea about it.'

'Why?' said Letitia sharply.

'Oh, the odd thing he's said. One night, when we were talking, just after I got home. About how there seemed to be a mystery about it all. How various people still gossiped about it. About all of us. He clammed up after that, wouldn't say any more. But I shall just pester him if you won't tell me.'

Letitia looked at him for a long time. Then she sighed and stood up.

'Where are you going?'

'To pour myself a stiff drink,' she said. 'And one for you. I will tell you. If only to stop you worrying James with it. I had no idea that gossip was still going on. Of course he would never ask me, he's much too shy. You do have a right to know, I suppose. And it does concern you. You, but not James. So I would much rather you didn't talk to him about it. Will you promise me that, Julian?'

'Of course.' He watched her as she sat down again. 'I'm very intrigued now, Mother,' he said, as lightly as he could, knowing, sensing what he was to hear was hugely important for both of them. 'I can't imagine what you're going to tell me.'

45

'No,' she said, 'no you couldn't possibly.'

He listened, as she told him, in complete silence; afterwards he sat for a long time, just holding her hand and watching the fire, marvelling at her courage and at the human capacity for love and its power to keep silent.

Chapter Two

London, 1948–51

Julian and Letitia Morell settled into life in London with a kind of joyous relief, falling hungrily on its pleasures and feeling they were both for the first time in their proper habitat. They bought a pretty little terrace house in First Street, just off Walton Street ('I can smell Harrods,' said Letitia contentedly), four tiny floors, one above the other. Property prices were just setting off on their dizzy postwar course and they got it just in time; it cost two thousand pounds and they were lucky. It was charmingly shabby, but quite unspoilt; it had belonged to an old lady, who had resolutely refused to leave it until the very last All Clear sounded, when she had finally agreed to join her family in the depths of Somerset and promptly died. They acquired much of her furniture along with the house, some of it treasures, including some extremely valuable Indian and Persian carpets, but for the most part rather too heavily Victorian for the light sunny little house. Almost everything at Maltings was too big and although James was guiltily generous, urging them to take anything they wanted, neither of them felt they should bring too many remnants of their old life into the new. Letitia brought the Sheraton escritoire and four exquisite eighteenth-century drawing room chairs left to her by her grandmother and Julian salvaged a Regency card table which had belonged to his father before his marriage and an ornate seventeenth-century bracket clock which had always looked rather overdressed on the fireplace at Maltings. 'It's a towny clock,' he said to Letitia, 'we should take it where it will feel more at home.' Apart from that, he left everything, except a set of first-edition prints of the *Just So Stories* which had been a present from his godfather, and which he said reminded him of one of the happier episodes in the war.

They managed to find a few pretty things – a brass-headed bed for Letitia, who said she had always longed for one, a small Hepplewhite-style sideboard, and an enchanting love seat for the drawing room – all at country-house sales. The London shops were beginning to look a little less stark, but there was nothing either Julian or Letitia really felt right for their playhouse, as Letitia called it, so they hunted for curtains and fabrics as well. Letitia rescued her old Singer machine from Maltings and set to work, cutting down and adapting huge dusty brocades they acquired at a sale, and hanging them at her new drawing room windows.

They were altogether perfectly happy: it was Royal Wedding Year and Princess Elizabeth was planning her wedding to the dashing Prince Philip; London was in party mood, and very busy in every way; bombed theatres (most notably the Old Vic) were being rebuilt, and galleries and museums reopened, holding out their treasures proudly for inspection again, after years of fearful concealment. The social scene was frantic, as people struggled to re-create a normal pleasurable life; Julian and Letitia lunched, shopped and gossiped, went to the theatre (Letitia daringly bought seats for *A Streetcar Named Desire*, but actually confessed to preferring *Brigadoon*), and the cinema (Julian's own special favourite being *The Secret Life of Walter Mitty*, which he saw three times), and listened to concerts. Julian also launched himself on a lifetime passion for cars, and bought himself a prewar Wolseley saloon, scorning the Utility-style modern models, and feeling, as he settled into its soft deep leather seat, and behind its huge steering wheel, that this was for him precisely what First Street and the proximity of Harrods was for Letitia: a wholly desirable place to be.

And they entertained and were entertained tirelessly, a charming if slightly eccentric couple, providing in one deliciously simple package a single man and the perfect excuse to invite him anywhere. No hostess need fear she might appear herself to be pursuing Julian Morell, so charming, so hand-some, so delightfully available, but still not quite yet a properly known commodity, or to be hurling him rather precipitately at her single women friends, when he could so easily and without any embarrassment be invited to dinner with his mother. And then such was Mrs Morell's grace, wit and beauty that no dinner table could be other than adorned by her, no young people could consider her an assault on their fun.

It became a game in the early days, before the Morells were properly well known in London, for a hostess to tell her guests that she had invited a charming, single man to dinner, but that she had been obliged to ask his mother as well, as she was all alone in London; and then to watch the faces of her guests – particularly the men – braced with bright smiles, soften into pleasure, admiration and undisguised relief as Letitia came into the room. Another version of the same game, and one Letitia and Julian tacitly joined in, was for them to be introduced as Letitia and Julian Morell and to leave the rest of the gathering to try to fathom quite what their relationship was. Sometimes when the stakes were high, and there was a particularly pretty girl or attractive man at the table (for Letitia was enjoying her new social success quite as much as Julian), they would draw the thing out until well into the second or third course, waiting for precisely the right moment to drop the words 'my mother' or 'my son' into the conversation, and then savouring the various degrees of amusement, pleasure and irritation that followed. It was hard to say which of them was enjoying themselves more.

Letitia, looking back at the long, lonely years at Maltings, the stiff country dinner parties, the boring conversations about cattle and yield, land and horses, stock prices and servants, the red-faced men, stuffy when sober, lecherous when drunk, and their loyal, large braying wives, wondered how she had borne it. Suddenly the world was full of charming, amusing people and gossip; she would sit at supper, quite unable to swallow sometimes for pleasure and excitement and fear of missing a gem, or better still the opportunity to pass one on. She had a genius for gossip herself, she filed things away neatly in her head, cross-referenced under people and places, a treasure trove of meetings, conversations, glances, jokes, and she would produce a piece of it at exactly the right moment, knowing precisely how to silence a table with a wicked announcement, or how to intrigue a group with a perfectly innocent observation. She did it not only cleverly, but with great charm; she flattered those whose reputation she was shredding, bestowing virtues and beauty upon people who possessed neither and giving her conversations a deceptively benign air.

'That little Serena Motcombe,' she would say, 'such a lovely girl, you know she paints quite beautifully, I saw her at lunch last week with Toby Ferranti, he was looking quite marvellous and did you know that Lady Brigstocke is learning to ride, she looks wonderful, I saw her in the Park on Tuesday with David Berner, I believe he's trying to get back into polo, and of course William Brigstocke is the most marvellous player . . .' and so it went on and on, a glittering wicked chronicle. But it was not malicious; Letitia had a shrewd eye and a tender heart and where she saw true love, real pain, she was friend, confidante, ally and counsel; she would provide alibis, divert suspicion, and even provide venues for meetings that could take place absolutely nowhere else.

She was having a glorious time.

So was Julian. He was now twenty-seven, with that ability to disturb that truly sexually accomplished men possess; another dimension beyond good looks, attractiveness or even ordinary sexuality. His entry to a room caused women to fall suddenly into confusion, to lose the place in their conversation, to glance at their reflections, to smooth their hair; and men to feel threatened and aggressive, to look sharply at their wives, to form a closer group, while greeting him at the same time most warmly, shaking his hand and inquiring after his health and his business.

With good reason; Julian was a most adroit adulterer, seducing quite ruthlessly wherever he chose with a careless skill, and he greatly preferred the company and attentions of married women, not only because of their greater experience in bed but because of the excitement and danger of getting them there. There was more than one marriage in London in the savage winter and glorious spring of 1948 ripped apart as a wife found herself propelled by a force she was quite unable to resist into first the arms and then the bed of Julian Morell.

There was nothing original about Julian's approach; but he was simply and pleasurably aware of the fact that women became suddenly and uncomfortably sexually tautened by the most mundane conversation with him, and that by the end of a dinner party at his side or even an encounter at a cocktail party, or a theatre interval, would feel an extraordinarily strong urge to take their husbands home to bed and screw them relentlessly. (Indeed, husbands in the early stages of their wives' affairs with Julian Morell had rather more reason to be grateful to him than they would ever know.) This made his progression into lunch and from there into long afternoons in bed extraordinarily easy. He knew exactly how to distract and discomfort women, how to throw them into a passion of emotional desire; long before he turned his attention to their physical needs, he would talk to them, and more than talk, listen, laugh at their jokes, look seriously on their concerns, encourage their thinking. He would send flowers with funny, quirky messages, make outrageous phone calls pretending to be someone else should their husbands answer the phone, hand-deliver silly notes, and give small thoughtful presents: a record of some song or piece of music they had heard together, a tiny antique pill box with a love letter folded up tightly inside it, a book of poetry with some particularly poignant piece carefully marked – the kind of things, in fact, that most women eating out their hearts in the sweet agony of an illicit love affair yearn for and which most men entirely fail to give them or even consider.

He was a brilliant lover in precisely the same way: it was not just his sexual skills, his capacity to arouse, to deepen, to sharpen sexual pleasure, to bring the most tearful, the most reticent women to shatteringly triumphant orgasm; it was his tenderness, his appreciation, his patience that earned him their gratitude, and their love.

The gratitude and the acquiescence were one thing, the love quite another; in his early days Julian found himself in quite extraordinarily delicate situations as poised cool mistresses suddenly metamorphosed into feverish, would-be wives, ready to confess, to pack, to leave husband, children and home and follow him to whichever end of the earth he might choose to lead them. It took all Julian's skills to handle these situations; gently, patiently, through long fearful afternoons in slowly darkening bedrooms (it was another factor in Julian's success that he was at this point in his life partially unemployed) he would persuade them that they would be losing infinitely more than they would gain, that he was making a sacrifice just as big as their own, and he would leave them feeling just sufficiently warmly towards him to prevent them speaking too harshly of him, and just humiliated enough to be unwilling to reveal the extent of their involvement to any of their friends.

For his first six months or so in London this was the high wire he walked, permanently exhilarated by his success, his only safety net his own deviousness. After that, he grew not only more cautious but busier, involved in the birth of his business and the development of his talents in rather more conventional and fruitful directions. It was a perfect time for him; the boom he had prophesied had finally arrived, and there was a bullish attitude in the country. Investment was available for sound propositions, ideas were the top-selling commodity.

Perhaps most happily for Julian, fashion was being reborn. Not just clothes, not foolish frivolity, nor even a burgeoning industry, it was a serious matter, one worthy of sober consideration and artistic merit. The Royal College of Art had opened its school of fashion design in 1948 with Madge Garland, an ex-editor of *Vogue*, as its professor. People talked about fashion and the design of clothes as something seriously important. Moreover, it was big business. The effect of M. Dior's New Look had been staggering. Not only was it revolutionary in look, but in attitude. In three dizzy hours in the February of 1947 it spelt the end of economy as a virtue and of fashion as a sin; after six years of skimpy skirts and square shoulders, here were clothes that caressed the body, clung to the waist and swirled around the ankles in glorious extravagance. Women didn't just like it, or even want it, they yearned for it, they demanded it, they had to have it. The rich flocked to Paris; the ready-to-wear houses copied it within days and it sold and sold and sold.

It was considered unpatriotic, which only lent it more glamour; questions were not quite asked in the House, but Sir Stafford Cripps called a meeting of the major British designers to try to persuade them to keep the short skirt popular, and another of fashion editors to tell them to instruct women to ignore the long; and Mrs Bessie Braddock, the stout and aggressively unfashionable Labour MP, took women to task for caring so passionately about something so frivolous. Princess Margaret promptly negated any impression Mrs Braddock might have made by appearing constantly in the New Look. It all added up to a defiant, almost reckless approach to anything to do with clothes and looks; and made it an excellent time to be involved in cosmetics.

The Morell empire began life as a cough mixture. It was a perfectly ordinary cough mixture (called unimaginatively, if graphically, Morell's Cough Linctus), in three flavours: lemon, cherry, and blackcurrant, but it had two important selling points. The first was that it tasted extraordinarily good, and children therefore loved it; the second was that it worked. Given to tired children in the night by tireder parents, it had them asleep again in ten minutes, their coughing silenced, their throats soothed. The reason for both factors was in the formulation, for which the parents and the children had to thank an old man working in the back room of a *pharmacie* in a small town near Deauville, but this was long before a Trades Description Act could prevent anybody from saying anything very much, and Julian had an ingenious and laterally thinking mind. Thus the linctus bore the legend 'specially formulated for night-time coughs'.

There was no question of there being any money for advertising, and the labels stuck on the bottles by the hands of the bored housewives of West Ealing, where Morell Pharmaceuticals had its headquarters in an ex-WRVS canteen, were simply printed in white on red, with no embellishments of any kind except a border of medicine spoons twisted together, which was to become the Morell company logo. Nevertheless, the simple message was successfully and powerfully conveyed.

Julian sold the product into the chemists' shops himself, driving huge distances in his Wolseley saloon, its big boot and passenger seats crammed with samples. The pharmacists, used to being fobbed off by crass young salesmen, were charmed by the intelligent, courteous man who could discuss formulae with them and who would always meet orders, even if it meant him personally driving hundreds of miles overnight to do so; originally reluctant to stock the medicine, those who did so invariably came back for more, and because of the conversations they had had with Julian about formulae, would recommend it to distracted mothers and worried grandmothers and anxious nannies with rather more confidence than usual.

The worried mothers, having experienced its considerable effectiveness and coughs being a constantly recurring problem in the pre-antibiotic era, came back for more and still more, recommended it to their friends, and took to keeping a spare bottle permanently in their medicine cupboard, a suggestion added to the original label as a result of one of Julian's overnight delivery drives, the time he always had his best ideas.

They trod a delicate path, he and Letitia; their capital had all gone and they lived very much from hand to mouth. The pharmacists were slow to pay, and he had difficulty getting credit for his raw materials. They fortunately had paid cash for their factory building, and had First Street on a mortgage; but for two months they were unable to meet the payment on that. 'It's too ridiculous,' said Letitia cheerfully, over breakfast one morning, looking up from a pained letter from the building society, 'here we are, dining out every night with the very best people in London – just as well or we'd be quite hungry a lot of the time – and we are threatened with having the roof removed from over our heads.'

Julian looked at her warily. 'What do you mean?'

'What I say, darling. The building society are threatening to repossess the house.'

'Oh God,' he said. 'What on earth do we do now?'

'You don't do anything,' said Letitia firmly, 'just get on with delivering today's orders and pressing them all for payment. I'm the financial director, I'll go and see the bank.'

Which she did; Julian never quite knew what she said to the manager, but he saw her leaving the house, a suddenly much smaller and drabber figure in her oldest clothes, her face devoid of make-up, a plentiful supply of lace-trimmed handkerchiefs in her shabbiest handbag, and returned to his duties as sales manager feeling the future of the company and the home of its directors were in very safe hands.

Before going out to dine with the Countess of Lincoln that night, they drank to their modestly generous new overdraft facility in gin and tonic minus the gin, and Letitia assured him they had a breathing space of precisely two months and one week before their cash-flow situation became critical once more.

'And now I am going to go and get ready; I've bought a most lovely new dress, with a hundred yards of material in it and a pair of those marvellous platform soles exactly like Princess Margaret's, just wait till you see them.'

'Mother, how can you possibly afford new clothes when we can't buy gin or pay the mortgage?' said Julian, laughing.

'Oh, darling, I have my account at Harrods and they are dreadfully patient about payment, and we certainly can't afford to go round looking as if we haven't got any money.'

'Mother,' said Julian, 'I don't know what you're doing working for this company. I'm surprised you're not chairman, or whatever a woman would be, of the Bank of England.'

'Oh,' said Letitia, 'I very likely will be one day. I'm just doing my apprenticeship. Now, what you have to do, Julian, is take a very hard look at those customers of yours and which ones aren't paying you quickly enough. We can't afford charity.'

Julian was certainly not over charitable with his customers, nor was he yet in a position to refuse delivery to slow payers (although he had learnt which of his customers warranted more time and attention than others); but he was learning pragmatism in places other than the bedroom. One of his very first orders came from an old man called Bill Gibson in a small chemist shop in North London; he had taken two cases of the cough linctus and paid Julian on the spot; moreover he had told other friends in the business to see him and take some of his wares as well. Julian owed him a lot and he knew it. Bill had a struggle to keep his shop going, but it was the only living he had, or knew how to manage, and he had no pension to look forward to, it was literally his lifeblood. Besides he loved it, and was proud of it, it gave him a footing of immense respectability and responsibility in the neighbourhood and since the death of his wife it was literally all he had. He lived in permanent dread of his landlord realizing the asset he had and selling his premises over his head.

Six months after launching his company, Julian had still not managed to break into any of the big or even even medium-sized chemist chains; he knew that not only would it make all the difference to his cash flow as well as his order books, it would give him a stature in the industry that so far he lacked.

One night over dinner he met a man called Paul Learmount, who was building up a nice line of business in outer London, buying run-down shops at cheap prices and converting them into cut-price chemist shops; he was looking for another in Bill Gibson's area, did Julian know of any? Julian said he did, that he happened to know a place that exactly fitted Paul's description, and moreover he could put him in touch with the landlord. Four weeks later, Bill Gibson was served notice on his premises, a brash young manager arrived to refurbish the shop, and Julian got a huge order from Learmount's central buying office.

He took Bill Gibson out to lunch, commiserated with him over his bad luck and insisted on giving him a cheque for fifty pounds to keep him going 'until you find your feet again. I'll never forget what I owe you, after all, Bill.' To his dying day, Bill Gibson spoke glowingly of Mr Morell and the way he never forgot to send him a card at Christmas time.

Within another three months demand was exceeding supply to an almost worrying extent; Julian failed to meet a couple of orders, nearly lost a crucial account, and realized he had to double both his manufacturing staff and his sales force.

This meant hiring two people: a salesman, to cover the half of the country he couldn't efficiently reach himself, and a second pharmacist. His original pharmacist, a laconic Scotsman called Jim Macdougall, worked tirelessly, twice round the clock if necessary, performing the extremely repetitive task of filling up to five hundred bottles of linctus a day without complaint on the most primitive equipment imaginable, as well as working in his spare time on Morell Pharmaceuticals' second product, an indigestion tablet.

The assistant Julian presented him with was a pretty young war widow called Susan Johns.

Corporal Brian Johns had been parachuted into the woods near Lyons late one night while Julian had still been living at the chateau. He had been involved in the pick-up and was responsible for arranging Johns' transport to a nearby farm, and his liaison with another agent. Johns was only twenty, nearly two years younger than Julian, married with two little girls, and a brilliant radio operator; he was bringing forged papers from London with him for French agents.

Julian was looking forward to his arrival; he had been feeling particularly lonely and homesick, his work had grown increasingly tedious and futile-seeming, and the thought of some English company was very pleasant.

He waited where Johns was to come down; it was a horribly bright night, but the drop had been postponed three times, and the need for the forged papers was desperate. Fortunately a bombing raid just south of Lyons had distracted the patrolling Germans for most of the night; Corporal Johns reached the ground unobserved by anyone except Julian. That was, however, the last of his good fortune. He landed awkwardly and fell heavily on some rocks; Julian heard him swear, then groan, and then nothing. He had broken both his legs; he was, for a while, mercifully unconscious. He came to in agony to see Julian bending over him.

'Johns?'

'Yes.'

'Sorry, but I have to do this. Is your aunt still alive?'

'She is, and has moved down to Nantes,' said Johns, answering the coded question, and promptly passed out again.

Julian managed to get him to the farm. It was a mile and a half away, half carrying and half dragging him, and it took a nightmare three hours. He had never seen anyone in such pain, never personally felt such fear; the woods were frequently patrolled and he knew if they were caught they would face, at the very best, death. Johns was unbelievably brave, but from time to time a groan escaped him and once, when Julian tripped into a rabbit hole and let him fall to the ground, he screamed. They lay in the undergrowth for what seemed like hours, sweating, listening, shuddering with fear; Julian, glancing at Johns' face in the moonlight, saw tears of pain on it, and blood on his lip where he had bitten it almost through in an effort to control himself, and for the thousandth time since he had arrived in France marvelled at the power of human courage and will.

He found more of it at the farm, which was already under surveillance; they took Johns in without a moment's hesitation, hid him in a barn, poured a bottle of brandy into him, and did what they could with his poor, shattered legs. They dared not get a doctor, but the farmer's wife had some nursing skills; she made some splints and set them as best she could. Julian, forcing himself to watch as Johns endured this fresh agony, reflected that if his horse had been in such hopeless pain, he would have shot her without hesitation.

For two days Johns lay in the barn; Julian spent a lot of time with him. Plans were being made, an escape route being established, for his safe removal from the farm, and from France, but it meant danger for a lot of people, and Johns knew it. The Gestapo had already searched the farm twice in the past week and every peaceful hour that passed merely led them inexorably towards the next time.

Johns was plagued by guilt as much as by pain. 'I'm so fucking bloody stupid,' he kept saying, 'so fucking, fucking stupid.'

Julian, unable to offer any relief from either the guilt or the pain, except ceaseless administration of the rough French brandy which only succeeded in the end in making Johns violently ill, encouraged him to talk, listening for long hours to rambling stories of Johns' childhood (not long behind him), of his marriage to his childhood sweetheart, Susan, and the birth of their two little girls. In the three years since the beginning of the war, they had spent six weeks together. He gave Julian her address and made him promise to go and find her 'in case I don't get back.'

'Oh, don't be so bloody stupid,' said Julian, 'of course you'll get back. They're working on the final details now. Another day or two and you'll be back in a British hospital with an endless supply of morphine.'

'Sure,' said Johns, and Julian knew he didn't believe him.

He was silent for a bit, and then he said, 'Do you know what I'd really like, sir?'

'A bit of crumpet?' said Julian in what he knew was a horribly inappropriate bit of flippancy.

'Well, that too, sir. Don't think I'd do anyone much justice, though. But even more than that, sir, I'd like a cup of tea. Strong, and lots of sugar. Could you manage that for me, do you think? I'd be very grateful.'

'Of course,' said Julian, relieved to be able to do anything so constructive.

He came back to find Johns looking calm and composed, almost peaceful. 'Feeling better?'

'Yes, sir, yes I am. In a way. You've been very good to me, sir. I do appreciate it. I'm a bit of a liability, aren't I?'

'Well,' said Julian, smiling at him, 'I can't pretend you're an enormous help at the moment. But don't worry, Johns, you will be. We'll get our pound of flesh. And I expect one hell of a bender at your expense when we finally get back home.'

'Right you are, sir. You're on.'

He looked at Julian, and Julian looked at him, and they both could see with awesome clarity what the other was thinking.

'I think I might have a nap,' said Johns, suddenly brisk. 'I think I'd like to be alone for a bit, sir, if you don't mind.'

'Sure,' said Julian. 'Sorry to keep rabbiting on.'

'Oh, no, don't apologize, I've enjoyed this evening.'

Jesus God, thought Julian, the poor sod's in absolute fucking agony, shitting himself with pain, and he manages to tell me he's enjoyed himself.

'Good,' he said, 'anything else I can get you?'

'Well, yes, sir, there is. My rucksack. There's just a few things in it I'd like to go through. Pictures of Susie, and the little ones. Odds and ends. Would you mind? It'd help me to settle.'

'Of course. I buried it at the back of the barn. Won't be a tick.'

He gave it to Johns; he knew what was in it, what Johns really wanted, and Johns knew that he knew. 'Good night, Johns. God bless you.' He was surprised to hear those particular words come out; it was not a phrase he was in the habit of using. But it meant comfort and home; it was childhood and happiness; it was safety and courage.

Johns smiled. 'I hope so, sir.'

Julian heard the pistol go off before he reached the house; he stumbled as if he had been hit himself, and felt hot tears in his eyes. 'Stupid fuckers,' was all he could say, 'stupid, stupid fuckers.' And he said it over and over again in a kind of blind, hopeless fury as he dug a grave and buried Johns. When he had finished he sat and looked at the sky for a long time, and promised himself that the very first thing he would do when the war was over was find Susan Johns and tell her that her husband had been the bravest man in the whole of France. He wrote when he returned to England and told her that her husband had been shot by the Germans and hadn't known anything at all about it; it seemed the only way he could salvage any comfort for her, and indeed even when he knew her quite well, he never told her the truth.

He had quite a lot of trouble finding her when he came home. The street she had lived in, the address Johns had given him, had been completely levelled, but he doggedly followed a trail which the woman at the corner shop gave him, and finally found her living in Acton with her two little girls, doing shift work at a soap factory. He kept in close contact with her; he liked her, she was pretty and immensely brave. She was also very bright. When he first found her she was deeply depressed, due as much, he thought, to her enforced cohabitation with an appalling mother as the loss of a husband she had hardly known; he would take her out to tea at Lyons' Corner House where she ate hugely and unselfconsciously ('You would too,' she said when he first commented on her enormous appetite, 'if you had to live on what my mum produces. A hundred and one ways with dried egg, and they're all the same'), and encouraged her to talk about her life, about her two little girls and the hopelessness of her situation, and what she would have liked to do if things had been different; surprisingly it was not to live in domestic bliss with her Brian (or another Brian) for evermore, but to get a job working as a pharmacist.

'I liked chemistry at school, and I always fancied playing around with all those bottles, and mixing medicines.'

'Well, why don't you try to do it now?' he said, watching her with a mixture of admiration and amusement as she spread jam on her fourth toasted teacake.

'Because I couldn't cope with all the drama,' she said. 'Mum would go on and on, saying I'd got a perfectly good job already, and what did I want to change it for, and moan because it would mean more work and worry for her while I was getting it together, and anyway I might not be any good at it, and then where would I be? On the National Assistance. No, 'fraid it's not to be. But I would have liked it. Can I have one of those cream cakes, please?'

'Of course. Well, I promise you one thing, Mrs Johns. I may have just the job for you myself one day, when my company gets off the ground, and then I shall come and offer you riches beyond the dreams of avarice to do it for me.'

'Oh, yeah?' she said, grinning at him, and pausing momentarily in her task of choosing precisely which of the four cakes before her was the jammiest and the sickliest. 'Pull the other one.'

Julian was surprised by how hurt he felt. 'I mean it. Just you wait and see.'

'OK. I'll have the doughnut, please.'

It was with a degree of self-satisfaction therefore, and a strong temptation to say that he had told her so, when he took her out (to the Kardomah this time) and offered her the job as laboratory assistant in Morell Pharmaceuticals. But if he was expecting her to be impressed and grateful, he was disappointed.

'Thank you for asking me,' she said, spreading her teacake with honey and tipping half the sugar bowl into her cup (her mother's cooking had not improved along with the raw ingredients available to her), 'but I really don't think so. I don't think I could.'

'Oh, nonsense, of course you could. It's not difficult and it's a lot more interesting than putting soap into boxes –'

'Cartons,' said Susan pedantically.

'– and you'd enjoy it.'

'Oh, I don't mean I couldn't do it, of course I could, and I daresay yes, I would enjoy it, but how would I ever get there every day? And how do I know you won't go bust and leave me out of a job? And what would I tell Mum? She wouldn't like it.'

'Tell Mum she isn't going to get it,' said Julian lightly, and was vaguely surprised and pleased when she laughed. 'You can get there on a bus, it's not far, and whenever I can I'll give you a lift, I can easily come your way. You don't know I won't go bust, but if you work your backside off and help me, I probably won't. Come on, Susan, it'll cheer you up and it's a terrific opportunity for you. You could end up as managing director of Morell Pharmaceuticals.'

'Oh, yeah,' said Susan, 'and pigs might fly. Girls don't get to be managing directors, Mr Morell, at least not if they went to secondary mods and have two kids to worry about.'

'Well, that's just where you might be wrong. I believe in women. I think they're terrific.'

'Yeah, I bet you do. Between the sheets.'

'No, Susan.' Julian was angry suddenly. He pushed his hair back and stirred his tea so hard it slopped into the saucer. 'That's very unfair. If I thought women were only good for sex, I wouldn't be offering you a job, would I? I'd be looking for a man. And trying to seduce you instead of employing you.'

Susan looked him very straight in the eyes. 'You wouldn't bother seducing me,' she said. 'Girls like me don't belong in your world.'

'Susan,' said Julian, 'I would very much like to bother seducing you. I think you're lovely. I think you're brave and pretty and clever. But I wouldn't insult you, that's the point. I want you to do something much more important than going to bed with me. I want you to work for me. How do I make you understand?'

Susan smiled suddenly. 'You just have. And thank you. That's the nicest thing anyone ever said to me. Ever. Except for Brian when he first asked me to marry him. All right, let's get down to business.'

'Does that mean you'll come?'

'I don't know. How much are you going to pay me?'

'Four pounds a week.'

'Not enough.'

Julian was impressed.

'It's the going rate.'

'Yes, but it's a risk.'

'All right. Five pounds. But that's bloody good and you'll have to earn it.'

'I will. Don't worry.' She was silent for a bit, thinking. 'OK. I'd like to come very much. Thanks. Now I must go and collect Jenny and Sheila. They're with the child minder.'

'Is she good?'

'She's OK. I don't have much choice. She's kind enough. You can't hope for much more.'

'And how are they?'

'All right. Jenny's a bit delicate. She's got a cough. It keeps both of them awake at night. And Sheila has a lot of tummy upsets.'

Julian handed her two bottles of Morell's Cherry Linctus. 'Try this. I think you'll find it'll help.'

'Thanks. When do I start?'

'Monday week. That'll give you time to give in your notice. Honestly, Susan, you are doing the right thing. Shall we drink to our association?'

'Not with alcohol, I hate what it does to people. So let's stick to tea.'

'All right,' said Julian. 'I don't think the Kardomah has a very good wine list, as a matter of fact.' He smiled at her and raised his cup. 'To you. And me. And Morell Pharmaceuticals. Long may we all prosper.'

Susan clinked her cup against his. 'Cheers. And thank you. Especially for saying you'd rather I worked for you than went to bed with you. That's really nice.'

'That's all right,' said Julian, slightly surprised by the pleasure she took in what she might well have considered a rather dubious compliment. 'I promise you, Mrs Johns, that I will always maintain our relationship on that basis.' He wondered if it was a promise that he would regret making.

Susan Johns proved to be a moderately good chemist and a brilliant administrator. From the day she arrived at the lab, everything fell into a state of perfect order. Jim Macdougall, who had gone into paroxysms of anxiety at the news that Julian had hired a woman, and a young one at that, was by the end of the first week grudgingly acknowledging that she had her uses, and by the end of the second totally, and by his own admission, dependent on her.

'The lass is a marvel,' he said, 'she has a complete inventory of all our stock, she has tabs on what we need to replace; she has a new ordering system, she has every invoice cross-referenced under product and outlet – she worked out that system with your mother, by the way – she seems to understand exactly what our priorities should be, and she works unbelievably hard. And doesn't even stop for a lunch break.'

'What a paragon,' said Julian, laughing, careful not to

remind Jim that he had given Susan a week and prophesied endless disasters as a direct result of her arrival, including the botching of formulations, loss of customers, and the clear possibility of the whole place being burnt down. 'Does she have any vices at all? Don't you think she might be making off with the tea money, or smuggling out cases of cough linctus to sell on the black market?'

'Oh, aye, she has her faults,' said Jim, quite unmoved by this attack. 'She's a clock watcher for one, which is one thing I can't abide. Off on the stroke of five, no matter what has to be done.'

'Yes, but she has to collect her children from their child minder,' said Julian, 'and you just said yourself she worked through the lunch hour. So you can't really complain about that.'

'I'm not complaining,' said Macdougall indignantly, 'just telling you how the lassie works. And then she does eat a lot of the time. She may not take a lunch hour, but she's always picking at something. If it's not sandwiches, it's crisps, and if it's not crisps, it's sweets. It's a marvel she's not the size of a house. Little slip of a thing, you'd imagine she lived on air.'

'Well, neither of those things sounds very serious to me,' said Julian. 'And I'm delighted she's working out so well. Do you like her? Is she nice to work with?'

'Oh, aye, she's very nice. Not much of a talker, keeps herself to herself, but then that's rare enough in a woman, and something on the whole to be thankful for. No, I'll admit I was against the idea, but I was wrong and I'm delighted to say so.'

'Good,' said Julian, 'she likes you too. She says you're a good bloke. Which is high praise, I can tell you. She certainly wouldn't say that about me. Now, Jim, I want to talk to you about something else. How's the indigestion tablet coming along?'

'It's fine. Real fine. I have the prototype ready now, and we could start selling it into the pharmacies in a month or two, I reckon.'

'How are we on the packaging? Are those boxes really going to be adequate, or should we go into bottles?'

'Well, bottles will be safer, and will keep the tablets in better condition. But they'll cost twice as much.'

'We're up to our necks in debt already. Can't we get away with paying those wretched women a bit less to pack the stuff?'

'No, you bloody well can't.' It was Susan's voice; she had come back, to collect some order books she had promised Jim to go through that night, and which he'd been unable to give her earlier; she had one child in her arms, and was trailing the other by the hand. All three looked half asleep.

'Susan,' said Julian, 'what on earth are you doing here with those children at this time of night? It's nearly seven.'

'I know, and I was going to do it tomorrow, but then I thought the orders were so important, and Mum's out tonight, so I'll have a bit of peace and quiet and I could really make a big impression on them.'

'Have you trekked all the way back here from Acton? On the bus?'

'Yeah, well, it didn't take that long. I saw the bus coming, so I thought what the hell, might as well. Sheila was asleep anyway. And I'm glad I did come back, otherwise I wouldn't have heard you plotting to do those poor bloody cows out of their money.'

'Oh, don't be ridiculous, Susan,' said Julian in exasperation. 'Nobody's planning to do anybody out of anything.'

'Planning to try, though.'

'Not at all. Simply trying to make the company a little more cost effective. And Susan, this really is none of your business. I don't think you should get involved in wage negotiations. You can't begin to understand any of it.'

Susan eyed him contemptuously. 'Don't lie to me, Mr Morell. And don't insult me either. I understand all about it and I think it's disgusting. There you sit, you and your mother, in your charming little house in your posh little street, driving around in your smart cars, complaining that you can't get any decent champagne, and that Harrods won't deliver before nine o'clock in the morning, and you begrudge a few women the chance to get their kids a new pair of shoes before the last ones actually fall to pieces. Some of those bloody women, as you call them, haven't had a decent meal in months; some of them are doing two jobs, filling your rotten bottles in the day, and doing factory cleaning at night, just so they can stay in their homes and not get turned out for not paying the rent. Some of them have got three kids and no husband, they either didn't come home because they'd been killed, or they went off with some popsie they met while they were away, while the poor stupid loyal wives stayed at home, minding the baby and saving themselves for the hero's return. Just do me a favour, Mr Morell, and find out what life's really like. Try living on a quarter, an eighth of what you've got, and see how you get on. You wouldn't last a day. Come on, Jenny, we're going home.'

She turned and walked out; Julian looked after her appalled, and then turned to Jim, who had a strange expression of admiration and trepidation on his face. 'What the hell do I do with her now? Fire her?'

'I don't think you'll get a chance to fire her,' said Jim. 'Your problem will be persuading her to stay.'

'I don't want her to stay,' said Julian, scowling. 'That was bloody, outrageous, rude, inexcusable behaviour. How dare she talk to me like that?'

'She'd dare talk to anybody like that,' said Jim. 'She's got guts, that girl. And besides, it was true. All of it. Those women do have a dreadful life, some of them. And you don't even begin to know what it's like for them.'

'Oh, rubbish,' said Julian wearily. 'Who created the opportunity for them to work in the first place? Me. Who risked everything, to get the company going? Me. Who works all night whenever it's necessary? I do. Who drives the length of the country, until I'm practically dead at the wheel? Don't you take up all that pinko claptrap, Jim. Someone should give people like me some credit for a change.'

'Why?' said Jim. 'Why should they? You enjoy it. Every bloody moment of it. And she's right, that girl, you may work very hard, but you enjoy a standard of living most people can't even begin to imagine. And you have the satisfaction of knowing all the work you put in is building up your own company. You don't need any credit. You have plenty of other things. Now if you've got any sense you'll go after the lass and apologize. Or you'll lose one of the two best people you've got in your company.'

He grinned suddenly. Julian scowled at him again.

'Oh, all right. But she can't go on talking to me like that. Well, not in public anyway. She's got to learn to draw the line. I won't have it.'

'Oh, stop being so pompous, man, and get a move on. She'll be on her bus by now and you'll never see her again.'

*

Susan was indeed on the bus, but Julian's car was waiting for her outside the shabby little house in Acton when she struggled wearily along with the children an hour later. He got out and walked towards her.

'Piss off.'

'Look,' said Julian, 'I came to apologize, to say I'm sorry I offended you. There's no need for that.'

'There's every need. I don't want to talk to you.'

'Why not?'

'Because I don't want to have any more to do with you. I should never have got involved in the first place. I don't like your sort and I never will. So just go away and leave me alone. And pay me for the work I've done this week.'

'Susan,' said Julian, surprising himself with his own patience, 'my sort, as you put it, is giving you the chance of a lifetime. To get out of this miserable dump and make something of yourself.'

'Don't you call my home a dump.'

'It's not your home, and it is a dump. Working for me, you can have your own home, and lots of other things too. A career. A life of your own, that you can be proud of. Think of Jenny and Sheila. A good education.'

'If you're suggesting I'd want to send them to some bloody private school you can forget it. I wouldn't have them associating with those sorts of kids.'

'No, of course I don't,' said Julian, encouraged that she had moved outside her outrage and into a more abstract argument. 'But you can live in the sort of area where the schools are better. You can buy them books. Send them abroad in due course. Let them choose their own destinies. And,' he added with a dash of inspired deviousness, 'show them what women can do. On their own. Make them proud of you. Set them an example.'

Susan looked at him and smiled grudgingly. 'You're a clever bastard. All right. I'll stay. But only if you give the outworkers a rise.'

'Can't afford it.'

'Of course you can.'

'Susan, I can't. Ask my mother.'

'OK. But as soon as you can then.'

Julian sighed. 'All right. It's a deal. But I certainly didn't think I'd find a trade union in my own company at this stage.'

'Well, you didn't think you'd be working with someone like me. Do you want to come in and have a cup of tea?'

'No thanks. I'm –' He had been about to say 'going out to dinner' but stopped himself. 'Going home. I'm late already, and I've got a very early start. Good night Susan. See you tomorrow.'

'Good night. And –'

'Yes?'

'Well, thanks. Sorry I was rude.'

'That's all right. You'd better get those children to bed.'

He drove away feeling curiously disturbed. It wasn't until he was getting into bed after an excellent dinner with Letitia and an old school friend that he realized that the intense outrage and anger Susan had caused him had been mingled with another sensation altogether. It was sexual desire.

Morell's Indigestion Treatment, as Julian finally called it (the name implying something more medically ethical and ongoing in its benefits than simply an antacid tablet), was a huge success. All the chemists who already stocked the cough linctus took it immediately, recommended it to their customers, and ordered more. Printed on the cardboard pill boxes, under the name, was the message 'Keeps the misery of indigestion away' and on the bottom of the box was a helpful little paragraph instructing sufferers to take the tablets before the pain struck, not to wait until afterwards, as it doubled the efficiency of the medication that way.

Within weeks orders had doubled, trebled, quadrupled; Julian was physically unable to deal with the deliveries, and hired two salesmen/drivers (in whom he invested sufficient time and money to enable them to talk to the chemists with at least a modicum of authority), and Jim and Susan were equally unable to cope with the manufacture, and to oversee the filling and packaging arrangements. The company acquired a second building in Ealing, twice the size of the first, and invested the whole of the year's profits paying builders and laboratory outfitters double time to get it operational in a month. Over half the women outworkers were taken on full time in the new factory and Susan Johns became, at the end of her first year, factory manager. It meant she no longer did much of the laboratory work, but Jim had two other assistants working almost full time on research and manufacture, and Susan's real talent was for administration, not formulation.

She and Letitia were a formidable team; Letitia found Susan not only interesting but challenging to work with, she had a mind like a razor, a great capacity for hard work and, even more unusually, an ability to exact a similar dedication from other people. Letitia liked her, too; she found her honesty, her courage, and her absolute refusal to accept anything without questioning it, interesting and engaging, and she was slightly surprised to find herself amused, rather than irritated by the way Susan regarded Julian with just a very slight degree of contempt. This was entirely missing from the attitude Susan had towards her. She liked Letitia enormously, and rather to her own surprise found her blatant snobbery amusing and unimportant; probably, she told herself, because it was so blatant. 'She's honest about it,' she said once to Julian when he teased her about it, 'she's not a hypocrite, she doesn't go round patronizing everyone, pretending she thinks everyone's equal, she really believes they aren't. Well, that's all right. She's entitled to her own opinion.' Julian laughed, and told her she was a hypocrite herself, but she was unmoved; Letitia was her heroine, she admired her brain, enjoyed her guts and her sense of fun and was constantly delighted by the fresh thinking and innovative approach Letitia brought to the company. Letitia was fascinated by new financial systems; she spent hours reading reports from big companies, she lunched with financial analysts and accountants, and hardly a week went by before she introduced some new piece of sophisticated accountancy, and drove Julian almost to distraction by constantly updating and changing her methods.

'I really can't see what's wrong with the way you've done things so far, Mother,' he said slightly fretfully one evening, as he arrived home exhausted after a long session with the buyer for a chain of chemists in the West Country and found her deep in conversation with Susan over the latest refinements to her system and the effect it was going to have on the next year's wage structure. 'I spend my life trying to follow your books and work out fairly crucial basic things like how much money we've got in the bank and I have to plough through three ledgers before I know if it's OK to buy myself a sandwich.'

'Well, I can always tell you that,' said Susan briskly. 'I understand all the financial systems perfectly well. And buying anything, even sandwiches, is my job, not yours. So there really isn't any problem.'

'Absolutely not,' said Letitia. 'Susan's quite right, Julian, you just stick to your part of the operation and let us worry about ours. If Susan can cope with my systems, then it doesn't matter if you can't.'

'Well thanks a lot,' said Julian tetchily, pouring himself a large whisky. 'I had no idea I played such a small part in this organization. You two seem to have something of a conspiracy going. Do let me know when I'm to be allowed to do something more challenging than planning the salesmen's journeys.'

'Oh, don't be childish,' said Letitia, 'you're obviously hungry. It always makes him fractious,' she added to Susan. 'Why don't you take both of us out to dinner? Then we can try and explain whatever it is you don't understand, and I can put in my request for a new accounts clerk at the same time.'

'Dear God,' said Julian, 'your department will be the biggest in the company soon, Mother. What on earth do you need a clerk for?'

'To do a lot of tedious repetitive work, so that I can get on with something more constructive.'

'I think you're just empire building,' said Julian, laughing suddenly. 'It's a conspiracy between you and Susan to get more and more people employed in the company, and keep my wages bill so high I never make a profit. Isn't that right, Susan?'

'Well, people are the best investment,' said Susan, very serious as always when her political beliefs were called into a conversation. 'And there's no virtue in profit for its own sake.'

'Rubbish,' said Julian. 'Come out to dinner with Mother and me and I'll show you the virtue of spending a bit of it.'

'No, honestly I can't,' said Susan, 'I must go home. It's getting late.'

'Well at least can I give you a lift?'

'No, it's all right, thanks.'

'Well, let me get you a taxi.'

'No. Really. It doesn't take that long from here by bus.'

'Susan, it takes hours,' said Letitia. 'For heaven's sake, let Julian take you home.'

'Oh, all right. I would be grateful.'

Julian looked at her. She seemed terribly tired. She was basically in far better health than she had been, and was altogether strikingly changed; she had filled out from her painful thinness, she had been able to buy herself a few nice clothes, she had had her hair cut properly, the cheap perm was gone and so was the peroxide rinse, and she wore it swinging straight and shining, a beautiful nut brown, just clear of her shoulders; her skin looked clear and creamy instead of pasty and grey. But the biggest change in her was the air of confidence she carried about with her. He could see it in her clear blue eyes, hear it in her voice, watch it as she walked, taller, more purposefully.

'That girl,' Letitia had said, looking at her across the factory one day, 'is turning out to be something of a beauty.'

'Yes,' said Julian, 'I know.'

She had looked at him sharply, but his face was blank, his attention totally fixed apparently on some orders. Thank God, she thought, that would never, ever do.

'Tell you what,' said Julian as the car pulled out into the Brompton Road and headed for Hammersmith Broadway, 'how would you like a car to use? You could have one of the vans, we've got a spare, and it would make such a difference to you.'

'Oh, I couldn't possibly,' said Susan. 'Company car? Not my sort of thing, Mr Morell.'

'Oh, for heaven's sake, why not?' said Julian irritably. 'I'd like it even if you didn't. I'm always either worrying or feeling guilty about you, or having to drive you home.'

'Good,' said Susan, 'helps keep you in touch with reality.' But she was smiling.

'Look,' said Julian, 'if you like, if it'll make you feel any better, you can pay me for the use of it. A bit. Give me what you pay on bus fares. And do the odd delivery, if it fits in. You work such long hours, Susan, you really do deserve it. And it would help with getting the kids to the minder in the morning. Go on.'

'No,' said Susan, 'honestly I couldn't. I may deserve it, but I can't afford it. I can't afford to buy a car for myself, I mean. And so I don't think it's right for me to have one I'm not paying for. It would make me feel uncomfortable. And what would the other girls think?'

'They'd think you were bloody sensible,' said Julian, 'and if they could hear this conversation they'd think you were bloody silly.'

'Well, I can't help it. It feels wrong.'

'Look,' said Julian, 'how about this. I want you to have a rise. Have the van instead.'

'I've just had one. Anyway, I can't drive.'

'You can learn. I'll teach you myself. Oh, for Christ's sake, you are the most ridiculous woman. Here I am trying to improve your standard of living and you throw it back in my face. Don't you want to get on in the world?'

'Not if it means moving out of the bit of it I belong to. Losing touch with my own sort of people. That's the most important thing in the world to me, Mr Morell. I can't sell out on that.'

'But you're already doing a lot for your own sort of people as you call them, by getting on yourself. Surely you can see that. And I think it's time you started calling me Julian.'

'Oh. Oh, OK. But not in the office.'

'All right. If you say so. But please think about what I've said.'

'I will. And thank you.'

She came into his office a few days later, looking slightly awkward. 'Mr Morell, I've thought about everything you said. I agree. I've been very shortsighted. I'd like to take the van, please. On one condition.'

'What's that? There can't be many executives who lay down conditions for accepting their own perks.'

'You put the girls' overtime rates up, just a bit.'

'Dear God,' said Julian, 'so your company car costs me about six times what it would have done. Why on earth should I do that?'

'Because it's fair. Because you can afford it. And because you won't have to waste so much of your time and energy worrying about me on the bus.' She was smiling at him now, a confident, almost arrogant smile; but there was, for the first time, real friendship in her eyes.

Julian didn't smile back; he looked at her very seriously and sighed and buzzed through to Letitia who sat in a small anteroom outside his own. 'Could you ask that infernal financial system of yours if we can afford to put the overtime rates up very slightly? Say two bob an hour?'

By the beginning of 1950 Morell Pharmaceuticals had expanded sufficiently for Julian to launch into his next phase.

He had sold both the factories for a sufficiently large amount of money, in the first of the great property price booms, to purchase a building in a small industrial estate near Hounslow. It housed two laboratories, a filling plant, a storage area and management offices. Management now incorporated a sales force of four.

His pharmaceutical range had extended to include six more simple, effective products, including a successful antiseptic lotion which incorporated a very mild topical anaesthetic in its formulation and therefore was far less unpleasant when dabbed on a grazed elbow or knee than other products on the market; it was no longer necessary to persuade chemists to stock Morell products, he was permanently bombarded with requests for them, and for information on any new ones which might be in the pipeline. Indeed he had received the unique accolade in the pharmaceutical industry of being approached by the head office of Boots the Chemist, rather than being forced to wait patiently in line for the honour of being granted an appointment.

Nevertheless, he stayed with his basic principle of knowing what he was talking about and knowing that his sales force knew it too; it was not only the thing which earned him the industry's respect and custom, it was the way he kept tabs on what was happening in other companies, and it gave him some of his best ideas. A chance remark from a pharmacist over a cup of coffee, about how a customer had said she wished there was a toothpaste that would persuade children to clean their teeth, led with dazzling speed to Morell raspberry flavoured toothpaste; another over how most of the laxatives on the market were so unpleasant to take, and Morell Pharmaceuticals had come up with Herbal Tea Laxative, 'the Comforting Way to Regularity.'

*

But Julian was wearying of patent medicines; he wanted to move into the field that had excited him more from the very beginning: cosmetics. And the cosmetic market was ready for him. There was as much excitement and interest in what women wore on their faces as on their bodies; fashion in make-up had changed as much as in clothes. During the war the only cosmetics a woman carried in her make-up bag were a powder compact and a lipstick, and possibly some 'lick and spit' mascara; now suddenly make-up had become much more complex. Foundation had become thicker, and less naturally coloured; rouge was being applied more skilfully and artistically (and was suddenly more respectable); lipsticks were no longer just pink and red, but every shade of coral, lilac and crimson in between; and eyes had become the focus of the face, with the dramatic, doe-eyed look, prominent feature of the high-class glamour peddled in the pages of *Vogue* by such high-class peddlers as Barbara Goalen, Zizi Jeanmaire and Enid Boulting. There was also (in keeping with the new extravagance in the air) a strong movement towards skin care in all its mysticism; women long urged (in Miss Arden's immortal words) to cleanse, tone and nourish their skins, were now feeding it with different creams for night and day, relaxing it (with face masks), and guarding its youth (with formulae so complex it required a degree in chemistry to make head or tail of it, but you could put it on your face anyway, and believe). And belief was what it was really all about.

Julian Morell's talent for understanding women, what they wanted, and above all what they could be made to believe, found itself suddenly most gainfully employed. What he knew women wanted above everything else was to feel desirable. Not necessarily beautiful, or clever, but desirable. To feel, to know that they could arouse interest, admiration and above all desire was worth a queen's ransom. And those were qualities which he knew could not, should not, be bought cheap. The more rare and luxurious a cream, a look, a perfume was, the more rarity and luxury it would bestow. Anoint your skin with ultra-expensive oils and creams, surround yourself with a rich, expensive fragrance, colour your lips, your eyes, with unusual, expensive products, and you will feel and look and smell

73

expensive. The other thing about cosmetics (and what distinguishes them from clothes) is that every woman personalizes them, makes them her own. A moisturizer, a fragrance, a colour becomes, in however small a way, changed, part of a woman's own chemistry and aura and sex appeal. No colour, no perfume is precisely the same on any two women. It was this concept, together with that of desirability, that went into the formulation and personality of the first products in the Juliana range.

He started boldly. He knew if there was to be an impact of any magnitude on the market, it could not be achieved in the same quiet way as he had launched his medicines. There had to be a noise. The range had to have a personality. There did not have to be many products, initially, but there did have to be an advertising campaign. Women had to know it was there in order to buy it.

Formulating the range was the least of his problems. He knew exactly what he wanted in it – an expensive and complex skin-care range, with a strong selling concept, a streamlined colour collection, and a fragrance that was not only individual and sophisticated, but long-lasting. Everyone tried to talk him out of the idea of doing a perfume; the only ones with any cachet (everyone said) were French, and he would be wasting his time and money launching an English one. 'It won't be English,' said Julian, 'it will be French. And the range needs it.'

He hired, to help him create all these things, a man called Adam Sarsted, a brilliant lateral thinker and chemist, who had gone into pharmaceuticals from Cambridge, and spent a few months working for Beecham's on their new toiletries division; he had heard Julian was looking for someone, went to see him, fell in love with his entrepreneurial approach and took a drop in salary to work with him. Together they created Juliana, not just the products, but the concept. The concept was Julian's, born of a chance remark of Adam's.

'Christ,' he said, late in the lab one night, after a prolonged session with Julian earnestly rubbing skin food and face masks into one another's faces and studying the results. 'All this, just for a lot of bloody silly women, with nothing else to worry about, and who think it's essential they spend masses of their husbands' money on their faces.'

'My God, Adam, that's it!' said Julian, pausing in his study of himself in the mirror with peach kernel treatment on one side of his face and cucumber on the other. 'Christ. How fantastic. I thought I'd never get it. You're a genius. Wonderful. Thank you.'

'What for?'

'For a singularly great thought. I was waiting for a concept. A selling point for this range. You've just given it to me.'

'I have?'

'You have. Don't you see, you just said it. What Juliana is or will be is essential to women. They'll have to have it. Won't be able to get on without it. It kind of knocks the rest, ever so slightly, makes them feel they're depriving themselves if they don't buy it. God, it's brilliant.'

'Christ,' said Adam, 'sometimes I know I should have stuck to ethicals. Can I have a rise?'

'Absolutely not. But I'll buy you dinner. And we can drink to your concept. Come on, I'm sick of this. Let's go and talk some more.' He pulled on his coat, held Adam's out to him. 'Let's treat ourselves, this is a great occasion. It isn't often a great new cosmetic range is born. I'll take you to the Savoy.'

Adam looked at him and grinned. 'Fine. I'd like that. The only thing I'd suggest, Julian, is that you might get a better table if you wipe Peach Kernel off your face first, and possibly Mauve Madness off your eyelids as well.'

Julian's biggest problem, and he knew it, was selling Juliana into the stores. The rest seemed comparatively easy. He raised the money (through a merchant bank, impressed by his record over the past two years); he saw Adam's occasionally undisciplined formulation safely into perfectly ordered ranges of cleansers and moisturizers, tonics and masks; and he created an advertising campaign with the help of a brilliant team at Colman Prentice and Varley, who took his concept of Essential Cosmetics and turned it into one of the great classics of cosmetic advertising, called the Barefaced Truth, a series of photographs of an exquisitely unmade-up face, the skin dewily, tenderly soft, the implication being that with the help of Juliana and its essential care, any face could be as lovely; the advertisements appeared on double page spreads in all the major magazines and on posters over all the major cities and made the elaborate make-up of the models advertising other ranges look overdone and tacky. He packaged the range, against the advice of his creative team, in dark grey and white; it looked clinical they said, not feminine enough, it did not carry any implications of luxury. But set against the pale creams and golds and pinks of the competition on the mock-up beauty counter Julian kept permanently in his office, the Juliana range looked streamlined, expensive and chic; the creative team admitted it had been wrong.

The perfume, which Julian named simply *Je*, researched outstandingly. Adam Sarsted went to Grasse and worked for weeks with Rudolph Grozinknski, an exiled Pole, one of the great Noses (an accolade awarded to few) of his generation, and together they created a fragrance that was rich, musky, warm: it exuded sex. '*Je*,' ran the copyline under a photograph of a woman in a silkily clinging peignoir, turning away from her dressing table and looking into the camera with an unmistakable message in her eyes, 'for the Frenchwoman in you'.

When it was researched, over ninety per cent of the women questioned wanted to know where they could buy *Je*.

But all this was effortless, set against getting the range into the stores. The most exquisite colours, the most perfectly formulated creams, the most sensational perfume, will never reach the public unless they can buy it easily, and see it displayed extensively in the big stores. In London Harrods, Harvey Nichols, and Selfridges are *de rigueur* stockists for any successful range; in Birmingham Rackhams, in Newcastle Fenwick, Kendals in Manchester and in Edinburgh Jenners. A newcomer imagining he can impress the buyers for these stores and persuade them to give away a considerable amount of their invaluable counter space can only be compared with a ballet student expecting a lead role at Covent Garden, or an unseeded player staking a claim on the Centre Court at Wimbledon.

Nevertheless Julian knew he had to do it; his first advantage was that, with a very few exceptions, his prey were women. His second was that he had a strong gambling instinct. He took the buyers out to lunch, individually, and rather than risk insulting them by attempting to charm them in more conventional ways, he asked their advice on every possible aspect of his range; on its formulation, its positioning, its packaging, its advertising, and then paid them the immeasurable compliment of putting some bit of each piece of their advice, in however small a way, into practice. It was to the buyer at Harrods that *Je* owed its just slightly stronger formulation in the perfume concentrate, to the buyer from Fenwick Newcastle that the night cream was coloured ivory rather than pink, and to the buyer from Selfridges that the eye shadows were sold in powder as well as in cream form. He then told them that if they would give him counter space, in a modestly good position (not demanding the prime places, knowing that would alienate them), he would remove himself and his products if they were not meeting their targets after eight weeks. The buyers agreed; Julian then gave several interviews to the press explaining exactly what he was doing, and what a risk he was taking, and the women of Britain, moved by the thought of this handsome civilized man (who talked to them in a way that made them feel he knew and understood them intimately – not only through his advertising campaign and his public relations officer but in his interviews with Mrs Ernestine Carter in the *Sunday Times* and Miss Anne Scott James of *Vogue*, to name but a couple) placing his fortune on the line in this way, went out in sufficiently large numbers to inspect the range, to try it, and to save him from financial ruin. By the end of its first week in the stores Juliana had doubled its targets and by Christmas it had exhausted all its stocks.

'Where's Susan?' said Julian irritably to Letitia one morning in the following July. 'The cosmetic factory is still only running at eighty per cent capacity, and I want to know when she thinks it's going to be at full strength.'

'She's just come in,' said Letitia, 'in something of a tizz, I would say. Very unlike her to be late. Something must be wrong.'

Susan was sitting in her office eating a doughnut with savage speed. Julian looked at her anxiously.

'You OK?'

'I'm just furious, that's all. I'm sorry I'm late, Julian, but I had to go and see Mum's landlord. She had a letter this morning, saying she had to be prepared to move out within three months, as he wanted to sell the house.'

'Well, that's nonsense. Surely she's protected by law.'

'No, she isn't. The house used to belong to his father, he was a dear old chap, came round every week for the rent, nice as pie. But he died, and the son's been looking at all the tenancies, and because his dad never worried about making things official and proper leases, and Mum was just glad to get the place after the war, she just signed something without going into it very thoroughly. All it is is a tenancy agreement with a one-month-notice arrangement. I went and shouted at him, but he said he was doing her a big favour giving her three months, and told me to get the hell out and stop wasting his time.'

'Brave chap,' said Julian, grinning at her. 'Sorry,' he added hastily, watching her face freeze. 'Can I help?'

'I don't think so. I just can't think what she can do. It sounds awful, I know, but I just don't want her with us. But I don't see any option to her living with us again unless she goes and shares with her sister, and they can spend just about fifteen minutes together before they start bickering.'

'It doesn't sound awful at all,' said Julian, who had met Susan's mother and felt he had never come across such an unpleasant woman with the possible exception of a female commandant in the Gestapo who had conducted his preliminary interrogation when he had been captured during the war. ('And the Gestapo woman had the mitigating virtue of being rather beautiful,' he said to Letitia, when describing his early encounters with Meg Tucker. 'This woman isn't just unattractive, she's positively repellent. I cannot imagine how she produced Susan.')

'Look, Susan, I really do need to talk work to you now, but let's have a drink after we've finished and I really will do anything I can to help. Will the kids be OK for half an hour?'

'Oh, I think so. Anna next door will have them in if I ring her. Thank you, Julian. I really do need someone to discuss it with.'

Susan had moved out of her mother's house a year earlier, and bought a tiny little terrace house in South Ealing, with the help of a sudden and rather suspiciously timely payment from the War Office. (Not even Susan could see how Julian could have forged a letter on War Office paper; she underestimated what he had learnt in the Resistance movement.)

Jenny and Sheila were now ten and eight years old

respectively, pretty but rather surly little girls – probably, Julian thought, as a result of spending too much time with their grandmother. They went to school within walking distance of the house, and Susan generally found life quite astonishingly easier. It took her just ten minutes to drive her van to the factory in the morning; she was earning, despite her strenuous efforts to keep her salary in line with what she considered equitable, quite a lot of money; she could afford to pay the girl next door to look after the girls after school and in the holidays, and was currently planning a package holiday with them on the Costa del Sol. She was endlessly teased about this, not only by Julian and Letitia, but Jim and Adam as well, who never missed an opportunity to point out to her that there were hundreds of people all over the country who couldn't even afford a weekend in the Isle of Wight never mind jetting off (as they all put it) to the Mediterranean, but for once she was not even contrite. 'I've never had a holiday, and we all need it,' she kept saying defiantly, poring over her travel brochures.

A week after the disagreeable Mrs Tucker had first been served with notice to quit her flat, Susan came flying into Julian's office, flushed and radiant.

'You'll never believe this,' she said, 'but we've had another letter from the landlord, telling Mum she can stay. He's even sent her a new lease offering her a tenancy for an unlimited period. I just can't believe it. Isn't it marvellous?'

'Marvellous,' said Julian, smiling at her, just a little complacently.

'Did you –' Susan stood very still, looking at him in awe. 'Did you have anything to do with this?'

'A bit.'

'But you couldn't have.'

'OK then, I didn't.'

'Well, what did you do?'

'Talked to a few people.'

'What sort of people?'

'Oh, you know, mildly influential people.'

'Like?'

'Well, like a friend of mine who belongs to the local Freemasons', which our chum the landlord is desperate to join. A reporter on the local paper. Those sort of people.'

'But what did you actually —'

'Susan, darling, I think the less you know about it the better. Otherwise you might say something to your entirely charming mother, or perhaps to anyone who might be interested in your knowing anything about it all.'

Susan looked at him thoughtfully. 'It all smacks of corruption a bit, if you ask me.'

'I'm not asking you. And hopefully nobody else will. Now if I were you I'd just help your mother sign the lease and get it back to the landlord quickly before he changes his mind.'

'Oh, Julian . . .' She stopped, and looked at him very seriously. 'I do know how good you are to me. And I never seem to thank you properly. How can I?'

'Have dinner with me tonight.'

They were both surprised, shocked almost, by the invitation. Julian, who had been subconsciously avoiding any kind of close contact with Susan for as long as he could remember, and had planned to spend the evening with an old friend looking at horses at a stable in Buckinghamshire (he felt he deserved some slight reward for his unstinting labours of the past three years) wasn't sure if he was pleased or sorry he had issued it, but having done so saw it determinedly through. 'Please, Susan. I'd really like it.'

Susan flushed, looked down at her hands, and then very directly at him. 'I don't really think it's a very good idea.'

'Why not?'

'Well — because — well, people might talk.'

'Angel, people have been talking about us for years. We might as well give them at least something worth talking about. Besides, I only want a bit of peace and quiet with you so we can discuss Letitia's wretched new costing system and how much we want the sales force to use it.'

'Oh, well,' she said, choosing to accept this arguably unflattering explanation, 'that's all right then. Thank you, I'd like it very much.'

'Do you want to go home and change? Or shall we go from here?'

'If we're only going to talk about costing systems,' said Susan briskly, 'I don't need to get all dolled up, do I? I'll phone Anna and see if she can babysit. If she can't I'll have to ask Mum.'

Julian devoutly hoped that Anna would be able to oblige.

'Where are you off to, darling?' said Letitia as he came into her office at half past five to say goodbye.

'Oh, I'm taking Susan out for a bite to eat. We're discussing the sales people's return sheets.'

Letitia looked at him very seriously.

'Julian, don't. Please.'

'I don't know what you mean,' he said, irritably defensive. 'Mother, just leave me alone, will you? Good night. I won't be late.'

'You do know. And I sincerely hope you won't be.'

Julian slammed the door of her office and wondered, not for the first time, if perhaps he ought to think about getting a house of his own.

Susan was waiting for him in the car park.

'Before we have dinner,' said Julian, 'I want to take you somewhere else. To meet a friend. Won't take long. I tried to put her off but I couldn't. Out near Slough. I need to be there by seven. But we should make that.'

'What sort of a friend?' said Susan, ever so slightly sulky. 'What does she do?'

'Runs around.'

'I see.'

It was a perfect July evening: the sky was that peculiarly clear light turquoise that follows slightly hazy days, and spangled with tiny orange and grey clouds. It had been hot, but there was a breeze tossing the air about; Julian rolled back the sunroof of his new four wheeled toy, a cream Lagonda, and smiled briefly at Susan.

'Now,' he said, 'if you look in that pocket there, you should find a map. Can you map read?'

'Course.'

'Good. Now it's near Stoke Poges, this place. Near Burnham Beeches. Got it?'

'Yes. You want to head out of Slough on the A4. I'll tell you after that.'

'OK.'

They pulled into the drive of a large, low house just after seven.

81

'Damn,' said Julian, 'I think he's gone.'

'I thought it was a she we've come to see.'

'It is. But there's a chaperon involved. Ah, there he is. Tony, hello. Sorry we're late.'

'That's OK. Traffic's awful, I know. She's round here, your lady friend. She really is gorgeous. You're going to love her.'

'Perhaps I'd better stay here,' said Susan crossly.

'Oh, don't be ridiculous,' said Julian, 'you'll like her. Tony, this is Susan Johns. My right-hand woman in the company. Susan, Tony Sargeant.'

Susan nodded slightly coolly at Tony. She felt increasingly silly and miserable as she followed the man into a stable yard.

'There,' said Tony, stopping by a bay with a very dark mane, 'this is She. Gloriana. Absolutely made for you, Julian. Superb hunter, very strong, but graceful too. She's a honey. I'd love to keep her myself, but I don't need another mare.'

'She's got a very nice head. Lovely expression,' said Julian, 'let's have a look at the rest of her.'

Tony led the mare out into the yard. She was restive, dancing about at the end of her rein. 'How old is she, did you say?'

'Four.'

'She looks younger.'

'No, just four. She is quite slightly built. But she's terrifically fast. And strong. She'd make a superb National Hunt horse, if you wanted her for that. Do you want to ride her now?'

'No. I haven't got any of the stuff with me,' said Julian, eyeing Susan who had wandered off down the other end of the yard. Her initial relief at discovering the mysterious female was a horse had given way to boredom and irritation. 'Anyway, I can't stop now. But she is beautiful, I agree. I'll come back and ride her at the weekend, if that's OK. And thank you very much.' He stroked the horse's neck tenderly; scratched her ear. She snorted with pleasure. 'He's got a way with women,' said Tony to Susan, laughing.

'I daresay,' she said shortly. 'It's not a side of him we see much of at work.'

'Oh, come on, you misery,' said Julian, taking her hand. It was the first time he had ever touched her. She shivered; she couldn't help it. He noticed, and dropped her hand again, quickly. 'You must be hungry.'

'Sorry about that,' he said, as the Lagonda swung out into the lane. 'Very boring for you, I'm afraid.'

'It was a pretty cheap joke,' said Susan. 'Making me think we were going to meet some woman.'

'Susan!' said Julian, 'I do declare you were jealous.'

Susan looked at him very seriously. 'Not jealous, Julian. But I don't like being made a fool of. Even in very small ways. OK?'

'OK. Sorry. Now get that map out again, and find somewhere called Aston Clinton. That's where we're going. To a restaurant called the Bell. You'll like it. And I won't make a fool of you ever again. Promise.'

The Bell was not very full. They sat outside in the garden to savour the evening and the menu, and Julian ordered a bottle of champagne.

'I don't know how you think you're going to drive home,' said Susan, 'I'm not going to have any of that, and you'll get awfully drunk.'

'Oh, go on,' said Julian, 'just this once. For me. Try it. You'll love it, honestly you will.'

'No,' said Susan.

'All right. But you're missing one of life's great pleasures. Tell you what, I'll get some orange juice and have it as Bucks Fizz and then maybe you'll be persuaded to try it.'

'Maybe. But I don't think so. Tell me, what would you say life's other great pleasures are? For you?'

'Oh, horses. Cars. Women. Making money.'

'What a corrupt list.'

'I'm a corrupt person. You should know that by now.'

'No,' she said, very serious. 'I don't. Not personally. I'm prepared to believe it, but I don't have any evidence of my own. Could I have some crisps?'

'I'll try,' said Julian, wondering if they knew about crisps at the Bell.

The barman looked disdainful but provided a bowl of nuts, which Susan demolished in minutes, and while she was waiting for a second, and a replenishment of her orange juice, took a sip of Julian's Bucks Fizz.

'Yes,' she said, savouring it carefully, 'it is quite nice. It's a little bit like orange and soda, isn't it? You should try that, you know. Much better for you.'

'Well, I suppose I might,' said Julian, allowing himself for a moment to contemplate the terrible prospect of drinking orange and soda at parties. 'Now shall I get a glass for you to have a bit more?'

'No, thank you. I'll just have the occasional sip of yours. I didn't know you liked horses.'

'You don't know a lot of things about me. I love horses. Always have. Until we came to London, I rode all the time.'

'I suppose you went hunting and that sort of thing.'

'That sort of thing.'

'I see.'

'Do you disapprove?'

'Yes, I do. But it's nothing to do with me.'

'True. And your disapproval is nothing to do with me, so I won't try to convert you.'

'No, don't. You'd be wasting your breath.'

She took another sip of his drink. 'I could get to like this, though.'

'Be careful, Susan. One vice leads to another. Talking of vice, when are you off to the Med?'

'Oh, I'm so tired of everyone going on about that. In a fortnight. The girls are so excited.'

'I bet. Are you – is anyone going with you?'

'What, Mum do you mean? No, just the three of us.'

He hadn't meant Mum, but he was strangely relieved that nobody else was going either.

'Also, could I have a week off in October?'

'Good God, woman, your life is one long holiday. What on earth for?'

'Well, it's the Labour Party Conference, and I want to go.'

'What, up to Blackpool?'

'Yes.'

'What an extraordinary girl you are.'

'Not at all. You'd be surprised how many perfectly ordinary people go to party conferences. More than go hunting, I would say.'

'OK. Yes, of course you can have the week off. Can anyone go? I might come with you.'

'Of course you can't come. They wouldn't let you over the

threshold. And anyway, you have to be a delegate from the Management Committee of your Ward.'

'And are you?'

'Yes. I'm not doing very much, but I would really like to get involved with the women's side of it. They're a very strong force in the Labour Party, you know.'

'Indeed?'

She flushed. 'I didn't mean to bore you.'

'You didn't,' he said, 'not in the least. I like listening to you talk. I like trying to understand you. The only thing I don't like is the thought of you getting too involved with the Labour Party and having no time left for me. For us.'

'I don't think there's a serious danger of that.'

'Good,' he said, 'because I should miss you more than I could say. Now then,' he went on, deliberately moving the mood away from the sudden tension he had created, 'what do you want to eat?'

Susan took another sip of Bucks Fizz, partly to please him, and partly because it was making her feel pleasantly relaxed, and picked up the menu. 'A lot.'

She ate her way through a plate of parma ham and melon, and then some whitebait, before turning her attention to the main course; they shared a chateaubriand, and she ate all of Julian's vegetables as well as her own and worked her way through three bread rolls and a packet of bread sticks.

'You really have got the most extraordinary appetite,' said Julian, looking at her in admiration. 'Have you always eaten that much?'

'Always.'

'And never got fat?'

'Never.'

'Strange.'

'I sometimes wish I could be a bit more – well, round,' she said, 'men like it better that way.'

'I don't,' he said, 'I like thin ladies. Preferably with very small bosoms.'

'Then I should please you,' she said, laughing.

'Yes, you would.'

There was a silence.

'And what else do you like in your ladies?'

'Oh, all sorts of things. Long legs. Nice hair. And minds of their own.'

'Husbands of their own, as well, from what I hear.' She meant it lightly, but he scowled. 'I'm sorry, Julian, I didn't mean to be rude. I shouldn't have said that.'

'Well,' he said, pouring himself another glass of wine, 'I daresay I deserved it. It certainly used to be true. I don't have time for any kind of ladies these days, married or otherwise. Except my mother. And you of course.'

'Tell me why you like married ladies.'

'More fun,' said Julian lightly. 'Less of a threat.'

'To what?'

'My bachelor status.'

'And what's so great about that?'

'Not a lot,' he said with a sudden, small sigh. 'It gets bloody lonely at times. Don't you find that? Don't you still miss Brian?'

She looked at him, very directly. 'Actually, no. I know that sounds awful. He was very sweet, but we never had a life together. I don't even know what it might have been like. Living with him, I mean.'

'And since then? Anybody?'

'Nobody. No time. No inclination either.'

'None at all?'

She looked at him sharply, knowing what he meant. 'Not a lot.'

'I see.'

'I don't think you do. But never mind.'

She wondered if he would think she was frigid, devoid of desire, and if it mattered that he did; whether she should try to explain, make him understand that the only way she could cope with her aloneness, the stark emptiness of her most private, personal life and her fear that she would forget altogether how to feel, how to want, how to take and be taken, was simply to ignore it, negate it, deny its existence; and decided it was better left unexplored as a subject between them, that she did not trust either herself or him sufficiently to take the risk.

'What I'd really like now,' she said briskly, 'is some pudding.'

He called the waiter over. 'Pavlova, please,' she said, and upset the waiter visibly by ordering ice cream with it. 'And could I have another Bucks Fizz, please? I'm thirsty.'

'There is a possible connection,' said Julian, laughing, 'between the fact you've now had three of them, and your thirst. But never mind.' He raised his glass to her. 'It's been a lovely evening. Thank you.'

'It's me that should be doing the thanking. As usual. I wish I could do more for you.'

'My darling girl, you do a monumental amount for me. That company runs entirely on your efficiency. We would all be absolutely lost without you. I am deeply indebted to you. I mean it.'

A very strange feeling was running through Susan. It was partly being called Julian's darling girl, and partly the effect of the Bucks Fizz; but more than anything, she realized it was simply a sort of tender intimacy that was enfolding both of them, a mixture of friendliness and sexual awareness, and a feeling of being properly close to him and knowing him and liking what she knew. The big low-ceilinged room was full now, there was a low hum of conversation and laughter surrounding them, candlelight danced from table to table, an entirely unnecessary fire flickered in the corner, and outside the sky was only just giving up its blue. She felt important, privileged, and strangely confident and safe; able to be witty, interesting, challenging.

This, she suddenly realized, was much of what having money was about; not just the rich smell of food, your glass constantly refilled; a waiter to bring you everything you wished. It was warmth, and relaxation; a shameless, conscienceless pursuit of pleasure; and it was having time to talk, to laugh, to contemplate, to pronounce, and all of it smoothed and eased by a mood of self-indulgence and the suspension of any kind of critical faculty for yourself and what you might say or do.

She looked across the table at Julian, graceful, relaxed, leaning back in his seat, smiling at her, his dark eyes dancing, moving over her face, utterly relaxed himself, his charm almost a tangible thing that she could reach out for and she felt an overwhelming urge to kiss him; not in a sexual way, not even flirtatiously, but rather as a happy child might, to express its pleasure and its gratitude at some particularly nice treat. She smiled at the thought.

'What are you smiling at?'

'I was thinking,' she said with perfect truth, 'that I'd like to kiss you.'

'Oh?' he said, smiling back, 'well do go ahead.'

'I can't. Not here.'

'Why not?'

'The waiters wouldn't like it.'

'The waiters,' he said, and they chanted together enjoying their old joke, 'aren't going to get it.'

'Am I?' he said, suddenly serious, pushing the thought of Letitia firmly from his mind.

'Oh, Julian, don't spoil a lovely evening.' She spoke simply, from her heart; she was suddenly very young again, very vulnerable.

'Well,' said Julian, his eyes dancing, 'I've had some put-downs in my time, but most of them were a bit more tactfully expressed than that.'

'Oh, don't be ridiculous,' said Susan irritably, upset at the fracture of her magic mood, 'as if you cared what I said to you.'

'Susan,' said Julian, suddenly taking her hand, 'I care very very much what you say to me. Probably more than anything anyone else says to me. Didn't you realize that?'

'No,' she said, 'no I didn't,' and an extraordinary charge of feeling shot through her, a shock of pleasure and hunger at the same time, confusing and delicious, turning her heart over, and leaving her helpless and raw with desire.

She looked at him, and he saw it all in her eyes; and for a moment he wanted her more than he had ever wanted anyone. He looked at her eyes, soft and tender in the candlelight, at the frail, slender, sensuous body, the tough, brave, hungry mouth; he contemplated having her, taking her, loving her; and he remembered the promise he had made to her so long ago, and in one of the very few unselfish acts of his life he put it all aside.

'Come along, Mrs Johns,' he said lightly, 'we must get you home. It's late, and we both have a long day tomorrow. I'll get the bill.'

Susan stared at him, staggering almost physically from the pain of the rejection, and what she saw as the reason for it. Her eyes filled with tears; the golden room blurred.

'Excuse me,' she said, standing up, 'I must go to the toilet.

The lavatory as you would say. I'd never get it right, would I, Julian?'

'Probably not,' he said with a sigh, 'and it wouldn't matter in the very least. Not to me. Maybe to you. You've got it all wrong, Susan, but you'd never believe me.'

'I'd be a fool if I did,' she said. 'Let's go.'

It was weeks before she would talk to him alone; months before their friendship was restored. But finally, she came to understand. And she was grateful for what he had not done.

Chapter Three

London, 1953–7

Julian Morell had just banked his first million (having floated his company on the stock exchange a year earlier), when he met Eliza Grahame Black.

He was then thirty-three years old, and besides being extremely rich and hugely successful, was acknowledged one of the most charming and desirable men in London. Eliza was seventeen, and acknowledged the most beautiful and witty debutante of her year. Julian needed a wife, and Eliza needed a fortune. It was a case of natural selection.

Julian needed a wife for many reasons. He was beginning to find that having mistresses, whether short or long-term, married or single, was time-consuming and demeaning; he wanted to establish himself in a home and a household of his own; he wanted a decorative and agreeable companion; he wanted a hostess; he wanted an heir. What he was not too concerned about was love.

Eliza needed a fortune because everything in life she craved for was expensive and she had no money of her own. Being a conventionally raised upper-class girl of the fifties, she was anticipating earning it in the only way she knew how: by marrying a rich (and preferably personable) man. She was not too concerned about love either.

Eliza's father, Sir Nigel Grahame Black, was a farmer; he had five hundred acres in Wiltshire and a modest private income, one of his sons was training to be a doctor and the other a lawyer. Eliza came a long way down on the list of demands on his purse, and indeed financing her London season had been largely made possible by her godmother, Lady Ethne Powers, an erstwhile girlfriend of Sir Nigel, who had looked at the potential for investment in her charge (sixteen years old, slender, silvery haired and fine featured, with pretty manners and huge sense of fun) and handed him a cheque for a thousand pounds along with a cup of tea and a cucumber sandwich in her garden the previous September. 'Give that child a really good Season and she'll be off your hands by this time next year,' she said.

She was right. Dressed charmingly, in clothes made for her by Ethne's dressmaker, Eliza danced, chattered and charmed her way through the Season, and found her way into every society column, every important party and dance. She adored it all; she felt she had gone straight to Heaven. She was a huge success with the young men she met; but then that had been something of a foregone conclusion. What surprised everybody, not least Eliza herself, was that she also got on extremely well with the other girls, and even succeeded in charming their mothers, something of an achievement given the fact that she was considerably prettier and more amusing than a great many of their daughters.

This had a lot to do with the fact that she was simply not in the least spoilt. She might have been the youngest in her family, the only girl, and enchantingly pretty, but her mother put a high value on practical accomplishment and a low one on personal appearance; consequently Eliza found herself more sighed than exclaimed over, as her total lack of ability to cook, sew, pluck pheasants, grade eggs, hand rear lambs and indeed perform any of the basic countrywomen's skills became increasingly apparent. She did not even ride particularly well; nobody looked more wonderful hunting, but it was noticeable that she was invariably near the back of the field. Such virtues as she possessed – her beauty, her wit, and a stylishness which was apparent when at the age of twelve she took to wearing her school hat tipped slightly forward on her head, and lengthening all her dirndl skirts in deference to M. Dior and his New Look – her family put no value on whatsoever.

Consequently, Eliza grew up with an interestingly low opinion of herself; she did not lack confidence exactly, she knew she looked nice, and that she had a talent to amuse, but she did not expect other people to admire or appreciate her; and when she suddenly found herself that year so much sought after, regarded as an ornament at a party, an asset at a dinner table, it seemed to her entirely surprising and unexpected, a kind of delightful mistake on everybody's part, and it did not go to her head.

Everything to do with the Season enchanted her in that Coronation year, when the whole country was in party mood; day after dizzy day whirled past, she was drunk with it, she could not have enough.

Strangely, her presentation at Court was the least clear of her memories; it was a blur. She could remember the long long queue in the taxi in the Mall, being ushered into the palace, into the anteroom even, but she could never even recall what she wore, nor what Lady Powers wore; who sat next to her on the long wait, whether she talked, whether she giggled, whether she was nervous. She remembered the Queen, looking so very much smaller than she had expected in the throne room, and the Duke of Edinburgh trying not to look bored beside her; and she did always remember making her curtsy because she slightly overdid it, and sank just a little too low, and then it was hard to get up gracefully and she wobbled and was terrified she was going to fall over; but apart from that she could recall very little, apart from an achingly full bladder throughout the entire procedure. 'Such a waste,' she would often say to her friends, years later, 'being in the presence of the Queen of England, and just longing for it to be over so I could go and have a pee.'

But other things she did remember with extraordinary clarity: Queen Charlotte's Ball (The Harlot's Ball as it was christened by the Debs' Delights with what they considered huge wit). Henley, where she was photographed a dozen times for a dozen newspapers ('Beautiful Eliza Grahame Black, one of the brightest stars of this year's Season, arrived at Henley looking particularly appropriate in a white dress with an outsize sailor's collar and a straw boater that rivalled those of her three

escorts', rambled the gushing diarist of the *Daily Sketch*).
Ladies' Day at Ascot, perhaps most exciting of all, where she
picked three winners and found herself standing next to
Princess Margaret and the dashing Billy Wallace in the Royal
Enclosure, both of whom smiled most graciously at her. It was
an enchanted time; she could do no wrong, it seemed, fortune
smiled on her along with everybody else, and finally, in a last,
magnificent gesture, tossed a seriously rich man into the guest
list at her own dance.

Eliza's dance was held in Wiltshire on the second Saturday
in July; she wore what she and Ethne termed a proper frock – a
shimmering, embroidered cream organza crinoline from
Worth. She wore fresh cream and pink roses in her silvery hair,
a pearl necklace given to her for her presentation by her
grandmother, drop pearl earrings a gift from her godmother on
the night of the dance. It was a lyrically perfect evening; the
huge marquee was decorated with banks of white roses; there
were two bands, one jazz, one swing; there was as much
champagne as anyone could wish for, a superb supper served at
midnight, breakfast at dawn; three papers sent photographers,
there were several minor royals, and every one of the three
hundred people invited arrived. 'I do hope you realize this has
cost me a fortune which I certainly don't have,' moaned Sir
Nigel to Ethne, watching the interminable line of cars driving
up and parking in the paddock beyond the house.

'Oh, don't be so dreary,' said Ethne, 'this is an investment,
Nigel, and probably a much better one than that new strain of
cattle you've just put yourself really in debt for. This evening is
going to pay dividends. I don't know how you can look at that
daughter of yours and begrudge her a penny. She's an
enchantment, and you ought to be very proud of her instead of
regarding her as some kind of useless millstone round your
neck. Just look at her, did you ever see anything so lovely?
Honestly, Nigel, she'll make a brilliant marriage. Mark my
words.'

At this moment, most remarkably and punctually on cue,
Julian Morell arrived.

He was not in the habit of attending debutante dances, but his
brother James and his wife, as near neighbours of the Grahame

Blacks, had been asked to make up a party, and had hauled him out of London for the occasion.

He came reluctantly, not expecting for a moment that the evening would have any more to offer him at absolute best than some second-rate champagne and some modestly agreeable dancing partners; but he was fond of his brother, he had nothing else to do and besides he was running in a new car, a Mercedes convertible, and the long drive to Wiltshire would serve the purpose well.

Nevertheless, as he arrived he looked with some foreboding at the house and the marquee, wondering if it could actually offer him anything at all that he might actually want.

It could and it did; it offered him Eliza.

She stood out, at her party, like a star, a jewel; Julian took one look at her, laughing, dancing in the arms of a pale, aristocratic boy; and felt his heart, most unaccustomedly but unmistakably, in the way of the best clichés, lurch within him.

'Who is that girl?' he said to his brother who was settling the rest of the party at a table, 'the one in cream, with the fair hair?'

'That's Eliza, you fool,' said James, 'this is her party. I thought you'd met her at our place. You've certainly met her parents, her father's the local MFH, nice chap.'

'No,' said Julian, 'no, I haven't met her, I would remember her if I had.'

He sat down and watched Eliza for quite a long time, sipping what he noticed despite his misgivings was excellent champagne, studying her, savouring her, before he made his way over to Lady Powers who was engaged in much the same activity, standing on the edge of the dance floor, briefly unoccupied.

He had met her once or twice in London; he smiled at her now and took her hand, bowing over it just slightly.

'Lady Powers. Good evening. Julian Morell. You played an excellent game of bridge against my mother once: too good, she never forgave you. How are you?'

Ethne Powers looked at Julian and recognized instantly the return on her investment.

'She's pretty, isn't she, my goddaughter?' she said after they had exchanged gossip, news of Letitia, of Julian's company, of the recent flotation which Julian was charmed to discover she had read much about. 'Would you like to meet her?'

'Oh, I would,' said Julian, his eyes dancing, knowing precisely what was going through Lady Powers' mind, enjoying the game, 'I would very much. And yes, she is extremely pretty. What a lovely dress. Is it Worth?'

'Yes, it is,' said Lady Powers. 'What a very unusual man you are. How do you know about women's dresses?'

'Oh, I make it my business to,' said Julian, and then (lest the remark should sound in some way coarse, unsuitable, too much of an alien world to this one), went smoothly on, 'it suits her very well. Shall we catch her now, in between dances?'

Eliza was flushed and excited now. Two of the roses had fallen from her hair and been thrust into her bosom by some over-enthusiastic partner. She looked quite extraordinarily desirable, a curious mixture of hoyden and high-class virgin.

Lady Powers moved over towards her and raised her not inconsiderable voice. 'Darling. Come over here, I want to introduce you to someone.'

Eliza looked up at Julian and knew she had, quite literally, met her match. He stood out, much as she herself did on that evening, as someone of outstanding physical attractiveness and style. He wore his white tie and tails, as he did everything, with a kind of careless grace; his face was tanned, his dark eyes, skimming over her unashamedly, brilliant and alive with pleasure. As he took her small hand in his she felt his energy, his unmistakable capacity for pleasure, somehow entering her; she met his gaze with frank, undisguised interest.

To her enchantment, after he had bowed briefly over her hand, said 'Miss Grahame Black' and smiled at her, he raised her hand to his lips and gave it the lightest, slightest kiss; something inside Eliza quivered, she felt awed and excited.

'How strange, how sad,' he said, 'that we have never met before. Could you spare me a dance? Or would that be too much to hope for?'

'Not quite too much, although not quite straight away,' she said –bravely, for all she wanted was to fall into his arms and stay there for the rest of the night, and was fearful that he might not wait for her if she did not. 'I've promised the next one and the one after that, but then it would be lovely.'

'I shall wait,' he said solemnly, 'and perhaps your godmother will keep me company until then. If not, then I shall simply have to be lonely.'

'Oh, fiddlesticks,' said Lady Powers, 'there's not a woman in this room who wouldn't like to dance with you. Who did you come with anyway?'

'My brother, James, and his wife, Caroline. Oh, and the Hetheringtons and the Branksome Joneses. Caroline's parents, the Reever Smiths.'

'Good God,' said Lady Powers. 'How perfectly appalling for you. Perhaps you'd better stay with me. Come along, let's find you a drink, and then you can give me a dance.'

'That would be delightful.'

But for the rest of the night he danced with Eliza; she was a beautiful dancer, graceful and musical, with a taut suppressed energy that he felt augured well for her sexuality. She was tiny, he realized as he took her in his arms for the waltz; she stood well below his shoulder, it added to her child-likeness. But then she was only seventeen. It was a long long time since he had had anything to do with any woman as young; scarcely a woman either, certainly a virgin, he would have to tread with care.

Eliza was very much a virgin: she had been repeatedly kissed and occasionally fondled rather as if she was a puppy by the over-enthusiastic under-skilled boys she had met and danced with during her magical summer but that was as far as her sexual experience extended. She had spent her entire life in the company of women; her two brothers had never had any time for her, and although their friends had occasionally remarked on Eliza's prettiness and her charm, had been very much discouraged from pursuing matters in any way.

The fondling boys had seemed to her mere accessories, to be worn rather like a hat or a necklace, to set her off to her best advantage, they had touched no chord of feeling of any kind. She had never met a man who had inspired the kind of all-consuming, hungry yearning that most girls – and particularly very innocent girls – fall prey to. She did not spend long hours imagining herself in the arms of anybody in particular, did not dream of any declaration of passionate and lifelong devotion,

95

had not come across anybody at all who made her blush, stumble over her words, whose name made her start, whose image haunted her dreams. The only men she did daydream about were totally beyond reach (most notably Mr Frank Sinatra and Mr Gregory Peck), but she was emotionally, as well as physically, totally untouched and her fantasies were more to do with being discovered and starring in films with them than being crushed to their manly breasts and swept off to nights of passion.

She found, as did so many very young girls of her background, the thought of nights of passion intriguing but a trifle incomprehensible. Having grown up on a farm, she had no illusions about precisely what took place between the male and female animal, but she found it very difficult to equate that with pleasure and what might take place between her and one of the fumbling boys. The nearest she had ever come to a truly pleasant physical sensation was climbing the ropes at school; then, several times, she had experienced an explosion of pleasure so great she had found it hard to walk normally and casually when she got to the ground. She had asked her best friend if she knew what she was talking about and the best friend said no, so she had assumed there must be something odd about her, and (while continuing the climb the ropes rather too vigorously from time to time in pursuit of the pleasure), had kept quiet about it; it was only at a giggly girls' lunch during her Season that someone had referred to a 'real climbing up the ropes feeling' and she had realized with a surge of relief that she was not a misfit and indeed possibly had much to look forward to at the hands of the fondlers. But it had not come. Yet.

Dancing with Julian that night, during the extraordinary series of emotions that shot through her, she thought briefly, and to her own surprise, of that conversation and realized that along with happiness, emotional confusion and excitement, and a strange sense that she was no longer in command of herself, certain unexpected and unfamiliar physical sensations were invading her as well. She smiled to herself at the thought, and Julian noticed.

'What are you thinking about?'

'Oh,' said Eliza lightly and with perfect truth, 'school actually.'

'How very unflattering. Here I am, dancing to the very best of my ability and trying to engage you in interesting conversation, and all you can think about is school. Did you like school, Miss Grahame Black?'

'I loathed it.'

'Where did you go?'

'Wycombe Abbey.'

'Oh, well you would have done. I disapprove of boarding school for girls myself.'

'So do I.'

'Then,' he said lightly, 'our daughters will all go to day schools or stay at home with governesses. All right?'

'Absolutely all right.'

It was a conversation she was often to remember in the years ahead.

Julian was completely unlike anyone Eliza had ever met. It was not just that he was so much older than she was; it was his clothes, his cars, his lifestyle, the things he talked about, the people he knew; and, perhaps most alien to her background and upbringing, the acute importance of money and the making of it in his life. He was obviously immeasurably richer than anyone she had ever met but that was less significant than the fact that he had made his money himself. Eliza had grown up in a society that did not talk about money; and that regarded the making of it in large quantities as something rather undesirable; it betrayed an adherence to a code of values and a set of necessities that found no place in upper-class rural life. Nevertheless he was not what her mother described (in a hushed voice) as a nouveau (had he not after all lived five miles away from her most of his life, been to Marlborough like so many of the fumblers, and ride to hounds and dress with impeccable taste?) So it was hard to define exactly what made him so exciting, gave him just the faintest aura of unsuitability. She only knew that getting to know him was like discovering some totally new, hitherto unimagined country. And she got to know him (as she thought) extremely well and very quickly. He simply never left her alone. At the end of her dance he had said goodbye, very correctly, with the most chaste of kisses on her forehead (much to her disappointment) and driven off to

97

London; she watched the tail lights of the Mercedes disappearing into the darkness and fell into a desperate anxiety that she would never see him again. But he phoned her next morning, thanking her for a wonderful evening, and asking her to dinner on the Monday night.

'I'd love to,' she said, her heart soaring and singing above her hangover, 'I – I shall probably be back in London with my godmother. At the Albany. Shall I give you the number?'

'I have it,' he said. 'I made sure of it before I left.'

'Oh,' she said, smiling foolishly into the phone at this small, important piece of information, 'well, then, perhaps you could ring me in the afternoon and arrange when to pick me up.'

'I will,' he said. 'How are you this morning?'

'I feel terrible,' she said. 'How about you?'

'I feel wonderful,' he said. 'It was the best evening I can remember for a very long time.'

'Oh, good.' She could hear herself sounding gauche and uninteresting. 'I enjoyed it too. Well, thank you for ringing. I'll look forward to tomorrow.'

Julian took her out to dinner that first evening at the Connaught. Her godmother had taken her once, as she had to most of the best hotels and restaurants in London; she said it was important for any girl not to be unfamiliar with places she might be taken with men, particularly the more expensive ones, it put them at a disadvantage. But being at the Connaught with Julian was not too like being there with her godmother.

The Connaught, Julian had often thought, and indeed put the thought to the test, had been designed with seduction in mind. It was not just its quite ridiculous extravagance, the way it pampered and spoilt its customers even before they pushed through the swing doors; nor the peculiar blend of deference and friendliness shown by the staff to its more favourite customers; nor its spectacular elegance, nor that of its guests; not even the wonder of its menu, its restrained adventurousness, the treasures of its cellar, the precisely perfect timing of its service; it was the strange quality it had of being something, just a little, like a private house, it had an intimacy, a humanity. He had often tried to pinpoint the exact nature of that quality; as he got ready for dinner with Eliza, contemplating the undoubted pleasure to come, he realized suddenly what it was.

'Carnal knowledge,' he said to his reflection in the mirror, 'that's what the old place has.' And he smiled at the thought of placing Eliza within it.

They talked, that night, for hours and hours. Or rather Eliza did. She forgot to eat (her sole went back to the kitchen virtually untouched, to the great distress of the chef, despite Julian's repeated reassurances) and she hardly drank anything either. She had no need to; she was excited, relaxed, exhilarated all at once simply by being where she was, and the enchantment of being with someone who not only seemed to want to hear what she had to say but gave it serious consideration. Eliza was used to being dismissed, to having her views disregarded; Julian's gift for listening, for easing the truth from women about themselves, was never more rapturously received – or so well rewarded.

He sat across the table from her, watching her, enjoying her, and enjoying the fact that he was disturbing her just a little, and he learnt all he needed to know about her and more.

He learnt that she was intelligent, but ill-read and worse informed; that she loved clothes, dancing and the cinema; that she hated the theatre and loathed concerts; that she liked women as much as men; that her parents had been strangely unsupportive and detached; that she had been curiously lonely for much of her childhood; that her beauty was a source of pleasure to her, but had not made her arrogant; that she was indeed utterly sexually inexperienced and at engaging pains to conceal the matter; and that she was a most intriguing blend of self-confident and self-deprecating, much given to claiming her incompetence and stupidity on a great many counts. It all added up to a most interesting and desirable commodity.

Eliza learnt little of him, by contrast; trained by her godmother to talk to men, to draw them out, she tried hard to make Julian tell her about his childhood, his experiences in the war, his early days with the company. She failed totally; he smiled at her, his most engaging, charming smile, and told her that his childhood had no doubt been much like her own, as they had been such near neighbours, that she would be dreadfully bored by the rather mundane details of how his company had been born, and that to someone as young as she

99

was, the war must seem like history and he had no intention of turning himself into a historic figure.

Eliza found this perfectly acceptable; she was still child enough to be told what she should think, and be interested in, and if he was more interested in talking about her than about himself then that seemed to her to be a charming compliment. It did not occur to her that this aspect of her youth was, for Julian, one of her greatest assets. And she was a great deal older and wiser before she recognized it for the ruthless, deliberate isolation of her from his most personal self that it was.

What he did make her feel that night, and for many nights, was more interesting, more amusing and more worldly than she had ever imagined she could be; and more aware of herself, in an oddly potent way. She had always known she was pretty, that people liked to be with her; but that night she felt desirable and desired, for the very first time, and it was an exciting and delicious discovery. It wasn't anything especially that Julian said, or even that he did; simply the way he looked at her, smiled at her, studied her, responded to her. And for the first time also, since she had been a very young child, she found herself thinking of, yearning for even, physical contact: to be touched, held, stroked, caressed.

Julian kissed her that night; not chastely on the forehead, but on the mouth; he had had great hopes of that mouth, so full, so soft, so sensual-seeming, and he was not disappointed. 'You are,' he told her gently as he drew back, more disturbed than he had expected to be, wondering precisely how long he would be able to defer her seduction, 'most beautiful. Most lovely. I want to see you again and again.'

He did see her, again and again. Every morning he phoned her, wherever she was, either at home in Wiltshire or at Ethne's flat in the Albany. If she was in London he insisted on her having lunch with him; he would spend hours over lunch, there was never any hurry, it seemed (or hardly ever); he would meet her at half past twelve, and there was always a bottle of Bollinger or Moët waiting by the table when she arrived, and he would sit listening to her, laughing with her, talking to her until well after three. In the evening he met her for drinks at seven, and then took her out to dinner and then to dance at nightclubs; she liked the Blue Angel best in Berkeley Square where Hutch sat at the piano and played whatever he was asked in his quiet, amused and amusing way, the classics of Cole Porter and Rodgers and Hart, and the great songs of that year, 'Cry Me a River' and 'Secret Love'; but Eliza often asked him to play her own favourite, 'All the Things You Are', and sat and gazed, drowned, in Julian's brilliant dark eyes, and discovered for the first time the great truth of Mr Coward's pronouncement about the potency of cheap music. They drank endless champagne and talked and talked, and laughed and danced until far far into the night on the small, crowded floor, in the peculiarly public privacy created by warmth and darkness and sexy music.

And every night Julian delivered Eliza home to her god-mother and her bed, and drove back to Chelsea and his, after doing no more than kissing her and driving her to a torment of frustration and anxiety. He must, she knew, have great sexual experience; he could not possibly, she felt, be satisfied with mere kissing for very long, and yet the weeks went by and he demanded nothing more of her. Was she too young to be of sexual interest to him, she wondered; was she simply not attractive? Was he (most dreadful thought of all) merely spending so much time with her in the absence of anyone more interesting and exciting? She did not realize that these were precisely the things he intended her to think, to wonder, to fear; so that when the time had finally come for him to seduce her, she would be relieved, grateful, overwhelmed and his task would be easier, more rewarding, and emotionally heightened.

Meanwhile, almost without her realizing it, he aroused her appetite; he did not frighten her, or hurry her, he simply brought her to a fever of impatience and hunger, awakening in her feelings and sensations she had never dreamt herself capable of, and then, tenderly, gently, lovingly, left her be. And he had decided to marry her before he finally took her to bed.

There was much speculation about Julian's engagement to the almost absurdly young Eliza Grahame Black. Why (London society wondered to itself, and particularly female London society) should a man of such urbanity, worldly knowledge, sexual sophistication, decide to marry a girl sixteen years younger than he was, almost young enough (as London society kept remarking) to be his daughter, with no more experience of life than the rather limited variety to be gained in the school dormitory and the debutante dance. She might be, indeed she was, extremely beautiful and very sweet, but the marriage of such a person to Julian Morell could only be compared to setting a novice rider astride a thoroughbred and sending it off down a three-mile straight: the horse would do precisely as it wished, and would not pause to give its rider the merest consideration. And perhaps (remarked London society, nodding wisely over a great many cocktails and luncheons and dinners), that was precisely the charm of the match.

The Grahame Blacks received Julian's request for their daughter's hand with extremely mixed feelings. Clearly it was a brilliant marriage, he could offer her the world and a little more; moreover he gave every sign of caring very much for her. Nevertheless, Mary had severe misgivings. She felt Eliza was to be led into a life for which she was not prepared and was ill suited; and although her perspective of Julian's life was a little hazy, she was surprisingly correct.

Julian's friends were all much older than Eliza, most of them had been married for years, and were embarking on the bored merry-go-round of adultery that occupies the moneyed classes through their middle years. They tended to regard her, therefore, as something of a nuisance, an interloper, who had deprived them of one of the more amusing members of their circle, and in whose presence their behaviour had to be somewhat modified.

They were not the sort of people Eliza had grown up with, friends of her parents, or even the more sophisticated friends of her godmother; they were, many of them, pleasure seekers, pursuing their quarry wherever they might find it: killing time, and boredom, skiing for weeks at a time in Klosters or Aspen Colorado, following the sun to the Caribbean and the Bahamas, racing at Longchamps, shopping in Paris, Milan and New York, educating their children in the international schools, and spending money with a steady, addictive compulsion. All this Eliza would have to learn: how to speak their language, share their concerns, master their accomplishments, and it would not be easy.

Also, once the first rapture of the relationship was over, Eliza would plainly have to learn to live with Julian's other great love, his company; he was an acutely busy man, he travelled a great deal, and his head and to a degree his heart as well as his physical presence were frequently elsewhere. Eliza was very young and she did not have a great many of her own resources; her parents could see much boredom and loneliness in store for her.

There was also that other great hazard of the so-called brilliant marriage, the disagreeable spectre of inequality. It is all very well, as Mary Grahame Black pointed out to Lady Powers, catching a man vastly richer than yourself; but for the rest of your life, or at least until you are extremely well settled into it, you are forced to regard yourself (and certainly others will regard you thus) as fortunate, and worse than fortunate, inferior. Lady Powers pooh-poohed this (mainly because there was nothing else she could do) but she had to concede that it was an element in the affair, and that Eliza might find it difficult.

'But then, every marriage has its problems. Many of them worse things than that. Suppose she was going to marry somebody very poor. Or dishonest. Or . . .' she dredged her mind for the worst horrors she could find there, 'common. The child is managing to hold her own brilliantly at the moment. She will cope. And she does look perfectly wonderful.'

This was true. Eliza did look perfectly wonderful. There was no other way to describe it. She didn't just look beautiful and happy, she had developed a kind of gloss, a sleekness, a careless confidence. The reason was sex.

Eliza took to sex with an enthusiasm and a hunger that surprised even Julian.

'I have something for you,' he had said to her early one evening when he came to pick her up from the Albany. 'Look. I hope you like it.'

He gave her a small box; inside it was a sapphire and diamond art deco ring that he had bought at Sotheby's.

'I thought it would suit you.'

'Oh, Julian, it's beautiful. I love it. I don't deserve it.'

'Yes, you do. But you can only have it on one condition.'

'What?'

'That you marry me.'

Eliza looked at him, very seriously. She had thought, even expected that he would ask her, even while she had been afraid that he would not, and the moment was too important, too serious to play silly games.

'Of course I will marry you,' she said, placing her hand in his in a gesture he found oddly touching. 'I would adore to marry you. Thank you for asking me,' she added, with the echo of the well-brought-up child she had so recently been, and then, even as he laughed at her, she said, with all the assurance of the sensual woman she had become, 'but I want you to make love to me. Please. Soon. I don't think I can wait very much longer.'

'Not until we are married?'

'Certainly not until we are married.'

'I hope you realize this is what I should be saying to you, rather than you to me.'

'Yes, of course I do. But I thought you probably wouldn't.'

'I have been trying not to.'

'I know.'

'But I wanted to. Desperately. As I hope you knew.'

'Well, you can. I wish you would.'

'Eliza.'

'Yes?'

'Will you come to bed with me? Very very soon?'

'Yes,' she said, 'yes, yes I will.'

She was ardent, tender, eager to learn, to please, to give, and most important to take. Where he had expected to find diffidence, he found impatience; instead of shyness, there was confidence, instead of reticence a glorious, greedy abandon.

'Are you quite sure you haven't ever done this before?' said Julian, smiling, stroking her tiny breasts, kissing her nipples, smoothing back her silvery hair after she had most triumphantly come not once but three times. 'Nicely reared young ladies aren't supposed to be quite so successful straight away, you know, they need a little coaxing.'

'It isn't straight away,' said Eliza, stretching herself with pleasure, 'it's the – let me see – the fourth time we've been to bed. And you've been coaxing me, haven't you, for weeks and weeks.'

'You noticed.'

'Of course. Most of the time,' she added truthfully, 'I couldn't notice anything else.'

He laughed. 'You're wonderful. Really, really wonderful. I'm a very lucky man. I mean it. And I adore you.'

'Do you really?'

'I really really do.'

They were to be married at Holy Trinity Brompton at Eliza's own insistence; it nearly broke her mother's heart not to have the wedding in the country, deeply grieved her father, and even Lady Powers was hard pressed to defend her, but Eliza was adamant; she had fallen in love with London and its society and nothing on earth, she said, was going to persuade her to drag her smart new friends down to the wilds of Wiltshire for a hick country wedding.

What was more she wanted a dress from Hartnell for her wedding and that was that; she wasn't going to be married in a dress made by anybody less. Lady Powers told her first gently, then sharply that her father could hardly be expected to pay for such a dress, and Eliza had answered that she had no intention of her father paying for it, and that Julian was perfectly happy to do so.

'I imagine your father will be very hurt,' said Lady Powers. 'I think you should talk to him about it.'

'Oh, you do all fuss,' cried Eliza irritably. 'All right, I'll tell him next weekend. I must go and get dressed now. Julian's taking me to *South Pacific* tonight, we were just so lucky to get tickets.'

Sir Nigel *was* very hurt about the dress; and the location for the wedding; Eliza stormed upstairs after dinner, leaving Julian to salvage the situation as best he could.

'I know you don't like the idea of this London wedding, and I quite understand,' he said, smiling at them gently over his brandy. 'To be quite honest I'd rather be married in the country myself. But I'm afraid all this London business has gone to Eliza's head, and I suppose we should humour her a little. After all it is her wedding day, and I very much hope she won't be having another, so maybe we should put our own wishes aside. As for the dress, well I really would like to help in some way. I know how devilishly expensive everything is now, and the wedding itself is going to cost such a lot and you've been so good to me all this year; let me buy her her dress. It would be a way of saying thank you for everything; most of all for Eliza.'

The Grahame Blacks were more than a little mollified by this, and accepted reluctantly but gracefully; but Mary, lying awake that night thinking about Julian's words, tried to analyse precisely what it was about them that had made her feel uneasy. It was nearly dawn before she succeeded, and then she did not feel she could share the knowledge: Julian had been talking about Eliza exactly as if he were her father and not in the least as if he was a man in love.

There was another person deeply affected by the prospective marriage, and that was Letitia.

Letitia was losing more than a son (and gaining a daughter was little compensation); she was losing her best friend, her life's companion, her housemate, her escort. The only thing she was not losing was her business partner, and the thought of that, as she contemplated Eliza's invasion of her life, was curiously comforting. She did not exactly feel sorry for herself, that was not her style, but she did have a sense of loss, and what she could only describe to herself as nostalgia. The playhouse would be hers now, to live her own life in, and that would have its advantages, to be sure; but the fun, the excitement, the closeness she and Julian had shared for five dizzy years was clearly about to be very much over.

She viewed the marriage with some foreboding; she found it hard to believe that Julian was in love with Eliza, she had never known him to be in love with anyone, and that he should suddenly discover the emotion within the arms of a seventeen-year child, however appealing, seemed highly unlikely. When she taxed him with it, he had looked at her with dark, blank eyes and said, 'Mother, you said yourself it was time I got married. Don't you remember? And you were absolutely right. I'm simply doing what you tell me, as usual.'

'But not, I hope,' said Letitia, refusing to rise to this irritating piece of bait, 'to the first person who accepts you? She is very very young, Julian, and not greatly experienced.'

'She is the first person who has accepted me,' he said lightly, 'but she is also the first person I have asked. I like her youth and I like her lack of experience. I find them refreshing and charming.'

'Well, if that's all you find them, all well and good,' said Letitia.

'What else would I find them?'

'Oh, untroublesome. Malleable. Grateful perhaps.'

'What an extraordinary remark,' he said.

Letitia let the subject drop.

She did not exactly dislike Eliza, indeed she grew, in the end, quite fond of her; she admired her beauty, appreciated her style, and found the way she was quite clearly setting out to be A Good Wife oddly touching.

Eliza, rather unexpectedly, admired Letitia greatly, indeed had something approaching a schoolgirl crush on her. She thought she was wonderful in every possible way, and told Julian that when she was old (Julian was careful not to relay this particular bit of the conversation to Letitia) she hoped she would be exactly like her. Nevertheless, she was greatly in awe of her, and in her more realistic moments recognized that as mothers-in-law went, hers was more of a challenge than most.

Letitia was sympathetic to this; she could see precisely how daunting she would have been to any bride, but particularly someone as young and unworldly as Eliza, but the more she tried not to daunt, the more she was aware of seeming patronizing and irritating. She was also concerned that Eliza seemed not to have the slightest idea how important Julian's company was to him, and what a vast and consuming element it was in his life; he had been neglecting it rather over the past three months, but she knew that would simply mean that when the honeymoon was over – literally – he would be more absorbed and occupied with it than ever. He was clearly not going to spell that out to a tender and ardent bride, but somebody had to, in the bride's interest; Letitia decided to take the bull, or rather the heifer, by the horns, and confront Eliza with the various unpalatable truths, as she saw them.

She invited Eliza to lunch at First Street, a few weeks after the engagement was announced, ostensibly to discuss wedding plans; dresses, bridesmaids, music and flowers occupied them through the first course, but halfway through the compote she put down her spoon, picked up her glass and said, 'Eliza, I wonder if you realize quite what you are marrying?'

Eliza, startled, put down her own spoon, looked nervously at Letitia and blushed. 'I think I do,' she said firmly. 'I hope I do.'

'Well, you see,' said Letitia, equally firmly, 'I'm afraid you don't. You think you are about to become the wife of a rich man who will be giving some of his time and attention to his company, but most of it to you. I'm afraid it will be rather the other way round.'

Eliza's chin went up; she was not easily frightened.

'I don't know quite what you mean,' she said, 'but of course I realize that Julian is a very busy man. That he has to work very hard.'

'No,' said Letitia, 'he is not just a very busy man. He is an obsessed man. That company is everything – well, almost everything – to him. How much do you know about it, Eliza? About Morell's? Tell me.'

She sounded and felt cross; anyone who could approach marriage to Julian without a very full grasp of his business seemed to her to be without a very full grasp of him; realizing that Julian had talked to Eliza even less about it than she had thought, she felt cross with him as well.

'Quite a lot,' said Eliza. 'I know he's built it up from nothing all by himself and that the cosmetic range is very successful and that he's hoping to start selling it in New York soon.'

'I see,' said Letitia, not sure whether she was more irritated at hearing that Julian had built up the company all by himself, or that he was planning to go to New York, a piece of information he had not shared with her.

'And do you know about any of the people who work for us?'

'Well, I know there's a wonderful chemist called Adam – Sarsted – is it?'

'Yes,' said Letitia. 'Some of us are less impressed by his wonderfulness than others. Go on.'

'And I met a clever woman called Mrs Johns. She frightened me a bit,' she added, forgetting for a moment she was supposed to be presenting a cool grown-up front.

'She frightens us all,' said Letitia cheerfully, 'not least your fiancé. Now then, Eliza, there's a bit more about the company that you should understand. First that it is just about the most important thing in the world to Julian. It is mistress, wife and children, and you must never forget it.'

'What about mother?' said Eliza bravely.

'No, not mother. Mother is part of it' (Good shot, Eliza, she thought).

'Which part?'

'A very important part. The part that pays the bills.'

'So what exactly do you *do* there?'

'I'm the financial director, Eliza. I run the financial side of it. I decide how much we should invest, how much we should pay people, what we can afford to buy, what we can afford to spend. In the very beginning, there was only Julian and me. We've built it up together.'

'So it's not Julian's company? It's yours as well.'

'Well, it is largely his. I have a share in it of course, and I know how important my role is. But the ideas, the input, the – what shall we say – inspiration, oh dear, that sounds very pretentious, doesn't it? – are his. The company certainly wouldn't have happened without him. But it wouldn't have kept going without me either.' She spoke with a certain pride, looked at Eliza a trifle challengingly. 'We started it,' she said, 'on what capital we could rake together, and an overdraft. We worked very hard, terribly long hours. It was all great fun, but it was very very demanding and at times extremely worrying. Did Julian tell you none of this?'

Eliza shook her head.

'I'm surprised. He usually can't stop talking about it. There was just the three of us, then; Julian, who sold all the products, just the patent medicines, no cosmetics in those days, to the chemists, driving all over the country in his car; Jim Macdougall working on formulation; and me managing the money and keeping us from bankruptcy. Just. Susan joined us after the first year or so. She is a remarkable young woman, and Julian is deeply dependent on her.'

'What – what do you mean?' said Eliza in a small alien voice.

'Oh, nothing that need trouble you,' said Letitia briskly. 'I don't mean he's in love with her.' She was silent for a moment, remembering the point at which she had feared that very thing. 'But she is part of the company, a crucial part, and therefore a crucial part of his life.'

'What does she do?' asked Eliza.

'Oh, she runs the company. From an administrative point of view. Keeps us all in order. Everything under control. Julian made her a director last year. You didn't know that either?'

Eliza shook her head miserably.

'Well,' said Letitia comfortingly, 'he's obviously been much too busy discussing your future to talk about his past. But anyway, Susan and I work together a great deal, as you can imagine. The financial side of the company and the administration are very intertwined. Obviously. So you see, the company is a huge part of my life, as well as Julian's. I just wanted you to understand that, before you became part of the family.' There, she thought, I wonder what she will make of all that.

'Do you think,' said Eliza, a trifle tremulously, 'that I could get involved with the company too? Work there, I mean?'

'Oh, my darling child,' said Letitia, unsure whether she was more appalled at the notion, or at what Julian's reaction would be, 'I shouldn't think so. Julian obviously doesn't want you to have anything to do with it. Otherwise he'd have suggested it by now.'

'I suppose then,' said Eliza, in a rather flat sad voice, 'that's why he hasn't told me anything about it all. To keep me well out of it. He probably thinks I'm too stupid.'

'Eliza, I can assure you that Julian doesn't consider you in the least stupid,' said Letitia firmly. 'Quite the reverse. I don't quite know why he hasn't told you more about the company, and I think you should ask him. But you can see how important it was that I should explain. Because when things are back on an even keel, and you are settled into a normal life together, you will find that Julian devotes a great deal of his time and attention to the company – a great deal – and I don't want you to think it's because he doesn't love you, or doesn't want to be with you.'

'No,' said Eliza, sounding very subdued. 'No, but of course I might have done. So thank you for telling me. I'll talk to Julian about it all anyway. I think I should. That was a delicious lunch, Mrs Morell, thank you very much.'

'It was a pleasure. You can call me Letitia,' said Letitia graciously. 'Come again. I enjoy your company.'

'I will. Thank you.'

She watched Eliza walking rather slowly up the street, wondering just what size of hornet's nest she had stirred up.

It was quite a big one. Eliza had a row with Julian about what she saw as a conspiracy to keep her from a proper involvement with his company; Julian had a row with Letitia about what he saw as a piece of unwarranted interference; Lady Powers telephoned Letitia and gave her a piece of her mind for sending Eliza away seriously upset; Eliza had a fight with Lady Powers for interfering in her affairs. Out of it all, only Eliza emerged in a thoroughly creditable light. Julian appeared arrogant and dismissive; Letitia scheming and self-important; and Lady Powers overbearing and rude.

The worst thing about it all, as Eliza said in the middle of her heated exchange with her godmother, was that they all appeared to regard her as a child, somebody unable to think, act and worst of all, stand up for herself.

'I am not a child, I am a woman, about to be married,' she said. 'I would be grateful if you would treat me as such.'

But it was one thing to say it, and another to confront, in the privacy of herself, the fact that she so patently appeared to everyone, most importantly the man who was about to be her husband, in such an insignificant light. It hurt her almost beyond endurance; in time she forgave them all, even Julian, but it changed her perception of him, however slightly, and she never quite trusted him again.

Susan Johns was not quite sure what she felt about Julian's marriage; a range of emotions infiltrated her consciousness, none of them entirely pleasing. What she would most have liked to feel, what she knew would be most appropriate, would have been nothing at all, save a mild rather distant interest; the savage jealousy, the desire to impinge herself on Eliza's consciousness, the scorn and disappointment at Julian's choice of a wife, these were all undignified, unseemly and uncomfortable. He had told her over lunch one day; he had taken her to Simpson's in the Strand, where he assured her she could eat a whole cow if she liked; over her second helping of trifle, finally unable to postpone the moment any longer, he had told her.

Susan pushed her bowl to one side, fixed him with her large, clear blue eyes and said, 'What on earth do you want to do that for?'

Thrown, as always, by a direct question, he struggled visibly to find a route around it. 'My dear Susan,' he said, 'what an inappropriate response to such romantic news. Are you going to tell me what it's all about?' He smiled at her carefully; she met his gaze coldly.

'Don't switch on your famous charm, please. It makes me uncomfortable. And I'm not hostile. Just – well, surprised I suppose.'

'What by? I need a wife.'

'Yes,' she said, and there was a cold wall of scorn in her eyes. 'Of course you do.'

'Well?'

'I just don't happen to think that's a very good reason for marrying someone.'

'Susan, I'm not just marrying someone. I'm marrying someone who is very important to me. Someone I want to share my life with. Someone –'

'Someone who'll be good at the job?'

He looked at her, and for a moment she thought he was going to lose his temper. He suddenly smiled instead. It was the kind of unpredictability that made her go on, against all the evidence, setting a value on him.

'Yes. If you like.'

'Well, I hope you'll be very happy,' she said, scooping up what was left of her trifle.

'You don't sound very convinced.'

'I'm not.'

'Why not?'

'Because,' she said, looking at him very directly, searching out what little she could read in his dark eyes, 'you haven't said anything at all about love.'

The house Julian bought for them was undoubtedly one of the most beautiful in London, one of the Nash terraces on the west side of the Regent's Park, huge and spacious, with a great vaulted hall and staircase and a glorious drawing room filled with light that ran the entire width of the first floor and overlooked the park. Eliza discovered in herself a certain flair for interior design, albeit a trifle fussy for Julian's taste, and instead of calling David Hicks into her house to style it, like most of their smart friends, she set to work herself, poring over magazines and books, roaming Harvey Nichols and Liberty and antique salerooms herself, choosing wallpapers and curtain fabrics, innovatory colour schemes and clever little quirks of decor (setting a tiny conservatory into the end of the dining room, placing a spiral staircase from the top landing up to the roof) that made the house original and charming without in any way damaging its style. The main bedroom above the drawing room was her special love; she shared with Julian a passion for the deco period and there was nothing in their room that wasn't a very fine example of that style – a marvellous suite of bed, dressing table and wardrobe by Ruhlmann, in light rosewood, a pair of Tiffany lamps by the bed, a priceless collection of Chiparus figures on the fireplace; a set of original Erté drawings given to her by Letitia who had once met and charmed the great man; and a mass of enchanting details, cigarette boxes, ashtrays, jugs, vases, mirrors. The room was entirely white: walls, carpet, curtains, bedspread ('Very virginal, my darling,' said Julian, 'how inappropriate'). It was a stage set, a background for an extraordinarily confident display of style and taste.

On the spacious half landings she created small areas furnished with sofas, small tables, books, pictures, sometimes a desk, all in different periods: thirties for the nursery floor, twenties for the bedroom floor, pure Regency for the one above the drawing room. And on the ground floor, to the left of the huge hall, she created her very own private sitting room that was a shrine to Victoriana; she made it dark, and almost claustrophobic, with William Morris wallpaper, a brass grate, small button-back chairs, embroidered footstools, sentimental paintings; she put jardinières in it, filled with ferns and palms, a scrap screen, a brass-inlaid piano; she covered the fireplace with bric-a-brac, collected samplers, draped small tables with lace cloths, and in the window she hung a small bird cage in which two lovebirds sang. It was a flash of humour, of eccentricity, and a total contrast to the light and space and clarity of the rest of the house. Julian loathed it and refused to set foot inside it.

'That's all right, my darling,' said Eliza lightly, 'that room is for me anyway, it's my parlour. Leave me be in it.'

'For what?'

'To entertain my lovers, of course; what else?'

Then she was very busy buying clothes for herself; she did not only go to the English designers and shops, but took herself to Paris twice a year to buy from the great names, from Dior, Patou, Fath, Balmain, Balenciaga. She was clever with clothes; she had a very definite almost stark taste, and a passion for white and beige. She could look just as wonderful in things from the ready to wear boutiques in Paris as well; her beauty was becoming less childlike, but she was slender, delicate, a joy to dress, a favourite customer.

Then there was the social life; she and Julian began to give parties that became legendary, and she discovered she had a talent as a hostess, mixing and matching likely and unlikely people brilliantly. Her dinner parties were famous, a heady blend of names, fine wine and food and scandalous talk; Eliza Morell, like her mother-in-law, had an ear and an eye for gossip and a wit to match it.

She developed an admittedly rather gossip-column-style interest in politics and a liking for politicians, and the gossip of Westminster as well as of London society. She preferred socialists to Tories, she found them more interesting and charismatic; and she was amused by their intellectual approach to socialism which seemed to her to have so extremely little to do with reality. She met Michael Foot and his wife Jill Craigie at a party and liked them very much; they were in turn rather charmed by her, and accepted her invitation to dinner. Through them she met some of the other leading socialists of the day: Crossman and Gaitskell and the dashing Anthony Wedgwood Benn. Julian found her interest in such men and matters intriguing, amusing even, but he couldn't share it. He told her that all politicians were self-seeking and manipulative ('I would have thought you would have much in common with them, my darling,' Eliza had replied lightly); the company he sought and valued, apart from amusing and pretty women, were businessmen whose time and energies were directed fiercely, determinedly and tirelessly to the process of making money, building companies, creating empires. They seemed to him to be the real people concerned with reality; they did not theorize, they had no time to, they acted, they fought, and they won.

What he did not understand about Eliza's interest in politics was that it was an area that, in their marriage, she could stake a claim in, something she could know about and enjoy that he did not. Letitia had been quite right, she did feel excluded, ostracized even, from the company, and she was often, before she made friends of her own, lonely, and worse than that, diminished. She tried to become involved, to make Julian discuss matters with her, take her on trips, but he discouraged her, first gently, then more vigorously: 'The business is mine, Eliza my darling, my problem, my concern; yours is our home, and our life together, and in due course I hope, our family. I need a refuge from my work, and I want you to provide it; I really would not want you to be distracted from anything so important.'

'But I feel shut out,' said Eliza fretfully. 'Your work is so important to you, I want to share it.'

Julian looked at her almost coldly. 'Eliza, you couldn't. It's too complex, and it is not what I want from you. Now please, let us not have any more of this.'

And so she gave up.

She learnt very quickly too that she was not going to find very much true friendship from within Julian's circle. The women were all ten years at least older than her, and although charming and outwardly friendly found very little to say to her; they were worlds of experience away from her, they found her lightweight, boring even, and although the Morells were very generously entertained as a couple and people flocked to their house and their parties, Eliza found herself excluded from the gossipy women's lunches, the time-killing activities they all went in for – riding in the park, playing tennis, running various charity committees. She had two or three friends from her debutante days, and she saw them, and talked to them, but they had all married much younger men, who Julian had no time for and did not enjoy seeing at his dinner table, and so she kept the two elements in her life separate, and tried not to notice how lonely she often felt. But her political friends were a great comfort to her, she felt they proved to herself as well as to Julian that she was not simply an empty-headed foolish child, incapable of coherent thought; and she also found their company a great deal more amusing and stimulating than that of the businessmen and their wives, and the partying, globetrotting socialites that Julian chose to surround himself with.

By the time they had been married a year, Eliza was learning disillusionment. In many ways her life was still a fairy tale; she was rich, indulged, admired. But her loneliness, her sense of not belonging, went beyond their social life and even Julian's addiction to his work. She felt excluded from him, from his most intimate self; looking back over their courtship, she could see that while he had listened to her endlessly, encouraged her to talk, showed a huge interest in everything to do with her, he rarely talked about himself. In the self-obsession of youth and love she had not noticed it at the time; six months into her marriage, she thought of little else. She would try to talk to him, to persuade him to communicate with her, to share his thoughts, his hopes, his anxieties; but she failed. He would chat to her, gossip even, talk about their friends, the house, the antique cars that were his new hobby, a trip they were planning; but from anything more personal, meaningful, he kept determinedly, almost forbiddingly silent. It first saddened, then enraged her; in time she learnt to live with it, but never to accept it. She felt he saw her as empty-headed, frivolous, stupid even, quite incapable of sharing his more serious concerns, and it was a hard thing to bear. In theory he was an ideal husband: he gave her everything she wanted, he was affectionate, he frequently told her she was playing her new role wonderfully well, commenting admiringly on her clothes, her decor, her talent for entertaining, her skill at running the household; and he continued to be a superb lover; if only, Eliza thought sadly, the rest of their life was as happy, as close, as complete, as the part that took place in their bedroom. Even that seemed to her to have its imperfections, its shortcomings; the long, charming, amusing conversations they had once had, when they had finished making love, were becoming shorter, less frequent; Julian would say he needed to sleep, that he had an early meeting, a demanding day's hunting, that he was tired from a trip, and gently discourage her from talking.

She had nothing to complain about, she knew; many, most women would envy her; but she was not properly happy. She did not think Julian was having an affair with anybody else, although she sometimes thought that even if he did she could feel little more excluded, more shut out than she did already. But she did not feel loved, as she had expected, hoped to feel; petted, pampered, spoilt, but not loved, not cared for, and most importantly of all, not considered. It was not a very comfortable or comforting state of affairs.

She was surprisingly busy; as well as running the London house, she and Julian had also bought a house in West Sussex, Lower Marriotts Manor, a perfect, medium-sized Queen Anne house; it had fifteen bedrooms, a glorious drawing room, and a perfect dining room, exquisitely carved ceilings and cornices that featured prominently in several books on English architecture, forty acres, a garden designed by Capability Brown, and very shortly after they bought it, a stable block designed by Michael McCarthy, an Irish architect who had made a fortune out of the simple notion of designing stables for the rich that looked just a little more than a set of stables. The stables and yard at Marriotts were a facsimile of Queen Anne stables, lofty, vaulted and quite lovely. The horses which Julian placed in them were quite lovely too, five hunters and five thoroughbreds, for he had developed a passion for racing, and was planning to breed as well. Eliza had a horse of her own, an exquisite Arab mare called Clementine (after the Prime Minister's wife) who she flatly refused to take on to the hunting field.

'I want riding to be a pleasure,' she said to Julian firmly, 'for both me and Clementine, and we are both much happier out on the downs on our own.'

'My darling, you can ride her round and round the front lawn, if that will make you happy,' he said, 'as long as you don't begrudge me my hunting. So many wives get jealous.'

'Oh, Julian, I have quite enough to keep me jealous without adding hunting to the list,' said Eliza lightly; Julian looked at her sharply, but her face was amusedly blank, her eyes unreadable.

Hunting weekends at Marriotts were legendary; right through the winter the Morells entertained, large house-parties to which came not only the hunting community but Julian's business associates, many of whom had not been any closer to a horse than donkey riding in their childhood, and their socially climbing wives, all thrilled to be included in what they felt was a very aristocratic occasion, but totally unequipped to participate. Because she did not hunt herself, Eliza found herself forced to entertain these people, and on many a magically beautiful winter afternoon, the red sun burning determinedly through the white misty cold, the trees carving their stark black shapes out of the grey-blue sky, when she longed to be out alone with Clementine she found herself walking along the lanes with two or three women, listening to their accounts of purchasing their winter wardrobes or their cruise wear, or playing backgammon indoors with their loud-voiced, red-faced husbands.

She loved Marriotts, rather to her own surprise; she had thought to have become a completely urban person, but she found herself missing the rolling downs of Wiltshire, the huge skies, the soft, clear air, and she looked forward to the weekends more than she would have imagined – especially the rare occasions when she and Julian were alone, and could ride together on Sundays, chatting, laughing, absolutely at peace, in a way that was becoming more and more rare.

In the summer of 1955, though, she had to stop riding altogether; she was pregnant.

Eliza had very mixed feelings about her pregnancy. She didn't like babies at all, or small children; she had no desire whatsoever to feel sick or grow fat, and she resented the curtailment of her freedom for nine months. Nevertheless she had not been brought up the daughter of even a minor strand of the British aristocracy without knowing perfectly well that it was the function of a wife to bear sons, and especially the wife of a rich man; she had a strong sense of the continuity of names and lines and she was still country girl enough to be totally relaxed and indeed cheerful at the actual concept of giving birth and mothering.

As it happened, relaxed and cheerful though she might have been, she was so tiny, so sliver-thin, that Rosamund Morell was born by Caesarean section after almost two days of quite excruciating labour, and Julian was told firmly and bluntly by the obstetrician that he was lucky his wife had not died, and that another child would undoubtedly kill her. Rosamund was therefore an important baby; the heiress apparent to a fortune, and an empire, with no fear of being usurped by a brother at any future date, and the unrivalled focus of her parents' love and attention.

The Connection One

Los Angeles, 1957

Lee Wilburn had just come in from the beach when the phone rang. It was long distance. 'Santa Monica 471227? Mrs Wilburn? Will you take a person to person call from London? From Mr Hugo Dashwood?'

'Yes, yes I will,' said Lee, pushing her hair back from her face, feeling her heart pound, her knees suddenly limp.

'Lee? Hello. It's Hugo Dashwood. How are you?'

'I'm fine, Hugo, thank you, how are you?'

'Very very well. I'm coming to New York next week. Can I come over the following weekend and see you both? Will Dean be there?'

Lee thought very quickly. 'Yes, to both. You'll be very welcome. Come on Friday night if you can get away. I'll – we'll look forward to seeing you.'

'Yes, I should make it. I have an early meeting on Friday morning, then I could leave. I'll get a car from the airport, don't worry about meeting me.'

'OK. Bye, Hugo.'

'Goodbye, Lee. And thank you.'

She put the phone down; she was shaking all over. That had done it; there was no going back now.

She walked slowly through into the kitchen and poured herself a cold beer. Then she went into the living room, opened the full-length windows and looked out at the ocean for a long time. It was the most perfect of Californian evenings, the sky a bright, almost translucent blue, the sun sending a golden dusting on the sea. The beach was still busy, the white sand covered with people; the surf was gentle, almost slow-motion. Lee never got tired of this view, this time; relaxed and at peace from the sun and the sea, she would sit there, enjoying it, drinking it in, and go into an almost trancelike state, wishing she need never move again. A lot of her friends were taking up yoga and meditation but she never could see the point in that. Half an hour on the patio with a beer and the ocean, and she felt as relaxed as anybody.

The phone rang again, disturbing her peace; she frowned, went into the kitchen and picked it up, aiming her beer bottle at the trash can as she passed. It missed, and slithered into the corner.

'Hi,' she said into the phone.

'Lee? Hi, honey, it's Dean. You OK? I'll be home in a couple of hours. It's going to be a great weekend. You missed me? I sure have missed you.'

'You know I have, Dean,' said Lee, smiling into the phone, and it was true, she had. 'And I have your favourite dinner for you.'

'You're my favourite dinner. Now honey, you haven't forgotten I'll be away next weekend, have you? I've tried to wriggle my way out of it, but I can't. Is that really going to be OK?'

'I think I can just about handle it. We've got this one after all. Don't be late, Dean.'

'I won't.'

She put the phone down, left the beer bottle where it was (she was not an over-fastidious housewife) and went slowly through the hall and towards the stairs. She caught sight of herself in the long mirror at the end of the room: long streaky blonde hair, blue eyes, freckled face, wearing denim overalls and an old white shirt of her husband's. She looked like a college kid, not a married woman about to commit adultery . . . she grinned into the mirror and went on upstairs.

Standing in the shower, alternating the hot and cold water (it was good for the bustline and the skin – and the bowels, Amy Meredith had told her, for heaven's sake, now how could that be true? Stimulation, maybe –) soaping the salt out of her sun-drenched skin, she wondered what actually brought people to the edge of adultery, or tipped them over it and into the bed. Not unhappiness, she couldn't claim that; she and Dean were perfectly happy, had been ever since they married seven years ago. Boredom? No, not really. Of course after seven years drums didn't roll and stars leap out of the sky every time she saw him, and the earth didn't exactly rock around every time they had sex, which anyway wasn't very often these days, nor very satisfying either, but he was still fun, still jokey, and she still enjoyed his company. So – what? What excuse did she have? I'm just bad, maybe, she thought, stepping out of the shower and wrapping herself in a huge white towel. I'm greedy. I want more than I ought to have. It was not an entirely nice thought. She drenched her skin all over with body milk (otherwise it got so dry and flaky) and then sprayed herself liberally with Intimate, the new Revlon fragrance she liked so much; it was sexy and it stayed with you, didn't fade like a lot of those much more expensive ladylike scents. She felt very interested in sex at the moment. She supposed it was because of Hugo Dashwood and the way he was disturbing her; anyway, so far it wasn't doing Dean any harm, she could hardly keep her hands off him, and he wasn't to know that it was a different face from his own that swam into her head as he laboured over her, grunting with pleasure; a thinner, more handsome face, with brown eyes, and a beautiful dancing smile.

She studied herself in the mirror, as she stood there naked; her body was pretty good still, she thought, it didn't look twenty-nine years old, tall (five foot eight), slim (a hundred and ten pounds), with a stomach so flat it was practically concave, and surprisingly, lusciously full breasts. Her bottom was her greatest pride: flat and neat, firm as a drum; she worked hard on that bottom, she did exercises twice a day, and swam for at least half an hour. It wasn't a particularly sexy bottom – men fondling it hopefully at parties were slightly repelled by its firmness, its lack of yieldingness – but she didn't care, and besides her breasts made up for it. The line of her bikini was dramatic: clearly carved out of her suntan. It was quite modest, her bikini; she didn't really like the ones that were cut so low you could see the line of the buttocks disappearing into them. Kim Devon's was like that and Lee thought it was vulgar. She wondered if she ought to trim her pubic hair for Dean's return; it was looking shaggy, and he did like things to be neat. That reminded her, she must clear up the kitchen a bit, pick up that beer bottle, wash the floor. Although, she thought, smiling at herself suddenly in the mirror, she could easily distract him away from the kitchen floor.

Which did mean trimming the pubes, she supposed . . .

She and Dean had met Hugo Dashwood at a conference in New York on advertising a couple of months ago. It had been a real treat for her to go; Dean was away such a lot, in his job as representative for an own-label marketing company, and not to have to stay at home and on her own for once, and to see a bit of New York, was just too good to be true. The conference was at the Hyatt, and the delegates were all scattered round the city; Lee and Dean were staying just off Broadway; it was an undeniably tacky hotel, but as Dean kept pointing out to her it was all a freebie, and tackiness was the last thing in the world Lee cared about anyway.

The wives had their own programme for a lot of the time, and she had taken the Circle Line tour, gone up the Empire State and explored the wonders of Bergdorf's and Macy's (ducking out of the more cultural outings on offer, like the Museum of Modern Art and a tour of New York's churches) but on the first day there had been a buffet lunch, so that they could all get to know one another; she hadn't actually taken too much to many of them, older than she was, most of them, formally and forbiddingly dressed, and very self-consciously good American wives, talking with huge and ostentatious knowledge not only about their husbands' companies, but the advertising industry in general, exchanging telephone numbers and addresses, discussing their husbands' career patterns, comparing company benefits, and constantly interrupting the men's conversations to introduce them to their own newfound acquaintances. Lee could positively feel them looking her up and down, examining her and discarding her, as being young, flighty, and altogether too attractive to be included either in the earnest merry-go-round or the introductions to the men, and decided she preferred her own company; she was standing in the queue for the buffet waiting for Dean to finish an interminable conversation with someone about the rival virtues of supermarkets and drugstores as an outlet for cotton wool balls when a voice that was just like English molasses, as she confided to Amy Meredith later ('If you can imagine such a thing, all dark brown and treacly, but so refined'), asked her if she would be kind enough to keep his place while he went and retrieved the book he had been foolish enough to leave in the conference hall. 'I don't want to lose it, I am enjoying it immensely, and besides, I'm on my own here, I'm not fortunate enough to have a wife to keep me company, and I may need it if I can't find anyone to talk to during lunch.'

'Oh, my goodness,' said Lee, 'we can certainly help you there, my husband and I, but do go and get it anyway, before they clear it away. I'll hold your place.'

She looked at him thoughtfully as he disappeared into the crowd; he was exactly as she would imagine an upper-class Englishman to be (she could tell he was very upper class, he spoke with that David Niven accent everybody had in English films, with the exception of the comic characters, rather clipped and drawly at the same time). He was wearing a grey pinstriped suit, a white shirt, a white and grey spotted tie; he was tall and very slim, with long legs and the most beautiful shoes, in very soft black leather. His hair was dark and slightly longer than she was used to, and he had velvety brown eyes and the most beautiful teeth. She couldn't, she thought, have possibly asked for a more desirable lunch companion, and felt pleased that she had decided to wear her red sheath dress and pin her hair up in a French pleat, so that she looked more sophisticated rather than leaving it hanging down on her shoulders the way Dean liked it.

He was back in a minute, with a copy of *The Grapes of Wrath* tucked under his arm: 'I'm mugging up on my American social history,' he said with a smile. 'Marvellous book, I suppose you've read it?'

'Of course,' said Lee earnestly, remembering how she had picked her way painfully through it in high school, and rewarded herself for finishing each chapter with a chapter of *Gone With the Wind*; 'I loved it, of course.'

'Of course,' he said solemnly, 'and do you read a lot, Mrs –' he peered at her name badge – 'Wilburn?'

'Well,' said Lee carefully, 'quite a lot. Of course I don't have a great deal of time. But I do enjoy it. When I do.' Jesus, she thought, how do I manage to talk such crap?

'And why are you here?' he asked her, moving into safer territory. 'Are you one of the delegates?'

'Oh, no,' she said, charmed and amused at the same time, that he should think her of sufficient status and intelligence to warrant her own place at a conference. 'I'm here with my husband.'

'And what does your husband do?'

'He's a sales representative. He works for an own-label marketing company. He's very good at his job,' she added, mindful of her shortcomings as a professional wife.

'I'm sure,' he said, 'can you point him out to me? Where is he?'

'Over there,' said Lee, pointing to Dean who was furiously distributing his business cards as if they were leaflets on the subway, to a rather unenthusiastic-looking group. 'He'll be over in a minute. He wouldn't miss a lunch.' She looked at Dean rather thoughtfully, trying not to compare him unfavourably with the Englishman. She was very fond of him, but nobody could call him a dresser; he had bought a new suit in Terylene mohair for the conference, it hadn't looked too bad in the shop, but here it seemed rather too bright a blue, and it had a slightly tacky sheen on it. And then there was his tie: it was a real mistake, that tie, much too wide, with that awful splashy pattern on it – the English tie, she noted, was discreetly narrow. And she really must, the minute they got home, start doing something about his weight. He must be thirty pounds over now, and rising; apart from looking bad, with his beer belly sticking out over his trousers, however hard he tried to hold it in, it wasn't good for him. Amy was always going on about cholesterol and the dangers of heart disease, and telling her she should give Dean more vegetables and feed him bran for breakfast. And however trying he might be at times, she certainly didn't want to lose him; she must try to be a better wife.

She pulled her mind away from this reverie and turned back

to her new friend who was gently guiding her towards the heap of plates at the buffet table.

'Now look,' he said, 'we've reached the food. Should we get a plateful for your husband as well, do you think?'

'Oh, no,' said Lee, 'he likes to choose his own. He's terribly, terribly fond of his food. You just go ahead. I'll wait for him.'

'Nonsense,' he said. 'Having found a friend I'd like to stay with her. If I may. Until lunch is over at any rate. I hardly know anybody here. I haven't been in New York long.'

'Are you from London?' asked Lee, helping herself to a modest amount of chicken in mayonnaise, anxious not to appear greedy, and careful to choose something that she could eat easily with a fork. The last thing she wanted to do was drop food down her new red dress in front of this rather intimidatingly svelte creature.

'I am.'

'And why are you here?'

'Oh, to learn a bit about American business methods. I'm opening up in New York, and the more contacts and knowledge I have the better.'

'What's your business?'

'Direct selling, I suppose you'd call it,' he said. 'It's a bit of a new science in England, but it's catching on. And then I thought I'd bring some coals to Newcastle and try it here.'

'I see,' said Lee, trying desperately not to show that she didn't.

He read her face and smiled, understanding. 'Don't worry about it,' he said, 'old English saying. Let's just leave it at the direct selling. Toiletries mostly.'

'Oh,' she said, 'that's Dean's field too. He's coming now, look, he will be interested. Oh, now I don't know your name, I can't introduce you. Why haven't you got a label?'

'Allergic to them,' he said, 'we don't often have them in England. Silly, I know, they're a very good idea. Anyway, Dashwood is the name. Hugo Dashwood.' He held out his hand. 'Delighted to meet you.'

Lee took his hand and smiled and felt a delicious charge of warm pleasure shoot through her. My goodness, she thought, this guy could be dangerous. The thought was surprisingly interesting. 'Lee Wilburn,' she said, 'and I'm certainly delighted to meet you. Dean,' she called to her husband, who was scanning the room anxiously, his overladen plate tipped dangerously to the side, his tie dangling horribly near his potato salad, 'Dean, we're here. Come and sit down, we kept you a place. Now this is Hugo Dashwood, from London; Mr Dashwood, this is my husband Dean Wilburn. Mr Dashwood is in direct selling, Dean, in toiletries mostly. I was saying you would be really interested to talk to him.' She spoke with a certain satisfaction, feeling that for the first time, since the convention had begun, she had actually acquitted herself and performed as a conference wife properly should.

'Well, that is just wonderful,' said Dean, easing his two hundred pounds cautiously on to the spindly chair and tucking his tie carefully into his shirt buttons (Lee, who had long ago given up trying to stop him doing that, wished suddenly and fervently that she hadn't). 'It's real nice to meet you, Mr Dashwood. My company is very big in own-brand toiletries in the supermarkets, and I'd really like to tell you about that. How long have you been operating over here?'

'Oh, I've hardly begun,' said Hugo, 'I'm mostly involved in my business in England. But I like the market over here. It's very fast moving at the moment.'

'Oh, you can say that again,' said Dean, in between mouthfuls of Russian salad. 'Lee, honey, would you like to try and find me a beer? I don't go a lot on wine at lunch time. Do you, Mr Dashwood?'

'Oh, do please call me Hugo. Well, I don't like drinking at lunch time at all. I'd like a soft drink. But let me get you both a drink. Mrs Wilburn, what would you like?'

'Oh, a beer,' said Lee without thinking, and then could have bitten her tongue out. Beer! How unsophisticated, how gauche! Why couldn't she have said wine, or better still fruit juice? He would think her so hick, so crass, just like her husband, she thought sorrowfully, watching Dean wipe his plate with his bread, and then lick each finger in turn, before standing up and picking up his plate. 'I'm going to get myself some more food,' he said, 'I hate these buffet things. No substance. Hugo, how about you?'

'Oh, no thank you,' said Hugo, 'but I will get you your beer.'

'Er – Hugo – I won't have beer,' said Lee, 'if you could find me a soda water, that would be fine.'

'Oh,' he said, his dark eyes snapping at her with amusement and an unmistakable appreciation, 'I will if you like. But I would have the beer if you want it. You haven't got to work this afternoon, as we have.'

'No,' she said firmly, anxious to retain the more refined image she felt sure he would appreciate, 'I really wasn't thinking. Soda water, please.'

She sat sipping it, wishing it was beer, watching Hugo Dashwood listening courteously to Dean, and occasionally glancing at her with his warm, intensely interested eyes, and thought he was the most attractive man she had ever met in her entire life.

They became quite friendly after that, the three of them; they had supper together that evening, and Hugo joined them for breakfast the next day on his way to the conference, and they met in the bar of the Hyatt one evening when the last seminar of the day was over while Dean and Hugo unwound and Lee recounted the events of her day: a tour of the Radio City Concert Hall, and a trip around Tiffany's, which she had found disappointing. 'It just wasn't a patch on the jewellery shops on Beverly Drive, not glamorous at all.'

She enjoyed talking to Hugo; he had a way of listening that was flattering and that encouraged her to talk, and she enjoyed feeling his eyes on her. She could see he found her attractive, and it made her feel confident and rather grown up; he was so extremely sophisticated and so obviously clever, and she was, after all, a perfectly ordinary American girl; she might have majored in psychology, but she knew quite well she wasn't intellectual; she could chat away amusingly, and even manage the odd wisecrack when she'd had a beer or two, but that was hardly the sort of thing an urbane upper-class Englishman was going to fall for. Or maybe it was. Anyway, in the meantime it was a wonderful few days. Lee felt more alive, more aware of herself, and a lot more sexy, than she had with Dean in a month of Sundays.

On the fourth and last evening of the conference there was a cocktail party. Lee had dressed for it with great care in a pink

127

shot-silk sheath dress that clung to her body and stopped just below the knee to show off her long, long slender legs. She had bought it in Macy's that morning, and a pair of extra-high-heeled shoes to match; her blonde hair was drawn back with pink combs, and hanging in a straight shining sheet down her back. She was excited and nervous, looking across the room restlessly for Hugo from the moment they arrived. He wasn't there, and an hour later, as the party began to wind down, he still hadn't appeared; she was disappointed and miserable, and found it depressingly hard to concentrate on what the inter-minable line of husbands and wives Dean was managing to get a hold of, and hand his cards out to, was saying. She had just told one woman how delighted she must be to have left their four children behind, and another how sorry she was to hear she had just installed a new kitchen, when she felt a hand moving gently up and down her arm, and a mouth pressed into her ear. 'You look wonderful. I'm awfully late. Have I missed anything important?'

She turned, abandoning both wives totally, her face alight. 'Hugo! I'm so glad you're here. No not a thing. It's been terribly boring,' said Lee cheerfully, and then realizing what she had said, blushed and tried frantically to retrieve the situation. 'Er, Hugo this is Mary Ann Whittaker, and this is – er Joanne Smith. This is our friend from England, Mr Hugo Dashwood.'

'Mary Ann White,' said the kitchen owner pointedly, holding out her hand. 'Which part of England are you from, Mr Dashwood?'

'London,' he said.

'Oh,' she said, 'we have some very good friends there. They have an upholstery business. You may have met them. Their name is Walker. They live in, now let me see, would it be Willesden?'

'It could be,' he said, 'there is such a place.'

'But you don't know them?'

'I don't think so,' he said. 'Of course there are a lot of Walkers in London. And it's a big place.'

Then suddenly, he put his arm round her shoulders and said to Mary Anne White, 'You must excuse us now, I'm afraid, we have to meet friends on the other side of the room,' and steered her away, and she turned to apologize and saw that he was grinning hugely.

'God in heaven,' he said, grasping a glass of wine from a passing tray, 'why can't more American women be like you?'

'I am really sorry,' said Lee, 'to have got you into that. I would like to say, in defence of my race, that she was a bad sample, but I don't think I can. Where is Willesden, anyway?'

'Oh,' said Hugo, 'a very long way away from the centre. Don't apologize, I enjoy such encounters. They amuse me. My only regret is it kept me from talking to you. Here's to you, Mrs Wilburn, and what I hope will be a lasting association.'

Lee looked at him, meeting his dark vivid eyes with her clear blue ones, very steadily. 'I hope so too,' she said, composed, in command of the situation suddenly, 'and if you ever come to California, then you must come and stay. We live in Los Angeles, right on the ocean at Santa Monica, it's a great place to come at weekends.'

'I'd love to,' he said, 'now Dean has given me his card. Several, actually,' he added, and grinned, but it was a kindly, unmalicious grin. 'I don't have any at the moment, I've run out, but if you really need to, you can get me at this number, it's my office in New York, but I'm hardly ever there, so not very satisfactory, I'm afraid. Anyway, I'll certainly ring you. I've never been to Los Angeles and I've always wanted to go, so now I shall have a double reason for visiting.'

'Good. Do you want to eat dinner with me and Dean tonight? We wondered if you'd like to join us?'

'I can't, I'm afraid. I have another engagement. But thank you for asking me.'

'That's all right.' She felt ridiculously disappointed, her evening suddenly emptied of substance, her pink dress foolishly profitless; he looked at her sharply and then smiled and tipped up her face towards him.

'Don't worry,' he said, 'we will meet again. I couldn't bear the thought that we wouldn't. I think you are perfectly lovely, and Dean is a very lucky man. And that dress is extremely distracting. It's just as well we're not going to have dinner together, I wouldn't hear a word anybody said. Now I must go, I only popped in to say goodbye. Say goodbye to Dean for me, will you? I don't want to interrupt him.'

'I will,' she said, 'and thank you for coming. It was nice of you to bother.'

'No,' he said, 'not nice at all. I wanted to see you.' He paused for a moment, looking at her very seriously. 'I find you rather desirable. Now I must go. Goodbye.'

He kissed her lightly on the lips, a gentle, glancing embrace, and then smiled at her and turned away. Lee stood there quite still, a hot fierce lick of desire stabbing at her, so physically disturbed she hardly knew what she was doing. She went to the ladies' room and shut herself in the cubicle, and sat down quietly and very still on the toilet seat waiting for the throbbing in her body to subside. After a while she felt calmer and went outside and bathed her forehead and her wrists in cold water. Next best thing to a cold shower, she thought to herself cheerfully and grinned at her reflection. Only men were supposed to get these great onslaughts of sexual desire, to have to hide their hard-ons, to work off their discomfort. Yet she had known them all her grown-up life – ever since she had started to develop a bust, and noticed how interestingly her body was changing, and had found what acute pleasure could be achieved by touching and exploring herself with her fingers, by finding the small hard tender centre of her feeling that was her clitoris and gently, very gently but insistently working and stroking at it, and feeling herself grow wet, liquid with delight, until a hot, consuming sensation rose and rose in her and then exploded with such force she could almost see it before her tightly closed eyes. She tried not to do it too often, because it was so delicious she felt sure it must in some way be wrong and it was something nobody had ever told her about; her mother had patiently talked to her carefully and gently for hours in the most incomprehensible way about how babies were made, and what to do should she find blood in her knickers, but had never mentioned, never hinted at, the concept of pleasure.

As she grew older, though, the feelings came of their own volition, she did not have to do anything to arouse them; uncomfortable, disturbing, she had to release them as soon as she could, otherwise they dominated everything she was doing or thinking. Worried that there might be something wrong with her, she asked her best friend, Betsy Newman, if she had experienced anything like them; Betsy said no, she never had, but she had once heard her big brother Ralphy talking to his friend about girls, and he had described something Betsy couldn't understand but sounded a bit like what Lee was talking about.

Lee felt a bit better after that; when she was sixteen and went to high school she made a new friend, a beautiful girl called Laura, who asked her quite casually in the shower one day after basketball how often she masturbated, and if she had ever had a boy do it to her; Lee, misunderstanding, said certainly not, that was the straight way to pregnancy and generally wrecking your life, and Laura had laughed and said no, had a boy done it with his hands. Lee said she hadn't and Laura said she really should, it was great and it kept the boys happy too; on her next date, Lee allowed Brett Mitchell to caress her breasts and on the one after that, to explore her desperate, hungry vagina. In return she offered to attend to his penis in much the same way. They were both amazed and delighted by the pleasure they gave and were given.

A year or so later Lee surrendered herself to more conventional sexual experiences; most of the girls she knew remained virgins until they were married, but Lee couldn't wait. She was intrigued, excited, exhilarated by sex; she loved it, she needed it, and if she didn't get it, she became irritable and depressed. It seemed to her worth the attendant risks, of expulsion from college if you were caught in flagrante, and of pregnancy even if you weren't; but she was never caught, and she told everyone the danger of pregnancy was seriously overrated, all you had to do was use a sheath and maybe count a bit as well, and not do it right in the middle of your cycle, and you would be perfectly all right.

'Or maybe I've just been lucky,' she would say. Five years into her marriage with no baby in sight, even though she and Dean hadn't used any kind of contraception for years, she realized she maybe hadn't been so lucky after all.

Hugo Dashwood spent a weekend with the Wilburns about a month later; Dean and Lee took their duties as hosts seriously and showed him the sights of LA, in a tireless, enthusiastic forty-eight hours; they took him to Graumann's, and to Griffith Park and the Observatory; they took him to Beverly Hills and showed him the film stars' mansions; they took him to Muscle

Beach where he laughed at the desperate seriousness of the men posing and pumping ('Look,' said Lee in awed tones, pointing to one particularly impressive rippling blond mountain, 'it's Mickie Hagerty') and to Malibu where they sat in a beach bar and he marvelled at the compulsive joy and excitement of the surfers and the sea. 'I just love it,' he said when they finally got back to the Santa Monica house on Sunday afternoon. 'I would adore to live here.'

'Well, come,' said Lee, flinging herself on to the swing seat on the patio and tearing the top off a bottle of beer. 'Bring your wife over. It's not expensive. There's all the opportunities in the world. New people coming in all the time, with the new engineering industries. And this particular bit where we live, here, do you know, they're so desperate for young people to come and live, because everyone wants to be inland, up in the hills, we got free rent for a year and a free television, as bait.'

'I wish I could,' said Hugo, 'but I have enough problems coping with living in London and getting a business going in New York. Any more complication would finish me off altogether.'

'How's it going?' said Dean lazily. His eyes were closed. He had drunk several beers and the sun and the alcohol had got the better of him.

'OK. It's tough over there, as you know. But I think it'll work. My main base will always be London, though.'

'Why doesn't your wife ever come over?' asked Lee. The last thing she wanted was the minutiae of Hugo's marriage, but she found ignorance still more painful than knowledge. The knowledge she had was minimal, not because he did not answer any questions, but because she did not ask many (not wanting to know the answers); neither did Dean because he wasn't interested, and Hugo didn't volunteer a great deal of information. (Lee was a little disappointed to learn that Hugo wasn't as aristocratic as she had imagined; middle class, he told her he was, and the product of a grammar school rather than Eton as she had visualised.) They knew he had a wife, whose name was Alice; that they had been married five years; that she did not get over-involved with the business, largely through lack of time; that there was a child; and that as families went it was a fairly happy one. More than that Lee could not bear to hear; she pictured Alice as buttoned-up, frigid English, with a plummy voice and a cold stare, and the vision kept her calm and conscience-free. It was based on nothing Hugo had said or even implied.

'She's busy. She has a lot to do. The house is in a dreadful state, and then we have the child, she can't keep whipping across the Atlantic for the dubious pleasure of waiting in a hotel room for me to come back from work every day.'

'Will you get somewhere permanent to live, do you think, in New York?'

'Not worth it at the moment. I don't plan to stay on a long-term basis. I want to find someone who can run the business for me. If it really takes off, then obviously I would take a place, but at the moment it's cheaper to stay in hotels when I do come. I'm still doing a suck-it-and-see operation, as we say in Britain.'

Dean was now snoring, his mouth hanging open, his empty beer bottle dangling loosely in his hand. Lee took it gently, looking at him in some distaste, and set it down on the ground.

'He's always like this after the sun. He can't take it, really. Not like me. I love it, it makes me feel just – oh, wonderful.'

She stretched herself out on the seat, arching her body; seeing Hugo looking at it, at the long, slender line from her breasts down to her legs, she stayed still for a moment, holding the pose; then she relaxed and smiled at him.

He smiled back. 'You should go and do that at Muscle Beach. You're much prettier than all of them. Tell me how the sun makes you feel.'

'Oh, you know, kind of warmed through. Happy, peaceful, good all over.'

'Sexy?'

She was surprised by his directness. He was normally rather Englishly reserved. 'Yes,' she said, 'yes, very.'

'I thought so.' He was silent.

'You look tired,' said Lee, jumping up, easing out of the tension. 'Let me get you a drink. What time do you have to be at the airport?'

'My plane leaves at nine. Could you ring for a taxi?'

'I'll take you. Dean has his Sunday homework to do, he's always busy on Sunday night. I get lonely. It'll be a pleasure. Beer?'

'Do you have any whisky?'

'Bourbon.'

'Fine.'

She was gone for a while, finding the bourbon, cracking the ice; when she came back he had drifted off to sleep too; she sat there, very quiet and still holding his drink. He opened his eyes with a start, looked towards Dean, who was utterly soundly asleep, and then took her hand, and raised it to his lips and kissed it and smiled at her; and then took the drink from her.

'Tell me, Mrs Wilburn,' he said, 'why have you not had any children?'

'Oh,' she said, turning away from him and looking out to sea, 'it just hasn't happened, that's all. I'd like them, we both would, but God and Mother Nature don't seem to agree with us.' And without warning her eyes filled with tears.

'Oh, darling, I'm sorry, so sorry,' said Hugo, using the endearment unself-consciously, entirely naturally. 'I'm an idiot to have asked, I shouldn't have.'

'It's all right,' she said, smiling at him slightly shakily, 'in a funny way I think Dean's quite pleased. I think. It means I can concentrate completely on him.'

'Well,' he said, 'he has a point.'

'Do – do you enjoy being a father?'

'Oh yes. But it has its drawbacks. They're very demanding.'

'And does – your wife like being a mother?'

'Yes, I believe so. She finds it difficult at times, of course. All women do, I imagine.'

'Yes, I imagine they do,' said Lee bitterly.

'I'm sorry,' he said, 'that was tactless of me. I didn't mean to hurt you. Look, don't worry about driving me to the airport. It's silly. I can get a taxi.'

'No, honestly, I'd like to take you. I like driving. And I love airports. Let me have a shower and fix Dean a steak, and we'll go.'

He looked at her, and gave her his slow dancing smile. 'All right.'

The road to the airport was busy; the city was growing relentlessly and even the new freeways seemed inadequate. They sat in silence, crawling along, listening to the radio. Pat

Boone was throwing his heart and soul into 'April Love'. It was hot. Lee sighed, pushed the hair off the back of her neck, threw her head back. 'Just think, you'll be cold tomorrow. March in New York. And what about England?'

'Cold.'

'Well,' she said, 'I'd rather be here.'

'Lee,' he said.

'Yes.'

'I do find you very interesting, and very very beautiful. I would like to know you better. Could you remember that?'

She turned and looked at him. 'I think so.'

'Good.'

The traffic had slowed to a complete standstill. The radio was now playing a selection from *West Side Story*; Hugo leant over to Lee, turned her towards him. 'Kiss me.'

She kissed him. She didn't usually like kissing, it was somehow rather tedious, and men got so worked up about it, breathing heavily and slavering away. Kissing Hugo Dashwood wasn't too much like that. He kissed with what she could only call style, thinking about it afterwards; very slowly, very strongly and deliberately, pausing every now and again to stroke her hair, her neck, his hand lingering gently, tenderly, on her breast, and he did not just kiss her mouth, he kissed her eyes, and her chin, and her throat. Lee felt as if she was floating, drifting in some delicious, tossing liquid, rising and then sinking, let loose in desire. She sighed, pulled away from him for a moment. He took her face between his hands.

'What do you feel?' he said.

'Everything,' she said simply. 'Absolutely everything.'

'Ah,' he said. 'Good.'

Around them cars were hooting, other drivers shouting. 'Get a goddamned move on,' and 'Get off and do that off the fucking road.' The disc jockey had just started to play 'Good Night Little Susie'.

Hugo sighed, then laughed and drew away from her. 'We'd better go or we'll be arrested.'

They drove in silence the rest of the way. When they got there he simply kissed her cheek briefly and got out. 'Good night, Lee. I shall hope to see you soon. Thank you for a wonderful weekend.'

'Good night, Hugo.'

She watched him until he disappeared into the crowd and then drove home, very fast, which was the only other way she knew of relieving sexual tension; when she got home she went into the shower for a long time and came out calmer.

She was never able to hear 'Good Night Little Susie' again without becoming seriously sexually aroused.

She did wonder if she should tell Amy or Kim what she had orchestrated so cleverly for the next weekend; they were both such good friends, they wouldn't tell, they would be thrilled for her and she felt an overpowering need to talk about Hugo and how she felt about him. With Amy in particular she had the most terrific and explicit conversations about sex and men in general, their husbands in particular; Amy had a husband who was the opposite of Dean, and couldn't let her alone; he would disturb her as she cooked and sewed, made up her face and even went to the lavatory (that, indeed, she told Lee, seemed to excite him more than anything). Lee could see that could be worse than permanent frustration, and that a rampant Bob Meredith would not always be a welcome element in a quiet baking session or even a spell on the toilet; on the other hand, Amy plainly did not have the first idea of the constant hot hunger in her body, or the fretful misery of a half-accomplished orgasm. It would be such fun to talk to them about Hugo; to describe him and how sexy he was, how much she fancied him, how intelligent and how special he made her feel, how skilfully she had made her plans, how nervous and excited she felt about the weekend. But then on the other hand, it was safer not to tell anyone; neither of them lived in Santa Monica, none of her friends did, and nobody at all would know who she had there with her. It had to be better that way. And so she waited, fearful, excited; she doubled her exercise routine, she swam and sunned herself; she tidied the house compulsively; she changed the bed; she counted the hours, the days; she bought the London and the New York *Times* so that she might make intelligent conversation; she even, on the afternoon before he was due to arrive, shaved her pubes. And then she could do no more, and so she simply waited.

She was on the patio when he arrived. She was wearing a T-shirt and a pair of white slacks; unusually (for she felt uncomfortable, uneasy without them) she had left off her bra and her pants; she had drenched herself in Intimate; her hair was slightly damp from the shower; she looked just about seventeen.

'Lee, you look like an angel,' said Hugo, kissing her formally on the cheek. 'An all-American angel. It's so nice to see you.'

'It's good to see you too,' said Lee, smiling at him, 'can I fix you a drink?'

'That would be nice. A beer I think. Is Dean not home yet?'

'Not yet,' said Lee, going quickly into the house; she re-emerged with the beer and a glass, and poured it for him, thinking that she could never remember how amazingly good-looking and sexy he was, and feeling all over again inadequate and crass.

'How was your flight?'

'All right. Long.'

'Are you hungry?'

'Not really. I can wait. Why don't you have a drink too?'

So Lee fetched another beer and sat down beside him on the patio, on the swing seat, and they looked together silently at the ocean; she did think of asking him what he thought might happen over the Suez crisis, just to show she knew there was one, or even if he had seen *West Side Story* yet, but it didn't really seem very appropriate, so she just sat there; then: 'When will Dean be home?'

'Not tonight.'

'I see.'

That was all he said; no corny responses, no come-on, no surprise. Just 'I see.' Very English.

'Would you like your dinner now?'

'Yes please, I would.'

So they sat inside eating steaks and salads and drinking red wine, just chatting like any married couple, like she and Dean did in the evening and it wasn't especially exciting or erotic or anything, just very very nice.

'I'm tired,' he said at last, 'can I go to bed now?'

'Of course,' she said, 'I'll show you your room.'

'Don't worry,' he said, 'I'll find it, it's the same one, I

suppose? You tidy up down here. I'll look after myself. Good night Lee.'

She felt half rebuffed, anxious; was he telling her he didn't want her, she wondered, that she was being foolish and presumptuous? And saying she should tidy up, had he noticed the overflowing trash can, the dishes heaped in the sink, the magazines dumped behind the couch; she was sure Alice would keep the house neat as a pin all the time, he probably hated it here and her casual ways. She smiled at him nervously.

'I'll fix you some coffee,' she said.

'No, don't,' he said, 'it'll keep me awake, but I'd like some water and a brandy maybe to go with it. Perhaps you could bring it up to me in a minute.'

And she knew then she wasn't being foolish and presumptuous, that he wanted her as much as she wanted him, that he was simply a courteous, thoughtful man, giving her every chance to let herself off the hook should she change her mind – or indeed should he have misread it.

She put a jug of iced water on a tray and a bottle of brandy and a glass, and went quietly up the stairs in her bare feet. Outside his room she listened: silence. She knocked gently and went in; at first she thought he was asleep. She went over to the side of the bed and put down the tray very quietly. As she turned to leave the room, his hand came out and caught hers.

'Don't go,' he said, 'unless you really want to.'

'I don't,' she said and sat down on the bed; he looked at her for a long time, very seriously, and then put out a hand and traced the outline of her face with his finger.

'You're so lovely,' he said, 'so very very lovely.' And then he pushed his hand under her T-shirt and stroked very very gently her breasts, and then he leant forward and kissed her on the mouth, gently, repeatedly, as he had in the car.

Lee sat still and silent; she felt her nipples grow erect, a monstrous aching deep within her, but she did not move.

'Lie down,' he said, 'lie down beside me,' and her eyes never leaving his face, she slid her T-shirt over her head, unbuttoned her trousers and stood naked before him, smiling.

'No underwear, Mrs Wilburn? Is this for my benefit, or would that be presumptuous of me?'

138

'It would,' she said untruthfully, 'I never wear any. I don't like it.'

'I think you're lying,' he said, reaching out and stroking her stomach, 'I don't believe those wonderful breasts could survive without the help of a bra. Dear God, have you no pubic hair?' he added, sitting up and peering at her with genuine interest.

'I shave it,' she said, 'Dean doesn't like it. I thought you wouldn't either.'

'You were wrong,' he said, 'but it doesn't matter. Here.' And he put his hand behind her buttocks, pressing her towards him, burying his face in her stomach, kissing her where the hair should have been, licking her, searching out her clitoris with his tongue.

'It's different,' he said, smiling up at her. 'I'm not sure if I like it but it's different. Is that nice? You must tell me.'

'Oh, God,' said Lee, and it was almost a groan, 'it's nice. Don't, don't stop.'

'Oh, I think I will,' he said, 'in a minute,' and he went on and on, until she cried out with pleasure and an exquisite pain, and fell on to him, lying above him, kissing him, licking him, biting him, thrusting herself on to him, and feeling suddenly the immense strong delight of his penis going deep deep within her, answering her need, gratifying her awful, aching desire. She lay there, tearing at him, like some hungry animal, rising from him, arching away, and then lunging down again, over and over again, shuddering with pleasure and need; she came once, and then again, and still she was hungry, still wanted more; he turned her on to her back, driving into her fast and hard, almost hurting her, stirring places and pleasures she had never known; she felt the waves growing, then breaking, and as she clung to him, calling out in an agony of release, he shuddered into her, with a huge groan of delight and relief.

And afterwards, they lay together and he took great handfuls of her long blonde hair and wound it round his fingers and kissed it and kissed her everywhere, on her eyelids, her nose, her lips, her breasts, saying her name over and over again. And then she felt him growing hard again, and her own need growing too, then he took her with him, further, higher than she would ever have imagined possible; and finally they slept, completely peaceful, for a long, long time.

It was midday when they woke; Hugo looked at his watch, groaned and shook her.

'Lee, it's after twelve, for God's sake wake up, when is Dean getting home?'

And she looked at him through a haze of love and sleepiness, her body sated and yet hungry again, and smiled and kissed him and said, 'On Friday night.'

They stayed there all weekend, occasionally going downstairs for food and wine and once to swim; they made love until their bodies ached with exhaustion and even Lee could ask for no more.

On Sunday afternoon they finally got up and showered together and dressed and sat quietly in the kitchen, drinking coffee and looking at one another.

'I have to go quite soon,' he said.

'When?'

'My plane leaves Los Angeles for New York at nine. I've ordered a car for six.'

'Let me come with you.'

'No.'

'What do you want me to do?'

'I don't know,' he said and she knew it was a lie.

She knew what he wanted. He wanted her to stay with Dean, and to be there when he needed her. It was a hard bargain. But she knew she had to settle for it. She had no choice. It was that or absolutely nothing at all.

In time, she could see, she would grow angry, resentful, but now, so filled with him, filled with pleasure and love, she could accept it easily and gracefully.

'I'll come to the airport with you,' she said quietly, and was rewarded by seeing the respect in his eyes.

Chapter Four

New York and London, 1956-9

Whenever Julian Morell was asked by the press, or eager young men with visions of following in his footsteps, how he had conceived each stage of his empire, he gave the same answer: 'It's all there,' he would say, tapping his head gently, smiling (most charmingly at the journalists, slightly more coldly at the eager young men), 'in your mind, maturing, honing down. All you have to do is release it. And know when to do so, of course.'

He did sincerely believe this; he had never consciously sat down and thought anything through, worked anything out; he had immense respect for the power of experience, instinct and logic to merge into something original, desirable and commercially sound and in his own case at any rate, the respect was totally justified. Certainly the phase of his empire that occupied much of his attention for much of the late fifties was not something that sprang from any brainstorming session or carefully formulated marketing plan. Nevertheless it was absolutely right for its time, with that perfect blend of the original and the familiar that leads the onlooker to believe that it was precisely what he or she had been waiting for and wanting for quite some time.

He was wandering through Harrods when the idea actually surfaced, looking at the cosmetic counters, chatting to the Juliana consultants and reflecting on their very pleasing sales figures; he suddenly had a vision of a very different kind of establishment: rather more than a beauty salon, a little less than a store: something small, intimate and totally extravagant. It should be, he thought, about the size of a large house, on two or three floors, rather like that of an infinitely luxurious hotel in feel, supplying his perfume and cosmetics and all the allied beauty business paraphernalia -treatment rooms, masseurs, steam baths, saunas, beauty therapists, hair stylists - that had become a most necessary accessory to well-heeled life on both sides of the Atlantic. But it would offer other things too, things to buy, all compatible with a mood of self-indulgence, the atmosphere rich and rare, a place that enticed, beguiled, encouraged women into extravagance.

Each department should be small and exclusive, leading

from one mood and set of desires to the next: logically extending from cosmetics to lingerie, dresses to furs, hats to shoes. Shopping there would not be a chore, or even a business, it would be a beautiful experience and his establishment would provide a series of different settings for the experiences, a world apart, an excursion into a charmed life; and it would not consist of departments and counters and salesgirls and tills, it would be carefully designed into spaces and areas and moods.

Women would come in initially for the cosmetics and the beauty treatments, that would be the lure; but then they would stay; and it would be the beautiful things they could acquire that kept them there: it would all be glittering, and unashamed luxury, outrageously expensive, and totally unique, so that a customer, should she only have bought a silk scarf, a leather belt, would feel she had acquired just a tiny portion of that charmed and charming life.

All these things Julian thought almost without realizing he had thought them; later, talking to Philip Mainwaring (the marketing manager for Juliana he had decided with some misgivings to employ) he found himself describing them in the finest detail. Philip listened politely, as he was paid to do, found himself more impressed than he really wanted to be – he found Julian's capacity for creativity made his job pattern more complex and difficult than he had ever envisaged when he took it on – and tried, like the good businessman he was, to talk him out of it.

'I can't see it working here,' he said, 'not yet. London has come a long way in the last three or four years, but I don't know that it's ready for that kind of concept.'

'It's not that new a concept,' said Julian, 'I mean it's not that far removed from the Elizabeth Arden's Red Door idea, but I see it as being much nearer a store. With a wider range of merchandise perhaps.'

'Your other retail outlets wouldn't like it,' said Philip gloomily, 'have you thought of that?'

'Can't see why not. I mean yes, we'll be in competition with them in a way, but it doesn't make Juliana less good a selling proposition. Arden still sells everywhere, after all. And the salon side of the business would provide a perfect cover, if you

142

like, so that we're not actually trying to beat the stores at their own game. We're just giving women what they want, and a lot more besides.'

Philip looked at him thoughtfully. 'I still don't feel it's right for London. Not yet. Have you thought about doing it anywhere else?'

'No, not really. You mean somewhere like Paris?'

'No, New York. It's so busy over there at the moment. There's so much money about. And there's nothing they like more than a new idea.'

'Well,' said Julian, 'I don't know New York at all. But I'm ready to have a look at it. You could be right.'

'How would you stock it?'

'Obviously we'd have to employ buyers. Who'd buy stuff from designers and so on in the normal way. And we could have our own designers as well. Exclusive to us. Sign them up.'

Philip shuddered. 'It sounds horrendously expensive.'

'That's not an argument against it. We can raise the money easily. Morell is on an extremely sound footing. OK. I'll have a look at New York. I'm going over next week anyway, to see how much headway we're making with Juliana. Come with me. I need your opinion on some of those people over there anyway. There's a new woman on the scene called Estée Lauder. She has some interesting products, and her marketing is just extraordinary.'

'OK,' said Philip. 'I'd like to come. Thanks.' He looked at Julian and grinned. 'What does our financial director have to say about all this?'

'Haven't told her,' said Julian shortly. 'I think I'll sort out the money first.' He returned Philip's look a little coldly. He found the attitude of his younger staff towards Letitia's position in the company (that she must only be there out of some kind of misguided family feeling, that he must have a relationship with her that was odd to put it mildly) at best irritating and at worst insulting. It seemed to him patently obvious that a company as successful as Morell's was clearly in excellent financial hands and there was no more to the matter than that. Letitia now had a department of five which she ran with crushing efficiency; she was an innovative and exacting force in the business, and Julian's only anxiety about her was that she was nearly sixty now and could surely not work on into the unforeseeable future. He said as much to Susan Johns one day over lunch at the Caprice; Susan laughed and said she was quite sure that Letitia would outlive them all.

'Including you,' said Julian, watching her happily devouring a double portion of profiteroles. 'You'll have a heart attack any day now. Do you want some more of those?'

'Wouldn't mind. Do you think they know about second helpings here?'

'They should if they don't. Have you ever put on any weight, Susan?'

'Never.'

'You're very fortunate,' said Julian with a sigh, looking at the dozen or so outrageously expensive grapes which he was eating for his own dessert. 'I have to be extremely careful what I eat these days. Middle-age coming on, I suppose.'

'Oh, don't be ridiculous. Anyway if you're middle-aged so am I.'

'How old are you, Susan?'

'Thirty-five.'

'You really were a child bride, weren't you?'

'I was. Seventeen years old. Criminal really.'

'Yes,' said Julian, looking sombre. 'It's too young.'

Susan, reflecting on the fact that Eliza had only been eighteen when Julian had married her, decided they were on slightly dangerous ground and briskly changed the subject. She had gathered from the occasional remark of Letitia's that the Morell marriage was not quite as idyllically perfect as it had promised to be and it was a subject she preferred to keep not only from talking, but also thinking, about.

'I hear you're going to New York.'

'Yes. Do you know why?'

'I imagine to sell Juliana into the stores there.'

'Yes. And I have another project too.'

'Am I allowed to hear about it?'

'Well,' said Julian, signalling to the waiter to bring some more profiteroles, 'I suppose as a director of the company you have a right to hear about it. But there is a condition.'

'What's that?'

'You don't tell my mother.'

Susan looked at him and shook her head in mock disapproval. 'My goodness. It must be bad.'

'Not bad. A bit risky, perhaps.'

'All right, I promise. You need one sensible opinion. Come
on, tell me.'

He told her. Of his vision; of how he saw it adding breadth
and quality to Juliana's image; of the kind of feel it would have;
the sort of women who would be attracted to it; the people he
would hope to have working on it and designing for it; where it
might be, how it might look. Eliza would have given all she
owned to be entrusted with half, a quarter of such a confidence.

'It's a new phase altogether, a new venture. I feel I need one.'

'Why?'

'Oh, you know, boredom, restlessness. I always want to be on
to the next thing. What do you think, anyway?'

'I like it. I think it's terrific.'

'Good God.' He was surprised.

'Didn't you think I would?'

'No, not really.'

'Why not? Not my style, I suppose. Too upmarket.'

'Now don't start getting touchy, Susan.'

'I'm not. I'm just teasing you.'

'Good. No, but seriously, I'd have thought it was a bit out of
order, from your point of view. Expensive. For the company, I
mean, new ground. All that sort of thing.'

'New ground is its lifeblood. But it will be expensive, won't
it? How are you going to finance it?'

'I think I can get the money in New York. If not, I'll raise it
here. I'm sure I can.'

'What does Eliza – Mrs Morell think about it?'

'I haven't talked to her about it,' said Julian shortly.

'I see.'

'I'm going to have a brandy. Do you want anything?'

'Of course not. I never drink at lunch time.'

'Or any other time, I know. Except Bucks Fizz of course.'

'Yes,' she said smiling at him, able at last to remember that
evening with pleasure rather than pain. 'But not at lunch time.
Anyway, you go ahead. I'll have a cup of tea.'

'Now that really will upset the Caprice. How's the Labour
Party?'

'It's fine. I – I hear Mrs Morell is taking an interest in it.'

'Oh,' said Julian lightly, 'only its politicians. She likes having them at her dinner table.'

'What is Foot really like?'

'Absolutely charming.' He was clearly impatient of Eliza's political leanings. 'What about you? Are you going to end up an MP, do you think?'

'I don't know,' she said very seriously. 'I'd like to, I really would. I do love politics, and I'd enjoy getting something done about some of the things I care about. But I don't know if I'd ever manage it, they're not too keen on women in the Labour Party, you know, although they certainly ought to be. It would be such a huge struggle to get adopted even, years of fighting and in-fighting, and I'm not sure if I'm ready for that. And it would mean my giving up my job, probably, and I certainly don't know if I could face that.'

'Well, I certainly couldn't,' said Julian.

He spoke very seriously. There was a silence.

'Well, anyway,' said Susan lightly, 'it's out of the question at the moment. The girls are still at home. Maybe when they're grown up.'

'Maybe. I must say I can't quite adjust to the thought of you shirking a fight. You used to thrive on them.'

'I know. But I'm older now. Maybe a bit wiser. Anyway, for the next two or three years my work on the South Ealing council will keep me quite busy enough. Then I'll see.'

Julian looked at her. She was one of those women who improve with time, who grow into their looks and their style. When she had been young, her features had been too angular, too harsh for beauty, prettiness even, and she had had neither the money nor the skill to improve upon the raw material. She was still very thin, and not classically beautiful, but she had developed an elegance, she wore clothes well; her hair hung smoothly on her shoulders, a beautifully cut bright brown. She dressed simply but with distinct style; today she was in the shirt dress so beloved of the fifties, in soft navy wool, with a full skirt that swirled almost to her ankles, and pulled in tightly at the waist with a wide, soft red leather belt, and plain red court shoes. Her skin was pale, but clear, her eyes a dazzling light blue; on her mouth, her most remarkable feature, she wore a shiny, bright pink lipstick. She looked expensive, glamorous even; what was missing, Julian thought to himself, was jewellery, she never wore any, and her look needed it, it would suit her and her stark style.

'You look terrific,' he said with perfect truth. 'Is that the new autumn coral?'

'It is. Mango, it's called. I like it best out of the range. Mum says it's tarty, so I know it must be good and strong.'

'It's terrific. Sarsted's doing a good job, don't you think?'

'Very good.'

'And how is Mum?'

'Much the same.'

'Oh dear.'

'Well, I don't have to live with her any more.'

'Susan,' said Julian suddenly. 'Why don't you come to New York with me? I could use your opinion, and it would be fun.'

Susan looked at him very steadily for a long time.

'No, I don't think so,' she said at last.

'Why not?'

'You know why not.'

'I don't.'

'Yes you do.'

'Don't you want to come?'

'Oh, Julian,' she said, with a sigh that seemed to consume her entire body, 'I'd love to. You know I would. But I can't. And I do think it's a terrific idea, your store. Now let's get back. It's late.'

'I do hope,' he said, half smiling, half serious, 'you know what you're turning down. A whole new chapter in your life.'

'Julian, don't play games with me.'

'I'm not playing games,' he said, 'I mean what I say. I think I'll need you there.'

She looked at him sharply, trying to interpret his words, to disentangle his motives. It was not easy, and most people didn't begin to try; he had a capacity to talk on two or even three levels at once, leading people deliberately to think that he was talking business when he meant pleasure, that he was serious when he was not, that he was careless when he was deeply concerned. He had brought it to a fine art; he used it to trap people, to confuse them, to disorient them; and it meant he could play cat

147

and mouse in a business or a social or sexual context until he had manoeuvred his opponents into a position from which it was very hard for them to escape, without looking foolish. Susan was one of the very few people who was unfazed by this; she dealt with it as she did with everything: directly.

'Julian, if you're tempting me with promotion, some lofty new position, I would like it spelt out before I waste weeks of my very busy life finding out exactly what it might be, and if you're tempting me with yourself I can resist. Just.' She smiled at him. 'So either way, probably we should get back to the office.'

He sighed. 'Will I ever get the better of you, Susan? Persuade you to do something you don't totally approve of?'

'Certainly not. Are you coming back? Or are you going to waste even more company time than you have already?'

'You go on,' he said, 'I'll follow.'

When her taxi was out of sight he walked along Piccadilly, up Regent Street and into Mappin and Webb. He spent a long time there, looking, selecting, and rejecting; finally he chose a two-strand pearl necklace with a diamond clasp and a pair of pearl and gold stud earrings. When he got back to the offices he went into her room and put the box on her desk.

'What's that?'

'Thank-you present.'

'What for?'

'For liking my idea. For not coming to New York. And because you deserve it. No strings. But I shall be very offended if you don't take it.'

Susan opened the box, looked at the pearls in silence for a long time, and then at him. Her eyes were very bright and big, and suspiciously moist. 'You won't have to be offended. Of course I'll take them. And wear them every day. They're simply beautiful. Thank you very much, I – I just don't know what to say.'

'Well,' said Julian lightly, 'you are simply beautiful too. So you suit one another, you and the pearls. I'll keep you informed about New York. Just in the hope you might change your mind.'

But they both knew she wouldn't.

New York in the autumn of 1956 was a heady place. It had taken a long time to recover from the depression; in 1939 half a million people in the state were still receiving public assistance. But by the mid-forties the big business giants – IBM, Xerox, General Electric – were all becoming corporations; a new governor, Thomas Dewey, had set schemes for state universities and new highways into motion – six were built in the decade following the war – and Harriman and Rockefeller poured money into the state. In 1955 the new state thruway from New York City to Buffalo was opened, and soon after that construction began on the St Lawrence Seaway.

The new highways meant the real birth of the commuter to New York, and the birth of the suburb; paving a way for ambition, opportunity, and the American dream; they also paved an increasing drift, for the less fortunate, to the ever-growing ghettos. But in the commercial heart of the city there was money, real money, more and more of it, up for grabs. And Julian Morell was in grabbing mood.

He stayed, with Philip Mainwaring, at the Pierre Hotel, shrine to luxury and a slightly old-fashioned glamour, just on Central Park – and an inspiration for their cause, filled as it was with spoilt, lavished-upon women and extravagant, indulgent, men.

They had a huge success with Juliana; Bergdorf's, Bonwit's and Sak's all bought it, and promised Julian special displays and promotions when he launched his new young perfume, *Mademoiselle Je*, in the spring. He set up a recruitment drive for consultants selling his range in the stores, interviewing them every morning in his suite; he was looking not just for women who could sell the products but who could communicate with the customers, sympathize with their anxieties, reassure them, make intelligent suggestions. It was a difficult task; he was looking for a type of woman who would not normally consider selling cosmetics behind a counter. He had managed to find them in London, but it was more difficult to find this particular breed in New York, mecca of the hard sell. At last, after days of intensive interviewing, Julian found a handful and hired them at just over half again the salary all their rivals were getting and said he would pay them no commission. 'That way,' he said to Philip, 'they aren't hammering away pushing unsuitable stuff at women who don't want any more than advice. It works in London; it'll work here.' Then he turned his attention to looking for his building.

They worked their way steadily through central New York for days, marvelling at the soaring erratic beauty of the place; up and down the huge avenues. Sixth and Fifth, Lexington and Park; down the side streets; examining new buildings, conversions, buildings in use as offices, even already as shops. It was exhausting, depressing and began to feel hopeless.

'Maybe,' said Philip as they walked slowly back to the Pierre one evening, 'we should think of building.'

'No,' said Julian, 'no, I know we shouldn't build. I know we need something with a past.'

'Julian, we must have looked at everything with a past in New York City and a lot without a future,' said Philip, 'this place doesn't exist, you have to rethink.'

'No,' said Julian, 'I'm not going to rethink. We'll find it. There's no rush. Come on, let's have a martini, it'll cheer you up, and then I'll see if anything's come in for us during the day.'

He ordered two martinis and went to the desk to pick up his mail: a huge armful of real-estate agents' envelopes. He carried them over to Philip in the bar, laughing. 'Come on, Philip, plenty to do. We needn't be bored.'

'I long to be bored,' said Philip gloomily, downing his martini in one.

'Oh, nonsense. Where's your spirit of adventure? Have another one of those to stiffen your sinews a bit and – Oh, look, here's something from a residential agent. That's interesting.'

He opened the envelope. A photograph fell out of a beautiful house, about a hundred years old, tall and graceful, five storeys high, with beautiful windows, classic proportions. It was just off Park Avenue on 57th, and it was being offered for sale as a possible small hotel. Julian looked at it for a long time in silence.

'That's it,' he said, 'that's my building. Jesus, that's it. What do they want for it?'

'Julian, that's a house,' said Philip. 'You can't convert that into a shop.'

'Of course I can,' said Julian, smiling at him radiantly, 'a house is exactly what I want. I don't know why I didn't realize before. Come on, Philip, let's go and look at it now.'

'But it's dark,' said Philip plaintively, 'we won't be able to see it.'

'Oh, for heaven's sake, man, don't be so negative. Haven't you heard of electric light? It's all the rage. Come on, we can do it easily before dinner.'

They got in a cab and travelled the few blocks down to 57th. There they got out and walked slowly along the street until they reached the house. It was nestled between two other, taller buildings, a small elegant jewel. A light hung over the front door like a canopy, showing off its perfect shape, its delicate fanlight. It was a very lovely house. Julian looked at it in silence; he crossed the street and looked at it still longer. Then he crossed again and knocked at the door.

It was over two years before the store opened. An expensive two years.

The first thing Julian had to do was find the money to buy the house, and to do the conversion. Most of the larger banks were not over-helpful. Morell's, and indeed Juliana did not have the substance, hold the authority in New York, that they did in London. Julian tried the merchant banks in London, but they were reluctant to put money into an untried venture in New York.

He was just about to try to raise a personal loan when he was put in touch with a young man called Scott Emerson, who headed up one of the investment divisions at the Chase Manhattan Bank and who was earning a reputation as having a shrewd eye for a clever investment. Julian went to see him, armed with photographs, cash flows, prospectuses, his own company history and his burning, driving enthusiasm; he came away with a cautious promise – 'a definite maybe' Julian told Susan and Letitia on the phone to London – and a life-long friendship. Scott lived with his wife Madeleine and their two children ('Nearly four,' he told Julian proudly over lunch that first day. 'Madeleine's expecting twins') on Long Island; he invited Julian to spend the weekend there, and Julian fell promptly in love with American family life. Unlike most Englishmen, he found the way American children were encouraged to talk, to join in a conversation, to consider themselves as important as adults, charming and interesting; he thought of his small daughter brought up by Eliza and her nanny in the nurseries at the top of the house, and resolved to change things.

'You must bring Eliza to stay here next time you come,' said Madeleine, smiling at him over Saturday breakfast. 'We would just love to meet her, she sounds so interesting and so young. It's quite an undertaking, marrying a man with such a huge and demanding business at her age. She's obviously a coper.'

'Well, she's very busy,' said Julian, carefully ignoring the comment on Eliza's capacities as a wife. 'Our child is very young. But yes, I'm sure she'd like New York, and of course to meet you. Perhaps for the opening of the store.'

'Well, that's –' Madeleine had been going to say 'two years off' but decided against it – 'a really good idea.' Something in Julian Morell's face told her he was not a man to argue with, especially on the subject of his wife.

'How old is your daughter?'

'She's nine months old,' said Julian.

'Well, that's a lovely age,' said Madeleine. 'I wish they could stay like that. Our C. J. is just a little older. He'll be down in a minute, his nurse is taking him out for a walk. Maybe when they're older he and your Rosamund can be friends. I'd really like that. Oh, look, here he is now. C. J. come and say hallo to Mr Morell.'

The nurse, smiling, carried C. J. over to Julian; the child looked at him solemnly and then buried his head in her shoulder.

'Oh, dear,' said Julian, 'don't I even get a smile?'

Madeleine held out her arms, took the child; he turned and smiled suddenly at Julian. He had brown hair, and large brown eyes; they held a slightly tremulous expression. Madeleine kissed him and then handed him back to the nurse. She went out, talking quietly to the baby under her breath.

'He's sweet,' said Julian. 'What's his real name?'

'Well, he was christened Christopher John, but the nursemaid we had then called him C. J. and it kind of stuck. He's so terribly different from his sister, it's funny how you can tell so early. He's quieter, and he doesn't try and push the world around like she did at that age. I don't think he's ever had a temper tantrum. She'll be running for president by the time she's seventeen. But he's such a nice little boy. I suppose he may toughen up.'

Julian thought of C. J.'s soft brown eyes, his shy smile, and thought it would be rather a pity if he did.

Julian spent most of those two years in New York working harder than he had ever worked in his life, even during the very early days of the company, in a total commitment to seeing his vision become reality. It was not unusual for him to work right through the night, and occasionally half of the next one as well; he missed meals, he cancelled social engagements, and he expected precisely the same dedication from everyone working with him.

Nathan and Hartman, considered to be the finest architects in New York, had initially been hired to work on the store, and were fired within weeks because their plans didn't meet with Julian's absolute approval; a second firm met the same fate. Then a young French architect, Paul Baud, arrived at the Pierre one evening and asked to see Julian. He had a small portfolio under his arm, and he looked about nineteen. Julian had sighed when he heard he was downstairs; then he said he would give him five minutes and if he hadn't convinced him by then he would have to go away again. Baud drew out of his portfolio the plans for a tiny hotel in Paris and a small store in Lyons which was the only work he had ever done, and spent the entire night in the bar at the Pierre with Julian, drawing, talking, listening. Then he went away for a week and came back with the plans complete. Julian hardly altered a thing.

He went to Paris for his beauty therapists, knowing that only there would he find the crucial combination of knowledge, mystique and deep-seated belief in the importance of beauty treatment that would have the women of New York paying visits three or four times a week to his salons. He installed on the fifth floor an extraordinary range of equipment and treatments, massage machines, passive exercisers, seaweed and mud baths, steam cabinets, infra-red sunbeds, saunas, and a battery of masseurs, visagistes, hair stylists, manicurists, dietitians. There was a small excessively well-heated swimming pool, a gymnasium, a bar that sold pure fruit and vegetable juices, and a few dimly lit cubicles fitted out with nothing but beds and telephones, where the ladies, exhausted from a morning's toil, could sleep for an hour or so before setting forth to buy the clothes, jewellery, perfume and make-up to adorn their tortured, treated, bodies.

Buyers were brought in from all over the world: from Milan, Rome, London, Paris, Nice, San Francisco: men and women who did not just know about fashion and clothes but had it in their blood, who could recognize a new line, a dazzling colour, a perfect fabric as surely as they could tell their own names, their own desires.

Julian hired a young greedy advertising agency called Silk diMaggio to promote the store, ignoring the sober advice of Philip Mainwaring to go to Young and Rubicam or Doyle Dane.

Nigel Silk was old money, new style, born of a Boston banking family, who had perfected the art of appearing establishment while questioning every one of its tenets; he was tall, blond – 'By Harvard out of Brooks Brothers,' Scott Emerson described him – charming and civilized.

Mick diMaggio, on the other hand, was no money at all, the youngest of the eight children of a third-generation Italian immigrant, who ran a deli just off Broadway. Mick talked like Italian ice cream spiked with bourbon, and wrote the same way; Julian looked at the creative roughs he produced for the poster campaign – a young beautiful woman, lying quite clearly in the aftermath of sexual love, under the headline 'The absolute experience' – and threw up his hands in pleasure.

'This,' he said, 'will empty Bergdorf's.'

They were a formidable team.

One of its most formidable parts was Camilla North.

Camilla North was born ambitious.

So eager had she been to get out into the world and start achieving that she had actually arrived nearly four weeks early; she was walking at seven months old, talking at nine; she was at dancing class at two, riding at three and reading and writing at four.

By the time she was ten she had become a superb horsewoman, an accomplished dancer, and was gaining honours in examinations in both the piano and the violin; by way of recreation she was also learning the classical guitar. She promised to be a brilliant linguist and mathematician, and was the only pupil at her exclusive girls' school ever to have gained a hundred per cent mark in Latin at the end-of-year examinations three years running.

The interesting thing about Camilla was that she was not actually especially gifted at most of the things she excelled at; she had talents, minor facilities, but because she had a fierce, burning need to do everything better than anybody else, she was prepared to put sufficient, monumental even, effort into it to fulfil that need. A rare enough quality in an adult, it was an extraordinary thing to find in a child; her piano teacher, coming to the house to give her her lesson, frequently found her white with exhaustion, on the point of tears, labouring over some difficult piece or set of scales; her mother would often tell people in a mixture of pride and concern that ever since she had been a tiny child she had got up half an hour earlier than she need, in order to practise her ballet; she was hardly ever to be seen simply fooling around and enjoying her pony, but spent long hours practising her dressage skills, endlessly crossing and traversing the paddock, changing legs, pacing out figures of eight; she even insisted on learning to ride side-saddle; and if she was ever found to have fallen asleep over a book, it would be her Latin grammar and not a story book.

She even extended this capacity to what would normally be regarded as fun; when she first was given a bicycle she went out to the back yard with it and said she wouldn't come in until she could ride it. Five hours later she was still out there, in the dark, both knees cut, both elbows badly bruised, a fast swelling lip where she had struck it on the handlebars – and an expression of complete triumph on her face as she rode round and round the lawn.

Nobody could quite work out what drove her. She was the much-loved oldest child and only daughter of Mary and William North; amateur psychologist friends of the family said she was trying to hold her own against the competition on offer from her three younger brothers but as none of them were nearly as clever or as successful as she was (although it had to be said none of them worked nearly so hard) this did not seem an entirely satisfactory explanation. Neither did it seem to be genetically determined; William North was old money; a charming, and gentle-mannered man, with a large and successful law practice in Philadelphia that he had inherited from his father. He worked hard and he was a clever man, but his instinct in confrontation of any kind was to withdraw, and he had no serious desire to see his firm taking on the world – or even the rest of Philadelphia. Mary North was even older money, still more charming and gentle-mannered, with no serious desire to do anything at all except keep her household running smoothly and happily; she was slightly frightened by her restless, brilliant little daughter and felt more at ease with her sons. But William was fiercely proud of her; they were very best friends, and would sit for hours after dinner, discussing politics, playing chess (this was the only time Camilla could bear to lose at anything) or simply reading together, while the boys loafed around, watching television and playing rock and roll records.

Camilla went, inevitably to Vassar, a year young; she graduated, summa cum laude, in languages, and also studied fine arts. She left in 1956, with a reputation as the most brilliant girl not just of her year but several years; and also as the most beautiful.

Camilla sometimes wondered what she would have done if she had been born plain. Being beautiful was as important to her as being clever; she simply could not bear to be anything but the loveliest, and the best-dressed woman, in a room. Fortunately for her she almost always was. She had a curly tangled mane of red-gold hair, transparently pale skin, and dramatically dark brown eyes. She was very tall and extremely slender; she had in fact a genetic tendency, a legacy from her mother, to put on weight, and from the age of twelve when she had heard somebody say she was developing puppy fat, she had been on a ferocious diet. Nobody had ever seen Camilla North put butter on her bread or sugar in her coffee; she never ate cheese, avocados, cereal or cookies; she weighed herself twice a day, and if the scales tipped an ounce over eight stone, she simply stopped eating altogether until they went back again. She quite often went to bed hungry, and dreamed about food.

She always dressed superbly; sharp stark slender clothes, in brilliant red, stinging blue, or emerald. At college she had been famous for her cashmere, her kilts, her loafers, a supreme example of the preppy look; but as soon as she left, she abandoned them and moved into dresses, suits, grown-up clothes, the severity always relieved by some witty dashing accessory, a scarf, a big necklace, a wide leather belt in some brilliant unexpected colour. She loved shoes; she had dozens of pairs, mostly classic courts with very high heels which she somehow managed to move gracefully in; but she looked best of all in her riding clothes, in her white breeches, black jacket, and her long, wonderfully worn and polished boots, her red hair scooped severely back. She occasionally hunted side-saddle; it was an extraordinary display of horsemanship and she looked more wonderful still, in a navy habit and white stock, a top hat covering her wild hair. So much did she like her habit that she had a version of it made in velvet for the evening; she wore it without a shirt, and with a pearl choker at her throat, her hair cascading over her shoulders; it was a sight that took men's breath away, and it was this that she was wearing when she first met Julian Morell.

She was living in New York by then, in a small, walk-up apartment in Greenwich Village. It was several months since she had left Vassar, and she had not yet found a definite job to do. She had found the debutante and the social scene boring, and she had, besides, considerable hopes and ambitions for herself; she came to New York to seek her fortune, preferably in the field of the arts. She had hopes of working in the theatre, as a designer; or perhaps in the world of interior design. She met Paul Baud at a party; he was immediately impressed by her, and told her he was looking for designers for a new store; why didn't she let her talents and imagination loose on a department or two. It was a new concept for Camilla; she sat at her drawing board virtually without food or rest for almost thirty-six hours before she was even remotely satisfied with what she had done. She delivered the drawings to Paul's office without even asking to see him, so sure was she that she would never hear from him about them again.

   She had chosen to live alone, against considerable opposition from her parents, for two reasons; one was that she liked her own company. The other was that she had hardly any friends. Camilla had no idea how to make friends. All her life she had been entirely occupied with struggling, striving, working; she had never had a best friend to talk to, giggle with, confide in, not even as a small girl. She had gone to children's parties, she was pleasant and friendly and nobody disliked her, but nobody liked her particularly either. She was too serious, too earnest, there was too little common ground. Later on, in her teens, she went to fewer parties, because she tended to get left out; she didn't mind, because she was so busy. But at college she became much sought after, because of the way she adorned a room, set a seal on a gathering; she was not exactly popular, but she was a status symbol, she was asked everywhere.

Nevertheless she remained friendless, solitary; and she had no gift for casual encounters. On Sundays for instance, when the other girls went for walks or spent long hours chatting, giggling, talking about men, making tea and toast, she would sit alone in her room, studying or reading, declining with a polite smile any invitations to join them.

She was perfectly happy; her friendlessness did not worry her. It worried and surprised other people, but it was of no importance to her. What would have surprised other people, also, and was perhaps of a little more importance to her, was that at the age of twenty-one she was not only a virgin, but she had never been in love.

Julian was immediately impressed by Camilla's drawings, brought to him by Paul late one Friday evening; feverish with excitement about his project, desperate to progress it further, he asked to meet her immediately. Paul phoned the number of Camilla's apartment in Greenwich, and got no answer; urged on by Julian's impatience to see her, he tried her parents' number. Yes, they were told, Miss North would indeed be back that night; she had gone to the opera with her parents and was coming home for the weekend.

Julian looked at Paul; it was nine o'clock. 'Let's go and meet her at the opera,' he said. 'Then I can arrange to see her over the weekend.'

They waited patiently in the foyer of the opera house; they heard the final applause, the bravos, to Callas's great Carmen, and as the doors from the auditorium finally opened Julian felt in some strange way this was an important moment; as much for him as for his store. Then the great surge of people began to come out and he wondered if what he was doing was not rather foolish. How could they expect to find one girl he had never seen, and Paul had met briefly only once, in this melee? It was hopeless.

But he had reckoned without Camilla's great beauty, and the talent she had for parting crowds; as she walked through the foyer of the opera house in her blue velvet habit, pearls in her throat and in her wild red hair, her brown eyes tender with pleasure at the music she had just heard, people stared; and they did not just stare, they drew aside just a little to look at her. Julian, standing at the main doors, looking in, found himself suddenly confronted by her coming directly towards him. Not knowing who she was, he forgot Camilla North, and gazed at her, then smiled; drawn to her, moved by her beauty and her grace. She looked at him, recognizing, acknowledging, his appreciation, and then turned and said something briefly to her father who was just behind her.

Paul stepped forward. 'Miss North. Good evening. I am so sorry to intrude upon your family evening. But I liked your drawings so much and Mr Morell, here, was anxious to meet you as soon as possible to discuss them.'

Julian, astonished and amused that this beautiful creature could be his prey, held out his hand to her. 'Miss North. I am Julian Morell. Let me add my apologies to Paul's. And extend them to your family. It is an unforgivable intrusion. But I am in a fearsome hurry with my project. And I think we can work together. I wondered only if we could arrange a meeting over the weekend.'

Camilla looked at him, and recognized immediately a kindred spirit, a fellow fighter, an accomplice in the struggle to do not merely better but best. Where many people would have considered his behaviour in haunting the foyer of the opera house all evening a little excessive, ridiculous even, when a phone call on Monday morning would have done nearly as well, to her it seemed entirely reasonable. She smiled at him and took his hand.

'Mr Morell, I am delighted to meet you. How very very flattering that you should hunt me out. These are my parents, William and Mary North, Mother, Father, this is Julian Morell, who I hope very much to be able to work for, and Paul Baud, his colleague. Paul, Mr Morell, would you care to join us for supper? We are going to Sardi's, and it would be so nice to have you with us.'

It was interesting, Julian thought, that she did not defer to her parents in this suggestion; the evening was hers and she had taken charge of it. He noticed too, and liked, her formal manners, her serious self-confidence; he could work with her, and work with her well.

'That would be delightful,' he said, 'providing we shall not be intruding?'

'Not at all,' said William North, 'please do come. So nice to meet an Englishman too.'

Camilla, sitting next to Julian and opposite Paul Baud, discussing initially the opera, New York, the latest exhibition at the Metropolitan, felt acutely aware that she had crossed a threshold, that this was the most important evening she had ever spent. And the feeling was not entirely confined to her career.

She and Julian worked closely together for weeks before anything more intimate took place between them than drinking out of the same cup of coffee. Professionally they were completely besotted with one another: they recognized each other's talents, admired each other's style, inspired each other's creativity. Julian, initially overwhelmed by Camilla's capacity for work, by her perfectionism, by her ability to work to the highest standard for countless hours without food or rest, very swiftly came to take it for granted, and simply to accept her and her talents as an extension of his own. Camilla accepted this as the highest compliment and regarded his impatient arrogance, his insistence on achieving precisely what he wanted, his disregard for any other views but those which concurred with his own, as an essential element in her work for him.

She had initially been hired to design the lingerie and jewellery departments; while she worked on those Julian instructed Paul to search for others to set their mark on the more specialist area of the beauty floor, the precise demands of the fur department. But looking at the drawings she produced, the soft, sensuous fantasy she set the lingerie in, the rich, brilliant hard-edged greed she created for the jewellery, he abandoned his search and told her she must do the rest. While they worked in the close tension so peculiar to a shared ideal, she grew to know everything there was to know about him, as a person; she knew when he was angry, when he was discouraged, when he was afraid of what he had taken on; she could tell in moments whether he was worried, excited, pleased. She could see he was arrogant, demanding, ruthless; she found it absolutely correct that he should be so.

She was, she realized, for the first time in her life, absolutely happy.

She was a little less happy after she had been to bed with him. Camilla had for quite a long time realized that she had to go to bed with someone, before very much time elapsed. It was one thing maintaining your virginity through college, and indeed in the fifties that was what any well-brought-up girl was expected to do. They might not all live up to the expectations, but a lot did. But living as a successful career woman in New York City, and maintaining it, was something altogether different. There was something faintly un-chic about it, something gauche and awkward –almost, she felt, slightly ridiculous. The trouble was, if a man was to relieve her of it, he had to know it was there; if he was to know it was there he had to be told (or to find out for himself under rather difficult circumstances) and how, she wondered, did you do that? How did you say to a would-be lover, who had been drawn to you by your sophistication, your woman of the worldliness, who assumed that you were as accomplished in bed as you were in your career: Look, I'm sorry, but I don't actually know how to go about this? She supposed to a certain extent that you would know how to go about this, that your instincts would guide you, and she had very carefully read, in her painstaking way, a great many books on the subject, she knew a great deal of the theory, about positions and foreplay and virtually everything there was to know about contraception: (and there was another thing, she had been carefully fitted for a dutch cap by a very fashionable New York gynaecologist, that was the modern, chic answer to such things, and it lay unworn in its pink tin in her underwear drawer, waiting to be used) but she still couldn't imagine anybody being deceived into thinking she really knew what she was doing. And it was important to Camilla that she appeared to know exactly what she was doing, all the time.

She also, she had to admit, still found it a little hard to imagine that it could be as wonderful as it was supposed to be. Because of her friendless adolescence, she had totally missed out on the giggly intimate exchanges of sexual knowledge, and the lack of it; she had continued, as children do, to regard the whole thing as something people had to do rather than that they wanted to. Even now, when from time to time, usually in the company of some attractive man, she did feel slightly pleasurable stirrings of what she could only assume were sexual desire, she couldn't imagine being so overcome by them that she would get carried away, and risk pregnancy, scandal, and even being cited in the divorce court.

Just the same, she obviously had to do it, and do it soon; and Julian Morell seemed to her the ideal accomplice in the matter. He was much older than she was, so he would be experienced and presumably skilled; he would be more likely to be understanding and even charmed by her lack of experience; she knew he found her extremely attractive; and her opportunities for seducing him were legion. She did not give his wife a great deal of thought. She was three thousand miles away, and it was clearly a marriage of convenience, otherwise she would come to New York much more often; and besides this was 1957, it would be an adult relationship, and she had no intention whatsoever of breaking up the marriage.

She laid her plans with care.

None of it, however, had quite worked out how she had expected. She had managed to present him quite late on Friday evening with some drawings that were just sufficiently below her usual standard to require further discussion and work; she had suggested they talked over dinner at a new Italian place in the Village near her apartment; she had asked him to see her home (as it was Friday night and there were more than the usual number of drunks about); she had made them both coffee and poured them both brandy (which he had drunk rather less enthusiastically than she had) and then sat, edgy and dry mouthed, hoping rather desperately that some overpowering natural instinct would propel them both into the studio couch (made up freshly this morning with some new thick linen sheets she had bought from Saks) without her having consciously to do any more about it.

Julian had not seemed, however, in the least danger of being overpowered by anything; he sat totally relaxed, leafing through the pages of *Vogue* and *Bazaar*, pointing out the occasional reference to himself, to Mrs Lauder's new range, to a forthcoming promotion from Mr Revson; finally he had leant back on the couch, looked at her and said, 'What's the matter, Camilla?'

'Nothing,' she said, 'nothing at all.'

'Oh yes there is,' he said, 'first you present me with some damn fool designs and pretend you can't do any better. Then you tell me you're afraid to come home on your own, when you're the most independent woman in New York and that includes the Lady on Ellis Island. Now you're shaking like a teenager on her first date. What is it?'

She had said nothing, nothing at all, that she was simply tired; and he had laughed and said she was never tired; and had taken her hand and said, 'I may be being presumptuous but are you out to seduce me?'

And she said, half angry, half ashamed, no of course she wasn't; that it was time he left, it was late; and he said he would certainly leave if she liked, only he would much rather stay if she would like that; and then she started to cry, and said please, please go, and then he had put his arms around her, to comfort her, and that had been cosy and comforting and reassuring, and she had stopped feeling frightened and silly; and then somehow everything had changed and he was kissing her, really kissing her, and holding her and stroking her, and at first it was nice, and then as she realized what was happening, she stopped being relaxed and she tautened and shivered violently; he had drawn back from her and said, 'Camilla, what is it, what's the matter?' and she had suddenly taken a deep breath and said, 'I've never done it before.'

She would never forget to her dying day the look of absolute amazement on his face; how he had sat back from her, just staring at her, and she had been sure he was going to be angry, or amused; and then he had said, very gently, reaching out and touching her face, 'Then we must take great care that you will want to do it again.'

After that it had been all right; she had had a moment of panic when she had suddenly remembered the cap, sitting expectantly in its drawer, but by then she was undressed and so was he (and neither he nor *it* had looked nearly as alarming as she had expected) and she was feeling relaxed enough to be able to say she had to go to the bathroom; and when she came back he had been waiting for her with an expression of such tenderness, such patience that she had stopped being frightened altogether.

Nevertheless, she had not found it as wonderful as she had hoped; indeed it had been rather more as she had feared; and she had felt strangely detached, almost disembodied, as if she had been watching above the bed as he fondled her and kissed her, and stroked her breasts and kissed them; and kept asking her if she was happy, if it was all right; and finally, as the moment arrived, as he gently, tenderly entered her, patiently waiting again and again for her to follow him, as he began to move within her, as eventually the movements became urgent, bigger, more demanding, as he kissed her, stroked her, sought out her most secret, tender places: as he shuddered tumultuously into her, murmuring her name again and again, all she could feel, all she could think as she tried dutifully, earnestly to respond, was a sense of huge relief that it was over at last. Afterwards, of course, she had lied; she had said it had been lovely, that no, she hadn't quite come, but she had felt marvellous, that (and this much at least was true) it couldn't have been more wonderfully, more gently accomplished, and that she was truly truly happy. They had fallen asleep then; later, waking thirsty and uncomfortable, unaccustomed to the restless invasion of her quietly peaceful bed, she had got up and gone to the kitchen for a drink of water; when she came back he was awake, waiting for her, his hand outstretched, asking her back to bed; and he had done it again, less carefully, more urgently, and it had been a little nicer and she could almost have said she enjoyed it. And when she awoke in the morning, and got up and showered, and made him coffee and sat drinking it with him, she had felt quite wonderful, to think at last, at long last, she was like everyone else, every other woman; no longer set strangely and awkwardly apart.

What Camilla had not been quite clear about was whether she was now actually Julian's mistress. It was one thing being seduced by him, that was what she had absolutely wanted; what was quite another was being emotionally and physically involved with him long term, and she was not sure if she wanted that at all.

There were many things she did want from him: recognition, power, prestige; but these sat curiously at odds with other such things as love, tenderness and physical pleasure. Indeed, as she lay in her bed in her parents' home on the Saturday night, after parting at midday from Julian, she had wondered, with a touch of panic, if she had actually done the right thing; if in asking him for sex she had forfeited her career. He must, indeed he had told her so, now see her rather differently; no longer the cool, self-confident Camilla North, possessor of a formidable talent, but a tender, tentative lover; possessor (as he himself had said, as he kissed and caressed it joyfully), of a formidable body. What was that going to do to her position, her future, in the company? Had she in an uncharacteristically feckless, reckless act, thrown away what mattered most to her in the world: her own success?

But it was actually quite all right. She need not have worried: on either count as it turned out. Julian simply could not afford to lose her, as a considerable force within the company – and at that particular point in time he did want to have any long-term commitment. His marriage was still alive, and if not well, certainly not sick enough to abandon, and he most emphatically did not want to subject himself to the scandal and trauma of a divorce. He had made these things charmingly and patently clear to her over lunch on the following Monday; he had told her she was the loveliest thing that had happened to him since he had arrived in America, that if she had enjoyed Friday's encounter even half as much as he had, then she was a very lucky girl, and he hoped that she would invite him to dinner again very soon; and then, lest she might find this ever so slightly dismissive, he had told her that he would like her to work closely with the advertising agency in future, as he wanted her input and visual judgement in that area.

'This has nothing whatever to do,' he added, raising his glass to her and smiling, 'with the great pleasure you were able to give me the other evening. It is because I think, I know, that you

165

are an extremely talented person, and I want your expertise wherever it is needed. Also I happen to consider that your talents don't stop at what is known as the creative area. You have a commercial sense as well.'

Camilla's heart had thudded, her pulses had raced, far more pleasingly, more passionately than they had when she had been in bed with him. This, she thought, meeting his eyes with an expression of absolute pleasure and confidence, was what was really important to her. Everything else came an extremely bad second.

Nevertheless, over the next few weeks she and Julian were together almost all the time – day and night.

She felt absolutely no guilt whatsoever about Eliza: her attitude towards her was completely dispassionate. She could clearly see that Julian did not love her and she felt besides that Eliza did quite well enough out of her marriage as it was, without demanding or even requiring fidelity from her husband. She studied her with great interest when Eliza finally came to New York, rather as a biologist might a rare, hitherto undiscovered species; she noted her great beauty, her unmistakable chic, her rather naïve if sparkly manner; she probed her conversational skills, she analysed her cultural and intellectual abilities, she examined her grasp of the affairs of Julian's company and found her wanting on almost every count. It seemed quite incomprehensible to her that a woman in Eliza's position should not be totally au fait with every possible aspect of her husband's world: not only in the broader matters, in the workings of the cosmetic and retail industry, but also in the minutiae of the people he employed and their role within the company. That seemed to Camilla to be the very least a wife should offer her husband; if she did not, then she deserved absolutely everything she got.

It did not occur to her that Julian saw to it quite deliberately that Eliza was able to offer almost nothing.

Eliza, left alone in London, was not only lonely; more miserably, more significantly indeed, she felt isolated, shut out; she tried very hard at first to persuade Julian to tell her about his project in New York, she asked him endless questions, even tried to make suggestions of her own about what the store might be like, what it might sell, what she would like herself to find in such a place. But Julian would not be drawn, answering her questions as briefly as possible, ignoring her suggestions, and totally rejecting any requests she made to accompany him on one of the many trips. He would phone her quite often when he was there, asking how she and how Roz were, he would send her funny cards, he would have flowers delivered, and he would return to her with his arms full of presents, impatiently ardent, with a string of funny stories and amusing gossip; but of what he had really been doing, actually achieving, she learnt almost nothing. In the end, inevitably, she came to reject the presents, to resent the gossip, and to find the ardour unwelcome.

'Eliza,' said Julian in an attempt at lightness as she turned away from him for the third night in a row, 'forgive me if I'm wrong, but you seem to find me marginally less attractive than you did a short while ago.'

'Yes,' she said flatly, 'yes I do. I'm surprised you have taken so long to be aware of it.'

'Do I have to look to myself for the reason? Am I growing fat? Boring? Perhaps if you would be kind enough to enlighten me I might be able to do something about it.'

'No, Julian,' said Eliza, turning over on to her back and looking at him, her green eyes hard and oddly blank, 'you're not in the least fat, and I don't suppose you're boring. Although it would be a little hard for me to tell.'

'I don't quite know what you mean.'

'Oh, for Christ's sake,' she said. 'Don't be so dense. I see so little of you, and talk to you so seldom, how can I possibly know what you're like any more?'

'That's not fair. You know how busy I am. And I took you out to dinner this evening, and devoted myself very thoroughly to your interests. Which were, I have to say, a little less than riveting. A nursery school for Rosamund, I seem to recall, and the advisability of refurnishing Marriotts throughout. Oh, and of course your latest purchases from M. St Laurent.'

'Shut up, shut up!' cried Eliza, sitting up, her eyes stinging with sudden tears. 'How can you possibly expect me to have anything to say to you that you might find interesting when I don't have the faintest idea what you're doing from one week's end to the next?'

'Other wives seem to manage. To occupy themselves with something more than total trivia.'

'Julian,' said Eliza, controlling her voice with an effort, 'I don't want to have to occupy myself, as you put it, with anything. I want to be busy with you. With our marriage. I want to be involved.'

'Eliza, we've been through this before. I have not the slightest desire to have you mixed up with my company. I want a wife, not a business partner.'

'And how can I be a wife when I don't even know what kind of areas your business is extending into? I don't want to work for your lousy company, but I would like at least to be able to answer people when they ask me what you're doing in New York, and whether the cosmetics are doing as well there as they are in London. I've never even been to New York, I don't know what it looks like, and I'm expected to be able to comment on the comparative merits of Bergdorf's and Saks. How can I begin to understand what might be worrying you, interesting you, exciting you, when you answer me in monosyllables and treat me as if I was some kind of half-witted child? You diminish me, Julian, as a person, and then you expect me to be wholly responsive to you in bed. Well, I can't be. Don't ask me any more.'

There was a silence for a moment. Then Julian got up and walked over to the door.

'I think I'll sleep in my dressing room,' he said, 'I won't say if you don't mind, because clearly you wouldn't.'

'Don't you think?' said Eliza sitting up in bed, tears streaming down her face now, 'don't you think there is at least something in what I say?'

'No,' he said very finally. 'No, I don't. I married you because I thought you could offer the kind of undemanding support and understanding I desperately need. I was obviously wrong.'

'You were,' said Eliza, a cold calm descending on her, 'and I wish to God you had looked for it in somebody else.'

'Well,' he said, 'on that note I will say good night.'

She thought with some satisfaction that for the first time she had managed to hurt him, however slightly.

He never apologized or referred to the conversation again. But he came in two days later with an envelope which he tossed

168

down on to the dinner table, and looked at her with a slightly odd expression in his dark eyes.

'I wondered if you might like to come to New York with me next time I go. I'm thinking of getting an apartment there and it would be very nice if you could help me with it. There are a few photographs in there of the site for the store. I thought it would amuse you to see them.'

Eliza looked at him, unsmiling, slightly wary. 'I'd like that very much. Thank you.'

'Well,' he said with a sigh, 'I hope you're not disappointed.'

She wasn't. She thought New York was wonderful. She loved the wide, windy streets (it was autumn), the sculptured beauty of the skyline, the pace of life, the glamour, the shops. Most of all the shops. They drove up Fifth Avenue the first evening past Lord and Taylor's, Saks, Tiffanys, Henri Bendel, Cartier, Bonwit's, and at every one she grew more excited, twisting and turning in her seat like a small child at a party. Then she caught a glimpse of Julian's face, oddly severe, almost pained, and remembered she was supposed to be presenting him with a more sophisticated, intelligent front.

'I'm sorry, Julian. I'll calm down tomorrow. But it's like seeing a fairy tale come true, and I know that's a cliché, so don't tell me, having heard of all these places for so long and suddenly they're really there. And this is where your store is to be?'

'Yes,' he said, motioning the driver to pull in, pointing out to her the corner where the building stood. 'Look, there, see, that place there, just past Gucci.'

'Oh,' she said, 'yes, I do, and it's lovely. But isn't it –'

'Isn't it what?' he said, and there was ice in his voice.

'Well, a bit small.'

'Eliza, that was the whole idea. That it should be small. Not large and lavish and predictable. I thought you realized that, at least.'

'No,' she said, her voice small, her excitement gone. 'No, I didn't, I'm afraid. I'm sorry.'

In the morning, his mood still distant, he took her round the building briefly, then said he had a series of meetings and would see her for cocktails.

'Not lunch?'

'No, Eliza, not lunch. I have to take three buyers out.'

'I could come too.'

'No, you'd be a bored.'

'Julian, I promise you I wouldn't be bored.'

'Eliza, I'm sorry, I just don't think it's a very good idea. You have plenty to do. You can start looking at all those apartments. Make a shortlist, and then I'll look at them.'

'Look on my own?'

'Yes.'

She sighed. 'All right.'

She worked hard that day; she looked at seven apartments, drew up a comprehensive list, with an outline of the advantages and drawbacks of each one, and presented him with it at dinner.

'There you are, Julian. I think the one on 57th is the best. Lovely and near your building – what are you going to call it, by the way?'

'What do you mean? Juliana of course.'

'But it's more than Juliana. I think it should have a name of its own. That will give it an identity.'

'Eliza,' said Julian with a sigh, 'Juliana has plenty of identity.'

'Yes, but it's a cosmetic. The store will have much more to offer than that.'

'And what sort of name do you think it should have?'

He spoke as if to a child, humouring her, not as if he wanted to hear the answer.

'Oh, I don't know. Something beautiful. Something classical maybe. Something out of mythology perhaps.'

'My darling, I don't think you know what you are talking about. It really would be much better if you confined your efforts to finding our apartment. But thank you for the thought.'

Even when he had actually called the store Circe, he failed to give her any credit for it whatsoever.

The store finally opened in the spring of 1959 with a party that was lavish even by New York standards. It was devastatingly beautiful throughout, a shrine to luxury and vanity; it was also an extraordinary tribute to Julian Morell's taste, commercial instinct and crushing determination to get what he wanted.

The party he threw to open it was more like a theatrical production than a commercial launch. Lucky (as he so often was) with the weather, it was a tender spring evening, and still just light when the huge white doors of Circe were opened to New York for the very first time. A wide awning stretched from the door right across the sidewalk; looking up through it, all that could be seen from the street were banks of white lilies and what appeared to be a million dancing candles. A string quartet played at the top of the beautiful double curving staircase, a jazz trio on the second floor, amidst a tumble of furs, and in the main room on the ground floor where the huge cases of jewellery, all the colours of some exotic darkened rainbow, shimmered against the candlelight, a pianist in white tails sat at a white grand piano and played the music of Cole Porter, Rodgers and Hart and Irving Berlin.

Champagne flowed ceaselessly, recklessly, into white glass flutes; the cocktail waiter from the Savoy had been flown in from London for the occasion and the canapés were entirely black and red caviare, smoked salmon, Mediterranean prawns, monster strawberries dipped in chocolate.

'Well, it was certainly worth coming for these, anyway,' remarked Susan Johns to Letitia through a mouthful of several of them. 'What a party, Letitia. Is New York always like this?'

'A bit,' said Letitia, who was enjoying herself more than she could remember for years, and had already received several invitations to supper after the party from attractive smooth-faced, grey-haired suntanned almost indistinguishable gentlemen. 'I must say, Susan, I was a little opposed to this store, but I do think I was probably wrong. Julian has done something quite remarkable. I think it will be a great success.'

'Let's hope,' said Susan. 'It's cost enough. And in terms of Julian's time as much as money. Letitia, is that perfectly beautiful woman over there, talking to the pianist, Camilla North? The designer lady? The one we've heard just a bit too much about lately?'

Letitia looked over at the piano and at the undeniably beautiful Miss North, tall and very slender, with a mass of wild red hair and large brown eyes, dressed in a long slither of black satin that clung somewhat tenuously to her surprisingly full bosom.

'Yes,' she said, 'yes, that's Camilla. And she is beautiful, I agree. Very clever too, I believe. But if you're thinking what I think you might be thinking, you're wrong. No sense of humour whatsoever and a dreadful tendency to bang on in that heavy American way. She is absolutely not Julian's type.'

Eliza, who had decided that evening once and for all that she was not Julian's type either, was trying very hard to enjoy the party. And failing. Miserably. Everything had gone wrong from the moment she arrived, when the ghastly Camilla North had said in her earnest way, 'What a lovely dress, Mrs Morell. I always loved Chanel,' in tones that most clearly implied Chanel was best left in the past; Eliza, not easily demoralized in matters of dress, had felt an almost overwhelming urge to rush back to the apartment and change. From there it had been downhill all the way; everyone seemed to be friends, colleagues, to have worked on the project, to know a million times more about it than she did. She had tried very hard to keep abreast of Circe's development; had pestered Julian to talk to her about it, had visited it whenever she came to New York in the process of doing up their new apartment in Sutton Place ('You'd love it,' she had said to Letitia, 'it's exactly like London there right on the river') but it had been difficult, humiliating even, to have to keep asking people about it, to question them and betray her own ignorance.

But looking at the store that evening, in the company of Paul Baud who had taken it upon himself to look after her, she was still amazed, dazzled by Julian's achievement: by the design of each department, the way each was so different, yet blended so perfectly into the whole; at the selection of merchandise, the range of exclusive designers on offer, the wit and style of the accessories, the imaginativeness and scope of the beauty floor, the grace and charm of the entire building. 'It's truly beautiful, Paul,' she said, 'you must be very very proud.'

'Thank you,' he said, smiling at her, 'not proud perhaps, but pleased of course. It was a wonderful opportunity for me. Your husband is a very good person to work with. So – let me think, what am I trying to say – so easy to talk to, to explain things to, so understanding, such an – an inspiration. It is very unusual, I think, for a business person to be so in tune with the creative side of things.'

'I'm sure,' said Eliza, trying to reconcile this patron saint of communication with the man she had been endeavouring to talk to for nearly five years.

'Camilla says the same thing, very very often,' said Paul. 'She says it is quite extraordinary to work with a man who so appreciates so quickly what you are trying to do. She has adored working with him, I know.'

'Oh, good,' said Eliza sweetly, 'I'm so glad. Shall we go and find some food, Paul? I'm hungry.'

'Oh, I'm sorry, keeping you up here away from the party,' said Paul, looking stricken. 'Come, we'll find some food and some more champagne, and then perhaps you will dance with me. I do admire your dress. Chanel is my favourite designer of all time. And it is nice to see a woman not in black this evening.'

'Thank you,' said Eliza, feeling just slightly soothed.

'Come, then. And perhaps you will tell me about the people in the company in London, while we go down, particularly the *grandmère*. She is beautiful, that one. She has style.'

'Don't let her hear you referring to her as the *grandmère*,' said Eliza, laughing. 'But yes, she is beautiful. And clever, too.'

'So I believe. And the other lady? The one with the glorious legs. She looks as if she might be a dark mare – is that the expression?'

'Nearly,' said Eliza, laughing, 'that's Susan Johns. I'd never honestly noticed her legs. But she is terribly clever too. And maybe a bit of a dark mare. She virtually runs the company in London while Julian is away.'

'She has chic, that one,' said Paul. 'I admire her look.'

It had never occurred to Eliza that Susan had a look. She resolved to study her more closely in future. The world suddenly seemed full of beautiful, clever women, all of whom appeared to know her husband a great deal better than she did. She sighed.

'What is it, Mrs Morell? Did I say something wrong?' asked Paul anxiously. He hoped he was not upsetting his patron's wife on such an occasion; that would never do. Only that evening Julian had said he would like to think about opening a Circe in Paris. It would be terrible not to get the contract because of a little tactlessness or indiscretion. Besides, he had a kind heart; and he found Eliza charming. She was beautiful, he thought (only there was a sadness in her huge green eyes that puzzled him); and she looked ravishing in her white beaded shift dress, so elegant, so discreetly noticeable. Most of the Englishwomen he had met were loud and badly dressed; not chic or *sympatique*.

'Come,' he said, 'let us find the champagne. And we can study the celebrities on the way. So many, we have done well.'

They had; moving so gracefully up the stairs she appeared to float, they passed Audrey Hepburn, stunning in a black Givenchy sheath dress, a drifting mass of black ostrich feathers on her head; Zsa Zsa Gabor rippled through the crowd, in a cloud of red ruffles; Cary Grant smiled his way round the room.

'Camilla invited Jackie Kennedy. She knows her, it seems. She might come. But I fear not now. They are out of town. They say he has a very good chance of becoming president. I hope so,' he added fervently. 'It would be nice to have some chic in the White House. I would certainly vote for him, if I were allowed.'

Eliza liked the idea of a president elected in the cause of chic. 'Then I hope for your sake he gets in,' she said. 'Come on, Paul. Let's dance.'

When the party finally ended, with a rain of golden fireworks over the city from the roof garden, they had gone out in a huge party to Sardi's, with the Emersons, Paul, Camilla North, Letitia, Susan, and the Silks and the diMaggios.

Eliza, who had drunk a great deal of champagne by now, in sheer nervousness and desperation, and was sitting in between Scott and Mick, talked and giggled loudly a great deal, flirted with them both outrageously at first and then, as she became increasingly drunk, more and more recklessly garrulous, suggested to Scott that she should have a place on the board, that Mick might like to give her a job in his studio, and even that she might open up her own department at Circe, selling children's clothes. Everyone humoured her, fielded her suggestions gracefully, laughed at her jokes, but that could not hide the fact that she was, of all the people present, with the possible exception of Madeleine Emerson, a total outsider, and an awkwardness in the party. And despite the champagne, she knew it very well herself.

While they were waiting for their dessert she got up and walked round to Julian; he had been engrossed in conversation with Camilla for some time, and she felt an overpowering urge to disrupt them.

'Darling, move over,' she said, 'I want to share your chair.'

'Don't be silly, Eliza,' said Julian coldly, 'there isn't room.'

'Then let me sit on your knee. Just for a minute. I've hardly been near you all evening.'

'Eliza, please.'

'Oh, Julian, don't be so stuffy. All those celebrities must have gone to your head.' She picked up his glass and drained it. 'But we're with friends now. Aren't we? Or aren't we?' She looked round the table. 'We're all friends aren't we?'

Nobody spoke. 'Of course we are. Great friends. So come on, Julian, be friendly. I'm your wife. Remember? Move up.'

Camilla stood up and smiled at her graciously. 'Here, Eliza, do take my chair. I'm going to the ladies' room anyway.'

'Thank you,' said Eliza, 'thank you very much. How kind of you. How very very kind. Julian, Miss North is very very kind. And beautiful, don't you think? Yes, of course you do. You always notice beauty, don't you, my darling. Lots of beauty here, isn't there, among our friends. Well, just your friends, really, until tonight. You've been keeping them to yourself. I hope they're my friends too, now.'

The table had fallen into a ghastly silence. Julian stared at his plate, white faced, pushing back his hair compulsively. Eliza picked up Camilla's glass and raised it. 'A toast,' she said. 'To Circe. I named it, you know, in a way. It was my idea to give it a classical name. Julian's forgotten, of course, but we're all friends, so I can tell you. To Circe, then. Raise your glasses.'

Mick diMaggio, who had been watching Eliza intently, half admiring, half fearful for her, suddenly raised his glass. 'I echo the toast,' he said, 'to Circe. And to Eliza, who named it – her. And to all of us – friends – who sail in her,' he added quickly. It was a charming and graceful gesture; it eased the situation totally. 'To Circe,' they all said, even Julian managed a shadow of a gesture, mouthed the words.

Susan, who had been watching the scene with particular

horror, her heart constricted with panic and sympathy for Eliza, spoke suddenly. 'It is such a good name,' she said. 'Who *was* Circe, anyway?'

'She was a magician,' said Nigel Silk, in his impeccable Boston tones. 'She turned Ulysses' companions into swine.'

'A sorceress,' corrected Camilla.

'Same thing,' said Nigel.

'Not quite.'

'What's the difference?'

'Oh, my goodness,' said Letitia under her breath to Madeleine, 'Vassar versus Yale. Who would you put your money on?'

'Vassar, I think. More staying power.'

The conversation had become mercifully more general. Camilla and Nigel were engrossed in a dazzling display of mythological knowledge and had moved on to the influence of Sappho on modern poetry; Letitia was making Mick diMaggio laugh as she described how no fewer than three of her would-be suitors that evening had asked her if she could introduce them to the Queen; Madeleine Emerson had managed to engage Eliza in conversation about interior designers in London, and the possible career she was planning for herself among their ranks. Susan looked at Julian, silent and withdrawn, and felt suddenly and inexplicably sorry for him. She went and sat down next to him.

'It's been a lovely evening. A very special occasion. You must be really happy.'

She had chosen her words carefully.

'I was,' he said shortly, as she had known he would.

'Oh, Julian, don't be silly. It didn't matter. She'd had a bit too much to drink, that's all.'

'She looked stupid. Ridiculous.'

'And your wife is not allowed to look stupid?'

'No. She isn't.'

'Never?'

'Never. And certainly not on an occasion like this.'

'Well,' said Susan, 'I'm glad I'm not your wife.'

'Sometimes,' said Julian, 'I wish you were. As you very well know.'

'Maybe. But I can assure you if I was I'd look stupid a great deal more often than Eliza does. She's a great asset to you, Julian, and she'd be more of one if you'd let her be.'

'What do you mean?'

'I mean you shut her out.'

'How do you know? Has she been talking to you?'

'Of course not. She hardly ever talks to me, about anything. I wish she would. I like her. But anyway, she's very very loyal. More so than you deserve.'

'Thanks.'

'I know you shut her out because I have eyes in my head. It's extremely obvious, Julian. You never talk to her. You don't tell her anything. It's ridiculous. She could be such an asset to you. You *should* talk to her and you should listen to her. Then this sort of thing wouldn't happen. It was very sad, seeing her tonight, pretending she knew more about everything than she did, talking away, covering up for herself.'

'Stop lecturing me, Susan.' But he looked less angry, more relaxed.

'It's a bloody sight more interesting lecture than the one that's going on on my left.'

'Oh, Lord.'

Camilla and Nigel had left mythology for primitive American art; Letitia, who was now nearly as drunk as Eliza, was regaling Mick diMaggio with her stories of the Prince of Wales; Scott Emerson was nodding gently over his bourbon.

'I think,' said Julian sotto voce to Susan, 'that it's time to go home.'

'I agree. Now promise me you won't be angry with Eliza.'

Julian sighed and raised his hands in mock surrender. 'All right. I promise. Why is everyone on her side? You, Madeleine, Mick.'

'Perhaps,' said Susan with some asperity, 'because we're sorry for her.'

Eliza, waking in the morning to a hideous hangover and an empty apartment, knew they had been sorry for her, and decided it would never ever happen again. If she could not persuade Julian to share his life with her, then she would have one of her own, and make sure she didn't share that one with him.

She had apologized to him on the way home for behaving badly, and he had said shortly that it hadn't mattered so very much as they had after all been with close friends, and clearly wished to end the discussion. But he had slept in his dressing room, after giving her the briefest good night kiss, as increasingly often now he did.

She booked her flight home immediately, instead of waiting another week; she phoned Madeleine to tell her.

'Eliza, I hope this isn't because of last night,' said Madeleine, 'because that would be very silly.'

'Well,' said Eliza in a rather tight voice, 'it is and it isn't.'

'But darling, it just didn't matter, and nobody minded if that's what you mean. Nobody.'

'Yes, they did,' said Eliza, 'I minded. I made a fool of myself. And in front of a lot of people who matter to Julian. People I hardly know. People like the Silks and – and Camilla North.'

'I see,' said Madeleine quietly.

'But thank you for being on my side. You were wonderful. And when you come over next month, you will come and stay, won't you?'

'Of course we will. Now Eliza, promise me you're not going to rush off back to London and do anything silly.'

'Oh, Madeleine,' said Eliza with a sigh, 'I've spent the last five years trying to be sensible. It doesn't seem to have worked. I feel a bit disillusioned with it all. I just want to get home.'

'Eliza, you sound so sad,' said Madeleine. 'Please, please believe me, I know Julian cares about you very much.'

'Maybe he does,' said Eliza with a sigh, 'but he has a very strange way of showing it.'

'Well, I know so,' said Madeleine. 'He talks about you so much. And if – if you're worried about – well – Camilla North, you shouldn't be. They just work together. I'm quite sure there's no more to it than that.'

'Oh goodness,' said Eliza, dangerously bright, 'Camilla North is the least of my worries. It's nothing like that, Madeleine. Really. I just need to get away from it all. I feel like an outcast here. Can you understand that?'

'Yes,' said Madeleine, 'yes I think I can.'

'And besides,' said Eliza, 'you never know, I might even find a job of my own to do. Who knows what Fate might have in store for me?'

The Connection Two

Los Angeles, 1957–8

Lee was discussing sex with Amy Meredith when she realized her period was late.

She had never been much in the habit of noting down dates; she had long given up serious hope of a baby. Unlike some of her friends she never had any bad cramps, so she didn't have to plan around it – when it happened it happened, and that was all there was to it.

They were lying on the beach, she and Amy, one afternoon, not talking about anything in particular, and she was just debating for the hundredth time whether she should tell Amy about Hugo, it might help bring him a bit nearer, ease the loneliness and the growing hurt that he had only phoned twice briefly in the past four weeks (although he was coming down to stay in a fortnight), when Amy had said she mustn't be back late because Bob was bringing a client home for dinner.

'Dreadfully boring it'll be too,' she said, turning over on to her back and rearranging her hair on the towel, 'the wife is coming as well, and it'll be new drapes and the PTA right through to dessert. The only advantage is that Bob will probably get seriously drunk and then I'll have a bit of peace tonight.'

Lee laughed. 'Amy, is it really so bad?'

'Well, it mightn't be if it wasn't quite so predictable. I mean, you say Dean doesn't do it enough, but at least you have the luxury of being able to go straight to sleep from time to time.'

'Well, yes,' said Lee, 'but then you see I sometimes want it so much I can't get to sleep anyway. Maybe we should swap for a bit.'

'I honestly just can't imagine actually really wanting it,' said Amy. 'I mean, I don't think I'm properly frigid, but all those years of force feeding do put a girl off. The only time I get any peace at all is when I get the curse. He really doesn't like that. How about Dean?'

Lee looked at her, and smiled, shaking her head, and then froze suddenly into absolute petrified stillness. She felt as if she was falling helplessly, sucked down into some fearsome vortex. She put out her hand on the sand to steady herself; the beach seemed to rock. She shut her eyes tightly for a minute and then opened them again; the sun looked harshly, whitely bright, the heat all of a sudden unbearable.

She looked at Amy, and a huge fist-sized lump grew in her throat; she tried to swallow, her mouth felt dust-dry.

'Lee, for heaven's sake, what is it? You look awful, terrible. Do you feel all right?'

'Yes – no – that is, oh, shit, Amy, what have I done? What have I done? Amy, do you have a diary, here give it to me, quick, quick, oh Jesus, Amy, I feel . . .'

Her voice trailed away; she was feverishly counting, checking off weeks. She threw the diary on to the sand, looked at Amy, her cheeks flushed, her eyes big and scared.

'Amy, I'm late. Really late. Nearly three weeks.'

'Well, honey, isn't that good news? Don't look like that. You and Dean have always wanted a baby. What's the panic? Anyway, it probably doesn't mean a thing anyway. Do you have any other symptoms?'

Lee shook her head. 'No, I feel perfectly normal.'

'Well then. Calm down. When I was trying to have Cary I was late every other month for nearly a year, until it actually happened. But I honestly would have thought you'd be pleased. I mean it certainly doesn't matter. It's nothing to panic about. Christ, I thought you were going to die on me then.'

Lee managed a shaky smile. 'So did I. It must have been the sun.'

'Lee Wilburn, when did the sun ever give you the vapours?' She looked at her friend sharply. 'Is something worrying you, Lee? I mean, you know, something that you should tell me?'

Lee looked at her, and longed to tell her everything, and knew she never could. If nobody knew, then nothing could happen to her. If she kept quiet, she would be safe. Probably in any case Amy was right, and it was just nothing; and if it wasn't, if the unthinkable had happened, if she had to think it, then it was far far better nobody knew. It wasn't that she didn't trust Amy, it was just that it was too much of a burden to lay on her, to ask her to carry. Besides, if she didn't tell, anyone, anyone at all, then she could just make herself believe, make it true even, that the weekend with Hugo hadn't happened, that the terrifying consequences of it couldn't happen either.

She began to feel calmer; that was it, she could see now, of course, how stupid, if she was – well, if there was a real reason for her period being so late, then it must surely be Dean who was responsible for it. She had been sleeping with him extremely regularly for years and years, just as regularly over the last few weeks, how silly to think there could be any other explanation. She lay back on the sand again, feeling her panic ebb away; then a new one started to rise, smaller but just as fierce. She hadn't slept with Dean that much lately. He had been so tired, so worried about his job, drinking too much; night after night he had just gone straight to sleep, snoring loudly, leaving her lying beside him, thinking of Hugo, fantasizing. But once or twice – surely – yes, of course, at least once – well, that was enough. She could persuade Dean of anything, anything at all. Only – she shivered suddenly, remembering what Doctor Forsythe had said last time she had been to see him about her inability to conceive. 'Time it very carefully, Lee. It's no use just leaving it all to Mother Nature. She's not always too reliable. Be sure you make love right bang in the middle of your cycle. Every one of the three or four days. And take your temperature to check it. That's very important.'

She had made a lot of that to Dean, she remembered; ironically seeing it as a surefire way of getting sex now and again. He had taken it very seriously, too; and it had become something of a habit with him, even though it hadn't worked, every month he would ask her to make sure to tell him when the time was, to take her temperature, so that they could be quite sure, say, 'Come on honey, baby-making time, we have to keep trying, he'll be along sooner or later.' And this month, he hadn't; he had said he was sorry, he was too tired, too distracted, maybe next time; and then he had felt bad about it, apologized to her a few days later. He would remember that; Lee shut her eyes again, feeling suddenly sick. She sat up, smiling shakily at Amy. 'Sorry about that. I can't think what came over me. Let's get back anyway. It's late, and you have dinner to cook.'

'Now are you sure you're all right?' said Amy solicitously, as she dropped Lee off at her house. 'You look a little pale. Honestly, Lee, I tell you, I would just love it if you were pregnant. Now you go in and put your feet up and have a drink of milk. I'll call you in the morning.'

Lee didn't have a drink of milk. She poured herself a large gin. Over the next few days she drank a lot of large gins. She had heard it could help. She followed all the other old wives' advice too; she took endless unbearably hot baths; she bought a skipping rope and did five hundred jumps a day; she jumped down the stairs. She even went to a drugstore down at Venice, where they wouldn't know her, and spun them some cock and bull story about her period being a few days late, and she wanted to hurry it along because she was going on vacation. The pharmacist gave her a funny look and sold her some pills for twenty dollars which she had to take every day for three days; all they did was make her feel violently ill and throw up all over the back yard.

Dean was mercifully away for a few days; she moped about the house avoiding everybody, even Amy. Especially Amy.

Every hour on the hour she went hopefully into the toilet; her pants remained stubbornly white. She dreamt twice her period had started; awaking, she shot out of bed, joyfully convinced it was true and then crawled back in again, shivering with disappointment and fear. She made bargains with God: If I'm not pregnant, I'll never speak to Hugo again, give up beer, keep the house clean and tidy.

She became superstitious: if there are any melons left in the market by five o'clock, if those lights change to green by the time I get there, it'll start. It didn't.

At the weekend Dean came home, tired, depressed; sales were not good. Desperate for her alibi, she tried to force him to make love to her, and failed utterly.

'Honey, I'm tired, just leave me alone, will you. I need to sleep.'

She turned over on her pillow and wept.

In the middle of the following week she began to be sick. She was sick not just in the morning, but three or four times a day; she seemed to spend her entire life these days in the lavatory. Her breasts were sore; her head ached.

'There's no doubt you're pregnant,' said Amy, who had taken to dropping by every morning to check on her and cheer her up. 'I know it's hell, but it's such good news too. And you'll feel great in a little while. Now listen, you have to start on extra vitamins, right away, and cut out the booze, of course, just orange juice; lots of fruit, and for goodness' sake you will cut out any medication, won't you, stop taking all those aspirin you're so fond of. They're dreadfully toxic. And you should take bran every morning too, pregnancy is terribly constipating. And lots of rest. Have you told Dean yet?'

'No,' said Lee listlessly.

'Well he must have the brains of an ox not to have worked it out for himself. I suppose he's got a lot on his mind. Do tell him, honey, he'll be so pleased, and he can look after you, help a bit. This place looks terrible, Lee, even by your standards. When did you last clean that sink?'

'I can't remember,' said Lee.

'It shows. Well look, let me do it for you. And then I'm going to take you for a walk to the beach. You look as if you could do with some fresh air.'

Lee did as she was told. She didn't have the strength to do anything else. She had just finished a prolonged bout of throwing up when Hugo phoned. She crawled over to the couch and sat there, trying to sound normal, as he chatted away about New York, and how much he had enjoyed his last trip, and was it still all right for the following weekend?

Torn between a longing to see him and a strong desire to tell him to fuck off, she sat silent; she knew what he was doing, the bastard, he was leaving all his options open, maintaining contact with her while making it perfectly plain he only wanted their relationship to continue on the most superficial level, that next time at least he wanted to be sure Dean was there as well, lest she might start to think he was taking things too seriously. She suddenly felt violently sick again.

'I have to go now,' she said and put the phone down, rushing to the bathroom, vomiting again and again, and then she sat there, on the floor, resting her head tiredly on the toilet, hot tears trickling down her cheeks, hating him, longing for him, wishing most fervently that she could die.

The phone rang again. It was Hugo.

'Lee, are you all right? You sound awful.'

'Oh, yes,' she said lightly, 'just a bit of a cold, that's all.'

'So is next weekend all right?'

'What?'

'Lee, are you sure you're all right?'

'Hugo, I'm all right.'

'Good. Then can I come next weekend?'

'Oh, yes, sure. Sorry. That'll be nice.'

They arrived together, he and Dean; she had made a huge effort, tidied up, made up her face, drunk lots of glucose water to help with the vomiting.

'You look wonderful, honey,' said Dean, hugging her, 'doesn't she, Hugo?'

'Marvellous,' said Hugo, but his eyes went sharply over her, and she was afraid he must guess.

Later, Dean went to bed early; she tried to make an excuse to follow, but Hugo put out a hand and caught hers.

'What's the matter?'

'Oh, nothing,' she said harshly, 'nothing at all. Why don't you just leave me completely alone, Hugo, instead of nearly. It would be much easier for you, I would have thought.'

'Don't be silly,' he said gently, 'I couldn't imagine not seeing you any more. It's difficult, that's all. And a little bit dangerous. You must understand.'

'Oh,' she said. 'I understand all right. Good night, Hugo. You're in your usual room.'

She got just a tiny bit of satisfaction from the expression on his face. He didn't look merely hurt; he looked worried as well.

She woke up early and shot into the lavatory; the glucose water had failed her. Wandering miserably into the living room a few minutes later, sipping a glass of water, she found Hugo, standing by the patio windows.

'Oh,' she said, 'hello.'

'You're not well, are you?'

'I'm perfectly well, thank you.'

'You don't seem well.' He crossed to the couch, sat down, patted the seat next to him. 'Come here. Come on. Darling, please. Don't be so hostile. What is it? Aren't we to be friends any more?'

Lee turned to look at him, and there was all human knowledge and experience in that look: humour, love, scorn, despair; then she sighed and said simply, 'I'm pregnant.'

Hugo was quite quite silent for a moment; then he looked at her intently, searching, exploring her face, her eyes.

He took her hand.

'And is it mine? It's mine, isn't it?'

'No,' said Lee, 'no, no it isn't. It's not yours, it's Dean's.' She pulled her hand away, and she felt the tears hot behind her eyes. Dear God, she thought, don't let me cry. Not now. Not in front of him.

'Lee,' said Hugo, 'Lee, look at me.'

'No,' she said, 'don't. I can't. Leave me alone. The baby is Dean's.'

'But you said . . .'

'It doesn't matter what I said. Obviously I was wrong. This baby is Dean's. I know it is. I know.'

'How do you know?'

'Oh, Hugo, stop it. I can count, that's how I know.'

'I see.'

She watched him; trying to analyse what she really wanted, what she really felt. She had so longed to see him again, that was why she had allowed him to come, but she couldn't imagine why. She had thought that perhaps in some miraculous way he would be able to help, make her feel better, but she had been wrong. There was no way he could help her, and he was making her feel worse. They could hardly disappear into the Californian sunset together. And she had to stick to her plan, of not admitting even to herself that the baby's father might be anybody but Dean. In time, she knew, she could make herself believe it. Sometimes, already, she managed to persuade herself that it was just possible. One word, one hint to Hugo, and she was lost.

He looked up at her, his eyes full of anxiety. She trembled. A tender word, now, and she might give in. Fear made her harsh.

'Just leave me alone, will you? I'd like to go back to bed. I don't feel too good.'

'What does Dean think?'

'I haven't told him.'

'Why not?'

'I don't know.'

'I know.'

'You don't.'

'But Lee, if it is Dean's baby he would be over the moon. He's always wanted kids. He was born to be a father. You should tell him.'

'I will, I will. But I . . .'

'Yes?'

'I wanted to be sure.'

'Of what?'

'Of being pregnant.'

'Oh, Lee, that's ridiculous. You look terrible.'

'Thank you.'

'You know what I mean. And you woke me up vomiting this morning. He's not stupid.'

Lee turned to look at him. 'He is, quite. In some ways. I just told him I had a stomach bug. He believes anything I say. Anything,' she repeated with an odd insistence.

'And can't he count either?'

'He's been away a lot. I'll tell him soon. When I see the doctor.'

Hugo was silent again.

'And is that all you have to say to me?'

'Yes, it is.'

'You won't change your mind?'

'No. Why should I?'

'Well, I'm sorry. More than I can tell you.'

Lee suddenly started to weep, huge shuddering sobs, burying her face in her hands. He took her in his arms then and comforted her as best he could, stroking her hair, holding her to him tightly, just murmuring quietly as if to a small child. She stopped crying, blew her nose hard, and pulled away from him, curling herself up into a small ball in the corner of the couch.

'It would kill him, you see,' she said very quietly, 'if – if he had any idea, the faintest idea that it wasn't his baby. He wants kids so much. He'd like a dozen. It would be far, far worse than if he thought I'd just slept with someone. The fact that someone else could make me pregnant. He just couldn't bear it.'

Another silence. Then: 'Did you think about abortion?'

She looked at him hard, aware that he was leading her into a trap.

'Why should I have an abortion? It's Dean's baby. I'm really very happy about it.' She smiled, a bright tremulous smile. 'I'm just a bit over-emotional. But I tell you something, Hugo, if you ever imply, by so much as a look, that you think it might – might not be Dean's baby, I shall come to England and I shall find your wife and I shall tell her everything.'

'Oh, Lee,' he said, with a heavy sigh, 'I won't. Of course I won't. I'll do whatever you want. But you know I'm there if you need me.'

Lee wasn't going to let him get off that lightly.

'I'm afraid,' she said, walking towards the door, and turning to look at him with infinite scorn, 'I know nothing of the sort.'

She began to feel better quite soon after that. She couldn't quite figure out why, but she supposed that having confronted Hugo, laid that ghost, she could only go forward, believing in what simply had to be the truth. Dean was so beside himself with pride and joy when she told him, he didn't even pause to consider that their sex life had been a trifle spasmodic over the past couple of months. He even remarked quite spontaneously that it had been worth all the temperature-taking and counting.

He talked non-stop about the baby, what they would do together, he and his boy (he seemed to have no doubts at all about its sex), how they would fish together, play football, camp, ride, hike. Lee listened quietly. She was calm now, serene, happy. She looked beautiful. Pregnancy suited her.

Amy had taken her health in hand, and had her on an entirely wholefood diet, and a formidable array of vitamins and minerals to top it up. Lee swallowed them all obediently; she couldn't quite see how seaweed and whale oil were going to do anything for her baby, but it was easier not to argue. Amy also insisted on her going to yoga classes, so that she could enjoy a painless, natural birth. Lee had serious doubts about how a birth could be both, but she went to the classes anyway. She enjoyed the meditation part of it, and the part of the sessions which were set aside for visualization; you were supposed to visualize the baby emerging painlessly and easily from your body, but she used the time rather differently, and would sit in a trancelike state, fervently visualizing a baby girl with blonde hair and blue eyes, emerging as painfully and awkwardly as she liked; fervently dismissing any stray picture of a dark-eyed little boy that might drift into her head.

It had just become fashionable for fathers to be present at the birth. Dean was initially very enthusiastic, and attended classes with the other husbands, practising different breathing levels with Lee and learning how to rub her back, but after watching a film called *Happy Birthday* put on by the obstetric unit at the hospital for prospective parents, he became very quiet and told Lee in the car on the way home that he thought after all a father's place was in the waiting room. Both the yoga teacher and the Natural Childbirth teacher were shocked and distressed and tried to persuade him to participate, assuring him he was going to miss the most important and beautiful experience of his entire life, but Lee didn't mind; she thought she was going to have quite enough to put up with without Dean rubbing her back all the way through, which he did extraordinarily clumsily, and worrying if he was going to faint at the crucial moment.

In the event, she gave birth to her son with the minimum of trouble, albeit three weeks late; they placed him in her arms, and she looked down at the blue eyes, and stroked the blond downy head, and reflected that either she had been hallucinating in ever thinking that Dean might not have been his father, or that visualization was an extraordinarily powerful force.

Hugo Dashwood, arriving at his New York hotel one day in early January, found a card waiting for him with a California postmark. 'Miles Sinclair Wilburn has arrived,' it said. 'Born January 2nd, 8.30 p.m. Weight 8½ pounds. A big 'un. Mother and baby well. Come and meet him soon.'

Chapter Five

London, 1959

What Fate had in store for Eliza was not a job: it was something rather less predictable and came in the truculent form of Peter Thetford.

Peter Thetford was thirty-two years old, and trying rather too hard to reconcile a burning socialist ideology with a strong desire not only to achieve political power but to savour the good things of life, so far fairly sternly denied to him.

His father had been a Nottingham miner; Peter had been his fifth child, and had won a scholarship to the local grammar school, where, mixing with middle-class boys, he became totally obsessed with the essential injustice of British society and its caste system. He found the barrier thrown up between him and David Johnson, the local doctor's son who sat at the next desk, not so much insurmountable as incomprehensible. He could play soccer with David, and score goals alongside him, could thrash him on the assault course in the cadet corps, get higher marks at mathematics, and alternate term by term with him, winning the form prize. Yet when he sought his friendship, tried to communicate with him, tell him filthy jokes, discuss the female anatomy, borrow the dog-eared centrefold spread of *Playboy* which went the rounds of the form every month, tried to join David in the group that went to the local youth club every Friday, he met a polite, slightly stilted rejection.

Then at Cambridge, where he won an outright maths scholarship, he comprehended it better and loathed it more. It enraged and embittered him that there was no equal ground between him and Anthony Smythe Andrews who had come up from Eton, and who was also reading economics; no way they could communicate except on the most self-conscious and false terms, and yet he was cleverer than Smythe Andrews, he worked harder, he had read more, they had passed the same exams, and indeed he knew he had done better, simply to get the scholarship from a position well back from most people's starting line.

It was no use fighting it, he could see that, or at least not at Cambridge; no use trying to climb the fence, to become Smythe Andrews' friend, because there was absolutely no basis for friendship. Smythe Andrews despised him, and he despised Smythe Andrews, not because either thought the other stupid, unpleasant or rude, but because each had roots in something the other could not begin to comprehend and indeed was deeply wary of.

Anthony Smythe Andrews knew he was Peter Thetford's superior because he was born to a different class, spoke in a different voice, used different words and had different friends, who were all exactly like him; and when Peter Thetford won the Economics Exhibition at the end of the first year, and Smythe Andrews failed his first Tripos, it was Smythe Andrews who remained the superior.

The sense of isolation Thetford knew at Cambridge also had a profound effect on his sexual attitudes. There were very few working-class boys at the university in the late forties, despite Oxbridge, and certainly no working-class girls. The girls were an extraordinarily elite clique, all from intellectual, upper-class backgrounds, most of them witty and clever, eccentrically dressed, outrageously self-confident, with the power to pick and choose from quite literally hundreds of rich, amusing, charming young men. The social climate was heady, hectic, modestly promiscuous; the fact that you were sent down for being caught in bed, or even in the room of a member of the opposite sex after ten o'clock, was a considerable, but not total, deterrent.

It took a strong intellectual and sexual confidence to break into that set, if you were not born to it; Thetford had neither. The girls would in the early days politely dance with him, if they were asked, talk to him in the dining room, even invite him to an occasional tea party; but they were not, he recognized quite quickly, going to enter into any more intimate relationship than that.

Consequently he was lonely, isolated, and quite often angry; he would sit alone in his room studying at night, surrounded by the sounds of social and – more dreadfully isolating still – sexual pleasure down the corridors, and wonder not only how he could bear it, but why he should. His virginity accompanied him back and forwards to Cambridge each term, an increasingly embarrassing burden which he was finally able to lay down in the bed of an art student he met at a Christmas party in Nottingham; they wrote to each other for a brief time into the following term, both anxious to pretend that they felt more than they did and that it had not just been a one-night stand. Shortly after he came down from Cambridge he met Margaret Phipps, a student teacher, for whom he felt quite a lot and in whose arms he enjoyed considerable pleasure; and in due course he married her. But he continued to regard sex as something inextricably bound up with class; as privileged territory, with access automatically granted to the rich and successful, the expensively educated, the socially secure; and denied, unless with an attendant load of responsibility, to those who were none of those things.

Then he met Eliza Morell.

Eliza had been invited by Hugh Gaitskell to a party at the House of Commons ten days after she got back to London, and had been strongly disinclined to go, when Julian called from New York to say he would be away for a week longer than he had thought and that he was coming home via Paris in order to look at sites for a second Circe with Paul Baud.

'Is that all right, darling? I can go later, if you'd rather.'

He sounded anxious, conciliatory. Guilty conscience, thought Eliza, good.

'Of course it's all right. Well, Julian, I'll see you – when? Three weeks?'

'Four. But Scott and Madeleine will be over before that, so they'll be company for you.'

'Julian,' said Eliza, her voice trembling with outrage, 'I am not so bereft of company in London that I have to wait for it to arrive from the United States. I'll see you when you get back. Goodbye.'

'Goodbye Eliza. Give my love to Roz.'

'I would, if I thought she would know who it was sending it.'

'Eliza, don't.'

'Goodbye Julian.'

She put down the phone, looked at herself in the mirror, and sighed heavily. Then she picked it up again, arranged to have her hair done, and dialled through to Nanny Henry on the house telephone and told her she'd be out that evening.

'This,' she said to her reflection, 'is the first day of the rest of my life. As they say in America.'

She went out feeling more positive than she could remember for months.

It was a good party. Eliza, her hair dressed by M. René of South Audley Street, piled high in the new fashion, and with a huge fake pearl pinned into the tumble of curls at the front, and dressed in a navy pleated silk on-the-knee dress from St Laurent with a wide cape collar, and extremely high-heeled, yellow satin shoes with pointed toes, was surprised to find she was enjoying herself greatly. The room was full of friends, all longing to hear about her trip, all blissfully unaware of what a fiasco it had been; she talked and laughed and told them how she and Julian had entertained most of New York at the opening of Circe and how she had met Cary Grant and almost curtsied to him in her excitement, and what a wonderful city it was, and how they must all come and visit them now that they had an apartment there, and how she would have stayed much longer if she hadn't been missing Roz, when she suddenly became aware of a pair of dark blue eyes boring into her from across the room. The eyes were set in a face that was pale and rather thin with dark hair that was just a little too long flopping over the forehead; a face that wore an expression that was an extraordinary mixture of disdain and admiration; a face that was clearly not going to smile, or indeed soften unless she gave it considerable cause to do so.

'John, who is that man over there, the one staring at me; the one with the ghastly blue suit.'

John Wetheringham, a senior civil servant, who was very fond of Eliza but feared sometimes for her worst social excesses in the presence of some of the more fervent socialists in the land, put a warning hand on her arm. 'You mustn't talk disparagingly about the Labour Party's suits, Eliza. Not at a party given by their leader, anyway. That's Peter Thetford. New MP for Midbury in West Yorkshire. Gave a very good speech on education the other day. Promising young chap. Want to meet him?'

'Oh, in a while,' said Eliza. 'Don't worry, I'll introduce myself. I just want to have a quick word with Mary Lipscombe first. Nice to see you, John. Come and have a drink one night, you and Jenny. I'll give her a ring. I have some friends coming to stay in a few weeks from the States, you'd like them.'

'That would be lovely,' said Wetheringham. 'Julian not back yet, then?'

'Heavens no. He's becoming more American than the Americans. Can't keep away.'

Wetheringham looked at her sharply. She looked wonderful, he thought, but very thin. 'Come and have a meal with us one night, then,' he said. 'Jenny would like it. I'll get her to ring you.'

'Wonderful. Bye, John.'

She wandered across the room in search of Mary Lipscombe, failed to find her and saw Peter Thetford's narrow back, encased in its too-blue suit, directly in front of her. She tapped it.

'Mr Thetford. At last. I've been longing to meet you. I'm Eliza Morell, a friend of Hugh Gaitskell. How do you do?'

Thetford turned to look at her, excused himself from his companion and said abruptly, 'Do you always interrupt conversations whenever it suits you, Mrs Morell?' His voice was extraordinary, it was deep and scratched, and sounded somehow injured, as if it had been dragged across hot gravel; his accent was strong, and northern, but strangely musical. It was a sexy voice, it was bigger than he was.

'If I want to talk to someone enough, yes. Sorry. Rude of me. Bad habit. But you didn't look frightfully engrossed.'

'I was, actually.'

'Then you must continue. I expect I can find someone else to interrupt.'

'No,' he said, 'don't go. I'm sorry. I didn't mean to be rude either.'

'Well,' she said lightly, 'we're quits. Now then, why haven't I seen you at one of these lovely parties before?'

'I don't go to many parties,' he said, 'I'm a very busy man.'

'Oh, people always say that when they want an excuse, but I can tell you most of the busiest men I know spend a lot of time at parties. It's how they meet other people, you see. Contacts. That sort of thing.'

'I don't really set a lot of store by contacts.'

'Well, that's extremely silly of you. Contacts make the world go round.'

'Not mine.'

'That's what you think. But they do.' She smiled at him radiantly. 'Haven't you got a drink? Let me find you one. Champagne?'

Sipping the champagne, studying her further, his sexual hackles as always rising when confronted by the smell of real money, Thetford wondered a trifle contemptuously why she was bothering. She must know he wasn't important, he wasn't rich, he certainly wasn't known for his wit and charm; nothing that had taken place in his life thus far had suggested he carried an aura of sexual irresistibility about with him; and yet, here she was, a beautiful and patently rich and socially important woman, making a most visible and strenuous effort to amuse and interest him.

'I know what you're thinking,' said Eliza briskly, looking very directly into his dark blue eyes.

'I don't think you do.'

'Oh, yes I do. You're wondering why a rich bitch like me should be taking so much interest in a yet-to-make-it person like you. Aren't I right?'

'Yes,' he said, slightly disconcerted. 'Yes, you're right.'

'Well, I'm not sure either,' she said, and laughed. 'But I was looking at you across the room, and I thought you looked interesting. And I see I was right.'

'In what way am I interesting?'

'Well, you don't try very hard to be charming.'

'That's true. I find deliberately charming people very tiresome.'

'So I see.'

'How does that make me interesting?'

'Well, you see, I spend most of my time with very deliberately charming people.'

'So I am a novelty?'

'Yes.'

'In other ways too, no doubt.'

'What do you mean?'

'Well, despite your fraternization with the Labour Party, I

don't suppose you spend much of your time socializing with the working classes.'

'No,' she said, 'I don't.'

'Well,' he said, 'I should be a nice bit of social experimentation for you then.'

'Oh, for heaven's sake,' she said, 'don't be so touchy.'

'I'm afraid I find it very difficult not to be. I've spent my life working my way out of the disadvantages of being working class, of being a social experiment if you like, and it hasn't been very easy. Or pleasant even.'

'Well,' she said, draining her glass, 'I daresay not. But that really isn't my fault. Don't get cross with me about it. I just thought we could have a nice conversation. I was obviously wrong. Good evening, Mr Thetford.'

She turned away; he put his hand out and gently touched her arm.

'Don't go. I'm sorry. I didn't mean to be rude. I get a bit carried away sometimes. It's being in politics. It's bad for the manners.'

Eliza looked at him. 'Obviously. Let's start again, then. Tell me about your politics.'

Beguiled by her beauty as much as her patently genuine desire to be with him, charmed and flattered out of his suspicion, he told her. He told her what he cared about and why; he told her of his dream of an equal beginning for everyone; he described a school to which every child would go, rich and poor, clever and stupid, each learning and gaining from the other; he told her of his own childhood, of his father, dying from lung disease at only fifty-six, of his mother's tireless battle to see her children educated out of the mines. He told her of his passionate commitment to the National Health Service, of his fears that it would not continue to function, of his rage at the way consultants were still spending so much of their time with their private patients. He told her his dream was to be Minister of Education, to change the face of English schools; he talked and he talked and she listened in silence and they suddenly realized the room was emptying, and they were almost alone.

'Oh, goodness,' said Eliza, 'it's nearly eight o'clock. What are you doing now?'

'Going back to my bedsit in Victoria, I suppose.'

'Don't you have a wife?'

'I do. But she's in Manchester.'

'Why?'

'We live there,' he said sounding impatient. 'She teaches at a school there.'

'Well,' she said, 'how would you like me to take you out to dinner?'

Thetford was so startled he dropped the remains of a smoked salmon sandwich he was holding.

'Oh, what a ridiculous waste. Probably all you were going to get for supper anyway. Now look, you'll just have to take me or leave me, but I'd much rather you took me. My husband's in New York and I've got no one else to eat with tonight.'

'Well, I really don't think –' said Thetford, fingering nervously at his tie.

'Don't think what? Oh, for heaven's sake, I'm not going to march you off to the Ritz or seduce you in a private room at the Café Royal. We'll go to a pub. And it won't take long.'

'Oh . . .' The scratchy voice elongated the word. Then he looked at her and smiled, a sudden, heartbreakingly open smile. 'Why not?'

'My goodness,' said Eliza, walking through the door ahead of him. 'Don't do that too often or I *shall* take you off to a private room.'

'Do what?'

'Smile.'

'Ah.'

Margaret had often told him he had a very seductive smile. He had never really believed her.

It wasn't quite a pub she took him to, it was Moony's in the Strand, and they drank Guinness and ate oyster and steak pie and it took a very long time indeed. Peter, having exhausted his political platform for a while, told her about his own family: about Margaret, and her own educational ideologies and how she tried very hard to put them into practice against some opposition from her headmistress, who was very traditionalist, and tried to run her little primary school as if it was Eton or Winchester; about his two little boys, David and Hugh, who

196

were both already showing signs of being very clever indeed; about the new semi-detached house they had just bought and which his mother regarded as a palace; about his mother and what an anxiety she was, living on her own now, with arthritis and diabetes, but refusing to give in and be a burden on her children.

'I'm sorry,' he said suddenly, 'I haven't stopped talking for hours. I don't often get such an opportunity to be listened to.'

'I thought that was the whole point of politics,' said Eliza, 'having people listen to you all the time.'

'No, no, not at all. The other politicians all talk at the same time, and never stop for a moment, and the public are always talking back at you, contradicting you. It's permanent bedlam.'

'But you like it?'

'Yes,' he said simply, 'I love it.'

There was a pause. 'What about you, then?'

'Oh, dear,' she said, 'I was afraid you'd ask. Less said the better, I'm afraid.'

'Come on. I can take it.'

'Oh, well, you know, public school. Rich husband. No job. Vote Tory. Big house. Expensive clothes. Dreadful. Sorry.'

'You're intelligent, though,' he said. 'Wouldn't you like to have a job, for instance?'

'Yes,' she said shortly.

'Sore subject?'

'Very.'

'Why do you vote Tory, for heaven's sake?' he said, partly because he wanted to know, because he simply could never understand anyone doing such a thing, and partly to get back on to safer ground.

'Oh, it's all that early conditioning. Some kind of divine force guides my hand to the right name on the ballot paper. I honestly would expect to be struck down in the polling booth if I voted Labour. Don't tell Hugh, though. And I certainly don't think much of the Conservatives. Although Macmillan's a sweetie.'

'Mmm,' said Thetford, who did not think of Macmillan in quite that way himself, 'how on earth did you get mixed up with people like Gaitskell?'

'Oh, met the Foots at a party, and it went on from there. I'm very intrigued by people like them, and by Wedgwood Benn. I think they're wonderful, but they do seem to me to be slightly hypocritical, living in those big houses, and Tony's got a huge estate in Suffolk, you know, I mean you have a right to be socialist, but I'm honestly not sure they do.'

'What does your husband do?' asked Thetford, anxious not to get drawn into that particular high-Tory by-way.

'Oh, God, everything. Has a company that makes medicines. And cosmetics. And he's just opened a store in New York. That's why he's there.' She was silent.

'Is he nice?' asked Thetford. 'Do you like him?'

He was as surprised by this inquiry as she was; Margaret often said his idea of a really personal question was whether someone would rather walk or drive to the polling booth; but Eliza's candour was curiously relaxing, and besides, some curiously potent force was impelling him to explore her and her situation.

'Well, he isn't exactly nice,' said Eliza. 'But he is very interesting. And I do like him. I think. But I don't see much of him. And I don't think he likes me as much as he did. And I think he's probably got someone else in New York anyway.'

'Why?'

'Don't know. Nothing tangible. I just feel he's not with me half the time.'

'Well, he isn't,' he said, deliberately misunderstanding. 'And what do you feel about that?'

'About the someone else? Oh, I don't know, really. I'm not devastated, if that's what you mean. But it hurts. Of course it does. A lot of the other things he does hurt too.'

'Like?'

'Oh, too complex to explain. He's a very complex man. Would you have an affair with someone who wasn't your wife?'

He looked at her very intently. 'I don't know. I haven't been tempted yet.'

'Really?' she said. 'I'm surprised. Well, anyway,' she added, breaking an oddly forceful silence, 'I think I can live with it. Now what about some treacle pudding?'

They ate some treacle pudding and then they went out into the Strand and she hailed a taxi. 'It's been lovely,' she said, 'thank you for coming. Ring me.'

'I don't have your number.'

'It's in the book. Morell. Hanover Terrace, Regent's Park. Not a very equal sort of an address, I'm afraid.'

When she got home, the phone was already ringing. It was Thetford.

'I was just testing your phone.'

'I see.'

'You did say I should ring.'

'I know. Where do you live, did you say?'

'Oh, in Victoria. In a very dreary MP flatlet. I only go home weekends.'

'Lots of lonely evenings?'

'Lots.'

'Come to dinner here next week. No, it won't be a dinner party. Or a seduction. We'll have a chaperone. Name of Rosamund.'

Thetford felt suddenly and sharply and with a sense of piercing anticipation that he was in entirely uncharted territory. He knew what it was. Not the house in Regent's Park, nor even the tacky relaxed indulgence of Moony's. The vision that was beckoning so deliciously and irresistibly at him was of the land of entirely pleasurable and irresponsible sexual opportunity.

Rosamund turned out to be not much of a chaperone. By the time they had finished the first course (smoked salmon 'to make up for the bit I made you drop') she was squirming about and throwing knives on to the floor. Eliza sighed, scooped her up and buzzed on the house intercom.

'Nanny? I think really that Roz had better go to bed after all, she seems awfully tired. Call me when she's ready and I'll tuck her up.' She disappeared briefly with the child, and came back smiling briskly.

'That's better. Goodness, they're tiring, aren't they? Don't look so nervous. Nanny's still here, and so are the Bristows, down in the garden flat. We're not alone.'

'Who are the Bristows?'

'Oh.' She looked at him slightly awkwardly and then laughed. 'Oh, hell, better get it over with. Staff. Mrs B. sees to the house and most of the cooking; Mr B. looks after Julian mostly.'

'In what way?' asked Thetford, genuinely intrigued.

'Oh, you know, his clothes, that sort of thing. And he sees to running repairs on the house. And the cars. We don't actually have a chauffeur as such, because Julian loves driving so much, but of course he can't always.'

'Of course not.'

'So he sees to them all.'

'How many have you got?'

'Oh, gosh, I don't know, three really, mine, and Julian's latest toy, which is some rare American thing, and the Rolls for just going out, you know, and then Julian has about half a dozen antique ones down in the country. He collects them.'

'What's the country?'

'House in Sussex we've got. Sorry.'

'That's all right. So he has a sort of nanny of his own, this husband of yours?'

'Yes. You could call him that. What a lovely idea.'

There was a silence.

'Oh, goodness,' she said, 'I haven't given us our food. How silly. Boeuf bourguignon. Do you like it?'

'Oh yes,' he said, deadpan, 'it makes a change from tripe. Just now and again.'

'Shut up. What's tripe like, anyway?'

'Putrid.'

'I thought it would be. Tell me,' she added, pouring wine into his glass, 'who looks after your children while your wife is teaching? Do you have a nanny?'

'No,' he said, 'we don't have a nanny. They go to a child minder. You won't have heard of child minders, perhaps. They cost a little less than nannies.'

'Oh, goodness, don't start all that again,' she said with a sigh. 'I'm sorry, I didn't think, I can't help being tactless.'

'I can see that,' he said, and smiled. 'It's all right. I'm getting the hang of it. I'll be eating my peas with a fork in no time now.'

Nanny Henry came into the kitchen. 'She's ready, Mrs Morell, if you'd like to come up. Or shall I. . . ?'

She looked doubtfully at Peter.

'No, Nanny, absolutely not. We'll both come up. This is Mr Thetford, Nanny, an old friend.'

'Pleased to meet you, sir,' said Nanny Henry, looking at Peter with extremely ill-disguised distaste. Peter smiled at her and followed her upstairs.

'She thinks I'm rough trade,' he hissed, turning to Eliza who was behind him.

'She's right,' whispered Eliza, 'and she's not used to it, I can tell you.'

The nursery was at the very top of the house. Roz lay in her bed, virtually submerged with teddies, sucking her thumb. She was not as pretty as Peter had expected; she was dark and her eyes were green and solemn in her pale little face.

'Good night, my dearest darling,' said Eliza, bending over the little bed, 'sleep very very tight.'

'Story,' came the imperious voice.

'Oh, darling, Mummy is very busy.'

'No you're not. I want a story.'

And so they stayed and Eliza told her a story, a charmingly dizzy tale about a bear that ran away, and Peter leant against the wall and listened and thought at one and the same moment how easy it was to make up charming stories when you hadn't had to bath a child and put it to bed in between cooking the supper and tidying up the house and how totally enchanting Eliza looked as she told the story, and how he could have stood there for many hours just listening to her and watching her.

At the extremely happy end of the story, Eliza kissed Roz and then turned to him.

'Would you kiss her too? She's a bit starved of affection at the moment.'

And Peter moved over and kissed Roz's cheek, and she turned over immediately and buried her face contentedly in her teddies, her thumb in her mouth; Eliza turned the light out and beckoned to Peter to follow her out of the door.

It was a strangely intimate moment; as they left the nursery, she took his hand and led him to the top of the stairs; he paused, half tempted, half terrified by her closeness, her readiness, her beauty, and he said to her, 'How often have you done this sort of thing?'

'Oh,' she said, understanding completely what he meant, 'never. Never before. I've never wanted to. It's never seemed right.'

'And what,' he asked, brusque, impatient with himself and his insecurities, 'is so different about this, about me?'

'You, I suppose,' she said simply. 'You're different. I trust you. You talk to me. Now let's go down and finish our dinner, and that perfectly gorgeous burgundy that Julian would begrudge us so much.'

Nanny Henry heard them go downstairs with some relief. She didn't like the idea of hanky-panky on her nursery floor.

After that they spent a lot of time together. Innocent, unadulterous time. No hanky-panky at all. A private detective set to follow them would have found their behaviour rather puzzling, and his work extremely dull. Peter Thetford had most of his mornings free before going to the House; they went for walks in the park, for drives in Eliza's car; took picnics to Hampstead Heath, and accompanied Roz to the zoo. They lunched together early, often at Hanover Terrace, sometimes with Nanny and Roz, occasionally alone; (but never, Eliza was careful to ensure, mindful of Peter's insecurities, anywhere smart or expensive). Peter talked a great deal and Eliza listened.

It was on this that the success of their relationship was founded; they liked each other very much, and they were both intrigued and excited by the utter unfamiliarity of one another, but the novelty of being talked to at length, of being trusted with important conversation, overwhelmed Eliza.

'You cannot imagine,' she said to him one day after he had given her an exhaustive account of a debate on the crisis in housing in the House the night before, 'how wonderful I find all this. Being told things. Not being fobbed off. Promise me not to stop.'

'I promise,' said Peter. It seemed fairly wonderful to him too; Margaret rarely had time to listen to him, and when she did, it was with half an ear on the children, most of the other half on what she was about to be saying back to him.

'Have you told your wife about me?' asked Eliza idly one morning as they wandered round the boating lake with Roz between them.

'Yes and no.'

'What does that mean?'

'I've told her I met you.'

'Is that all?'

'Yes.'

'Why?'

'She wouldn't understand.'

'Julian wouldn't either,' said Eliza. 'I hardly understand it myself,' she added with a sigh. 'But at least we have nothing to hide.'

A few days later there was rather more both to understand and to hide. Eliza had been both relieved and puzzled by Peter's lack of sexual assertiveness. She was so accustomed to infidelity in the marriages of most of her friends, she took it so for granted, it was so much part of a natural progression, an inevitable process, as love turned to indifference and indifference to boredom, boredom to diversion, that she found it extremely difficult to understand how a man who had been married for seven years, who was so undoubtedly sexually motivated, and who was equally undoubtedly sexually attracted to her, could spend considerable amounts of time with her and not so much as try to kiss her. She would have liked him to kiss her, and indeed to suggest doing rather more; it would have soothed her hurt feelings, stroked her ego, reassured her about her own desirability. She was also, she had to admit, feeling randy. It was several weeks now since she had had sex with Julian, and although she had learnt to take her pleasure in a rather irregular rhythm these days, her unhappiness and insecurity had made her uncomfortable and hungry. She found the thought of being in bed with Peter extremely arousing; there was a certain quality about him, an aggression, an awkwardness, which was sexually intriguing. She had been absolutely faithful to Julian, largely because she was frightened not to be. She had had the odd flirtation, the occasional passionate lunch, been kissed quite thoroughly from time to time; but that was all, and she surprised herself as well as her friends. But she did now want quite badly to be unfaithful. She wanted to know another man; it was as simple as that, and she wanted it not because she was bored or even unhappy, but because she felt so desperately inexperienced and so hopelessly vulnerable.

What she could not know, because he concealed it so carefully beneath his facade of aggression, was that Peter Thetford was terrified of making love to her. He was extremely inexperienced himself; he had only slept with two women in his life, Margaret and the art student, and the nearest he had ever come to unfaithfulness had been a prolonged and drunken necking session with a journalist at one of the Labour Party conferences. Margaret was a conventional but undemanding wife in bed; confronted by any attempt on his part to explore, to innovate, she became irritable and uneasy. Consequently, Peter's sexual performance was practised but proscribed; he was, however, quite highly sexed and he thought about it a lot and fantasized considerably; (he had developed a slightly unfortunate tendency to do this in the middle of his constituency surgeries when boredom was running particularly high; and would find himself sharply distracted from some tale of unjust landlord, or pillaging allotment holder, by a sexual image of such vividness that he had to pull several files on to his lap to cover his erection). But fantasies were one thing, reality another; he felt sick with terror as well as desire every time he contemplated Eliza's sensuous mouth, her slender graceful body, and the undoubted hunger in her large green eyes. There was also her social status. Knowing her better, liking her more and more, he was still both overawed and angered by it. She had been born to class, confidence and money, and had acquired far more; his hostility to that, and his fear of it, held him back day after day. She was on the other side of all those closed doors and he still could not imagine himself walking through them.

And so he did nothing; and Eliza became increasingly frustrated and baffled – without being quite desperate or confident enough to initiate matters herself.

Besides, while Peter Thetford asked no more of her than her company, and her untiring ear, she was at least not threatened: she was safe. Safe from gossip, safe from rejection, safe from fear. There was the odd remark, the occasional rumour in those talkative weeks, but as they did nothing but wander about London, in the most public possible way, not even holding hands, for all the world to see, it was hard for anyone to work up much interest in their story. Even Letitia, arch gossip that she was, and deeply suspicious, could make nothing of the relationship; Eliza brought Peter Thetford to tea with her at First Street; for two hours he lectured them both on the subject of comprehensive schooling, produced pictures of Margaret,

David and Hugh for Letitia to see, invited her to a debate on the possibility of decimal currency the following week and then left alone to write a speech on teachers' salaries.

'I find it hard to believe,' said Letitia to Susan (who was passionately intrigued by Eliza's latest foray into socialist politics) later that week, 'but I honestly don't think he's laid a finger on her. Most extraordinary. He's very nice really,' she added, forgetting who she was with, 'in spite of his background. And I'm told he's very clever. Dreadful suit though.'

'I know you can never quite believe it, Letitia,' said Susan mildly, 'but quite a lot of people are nice in spite of their backgrounds. I've met several perfectly decent people in my time, you know, who had to wipe their own bottoms without a nanny to help them, from a very early age, never went away to school, never buggered the new boys . . .'

'Oh, my darling, do forgive me,' said Letitia. 'I am so tactless. Oh, dear, what can I say? You know I don't mean it.'

'Of course I do,' said Susan, and laughed. 'But you'd better not make those sort of remarks in front of Mr Thetford. He wouldn't know anything of the sort. Red rag to a bull, I'd say that would be.'

Ironically it was precisely that sort of remark that finally got Peter Thetford into bed with Eliza Morell.

They were in the garden of Hanover Terrace with Roz, one afternoon, about three weeks after they had met. Eliza was trying to make a daisy chain with a marked lack of success. 'Here,' she said, turning to Peter and laughing, 'see if you can do it. Nothing brings back childhood like daisy chains, don't you think? Daisy chains and tea on the lawn.'

It was an innocent remark and she meant it quite simply; but Peter was tired, he had had a worrying conversation with his agent about a forthcoming by-election and a rather too promising Tory candidate; he had to go up next day on the milk train to Manchester and take his surgery without so much as time for a cup of tea when he got there; his head ached, his speech was still not right, and he felt he was making absolutely no headway with Gaitskell in his long-term plan to move into the Department of Education. Eliza's remark seemed frivolous and fatuous.

'Your childhood maybe. Mine was rather different, you may remember. Tea was a big meal at six o'clock, round the table, with Father often still not washed after coming home from the mine, coughing his lungs up and spitting into his handkerchief. Not a daisy chain in sight.'

'Oh, for Christ's sake,' said Eliza, 'I am so tired of that bloody background of yours. I'll tell you one of the most important differences between your class and mine; we don't keep on and on about it. It's so boring. Don't you think it's time you learnt to behave properly?'

Peter looked at her and all the memories swam into his head: hot angry memories, of rejection, of loneliness, of a realization he was different, odd, not up to standard. Of other people laughing, talking, closing doors, leaving him behind. Of beautiful girls, self-assured, sexually arrogant, gently but cruelly turning him away.

He felt a shudder go through him, a savage angry shot of desire; he looked at Eliza, and he knew he had to have her, master her, bring her down; he stood up suddenly, his face livid, picked up little Roz and carried her inside.

'What the hell are you doing?' said Eliza, scrambling up after him, following him up the stairs, frightened, calling for Nanny.

Thetford took Roz to the nursery and ran back downstairs; Eliza was standing in the hall. He took her hand, dragging her towards him; she looked at him half frightened, half excited. 'Leave me alone,' she said, but he knew she didn't mean it, she stopped almost at once even pretending, simply turned, and led him quickly, silently, across the hall and into her parlour and closed the door.

He stood back and looked at her; then reached out and unbuttoned her shirt; slipped it off her shoulders and bent and started kissing her bare breasts. He kissed them slowly, tenderly, licking the nipples, sucking them, working them with his tongue; on and on it went, insistent, hungry, patient; Eliza standing there, her head bent over him, her fists clenched with hunger and pleasure, felt soft, fluid with desire. He wrenched off her skirt, her pants; he was kneeling now, kissing, fondling her stomach, her thighs, his tongue suddenly, cunningly darting into her; she moaned, cried out, trembling violently with excitement, fear, desire.

'Please,' she said, 'please, please, now.' But he stayed there, kneeling, still dressed, just tonguing her, stroking her buttocks, exploring her with his hands, until she spasmed, suddenly, and was still.

Then he took her, again and still again; he was rough with her, almost brutal, tearing into her as if he wished to break her; and she became in the end exhausted, tearful, she lay back away from him, silent, her face turned into the floor. He came then, finally; allowed himself to let go; and he lay on her, heavy, sweating, panting, in a sweet, savage triumph, feeling that at last he had avenged himself and the injustices of all those long, enraging years.

'You bitch,' he said, 'you rich bitch,' but he was smiling now, gently, tenderly easing himself away from her, stroking her hair, kissing her tear-wet cheeks.

'You bastard,' she said, and smiled in reply. 'You poor, working-class bastard.'

'I'm sorry,' he said, restored to himself. 'I was rough. Did I hurt you? Shall I go away?'

She resettled herself beneath him, around him, in a gesture of most joyful pleasure.

'No,' she said, her hand moving firmly, questingly around his buttocks, 'I want some more, please.'

They spent much time in the parlour after that; and it was there that Julian found them together early one morning, after he had flown in a day earlier than anyone had expected.

The Connection Three

Los Angeles, 1965

'If ever a child looked exactly like his daddy, it's Miles, Mrs Wilburn. He certainly is a lovely little boy.' Father Kennedy at the Santa Monica Catholic church on California Avenue was chatting to the faithful after mid-morning mass; he liked to establish friendships with his flock, make them feel he was an approachable figure they could turn to in trouble. Not that he could imagine Mrs Wilburn would ever need anyone to turn to, she seemed such a nice, steady, competent person, not the sort to fool around or leave her little boy to come home to an empty house because she went to work like some of the mothers in the area. With her looks she might even have been tempted to try for extra work in the studios, but she didn't. She stayed at home and kept house for Miles and her nice rock-solid husband. Not that he attended church as often as he might, but he was a nice enough person, he came to Thanksgiving and Christmas, and at least one parent was attending regularly and raising the child in the faith.

He suddenly realized that Mrs Wilburn was looking at him slightly oddly, nervously even, and he wondered what he had said, but then she relaxed and smiled at him, her lovely warm, friendly smile. What a pretty woman she was.

'Thank you, Father. Yes, he certainly is. Of course he's a handful, very very lively, but you would expect that, wouldn't you?'

'Well, you certainly do, Mrs Wilburn. Boys should be boys. How old is he now? Is he in school yet?'

'He's nearly eight, Father. Yes, he's been in St Clement's Grade School for two years. I can't say he seems to be a genius, but there's plenty of time, I guess. All he thinks about is sports, he just can't wait to join the Little League. And Dean – my husband – can't wait for that either.'

'Well, it's nice to see a father taking so much interest in his child.'

'It certainly is. I never see them at weekends, they go off fishing together and watching the football games. Sometimes I feel quite left out.'

She smiled gaily, to let him know she wasn't serious.

'You should have another child, Mrs Wilburn. A girl maybe. To keep you company.'

He smiled back, letting her know he wasn't serious either, that he wasn't insinuating that she was doing anything wrong, breaking the laws of the church.

Nevertheless he had wondered. She was young, such an ideal mother, now why had there not been another child?

A shadow passed over her face. 'I can't tell you how much I'd like that, Father.'

He felt remorseful at opening what was obviously a wound. He patted her hand. 'Well, God works in a mysterious way, Mrs Wilburn. Who knows what may happen in his own good time?'

'Yes, Father. Perhaps. Good morning. Miles, come along. Your daddy will be waiting to take you fishing.'

But she knew, thought Lee as she headed for home that bright October morning, she knew what might happen, what would happen in that particular direction: nothing, nothing at all. Dean, encouraged by his first success at fathering a child, had never given up hope, but the years had gone by and Miles had remained the only one. She didn't think actually that Dean minded that much. He was so absolutely and utterly wrapped up in Miles, he loved him so much, it quite frightened her. Another woman in another situation might have been jealous, as she had joked to Father Kennedy; so absolutely second place did she come to the little boy. As it was she was just thankful, deeply deeply thankful that not so much as a shiver of suspicion or mistrust darkened Dean's relationship with his son.

And they were a very happy little family. There was no doubt about it. And Miles was a very bright, nice little boy. He was naughty, a bit wild, and a bit devious maybe, and very lazy when it came to school, she could see trouble ahead there; it was annoying because he was obviously clever (a bit too clever, she sometimes thought uneasily). He picked things up in a trice if he wanted to, and he had a real flair for numbers, he positively enjoyed adding them up in his head, which he did terrifically fast. When they went to market sometimes, and he was waiting for her to check out her shopping, he would stand on one of the other aisles, watching the cash register totting up the totals, silently mouthing the figures as they went up and announcing the final sum to the impressed women before the girl at the check-out did. It became a kind of party piece, people would talk about it, and point him out, smiling, and the check-out girls would say, 'Hey, that's really neat,' and tell him what a clever kid he was; Miles liked that, it was one of the things Lee worried about, he loved being the centre of attention, being admired, having a fuss made of him, not in the regular way kids did, of enjoying a bit of spoiling, but actually being in the limelight, being stared at, having an audience. She hoped to heaven he wasn't going to grow up wanting to go into the film business; a lot of mothers would encourage that, of course, but the only thing Miles seemed likely to want to star in at the moment was the baseball team, and that was good and healthy.

'Mom,' said Miles hopefully, pulling on her hand as they walked down the hill towards their house, 'do you think we could have lunch on the pier today?'

'Miles, you know your daddy was planning to take you fishing. Don't you want to go?' said Lee in astonishment. Usually there was nothing Miles liked better than a day's fishing off Malibu with Dean.

'I'm kind of tired of it, we go so often. And Jamie is going to the pier today with his folks, and he says he has something real neat he wants to show me and I would like that. Please, Mom, could you ask Dad?'

'Well, I don't know,' said Lee doubtfully. 'He'll have everything ready for you to go, he was getting the rods out when we left.'

Miles scowled. 'I don't see why I should have to go. That would be two things in one day I didn't want to do.'

'Well, Miles, there's nothing anywhere that says you should only do what you want to do. That would be very bad for you. What was the other thing?'

'Going to mass of course.'

'Now Miles, that is just ridiculous. Of course you have to go to mass.'

'Jamie doesn't have to go to mass.'

'I know, but Jamie's family isn't Catholic.'

'Why do we have to be Catholic?'

'We don't have to be Catholic, Miles, we just are. It's something you're born with, that you grow up to because your parents are.'

'Dad doesn't go to mass.'

'He does sometimes. Now stop this argument, Miles. It's just silly.'

Lee always grew uncomfortable when anyone started to comment on her religion, especially Miles or Dean. It was one of the bargains she had made with God: if and when Miles had been safely and unquestionably California born, then she would become a regular attender at church again, and she hadn't broken her side of it, she had gone not only to mass on Sundays but confession every Friday too – although there were some things of course that she was never going to confess to anybody, not even God, never mind Father Kennedy who was a bit of an old gossip, she always suspected. Dean had remarked on it at first, teased her even, at her apparently unprompted conversion to devout Catholicism, but Lee had reminded him she had always been a Catholic, just lapsed a bit, and said with some truth that she was so pleased and thankful for Miles' safe delivery that she felt duty bound to let God know it.

When they got home Dean was indeed ready, all the rods packed up in the hall, beaming delightedly as Miles appeared.

'There you are, son. Ready to go?'

'Yes, he is,' said Lee, just slightly challenging. 'Just let him go and change, Dean, he won't be five minutes.'

Miles looked back at her defiantly, his blue eyes so like her own, and yet so different: a darker, harder blue, suddenly hostile.

'Do we have to go, Dad?'

Dean looked amazed and hurt. 'What do you mean, Miles? Of course we have to go. We want to go. Don't we?'

'Not specially, Dad. Not today.'

'Miles, go and change,' said Lee quickly. 'Go on, run along.'

'Do I have to?'

'Yes, you do. Whatever you do, you have to change. I'll talk to your dad.'

'What on earth is that about?' said Dean, his plump face bewildered, a little hurt. 'When did he ever not want to go fishing?'

'Quite often, possibly,' said Lee. 'He's never mentioned it before, that's all. He never has to me either. But Dean, I think maybe he'd like a change sometimes. Do something different. All of us together, maybe. Today he asked me if we could go to the pier. Jamie's going. I can see that would be nice for him once in a while. He loves going fishing with you, of course he does, but maybe every Sunday is a little too much. Don't be upset. Would you mind not going today?'

'Yes, I would,' said Dean truculently. 'All morning I've been waiting, getting the rods ready. I've been looking forward to it.'

'Yes, well Miles hasn't,' said Lee firmly. 'It's his Sunday too. I think you should listen to him once in a while.'

'Since when did little boys get listened to?'

'Since there were little boys, maybe. I bet you got listened to.'

'I did not.'

'Well, you should have been.' She gave him a kiss. 'Go on, Dean. Stay home with me. Just this once.'

He softened, grinning at her. 'OK. You'll have to make it up to me later, mind.'

'I will,' said Lee.

Santa Monica pier was a good place to go on a Sunday. 'It's always like Thanksgiving here,' Miles had once said when he was a little tiny boy, and it was true, people seemed permanently happy, relaxed, in a good mood. Dean, warmed out of his sulks, took Miles on the dodgems and challenged him to a turn on the shooting gallery, and they all leant over the rail and watched people going out with Mike Tomich's water ski school.

'I'd really like to do that,' said Miles. 'Dad, can I have a turn at that?'

'You certainly can not,' said Dean, instinctively putting out a protective hand and drawing the little boy closer to him. 'That's real dangerous, Miles, not for little boys.'

'I like things that are real dangerous,' said Miles cheerfully. 'When I grow up I'm going to be a stunt pilot for the movies.'

'You most certainly are not,' said Lee. 'I never ever would allow such a thing.'

Miles gave her one of his slow thoughtful looks. 'You won't be allowing me or not allowing me anything, Mom. I'll be doing what I like. I might even be living thousands and thousands of miles away.'

Lee shivered suddenly; the day seemed to darken. 'If you live thousands of miles away,' she said sharply, 'you won't be able to be a stunt pilot for the movies.'

'I will too,' said Miles, and scowled at her.

'Hey,' said Dean, 'come on, I thought we here to please the two of you. Let's go down to Muscle Beach and watch the acrobats.'

They went down the steps under the pier and fought their

way through the crowds near the Muscle Inn; massive men, their muscles like skeins of throbbing rope, were posing on the sand, lifting up girls who asked them to as if they were rag dolls, practising their strange craft with unsmiling fanaticism. Dean bought beers for himself and Lee and gave Miles an ice cream. The beach was packed; it was hot for October, even by Californian standards. 'I should have brought my suit,' said Lee, 'I might go home and get it. Dean, can we have lunch at Sinbad's? I know that's what Miles is hoping for.'

'Sure,' said Dean, mellowed into total good humour by the holiday atmosphere and the beer. 'When is he going to meet his friend?'

'I don't know,' said Lee. 'Miles, when did you plan on finding Jamie?'

'He said he'd be down after lunch. With his mom and dad. Can we go to Sinbad's, Dad?'

'Sure. If we go now we'll get a table.'

They sat in Sinbad's on the pier, eating swordfish steaks; Miles had his favourite, the speciality of the house, au gratin potatoes mixed with dry slices of bananas. Dean had french fries with his, and coleslaw and pickles and sweetcorn; then he ordered chocolate brownies with strawberry sauce and whipped cream for himself; Lee and Miles had sorbets.

'You eat too much, Dean,' said Lee, patting his stomach affectionately. 'You should cut down a little. It isn't good for you.'

'Ah honey, don't spoil a nice day nagging.'

'I'm not nagging, Dean. Just saying you eat too much.' She kissed him quickly on the cheek, anxious he shouldn't think she was seriously criticizing him. 'It's only because I care about you. Sorry, Dean. Look, Miles, there's Jamie. There, walking down the pier now.'

'Hey,' said Miles, 'hey look, he has a skateboard. Oh, wow, oh, wow, would I like one of those! Can I go get him, Mom?'

'Sure. Tell him to come here and say hello. Fetch his mom and dad.'

'And when,' she said, laughing to Sue and Gerry Forrest, 'did you thoughtless folks get Jamie that? Now every kid on the block will have to have one. Did he get top grades in school or something?'

'It was a birthday present from his godfather,' said Sue. 'I don't think I've ever seen him so excited about anything. He even took it to bed with him last night. He already has about a hundred and fifty bruises.'

'Can we go down on the boardwalk and try Jamie's board?' said Miles. 'Please, please. He says I can have a go on it. *Please.*'

'OK,' said Dean. 'We're coming. But don't blame me if you fall and skin your knees, Miles. I'm sure it isn't very easy.'

Miles made it look very easy very quickly. He took two tumbles in swift succession, and then suddenly got his balance and was away, swooping down the boardwalk, whooping with excitement.

'Hey,' said Jamie, 'he's real good. I took much longer than that. Miles, come back, come back,' he yelled, and started running after Miles down the boardwalk; but Miles was far ahead, not stopping, gliding easily away, occasionally wobbling a little, a small, joyous, oddly graceful figure. At last he came back, panting, flushed, his eyes huge and starry.

'Oh wow,' he said, 'was that neat. Was that neat. O, wow. Dad, can I have one, will you buy me one, please please I'll be so good, I'll do my homework and I'll get good grades and I'll help Mom with the dishes and I'll . . . I'll . . .' ('come fishing with you,' he was about to say, but stopped, realizing it was not quite the most tactful thing to say and that anyway, if he had his way, he would never again sit on a boring lake with a boring fishing rod when he could be swooping along with the wind in his hair and the sun on his face, vying with the birds for speed).

'You can not,' said Dean firmly. 'Not yet anyway. I don't believe in letting little boys have things just whenever they want them.'

'But can I have one for Christmas? That isn't so far off?'

'Maybe. I'll have a word with Santa nearer Christmas time.'

'No, I didn't mean wait till Christmas, I mean have it now and not have a Christmas present. Please, Dad, please.'

'No, Miles,' said Lee sharply, 'you can't.'

'But why not? I want one. I want one real bad.'

'Lots of us want things real bad,' said Sue Forrest, smiling, 'but it doesn't always get them for us.'

Miles looked at her thoughtfully and then turned again to his mother with his sweetest, most appealing smile. 'Please, Mom. It would make me real happy.'

'Miles,' said Lee, 'will you shut up. We said no. Now stop it.'
She was always a little alarmed by the way Miles went for what
he wanted. He didn't usually ask for much, but if something
mattered to him he pursued it with a mixture of such charm and
absolute determination, it was very hard to move or resist him.

'Jamie,' said Sue, eager to end a tedious family scene, 'let
Miles have another go on your board.'

'I don't want him to,' said Jamie. 'He'll go off with it again.
It's my board.'

'Yes, but you've had it for quite a while now, dear. All
yesterday, all this morning.'

'That's not very long. Anyway, I need to practise.'

'Jamie, that's not very generous.'

'I don't care.'

'It's all right,' said Miles suddenly, appearing to give in. 'You
take it, Jamie. You're right. You do need to practise. I kind of
got it quicker than you.'

The little shit, thought Sue, looking at Miles' sweet smile.
Who taught him to hurt like that?

'Well, that's real nice of you, Miles,' she said with an effort,
'but I'm sure you boys can share the board nicely. We'll just sit
here by the walk and watch you.'

But after half an hour the contrast between Jamie's incessant
painful clumsiness and Miles' swift, easy confidence was more
than any of them could bear. They all agreed to go home and
watch the baseball game on TV.

Over dinner Miles tried again.

'I'll pay you interest on the loan for a skateboard,' he said
suddenly.

'Oh, Miles, don't be silly, what on earth do you know about
interest?' said Lee.

'Enough to know it makes lending money worth while. You
lend me ten dollars for a skateboard and I'll pay you back fifteen
in a year. That's a fifty per cent profit you'd be making over
twelve months. It's a good deal.'

Lee laughed suddenly, ruffling his hair. 'Maybe it is. But
where would you get the money to repay a loan? And I don't
have ten right now. Not to lend, anyway,' she added with a sigh.
'Now be a good boy, Miles, and help me with the dishes.'

'I don't see why I have to. Why should I?'

'Because it would be nice for me,' said Lee, sharply hurt.

'I don't see why I should make things nice for you if you don't make them nice for me,' said Miles.

'Miles,' said Dean, looking up from the *Times*. 'Miles, you just apologize to your mother this instant. And get right on helping her.'

'I don't see why . . .' Miles was interrupted by the phone. Dean picked it up, still glaring at him.

'Dean Wilburn. Yes. Oh, Hugo, hi. How are you? Good good. Great to hear from you. Yeah, I'll hold.' He covered the mouthpiece and turned to Lee. 'I was wondering when we'd be hearing from him again . . . Hugo, yes, hi. Sure, sure, we'll be here. We'd love to see you. Lee would be thrilled, stay for a few days if you can.'

'Not too many,' said Lee sharply. She dreaded Hugo's visits. They hung over her uncomplicated sunlit life a dark, uneasy shadow: not very frequent, to be sure, but inevitable, an irregularity in the year's calendar, every two or three months. The very thought of them made her throat dry, her stomach contract, made her want to run, to hide, taking Miles with her. What she felt for Hugo these days was a fierce dislike, a deep resentment, mixed still with a sharp tug of sexual attraction. The mixture of emotions made her sullen, withdrawn, aggressive. She was always amazed he didn't seem to care and Dean didn't seem to notice. She lived in a state of permanent terror all the time he was in the house that he would say or do something, anything, that would arouse Dean's suspicions; she was forced to admire, however grudgingly, his skill at deceit.

Nevertheless, skills faded, watchfulness could slip, memories falter; every second he was in the house she was sick with fear. He had not been for some time, not since May; he had been busy, he said, in England, neglecting his American company. They had had a couple of notes, there had been a card and a five-dollar bill for Miles on his birthday, a postcard from Scotland where he and Alice and the children had been having their holiday, and that had been all. She prayed fervently, every Sunday, every day almost that he would not come again; but the God who had given Miles blue eyes and blond hair plainly felt he had done enough for her and had not seen fit to hear or at any rate answer that particular prayer.

'Next Friday then,' Dean was saying, 'great. Lee will meet you, I'm sure. What's that? OK, I'll tell her to have dinner for you. Bye, Hugo.'

He put the phone down, beaming with pleasure; he enjoyed Hugo's persistent friendship, felt it marked him out as a person of some interest and stature.

'He's coming next weekend, honey. On Friday. About dinner time. Won't that be nice?'

'Very nice,' said Lee, walking to the fridge and getting out a bottle of beer, hoping Dean would not notice her shaking hand, her taut voice.

'And Miles, I want you to be on your best behaviour next weekend,' said Dean. 'Mr Dashwood is coming from England and you know how he always likes to see you and hear about your schoolwork and so on. You be in real early for dinner on Friday and stay home Saturday, OK? No going out to play with Jamie or anyone. English kids are so polite. I don't want you letting American ones down.'

'I don't really like Mr Dashwood,' said Miles, scowling. 'I don't want to stay home and talk to him. Always asking me how I'm getting on and what grades I got and what I'm reading, and having to sit quiet at table while he drones on about his dumb kids in England. He's so – so nosy.'

'Miles, don't be ridiculous,' said Lee sharply. 'Of course Mr Dashwood is interested in you, he's known you all your life.'

'Yeah, well I wish he hadn't. And I'm going out with Jamie, no matter what you say.'

'Miles, I am getting just a little bit tired of your behaviour,' said Lee. 'Just cut it out, will you. Mr Dashwood is our guest and he's always very good to you and you have a duty to be courteous to him.'

'I don't see . . . why . . .' Miles' voice trailed gently off into an exquisite, thunderstruck silence. 'Gee,' he said. 'Gee whizz, I'll be nice to him. I'll stay home Saturday, I sure will.'

'Good,' said Dean. 'That's better. That's my boy.'

Lee looked at Miles sharply. He caught her eye and smiled at her, his sudden enchantingly sweet smile, his blue eyes wide, guileless.

'I shall really like to see Mr Dashwood,' he said slowly. 'He's real kind to me. I'd forgotten for a minute how kind he was.'

'Miles,' said Lee. 'If you as much as say one word about wanting a skateboard to Mr Dashwood, I shall tan your hide. Real hard. I mean it.'

'Don't worry,' said Miles, 'you won't need to. I won't say one word. I swear it. But he'll give me one just the same, I guess. He loves giving me things. Things I'm interested in. He's interested in everything I'm interested in. He even said he'd take me on trips if I wanted to go. To England. He told me so.' He stood up. 'I'll help you with the dishes now, Mom.'

'OK,' said Lee. She stood up, suddenly feeling sick.

'Lee, are you all right, honey?' said Dean. 'You look a bit pale.'

Lee looked at him, and rushed to the toilet. She vomited violently and sat there on the floor, her head resting on her arm, for a long time.

Dean banged on the door. 'Honey, are you OK? What is it?' She came out slowly and sat down heavily on the couch.

'Oh, it's nothing, Dean. Must have been the swordfish. I'll be OK. I'll just go lie down for a while.'

She lay on the bed, twisting and turning, with waves of panic and dread going through her, rather like the fierce deepening waves of childbirth. She had been wrong, so wrong, to think that she could get away. Because Hugo was there. In the house. Growing up. Becoming more and more visible every day of her life.

Chapter Six

London and New York, 1965–7

Roz could remember exactly when she had discovered her father didn't love her. She had been six years old at the time and it was fixed in her memory as indelibly and certainly as her own name, and the fact that she was too tall for her age, and the least pretty girl in Miss Ballantine's dancing class, and therefore the one chosen to be the prince in the charity concert and not one of the pink and white princesses. And it had been no use her father telling her over and over again that he did love her, and trying to prove it to her with expensive presents and treats and holidays, just as it had been no use Miss Ballantine telling her she had been cast as the prince because she was better at dancing than all the others; she believed neither of them, and indeed she despised them both for trying to convince her of something that she and they knew perfectly well was so patently untrue.

She knew he didn't love her because she had heard him say so. Well, perhaps not in so many words, but he had certainly admitted it. He had been having a row with her mother, shortly after she had married Peter Thetford; they had been shouting at one another in the drawing room of the house in Holland Park which Roz and Nanny and Eliza and Thetford all lived in, and which was so small you couldn't help overhearing everything, and she certainly hadn't intended not to overhear the row anyway. Rows were a good way of learning things. It was during a row between her mother and Thetford that she had learnt that he regarded her as a stuck-up bitch, and during another that he thought she had robbed him of any possibility of becoming a major force in politics (whatever that might mean). This particular row started when her father returned her to the house in Holland Park after she had spent the weekend with him. She never knew if it was worth the happiness of those weekends for the misery of their endings; they had such fun, the two of them. Sometimes in London, when he took her out shopping and bought her clothes that her mother strongly disapproved of, and to meals in smart restaurants like the Ritz, and let her stay up late, but more often they went to the country, to Marriotts where he was teaching her to ride, and had bought her her own pony called Miss Madam, because that was what Nanny Henry was always calling her. Nearly as excitingly, he took her for rides in some of his very special cars, the old ones with lamps sticking out of their fronts and roofs that opened like the hood of a pram, the Lanchester, and the Ford Model T and the Mercedes 60; he told her that as soon as she was big enough, probably about twelve years old, he would let her drive one of them round the grounds of Marriotts, and that she would find out what driving a real car felt like.

They had the most wonderful time, those weekends; to have her father to herself seemed to Roz the most perfect happiness. She was very fond of her mother, indeed she supposed she loved her, although she hated Peter Thetford so much she found it very hard to forgive her mother for wanting to go and live with him, and forcing her to go and live with him too. But her father had always seemed to Roz the most perfect person; he was so good-looking, so much more good-looking than most of her friends' fathers, and he wore such lovely clothes, and he was so good at telling her stories, and making her laugh and just knowing what she would most like to do. But more important than all those things, he seemed to value her company and her opinions; he never sent her off up to the nursery if she didn't want to go, he would explain things to her about his company and the sort of things he was doing and wanting to do when she was a little tiny girl, and he told her it was never too early to learn and that one day it would be hers, because he was never ever going to have any other children, and that Roz was his heir.

'Don't be ridiculous, Julian,' her mother had said the first time he had ever said this, when she had only been four years old, 'how can you expect her to understand such a thing, and anyway, she's an heiress, not an heir.'

And her father had looked at her, not her mother, and smiled, and said, 'No, she is my heir. Roz will inherit the company, because she is my child and extremely clever and her sex is quite immaterial.'

She hadn't understood all the words, but she certainly understood the meaning; that whatever happened, one day her father's company would be hers, because he thought she was the right person to have it, and no one, no one at all, was going to be able to take it away from her. It was something that made everything else worth while, the awfulness of her parents not being married any more, and seeing so much less of her father, and having to live with Peter Thetford and sometimes even his horrible little boys, with their very short hair and loud rough voices, the kind of boys Nanny Henry called her away from in the park, and also of not being able to live all the time with her father: the certain knowledge that he loved her so much and considered her so special.

And then it was taken away from her.

They had got back from Sussex quite late one Sunday evening; her father had returned her to the doorstep, said she was very tired, and her mother had sent her up to Nanny Henry to get ready for bed.

'Do you want a drink, Julian?' she heard her mother say, and her father said yes, that would be very welcome, and where was the master of the house.

'He's driving the boys back home.'

'Long way.'

'Yes, but Margaret won't have them put on the train, and she's not prepared to come down and get them, so he doesn't have much choice.'

'I see. And how is the most promising young man in politics since Lloyd George? Or would Aneurin Bevan be more appropriate?'

'Don't be unpleasant, Julian, please. Peter is a very clever politician. And he's doing well. Very well.'

'Really? I had heard rather the reverse.'

'Had you? Well your informant was clearly in the wrong.'

'And how are you, Eliza?'

'I'm extremely well. Very happy.'

'Good. You don't look it.'

'Julian, you have no idea how I look when I'm happy. It was not a state I enjoyed very often during our marriage.'

'Well, we won't discuss that now. Roz doesn't seem to like Thetford very much.'

'What on earth do you mean?'

'What I say.'

'How do you know?'

'She told me.'

'How dare you encourage her to talk about such things? To be so disloyal?'

'I didn't have to encourage her. And I think we should not get on to the topic of disloyalty. Otherwise I might find a few stones to sling at you of that nature.'

'Oh, go to hell.'

'Eliza, I do assure you there was no question of my prompting Roz in any way. She says spontaneously, and quite frequently, that she hates her stepfather and she'd like to come and live with me.'

'And?'

'And what?'

'What do you say back?'

'What can I say? I can't encourage her in that fantasy, can I? I've tried to make her feel more warmly towards him. Without success.'

Roz, listening on the first-floor landing, praying Nanny Henry wouldn't stop watching *Sunday Night at the London Palladium* on her television and realize she was home, couldn't actually remember her father ever trying to do anything of the sort; he sneered at Thetford a lot, and said how dreary he was, and how he wouldn't know one end of a horse from the other and that sort of thing, but otherwise he was never mentioned between them, it was too depressing on her weekends away.

'Julian,' she heard her mother say, just casually, 'Julian how would you feel about having Roz to live with you?'

Roz's heart lifted, leapt; she had to bite her fists to keep quiet. She knew how her father would feel; he would love the idea as much as she did. She had always thought her mother would never consider such a thing. If she was willing to let her go back home, as she still thought of Hanover Terrace, then obviously her father would take her. She waited to hear him say it. To say, 'Well of course I'd love it,' or something like that. But there was a long, an endless silence. Then:

'Eliza, exactly what do you mean?'

'I mean what I say. I just think it might be better.'

'For her?'

'Well, yes. Of course for her. I mean she isn't happy here, you're quite right. And she doesn't get on with Peter. She's very awkward. She causes a lot of friction. There's no doubt about it. She's rude about the boys, won't have anything to do with them –'

'Good. Vile little tykes.'

'Julian –'

'Sorry.'

'Well anyway, it's all very difficult.'

'For you?'

'Well, yes. And for Peter. And I thought – well, of course I'd miss her, but, Julian, things aren't going terribly well. If she was with you more, here less, just for a bit, then it would give us more of a chance. Nanny could come of course –'

'Of course.'

'I mean, I could have her when Peter wasn't here. It would be better for her.'

'Really? And for you. And most of all for him. Jesus, Eliza, what a hypocrite you are.'

'Oh, I knew you wouldn't understand.'

'Oh, I understand, Eliza. Very well. Roz is making your idyllic new life difficult, and so the best thing is to get rid of her.'

'I'm not trying to get rid of her.'

'You could have fooled me.'

'No, Julian, I'm not. But she does so much prefer you. She adores you. You know she does. And I just can't do anything right for her. She's –' and Roz could hear the suppressed laughter in her voice, slightly shaky, but nonetheless there, 'she's just like you.'

'Really? In what way?'

'Oh, every possible way. Hard to please. Impossible to reason with. Shutting people – me out.'

'Poor child. You make her sound very unattractive.'

'Well, she isn't very attractive, is she? At the moment? Be honest. She's so morose and awkward.'

'She seems fine to me. I would agree she isn't very physically attractive at the moment. She's going through a very plain phase, and she's so big for her age. It's a shame, poor child. She has enough problems.'

'Yes, well, that will pass, I'm sure. So what do you think, Julian? Would you – could you have her for a while?'

Time had stopped for Roz, sitting on the landing in a frozen stillness, her legs cramped underneath her, her fists still crammed into her mouth to stop her making a sound. Surely this was it, the long boring conversation would finish, and her father would say yes of course he would have her, and probably tell her to pack up her things immediately, come back with him now. That was all that mattered, really; it had been very unpleasant hearing him say she was plain (she didn't mind her mother saying she was unattractive), but she had known really anyway, and if she could only go and live with her father, she would become more beautiful straight away. All the people surrounding him were, it was a kind of magic he seemed to work, and she would be happier and she would smile more so she would look prettier anyway. So all he had to say was yes: so why wasn't he saying it?

'No, Eliza, it's absolutely out of the question.' (What? What? Roz thought she must be hearing wrongly, that she was imagining his words.) 'I couldn't have her even if I wanted to, and frankly I don't. I –'

But Roz heard no more. She got up, very quickly, and crept up to her bedroom and lay down on her bed fully clothed, with the eiderdown pulled over her, waiting for the tears to come. But they didn't. She just lay there, silent, and as she lay, her numb legs, which she had been sitting on for so long, came back in a stabbing agony to life. The pain was so bad, she found it hard not to yell out. But it was nothing, nothing at all, compared to the awful, deathly cold hurt throbbing in her head and her heart.

She had learnt to live with it, of course. You could learn to live with anything. Obviously there was a reason for him not loving her, and she spent a lot of time trying to find it. Was it that she was not pretty? It could be. Her mother was so beautiful, and so was her grandmother, Granny Letitia, and her father was extremely good-looking; it must be horribly disappointing for them to have someone in the family who was so plain. Of course her father wouldn't want a plain, an ugly person living with him; he couldn't be expected to. Then maybe it was because she wasn't clever enough. He was so extremely clever himself, and if he was going to leave her his company (only maybe he wasn't now, maybe he had changed his mind) she needed to be extremely clever too. Of course he hadn't said yet that he wasn't going to give her the company, but if he didn't think she was good enough to live with him, then he probably wouldn't think she was good enough to have the company either.

Or maybe it was because she wasn't a boy. He had never said he minded, but Nanny Henry (and quite a few other people, mostly Nanny's friends, but also the Thetford boys, and some of her mother's luncheon companions, the ladies who arrived at half past twelve and stayed often till about four, drinking wine and eating almost nothing and laughing and talking endlessly) had said it would have been much better if she had been a boy and could take over the company. Or – and this was the most frightening thing of all – maybe he was planning marrying someone else, and having another baby with her. And maybe that baby would be a boy, or a pretty girl, or really really clever and then the company would go to him or her instead.

Nothing that had happened to Roz could compare with this in awfulness; not even the day that her father had taken her on his knee and held her very tight and said he was terribly sorry, but he and her mother were going to be living in separate houses from then on, because they didn't get on very well any more, or when her mother had told her that she and Peter Thetford were going to get married and be together always. And the worst thing about it of all, she knew, was not finding out that her father didn't love her; it was finding out that she couldn't love him in the same way either.

She couldn't talk to him about that of course; she couldn't talk to him about any of it. She simply shut him out, and tried not to let him see how badly she felt. She didn't want him to know what power he had to hurt her; she wanted him to think she didn't care what he did. He could buy her as many dresses as he liked, and take her on trips to New York and Paris, and throw extravagant parties for her on her birthdays (one year he took her and her six very best friends to Le Touquet for the day in his own plane which he piloted himself, and bought them all lunch in a very smart restaurant there; another he hired the ballroom at the Ritz, and everyone wore long dresses, even though they were only ten, and instead of a conjuror which most of the girls had, they had a pop group who played all the top hits, and instead of it being in the afternoon it was from six o'clock till ten o'clock at night). He never stopped trying to please her; he got tickets for shows like *Camelot* and *Beyond the Fringe* and arranged for her to meet the cast afterwards, and to premieres of films like *Lawrence of Arabia* and *West Side Story* and even occasionally to the parties afterwards where the stars went; he took her out to expensive restaurants (by the time she was ten Roz had eaten in practically every restaurant recommended by Egon Ronay – and complained in most of them); he took her to Disneyland; he did (as promised) let her drive some of the cars round the grounds of Marriotts on her twelfth birthday; he bought her not one but two ponies to replace Miss Madam when she was eight, one grey and one chestnut, because she said she couldn't make up her mind between them, he had her to stay with him in New York most school holidays; and she had only to mention most casually that she wanted a puppy, a kitten, a new bicycle, a new stereo, and it arrived. And Roz would say thank you politely, formally, but never warmly, never showing her pleasure; and she got great satisfaction from seeing the disappointment, the hurt in his eyes. She knew he was desperate to please her, that he was frightened of making her unhappy, and she enjoyed the knowledge. It was the only thing that made her feel safe.

When Roz was nine years old Peter Thetford moved out of the house in Holland Park. She had stood at the window of her bedroom and watched him piling his things into the taxi that morning, and quite literally danced with pleasure. Her joy came quite as much from the fact that he was gone from the house as that her mother would be on her own, and it seemed to her just possible that she and her father might start living together again. The disappointment when they did not was almost as bad as the hurt when they first separated. 'But why?' she asked Eliza over and over again, crying in bed the night she finally asked if this might be possible, and beating the pillow with rage and despair when she was told it was not. 'Why not? You've had a turn at being married to someone else, and you didn't like it. Why not go back to Daddy?' And Eliza had tried to comfort her, holding her, wiping her tears. 'Just because I wasn't very happy with Peter, darling, doesn't mean I can just go back and be happy with Daddy. Life isn't like that. But we shall have more time together, and you must keep me company now I'm on my own again.'

And Roz, remembering all the evenings she had begged her mother to stay in with her and not go out with her friends or with Peter, and Eliza had gone just the same, said, 'Oh you'll find someone else to keep you company, I expect,' and turned her face into her pillow and cried endlessly and refused to be comforted.

Her father had said much the same thing: that he and her mother just couldn't get along any more and it was better they lived in different houses even though Peter had gone; and he said perhaps Roz would like to stay with him a bit more often now that she was a bigger girl and that he got lonely sometimes too.

'No,' Roz said, seeing a chance to hurt him, to show that she was in command of the situation, not him, 'no, I want to be with Mummy, she needs me. Besides,' she added, looking at him out of her green eyes with a blank expression so like his own, 'you have Camilla to keep you company, don't you? Poor Mummy hasn't got anyone.'

Roz hated Camilla. She had hated her from the very first time she met her, when she had gone to stay with her father in New York when she was just seven years old. At first she had thought she was just a friend of her father's, one of the many ladies he took out to dinner or the theatre and then didn't see again – or not very often. But Camilla didn't go away. She went on being around, first in America and then in London until Roz couldn't remember a time when she hadn't been there. One of the things she had most hated about her was how beautiful she was, with her goldy red hair and her bright red lips, and her long red nails; she could see that was why her father must like her, and it seemed so unfair that someone could be liked so much straight away just because they were beautiful.

Camilla came out to lunch with them twice in New York that first time, and although she worked very hard being nice to her, asking her endless questions about her friends and her school and her pony, Roz could see perfectly well she was bored, she had that look on her face that grown-ups always had when they weren't listening to what you said, a sort of fixed smile with her eyes wandering round the room a bit. She didn't like the way that her father looked at Camilla either, or the way Camilla put her hand over his and kissed his cheek, or talked for a very long time very seriously about something that had happened in a meeting that morning. Another night she went out to dinner

with them; she was looking particularly beautiful, Roz thought
– although she didn't like to have even to think it – wearing a
great big shaggy sweater in lovely blues and greens, with a
V-neck, and rows and rows of beads, in a pair of very thin black
velvet trousers, and sort of slipper-like shoes. Her father had
laughed and told her she looked like a beatnik, and Camilla had
got very serious and told him he was out of date, beatniks had
been around five years earlier, and he had told her not to be so
tedious, which had pleased Roz very much. They went to a
restaurant called Sardi's, which Roz liked much better than all
the expensive places they had been to; she had a hamburger
and a knickerbocker glory and felt quite happy until Camilla
started talking to her again, and said she had a present for her
and gave her a little box with a silver dollar in it made into a
brooch.

'That's lovely, Camilla,' her father said, 'isn't that kind of
Camilla, Roz, what do you say? Put it on, darling, and let's see
how pretty it looks.'

'Thank you, Camilla,' said Roz carefully, aware that once
again someone was trying to buy her and trying to make her like
them, 'but I won't wear it now, it doesn't go with this dress.'

'Roz, you don't know what does and doesn't go with dresses.
Put it on,' said Julian. He tried to sound light and amused, but
she could see the anger in his eyes and she felt just slightly
frightened.

'No,' she said, bravely. 'No, I don't want to.'

'Roz,' said Julian, and he had stopped even pretending to be
amused. 'Put it on.'

'No,' she said. 'I won't.'

'Oh, Julian,' said Camilla quickly, 'don't make a thing of it. If
Roz doesn't want to wear it I don't mind. And she's quite right,
aren't you, Roz, it doesn't go with that dress. What a clever little
girl you are.'

Something snapped in Roz; she could feel a hot rage
sweeping over her, could feel Camilla thinking she was getting
round her.

'I'm not clever,' she said. 'I just don't like the brooch. And I
don't want to wear it. I feel sick and I want to go home.'

'Don't be ridiculous, Roz,' said Julian. 'Apologize to Camilla
and eat your food. We are not going home.'

'I shall be sick.'

'No you won't. Now eat it.'

Roz ate in total silence; when she had finished the last mouthful she took a deep breath, and by sheer effort of will vomited the entire meal on to her plate again. It was a trick she was to learn to perfect over the years.

Looking at her father across the table, she was rewarded by an expression on his face she had never seen there before. It was defeat.

But she did not get rid of Camilla.

Later, Camilla often came to London, and stayed at the house in Regent's Park, or even came down to Marriotts. Roz minded her being at Marriotts even more than in London, because she always thought of it as her father's and her house, and Camilla absolutely ruined it. She was so boring about things and went on and on about whatever Roz said, even if it was a joke, or if they were playing a game like draughts, spending hours studying her moves, and if they went riding together, the three of them, Camilla was forever telling her little things she was doing wrong, like not sitting into the canter enough, or letting her pony trail his legs over a jump. She was meant to sleep in one of the guest rooms, but Roz had seen her coming out of her father's bedroom more than once. She knew what happened when a man and a woman were in bed together, intercourse it was called, her friend Rosie Howard Johnson had told her, and she had also told her it could lead to the woman having a baby; Roz didn't mind too much about the intercourse but the thought of Camilla having a baby made her feel very sick indeed. Apart from the fact it might be a boy, and that he might get the company, her father might love the baby more than he loved her. If he loved her at all. Sometimes for days at a time Roz managed to make herself forget that she had heard him refusing to have her to live with him, but when she thought about him sort of living with Camilla and possibly even having a baby with her, the pain came back so badly it made her breath go away and she felt as if she had fallen and winded herself.

Right from the very beginning of her relationship with Julian,

Camilla's main problem had been Roz. She could handle the highly charged matter of having both to work with Julian and sleep with him, and the inevitable speculation and tensions it caused; she could handle the fact that she knew she was not the only woman in his life; she could handle her slightly ambivalent attitude to her sex life. And she had no problem at all handling the question of Eliza. Through the divorce, which did not surprise her in the very least (except perhaps in that someone as frivolous and non-intellectual as Eliza should have captured the attentions of a politician), Camilla supported Julian admirably; she allowed him to talk as much as he wished: to question his behaviour, to examine his feelings, to express regret, anxiety, remorse (which he did occasionally and rather dutifully, as if he knew it was expected of him); she was careful not to criticize Eliza, and was even more careful to avoid any hint of an idea that now he was free he might wish to enter into a more serious relationship with her. And she took great care to allow him to spend more time with her than usual between the linen sheets, and to consciously express more affection and tenderness there than perhaps she had done in the past. In brief, she was the perfect mistress. But she was not the perfect stepmother.

Roz quite clearly resented her, feared the impact she might make on her life, and in fact (Camilla had to admit to herself) thoroughly disliked her. She was polite to her – just – but no more, she rejected her overtures of friendship, she cut any conversation with her down to a minimum and she made it perfectly plain that whenever Camilla was with her and her father she would much prefer it if she was not. Julian had taken an indulgent attitude to this at first, saying easily that Roz would soon get to know Camilla better and feel less threatened by her; later on, weary of the constant hostility between the two of them, unable to ease it in any way, he refused to discuss it or even acknowledge its existence.

The fact that she was not a pretty child didn't help; she was not appealing, she did not enlist sympathy, she was big for her age, not fat, but sturdily built, dark-haired and slightly sallow-skinned, with a rather large nose and a solemn expression. The only thing that gave her face any charm at all was her eyes, which were green like her mother's, large and expressive. But the expression in them was very frequently not in the least charming; she had a capacity to fill them with a kind of brooding intensity which she would fix on Camilla, or make them, like her father's, an inscrutable blank.

She was obviously a clever child, and she seemed very self-confident. Camilla, studying her carefully, could see few signs of insecurity. She knew quite a lot about disturbed children, as she had done a psychology project about them at high school and had worked at a day centre in one of the poorer areas of Philadelphia; her thesis had won the psychology prize and left her with an abiding interest in the subject. Julian's lecture on being tactful and patient with Roz had left her irritated. He had gone to some lengths to explain that at no time during Roz's visits was she to stay over at the apartment or to appear anything more than ordinarily friendly towards him. Camilla had told him shortly that he would be fortunate if she appeared friendly towards him at all, ordinarily or otherwise, if he persisted in treating her like some kind of insensitive moron. In fact she avoided him altogether until Roz had been in New York for several days.

Later, as Roz got older and she herself became more involved with Julian, the problem increased. Roz was increasingly difficult to handle; both her parents spoilt her and were afraid of upsetting her, and Camilla could perfectly well see that she was fast reaching a point where nobody would be able to handle her at all – she was like a badly trained overexcited thoroughbred, she told Julian, and she needed a good long session on the lunge rein at regular intervals. She had been rather pleased with this analogy, but Julian clearly hadn't liked it at all and told her shortly that handling children was extremely easy for people who hadn't got any.

Camilla observed with a mixtue of irritation and admiration Roz's manipulative skills; she heard her on the phone one evening, telling her mother that she had been having the most wonderful time with Daddy and Camilla and didn't really want to come home until the next day when in fact they had all spent a rather depressing afternoon skating at Queen's and then having supper at a dreadful place called the Carvery where you could take as much of everything as you liked and which was supposed to be Roz's favourite place. Roz had sat out most of the skating saying her ankles hurt, and had refused to eat anything at the Carvery except ice cream and roast potatoes.

Roz was just about nine at the time; Camilla rather bravely volunteered to take her home in the morning by taxi as Julian had several meetings, and on the way she asked Roz to show her Harrods and offered to buy her something. Roz had said she hated Harrods, it was a boring shop and anyway her mother had bought her so much lately she really couldn't think of anything else she wanted; but then, as Camilla delivered her to a rather cool Eliza, Roz had said thank you very very much and could she please please go out with her another day and buy her a present for always being so kind to her in New York.

What Camilla felt within her most secret self – the self she crushed ruthlessly into submission most of the time and which only surfaced during the middle of the night – (like most obsessive over-achievers Camilla was a poor sleeper) was that her own rather irregular situation with Julian made her relationship with Roz worse. Had she been married to him, or even his permanent, long-term mistress, sharing his homes as well as his bed, then she felt that Roz would come to accept her, and she could have established a relationship with the child which had some stability. But Julian did not want that; he made it perfectly clear, they had a great many long conversations about it (usually at Camilla's instigation) and agreed over and over again that the success of their relationship was based on their total freedom, and the lack of anything in it that smacked of obligation. Camilla was always at even greater pains to assure him and herself that this was precisely what she wanted; she liked him, she told him earnestly, and more than that, she was very fond of him, they had a superb working relationship and an equally superb sex life, they shared many other pleasures and interests, riding, design, fashion, and it would have been very foolish, very foolish indeed to have introduced any form of long-term commitment into what was a totally pleasurable and undemanding arrangement. But the fact remained that in the middle of the night, when the secret self was asserting itself and having its rather obstreperous say, Camilla knew much of this was quite untrue. She was indeed very fond of Julian, very very fond, and if she had been caught unawares and asked directly if she loved him she would have said yes. More importantly than that, there was a lot about him that she didn't actually like very much, and particularly in the work situation. She found his ruthlessness with people, the way he used them and discarded them, very hard to accept: he would take an idea from someone and claim the credit for himself if it succeeded and make sure that everyone knew whence it came if it failed; and she found his deviousness almost intolerable. He had what amounted to a near compulsion to confuse people, to inform the creative team of some part of his plans and the sales team another, so that only he could bring the whole together. It caused uncertainty, ill feeling and mistrust among his staff; but what it did do was ensure his continuing indispensability, it kept him totally in control. Camilla saw through this, and despised it; she even challenged him on it. But he had a great talent for turning away criticism and disapproval; he would smile at her and tell her she was far too astute for her own good, that if there was one person in the entire company apart from himself who he could trust to know everything it was her, and although she knew this to be untrue she was quite unable to prove it.

Then there was their sex life; Camilla continued to try very hard to enjoy sex, and to improve her performance constantly for Julian; she never refused him if he wanted to go to bed with her, and she always told him afterwards that it had been absolutely wonderful. She hardly ever had an orgasm, or even came near it (although she became adept at faking); her sex therapist told her it was because she would not release her emotions, that she was afraid of her body taking her over, and gave her all sorts of exercises to do, both physical and mental, but it didn't do any good. Fearing that it might be Julian's fault and that they were incompatible, she took another lover from time to time, but it was no better, worse if anything; so then she was left fearing she must be frigid, which was worse still.

She knew what an orgasm felt like because her therapist had taught her to achieve it herself, but even that seemed to her a purely mechanical pleasure, rather like having a drink of water when she was very thirsty, or scratching an itch, it never approached the glorious abandon and heights that she read of and indeed which Julian seemed to experience when they were in bed together.

She had moved in 1963 from her apartment in the Village and had bought a studio in the upper Seventies; near enough Sutton Place and Julian for convenience, not too near for either of them to feel stifled. She loved the area, the quieter, sunnier streets, the expensive shops, the wealth of museums and galleries, the smart restaurants, the pastry shops, the sidewalk cafes, the entire atmosphere so much more cosmopolitan and civilized than the roaring, grabbing street life of mid-town Manhattan.

Her position in the company was unchallenged, and the most envious, the most malicious person could not but have acknowledged it had been earned, that her success was not dependent on her relationship with the chairman. After Circe's launch, Julian made her design director of the company (stores division); when he opened another Circe in Paris in 1961 he put her on the main board. Two years after that he made her advertising director as well, and creative director of the company worldwide; this meant she had to spend several months of the year in London as well. She bought a tiny flat in The Boltons, and shared her life with Julian exactly as she did in New York; undemandingly, charmingly and affectionately. But she was very clearly, as even Letitia (who loathed her) acknowledged, in London to work and not as his mistress.

She was brilliant, innovative and (most unusually) had a shrewd commercial sense as well; she never put forward a proposal for a new line, a relaunch, an advertising campaign without costing it out very carefully, without examining it in all its aspects, and she was equally clever at recognizing the virtue of an idea, a scheme, a suggestion from someone else; she knew how to delegate and she knew how to lead and inspire. She was an invaluable asset. And Julian needed her, very badly.

Circe had been a huge, a breathtaking success; it stood, a glittering jewel, in the very top echelons of the world's stores; it did not so much rank with Bonwit's, Bergdorf's and Saks in New York, Fortnum and Liberty in London, it had a glamour and style above and beyond all of them, for it had exclusivity, a sense of intimacy that set it closer to the smaller, more specialist establishments, to Gucci, Hermes, the Dior boutiques.

The Paris Circe, opened two years after New York, stood on

the Faubourg St Honoré, very similar in feel, a building that had, in living memory, been a house.

But it was the cosmetic company itself which was still at the heart of the Morell empire; and it needed ever more intense attention. Competition in the industry was getting increasingly ferocious in the sixties: Charles Revson was probably at the height of his creative and innovative skills, launching new colours with the brilliance and panache of an impresario: the show was a non-stop extravaganza with one brilliant promotion staged after another: six, eight brilliant launches a year, all with dazzling, emotive, pulsey names. The man who gave the world Fire and Ice, Stormy Pink, Cherries in the Snow was setting a formidable standard; he was also innovative with his products, there was powder blusher, frosted nail enamel, 'wet-look' lipsticks and above all a mood of constant excitement and innovation. Then there was Mrs Lauder, rocking the cosmetic world with her high-priced and exclusive range: Re-Nutriv Crême and Extract with its twenty secret ingredients, selling for the awe-inspiring sum of one hundred and fifteen dollars a jar.

The cosmetic industry was discovering science in a big way: Helena Rubinstein had launched a 'deep pore' bio facial treatment; Elizabeth Arden had Crême Extraordinaire 'protecting and redirecting'; Biotherm had incorporated plankton 'tiny primal organisms' for the skin in their creams.

It was a challenging time in the industry and nobody could afford to rest on their laurels, however exquisitely coloured and beautifully perfumed the leaves. Julian responded with a range from Juliana called Epidermelle which offered a new complex cream containing placental extract for its 'cell revival programme' and fought back on the colour front with a series of promotions based on the concept of the new frenetic fashion of the sixties – his range of first mini and then micro-mini colours, pale, pale, transparent lipsticks, and ultra pearlized eye shadows sold out in days and his eye wardrobe, the collection of false eyelashes, thick and thin, upper and lower, launched to adorn the little-girl wide-eyed faces of the sixties dolly birds, with their waist-length hair and their waist-high legs, was the sensation of the cosmetic year in 1965.

Nevertheless, Letitia's prophecy that Julian would need to

find more and more brilliant chemists had indeed come to pass. He had actually hired not one but three; each overseeing their own branch of a large development team: two American, one French, and the rivalry between them was intense (each having deliberately been given the impression that the others were just slightly more brilliant, talented and experienced) and a great spur to creative activity. He had opened a large new laboratory in New Jersey, and greatly expanded the one in England, having moved to new premises in Slough with Sarsted in charge.

However, most of the major cosmetic concepts for Juliana came from none of the chemists but from Julian himself. They were the result of several things: his extraordinarily astute understanding of women and what they wanted; his endlessly fertile mind; and a capacity above all to think laterally about what were apparently small and unimportant incidents.

He was sitting with Camilla in the New York office over a working lunch one day, discussing the decor of the salons in the Paris store, when Camilla said she would go and get some mineral water to drink. She stood up, looking in the mirror on Julian's wall as she did so.

'Oh, I look awful,' she said. 'This colour has changed on me so badly, the formula just doesn't suit me, the lipstick has gone really dark. I look ten years older.'

'I hope it's not one of ours,' said Julian absently; then he suddenly froze, staring at Camilla with an expression of intense excitement. 'Good God,' he said. 'Dear Christ. God in heaven. Shelley!' he shouted at his secretary down the intercom, 'get me Tom Duchinsky in the lab right away.'

'Good God,' said Camilla, half amused, half startled. 'Do I really look so awful?'

'No, Camilla, you look wonderful. Wonderful. As always. Listen, listen – oh, Tom, is that you? Tom, listen to me. You know how lipsticks and eye colours – lipsticks particularly – change on the woman? Due to the acid content of her skin? Do you think you could formulate some quite basic colours that could make a virtue of that fact? That were sufficiently neutral and formulated so that they responded to the woman's chemistry. Developed on her? Do you see what I'm getting at?

You do? Good. I'd have fired you if you hadn't. What's that? Of course it hasn't been done. Well, it happens all the time, but it's a vice, not a virtue. I want to turn it into a product benefit. And for eye shadows as well. Listen, give it some thought. Camilla and I will be over there in an hour.'

'No we won't,' said Camilla crossly. 'Julian, I have work to do on the new advertising, I can't afford to spend the afternoon in New Jersey.'

'Rubbish,' said Julian. 'If it wasn't for all the new products, you wouldn't have anything to advertise. Come on, I'll drive us. In the Cord. You know you can't resist that.'

'Of course I can,' said Camilla, crosser still. She found Julian's endless preoccupation with cars intensely irritating, and was constantly telling him he would have been far better off with a perfectly ordinary limo and a chauffeur rather than insisting on driving himself round the streets of New York and London in the various exotic vehicles he fell in love with. The white thirties supercharged Cord was his latest piece of folly, as she saw it, with its monster curving mudguards and very long bonnet, set in front of a modestly shaped body; Julian told her as they pulled out from the garage built beneath Circe that he loved it more than anything in the world, with the possible exception of his new brood mare. Camilla was never quite sure whether this kind of remark was made as a joke or not; but there were times, and today was one of them, when she found it very hard indeed to smile.

Later that year they took a trip to Florida, and stayed in Key West; it was the first time he had suggested they vacationed together and Camilla saw it as important to their relationship. Lying in bed on the third humid night, she was dutifully struggling to arouse the energy to respond to Julian and his protestations of desire when he drew back and looked at her.

'What's the matter,' he said, half amused, 'don't I excite you any more?'

'Of course you do,' she said, 'it's just so very very hot. Let me go and take a shower, and revive myself.'

She went and stood in the tepid water for a long time, doing some of the mental relaxation exercises her therapist had taught her, breathing deeply and emptying her mind, and some of the physical ones too, earnestly clenching and unclenching her vaginal muscles, hoping to find in herself some semblance of desire. She had her eyes closed; she suddenly heard the shower curtains part, and saw Julian looking at her with an expression of great amusement.

'What on earth are you doing?' he said. 'If I didn't know you better, I would say you were up to all kinds of solitary vices in here.'

'Certainly not,' said Camilla, nearly in tears at being caught in such foolishness, 'I'm just trying to relax, that's all.'

'Well, you had an expression of great concentration on your face. Not relaxed at all. Come on, darling, let me dry you down, and make you feel really good.'

He wrapped her in a huge towel and led her to the bed, and massaged her gently through it; then he removed it and took up her body oil and began to massage it into her breasts, her stomach, her thighs.

'Nice?'

'Lovely,' said Camilla firmly, closing her eyes, forcing her mind back on to her relaxation therapy, saying, pleasure pleasure pleasure over and over again silently, like a mantra.

'You feel better. Softer . . . This oil doesn't smell very good,' he said suddenly, 'funny, how perfumes seem to change in bed, in this kind –' he bent and kissed her breasts – 'this kind of situation. I wonder – Good God, yes, I wonder . . .'

'What, Julian? What do you wonder?'

'Oh, nothing. Nothing worth talking about now.'

'Tell me,' said Camilla, who would have thought anything at all worth talking about then.

'No, really nothing. All I want to do now is just take you over and love you until it's light again.'

Camilla yawned and then hastily stifled the sound, hoping he would think it was a sigh of passion. It just all sounded terribly exhausting.

Signature Colours, the dazzling new range of lipsticks and eye shadows that were designed personally to suit every woman, to adjust to her own individual chemistry, and the new Juliana fragrance Affair, spearhead of an important new element in the Juliana range, were both great successes financially and creatively, launched simultaneously in the spring of 1966 in New York and London. Affair was one of the new all-over fragrance concepts, designed to flatter and adorn the entire body. There was a bath oil, a shower gel, a body lotion, the usual battery of perfume concentrates, and eau de toilettes; and a new product altogether, a body fragrance for the night. 'Night-Time Affair', it said on the packaging, 'to be stroked and massaged into the skin, last thing at night, to surround a woman and her body with the lingering sensuous echoes of Affair until morning.' The implications were very clear.

Mick diMaggio produced an advertisement that was so near to being an explicit piece of soft porn – a woman's body, a man's hand, and a bottle of Night-Time Affair fallen on to the rumpled sheet beside them – that two publications (although assuredly not *Vogue* and *Harpers Bazaar* who both adored it) refused to run it; in its first week Night-Time Affair sold out in every store in New York.

Sometimes Camilla North wondered if there was any aspect of her life with Julian Morell that would not become a product.

When Roz was ten years old her parents decided to send her to boarding school. This was partly because they both felt she needed the discipline and stability it could provide and partly because neither of them was prepared to try and provide it at home. Julian was riding on the crest of wave after wave; dizzy, exalted with his own success, jetting from London to New York and back again almost weekly; he was investigating the possibility of launching Circe in Madrid and Nice, he was exploring hotels, he was investigating a chain of health farms, and he had no time at all to spare for an awkward little girl who was more demanding than all his business interests put together. Had she been more attractive, more appealing, he might have taken her with him sometimes, but she was still a large child, solemn, heavy featured; Eliza worked hard on her wardrobe and her hair, but she never looked pretty as so many of her friends did, and her manner was not appealing either, she was truculent and argumentative and she made no attempt to talk to people if she did not like them.

Eliza was also extremely busy, having a great many well-documented affairs both with members of the British aristocracy and the cosmopolitan set: with the twin aims of having a good time and finding a husband. She was achieving the first, although not the second; the English aristocrats, while delighted to enjoy her favours in their beds, did not really wish to marry the twice divorced Mrs Thetford, and the cosmopolitan set, while appreciating her beauty and her style, found her in the last resort too English, she lacked their sybaritic indolence, the absolute devotion to the pursuit of pleasure that they required of her. Nevertheless, her days and her energies were extremely occupied; like Julian, there was no place in them for a daughter who did her very little credit. Boarding school, it was agreed, was the best place for Roz. It fell to Julian to tell her.

'Mummy and I think,' he said to her, over lunch one day at the Ritz (it had become a ritual at the start of each school holidays that he took her there), 'that you should go to boarding school.'

Roz dropped her knife on the floor, panic rising in her throat. 'I don't want to go to boarding school,' she said firmly, anxious not to allow him to see how frightened she was. 'I like being at home.'

'Well, darling, you might like it, but we think it would be better for you to go away. You'll like that even better.'

'I won't. Why ever should I?'

'Well, because you're all on your own, it isn't as if you have any brothers and sisters and Nanny really is getting very old and she can't stay looking after you for ever, and Mummy and I worry about you being lonely.'

'And since when,' said Roz rudely, 'did you and Mummy decide things together for me? I'd have thought you'd want to do the opposite of what Mummy thought.'

'Rosamund, don't be rude,' said Julian briskly. He only ever called her Rosamund when he was very cross with her.

'I don't see,' said Roz, determined not to be frightened away from her position, 'why I shouldn't be rude. You seem to want to get rid of me. Why should I be polite about it?'

'Darling, we don't want to get rid of you. We think you'd like it.'

'No you don't. You don't know what I'd like. You don't spend enough time with me to find out. And you do want to get rid of me, so you can go to New York whenever you want, and out to dinner all the time, and Mummy can go rushing off to France and things with her boyfriends, and have them to stay without having to worry about me being rude to them. You both want to get rid of me. I know you do.'

'Darling,' said Julian patiently, choosing to ignore her attack rather than defend himself against it, 'you're wrong. We love you very much. But going to boarding school is what an awful lot of girls your age do. Isn't Rosie going?'

'I don't know. I don't think so. She wants to go to St Paul's. And so do I.'

'You don't know anything about it.'

She could see he was beginning to lose his temper. She enjoyed that, urging him nearer and nearer the edge. When he pushed his hair back, she knew she was nearly there. She gave a final shove. 'Anyway, I'm not going just to please you.'

She watched his lips go rather tight and white round the edges. She had done it. But he still didn't say anything really angry. 'Well, what you're going to do, Roz, is take your Common Entrance next January and we'll go and look at a few schools.'

'I'm not going.'

'Rosamund,' said Julian, 'you will do what you're told.'

'No,' she said. 'I won't.'

She sat in the Common Entrance examination and didn't write a word. The headmistress sent for both her parents: her father came and took her home with him. She had never seen him so angry.

'I hope you don't imagine,' he said, 'that you are going to get your own way in this. All this sort of behaviour does is convince me you are grossly spoilt and you need the discipline of boarding school.'

Roz shrugged. 'You've spoilt me. It's not my fault.'

'No,' he said. 'No, you're right, it isn't. None of it is. But I am not going to allow you to ruin your life because we have been stupid enough to do it for you so far. You are going to boarding school, Roz, and that is the end of it. Had you behaved more reasonably I might have considered day school. Now it's out of the question.'

'No one will take me. Not now I haven't done the exam.'

'Oh, but they will. Your headmistress says you are an extremely clever child, and she is personally writing to the heads of the schools we have chosen for you, with some examples of your work, and you will sit the individual entrance exams.'

'I won't do them either.'

'Yes, Rosamund, you will. Otherwise you will go to a school that doesn't require any kind of exam. The sort that exists to help difficult children like you.'

'I'll run away.'

'Do. You'll be taken back.'

Suddenly she stopped being brave, allowed the tears to flow, and once the tears started, the screams followed, the ones she had been silencing for years and years; her father looked at her in horror for a moment then stepped forward and slapped her hard across the face. It hurt horribly; she hit him back.

'I hate you. I hate you all. You and Mummy and Thetford and Camilla. You all hate me. You want to be rid of me. Send me away so I don't interfere in your own precious lives. So you can all do what you like and Mummy and her boyfriends and you and Camilla can – can have – have – ' 'intercourse' she had been going to say, but her courage failed her, and she stood silent, white, her eyes huge, tears streaming down her face, sobs shaking her body.

Her father stepped forward and took her in his arms, and held her close for a long time, soothing her, stroking her, kissing her hair, telling her it was all right, that he loved her, that they all loved her, that they didn't want to send her away, that it was for her own good, they thought she was lonely and unhappy and getting more so.

She didn't believe him, she couldn't remember when she had last believed anyone, when they told her such things; and she didn't argue any more or say the reason she was lonely and unhappy was because they had no time for her; but she could see she was beaten. Slowly, very slowly she stopped crying.

He held her away from him, looked down at her, wiped her eyes on his hanky.

'Better?'

She nodded.

'Good girl. I'm sorry, I'm so terribly terribly sorry, Roz, that we've hurt you so much. We didn't mean to.'

'Didn't you?' she said.

'No. You have to believe me.'

She had learnt that when her father said that he was invariably lying; she pulled herself out of his arms and went over to the window. She couldn't ever remember feeling so bad. She wondered how they could possibly go on and on being so cruel to her. It was interesting that her father at least realized it.

She suddenly remembered a request she had been storing up for several weeks. This was clearly a good time.

'Daddy,' she said, 'can I have a new horse? A hunter?'

'Of course you can,' he said. 'We'll go to some sales this holidays.'

Once again she had been bought off.

They decided on Cheltenham Ladies' College for her; Roz loathed it. She loathed everything about it from the very first day; the awful dreary green uniform, the way they were all scattered round the town in houses, and marched through it in crocodiles, the endless games, the misery of communal bathing and dressing, the aching horror of homesickness, the hearty jolly staff, the way everyone acted as if they were terribly lucky to be there, the awful food and most of all the feeling of dreadful isolation from the real world. She wasn't popular because she didn't conform; she wasn't friendly and jolly and eager to get on with, she was aloof and patently miserable and refused to join any clubs or societies or even do any extra lessons. She did what she was required to do; she went there and she stayed there and she worked very hard, because it was the only thing that seemed to make it bearable, and she was always top or nearly top of everything, but beyond that she wouldn't cooperate. She would go, but she was not going to be happy. That was asking too much.

Camilla had interceded on Roz's behalf over the matter of boarding school; she told Julian that if there was one thing a rejected child didn't need it was to be sent away from the rejecting parents and that she should be allowed to stay at home and go to day school; Julian told her that he wished she would keep her damn fool psychology to herself. Camilla had an uneasy feeling she had probably made poor Roz more and not less likely to be sent away.

After Roz had actually started at Cheltenham her hostility to Camilla became greater. She was illogically afraid that in her absence they might suddenly decide they were able to get married and have a baby.

Camilla, sensing at least some of this, decided she should talk to Roz, bring some of her fears into the open (knowing that honesty and openness were crucial in these matters). She felt that if Roz realized there was no likelihood of her ever marrying her father, she would be more friendly, and open up a little, come out of her hostile little shell. During the Christmas holidays, when Camilla was in London, working over and anglicizing the advertising campaign, she invited Roz to tea with her and told her she would like to hear about her new school. She made little progress; Roz sat in a sullen silence, pushing her teacake round her plate in a manner very reminiscent of her father. Camilla suddenly took a deep breath and said, 'Roz dear, there's something I would like to discuss with you.'

'What?' said Roz rudely.

'Well, I have always imagined that you felt rather as if I was trying to come between you and your father.'

'No,' said Roz, 'not at all. Nobody could do that.'

'Well perhaps not come between you. But that you thought that if I was going to marry your father, then I might be – well – a threat.'

Roz was silent.

'Well, the thing is, dear, that I have no intention of marrying him. Not because I am not very fond of him, but because neither of us really wants that kind of commitment.'

'Why not? Isn't he good enough for you?'

'Of course he is. Too good in lots of ways. But you see, some women, and I am one, feel that there is much more to our lives than marriage. We are people in our own right, we may want to have relationships with people, but we don't want those relationships to take our lives over. We want other things. My career has always been terribly important to me, and I would never combine it with marriage, I would feel I had to neglect either the career or the husband. That doesn't mean, of course, that we can't feel very lovingly towards people and enjoy their company. So you see, Roz, there is absolutely no danger of my ever becoming your stepmother, and moving into your home on a permanent basis. I thought that might make you feel more friendly towards me.'

Roz's sullen, pinched face told Camilla that friendship was not forthcoming.

The other large thorn in Camilla's side at this time was Letitia. Camilla loathed Letitia. Whenever she allowed herself to consider, however briefly, whether she might, after all, like to be the second Mrs Julian Morell, she reflected upon the reality of becoming Letitia's daughter-in-law and quite literally shuddered.

She loathed Letitia on two counts: personal and professional. She found it quite extraordinary that this old lady (Letitia was now sixty-nine) should still hold a position of considerable power in the company, and she could not help but feel that Julian was being less than professionally fastidious to allow it. Although Letitia was no longer involved on a day-to-day basis, having retired with a stupendously extravagant party at the age of sixty-five, at which she had danced the Charleston into the small hours at the Savoy, she was still a director of the company, with a most formidable grasp of its workings, a sure steady instinct for financial complexities, and an equally strong feeling for the cosmetic industry in general. The new financial director, Freddy Branksome, said that the day he was no longer able to consult her on company matters, he would take an early pension and go; to an extent he was being diplomatic, but the fact remained that he did give considerable credence to her views, and liked to have her at all major financial review meetings. Camilla found this incomprehensible, and was perfectly certain that both Julian and Freddy must simply be flattering a vain and difficult old lady. It simply did not make sense so far as she could see, that a woman with no formal education, no training in business affairs or company management, could possibly be of any value to a multi-million-pound company. She had tried to say as much to Julian, but he had become extremely angry, told her to keep her business-school nonsense to herself, and that Letitia had more nous and flair in her little finger than the entire staff of the Harvard Business School.

'When I need your opinion on company structure, Camilla, I will ask for it. Otherwise I would be intensely grateful if you would keep your elegant nose out of things which have nothing whatever to do with you.'

Camilla had said nothing more. She never minded when Julian attacked her views on management and policy. She knew perfectly well his touchiness on the subject and his suspicion of any formal scientific approach sprang from insecurity, but she did think it was a pity he refused to study modern business theory with a sightly more open mind. She supposed it all came from the well-known English passion for the amateur; in time, no doubt, Julian would come to see his methods were simply not professional enough for the hugely competitive business environment of the sixties.

But if she found Letitia's professional relationship with Julian difficult to cope with, his personal one was almost impossible. He seemed to regard her more as a mistress than a mother; whenever he got back to London he seemed more eager to see Letitia even than his daughter ('I am,' he said cheerfully, when she taxed him with this quite early on in their relationship, 'she's better tempered.') And would take her out to dinner, to lunch, and quite often away for the weekend, down to Marriotts, leaving Camilla (should she have accompanied him on a trip) fuming alone in London, rather than face the disagreeable prospect of spending forty-eight hours alone with them, listening to their silly jokes, their convoluted conversations, their detailed accounts of how each of them had spent the intervening few weeks. She knew Letitia found her tiresome; what enraged her was that she made so little effort to disguise the fact.

Camilla had tried terribly hard at first, she had been courteous, patient and polite; she had talked about Julian at great length (knowing this to be the key to a mother's heart), she had been very careful not to imply any suggestion that she might be trying to encroach on their relationship in any way; and she had made it as clear as she could, without being actually rude or crass, that she had no intention of marrying Julian, that she saw herself purely as a professional colleague.

On her trip to London in the summer of 1967 she decided once again to try to form an adult, working relationship with Letitia; she phoned her and invited her to lunch at the Savoy, which she knew was her favourite place. But Letitia said no, she was on a strict diet and why didn't they meet in the Juliana salon, for a fruit juice and a salad; Camilla, always grateful to be able to avoid gastronomic temptation and for an opportunity to indulge her body in some therapy or another, agreed and booked herself into the salon for a massage and a sauna for the hour before lunch.

She was now thirty, and against the atmosphere of frenetic pursuit of youth that was taking place in that year, she felt old. London was full of girls who looked just past their seventeenth birthdays, with silky straight hair tumbling down their backs, bambi-wide eyes, and skirts that just skimmed their bottoms. Jean Shrimpton's face, photographed by David Bailey, gazed with a sexy tenderness from every magazine cover, every hoarding; Marianne Faithfull, Sandie Shaw, Cathy McGowan lookalikes stalked the streets, rangy, self-confident; and through the open window of every car in the capital the Beatles and the Stones sang 'Yesterday' and 'Ruby Tuesday' and 'Penny Lane'. It was no time to be over twenty-five.

Camilla sank gratefully on to the massage couch, accepted the sycophantic exclamations over her slenderness from the beauty therapist, and then feeling just pleasantly traumatized from the massage and the attentions of the G5 machine to her buttocks, walked into the sauna, removed her towel and lay flat on her back with her eyes closed.

She was feeling just slightly sleepy when the door opened; Letitia's voice greeting her made her sit up startled, looking frantically round for her towel, and in its absence, wrap her arms round her breasts. Quite why she didn't want Letitia to see her naked she wasn't sure; but it seemed in some way an intrusion into her relationship with Julian; she felt Letitia was not looking merely at her body, but at what it might offer her son, and that she would find the sight immensely interesting; and she didn't like the feeling at all. Letitia was dressed in a towelling robe, with a turban wrapped round her head; she did not remove either, merely sat down on the wooden seat opposite Camilla and smiled at her graciously, her eyes skimming amusedly and slightly contemptuously over her body. Camilla, with a great effort of will, removed her arms and met Letitia's eyes.

'Good morning, Letitia,' she said. 'How nice to see you. I am so looking forward to our lunch.'

'I too,' said Letitia. 'And now we shall have even longer together. How well you look, Camilla.' And her gaze rested again, lingering, interestedly on Camilla's breasts and travelled down towards her stomach and her pubic hair.

Camilla swallowed hard, closed her eyes, did a relaxation exercise briefly, and said, 'Maybe I should go and get dressed, Letitia, I've been here ages already.'

'Really?' said Letitia. 'They must have been mistaken, they told me you had only just arrived. Don't mind me, dear, I have plenty to think about, just relax.'

'Well,' said Camilla, 'perhaps I will stay a little longer. Have you been shopping, Letitia?' she added in a desperate attempt to get the conversation on to a comfortingly mundane level.

'No, dear. I don't often shop these days. The shops come to me. No, I've been to see Julian. To discuss next year's budgets and so on. So nice the company is doing so extremely well, don't you think?'

'Marvellous,' said Camilla.

'Such a clever man, my son, isn't he?'

'Very clever.'

'And you, Camilla, you have done a great deal for the company. I hope he gives you sufficient credit for it.'

'Oh yes,' said Camilla, startled by this sudden rush of friendliness and the unexpected tribute, 'yes, he does.'

'Good. You are unusually fortunate in that case. And in other cases as well, of course.'

'Er – yes.'

'You seem to enjoy a very special relationship with Julian.' Her gaze again travelled down to Camilla's breasts. Camilla made a superhuman effort not to cover them up again.

'Well, yes. Well, that is to say – I thought . . .'

'Yes, my dear?' Letitia's voice was treacly sweet.

'Well, that was one of the things I wanted to talk to you about.'

'Really? What exactly do you mean?' A wasp was buzzing languidly now near the treacly tones.

'Well, you know, Mrs Morell, I have always hoped we could be friends. But I imagined you thought that I might be in some way becoming very involved with Julian personally, and that you might find that difficult to handle.'

'What a strange expression,' said Letitia sweetly. 'No, I don't think so, Camilla dear, I very rarely find things difficult to handle, as you put it. It is one of the advantages of growing older, I suppose. Now what exactly do you mean? That I would be jealous of you?' And her gaze flicked down again.

'Oh, no, of course not,' said Camilla earnestly, 'and that is exactly what I want you to understand. There is nothing to be jealous of, in that my relationship with Julian is really very much more professional than personal. I see him primarily as a colleague, an employer, rather than a man.'

Letitia leant forward, an expression of acute puzzlement on her face. 'Camilla, are you trying to tell me that you do not find my son sexually attractive?'

Camilla was so shocked that she did something she had not done for years, and blushed; furious with herself, desperate to escape from the claustrophobia of the sauna and Letitia's amused, insolent eyes, she stood up and reached for the towel which had fallen on the floor, bracing herself for the full frontal confrontation.

'How thin you are, dear. Perhaps you should eat a little more. Now I can assure you,' the silvery, flute-like voice went on, 'you are very much alone, if that *is* the case. Most women can't wait to get into bed with him.'

Camilla rallied. 'I do find him attractive,' she said, wrapping herself thankfully in her towel, 'but I happen to think that some relationships can transcend the physical.'

'Balls,' said Letitia. She smiled at Camilla sweetly.

'I beg your pardon?'

'I said "balls", dear. An old Anglo-Saxon expression. It means rubbish. Balderdash. Poppycock. Oh dear, you won't know what those words mean either. Your country's vernacular is, if I may say so, extremely limited.'

'I do understand you, Mrs Morell. But I really can't agree with you.'

'Really? Then what do you do when you are over here, staying at my son's house? Talk to him all night long? Hold animated discussions about sales psychology and corporate identity, and the design ethic, and all those other things you take so seriously over there? I find that very hard to believe.'

Camilla struggled not to lose her temper.

'No. Of course we have a – a physical relationship.'

'I see. But you don't enjoy it. Is that what you are trying to say?'

Camilla flushed again; she pulled her towel more closely round her.

'No. It's not what I am trying to say.'

'Then try harder, my dear. I am only a very simple old woman. I can't quite follow your articulate Americanisms.'

'What I am trying to say,' said Camilla, 'is that although I do, since you force me to express it, enjoy my personal – physical – relationship with Julian, what is really important to me is our professional one. I can't imagine my life without that. However much I might admire and enjoy him as a person.'

'I see,' said Letitia, 'how very interesting.'

'Why is it so particularly interesting?' asked Camilla boldly.

'Well, dear, forgive me, but it seems to smack of using him to me. Of using your considerable feminine charms to inveigle him into employing you in his company.'

'Not at all. I worked for Julian for quite a long time before we – I – he –'

'Had sexual intercourse with you? How charming,' said Letitia.

Camilla had had enough. 'Mrs Morell, forgive me, but I am finding this a little embarrassing. Perhaps you would excuse me, I have a lot of work to do.'

'Oh, my dear, I am so sorry!' cried Letitia, an expression of great distress on her face. 'How thoughtless of me. Of course I have no right to talk to you like this. It is absolutely no business of mine. It's just that Eliza and I were so very close, still are, and I find it hard to be formal when I talk about my son. Now, why don't we both get dressed and move out to the juice bar and you can tell me exactly which aspect of the company you are currently engaged in, to keep you so busy, and over here so much.'

'Well,' said Camilla carefully, determined not to lose her temper. 'As you may not know, Julian has put me in overall charge of the advertising, both here and in New York. Not the creative concept, of course, although he likes me to be heavily involved in that, but I have a major responsibility, reporting only to him, on campaign planning, budgets, media schedules, and of course, overseeing the advertising, in all its aspects here. The campaigns don't alter very much, but they need to be carefully anglicized, and we are always ready to consider creative concepts this end. So I have a lot to do this week. I – we – have also to get to know the people at the new agency, and see how we are going to work with them.'

'I see,' said Letitia thoughtfully. 'Tell me, is Julian no longer able to afford to employ an advertising manager in New York?'

Camilla looked at her, her eyes wary.

'Of course there is an advertising manager. But he reports to me. He is not on the main board. I'm surprised you didn't realize that, Mrs Morell. But I suppose Julian finds it difficult to keep you informed on every detail of the company these days. It must be so different from the old days when he ran it virtually single handed, and you helped him.'

Letitia stood up and smiled at Camilla graciously. 'He did not run it single handed, my dear, and I did not help him. We did it together. It could not have survived any other way.' She looked at Camilla and then suddenly raised a limp hand to her head. 'I am so sorry, but I very much fear I may have to cancel our luncheon after all. I have a very severe migraine coming on. The only thing is simply to get home and lie down in a darkened room. Do forgive me.'

'Of course,' said Camilla, relief and rage struggling with each other, 'can I get my driver to take you home?'

'Oh, no, dear, mine is waiting. He's been with me for years, you know. Ever since the company began. So loyal, all my staff. Goodbye, Camilla, I think I'll just get dressed again and hurry off. I do hope you will find someone else to join you. I don't suppose you have managed to find many friends in London, as you are so dreadfully overworked.'

Talking to Eliza that evening over dinner, regaling her most wickedly with every lurid detail of the encounter, Letitia said, 'I do hope for all our sakes, Eliza, he never does marry that dreadful creature. Our lives will become a great deal less agreeable if he does.'

The Connection Four

Los Angeles, 1968

Lee looked at Dean across the breakfast table and wondered for the hundredth, possibly the thousandth time, what she could possibly do to make him eat less. He was, at forty-two, seriously overweight: the last time she had managed to get a look at the scales when he had been on them they had lurched up to two hundred and forty pounds; that was an awful lot for a man who only stood five foot ten in his socks. It wasn't just that he looked – well, certainly not the most attractive man she had ever seen, his shirts straining desperately round his huge belly, his trousers slung awkwardly and uncomfortably beneath it ('You'll need them specially made soon' she had said tartly, the last time they had been shopping for some together, 'Or some maternity ones, like I used to wear with an elastic panel in the front'). She felt his weight was a serious threat to his health, and had only last week tried to tell him so, and suggest he cut down on the hamburgers and the fries and the beer, but he had laughed easily, and slapped his gut with his soft, dimpled hand and said he and his belly were old friends, and he was damned if any diet was going to come between them.

'Well,' she said, 'if you get to grow any bigger, you won't have any other friends. You look terrible, Dean.'

'Miles,' he said to the little boy, who was sitting in the living room reading comics and munching his way through a bumper bag of potato chips, 'do you think I look terrible?'

'No, Dad,' said Miles without even looking up.

'There you are,' said Dean, 'two friends. Miles doesn't mind me being a little overweight, do you, son?'

'No, Dad.'

'Honey, you shouldn't worry so much about these things. It's that Amy Meredith with all her cranky nonsense about wholefood and not eating red meat, I never heard of such nonsense, man was meant to eat meat, he used to live on nothing else, a bison for breakfast on a good day, now you go tell Amy Meredith that.'

'Well, I will if you like,' said Lee, 'she won't want to hear it, but I will. And you're wrong anyway, man was a hunter-gatherer, he ate nuts and grains as well, and vegetables. And besides if we're going to get into all that stuff, when man was eating bison for breakfast, he was also going out and killing the bison, and getting quite a lot of exercise that way. The only thing you do to hunt your food is walk over to the refrigerator and open the door. Please, Dean, do at least think about a diet.'

'OK,' he said, grinning at her. 'I'll think about it. For five minutes every day. Before dinner. Now why don't you start worrying about something more sensible, like your own figure. You're skin and bone, honey. If anyone looks awful, you do.'

'Well thanks,' said Lee, giving up on the discussion, shooing Miles outside and turning her attention to sorting the laundry. 'But at least I won't be dying of a heart attack.'

'No, malnutrition. With all those goddamned dance and yoga classes you go to, you could eat twice as much as you do. I'd like it if you were a bit rounder, honey. Bit more to get hold of. And roll around in the hay with.'

Lee thought of his massive weight descending upon her in bed, and the way, these days, she had to lie on top of him if he wanted to make love to her, and looked thoughtfully at him. Maybe this was her chance.

'Dean, if you get to weigh any more at all you won't be able to roll around in the hay at all. And I certainly won't be rolling underneath you. So think about that.'

'Oh, hell, honey, we manage.'

'We don't, actually,' she said shortly, 'or rather you don't. Not very often. I mind about that, Dean.'

'Hey!' he said, beaming at her affectionately, 'what about that? Eighteen years we've been married, and my wife still wants to get me into the sack. You always were a bit of a hot pants, weren't you, honey?' He got out his handkerchief and wiped the sweat off his forehead. 'Jesus, it's hot. Aren't you hot, Lee?'

'Not terribly,' she said. 'You're feeling hot because you're so overweight. If I was lugging around two hundred pounds all day, I'd get hot. Now Dean, will you please, please think about a diet? Go see Doctor Forsythe if you don't believe me.'

'I might.'

But he didn't.

That particular morning Lee didn't in any case want to get involved in a discussion with Dean about his weight. She had a lot to do. It was nearly the end of the school year and there was Miles to get ready for summer camp; she and Amy had their ballet class, and then after that they had planned to go to the beach. Sometimes Lee wondered if there mightn't be more to life than going to ballet classes and going to the beach, she felt somehow she was missing out on the real world, but she couldn't see what she could do about it now, nobody was going to take on a forty-year-old housewife and give her a job, and besides there was Miles to take care of, he was still only ten, and she didn't believe in giving kids latch keys to let themselves into the house with after school, that was where the trouble started and they got in with a bad crowd.

She wondered, as she watched Miles get into the car beside Dean, to be dropped off at school, if the way she felt a lot of the time could be described as happy. It was all a bit monotone, without any highs, or even promises of highs in the far-off distance: just a long, level road stretching ahead. On the other hand, she certainly wasn't unhappy, she had most of what she had always wanted: a family at last (albeit only a small one), a nice house and peace of mind. She valued peace of mind very highly; the only thing that threatened it was when (increasingly rarely) she saw Hugo Dashwood.

Dean was still always delighted to see Hugo; he admired him and his English style hugely, and since he had discovered that Hugo had not after all made such a success of his business, had warmed to him still more. Dean had not made too much of a success of his business either; he got by, he had provided for his family and hung on to his job, even made chief district sales rep, but he wasn't exactly Henry Ford. It made him feel comfortable that someone with all Hugo Dashwood's obvious advantages should not do so well either. Anyway, Lee thought with some relief, there was no danger of Hugo coming for a bit yet; he had said he was spending the rest of the summer in England, and would contact them in what he called the autumn; she was safe for a while: safe from his probing eyes, his interest in her, his insistent friendliness, his ridiculously pressing attentions to Miles.

Miles at ten could not have been more of an all-American boy, she thought fondly; with his blond hair, his snub nose, his passion for the beach and for baseball, his hatred of anything that might smack of book-work. Nobody, nobody at all, could doubt for an instant that he was an all-American boy; in fact, why on earth did she have that thought so often, when there was no reason why they should?

Lee had managed by now to persuade herself that the relationship with Hugo had never happened; she had done this by every means she knew, from simply determinedly putting it out of her head, to (when that was not quite enough) using the meditation and visualization techniques she had learnt in her yoga classes. Most of the time she never even thought about it; it was dead, buried, like a person she might have met long ago; but every now and again, usually when she couldn't sleep, it would rise up inside her, the memories, the knowledge, and a suffocating stifling panic, and she would have to get up and get herself a cup of tea, and sit very still, in her yoga lotus position, willing herself into calm. And in the morning, when the sun was shining and Miles was playing in the yard and Dean was tucking into his double egg and bacon breakfast, grunting contentedly at her as she set it before him, she would be able to smile at her fears and wonder how had she ever worked herself into such a state, and tell herself that nothing could hurt her now.

Only she was wrong; and it could.

The phone was ringing as she and Amy got back to the house from the beach. 'Mrs Wilburn? This is the hospital. Casualty. We have your husband here.'

'Oh my God,' said Lee, clutching Amy's hand and dropping all her things, 'it's happened. Dean's had a heart attack.'

'No, no, Mrs Wilburn, it's all right. Nothing terribly serious. But could you get down here right away, please.'

'Of course,' said Lee, 'I'll be right there. Amy, will you drive me to the hospital? Dean's in Casualty.'

'Oh God,' said Amy. 'Oh, God. Lee, I told you he should go on a diet.'

'Shut up, Amy, for Christ's sake. I know, I know he should have gone on a diet. Did you ever try telling the sun to cool down? Anyway, he hasn't had a heart attack. I don't know what it is.'

'Whatever it is, his weight will exacerbate it,' said Amy. 'There is a constant strain on his heart and all that cholesterol he consumes will have totally damaged his arteries.'

'Amy, will you for God's sake stop giving me a lecture on health care, and get into the car. Oh, wait, Miles will be home soon. He doesn't have a key.'

'I'll come back and let Miles in, if you look like being a long time,' said Amy. 'Come on, let's go.'

'Oh, Amy,' said Lee, her voice trembling, 'what if he dies? What will I do? I'll feel so guilty. All those eggs. All that red meat. It'll be my fault.'

'He won't die,' said Amy firmly. 'Apart from anything else, Heaven couldn't hold him. Half the people already there would have to leave. They said it wasn't too serious. Hang on to that. Christ, I wish they'd do something about this traffic.'

Dean was lying in a room in Emergency when they got there. He looked pale and sweaty; a pretty nurse was taking his blood pressure.

'Hi,' said Lee, 'I'm Mrs Wilburn. They said to come on up.'

'Yes. That's right, Mrs Wilburn,' said the nurse. 'I'll go find the doctor. He said he wanted to see you.'

'How is he?' asked Lee, gently taking Dean's fat, moist hand in hers.

'Not too bad, I think. The doctor will be able to tell you, though.'

She disappeared. Lee kissed Dean's forehead. 'What happened, Hon?'

'I'm not sure. I was just leaving the diner, after my lunch, and suddenly I felt very sick and swimmy. Sweaty too. Next thing I knew I was lying on the floor of the diner, and then they brought me here.'

'What'd the doctor say to you?'

'Not a lot.'

'Does he think it's a heart attack?'

'No. That's what I thought, of course, but he said no it wasn't. He said he wanted to talk to you.'

'Oh, how do you feel?'

'So so. A bit shaky. A bit sick.'

A doctor walked into the cubicle.

'Mrs Wilburn?'

'Yes.'

'I'm Doctor Burgess. Could I have a word with you outside, please?'

'Yes, of course,' said Lee. She suddenly felt very sick herself. Amy was out in the corridor. 'Amy, could you possibly go and meet Miles, do you think? And maybe bring him back here?'

'Sure,' said Amy. 'Everything OK?'

'I think I'm just going to find out.'

'Well,' said the doctor, 'first of all, let me reassure you. He has not had a cardiac. But you're very lucky he didn't.'

'So what was it?'

'He's simply had a blackout. His blood pressure is phenomenally high. And it was no doubt increased by the beer he had for lunch and the heat, and I imagine stress of his job. Now that in itself is not very serious. He's fine now. But what you have to understand, Mrs Wilburn, is that if he goes on the way he is he will have a cardiac, and very soon. He is grossly overweight, his diet is frankly disastrous, and one more incident like this and I wouldn't like to answer for the consequences.'

'I see,' said Lee. She felt very small. 'Doctor, I have tried to make him diet. And exercise. But he won't.'

The doctor smiled at her. 'If I had a ten-dollar bill for every wife who has said that to me over the past five years I could retire right away up to the Hills. Mrs Wilburn, you have to make him. I think he'll be more cooperative now.'

'Yes,' said Lee, 'maybe for a while, but once the fright is past, he'll just relapse into his old bad ways.' She felt faint herself, suddenly. 'Could I sit down?'

'Of course. I'm sorry. Water?'

'No, it's OK.'

Doctor Burgess looked at her thoughtfully. 'You're very slim yourself. Very fit looking. You obviously know about what you should and shouldn't do.'

'I do, of course I do. And I am so careful with my little boy. But Dean – my husband – he just lives for his food.'

'Well,' said Doctor Burgess. 'He'll die for it if he isn't careful. What about exercise. Does he take any?'

'No.'

'None? Not even walk?'

'Least of all walk,' said Lee, and sighed.

'How long has he been this big?'

'This big for about five years. Always inclined to be that way.'

'I see. Does he suffer from stress?'

'Not too seriously. He takes life pretty much as it comes.'

'Well, that's something. Does he drink a lot?'

'Yes. A lot of beer.'

'Anything else?'

'Bourbon.'

'I see. Does he smoke?'

'Yes. But not too much. After dinner. After lunch.'

'How is his health generally?'

'Not too bad. He doesn't get colds and all that stuff.'

'Headaches?'

'Yes, a lot of headaches.'

'That's the blood pressure. How does he sleep?'

'Very well. Too well.'

'How's his libido?'

'I beg your pardon?'

'How often does he want to make love?'

'Oh,' said Lee, 'not very often.' She knew why he had asked that. Amy had told her that very overweight men often lost their sex drive.

'Do you have children?'

'Er – only one.'

'Was that deliberate?'

'Well – no. Not exactly. We – he – well, it never happened again.'

'Did either of you have any investigation into that?'

'Yes. A long time ago.'

'How long?'

258

'Before my – our little boy was born.'

She began to feel her midnight fears closing in on her, beginning to threaten her. 'Is that – relevant?'

'What? Oh, no, not really. Well it could be. Certainly the loss of libido. Now look, Mrs Wilburn, I think what I'm going to do is keep him in hospital overnight and then, providing he's OK in the morning, and the blood pressure is down, he can go home tomorrow. But he has to go on a very fierce diet, he must lose at least seventy pounds, and he must start taking some sensible exercise. Nothing too radical, just some steady walking would be ideal at first. Now I'm going to talk to him very seriously about his weight, impress upon him how crucial it is. I'll give you some diet sheets and I want to see him here in a week. And I'll talk to your family physician and explain the situation and make sure that he keeps an absolutely regular check on your husband. He should have his blood pressure and his heart rate taken every week at least. All right? Are *you* all right now?'

'Yes,' said Lee. 'Yes, thank you.'

But she wasn't. She was seriously frightened.

Dean embarked on his new regime with immense seriousness. He cut out alcohol, gave up smoking and almost stopped eating red meat and butter and fries. Once a week he allowed himself a steak. He said he had to have some pleasure left in his life. He went for a walk right around the neighbourhood every evening after dinner and even bought a dog, a roly poly golden retriever called Mr Brown, to keep him company.

Within one month he had lost fourteen pounds, his blood pressure was down and his headaches were improving. After two, he had lost twenty, his headaches had gone. He looked ten years younger and, he said to Lee one night in bed, he certainly felt it.

'I hate to admit this, Hon, but I think the old doc's probably right. He said I'd be feeling as randy as a young man again if I lost this weight, got myself back in shape, and I do. Come over here, and let me show you how much I love you.'

He was showing her how much he loved her quite often after that. If some hovering dread hadn't been permanently with her, Lee would have been pleased. As it was, she was fearful; and she didn't know why.

'You never know, Honey,' said Dean, rolling off her one night and kissing her contentedly, 'this whole thing may have been a blessing in disguise. We may manage to provide Miles with a little brother yet.'

'Oh, Dean, don't be silly,' said Lee quickly. 'What difference can losing a little weight make to your fertility?'

'Oh, you don't know, Honey, quite a lot. The doctor said obesity and high blood pressure could certainly affect your performance, and who knows but it might not affect that as well. He thought it perfectly possible.'

'Have you been – discussing – that with him?' asked Lee.

'I certainly have. Why not? He asked me if there was any aspect of my health that bothered me, and I said, two things: one, I didn't seem able to get it up any more – well, that's cured, isn't it – and the other, we had always had trouble conceiving children.'

'But Dean,' said Lee, feeling sweat cold on her forehead. 'You know that was my fault. Not yours. Doctor Forsythe always said . . .'

'Well, seems he might have been wrong,' said Dean. 'I don't know, of course, nobody does, but Doctor Burgess says it could be me. Anyway, it doesn't matter. Time will tell.'

'But Dean, I'm forty. Too old to have any more children. Even if – well, I could. And besides, Miles is ten. It wouldn't work.'

'Nonsense. My mother was forty-seven when I was born. Fit as a flea. And it would do Miles good. He's spoilt. No, I think we should let Nature take its course. I really like the idea of being a dad again.'

'I see,' said Lee quietly. She didn't sleep until dawn broke.

Three weeks later Dean came back from his check-up looking particularly cheerful. 'Lee, I've taken a decision today.'

'What's that?'

'I'm going to have some investigations done.'

'For heaven's sake what into?' said Lee irritably.

Dean looked at her sharply. 'What's the matter, Lee? You don't look too good. Now listen, we have to take care of you. Because I think we might well be able to be parents again.'

'Oh, Dean, no, not that again. Please.'

'Lee, why on earth not? You've loved having Miles. Why not another baby?'

'Dean, I don't want another baby. I'm forty. There are – risks.'

'I know, I know. But if Doctor Burgess says they weren't too serious, then how would you feel?'

'Miserable,' said Lee. She spoke without thinking.

'Honey, I just don't know what's come over you. I thought you'd be over the moon about all this.'

'About what? There's nothing to be over the moon about.'

'Well, there being a possibility that we could have more children.'

Lee looked at him wearily. 'Dean, it's a very remote possibility.'

'Not necessarily. Anyway Doctor Burgess is arranging for me to have a sperm count. That'll take us to first base. Then we can talk some more. You can't object to that, can you?'

'I suppose not,' said Lee listlessly. She felt extremely sick. Dread had settled itself heavily and comfortably on to her shoulders. Nothing would shift it now.

It was a week later when Dean arrived home at lunch time. Lee heard him shut the front door rather slowly and carefully. She was spraying the leaves of the plants in the living room; he walked in and sat down on the couch. He looked at her, his eyes blank, his face dragged, empty of any emotion.

'Dean, what is it? Whatever is the matter?'

'Oh,' he said, speaking rather slowly. 'I think you know really, don't you? You know what the matter is.'

'Dean, you're talking in riddles. Of course I don't.'

'I think you do. I had a sperm count three days ago. You know what the result is, of course?'

'Of course I don't. Don't be so ridiculous. Why should Doctor Burgess tell me? What did it say anyway? What was it?'

'Don't play games with me, Lee. You know what it was. It was nix, wasn't it? Zero. Negative. Zilcho. I have no sperms. Doctor Burgess said I was absolutely sterile.'

'Well, probably that was being so overweight – so unwell for so long.'

'Is that what you think?'

261

'What else can I think?'

'I'll tell you. You can think the truth. That I've always been sterile. That I could never have fathered a child. That's what Doctor Burgess said.'

'Well, clearly,' said Lee, 'Doctor Burgess doesn't know too much what he's talking about. What about Miles?'

'Yes, Lee, what about Miles?'

'What do you mean?'

'I mean who did father him?'

'Oh, don't be so ridiculous. You know perfectly well you fathered him. He looks just like you.'

'No, he doesn't. He looks just like you. Lucky that, wasn't it? Supposing he'd had red hair? Brown eyes?'

Lee shivered. 'Dean, this is ridiculous. I'm going to call Doctor Burgess. I just don't believe any doctor would have said you – any man – could never have fathered a child. Is that really what he said?'

Dean suddenly broke down, sobbing like a baby. 'No. Yes. Oh, I don't know. He said I was very very lucky I had managed to father a child. Because the sperm count was so low. I said what would he have said the chances were. He said he couldn't say. I said what was the count. He said I wouldn't understand. But that it was very low. He was clearly very embarrassed. Lee, I'm not a fool. I can see when I'm being lied to. Now will you for Christ's sake tell me who Miles' father is? Who you were fucking then. Who you've been fucking since. Come on, Lee, I need to know. We're not leaving this room until you tell me.'

Lee rallied. She took a deep breath, sat down on the couch beside him. 'I haven't been fucking anybody. Anybody at all. Not even you very often. Until just recently.'

She sounded bitter.

'Don't try to change the subject.'

'I'm not. It's the truth.'

'I don't believe you.'

'You don't have to.'

Dean's eyes suddenly filled with tears again. He gripped her small, thin hand with his huge one. It hurt. Lee winced.

'I do have to, though. I do have to believe you.'

'Well, for Christ's sake then, Dean, do believe me. Please. I'm telling you the truth. You are Miles' father.'

He looked at her for a long time. She did not falter.

Please, please God she thought, please let him believe me.

'I can't,' Dean said at last. 'I can't. I want to but I can't. Lee, you simply have to tell me. Who was it?'

Lee stood up abruptly. 'This is getting ridiculous. I'm going to fix you some lunch. Maybe you'll feel calmer then.'

'I don't want any lunch. Sit down.'

'No.'

'Lee, will you for fuck's sake sit down. Jesus, I swear to God I'll kill you if you don't tell me the truth.'

'Dean, I don't think I can stand this much longer.'

'*You* can't stand it.' He laughed shortly, a harsh, cracked sound. 'You can't stand it. That's rich. How sad for you. How painful. I am so sorry.'

He crossed to the bar and poured himself a huge slug of bourbon. Lee looked at it.

'Dean, you shouldn't be drinking that. You know you shouldn't.'

'Don't you tell me what I should do. You have absolutely *no* right. No right at all. I'll do what I like.'

'OK.' She shrugged. 'It's your funeral.'

She was to remember saying that for a long time.

They sat in silence, scarcely moving for nearly an hour. It was very hot in the living room; Dean wouldn't let her open a window. Most of the time they were silent; just sitting there. Dean drank; Lee watched him.

Every so often he would say, 'Who was it, Lee?'

'Nobody,' she would say. 'Nobody. Let me go.'

'No. You're staying here.'

Once she tried to walk out, but he stood in front of the door, barring her way. He was very drunk now, red in the face, sweating heavily. He had stopped crying, or even shouting at her; he was simply waiting, watching her, willing her to crack.

She asked him if she could go out to the toilet; he accompanied her, stood outside the door. Then they went back to the living room. It smelt, stale, sweaty, alcoholic. Lee began to feel ill. She sat down on the couch.

'Dean, I feel sick. Could you get me a glass of water?'

'Sure.' As he went out, he unplugged the phone, took the set

263

with him. When he came back he handed her the glass, tipped up her chin and looked down into her face.

'You may as well tell me. I'll get it out of you in the end.'

She drank the water. 'There's nothing to tell.'

'You're lying.'

'I'm not.'

It was exactly like all her nightmares.

At half past three Miles came home, banging on the door, calling out, 'Mom, Mom,' when she didn't answer.

She looked at Dean. 'You'll have to let him in.'

'OK.' He suddenly gripped her wrist, twisting it round. 'Now you just keep your goddamned mouth shut. Or I swear to God I'll tell him as well.'

He went out to the door. 'Oh, hi, Dad,' she heard Miles say, 'where's Mom?'

'She isn't too well. She's lying down upstairs. Listen, can you go play with someone for a bit?'

'Sure. I'll go to Freddy's. His mom's real nice. She'll understand. Can I take my bike?'

'Sure.'

'Bye, Dad.'

'Goodbye, Miles.'

He came back into the living room.

'You gonna tell me?'

'No.'

Suddenly he raised his fist and struck her across the face, she felt an explosion of searing aching pain across one eye, and tasted the sweet salty flavour of blood trickling from her mouth. For the first time she was seriously frightened.

If only, if only Amy would come, she thought, she would know, she would guess something was wrong. She would get help. But Amy was away staying with her mother.

'It's no use thinking I'm going to get tired,' he said. 'That I'll let you go. We're staying here till you tell me.' He looked at her shrewdly, thoughtfully, 'What was it like?' he said. 'Fucking someone else? Was it as good as doing it with me? Did you think about me?'

'Don't be a fool,' she said. 'Stop asking me these questions. I can't answer them. You know I can't.'

'Oh, no,' he said, 'you're wrong. I know you can. What was it like, Lee? Was his dick bigger than mine? Did you come? How many times? You always were a sexpot.' He poured himself another glass of bourbon. It had emptied the bottle. He looked down at her, angry, contemptuous. 'You whore,' he said, and all that was in his voice was disgust. 'You fucking, fucking whore.'

Lee sat quite still, on the couch, curled up, her head buried in her hands. Some time, surely to God someone would come.

Later, goodness knows how much later, she heard footsteps on the front steps. The bell went. She stood up.

'Shut up,' said Dean, pushing her down. It went again and again. Then she heard Freddy's mother's voice.

'Mrs Wilburn! Mr Wilburn! Are you there?'

'You'll have to go,' she said to Dean. 'She won't go away. She'll call the police if she doesn't get an answer.'

Dean went to the door. He didn't open it, just called through it.

'Yes? Who is it?'

'It's Molly Wainwright. Is everything all right?'

Lee heard him open it a crack. Maybe Molly Wainwright would smell the bourbon on his breath, guess something was wrong.

'It's fine. My wife's just gone to sleep.'

'Well, I just called to say would you like Miles to stay over? Then Lee can sleep through till morning, and she won't have to worry about taking care of him or getting him off to school.'

Dean cleared his throat. Lee could hear him making an intense effort to speak normally. 'Thank you, Mrs Wainwright. That'd be fine.'

'Could I have his things, do you think?'

'Er – what things?'

'His pyjamas and so on.'

'Well – I – that is – I'd rather I didn't disturb my wife right now. She – only she would know where they are, you see. Could you lend Miles something, do you think?'

There was a long silence. Surely she'll think that's odd, thought Lee. She wondered, if she made a dash into the hall, Mrs Wainwright would hear her. But some strange lethargy

265

gripped her; her legs felt weak, her eyes were half closed. She knew she couldn't make the effort.

'Oh – well, all right.' Mrs Wainwright sounded slightly dubious. 'Is there anything I can do, Mr Wilburn? Fix Mrs Wilburn some soup or something?'

'No. No thank you,' said Dean. 'Now if you'll excuse me I must get back to my wife.'

'Is she very sick?'

'No, no, she just has a migraine.'

'Well, if you need me you know where I am.'

'Sure.'

Lee heard the door slam; Dean walked back into the room.

'OK,' he said. 'Now we have plenty of time. I'm certainly in no hurry. I'll just open this other bottle of bourbon and then I'll come and sit beside you.' He poured two glasses and offered her one.

'Here.'

'No thank you.'

'Take it.'

'I said no thank you.'

'And I said take it. Now take it, for Christ's sake. And drink it. I don't like drinking alone.'

She took a swig. It was strangely comforting, burning warm in her throat, numbing the pain of her cut mouth.

Dean suddenly put down his glass, and touched her face. 'You're a pretty woman, Lee,' he said. 'Very pretty. You're still pretty. I still get the hots when I look at you.'

Dear God, she thought, how do I handle this one? She smiled at him, trying to lighten his mood. 'That's nice,' she said. 'That's really nice.'

She took another gulp of the bourbon. 'So is this. I'm beginning to feel better.'

It was a mistake. He knocked the glass out of her hand, his face suddenly crumpled unrecognizably in rage. 'I don't want you to feel better. Not one bit. I want you to feel worse. Terribly, dreadfully worse. You filthy, lying bitch. Fucking with other men. Having another man's baby. Making me think it was mine. Whose was it, Lee? Whose was it?'

'Dean, I can't go on with this much longer. It was your baby. Miles is your baby.'

'Make me believe you then,' he said, coming closer to her, grabbing hold of both her wrists, searching her face. 'Was this how he was conceived? Was it? Like this?'

He kissed her suddenly, hard on the mouth, then threw her back on the couch; he held her down with one hand, ripping her pants off with the other. 'Come on, Lee, show me. Show me how you did it. Show me how you did it with him.'

He smelt disgusting; of drink and sweat; Lee turned her head away from him, shutting her eyes. 'Don't. Please don't.'

'Oh, but I want to. I will. Let's see what you can do.'

And then it was total horror; he unzipped his fly, and fell on top of her, stabbing at her with his penis; clawing at her thighs, her buttocks with his hands, kissing her again and again, pausing gasping for breath, he entered her clumsily, impatiently, and began to thrust into her, harshly, heavily. She could hardly breathe, she was crushed beneath his huge weight, she seemed to be drowning in the darkness, the pain and the foul smell. He pulled out suddenly and drew back from her, looking at her, a hideous smile on his face. 'Is this how you like it, Lee? Is this how you did it? Tell me, tell me you like it. Tell me, Lee, I want to know.'

She was so afraid she couldn't speak; lay looking up at him, her eyes huge, desperately trying to say something, anything; no words would come.

'You silly, silly bitch,' he said, 'why won't you tell me?' And then he entered her again, brutally, hopelessly, and it seemed to go on for ever, and she lay there, hanging on somehow to her sanity, her courage, willing it just to be over. And when finally it was, he lay there, weeping again, and saying, 'I'm sorry, I'm sorry,' and she stroked his head and said, 'It's all right, it's all right,' and they stayed there for a long time.

Finally he said he would get her a drink, some tea or something; yes, she said, tea would be nice, and sat there trembling, not knowing what to do while he went to the kitchen. She drank the tea, and persuaded him to have some; he seemed calmer, she was beginning to think she might be able to move from the room. Then:

'I haven't given up,' he said softly.

'What do you mean?'

'I won't let you go. Not until you tell me. I have to know.'

267

'Dean, please believe me. There is nothing to tell.'

'I don't believe you,' he said, perfectly normally, quite quietly, and then crossing to the bar, he took a bottle of beer out. 'Are you going to tell me?'

'No.'

'You are,' he said, and suddenly smashed the beer bottle on the edge of the bar, knocking two glasses off at the same time, and came at her with the jagged edge. 'Tell me, Lee. You have to tell me.'

Lee felt suddenly calm. She saw quite clearly that she was going to have to tell him something; otherwise she would be dead by morning; but she also saw that if she did it right now, he would probably kill her anyway. She faced him, steady-eyed.

'Dean, don't. You'll be up for assault, possibly murder. I won't tell you anything until you're behaving rationally. Put that down.'

He did put it down, as she had known he would, and sat down suddenly again, looking around him in a slightly puzzled remorseful way, surveying the mess, the beer over everything, the broken bottle, the smashed glasses.

'Sorry,' he said as if he had just knocked a cup of coffee over. 'Sorry about that. Now, you were saying?'

'Have some more tea, Dean.'

'No thank you.'

'It'll make you feel better.'

'All right.'

He picked up his tea cup. 'I'm ready. For anything.'

Lee took a deep breath.

'OK. Here it is. It was only once. Long long ago. It wasn't an affair. Honestly. I didn't love him. Just – just a one-night stand.'

'I see.'

'But – well, yes, I got pregnant. I didn't think I could. I thought it was me that couldn't conceive.'

'How unfortunate for you.'

'Yes, well. Anyway, that was it. I never ever slept with him again.'

'Did you see him again?'

'Hardly.'

'Who was it then?'

'I can't tell you that.'

'You have to.'

'I won't.'

'Then,' he said, 'I shall tell Miles.'

'Why?'

'Because,' he said, looking at her with infinite distaste, 'you deserve it. And he would have a right to know.'

'But you won't if I tell you?'

'Possibly not. It would depend who it was.'

'That isn't logical.'

'I know. This isn't a logical situation. Do you want me to tell him?'

'Of course not.'

'Then you tell me.'

Lee looked at him. There was a long silence. Then: 'All right. It was Hugo. Hugo Dashwood.'

'Dear God,' said Dean. 'How bizarre. How unsuitable. The perfect English gentleman. Fucking my wife. Giving her a bastard baby. And never having the decency to own up.'

'He didn't know.'

'He didn't?'

'No. I never told him.'

'Good God.' He turned and looked at her. All the violence, all the anger had suddenly drained out of him. He looked suddenly years older, very frail and vulnerable. 'You're quite a woman, aren't you? All these years. Never told him.' There was another long silence. 'Imagine it being Hugo,' he said. 'The last person I'd have suspected. Not British, that sort of thing. Not British at all. I always liked old Hugo too. Thought he was my friend. Oh, well. At least I know. I feel kind of better now. You should have told me before. Right in the beginning.' He sighed. 'I feel very tired. I think I'll go up to bed. Good night, Lee. I'll sleep in the guest room.'

'All right,' she said, disconcerted by this sudden return to normality. 'Shall I bring you some more tea?'

'No. No thank you.' He sighed and stood up, doing up his trousers, straightening his shirt. His eyes were full of tears; he put his hand up and brushed them away. 'I still love you,' he said. 'Very very much. I always knew you were too good for me. Good night, Lee.'

'Good night, Dean,' she said, afraid to break the spell. 'Good night.'

He went upstairs. She heard him going into the bathroom, heard the guest room door open, the bed groan as he fell on to it. Somehow, within her aching, trembling body she found the strength to pick up the empty bottles, to straighten the cushions, to turn off the light. It was only half past ten; it felt as if days had passed.

As she went up to her room she could hear his snores begin; he would not wake now. She would decide what to do in the morning. She went to bed.

In the night the snoring stopped. Going in early in the morning, to see if he was all right, she found him absolutely waxen – white and still, scarcely breathing, beyond help. He had taken her bottle of tranquillizers from the bathroom and swallowed the lot, washed down with the remainder of the bourbon. The verdict at the inquest was suicide whilst temporarily deranged.

Whichever way you looked at it, she thought, she had killed him.

Chapter Seven

London, 1970–71

Roz was in love.

She was not in love, as most of the girls at Cheltenham were, with one of the spotty boys of fifteen or sixteen, one of the band of girls' brothers, who accompanied their parents down to school on Open Day or to collect at the end of term: brothers were, as far as Roz could see, arrogant, stupid and tedious, with nothing to say to anyone except 'Good term?' or 'Er – hallo' according to whether they were greeting their sister or their sisters' friends. Nevertheless their prospective arrival caused much giggling, and brushing of hair and excited anticipatory remarks like 'I bet he won't remember me,' or 'Gosh, my brother's not a patch on yours,' and the young Ladies of

Cheltenham went through a formalized mating ritual on their arrival which consisted in the main of their faces blushing scarlet, their voices rising an octave or so, and their eyes rolling rather strangely as one brother or another was introduced to, or reminded of, them; and if things were going really well, proceeded to suggest that perhaps they might see them during the holidays, at some intimate event like a horse show or a family skiing trip.

Roz did blush at least a little when confronted by her love, but her voice did not rise, and her eyes did not roll strangely, she was able to look at him, and even answer him when he spoke; but the things that happened to her heart in his presence were much the same as those that happened to the young ladies: it leapt, it lurched, it rose in her throat and threatened to deafen her with its pounding.

And her love, while not being aware of her feelings, was certainly not indifferent to her: he spoke to her, he inquired after her health and her progress, he remarked on how tall she had grown, and quite often on how much he liked what she was wearing. This was not, it has to be said, because he returned her affections: it was because he was employed by her father and he was in love with her mother.

David Sassoon was the only son of a modestly successful, fiercely proud, Jewish businessman, and having been quite exceptionally good-looking and sexually precocious, he had been expelled from a minor public school, St Michael's in Gloucestershire, for being found in flagrante with one of the housemaids at the age of fifteen. This had nearly broken his father's heart, and he had been sent to the local secondary modern in North London to complete his education and learn a few more lessons besides, including, his father hoped, that of humility and the folly of lost opportunity.

David was not, however, so easily defeated; he passed his School Certificate with distinction and became, against every possible odds, the hero of his year; the boys were impressed by his ability to beat even the most savagely raised bully in a playground fight, and the girls by an equally daunting ability to make three hours in the back row of the cinema, or a sojourn in the park with a couple of bags of chips, an experience of high sensual pleasure.

After school he went to St Martin's School of Art where he took every possible prize and graduated with the highest possible honours, and got a job in a large and fashionable design studio in London; six months after he arrived he was put to work redesigning the packaging for a range of preserves for one of the huge grocery chains. His designs were promptly accepted and put on display; he was then asked to look at the image of the canned goods.

The product manager of canned goods was a beautiful, and recklessly sexy, girl called Mary; before long Mary had not only taken David into her bed and her elegant young person, but had become pregnant by him. What nobody had thought to inform David of, least of all Mary, was that her father was the chairman of the supermarket chain.

This being the late fifties, and abortion being not entirely easy to organize without the passing over of a considerable sum of money, Mary felt obliged to confess all to her father; the consequence was that not only was David fired from the account, but the design company as well, and found himself looking for a job without any kind of reference.

Fortunately for him, Mick diMaggio, on a trip to London, happened to be in the Juliana offices one day when David was making his somewhat wearisome rounds of the studios and offices of London; Mick told Julian he should hire him immediately, Julian said he didn't give a monkey's why David didn't have any decent references as long as he had not actually been caught with his hand in the till; and David took the job as assistant design manager in the packaging department with a huge sigh of relief and a resolve never to be found again with his hand in anything, including a till, unless he was one hundred per cent certain he could not be reproached for it. He had learnt something else about himself through this rather salutary experience: that he was savagely, almost ferociously, ambitious. He, and his work, he now knew, had to be very, very successful indeed – so successful that nothing of a personal nature could threaten it.

Some designers work with their creative instincts alone, some give more emphasis to commercial demands. A few manage to use both, and throw something else in as well: Mick diMaggio himself, looking at David's work, put a word to it:

guts. David Sassoon took risks on the drawing board. He used colours, shapes, typefaces that had not been seen in association with cosmetics before. They were not brash, or vulgar or in any way shocking, they were beautiful and desirable, but they were also absolutely stunningly new, fresh, rethought. Under David, Juliana took an entirely new look, while perfectly retaining its air of exclusivity, extravagance, desirability. A new Sassoon-styled counter display for Juliana making its appearance at Harrods or Harvey Nichols was a major attraction in itself, and the windows he created every Christmas to promote *Je* and *Mademoiselle Je* in all the big stores, including Circe in both New York and Paris, owed more to the cinematic style of Mr Busby Berkeley than anything taught at art college about window display.

Five years later David was creative director of Juliana, reporting directly to Julian and with a seat on the main board; he had a flat in the King's Road and a white Mercedes convertible, he spent his nights dancing at the Saddle Room and the Ad Lib, high temples of the shrine immortalized in *Time Magazine* as swinging London, with a string of beautiful girls, each one with longer hair, legs and eyelashes and shorter skirts than the last. He knew everybody in London worth knowing: the terrible trio of photographers – David Bailey, Terry Donovan, Brian Duffy – and their ever-changing coterie of divinely long-legged huge-eyed companions; he knew Barbara Hulanicki and her husband Stephen FitzSimon, and indeed had worked with them on some early designs for the first Biba; he knew Cathy McGowan, the star of *Ready Steady Go*; he knew all the most brilliant fashion journalists of the day, Grace Coddington of *Vogue*, Anne Trehearne of *Queen*, Molly Parkin of *Nova*; he knew Mary Quant and Alexander Plunkett Greene; he knew Twiggy and Justin de Villeneuve.

He bought his clothes from Blades, he had his hair cut personally by Vidal Sassoon, who was, they were both at great pains to assure everybody, absolutely no relation, he ate at the Arethusa club, and at Nick's Diner, the ultimate gourmet experience in the Fulham Road for young London; his life was a hyped-up fairy story of success and fame, and he was deeply in love with it.

He was also exceedingly good-looking. He had dark curly

hair, a slightly swarthy freckled skin, and dark eyes that it was impossible to meet without feeling infected by the naked, unashamed, joyful carnal knowledge that filled them. He was fairly slim, and although he was not very tall, only about five foot ten, he was a curious combination of both graceful and powerful, which emphasized his extraordinary sexuality. David Sassoon did not just look sexy, as one tender young model of seventeen confided to another in the ladies' room at the Ad Lib club one night, he felt sexy. 'And I don't mean he has hard-ons all the time, he just only has to touch your hand and you start thinking about what it would be like to be in bed with him.'

Nevertheless, his reputation was surprisingly blemish free. He flirted with, he courted, he enjoyed women; but he very rarely took them to bed until he knew them almost as well as they knew themselves.

This was partly because of a deeply held belief of his that women were only satisfactory as sexual partners if they felt at ease; and partly because he was absolutely terrified of finding himself unwittingly in yet another compromising situation. In David Sassoon's opinion, and indeed his experience, sod's law operated more painstakingly in the bedroom than anywhere else; and he had no desire to see his meteoric career blacked out by the consequences of a night's pleasure, however intense, in the company of a lady who might be the wife, daughter or mistress of someone who employed him.

Eliza Thetford, however, having seen David across the room at a party Julian had thrown to celebrate the launch of his first health farm (now that he was no longer married to her, and indeed was at one husband's remove from her, Julian perversely greatly enjoyed her company and her attendance at his parties) had set her sights on him rather firmly. She was talking to Letitia at the time, with whom she was still the very best of friends, when she saw him, and decided she would greatly like to get to know him.

'Letitia,' she whispered, 'who is that perfectly glorious man with the black curly hair and the divine beige suit? The one who looks a bit like Richard Burton, only with dark hair.'

'Oh,' said Letitia, following her gaze and then looking back at her amusedly. 'That's Julian's latest discovery. His new creative director in London. Awfully clever. A bit abrasive. His name's David Sassoon. Do you want to meet him?'

'Of course.'

'He's very dangerous.'

'In what way?'

'You know perfectly well what way.'

'Then I certainly want to meet him.'

'On your own head be it.'

'It's not my head I want it to be on.'

'Eliza! How coarse!' But she was laughing.

David Sassoon in fact proved the opposite of dangerous at first. Eliza was disappointed. He bowed over her hand, looked into her eyes with his burning brown ones, and immediately made her feel half undressed; he chatted amusingly with her, danced with her once or twice, told her she was the most beautiful woman in the room, and that he included the ravishing Miss Julie Christie and the divine Miss Penelope Tree in that statement, and then vanished without trace. 'Rather like a male Cinderella,' said Eliza plaintively to Letitia at the end of the party. What David was doing, however, was what he had been doing all his life, safeguarding his own position – or not shitting on his own doorstep as he described it eloquently if inelegantly to his best friend and workmate over lunch next day.

'I fancy that lady rotten. She's gorgeous, she's sexy, she's been around, and yet right now she needs a jolly good old-fashioned fuck. And I'd like to give it to her. But she's been the boss's wife and I'm not going to get into that. Or her,' he added with a grin.

But he had not reckoned on Eliza's skill at getting what she wanted.

Coming back from a difficult two days in Paris trying to impose his will on the cosmetic buyer for Galleries Lafayette, David found a message on his desk. 'Mrs Thetford phoned.' He ignored it.

She rang again, two days later. 'This is Eliza Thetford. Do you remember me? Sorry to hound you. I wondered if we could have lunch.'

David took a deep breath. 'Mrs Thetford, of course I remember you. I'm charmed and flattered, but I think I should say no.'

'Why?'

'Your husband might not like it,' he said and then, furious with himself, realized what he had said and how unutterably crass it must have sounded.

Her voice was amused down the line. 'I don't have a husband, Mr Sassoon. I've long since divorced him. And he's much too busy getting into the Cabinet to worry about my having lunch with you.'

'I'm sorry. You must think I'm quite mad.'

'No. A little neurotic perhaps, but not mad. And I can see what you're really worried about. But my first husband also doesn't mind in the least what I do, or with whom I do it. And even if he did I have nothing more incriminating in mind for us than a business discussion. So when shall we meet?'

David knew when he was beaten. 'Thursday?'

'Thursday would be lovely. The Walton Street Restaurant at one?'

'Fine.'

She was waiting for him when he got there, sitting at a table in the window; the moment he saw her, looking at him with the extraordinary combination of innocence and blatant sexuality that she so uniquely conveyed, he knew he was lost, that whatever he might resolve or think to the contrary, if she wanted him then she could and would have him.

Eliza wanted him; and she had him.

The business discussion she had managed to create (whisper thin, a request that he should advise her on her new prospective career as an interior designer) was over in half an hour; for two more they danced an elaborate sexual quadrille around each other, and finally fell into each other's arms, bodies and Eliza's bed in the Holland Park house as the October dusk gathered and the clock was striking five o'clock.

David stayed there for several days; he did not go to work at all on the Friday, and right through the weekend they talked, and made love with ever increasing delight, and drank quite a few bottles of wine, and even ventured out once to walk in

Holland Park and to top up the contents of Eliza's fridge, which were extraordinarily meagre ('I have to keep thin somehow,' she said), and told jokes and played the music of Stevie Wonder, whose raw, sexy voice seemed totally in accord with the delightful discoveries they were making about each other, and spent quite a lot of time simply looking at each other in silence, happy and almost awed by the perfect pleasure they had found in one another's company.

'I have to tell you,' David said quite late on the Sunday night, as they lay in bed and he was smiling at her, and dipping his fingers in his glass of wine, wetting her nipples and kissing them, 'I have to tell you you seem to be threatening to become important to me.'

'I should think so,' said Eliza half indignantly, pushing him away and sitting up, 'I don't do this with just anyone, you know.'

'No, I can see that. Just the best. But anyway, there's no need to get upset. I think we have to spend some time together. Do you see any problems there?'

'Not for me. Are there any for you?'

'A few. The main one as I see it is your husband – your ex exhusband, that is. Are you quite sure he isn't going to object to any of this?'

'Of course not,' said Eliza, lying down again, 'why should he?'

'I don't know. He's a funny guy. Very possessive. Within the company. He doesn't like interdepartmental liaisons for a start.'

'He's got a nerve,' said Eliza. 'Carrying on with Camilla the way he does.'

'I know. But he is the boss. I suppose that gives him the right to have a nerve or two. And he has come down very hard on a couple of people having affairs on office territory. He dresses it up, of course, said they were wasting company time. But the real reason is he doesn't like it. He gets kind of jealous, as far as everyone can make out.'

'Well, that's all right,' said Eliza. 'I don't work for the company.'

'I know. But you used to be his wife. It just worries me a bit.'

'You're really jumpy about him, aren't you?' she said, looking at him interestedly.

'Yes, I am. He's put me where I am today, as they say in the movies. I told you, I've had quite a few chances mucked up by my sexual indiscretions. I can't help it.'

'Well,' she said, 'I don't know if I like coming such a very bad second to your career.'

'I'm sorry. I didn't mean it to sound like that. Let's put it this way. There's quite a strong body of opinion in the company that your husband still cares very much about you and what you do. If I was your ex-husband I would too.' He bent and kissed her breasts again. 'I just think we should be careful, that's all. He's a powerful and quixotic fellow. He could hurt both of us.'

'I honestly think the body of opinion is quite wrong,' said Eliza, 'but anyway, all right, if you think we should, we'll be discreet for a bit. Just for a day or two. Now put that glass down, and concentrate on me for a bit. It's dark outside now, and the shutters are closed. Or would you like me to check there's not a private detective hanging about underneath the lamp post?'

They were very discreet for a while. David kept his flat, and only stayed with her one or two nights a week ('It's more exciting and romantic that way anyway,' he said) and Eliza, deeply in love by now for the first time since Peter Thetford, managed to restrain her strong inclination to ring every single one of her girlfriends and tell them, and even invented a completely fictitious new boyfriend for them who she said they couldn't meet because his wife was madly jealous and had threatened all kinds of dreadful revenge. She rather enjoyed this and elaborated on it so much that in the end she had both herself and the lover threatened by the wife at gunpoint before finally the real story and the gossip broke and William Hickey informed the waiting world, or at least such part of it as read his gossip column in the *Daily Express*, that the beautiful Eliza Thetford had become very friendly with one of her ex husband's senior executives and was engaging his help in setting herself up as an interior designer.

But Julian showed no signs of jealousy when he phoned her to discuss who should pick Roz up for the Christmas holidays.

'I hear you have enlisted Mr Sassoon's services as an agent,' he said. 'Charming fellow. I'm sure he'll be very helpful.'

*

278

Roz looked at her mother as she climbed out of the red E-Type Julian had given her as a Christmas present (he said it was bad for his image to have his wife going round London like a pauper) and thought she had never seen her looking so happy or so beautiful.

'Hallo, Mummy.'

'Hallo, darling. You look – well.'

Only Roz, in her acute paranoia about her looks, would have noticed the pause; but she did and she knew what it meant. It meant that her mother couldn't find anything else to say about her appearance (taller: only slightly thinner: shaggy-haired). She looked at her blankly.

'I don't feel very well, actually. I feel sick.'

'Oh darling, I'm sorry. Will you be all right in the car?'

'I expect so, yes, if we can have the windows open.'

She knew her mother hated that; it blew her hair about.

Eliza sighed. 'All right, darling. Where are your things?'

They drove back to London in comparative silence, having exhausted the topic of Roz's term, report, exam results; Eliza was wondering how to broach the news of David, and that she was hoping Julian would have Roz for Christmas.

'Looking forward to Christmas, darling? I've got you a nice present.'

'Depends what's happening. Is it Wiltshire, or have you persuaded Daddy to take me to the Bahamas?'

'Darling, I haven't persuaded Daddy to do anything. I want you with me, of course. It's what would be more fun for you.'

'God, I don't care,' said Roz. 'Wiltshire, I suppose. I can ride there.'

'We must get your hair cut tomorrow,' said Eliza absently. 'I'll book you into Leonard. And then get you some clothes. Would you like that?'

'Not really. You know I hate shopping.'

'Yes, but darling, you do need some new things. You've grown a lot.'

'No I haven't.'

'Well anyway, I'm sure you need a couple of things. Now, Roz, I have something to tell you.'

'Yes?'

'I have a new – friend.'

'Really?'

'Yes. He's called David Sassoon. He works for your father. He's very nice, and I think you'll like him.'

'Is he living with you or just sleeping with you?'

'Roz, I wish you wouldn't talk like that. It isn't very attractive.'

'Sorry.'

'No, he isn't living with me. But we are very – fond of each other. And he wants to meet you.'

'Oh.'

'So he's coming round this evening. Just for a meal with us both. I hope you like him.'

'I don't really feel well enough to have a meal with anyone, Mummy. I seem to have some kind of a tummy bug. I might just go straight to bed when we get home.'

'Now Roz, that's a pity. David is coming specially to meet you. Don't you think you could make an effort?'

'Well, I'll try. But I certainly don't feel up to getting all dressed up if that's what you're hoping.'

'No,' said Eliza, 'I wouldn't ever hope for very much from you, Roz. Now I'm sorry but we really will have to have that window shut.'

'All right. I just might be sick, that's all.'

She was sitting by the fire in the drawing room, still in her school uniform, when David arrived; she heard her mother open the front door, and settled herself deeper into her chair, picking up the latest *Vogue* which was lying on the coffee table; she didn't even look up as they came into the room.

'Roz,' said her mother, and she could hear the familiar over-conciliatory note in her voice, 'Roz, darling, this is David. David Sassoon. David, this is my daughter Roz.'

And she had looked up and met his eyes, his dark, amused, oddly intimate eyes, and her heart had felt as if it was rocketing up and down inside her, and she felt slightly dizzy at the same time, and she would have given anything, anything at all, to have been wearing her new long grey crushed velvet skirt from Biba, and the pink suede boots, and to have brushed her hair properly and to have put some Top-ex on the spot on her chin; and he said, 'Hallo, Roz, it's so nice to have a face to the name. I see you're reading *Vogue*, what do you think of those pictures, do you like them, they were taken by a great friend of mine?' and overwhelmed by his smile and his jokey voice that sounded as if he was going to laugh any minute, its touch of carefully cultivated cockney, and the fact that anyone at all should ask her opinion about anything other than whether this term had been better than the last, she fell hopelessly and irremediably in love.

Later they all went out to supper to Nick's Diner; she felt better, she told her mother, she had probably just been hungry, and she put on her velvet skirt and the boots, and did the best she could with her hair, and asked her mother if she had arranged her appointment for the next day at Leonard's, and sat between them listening politely, offering her opinion if it was asked, which it was quite frequently by David, and even from time to time making them both laugh, and had the best time she could ever remember. She studied David intently all evening: drinking him in, feeling she could never have enough just of looking at him; the riotously curling hair, just short of his collar, his dark almost swarthy skin, the freckles everywhere on his nose, his eyelids, his forehead; his perfect teeth, and his great grin of a smile, that was always accompanied by that look of his, his eyes sweeping over your face and settling on your lips, as if he might be thinking about kissing you; and his clothes, oh, she loved his clothes, the printed cream and black silk shirt, and the black flaring trousers that fitted so extremely well over his hips (Roz tried not to look at his hips, or to contemplate what else those trousers were concealing) and his black velvet jacket, with the lining that matched his shirt. Roz could hardly swallow that evening, for emotion and excitement, but that was all right, she said she was still feeling a bit funny, but she did at David's instigation have a glass of wine, and that on top of her empty stomach and her excitement conspired to make her a bit giggly and more talkative than usual, and then when they were going home in David's car, to fall into a half sleep. But not so that she could not hear what was said.

'She's had a lovely evening,' said Eliza, looking over her shoulder, 'she's absolutely out cold. I've never known her so talkative. You've obviously made a big hit. Thank you for letting her come.'

'I enjoyed it,' he said. 'Don't thank me. I like her, she's an amusing kid, and I don't know why you keep saying she's plain, she has a great face, I'd like to get her photographed, Terry would love her look.'

'Well, he's not going to get a chance to love it,' said Eliza briskly. 'I know all about your friend Mr Donovan. And I must say you're getting a bit carried away, David, she might look a bit better than she did, but I wouldn't say she was model material.'

'Not model, darling, but very interesting-looking, very striking. Anyway, what are we going to do now?'

'I think maybe,' said Eliza with another look at the inert form of her daughter, 'you should go home tonight. I want her to get used to the idea slowly. Would you mind terribly?'

'Of course not. I'm an easy-going guy. You should know that by now.'

'You're wonderful,' said Eliza. 'Come on, give me a kiss before our chaperone wakes up.'

Roz floated through the next day in a dream. David Sassoon, the most attractive, the most sophisticated man she had ever met, had said she was not plain, that she had a great face and that she was amusing into the bargain. She thought she had never been so happy. She smiled at her mother over breakfast, asked her if they could go shopping after the hairdresser, and then phoned her father and asked him if he would take her out to supper that night. She had never done such a thing before; she had never, convinced of her own nuisance value, and her own unattractiveness as a companion, had the confidence. She could hear him smiling down the phone.

'Yes, Roz, it would be a pleasure. Now would you like just me, or shall I ask Camilla? She's here.'

'Oh, no,' she said quickly. 'Let's make it just the two of us. Please.'

'Fine. Dress up then. We'll go to the Ritz. As it's the holidays.'

She walked into the Ritz feeling like a real model. Leonard had cut her hair in the new wispy layered look, with little petals of it overlapping one another all over her head and down on to the nape of her neck. Then they had gone, she and her mother, to the Purple Shop and bought her a pair of black velvet breeches, and a glorious red silk shirt, and some high boots, and a wonderfully flouncy red and purple skirt, like a gypsy's and then they had gone on to Biba and bought a long, long black velvet dress, with buttons down the front, which her mother said was much too sophisticated but which she knew showed off her new flatter stomach very well, and a long black coat right to the ground, from next door in Bus Stop, and a huge black hat with a floppy brim, and then she had bought a set of eye pencils and spent the whole afternoon practising drawing round her eyes with them, and then the most marvellous thing had happened, David Sassoon had arrived and found her rubbing at them furiously in the kitchen because the light was better there, and he had said, 'Here, let me do that, if there's one thing I can do it's draw,' and he had held the back of her head very gently with one hand, while carefully outlining her eyes with a dark blue pencil, looking at her very intently all the time, until Roz thought she would faint with emotion, and then telling her she looked gorgeous, and when she walked out to her father sitting in his new black Bentley, with its tinted windows, wearing the skirt and the red shirt and the boots, with her eyes looking all smudgy and big, and her new haircut and she saw him looking at her in genuine astonishment and admiration, she knew that for the very first time since she had heard him saying he didn't want her to go and live with him, she didn't have to feel apologetic about herself.

Later over dinner, he asked her how she liked David: he seemed quite nice, she said carefully, much nicer than the last one, and he said, good, and that he liked David very much and he was delighted that her mother seemed happy; but Roz noticed that he pushed his hair back quite a lot during this conversation, and that he didn't really seem very delighted, and didn't want to talk about it for long. Testing him she said casually, 'I wonder if they might get married,' and he looked very odd indeed, and almost angry, and said, 'Oh, I shouldn't think so. I don't think that would be a good idea at all,' and changed the subject very quickly and asked her if she would like to come for Christmas with him to the house at Turtle Cove on Eleuthera in the Bahamas that he had just bought, to spend Christmas.

'And Camilla?' Roz asked.

'No,' he said, looking almost angry again, 'no, Camilla is spending Christmas with her family.'

'So would it be just the two of us?'

'Yes. I'd really like you to come, darling. We'd have fun.'

And Roz, realizing that also for the first time in her life her father really needed her and was depending on her company, looked at him over her forkful of chicken and said, 'I'm really sorry, Daddy, but I promised Granny and Grandpa just today that I'd go and stay in Wiltshire with them.'

'Couldn't you change your mind? Tell them you have to keep your old father company?'

'No,' she said, 'no, I'm afraid I couldn't, I don't want to let them down.'

The expression of hurt on her father's face added greatly to the pleasure of her evening.

For the first time in her life Roz went back to school feeling quite happy. It wasn't that she wanted to go back to school, but she had had a nice holiday, she had had fun, just like the other girls. She actually found herself joining in the conversation, saying, 'Well, we did this' and 'I got that,' instead of remaining aloof and apart from them. She supposed it was love that made her feel so good. Everyone knew it changed people for the better.

What was more, she was beginning to think that David did return her feelings a bit. He had that way of looking very deep into her eyes when he was talking to her, and smiling very intently at her; and he always noticed what she was wearing and how she looked and remarking on it, and telling her she looked gorgeous; and he seemed to like talking to her, and hearing her opinion on things; and at the New Year party Granny and Grandpa had given in Wiltshire, he had danced with her several times, and once it had been a real slow dance, and he had held her quite tightly and actually rested his head on her hair and squeezed her hand at one point. Roz had felt so extraordinarily emotional when this had happened, and sort of tingly and tense inside, that she had gone away and sat in her bedroom afterwards, just to think about it and enjoy the memory; and although when she came down again he had been dancing with her mother and holding her, and looking into her eyes, it hadn't mattered because she knew what he felt for her was different and special. When she went back to school he had kissed her goodbye, just lightly on the lips, but she had been quite quite sure he had pressed against them just for a moment, and then he had said he would miss her and he would look forward to seeing her at half term.

'In fact,' he said, 'I'll come and pick you up, if I can, with your mum. So I see you as soon as possible. Would you like that?'

She lived for half term, counting the weeks, the days, the hours; and then the most perfect thing happened, when the day finally arrived and she was looking out of the window for the car, it was his car that pulled into the front of the school, and he got out of it all by himself, looking absolutely marvellous in blue denims and a navy donkey jacket, with his hair even longer, and she rushed down and out to him, and he held out his arms and gave her a huge bear hug and said, 'Your mum is terribly terribly busy pleating up somebody's curtains and I offered to come and get you. I hope that's all right.' And Roz looked at him radiantly and said yes of course it was all right, it was marvellous and he said she looked even slimmer and she would soon be too tall for him altogether, and she went and got her bag and got in the car beside him, and hoped just everyone in the school was looking.

All the way back in the car the radio was playing, the most marvellously appropriate songs like 'Let It Be' and 'Everything is Beautiful' and 'We've Only Just Begun' and Roz sat silent and every so often risked a look at him, and he would grin at her and say 'All right?' and she would say 'Yes, perfectly,' and much too soon they reached London and Holland Park and her mother came rushing out of the house and said 'Hello, darling, I do hope you didn't mind terribly David coming instead of me,' and Roz said 'No, of course not,' and thought with great satisfaction how deeply miserable her mother would be when she realized that her lover had grown tired of her and was in love with her daughter instead.

She didn't see all that much of him over half term, he was very busy, but she didn't mind, she had the journey to remember; on the second night her father invited her to supper and to stay the night at Hanover Terrace, with a rather quiet

Camilla, and was very polite and charming to her and told her she was looking terrific, and said he would take her to Marriotts at the weekend for some hunting if she would like that, and Roz had said no, she was sorry, but she and her mother and David had all sorts of plans.

Later, when they thought she had gone to bed, she overheard him and Camilla arguing. She crept out on to the corridor to listen.

'I'll tell you what I think,' Camilla was saying, 'I think you're still in love with her.'

'Oh, don't be ridiculous,' her father said. 'Of course I'm not. I probably never was in love with her.'

'Then why are you so insanely jealous of David Sassoon?'

'I'm not.'

'I think you are.'

'I just don't like the way he's taking over my family. My daughter seems as besotted with him as my wife.'

'An interesting Freudian slip, Julian. Your ex-wife.'

'All right, Camilla. My ex-wife.'

There was a short silence. Then: 'A lot of people in the company are saying they'll get married. How would you feel about that?'

'Oh,' she heard her father say, and the lightness of his tone did not fool Roz in the very least, 'I'd find a way of putting a stop to it, I expect.'

David did not come to collect Roz from school for the Easter holidays; Julian came instead in his latest acquisition, a dark blue Bentley Continental. Roz tried not to be disappointed and to tell herself how much she would have longed for such a thing only a year ago.

'Hallo, Daddy. That's a nice car.'

'Isn't it? I knew you'd appreciate it. I've come because Mummy's away for a couple of days –'

'With David?'

'No,' said her father, pushing his hair back, 'no, not with David. David is doing a little work for a change. Mummy's in Paris – working, she tells me. She'll be back the day after tomorrow.'

'Oh.'

'So you're coming home with me. Only, tomorrow I have to go out to a dinner, so you'll be on your own, I'm afraid. I'm sorry. Mrs Bristow will look after you.'

'That's all right.' She smiled at him.

A plan was forming in her mind.

'David? Hallo, it's Roz.'

'Roz, hallo darling. I didn't realize you were home.'

She was disappointed.

'Well, I am. And I'm all alone tonight. Daddy's out at a dinner.'

'That makes two of us.'

'Yes, I know. Well, I wondered if – well if you'd like to take me out to supper.'

There was a moment's silence. Then: 'Yes, of course I would. What about Parson's? You like that, don't you?'

Parson's was where the *haut monde* ate spaghetti in the Fulham Road.

She smiled into the telephone. 'Yes, please.'

She could hardly swallow a thing. David was concerned.

'Roz, you're not eating. Aren't you well?'

'I'm fine. Just not hungry. Too much school food.'

'Well, you look terrific on it. Or rather not terrific. Very slim.'

'Thank you. Could I – could I have some wine?'

'Of course.'

He filled her glass and watched her drain it almost at once. He shook his head, looking deep into her eyes with his half smile. 'What would your mother say? Taking you out and getting you drunk?'

'I don't suppose she'd care. She doesn't care about anything I do.'

'Don't be silly. She loves you very much.'

'How do you know?'

'Because she told me.'

Roz was silent.

'Roz, look at me.'

She looked. She saw his eyes looking at her with great concern and tenderness. Her heart turned over, her tummy felt fluid with excitement and love.

'Roz,' he said.

'Yes?'

'Roz, you have this crazy idea, don't you, that nobody cares about you?'

'Yes, and it's true.'

'It's not, you know. We all do. Your mother. Your father. Me –'

'You?'

'Yes. Me.' He put his hand over hers on the table. 'You're very special, you know. A very special person. I'm extremely fond of you.' He smiled into her eyes.

The room blurred. Roz realized her eyes were full of tears. She swallowed.

'Darling,' he said, realizing, 'darling, don't cry.' And he reached out his hand and wiped away her tears, very gently.

'Oh, David,' said Roz, terrified of breaking the spell, 'David, please will you take me home.'

'Yes,' he said, puzzled, 'yes of course I will.'

In the car she didn't speak; when they got to Hanover Terrace she turned to him. He was looking almost unbearably handsome and sexy; his eyes moved over her face, lingered on her lips. Roz knew this was the moment: that she had to speak: that he would never have the courage to speak, to make the first move when he had no idea of her feelings, when he thought she simply saw him as an older man, her mother's boyfriend.

'David,' she said, and a huge lump of terror rose in her throat; she swallowed hard, 'David, I – I –'

'Yes, Roz?'

Words were no good; she had to show him how she felt, give him the opportunity to speak, to show her that he loved her too. She leant forward, put out her arms, kissed him on the mouth, wondering even as she did so if real kissing had to mean putting your tongue in the other person's mouth or if there was some other way round it; waiting, wondering, every fibre of her alive, excited, tremulous, she felt almost at once that something was wrong. His mouth was dry and still under hers, his arms did not go round her; he drew back in his seat, and when she opened her eyes and looked at him his gaze was fixed on her in horror and alarm.

'Now, my darling, look,' he said, in an attempt at lightness, 'you don't want to get mixed up with an old man like me. Pick on some lucky fellow your own age.'

'But David,' she said, and her voice was almost pleading. 'David, I love you. And I thought you loved me. You said –'

'Roz, darling, I'm sorry. I do love you. Do care about you. Very much. But not – not in that way. I'm so sorry. Sorry if you misunderstood. I – I obviously said too much.'

'Oh,' she said, and a wave of pain went over her, filling every corner of her with hot, ashamed, shock. 'Oh, no.' And then desperate, frantic to save herself and her pride, she managed to smile, to laugh even a tiny forced laugh, and she drew back, groping for the door handle. 'Well, of course you didn't. I knew, perfectly well, I was just joking myself. I wouldn't dream of coming between you and Mummy.'

'No,' he said, grasping at this, smiling falsely, foolishly with relief, 'no, I know you wouldn't. We've been such friends, and we always will be. I hope . . . I do hope.'

'Of course,' she said, 'of course we will. I mean – well, I expect you'll be marrying Mummy soon, well, I hope so anyway.'

'Well,' he said, eager to turn the situation round from its horror, awkward, crass in his anxiety, 'you could be the very first person to know. Apart from me. I haven't even asked her yet. What do you think she'll say?'

And Roz, unable to bear it any longer, jumped out of the car and shouted at him from the pavement, 'I hope she'll say no. All right? No, no, no!'

And she slammed the door and ran into the house.

Next night, a little pale, but dry-eyed and composed, she ate dinner alone with her father.

'All right, darling? You don't seem quite yourself.'

'Yes, I'm fine, Daddy.'

'I hear you were out last night. Where did you go?'

'Oh, to Rosie's house.'

'I see. How is Rosie?'

'She's fine.'

'Good.'

'Daddy – '

'Yes?'

'Daddy, I don't know if I ought to tell you this, but it's awfully exciting, I think David and Mummy are going to get married. It would be perfectly lovely for me, I would have a proper family again. What do you think about it?'

Two days later David Sassoon, rushing out of his office mid morning to meet Eliza Thetford at the airport, and to tell her that for the first time in his life he felt ready to commit himself and wanted to marry her, saw a newly delivered letter on his desk marked Private and Confidential. It was from Julian, and it offered him the position of design director of the company worldwide at virtually double his present salary, with immediate effect. The job was based in New York.

The letter finished by saying that David's bachelor status had been a minor but important factor in helping Julian to reach the decision, given that the job would entail a great deal of travelling, and in the first year at least a crushing workload.

The Connection Five

Los Angeles, 1970–71

It really was only a little lump. Lee, feeling it again and again, morning after morning, convincing herself it had grown no bigger, promised herself that next time she had to see the doctor about anything important, she would just mention it and then he could assure her it was nothing, and then she could forget about it. She couldn't spare either the time or the money to go about something that really was absolutely unimportant. Mr Phillips was a very busy man, and he was so extremely good about her being away when she had to take Miles to the dentist or watch him play baseball, or go and see his teacher for one of the interminable chats about his outstanding abilities and his equally outstanding laziness. Just thinking about Miles and his laziness made Lee feel tired and limp herself. Not that she would call it laziness, exactly; more an absolute refusal to put his mind to anything that did not engage it. He had not been known to write an essay more than one page long, he never read anything more challenging than the sports pages in the newspapers and the *Little League Newsletter*; he regarded history with contempt and science with amusement; he gave the occasional nod in the direction of languages and had a gift for mimicry that made his accent in both Spanish and French virtually flawless; but when it came to maths he set himself to his books and his homework with a ferocious determination, he was always not only top of the class but top by a very long way, and had rarely been known to get a mark lower than ninety per cent, grade less than A, and for some reason he also worked very hard at geography. When pressed by his mother as to the reason he would fix her with his dancing, slightly insolent dark blue eyes and say, 'There's a point to it.'

'Yes, but Miles, there's also a point to being able to string more than three sentences together on a page,' Lee would say.

'Not really,' he would say, 'what's the telephone for?'

'But Miles, you have to write letters in business and things like that.'

'Mom, I don't intend to go into business. Not the kind that needs letters writing anyway.'

After a few more protests, Lee would give up, too tired, too busy, too weary of the battle to pursue it any longer.

She was very often – more and more frequently, in fact – very tired. She found looking after Miles, trying to bring him up on her own, and earning a living for them both and keeping the house nice, extremely demanding. There simply weren't enough hours in the day.

They had stayed in the house purely on the strength of Hugo's generosity. She had hated taking money from him, but there had been simply no one else to turn to. Dean's life insurance had been useless, since he had committed suicide, and she and Miles would have been destitute. Had there been no Miles she would have slept on the beach gladly, along with the other vagrants, rather than ask Hugo for a dime, but there was Miles, and now that Dean had died she had dared to delve into her subconscious and acknowledge that not only was Miles a burden she could and should lay on Hugo, but the responsibility for Dean's death stood at least in some part at his door as well.

She had hated telling him, hated contacting him, but she had felt, in her unutterable grief and guilt and loneliness, driven to him; it was the first time in ten years she had ever dialled the number in New York, and even then she had rung off three times as the phone was answered before asking for him.

And then he had not been there; the woman had said she would take a message, but she didn't know when he would get it, and then when Lee said it was very very urgent, and was he in England, the woman had said grudgingly, well, she could pass on the message to another number, in New York, but she couldn't give the number to Lee.

'Please,' said Lee desperately, 'please give it to me, I am an old friend,' (urging the words out of herself with huge, terrible difficulty) and the woman said she didn't care if she was the President himself, she wasn't allowed to give the number. 'Well, give him a message then, please –please,' said Lee.

'OK, OK,' said the woman, and Lee could hear her raising her eyebrows and shifting impatiently on her chair. 'I said I would. What'll I say?'

'Oh,' said Lee, 'say just could Hugo Dashwood please call Lee Wilburn urgently.' And she put the phone down feeling more alone than ever, sure that Hugo must be thousands of miles away in England with Alice and that even if he wasn't he would make little effort to help her. And indeed why should he, she reflected, when she had been so persistently hostile, so harsh to him for the past ten years, refusing him any kind of friendliness, crushing his overtures to Miles, blocking his access to the heart of her family.

But she was wrong, and he did; he was with her in twenty-four hours, gentle, supportive, comforting. He booked into a hotel (to confound the gossips) and visited her daily. He helped her with the funeral arrangements, he sorted through her papers, he checked on her financial affairs.

'You're going to need help, Lee,' he said on the third day, looking up from a sheaf of papers. 'Dean has left virtually nothing. There's a small pension. That's all.'

'So what shall I do?' she said, fearful, tearstained, shredding Kleenex after Kleenex into her lap, looking at him in a kind of helpless panic.

'Take some money from me.'

'No. I can't.'

'Why not?'

'I just can't. We're not your responsibility, and besides, you don't have any money.'

'You are my responsibility, and I do have some money.'

'But you told Dean –'

'What?'

'That things weren't going well for you. That you were having a difficult time.'

'I was lying.'

'But why?'

'Lee, use your common sense. Dean was not exactly a success, was he?'

'He was too,' she said, instinctively indignant, defending the Dean who was far beyond humiliation.

'Well, all right,' he said, 'maybe he was. But not such a success as I am. I didn't want to rub his nose in that. I was his friend. Friends don't do that sort of thing. Bad form. In England anyway.' He was smiling gently.

She looked at him scornfully. 'They do other things that are bad form, I gather. Sleep with other men's wives.'

'Look, Lee,' said Hugo, suddenly angry. 'I know I did wrong. But so did you. And you've done precious little to let me help put it right. So just shut up. And let me do it now. You need me, Lee. Don't drive me away.'

She looked at him, through the blur of fresh tears, and felt remorseful. It was true. He would have helped. He had done everything he could, everything she had allowed him to, keeping in touch, giving extravagant presents to Miles, making sure she was all right, all down the years.

'I'm sorry,' she said. 'You're right. And it was mostly my fault. I shouldn't have blamed you so much.'

'Yes you should,' he said, patting the seat beside him on the couch. 'But you can stop now. Come here and let me hold you. It's all right,' he added as she stiffened in fearful wariness. 'I'm not going to seduce you. I think we've both lived well past that. I just think you need some arms round you.'

And she had crawled into his arms, and lain there, crying for a long time, and he had stroked her hair and kissed the top of her head, and soothed and gentled her, and in the end she did feel a little better.

'Hugo, how will I ever get through this? Forgive myself? Live with knowing what I did to him?'

'Oh,' he said, and there was an odd expression in his eyes. 'Time will do it for you. It is amazing what one does learn to live with. Come to terms with. Forget. No, not forget, but allow to fade. You will never get over it. Not in the way you mean. But a day will come when you will be able to remember Dean with a kind of happiness, and to know that you gave him a lot of happiness too. Don't let yourself forget that, Lee. You made him very happy for eighteen years. That's a long time, and it's a lot to do for someone.'

'But what an end to it. What a terrible, terrible end.'

'Yes, but at least there was never any suspicion, any pain, before. That would have been much worse. Remember the coroner's verdict. Temporarily deranged. It was very temporary. Hang on to that. Death isn't so bad. Not when it's over.'

She looked at him and smiled shakily. 'How do you know? Have you been there?'

'No. But I've watched people who have.'

'When?'

'In the war.'

'Ah.'

'Now then,' he said, suddenly brisk. 'Miles can't stay with the Wainwrights for ever. He needs to be with you. When are you going to get him back?'

'Not for another day or two, Hugo. I can't cope.'

'All right. But don't leave it too long.'

'How – how long can you stay?'

'Oh, another forty-eight hours. Then I have to get back. Incidentally, Lee, I know you had to tell the coroner you were having an affair, but are you going to tell anyone else?'

'Why?' she said, suddenly hostile again. 'Are you afraid you'll get landed with it?'

'No,' he said with a great weariness, 'I don't give a damn if I get landed with it. I just want to know. So that I know what to say. To Mrs Wainwright and Sue Forrest and your nice friend Amy. I'll go and hire a poster site if you like and write in letters three feet high: . . . "Hugo Dashwood is responsible for Dean Wilburn's death". . . . If that will make you feel any better. But I need to know what you want me to say. And do.' He sighed.

Lee was filled with remorse again.

'Hugo, I'm sorry, I'm sorry. Please forgive me. I – I guess I'm not quite myself.'

'On the contrary,' he said, smiling down at her and wiping a fresh rivulet of tears from her face with his handkerchief, 'I think, on the evidence of the past ten years, you are being absolutely yourself. Your awkward, stroppy self.'

'But I'm not usually awkward and stroppy. It's only – only –'

'With me?'

'Well – yes.' For the first time that day she smiled. He smiled back.

'Tell you what we both need. A drink. Do you want some of that disgusting beer of yours?'

'Yes, please.'

'Do you have any wine in the house?'

'No. Sorry. Lots of bourbon.'

'I hate the stuff. But it'll do.'

He fetched them both drinks. They sat outside on the patio looking at the ocean and the pier. Lee sighed.

'In answer to your question, Hugo, I haven't told anyone I was having an affair, but most people have put two and two together. They've assumed that's why he did it. I think I'm going to be a pretty unpopular lady.'

Hugo raised his glass. 'To the prettiest unpopular lady I know. Don't worry, darling. People have short memories.'

He was right. She had a bad six months, and then gradually, in the light of her blameless behaviour, the absolute lack of any kind of lover appearing in her life, her patent desire to look after Miles and bring him up well on her own, in spite of her difficulties, people forgave her whatever they imagined there was to forgive. And Hugo was right, and she did begin to remember Dean more happily and to feel she had done at least a few things right. She did not, as she had feared, go mad with remorse. And life did begin to seem a little more worth living.

She managed to get a job quite easily. She took a quick brush-up course in shorthand typing (paid for by Hugo), and very swiftly found herself working for Irving Phillips, a litigation lawyer who was building himself up a practice in Beverly Hills with impressive speed. He was only five years out of law school, but ruthlessly ambitious and riding high on California's ever-growing wave of aggressive litigation. He had interviewed Lee and a long line of glamorous twenty-two-year-olds who were far more decorative and impressive than she was, Lee had thought despairingly as she watched the one preceding her leave his office and the one following her go into it, but he had hired her without hesitation.

'I want someone who's got a reason to work,' he said to her simply, 'someone who needs the job, and isn't just waiting for some man to come along and keep her.'

'You do realize,' said Lee anxiously, emboldened into honesty by his confiding manner, 'that I've got a little boy. I may have to leave early sometimes, not often, but sometimes, to watch him play in a match or a school play or something. I don't want to come into your firm under false pretences.'

'Lee Wilburn,' Amy Meredith had said when she heard this, 'you're mad. Out of your head. You're lucky he didn't show you the door then and there.'

'Well, he didn't,' said Lee, 'he actually said he liked the fact I'd been so honest, and it made him feel more sure than ever he wanted to hire me. I said I'd work early, late, any time, to make up any leave I took, and I said I'd take work home, and he said, well, that was just fine.'

'Hm!' said Amy. 'Sounds like you'll be exploited if you're not careful. Or else he's got his eye on you for extra office activities. I don't like the sound of it at all.'

But Amy had been wrong, and it had worked out beautifully. Lee did work very hard, and very often took work home and was at her typewriter until long after Miles was asleep at night, and even worked on Saturdays sometimes, if Miles could be taken care of; but in return Irving Phillips paid her extremely generously, and never, ever carped if she had to be away. She was valuable to him, and he knew it; she was bright enough and personable enough to run the office single-handed if he and his assistant were not there, she very swiftly picked up a working knowledge of legal terms and procedures, she never forgot a client's name, or any detail of a case, however small, and those things were worth infinitely more to Irving Phillips than a spot-on regular five-day attendance in the office that ended at five thirty on the dot, and carried no remnant of one day's work over to the next. And there had certainly been absolutely no suspicion ever of him wanting to do anything remotely unbusinesslike, as Amy had so darkly prophesied; there was Mrs Phillips, Mrs Sarah Phillips, who was dark and pretty and devoted to her Irving, and the two little Phillips boys, and all their photographs were all over his desk, and he called home at least twice a day, and he genuinely seemed to be just about the nicest most straightforward person anyone could wish to work for.

And then Hugo had been really good to her. Lee was amazed by how good he had been. He visited them at least every three months, sometimes more often; he had insisted on paying off the outstanding mortgage on the house, so that she lived there for nothing; he made her an allowance. 'For Miles, not you,' he said firmly, 'so don't go getting proud on me,' and he called her at least once a week to check that everything was all right. She was intrigued to find that she felt nothing remotely sexual for him, any more, nor he apparently for her; they had become (not without some difficulty, she reflected with a wry amusement) that rarest of rare things, platonic friends. They had very little in common in most ways; he was, she knew, far more cultured, educated, sophisticated than she was, but somehow they always had a great deal to talk about, they would sit and chat for hours over dinner or walking on the beach, about anything or everything that happened to catch their attentions. Hugo told her she made him feel relaxed and easy; he said that when he was with her the stresses and pressures of his other life faded away; he felt like a different person.

'Just as well,' she said, teasing him, 'otherwise you might start feeling guilty or confused.'

'No,' he said, 'not with you. I never feel anything bad with you. I just feel peaceful and happy.'

She felt that was nice; something she could give him in return for all he did for her. She still knew amazingly little about him (mostly because she hardly ever asked, and he was not unnaturally unwilling to talk about his other life); he said he was absolutely certain that Alice suspected nothing, that she

297

was very busy with her own life as a teacher, and bringing up the little boys, and she was used to him being away a lot, he always had been. Lee had once, driven by a mixture of desperate curiosity and something strangely akin to jealousy, asked him to tell her exactly what Alice was like, what she looked like, and the sort of person she was, and he had been angry, in a quiet, white-lipped way, and told her not to be destructive and stupid, and that Alice was no concern of hers; she had apologized at once, and later he had too, and said that he could see it must be tantalizing for her, but that it really was better that she knew as little as possible, and she had agreed and said again she was sorry, and that had been the last time they had ever talked about it, and almost the last time Lee had ever seriously thought about it. In the early days she had spent a lot of time thinking about Alice, imagining how beautiful she must be, and how efficient and how sexy, but now she filed her neatly away just as she did Irving Phillips' letters and documents, she knew where she was and she could get her out if necessary, but her place was at the very back of a closed drawer.

Although she did not fancy Hugo any more, she occasionally was tempted to start a relationship with other men; she was not nearly as sexually aware as she had been, but she was still a sensual woman, and she missed that side of her life quite badly at times. And when she met a man – at a PTA meeting, or at the baseball games, or in Irving Phillips' office – who looked at her in a way that made her senses stir, made her feel aware of herself and her sexuality again, it was as if a small sleeping bird, settled somewhere deep within her, had stirred and fluttered its wings, and for days after that she would be troubled and restless; she would have wild, sexual dreams, and wake up in the middle of an orgasm, or she would lie awake, tossing and turning, masturbating, coming again and again, but still empty, still hungry. Nevertheless, she never pursued any relationship with any man; she was too afraid. Afraid of involvement, afraid of distressing Miles (who had weathered Dean's death so extremely well), afraid of upsetting Hugo, who deserved some kind of fidelity, however one-sided their arrangement might be, afraid of pregnancy, afraid of love. She had friendships, she had a modest social life, and was very active on the PTA and the Little League, and that she found was surprisingly enough, most of the time.

And so Lee's life had assumed some kind of order and pleasantness; she felt she could look upon it if not with happiness, then certainly not with misery, and indeed rather less anxiety than had been haunting her for the last twelve years.

Her only serious anxiety these days was Miles.

Miles at twelve years old was an interesting child. Too interesting. Lee, analysing it (as she so often did) in the middle of the night, very soon after she had first felt the lump in her breast and totally failed to recapture any semblance of sleep, decided that was why she worried about him. It wasn't that he was particularly naughty, he didn't play hookey from school (or at least only once, at Christmas, the one after Dean died, and he had got a job delivering parcels to earn some Christmas money, and who could blame a little boy seriously for that?) He wasn't cheeky, he didn't hang around street corners after school, he was nearly always there when she got home, or with the Forrests or the Wainwrights, with a note pinned on the door saying exactly where, he didn't even tell lies or knock the furniture around like most twelve-year-olds. He simply went his own sweet way, and did what he wanted; or rather, being only twelve and a trifle limited in his lifestyle, firmly refused to do anything he didn't want. And this did not stop at his school work.

Lee had almost given up now trying to persuade him to go to church with her; every once in a while, when he really wanted to please her (and, she suspected, really wanted something to please himself) he would go along to mass on Sunday morning, swallowing Father Kennedy's smiling admonitions about his absence with remarkably good grace, but generally he would simply give Lee his sweet, unanswerable smile and say no, he didn't plan on coming today. Initially she had tried threatening him with the wrath of either God or the Church or both, but he had shrugged and smiled and returned to his comic or his TV programme without so much as a word of argument. She had even asked Father Kennedy if he would speak to him, and Father Kennedy had come round to the house once or twice, and Miles had listened to his small gentle lecture about the mortal sin of not going to church, and looked gravely at Father

Kennedy and said, 'Thank you for explaining that to me, Father,' and absolutely refused to discuss the matter any further. Afterwards, when the priest had gone, Lee reproached Miles and said how could he be so rude and unresponsive and Miles said he was sorry, but there was nothing to discuss. 'But why isn't there?' Lee said. 'At the very least, God forbid, you could have argued with him. Put your view.'

'Mom, there wouldn't have been any point,' said Miles, 'he wouldn't have seen it. Waste of breath.'

That was his attitude to most things. If he didn't like something, or the idea of doing something, he just cut it out of his life, or did the minimum – like his school work. He didn't argue and make a fuss, he simply didn't do it. As he was now taller than Lee there was very little she could do about it. There was very little anyone could do about it. His teachers could punish him, and keep him in after school and give him lines, but those were punishments for bad behaviour and Miles did not behave badly. He was always polite and charming to his elders, he gave his work in on time – such as it was – he attended lessons, he sat quietly, he was not disruptive. But his grades were awful – except at maths and geography.

The other reason the teachers found it hard to get too angry with him was that he was such an asset to the school. He played games superbly. He was best pitch anyone in the school could ever remember, and although it wasn't his game, he was a fine soccer player too. He was the star of all the athletics teams; he could run like the wind, and jump in a way that defied gravity. He had beaten every speed and high-jump record in the school's history. In matches against other schools, if Miles Wilburn was in the team, St Clement's won.

He was also a very talented actor. While other kids giggled and got embarrassed, or alternatively overacted, Miles simply became the person he was playing. The boy in jeans and T-shirt could become, in an instant, with an imperceptible shift of personality, a prince, a king, an old man, even a young woman. Miles' impression of Marilyn Monroe was a joy to behold.

Lee worried about that talent in a way, because she was so afraid Miles would want to go into the film business and start hanging round the studio lots, but he showed not the slightest tendency to do anything of the sort. He enjoyed drama at school, but only in a passive way; he did not, as stagestruck kids so often did, form companies and put on productions, or want to take extra drama lessons. It was more as if he was aware of his talent and was waiting to use it when the time came: not on the stage at all, perhaps, or in front of the cameras, but in life itself. Indeed he used it in this way already: watching Miles switch from naughty small boy to thoughtful student when his grandmother visited, for instance, to avoid a time and energy-wasting confrontation with her, or as dutiful respectful Young Person in the presence of Hugo Dashwood, was enraging but amusing. Hugo was not deceived, Lee could see, by the impersonation of dutiful and respectful Young Person, mostly because he had heard too much of the other side of Miles from her, but he went along with the charade; he was obviously very fond of the boy, and enjoyed his company. She was not quite sure if the enjoyment was two-sided.

Miles was also now quite exceptionally good-looking. He was very tall for twelve, nearly five foot ten, with golden blond hair, a classically straight nose, a rather sensuously full mouth and dark, extraordinarily luminous blue eyes fringed by long, curly black lashes – 'Like a girl's,' said Jamie Forrest in disgust. Jamie, like most of the other boys, liked Miles, hero worshipped him almost, for his prowess at sport, but were fiercely jealous of him for his looks, the way he got away with things, and the way that, already, the girls were falling over themselves to get near him.

Miles was not only tall and good-looking, he had a way with the girls. He would sit looking at them very intensely, listening to them chattering and giggling, and they would gradually fall silent, discomforted, suddenly self-conscious and acutely aware of his attention. Then he would smile at them, his slow, heartbreaking smile, at whichever one (or two, or even three) had taken his fancy, and wander over to them, and start talking to them.

Jamie and Freddy Wainwright and all the other boys never could imagine what he could talk to them about; everybody knew girls had nothing in their heads except clothes and make-up, and weren't interested in soccer or baseball, which didn't leave a lot of room for conversational manoeuvre, but Miles managed. In no time at all the girls were laughing with him, and talking nineteen to the dozen, and he was laughing and talking back. When they asked him he would shrug and say, 'Oh, you know,' and they didn't like to say no they didn't because it sounded so hopelessly crass, so it remained a mystery. What they did know was that the prettiest girls in the school, and the sexiest, like Joanna Albertson who already had size thirty-four-inch tits, and Sonia Tullio who had legs as long as a colt's and eyes full of what the dumbest boy could see was carnal knowledge, made it very plain that the person they wanted to walk along with, and have carry their books for them, and meet on the beach on Sundays, was Miles Wilburn. And it was very irritating.

And so Lee worried. She worried that Miles' grades were never going to get any better and that was really scary, because everyone knew that the war in Vietnam was escalating and any boy whose grades were below a C in college got sent out there, and OK, Miles was only twelve, nearly thirteen actually now, but six years could go really fast and the rate that war was going and the rate young men were getting killed they might even bring the enlistment age down; and she worried that Miles was just too clever for his own good, and too good at manipulating people and getting them to do what he wanted; and she worried that he might suddenly take it into his head to want to be an actor after all; and she worried that he was sexually precocious, and the way the girls were all running after him, he would get one of them into trouble. But most of all she worried that he seemed to her in every way to be getting more and more like Hugo.

And that was a worry she couldn't share with anyone.

'I think' – and the doctor's voice was dangerously, threateningly casual – 'I think we'd better have a look at this little lump, Mrs Wilburn. I'm sure it's nothing, nothing at all, just a cyst, but it's as well to be on the safe side. We can take it out very easily, you'll only need to be in hospital for a couple of days, and send it off to be analysed and then we won't have to worry any more.'

'I see,' said Lee. The room spun threateningly, darkened with panic; she felt horribly, sickly afraid. 'But if you're sure it's nothing, why do we have to bother? I mean, are you really sure?'

'As sure as I can be without actually looking at it. I mean, it's very small and you say it hasn't got any bigger?'

She shook her head vigorously, pushing back the doubt.

'And you breast fed your baby, didn't you?'

'Yes, I did.'

'Yes, well that's a good thing, a very good thing. How's your health otherwise? Periods regular, all that sort of thing?'

'Yes,' said Lee, wondering briefly whether to mention an increase in pain and frequency, and rejecting it. After all she was forty-two years old, and it was probably the change beginning; doctors were notoriously unwilling to sympathize with women on that.

'Well, let's see, the sooner the better. I think I'd like to bring you in next week, and then we can get the whole thing over and done with before Thanksgiving. Can you get time off from work?'

'I think so.'

'And what about your little boy? Can he go to friends?'

'Oh, yes. That's no problem.'

'Good. Well, I'll have a word with my secretary, and let you know. I expect by this time in a fortnight, you'll be out and about and feeling just wonderful. Now I don't want you to worry, Mrs Wilburn. I'm just taking precautions.'

'Oh, I won't worry,' said Lee. 'Thank you very much.'

So what was it like, to lose a breast? What did it look like, before the wound healed? Was it a huge, gaping hole? How did they get the skin over it? How hideous did it look, even when it had healed? What would you do, under your clothes? Stuff out a bra with socks or something? Or would they give you something? Would people know? How could you bear to touch yourself? Look at yourself? Could you ever go on the beach again? Thank God Dean was gone. He would have hated it, loathed it, been revolted by it. What about Miles? How would he cope with the thought of a maimed mother? What would it do to his sexual development? What would the other kids say? They would be bound to hear.

How much would it hurt? Would the pain be awful? Would they give you morphine just when you asked them, or would you get it anyway? Would she be able to bear it? Would she scream? Was it that kind of pain? Like childbirth, ripping-apart pain? Only that was bearable because it was good pain. This was evil, destructive, deadly pain. Suppose it was in other places already, the cancer? In her uterus, in her stomach? How could they treat that? They could take the uterus out, but what of the stomach? Would she have to have one of those bag things like old Mrs Thackeray, that gurgled all the time? Better to die. No, not better to die.

Who would look after Miles if she died? Hugo couldn't, that would be asking too much. Her friends couldn't. Dean had no parents. She only had her distinctly difficult and eccentric mother, who lived in Ohio and only came to visit once a year at Thanksgiving, and anyway, she was sixty-five. He would be alone. Would he have to go to an orphanage? One of the refuge places? How would he ever grow up adjusted now, with two parents dead? Who would ever drive him to do his school work, see he didn't get too full of himself, discipline him, love him, praise him, cuddle him?

At half past six next morning, when the sun was just beginning to break into the shadows of the Santa Monica Mountains and tinge the sea with a faint shy blush, Lee was still awake.

The lump proved to be absolutely harmless. 'Just a tiny cyst,' said the doctor, smiling at her in pleasure and self-justification. 'You see how right we were to take it out.'

'Oh,' said Lee, tears of relief and weak joy pouring down her face, 'oh, thank you, Doctor Forsythe, thank you very, very much. When can I go home?'

'Tomorrow. Only you must take it easy. You've had a general anaesthetic. Promise me you won't go rushing off stocking up for Thanksgiving.'

'I promise. I promise.' She was laughing and crying at the same time.

That night Miles came to see her with Amy. They both had armfuls of flowers.

'It's all right,' said Lee, beaming at then ecstatically. 'Everything is all right. It was nothing. Just a cyst. Isn't that just the most glorious news ever? I don't have cancer. I'm not going to die.'

'Hey Mom,' said Miles, reaching for her hand, 'you never told me that was on the cards. You said it was just nothing.'

'Well, it was nothing,' said Lee, stretching forward and kissing him, 'nothing at all. Thank you for the flowers, honey. Are you OK?'

'Yeah, I'm fine.'

'Did you go to school?'

'Of course I went to school, Mom. Don't insult me!' He was laughing at her.

'I'm sorry.'

'I have two messages,' said Amy, who had stayed over the night before to keep Miles company. 'One from your English gentleman friend. He said he just called to say hallo, and how were you. I said you were fine, just having minor surgery, and you'd be home tomorrow. He said he'd call you then. He must be pretty keen on you, Lee, to keep calling you from New York.'

'Oh, not really,' said Lee airily. She was not to be drawn on the subject of Hugo, not even by Amy. She knew Amy was consumed with curiosity on the subject, but she just left her permanently consumed. She knew this hurt her friend, but she couldn't help it. Miles and Hugo himself were more important to her than anyone in the world. And every single person who knew anything more about Hugo than that he was an old business friend of Dean's, which was what she told everyone, made the situation a hundred per cent more dangerous.

'Who else phoned?'

'Your mom.'

'Oh, God.'

'Yeah. I told her the same, and she said she would be down next week for Thanksgiving and she'd look after you then.'

'Oh, great,' said Lee. But she didn't really mind. She didn't mind anything. She was not going to die.

Forty-eight hours later she was pushing her cart through the market, getting the weekend groceries, when she suddenly felt a huge and terrible weakness, and a hot, fierce pain in her belly. She fainted and came round, in the manager's office, a wad of towels between her legs. She was haemorrhaging.

That night she had a hysterectomy; a malignant uterine tumour had been discovered.

Lying, weak and tearful, in the bed she had left so happily three days earlier, she asked Doctor Forsythe what might lie ahead. 'Is – is that it? Might the cancer be anywhere else?'

'It might,' he said, patting her hand gently. 'But uterine cancer is the easiest to contain. We may be lucky.'

She noticed he did not meet her eye.

'Amy,' she said next day. 'Could you call this number? Just leave a message to say I called.'

'Sure.' Amy looked at it. 'New York, huh? Is this your beau?'

'He's not a beau,' said Lee, managing to smile faintly. 'Just call him, Amy. No, on second thoughts, don't. I don't want to worry him. But Amy, I do think you'd better call my mom. Get her down sooner. I won't be home for a week or so. She's coming anyway, so she can't complain. Miles won't like it, but he'll have to put up with it for a bit. And could you tell Mr Phillips too, that I won't be back for a week or two?'

'Honey, you won't be back that soon. You have to rest up for a long time after a hysterectomy. Otherwise you just won't get well again.'

'Well, never mind,' said Lee. 'We'll just take it one day at a time. Tell him two weeks for now. OK?'

'OK,' said Amy.

She was home in two weeks; relieved and happy to be there, she lay obediently on the couch all day, directing operations, running her small household. Her mother, eccentrically vague but deceptively spry for her sixty-five years, needed directing, but coped physically extremely well. She kept telling Lee she couldn't stay long, and that her hens and her goats needed her more than Lee did, but she promised not to go home until things were back under control. It was a promise she had some difficulty keeping.

Six weeks after her operation, when Lee was just beginning to feel stronger, and thinking that very soon she would be able to go back to work and let her mother return to the goats, she developed a stomach bug.

'It's just because I'm run down,' she said shakily to Amy, returning to her couch after a prolonged session in the toilet. 'I'll be better soon.'

'You'd better be,' said Mrs Kelly from her corner, where she was working on a petit point picture of some hens in a barnyard, 'I have to get back to my family real soon.'

'Mom, we're your family,' said Lee mildly, sinking back on her pillows with a grimace of pain, 'surely we matter more than a few old hens.'

'That's arguable,' said Mrs Kelly, 'and they're not old, they're young and at the peak of their laying capability. I dread to think what young Terence is doing with those darlings; giving them under-cooked bran mash, cutting down on their greens. Oh, it just turns my mind thinking about it.'

'Mrs Kelly, I'm sure the hens are all right,' said Amy, 'but if you're really worried why don't you go home and I'll stay with Lee till she's over this. It won't be more than a few days.'

'No,' said Mrs Kelly firmly, her face starched into a martyred mould. 'I promised my daughter I'd stay till she was on her feet, and I will. I'm not a one to go back on a promise. Besides, Amy, I've noticed you are far too indulgent with Miles, that boy is running wild and I see it as my duty to bring some discipline into his life. He may not like it, but he will thank me when he's older. No, my hens will just have to wait. It's tragic, when I think how much they must be missing me, but there it is. I know my duty.'

'OK,' said Amy, diplomatically tactful for the sake of her friend. 'That's really nice of you. Lee, can I get you anything, honey? Some iced herbal tea? Some lemonade? I've made some fresh. I know exactly what's the matter with you, Lee Wilburn, you're just stuck full of additives and preservatives, you've been living on that stuff for far too long. You need a totally organic diet for a while and you'll be just fine.'

'Quite right,' said Mrs Kelly. 'I wouldn't give my hens chemically produced food, wouldn't dream of it. It affects them and it affects their eggs. It's a whole dreadful cycle. Amy's right, Lee, your diet is just awful, no wonder you're ill.'

'Oh, could you both just shut up and help me back to the toilet,' said Lee, her face twisted with pain. 'I'm getting rid of every bit of artificially grown food in my body just as fast as it'll go. Please, Amy, please!'

'I think,' said Amy later to Mrs Kelly, looking at Lee's ashen, slightly waxy face as she dozed fitfully on the couch, 'we should get hold of Doctor Forsythe. I think this is more than additives.'

It was. Doctor Forsythe had Lee back in hospital, ran some tests and scans, and pronounced cancer of the liver and the bowel. 'Inoperable. I'm sorry, Lee. So very sorry.'

He held her hand. She clung to it, as if she could drag some of his own strong life into her.

'It's not your fault,' she said, politely, as if seeking to put him at his ease.

'No. Nor yours.'

'Of course not.' She was surprised.

'Oh, you'd be surprised. A lot of people feel guilt. Feel they could have prevented it. Feel there was something they should, and indeed could, do.'

'Yes,' said Lee. 'Yes, Amy will say it's the additives.'

'Ah,' he said. 'Yes, a favourite scapegoat right now.'

There was a silence. He looked at her tenderly.

'You haven't had much luck lately, have you, Lee?'

'No,' she said, 'I haven't. Will – will it . . .'

'Hurt? No, no more than you can bear. Pain control has become very good. You have only to ask.'

'And how long?'

He looked at her very steadily. 'Not long. Perhaps three months.'

She gasped, reeled back as if he had hit her. Then she started to cry, huge wracking, childish tears, on and on; she hit the pillow, bit her fists, screamed. 'It's not fair, it's not fair, I've tried so hard, so hard, why should it be me, why why why? I hate it, I hate it, I hate everybody, everything. Go away, go away, I hate you, why couldn't you have seen it, helped me, done something, you told me it was nothing, just a cyst, and now I'm dying and you can only give me three months. You're cruel and you're an idiot, you're a lousy, fucking, useless doctor, and I hate you. Go away, go away.'

He didn't go away, he stayed and listened to her, and when she would let him, held her, held her hand, held her in his arms, like a lover, like a father; gradually she calmed.

'I'm sorry.'

'I know. Can I do anything?'

'Yes. Could you ask Father Kennedy to come and see me? And could you ring this number, this man, and ask him to come? Explain why. Soon. Please.'

Father Kennedy came first. Lee was frightened, as only a sinning Catholic can be frightened.

'Father, I have to confess.'

'Very well.'

'No, not in church, here now. Will you listen?'

'I will.'

She told him. She told him everything, about Hugo, about Miles, about Dean. He listened.

'May God forgive you.'

'Do you think he will?'

'Christ came to the world to save sinners.'

'I know. But sinners like me?'

'Exactly like you. And me. We are all sinners.'

She looked at him and smiled. 'Father, I don't think you rank as a sinner.'

'In the eyes of God I do.'

'Well, he must have pretty sharp eyes.'

'Merciful eyes also.'

'Father, will you come?'

He understood at once.

'Of course. Whenever you feel it is time.'

'Suppose I don't know?'

'You will.'

'Will you tell Doctor Forsythe to call you? Just in case?'

'Of course. He always does.'

She was comforted.

'Father, what can I do about Miles? I only have my mother, and she is so – well, so unsuitable.'

'She is his grandmother, though. And she is willing to take care of him.'

'How do you know?'

'She told me.'

'Heavens above,' said Lee, shocked out of her submissiveness. 'When?'

'She came to see me. She said she thought it was her duty. Lee, I wouldn't call her unsuitable. She's a good woman. She's strong, for her age. And she loves Miles. She might even be good for him. A little old-fashioned discipline.'

Lee frowned. 'I know everyone thinks I spoil Miles. But it's almost impossible not to.'

'I know.' He patted her hand. 'He is a beautiful and charming boy.'

'But he's so young. Such a baby. So little to be left alone. I can't bear leaving him, Father, I just can't. Never to see him grow up, how will he manage without me?'

He watched her, weeping silently, struggling to control herself.

'He won't be alone, Lee.'

'Oh,' she said, angry suddenly. 'Oh, I forgot. Of course, God will be there. He'll see to his packed lunch, and comfort him when he skins his knees and cheer him on when he plays baseball and watch he isn't out after dark, and listen to him when he's worried, and have fun with him on Sundays, and ask his friends round and cuddle him and tell him he's a great guy when things go wrong and be on his side when the teachers pick on him, and try to make sure he gets to college so he doesn't have to go to Vietnam. Oh, good, I don't need to worry at all.'

'God will do some of those things, Lee. Your mother will do others. Some he will have to manage on his own. You must have faith, Lee, to save your own happiness during these weeks. They're too precious to waste in misery and doubt.'

'I just don't know how you can talk like that. Think like that.'

'Talking is easy. Thinking, believing is more difficult.' He smiled at her. 'Tell me, is your English friend coming to see you?'

'Yes. Tomorrow he arrives. I suppose you think that's terribly wicked.' She looked at him, half tearful, half hostile.

'No. I don't think love and comfort are ever wicked. Given in the right way at the right time. I'm glad he's coming. Perhaps I shouldn't be, but I am.'

'Thank you, Father.' She smiled at him, easier, happier again. 'Thank you. Please come again. Before – before you have to.'

'I will. Often. I shall enjoy it. The company of a pretty young woman is always pleasant.'

She looked in the mirror at her pallid face, already tinged with yellow, her distended stomach, and grimaced. 'Pretty!'

He bent and kissed her cheek. 'Very pretty. Now rest. And enjoy your visitor.'

*

Hugo was shocked at the sight of her. She could see it in his eyes. He hadn't seen her since she had had the cyst out – well, it had only been six weeks altogether – and he winced as he looked at her. It hurt her.

'Hi, Hugo. Here I am then, your golden California girl, turned a little tarnished. I'm sorry I look so hideous. I can't help it, I'm afraid.'

'You don't look hideous. You couldn't. Not exactly glowing, but not hideous.'

She was sullen, hostile.

'Don't lie to me. I look hideous.'

'OK,' he said agreeably, 'you look hideous.'

'You didn't have to come,' she said, and started, once again, to cry. Every fresh visitor, fresh intruder into her safe, sick world, made her cry, forcing her as they did to confront her sickness, her imminent death.

'No, I didn't,' he said. 'But I did come. I wanted to come.'

'Good for you.'

She was silent. Then: 'Have you come from England or New York?'

'England.'

'Ah. How's Alice?'

'She's fine.'

'How very nice for her,' she said bitterly. 'How very nice.'

'Lee, don't.'

'Don't what? Don't care?'

'Don't be angry.'

'But I am angry,' she cried, 'you would be angry too. Losing half your life, losing your child, being in pain, being afraid, of course I'm angry, fuck you, I'm furious.'

'I'm sorry.'

'Yes, I expect you are. I expect you thought you'd find some peaceful, madonna-like figure lying back on her pillows, smiling serenely, telling her rosary. Well, death isn't like that, Hugo, I've learnt. It's hard and it's painful and it's elusive and it's ugly. And it makes you angry. So angry.'

'I know,' he said.

'You don't.'

'Yes, I do. I told you once, don't you remember?'

'What?'

'That death wasn't so bad.'

'Oh,' she said, 'oh, yes, yes, I do. Tell me about it, Hugo, tell me about the people you have seen die.'

'Mostly men,' he said. 'A few women. In the war. People are nearly always brave. Almost welcoming. Usually very calm.'

'And afterwards?'

'Great, great peace. A peace you can feel. A stillness.'

She reached out for his hand and gripped it.

'I'm so frightened.'

'I know. So am I.'

'What of?'

'Of losing you.'

She was amazed. 'Losing me?'

'Yes. Losing you. I can't imagine life without you now. You are the only truly happy thing I have. I love you. I love you so much.'

She lay on her pillows, her eyes fixed in genuine, awestruck astonishment on his face. 'I never knew.'

'I know you didn't. God knows why you didn't. Didn't I behave as if I did?'

She thought, looking back over the lost, happy years. 'Yes. Yes, I suppose you did. I never saw it, but yes you did.'

He smoothed her thin hair back from her forehead. 'And you don't look hideous. Truly. You look lovely.'

She looked at him and smiled, took his hand.

'I wish I'd known.'

'Why?'

'Well – I would have been nicer to you for a start.'

'You've been very nice to me recently.'

'I know, but I was so horrid all those years.'

'True.'

'I was just so afraid – well, it doesn't matter.'

'I know. That I would come and claim Miles.'

'Yes.'

'As if I would have done. Loving you. Loving him.'

She looked at him. 'Do you love him?'

'Very much. I think he's interesting and clever and charming. Like me.'

'No, seriously.'

'Seriously I think he's all those things. Seriously I love him. And I'll do everything I can to take care of him.'

'But you won't . . .'

'No. Never. Don't worry.'

'He'll need taking care of. My mother is going to move down. She'll see he does his school work and doesn't go on the streets, but she won't truly understand him and what he needs. She can't.'

'I'm sure Amy will do a lot. And his other friends and their families.'

'At first. But they have their own families. And they'll slowly stop thinking about Miles. In that kind of way.'

'Well, I will do my best.'

'What will you do? What can you do?'

'Oh, lots of things. I even thought about adopting him. Don't look at me like that, I'm a good liar and I would have thought of something.'

'Are you a good liar?'

'Excellent.'

'I'm not. Sometimes I wish I was.' She sighed and looked at him with a rueful smile. 'Miles is a wonderful liar. I can't even tell when he's doing it.'

'Well, it can be useful. Anyway, I thought I would make a settlement on Miles, a lump sum, to be held in trust for him. The income will be useful to your mother now. At least they won't have any material worries.'

'Hugo, how can you afford that sort of thing? Are you very rich?'

'No. Not what I would call very rich. But I do have some money and I think I owe it to him.'

'And who will look after this settlement? See he gets it?'

'My lawyer in New York.'

'Could my mother have his name?'

'Of course.'

'Thank you.'

'And then later, I will see he goes to a good college. That will postpone his draft as long as possible. I know that worries you. And then, I will also see he gets a job. A good job. Maybe he could work for me. I don't know. But I won't let him hang around the town, sharing peace and love with the flower children. Or taking drugs. I promise you. And I will come and see him very often, and talk to him, and make sure there aren't any serious problems, and that he isn't seriously unhappy. That your mother is meeting all the needs she can. That he isn't too lonely. Too lost.'

Lee was crying again. 'I'm sorry. I can't bear the thought of leaving him. It's the worst, the only thing I really care about.'

'I know.'

She was silent for a while. Then: 'Why do you love me? I mean what is it about me? I don't really understand. I thought it was just sex.'

'It was at first. I thought you were the most beautiful, desirable, sexy woman I had ever seen. You were certainly the sexiest woman I'd ever been to bed with.'

'Really?' she said in genuine astonishment.

'Yes, really.'

'But how? I mean in what way?'

'Hard to define. I suppose because you didn't think about it. Didn't analyse it. Just wanted it terribly badly and did it.'

'And could you tell I wanted it? I mean early on?'

'Oh yes,' he said, kissing her hand, fixing her eyes with his own. 'From that very first day, that very first lunch. I thought, now there is a lady who would be a terrific, gloriously outrageously wonderful lay. And I was right.'

'OK. So that was the sex. But the love?'

'Oh, the love. That's quite different.'

'How?'

'I had to love you without ever getting near you again. So I had to find other things to love. It wasn't hard.'

'What were they?'

'Your courage. Your honesty. Your straightforward, sock it to me, let's get on with life attitude. And then later, more recently, still your courage, which has been phenomenal, but also your capacity for happiness. For pleasure. The talent you have for caring for people. I think,' he said slowly, stroking her hand very gently, 'I am very lucky to have known you. And to have fathered your – our child. I count it as a great privilege. And it is the source of great happiness in my life.'

'Oh, Hugo,' said Lee, a great sob breaking into her voice, lying back on her pillows, closing her eyes, 'leave me alone now. Come back tomorrow. I can't bear it.'

'All right,' he said standing up. 'I'll go. And I will be back tomorrow.'

'How – how long can you stay?'

'A while. As long as you need me.'

'All right.'

'Now Mom, are you absolutely perfectly sure about all this?'

'I'm as perfectly sure as I can be,' said Mrs Kelly with a martyred sigh. 'The way I look at it, I don't have much choice.'

'Well you are sixty-five. That's quite an age to be caring for a little boy.'

'And what a little boy. If you'd raised him a little more strictly it might be an easier task. I always told you you spoilt him. Now I have to pick up the pieces.'

'Oh, Mom, don't. And he's a good boy. Please remember that. Please. And he needs love.'

'I know.' Her face softened. 'It's all right, Honey, I will love him. I do love him. You don't have to fret.'

'I can't help fretting.'

'Yes, well, it don't help anyone. Least of all you.'

'No, I suppose. Now Mom, I want to talk to you about money. There really isn't a problem there.'

'Why not? Dean never made any money.'

'No, but – well, he had a good life policy. Hugo – Mr Dashwood, you know – he helped me invest it and it is worth quite a lot now. He suggests we put it in trust for Miles, for when he's twenty-one, and the income will be very useful to you in the meantime.'

'It must be a very good life policy. How come you got it when Dean killed himself?'

'Oh, it was a special one,' said Lee quickly. 'And also, Mom, if you have any problems, money or legal ones, you can contact Mr Dashwood. He lives in England, but he has a small office in New York. They can take messages. You can always contact him, if it's urgent. Only don't do it all the time.'

'I certainly won't,' said Mrs Kelly. 'I wouldn't want to. I don't like the English. Stiff, unfriendly lot. Living in the dark ages most of the time.' She looked at Lee sharply. 'Mr Dashwood seems to be a very good friend to you, Lee.'

'He is,' said Lee firmly, 'and he was a real good friend to Dean too. Dean – helped him once, when he was starting out. He's always said he'd like to repay that.'

'I see.'

'And you really really don't mind coming to live over here?'

'I mind like hell,' said Mrs Kelly. 'Like hell. And how I can face saying goodbye to those hens I don't know. But I know my duty. I always have. I would never forgive myself if I failed in it now. And this is where Miles should be. I can see that. So what must be must be. But it isn't easy.'

'No,' said Lee. She closed her eyes.

Her mother looked at her. 'Are you OK?'

'Just about. It's nearly time for the morphine. That's a bad bit of the day.'

'Poor kid,' said her mother. It was the first and indeed the only time she had ever evinced any sympathy for Lee whatsoever. Lee knew what it meant. She smiled at her mother and took her hand.

'I really am very grateful to you.'

'Hmm. Well, I just hope I last the course.' There was a pause. 'Lee, that affair you were having – before Dean died, the one that caused it – is that right over now? I never asked you, never wanted to know. But now I need to, I guess.'

'Oh, yes,' said Lee. 'Absolutely over.'

'Amy, you will keep an eye on Miles, won't you?'

'Of course I will. You know I will.'

'No, but you'll keep keeping an eye on him. You won't forget.'

'For God's sake, Lee. We go back a long way. I won't forget.'

'He'll need you so badly.'

'I know.'

'Just – just hug him sometimes. And have some fun with him.'

'I will. Don't worry about it.'

'I can't help it.'

'I know.'

'Hugo will be down from time to time. Keeping an eye on things. He's – he's very fond of Miles.'

Amy looked at her deadpan. 'I can see that.'

'Yes, well.'

'He's very fond of you too, I guess.'

'Yes, he is.'

'You're not going to tell me, are you, Lee?'

'No,' said Lee simply.

'Yeah, well, I have eyes in my head. And a brain. Oh, don't look at me like that, Lee. I won't say anything. I can't say anything. I don't know anything to say.'

'No,' said Lee. 'No, you don't.'

'Is – is everything all right with your mom? Money and so on.'

'Oh, yes,' said Lee. 'No worries about money. There's the insurance and everything. The house is mine. No mortgage.'

'Some insurance policy,' said Amy.

'Yes.'

'How do you feel?' said Amy, looking at her tenderly.

'Lousy.'

'You look lousy.'

'Thanks.'

'Does it hurt a lot?'

'Sometimes. The drugs are very good. Mostly it's just terrible discomfort. And weakness. Weariness. And I can't sleep.' She gripped her friend's hand. 'Oh, Amy, I'm not even scared any more. I just want it to be over.'

'It will be, Honey. Soon.'

'Miles, look at me. No, on second thoughts, don't. I'm not a pretty sight.'

'You look OK.'

'Thanks Hon.'

'That's OK.'

'Now listen to me, Miles. We have to have a talk.'

'OK.'

'Now you do know, don't you, that I won't be here much longer.'

'Yes, I do.'

'Now we have to be grown up and sensible about this, Miles. No point crying or making a fuss, like I used to tell you about your school work. It has to be done.'

'That's different from my school work. I manage to duck out of that. I can't duck out of you dying.'

'No,' said Lee, thinking she would stifle under the weight of the huge tearing pain in her heart as she looked at him, so much worse than any physical pain she had endured over the past three months. 'No, you can't. And I can't duck out of it either.'

'Are you scared Mom?'

'A bit. Not really any more.'

'I'm scared.'

'What of?'

'Of being without you.'

'Oh, Miles.' She closed her eyes, swallowed, fought to hold on to herself. 'Miles, don't be scared. You're allowed to be sad, but not to be scared. You'll manage. You're so brave. And so tough.'

'Like you. You're the bravest person I ever even heard of.'

'I try to be,' said Lee.

'Was Dad brave? I don't really remember.'

'Very brave.'

'Why did he die, Mom? I never understood. I think you should tell me. I know he killed himself. Billy Fields told me he heard his mom tell his dad that Dad killed himself. And I saw a newspaper cutting that somebody else found in their attic. And I just can't think why. All I can remember is us being a really happy family.'

'Well, we were,' said Lee staunchly. 'And don't let anyone ever tell you any different. We were very very happy. Your dad was happy. Until – until that last day. Then he did something silly. Something foolish. And it went rather badly wrong.'

'What?'

'Well, you see' – God help me, thought Lee – 'you see, although your dad was very clever and very good, he didn't make that much money. He was quite successful but not terribly terribly successful. And he minded about that very much. And he heard that an old friend had done terribly terribly well, and he got very depressed, and he felt he was a failure. And he also got very drunk. And then he went up to bed and took some sleeping pills. Only, mixed with the drink and his bad heart, it killed him.'

'I see. How sad.'

'Yes, it was terribly sad. Dreadful. But I have learnt to think about when we were happy. As you do. Just keep thinking about that, Miles. Don't let anyone take it away from you.'

'I won't. Anyway, I feel better now. I wish I'd asked you

318

before. I'm glad you told me.' He looked at her, his frightened, loving heart in his dark blue eyes. 'Oh, Mom, what am I going to do without you to make me feel better?'

Lee couldn't speak. She held out her arms, and Miles, big boy that he was, crawled into them. She smoothed back his hair, kissed his head, stroked his face.

'I'm sorry I don't work at school much, Mom,' he said after a while. 'Was that what you wanted to talk to me about?'

'Partly,' said Lee, grateful to get the conversation on a less emotional level. 'Not because I'm cross with you. But because I have such hopes, such high hopes for you. You're so clever, Miles. Cleverer than me or Dad' (Oh, God, she thought, I shouldn't have said that) 'and you can do so well. So terribly well. Don't throw it away, Miles. You must work hard. Don't let me down.'

'You won't be there,' he said with simple logic. 'You won't know if I've let you down.'

'Now look,' said Lee, half laughing, half crying, 'is that going to make me feel any better right now, Miles Wilburn? Worrying about you, all day and all night? I want to – to go away feeling proud and confident and happy about you. That's the very last thing you can give me, and it will be such a lot.'

'OK,' said Miles. 'I promise. I'll work hard. Do you want me to be President? I'll try if you want.'

'It might do for starters.'

'OK.'

'And I want you to be real nice to Granny Kelly. It won't be easy for her. She won't have her friends or her hens or anything.'

'I wouldn't mind her hens. I like hens.'

'Yes, well there's no space for hens in our back yard.'

'I don't know,' said Miles, brightening up, 'there might be.'

'Well,' said Lee, with the first thankful sigh she had heaved for weeks, 'that is nothing to do with me, that is entirely between you and Granny Kelly.'

'OK.'

'Now, Mr Dashwood – '

'Mom, I wish you'd call him Hugo to me. He calls himself Hugo.'

'All right, Hugo. He has very kindly said he will keep an eye on you and Granny Kelly, so if you have any big problems, at school, or about money, or if you think Granny isn't coping, you can talk to him. I'll give you his number in New York – he won't answer it, it's not his home, but a secretary will take a message.'

'OK. Where is his home exactly?'

'In England.'

'I know, but where?'

'I'm not sure. In London, somewhere.'

'He seems real fond of you, Mom.' His eyes were probing on her.

'Yes,' said Lee, 'well, he's been a good friend for a long time.'

'But he's not the friend who was more successful than Dad?'

'What? Oh, good gracious no.'

'I just wondered.'

'And day to day problems, you just go to Amy.'

'But,' he said, and tears filled his eyes and spilled down his cheeks, 'it's the day to day problems I'll need you for.'

And then Lee started to cry too, and he climbed right up on the bed beside her, and lay clinging to her, sobbing, sounding as if he was three years old.

They stayed there for a long time. And then she said, finally, exhausted, drained of strength and emotion, trying desperately, helplessly to comfort him, to give him something he could take away with him, 'Miles, my darling, stop, stop crying, this isn't going to do anything, anything at all for either of us.'

'Oh, but it is,' he said, nestling his blond head further on to her pillow, 'I can remember it for always.'

She died early next morning, her sheets still crumpled from where he had lain.

Chapter Eight

London and France, 1972

Things were definitely getting better. Roz felt life was beginning to go her way.

In the first place she had escaped from Cheltenham, and was spending her two sixth-form years at Bedales: co-educational, progressive, civilized. It suited her well; there was scope for her fiercely individual mind, her rather puritan approach to her work, her disregard for the normal social conventions required of a girl of her age.

'The worst thing about Cheltenham,' she said to Letitia, one of the few people she trusted enough to talk to, 'was that if you weren't like the others, all giggly and jolly and gossipy and mad on games, it was hopeless, you were just all alone in the world, but if you didn't want to be alone, you had to pretend to be like them. Pretending was worse than being alone, though,' she added.

'Poor Roz,' said Letitia, 'five years of that sort of thing is a long time.'

'Yes,' said Roz shortly. 'Well, I daresay it did me some good.'

'I hope so, darling. I'm never quite convinced about the therapeutic value of unhappiness. Anyway, I'm glad you like it so much better where you are now. You're looking wonderful,' she added.

Wonderful was perhaps an exaggeration, and Roz knew it; but she also knew she did look better all the time. She was still far from pretty, and probably always would be, but she didn't think anyone any more could call her exactly plain. She was taller, quite a lot taller than any other girl in her year; nobody could quite work out where her height came from –Julian was only six foot, and Eliza was tiny, just about five foot (and half an inch, she always insisted). But there it was, Roz was five foot nine already and still growing, and she was large framed too, with wide shoulders and, to her constant misery, size nine feet. 'Just you try getting fashionable shoes in that size,' she said darkly to anyone who told her it didn't matter. But there was not an ounce of fat on her, she was lean and rangy-looking, apart from a most gratifyingly large bosom. Her face was interesting, dramatic, her rather hollow cheekbones and harsh jaw accentuating her large green eyes, her slightly over-full mouth. Her nose caused her much anguish, it was big, but it was at least straight and not hooked or anything awful, she kept reassuring herself; and her dark hair was thick and shiny, even if it was as straight as the proverbial die, and wilful with it. She wore it long now, and tied back in a long swinging pony tail; it wasn't a style that flattered her but at least it kept it under control, and stopped it sticking out the wrong way which it did unless she spent hours on it with the styling brush and the hair dryer, and even then it often got the better of her and she would end up in tears of frustration with one side neatly turned under and the other flying relentlessly outwards. Of the many things for which she loathed Camilla North her exquisitely behaved red hair came almost top of the list. She had done very well in her O levels, and got eleven, nine of them As; she was doing maths, economics and geography A levels, and in her first term at Bedales had beaten all the girls and all but two of the boys in the pre-Christmas exams. She planned on going to Cambridge to read maths; her tutor had told Julian that she would probably get in on fifth term entry, rather than doing a third year in the sixth. Nothing pleased Roz more than showing her father how clever she was; it made up for not being pretty, not being a boy, not really being the sort of daughter she knew he would have liked. And loved. He obviously liked her more than he had done, he sought her company, even showed her off at times, but it was detachedly, rather as if she was some clever person he had employed rather than his own daughter. She supposed, rather resignedly these days, that she neither looked nor played the daughter part correctly. He was never physically affectionate towards her, never petted her, never teased her; and he had still never asked her to go and live with him permanently, even though her mother was away more than not these days, pursuing first one and then another awful playboy round the world; she had given up all pretence of having a career and was shamelessly (as Roz put it to Rosie Howard Johnson, still her closest and indeed her only friend) being kept by one rich man after another.

And then, Camilla was definitely fading from the scene. It had been months now since she had been even in the guest room at Hanover Terrace, never mind tiptoeing along the corridor to Julian's bedroom, and certainly never at Marriotts; and besides she must be getting on a bit now, in her mid thirties, getting well past her fertility peak, and even safely into the danger zone of prospective foetal abnormalities (Roz had become an expert on such matters, feverishly reading every article and book on the subject she could find).

But there was one willowy and rather distressingly beautiful fly in the ointment: the spirit of Juliana incarnate, one Araminta Jones. And although she was less worrying and certainly less ghastly than Camilla (and had the most enragingly neat, golden brown head of hair), Roz would still have been a lot happier if she had not been around.

The seventies saw the real birth of the personality cult in cosmetics: when one face, one spirit, one aura personified and sold a brand. For Charles Revson and Revlon it was Lauren Hutton; for Mrs Lauder it was Karen Graham; for Julian Morell and Juliana it was Araminta Jones.

When a middle-aged, overweight matron, anxious she might be losing her husband to his twenty-year-old secretary, bought a Revlon lipstick or eye shadow, she felt somehow magically transformed into Lauren Hutton, all college-girl charm, long-legged, radiantly gap-toothed; when a gauche, unremarkable young wife used a Lauder cream or sprayed herself with Alliage before entertaining her husband's important clients, she felt she had acquired some of Karen Graham's old-money glamour and confidence; and when a plain, nervous woman made up her face with Juliana colours and surrounded herself with a cloud of *Mademoiselle Je* before she went to a party, she felt herself suddenly acquiring the upper-class Englishness, the sexy sophistication of Araminta Jones. Miss Jones, like Miss Hutton and Miss Graham, was not just a face or even a body, she was a package, a lifestyle, a way of dressing, of walking, of thinking. You could tell, just by looking at her (and of course by some very clever publicity) that she was well educated, perfectly bred, that she wore designer label clothes, drove an expensive car, knew one end of a horse from another, ate in the best restaurants, holidayed in Bermuda, skied in Aspen, drank nothing but champagne, and had been pro-grammed for success from birth.

The bad news about her, from Rosamund Morell's point of view, was that most of these things were fact, and Julian Morell, having discovered her (and bought her, for what amounted to millions of dollars), was showing every sign of being rather seriously besotted with her. And Araminta was most definitely of childbearing age. On the other hand, it seemed to Roz, her father was definitely getting on a bit, into his fifties, and surely nobody of twenty-two in their right minds would want to get mixed up with someone so seriously old. Araminta, she was sure, was simply stringing her father along, knowing precisely on which side her wafer-thin slices of bread were buttered, taking him for every penny she could get, and would be off without a backward glance from her wide, purple eyes if someone younger and more suitable came along.

Roz had chosen to forget her own brief foray into Love with an Older Man; what was more her opinion of the male race, already low, had taken a further dive at David Sassoon's defection to the United States and from her mother's bed the moment success and fame beckoned in even larger quantities than were already in his possession. She had suffered a qualm or two of conscience witnessing Eliza's awful grief over the defection; had tried not to listen, her hands over her ears, to the hideous, ferocious scene as David tried to justify it ('Darling, I can't afford not to take it, he'll destroy me, give me a chance to make it out there and I'll set up on my own, and we'll be married,') – on and on it went, hour after hour, all one night, and in the morning he was gone, leaving Eliza swollen-eyed, ashen, and somehow suddenly smaller than ever, and very frail. Roz had known she had had at least something to do with that suffering, that frailty, and tell herself as she might that had David really loved her mother he would not have gone, she knew that had she not spoken as she had to her father over those months, David would not have had the opportunity to go. However, she told herself, her mother had caused her a great deal of suffering in her life and certainly didn't seem to have felt guilty about it; moreover, Eliza was tough, she was resilient, and she just didn't need a man who put his worldly success so firmly before his emotional life.

Roz had grown very skilful at such rationalization.

Freddy Branksome, financial director of Morell's, came into Julian's office one morning in early 1972 and shut the door firmly behind him.

'I think we might have a problem,' he said.

Julian, who had been studying with some pleasure the latest pictures of Araminta Jones by David Bailey for the autumn advertising campaign, and reflecting with greater pleasure still upon the circumstances in which he had last gazed into those vast, black-lashed, purply-blue eyes, recognized the tone in Freddy's voice that demanded his undivided attention, and set the contacts aside.

'Yes, Freddy?'

'I've been looking at the share register. I don't like it. There's been a lot of buying by some set-up in Zürich. Big blocks. I smell trouble.'

'Can you check it out?'

'I'm trying.'

'Takeover?'

'Not yet. But we could be heading for a bid.'

'Christ, I wish this company was still mine.'

'Yes, well it's a bit late for that. You went public twenty years ago or so. You've still got thirty per cent. That's not a bad stake, in a company this size.'

'Not enough though, is it? Not when this sort of thing happens.'

'Well, it hasn't happened yet. I'll keep working on it.'

A week later he was back in Julian's office. 'More buying. Just in dribs and drabs. Something like twenty per cent of all the shares now. I can't make it out.'

'But there's nothing tangible?'

'Not yet.'

'Maybe it's nothing to worry about.'

'Maybe. You OK, Julian? You look rotten.'

'Thanks a lot. I feel fine.'

'OK. Sorry I spoke.'

Araminta Jones lay looking at the ceiling above Julian Morell's huge bed in Hanover Terrace. This was the third time he hadn't been able to deliver and it was getting very boring. Just once was all right, it was almost exciting in a way, trying and trying, working on them, using everything you had, talking dirty, porno pictures, offering every orifice; she'd suggested whips and all that stuff, but nothing had worked, and she was getting just totally frustrated. In a minute, she thought, she'd get up and go home, and ring up that nice boy who'd been in the agency today and see what he could do for her. Julian was OK, very charming and all that, and the bracelet had been gorgeous, she'd always loved sapphires, and she loved the idea of the Bahamas. But on the other hand, with what he paid her she could afford to go herself, and take someone young and horny with her. Christ, it was hot. Why did these old guys always have to have their bedrooms like ovens? She wondered if he was still awake. If he wasn't, she could just creep off and spin him some yarn in the morning about having an early call, and needing to get her stuff together. She shifted experimentally, turning her back to him; Julian's hand came over her shoulder and stroked her breasts tentatively.

'I'm sorry, Araminta. Again. I suppose I'm just worried.'

'What about?' (As if she didn't know.)

'Oh, the company. We have a few problems.'

'Not with the new campaign, I hope. I don't want to have to re-shoot. I'm going to New York next week.'

'No, not the campaign. I didn't know you were going to New York. I might come with you. Maybe then we could go down to the Bahamas. A holiday is probably exactly what I need.'

'Maybe.' (They all said that.)

'Julian,' said Freddy Branksome a week later, 'I really don't think you ought to go to New York for a day or two.'

'Why not?'

'Because of this situation with the shares. It's still going on. Still worrying me.'

'OK, I'll hang on a bit.'

'Any more news on the shares, Freddy?'

'Well, it's one buyer. French. I've established that much. I think we could be in for a rocky ride.'

'But you still don't know who?'

'Well, it's unlikely to be an institution. It could be of course, could even be a rival cosmetic company. But I don't think so. It's an individual, as far as we can make out. Got any particular enemies at the moment, Julian?'

'What's that? Oh, no, I don't think so. No more than usual.'

'Good.'

In the main bedroom of his château in the champagne-producing area of the Loire, the Vicomte du Chene was looking tenderly at the slender, wonderfully sensuous body of his new wife. 'My darling darling,' he said, punctuating the words with repeated and ever-longer forays with his tongue into her genitals, and postponing in a delicious agony the moment when he could allow himself to enter her with his eager (if somewhat modestly made) member, 'you are so lovely, so very very lovely. You have made me the happiest man in France. I cannot believe that you have consented to be' – very long pause – 'my wife.'

'Oh, Pierre, you're so sweet. It's me that is fortunate. And the happiest woman in France. And thank you for the marvellous – wedding present. We can have such fun with it. It was so terribly generous of you.'

'My darling, a few shares. It was nothing. In return for your love. And perhaps – '

'Yes?'

'Well, the little matter of course of an heir. To the vineyards. My only unsatisfied ambition now.'

'I know. Of course. And I'm sure we can fulfil it. Together. Like this . . .'

'Indeed, my darling. Just a matter of time. And – such pleasantly, wonderfully spent time. If it took all eternity it would be too short.'

His bride stretched herself out beneath him, opening her legs, encasing his penis lovingly in her hands, guiding it, urging it into her body. 'Yes, my darling,' she murmured, raising her hips, pushing herself against him, trying with all the skill she had been born with and learnt, to help him to maintain his erection for a few moments at least, to bring him just a little more slowly to orgasm. 'It would. Now – now – no, my darling wait, please – aah,' and she relaxed suddenly, clenching and unclenching her vagina in a fiercely faked orgasm, as the hapless Vicomte's little problem of premature ejaculation once again came between her and her pleasure.

'Ah,' he said, 'how was it for you?'

'Marvellous. Quite marvellous.'

'My darling. My own darling,' he said, kissing her repeatedly in a gush of gratitude. 'How fortunate I am. How very very fortunate.'

Eliza du Chene, looking up at the ceiling, a yearning void somewhere deep inside her, hoped fervently that the price of revenge and becoming a major shareholder in her ex-husband's company was not going to become unbearably high.

'Roz darling, hallo, it's Mummy.'

'Oh, hallo.'

'How are you, darling?'

'Fine. Quite busy. Mummy, they really don't like us having personal calls. Unless it's an emergency. They asked me to tell you.'

'Oh, well I'm sorry. It's not an emergency exactly, but I did need to speak to you. I've just got married again.'

'How nice.'

'Roz, you could be a bit more enthusiastic for me.'

'Sorry. Of course I'm pleased. If you are. Will I like him?'

'I hope so, darling. He's French. He has the most divine chateau in the Loire Valley, and absolutely acres of vineyards, champagne mostly.'

'Well, that'll be convenient.'

'Yes.'

'So what's his name, my new stepfather?'

'Pierre. Pierre du Chene. He's a vicomte.'

'Oh, I see.'

'What do you mean?'

'Oh, nothing.'

'Well anyway, darling, of course I would have liked you to be at the wedding, but – well, I hardly had time to get there myself.'

'I see. It does seem a bit sudden. Couldn't you have told me before?'

'Not really, darling. I've been swept off my feet, as you might say. He was just desperate to get it settled.'

'How romantic. Oh well, never mind.'

'Roz, don't sound like that. I want you to be happy for me.'

'Mummy, I'm trying. It's just a bit of a shock, that's all. OK, here goes. Let's see if I can find the proper words. Mummy, that is absolutely marvellous, thrilling news, how wonderful, I hope you'll be very very happy. Will that do? Now I must go. Have a good honeymoon. Does Daddy know?'

'Not yet. Roz, darling, you mustn't be upset. We want you to come and stay here very very soon. Next holidays. I know you're going to love him. Goodbye, Roz.'

'I hope so. Goodbye, Mummy.'

Roz put the phone down and waited for the familiar bleak, shut-out feeling to engulf her. It didn't take very long.

'There's a Vicomtesse du Chene on the phone, Mr Morell.' Sarah Brownsmith, Julian's new secretary, spoke nervously. Julian's temper had been extremely uncertain over the past few weeks.

'Who? Never heard of her. Ask her what she wants.'

The line went blank for a while. 'She says she's one of your shareholders. One of your major shareholders. She wants to ask you some questions about the company.'

'Tell her she can't. Tell her it's nothing to do with me.'

The line went blank again. 'I'm sorry, Mr Morell, but she's very insistent. She says when you speak to her you'll know what it's about.'

'What? Oh, all right. Put her on. But tell her I've only got one minute. Tell her I've got to catch a plane.'

'Really, Julian. You can do better than that. Surely everyone knows by now you've got your own plane.'

It was Eliza's voice. Julian knocked over his coffee.

'Eliza. What on earth are you doing on the phone? I was expecting some damn fool Frenchwoman.'

'No. A damn fool Englishwoman. With a French husband.'

'What?'

'The Vicomtesse du Chene. *C'est moi*. It's me.'

Roz loathed Pierre du Chene. She thought he was disgusting. He was physically disgusting, short and dark and with an awful smell, a nauseating blend of garlic and strong aftershave, and in spite of that a kind of lingering fragrance of BO as well. And he had those awful sleazy eyes, which were always on her, watching her, half smiling, and often if she caught him unawares, she found them fixed not on her face but on her breasts, or her stomach. He had a little squashed monkey's face with a kind of snub nose, and a moustache, and his breath smelt horrible too, and when he kissed her, which he did at every possible opportunity it seemed to her, she thought she would be sick. And his personality was also disgusting, smarmy and ingratiating, chatting her up, telling her how clever she was, how pretty, pretending a great interest in her school, her friends, anything at all that he thought would win her over. Roz thought if she told him she collected dog turds, he would have exclaimed at her originality and offered to go and find her a few interesting specimens.

She just hadn't been able to believe her eyes when he came out on to the terrace of the chateau when she had first gone there in the Easter holidays; her mother had met her at Tours in the most beautiful white Rolls Corniche with a chauffeur who was very handsome indeed; Roz had thought for a wild moment that he had been the Vicomte but then they had driven back along the wide straight roads up towards Saumur, Eliza talking endlessly and over-brightly about how perfectly wonderful everything was, and what fun they were all going to have, and how much Roz would love Pierre, and there was a horse she could ride, and Pierre was dying to ride with her, he was a superb horseman, and the chateau, well – the chateau was just the most beautiful place Roz could ever imagine, exactly like the Sleeping Beauty's castle, and Pierre was just the best fun in the world, terribly cultured, and amusing, and she had never been so happy in her life.

Roz, looking at her, thinking she looked rather thin, and pale even, was a little surprised at this, but she had long since given up trying to understand her mother. Then: 'There is just one thing, darling, I'd better tell you, in case he mentions it, well that is, he will mention it. Pierre is fearfully keen for us to have children, or at least an heir, well, you'll understand when you see the estate, and of course I would love that too, and I hope it will happen, but – well, just don't be surprised, that's all. You probably think I'm much too old to have babies, but of course I'm not, I'm only thirty-six, that's nothing really, I just thought I'd better tell you, as I don't suppose you thought it was something your old mother might ever do again. All right?'

'All right,' said Roz, extremely confused by this, not sure what she was meant to do or say, but whenever she looked at the awful monkey-like form of du Chene now, smelt his breath, saw his awful furtive eyes, she shuddered – and more than that, shuddered for her mother having to go to bed with him, never mind carry his child.

Du Chene didn't actually start on her until the summer. Even then at first, like all comparatively innocent young girls in the hands (literally) of their elders, she thought she must be mistaken. It began with just a pressure on her leg under the table, a squeeze of her hand when she passed him in the corridor; progressed unmistakably to the patting of her bottom, the massaging of her shoulder as he passed her chair, his hand lingering, straying down towards her breast; then one evening after supper, when her mother had pleaded a headache, and they were sitting alone in the small drawing room, she reading, he studying papers, he looked up at her and said, 'You're looking very lovely, my dear Rosamund.'

'Thank you, Pierre. I expect it's the French air.'

'Oh, no,' he said, 'no, it is your own lovely look, your eyes and your skin, and of course your legs, your legs are so tanned now. You should wear shorter skirts so that they can be admired.'

'Thank you, Pierre, but I don't like short skirts. I'm a little tired now, I think I might go up to bed.'

'Very well, my dear, of course you must if you are tired. We cannot have you missing your beauty sleep. Come and kiss me good night.'

'No, Pierre, I won't, if you don't mind.'

'And why not? I am after all your step-papa. Come, my dear, a little daughterly kiss.'

'No, really, Pierre. Good night.'

She got up, but she had to walk past him; he shot his little brown hand out, and caught hers. 'Such a – what do you say – a tease. It only makes me more excited, my dear.'

Roz shook her hand free. 'Leave me alone.'

She walked swiftly past him, but he still managed, as his hand released hers, to stroke her bottom, then he jumped up, and with an unbelievably swift dart was in the doorway, barring her way. 'Just a little kiss. A *petit petit* kiss.'

His breath was foul; Roz turned her face away. But he caught her wrists, pulled her towards him; he was just slightly shorter than her, but he pushed her against the doorway, and started pressing his wet mouth against hers, prising her arms above her head and holding them there. Roz acted swiftly; she raised her right knee and thrust it hard into his groin. He groaned softly and let her go; but when she looked back at him, as she fled across the hall, his eyes were bright and his cheeks flushed with excitement.

Next morning he did not ride with her and after she had stabled her horse she came into breakfast nervous as to what he might say; but he was as always immaculately polite, almost distant, and nodded to her as if nothing had happened between them at all. But Eliza appeared at lunch heavy-eyed and listless, and hardly spoke.

Roz began to worry about her; she suggested twice that she might come back and stay with Letitia in London for a while, but Eliza said gaily that it was out of the question, that she wouldn't dream of leaving Pierre even for a short while.

'Well, Mummy, I think if you don't mind, I might go back a bit earlier. Rosie has asked me to go and stay with them in Colorado, her new stepfather has a ranch there, I'd love to go. Would you mind?'

'No of course not,' said Eliza, her eyes almost frighteningly bright. 'You go, Roz darling, and have fun. When do you want to leave?'

'Oh, I don't know, maybe on Sunday. Whenever it suits you.'

'Fine. Now I think I'll go and have my rest. I seem to be getting old, all I want to do is sleep these days.'

'You're not – ?' Roz couldn't bring herself to say it, to acknowledge what her mother must be doing, endlessly, horribly with du Chene.

'Oh, no, darling, not yet, give me a chance. These things take time, you know.'

'Do they?' said Roz.

The night before she was due to leave, the three of them ate outside; whatever else, Roz thought, this place greatly resembled Paradise. The air was sweet and full of the sound of the poplar trees and the crickets' evening chorus; she looked up at the towers of the chateau against the darkening sky, and across to where they were reflected in the great lake. In the hedges near the terrace there was the light of a thousand glow-worms; the new moon, a sliver of silver, was climbing the sky.

'Look,' said Roz, 'look at that moon. Isn't it perfect?'

' "Softly she was going up, and a star or two beside," ' said du Chene suddenly. 'Is not that a most beautiful English poem?'

Roz looked at him, surprised. 'It is. I didn't know you read English literature, Pierre.'

'Oh,' he said, 'I am full of surprises. I can quote you the whole of "Oh to be in England" by Robert Browning, as well.'

'I bet you can't,' said Eliza.

'Yes I can,' he said and proceeded to do so, rather beautifully. 'You see,' he said to Roz, 'I am not the ignorant French peasant you thought.'

'I didn't think you were anything of the sort,' said Roz quickly.

'Good,' he said and smiled at her, patting her hand.

Roz pulled it away and felt him turning his attention to her thighs instead. Oh well, she was going home next day.

She went to bed early; she had just turned out the light and settled into the huge bed when there was a tap at the door.

'Mummy?'

Silence. Another tap, more urgent.

Roz climbed out of bed and went over to the door, which she always kept locked against the threat of du Chene's attentions. 'Who is it?'

'Rosamund, it's Pierre. Open the door and come with me quickly. It's your mother, I am worried about her.'

She unlocked the door; saw his face; tried to shut it again too late. He was inside the room, pushing her backwards towards the bed; he was wearing only a robe and it was hanging open. Roz tried not to look at him, just concentrated on fighting him; she was a big girl and strong, but he was stronger. He had her on the bed in no time, pushing her down on to it, pressing his slobbery mouth on to hers, pushing up the hem of her nightdress with his free hand. Then she felt the hand exploring her thigh, and creeping up, up towards her pubic hair; a hot panic engulfed her, she tried to scream, but his mouth was over hers, attempted to kick him, but she couldn't move.

'Arrogant English bitch,' he said suddenly, almost cheerfully, and stood up, shrugging out of his robe. Roz shut her eyes; she didn't want to see. Then in the split second she was free, she raised one long strong leg and kicked him, hard in the chest; he staggered and fell backward and lay splayed on the ground, his hands clutched over his penis; he looked more than ever like one of those rather sad-faced small monkeys that hide in the corners of their cages at the zoo.

'Get up,' said Roz, 'get up and get out. You're disgusting.'

'Oh Rosamund,' he said, 'don't be unkind to me. I love you.'

'No you don't,' she said. 'You're supposed to love my mother.'

'No, I love you.'

'Rubbish. Now are you going to go, or shall I call her?'

'I'll go.' He scrambled up, still covering his parts, and groped for his robe.

'I only wanted to stroke your pussy,' he said plaintively. 'Your beautiful English pussy.'

'Oh, fuck off,' said Roz, and then remembering his reaction when she hurt him the night in the drawing room, afraid that he would become aroused again if she went on being hostile, took him by the shoulders and marched him to the door.

'Come along. Time for bed. Good night, Pierre.'

He went meekly enough, but at the door he turned once again, with an expression of great sadness. 'Forgive me,' he said, 'I didn't mean to harm you. It's just that you are so beautiful.' Roz relaxed her guard and suddenly his hand was inside her nightdress, feeling for, squeezing her nipple. 'Beautiful,' he said, his face millimetres away, 'beautiful bitch.'

'Fuck off,' said Roz again, pushing his hand frantically away.

'That is precisely what I want to do,' he said, pushing it back again, working it down towards her stomach this time. 'Do you feel nothing for me at all?'

'Yes,' said Roz. 'Revulsion. Shall I knee you in the groin again, Pierre, or are you going?'

He looked at her, breathing heavily, his face flushed, his eyes still oddly sad.

'I will go,' he said, 'this time. But I shall not forget you. There will be other holidays.'

'There won't. I shan't come. I shall tell my mother in the morning. She'll probably come home with me.'

'I'm afraid,' he said, 'that your mother will not be surprised.'

'What?' said Roz, too horrified to be afraid any more, pushing his hand away from her repeatedly, 'you mean she knows?'

'Not about you. No, of course. But my very healthy appetite for – well, for young ladies.'

'I don't believe you. She wouldn't put up with it. She wouldn't stay.'

'My dear child,' he said, finally dropping his hand, fastening his robe, 'she has no choice. Ask her about her wedding present when you tell her about tonight. Good night, Rosamund. Sleep well.'

He raised her hand and kissed it, formally, courtly. Roz stared after him, then went back into her room and slammed, locked the door. She leant against it, feeling first shaky, then sick. She longed to go to her mother, to be with someone, but she would be with du Chene, it was impossible, she had to cope with this, get through the night on her own. She went through into her bathroom and ran a deep very hot bath and lay in it a long time, trying to calm herself, to control her panic, her sense of revulsion, of invasion. And what had he meant? What wedding present?

Roz hardly slept; every time she closed her eyes she saw, felt, du Chene, his horrible clawing hands, his frightful slobbering mouth. She had never thought about sex except in rather abstract terms, or alternatively very romantic ones, in the height of her passion for David; now its worst implications had been literally forced upon her and she felt damaged, grieved.

Towards morning she finally fell asleep and dreamed, a confused, half nightmare, that she was tied down, on her bed, and he was coming at her, smiling, his robe flapping loose; she felt his hands pushing at her, probing her pubic hair, and then further, further up, and she woke up, her head tossing from side to side, her face wet with tears, and her own hands clasped together over her vagina.

She got up, dressed, packed, went downstairs to the kitchens and made herself some coffee; she was terrified he would appear, but then she saw him walking to the stables and relaxed a little. Now that it was morning, and life was becoming normal again, the nightmare was receding, had become something she could put away, keep under control, like so many of the unpleasant events that had punctuated her life.

335

What in some ways she wanted, longed to do was go to her mother, talk to her, tell her, but something stopped her. In the first place she felt it would simply prolong her agony, deepen her own distress.

The other thing was the deeply disturbing fact that her mother was married to this man, she must surely know what he was like, or certainly suspect, indeed he had said last night that her mother knew about his behaviour.

Roz went upstairs, finished her packing and then went along to her mother's room. Outside the door she took a deep breath, visibly squared her shoulders, and knocked.

'Mummy? Can I come in, I want to say goodbye.'

Roz went home to England, told her father she had had a marvellous time in France, and that her mother seemed very well, spent a month in Colorado with Rosie Howard Johnson, and then went back to school.

Everything, she kept telling herself, was fine. She was doing well; she had had a brilliant time with Rosie, and to begin with with Rosie's eldest stepbrother, Tom, who was eighteen and just going to Harvard; he had clearly liked her very much, had gone out of his way to spend time with her, and she had liked him too. The only thing was that every time he kissed her, which he did two or three times, Roz began by enjoying it very much, and the whole flood of new and intense feelings which seemed to accompany the process, and then suddenly the vision of du Chene and his awful little body, and the feel of his hands on her, would rise up inside her head and she would feel sick and repulsed. She didn't say anything to Tom Bennett, obviously, and tried to suppress the repulsion and recapture the other feelings, but it really didn't work, and instead of hoping he would kiss her, she began to dread it. As a result Tom decided she was a cold fish, and left her alone.

Roz didn't think too much about it at first, but then as the term went on she began to have nightmares, to wake up, as she had that first morning, crying, clutching herself; and the nightmares began to grow in intensity. She started sleeping badly; she would put off going to bed until later and later, and then, dreading the dreams, slept very shallowly, trying to ward them off. Her housemistress noticed the way she was looking, and asked her if she was feeling all right; Roz said yes, perfectly, and worked even harder, acted even tougher; and then one morning, right in the middle of a maths tutorial, she felt terrible, started to cry, and couldn't stop.

After an hour or so the matron, alarmed, phoned her father; he was in New York, Eliza was of course in France, Letitia was on holiday in Florence, and Sarah Brownsmith, completely at a loss as to what to do, consulted Susan Johns, who was at least, as she said to Susan apologetically, at least a mother herself.

As a result Roz found herself opening the can of worms and releasing them all over Susan that evening in the little house in Fulham where Susan now lived and where she had taken Roz (with the school doctor's rather relieved permission) for a few days.

Roz had always liked Susan, but that night she learnt to love her. Susan did not do any of the things her father, or indeed her mother would have done. She did not become hysterical, or act particularly appalled, or threaten to inform the police, or attach the merest suspicion of blame to Roz, and naturally enough, not being Roz's mother or father, did not go through the nauseating process of debasing herself, claiming it was all her fault, and offering her the world in order to help her recover.

She merely listened, quietly and calmly, handing Roz interminable tissues, holding her in her arms occasionally when the tears became so overpowering she was unable to speak, asked sensible questions, made her lots of cups of tea, offered her a drink, and even managed to make Roz laugh by forcing her to repeat, her own lips twitching slightly, the description of du Chene lying naked on the floor, covering his private parts with his little monkey hands.

'Well,' she said when Roz had finally finished, and finally stopped crying too, and was sitting exhausted but calm in the corner of her sofa, 'none of it sounds too bad. Don't misunderstand me, I can see it was perfectly awful, and I think you've handled it wonderfully, I think you've been amazingly mature about it all, but I just don't think you have to go on worrying about it. Your big mistake was not telling your mother that morning, just talking about it straight away, so it didn't have to fester away for months –'

'But I told you,' said Roz, tears welling up in her eyes again, 'I couldn't tell her, she's having a bad enough time as it is, without that sort of thing to worry about, and anyway –'

'I know. You didn't want to have to relive it.'

'No. I couldn't face it. I'd just got away from him. It.'

'Even so, all you've been doing is relive it ever since, instead.'

'Yes. Sometimes I can't think of anything else. It's so horrible.'

'Of course. Very horrible. Don't get me wrong, I can see exactly how horrible it was –'

'Can you? Can you really?' Roz looked at her with suddenly hostile eyes. 'I don't think you could. Nobody could, who hadn't gone through it.'

'Roz,' said Susan briskly, 'when I was only about twelve, my uncle used to get drunk and wait till my mum and dad were out and touch me up in the front room. I didn't know what to do, who to tell, I felt somehow I ought to like it because he was a grown-up so it must be right. Sometimes, I assure you, even now I can remember how that felt.'

Roz looked at her with a kind of desperate hope.

'Really? And you've – well you've got to – well –'

'Like men? And sex? Yes, of course. Maybe it took me a bit longer than it would have done, but once I found someone I could trust, it was fine. You'll find the same.'

'I hope so.'

'The really important thing was that he didn't really do anything. He could have raped you. But I suppose you've thought about that, imagined it, endlessly, thought how it could have happened.'

Roz smiled. 'You really do understand, don't you?'

'Of course I do. Most women would.'

'Mummy wouldn't.'

'Oh, I expect she would.' There was a silence. 'Do you really think she's in a mess?'

'Yes. I do. I think he's giving her an awful time. She's odd. Terribly subdued. And once or twice, she had a bruise on her face. Of course she said she'd fallen over or something, but I think he's knocking her about. But because I feel it's partly my fault, you know, about David and everything, I just can't – couldn't – tell anyone.'

'I really don't think it's anything to do with you. All right, you might have got your father a bit worked up about Sassoon, but he's not some kind of saint you suddenly corrupted. He's a quixotic, powerful man, used to having his own way; you can't be blamed for that.'

Roz looked doubtful. 'I don't think that's right.'

'OK. Maybe you should take that bit of blame. But that was two years ago; your mother didn't rush off and marry the awful little monkey on the rebound. She's a grown woman, Roz. She's very sophisticated, very strong willed; you really can't be held responsible for her actions. I'm very fond of your mother, but I'd be the first to say that nobody could possibly make her do or not do anything once she's made up her mind about something. I think you should put that right out of your head.'

'Oh.'

Roz felt as if a great boulder had been rolled away from her path, a boulder that had been blocking out the light, preventing her from going forward, keeping her crammed into a tight airless hole. She sighed suddenly, and smiled at Susan, a radiantly happy, almost childlike smile. It was oddly moving.

'You've been so nice to me. You've helped me so much. I wish you were my mother.' This tribute, combined with the smile, affected Susan strongly; she felt tears at the back of her eyes.

'My dear girl, you have a most remarkable mother.'

'I do? No. A remarkable person, maybe. Not much of a mother though.'

'Roz, you don't know –'

'I do know. But we won't go into that now. I'm awfully tired. When did you say I'd be back at school?'

'When you were ready. Take a day or two off, I would. You can stay here with me. Is your friend Rosie home?'

'No, she's at school in Paris now.'

'Why didn't you tell her about it all?'

'Oh, I don't know. I just didn't want to talk about it. It's too – oh, I don't know, personal. And I'm not much good at confidences.'

'No. Nor me. The only person I talk to a lot these days is your grandmother.'

'Not your daughters?'

'No. I hardly ever see them. Jenny's married and Sheila's teaching in the North. They say I'm changed. I expect they're right.' She sighed.

'I like talking to Granny Letitia too,' said Roz. 'She's wonderful, isn't she? I'm sure she's immortal, she never seems to get any older.'

'Oh, she does to me,' said Susan, 'but you see I knew her when she was quite young, not much older than I am now. Oh, Roz, we had such fun.'

'What was my father like in those days?' asked Roz suddenly.

'Oh, much more light-hearted. But otherwise much the same. Terribly ambitious. A workaholic. Lots of lovely ladies, of course.' She spoke very brightly. Roz looked at her.

'I suppose he was terribly attractive.'

'Oh yes. Terribly. Well, he still is, of course.'

'I suppose he must be. Otherwise Araminta wouldn't be carrying on with him.'

'Oh, I think that's purely because of her contract. Between you and me.'

'But she doesn't have to sleep with him.'

'No. But going round with him, being his mistress gives her a certain cachet. It all helps her image. And his, of course.'

'Yes. Yes, I suppose so. Do you mind?' asked Roz suddenly.

'Mind what? Araminta being your father's mistress? No, of course not. Why ever should I?'

'Don't know. Sorry.'

'Now listen, are we to tell your parents about all this or not?'

'I'd rather not. But I am a bit worried about my mother. I mean, as well as the fact he might be knocking her about, there's this really weird business about her having a baby. I told you. With – with the monkey. It seemed to be really obsessing her. I still don't know what to do.'

'Well look,' said Susan, 'will you trust me to handle it? I won't make a big deal of it, I'll play it down, but I'll have to tell your father something, the school is bound to mention it, and then I can suggest your mother might need help. Then it'll be out of our hands. All right?'

'All right. Thank you.'

'I'm not suggesting that one chat with me is going to sort you out completely. You may still have nightmares for a while, you may not like being kissed by your next boyfriend either. But I do feel sure it'll get better. Just concentrate on that picture of the monkey on the floor, clutching his balls, and try and laugh about it. It'll help.'

'I will. You're wonderful, Susan.'

'Not really. One more thing, if you do go on feeling really bad, let me know and we can sort out someone cleverer than me to talk to.'

'A shrink, do you mean? No thanks. Half the girls I met in America go to shrinks. It's pathetic. I like to handle my own problems.'

'Well, so do I. But just occasionally, we all need a bit of help. Now I think we should both go to bed. Good night, Roz.'

'Good night, Susan. And thank you again.'

Roz fell asleep feeling relaxed and confident, and thinking how wise and honest Susan was; the only thing she had not believed was when she had said she didn't mind Araminta being her father's mistress.

'Julian,' said Susan, 'I know you're not going to like this, but there's something you have to know.'

Julian left for France forty-eight hours later and returned with the shares back in his possession; a week later Eliza came home, very thin, rather pale, but patently extremely cheerful, and told Roz she was divorcing du Chene.

'Julian,' said Susan, 'what on earth have you been doing? How did you manage that?'

'Oh,' he said, 'it's much better you don't know. You would be even more disapproving of me than you are already. Which I wouldn't like. Let's just say I gave that little squirt a very nasty hour or so, and he came to see that it was greatly in his interest to do what I asked.'

'I suppose you blackmailed him?'

'Mrs Johns! What an ugly concept.' He paused, then smiled at her.

'You did, didn't you?'

'Well, let's say I pointed out to him how very anti-social his behaviour had been. Was.'

'And Eliza?'

'Well, Eliza of course was delighted to find herself free.'

'Yes, but –'

'But what? You said I should help her. I do a lot because you say so, Susan. I'm always telling you that.'

'Did you tell Eliza about Roz?'

'Of course. She was appalled. She really had had no idea. If she had, then I'm sure she would have left him immediately. But we agreed that she should never discuss it with Roz. On your advice. Again.' He was silent for a moment. 'We seem to do everything you tell us, my family and I.'

'What about this nonsense about Eliza having a baby? Did you get to the bottom of that?'

'Well, yes, I suppose so.'

'And?'

'Do you really want to know? It will confirm all your darkest suspicions about the decadent upper classes.'

'They don't need confirming.'

'Well, Eliza had led the Vicomte to believe she could give him an heir. Of course she couldn't. Nobody knew that but me, and her, and possibly her mother. She was sterilized after Roz was born. The doctor said another baby would kill her. It seemed the best solution.'

'So?'

'Well, obviously, had the Vicomte known that, it might have put a slightly different complexion on – our conversation. Particularly for Eliza.'

'Why?'

'Well, because she'd married him under false pretences, which meant I could get the shares back just slightly more easily.'

'Why? I still don't understand.'

'Well, you see, they were in Eliza's name. They were a wedding present from him to her. I don't think she really wanted to part with them even then. But she did agree that I should have them. Under the circumstances.'

'So you bought the shares from Eliza? I hope you paid her properly for them.'

'Of course I did. Exactly what du Chene paid for them.'

'But that was a year ago. They're worth far more now.'

'I know. But I think she owes me some – what shall we say – interest.'

'Julian, that is outrageous.'

'Susan, it's no such thing. Her behaviour was outrageous. She's a very rich woman now, which is nice for her. Just not quite as rich as she might have been.'

'I still think it's outrageous.'

'Well,' he said, 'you're entitled to your opinion. But remember that I have rescued her from a very nasty situation. One that she got herself into.'

'What I can't work out,' said Susan, giving up the struggle, as always, to talk ethics with Julian, 'is why didn't she walk out months ago, if the shares were hers?'

'She didn't dare. He threatened to tell everyone exactly why she'd married him if she did. He could have made her look very unpleasant indeed. Eliza is quite anxious about her reputation, you know. Interestingly so. And she has this quaint old-fashioned sense of honour. You would understand that, no doubt. She felt she owed it to him to try and make the marriage work. God knows why. She's had a hideous time.'

'Was he beating her up?'

'No, not really. But other things.'

'What sort of things?'

'Minor perversions. Of course once she'd told me about them, he became even more anxious to cooperate.'

'God, you're devious,' she said.

'No,' he said, 'just pragmatic.'

A few weeks later, in one of the few non-pragmatic actions of his life, Julian Morell asked Susan Johns to marry him. Not without considerable regret, she turned him down.

The Connection Six

Los Angeles, 1973–6

Mrs Kelly looked anxiously across the table at Hugo Dashwood. She found it hard to talk to him, harder to ask him for help, but Lee had told her, insisted that she could and should, and he himself on his regular visits to Santa Monica had always stressed the same thing.

'It's nothing I can put my finger on, Mr Dashwood,' she said. 'But I just don't feel happy about him. He isn't working at high school, but then lots of boys of fifteen don't. And he seems a mite too interested in girls, but then at his age I suppose he would be.'

'Does he have a regular girlfriend?' asked Hugo. 'Or does he just go around with a crowd?'

'Oh, he has a girlfriend,' said Mrs Kelly with a sniff. 'And I can't say I like her. She's a Latin type; eyes that know it all. You know?'

'I think so. Does he bring her here?'

'Well, he certainly does. I've always encouraged him to bring his friends home, because everybody knows that's how kids stay out of trouble. So he brings her home most Saturday nights.'

'Not for the night?' said Hugo, misunderstanding, appalled.

'Of course not. That boy is a Catholic, and I see he goes to mass every Sunday and knows what's what. I don't think he would do anything –anything wrong. But she would. That girl would.'

'What's her name?'

'Donna. Donna Palladini.'

'So what exactly is it that worries you?'

'I told you, Mr Dashwood, I just don't know. I think it's that he's a drifter. No sense of purpose. Now, Lee was determined he should go to college. He wants to go to college, he says. Even though the draft business is receding, thank God, and you don't have to hide inside college any more, he still wants to go to. But he doesn't seem to understand you have to work to get there. He never does anything. You know what his grades are like. Straight As in maths and geography and Spanish, and Ds and Es in everything else.'

'Well look,' said Hugo, 'it doesn't sound too worrying. Let me talk to Miles. I'm here for a day or two. Where is he?'

'Friday afternoon – oh, he'll be playing water polo. He's in the team. He's very good, I believe. And they have a great water polo team at Samo High. I mean not everyone can get in it.'

Hugo smiled gently at her pride in the boy who worried her

so much and went for a walk along the Palisades, until Miles returned. It was a ravishing May afternoon: hot, clear, brilliant. The surf was up, the sea looked unreal in its blueness. The white beach was modestly littered with people. Cyclists zoomed along the boardwalk; tiny whirling toys from where he stood high above them. He wondered if Miles ever rode the bike he had given him last Christmas; he hadn't seemed very interested, merely politely grateful.

He decided to drive up to the school and watch for Miles to come out. He wouldn't declare himself, show himself to be meeting him, just observe him. It might be interesting.

He got back in the car and drove along Ocean Avenue and turned into Pico. The school was quiet; most of the kids were home already. He parked fifty yards down the street and waited.

Miles came out in a crowd, his arm round the shoulders of a very pretty girl. Hugo thought she was one of the prettiest girls he had ever seen. Dark, tall, slender, with big breasts and long long legs; she was quite outstanding. But then so was Miles. Tall already as a man, with golden-blond hair (a pity he had to have it hanging on his shoulders, but that was not an irremediable problem) and piercing dark blue eyes in his tanned face: he looked wonderful. Hugo felt a stab of pride and another of envy – of his youth, his lack of responsibility, his blatant, come-and-get-me sexuality. And he was only fifteen! No wonder old Mrs Kelly was worried.

Miles was dressed all in white – long white shorts, a white sweatshirt and white loafers. It all emphasized his golden, utterly desirable youth.

The others were going the opposite way; Miles and Donna waved to them, and set off towards the ocean and Miles' house. They stopped suddenly, looked into each other's eyes, and Miles bent and kissed her briefly. They were a charming couple. Hugo found it hard to fault them. He let them walk home, waited ten minutes then turned the car round and drove back to the house.

Miles and Donna were sitting on the patio when he got there. Miles looked at him warily; he had only half expected him. He had grown to associate him with trouble. He did not get up, or greet him formally.

'Hi, Hugo.'

'Good afternoon, Miles.'

'Donna, this is an old friend of my mom's, Hugo Dashwood. Hugo, this is Donna Palladini.'

'Hi, Mr Dashwood.'

She seemed nice. Hugo smiled at her.

'How do you do.'

She smiled back. 'I love your accent.'

'Thank you. Of course we think we don't have one. That it is you who have the accent.'

'Is that right?'

'It is. Miles, how was the match? I didn't know you were in the water polo team.'

'It wasn't a match, just a practice.'

'I see.'

'Miles is real good,' said Donna. 'The best. Captain next year, they say, don't they, Miles?'

'I don't know, do they?' He was reluctant to appear successful in front of Hugo, who he knew wanted that so badly.

'Miles, you know they do.'

'Well, that's wonderful, Miles. I'm delighted. I'd like to watch you play one day, if that's possible.'

'Are you related in some way to Miles?' said Donna. 'An uncle or something?'

'No. Why do you ask?'

'Oh, I just wondered. You seem to talk like an uncle or a grandpop or something. You know.'

'I know,' said Hugo. 'But no. And certainly not a grandpop.'

'Oh, I didn't mean to be rude.' She looked stricken.

'You weren't.'

A silence fell.

'Well, I guess I'd better be getting along,' said Donna.

'Donna, don't go,' said Miles, putting out a brown arm. 'What's the rush?'

'Oh, Mom's expecting me. She'll be worried.'

'OK. I'll see you out.'

Hugo heard them talking quietly in the hall. 'I don't want to intrude,' Donna said. 'He feels like family.'

'He is not family,' Miles hissed. 'No way. Don't go, Donna.'

'I have to. I'll see you tomorrow.'

'OK.'

Miles walked back into the patio. He didn't look at Hugo, just sat down on the swing seat and picked up a surfing magazine.

'Do you like surfing?'

'Uh-huh.'

'Do you do much of it?'

'A bit.'

'Donna seems a very nice girl.'

'She is.'

'Have you been – together – for long?'

'Hugo, I don't want to be rude, but that really is none of your business.'

'Miles, you are being rude. I was only being friendly.'

'Sorry.'

'So have you?'

'Have I what?'

'Been with Donna long?'

'She's in my class at school. Always has been. So in a way, yes.'

'I see.'

Miles, sensing Hugo's sudden hostility, made a huge effort. 'Would you like some tea?'

'Yes, please, I would.'

'OK, I'll get some.'

He came back with some iced tea; the Californian standard version. Hugo loathed it, but didn't want to reject the peace offering. 'Thank you. How nice.'

'That's OK.'

'How's school?'

'OK.'

'How are the grades?'

'Much the same.'

'Not so OK.'

'Depends which ones you're looking at.'

'I suppose so. But Miles, next year you're going to senior high school, and then it's only two years to college. Don't you think you should try to pull up your grades all round? You know you're capable of it.'

'Yeah, I know. Don't worry, Hugo, I will. When the time comes I'll pull out all the stops.'

347

'It may be a little late by then. You'll have missed out on a lot of groundwork.'

'No, I can make it up.' He yawned. 'Hugo, again, I don't want to be rude, but my grades really aren't anything to do with you.'

'Well, Miles, they are in a way. I promised your mother I would keep an eye on you, and your grandmother turns to me in a crisis, and altogether I do feel responsible for you. If you flunk out now, and don't get into college, I shall have to find you something to do. Or I shall be letting your mother down. So don't make me do that, please.'

'OK.'

It was altogether a rather unsatisfactory conversation.

'I think it's his friends,' said Mrs Kelly. 'They're all like that. No manners. Hang around the beach bars all the time. Never do anything constructive. I don't think it's healthy.'

'I wondered if it mightn't be better for Miles if you moved out of Santa Monica.'

'What, right away? Oh, I don't think that's a good idea. He would be really unhappy. He likes school. He loves the sport. He'd resent it bitterly.'

'No, not right away, just out a little way. Out of the town. Say to Malibu. He loves the surf, he told me so, and he could stay at the school, you'd have to drive him in for a year or two, but you could monitor his friendships a lot more closely and he just couldn't spend a lot of time with some of these undesirable, layabout types.'

Mrs Kelly looked at him shrewdly. 'That's kinda sensible, Mr Dashwood. I like that idea. But I certainly don't have time to look for anywhere.'

'No, I'll look. Don't worry about that. You wouldn't mind though? You wouldn't feel you were losing your friends and social life?'

'Don't have any. Don't like the folks down here. Never have. Affected, I call them. No, I wouldn't mind a bit. And I think it would be good for Miles. I really do.'

Miles was furious. Hugo drove him out along the Pacific Coast Highway, to show him the house he had chosen, an architect-designed wooden building, tucked high into the hillside off one of the small canyons, a few miles along from Malibu Beach. The view was staggering, a great sweep of ocean and head after head, taking in sunrise and sunset; Miles looked at it coldly.

'I don't want to move. I like it in Santa Monica.'

'But Miles, this is a nicer house, and you have more room and you can surf whenever you want to –'

'I can surf in Santa Monica.'

'But the surf here is world famous.'

'I don't want world famous surf. I like the surf at home.'

'And you will still be at Samo High. You can still see your friends.'

'Not so easily. I'll have to go to school with Gran in the car and get laughed at. I just won't come. I'll stay with Donna. Her mom is always saying I can stay there.'

'Miles, next year you're sixteen,' said Hugo, desperate at the hostility in Miles' face. 'I'll buy you a car, then you won't have to go with Gran.' He could immediately see the folly of that one; the whole idea of moving was to make Miles' friends less accessible to him. But it was too late; he had said it now.

Miles looked at him shrewdly. 'Can I choose what sort?'

'Within reason, yes.'

Miles shrugged. 'I still don't see why we have to come. And it won't change anything. But I guess I have to say yes.'

What nobody quite realized, not even Mrs Kelly, who cared for him, not even Donna, who loved him, was that Miles' refusal to work at anything which seemed remotely unimportant and uninteresting was a direct result of his grief for his mother. She had taken with her, when she died, Miles' sense of direction. He had coped with his grief, his loneliness, his need to look after himself, but he had been left a very bewildered little boy; he could get through the days, get himself to school, go out to play, talk to his friends, but anything which required any degree of effort was beyond him. For at least a year he survived on the most superficial level, with only his grandmother to provide all his emotional needs. She did her best, but she was a brusque, impatient woman; Lee had been endlessly affectionate, caring, thoughtful for him, and fun.

By the end of the first year, he had learnt to manage without cuddles, treats, a concerned ear, a sense of someone being unequivocally on his side, and he had developed a calm self-sufficiency; but he had no emotional or intellectual energy to spare. Consequently, anything demanding he set aside; and by the time he could have coped with it, the pattern was too deeply established to change. And so he went on, as he had always anyway been inclined, doing the things he liked and which seemed to matter to him, and ignoring the things he did not; it gave him a very clear and pragmatic set of values. And there was no way he was going to set them aside and start working at literature or history because Hugo Dashwood or indeed anyone else told him to.

Two years later, he was not entirely sorry they had moved. It gave him a certain cachet at school, living out at Malibu. And it was a nice house. And he had the car, The Car, jeez it was a good car, a 1965 Mustang, and the old Creep had bought it for him just like that. He and Donna had had a high old time in the back of that car. Just thinking about being in the back of the car with Donna gave Miles an erection. He still hadn't exactly done it, not all the way, but Donna was so sweet he just couldn't push her, and she was so patient and let him touch her up and wank at the same time, and kiss her breasts and everything. In any case, however much he complained to her, he knew that in his heart of hearts he wouldn't want a girl who'd let him go all the way. The only girls that did that were tarts, and there was no way he was going to go round with a tart. Not now he was captain of the water polo team, and one of the best young surfers on Malibu beach. He had a position to consider. Not just anyone would do for him.

And the way she'd looked at the Prom, the other night, in a kind of a gypsy dress, all red, off the shoulders, with a flounced skirt – well, Miles knew he'd certainly got the most beautiful girl in Santa Monica that night, and that he was the envy of not just his year, but the year above, the one graduating. He'd even wished for a minute he hadn't insisted on wearing tennis shoes with his tux, just to make the point he was a rebel – but there it was, he had, and he certainly couldn't go all the way home to Malibu to change.

The summer stretched before him now; three whole months of surfing, and no school work or grades to worry about. The old Creep wouldn't be over, because he only seemed to appear at important times, like the new school year, or Christmas; he'd tried to come and watch a water polo match once, but Miles had changed the date so many times, in his letters, that the Creep had given up, and said he'd try to come another year. He supposed he'd have to write and tell him his grades, otherwise he'd be on the phone, and then there might be a lecture, but he'd pulled up a lot lately, and he was still getting As for maths and languages. And Cs and Ds for the rest. Not bad, for absolutely no work.

So tonight he'd drive into town, pick up Donna, and they'd maybe see a movie with some of the others, and then when they'd finished there they'd go off and neck for a while, and then drive down to the ocean and get some cheese cake and coffee at Zucky's, because necking made you hungry, and then after that park down near the ocean, and neck some more. And then they'd have to take the girls home, and probably they'd all go over to Tony's No. 5, and have some chilli fries and boast about their conquests on the back seats and finally get tired of all that and go home to bed. Miles smiled with pleasure and anticipation. Life seemed pretty good.

She was on the beach at Malibu when he rode down on his bike later that afternoon. Just stretched out on the sand, with what was obviously a family picnic hamper by her. Miles thought he had never seen anyone so beautiful. She was blonde, curly hair tied back in a pony tail with a blue ribbon, a tipped-up nose all freckled with the sun and a curvy smiley mouth. She was deliciously pale brown all over – well, all the over that he could see – and she was wearing a pale sea-green bikini, cut so low on the bottom that he could just see the palest fluff of a curl of pubic hair. Miles swallowed, felt an erection growing inside his surfing shorts and hurried on.

When he felt better, carrying his surf board for protection, he walked back past her. She was still alone. He looked down at her and smiled. 'Hi.'

'Hi.'

'Are you alone?'

'Only for a moment. My parents are having a drink in Alice's, and my brother is out there pretending he can surf.'

She looked at the surf board. 'Do you pretend or can you really do it?'

'Oh, I can do it. And I can surf.' He grinned at her; she blushed and looked away, embarrassed at the double entendre.

'Oh, I'm sorry. I didn't mean to offend you. I get kind of used to just talking to the surfies here. I'll go away if you like.'

'No don't, it's all right. I was awfully bored. Do you live around here?'

'Yeah, up in one of the canyons. Right up there.' He pointed.

'It looks wonderful. So romantic. What do your parents do?'

'Oh, they're both dead. I live with my gran.'

He was so used to the fact by now he never thought of it upsetting anyone; he was startled to see her eyes fill with tears.

'Oh, how sad, I am so sorry.'

'Well, it was sad, but I was real small when my dad died, and only twelve when my mom went, so I've got used to it now. Kind of,' he added hastily, not wanting to appear hard-hearted. 'What about your folks?'

'Oh, they're both in the film business. My dad is a director and my mom is a costume designer.'

'I see. And where do you live, do you live in LA?'

'We certainly do.'

'Whereabouts?'

'In Beverly Glen.'

Miles nearly dropped his surf board. Not in his wildest imaginings had he ever thought of even talking in a friendly way to a girl who lived on Beverly Glen. Beverly Glen, where some of the richest, most cultured, high-class people in Los Angeles had their homes. Beverly Glen. Real money, real real money.

He realized she was looking at him oddly. 'Sorry. I guess I looked kinda surprised. I don't meet many folk from Beverly Glen.'

'Oh, we don't live at the real ritzy end. Just a couple of blocks up from Santa Monica Boulevard. I mean it's nice, but it's not Stone Canyon.'

'Oh,' said Miles.

'What's your name?'

'Miles. Miles Wilburn.'

'Joanna. Joanna Tyler.'

'It's been real nice to meet you, Joanna.'

'And nice to meet you too. Are you hurrying off somewhere?'

'No. But I guess your parents might not like you to be talking to a poor orphan from Malibu.'

'Oh, don't be silly. My parents believe in democracy. My father is a socialist. That's why they don't send me to boarding school, and that's why we're here on the public beach and not on one of the snotty private ones, owned by half of Hollywood.'

'So where do you go to school?'

'Marymount High.'

It was several cuts above Samo, but it was still a public school. Miles felt bolder.

'Will you be coming here again?'

'I don't know. Depends how my brother gets on pretending to surf. Oh, he's coming now. Tigs! Tigs! How'd you get on?'

Tigs, thought Miles. What a bloody silly name. He smiled earnestly at the boy who was approaching them, carrying a brand-new surf board awkwardly.

'OK,' he said. 'It's not as easy as it looks.'

'I told you it wouldn't be,' she said. 'Tigs, this is Miles. Miles, Tigs, Short for Tigger, short for Thomas.'

Miles couldn't see how Tigger could possibly be short for Thomas, but didn't like to say so. He shook Tigs' outstretched hand.

'Hi.'

'Miles can really surf, Tigs. He could give you a few tips, I expect.'

Tigs looked at Miles longingly. 'Could you really? I'd be extremely grateful.'

He sounded a bit like the Creep, Miles thought, or maybe it was the accent. He sounded East Coast, it was different from his sister's. Anyway, he didn't seem too bad, and if it was going to make him a friend of Joanna's, he would spend all day and all night teaching Tigs to surf.

'Sure. Any time. Want to try now?'

'In a minute maybe. When I get my breath back.'

'Miles lives right here,' said Joanna. 'In the mountains. Wouldn't that be great, Tigs? Tigs is a year older than me,' she went on. 'He's at college now. Or nearly. Next year.'

'Where are you going?' said Miles.

'Colorado.'

353

'Ah.'

'Tigs loves to ski,' said Joanna 'and it's not too far away from here, you see. Not like New York. So it seemed like a good idea.'

'Yes.'

'Are you going to college?' asked Tigs.

'I guess so.'

'Which one?'

'Oh, I guess Santa Monica College. That's not too far away from here either.' He grinned at them both. 'Shall we try the surf now?'

'Sure.'

There were several things Miles was sure he could do better than Tigs; surfing was only one of them.

If this was love, Miles thought, it was very uncomfortable. What he had felt for Donna had been much nicer. He had been able to concentrate on other things, and had never worried about what he ought to say or wear or do when he was with her; life with Joanna was initially one big anxiety.

But it was worth it. Every time he looked at her exquisite little golden-brown face, her freckle-spangled nose, her surprised blue eyes, he discovered afresh where his heart was, for it turned right over, not just once but several times.

What was quite amazing was that she obviously liked him back. Very much. Probably she didn't love him, Miles couldn't in his wildest, most self-confident dreams think that, but liking him was enough for now. He could tell she liked him because she was so friendly; that very first day she had insisted on him being introduced to her parents, and they were really nice too; her father was a tall, gentle man with golden hair and a shaggy beard, and her mother was small and sparkly like Joanna, with dark curly hair and a body that certainly didn't look like it had borne two children. They had been terribly nice to Miles and talked to him for a while, and then insisted he came and joined them for a drink in Alice's, and when Tigs had asked him if he would maybe give him another surfing lesson soon and Miles had said 'Yes, sure,' they had said Tigs must bring Miles back afterwards for supper or a barbecue or something. Tigs was absolutely hopeless in the surf; he simply had no feeling for the sea, no concept how to even catch a wave, never mind get up on the board, but Miles didn't care; indeed, the longer Tigs took to master the whole thing – and from where Miles was sitting, it looked like a lifetime – the longer he would need to ask Miles for help. So that was all right.

He had been up to their house on Beverly Glen several times now; Joanna had been right, it hadn't been one of the mega mansions, but it was still about five times bigger than any house Miles had ever been inside: a charming colonial style white house, with God knows how many bedrooms, every one with its own bathroom and Jacuzzi, and a sunken hall and living room with marble floorings, and what was obviously antique furniture, and a coloured maid who opened the door in a uniform, and a kitchen that looked straight out of *House and Garden*, and an enormous yard and a massive pool, and a tennis-court and three garages. Both Joanna and Tigs had cars: twin VW Convertible Rabbits.

But the Tylers, for all their money, were just the nicest people Miles thought he had ever met; friendly, chatty, unsnobby, and so welcoming and generous.

His grandmother had been very sniffy about the friendship: 'People like that think they're doing you a real favour,' she said, 'letting you into their homes. Don't you get taken in, you'll end up hurt and patronized.'

But Miles didn't see he could possibly end up hurt; the Tylers just seemed to like having him there. The house was always full of people anyway, friends and neighbours. He very quickly learnt where Joanna got her friendliness and charm; it came from growing up in a household that was one long party. He found himself there more and more, and not just after he had given Tigs a surfing lesson; they invited him over every Sunday for barbecue lunch, and Joanna very often asked him to come and play tennis; he had never learnt the game, but he was naturally gifted at all sports and in weeks was playing better than a lot of the other kids who were there.

Not all of them were as nice to him as Joanna and Tigs; they clearly regarded him as an upstart, an intruder in their golden world. Miles didn't care. He didn't care about anything at all as long as he could be close to Joanna. And besides, he learnt fast. He had a surprisingly acute social sense, and charming manners when he put his mind to them; he swiftly absorbed the small differences of behaviour between himself and Tigs: the way you stood up when an adult came in the room. Called older men sir (but not older women ma'am), let girls go in front of you through doorways, pushed their chairs in for them at table, used a linen napkin, and ate a little less as if your life depended on it. He learnt to keep quiet about Samo High, or at least when he could, and talked vaguely about maybe Berkeley when people asked him about college. He found Malibu was a usefully neutral address; a house in Latego Canyon was much better than downtown Santa Monica. Moreover he found, somewhat to his own discomfort, that he felt more and more at home, more comfortable with the Tylers and their friends; he did not feel an intruder, a cuckoo in the nest, but as if he was actually a fledgling from Beverly Glen and its environs himself. He began, not so much to look down on his old friends and his grandmother, but to regard them with the same kind of detached interest he had originally given the Tylers, as if they were different from him in some way.

It had all meant breaking up with Donna, and that had been perfectly awful; she had looked at him with infinite scorn in her dark eyes and said, 'OK, Miles, if that's how you want it, go and learn to be a rich girl's pet. Only when she gets tired of you, don't come running back to me, that's all. And she will.' And she had left him, then and there, slammed out of the car, not upset at all as far as he could see, just angry and contemptuous, which had been worse in a way.

He had been with Donna for a long time; everything he knew about girls and their bodies he had learnt from her. How soon you could kiss them, how to make them want you to do a bit more, how to stroke their breasts gently, not maul them about and put them off; what a vagina felt like, how to find the bit that got them excited, when to approach it; how to know when they had their periods and to show you knew without actually saying anything; how to reassure them that you weren't going to try and force them to go all the way, while actually trying like mad to persuade them. He owed Donna a lot and he knew it, and he felt terrible about leaving her; but love was love, and what he felt for Joanna was utterly different and he had to be free to pursue her – and it.

Miles at seventeen was not only good-looking and attractive; he had a certain confidence about him, a kind of subtlety to his sexuality that persuaded girls he knew his way around more than he did. Girls who didn't know him always imagined that he had been to bed, gone all the way, lots of times; he seemed so much more sophisticated than most of the sweaty, fumbling boys in his year. Donna of course put them right, because she didn't want anyone thinking she was a tart and been to bed with him, and nor was she having people thinking anyone else had been to bed with him either. But nevertheless the initial impression was one of experience.

And this was certainly the impression Joanna got. She was totally inexperienced herself; apart from a few fumbles in cars after parties, or in the garden or maybe occasionally even a bedroom, and a lot of kissing of course, she had no idea what sex meant. She knew the theory, of course. Her mother was a liberated and civilized woman, and she had had all the right conversations with Joanna, and given her all the right books to read as well, but until she had met Miles, Joanna had never felt so much as a flicker of sexual desire. That had now, however, radically changed. She could scarcely these days think of anything else. The very first time he had kissed her, slowly, deliciously, confidently, she had felt hot, startled, charged; she had woken in the night, with all kinds of strange sensations in her body. Exploring it and them cautiously, she discovered vivid pleasures and sensations; she fell asleep dreaming of Miles, and awoke longing only to see him again, to be held by him, kissed by him.

Gradually he showed her all the things he had learnt with Donna; never pushing her, never worrying her, always reassuring her that he would never, ever do anything she didn't want, or that would be dangerous. Through the summer, Joanna learnt a great deal about not only her own body, but Miles', what she could do to excite him, how to get him to excite her, how to prolong the feeling until it was almost unendurable, and then how to relieve it, and the delicious explosions of pleasure they could give one another. Of course, in a way she could see it would be nice to do it properly, to end all this messiness and fumbling, and quite often she did wonder if she ought to go and see nice Doctor Schlesinger and ask her for the pill, and she knew she would give it to her without lecturing her or anything; but she had always promised herself that she would only go to bed with a boy if she really loved him, and she wasn't quite quite sure if she loved Miles yet. So she waited.

Tigs, she knew, mistrusted Miles; he thought he was a fortune hunter. This upset Joanna, because she found it insulting to both her and Miles; she worked very hard to make the two boys friends, but it never quite worked. Tigs despised Miles for his humble origins, and Miles despised Tigs for his incompetence at anything physical – including pulling the girls – and it was a gulf too big to bridge.

In September Tigs went off to college, and Joanna and Miles grew closer. He drove to see her not just at the weekends, but several evenings during the week; when both of them should have been studying. He would eat his meal and then get into the Mustang and drive out along the highway and drive all the long long way up Sunset, round and round the curving suburban roads, watching them get ritzier and ritzier, through Brentwood and Westwood, finally actually passing the ultimate landmark, bringing him close to Joanna, Marymount High, and thence into Paradise and the white house on Beverly Glen.

They were both now in their last year at high school; seriously distracted from their studies. They could think of very little but each other and of sex; where the one ended and the other began neither was certain. William and Jennifer Tyler watched them with a fairly benign anxiety; they liked Miles very much, they did not share Tigs' view of him, but they were not happy with the fact that Joanna was doing virtually no work, and her grades were dropping steadily.

Finally they intervened, and told her she was not to see Miles except on Sundays until Christmas; if by then her grades had pulled up, they would review the situation. Joanna stormed and cried and accused them of being snobs and prejudiced; to no avail.

'Darling, we love Miles. We really do. More than almost any of the boys who come here. But he is a serious distraction. And your work is important.' Jennifer looked at her daughter shrewdly. 'The last thing we want is to send you away to school now. But if these grades don't improve, that's what we'll have to do.'

'You wouldn't be so cruel. You couldn't!' cried Joanna, her eyes big with fright.

'We could. Now we're not asking a lot. Only giving him up during the week. Get your head down and prove we can trust you.'

Joanna wondered how they would feel if they knew they couldn't trust her in other ways too. In September she had made the trip to Doctor Schlesinger, and thence to bed proper with Miles; after a slightly difficult painful start, he had proved marvellously clever and skilful, and she sensual and responsive; they spent evening after evening in her little suite, enjoying the most triumphantly pleasing sex, relaxed in the knowledge that her parents, too sensitive and liberated to interfere, would merely walk past the closed doors and never dream of knocking or coming in.

And then they discovered a new pleasure. Accepting the disciplines, the limits set on their meeting, with fairly good grace, they began to experiment with drugs. Miles had been smoking pot for some time; it had been going round his crowd at school for years, regarded as something almost wholesome. 'It's organic,' Donna had assured him earnestly, passing him his very first joint; and on one or two memorable occasions he and Joanna had tried LSD. Miles had found it at once terrifying and exhilarating; the way it invaded his senses, took him on a journey through colours and shapes and sensations, would have ensnared him very quickly had it not been for a (literally) sobering incident which frightened him more than he ever quite cared to admit.

All the kids at all the Hollywood parties smoked pot; their parents, who smoked it also at their parties and dinner parties, for the most part turned a blind eye. But then one night, all the crowd Miles and Joanna went around with were busted at a party just after the New Year. The Tylers and Mrs Kelly were both woken in the night by the police, along with a lot of other respectable and shaken parents, and told their children would be charged. They had to pay a bail of five hundred dollars for each of them, and also pay the lawyer who made a most luxurious living for himself entirely out of defending Beverly Hills kids against drugs charges.

The Tylers forbad Miles ever to see Joanna again; Mrs Kelly

virtually placed Miles under house arrest, contacted Bill Wilburn, a cousin of Dean's who lived in San Francisco, for further legal advice and support, and took the unprecedented step of phoning Hugo Dashwood to enlist his help.

Bill Wilburn didn't like Hugo Dashwood. He had met him at Lee's funeral, and found him stiff and overbearing. He couldn't see what his cousin could have liked about him, and he resented the rather proprietary interest he took in the family and particularly in Miles. When he discovered Miles' nickname for him, he had had some difficulty in not laughing out loud, and although he had rebuked the boy for being cheeky, he had twinkled at him at the same time. Now, confronted by him across the family crisis, he felt the same old hostility rising.

'Good of you to come, Mr Dashwood. But I think we can handle this ourselves, just keep it in the family.'

'I like to think of myself as family, Mr Wilburn. Mrs Kelly has asked me to help.'

'Whatever you might like to think, Mr Dashwood, you're not. And I can't see how you can help.'

'You may need money.'

'We may.'

'Well, let me provide it.'

'Why should you feel you should do that?'

'I made a promise to Lee to keep an eye on Miles. I want to keep that promise.'

'I see.'

'And I am quite prepared to talk to Miles. To try and help sort things out.'

'I don't know that would be very constructive right now,' said Wilburn, remembering Miles' nickname for Hugo. 'He's very withdrawn.'

'I daresay. But he has to realize he can't stay withdrawn. He has to make amends. He has to start rebuilding his life.'

'Mr Dashwood, I'm not making excuses for Miles and I agree with you in a way, but he's had a terrible shock and he's in a strange state. I would advise against interfering just now.'

'Mr Wilburn,' said Hugo, his mouth twitching slightly with suppressed rage, 'I think the situation warrants interfering. Anyway, we can come back to that. What is the legal situation?'

'It's not too bad. There are charges against all the kids. There'll be a stiff fine, and a record, I guess. Not good, but not disastrous.'

'Do they have to appear in court?'

'Yup.'

'When?'

'Next week.'

'I'll stay till then.'

'You don't have to.'

'I want to.'

The children were each fined a thousand dollars. Any repetition of the offence, they were told, would result in a jail sentence. The judge read them all a lecture and they were driven away from the courtroom by their parents, subdued and silent. Miles was driven away by Hugo.

'Now, Miles, I don't want to pile on the agony and say what the judge did all over again.'

'Please don't.'

'But I have spoken to you before about your behaviour generally, and I simply don't like it. I don't like the direction you are going in.'

'I don't care what you like or don't like. It has nothing to do with you.'

'That is your opinion.'

'It's a fact.'

'Only as you see it.'

Miles was silent.

'Now then, I have some suggestions to make to you. Miles, look at me.'

Miles turned and looked out of the window.

'Miles,' said Hugo, 'if you are not very careful, I shall have you sent right away, and you will never see any of your friends here for a very long time.'

'You couldn't.'

'I most certainly could. Your grandmother is your legal guardian, and she is most emphatically in favour of the idea. Now will you please do me the courtesy of listening to me properly.'

Miles turned with infinite slowness and presented an insolent face to Hugo. 'OK.'

'Right. Now the first thing I want is for you to promise me never to see this particular crowd again.'

Miles looked at him and grinned. 'Funny, isn't it? You dragged me away from my Samo High friends because you thought they were a bad influence. Then I get in with some nicely raised rich kids and look what happens. All kinds of trouble.'

'Yes, well, I'm afraid neither a modest nor a rich background is a guarantee against wrongdoing. Anyway, do I have your word on that?'

'I guess you do for now.'

'What do you mean?'

'Well, we'll all be kept under lock and key. They're all mostly at boarding school, and Joanna's parents have forbidden me to see her —' He was silent, his face morose as he remembered his last conversation with Joanna on the phone, her voice shaken with sobs and fear. Not only had her parents been shocked and horrified by the drugs case, they had betrayed all their own liberal ideals and thrown the book at Joanna when her store of contraceptive pills had been found, during the course of a search of her room.

'Miles, I don't want a promise with a time limit. These people are not good for you. I forbid you to see them any more, ever.'

He shrugged. 'OK.'

'Now I have been thinking. You're a clever boy and I think you could get into a good college. I am prepared to send you to one, a really good one, on the East Coast maybe. Babson, or Pine Manor. It would be a wonderful opportunity for you. You would have to work very very hard to get in. There would have to be private tuition every night until you went. God knows if you could even get in. But I'm prepared to make the push if you are. Your sporting background might help.'

Miles was looking at him thoughtfully. 'I don't want to go to some snooty East Coast college. Could I maybe go to Berkeley?'

'You maybe could. You maybe couldn't. You don't seem to understand how difficult this is going to be. Are you prepared to make the effort or not? And to agree to my other conditions?'

'Which are?'

'Miles, I am finding it very difficult to keep my temper.'
'Sorry.'

'To stop seeing your current friends. Not to see Joanna – at least until the academic year is over and then only if her parents are agreeable. To stay in and study every night, and only to go out one evening a week. And only to surf once a week.'

Miles looked at him open mouthed and saw the life he loved slipping away from him. The sweet golden days on the beach, in the sun, waiting for the wave, with the other surf bums; lunch at the omelette parlour at Malibu; driving up Sunset in the dusk, his heart thumping, thinking of Joanna; sitting in the parking lot with her on Mulholland Drive, seeing the sun drop almost sensuously into the ocean, while the sky turned from blue to blush to dark; being with her while she played tennis and swam and lay in the sun, her lovely sun-kissed face smiling at him with the look of love; the long, discovery-filled evenings in her conveniently big bed, as he explored her small, eager, erotic little body and the joys of joining it with his own; talking to her endlessly over a joint, finding more and more to learn and love about her; the long easy days at school with his friends, just skidding by on the work, starring at sport, the hero of his year. All to be taken from him, by this rich, interfering Creep. God, why did his mother have to get so friendly with him.

Nevertheless – Berkeley! That would be cool. That would impress the world. That would even maybe impress Joanna's parents. Miles sighed. It was probably worth it.

'OK,' he said to Hugo as the car pulled up in front of the house. 'I agree. And –' he wrenched the word from himself with an almost physical effort – 'thanks.'

'That's all right. I want to be proud of you.'

Miles thought he might be sick.

'Old Dashwood wants to send me to a smart college,' he said next day to Bill Wilburn, who had just read him a lesser lecture and drawn a cheque from his mother's estate to pay the fine (he had refused Dashwood's offer, saying this was an expense Miles should ultimately shoulder).

'Really? Where?'

'Oh, he mentioned some swanky East Coast places. I said I'd like to go to Berkeley. He said OK.'

Bill put down his pen and looked at Miles in genuine astonishment.

'That would cost thousands of dollars.'

'I know. He seems to have them.'

'But why should he spend them on you?'

'Don't know. He seems to feel strongly about what I do.'

'Well, you're a very fortunate young man.'

'Yeah, I guess so.'

'What makes you think one of these colleges will take you?'

'Oh,' said Miles with the supreme confidence of one who has only failed because he has chosen to. 'They'll take me.'

'Well, that's fine then.' Bill appeared to have dropped the subject, but his mind was seething. What in God's name was this guy about, spending that kind of money on some kid who was nothing to do with him? It didn't make any kind of sense. He decided to do a little investigating before he went back to San Francisco.

'Mrs Kelly, do you have all the old papers of Lee and Dean's, you know, wills, financial matters, all that kind of thing? I'd sure like to look at them. Just in case this matter gets taken any further.'

'Yes, I do. They're all in my room. I'll get them for you. Do you think it might, then?'

'What? Oh, get taken further? No, but it's as well to be sure. Thanks. Oh, and how much did Lee ever say to you about this Dashwood character? Just how good a friend was he?'

'Nothing like that,' snapped Mrs Kelly. 'Lee never looked at another man, after Dean. There was nothing between those two at all. Although I don't mind telling you, as you're family, I wondered about it myself. He's been around ever since I can remember. Before Miles was born. I even asked her about it when she was dying. Dean once did him a good turn, she said, and he always said he'd wanted to repay him, and when Dean died he came to see Lee and was a real comfort to her. But not in that way. Not how you might think.'

'OK. I just wondered. He seems to feel pretty possessive about Miles.'

'Yes, well he promised Lee to see after him. To see he turned out right. I'm an old woman, there's a limit to what I can do. And I've been real glad of his help, so don't you go criticizing him now. He's been very good to us.'

'I won't say another word. Now let me have those papers.'

'I want them back.'

'You can have them back tomorrow.'

The papers were scanty: Dean's will, Lee's will; funeral expenses; Miles' birth certificate, doctors' bills for Lee.

Doctors! thought Bill. They always hold a lot of information. He noted the number of Doctor Forsythe, and put the rest of the papers back in the file.

'That was a terrible tragedy.' Old Doctor Forsythe's eyes darkened, thinking about it. 'She was so young and so lovely.'

'She was.'

'And she had a lot to bear. That was a dreadful thing, her husband dying.'

'Killing himself.'

'Yes.'

The old man looked pained.

'Do you – do you have any idea quite why he did it?'

'No. Who can tell? His work wasn't going well. He wasn't a fit man. I imagine he just couldn't stand the strain any more.'

'Were you looking after him all the time?'

'No. As a matter of fact he was seeing a young doctor at the hospital for a few weeks before he died. He'd had a bad scare, a blackout.

'Which hospital?'

'St John's.'

'Do you know who the doctor was?'

'Let me see. Of course I don't have notes on him any more, the poor soul. I imagine it would have been the cardiac unit. Try Doctor Burgess.'

'I will.'

'Oh, yes, I remember Mr Wilburn. A dreadful tragedy. He was doing so well, that was the irony.'

'In what way?'

'Well, he'd lost quite a lot of weight. He was getting fitter. And so hopeful.'

'About what?'

'Well, life in general. Of course the one thing he most hoped for wasn't possible. I –' He hesitated.

'What?'

'Oh, I shouldn't be telling you, it's confidential.'

'Doctor Burgess, how can it be confidential now? The man's been dead seven years. And I'm a relative.'

'Even so. Oh, all right. What he wanted desperately was another child. Seemed to think that if he got fit and gave up drinking, all that kind of thing, it might happen.'

'So? Mightn't it?'

'Not for him.'

'Why not?'

'Well, because he was absolutely sterile. Totally. A zero sperm count. It puzzled me a lot.'

'Why?'

'Well, because as far as I could see, from the nature of the tests we ran, it must always have been the same. I could not imagine how he could ever have fathered a child. I said so to him. I told him he'd been very very fortunate. That his son was one of Nature's little miracles.'

'Really? Lee never told me any of this.'

'Lee? Oh, the wife. Well, why should she? You're only a cousin by marriage. These things are hurtful and difficult in a relationship. Besides –'

'What?'

'Oh – forgive me. It's just that some people might – might misinterpret it. Think –'

'Think what?'

'Well, that perhaps your cousin hadn't been the boy's father. People are very cynical, you know. Eager to think the worst.'

A loud noise like cymbals was beating in Bill Wilburn's ears. He seemed to be seeing the doctor down the end of a long tunnel. Phrases kept repeating in his mind, tumbling in a wild pattern like a kaleidoscope. 'Perhaps your cousin hadn't been the boy's father . . . one of Nature's little miracles . . . a dreadful thing, her husband dying . . . been around ever since I can remember, before Miles was born . . . thousands of dollars . . . he seems to feel strongly about what I do.'

He swallowed hard. 'Thank you, Doctor.'

366

'My pleasure.'

Bill Wilburn went for a long walk along the Palisades. The more he thought about it, the more sense it made. Hugo Dashwood was Miles' father. And didn't want him to know. Probably had made some kind of damn fool promise to Lee. Well, it was probably better. There was no point telling the boy now. It would only upset him, make him feel bad about his parents.

Should he do anything, say anything? No, it was all much too delicate. Better to stay quiet. If it was ever really necessary to come forward, he would. If there was any more trouble. Or if anyone ever really needed to know.

Chapter Nine

London and Eleuthera, 1973–6

Roz had never expected to feel pity for her father; nevertheless that was the emotion she was currently experiencing whenever she thought about him. And as always she thought about him a great deal. Everything seemed to have gone wrong for him, and, what was worse, his misfortunes were enduring a rather high profile. Araminta Jones had pulled on her hot pants and thigh-high boots one morning and stalked out on him finally, her exit from both his life and the company having been preceded only a few months by that of Camilla, who told him in uncharacteristically few words that she was not prepared to play understudy to anybody and certainly not a self-obsessed girl of twenty-three with the brains of a flea. Moreover – she had also told him, in only slightly more words – she was not prepared to work any longer towards the success of his company, and was setting up her own advertising agency in New York. There was considerable speculation as to which of her two defections had hurt Julian more. He had also apparently lost the close and happy relationship he had had with Susan for so many years; they were almost estranged, communicating rather stiffly and formally when it was absolutely necessary. It seemed to Roz that he could never have needed her friendship more.

The new ethical pharmaceutical wing of the company, founded upon millions of pounds' worth of investment and a fanfare of publicity, had had a spectacular flop with its first big product launch; and the fact that Eliza was in the throes of a wildly successful, much-chronicled love affair with the son of one of the richest of the oil-rich sheikhs did not help either.

There was another, more intimate problem Julian was undergoing at the moment, which Araminta could have borne testament to but mercifully did not, and which Susan's rejection had exacerbated; the end result was that he looked exhausted and haggard, and was bad tempered and totally unpredictable both at home and work.

It was Letitia who alerted Roz to the problems – with the exception of the intimate one, which not even she could have known about, or even suspected – and suggested she should talk to him about them.

'I can't possibly, darling, he'll just feel I'm interfering as usual. But you could, he needs to talk to someone, he's awfully low. And after all, you're eighteen now, quite grown up, and he loves you so much, you could be exactly what he needs.'

'I don't know about that,' said Roz shortly. 'Loving me, I mean. But of course I'll talk to him. I'm going to stay with him at Marriotts this weekend. I'm so absolutely sick and tired of Mummy and her lovesick Arab, so it'll be an ideal time.'

'Thank you, darling. And you're wrong, you know. He does love you, more than anyone or anything else in the world.'

'Does he?' said Roz, looking at her rather coolly. 'Well, maybe. He has had a very strange way of showing it, that's all I can say.'

Letitia sighed. 'I know. Poor Roz. I'm afraid you've had a very difficult time.'

'Oh well,' said Roz briskly. 'I expect it's done me good. Some people would say I'd had a marvellous life. Just a poor little rich girl, that's what I am, I suppose.'

Her father did seem acutely depressed. He drove her down to Marriotts in his new Mercedes (one of the things which had been most revealing about his low morale had been the fact he hadn't bought a rare car for six months), hardly speaking. Roz, who was not a chatterer herself, sat in silence beside him and wondered what on earth she could do for him. Apart from anything else, she reflected, it was going to be a very dreary weekend. She might even have to send an SOS to Rosie to come and join them.

Poor Daddy. Well, he was getting on a bit now. Seriously old. Nearly fifty-four, he still looked very good, of course, his hair was hardly grey at all, and he had never put on any weight. He dressed well, too, she had to admit; always in very classic clothes, but with a dash of style to spice them up a bit; right now, she thought, in his cream silk shirt, open at the neck, his beige linen trousers, his brown Gucci loafers, he looked really terrific. She told him so.

He smiled. 'You don't look so bad yourself. Although a bit as if you ought to be scoring a century in that sweater. I like those wide trousers, they remind me of when I was young.'

Roz took this to be a clue: he really must be feeling his age. And it was no wonder Araminta had finally gone off with her ghastly photographer boyfriend, she was only about twenty-four herself. It had been bad that, not least because it had affected her contract with Juliana. Nigel Dempster had imparted the news to a few close friends and several million of his readers in his column only that week.

'About Face', the story had been headed, and gone on to say that the 'ravishing Araminta Jones, the model daughter of "Buster" Jones, food broker millionaire, who has embodied the high-class image of Juliana cosmetics for over three years now, and been a close friend and constant companion of its chairman and founder Julian Morell, has left these shores and the modelling business to seek a second fortune, as an actress in New York. Her friend, the photographer Barry Binns, East End Boy made very good, has a studio in New York, and the two are planning to take the new world by storm together. This is a double blow for Mr Morell, as Miss Jones has managed to find a let-out clause in her contract and has informed him that she is no longer available to work for him. She tells me, however, that there has been no ill feeling between herself and Mr Morell, and that he completely understands her ambitions to further her career.'

Well, Roz thought, it might not be an ideal subject, but it was something to start on. 'I hear Araminta has left you,' she said casually, pressing the button to lower her window.

'She hasn't left me, as you put it,' said Julian irritably, 'she was never with me. Roz, please don't let that window down, it's so dusty and fumy on this road, the air conditioning is perfectly adequate.'

'Sorry. Of course I didn't mean you personally, I meant the company. Does it matter terribly? I suppose it will hurt Juliana badly?'

'Of course not. A company as large and important as Juliana hardly needs the attentions of some self-centred fool of a model girl to keep it afloat. Of course it's annoying, we shall have to find someone else, but we can make something of that publicity-wise.'

'Oh well, that's all right then.'

'Yes.' He was silent for a while, then said suddenly, 'How's your mother?'

'She's fine.'

'I hear she lost a great deal of money on that film she got involved in.'

'Yes, well she was really silly to be taken in by that phony director guy. Anyone with half a brain could see he wasn't ever going to get all those people like Dustin Hoffman and Ryan O'Neal, and then when he didn't, and all the others pulled out, it was too late, and she'd handed over the mega bucks. She says she doesn't care, it suits her to be poor. And she still thinks it will all come good.'

'I really don't think,' said Julian drily, 'your mother has the faintest idea what it means to be poor.'

'No. Do you?' She looked at him with the blank, slightly amused stare so like his own; he met it briefly and smiled for the first time that day. 'Better than she does. But no, not really.'

'Anyway, she's frightfully happy with Jamil. She says this is the real, the great love of her life, and nothing else matters.'

'Tell me about Jamil. Is he fun?'

'Great fun. Terribly good-looking. I don't usually like Arabs, but he is gorgeous, just like Omar Sharif.'

'How nice. Does he do anything? Apart from gamble at Les A every night, and pay court to your mother?'

'Not a lot. At the moment, he's buying a house here and some horses, he's the most marvellous horseman, we ride together in the park sometimes. He plans to settle here. His great ambition is to send his eldest son to Eton, and he wants to live like an English gentleman. Mummy's teaching him.'

'Well,' said Julian, 'that must be extremely nice for them both.'

'Yes, and one day, he wants to have a pharmaceutical company. He says he wants to put his money to good use. And establish a foundation. You know, like Wellcome, or Glaxo or something. Or yours, I suppose,' she added with an attempt at tact.

'Yes, I do know.'

'He's very very interesting. I really like him. He says if he does get a company established, there will always be a job for me. I'd really like that. I find that field very interesting.'

'Rosamund,' said Julian, 'you know perfectly well you will always have a job. More than a job. Let's not talk about you working for anyone else, please. Morell's will be yours one day, and it is clearly absurd for you to even consider any alternative, however short term.'

Roz opened her mouth to say she sometimes thought she would very much like to consider it, and then, in a rare moment of sensitivity, shut it again.

The weekend was not a success. Roz had no practice, no experience of intimacy, she had coped with the neglect of her parents over the years by distancing herself from them, and she was incapable now of reaching out and extending love and comfort to her father when he had so relentlessly deprived her of it. She tried again asking how he felt, even ventured an inquiry after Camilla, who had visited him in London recently, but he made it plain he did not want to discuss anything more personal than his new brood mare's recent confinement, and her plans for the rest of the summer.

'I'm going to Colorado with Rosie again, as you know, and I thought I'd spend a few days in Wiltshire, and then Susan suggested we went to one of the Greek islands for a week.'

'Susan! Susan?'

'Yes. Why are you so surprised? You know how much I like

371

her. She's probably my favourite person in the whole world, apart maybe from Granny Letitia.'

'Thank you, Roz. Look, if you don't mind I'd like to get back to London this afternoon, not wait till Monday morning. I have things to do.'

'Fine.'

They drove back even more silently than they had come. Roz, only dimly aware of how badly she had rubbed salt into almost every one of her father's wounds, set off on a shopping spree to furnish her wardrobe for the general delights of Colorado and the more specific ones of Rosie's stepbrother with great relief; Julian withdrew still further into his depression and ill temper and after two weeks of living like a recluse in his study at Hanover Terrace, firing a constant barrage of buckshot into the company in the form of memos, cancelling, changing, criticizing, rejecting, everything anyone was doing or had done, took himself off to his house on Eleuthera in the Bahamas to everyone's intense relief.

When he returned, he had Camilla North with him, and soon after that several trunkloads of her possessions were moved into the house in Hanover Terrace, including a large container full of her linen sheets.

People reacted in very different ways to the fact that Camilla North was at last formally established as Julian's mistress. Letitia was outraged; Susan was hurt almost beyond endurance; Eliza was amused; but the person most deeply affected, and indeed shocked, was Roz.

Roz had thought herself freed from Camilla, that the woman's absence from her father's life had been at his volition, the result of having finally come to his senses. She did not know that the boot had actually been on Camilla's slender, aristocratic foot, and had been planted firmly behind her father when Araminta Jones entered his life; she had heard how Camilla had resigned from Morell's, and set up her own very successful advertising agency in New York with some amazement (blinded as she was to Camilla's talents by her strong dislike); and she had thought that that had been the end of a rather long and dreary chapter in her life. Now she had to face not only Camilla's presence again, but the fact that her father clearly wanted it, enjoyed it, and indeed could not manage without it. It changed the part of her life that she spent with her father greatly for the worse; it changed her perception of him in much the same way; and it reinforced her determination not to work for him after she had left Cambridge, as everyone insisted on assuming. Camilla was not, to be sure, working in the company any more, and was spending at least three quarters of her time in New York, although there was talk of her setting up a London branch of North Creative, but the fact remained that there she stood, a beautiful, self-satisfied, humourless testimony to Julian's dependence on her, and Roz did not know how to bear the thought of it.

Camilla on the other hand was perfectly happy. For the first time in her life she had a cause, she was genuinely needed, and she was finding it intensely rewarding.

The cause was Julian's impotence.

God alone knew (and Julian) what it had cost him to tell her about it. Camilla found the thought quite overwhelming; and unemotional as she was, she had felt tears pricking at the back of her eyes as she sat, hands in her lap, listening carefully to him as they sat on the veranda of the house in Turtle Cove, Eleuthera.

He had phoned her at her parents' house in Philadephia, where she had been staying for a week, avoiding the intense heat of New York, and first asked her, then begged her to come down and stay for a few days.

'I need you, Camilla,' he had said, and she could hear the genuine emotion in his voice (so rarely there). 'I need you very badly. Please, please come.'

And so she had flown down to Nassau, and he had met her there in the small plane he kept on Eleuthera, and taken her to Turtle Cove and shown her very formally into the guest bedroom, and said he would be waiting for her on the veranda with some extremely good and cold champagne when she was ready; she emerged quite quickly, looking ravishing, in a jade green silk pyjama suit from Valentino, her red hair drifting on her shoulders, and after she had had half a glass of the champagne, and he had had about three, he began to talk to her about his problem.

It had begun while he had been with Araminta, so demanding, so selfish (and so young, Camilla thought to herself sagely); just occasionally, but of course it was a cumulative thing, once the fear was there, the knowledge that it might happen, it happened again and again. Araminta had not been good about it, not reassuring at all, and then there had been the crisis with the company, the anxiety over the shares and a possible takeover bid; it had got worse.

'Didn't you take any advice, have any therapy?' asked Camilla. 'It's so important, Julian, to get help immediately in these matters, not to try to handle it yourself, you can do untold damage, reinforce the problem . . .'

And yes he said, interrupting her, yes he had, as a matter of fact, and only Camilla would know how serious that meant the situation had been, regarding these things as he did with such deep distaste and distrust, he had seen a marvellous woman, and she had been very helpful, and he had begun to see an improvement, and then in the latest series of debacles, the failure of the pharmaceutical launch, Susan's rejection of his proposal (he spared himself nothing in this story, Camilla noticed, not sure whether she was more gratified that he was so totally debasing himself or her, or outraged that he should have asked Susan to marry him), Eliza's new and patent happiness with the monumentally rich and powerful Jamil Al-Shehra, Araminta's departure from his life and his bed, it had begun again, it was a nightmare of despair and fear; he had become afraid even to try now, and somehow, he felt, indeed he knew, he said, that Camilla, with her great understanding of him, and her unique position in his life, and also her very careful and serious approach to sexual matters, was probably the only person in the world who could help.

He sat looking at her in silence then, so unnaturally and strangely anxious and diffident, after what she felt was probably the most, indeed the only, honest conversation he had ever had with her, and Camilla's heart had turned over, and she had felt herself filled with a great warmth of tenderness towards him, and what she supposed was love, and she had smiled and leant forward and kissed him on the cheek, and said, her brown eyes even more than usually earnest, 'Julian, I don't know when I've felt happier or more honoured.'

She felt something else, as well, something that she had very rarely felt in her life, with Julian or indeed anyone: a sudden, lightning bolt of sexual desire.

Camilla knew a lot about impotence. She had studied it very carefully as a subject over the years, because everybody knew that powerful women were a threat to men, they emasculated them, and while power in a man was an aphrodisiac, in a woman it was the reverse. And being a powerful woman, she had always recognized it as a syndrome and a potential factor in her relationships, and something she should be prepared to have to face. She had not, however, ever expected to have to face it in connection with Julian Morell.

She knew a great many possible approaches, both psychological and physical; she knew it was the most difficult problem of all to handle, and quite extraordinarily delicate; and that quite possibly Julian would have to go into therapy whether she could personally help him or not. However, there was obviously no physical reason for it, the root cause was manifestly stess, caused by professional failure and reinforced by an unsympathetic response from his partners; there seemed some hope therefore, she felt, that she might be able to help to at least a limited degree.

That night, therefore, after a light dinner, accompanied by only a little alcohol (both at Camilla's instigation), she joined him in the master bedroom, and attempted to put some of the theories into practice.

'The most important thing is,' she told him earnestly, as she drew the sheets over their naked forms, and pulled his head gently towards her lovely breasts, 'that you shouldn't even begin to think about having an erection. We should just enjoy the feel of our bodies being together and the sensations of closeness on every level, nothing else.'

For three nights she achieved nothing; Julian was increasingly tense and fearful, almost in tears. Camilla, moved by his swift descent from powerful arrogance to helpless humility, tried to remain calm, positive, soothing. They spent their days swimming, sunbathing, sailing; Julian, touched by her devotion and patience, told her repeatedly how much he needed her, wanted her, had missed her. Camilla was perfectly happy. Then on the fourth night he had become angry as she lay beside him, trying to soothe his fears, comfort him out of his misery.

'Christ, Camilla,' he said suddenly, 'just leave me alone, will you. This is a nightmare, I should never have asked you to come, I'm sorry.' And he had turned away and shaken her arms off him; and a great white anger had come over Camilla, a sense of outrage that he should reject her, even while she understood the reason so well, and a hunger for him, and for sex, so violent she cried out with it; and he had turned again and looked at her with astonishment in his eyes and said, 'Camilla, what is it, whatever is it?'

And she had said, driven out of her usual reserve, her careful, watchful self-restraint, 'Christ, Julian, I want you, that's what it is, for the first time in my life I really want you.'

'What on earth do you mean?' he said. 'We've been having sex for years, marvellous sex,' and she had said no, no, they hadn't, it had been marvellous for him, but not for her, she couldn't believe he hadn't realized, she had never had an orgasm, with him, or with anyone, all her life the whole thing had seemed pointless, futile.

'Do you mean?' he said, 'that you've been faking all these years?'

'Yes,' said Camilla, almost screaming in her sudden sense of outrage, 'yes, yes, yes. I have been faking, faking orgasms, faking desire. Just to satisfy your monster male ego.'

And he sat bolt upright and smiled at her, looking suddenly quite different, younger, more alive. 'You bitch,' he said, 'you clever, devious bitch. I can't believe it of you. I don't believe it. Come here, Camilla, come here, lie down, here, please now, just forget all your theories and your therapies, and bloody well let me help you find out what sex is really all about.'

And Camilla, feeling him sinking into her strongly, insistently, reaching her, drawing her into a new wild confusion of liquid pleasure, thought confusedly that this was all wrong, that she should be helping him, healing him, and instead he was helping her, leading her into a new country of hot, soaring peaks and bright exploding waterfalls, and she was lost suddenly, she did not know who she was or what she was doing, and she was moving, following him, climbing him, falling on to him, tearing at him with her hands, her mouth, pulling away from him, feeling him plunging deep deep into her again, talking to him feverishly, moaning, crying out, she could have gone on, she felt, for ever, pursuing this brilliance, this huge mounting shuddering delight, she was totally abandoned to him, and he to her. And when it was over, and they lay quietly apart, still trembling, stroking one another, Camilla wept very gently with pleasure and at long last release, and she looked at Julian, lying there with his eyes closed, an expression of great peace on his face, and saw that his cheeks too were wet with tears.

Julian came up to Cambridge and took Roz out to lunch to tell her that Camilla would be moving into the house in Hanover Terrace, and that from now on she should regard Camilla as at least her unofficial stepmother.

Cambridge life was suiting Roz; she looked relaxed, and somehow younger; she was dressed in the current craze of layers in a dark, floral print: a long smock over a long full skirt, with a matching turban over her dark hair, and platform-soled blue suede boots.

'You look very nice,' Julian added, as a rider to his speech about Camilla. 'University life obviously suits you.'

'Yes,' she said briefly, ignoring the compliment. She looked at him stony-faced and said, 'Why not official? Why don't you marry her and be done with it?'

'Well,' he said, 'I would quite like to marry her, as a matter of fact, but Camilla doesn't want to marry me. Which puts me in my place, I suppose.'

'Why not? Why doesn't she want to marry you?'

'Camilla values her independence. She is a liberated woman. Like yourself.'

'I don't call it very independent, moving into someone else's house. Letting them keep you.'

'Roz, I'm not going to keep her. She has her own business. She is a rich woman in her own right.'

'Oh. So isn't she going to come back to working for you?'

'Unfortunately not. I wish she would, because she is extremely talented. I miss her input into the company. Her agency will, however, be working on some advertising for us.'

'Oh. How old is Camilla?'

'I'm not sure. Let me see, I suppose she must be thirty-six or thirty-seven. Why?'

'Oh, nothing.'

'Roz.'

'Yes?'

'Roz, I do hope you and Camilla will learn to be better friends this time round. I'm so extremely fond of you both, it would be nice for me to see you getting on better.'

'Daddy,' said Roz, 'you may be able to fix most things, but you don't seem to understand that you can't order people to like each other. I don't want to be Camilla's friend and I'm sure she doesn't want to be mine.'

'Roz,' said Julian, and there was genuine anxiety in his eyes, 'why do you dislike Camilla so much?'

'I suppose,' she said, watching him carefully, enjoying his insecurity, 'because you've always spent a great deal more time and effort fussing over Camilla than you ever have over me.'

'Roz, that's not true.'

'It's perfectly true.'

'Well,' he said, at an attempt at lightheartedness, 'let's not argue about that. I'm sorry you don't like Camilla, and that you're so unhappy about it, but you have your own life now, so maybe I don't have to worry about you and your unhappiness with things quite so much.'

'I don't remember,' said Roz, swallowing hard to prevent a rather insistent lump rising in her throat, looking at him with hard, blank eyes, 'you worrying about me and my unhappiness very much when I didn't have my own life.'

'Now Roz, that isn't fair.'

'Isn't it?'

'No. I have always put you first.'

'Goodness. I didn't realize.'

Julian kept his temper with a visible effort.

'How's life at Cambridge?'

'It's great, thank you.'

'Good. Well, I shall need that brain of yours in the company. I'm glad it's being so well trained.'

'Daddy,' said Roz. 'I've been meaning to tell you for months now. I really don't have the slightest desire to work for you. I want to make my own way. Do things on my own terms.'

She didn't mean a word of it, she had never wanted the security more, of knowing that he valued her, that the company would one day be hers. But it was worth the risk of losing it, just to see the fear and the hurt in his dark eyes.

Chapter Ten

London, 1979

One cold wet morning in November 1979 Julian Morell walked into his office, slammed the door and then immediately buzzed on the intercom for coffee. Sarah Brownsmith looked at the phone and sighed. This was obviously one of the days (increasingly frequent, she noticed) for keeping a very low profile indeed.

Julian was running on a fuse so short it ignited almost spontaneously. Everybody had remarked on it, so Sarah did not feel she had to blame herself. Freddy Branksome seldom passed her these days on his way through to Julian's office without raising his eyes to heaven; Richard Brookes, the company lawyer, whose languid academic exterior concealed a mind that went to work with the speed of a black mamba, had taken to working at home every morning in an attempt to lessen Julian's opportunities for summoning him. And David Sassoon, newly returned from New York, was threatening to go back again, or to leave Julian's employ altogether despite having had both his department and salary doubled in size and possessing the quite exceptional company perk of a helicopter for his exclusive use.

Only Susan Johns seemed perfectly happy, running her side of the company with as much efficiency, skill and innovative thought as ever, and conducting her relationship with its chairman with her usual calm, irreverence and humour. There were rumours in the company of a relationship between Susan and Richard Brookes, and certainly they spent a great deal of time together, and appeared very fond of one another, but Susan was, as Paul Baud had remarked so long ago, a dark

379

mare, and thirty years of working with Julian Morell had taught her the very high value of discretion.

Julian Morell, on the other hand, seemed to have forgotten its value altogether. There was a lot of ugly gossip about him and Camilla North, both in and out of the press. Camilla was spending at least two thirds of her time in New York, leaving her agency in London in the very capable hands of its managing director, a terrifyingly chic and competent New Yorker called Nancy Craig who at only twenty-nine seemed set to take on the entire advertising world – and anything else that happened to take her fancy into the bargain. There had been some interesting rumours about Julian Morell and Nancy Craig.

The last year had seen a considerable change in Julian. He was, Sarah Brownsmith supposed, struggling to find the right word, depressed. Not so much bad-tempered, although he frequently was that, not worried, just depressed. Even the considerable feat of re-acquiring the remaining forty per cent of his company had not cheered him up for long. And that wasn't like him. Indeed it wasn't like him to be anything but extremely cheerful. Difficult, quixotic, but not depressed.

At the end of the summer he had taken off with Camilla to his house on Eleuthera, and everyone had breathed a sigh of relief. But he returned sooner than expected, with a new business project (paper production) and without Camilla who did not reappear in London for another week.

Sarah reflected that his personal life at the moment must be the opposite of restful and happy . . . he was nearly sixty; he was unmarried; his brother, James had died a year earlier of a heart attack, which had clearly shaken Julian considerably, although they had not been close for years; his relationship with Camilla was volatile to put it mildly; and he had no real heir unless you counted that spoilt monster of a daughter.

Sarah could not stand Roz. She drifted in and out of her father's life whenever it suited her, cool, remote, demanding, and as far as Sarah could see, he tried endlessly to please her for extremely limited reward: he bought her everything she wanted (the latest offering had been a yacht which she kept moored on the waterfront near her father's hotel in Nice), allowed her the run of his houses and hotels all over the world, and would always cancel anything at all, however important, to have lunch or dinner with her when she deigned to visit him.

Sarah had just switched on the coffee machine that foggy morning, and she was wondering if she was brave enough to broach the subject of an extra week's leave at Christmas, when the phone rang.

'Julian Morell's office.'

'Miss Brownsmith. Good morning. How are you?'

The voice was pitched quite low for a woman; at once sexy and brisk. A voice men didn't know quite how to react to. It belonged to Roz, and Sarah's heart sank.

'I'm well, thank you, Miss Morell. And yourself?'

'Very well, thank you, Miss Brownsmith. Is my father there?'

Sarah felt Julian needed Roz on such a day like a dose of strychnine; nevertheless she was the only person in the world, apart from his mother and Camilla North, who she could not refuse to put through.

'He is, Miss Morell, but he's . . .'

'Tied up at the moment. Of course. What else? Is he free for lunch?'

'No, I'm afraid not.'

'Put me through to him, would you, Miss Brownsmith?'

Sarah did so. Two minutes later Julian pressed the intercom.

'Sarah, cancel my lunch with Jack Bottingley, would you. And book a table at the Meridiana. I'm meeting Roz there at one.'

Roz put down the phone. She was actually feeling a little nervous. It was one thing persuading her father to see her at the snap of her fingers, to give her whatever she desired as soon as she asked for it, but what she wanted from him today was something rather more considerable than a yacht, a horse, or a new wardrobe from Paris or New York. Moreover it meant going in for some considerable diplomacy on her part, some nibbling at least of humble pie, neither of which she had any talent for or practice in. Nevertheless it had to be done.

Roz had decided that the time had come to claim her birthright. She had wearied of pretending she didn't want it; of working, albeit hard, a trifle half-heartedly for other people, for Jamil Al-Shehra, for Marks and Spencer's, even for Camilla

North (who she had to admit had taught her a great deal). What she wanted to do now was work for her father, to serve her apprenticeship, and to start scaling the real heights. And she knew she would scale them fast.

In addition to her two years' work experience, as her father rather contemptuously described it, Roz had just spent a year at the Harvard Business School and it had been the happiest of her life and the most fascinating. Cambridge had seemed like prep school by comparison. Money, deals, politicking, power, it all fascinated her, made her heart beat faster, gave her a sexual thrill. That was what she wanted, great slices of it; she was prepared to work and sweat and suffer for it. She didn't want men falling at her feet or into her bed; she had sampled some of both, and it had left her for the most part bored and unimpressed. She wanted men where she decided to put them, preferably several seats beneath her on the board.

She knew, she felt in her bones that she would be able not just to deal with any business situation, but that she would win in it. When she looked at some of the hypothetical problems she had been set to crack at college, when she read the financial pages of the papers (which she devoured daily) it seemed to her she was almost clairvoyant; she could see not just to the end of a problem, a development, a takeover bid, but beyond it, considered not merely every angle that seemed relevant, but a dozen more that did not. She took not just facts and figures into her equations but people, situations, geography, history, even the seasons of the year and the time of day. She knew as surely as she knew her own name that she had a brilliant company brain; all she needed now was something to practise on. And she needed her father's help to get it. And she didn't relish it.

It was on occasions like this one that she stood back and saw very clearly exactly what her father was in real terms: a towering figure, one of the shrewdest, most ruthless men in the world, possessed of great power, and with a personal fortune that must come close to equalling Getty's; he had a brilliant and innovative business brain, a perfect sense of timing and almost flawless judgement. He was respected, revered, indeed often feared; and fear was the emotion Roz was experiencing now. She didn't actually think he would refuse her; that he would send her back to Marks and Spencer's, tell her to join the dole queue; but he was going to have an opportunity to extract his revenge for her awkwardness, for her rejection of him over the last few years, and she knew he was highly likely to take it.

Well, she had learnt a few skills which might help her, she thought, since leaving Cambridge, including a modicum at least of tact and the ability to project charm. Her truculence, although still very much a part of her, was well hidden, and she had learnt to smile, to listen, to look for the good in people and situations, rather than pouncing and pronouncing on the bad.

The trouble was, as she very well knew, her father would not be in the least deceived by any act she put on; he would translate any fiction she presented him with into fact, recognize her and what she was trying to do through any role she played; what was more he was quite capable of stringing her along, of pretending to believe the fiction, to be impressed by the role-playing and then suddenly, without warning, confront her with the truth of the situation as he saw it.

But she could see through him as well; her painful childhood had taught her that much. She knew when he was lying, when he was plotting, when he was feeling remorseful; she also, more usefully, knew how to hurt him, and when best to do it. It was a poor substitute for daughterly love, and she was well aware of the fact, but she had long ago learnt that was a luxury she could not afford. One day perhaps, when she had proved herself, when she was in a strong position, when her father was impressed by her and was less able to set her aside whenever it suited him, then perhaps she could trust herself to tell him how much she loved him, and how much she wanted him to love her. Meanwhile, she had to proceed with much caution and care.

She rifled through the rails of her wardrobe; selecting first a Margaret Howell suit and rejecting it (too severe), a Jean Muir dress and trying it on (too grown up) and settling finally on a Ralph Lauren skirt, shirt and sweater, all in tones of beige, (young enough to be appealing, expensive enough to look assured). Eliza had picked out the lot for her (she would never have had the vision herself), and it suited her very well. She pulled on some long brown boots, clipped back her long dark hair, sprayed herself with Chanel 19 and looked at herself for a long time. 'Just right,' she said aloud to the mirror, 'just right'; she looked well-bred stylish, with the faintest touch of college girl to make it more appealing. Her father would hopefully approve.

She put her diary, her credit cards, her wallet and her CV into a brown Hermes shoulder bag, slung her Burberry over her shoulders and went out to find a taxi.

Julian reached the chic whiteness of the Meridiana five minutes before her; ordered a bottle of Bollinger, greeted a few of the disparate people he knew there (Grace Coddington, fashion editor of *Vogue*, looking divinely severe in a Jean Muir dress, Terence Conran, charmingly jovial, a new cigar in one hand, glass of sancerre in the other, Paul Hamlyn), and watched his daughter swing in the door. He hadn't seen her for months; after Harvard she stayed with friends in New York, and had only been back in London for a week; she'd lost weight, grown her hair, and as she bent to kiss him, he noticed she had acquired a very expensive-looking necklace – thick gold inset with diamonds and emeralds, which he certainly hadn't bought her and her mother was unlikely to have given her – or that she would have bought herself. Interesting: who was she seeing with that sort of money?

'Roz,' he said. 'How nice! How are you? Let me take your coat. I've ordered champagne. I thought it was a celebration.'

Raphael, manager of the Meridiana, came bustling over to them. 'Miss Morell! How beautiful you look! How nice to have you back in London! Your father is a lucky man. What a charming luncheon companion, Mr Morell! Let me take Miss Morell's coat and what would you like to eat? The quails are beautiful and we have some very nice turbot, cooked in a wine sauce with truffles, and then there is some fresh salmon . . .' He launched into the restaurateurs' litany; Roz sat down, took the glass of champagne, ordered some parma ham and a plain grilled sole and looked at her father with genuine, if slight concern.

'You look tired, Daddy, have you been overworking?'

'I expect so. I enjoy it, you know. It makes a distraction from my social life.'

'Aren't you enjoying your social life?'

'Not much. How about you?'

'Not much either. How's Camilla?'

'Camilla is very well,' Julian said carefully, wondering how much she read the gossip columns. 'We had dinner with the father of a friend of yours the other night. Tom Robbinson. Weren't you at school with Sarah, or was it Cambridge? I know she was at your twenty-first.'

'School. Haven't seen her for ages. She was the despair of Cheltenham. She's getting married, isn't she?'

'Yes, after Christmas.

He sighed. The thought of weddings always depressed him. 'Nice necklace, Roz.'

'Yes,' said Roz, 'it was a present.'

Her tone closed the subject. Julian opened it again.

'From anyone I know?'

'No.'

'I see.'

'Someone I met at Harvard,' said Roz quickly, seeing her father was fast growing irritated by her lack of communicativeness. 'Someone called Michael Browning. He came down to give a lecture. He lives in New York. He's divorced. I just see him sometimes. Can I have some more champagne?'

'Of course,' said Julian. He looked at Roz thoughtfully. He knew Michael Browning well. He had made a fortune out of soft drinks in California, moved to New York and into supermarkets, and ran his business by instinct and the seat of his pants. Not the kind of man he'd really want sleeping with his daughter, which seemed likely if he was buying her that sort of present. But maybe it was a hopeful gesture on his part. At any rate clearly Roz wasn't going to give any more away just now. He changed the subject.

'How's Mummy?'

'Fine.' Roz sounded wary.

'And the charming Mr Al-Shehra?'

'Oh, charming as ever. He's a darling. So kind to me. He keeps a horse for me at the house they've bought in Berkshire, him and Mummy.'

'How nice of him,' said Julian shortly.

'I ride with him sometimes. In the park. He's absolutely superb.'

385

'I wondered,' said Julian, 'talking of riding, if you'd like to come down to Marriotts this weekend. I'm hunting on Saturday, if that appeals to you, and I'd like to show you some of my new acquisitions.'

'Will – will Camilla be there?'

'No.'

It was a very final word. Roz smiled at him. 'I'd love to. I haven't been to Marriotts for ages. I'm dying to see the new colt I read about in Dempster. What's he called?'

'First Million. I'm hoping great things of him.'

'Have you got anything I could ride on Saturday?'

'Of course.'

'Have you bought any cars lately?'

Julian smiled at her. Nothing made him happier than an interest in his collection.

'A very nice Ferrari. A Monza, 1954. Superb. And I've got a beautiful Delahaye in New York.'

'Could I drive the Ferrari?'

'Of course. Not to its capacity, unfortunately, in the Sussex lanes. It does one sixty.'

'Then I'll certainly come.'

'Good.'

Roz put down her fork. 'I've got something I want to talk to you about, Daddy.'

Julian looked at her, his eyes the familiar blank.

'And what is that, Rosamund?'

Things weren't going too well, Roz realized; he never called her Rosamund unless he was fairly displeased with her. She wished fervently she had been less awkward the last couple of times she had seen him.

'It's advice I really need, Daddy.' She had rehearsed this bit of her script carefully.

'About?'

'About a job.'

'A job? I see.'

He was looking at her with an odd rather shrewd amusement; Roz squirmed, but met his gaze steadily.

'Could you elucidate things a little more?'

'Well, you see, I've decided what I really want to get into is financial management.'

'Why does that appeal to you? Something like marketing is much more fun. You've made a start there. You should stay in that.'

'No, it's the finance side that really interests me. I love working out what makes companies successful and how to make them more so. And which companies would work well with others. Takeovers, mergers, all that sort of thing.'

'Does it?' Julian looked at her thoughtfully. 'Did you do much financial stuff at Harvard?'

'Not as much as I'd have liked. I'd gone in on the marketing side. By the time I fell in love with money it was a bit late. But never mind. That was only college. There's real life to come.'

'Indeed there is. So what do you want me to do?'

'Advise me.'

'Really! That will make a change.'

'Don't be silly. You know I always ask your advice about important things.'

'Perhaps. What particular advice do you want?'

'Well, I've been offered a job. It is marketing, but they've said I can move around. Really get to know the company.'

'Have you? By whom?'

'Unilever. That's what I need advice about. It's such a huge company. Michael – lots of people have said it might swallow me up. What do you think?'

'I don't think the job's good enough for you. You've got a good Cambridge degree, you've got some valuable experience, and you're an honours graduate from Harvard. You don't want to start working for some sweaty brand manager from East Anglia.'

'How do you know he'll be from East Anglia?'

'They always are.'

'Thats' – 'ridiculous' Roz had been about to say, but she managed to stop herself – 'really interesting.'

'What is?'

'That you don't think I should do it.'

'Why?'

'Because I don't think so either.'

'And what do you think you should do?'

Roz put down her knife and fork and looked him very straight in the eyes. 'Work for you.'

He hadn't expected that, and he was impressed by it. It took a kind of courage for her to lay herself so totally open. He had it in his power to reject her absolutely and she knew it, and knew moreover, that it was quite likely. Clearly she had even more guts than he'd thought. He put them to the test.

'I don't think it's possible.'

'Why not? Is it because I've –'

'Rejected me?'

He looked at her again with amused eyes.

'Yes. Oh, Daddy, I was just being silly. Young and silly. I'm sorry if it hurt you. It must have seemed very ridiculous. Ungrateful. But you must have known I didn't mean it.'

'You seemed to at the time. And you weren't all that young at the time. The last little conversation I remember was only about six months ago. How old are you now?'

'Twenty-three.'

'Well anyway –' There was a long pause. Roz braced herself to look at him. He was smiling. 'That's not the reason.'

'What do you mean?'

'I mean the reason I can't offer you a job is that we don't take Harvard people. Company policy.'

Roz went limp with relief.

'Daddy, that is just ridiculous. You're joking.'

'Not at all. I'm perfectly serious. I warned you before you went there. Only you were busy telling me it didn't matter.' He smiled at her again.

'Well it's mad.'

'Why?'

'Well, because Harvard people are the best. Brilliantly trained.'

'That's only your opinion.'

'No, it's not. It's a very valid, widely held opinion.'

'By whom? Other Harvard people? Your friends? Michael Browning?'

'No, people I've talked to. Companies I've applied to. They all want Harvard people. They say their power to analyse and apply theory to practice is outstanding. You're losing some of the best business brains in the country with a policy like that. Whose cockeyed prejudice is it?'

'Mine.'

'You should change it.'

'Convince me.'

'How?'

'From inside the company.'

'All right, I will.'

She had become so absorbed in the argument that she hadn't noticed where he was leading her. She stopped abruptly, looked at him furiously for a moment and noticed that his eyes were looking more benign than she had seen them for a very long time.

'Oh God,' she said, 'I wish you'd stop playing games with me.'

'I never stop that, Roz. As you should know. And besides, I really don't much like Harvard people. Over-analytical. But of course you're right, and one shouldn't allow one's prejudices to stand between one's company and talent. So let's see what yours can do.'

'You'll take me on then?'

'Yes I will. Of course. To nobody's great surprise, I'm sure. You'll have to work extremely hard. I'm not being accused of nepotism.'

'I will. I really will.'

'What segment of the company most appeals to you?'

'The stores.'

'No.'

'Why not?'

'Too specialized, and you won't learn enough.'

'I don't agree.'

'If you're going to work for me, Roz, you'll have to learn to accept what I say.'

'All right. For a bit. Cosmetics then, I suppose.'

'Now that is wise. When we get back to the office I'll phone Iris Bentinck and see what's going. She's the overall marketing director of Juliana.'

And occasional mistress of the Chairman, thought Roz. She wondered if he had any idea how much she knew about him.

'It might mean going to Paris or New York.'

'That's fine. I don't mind. Specially New York.'

'Really?'

Roz realized she had made a tactical error.

'Only because cosmetics are so much more buzzy in New York. I'd really much rather be in London.'

She ended up where she least wanted to be, and where Julian wanted her most. Paris. So far the score was fairly even.

Letitia Morell had three visitors that afternoon. There was nothing she liked better than entertaining, and at the age of eighty-one she still gave excellent dinner parties. She was wickedly amusing, she broke all the rules, thinking nothing of sitting a beautiful nineteen-year-old next to an elderly relic of the British Raj fifty years her senior, or a confirmed homosexual to a highly desirable (and desirous) divorcee and watching them all having the evening of their lives. People would go to some lengths to get a dinner invitation from Letitia Morell; drop hints, ask her to dinner repeatedly themselves, phone her casually on some weak pretext, but it was none of it any good. To qualify you had to be good-looking and amusing and preferably both. You could be poor, socially modest in exceptional cases, not always entirely well mannered. But you could not be dull.

She also found herself with one of the busiest luncheon engagement books in London. She was always so full of gossip herself, and so eager and amused to hear it; most days her pale blue Rolls-Royce with her patient chauffeur inside it was to be seen, parked long after three outside the Ritz, or the Caprice, or her latest find, Langan's Brasserie in Stratton Street, whose drunken and frequently disagreeable owner was so charmed by her that she claimed the distinction not only of a permanent table available to her, but of never having been insulted by him.

She still dressed beautifully; she found shopping a little tiring, but many of the designers were charmed and delighted to visit her in First Street with toiles and drawings and take her orders; and she was still very slim and trim, her latest passion (introduced to her by the Vicomtesse du Chene), being yoga. It was not at all unusual to arrive and find her dressed in leotard and tights, sitting in the lotus position in her drawing room.

It was thus that her first visitor, the Vicomtesse herself, found her that November afternoon.

'Darling! How lovely. Nancy, make us some tea will you? China, Eliza? And I think I'll go and change, I get cold in this ridiculous outfit after a bit.'

'Of course.' Eliza's smile was a trifle too bright. Letitia thought she had probably been crying.

'What is it, darling,' she said, returning in a navy cashmere two piece and beige calf-length boots, looking just about fifty-five years old. 'You're upset.'

'No,' said Eliza brightly. 'No, not at all. I'm getting married.'

'My darling! How marvellous. But how on earth have you managed that? I thought Arabian marriages were sacred. Should we be drinking champagne rather than tea?'

'No. Not yet. Well, it might help. Yes please. Yes, they are sacred. I'm not marrying Jamil.'

'Oh, my goodness. What an entertaining child you are. Nancy, will you please bring us a bottle of Bollinger from the fridge and two glasses. Have some yourself if you want it. Now then.' She raised her glass to Eliza. 'Who is it and why? And why have you been crying?'

'It's Peveril Garrylaig.'

'Good heavens. A proper title in the family at last. And a good one too. A countess. Oh, my grandmother would have been relieved.'

'Do you know him?'

'Well of course I do. I think he's charming,' said Letitia firmly, wondering what (apart from a title) the bluff, born-middle-aged, widowed Earl of Garrylaig could possibly offer Eliza that Jamil Al-Shehra could not.

'Well, then, you know what a charmer he is. I adore him. And he adores me. Of course it'll be a big change, living in Scotland, but I always did have a sneaking liking for the country, and the castle is just beautiful, Letitia, quite the most ravishing place, you will come and stay, won't you?'

'Darling, of course I will. All the time. Now then.' She looked sharply at Eliza. 'What does Mr Al-Shehra have to say about all this?'

'Oh, he's quite happy about it,' said Eliza briskly. 'Clearly we couldn't go on for ever how we were, and well – oh, Letitia, I can't bear it, I simply can't bear it, please please tell me I'm doing the right thing.'

Tears were streaming down her face; her green eyes searched Letitia's blue ones wildly, frantically, looking for relief from her pain and her grief.

'Tell me more, darling. When you're ready. I can't tell you anything until I know what it's all about.'

Eliza told her. She told her that there was no real future for her with Al-Shehra; that the most passionate love affair could not last for ever; that she was forty-three years old, and most assuredly not getting any younger; that she was afraid of being alone and lonely; that she wanted to be safe, with a status of her own again; that she was truly truly fond of Peveril or she wouldn't be doing it; and that she was so unhappy that she thought her heart was not just broken, but exploded into a million tiny fragments.

She did not tell her that Al-Shehra had wept in her arms the night before, that he had made love to her that morning so sadly, so tenderly, so exquisitely that she still felt faint remembering the sensations, and that it had taken every fragment of her courage not to change her mind.

'But you do see, Letitia, don't you, it was all right at first, the mistress of a wildly rich Arab potentate, or tycoon or whatever he is, all right when you're quite young, but think of being fifty, sixty, and still in that position, always terrified of new young women coming along, no status, no standing. I couldn't face it, Letitia, I just couldn't. I need to be married. I have to do this.'

'And when did the affair with Peveril begin?'

'Oh,' said Eliza with the shimmer of a smile. 'It isn't an affair, Letitia. Peveril is a gentleman. We shall go to bed on our wedding night and not before.'

'How charming. How refreshing. Well, all right, when did you meet him?'

'Last month. At Longchamps. Jamil wanted to take me to the Arc de Triomphe, and then he got gambling and I got cross and Peveril was there, with his sisters, one of them knew Julian, he'd been at her coming-out dance, and well – we started talking and he asked me if he could take me out to lunch one day in London, and it all went on from there.'

'It's not very long,' said Letitia, frowning.

'No, I know, and everyone's going to say that, but I have to get it settled quickly, and Peveril wants to, he's lonely and why should we wait?'

'To make sure you're doing the right thing?'

'No, I don't want to do that. Because I might not be. But if

I'm not I'll make it work just the same. Just you watch me. He's a good man, and a kind one, and I won't let him down.'

'No, darling, don't.'

It was the only rebuke or criticism Letitia uttered; Eliza took it with good grace.

'I deserved that. I deserve more. So please, Letitia, come on, tell me it's a good idea.'

Letitia took a deep breath.

'It is a good idea. I truly think so. Of course it has its dangers and they seem quite formidable, but you're clearly aware of them. I would be with you all the way. I have often wondered myself what might happen to you with Al-Shehra.'

Eliza kissed her. 'Thank you. You don't know what courage that gives me.'

Letitia looked at the lovely face in the darkening room, the heavy eyes, the drooping mouth. 'You will get over Jamil, you know,' she said. 'It will pass. It will take a long time, but it will pass. For weeks, months, you will think you can't take another day of the pain, and then one day, quite suddenly you will feel just a little better. Just a tiny bit lighthearted. It may not last, but it will come back, that feeling. More and more frequently. And in a year you will be sad, but not unhappy any longer. Don't rush the wedding though, Eliza. Wait a few months. You'll be asking too much of yourself. And it won't be fair to Peveril. Wait till the spring. He'll understand. There's a lot to do.'

'You've been through this, haven't you?' said Eliza. 'You've never told me, nobody has, but I can tell. You couldn't understand otherwise.'

'Yes,' said Letitia. 'I have. And it was a very, very long time ago. And I can still remember the pain. But all these years later, I do know that I did the right thing.'

Julian arrived at First Street half an hour later, beaming radiantly.

'Julian,' said Letitia. 'How nice. I've been thinking about you. Eliza's only just left.'

'How is Eliza?'

'Very well. Very happy.'

'Good. Well, I can't stop, but I have a little present for you,

Camilla brought it over from California, she's been vacationing there. Look, it's a solar-powered calculator.'

'Oh, how wonderful,' cried Letitia, delighted as a child. 'I've read about these. Will it work here? We don't have as much solar power as the Californians.'

'Of course it will, you idiot. It's light that does it. Look.'

'Marvellous! Thank you, darling. How is Camilla?'

'She's fine. Just passing through.'

'I see.'

'Don't look like that, Mother. Anyway, I have some nice news I wanted to share with you.'

'I thought you were looking rather more cheerful than you have lately. What is it?'

'I had lunch with Roz today.'

'Did you? How is the dear, difficult child?'

'Oh, looking wonderful. Very good. And greatly benefited from her year at Harvard.' A shadow passed over his face. 'Apart from getting in with a thoroughly undesirable fellow.'

'How much in?'

'All the way, I would say, from the look of her, and the necklace hanging round her neck.'

'Well Julian, she is twenty-three. Eliza was married and divorced at that age.'

'I know. But he's a bit of a rough diamond. American. Brooklyn. Very rich. Divorced. Very unsuitable. Anyway, there's nothing I can do about that and that's not the nice news. She's going to come and work for the company. She's got over that independence nonsense at last.'

'Now that is good news. I agree. Did she ask?'

'Yes, and very nicely. Quite humbly in fact. I honestly think she's grown up a bit.'

'Good. Where are you going to put her?'

'In Paris. Working on the cosmetics. With Annick Valery. I had a word with Iris Bentinck in New York this afternoon and she was perfectly agreeable.'

'Well she would be,' said Letitia briskly.

'What do you mean by that?'

'I mean she's your employee and your mistress, so she's unlikely to refuse to take on your daughter.'

'Mother, that's grossly unfair. I admit that in the past we had a liaison, but it was very short-lived. And it was ages ago.'

'And it's quite over?'

He met her eyes in amused surprise. 'Of course.'

'I see. Well anyway, what has Paris got to do with Iris? She's in New York.'

'Well, she's in charge of Juliana worldwide. As a courtesy I had to consult her.'

'I see. Well anyway, I'm delighted about Roz. Give her my love.'

'She's coming down to Marriotts for the weekend. Would you like to join us? Several people are coming, including Nancy Craig. She's very knowledgeable about horses.'

'No, I don't think so, thank you,' said Letitia. 'I think I may have things to do in London. Will Camilla be there? I don't suppose Roz will be very pleased if she is.'

'No, she won't,' he said shortly.

'Oh. I thought you said she was over here.'

'She is. But she's not spending the weekend with me.'

'Ah. Julian, just exactly what is going on with Camilla?'

'Nothing,' he said lightly, 'no more or less than there ever was. We have a perfect arrangement. It suits us very well. Well, as a matter of fact, we are changing things a little. Camilla is buying her own house. In Knightsbridge.'

'Really? Why?'

'Oh, it's entirely her idea,' he said easily. 'Like most things she does. One of her feminist theories. She says she doesn't enjoy the role of surrogate wife and she wishes to be geographically independent from me. She says she wants to be her own woman; one of her less attractive American expressions.'

'I see.'

He looked at her. 'Mother, don't look at me like that. Camilla is not some downtrodden housewife, you know. The move was her idea. I just told you. Things suit us very well.'

'They suit you very well,' said Letitia. 'Sometimes I wonder about Camilla.'

'Well,' he said, getting up, 'I must go. I'm going out to dinner.'

'Who with?'

'Oh,' he said, 'no one you'd know. Bye, Mother. Enjoy your calculator.'

'Goodbye, Julian.'

She looked after his tall figure with something close to dislike. She had never expected to feel sorry for Camilla, but just occasionally these days she did.

The last person to arrive was Roz. 'Well,' said Letitia, 'this completes the family party. First your mother then your father. How are you, darling?'

'Very well, thank you. I've had the most marvellous time in New York.'

'I know. Your father's been worrying about it.'

'Has he? What did he tell you?'

'Oh, nothing much. That you have a very unsuitable boyfriend.'

'Oh, he's so possessive. Michael isn't my boyfriend anyway. Just a friend.'

Letitia looked at the necklace that had so worried Julian and changed the subject.

'I gather that Camilla will be round a bit less.'

'Really?' Roz's face brightened. 'What's happened?'

'She's moving out of Hanover Terrace.'

'She's not! That's really good news. Oh, it's so exactly like Daddy not to tell me. I had lunch with him only today. How do you know?'

'Your father told me.'

'But why?'

'Oh, darling, I don't know. The official reason is that she wants to be her own woman. I think that was the phrase. Poor Camilla.'

'I never thought to hear you say poor Camilla. I suppose he's got some new bird.'

'I daresay. And I do feel sorry for her just at the moment. She's been very loyal to him, after all.'

'Granny Letitia, lots of people have been loyal to him. He's just not loyal back.'

Letitia sighed. 'You see your father very clearly, don't you, darling?'

'Yes, well, I've had ample opportunity to study him over the years. Not as much as most daughters, of course, but still enough. Anyway, I'm going to start working for him now.'

'I know. He told me.'

'And?'

'Well, I'm so pleased, darling. And so is he. Thrilled. He loves you very much, Roz. I wish you'd believe that. And he's always wanted this. I hear you're going to be in Paris.'

'Yes. I'd rather New York, of course.'

'No doubt,' said Letitia, with a gleam in her eye, 'that's why you're going to Paris.'

'Yes.'

Letitia looked at Roz and smiled. 'Well anyway, I do think you'll enjoy it and have a marvellous time. Do you want to have supper with me, darling?'

'No, really, I can't. I'm going round to see Susan. Another time perhaps, before I go.'

'Yes. You're very fond of Susan, aren't you?'

'Yes. Very, very fond. She's been really good to me. Ever since I can remember. Even when I was a really awful teenager, I always felt she was on my side. And she never dishes out all that nauseating horse manure about how much my parents adore me, and how lucky I am. She sees everything terribly straight. She was in New York last month,' she said suddenly, 'and met Michael. She really liked him.'

'Good,' said Letitia, 'if she liked him, he's probably nice. I wish Susan could get married,' she added with a sigh. 'She deserves some happiness.'

'Oh, I don't think she's unhappy. Anyway, she may be going to marry Richard Brookes. Oh, God, I shouldn't have told you. Now Granny, you're not to gossip about that. You're not to.'

'I wouldn't dream of it,' said Letitia, her purply-blue eyes very wide. 'But I am delighted.'

'So am I. Just thank goodness she didn't marry Daddy, that's all. Did you know he asked her?'

'Yes,' said Letitia, 'yes, she told me. Good gracious, you are close to her, aren't you?'

'Yes, I am.'

'And why do you think that would have been such a bad idea?'

'Well,' said Roz, 'don't you?'

'Yes,' said Letitia, 'yes, I'm very much afraid I do.'

The Connection Seven

Los Angeles, 1980

Miles had graduated from Berkeley, to his own surprise as
much as everyone else's, summa cum laude in Mathematics.

He walked across the college lawns, towards Hugo and Mrs
Kelly who had attended his graduation along with Father
Kennedy (an ill-assorted trio, he thought, but what the hell),
smiling happily. He looked superb; a beautiful, successful,
golden boy. He had had four glorious years; it showed.

'Hi.'

'Hello, Miles. Well done.'

'Thanks, Hugo.'

Mrs Kelly's eyes were full of tears. She was cross about
them, and sniffed fiercely. 'Congratulations, Miles. I wish your
ma was here.'

'So do I.' But he didn't look sad. He didn't feel sad. Not
really. It was too long ago. It was the future that mattered now.

Miles looked towards it, assured, successful, easy, and felt
deeply pleased with himself.

Later that night, when they were home and Father Kennedy
had gone back to the refuge, the three of them sat in the house
in Latego Canyon and watched the sunset.

'What next then, Miles?' said Hugo.

'Well, you tell me,' said Miles cheerfully.

'What do you mean?'

'Well, I kind of thought you would be helping.'

'In what way?'

'Getting me a job.'

'Oh, no, Miles, you've misunderstood me, I'm afraid. I've no
intention of finding you a job.'

'God, Hugo, why not? You're a rich man. You have a
company. Can't it find a space for me?'

'No. It can't.'

Miles was genuinely astounded; he looked physically
winded, betrayed.

'But why not?'

'Because I simply don't believe in that sort of thing.'

Miles shook his head, smiling.

'I'm just not hearing all this.'

'What do you mean?'

'I mean, all these years, I've been slaving away –'

'At my expense.'

'OK, but you offered. Slaving away, thinking it was all with a clear end in view. That you'd help me get a real good job.'

'I will help you, Miles. But I'm not giving you one.'

Miles stood up. He looked at Hugo with deep contempt.

'I just can't believe anyone can be so mean.'

'Miles!' said Mrs Kelly. 'How dare you. After all that Mr Dashwood has done.'

'What's he done?' said Miles. 'Signed a few cheques. Is he going to put himself on the line, present me to his company, his fancy friends and associates? He is not. I'm on my own now, Hugo, is that it?'

'Possibly. With a damn good college education behind you. I don't call that alone.'

'You've built me up, given me fancy ideas and a smart education, encouraged me to think I was worth something, taken me away from my friends, and now you're dropping me just back where I belonged. Well thanks a lot.'

'This really is the most extraordinary way to look at things, Miles.'

'Is it? I'd have thought it was your way that was extraordinary. To have the power to help and refuse it.'

'I'm prepared to do what I can. To speak to some associates, perhaps. To give you good references.'

'Oh, spare me. Don't bother. I don't want any lousy job anyway. I never did. It was all your idea. I'm going to see Joanna.'

'Perhaps she'll put some sense into your head,' said Hugo. He was white and shaken.

'Perhaps she will. But not the way you mean. Good night, Hugo.'

'I'm real sorry, Mr Dashwood' said Mrs Kelly. 'I would never have believed it.'

'No,' said Hugo, 'neither would I. Well, maybe Joanna will help. She's a very sensible young woman.'

Joanna didn't help. She couldn't help. Nobody could. Miles had invested four years of very hard work in what he thought was an easy option of a future, and now he felt cheated of it. And he had no intention of working any more.

He took to the beach. He joined the other surf bums who made it their life; he spent every day waiting for the wave. Or riding it. Occasionally earning a little money. He would pump gas. Deliver the odd grocery order. Serve in Alice's; maybe push a little grass. He smoked a lot of grass. Nothing more harmful than that; they all did. It was a strong brotherhood they had, the surfers. They had total loyalty to each other; none at all for the geeks, the incompetent newcomers who got in the way. Their only concern was waiting for the bitchin', the real quality surf, and enjoying it.

Joanna tried. She really tried. She argued, she pleaded, she threatened. She kept asking him why a person with a fine degree, a good brain, should just drop out, just like that. Let his folks down.

'I don't have any folks. Not really. And the ones who want to be, let me down.'

'Miles, that's ridiculous. Mr Dashwood did so much for you.'

'Nothing difficult. He won't help when it's really needed.'

She looked at him scornfully. 'You're really pathetic.'

'You have a right to your opinion.'

Joanna was working in the costume studio at Parmount. She loved it. She was happy, successful. She wanted Miles to be successful too. She hated what he had become. But she still loved him. She couldn't quite walk out on him. Besides, she felt, in a strange way he still needed her. He didn't.

Mrs Kelly tried too. 'Miles, for God's sake. Is this what I gave up my home and my friends for? So you could spend your life bumming about on that surf? Pull yourself together. Your mother would be ashamed.'

'I don't think so. I think she'd understand.'

Mrs Kelly thought of going back home to Ohio. She couldn't bear to see Miles throwing his life away. But like Joanna, she felt that deep down he needed her.

Hugo came from time to time. All that ever happened was

that he and Miles had terrible rows. Once Mrs Kelly had said couldn't he maybe do what Miles wanted, give him a job. Hugo said he couldn't. He really couldn't. Especially not now. Not after all Miles had said. But he would stay in touch. And he begged Mrs Kelly not to give up. He felt Miles needed her. Needed them all.

But Miles didn't need anybody. All he needed in the world was the surf and the sun, and his board, and the sweet dizzy feeling that was like sex, of elation and release when he caught a good wave and rode it in to the shore.

And nobody was going to take it away from him.

Chapter Eleven

London, Paris and New York, 1980–82

Annick Valery, who had expected to dislike Roz heartily, and to find working with her an unpleasant experience, found very little in her work to criticize and, even more to her own surprise, liked her very much.

The Paris office of Juliana was the least active, from a marketing point of view; most of the creative work on the cosmetics was done in London, with a considerable input from New York.

Roz found herself working as a junior brand manager on the colour ranges (as opposed to skin care and perfume), which meant to a large degree simply watching sales figures, overseeing the translation on packaging, checking distribution, watching and adjusting price levels, and rubber stamping media schedules. It was not inspiring, it allowed little if any scope for creative flair and it involved an enormous amount of tedious routine work. She could have sulked; she could have traded on her position and slacked; she could have thrown her weight around. She did none of those things; she worked very hard and efficiently, made modest suggestions about prices and packaging, always had her paper work up to date and made a point of spending at least one day a week behind the counter in one or other of Juliana's outlets.

Annick reported very favourably on her to Julian after the first six months, and passed on a couple of suggestions Roz had made which were clearly based on extremely sound judgement.

'She is a clever girl. She does not mind what she does. And she works very hard. She suggested to me that we price up all the lipsticks and make the eye shadows a slightly more budget line. And sell them together. Just as a promotion. I think it will work.'

'Why?' said Julian. 'Sounds a bit cockeyed to me.'

'Because she says women use up their lipsticks and want more. The eye shadow is never finished. So they will spend more replacing a lipstick they like and will buy more eye shadows, simply to get the new colours.'

'I don't follow.'

'But it is so simple,' said Annick, surprised at his denseness. 'If a woman likes a lipstick, it is because of not just the colour, but the texture, the perfume, even. So she will pay much more for it. It is a personal thing. Eye shadow is different. It is just the fashion, the colours. If you sell the two as a pair, you will persuade her to buy an eye shadow she is not perhaps ready for, especially if it is cheaper. And she will also pay more for the lipstick, because it comes as part of a package.'

'Yes, I see,' said Julian. 'It might work. Test market it in the next promotion.'

It did work. Sales increased by about ten per cent in all the stores offering the new see-saw prices, as Roz had privately named them.

'It's very good,' said Annick happily, to Roz, over the sales figures at the end of the first two months. 'You are a clever girl. Your father will be pleased with you, I think.'

'I hope so,' said Roz. 'He's the boss. Come on, Annick, I'll buy you lunch.'

Roz was enjoying Paris. She had a tiny flat just off the Tuileries; and with Annick's help she was learning to dress well. She had discovered the joy of French clothes, and the way French women, whether rich or poor, could put together and accessorize an outfit so that the end result was not just stylish, but witty as well, how the addition of the right, sharply noticeable hat, belt, tights or even earrings could make an unremarkable dress or suit look original and distinctive, how one simple dress could appear romantic, sharply chic or highly sophisticated, according to the wearer's hairstyle, make-up, accessories and even perfume; how colour should work in an outfit, turning up imaginatively and unexpectedly in shoes, a scarf, a brooch, so that no overall tone was ever quite left to dominate an outfit; how individual style was crucial, and the emphasis of natural assets rather than rigid enslavement to the length, shape, and mood of the season; all this and much more Roz learnt, and spent all of her modest salary and much of her immodest income (which came from the trust set up long ago by Julian and on which she had been drawing since her twenty-first birthday) at such pleasure palaces as the Pierre Cardin boutiques (often visiting with Annick the treasure trove of his markdown emporium on the Boulevard Sebastopol, where for strictly cash you could acquire the most stunning bargains), Dorothee Bis, Cacherel, and occasionally, when she was especially happy or excited, at Chanel, to gorge her taste buds on shirts, T-shirts, earrings, bags.

She began to look very chic; eighties fashion in any case became her well: the trouser suit which suited her rangy walk, the short skirts which showed off her superb legs, the strong, bold colours, the dashingly patterned knitwear which flattered her dark colouring, and the infiltration of the fitness craze into the fashion industry, via the 'sweats collection' of Norma Kamali, with her ra-ra skirts, leggings and sweatshirting tops with huge shoulder pads all perfectly suited Roz's dynamic, athletic style.

She had her dark hair cropped short, which emphasized her large green eyes, her big mouth, making no concessions to prettiness but everything to drama; she learnt to make up superbly, to wear strong colours on her lips and dramatic shapes on her eyes; she had her father's natural physical grace, she moved, sat, stood well, and she dieted and exercised ruthlessly, running in the Paris streets early every morning, working out in the Juliana salon most evenings, pushing herself harder and harder, until there was not an ounce of spare fat to be seen on her lean long body. She looked sleek, elegant, expensive. And the look pleased her.

Then she managed to enjoy her work, dull as it was; she felt she was learning things that really mattered; and she also had a very close and good friend. She liked Annick more than she had ever liked any other female, apart from Susan; she was very young, only two years older than Roz herself, fiercely ambitious and hard working (both qualities Roz recognized and respected), but work was very far from everything to her; she was amusing, she was irreverent, she was warm and supportive, and perhaps most importantly, she put no value whatsoever on Roz's background or position, she made it perfectly plain that she liked her for what she was, no more no less, and never even referred to her father, or why Roz just conceivably might be working with her.

And then there was Michael Browning.

Michael Browning was in love with her. Seriously in love with her. Roz could tell this quite clearly and the novelty of being loved wholeheartedly made her very happy indeed. It improved her temper, shrank the chip on her shoulder to manageable limits, increased her self-confidence, even in her appearance, and enabled her to regard the rest of the world with a little more tolerance.

'You're a bitch, Rosamund,' he had said to her frequently, from the very beginning of their relationship. 'A hard, bad-tempered bitch. And it turns me on. Don't change. I adore you.'

Being adored by Michael was a dizzy experience. He was thirty-five years old, a rough, tough Brooklyn diamond. His father had run an all-night deli, and Michael had worked in it from the age of fourteen. When sixteen he had observed the ever soaring sales of soft drinks, and wondered if there mightn't be room for a new one. He talked to a contact with a factory about it, and they came up with Fizzin' Flavours, a series of new imaginative mixtures in drinks: orange with lemon, black-currant with apple, pineapple with grapefruit. Mr Browning Senior shook his head over them, put them on a back shelf and they stayed there. Undeterred, Michael took six crates with him on vacation to California, and set up a stall near the boardwalk in Venice. They sold in a day, which he had known they would; next day people came back for more, which he hadn't been so confident about, and were disappointed at having to settle for 7-Up and Pepsi.

Michael flew home again, and went to see the bank; the manager lent him five hundred dollars against his father's surety. It wasn't much, but it filled a lot more crates; he shipped them down to Venice and sold them for more than half as much again as he had last time.

Then he went looking for another small soft drinks factory.

In five years Michael Browning was a millionaire with a chain of supermarkets, and married to a nice Jewish girl from Brooklyn called Anita, whom he had impregnated on their second meeting in his newly acquired penthouse just off Madison.

Both families were very happy, and given the size of the penthouse and Michael Browning's fortune, Anita's parents were easily able to ignore the fact that she looked just a little plump on her wedding day and that Michael Browning the Third was born a couple of months early.

Five years later Michael was a multi millionaire, heavily involved in oil, as well as food chains, and married to another rather less nice gentile girl from Washington, whom he had seduced on their second meeting in the Waldorf Astoria where he was chairing a conference.

Anita Browning took one look at the ravishing, ice-cool blonde on her husband's arm in the Cholly Knickerbocker column next day and knew when she was beaten. She took him to the cleaners for two million dollars and refused him access to Little Michael and Baby Sharon except at Thanksgiving, Christmas time, and an occasional weekend at her own specification if she particularly wanted to go off on her own. Michael minded this very much, but there was precious little he could do about it.

Carol Walsh left Michael Browning in 1975, wooed away from him by some older, more socially acceptable money; Michael was left with a profound mistrust of marriage, and a strong need for the company of women, the more beautiful the better. He did not have too much trouble finding them.

He was not very tall, just a little over five foot ten, and neither was he conventionally good-looking. But just looking at him, as Carol Walsh had remarked to her best friend the day after the seduction, made you think about sex. Michael Browning exuded sex, of a strangely emotional kind. He made women think not merely about their physical needs but their emotional ones; he made them aware not only of their bodies but their minds. As a result, he was extraordinarily successful, not only in bed, but in persuading women they would like to join him there at the earliest possible opportunity.

He was dark haired, with a slightly floppy preppy hair cut, 'Designed to bring out the mother of the bastard in us all,' Anita had been heard to pronounce in tones of absolute contempt a great deal more than once; he had brown eyes which looked as if they had seen and profited by every possible variety of carnal knowledge; a nose that only just betrayed his Jewish origins; and a slightly lugubrious expression which relaxed into good humour rather slowly, a little reluctantly even. This expression, an entirely natural asset, was neverthe-less of great value to Michael Browning in his relationships with women; they felt he must be sad, that he had some problem, some sorrow, and they went to some trouble to ascertain what it might be and whether they could help him with it. By the time they had discovered there was no problem, he could, should he so wish, persuade them to do almost anything.

And then there was his voice. Michael Browning's voice was unique. 'It sounds,' Roz had said to Annick, uncharacteristic-ally poetic in her attempt to describe it, 'like a voice that started out perfectly ordinary, and then had a punch-up with a dozen men and then got soothed again with honey and hot lemon, with a slug of bourbon thrown in for good measure.'

'Mon dieu,' said Annick. 'And what does it say, this voice?'

'Oh,' said Roz vaguely. 'Not an awful lot really.'

This was quite true. Michael Browning was not a raconteur, not a dazzler at dinner tables; he spoke with that particular form of Brooklyn succinctness which is so charming when a novelty and so wonderfully reassuring to those who have grown up around it. If he was asked a question, he would answer very fully, he was not a man for monosyllables, and he could be thoughtful and amusing in conversation. But women in love with him waited in vain to be told that they were beautiful, or charming, or all that he had ever wanted. He told them instead the simple truth: that they were a great piece of ass, that they were terrific company, that he wanted to go to bed with them as soon as possible, that this or that dress looked good on them. All in that gravelly, silken voice, while at the same time looking at them mournfully and interestedly with those dark brown eyes: 'As if he's never met anyone quite like you before,' Roz said on another occasion.

He did not dress particularly well; Roz joined a long line of women who tried to reform his wardrobe, with a total lack of success. He was quite simply uninterested; he bought his clothes in all the proper places – his shirts and ties came from Brooks Brothers, he had his suits tailored at J. Press, his shoes from Paul Stuart, and he acquired all the perpetually crumpled Burberrys, which he lost relentlessly, in London at Harrods. But he never looked stylish, and he always looked as if he had borrowed someone else's clothes, which didn't quite suit him, but rather surprisingly managed to fit him fairly well.

He lived in a penthouse duplex on Fifth Avenue, right on the park, one block up from the Pierre; it was much too big for him, but it was useful when Little Michael and Baby Sharon, and the ferocious English nanny who Anita insisted should accompany them, came to stay for the weekend. The duplex was a shrine to new money; it had marble flooring throughout, a pond and a waterfall in the lobby, a living area with a sunken floor and so many mirrored walls you hadn't the least idea where you really were, a master bedroom with not only a Jacuzzi, a sauna and a sunbed, but a small swimming pool adjacent as well, a large number of very expensive paintings by fashionable New York artists on every wall, a fully equipped gymnasium, a music room complete with a computer-drive piano and a computerized mixing deck so that Michael could indulge in his hobby of composing modern variations on the works of Bach, Mozart and even Wagner when he was feeling particularly creative, a playroom for Little Michael and Baby Sharon which made the toy department of Bloomingdale's look rather poorly stocked, and a roof garden bearing trees and shrubs so big they had to be hoisted by crane from Fifth Avenue fifty floors up the face of the building.

Perhaps the most surprising thing about Michael Browning was that despite his considerable wealth, his success, and the constant parade of women in and out of his life, he remained a comparatively nice unspoilt man. He had, of course, forgotten some of life's minor hazards; he did not have to worry about letters from his bank manager, nor do his own cleaning; he could go on vacation when he wished either alone or in the company of any number of beautiful women; he could acquire for himself anything at all that he wished for (a great deal, one of his greatest faults being an insatiable greed) and he could rid himself of anything he had ceased to like (be it a set of Louis Quinze chairs, a jet-propelled surf board from Hammacher Schlammer or a complete gold-plated dinner service, to name the three most recent) without giving a thought to how much money he might be losing in the process; but the fact remained, that despite a rather strong streak of self-interest, and a complete inability to deny himself what or whoever he wanted, he was kind, and honest.

He had an extraordinary and genuine interest in everybody; he could become as deeply engrossed in conversation with the teller at the bank about his vacation or the cleaning lady in his office about her grandchildren as he could in his own multi-million-pound deals. It was not in the least unknown for a new secretary to go in for dictation and spend the next thirty-five minutes showing him photographs of her parents' silver wedding, encouraged to describe painstakingly exactly what the cake had been like, and the precise age and state of health of her father's great aunt, who had somehow managed to take up a prominent position in nearly every shot. He did not do this sort of thing to charm people, as a means to an end; he simply had a great capacity for wanting to know about people, for finding out what they were really like, and very much enjoying himself in the process.

Which was precisely why he had fallen in love with Roz.

Roz had been responsible for his invitation to Harvard; she had suggested to one of her tutors that he would be an interesting person as a guest lecturer (having heard her father and Freddy Branksome both mention him) and had consequently also been assigned the task of meeting him in the shabby splendour of

Boston station, escorting him back to the college, and attending the luncheon (along with several other carefully selected students) in his honour. She had dressed for the occasion with great care; she was wearing a white gaberdine jacket and jodhpurs from Montana, with very pale beige flat-heeled suede boots; her hair was tied back on her neck with a silk scarf, she carried a large, beige canvas bag from Ralph Lauren. She looked expensive, classy, stylish. Michael Browning's first words made her feel less so. 'You wouldn't, I suppose –' he said, 'be the chauffeur from Harvard?' He had got off the train and stood looking around him in his rather hopeless way; at first she couldn't believe anyone so rumpled looking, so unimpressive, could possibly be the undisputed king of the cut-price foodmarket, self-made and self-hyped, she had heard and read so much about. However, there was nobody else leaving the New York train looking any more impressive, or rather nobody who was clearly looking for someone and waiting to be looked after, so she stepped forward and said, 'Yes, I'm the chauffeur. Mr Browning?' and he had looked at her very solemnly and said, 'Miss Morell?' and she had felt a strange lurch somewhere in the depths of herself and had led him to her car and driven him back to the college.

She knew precisely when she had fallen in love with Michael Browning, and it had not been the first time he had kissed her, nor when he had told her he wanted to go to bed with her more than he could ever remember wanting to go to bed with anyone; not even when he had told her she had a mind that was better and quicker than most of the men he most respected, or that if she should ever need a job, he would give her one at ten grand a year more than anyone else could offer. It wasn't even when he said that he hoped his small daughter would grow up into just such a woman as she was; it was when he said, 'Hey, are you Julian Morell's daughter?' and she had said, 'Yes, I am as a matter of fact,' and he had looked at her consideringly and very seriously, and said, 'That has to be quite an obstacle race.'

Roz had felt at that moment that after spending much of her life trying to explain things to people who spoke another language she had found herself in a country that spoke her own; who understood not just what she was saying, but why she was saying it; and she had actually stopped the car and looked at Michael Browning very seriously in a kind of pleased disbelief.

'Hey,' he said, 'did we run out of gas or something?'

'No,' she said, 'no, I'm sorry, it was just what you said.'

'About your father?' he said, and smiled at her again. 'Did I hit the button?'

'Very hard,' said Roz briefly, starting the car again.

'You're a terrible driver,' he said after they had gone a few more miles in silence. 'You drive like a New York cab driver.'

'Thank you.'

'Sorry. I didn't mean to be rude.'

'Well, you were.'

'I know. It happens all the time.'

'Can't you control it?' asked Roz, smiling in spite of her irritation.

'It seems not. I've been in analysis and had deep hypnosis and electric shock treatment and it just goes right on.'

'How unfortunate for you.'

'I get by.'

'So I understand.'

'I do find the English accent terribly sexy,' he said suddenly.

'Really?'

'Yes, I really do. It's so kind of lazy.'

'And do you find laziness sexy as well?'

'Oh absolutely. One hundred and one per cent sexy. I have to tell you, you could make me feel very lazy,' he added as an afterthought.

Roz felt confused, disoriented. The conversation seemed to be meandering down a series of wrong turnings, not at all the dynamic business-like route she had imagined.

'Do you like giving lectures?' she asked in an attempt to haul him back on to the main highway.

'I don't know. I never gave one before.'

'Oh.'

'It could be interesting. I'll tell you afterwards. Do I get to see you afterwards?'

'I don't know. I suppose so. Briefly.'

'Well,' he said, 'briefly will be better than nothing.'

The lecture, unrehearsed, unstructured, often funny, told the students more about food retailing than they had ever imagined they might need to know; afterwards he sought Roz out at the buffet lunch, gave her his card and told her to phone him next time she was in New York. Roz said she never went to New York.

Three days later she got a call from him.

'This is Michael Browning here. I thought if you were never going to come to New York, I would have to come to Harvard.'

'Why?' said Roz foolishly.

'Oh, just to take another look at you. Make sure I'd got it right.'

'Got what right?'

'Well,' he said, and there was a heavy sigh down the phone, 'it's those legs of yours, really. They're coming between me and my sleep. Were you born with them that long, like a racehorse, or did they just go on growing, like Topsy?'

'I think,' said Roz carefully, feeling oddly dizzy and happier than she could ever remember, 'they were quite short when I was born.'

'Well I would really like to take another look at them. And possibly the rest of you as well. Do you ever eat dinner?'

'Just occasionally,' she said.

When he was first getting to know her, Michael Browning had been unable to believe in the spoiltness, the truculence, the outrageous self-obsession of Roz.

He looked at her, and he wanted her, but he was not quite sure that he could take her on. Then he got to know her a little more, learnt of her wretched childhood, her totally unsatisfactory parents, the painstaking indulgence of her every whim that had gone on through fifteen years of recompense, and he had known that he could.

He treated her rough: at first. He told her she had no right, no one had any right to be so angry, so hostile, so aggressive, so self-pitying. He told her of girls he had grown up with, who had been raped by their mothers' boyfriends, their own fathers before they had reached puberty; who had had to go on the streets every night to fill their bellies; who had had their first unanaesthetized abortions at twelve, their fifth or sixth at fifteen, and dared her to go on being sorry for herself.

Then, having broken down some of her defences, he set to work on the rest. Roz was sexually, as well as emotionally, a mess. The fearsome attentions of the Vicomte du Chene apart, her history was unhappy.

By the time Michael Browning came into her life and her bed, she had a great need for skill and kindness as well as passion. He provided them; he coaxed her and cosseted her, teased her and tormented her, took her and fulfilled her, night after glorious night. He taught her to know what she wanted and ask for it; he taught her to please him, and to please herself; he taught her to think about sex and to give it her attention, just as she did to food and clothes and work. He turned her into a sexual being aware of her own sensuality and what she could do with it, possessed of great pleasures and new powers. Despite strong desires and instincts of her own, she was, she felt, his creation in bed; she sometimes wondered uneasily if he wished her to become his creation in other things.

He flew in to Paris from New York at least once a month for the weekend, amused and charmed, for the time being at least, by her bid for independence. They seldom left her apartment off the Tuileries those weekends; occasionally he would, in one of the grand gestures he so excelled in, take her off to the South of France, or to London, or to Venice, 'So that I can know you – in the Biblical sense – in another place. It might make a difference.'

Roz supposed she was in love. She had very little knowledge of love, although she had seen the worst excesses committed in its name; but if being filled with thoughts and concern and desire and joy by someone was love, then she felt she was experiencing it now.

She consulted another of her visitors, her mother, an expert she could only suppose, on the subject, but Eliza was charmingly vague.

'I can only tell you, darling, you'll know if it is. Not if it's not. Not the first time, anyway.'

'Oh, Mummy, surely you can be more precise.'

'No, Roz, I can't. There's nothing precise about love. That's what's so dangerous.'

Eliza was in Paris shopping. They were lunching in the Hotel

Maurice. Eliza was picking her way painstakingly through a tiny grilled sole; Roz was eating a steak tartare with rather more enjoyment. Eliza looked at her; she had never seen her so happy. Her skin, her eyes, even her hair glowed; she was wearing a smudgy pink cotton sweater with a pair of full linen trousers from Ralph Lauren; a long rope of pearls round her neck. Eliza, more formally dressed in a short black linen dress from Valentino, looked equally relaxed; newly married to her Peveril in that summer of 1980, she was surprisingly happy. Letitia had been right; the pain had eased.

It had been a quiet wedding in the private chapel at Garrylaig; Letitia had been there, and Roz, and Peveril's sisters, and Eliza's parents, and that had been all. Eliza had worn a ravishing ivory silk dress by Yves St Laurent, and had managed not to look ridiculous with wild roses in her silvery hair, and Peveril had worn his kilt and a look of such love that Letitia had felt her eyes fill with tears. Perhaps, this time, the child had done the right thing. She looked at Roz, who was also looking softer, tender, moved. Whoever this man Michael Browning was, he was undoubtedly doing her good.

Eliza was now intent on doing up the castle which had had no mistress for ten years. Quite what the Earl of Garrylaig thought of the new furnishings and pictures that were finding their way on to his austere walls was doubtful; he had already learnt not to criticize his new wife, and as prettying up the place, as he put it, seemed to keep her happy, he held his tongue as century-old brocades were packed away and replaced with silks and chintzes, and cavernous halls filled with seventeenth and eighteenth-century sofas, chaises longues and escritoires. He spent more time than ever in pursuit of the grouse and the deer; what did it matter, after all, he thought, as long as his bride was content and out of mischief. She looked after him beautifully, pandering to his every whim, and seemed to find him agreeable and attractive. Peveril was well content and found himself looking forward to bedtime more and more.

'You're a fine filly, my dear,' he would say, slapping her fondly on her tiny backside, 'very fine. I'm a lucky chap.'

Which indeed he was, and Eliza felt perfectly entitled to regular trips to London and Paris to spend his money and see her daughter, with whom she was suddenly finding it easier to communicate. She was rigidly faithful to Peveril, besides being truly fond of him, and she was enjoying being a countess and her new situation in life. She had fun shocking her Scottish neighbours and importing her London friends into the castle, and she was perfectly happy inflicting her slightly excessive taste on its decor.

'It sounds dreadful, Mummy,' said Roz after listening to her for most of lunch, describing the colour scheme for the main guest room, 'more suitable for Surrey than Scotland. Pink chintz in a castle; it's like poodle-clipping the deer. Whatever does Peveril think?'

'Oh, don't be so superior,' said Eliza, more than slightly miffed, for she greatly admired her own taste. 'Peveril likes everything I do for him. And he's thrilled with the way the castle's turning out. It was so horribly uncomfortable and bleak before. Well, you saw it; don't you honestly think so?'

'No, I liked it,' said Roz. 'I like austerity. And I think it has great dignity. You'll take all that away if you're not careful. Anyway, it doesn't really matter. How is my new stepfather?'

'It does matter,' said Eliza, 'it matters very much to me. I'm putting a great deal of time and effort into that place, Rosamund. I don't want doubts cast upon it by my own daughter. Anyway, I don't see much evidence of any interior design skills in your own home, my dear.'

This was true; Roz, who was at last demonstrating some taste, albeit modest, for clothes, cared nothing for her surroundings and would have agreed to spend the rest of her life in a twelve-foot-square attic, provided it was warm and clean, had she been asked.

'Oh, don't be so touchy, Mummy,' she said, 'I'm sure it's quite all right really, and I know Peveril thinks you're wonderful. Have another glass of wine and let's talk about something interesting.'

'Like what?' said Eliza, a trifle sulky.

'Me.'

'And what is so interesting about you?'

'Well, I need a bit of advice.'

'What about?'

'A man.'

'Ah. This Browning person.'

'Yes.'

'I don't really like what I hear about him, darling. He has an appalling reputation with women. What exactly do you want advice about?'

'Michael has asked me to marry him.'

'Oh, good God, don't,' said Eliza. 'Whatever you do, never marry his sort. It's quite wrong.'

'Mummy,' said Roz, half amused, half intrigued, 'what advice to be dishing out to your only daughter. Do I just continue as his mistress, then?'

'If you want to, if you enjoy it. You're so lucky these days, Roz, not having to have at least one ring on your wedding finger before you can go to bed with anyone. When I was a girl, virginity was still almost obligatory for a bride. Have fun, darling. But don't marry Michael Browning.'

'Why not?'

'Because you'll be divorced again in two years. Six months into the marriage and he'll have a new mistress. Believe me.'

Roz sighed. 'He says he loves me.'

'I'm sure he thinks he does.'

'He says I'm different.'

'We're all different. Take no notice.'

'He says he wants to settle down.'

'No man of thirty-five wants to settle down.'

'He says he wants more children. I'd like that.'

'Oh, for heaven's sake, Rosamund, I can't believe you can be so naïve and stupid! Why on earth do you want to go having babies at the age of twenty-four? It's absolutely ridiculous.'

'You were twenty when you had me.'

'I know, and it was a terrible mistake. The marriage was a terrible mistake. I was much too young. I hadn't lived at all. Nor have you. Just enjoy the man, Roz. Besides, I thought you were intent on building a proper career.'

'Well, I am. But Michael says he won't interfere. He says I can carry on with it.'

'Rosamund,' said Eliza darkly, signalling at the waiter. 'Michael Browning would be not interfering for about forty-eight hours. If that. I have learnt a few things in my misspent life. Now have some more wine,' she added, 'and darling, you'd better have some black coffee. You've got to go back to work. Please, please believe me, Roz. A career is far more important and worth while at your age – probably at any age – than a man.'

'But I can have both.'

'Darling, you can't. Perhaps if you married some milksop of a man who did exactly what you told him, and thought you should be allowed to do what you liked. But not people like Browning.'

'I don't see how you can be so sure,' said Roz sulkily. 'We've talked about it for hours and hours. Michael is very proud of me. He wants me to do well.'

'Rosamund, he won't want you to do well. Doing well will mean you not being there when he wants you. Men don't like that.'

'Don't they? I really think he might. Oh, I don't know,' said Roz with a sigh, draining her glass. 'I do absolutely adore him. And he is such fun.'

'Well, that's all right,' said Eliza. 'Just go on having fun with him.'

'Michael, I've told you, I just want more time to think about it,' Roz said earnestly. 'I'm not saying no. I'm not even saying probably no. I just need to think it through.'

'Oh, God,' said Browning wearily. 'Don't use your Harvard jargon on me.'

They were sitting in a café on the Champs Elysées having breakfast (croissants, orange juice and champagne), it was Saturday mid morning, and the sun was shining; Michael had spent the night on a plane and was tired and irritable and blind to the pleasures in front of him. He had dropped a box into Roz's lap as the waiter filled their glasses.

'That's for you, Roz. Part of a deal.'

'What kind of a deal?'

'You get that and I get you.'

Roz opened the box; inside was a diamong ring of monster proportions, a huge solitaire set in a rough-cut chunk of gold spangled with tiny sapphires. She looked at it thoughtfully.

'It's gorgeous. Simply gorgeous. I love it.'

'Put it on.'

'I can't. Not if it's what I think it is.'

'Rosamund, if you don't know what that is, you've even less

sense than I thought. It's a diamond. You will have heard of diamonds, I imagine. This is a big one. The goods. It's to show you what I think of you.'

'You know what I mean.'

'Yes, I know what you mean. And yes, it's that. It's an engagement ring, Roz, as you call them in England. I really do want to marry you.'

'Why?'

'Because I love you. God knows why, but I do.'

'I love you too. But things are fine as they are.'

'I wouldn't agree with that. I want them settled. I'm sick of jetting in here every other day. I want you with me.'

'Where do you mean?'

'New York.'

'I've just been offered a new job. In London.'

'London! Why didn't you tell me?'

'I didn't know. I was only offered it yesterday.'

'Well, turn it down. Or say you want to go to New York instead.'

'No, I can't.'

'What do you mean, you can't? Your father's got offices there.'

'Michael, my father isn't slotting me in somewhere just to suit me. He's given me a proper job to do. It's important. It's promotion.'

'Oh, for Christ's sake, Rosamund, how important is it to get promotion in your father's company?'

'It's terribly important, Michael. Terribly. I can't believe you don't understand. I really have earned it. I'm going to be marketing manager of all the Juliana colour products in the UK. It's a terrific job.'

'And I suppose the opposition was really stiff for this terrific job?'

'Oh, don't,' said Roz angrily. 'You don't know my father. He wouldn't give me any job he didn't think I could do.'

'I do know your father, and I think he would.'

'Well, thanks a lot.' Roz drained her coffee cup and called the waiter. '*L'addition, s'il vous plaît!*'

'Oh, for Christ's sake get off your high horse and have some more champagne.'

'No, thank you. I want to keep my head clear.'

She was finding the conversation difficult and terrifying. She kept hearing her mother's voice saying 'You can't have both' and pushing it resolutely to somewhere at the back of her head. It wouldn't stay there.

'Rosamund, I really want you to have a career. It's one of the things I value in you. I love the fact that you want to do well. But I want you to do well with me.'

'But Michael, I can't come to New York now. I can't give up my job, and be a proper good wife to you. Not yet.'

Michael picked up her left hand and slid the ring on to it.

'Please wear it.'

'I can't.'

'You can wear it, for Christ's sake. That doesn't commit you to a life sentence of picking out shirts for me at Brooks Brothers and doing the flowers for our dinner parties, which is what you seem to imagine I want.'

'No, I don't imagine that, of course I don't. But if I did marry you, if I was your wife, I'd want to be a proper one. I've seen too many wrecked marriages. And this way I'd be cheating. Well, I feel I would.'

'Well look, wear the ring. And say you'll marry me soon. I'm not insisting on next week. You can do this important job for a bit, if you really want to. I'll wait. Please, darling.'

'Michael, I'm not going to promise anything.'

'Why not? What harm's in a promise?'

'You have to keep them.'

'Oh, for God's sake, stop playing games.'

'I'm not playing games. I just –'

'What?'

Roz looked at him suddenly. He was white-faced with exhaustion; he had a night's growth of beard, his voice was shaking with rage and some other emotion, she wasn't sure what: in a moment of rare unselfishness, she realized she should stop hitting him when he was down.

'I just want time to think. Come on.'

She stood up and held out her hand. 'Let's go back to my flat and you can go to bed for a couple of hours.'

Michael's eyes flicked over her.

'You going to join me?'

418

'If you like.'

'I do like. I certainly do.'

At one o'clock he was still asleep. Roz rolled out of bed cautiously and crept out of the room. She felt exhilarated, recharged, absolutely alive. Sex with Michael Browning did that to her. Not just her body, but her emotions and her intellect had all been absolutely engaged, focused on the taking and giving of pleasure. She was left with a surge of adrenaline coursing through her; she felt she could quite literally have flown in the air.

She made herself a strong coffee and wandered into the bathroom, looked at her face, flushed, worked over with love, and smiled at it. Perhaps, perhaps, after all, Michael could be, would be, enough. She wished for that, at that moment, more than she had ever wished for anything in her life.

Then she looked at the great ring on her finger, where he had put it, and she thought about her father, about London, about her new job and the passion of excitement she had felt when he had phoned her about it: telling her she had earned it, that he was impressed with her work, that he knew she could do it, and do it well, and she knew that she could not, would not, give it up. Not for all the rings, all the money, all the sex, all the love in the world. It was difficult, because she wanted love, and she needed it; but the choice had to be made.

A milksop of a man, she thought sadly, hearing yet again her mother's voice. That's what I shall have to find.

In the event it wasn't really very difficult.

C. J. Emerson arrived at Harvard just as Roz was leaving, a charming, gentle young man whose only real ambition in life had been to study archaeology. His father, however, had rather different ones for him. He was only moderately successful himself, lacking the necessary drive and ruthlessness to head up empires and make fortunes; but he had had moments of inspired vision, and backed some brilliant investments: Scott Emerson's reputation on Wall Street was front rank.

None had been more brilliant than the one he had pushed through in 1957 when Julian Morell had come to him with his proposals for Circe; and the friendship forged then had remained through the years. They lunched, dined, talked and at times still worked together, they had visited each other's houses, become involved in each other's children.

Scott was impressed by Julian's immense success and fortune, he admired it, but he did not envy it. He had watched his personal unhappiness grow, seen his uncertainties and his agonies, observed his straightforward optimism become something darker and more complex; and he found himself (somewhat to his own surprise) increasingly content with his own more mediocre achievements, and his extraordinarily happy family life.

Scott Emerson in 1980, then, found himself viewing the thirty years to come in the same sanguine spirit as he had viewed the thirty that had so pleasantly passed. His daughters were all doing well; only his son was causing Scott the odd moment's anxiety. Or more than a moment, as he confided to his friend Julian Morell over lunch at the Oyster Bar at Grand Central station one spring day. The two of them sat and looked (each from their own standpoint) at the pretty girls around them, shedding like so many fluttering butterflies their coats, their boots, their scarves, their gloves and emerging in the delicious, slightly self-conscious sexiness of lighter, clingy dresses, of neatly cut, figure-hugging skirts and jackets, of higher heels and silky stockings. Scott looked and regretted, just perhaps for a fleeting moment, that such pleasures were purely visual; Julian enjoyed, for perhaps just a little longer, the reflection that the pleasures might be extended.

Settled into their martinis, their oysters ordered, the room surveyed, however, they turned their mind to more important matters: to the present, and the future of their families.

'C. J.'s a dreamer,' said Scott, gazing a trifle morosely into his martini. 'He's gone to Harvard, but his heart's not in it. Not really. He wants to be an archaeologist. I ask you, Julian, what kind of a job is that?'

'A fascinating pursuit,' said Julian, 'but I don't think I'd actually call it a job. More of a recreation. I didn't know you had such things in your country anyway, Scott. I didn't think there was anything to dig up.'

'Well, hell, of course there isn't, that's why it's such a crazy idea. He wants to travel, spend years on sites here, there and everywhere; do a postgraduate course at Oxford. That's no life for a young man, I told him so. Where's your ambition, I asked him, where are you aiming for in the world? I said he could have a job any time at the bank, but he wouldn't hear of it. It worries me, Julian, because I think he'll drift his life away if he's given the chance. And I won't have that.'

'No, you shouldn't,' said Julian. 'Young men should have proper jobs. I quite agree with you. Make their way in the world. Take life on. Plenty of time for dreaming when they're older. Nothing makes me angrier than this modern tendency to put the pursuit of happiness and self-fulfilment and some bloody silly ideals before the real stuff of life. I wouldn't have it if it was my son.'

He spoke with surprising passion; Scott looked at him sharply. He wouldn't have expected a man with no son, and no experience of such matters, to feel so strongly, to have given the subject so much thought.

'What about Roz?' he asked tentatively, wondering if she was failing her father in this matter, as she had in so many others. 'Is she frittering her life away, buying frocks and so on? How's she doing?'

'Very well,' said Julian, more warmly than he had spoken of Roz since she had been a little girl. 'She's working for me and she's working very hard. She's got brains and she's got push. She's very, very ambitious.'

'What a waste,' said Scott, half humorous, half genuinely envious. 'How ironic that you should have one daughter with all the traditional male virtues, and I should have one son with apparently none of them.'

'Well, work on him,' said Julian briskly. 'Don't let him throw his life away. Tell him there's plenty of time for archaeology when he's retired, in his vacations. Ideal sort of occupation then.'

'Oh, I have. I've tried that one. And he does try to see it my way. He's a good boy. And he's working quite hard at Harvard. But I worry about him long term.'

'Harvard might well sort him out. Roz loved it. Did her the world of good. I shouldn't worry too soon, Scott. Have another martini. Ah, here are the oysters.'

*

But six months later Scott was still worrying. C. J. had scraped his way through Harvard and was now sitting at home in Oyster Bay writing endless applications for jobs he didn't want. He was a tall, slender young man, with a pale softly freckled face and large dreamy brown eyes. He wore his clothes casual, his hair long, and he never seemed to be entirely present at any occasion.

He could be witty and entertaining, when he felt relaxed and appreciated, but his charm was low-key and diffident. At twenty-five he felt as confused about life and his future as he had at eighteen; and he could work up no feelings at all for money and business, profits and power. The prospect of having to find a job and work amongst such things, his father's assumption that he would change his mind and grow to like the idea, depressed him utterly; he loved his parents deeply and he wanted to please them, but it seemed to him this was too much for them to ask and for him to give.

He knew, deep in his gentle bones, that there was no real question of him actually being permitted to spend his life on the great digs of the ancient world, but he kept hoping against increasingly forlorn hope that a more pleasing occupation than wheeling and dealing on Wall Street might come his way. Publishing perhaps, he thought, or antiques; but he had made little headway with applications in that direction. You needed contacts in that world, as much as any other, he had discovered.

Nevertheless, he did finally get an offer of a job as junior editor with Doubleday at a modest salary. He looked up from the letter at the breakfast table, his brown eyes shining.

'I've been offered a job, Dad.'

'Have you now, son?' said Scott, putting down his coffee and beaming benevolently at him. 'What is it? Did that opening at Citicorp I gave you lead to anything?'

'Er – no, not exactly,' said C. J., who had kept that particular letter of rejection to himself for several days, bracing himself to tell his parents (he had had several and each one had upset them more than the last).

'No, actually, it's not banking, it's publishing.'

'Publishing,' said Scott. 'I didn't know you knew anything about it.'

'Well, I don't much,' said C. J., 'but I don't know anything about banking either. And I think I'd like publishing better. And this is a wonderful offer. I'm going to be an assistant editor at Doubleday's. It's a terrific opportunity. I'd really like to take it, Dad.'

Scott looked at him, and bit back the words of discouragement and disappointment that were struggling to get out. The boy had shown some initiative, after all, and Doubleday's were a good firm. He smiled at him.

'That's great, C. J. Well done. When do you start?'

'In a month, Dad. So you don't mind?'

'No, no son, not at all. I'm proud of you, you've got there on your own initiative, and that's a hell of a good thing to do. Write and accept it. Now here's a letter from Julian; what's he got to say, I wonder.'

He started to read and then drew in his breath sharply.

'C. J., listen to this. Julian Morell says he has an opening for you in his London office. He wants you to join the management team of the hotels division. He's hell bent on opening more of them, God knows why, and he's got guys working on it night and day. He needs people to do feasibility studies of various sites worldwide. You'd be working on that side. It's a hell of an opportunity, C. J. You'd do well. He says you could stay with him in London for a few weeks while you're finding somewhere to live. He'll pay you handsomely too. It says here, ". . . Tell C. J. he can have five grand and a BMW for starters." Now that really is great, C. J., isn't it? Listen, it would make me so happy to think that Julian and I could really put our friendship to work.'

'But Dad, I already have a job. I don't want handouts. It's very kind of Mr Morell, but I really would rather not take it. You just said it was very good that I'd got the job at Doubleday on my own initiative. And I don't want to go to London.'

'Why on earth not?' said Scott. 'I'd have thought it would be just the greatest. All those old buildings, and you could go do your digging at the weekends. I don't understand you, C. J., I really don't.'

'Dad, I know you don't and I'm sorry. But my life is here, and my work is here, and I want to stay. I don't want to work for Julian Morell.'

He was quite pale; he was so naturally conciliatory that every word pitted against his father felt like a self-inflicted wound.

'Well, think about it at least,' said Scott, disappointment and deflation echoing in his voice. 'Don't write to Doubleday's for a day or two, and I won't write to Julian.'

'OK,' said C. J. with a sigh.

'There's my boy. Now I have to go. I have a medical check this morning, this crazy ulcer is getting worse. Say goodbye to your mother for me when she comes down. See you later, C. J.'

'Yes Dad,' said C. J. absently. He sat reading and re-reading the letter from Doubleday for a long time. He was determined not to go to work for Julian Morell. But he trembled at the battles that lay ahead.

In the event there were no battles. Scott's ulcer proved to be cancer and C. J. could clearly not deprive him of the pleasure in the last year of his life of seeing his son go to work for his oldest and dearest friend.

But having put his shoulder to the wheel, C. J. did push at it with a vengeance. He worked hard at his new job, and put thoughts of archaeology and publishing resolutely behind him; hotels were clearly what Fate had had in mind for him and he went along with her as graciously as he knew how. And in actual fact he didn't mind it as much as he had expected. His father had been right in one respect; he found London wonderful. He began a love affair with the city that summer, that lasted for the rest of his life; it consumed his heart as well as his intellect. Where other young men pursued girls or worldly success in their spare time, C. J. pursued London. Every weekend he walked, exploring, looking, learning the place, familiarizing himself with every twist and turn of his beloved's form. He began with the centre, as it seemed to him, the City, and roamed the small lanes as well as the high, winding streets; wandering down tiny alleys, discovering shops, churches, workshops, that stood as if in a time warp. He walked by the river, under the bridges, explored the docklands; he went to all the markets in Whitechapel and Leather Lane and the Caledonian Road, buying, bargaining, being inevitably and hopelessly (but quite happily) cheated. He watched the newly opened hyper-chic Covent Garden taking shape, and mourned for the one he remembered from visits in his childhood, when the streets had been littered with vegetables and lorries piled high with flowers had held up the impotent traffic. He visited a strange pot pourri of places: the Museum of Childhood, the Battersea Dogs' Home, Pollock's Toy Museum. He spent a whole weekend in Fleet Street and its environs, absorbing the smell and feel of the place, watching its twenty-four-hour day pass from one early dawn as the lorries thundered out of the bays with their load of newspapers to the next. He could have written a thesis on the churches and cathedrals of the city, from the sweeping majesty of St Paul's and Westminster Abbey, to the high self-conscious fashionableness of Chelsea Old Church and St James's Spanish Place, which made him feel strangely at home and homesick for New York. He walked the residential areas: Belgravia, Chelsea, Knightsbridge, Fulham; he knew the layout of every big store and small smart shop in the city. He ate in every kind of restaurant, from the chic eateries of Fulham and Knightsbridge to the more physically satisfying all-night cafes of Fleet Street and thence to the great English establishments, to Simpson's in the Strand and Rules. He learnt the layout of the parks by heart: he visited Peter Pan in Kensington Gardens, the Orangery in Holland Park, spent days in Hyde Park, rowed along the Serpentine; he sat in St James's Park, and marvelled at the way it managed somehow to contain the English countryside, and he walked across Regent's Park, and spent a dizzy, happy day at the zoo.

All this he did alone, for who after all, in the first phases of a love affair, wants to share the beloved; London was company and happiness enough, and he did not ask for any more.

And then he did not actually hate the job quite as much as he had expected. C. J. was a carer, and hotels were in the caring business; having overcome his initial distaste, he found he could actually get quite interestingly involved in how best to ensure the maximum comfort, visual delight and pleasure of one person for twenty-four hours a day.

Julian Morell was swift to realize that where C. J. worked, people tended to think more visually, more imaginatively, and he encouraged and nurtured him. He was a brilliant employer; as with his own daughter, he gave C. J. no special privileges, attention or opportunities – until they were earned. And as in the case of his own daughter, they were earned quickly. In eight months C. J. was promoted to deputy marketing manager,

Morell Hotels Europe, at a hugely increased salary – every penny of which he earned.

Julian had taken a considerable gamble in giving him a job at all, but in the event it had paid off. And it was making Scott very happy as he lay failing in his huge bed in the house in Oyster Bay.

Roz was very unhappy. More than she would have believed possible. She missed Michael Browning with every fibre of her being; she hated every beginning of every day.

When they had finally parted (at her instigation and against appalling opposition from him) she spent forty-eight totally wakeful hours, wondering if she could stand the pain and the knowledge of what she had given up. She, who had been looking for love ever since she had been a tiny girl sitting on the stairs and had heard her father's voice rejecting her, had thrown it wantonly away. And not just love, but appreciation, acceptance, admiration, physical pleasure: simply so that she could be seen to be a worldly success, and to be taking up her position as her father's rightful heir. And it might well be worth it, indeed she had to believe it was, but the price was horrifically high. She had expected to feel bad; what she hadn't expected was to feel bad for so long. As the days became weeks, and the weeks a month, two, and her pain continued, she became angry and resentful.

It was very hard, even after this time, to stick to her decision; not to lift the phone, not to write, not to get on a plane. By one simple action, she knew, she could feel well, healed, happy again; but somehow she resisted. She had to.

At first she had expected him to make approaches to her, to try to make her change her mind. But such behaviour was not Browning's style. He was a proud man. If Roz told him she couldn't give him her life, then he was not about to crawl round her, trying to change her mind. They had one last night together, when he made love to her again and again, angrily, despairingly: 'This is what you are losing,' his body said to her through the long, endless hours, 'this pleasure, this hunger, this love,' and in the morning he had got out of bed and left her without saying another word to her, not even goodbye.

*

She had wept for hours. That was in itself a rare event; she surprised herself by her capacity to feel. Physical pain, this was; her skin felt sore, her head bruised, her joints ached. She couldn't think clearly, or concentrate or remember anything at all for more than sixty seconds. That went on for weeks. It was only when she flunked an important presentation that she remembered sharply and with a kind of thankfulness why she had subjected herself to this: precisely so that she could work and impress and succeed and excel.

She went home that night and took a sleeping pill, set her alarm for five-thirty. By six-thirty she had run three miles, showered and dressed; by seven she was in the office, dictating memos. That day she instigated a complete re-evaluation of all Juliana's outlets, made a review of the advertising and arranged presentations from five new agencies; called the studio in for a major briefing on re-packaging three of the lines, and tried to persuade her father of the wisdom of putting small, Circe-style boutiques in the hotels.

'I think it would work, Daddy. Let me give you some of my ideas.'

Julian looked at her white, drawn face and her dark eyes raw with the pain and saw how he could help her. 'Actually,' he said, 'I've been thinking about that for a while. I'm not convinced it's right, though. I'd like a document soon, Roz. I can't wait months. Can you let me have it in three weeks?'

She looked at him with weary gratitude. 'Yes, I think so. Yes. I can.'

He looked after her with great respect as she went out of the room. He was deeply thankful that the affair with Browning was over; but it wasn't entirely pleasant to see her so patently wretched.

Roz was too unhappy to think very rationally at the time, but later on it was to occur to her quite forcibly that she could perfectly well have done her new job in New York under the aegis of Miss Bentinck, rather than in London under her father, and continued to see Michael at the same time. It was yet another example of her father's power over her, and his insistence that she recognized and accepted it.

The document she delivered was excellent: clear sighted,

financially well based, persuasive. Julian, who had not had the slightest intention of putting any boutiques in the hotels, agreed to do a test in the Nice and the London Morell. As this came under C. J.'s domain, he called him in.

'Have lunch with Roz, C. J., and talk to her about her ideas. They're interesting. She thinks these boutiques should not be just expensive little shops but have properly planned merchandise with a fashion consultant in each one to coordinate accessories. It's a good idea. Let me have your views on it.'

C. J., who was pushing himself equally hard to try and numb himself against the pain of his father's death, hurled himself into the project with fervour. He didn't particularly like Roz, but he admired her and her ideas, and he enjoyed working with her; personally she terrified him, but on a business level she was a delight. Her brain was much more incisive than his, she could see her way through a problem or situation with extraordinary clarity. She was a brilliant analyst and a very clever negotiator. But she undoubtedly lacked flair and fashion instinct, her own appearance apart, and C. J. possessed both; they made an unbeatable team. It was a source of great sadness as well as huge pride to Madeleine that Scott missed seeing his son's promotion to junior vice president of Morell Hotels by just three months. Roz was given the same title at the same time. It was an interesting period in the Morell empire.

'C. J.,' said Roz one night, just after Christmas, 'why don't we go through these designers' names over dinner? I'm really hungry.'

C. J. looked at her warily. He was less frightened of her than he had been, but she was still far from the kind of dinner companion he would have chosen.

Nevertheless, it was a pleasant evening. They got through the list of designers (and a bottle of champagne) in half an hour and by the time the first course arrived they were sitting isolated from the in-buzzing and shrieking of San Frediano's restaurant in the Fulham Road in a kind of euphoric relaxation. Roz was enjoying herself for the first time in months.

'Oh, it's the best feeling in the world, this,' she said happily. 'Don't you think so, C. J.?'

'Being round half a bottle of champagne?'

'No, you fool, you know perfectly well what I mean. Finishing a difficult job, and knowing you've done it well. And knowing you've earned being round half a bottle of champagne. What a ghastly expression, anyway, C. J. Is that an Americanism?'

'My father told me it was an Anglicism,' said C. J., smiling at her. She looked very good; she was wearing a white silk shirt and a pair of tan leather jodhpurs with high boots; over her shoulders, slung casually, was one of Edina Ronay's fair-isle sweaters. She was leaning back in her chair, her long legs thrust out into the aisle between the tables, threatening to trip up the waiters as they hurtled past; almost for the first time he realized she was a very attractive woman in her strong, slightly forbidding way.

'How are you feeling about your father now?' asked Roz. 'Awful still?'

'Pretty awful.'

'I'm sorry.'

'Yeah, well, it's not so bad for me, I guess. It's my mother who's really doing the suffering. She's been so brave. She loved him so much. They were just all the world to each other. I guess not many people grow up looking at a happy marriage. It's a great privilege.'

'One I wouldn't know about,' said Roz, sad rather than angry for once about her parents' spectacular inability to form satisfactory relationships with anyone, let alone one another. 'Is she all right? How does she cope?'

'Not too badly. The girls are all in New York, and they see her a lot, and I go over quite often and call her all the time. But it's no use at all, really. It's Dad she wants. I'm just glad I was doing what he wanted me to do when he died.'

'That's a very unselfish sentiment. What a nice person you are, C. J.'

'You sound surprised.'

'Not about you. But I'm always surprised by niceness.'

'Why's that?'

'I haven't met an awful lot of it.'

'Are you feeling better?' asked C. J., anxious to change the direction of the conversation.

'What do you mean?' She looked suddenly defensive.

'Oh, I'm sorry,' said C. J., confused and nervous again. 'I guess I shouldn't have asked. Here's our food. Can we have some more champagne?' he said suddenly to the waiter.

'C. J.!' said Roz. 'What lavish behaviour.'

'My father always said champagne was cheaper than psychiatry,' said C. J., smiling at her, 'and it worked a darn sight better. I think he's right.'

'Do you need psychiatry? Do I?'

'I do,' said C. J., looking suddenly serious. 'Or something like it. I'd be in analysis if I was in America.'

'C. J., what is it? No, you don't have to tell me. I'm prying. I'm sorry.'

'No, I'd like to,' he said and to his total embarrassment and misery his eyes filled with tears. He blew his nose. 'It would be a relief, in a way. Although you're the last person I expected to tell.'

'Why?'

'Well, because you scare the shit out of me.'

'So I see,' said Roz, 'and it's deeply flattering. Now come on, C. J. Just forget I'm so terrifying and you don't like me and all that and just spill the beans.'

C. J. looked wretchedly down at the table. 'I – well, I think – that is, since Dad died – I – well, I don't have any sexual feelings at all. It scares me, Roz, it really does. I don't fancy anyone. I don't even want to fancy anyone. I'm not suggesting I'm impotent or anything drastic like that, I just feel – dead.'

'You mean sexually dead?'

'Yes.'

'What about emotionally?'

'What do you mean?'

'Well I mean, don't you think about girls and falling in love with them and all that sort of thing?'

C. J. looked at her, surprised. He had not expected Roz to look at his problem with such sensitivity and imaginativeness. 'Well, I worry about it. About not being in love. Not being able to be. But I haven't met anyone for ages who made me even think positively about it.'

'You mean you haven't met anyone you like enough, or fancy enough?'

'Both.'

'How awful.'

'It is.'

'No dreams even?'

'No dreams even,' said C. J. sadly, and then suddenly he smiled. 'What a strange girl you are, Roz.'

'What do you mean?'

'Well, you're so tough and clever and ambitious –'

'And terrifying.'

'And terrifying. And yet you seem to understand the most surprising things.'

'Like what?'

'Well, loneliness. Isolation, dreams. I mean that really is strange. For you to talk about dreams.'

'Oh, I'm a mass of contradictions,' said Roz, just slightly bitter. 'I've just been through the mill myself, C. J. That's how I know what you're talking about. I dream a lot. In fact I get all my sex in my sleep at the moment.'

'Well,' said C. J. 'At least you're getting some.' And totally unaware of the comedy of the situation, he heaved a shuddering sigh.

Roz sat there and a whole range of emotions filled her. She felt sadness for C. J. and pity; she felt remote and sad for herself; she felt a strong urge to giggle; and strongest of all and quite unbidden, she felt a great lick of desire. And she knew precisely what she would have to do.

'C. J.,' she said almost briskly, 'drink your coffee and take me home. I'm very very tired. Could you call a taxi, do you think, while you're paying the bill? I'm going to the loo.'

C. J. looked after her miserably as she disappeared. He had made a fool of himself, but at least she was clearly not going to attempt to comfort him or offer any advice. He should be grateful for that. And frightening as she was, he did know she wasn't a gossip. His misery was in safe hands. He paid the (enormous) bill, collected their coats and was standing in the doorway when Roz appeared, looking briskly cheerful, in a cloud of perfume. 'Got a taxi?'

'Yes.'

'Good.'

*

Inside the flat, which surprised him by its lack of style, its blanket decor of beige and white, its dull, born-again Conran furniture, its dearth of pictures and books, Roz kicked off her shoes, threw her coat on the sofa, put on a record – the LP of *Forty-Second Street* – and disappeared into the kitchen.

'Make yourself comfortable, C. J. That's what they say, isn't it? I won't be long.'

C. J. paced up and down the sitting room. 'Evening shadows fall!' cried the record player provocatively. He felt sick. He felt like a rabbit in a trap. He would have bolted if he'd had the courage, but he didn't. He wondered how he could have been quite such a fool, and had just decided to put in for a transfer to Sydney in the morning when Roz reappeared with two mugs of coffee.

'OK. Now I want to go over that list of designers just once more. I think we may have rushed it.'

C. J. felt a surge of gratitude. She was a clever girl. She knew exactly how to defuse the situation after all. He relaxed suddenly.

'I felt that.'

'What?'

'You relaxing.'

'Ah.'

'Now, don't go all tense again, C. J. Get the list.'

'OK.' He went out to the hall where he had left his briefcase. When he came back she stretched out her hand.

'Here you are.'

'Thanks. Now then,' she said, patting the sofa beside her. 'Let's see. Are you quite sure about Jean Muir?'

'Quite.'

'I'm not.'

'Why?'

'Too subtle. Zandra certainly. Belinda Belville almost certainly. But I'm doubtful about Jean. Give me your hand, C. J.'

He was so relaxed, he gave her his hand without thinking. Roz raised it to her lips and he looked at her, startled.

'Roz, don't.'

'Why not?'

'I don't like pity.'

432

'You're not going to get any.'

'Ah.'

The record had mercifully stopped; all he could hear, thundering somewhere inside him, was his heart.

'Kiss me.'

'Roz, I can't.'

'Why not?'

'You know why not.'

'I don't. Kiss me.'

'No.'

'Then,' she said taking his face in her hands, 'I shall kiss you.' And she leant forward very very slowly and kissed him very gently. 'Was that so dreadful?' she said, drawing back.

'Not dreadful at all.'

'I liked it too. I shall do it again.'

And she did.

'How was that?'

'It was great,' said C. J., and then suddenly drew back from her and collapsed into the corner of the sofa, roaring with laughter.

'C. J., what is the matter with you?'

'This is too ridiculous. It's like a re-run of *Some Like It Hot*. You know, when Tony Curtis has told Monroe he's impotent and she's really trying to get him going, and he keeps saying "Nothing" every time she asks him how he feels. It's just ridiculous!'

'Well, thanks,' said Roz, slightly nettled, but then she started to laugh too, and fell against him, and then she turned her head up to him, and pulled him down against her. And he kissed her again, and then again, and 'Still nothing?' she said, apeing Marilyn Monroe's baby voice, and 'Yes, something,' said C. J. in a thick American accent and then, his eyes still full of laughter, he pushed her upright and raised his hands and unbuttoned her shirt and began to slide it off her shoulder, and as he looked at her breasts naked under the silk shirt he felt at the same time a dreadful stab of terror and panic and a great lunge of desire, and he stopped smiling altogether and froze quite quite still.

'Oh, C. J., don't be afraid,' she said in a voice so soft he would not have believed it of her, and she took his head in her

hands and pressed it very tenderly against her breasts, stroking
his hair, and as he took one of her nipples in his mouth, played
with it, teased it, she began to moan, very very quietly. And then
suddenly he felt everything was totally out of control, and a
white-hot need came into him, that was blind, driving, deadly.
He was tearing at her clothes, and his own, and kissing her
everywhere, her face, her shoulders, her breasts, her hands,
and drawing her down on top of him. He felt her thin back, her
tight hard buttocks, and then her soft moistness, so tender, so
yielding at first, and then so hungry, and so strong; and he
turned her and entered her with a great surge of triumph; he
had only been in her for the briefest of times, it seemed,
settling, searching and feeling her juices flowing to meet him,
when it was over, in a shuddering agony of relief and the
months of misery and loneliness were wiped out and he lay
weeping on her breast. And Roz lay too, hardly begun to be
satisfied, aching with hunger, weeping for the loss of Michael
for the first time for months, but smiling nevertheless; and in
her ears she could hear, as if she was in the chair on the other
side of the room, her mother saying, 'Find some milksop of a
man who would do exactly what you told him.'

She looked up into his slightly anxious brown eyes and
smiled, and reached out a hungry hand, cupping his balls,
caressing them with light, feathery strokes. 'C. J.,' she said. 'Do
it again. Now. Before I scream.'

C. J. did it again.

C. J. did not do quite what she told him. At first. After a heady two
months, when they saw each other three times a week, in secrecy,
and went to bed together whenever they could (and during which
time she managed to improve his performance considerably), Roz
asked him to go to Paris with her one weekend, ostensibly on
business, booked them into the anonymity of the Paris Hilton, and
on Saturday morning, after some particularly satisfactory sex,
proposed to him. C. J. refused.

'You know as well as I do, Roz, it wouldn't work.'

'Why wouldn't it work?'

'Because you're the boss's daughter, for a start. And you'd
boss me to be going on with. And we're too unlike ever to make
a go of it.'

'You once said,' said Roz, bending down to kiss his flat stomach, 'that you wouldn't mind me being your boss.'

'Well, I wouldn't, in a business context. But I don't want to be bossed in my marriage.'

'Maybe I could learn not to.'

'No, I don't think you could.'

'C. J., I really think we could be very happy.'

'I don't.'

'But why not? I fancy you rotten. I enjoy your company. I' (and there was a fraction of a second's hesitation) 'love you.'

'No, Roz, you don't. And I don't love you.'

'I see.'

'Rosamund, I adore you. I think you're a terrific lay. I admire you. But I don't love you. You can't have thought I did.'

'God in heaven!' said Roz. 'How I hate being called Rosamund. It always heralds disaster. And I did think you loved me.'

'Roz, I never said –'

'Oh, go to hell,' said Roz angrily, climbing out of bed. She went into the bathroom, reappeared dressed and made up, and walked over to the door.

'Where are you going?'

'To see Annick. To discuss sales figures. That's all I'm really fit for, isn't it? Work. Let's keep things in order. Goodbye, C. J.'

'Roz, please!'

She was gone, the door slammed after her. She took a taxi to Annick's flat and stormed up the stairs.

'My goodness gracious, Roz, whatever is it? What is the matter?'

'Nothing! Everything!'

'Have a drink. Tell me.'

'Thank you. I'll have a brandy.'

'Before lunch! This must be bad.'

'Oh, it isn't really, I suppose,' said Roz, sinking into Annick's deep leather armchair with a hugh sigh. 'It's the old story. I want to marry someone and he doesn't want to marry me.'

'Not – not Michael Browning?'

'Oh, no,' said Roz, with a wry grin. 'He wanted to marry me. It's ironic, isn't it, Annick? He would have married me and it would have been disastrous for me. This one would work, and he won't. And I don't know what to do.'

'Forget him,' said Annick. 'There is no point in marrying someone who is not right for you.'

'I think he is, though, that's the point.'

'Well, *chérie*, even if he is you can't force him. And besides, Roz, why are you in such a hurry to get married? It is not so very long since you finished with Michael. You have your career. I don't understand.'

'I don't quite myself,' said Roz slowly. 'I only know I really really want to be married. I want to be wanted, and I want everyone to know I'm wanted. A lot of people thought Michael ended our relationship. I don't like that. And I'm afraid of being alone. Ever since Michael I've been afraid of being alone.'

'And your career?'

'Oh, that's no problem. Of course I want my career. But I want to be married too. I want it all, Annick. We all do, our generation. Don't you?'

'Perhaps.'

'Oh Annick, what am I going to do? How am I going to persuade him?'

'I don't know, *chérie*. Truly. After all, the good old days when women trapped men are gone, are they not?'

'How do you mean?'

'By becoming pregnant. *Mon Dieu*, how many men got caught like that. But not any more. And what a disastrous beginning for the marriage anyway. Now, have another glass of brandy, Roz, and tell yourself there are other pebbles in the river, or whatever it is you say.'

'Fish in the sea,' said Roz slowly. 'Thank you, Annick. Good advice. You're right, of course.'

She went back to the hotel that night and found C. J. had checked out. She was not over-bothered. She had a little time. Back in London she sought him out after a few days, apologized for making a fool of herself, and said they might as well be friends. Loving friends. C. J., relieved to see a peaceful end to the conflict, agreed. Within ten days she had seduced him again. After a month, they were back where they had been

– passionate lovers – with the difference that Roz confided in her father about the relationship.

'You won't believe this, Daddy. But we really really get on.'

'Darling, I'm delighted. Surprised. But delighted. My oldest friend's son. It's charming. I suppose I shouldn't be encouraging my daughter in an irregular relationship, but I'm so fond of C. J. and I know he'll take care of you.'

'Don't say anything to him, will you? He's so shy.'

'Of course not. But it is very nice news indeed. What delightful hands I am finding my company in.'

Roz had correctly anticipated her father's pleasure; but she had not quite thought through how deeply her future in the company might be affected by a marriage to C. J. The two of them – or rather the one of them, she thought wrily – could make an uncontested takeover for the whole thing in the fullness of time. Her father was sixty-two. He couldn't go on for ever. Any fear that somebody might emerge – the spectre of a son being born to Camilla, or indeed anybody, was receding steadily these days, thank God – would be greatly diminished if Julian's only child – she wondered idly, occasionally, why he always referred to her as his only daughter – was married to the son of his oldest friend and that son already a proven asset to the company. Roz smiled to herself over the glass of champagne her father had poured her. How very nicely everything would be working out.

Three weeks later they were having a lazy Sunday breakfast in C. J.'s flat in Primrose Hill when Roz put down the *Sunday Times* and looked at him just slightly nervously.

'C. J.,' she said, 'I have a tiny problem.'

'What's that?' said C. J. He was learning to be wary of her. 'Can I help?'

'I don't know. Probably not.' She paused and took a sip of coffee. 'My period's rather late.'

C. J. looked at her intently and rather oddly and put down his newspaper.

'What do you mean?'

'What I say. My period's rather late. Ten days, actually. What do you think?'

'I don't know,' said C. J. 'I don't know what I think. Or I hope I don't. Is it often late?'

'Well – sometimes. Not often. Bit worrying, isn't it?'

'I thought you were on the pill.'

'I am. But it's a low-dosage one and you do have to be terribly careful about not forgetting. Even taking it at the same time each day. Maybe I slipped up. I don't think I did, but I might have.'

'How do you feel?'

'Fine. Perfectly fine. Although –'

'Yes?'

'Well the only thing is, I'm terribly hungry all the time. But I certainly don't feel sick or anything like that. Oh, don't look so worried, C. J. I'm sure it's nothing. If it hasn't arrived by Friday I'll have a test done. Now let's get dressed and go for a walk or something. Don't you want to go and explore Spitalfields, or somewhere equally exotic?'

'What? Oh, no, it doesn't matter,' said C. J. absently.

'Well, anyway, you choose. I don't mind where we go.'

Coming out of the shower, she looked at C. J. He was staring out of the window, his face blank and white, his eyes somehow sunk into his face, darker than ever and full of fear.

The Connection Eight

Los Angeles and Nassau, 1981–82

'I just can't stand this any longer, Miles,' said Mrs Kelly. 'Either you get yourself a proper job or I'll tell the police about all that dope you're smokin'.'

Miles looked at her across the table and smiled his enchanting, irresistible smile.

'You wouldn't, Granny Kelly. I know you wouldn't. You couldn't.'

'I would and I could.'

'But you'd have to prove it. How would you do that? You'd

have to bring them down to the beach, or up to my room, and watch them catch me in the act.'

'I'd be prepared to do that. For your greater good.'

Miles smiled again. 'I just don't believe it. I just don't believe you'd come marching down to the beach with the law in tow and say, "Look, officer, there he is, that's my grandson, and he's smoking a joint right now." '

'Miles, I would.'

'Then I shall have to keep a very careful eye open for you.' He got up, kissed her fondly and walked towards the door.

'Where are you going, Miles?'

'To the beach. Where else? With a positive mountain of grass.'

'Miles, please come back. Please let's talk about it. It's not just the dope. I'm scared you're going to get on to stronger stuff. You're throwing your life away, Miles, and I just can't bear to see it.'

'Granny, I promise you I never touch anything else. Ever. I don't need it.'

'That's what they all say.'

'I know. And OK, maybe a couple of the guys take the odd snort. But not a lot of it. And certainly not me. I can't afford it. Now stop fretting.'

She looked at him as he stood there, leaning gracefully against the door frame. Whatever he was doing, he managed to look as if he was posing for a photograph in some glossy magazine, and yet it was entirely unself-conscious. His great beauty was like a present that he didn't really want, something he was very mildly pleased to have been given, and then put carelessly aside, unused. And yet it was not wasted, was not really unused at all; it opened doors for Miles, that beauty, made him welcome, sought after, everywhere he went. Women fell in love with it; and because of its singular nature, it did not repel men either, it lent Miles desirability. On a man with ambition it would have been dangerous; on Miles with his complete lack of concern for any kind of a future it was in safe keeping. He was now twenty-three, tall, a little over six foot two; his golden-blond hair hung over his narrow shoulders and halfway down his back; he was slim, but not thin, not gangly, and quite fine boned, with a long graceful neck and a

439

beautifully shaped head. He had a high, sloping forehead and a perfectly straight nose with very slightly flaring nostrils. His eyes were exceptional, dark, dark blue, flecked with brown, and his lashes so extravagantly long that women became irritated just contemplating them. But it was his smile that made his looks exceptional, and that saved them from the cliché: it was sweet, his smile and all embracing, but it also contained much humour and, above all, just a touch of self-mockery. You felt when you saw it, that smile, that you were part of a conspiracy, taken inside a charmed world; that you knew its owner and you liked him, and that he was anxious that you should not think he cared in the very least about how he looked or whether you might care either. He was constantly being approached by the photographers who came to Malibu, shooting fashion spreads or advertisements or commercials, to model for them; he had been asked not once but three times by movie people who had (in the way of all the best Hollywood fairy stories) watched him as he filled their cars, delivered their groceries, simply walked along Sunset with his swinging rangy grace, to come and test; several friends of the Tylers had suggested he go to castings for this and that film; but to them all he threw his most brilliant regretful smile and said that was really nice of them, and he was really really flattered, but he had no wish to be a model, and the film business did not interest him, and he was actually much happier doing what he did.

Which was almost absolutely nothing.

It was eighteen months now since he had graduated; after his first angry outburst he had relaxed into a lazy contentment. He no longer saw Joanna; as far as Mrs Kelly could make out he didn't see any girls at all. Or certainly not committedly. There were girls at the beach parties in the evening, but they were hangers on, they came and went, none of them were part of the surfing community, Miles brought none of them home. She felt sometimes that even if he could get committed to sex that would be better than nothing, and then she hastily stifled the thought and told herself that at least he was doing no harm the way he was.

Apart from the dope smoking, he seemed to be leading a blameless life. He never asked her for money; he wouldn't take any money from anybody. When he needed some, which wasn't very often, he earned it. He was strangely easy to live with; when she wasn't feeling irritated by his idleness, the wastage of his life, she couldn't help enjoying him and his relaxed, good-natured company. He spent many evenings just swinging lazily on the seat out on the lawn of the house high above the ocean, talking to her about anything that happened to engage him at the time, asking her opinion on things, listening carefully and consideringly to her answers; he did not exactly challenge her views, that would have been too exacting for his philosophy of minimum intellectual effort, but he would gaze at her from the depths of his blue eyes and say, 'Do you really really think that's right?' and she would say, nettled, 'Yes, yes I really do,' and he would raise his eyebrows mildly and smile at her, and shrug and resume his survey of the evening sky; and she would find herself against her will challenging her own views. He was kind to her, and thoughtful; he never stayed out late without telling her, he was almost always home to dinner, he brought her occasional presents, he took her for drives into Santa Monica. He did the marketing, and he did the garden; he stopped short of the housework or the cooking, but he would mend and fix things for her if she asked him. And he often told her she was the only person who had never let him down.

'Now Miles, that is ridiculous,' she had said, the first time he voiced this opinion. 'Joanna didn't let you down, the Tylers didn't let you down, Mr Dashwood didn't let you down when you got busted that time, and your parents both died, God help them, that isn't letting you down. How can you even think such a thing?'

And he had looked at her very seriously for quite a long time, and said that maybe they hadn't been able to help dying, although since his father had committed suicide even that was arguable, but the fact remained he had been left all alone when he was very young, to manage as best he could; that Joanna had not understood how he had felt about Dashwood's betrayal as he saw it, and that then she had tried to push and mould him into her own pattern, which was letting him down as he saw it; that the Tylers had done the same thing; and that as for Dashwood, all he had ever done was write a few cheques, and that they came pretty cheap.

'Miles, how can you say that, when all these years Mr

Dashwood has taken so much interest in you, visited you, encouraged you to make something of your life?'

'All he did,' said Miles, his eyes distant, 'was turn me into some kind of hobby. When it began to turn into hard work, he was gone.'

'Well, I don't see it like that.'

'Don't you, Granny? Ah well.'

And the subject, like so many, many others, was closed.

It was a year now since Hugo had visited them; he wrote frequently to Mrs Kelly impressing upon her that she must ask him for help if it seemed that he could give it, inquiring after Miles' progress (and, when the progress became clearly non-existent, his welfare), offering him constantly a large allowance the day he went out and got a job, and making sure that the regular payments into Mrs Kelly's bank accounts were kept up and that she was using them. But personal visits were too painful; Miles simply now went out. The last exchange between them had been ugly; Hugo had begun with coercion, and then moves to bribery and even threats (of withdrawing financial support entirely) in his attempts to make Miles use his education and his qualifications.

'I want to feel proud of you, Miles. Is that so much to ask?'

Miles had stood up, looked down at Hugo, an expression of absolute disdain on his face, and said, 'What right do you have to feel proud of me?' and walked out of the room.

One of Mrs Kelly's only confidants in her anxiety was the old priest from St Monica's, Father Kennedy. He had long since retired from the active administration of his church, and spent his days in the pastoral care of the long line of vagrants, homeless, single-parent families, alcoholics and drug addicts who came to the refuge he ran with the help of volunteers, students and the occasional rich widow anxious to reserve for herself a guaranteed corner in the kingdom of Heaven.

Mrs Kelly, who saw no reason to doubt that there would be a corner for her, after the requisite and hopefully short time in Purgatory, nevertheless worked at the refuge from time to time, out of the goodness of her heart, and indeed passed on the occasional percentage of the allowance made her by Hugo Dashwood when Father Kennedy, or rather one of his vagrants or their families, was in particular difficulties. She liked the atmosphere of the refuge, the strange marriage of earnest endeavour and fecklessness that existed behind its crumbling, peeling, walls; she was fond of many of the regular inmates who regarded it as almost as a permanent home, particularly the half-crazed but perfectly harmless drunks; and she enjoyed talking to Father Kennedy, who remembered Lee so fondly, and who had shared with the rest of them such high hopes for Miles.

Initially, when Miles had taken to the beach he had urged silence, counselled patience: 'He's a clever young man, Mrs Kelly, he will grow tired of the life.' But now, going on for two years later, he had to admit that the situation was becoming serious. 'It's a terrible thing to see such cleverness going to waste. And he is such a charming and such a personable young man. I can understand you feeling distressed. Your friend Mr Dashwood, now, is he unable to persuade Miles to take life a little more seriously?'

'Oh,' said Mrs Kelly grimly, 'quite unable. The least likely, Father. As I told you, Miles feels very strongly that he should have given him a job in one of his companies, he is a rich man – and to be honest, I can't quite see why he couldn't. But now it's become a matter of principle, and I don't blame him one bit. But Miles won't even see him, just walks out of the house. Mr Dashwood hasn't been to see us for a while now, and quite frankly I'm relieved. I feel I can't ask him for any more help, or even look him in the eye. It makes me feel just terrible to see that boy turn his back on him, after all he's done, and it's so out of character too, he's a charmer is Miles, even though he is so idle. But you can take a horse to water, Father, as you yourself know, and then it's up to the nag itself whether or not it takes a drink.'

'Indeed,' said Father Kennedy with a sigh, looking at his flock, who were so extremely eager most of them to take as many drinks as possible. 'There is nothing you can do when a strong will is pitted against you. But the boy is young, Mrs Kelly, there is time.'

'I don't know that there is,' said Mrs Kelly. 'Every day that passes he gets more settled, more happy with his life. And then it's the drugs. Father, he smokes marijuana all the time. Sooner or later there'll be trouble with the police, and you know he has a record already. And I'm so afraid he will turn to other stuff, to cocaine. He says some of the boys are taking it. I don't know what to do.'

'Can't you threaten him with the police if he doesn't stop?'

'I've tried. He says I'd never do it. He might be right. I'd certainly find it hard.'

'I think you should, Mrs Kelly. For his own sake, I think you have to do it.'

'Father,' said Mrs Kelly, 'could you shop your own grandson?'

'Mrs Kelly,' said the old man, 'these days I feel I could do anything to anyone, to save them from the dangers of these terrible things. And you're right, it won't stop at the joints. It will lead to the other stuff. And the police are tightening up their controls all the time. The boy will end up in jail. I would urge you very strongly to take the necessary steps. I will support you if you need me to.'

'Thank you, Father. I'll think about it.'

She did think about it, long and hard, and rejected, as Miles had known she would, any idea of shopping him to the police. Pride and embarrassment prevented her from bothering Hugo Dashwood. But she continued to worry at the problem night and day, like a hungry old dog with an overchewed bone. And in the end, she came up with a solution.

'Miles, I think we should move.'

'Granny Kelly, whatever for? Wherever to? You know I like it here. You know you like it here.'

'I don't like it that much, Miles. I've never made friends. I've never felt at home. Not really.'

'You have me. I'm your friend.'

'I know that, Miles, but you'd be mighty big-headed if you thought that was enough.'

He sighed, and smiled at her regretfully. 'I guess you're right. I'm sorry. But I really don't want to move.'

'I do. And maybe it's my turn.'

'Well, you could go and I could stay.'

'No, Miles, I want you to come with me.'

'Granny, I'm twenty-three. I can go – or stay – where I like.' He was smiling, but there was an edge to his voice.

'I know that, Miles. But I think you owe me something. Some loyalty. Some return.'

He was silent for a while. Then: 'Well, maybe. Where did you think of going?'

'The Bahamas.'

'The Bahamas! Why there?'

'I have an old friend there. In Nassau. I had a letter for her six months ago. She has a big house, it's beautiful Miles, you'd like it. She lives alone, and she's lonely. She suggested I went and stayed with her for a while. I didn't want to, because I didn't want to leave you. But I think I will. For a week or so at least, just to see if I like it. I asked her how she'd feel about us moving there and she said she thought it would work out real fine.'

'For you and her maybe. Not me.'

'Why not?'

'Granny Kelly, you know why not. I like it here. There's no surf in the Bahamas. I wouldn't know what to do.'

'You could get a job.'

'I could not get a job. I don't want to get a job.'

'Miles, have you never wondered what we really live on?'

'Well, you have some money, from my mom's insurance – my dad's, rather. And the house. And I bring in enough for food.'

'Yes, that's true. But if I chose to withdraw it from you I could. And you'd get pretty hungry and uncomfortable pretty fast.'

He went over to her and kissed her. 'You wouldn't do that to me. You wouldn't want me to be hungry and uncomfortable.'

'I just might. I'm pretty tired of being uncomfortable myself. I don't really like this climate that much. And I'm lonely, like I said.'

Miles sighed. 'I'm sorry you're lonely. It was really bad of me not to realize. I'll try to come home more.'

'Miles, I don't want you to come home more. I want friends of my own. Now I think we could have a good life in Nassau. It's a great city. I've been reading about it. There would be opportunities for you.'

'I don't want opportunities.'

'I know that, Miles. But I want them for you. Think about it. Please.'

'All right, Granny. I'll think.'
Thinking was cheap.

Partly out of a sense of guilt about his grandmother's
loneliness, partly out of a wish to make her think he was indeed
giving consideration to her plan, Miles stayed home next day
and dug the garden. The surf was virtually flat anyway.
Towards evening he took the truck and drove it down to the
beach to see his friends and say he'd be along next day. The
beach was swarming with police. He drove home again
thoughtfully.

Later that night two officers from the Los Angeles drug
squad called at the house. Miles went to the door.

'Evening, sir,' said one of them, a thickset, bullnecked man
with shifty, darting black eyes. 'Are you on your own here?'

'Good evening, Sergeant. No, I'm not. My grandmother's
here. She lives with me.'

'Could we come in?'

'Why?'

'We have reason to believe you may have drugs on the
premises.'

'Now what leads you to that line of reasoning, officer?'

'Those guys on the beach. Your friends.'

'Some friends,' said Miles lightly. 'Do you have a warrant?'

'We certainly do.'

'OK. You'd better come in.'

Mrs Kelly appeared from the kitchen wiping her hands on
her apron.

'Miles, what is it?'

'These gentlemen feel we may have drugs in the house,
Granny. Do you have a stack anywhere? I certainly don't.'

'This is not a laughing matter, sir,' said the sergeant with a
look of such menace that even Miles felt a heaving shudder
somewhere in the region of his bowels. 'You do have a police
record, Wilburn, you were convicted and fined over a drug
offence, as I am sure you will remember, and your friends did
lead us to believe, quite strongly, that you have drugs in your
house.'

'OK,' said Miles. 'Go ahead. You won't find anything.'

They started in his room, and wrecked it; they ripped open

pillows, quilts, curtains; they tore out drawers, tipped out cupboards, threw books, clothes, tapes, records on to the floor. They moved into the bathroom, emptied the linen closet, the dirty-clothes basket, tipped the entire contents of the medicine cupboard into a plastic bag.

Mrs Kelly, who had been watching half frightened until then, looked at them fiercely. 'You just watch what you're doing with that. There's things in there I need. All the time.'

'Are there now, ma'am? And what kind of things would that be?'

'My laxatives,' said Mrs Kelly firmly. 'Doctor Forsythe will have a great deal to say to you if I get bunged up again now. Nearly two weeks I went last time, and it was real bad, agony I was in, had to have an enema to shift it and I'm telling you I shall tell him you're personally responsible if it happens again. Which it will,' she added darkly.

The sergeant looked at her, and reluctantly opened the plastic bag again.

'Thank you,' she said. 'Now perhaps you'd be kind enough to help me sort them out as you've muddled everything up so badly. There's a packet of suppositories as well, which I also have to have with me all the time, so you can keep an eye open for them too.'

Miles hurriedly left the room.

But it was a small triumph, and one she paid dearly for, for they went through her room too, taking her mattress up, her curtains down, rummaging through her underwear drawers, tipping her jewellery box out on the bed. They cleared the kitchen too, every drawer, every cupboard, and then turned their attention to the living room, taking up every cushion on every chair, and turning out her beloved china collection from the corner cupboard on to the floor with a reckless, deliberate carelessness. When they had finished, and gone through every box and case and old jar in the garage too, taken the seats out of the car, the saddle off Miles' bike, they looked at the two of them with an expression of odd suppressed anger.

'Well, there doesn't seem to be anything. We might come back. Would you like us to clear up for you a bit now?'

'No,' said Mrs Kelly. 'I wouldn't fancy your clearing up. Just go.'

She was stiff-backed and tight-lipped until the car had vanished down the hill; then she suddenly collapsed on to one of the cushionless chairs, her eyes frightened and full of tears.

'Granny Kelly, don't,' said Miles, taking her in his arms. 'I'm so sorry. So terribly sorry.'

'But Miles, did you have any? Where had you put it?'

'Yeah, I had some hash. I put it down the toilet. That was all, though. They were looking for coke, but they'd have been really pleased to find the grass. It would have done them for now . . .'

'When did you do that? Why?'

'This afternoon. I saw them on the beach. I thought they might come.'

'Oh, Miles.'

'The bastards,' he said, in a sick quiet anger, 'the bastards.'

'They are, Miles, the police. They are pigs.'

'I don't mean the cops. I mean my friends. My friends, shopping me. How could they do that to me? After all we've been to one another? How could they?'

'I don't know, Miles.'

'You see. Everyone lets you down in the end. Lets me down, anyway.'

He looked down at her and kissed her wrinkled, sunburnt old forehead. 'Except you. What a performance, Granny. You were great. You made it almost worth it.'

'Not quite, though.'

'No.' He was silent for a while, looking at the mess. Thinking.

'Maybe,' he said slowly, 'maybe we should think seriously about going to Nassau.'

Nassau didn't suit Miles. He felt lonely, bored, hemmed in. He couldn't believe he could have been stupid enough to agree to come. He spent most of his days wandering through the back streets and the markets, wondering how he could escape back to California. It didn't seem on the face of it terribly easy.

They had left quite quickly, and very quietly. Only Father Kennedy had been informed of their destination, and that in the vaguest possible terms. Mrs Kelly had not sold the house or even put it on the market, simply put anything under covers and locked it up; she said she didn't feel it was really hers to sell, and that one day maybe she might want to go back. Miles had said that now he was over twenty-one wasn't it his, but she said no, Mr Dashwood had bought it for her, it was in her name, and there was no way she was letting Miles get his idle hands on it.

'And besides,' she said tartly, 'I wouldn't have thought you'd want to taint yourself with anything provided by Mr Dashwood, Miles Wilburn.'

Miles had shrugged. 'Maybe not.'

He had never gone back to the beach; he couldn't. The betrayal went deeper than that of friend by friend; it was brotherhood by brotherhood, the brutal denial of a whole, lovely, lifestyle. He could not believe that the fellowship, and what seemed to him the inherent goodness of life on the beach, could have been hacked to death in five brutal minutes by a load of cops, and that a dozen or so close brothers under the sunburnt skin could sell him down the river for nothing more than the half-baked promise of a more lenient sentence, a lower fine. He felt more than hurt; he was sickened. He had lost faith, trust; he didn't know where to go or what to do. And Nassau, suddenly, had seemed as good as anywhere – from a distance.

Flying in late one November afternoon, stepping out of the plane into the warm windy air, looking at the black faces everywhere, hearing their sing-song voices, discovering immediately a way of life that made California seem urgent and aggressive, he had felt briefly intrigued and charmed. Mrs Kelly's friend, Marcia Galbraith, had sent her car for them, driven by Little Ed, her chauffeur; Little Ed was six foot five tall and going on as wide; the name had been bestowed upon him by his father, Big Ed, who had been driver to Marcia's father until he died at the age of eighty-three. Little Ed was now sixty-seven. He took them on a brief tour of Old Nassau before delivering them to Mrs Galbraith's mansion; Miles and Mrs Kelly, looking out at the grand, colonial-style white and pink houses, the policemen in their banana-republic white uniforms with their pith helmets and gold braid, the tourists driven about in the open horse carriages, felt they had come to a new and romantic country and smiled happily at one another.

Inside the Galbraith mansion, hidden behind high walls near

the centre of the town, Mrs Galbraith waited for them, with afternoon tea.

It came served in a silver tea set and brought in by Little Ed's wife, Larissa. They sat in the shabbily grand drawing room filled with ornate furniture and painted cabinets, gilt chairs, overlooking a cool, shady garden, all palm leaves and extravagantly flowering shrubs, fluttering with small, brilliant birds, and drank china tea and nibbled wafer-thin cucumber sandwiches; later Marcia Galbraith showed them their rooms, equally shabby, equally grand, both with verandas set with rocking chairs, looking over the garden; they had big high beds, with posts and tapestries, horribly lumpy, piled with old, worn, chintz quilts; the walls were hung with portraits of Galbraith ancestors, and above their heads whirring fans with whirling arms shot the hot air round and round the room. The whole place had a strange, dreamlike quality; Miles felt as if he was watching a film or reading a book, and half expected it all to vanish and to find himself safely back in the house on Montego Canyon. Dinner would be at seven, said Marcia, no need to dress tonight, as they were tired; Miles went out for a walk and found himself near the water, looking at the high bridge over to Paradise Island and the modern, skyscraping buildings, and wondered what he would find to do here, to pass his days.

Dinner, served by Larissa, four courses, each separated from the last by a ritual with finger bowls and glasses of iced water to clear their palates, was tedious and endless; Marcia, who proved to be a little more than slightly senile, reminisced about her days in the last war when the Windsors had been resident at Government House, and she and her husband St George Galbraith had been frequent guests, and she had helped the Duchess – 'So charming, so very very kind' – with her Red Cross work. Miles and Mrs Kelly went early to bed.

But over the days that followed, Mrs Kelly settled down, settled in, began with astonishing speed to pick up her old friend's affectations, lethargic accent, ladylike ways. She bossed Larissa about, took up petit point, and went out shopping and exchanged her rather sexless, shapeless clothes for some girlishly flowing skirts and lacy blouses. She also managed to persuade Little Ed that some hens would be a useful addition to the household and could be kept at the bottom of the exotic garden.

'I feel,' she said happily to Miles, rocking a little too vigorously for a true lady, on her veranda after lunch one day, 'that I have come home.'

Miles kissed her hand, which seemed appropriate under the circumstances, and smiled down at her. 'Good,' he said.

After a few days, wretched with inactivity, he crossed the bridge and spent the day on Paradise Island. He sat on the silvery white beach and looked at the sea, so much greener than its Californian counterpart, so still, so dull, it seemed to him; he looked at the hotels, stacked one upon each other, with no breathing space between, he studied the people, the tourists, who looked mostly so rich and so old, and thought he had never been so lonely, or so unhappy. Later, he found there was more to like; but that day he was in despair.

Miles had never been bored. When he had been a small boy he had had his skate board and his bike, and the beach; when he had been grown up he had had his surf board and the beach; those things had filled his days, and he had never asked more of life. Now suddenly there were these long, achingly dull hours to fill. There were things that intrigued him, but they cost money, and he had none. He would have liked to ride the water bikes that skimmed across the greeny blue water like so many triumphant flying fish, but the hire fee was sixty dollars an hour. He was fascinated by the flashy gambling halls in places like the Nassau Beach Hotel, so big you could hardly see from one side across to the other, where you could fling pocketfuls of change into the fruit machines, or sit down to a serious game of craps, or play the roulette wheel – but he never won, and the little money he took there was gone in minutes. He liked the look of the younger women he saw sometimes, driving their stretch limos in and out of the hotels, and the hyper-smart Ocean Club, rich, sleek, glossy, not unlike the ladies who shopped on Rodeo Drive, and yet somehow in some strange way different, more restless-looking, less American, bored, sybaritic. They would always notice him, often smile, as he passed, but he could see no future in them, except maybe a highly risky one, and he had had enough of danger for now.

And Nassau was a dangerous place. You could feel it in the air. Beneath the surface of the old gentility and the new money, humming beguilingly in the warm air, lurking behind the huge smiles, the easy manners of the people on the streets, was a sense of crime. This was not a law-abiding place. The drugs industry was thriving; Miles had heard it said that up to seventy per cent of the money changing hands came from it. Drug-related crimes – robbery, murder, prostitution – throbbed in the arteries of the city.

And yet side by side with that was a lovely innocence. In the markets, where you could beat anyone down from ten dollars to fifty cents without a great deal of difficulty, the gospellers sang to themselves all day; women and children sat and gossiped and played the hours away; the old people were kind, generous, caring. In the Old Town the shops were modest, almost villagey; and there was a grace, a charm to life there that took a hold, quite without his realizing it, of Miles' heart. And so, for six months, he waited, not quite unhappy, but not happy either, watching his grandmother descend into delusions of gentility, and thence, in the company of her friend, senility, and wondered what on earth was going to happen to him.

And then he met Billy.

Billy de Launay was the son of Nassau gentry; his father was in the civil service, his mother had grown up in the Windsors' court, as a child. Billy had been sent to Hampden Sydney, where he had with great difficulty just mustered a pass in American History and was now home again, 'resting' as he put it to Miles, before he decided on a career worthy of his education and intelligence. It wasn't easy to find. Billy was not unlike Miles to look at, being blond and blue eyed; he did not have Miles' outstanding good looks, but he was very prepossessing nonetheless, with the old-fashioned slightly fey charm of his background and upbringing.

He and Miles met at a lunch party, given by the de Launays, to which Marcia Galbraith had been invited and to which she insisted on bringing her old friend and her old friend's grandson; the old ladies were both dressed in outlandish creations of flouncing lace, and carrying parasols, Miles good-naturedly out of character in white flannels and a navy blazer.

Billy de Launay came up to him, smiling broadly, and held out his hand. 'Hi. I'm Billy de Launay, you must be Miles Wilburn. I've been hoping you'd come. I'm just about starved to death of company here. Can I get you a drink?'

'Sure,' said Miles, smiling back at him.

'Bloody?'

'I beg your pardon?'

'Bloody. Sorry, Bloody Mary,' said Billy, wondering how anyone could have got this far in life and indeed to a party at his parents' house without knowing what a Bloody was. 'Vodka and tomato juice. OK?'

'Oh, yes, sure,' said Miles, smiling. 'Sorry. Love one. Thanks.'

'How are you enjoying Nassau?' asked Billy, detaching two Bloodies from the tray passing him and handing one to Miles. 'Having fun?'

'Not a lot,' said Miles, and then realizing this must sound rude, hastily added, 'I mean, in Nassau generally. This is a great party.'

'I don't think I'd go that far,' said Billy, laughing. 'We're a trifle short of young blood in Nassau. What do you do, or what are you going to do?'

'Don't know,' said Miles cautiously. 'I'm – waiting and seeing a bit.' He smiled his glorious smile at Billy. 'I think I have plenty of time.'

'You do,' said Billy, responding to this philosophy with gratitude and pleasure. 'We both do. Plenty. I keep telling Daddy there is absolutely no rush, that it's crazy to go into something I'm not sure about just for the sake of getting into order, but he doesn't see it that way.'

'None of them do,' said Miles, recovering swiftly from the cultural shock of hearing a six-foot twenty-three-year-old refer to his father as Daddy; Ivy League talk he supposed. 'They all feel we should follow them on to the conveyor belt the minute we're out of college and stay on it till we drop off. I think there has to be more to life than that.'

'Me too,' said Billy, beaming delightedly at him. 'Here, have another Bloody.'

'Thanks.'

'Where did you go to college?'

'Berkeley.'

'Uh-huh. What did you major in?'

'Math.'

'God!' Billy's gaze was respectful. 'And how did you graduate?'

'Oh,' said Miles with a shrug. 'Summa cum laude.'

'Jesus! Why hasn't some bank snapped you up?'

'I didn't want it to.'

'Did you even try?'

'Nope!'

'Good man! Your parents are dead, aren't they?'

'Yeah.'

'I'm sorry. That must be – well – hard.'

'Not really. It was a long time ago. My gran brought me up.'

'Is she your guardian?'

'Yeah. And some old guy put me through college, he was a friend of my parents.'

'He sounds like a good guy.'

'Kind of,' said Miles briefly. 'I didn't really like him.'

'He must be kind of sick you're not using your education.'

'Yes,' said Miles with relish. 'I think he is.'

Billy, realizing there was more to this story than he was going to hear just now, dropped the subject.

'Met any girls here?'

'Haven't met anyone under eighty till today.'

'Well there are a few. Pretty damn dull, though. Not many game ones.'

'That's bad.'

'Yeah, it is. The talent is over on Paradise Island. The older ladies, you know. Divine.'

'I have seen a few.'

'Well, hell,' said Billy, 'you don't have to stop at looking. They're really hot, half of them. Married to rich old guys who can't get it up half the time.'

'Uh-huh.'

'Honestly Miles, you can get most of them, just with a smile. With your smile,' he added, without even a touch of envy, 'you could get all of them.'

Miles decided he liked Billy more and more.

'But how do you meet them?'

'Oh, it's easy. Just hang around. Round the pool at some of the hotels, that's a good place. Up in the Mirage Club.'

'Yeah, but how do you get into those places?'

'Oh, it's easy. You just walk in. Settle down. Look like you're staying there. Dress the part. Club tie, battered old tennis hat, that sort of thing. I'll show you. The club's harder. I actually have had to pull out of there, there's a funny old French guy who runs it, who wears a morning suit every day, he's really spaced, and he's got to know me. And then once you're there, they just come flocking. It's so easy. After that it's parallel parking all the way.'

'Sorry?'

'Parallel parking. Fired up. Sex. All the way. You know?'

'Oh, sure,' said Miles, laughing. 'I know.'

Billy laughed too. Miles might be just a bit of a dork, he obviously hadn't been anywhere too smart to school, and he seemed to be a bit slow on the uptake a lot of the time, but he was a really nice guy, and living almost next door. There was nothing socially that Billy felt he could not fix. Miles was clearly good-natured and a quick study; he could teach him all the right things to say and how to behave. It was all too good to be true. Life was obviously going to look up a lot.

It did. The boys had a marvellous time. Billy had been absolutely right, and (just as Miles had himself suspected) many of the rich, bored ladies were indeed all too ready to spill their sexual largesse over the bodies of two charming and totally available young men. What was more, Miles discovered, their innocence was considerably in their favour. Women of thirty-five, forty, forty-five, painstakingly tutored in every possible variation, legitimate or deviant, of sexual behaviour were delighted to find themselves in bed with near virginal material. Miles, experienced for the most part in the straightforward, if greedy, sexual appetites of college girls and the beach groupies, learnt a great deal very quickly; he became expert in the ways of the flesh he had never dreamt of. He became skilled in cunnilingus; he discovered a woman's anus to be capable of huge pleasure; he learnt to enjoy fellatio. He became masterly at delaying his own orgasm, at tormenting and teasing, at talking a woman into a state of intense excitement and then leaving her for an hour, maybe two, and then returning, his smile just a trifle more triumphant than usual. He and Billy both became favourites; the hall porters and doormen at the hotels, initially suspicious, hostile even, swiftly learnt that their tips from this or that beautiful, bored woman would grow considerably in size in exchange for a little cooperation in the front hall, over the internal telephone, a message delivered, or even delayed, an alarm raised, should the true provider of the tips return unexpectedly early from his golf course or his business meeting.

The · boys worked usually separately; and resisted any attempt to engage them in group sex, or troilism; and they also set themselves against any attempt to persuade them to indulge in anything that approached perversion, as they saw it. Many was the afternoon they fled as a result of being presented with whips, ropes, rubber, women's clothes. They had their standards, as they saw it, they maintained some semblance of innocence, and they were united in the view that once they had set out on that slightly dubious road, there was no way back.

The main trouble was, from Miles' point of view, there was still no financial advantage from his occupation. There was absolutely no way either he or Billy were actually going to take money for their activities; they saw the whole thing as a lark, as fun, as something to do, and there was no way either the ladies would have given them any. Having an entertaining time with some charming boy who was clearly from a good family was one thing; paying for the entertainment would have put a very different complexion on it.

The boys were constantly being given presents: ties, silk shirts, belts, wallets, all very nice and good accessories in their work, particularly when they were moving on from one liaison to the next, but that was all. Nevertheless Miles did occasionally wish some of the presents could be turned into cash. The occasional belt or wallet provided him with a few dollars, but the market value for such things was poor; one particularly rich and, it had to be said, plain, lady had given him a Cartier watch one afternoon, but it was something Miles could not bear to part with. He had (he was discovering, and encouraged by his social education at Billy's hands) a serious liking for beautiful and prestigious things, he wanted more and more of them, and he would rather go without spending money for a month (as he frequently did) than part with anything of lasting value. Nevertheless it was frustrating. Because their work, as they called it, left their evenings free, they both liked to go and gamble; Billy had a little money, which he was generous with, but it never seemed to last for more than an hour, even on a good evening, and besides Miles had his pride. He had tried to persuade Mrs Kelly to give him a bit more, but she was increasingly withdrawn into her new persona of genteel widow, along with her friend. She had aged a lot in the year they had been in Nassau; relieved of the strain of caring single handed for Miles, and worrying about his future, she had suddenly descended into confusion and delusion. And she was after all nearly eighty; she had had a lot to cope with. Miles, who genuinely loved her, and was truly grateful to her, did not want to intrude on her new happiness. He could wait. It was not after all, he felt, her problem. He was a young man of rare integrity, as Billy and he often agreed.

The solution to their monetary problems came from a rather unexpected source: the doorman at the Bahamian Palace, who had grown fond of them, and saw them in a rather benevolent light.

'You boys play tennis?' he asked them one day as they wandered out blinking slightly into the sunshine after a long afternoon's work in the shaded air conditioning of two of the hotel's finer suites.

'I do,' said Billy, 'played for Hampden. How about you, Miles?'

'A bit,' said Miles. 'I could remember. Why?'

'They need a new tennis pro here. I'd apply if I were you. Probably take on the two of you. It wouldn't interfere with your other occupation, I wouldn't imagine. Might even help it along a little bit.' He grinned and winked at them. 'Go and see the manager now. He's by the pool.'

Miles and Billy played a test game, charmed the manager, who was pleased with the notion of what was clearly some old money on his staff, and Billy got taken on immediately. Miles was told to go and polish up his game and then he might be allowed to work with his friend on busy days. Given his facility for sport, he was on the courts at the Bahamian Palace in three weeks.

They benefited in two ways: they had an income, albeit a modest one, and they were able, as the doorman had prophesied, to pursue their prey with greater and more graceful ease.

Billy's parents were initially unhappy with the arrangement, but swiftly came round to the view that any employment was better than none, and at least were relieved of continuing to make Billy his modest allowance, which in their straitened circumstances was a relief; and Mrs Kelly was almost speechless with delight at the news, as presented by Miles, that he was working as sports and social manager of one of the island's most prestigious hotels.

Miles, in possession of money for the first time in his life, felt strangely exhilarated. He had never properly made the connection between work and money; had not thought of getting a job as the route to worldly delights. In any case, worldly delights had never interested him before; the surf had come cheap. But sitting in the gilded air of the Palace, taking in heady whiffs of the rich aroma of real money, studying the women he was making love to, who somehow managed to look rich even naked, looking at their jewels, their clothes, feeling underneath his skin the sensation of silk sheets, savouring the almost sensual pleasure of good champagne, he felt a swiftly growing desire for more and more of it.

He changed his outward appearance; basing much of his style on Billy's he cut off his long hair, he bought himself suits, and shirts and ribbon belts, and knotted silk cufflinks, and loafers and some L. L. Bean's Norwegian pullovers, and a whole set of Lacoste sports shirts, and even, in a fit of strange sartorial madness, sent for some madras bermudas from Trimingham's. He looked superb, an outstanding example of money of the very oldest kind.

He had proved, as Billy had suspected, a talented student of the social school Billy put him through; he learnt all the right preppy phrases and words and behavioural attitudes; he changed his accent slightly from his Californian drawl to something he based more on Tigs' than Billy's own; he learnt to display the peculiar WASP-mannered brand of ennui rather than his own rather more ingenuous Californian laid-backness.

And yet he remained true to himself and his roots. He never lied about his background, never disowned Granny Kelly, never set aside his happiness and his loyalty to Samo High and his days on the beach. He became something interesting and unique: a carefully stylish, rich blend of old-money behaviour and modest philosophies. Put together with his looks, and his charm, and a genuine sweetness of disposition, he found hardly a door anywhere that would not open for him. For the first time in his life he felt a sense of anticipation. He wondered where he might find himself next.

Chapter Twelve

Bristol and London, 1982

On the day they were to meet, both Phaedria Blenheim and Julian Morell woke up feeling exceptionally irritable.

Phaedria switched off her alarm, sank back deep under her duvet, and explored the events of the day ahead for possible reasons. There was only one and it came to her very quickly. It had been her day off, and she had lost it; a day out hunting with the Avon Vale had been replaced with an as-yet-unconfirmed interview with some boring old fart of an industrialist.

'Why me?' she had said furiously to her editor the night before, shaking her head at the can of beer he was offering her. 'You know it's my day off, I'm going hunting. Jane'll be here, and she can do it every bit as well as me, probably better because she'll care. I won't. Please, Barry, please don't make me do it.'

'I'm sorry, Phaedria, but Jane can't do it every bit as well as you. I need you there tomorrow. It's important. And you might like to remember I pay you to care,' he added a trifle heavily.

'But why? What's so special? Some boring plastics company. What's in that for the Women's Page?'

'Its chairman.'

'Its chairman? Oh Barry, come off it. Since when did the chairman of a plastics company have anything interesting to say to women?'

'Not just plastics, Phaedria. Pharmaceuticals. And cosmetics. And department stores and hotels. Don't you ever read press releases?'

'Of course not.'

'Well, you should. Read this one and stop looking so bloody constipated and have a drink. Sit down. Go on.'

Phaedria glared at him, slung her coat down on his spare chair, took the can of beer from him and leant against the wall, skimming over the release:

Morell Pharmaceuticals to open Bristol Plant. For Immediate Release.

The multi-million worldwide Morell Pharmaceutical Chain opens its new plant, the most technologically advanced in Europe, in Bristol in two weeks' time. The plant which is situated on the Fishponds Estate incorporates a factory, and a marketing and sales division, a research laboratory and a Conference Centre. It has been designed to entirely new specifications incorporating the very latest technology.

The Chairman of Morell Pharmaceuticals, Sir Julian Morell, knighted for his services to industry in 1981, will be coming in person to officially open the plant and will give a conference to selected members of the press at the same time. An invitation is attached.

There was much more about Sir Julian's other business interests, his pharmaceutical work and its vast benefits to mankind in general, and those in the Third World in particular, the drugs he had launched (most notably one of the first low-dosage oral contraceptives ten years earlier) and his various extraordinarily well-deserved awards for services to industry. Phaedria read the release stony-faced and looked at Barry.

'Still can't see it. It sounds totally boring. I'm going hunting.'

'Phaedria, you are not going hunting. You're going to get an interview with Julian Morell.'

'Barry, for Christ's sake, it's a press conference. Every half-assed reporter for miles around will be there asking him the same half-assed questions.'

'I know that, darling. You're going to get an exclusive.'

'And what will be so big about that?'

'Phaedria, you ought to read the papers a bit more as well as the press releases. Julian Morell is a great character. And a great womanizer,' he added, 'and he hasn't given an interview for ten years. He's developed a phobia about the press.'

For the first time Phaedria's expression sharpened. She slithered down against the wall and sat on the floor, taking another can of beer from Barry.

'OK. Tell me about him.'

'More or less self-made. Impoverished second son of the upper classes. Well upper middle. Started with a tiny range of medicines, just after the war. Went into cosmetics. Then plastics, pharmaceuticals, paper. Department stores. That's probably the big one. Never heard of Circe?'

'Never.'

'Well, there isn't one in London – yet. But there's one in Paris and Milan and New York. And Beverly Hills, I expect. Very very expensive. Makes Harrods look like Marks and Spencer, that sort of thing. Oh, and there's a chain of hotels.'

'Called?'

'Called just Morell. Like – well, like – just Hilton. Anyway, he's made a billion or two.'

'And what about the women?'

'Well, he's only been married once. Can't remember who to. But there's been a lot of mistresses, all beautiful, and a lot of scandal. He's always in the gossip columns.'

'Barry, I didn't think you read the gossip columns,' said Phaedria, laughing.

'A good journalist reads everything in the other papers,' said Barry slightly pompously. 'You have to. You need to know what's going on. I'm always telling you that, Phaedria.'

'I know,' said Phaedria, 'I know I'm bad. I just can't be bothered half the time. I'm not really a journalist at all, I'm afraid. Not like you,' she added, getting up and patting his hand fondly. 'All right, you've intrigued me. I'll go. I shall continue to complain, but I'll go. Now, have you fixed the interview?'

'No. They turned it down. That's precisely why I want you to go. I reckon you'll get one.'

'Why?'

'You know damned well why. Don't play games with me. Now go home and get some beauty sleep. You're going to need it.'

'Thanks,' said Phaedria. 'All right, I'll try. But I want another day off instead. And you can send Jane to the Mayor's Banquet, OK?'

'OK.'

'Don't forget.'

'All right, Phaedria,' said Barry wearily, 'I won't forget.'

'You probably will. But I'm not going to do it anyway. Night, Barry.'

'Good night, Phaedria. See you tomorrow.'

'Perhaps. I might elope with Sir Julian and never come back.'

'OK, that's fine by me, you can elope with him if you like, but get the copy in first. Bye, darling.'

'Bye, Barry.'

Barry looked after her thoughtfully as she walked out through the newsroom. She had been with him two and a half years now on the *Bristol Echo*, and she drove him to distraction. She was everything he disapproved of in a woman and a reporter and yet he lived in dread of her leaving. She was a talented writer and a clever interviewer; she could persuade new thoughts and pronouncements out of anybody. The most over-done, rent-a-quote actor, the most cliché-ridden, party-lined politician suddenly, under the scrutiny and influence of Phaedria Blenheim, found an original line, an unpredictable view, which they read themselves with surprise and pleasure – and refreshed and invigorated their own tired battery of quotes with it for months to come.

She was also extremely beautiful, which was clearly another asset; she could persuade any man to talk to her and pour his heart out, and she had little compunction about publishing all kinds of intimate little confidences and details which had been made to her 'strictly off the record this, darling,' taking the view that any public figure who was fool enough to trust a journalist deserved absolutely anything he got.

On the other hand she was quite right when she said she

wasn't really a journalist. Her knowledge of the world was extremely scanty; she scarcely knew who the Home Secretary was, and certainly not who ran Russia or China, or even Ireland, and more unusually in a woman, who Prince Andrew's latest girlfriend was, or whether Elizabeth Taylor was marrying for the fifth or sixth time. She was actually far more interested in horses and hunting than seeing her name in ever-bigger by-lines; her job financed her horse and her riding (just); Barry knew, and was alternately irritated and amused by the knowledge that she also capitalized on his rather indulgent attitude towards her to get days off when she wanted to hunt or attend a race meeting.

But she filled her pages (he had made her woman's editor a year ago) with original and charming ideas, and always delivered the goods every week (even if they were dangerously close to deadline) and he knew it would be a hundred years before anyone as talented came the way of his paper again. And Barry Morgan would do anything, go through fire and water, endure death by a million cuts, if it was to benefit his beloved *Echo*. The paper gave him back a hundredfold all the work and heartache and care he put into it, and every week, as the first one came off the presses, he would take it and unfold it and look at it with a sense of pride and wonder and something else that was strongly akin to love.

Phaedria had been a complete novice, not a journalist at all, when she came to work for him as a temporary copy typist. He had been very taken with her straight away (apart from her ridiculous name, but she couldn't help that after all); he found her attractive, she had a lot of dark hair and large brown eyes, and a rather stylishly severe way of dressing, and she worked hard and late if necessary; but the day she really won his heart was when she came into his office one evening with a piece of copy in her hand and a determined look on her face.

'Mr Morgan, I was just wondering if you'd let me have a go at re-writing this.'

'And what makes you think it needs re-writing?'

'It's awful,' said Phaedria simply.

'And why should you be able to make it less awful?'

'I'm good at writing.'

'Oh, yes?'

'Yes.'

He met her eyes with a grudging respect and took the piece of paper from her hand. It was an account of a production of *The Mikado* and she was right. It was awful. He grinned at her.

'All right, Miss Blenheim. Have a go at it.'

She came back half an hour later with the copy re-written.

'It's a bit better now, I think. Here you are.'

It was actually a lot better. It brought the entire evening – the production, the music, the audience, absolutely to life. Barry looked at her thoughtfully.

'Have you got a job lined up after you leave here?'

'No.'

'What are you thinking of doing?'

'I don't know. My degree's in English. There's a lot of us about.'

'Where did you get it?'

'The degree? Somerville.'

'Ah.'

He had a deep mistrust of graduates, and of Oxbridge ones deeper than most. They weren't merely self-confident, they were arrogant. They generally expected to come in and start writing an arts column immediately, and to take a deputy editorship as an encore three months later. But Phaedria didn't seem too much like that. She was very self-confident, but it was the confidence of her background (upper to middle, he'd put it at) rather than the intellectual variety.

'Where did you go to school?'

'In London.'

'St Paul's, I suppose.'

'Well, yes.'

He liked the way she played it down.

'Why did you come here then?'

'Oh, I like newspapers and magazines. I was a reporter for the university paper. I edited my school magazine. But I'm not sure if it's what I want to do for the rest of my life.'

'What else are you interested in?'

'Fashion. I wondered about buying.'

'While you're wondering, how would you like to try a stint here?'

'What as? A typist?'

'Well, typist, cum dogsbody, cum very occasional junior reporter.'

'I certainly would. I'd love it. Thank you very much, Mr Morgan.'

'You won't earn much.'

'I don't care.'

'Good.'

She had very quickly stopped being a typist and a dogsbody, forgot about fashion buying and became a full-time reporter. She worked very hard, she didn't mind what she did, and she was nice to have around. She was a touch abrasive, and she knew her value, but it did not make her arrogant, she mixed in with the others, she learnt to drink and swear and swop filthy jokes, she became in short one of the blokes. And she was extremely happy.

Barry grew very fond of her; often, when everyone else had gone home, they would go to the pub and talk. She was a good listener; almost without realizing it he had told her everything about his marriage, his career, his love for the *Echo*, and his one great terror in life, which was retirement.

It was a long time before he found out much about her. It came out gradually in bits and pieces, tiny pieces of confidences spilled over just one too many beers, or in the intimacy born of working closely together long and late. She was an only child and she had looked after her father ever since she was ten years old, when her mother had run away to South America with his best friend and had never properly communicated with either her husband or her child again.

Augustus Blenheim was an academic, and earned his living lecturing in literature and writing biographies of virtually unknown writers; it was him that Phaedria had to thank for her name. 'No it isn't Phaedra,' she would say patiently, a hundred, a thousand times over the years, 'it's Phaedria. Different lady.'

And then she would explain (or perhaps not explain, according to her audience) that Phaedria was one of the characters in Spenser's *Faerie Queen*, and the personification of Wantonness; why any father, most people would wonder, while keeping their wonderings to themselves, should inflict upon his daughter so strong an association with such a quality was a

465

considerable mystery. But Phaedria did not seem to have held it against him; it was a pretty name, and she liked it, and besides she loved him so much she would have forgiven him far more, and much worse.

They had lived together, father and daughter, in the same small house in Chelsea all their lives; and Phaedria had come home from school every day with a mountain of homework and had shopped and cooked for him before settling down to it. At the weekends they did the housework together, went to the cinema, visited friends (mostly academic or literary colleagues of Augustus's), experimented with recipes, played chess and talked interminably. They were all the world to one another; it was a perfect marriage. Phaedria had few friends of her own age, and she was perfectly happy with her father's. Occasionally one of the less reticent women in their circle would tax Augustus with Phaedria's rather unconventional social life, or suggest to her that she went to more parties and perhaps even on holiday with her contemporaries, but they would both politely say that things were perfectly satisfactory as they were, and ignore any attempts to change anything. Nobody ever managed, or even tried, to come between them.

The effect on Phaedria of all this was complex. It made her fairly incapable of relating to any male very much under the age of her father; it matured her in some ways emotionally and retarded her in others. It made her self-reliant; it meant she was not daunted by any person, however brilliant or famous, or any situation, however difficult or challenging; it also ensured that she remained a virgin.

Even at Oxford, when she finally began to make friends with men who were her contemporaries, she found herself completely incapable of entering into a sexual relationship with any of them. Having missed out to a large degree on any kind of emotional education, having had no mother, sisters or even friends to talk to about sex or love, or how she might feel about anything very much, she grew up self-contained, and innocent. She learnt the facts about sex from school and books; she had to handle her first period, her early sensations of desire, and the transformation of her own body from child to woman, entirely alone.

She entered her third year at Oxford intacta, with a

reputation for being fun, funny, clever and beautiful and absolutely not worth even trying to get into bed. Men initially saw her as a challenge, but confronted by her patent lack of interest in the matter, gave up. Nevertheless, she was popular; she had a capacity to listen and a lack of self-interest that made both sexes pleased to have her friendship. But she remained, unknown even to herself, very lonely.

And then she had met Charles Fraser-Smith, the darling of the gossip columns, blond, tall, heavily built, a superb rugger and polo player and a brilliant classics scholar; what nobody at Oxford ever knew was that he was homosexual.

From the beginning the slight aura of apartness they both carried with them, their talent for communication, their physical attractiveness, their ability to listen, drew them together. They spent more and more time with one another. They drank, danced, talked and walked together; what began as a joky, raucous evening after a particularly triumphant rugger match became the closest of friendships. They liked the same things, the same places, the same people; they enjoyed the same food, the same books, the same jokes, the same films. If one was invited to a party, the other would arrive; if one refused, the other would not attend. Phaedria introduced Charles to cooking, he introduced her to horses. He kept two polo ponies and a hunter at livery just outside Oxford and he taught her to ride. She fell in love with horses with a passion she had never felt for any man, and became a brave and skilful rider with remarkable speed. They rode out together early most mornings, initially with Phaedria on the leading rein, later cantering easily beside him; it was another factor in their relationship and the delight they took in each other's company. Their taste, their humour, their friends, their opinions were always compatible, usually indistinguishable, and they enjoyed being with one another more than anything else in the world. To see them apart was a rarity; what nobody was quite sure about was whether they were actually lovers.

One night, in Charles' room six months into their relationship, over a bottle of gut-rotting beaujolais left over from a party the night before, he suddenly sighed and took Phaedria's hand. She snatched it away.

'Don't.'

'Why not?'

'Because I don't want to.'

'Phaedria, I'm only trying to hold your hand.'

'Yes, and then you'll try and kiss me and then you'll try and get my knickers off,' said Phaedria with a sigh.

'I won't. I swear.'

'Why not?'

'Ah! I think I detect just a smidgen of a note of indignation.'

'You certainly don't.'

'What then?'

'Just interest.'

'How arrogant of you! Just why should I wish to get your knickers off?'

'Not arrogant at all. But most people do, I'm very sorry to say.'

'Well I don't.'

'I can't tell you how pleased I am, Charles, but I still find it – well, a bit interesting.'

'That I don't want to?'

'Yes.'

'Do you want me to tell you? Really?'

'Yes. Yes. I do.'

Charles took a long draught of the beaujolais, grimaced and got up. 'I'll have to have something a bit better to drink before I can face this, I think. Hang on a bit.'

'Gracious!' said Phaedria. 'It must be serious.'

He turned to look at her, a bottle of whisky in his hand. 'It is.'

He sat down again by the fire, handed her a glass of whisky, took her hand again. 'Phaedria, can I really trust you? I have never told anyone before, ever. This is quite a moment.'

Phaedria looked at him, her face very composed, her dark eyes brilliant in the firelight. 'Charles, you know you can.'

'OK. Here we go. Phaedria, I am not as other men. I feel the love that dares not speak its name. I'm a poofter, my darling, a queer, a nancy boy. Now what do you think about that?'

'I think it's wonderful,' said Phaedria simply.

'Well,' he said, smiling rather shakily at her, 'oh, well, that's all right then. Good God. What a relief.' He was silent for a moment, gazing into his glass. 'Oh Phaedria, if you knew how I've dreaded telling you and how much I've longed to. I've nearly done it a dozen times and then been too afraid.'

'You fool!' said Phaedria. 'What on earth did you think I was going to do. Rush out of the room screaming? Have the vapours? Honestly, Charles, how insulting. You're my best friend. And I really do think it's wonderful.'

'Oh,' he said, taking her hand again and kissing it. 'I do adore you. It's you that's wonderful.'

'Yes,' said Phaedria, 'I am. Now tell me all about it.'

They sat there all night talking; he had heard of her childhood, now she heard of his; insensitive father, doting mother, beating at prep school, buggery at Eton, and finally delicious seduction by a French actor he had met on a train on his way back from the Dordogne.

'And now what do I do, Phaedria? Can't face women, can't face men.'

'Literally,' said Phaedria, and giggled.

'No, but should I admit it, or fight it and hope it'll go away?'

'Well, I shouldn't think there's much hope of that. I should own up if I were you, and go and find someone to love. There's no real disgrace to it any more, surely.'

'Oh, Phaedria, I think there is. What do you think my family would say? How would the illustrious firm of stockbrokers who have already committed themselves to taking me on react? What would Dempster make of it?'

'A lot. But it wouldn't do any harm here, surely. There's lots of them – you – jumping in and out of bed with each other.'

'I know. I can't stand that set, though. And it would do me quite a lot of harm, actually. The real world would hate it. And it wouldn't do my sporting career any good either. Would I get my rugger blue? Not a hope.'

'Well, you'll just have to keep quiet then,' said Phaedria. 'I certainly will.'

'I know you will. I think you're marvellous. I really really love you.' He poured the last dregs of the whisky bottle into her glass. 'Will you be my friend, Phaedria? For better for worse? For richer for poorer?'

'In sickness and in health, *pro homo et hetero*,' said Phaedria, holding out her arms. Charles crawled into them. They were both very drunk. They slept for what was left of the night on the floor in front of the fire, and in the morning she was seen leaving his room. Their reputations were made.

After that they more or less lived together. An engagement was assumed inevitable. They would lie peacefully together at night, totally unaroused by one another, laughing at the drama they were creating. And every so often Charles would disappear to London for a night and come back just slightly morose; Phaedria was indulgently amused.

Then one Saturday Phaedria had a fall from her horse. She wasn't seriously hurt, but she was mildly concussed; she was taken to hospital, X-rayed and sent home pale and shaken. Charles put her to bed, made her some soup, read to her, and then suggested he went to his own room.

'No,' said Phaedria miserably. 'I want you here. Please stay.'

Charles lay down very gently on the bed beside her and took her hand. He kissed her forehead and stroked her hair. He nestled closer towards her; she turned towards him and he took her in his arms. He kissed her very gently on the lips; she looked at him and touched his face and smiled.

'I love you so much,' she said.

'I love you too.'

'Kiss me again.'

He did.

Something shot through Phaedria, something fiery and delicious and achingly painful; something confusing and hungry; something vaguely remembered, something suppressed, something denied. She pressed further against Charles, turned his head, kissed him full on the lips.

'Charles,' she whispered, 'Charles.'

'Yes, Phaedria?'

'Charles, could you try to pretend I was a beautiful young boy?'

'No, Phaedria. But I could think you were my best, my most dearly beloved friend, and do what I can for you.'

'Would you?'

'I will.'

It wasn't really so very good. Inevitably Phaedria found it painful, and Charles lacked almost every kind of experience that she needed. But as he sank down into her, moving as gently and as tenderly as he could against her tension and her resistance, and as she relaxed and softened, and as he kissed her and explored her new, untravelled depths, she felt a stirring and a fluttering, very very faintly, that promised to grow and grow; and she began to move too, desperate for more, greedy, frantic. And then Charles shuddered and came, and the echoes faded, the feast she was reaching for receded, and he was helpless for her, and kissing her and saying he was sorry; and there were tears in his eyes.

'Don't,' said Phaedria, 'don't, you did so much, you showed me such a lot, it was so wrong of me to ask. Thank you.' And she fell asleep smiling.

When she woke up he was sitting by the window, looking at her, bleak and anxious.

'I'm so sorry,' he said again.

'Oh, for heaven's sake,' said Phaedria, restored to her normal self-confidence and spirit, 'do stop it, Charles. This is no time for a tragedy. We did jolly well. And just think,' she added, 'at least I'm not a virgin any more. We're lovers. Isn't that terrific? We've made everyone's dreams come true.'

They never made love again, and Phaedria had never made love with anyone else. But she had not forgotten the echoes and the hunger, and she supposed that one day she might find someone to satisfy it.

They came down from Oxford, Charles with a First, Phaedria with an Upper Second, and a great sense of sadness. They knew their time together was over; they would always be friends, and have a large place in one another's hearts, but the real closeness, the sharing of a life, had to come to an end. It had had its roots in the fairy tale of Oxford life and now that the real thing had to begin, they had to part and start again.

Charles bought a flat in Fulham, fairly near Phaedria's father's house, and began work in the City; Phaedria settled back into her role of surrogate wife and, while she was wondering what she might enjoy, did a secretarial and a cookery course. Her father liked Charles, they all had dinner together once a week; and very often on Saturday they would ride together in Richmond Park, and when the next season began she would go and watch Charles play polo and spend the evening and occasionally the night with him. Her father never inquired into the relationship, or showed the slightest concern about it; the real world never seemed to him nearly as interesting as his current literary passion (at this particular time a painstaking study and biography of Prosper Merimee, a nineteenth-century French novelist and literary hoaxer, guaranteed to sell, Phaedria imagined, all of fifty copies) and he was simply content to see his beloved daughter so happily settled with so charming a partner.

Phaedria occasionally wondered if she was ever going to find a man who would charm, delight and amuse her as much as Charles did, who would be as important to her, who would love her as much, and at the same time fulfil her needs in a slightly more conventional way, but it seemed a prospect so remote, so extremely unlikely, set so far into the future as to be not worth troubling about. For the time being, she had Charles, she loved him and she trusted him, and she enjoyed being with him, and that was quite enough.

She felt she was happy.

One night, just about a year after they had come down from Oxford, Charles took her out to dinner; he was tense and awkward with her, and for the first time since they had met there was no fun, no gossip, no chat, no intimacy in any of it. After they had finished their meal Charles ordered brandies, sat back in his chair, looked at Phaedria very straight and said, 'I've got something to tell you.'

'I can see that. What is it? You seem like a man with a heavy burden.'

'I am.'

'Well, lay it down on me, for goodness' sake. There isn't much you could tell me that would shock me.'

'This will.'

'Oh, Charles, come on. What? What could it possibly be?'

'You'll hate it,' said Charles miserably, draining his glass and signalling to the waiter for another.

'I doubt it.'

'You will.'

'OK, then I'll hate it. I'm hating this more.'

'I'm getting married.'

Phaedria gasped. She couldn't help it. The shock was physical and frightful. She closed her eyes, swallowed, and then, with an enormous effort, opened them again. She felt sick, cold, frightened. She drained her glass and rested her head on her hands for a moment. Then she looked at him.

'You can't.'

'I can. I'm going to.'

'Why?'

'So many reasons. The usual ones. Cowardice. Ambition. Loneliness.'

'You could marry me in that case.'

'No, Phaedria, I couldn't,' said Charles, taking her hand. 'I love you. I couldn't inflict such a thing on you.'

'Oh, for Christ's sake,' said Phaedria, snatching her hand back again, her body rigid and tense, anger suddenly surfacing, 'stop talking in such riddles. I can't stand it. What's all this about?'

Charles sat with his head bent, staring into his brandy, and told her. His father, who still terrified him, and still provided most of his income, had heard a few rumours. Dempster had run a couple of stories about the surprisingly artistic Mr Fraser-Smith, and his lack of a regular girlfriend; someone had seen him coming out of one of the gay clubs; a friend of his father's had observed him dining late one night with a man who was most assuredly not one of Charles' usual circle. Old Mr Fraser-Smith had confronted Charles, questioned him closely and threatened him with public disgrace and disinheritance if he wasn't married in six months.

'Oh, for heaven's sake, Charles, call his bluff,' said Phaedria. 'This is the eighties. What does it matter?'

'I've told you how much it matters,' said Charles. 'A lot. I'm sorry, Phaedria. I'm ambitious. I'm extravagant. I need a lot of money. And like I said, I'm often lonely.'

'What a shame,' said Phaedria bitterly. 'What a lousy, bloody shame.'

'Phaedria, don't. Don't be angry.'

'For God's sake, Charles, I am angry. I'm more angry than I ever thought possible. We were friends, Charles, we were more than friends, we were everything. We loved each other. I trusted you. I trusted you with everything. I would never have betrayed you. Not for anything. And then you throw this lump of garbage at me, and tell me not to be angry. Jesus Christ. Who's the lucky girl?'

'You don't know her.'

'Well, that's a good thing. If I did I just might go and tell her the facts of life. She must be extremely simple.'

'She is.'

'Oh, Charles, how can you be so cretinous? What hope of happiness can there be in this? What are you doing to your life?'

'Preserving it.'

'You're not, you know. You're turning it rotten. It'll putrefy and stink. If I wasn't so sorry for you, so dreadfully, dreadfully sorry, I'd go and tell your father exactly what I think of him. And you. As it is I'll just leave you alone. All of you. To a lousy, fearful, hopeless future.'

She stood up. 'I'd like to tell you that I hope you'll be happy. But I can't. Because I know you won't. Goodbye, Charles.' She fumbled in her wallet and pulled out a twenty-pound note.

'This is for my dinner. I'd hate you to waste any of your precious money on me.'

Charles caught her arm. 'Phaedria, don't. Please please don't.'

'Charles, there's nothing else I can do. Now just let me go and get on with your own fucking life. And I do hope you manage to do a bit of that. Otherwise she'll need to be very simple indeed. Now let go of me or I might tell everyone in the restaurant what we're quarrelling about.'

She hadn't seen him since; three weeks later Dempster announced a huge and delightful surprise for the friends of Charles Fraser-Smith who had seemed destined to remain a bachelor for life; he had become engaged to Serenity Favell Jones, who had spent the last two winters as a chalet girl in Gstaad, and was now beginning a new career in an art gallery in London.

The wedding was planned for September, and the blushing bride was hoping for 'a huge family'.

At least Charles had the grace not to invite Phaedria to the wedding.

She did recover in time; she thought it impossible, but she did. For a long time she was so unhappy that she dreaded waking up every morning; she ached physically all over, she had no energy for anything, she put on weight, she had trouble sleeping.

Anything that reminded her of Charles, the sight of a blond head, an old E-Type parked by the road, a report of a polo match (the game was much in the news on account of the heir to the throne being so besotted with it), all threw her into such a pitch of misery and pain that she felt literally ill and faint. Most of her friends, assuming that her unhappiness was caused by having lost Charles to Serenity, tried to distract her with other men, throwing dinner parties and arranging trips to the theatre. It was dreadful. Her father, jerked into reality by her grief, abandoned Prosper Merimee for a few weeks, pronounced Charles a bounder and took her away for interminable weekends to divert her. In the end, she realized she had to get out of London.

She settled on Bristol because the parents of an Oxford friend lived there in a big house in Clifton, and let out bedsits to students. What she had seen of Bristol she liked; it was architecturally nice, very lively, and near enough to the country to be able to ride. She moved down with no clear idea of what she was going to do, but she had her typing and her shorthand skills, and she knew she could support herself. She did a series of temporary secretarial jobs, found some good stables, began to ride regularly and bought her own horse, slowly formed a new circle of friends and, without being fully aware of the process, began to heal. She knew she was better when she woke up one morning and began to think about a proper job. She had not got a good degree and had an expensive education in order to do typing and filing for a series of people who had less than half her brains.

Two things really interested her: one was fashion and the other was journalism. 'And you know the rest,' she said to Barry one night, over the hundredth or so half of bitter, 'and here I am.'

'And I'm delighted you are,' he said fondly, patting her hand. He had a great deal of time for her. She wasted no time whatsoever on self-pity.

Phaedria gave quite a lot of thought to what she would wear to persuade Sir Julian to talk to her exclusively. She was clever with clothes; she had never had any money to spend on them but she had that eye for shape and length, a flash of colour, an unexpected accessory, that ability to haul together three or four disparate items of clothing into something coherent and original, that is called style, and that is as ingrained and inborn an ability as it is to sing in tune or to spell correctly.

It was no use today, she thought, trying to dress up. Multi-millionaires would not be impressed by Wallis copies of Jean Muir or even Jaeger. Better dress down and chic, she decided, spraying herself in Guerlain's Jicky, the perfume she always wore, and pulling on a cream silk shirt and a pair of straight-legged Levis out of the wardrobe; she added soft brown leather calf-length boots, a wide brown belt and a soft leather jeacket she had got second hand in the flea market in Paris; and after a moment's hesitation she put on an antique gold chain and locket Charles had given her when they left Oxford and which she had never worn since the night he told her he was getting married. She felt the occasion warranted not only the locket but the emotional effort required to put it on. She hauled back her cloud of wild dark hair and tied it with a brown and cream Hermes scarf her father had given her for her birthday; and then after a moment's consideration set it free again; put on a very little brown eye shadow and a slither of lip gloss, and then slung a notebook, a pen and three pencils into the canvas and leather fishing bag she used for both handbag and briefcase.

'Right,' she said, smiling at herself pleasedly in the mirror. 'Sir Julian, here I come.'

Julian was still, in the middle of the morning, feeling acutely irritable. Sitting in the new, lush plush office of Brian Branscombe, recently appointed M.D. of Morell Pharmaceuticals, he poured himself a third coffee and looked morosely across the Avon estuary. He wasn't looking forward to the ceremony ahead. Not only was he host to a hundred or so local and not-so-local figures – the Mayor of Bristol, various bankers and businessmen who had been involved in the construction of the plant, and representatives of the pharmaceutical industry – but a strong contingency of journalists as well. He was very hostile to the press these days, hated even to see his picture in the papers and had done ever since the entry of Jamil Al-Shehra into his life, and he was particularly hostile to mass press conferences. On the other hand it was better than trying to deal with the interminable queue of journalists individually. There had been some request for an exclusive interview today: the women's page editor of some Bristol paper. He'd refused, as he had refused all such requests for some years; he'd met so many of the breed and hated it: middle-aged, hard-drinking, chain-smoking, life-beaten women with ginny voices and bags under their eyes. He was quite sure Phaedria Blenheim – what a ridiculous name, she must have made it up – would be exactly the same, and he had no intention of talking to her.

He settled down to the press release; his own PR outfit had prepared it and had done a fair job. Lots of finance stuff, lots of new technology, perhaps slightly too heavy implications of do-goodery (combating unemployment, intensive medical R & D), but it never really did any harm, and a gratifying shortage of anything remotely personal. Well, he would cut the tape, make a short speech, answer a maximum of six questions, attend the lunch briefly and be back in the helicopter by two o'clock, with an urgent meeting in London as his excuse. It didn't sound too bad. He even managed a smile as Branscombe came in, and stood up, buttoning his jacket and adjusting his tie.

'OK, Brian, let's go and get it over with. I do congratulate you on your work here. You've done a brilliant job getting it open on – sorry, ahead of – time. How did you do it?'

'Thank Mrs Thatcher,' said Branscombe with a grin, 'she's done more to motivate the work force than any person or thing since the industrial revolution. What with the fear of un-employment, and the reinvention of the work ethic, the managerial classes are laughing. Now do you feel you're sufficiently briefed on this conference?'

'Oh, yes,' said Julian with a sigh. 'More than. And Brian, can I make it absolutely clear, no exclusives. Whatever the excuse, or rationale, I refuse to speak to a single member of the press on a one to one basis today. I don't have the heart or the stomach. OK?'

'OK, Sir Julian,' said Branscombe. 'Understood. It's a pity from our point of view, but I do sympathize. I'll see you're clear by two-thirty.'

'Two,' said Julian, 'sharp. OK. Now let's go and get it over.'

He actually always gave a good performance on these

occasions. His charm and his capacity for lateral thought tended to cut neatly through the tedious razzmatazz of a mass conference. By the time he had unveiled the plaque (less pretentious than cutting tape, he thought to himself as he did it, but still bloody silly), made his short speech and answered five of the six journalists' questions he had promised himself, he felt himself on a downhill run; had actually picked up the sheaf of papers in front of him on the table and smiled charmingly at the assembled company and the Mayor and local dignitaries sitting behind him on the conference platform, when a female voice rang out through the hall.

'Sir Julian, could I ask you about women?'

The assembled company laughed; it was a neat line. He could not afford to be unreceptive. He put the papers down again, shaded his eyes against the flare of the lights, and smiled charmingly.

'I'll try to answer. Which particular aspect of the female race were you interested in, Miss – er?'

'Blenheim. Phaedria Blenheim. *Bristol Echo.*'

Ah, that one. The one who'd requested an exclusive. Clever stuff. She would need putting in her place.

'Could you stand up, Miss Blenheim? Or rather Ms, as I would imagine you would wish to be addressed.'

'Oh, no,' said Phaedria, standing up and smiling at him from the back of the hall, 'I much prefer to be Miss. I enjoy my status. I don't count myself among the more militant feminists.'

More laughter, but rather more muted. Most people were simply staring at her. Julian tried not to sound impatient.

'This is perhaps not quite the time for semantics, Miss Blenheim. Although I am sure we could have a very interesting discussion on the subject. What is your question, then?'

'My question is how many women will you be employing? In your management team here, that is, rather than on the factory floor.'

Julian smiled again. He still couldn't see her properly. But the voice (indisputably Oxbridge, although less ginny than he had imagined) was enough to tell him exactly what she was like: confident, assertive, and too clever for her own good, as his mother would probably have said had she been here.

'As many as earn their place in it, Miss Blenheim. I have a

good record in equal opportunity. I have several women on the boards of several of my companies, both here and in the United States. Including the major parent company. You really should do your homework a little more carefully.'

'Oh, but I have,' said Phaedria, 'and as far as I can see although your team on the board of Juliana and Circe is largely female, in the case of the hotels, and the pharmaceutical company, your record is less good. With the exception of Mrs Emerson, of course.'

A slight buzz went round the hall. Julian pushed his hair back. Brian Branscombe half stood up, but Julian shook his head at him, and smiled again into the lights. 'Do go on, Miss Blenheim. I had clearly underrated your capacity for research.'

'Thank you,' said Phaedria, 'I think I have made my point. The record in other companies and in particular in Europe is better. I thought perhaps as this was a new plant, you might feel you could be a little more bold.'

'How interesting,' said Julian. 'Well, Miss Blenheim, as you are clearly something of an expert on management matters, perhaps you would care to submit a proposal to me. In writing, of course. I would be most interested to read it. In the meantime I can only say that there will be several women on the management team here in Bristol and in due course they will be available for interview to you and your colleagues.'

'And you, Sir Julian. When will you be available for interview?'

'Miss Blenheim, forgive me, but I was under the impression that was precisely what was happening now.'

'No,' said Phaedria, 'this isn't an interview. This is a floorshow.'

She was walking down to the front of the hall now. Julian suddenly saw her emerging from the blurred darkness; she took form, became more than a voice, a purveyor of silly questions, aggressive observations, posturing clichés; he looked at her and his breath was momentarily caught. A great cloud of wildly tangled curly dark hair, pale oval face, luminous dark eyes; young, so young she looked, younger than his own daughter, younger than any woman he had looked at sexually for years. And that was how, he realized suddenly, he was looking at her: as a man appreciating, admiring, desiring, a woman. It happened with a speed, a force, that physically startled him; he felt suddenly confused, unable to remember what she had asked.

And Phaedria, sensing in some instinctive way the stab of emotion, the surge of interest, paused, looked at him more sharply and was moved by what she saw. Style he had, this man, and humour and a strange grace; but what hit her hardest was a sense of sexual energy, directed entirely at her. It was a cataclysmic moment that both of them would remember for the rest of their lives.

Brian Branscombe, finally deciding to arrest the tedious Miss Blenheim in her nicely shod tracks before she could do any more harm to his carefully orchestrated conference, stood up on the platform. 'Miss Blenheim, thank you for your question. I trust Sir Julian has answered it to your satisfaction. Ladies and Gentlemen, a buffet lunch is now being served in the hospitality suite. Unfortunately, Sir Julian has to leave for London very shortly after lunch, for an urgent meeting, but he will be joining us briefly. You can put any further questions to me, or our press officer. Thank you for your interest and time. Do please adjourn next door.'

The guests and the press moved as one hungry man towards the next room; only Phaedria remained, standing quite still, her eyes fixed on Julian's face.

'Miss Blenheim,' said Branscombe, a trifle impatiently, 'do please go next door and help yourself to lunch.'

'Well, I did wonder –' said Phaedria, motionless still, 'if I could have a few words . . .'

'No, Miss Blenheim, you cannot. I'm sorry. Sir Julian has to leave very shortly. Sir Julian, let me take your papers. If you will just follow me . . .'

'Just a moment, Brian. Miss Blenheim, was there anything else?'

'A lot,' said Phaedria briskly, seeming to wake, coming to herself again. 'I'd like to ask you about so many things, Sir Julian.'

'Miss Blenheim,' said Branscombe again, 'please. Sir Julian is on an extremely tight schedule. Do excuse us.'

'Miss Blenheim,' said Julian, ignoring him totally, 'I do have to go. It's quite true. But I would be happy to give you an interview. I wonder what your plans are for the rest of the day? If you have time, you could fly back to London with me now and I could give you an hour or so. And then I'll send you back again.'

'There's no need.'

'I pay the pilot,' he said, and smiled at her.

'Right,' said Phaedria, smiling back, 'I do have the time. I'll just call my editor. Thank you, Sir Julian. I do appreciate it very very much.'

'It will be my pleasure,' he said, and she thought she had never heard that word so blatantly caressed.

Branscombe, clearly irritated, showed her to his office, and she phoned Barry.

'Barry? It's Phaedria. Listen, I've got it. The exclusive. I'm flying back to London with Julian Morell now in his chopper. Stylish, huh? Expect me when you see me.'

'Phaedria,' said Barry in an agony of excitement and anxiety. 'I need that copy tomorrow, sweetheart. Don't forget.'

'Barry,' said Phaedria, 'I'm a pro. I told you, don't you remember? First I'll file the copy, then I'll elope with Sir Julian. You'll get it. Don't worry.'

He did. He got it that night. She phoned it from Julian's office. It was stereotyped, dull stuff. Barry read it disbelievingly. What he didn't realize was that Phaedria Blenheim, journalist, had, with one fierce, decisive gesture, signed off.

Phaedria had not really expected to like Julian Morell at all. She had thought he would be interesting and charming but arrogant and shallow. She found him interesting and charming, and unpretentious and thoughtful.

She also found him sexually attractive; her senses had not recovered from the shock they had received. She felt disturbed and irritated with herself at the same time; sitting looking at him across his desk, her stomach still unsettled from the helicopter flight, she found it impossible to relax, to set herself aside, to concentrate on him and what she could extract from him. She knew he was sixty-two, but she found it hard to believe; he looked easily ten years younger. His hair was only flecked with grey, his skin was lightly tanned, he was very slim. He was superbly, if a little predictably, dressed: classic grey

481

three-piece suit, grey and white striped shirt (with a button-down collar, she noticed: 'Are you the man in the Brooks Brothers shirt, Sir Julian?' she had asked, and yes, he said, yes he was, his son-in-law brought him half a dozen of the things every time he visited New York, which was fairly frequently. 'I wear them all once, and then file them away.') His tie was red, with a black line in it, very discreet; his watch a wafer-thin Cartier, his links plain gold; there was no suggestion of vulgarity, of showmanship, he simply looked a beautifully dressed, conservative Englishman.

He was good to listen to as well, she thought, his voice was light and level, not aggressively public school, nor flattened out mid-Atlantic. It had great charm, that voice: an ability to take certain words and phrases and warm them, lend emotion to them, or to toss humour into a remark, self-mockery even, without a fleck of emotion crossing the bland face, the dark, dark eyes.

He sat and looked at her with such pleasure, such patent interest that Phaedria felt exposed, vulnerable; short of leaving the room, there was nothing she could do to escape his examination. He had said little in the helicopter, he had studied papers, signed letters, having asked her to excuse him: 'Then when we get to my office, I shall be entirely at your disposal. Which I trust will please you.' They had landed at Battersea Heliport, and been met by a pale blue Rolls Corniche convertible; Phaedria was surprised by this, the first hint of any real ostentation in him that she had seen. 'Goodness,' she had said, 'what a nice car!' and yes, he had said, he liked cars, he always had, they were one of his hobbies, as no doubt she knew, being such a careful researcher. 'And do you like cars, Miss Blenheim?' No, she said, not really, they were just a means of transport to her, but his other passion, horses, now that was something which she did love, and his eyes had danced over her face, and he had started to talk to her about horses thinking to discover she knew nothing about them at all, pleased and surprised to find he was wrong, that she could converse about bloodstock and flat racing and hunting with confidence and knowledge.

'Do you have a horse, Miss Blenheim?'

'Yes, I do. A hunter. A six-year-old grey mare.'

'And what is her name, this young grey mare?'

'Grettisaga.'

'That is a very unusual name.'

'Yes. It's nice though, don't you think? I expect you know the tale well?'

'I fear not. Which tale?'

'The Grettisaga. It's a fourteenth-century Icelandic story. It has strong resemblances to Beowulf. William Morris has done a translation.'

'I see. You are clearly a very literary person.'

'Oh, not really. My father thinks I am woefully ill-read.'

'And who is your very well-read father?'

'His name is Augustus Blenheim. He's an academic. He writes books and lectures on literary figures only about two other people have ever heard of. His current obsession is Charles Maturin, he's an Irish gothic novelist. His dream is to be asked to make a television programme about someone, but I think it would be so minority viewing the channel showing it would go right off the air.'

'And I suppose you owe your very unusual name to your father?'

'Oh, yes,' said Phaedria with a cheerful sigh, 'of course. Do you know who Phaedria was?'

'Let me see. Did she not marry Theseus?'

'Fraid not. You've failed the test. No relation to her whatsoever. That was Phaedra. Phaedria was a character in –'

'I know,' said Julian suddenly, 'don't tell me. In – not Chaucer, no, Spenser, wasn't she? *The Faerie Queen*.' He smiled at her triumphantly. 'Do I pass?'

'Do you know what quality she represented?'

'No, I don't think I can go that far.'

'Well, then you do pass, but not very well. Although better than most. She was Wantonness.'

'I see. And how well does your name become you, Miss Blenheim?' He spoke lightly, he smiled charmingly, but Phaedria could feel him reaching out to her, making a small but irrevocable step towards intimacy, and she felt at the same time warmed and confused.

'That is a question I never answer,' she said. 'Whoever asks it.'

'Ah,' he said, 'an unoriginal one, clearly. Forgive me.'

'Very unoriginal. But yes, I do. Forgive you, I mean. Where are we going?'

'My office is in Dover Street. I'm surprised you didn't know that. Your research was so extremely thorough.'

'Yes. I'm sorry if I was rude. About your daughter and everything. I didn't exactly mean to be.'

'I forgive you. But why did you have to be at all? Exactly or otherwise?'

'I had to get you to notice me.'

He turned slightly in the car and looked at her for quite a long time; his eyes moving slowly from her hair to her face, pausing there, exploring her own eyes so tenderly, so questingly that she looked away, briefly, confused, lingering on her mouth, and then, quite briefly, but with an unmistakable confidence, at her neck, her breasts; and then he smiled and said, 'I don't think you had to be even inexactly rude to do that.'

'Not true,' she said, pulling herself together after what she felt to be an endless silence. 'Would I ever have made so much as another question if I hadn't been so – so bothersome?'

'Possibly not. And I would have regretted it greatly.' He looked away from her then, out of the window for a moment; they were travelling slowly along the Embankment; the river looked beautiful, goldenly grey in the winter sunshine. 'Do you like London?'

'Only quite. I prefer the country.'

'That's nice. I think I do too. Because you can ride?'

'Yes. And because I like space to myself.'

'That doesn't sound like a journalist.'

'Oh,' said Phaedria, 'I'm not really a journalist. My editor is always telling me that.'

'Really?' he smiled, genuinely amused. 'In what way are you not really a journalist?'

'Not interested in the world at large. Not really interested in newspapers. Only my bit of them.'

'Then why do you do it?'

'Because I'm good at it, and I like writing.'

'And interviewing famous people?'

'Everyone says that. No, not interviewing famous people. Most famous people are extremely boring.'

'On behalf of us all I apologize,' he said, and smiled his dancing smile. 'Or perhaps I am being presumptuous. Perhaps I don't qualify as famous in your book.'

'No,' she said, 'honestly you don't. Famous is – well, you know, really famous. Instantly recognised. Peter Cook. Clive James. Joanna Lumley.'

'I feel very humbled. But you're right.'

'I'm sorry. I didn't mean to be rude again.'

'You weren't. I was being arrogant. Have you interviewed all those people?'

'Yes.'

'And were they really boring?'

'Actually, those three weren't. Not at all. But they were exceptions.' She looked at him and smiled. 'I think you are probably another.'

'But I thought I wasn't famous.'

'Well, maybe you are a bit. But you aren't boring. So far.'

'Good.'

The car was swinging up Whitehall; the traffic, as it so often and inexplicably does in London, had cleared. Pete Praeger, Julian's chauffeur, bodyguard and probably the most discreet man in London, half turned his head. 'Straight to the office, Sir Julian? You don't want to stop anywhere for lunch?'

'No, thank you, Pete. Sarah has something waiting for me in the office. Sarah is my secretary,' he said to Phaedria. 'Terrifyingly efficient. We are all frightened of her. Aren't we, Pete? And do what she says.'

'We certainly do, sir. Will you need me any more today? You don't want me to bring you anything from the house?'

'No, I don't think so. But I have a dinner engagement. Can you come at seven to the office?'

'Yes, Sir Julian. Would that be in London, or out of town at all?'

'The Meridiana, Pete. And I won't be late.'

'Fine. Right, then here we are, sir.'

Phaedria, climbing out of the car, looked up at the offices with interest. She had expected some modern block; she found one of the original grey eighteenth-century buildings, with large white admittedly fake Palladian doors, and the original windows.

Julian pushed one of the doors open himself, standing aside to let her pass, taking his briefcase from Pete. 'In you go, Miss Blenheim. The lift's over there. Just a moment.'

He went and spoke briefly to the girl at the reception desk and then came over to her. They got in the lift. 'Top floor. My office is in what is known as a penthouse suite.'

'It sounds rather debauched.'

'I'm afraid it isn't. A great deal of very hard work goes on there, and that's all.'

'I see.'

Nevertheless, she was not surprised to find the suite, his personal offices, so stylish, so unbusinesslike: the lobby, with its sofas, its plants, its Tiffany-style lamps on low tables; the small rather more impersonal office beyond that where sat the terrifying Miss Brownsmith (who nodded briefly as they went through, skimming a thoughtful eye over Phaedria), and beyond that again, Julian's own office. Phaedria looked round it in delight, drinking in the white and chrome, the Symonds and Lutyens desk, the curving bookshelves, the lacquered standard lamps. 'What a beautiful room.'

'I'm glad you like it. Many people don't.'

'I'm amazed.'

'No, it's a little subtle, I find, for general consumption. People expect either very grand eighteenth-century style, a sort of cross between a boardroom and a brothel, or pure Conran. They can't cope with this at all.'

'Well I think it's marvellous.'

'I'm glad you like it. I am very fond of the art deco era. Probably because I was born in it. Although I fear it's beginning to be more historic than nostalgic.' He buzzed for Sarah Brownsmith. 'Ah, Sarah, could we have that lunch I hope you have been keeping for me. We're very hungry. Is there enough for two?'

'I think so, Sir Julian. Would you like wine, or just Perrier?'

'Oh, I think this is an occasion, I think we would like wine. No, more than that, champagne. Bring in a bottle of the Cristalle, will you, Sarah? And some Perrier as well, we have work to do. Miss Blenheim, I presume you would like a drink? Sarah, this is Phaedria Blenheim, a journalist from the *Bristol Echo*. She has come up to interview me. Now is there anything I need to know urgently, because I'll deal with it now, straight away, and then I want to be left alone for an hour or so. No calls or anything. This is an important interview.'

Phaedria met Sarah Brownsmith's politely amused gaze, resisted an almost overpowering urge to wink at her, and moved over to look out of the window down at Dover Street.

'Do you want lunch first, Sir Julian, or the messages?'

'Obviously lunch, Sarah, it's nearly half past three, and I have a guest. Just have it brought in, please, and then give me the messages quickly.'

Sarah Brownsmith's revenge for this small piece of arrogance was swift and heady. 'I'll give you all the messages,' she said, as Julian poured two glasses of champagne and held one out to Phaedria, 'then you can decide for yourself which are important. Miss North wants to know why you haven't rung her about tonight. She said to impress upon you that you were to be at the restaurant by seven sharp. Susan Johns says if you don't call her this afternoon about the marketing plans for next year she will resign immediately from – now what was it –' she consulted her notebook – 'ah yes, your bloody ego trip of a company. She said it was very important I gave you that message exactly.'

'Thank you, Sarah. Anything else?'

'Freddy Branksome said it was crucial you signed the audited accounts today, otherwise we should all be in jail by Christmas.'

'Yes?'

'Richard Brookes wants to know if you actually want to guarantee a lawsuit from Mrs Lauder, or if you would like to just consider renaming your new range. He must have a definite answer today.'

'Fine.'

'And your mother says if she doesn't hear from you by four she will be extremely displeased with you.'

'Thank you, Sarah. I hope you haven't forgotten anything.'

'I don't think so.'

'Good. Get my mother on the phone, will you?'

'Yes. And Miss North?'

'I will ring Miss North later,' said Julian lightly. He pushed his hair back. 'Thank you. Now, then, I don't want to be disturbed.'

'What about the accounts?'

'The accounts will have to wait. I believe the jails are very full towards Christmas. I doubt if they will have room for us.'

'Yes, Sir Julian.'

She closed the door behind her. Julian smiled at Phaedria. 'She is an excellent nanny. She likes to remind me I am imperfect and in need of discipline.'

'So I see.'

'And you also see what an extremely important person and how high-powered I am, and how my staff tremble at the sound of my name.'

'Yes. I do.'

The phone rang. 'Mother? Hallo. What? Yes, I know I didn't ring you last night, and I'm truly sorry. I was working with Freddy on the accounts. What? Well, we had a little supper later. No, Camilla was not with us. Well, your spies are lying. Now darling, I promise to come and see you tonight. Without fail. How are you? Good. I may have a friend with me. What? No, it won't be Camilla. I know she's bad for your health. Poor girl, I never can see what harm she does you.'

Phaedria, watching him closely, saw his face darken suddenly. 'Mother, I can't get into that now. I've got somebody with me. Yes, I have sent Roz some flowers. I know it's dreadful waiting for a late baby, but she'll survive. Other women do. She was a fortnight late herself. Serves her right. Bye, darling, I must go now. See you later. What? Oh, about seven.' He put down the phone, walked over to Phaedria and refilled her glass.

'Now then, Miss Phaedria Blenheim. What do you want to know about me?'

She had just finished telephoning her story through to the *Echo* from Sarah's desk when Julian appeared in the doorway.

'Was that all right? Was he pleased?'

'Very.'

'Good. My extremely valuable, moderately famous time has not been wasted, then?'

'Of course not,' she said, pushing the certain knowledge that she had done a lousy job to the bottom of her consciousness. She looked at Julian, about whom she knew so little more, and she did not wonder for a moment when she had not pushed him in the very least for information about himself beyond his companies, his money, his houses, his tastes. There was much she wanted to know about Julian Morell, much that she needed to know; about his first and only wife, and why he had never married again; about his daughter, and how, if at all, he rationalized having both her and his son-in-law holding significant positions in the company; about his very long association with Susan Johns and the closeness with him that gave her the right to insult him considerably and publicly through his secretary; about the demanding Camilla North, who was clearly not going to be met at seven o'clock sharp or indeed at any time during the evening; about his mother, who had worked in the company from its founding and was still, by all accounts, an active constituent; but it was not to be shared, any of it, either with her editor or her readers.

As for herself, she had time on her side; she could wait.

'I would like to buy you a drink,' he said, 'preferably several. But I have a slight problem.'

'I think you've already given me several drinks.'

'Maybe. But that was work. I would like to move you into the pleasure category now.'

There it was again; that gentle insistent pressure into intimacy. Phaedria started putting papers into her fishing bag, her head bent, glad to have a reason not to look at him, wondering confusedly at the warmth stirring somewhere in the depths of her body.

'I see.'

'Are you busy this evening? Do you want me to send you back? Because I will. You have only to say.'

'No,' she said, as he had known, as they had both known she would, looking up suddenly and meeting his eyes. 'No, I don't. I can stay in London.'

'Good. Now, then, I wonder how you'd feel about coming to see my mother before we go on for – what? Dinner perhaps?'

Sarah Brownsmith, working on the small computer on the other side of her office, wondered if Phaedria had any idea at all quite how much that invitation meant.

'You'll like my mother,' said Julian as the car made its slow, painful journey along St James's.

'Good. Will she like me?'

'I think so. I think definitely yes.'

'Then I shall like her.'

'And then, after that, I thought we would go out to dinner. If you have time. Where would you like to go?'

'I have time. Why not the Meridiana?'

'Why the Meridiana?'

'I imagine you have a table booked. You said you were going there this evening.'

'Oh, now here we have the journalist at work, do we not?' He sounded faintly irritated. 'Not missing a single thing. No, I don't have a table booked. I cancelled it.'

'Pity,' said Phaedria, undismayed by his change of mood.

'Why?'

'Because I like it.'

'Well, that is a pity, but anyway, we can't go there, because several people I know are going, and I don't want to see any of them. Where else do you like?'

'I love Chez Solange. I like Bentley's Oyster Bar. And I love Inigo Jones. In Covent Garden. Do you know it?'

'I do. How is it that you are so au fait with London restaurants? I thought you were a provincial girl.'

'Absolutely not,' said Phaedria firmly. 'I grew up in London, and my father is a great gourmet.'

'Are you a great gourmet too?'

'A small one.'

'Good. Then let us go to Inigo Jones. It's certainly an imaginative menu. I'll book a table from my mother's house. Tell me more about your father. Tell me about your mother. What does she do, if anything?'

'I haven't the faintest idea,' said Phaedria, and there was no bitterness, no emotion of any kind in her voice, just a blank indifference. 'She left us when I was ten. She wrote at Christmas for a few years. I think I last heard from her on my twenty-first birthday. She sent me a card.'

He looked at her with great interest. 'How appalling.'

'Not really. I had my father. We were perfectly happy.'

'You don't seem at all damaged by the experience.'

'Who knows? It's hard to assess, isn't it, that kind of thing? I might have been greatly damaged. But I don't think so.'

'I find that encouraging,' he said.

'Why?'

'Well, my own daughter has had – well, a difficult life. My wife and I divorced when she was very small. I have always worried about the effect on her. But perhaps she may prove as undamaged as you.'

'Perhaps.'

'She's about to have a baby,' he added.

'Yes, I know.'

'Dear God,' he said, half amused, half irritated. 'Is there anything about me you don't know?'

She met his gaze steadily, the warmth inside her stirring again. 'I think a lot.'

He smiled. 'Good.' Then he looked at her more seriously. 'This is very odd, what we are doing, you know. It has only just dawned on me how odd it is.'

'What?'

'Well, that you should be coming to meet my mother, and then agree to have dinner with me, when you should be safely back home in Bristol, typing your articles, or whatever you do in the evening. Is there nobody to worry about you?'

'Nobody.'

'Don't you have any friends?'

'Of course I do. But they don't monitor my every movement. Some evenings I see them, some I don't.'

'I see. So you live alone?'

'Yes.'

'Do you not have a boyfriend?'

'No.'

'Don't you think it might be a little rash, spending the evening with me? I might prove to be a lecher, or a miser or a bore.'

'You might. In each case, I could just go home.'

'To Bristol?'

'Of course not. To my father's house in Chelsea.'

'Then,' he said, smiling, his eyes dancing, 'I shall relax.'

'Mother, this is Phaedria. Phaedria Blenheim. She is writing a series of articles on leading Captains of Industry. She's started with me.'

'Really. How interesting. Which of the other Captains are you interviewing, Miss Blenheim?'

'Oh, Clive Sinclair. Richard Branson. Alan Sugar. John Bentley.'

She saw Julian looking at her with intense admiration.

'And for which publication?'

'The *Bristol Echo*.'

'How nice. And has my son given you some good copy?'

'Not yet,' said Phaedria. 'I'm hoping it will improve.'

Letitia sparkled at her. 'It probably won't. He can be very dull when he wants to be. And he lies a lot. Look out for that. What would you like to drink?'

'Oh, goodness, I'm not sure.'

'Well, if you're not sure, you'd better have champagne. Such a catholic drink, I always think. Julian, go and get a bottle, will you?'

She looked at Phaedria. 'How pretty you are. Now, Miss Blenheim, sit down by the fire, and let me look at you. She doesn't look like a journalist, does she, Julian? Too pretty.'

'Oh, some of them are,' said Julian. 'But not too many, I suppose. You're looking fairly pretty yourself today, Mother.'

Phaedria, startled by this word applied to a woman she knew to be over eighty, looked at her hostess with fresh eyes and realized he was right. Letitia Morell's skin was soft and glowing, even though a little wrinkled; her eyes were a clear violet blue; her pure white hair was thick and styled in a soft bob; she was wearing a scarlet crepe dress that Phaedria recognized as indisputably Jasper Conran; she wore low-heeled cream court shoes on her tiny feet and cream stockings on legs that were as shapely and slender as they had been when she had so famously danced the Charleston with the Prince of Wales on the glass dance floor of the Silver Slipper Nightclub in the twenties.

'Oh,' said Julian suddenly to Phaedria, 'I know where we should have dinner: Langan's. Mother, can I use the phone?'

'Oh, you won't get a table now,' said Letitia, getting up and walking briskly over to the phone. 'I'll ring and get you mine. What time?'

'Oh, I don't know. Nineish, I suppose.'

She stood there tapping her foot as the phone rang and rang

at Langan's, looking shrewdly at Phaedria and fearing for her and her young, vulnerable beauty in her son's hands. What next? Schoolchildren?

'There now,' she said, 'that's done. Nine. You can have my table. It's over in the corner. Well away from the window, excellent. I envy you.'

'Come with us,' said Julian, knowing how the invitation would please her, knowing that she would not come; and she, knowing in her turn exactly both those things, said no, really, she was tired; they chatted for a while, about company affairs, about Julian's growing ambition and continuing failure to find a site for Circe in London, and in deference to Phaedria's presence, about the opening of the Bristol plant, about Bristol and the lovely countryside surrounding it, about journalists they knew and she might, but did not, the beauty editors, Felicity Clark from *Vogue*, Leslie Kenton from *Harpers & Queen*, and the editors, Tina Brown, creator of the delicious new *Tatler*, Deirdre McSharry, already-legendary First Lady of *Cosmopolitan*.

'You must meet them all,' said Letitia firmly. 'You ought to be working in London, after all. I shall give a little dinner party for you.'

'Mother, don't frighten the poor girl,' said Julian. 'Come on, Phaedria, time to go, it's getting late.'

'I am not a poor girl, and I'm not frightened,' said Phaedria, firmly cool. 'And I don't need to be protected, by you or anybody. I would love to meet all those people, Mrs Morell, please don't forget.'

'I won't,' said Letitia, kissing her. 'You must learn not to be so bossy, Julian. Now good night, darling. Good night, Phaedria, may I call you that? Such a lovely name.'

'It's from *The Faerie Queen*,' said Julian.

'Well of course it is, I know that,' said Letitia briskly. 'Wantonness, wasn't she, Phaedria? You must get so tired of being asked if it suits you.'

'I do,' said Phaedria. She wasn't quite sure about the form her relationship with Julian Morell was going to take, but she was certainly in love with his mother.

Brought strangely closer by the interlude with Letitia, they sat

493

in Langan's, yet another bottle of champagne in the ice bucket beside them; Phaedria, half drunk, totally relaxed, sat with her elbows on the table, her chin resting on her hands, smiling at Julian.

'What a lovely lady.'

'She is. Although not always.'

'Isn't she? I can't believe that.'

'Oh, come now,' he said, 'nobody is lovely all the time. Or are you?'

'Me? I'm hardly ever lovely. Horrid most of the time.'

'I don't think,' he said, 'that I can believe that. You seem a consistently nice person to me.'

'Not at all. Look how stroppy and rude I was this morning.'

'That was just doing your job.'

'Doesn't that count?'

He seemed surprised. 'Of course not.'

'So you can be thoroughly unpleasant in the course of duty, and it doesn't really matter?'

'No, I don't think it does.'

She looked at him thoughtfully. 'I don't think I'd like to work for you.'

'Working was not what I had in mind for you.'

The warmth again; she looked down, confused, flushed.

'I was very impressed,' he said, 'by the way you summoned up all those names for my mother.'

'What names?'

'The Captains of Industry you are supposed to be interviewing.'

'Oh,' she said, smiling. 'I'm a good liar. When I have to be. Are you?'

'Not very.'

'Why did you have to tell her that story anyway?'

'Oh,' he said lightly, 'I thought it best for her to think our relationship was purely professional.'

'Why?'

'She doesn't trust me with young ladies. With any ladies. I didn't want a lecture in the morning.'

'Why not? I mean, why doesn't she trust you?'

'With good reason, I'm afraid. I have a bad reputation with women. Your research must have told you that.'

'A little.'

'Does it bother you?'

She looked at him very directly. 'Not really.'

'Good.'

'Now then, since you know so much about me, can I find a little out about you? And what would you like to eat? Shall we have oysters?'

'That would be lovely. Can I have a dozen?'

'You certainly can. Do you always have such a hearty appetite?'

'Fairly. But this has been a very long day.'

'Of course. I'm sorry, I didn't think. You must be tired.'

'Oh, no,' she said, 'I'm not tired at all. I don't get tired easily. I do feel a bit under-dressed, though. Everybody here looks so wonderful.'

'You don't look in the least under-dressed. I would say you look quite as good as anyone in this room. Do you like clothes?'

'Very much.'

'Good. I don't like women who aren't interested in clothes. It shows a lack of sensuality.'

This time the warmth was not something remote, or distant; it was a stab of fire. Phaedria drained her glass.

'And after the oysters?'

She looked at the menu. 'Steak tartare, please.'

'This is a very cold meal for November. Is that really what you want?'

'Yes.'

'Very well. We can have a big bowl of frites to warm you. And some – let me see, beaune. That would be nice.' He looked up. Peter Langan had lurched unsteadily over to their table.

'Evening.'

'Good evening, Mr Langan. How are you?'

'Fucking awful.'

'I'm sorry to hear that. It's very nice to be here.'

'I won't say it's nice to have you here, because I'd much rather have your mother. Have you ordered yet?'

'Not yet.'

'I'll send someone over. You look like you need some help. Nice shirt,' he added to Phaedria, and stumbled off.

'He's being exceptionally polite this evening,' she said, munching hungrily at the crudités the waiter had brought.

495

Julian looked at her in amused pleasure. 'I'm enjoying you,' he said.

'Good.'

'Now then, can we get back to you?'

'If you like. There isn't a great deal to tell. And of course, contrary to what you said, I don't know anything at all about you really.'

'Don't you?'

'I don't think so, no.'

'That's a nice necklace,' he said.

'Oh,' she said, and there was a shadow on her face that belied her bright tone. 'I've hardly ever worn it. It was a present from someone – ages ago.'

'Someone important?'

'Yes,' she said, 'someone very important. But it's over now.'

'How old are you, Phaedria?'

'Twenty-four.' She shook back her great mane of hair and looked at him very directly. 'How old are you?'

'Sixty-two.'

'Older than my father.' It was an oddly intimate statement.

'Does it matter?'

'What do you mean?'

'You know what I mean.'

'Yes,' said Phaedria. 'Yes, I do.'

He took her hand suddenly. 'I find you very beautiful. I find the way I am feeling very surprising. Please tell me about yourself.'

'All right. But you must talk as well.'

'Very well. We shall swop story for story, and see how we get along.'

He put out his hand and stroked her cheek, very gently; she turned her head and rested it in his hand. She smiled. 'I think I shall run out of stories first.'

'We shall see.'

They talked for hours. Warmed, relaxed by the wine, the strangely delicious sensations invading her body, his beguiling interest in everything she had to say, she talked of her childhood, her love for her father, their strangely intense relationship, her fear that her mother might return and invade it; of her days at Oxford, of her unwillingness to become involved with anybody, of her love for Charles. But she stopped there; she was not ready to betray him yet. She talked of her work, of the people she had interviewed – 'Everybody must ask you this,' he said, 'did you ever fall in love with any of them, have an affair?' and no, she said, never, you did not regard them as people at all, they were objects, part of the job – her ambitions, the delight she took in her work – and her occasional anxiety for the future and where her rather singular approach to life might lead her.

'It seems to me,' he said, 'that you have led a most blameless life.'

'Fairly. And you? You haven't done much swopping yet. Come along, tell me about you.'

'Well, not blameless,' he said, 'not blameless at all,' and he began to talk, as he had not talked for years, freely, easily, about Eliza, about Peter Thetford, about Roz, about the years in New York, about Camilla, about – very briefly – Susan. But, as for Phaedria, there were boundaries to the confidences, he was not prepared to go beyond the ones he had set.

He told her of his years in France during the war, of the early days in the company, he talked about his mother and the fun and the pleasure they had had in London in the early days, and how in fact it had never stopped.

And Phaedria listened, as she so skilfully did in her work, silently for the most part, attentively, occasionally asking a quiet, thoughtful question, and learnt more in two hours than most people did in two months, two years.

Suddenly he stopped, looked at her slightly warily, and smiled. 'You are a very dangerous person to talk to,' he said. 'You tempt one to say too much.'

'Can one say too much?'

'One certainly can.'

He was silent; then he reached out again and touched her face. 'What do you think?'

She knew what he meant.

'I'm not sure.'

'Ah.'

'Perhaps I should go.'

'Where?'

'Home.'

497

'Oh,' he said, 'don't go. Not yet.'

'Well in any case,' she said briskly, 'I have to go to the loo.'

'Very well, off you go, and I shall try and think of something to delay you before you return.'

Phaedria sat in the rather palatial Ladies' of Langan's, with its slight air of the boudoir, which had, as usual, a party of its own going on, the air thick with conflicting perfumes and the mirrors crowded with half made-up faces; girls sitting on the sofa gossiping, giggling. She sat apart from them, and brushed her hair, looking at herself in the mirror for a long long time. She felt excited, disturbed, alarmed; but happy. She was taking strange turnings, but she did not feel afraid; nor foolish; nor even surprised at herself. She could see quite well where this evening would very probably end, and despite a considerable sense of trepidation, she liked the prospect. How or why she liked it lay for the most part in the past, she supposed; in her odd childhood, her love for her father, her betrayal by Charles, but it also lay in the present, in the growing urgency of what she could quite clearly see was physical desire at its most beguiling, its most delicious, its most indiscreet. The centre of herself seemed to have shifted; she was thinking, talking, responding, feeling from somewhere deep within her newly restless, hungry body; for the first time in her whole life she felt she understood what a fearsome, reckless force sexuality could be. And she felt something else too, something tender, something happy, something loving; she liked this man, she liked his mind, she liked his voice, she liked his smile and his tenderness towards her, she liked the way he looked, the way he laughed, the way he sat, and walked and moved, the way he looked at her, the way he made her feel she mattered; she wanted to stay with him, to learn more of him, to be with him. He had given her courage; she wasn't afraid. She smiled at herself in the mirror, stood up and walked purposefully back down the stairs.

He was waiting for her at the table, looking almost anxious.

'I wondered if you'd run away.'

'No. I didn't want to.'

'I'm glad. What next?'

'You say.'

'Brandy?'

'No, thank you. I'd like some Perrier, though.'

'You shall have it.' He took her hand again, looked at her intensely with his dark, questing eyes, searching, half smiling, disturbing her.

Phaedria closed her eyes briefly and swallowed; she felt faint.

'Now, I have to ask you something. Something important. Something I have to know.'

'What?'

'Have you been to bcd with many men?'

'No.'

'Ah. Any men?'

'Yes and no.'

'Are you a virgin?'

'Yes and no.'

'My God,' said Julian, dropping her hand and laughing, signalling to the waiter, 'you're hard work. Are you always so mysterious?'

'I try to be. I don't like giving too much away.'

'You certainly succeed. Let me take you back to my place. I have some very interesting etchings.'

'No thank you,' said Phaedria, 'I really don't want to go back to your place. I hate men's places.'

'That's a very sweeping statement. My place is very nice.'

'I'm sure, but I don't want to go there.'

'There's the office.'

'Any etchings there?'

'Kind of. You've seen most of them.'

'I suppose so.' She looked at him with sudden interest. 'Do you have any pictures of the stores? And the hotels? I'd really like to see those.'

'Dear God in Heaven, I hadn't anticipated having to compete with my own company for your attention. Come along, let's forget the Perrier. Plenty in the office anyway.'

Pete had been waiting for two and a half hours outside Langan's; Julian looked at the car and sighed.

'I'd forgotten him. Poor old Pete. Ridiculous driving that short distance, but I can't dismiss him now. And I'd so wanted to walk with you.'

'Well, let's get him to take us somewhere else, and then walk,' said Phaedria.

He looked at her and smiled delightedly. 'What a clever girl you are. How I am enjoying myself. Pete! Sorry to have kept you so long. Look, just drop us off at the Connaught, will you, we want to have a nightcap there, and then we can get taxis. Quite late enough already for you.'

'Very good, Sir Julian.'

In the car he put his arm round her, kissed the top of her head, tipped her face up to his. 'I find you very special.'

Phaedria smiled into his eyes. 'I'm enjoying you too.'

'I plan for you to enjoy more of me.'

She felt an explosion, a melting somewhere deep within her; she got most reluctantly out of the car.

They pushed in through the swing doors, waited until Pete and the Rolls had disappeared and walked out again. The doorman at the Connaught looked at them suspiciously.

'Come on,' said Julian loudly, taking her hand, 'let's go and do that bank.'

Phaedria giggled.

They walked slowly down through Berkeley Square; a pale, wintry moon spattered on to the bare trees; it was cold, dank. She shivered.

He felt it and put his arm round her shoulders. 'Sorry. Lousy idea. I just wanted to walk with you.'

'It wasn't a lousy idea. And I'm not usually so feeble. But I haven't got much of a coat.'

'Oh, God!' He looked stricken, pulled his own off, and put it round her. 'There you are. And if we come to a puddle I'll lay it over it.'

'That would be a terrible waste of a very nice coat.'

'I don't agree. And I have plenty more.'

'I suppose you would have.'

They walked up Hay Hill in silence; occasionally he drew her closer to him, kissed the top of her head. She felt absurdly happy.

'I like the night time,' he said suddenly. 'You have so much more of the world to yourself.'

'Shall I go away, and leave the two of you alone together?'

'No. I can't think I would ever want you to go away again.'

'Well, I'll stay for now.'

'Please do.'

He unlocked the big white door, let them in, followed her into the lift. It was a small intimate space; he pulled her hard against him, turned her face up and kissed her suddenly, fiercely. At the top the doors opened abruptly, the lights on automatically; he looked down and saw her face, startled, raw with surprise and desire.

'You look very different from this morning.'

'I feel different.'

'Do you really want to look at photographs of my stores?' he asked, smiling gently, teasing her.

'No, not now.'

'You disappoint me.'

'Don't joke.'

She walked away from him with an effort, suddenly nervous, unsure of what she should do. He followed her, turned her round, looked at her and smiled. 'Don't be frightened.'

'I'm not frightened,' she said, 'but you will have to take care of me. I am half a virgin.'

'I promise I will.' He smiled down at her. 'I don't know exactly what you mean, but you can tell me later.'

He took off the coats; first his then hers, then, his eyes never leaving her face, unbuttoned her shirt, slid it off her shoulders. Her breasts were small, firm, almost pubescent; he looked at them for a long time, then bent his head and kissed them tenderly at first, then harder, working at the nipples with his tongue; Phaedria, her head thrown back, limp, shaken, forgot everything except her need to have him, to know him utterly, to give to him, to take, take, take. She moaned; he straightened up.

'Let's get undressed. We aren't giving our bodies much help.'

She lay on the carpet, shivering, watching him; she had been a little afraid that he would look less good, less youthful without his clothes, but he didn't, he was tanned, all over, his stomach flat, his buttocks taut and firm. His penis stood out starkly; she looked at it with frank interest.

'Now, you must have seen one of these before.'

'Yes, but it wasn't so big.'

'Ah,' he said, 'I expect you say that to all the boys.'

And he smiled, defusing her fear, and began to stroke her, gently, insistently, first her breasts, playing with the nipples, smoothing the skin; then on her stomach, stronger, harder, and then moved his hand into the mound of her pubic hair, gentle again, unthreatening, and then, as she began to move, involuntarily, responding to him, he sought for her clitoris with his finger, probing, questing, and smiled as he felt the swelling and the wetness.

He was kneeling above her now, bending now and again to kiss her; again and again she thrust herself up towards him, her arms stretched out, her hair spread about her, looking like some strange, pre-Raphaelite painting, an embodiment of desire.

He made her wait a long time, until she was quite quite ready for him; then very very slowly and gently, he began to enter her, pushing, urging, withdrawing every time he felt her tense. She was tight and tender, despite her desire, and still afraid, deep within herself; he waited for her again and again, following her pattern, understanding her ebbing and flowing, and gradually, very gradually she abandoned herself absolutely to him, relaxed beneath him, softened, opened deeper and deeper, and then suddenly she gathered herself and it was a different movement altogether, it was hungry and grasping and greedy, and then she cried out and trembled and clung to him, and he knew she was there, and that it was safe for him to join her. And afterwards she lay and cried, sobbed endlessly in his arms, and couldn't tell him why.

'I'm happy,' she kept saying, 'I'm happy, I can't bear it, please please don't go away.'

'I'm not going away,' he said, 'never. I shall be here with you always. Don't cry, my dearest, dearest darling love. I'm not going away. Shush, shush, Phaedria, don't cry.'

And in the end she stopped and turned towards him, her face all blotched and smudged with tears and exhaustion and sex, and smiled and said, 'How wonderful you are.'

'No,' he said, 'not wonderful. Not wonderful at all. I loved it. I love you.'

He had not said that for years; it frightened him, even as he spoke.

And Phaedria, who had said it only to Charles, and had been

betrayed and was frightened also, looked at him very seriously and said, 'I love you too.'

She moved in to the house in Regent's Park the next day.

The Connection Nine

Los Angeles, 1982

Father Kennedy was having serious problems with his conscience. Mrs Kelly had made it perfectly plain to him that she didn't want anyone knowing where she and Miles were going; indeed had entrusted him with the information under pain of great secrecy. It was essential for several reasons, she had said, that nobody knew; the police might come inquiring for Miles, those no-good friends of his from the beach might want to find him; and kind as Mr Dashwood was, she didn't really want him knowing either. If she and Miles were to make a clean start, then she didn't want him turning up, upsetting Miles, interfering. She felt bad about it in a way; on the other hand, she did feel, as she had confided to Father Kennedy more than once, that he could have done more to help, that he was just being plain stubborn now, digging his heels in as hard and as awkwardly as Miles, only Miles was little more than a child, and Mr Dashwood was old enough to know better. It could have made all the difference in the world to Miles, and his future, had he given him a job in his company, and it wouldn't have hurt any. Sometimes, she had said, she wondered if Miles wasn't right, and Mr Dashwood wasn't a little ashamed of him – and of her, as well.

Father Kennedy, having the advantage – or maybe the disadvantage – of knowing rather more about Hugo Dashwood and his relationship to Miles than Mrs Kelly, or indeed anyone else in the world, he imagined, found it very hard to understand why the man wouldn't help his own son; he had often thought about the puzzle over the years; ever since Miles had graduated so well and then wasted himself. Obviously it would be very damaging for the boy, even when he was grown up, to learn that his mother had had a sexual relationship with another man, and that the father he had been so fond of had not been his father at all. It would inevitably lead to the painful realization that the reason for his father's suicide had been his mother's adultery; the whole story was obviously much best kept untold. Especially as Miles disliked Hugo Dashwood so much. That was a sad thing, under the circumstances.

But on the other hand, that should not keep the man from giving Miles a job; he was clearly fond of him, proud of him, and besides, a man did not put a boy through college if he was ashamed of him, didn't like him. He was as good as the boy's guardian; why should he persist in this strange, stubborn attitude?

Father Kennedy could see all too clearly why the poor souls at his refuge should behave badly, refuse to help themselves, let alone others, but he could not see why a man who clearly had more than his fair share of the world's bounty in the palm of his hand should not pass a little of it on to his own flesh and blood. It wasn't as if Miles was an unattractive young man; quite the reverse, he would be a credit to anyone.

Well, as Father Kennedy had learnt as a very young priest, there was no accounting for human nature, and it was not for him to try; his duty as God's extremely humble servant was merely to accept it, and do for it what he could, within his own earthly limitations.

And now, here he was, confronted by Hugo Dashwood, just flown in from New York, clearly agitated, and demanding to know where Miles and Mrs Kelly had gone. And he really did not know what to do. This was always the difficult one: when knowledge came into your possession not through the confessional – when it was sacred, and not, on pain of death, to be released – but from conversation, confidences, when it could be argued it was yours to make a judgement on, to do with what you thought best.

And what would be best now? Did he respect the confidence of an old friend and do what she had asked, or did he use his knowledge of her whereabouts to rescue her grandson from a life of shocking idleness at best, and at worst, from the very serious danger of mortal sin?

'I need to find them,' Hugo Dashwood had said, sitting down

earnestly in front of him, and looking the very picture of remorse and anxiety. 'I have decided I have been terribly wrong, and I want to make amends, I want to offer Miles a job after all, before it's too late.'

'Well, I'm sure that is very heartening news,' said Father Kennedy, playing for time while his old mind roamed around his dilemma, 'and Mrs Kelly would be wonderfully pleased to hear it. I am not altogether certain how Miles himself would take to the idea now, though. It's a while now since he graduated, and I fear he has got rather seriously used to a life of idleness. If you will forgive me saying so, Mr Dashwood, I fear your change of heart may be a trifle late.'

'Well, you may be right, Father, but we shall never know unless I can find Miles and put it to him. If I don't then there is certainly no chance at all that my change of heart, as you put it, will benefit him.'

'And would it be too terribly inquisitive of me to ask whereabouts you would be offering him this job? Would you be taking him back to England with you, or to New York? Or would it be somewhere here in California?'

'Oh, I wouldn't take him to England. I think that would be too much of a culture shock for him. No, I have a small wholesale business in New York, supplying toiletries to the drugstores, soaps, toothpaste, that sort of thing, and I could fit him in there quite easily. I need some more younger salesmen, I think he would do well.'

'And do you think he would settle there? Do you think he would be happy?'

Hugo sounded impatient.

'It would be a marvellous opportunity. I think he would settle down quite quickly. It's what he wanted, after all.'

'It's what he wanted once. He was hurt not to get it at the time.'

'Father Kennedy, he is not a child. He has to learn the ways of the world. Things do not necessarily drop into our laps at precisely the moment we want them. They did not for me, and I am sure they have not always done so for you.'

Father Kennedy reflected, not for the first time, that the English had an unfortunate way of sounding pompous and distant when they probably meant to be neither.

'Indeed they have not. Nor for most of the people I have worked with all my life. And it does people very little good when things do drop into their laps. Struggle is spiritually enhancing, would you not agree, Mr Dashwood?'

'Oh, I would, Father.'

'You are not a Catholic, I think?'

'I am not.'

The old man was silent for a while, looking at him shrewdly, thinking. 'And what would become of Mrs Kelly if Miles were to go to New York?'

'I don't quite know. I would certainly try to look after her. She has been very good to Miles.'

'She has indeed. And she is anxious to protect him.'

'Father, I hope you are not implying Miles needs protection from me?'

'Not from you, Mr Dashwood. From unhappiness. From idleness, from falling into unfortunate ways.'

'Which I fear he has despite her efforts.'

'Indeed.'

Hugo leant forward earnestly. 'Father, I cannot tell you how very very much I want to re-establish contact with Miles. I want to make amends. I want to help him, to give him a chance, to make something of his life. I think it is time I managed to be more to him.'

Father Kennedy looked at him. 'I hope, Mr Dashwood, and forgive me if this sounds impertinent, I hope you would not be of a mind to change his perspective of life.'

Dashwood met his eyes steadily.

'I don't know exactly what you mean. But I give you my word I would do nothing, nothing at all, that would make Miles unhappy, that would make him think differently about his background, or change his mind about anyone who had cared for him.'

'I'm glad to hear that, Mr Dashwood. It puts my mind at rest. Miles is a loyal and a very well-adjusted young man. It would be a terrible shame if that was to change.'

'I agree with you.'

Father Kennedy stood up, his gentle old face calm and suddenly decisive. 'I don't think I can tell you where they are, Mr Dashwood. I think it would be a grievous betrayal of confidence. But I will write to Mrs Kelly, and tell her what you have told me. And then it will be for her to decide.'

'Do you not think, Father, that Miles should have a say in the decision?'

'I think we need have no fear that he will not. Mrs Kelly is fairly desperate to see him settled and doing well. I am quite certain she will consult him in the matter. I will write to her tonight.'

'Thank you.'

Father Kennedy wondered if he had made himself sufficiently plain to Hugo Dashwood. It was dangerous ground he had been treading. He hoped he was not falling into temptation and attempting to play God. He had an uneasy feeling that he had. He would spend some time in the church tonight, examining his conscience. He might even make his confession to that tiresome new young priest, who would no doubt give him some very tedious penances to do.

He reproached himself for his uncharitable thought. Father Howell was very young. It was wrong to judge him harshly.

He sighed. He sometimes felt he was getting further and further from a state of grace in his old age. It was a sorry state of affairs.

Chapter Thirteen

London and New York, 1982–3

'Shit,' screamed Roz. 'Shit. C. J., C. J. I can't stand it. Stop it, stop it, oh, Christ, it hurts. It hurts.'

She was in labour, and had been for twelve hours; ever since, as Letitia was to remark later, she had heard about the arrival of Phaedria in her father's life.

It was Eliza who had brought her the news, as she sat sulkily and vastly pregnant in the house she and C. J. had bought in Cheyne Walk. The drawing room was on the first floor; she had a chaise longue in the window, overlooking the river, and for days she had laid there, trying as her yoga teacher and her natural childbirth instructor had told her, to relax and think positive thoughts, to visualize her body opening gently and letting out the huge child it was nurturing. All she could visualize was her office, ever more disorganized, she felt sure, the many strands of her business life tangled, her staff taking matters into their own hands, making the wrong decisions, wrecking the painstakingly constructed edifice of her own particular empire.

Until the baby had actually been overdue, she had continued to go into the office every single day, but her gynaecologist had expressly forbidden it, telling her that her membranes were going to rupture any moment; Roz did not care whether they ruptured or not, as long as she went into labour, but she could see that it would not be very impressive or professional to sit or stand in a large pool of water in the boardroom, so she had reluctantly given in; making everybody's life a misery, insisting that papers, letters, marketing plans, budgets be shipped to her daily, countermanding other people's decisions, altering her own, dictating endless memos to her hapless secretary and circulating them to the entire company, putting forward proposals for new hotels, stores, cosmetics, even hospitals – 'Well, why not, Daddy?' she had said when Julian phoned her laughing to point out the folly of that particular plan, 'You have an excellent reputation in the pharmaceutical industry now, why not capitalize on it, hospitals are big business in the States' – and demanding to see every note, every minute of every meeting, every letter, almost a transcript of every phone call, that C. J. wrote, attended or made.

C. J. was wretched; while Roz had been active and in control of her life, she had paid lip service to making the marriage work, she had been polite to him, pretended to listen to his views, both professional and personal, had hired Robin and Tricia Guild to decorate their house, in the way he wanted (she having absolutely no interest in the matter) and even gone with him with a fairly good grace to stay with his mother in Oyster Bay for a week in lieu of a honeymoon – 'Well, after all, C. J., we certainly don't need one, too ridiculous' – and had continued to see that their sex life was as satisfying and as frequently conducted as it had been before their marriage. But now she had stopped trying; she was too angry, too miserable, she felt too ugly and sick and bored and uncomfortable to do anything but let her true feelings for him show. And her true feelings were a mixture of contemptuous fondness and an almost permanent irritation.

She managed to keep this hidden, with considerable effort, from her father, whose approval seemed (somewhat ironically, she felt) more and more crucial to her, and from her mother and grandmother, who had both told her in very clear terms that she was making a serious and a very destructive mistake in marrying C. J. in the first place. She had had no answer for Letitia, but she had looked at her mother in rage and despair and said, 'Mummy, I'm doing what you told me to, how dare you not support me now,' and Eliza, horrified by all the threads of all the lives she seemed to have so disastrously tangled together, had begged her to reconsider, and said over and over again that she had been wrong, that she should never have counselled any such action, that she would be no party to it. But Roz had gone ahead; whether Eliza agreed with her or not, marrying C. J., so far as she could see, was going to ensure her most of what she wanted from life: her father's approval, her future assured, and a husband and home of her own.

Unfortunately, she had not been able to see very far.

C. J., who had been able to see quite far enough from the very beginning, was in a state of rising panic. He was in an untenable situation, with no prospect of escaping from it. Julian had sent for him, the morning after Roz had broken the news of her accidental pregnancy; C. J., braced for a bawling out and in the slightly forlorn hope of dismissal from the company, had been confronted by a magnum of champagne, an outstretched hand and promotion.

'I couldn't be more delighted. Roz tells me you want to get married straight away. I think it's an excellent idea. I'm going to put you in as president of the Hotels division, reporting direct to me. You'll need more money, as a family man. God, I wish your father was still alive to see this.'

C. J., reflecting that none of this would have happened if that had been the case, agreed fervently, and then asked, slightly nervously, whether Roz was to be given a new job as well. 'I don't see her wanting to report to me.'

Julian laughed. 'Neither do I. Yes, I'm giving her a go at the stores. She's always wanted them. Starting her off as vice-president in Europe, and then when she's had the baby and is ready, she can move on. She won't want to do too much just yet.'

He was wrong, of course; Roz had wanted to do much too much. She was wild with joy and triumph at getting her hands on the stores at last. She worked fourteen, fifteen hours a day and demanded the presidency as her baby's birthday present. She got it.

Rather to her surprise, to everybody's surprise, pregnancy at least suited her well. She was never sick; she did not feel tired; she enjoyed the new sensations within her body, her comparative serenity, the feel of the baby kicking, her new statuesque shape; being so tall, she carried the baby well. Even more to everybody's surprise, she decided on a natural childbirth and went to classes, earnestly practising relaxation and breathing in different levels every day, attending yoga classes, seeking out a doctor who would allow her to deliver the baby in the way she had chosen, who would not insist on giving her drugs, or any unnecessary medical procedure.

'This is a natural process,' she told everybody firmly. 'I plan to experience it naturally. And handle it myself.'

Eliza, who still had rather uncomfortably vivid memories of Roz's own birth, was sceptical. 'Of course it might all work wonderfully, darling, but I do think you'll be glad of some kind of pain relief at least in the later stages.'

'Oh, I don't see why,' said Roz. 'Cordelia has seen countless babies delivered by her method and none of the women needed any drugs at all. You can be your own pain relief, Mummy. You didn't understand in your day.'

'Maybe not,' said Eliza. 'Who is Cordelia? A doctor?'

'No, she's my natural childbirth teacher.'

'Is she qualified to teach such things?'

'Of course. She works with midwives and doctors. It was her who recommended me to Mr Partridge. He is a very very advanced obstetrician, totally opposed to medical interference.'

'I would have thought that was a contradiction in terms,' said Eliza. 'And anyway, what is Cordelia's method? Does it all take place in darkness with waterbeds all over the place? I was reading about something like that last week.'

'Well, you read the wrong magazines. Not waterbeds, that's just silly, but some people do have their babies in warm water. But Cordelia's method is a bit more straightforward. Basically, you learn to listen to your own body, and follow what it wants. I mean, you might want to deliver your baby on all fours, or standing up. It's all much more natural than lying down, anyway.'

'It sounds rather tiring to me,' said Eliza. 'And this is what Mr Partridge thinks as well, is it?'

'Of course. And he has booked me into a private hospital, with a modern birthing room, C. J. can be there, and Cordelia as well, to encourage me. I'm looking forward to it.'

'Good,' said Eliza. 'I'm delighted.'

'Honestly,' she said to Letitia later, 'I think pregnancy has affected her brain. Roz, of all people. I'd have thought she'd have favoured a Caesarian. I didn't argue with her, you can try, but I think we're actually lucky she isn't insisting on having this baby in the middle of a field. Or Hyde Park,' she added. 'Oh dear, C. J.'s so unhappy about it too.'

Letitia, who felt that C. J. must be unhappy about a great deal more than the method by which his baby was going to enter the world, tried very hard to change Roz's mind as well, without success. Roz was convinced that her mother and grandmother had suffered in childbirth simply because of archaic conditioning, and was deaf to any advice they had to give her.

She would have her baby as she did everything else these days: the way she wanted.

'How are you, darling?' said Eliza, entering the drawing room at Cheyne Walk, her arms full of white roses.

'Lousy,' said Roz. 'Can't sleep. So uncomfortable. The baby's so big now it can't move at all. I feel as if I'm going to burst.'

'Well, never mind, darling, it's only twenty-four hours now at the most, and then Mr Partridge will take you in.'

'I know, but Cordelia is most unhappy about it. She says induction ruins the natural pattern of labour. I really think I might not let him.'

'Roz,' said Eliza firmly, 'with great respect to Cordelia, who I do hope I never have to meet, incidentally, she is not a doctor, and nothing will ruin the natural pattern of labour more swiftly for you than a dead baby. Do stop being so ridiculous.'

Roz looked at her mother, startled; she was not usually so firm. 'All right,' she said crossly, 'there's no need to start lecturing me.'

'Sorry, darling. Now listen, I have the most divine bit of gossip for you. You just aren't going to believe this.'

'What?'

'Your father has a new girlfriend.'

'Since when?' said Roz sharply.

'Since the day before yesterday.'

'Oh, Mummy, he's always in bed with someone or other. That's not gossip.'

'Well, I think it might be. She's living at Regent's Park already.'

'Good God. What on earth will Camilla have to say?'

'A great deal, I hear. Apparently she's flying back to New York this afternoon.'

'Well, who is this woman?'

'Hardly a woman, darling. Younger than you.'

'What?'

Eliza was so busy arranging the roses, she did not see Roz's face go white, her eyes blaze.

'Yes, really, that's what's so intriguing. She's twenty-four years old. Extremely beautiful, apparently. Sarah Brownsmith has met her, she came to the office. She's a journalist. She interviewed your father and never went home again.'

'Who told you all this?' Roz sounded strained.

'Well, lots of people. Letitia met her, he took her there for a drink. Well, that's pretty significant, wouldn't you say? She said she was charming, and very beautiful.'

'Yes, yes, so you keep saying. And?'

'Well, I rang Sarah, and managed to get a bit out of her, but you know how irritatingly discreet she is. So then I rang the housekeeper at Regent's Park, and asked if your father had any guests at the moment, and she said yes, a young lady. She has the most unusual name, she's called Phaedria, Phaedria Blenheim. And – and this is the most ridiculous thing of all, I'm sure it can't be true – but Angie Masterson was having a drink in the Ritz early yesterday evening, and Camilla was there, with a friend, and Angie said she looked absolutely dreadful, white as a sheet, not that Camilla would ever look really awful, and Angie heard her say, well she says she heard her say, "And he's talking about marrying her." Well, it's obviously nonsense, but I don't see why Camilla should make things sound worse for her than they really are. Can you imagine anything more absurd, he's sixty-two, marrying a child of twenty-four. Oh, it can't be true. Now, darling, what can I get you?'

'Nothing,' said Roz, who had turned very pale, her hands gripping the chaise longue. 'I don't want anything, I feel sick.' Tears had formed in her green eyes, and she was looking at her mother with a mixture of panic and misery.

'Roz, darling, what is it? Is it the baby? Shall I call Mr Partridge?'

'No,' said Roz, breathing heavily, the tears falling. 'It isn't the baby. Damn the baby. Oh, you wouldn't understand. Oh, shit, I can't stand it. Just go away, Mummy, and leave me alone. Actually I do want something. I want a drink. A big one.'

She was in labour by lunch time.

'Roz, Roz, you're forgetting everything you've learnt. Welcome your contractions, don't fight them, let your body enjoy them.'

Cordelia Fowler, Roz's childbirth teacher, had an earnest, pale plain face and long lank brown hair; she wore a long flowing cotton dress and Indian sandals. C. J., who was not given to aggressive feelings, was trying to resist a strong temptation to remove her physically from the room. Roz was less inhibited.

'For God's sake, Cordelia, shut up will you. This is plain, bloody agony, and you tell me to welcome it. I can't, I can't stand it. Just go away if you can't do anything to help.'

Cordelia was undisturbed by this attack. She smiled serenely. 'Roz, it's you who can help. You can help yourself. Lean into the contractions. Smile, relax. Visualize your body opening. Let your baby go.'

'Christ almighty, do you think I don't want to let it go? Oh, God, here comes another one.'

'Smile, Roz, smile.'

Roz leant forward, her face contorted with pain and rage, and slapped Cordelia sharply twice across the face. Then she lay back on her pillows and groaned.

'I think,' said Cordelia in a low voice to C. J., quite unmoved by this assault, 'she must be nearing transition. It's always an emotionally difficult time.'

'What does that mean?' asked C. J., his face white, sweat standing on his forehead.

'Oh, dear, I'd forgotten you didn't do the couples' course. If only you had. She needs your understanding so badly. Well anyway, it means the point in labour in between first and second stage. Just before the mother wants to push. Emotional liability is always a sign. I'll call the midwife.'

She rang the bell. 'Roz, I think you are getting to transition. Would you like to squat? It could help such a lot.'

'No,' said Roz, 'I would not like to squat. I would like a general anaesthetic and to wake up with my baby in a cot beside me.'

'Then visualize that,' said Cordelia earnestly, 'visualize pain blanking out, visualize your baby out of your body. Oh, Sister, there you are. I think she may be in transition.'

Sister advanced on Roz with a stethoscope; she placed it on Roz's stomach and listened to the baby's heart, then pulled on a pair of examination gloves.

'What are you going to do to me now?' said Roz ferociously.

'Just have a little look,' said Sister. 'Perhaps it would be better if your husband and your birthing companion stepped outside for a moment. Then if we're right, I can call Mr Partridge.'

'I don't know why he isn't here,' said Roz, 'we're paying him enough.'

'Mrs Emerson, you are having a straightforward labour, and down the corridor another lady is coping with a premature breech delivery. Mr Partridge has to stay with her until her own obstetrician arrives. He has examined you several times. He knows exactly where you are.'

'Oh, God,' wailed Roz, 'here's another!'

'Welcome it, Roz,' said Cordelia, gripping her hand, and then hurrying out of the door after C. J. 'Not long now.'

Roz flung herself back on her pillows again, fixed the sister with a baleful eye, snatched her stethoscope and flung it across the room. 'Don't you dare come near me. Don't. I want an epidural. Now. Quickly. I can't stand this any longer.'

Sister, who had spent ten years as an independent midwife, schooled in the most advanced methods of natural childbirth, had never come across a mother so totally out of control. She glared at Roz and picked up her stethoscope. 'You are doing yourself and your baby a lot of harm,' she said. 'This is no way to conduct a labour.'

'Have you ever had a baby?' asked Roz through clenched teeth.

'I have not.'

'Then I suggest you go and have one. And I hope you have some bloody silly woman beside you telling you to welcome it all. Go and get Mr Partridge. Now.'

Mr Partridge came in, a patient, sympathetic look on his face.

'How are we doing?'

'You may be all right,' said Roz. 'I am not. I want an epidural.'

'What a pity.'

'For whom?'

'For everybody. You. Your baby. Us. It would be so much better if you could do it all by yourself.'

'Mr Partridge,' said Roz, gripping her bedhead, 'I am in dreadful pain.'

'Ah, but it is constructive pain. Good pain. Think of it like that.'

'Constructive pain my ass. I want an epidural.'

'Well, let's have a little look and then we can decide. It might be too late.'

He bent to examine her, then stood up beaming happily, pulling off his glove.

'It is.'

'It is what?'

'Too late. You're fully dilated. Any minute now you'll be pushing. Then its just wonderful fun. You won't mind at all.'

Roz lifted one of her long legs and aimed it very hard at Mr Partridge's plump chest. He staggered and nearly fell; he looked at her with deep distaste.

'Now, Mrs Emerson, you must conserve your strength. You're going to need a lot for the next hour or so. It's a very big baby.' There was just a suggestion of menace in his eyes.

'Mr Partridge, I am going to start screaming now and I am not going to stop until you give me an epidural.'

'I can't.'

Roz began to scream. She screamed from rage as much as pain and fear and, somewhere within her tumult, a passion of misery at the news she had heard that morning. Why should she be going through all this, when in a year she might have a brother to take everything away from her? Another contraction gripped her; she couldn't take much more. Dear God, she thought as she sank into a morass of pain, let this baby at least be a boy. Please, please, a boy.

Miranda Emerson was born an hour later, a ten-pound, noisy, healthy baby. Roz had, as promised, continued to scream, kicked the midwife as well as Mr Partridge, sent Cordelia packing, bitten her husband's hand so hard she drew blood, and then suddenly at the end of it delivered her baby with extraordinary ease and swiftness and a beatific smile on her face.

'Isn't she lovely, C. J., isn't she absolutely lovely?' she said, sitting up in bed half an hour after the delivery, the picture of rosy health, Miranda in her arms. 'What on earth have you done to your hand, why is it all bandaged up?'

'You bit me,' said C. J., not a note of reproach in his voice. 'Hard. It bled.'

'Oh, God, I'm sorry. I really didn't know what I was doing. Did I bite that silly bitch Cordelia as well?'

'No.'

'Pity. I will if ever I see her again. What a load of balls. Pain management indeed. Never mind, it's over now. Don't you think she's beautiful?'

'She's lovely,' said C. J., looking slightly nervously at the small wrinkled face, the mop of black hair, the tiny waving hands. 'Lovely.'

'Did you ring Mummy?'

'Yes. She's very excited, she's coming over later.'

'Tonight? How lovely. I want everyone to see this baby. What about Daddy?'

'Yes, I spoke to him.'

'Where was he? At home?'

'Not at first. Some girl answered the phone. Said he would soon be back. She seemed to know about the baby. I don't know who she was. Then he rang here, and he's coming over in the morning. Sent lots of love.'

Roz scowled. In her euphoria she had temporarily forgotten the new mistress. A cloud of fear and rage was cast briefly over her happiness; she remembered with a rush how passionately she had needed the baby to be a boy; for a second she looked at her daughter with regret, then shook herself. Who needed boys? Women could fight as well as men. Miranda was hers, her own creation; she would train her from this moment.

'What did she sound like, this girl? How do you know she was a girl? She might have been fifty.'

'Didn't sound it,' said C. J. cheerfully. 'She sounded really young. She had a very pretty voice,' he added.

'Oh, great,' said Roz, tugging ferociously at the ribbons on her nightdress. 'I'm delighted.' Then she looked down at her daughter and her face lightened again. 'Look, C. J., she's woken up. Look at her lovely lovely blue eyes.'

She wasn't going to have tonight spoilt by Phaedria Blenheim. Of all the ridiculous names. There would be plenty of time to deal with her.

'I do think,' said Letitia to Eliza, 'that Julian has treated Camilla dreadfully badly. Moving this girl he hardly knows into his house.'

'Oh, I don't know,' said Eliza, who found it hard to feel charitable towards Camilla. 'I can't see it's that hard on her. It's not as if she's actually been living with Julian, she's kept that perfectly appalling little house going all this time.'

'There is a little word which my son, I fear, has not ever quite managed to get his tongue around,' said Letitia. 'It's "no". I'm afraid I find much of his behaviour very hard to excuse. Maybe he doesn't actually live with Camilla any more, but she was virtually driven out of the house by his behaviour. He has continued to use her when it suited him. And she has remained very loyal to him, never publicly complained about him. I don't like her either, but I think she has a code of honour. Which is more than I can say for Julian. I'm afraid I don't often feel very proud of him these days.' She sighed, and looked suddenly very sad; Eliza took her hand.

'Oh, Letitia, darling, don't start getting morbid. I really can't subscribe to this view that our children's faults are down to us. Julian is not a raw adolescent. He's been outrageously spoilt, not by you, but by life. It's hardly surprising he behaves badly.'

'Well, you may be right,' said Letitia with another sigh, 'but sometimes I wonder if –'

'If what, Letitia?'

Letitia looked at her, as if she might be about to say something; then visibly silenced herself. 'Oh, nothing. Just a silly thought.'

'Very silly, I would imagine. Anyway, I'm afraid I can't feel sorry for Camilla. I'm just terribly pleased she's left London. Now listen, you've met Phaedria, what's she like?'

'She's charming. Intelligent, quite self-contained, certainly not swept off her feet by him. And really most beautiful. Tall, very slim, with the most amazing hair, dark brown, all kind of pre-Raphaelite curls.'

'She sounds vile. And he really wants to marry her?'

'He tells me so. I do find the whole thing very hard to believe.'

Camilla, sitting on her plane, drinking distilled water and nibbling at raw vegetables – the only food she ever allowed herself on flights – found the whole thing equally hard to believe. She was hurt, she was angry, she was humiliated, but most of all she was, she discovered, slightly amused. It really was a trifle pathetic that a man of sixty-two should be swept off his feet by a girl young enough to be his daughter. Or his granddaughter.

Camilla knew exactly what had happened to Julian; she had spent a great deal of time discussing the syndrome with her analyst over the past eighteen months. It was the mid-life crisis. The male menopause. He was perhaps a little old for it, it usually struck in the mid forties or early fifties, but its manifestations – a panic rush into a new relationship, a desperate grab at youth – were classic and unmistakable. It usually coincided with the waning of the sexual powers and the new relationship was seen as a remedy, a revitalization. Camilla allowed herself a short and pleasant contemplation on Julian's sexual powers and their vulnerability and her own singular position with regard to them – and to wonder how he would manage without her in the future. Once or twice over the past years, when things had been rather less than one hundred per cent for him, he had turned to her again for help and she had given it generously, grateful, she had to admit to herself, for his unique need of her; there then would follow a period of great affection, and many promises of faithfulness. The promises were always broken, and Camilla always managed to persuade herself that the relationships were trivial, short term, and that she should not allow herself to over-react, to throw away so much that was good about her life with Julian Morell along with the little that was bad.

And usually she was right; the affairs did not last, and particularly not with the younger women he became involved with, who swiftly tired of being forced into a middle-aged lifestyle, however glamorous, and moved on. And there was absolutely no doubt in Camilla's mind that this would happen now. Phaedria Blenheim – very young indeed, even by Julian's standards – was clearly not going to spend the rest of her youth tied to someone so much older than herself, however rich he might be. No doubt she had found his wealth irresistible, she was from all accounts very hard up, but it was a commodity that very soon palled. In a year's time, her wardrobe full of couture clothes, her wrists and neck hung with jewels, her body expensively exercised and massaged and tanned, already bored with her old husband's old friends, Miss Blenheim would be looking, idly desperate, for a young lover, a friend, a soulmate, someone who spoke her language, shared her tastes, saw the world from her own viewpoint. And she would no doubt find him. Well, good for her.

She bit savagely on a stick of celery, remembering with fierce misery the session with Julian yesterday morning. He had been very frank, totally out of character; he had rung her quite early, about eight o'clock, apologized for not taking her to dinner the night before and asked her to join him for breakfast at the Connaught. She had gone along just mildly revengeful, but serene and in control nonetheless; he had stood up as she entered the dining room and looked at her very seriously. He was clearly tired; his eyes had the shadows of a sleepless night in them; and his mouth was tense, unsmiling.

'Camilla, good morning. Come and sit down. Breakfast?'

'Some honey in yogurt, please, and some decaffeinated coffee.'

He repeated her order to the waiter.

'Is the yogurt live?' she said.

The waiter looked at her with exquisitely polite disdain. 'I will inquire, madam. What shall I do if it is – dead?'

'Cancel my order,' said Camilla coolly. 'And bring me some freshly squeezed orange juice and strawberries instead.'

'Certainly, madam.'

'You're not eating,' she said to Julian in surprise. He usually ate well at breakfast time, the only meal in the day when he indulged himself.

'No, I'm not hungry.'

'Are you feeling unwell?'

'No.'

'Julian, I wish you'd consider a macrobiotic diet, for a short time at least. It would do your system so much good. So cleansing. So detoxifying. I have found an excellent dietician in Covent Garden. He draws up individual diet sheets according to lifestyle and metabolic requirement and –'

'Camilla, I really don't want to discuss my diet. I have something very serious to tell you. Something which may – which will – distress you. I'm sorry.'

She sat and looked at him, quite still, her face composed, devoid of emotion. She did, as she always did in stressful situations, one of her relaxation exercises – letting go slowly and completely from the belly inwards, breathing in very slowly through the nose and gently out through the mouth. It always worked; it kept her utterly in control.

'What is it?'

'I have to end our relationship. At once.'

'I see.'

His face was working, anxious, almost afraid. She had never known him so vulnerable.

'I have found – met – someone else.'

'When?'

'I beg your pardon?'

'When did you meet her?'

'Yesterday.'

'I see. Love at first sight.'

'Perhaps.'

'Well, this is not really very unusual, is it? I seem a little over-familiar with this scenario. Now, who is this person? Do I know her?'

'No, you don't. She's a journalist.'

'Will I have heard of her?'

'I very much doubt it. She is not at all well known. Although very talented.'

'Of course.'

'Camilla, I can see this must sound quite absurd. But I can only tell you that I feel I can't go on seeing you. Not now. It would be – dishonest.'

'Good heavens, Julian, what an interesting word to find on your lips. I didn't know you were familiar with it. She must be a very exceptional person, to lead you to think in such terms.'

'Yes,' he said, 'yes, I think she is.'

Camilla was having a little trouble with her relaxation therapy. She felt tense, shaky, rather faint. She took a deeper breath, closed her eyes for a moment, tried to wipe her mind blank.

The waiter returned, with her breakfast 'The yogurt is live, madam.'

'What? Oh, I don't want it. Take it away.'

'Do you want the strawberries instead, madam?'

'No,' said Camilla, teeth clenched, voice low, 'I don't want anything. Just some coffee.'

'Certainly, madam. Decaffeinated?'

'No.' She was almost shouting at him, in an agony of misery, 'I want real coffee. Full of caffeine. Strong. Black. With sugar. All right?'

'All right. Certainly, madam. I'll bring it at once.'

She looked at Julian and thought how much she had loved him, how much, at that moment, she hated him. 'How old is she, this person?'

He looked at her, then looked away. 'Twenty-four.'

'Twenty-four!' Camilla began to laugh, wild, hysterical

laughter. 'Twenty-four years old. How pathetic. Even by your standards. What a stupid, hopeless gesture. Julian, it's a classic. I suppose you realize that. A classic grab at youth. A negation of yourself, a rejection of where you really are, who you really are. I feel sorry for you, deeply sorry. And for her. How long do you think it will last?'

'A long time, I hope. I intend to marry her.'

Camilla sat staring at him, quite quite still, her face ashen, her eyes wide with horror. Her stomach heaved; she thought she might be sick. Then she leant forward, and in perhaps the first, the only truly spontaneous, unpremeditated action of her entire life, slapped him very hard twice across the face.

'You poor deluded bastard,' she said very clearly, so clearly everyone in the dining room could hear. Then she picked up her bag and walked quite slowly and deliberately out.

It was only when she was safely in a taxi that she began to cry.

The first person Roz had talked to, bared her soul to about Phaedria, was Susan. She found her very receptive.

Susan found herself reacting strongly and rather painfully to Julian's prospective marriage. She had imagined herself to be entirely free of any emotional involvement with him; she was happily involved with Richard Brookes, and was seriously considering marrying him ('Although at our age it does seem a little ridiculous,' she said, 'and I'm certainly not having anything but the smallest most badly publicized wedding'); she had watched Julian leading Camilla the elaborate and disagreeable dance she had visualized for herself over the years; and she had thanked God, and her own common sense and judgement, that she had escaped it. Then he sat her down in his office one morning (the same day as he had had the confrontation with Camilla at the Connaught) and told her that he was very much in love and planning to marry again, and she had felt sick, and savagely jealous.

She had managed to smile, to tease him mildly, to tell him he was too old for such nonsense, and that he should wait maybe another twenty-four hours before finally committing himself, but the words came out with difficulty, and the smile was frozen on to her mouth.

'I know it sounds absurd,' he said, kissing her fondly on the cheek, accepting her good wishes, 'I know I am old enough to know better, and that I am acting rather rashly, to put it mildly. I can only tell you that what I feel for Phaedria I have never felt for any other woman, so I can only presume it must be love. It has come to me rather late, but I have to be grateful that it is here at all. And you with your clear-sightedness and great knowledge of me should surely understand.'

'Oh, I do, Julian,' said Susan, a twist of pain in her heart as he acknowledged finally (and somewhat brutally) that whatever he had felt for her, it had not been love, 'I do understand. Does – that is, have you told Camilla?'

'I have,' he said with a heavy sigh. 'This morning. Over breakfast. At the Connaught,' he added, a trifle unnecessarily.

'I don't suppose it mattered much where you told her,' said Susan briskly. 'In fact, it might have been better to do it somewhere just slightly less public.'

'Yes. I think you're probably right,' he said. 'I'm afraid she was very upset. More than I thought she would be.'

'Julian,' said Susan, standing up, unable to bear it any longer. 'Sometimes I find it very hard to believe you think at all. Especially about people and how they might feel. I must go, we have a great deal of work on, and if you remember, you never did phone me yesterday about the marketing plans.'

'Oh, I'm sorry,' he said. 'I'll go through it all with you later.'

'Well, if you have the time,' she said.

As she looked back, she saw an expression on his face that was very seldom there: it was uncertainty.

She got over her shock and sense of misery quite quickly; she talked about it to Richard, who laughed and told her he thought Julian was no end of a fine fellow and that she was a miserable old hag.

'Nevertheless I think I have by far the better of it all,' he said, kissing her fondly. 'I'm very pleased indeed you didn't marry the old bugger all those years ago.'

'Richard, even if I had, this would still have happened,' she said. 'That's the whole point. If I wasn't so suspicious of Phaedria Blenheim, I would be very sorry for her.'

'Why should you be so suspicious of her? Poor young virginal thing.'

'Richard, if there's one thing Phaedria isn't, it's virginal. I'm sure she's been around a great many beds. Knows exactly what she's doing. Of course I'm suspicious of her. His money has to be a big factor.'

'Well, it doesn't have to be his money. Power, I'm told, is a great aphrodisiac.'

'Well, that isn't much better.'

'I think it is. A bit.'

'Richard thinks it's his power,' she said to Roz. They were lying on the sunbeds at the Sanctuary in Covent Garden.

'Well, I expect it is. And his money. Oh God, look at this stomach. It's so revolting.'

'Roz, you have no stomach. Don't be ridiculous.'

It was almost true. Roz's stomach had snapped back to almost its pre-natal tautness within days of the birth; her strong athletic body had dealt with pregnancy and childbirth with great efficiency.

'Well, I'm going back to work next week, and I'm not going to be seen looking like a Michelin woman. Especially not with Phaedria about. I'm sure she's extremely thin.'

'Yes she is, but for God's sake, Roz, you're not in competition with her. It's your father who's in love with her, not your husband.'

'I know,' said Roz, turning over suddenly; clearly not even Susan could begin to understand how she felt about Phaedria. She stood up, reached for her robe. 'Come on, let's get some fruit juice. Tell me more about what Richard said.'

'Well, he said exactly that,' said Susan, torn between sympathy and amusement at Roz's rather schoolgirl attitude towards Phaedria. 'He said he didn't think it was his money, or at least not only the money, it was the power.'

Roz said for many years how appropriate it had been for her and Phaedria to have met in the lavatory.

Two and a half weeks had passed since Miranda's birth and the arrival of Phaedria in her father's life; she knew she was being ridiculous in avoiding her, but every day she told herself that tomorrow she would be able to face it, or at least face arranging it, and every day she felt an even darker horror at the thought. Roz was not a coward, she flinched from very little; but the prospect of having not only to meet Phaedria, but to smile at her, to be nice to her, to express pleasure at having her in the family, seemed quite beyond endurance. And so she continued to hide, to make excuses, to find vague commitments; Letitia and Susan had pleaded with her, her father was on the brink of losing his temper, Eliza had given her a very sharp piece of her mind, and still she said no, she couldn't, she still felt unwell, weak, not up to such a confrontation, while looking radiantly healthy, attending her yoga classes, visiting the office for ever longer periods each day, and calling meetings at the house.

It was C. J. who finally persuaded her; he put down the phone at breakfast one morning and said, 'That was your father, he wants us to go and have dinner at the house tonight. I said I thought we could and you'd call him back.'

'I won't go,' said Roz, panic rising, 'I can't, I don't feel at all strong today, what about Miranda, how could you, C. J., just call him back, please, and say no, maybe at the weekend.'

'Rosamund, you look extremely well to me, you have a meeting in the office if you remember, which I imagine you won't want to cancel, and I haven't noticed Miranda preventing you from doing a great deal over the past two weeks. Now for God's sake pull yourself together, you're making yourself look a complete fool.'

Roz looked at him startled, impressed as always when he stood up to her; she managed to force a smile. 'All right, C. J. I certainly don't want to look a fool. I'll come.'

'Good. Call your dad back, will you. I have to go now.'

He walked out of the room without looking at her; Roz looked after him thoughtfully, and then picked up the phone and dialled Hanover Terrace. Her father answered it.

'Daddy? It's Roz.'

'Hallo, Roz.' He sounded brusque, impatient.

'Daddy, we'd really like to come tonight. I'm feeling much better. Thank you. I might have to bring Miranda, though. She's a bit colicky, and I don't want to leave her with Nanny.'

She could hear the warmth, the relief in his voice. 'Roz, I'm delighted. I'll tell Phaedria, she'll be so pleased. And of course bring Miranda. That will be lovely.'

525

'She might yell.'

'We won't mind a bit. Goodbye, darling. See you about eight.'

'Yes. Bye, Daddy.'

Roz put down the phone and went up to have a bath. She suddenly felt quite genuinely weak and shaky. On the way she looked in on Miranda, who was being bathed.

'You'd better yell good and hard tonight, baby,' she said.

The nanny, a young Norland-trained embodiment of efficiency, looked at her in surprise. Roz didn't bother to explain.

She went to her meeting in the office, a financial review of the stores' various performances in various cities of the world – New York still led the field, Paris was down, Milan up – and spent an hour with her secretary dictating letters and arranging a trip to Paris so that she could study Circe's performance for herself, and see Annick at the same time. She decided that she would go home and have a rest against the ordeal of the evening, and took the lift up to the penthouse to use the ladies' there while her car was brought round to the front of the building. As she stood in front of the mirror, brushing her hair, wondering if the half stone she had still retained was settled entirely on to her chin, the door opened behind her and a girl walked in. Roz glanced at her, half smiled and then looked at her more carefully, taking in properly what she saw: long, curling dark hair falling past her shoulders, a pale, rather serious face, and a slender red crepe dress with a gently swirling skirt that Roz recognized instantly as being from Jasper Conran's latest collection. The impact hit her gradually, like a slowed-down film; the girl's walk seemed almost to stop, her head to turn towards her inch by inch, the hair floating, drifting up in the air, a smile began, tenuously, cautiously to appear on her lips. Roz felt as if she was falling, the room swam; she closed her eyes, leant on the dressing table.

As if from a great distance she heard the girl say, 'Are you all right? Here, sit down, let me get you a glass of water.'

Roz straightened, hauled herself back to normality with a huge effort. 'I'm fine,' she said, meeting the brown eyes, the concerned face with a hard, distant stare. 'Absolutely fine. Thank you,' she added with an ill-disguised reluctance.

'Are you – you must be Roz? I'm Phaedria.' She was holding out her hand. Roz with enormous self-control took it.

'How formal! How do you do?'

'It feels a bit formal. How are you? Are you sure you're all right? How is the baby? I'm so looking forward to tonight.'

'I'm perfectly all right, thank you. So is the baby.'

There was a silence. Phaedria was looking at her uncertainly, searching for something else to say.

'I'm just going to have lunch with – with –'

'My father? How nice. Do give him my love.'

'Why don't you join us? It would be fun.'

'Oh, I don't think so,' said Roz, managing to smile now, graciously, sensing Phaedria's discomfiture. 'Thank you,' she added. There was a long silence.

'Well,' said Phaedria, 'I'd better go. He doesn't like to be kept waiting, does he?' She was floundering now.

'Perhaps not,' said Roz. 'He's never seemed particularly to mind waiting for me.' She smiled again. 'We'll see you tonight.'

'Yes. I hear you're bringing the baby. That will be lovely, I shall look forward to meeting her.'

'No, I'm not bringing her,' said Roz. 'I think after all it would be better if I didn't.'

She managed to imply it would be seriously bad for Miranda's health if Phaedria met her.

'Oh,' said Phaedria, 'oh, all right. Well, goodbye Roz. Nice meeting you.'

'Goodbye,' said Roz.

She watched Phaedria walk out of the cloakroom rather quickly, and smiled at herself in the mirror. It might be a long war, but she had certainly won the first skirmish.

The dinner was dreadful just the same. Roz had dressed to kill, fearing to look disadvantaged beside this paragon; she wore a black silk jersey dress from Chloe with the newly fashionable wide shoulders, and an above the knee skirt, which showed off her endlessly long, slender legs to their very best advantage. It did her very little good. Nothing, nothing at all could have prepared her for, or helped her through the agony of watching her father looking at Phaedria in adoration, asking her opinion on everything, encouraging her to talk, praising the way she had adjusted to her new life, organized the dinner that evening, charmed the housekeeper, done the flowers herself; dear God, thought Roz, any moment now he'll start saying how exquisitely she goes to the lavatory.

Roz knew her own performance was superb; she talked as charmingly as she knew how, questioned Phaedria graciously about her life as a journalist, admired the food and Phaedria's dress (another Conran, black crepe this time), teased her father (but only very gently) about his wicked past, and asked Phaedria most politely if she would forgive her if she and Julian talked shop very briefly after dinner. 'Literally shops. You know, I expect, that I'm president of Circe,' she said, smiling across the candlelight; and 'Of course,' said Phaedria, 'I do know. Yes, you withdraw, and I'll stay here and C. J. and I can tell dirty stories over the port.'

It was the first sign of retaliation; Roz looked at her sharply, startled, then smiled again.

'Do be careful,' she said. 'C. J. has a terribly weak stomach.'

The only thing she was quite unable to say was anything at all about when the wedding might be, or even to congratulate them; she tried, several times, but the words literally stuck in her throat, a hard, dry lump, and each time she had had to take a huge draught of the superb claret her father had brought out for the occasion, swallowing it desperately as if it was beer or water, and change the subject. However, she felt, as she kissed him lovingly on the steps of the house, and proffered her cheek to Phaedria, she had got through it all extremely well; but C. J., lying awake in the bedroom next to hers, that he now permanently occupied, thinking about her and the performance she had put on, heard her weeping for a long time, and wished, for all their sakes, there was something he could do to help.

'Phaedria, we have to think about the wedding.'

'Oh, good.'

'No, I'm serious.'

'So am I. I like weddings.'

'Now, we can play it two ways. We can sneak off and go to a registry office, and not really tell anybody. Or we can do it in style. Ask everybody. And it would have to be everybody. What do you think?'

'What do you want to do?'

'I don't mind. I want you to do what you want. I suppose I have a marginal preference for the sneaking off.'

'Let's do it in style.'

He was surprised. 'All right. If that's what you want.'

'When shall we do it?'

'Too late before Christmas now. If we're to do it in style. January. Here or in the country?'

'Oh, let's do it in the country. That would be much nicer. Then we can involve the horses.'

He laughed. 'They'll like that.'

The following weekend he took her to Marriotts for the first time. She fell in love with it. She wandered through its beautiful rooms, looking for a long time out of each window, so as to imprint each individual view on her mind; she insisted they eat lunch sitting at either end of the huge table in the dining room; she explored the attics, she investigated the cellars; she walked round the gardens, she exclaimed with delight at the stables, and she rode with him across the downs in the falling dusk, laughing, exultant.

'We must bring Grettisaga here. She would love it. Can I go and fetch her myself?'

'If you want to. Take Tony with you.'

'Who's Tony?'

'My groom. You can't manage on your own.'

'Yes, I can,' she said, and for the very first time he heard a tinge of irritation in her voice. 'Of course I can. I can drive a horse box. I've done it hundreds of times.'

'Phaedria, it really isn't very wise. It's a long way. Suppose you had a breakdown or a puncture?'

'I'd fix it.'

He sighed. 'Wait till next weekend, and I'll come with you.'

'No. I want her here sooner than that. Stop fussing.'

Later that night, as they lay in the big bed upstairs, with the shutters open, the ghostly moon falling across the pillow, she said, 'Julian?'

'Yes, darling?'

'What am I going to do about Roz?'

'What do you mean?'

'She hates me.'

'Phaedria! It's not like you to be hysterical.'

'Julian, I am not being hysterical.'

'Forgive me, darling, but I think you are. Those are very strong words. You've only met Roz twice. How can you possibly claim she hates you? It's nonsense.'

'Julian, I am capable of making a judgement. I can tell when people don't like me. And Roz doesn't. Well, she more than doesn't like me. Like I said, she hates me. She won't speak to me unless she has to. She won't even look at me. I've suggested lunch, I've asked if I can come to see her in the office, I've really tried. She won't meet me even a quarter of the way. And I find it very difficult.'

'She came to dinner with C. J.'

'That was to please you.'

He picked up her hand and kissed her fingertips. 'I think you're merely not having quite the success with Roz you've had with most other people. Which is natural really, in a way. She has a rather – intense attitude towards me, and she's bound to be a little wary. Now look, my mother adores you, Richard and Freddy are both dying of love for you, all the staff in Hanover Terrace dote on you, even Eliza wants to be your best friend. I haven't been on such good terms with Eliza for years. Can't you be content with that, and let Roz come round in her own time? She will. She likes you very much, she told me so.'

'Did she?' said Phaedria. 'How nice. Julian, please stop patronizing me. I am not a child, even if I seem like one to you.'

'Phaedria,' said Julian, dropping her hand and drawing slightly away from her. 'I think this is a little absurd.'

'Really? You call my objecting to a total animosity from Roz absurd? I'm disappointed in you, Julian.'

'I think,' he said, and she could hear the ice in his voice, 'we have enough real problems to confront without you manufacturing one over a non-existent hostility from my daughter.'

'It is not non-existent.'

'I happen to believe it is.'

'Then you should open your eyes a little wider. And perhaps you would like to tell me what real problems we have?'

'A great many. I'm amazed you have to have them spelt out. We have an age difference of nearly forty years. However much we may both deny it, there are awkwardnesses in that. I have a very large company to run which, if I may say so, you have not made much of an attempt to acquaint yourself with. I also have several households to maintain, and there are serious practical problems in that. You need to understand each one and its own particular system, you need to know the staff and to win their trust. You've made very little effort in that direction. You haven't bothered to buy yourself many decent clothes. You haven't suggested we do any entertaining. Your main concerns seem to be whether or not you can get a job on *Vogue*, and being reunited with your horse.'

Phaedria was silent for a while; then she got out of the bed.

'You bastard,' she said, 'you lousy bastard. I've known you just over three weeks and you throw that pile of garbage at me. How dare you?'

She walked over to the door, pulling her robe on.

'Where are you going?'

'Back to London.'

'Don't be absurd.'

She slammed the door.

She had no clothes to put on; she wasn't going to go back into the bedroom. She went into one of the spare rooms and found some jodhpurs –presumably belonging to Roz, she thought, dragging them on with vicious rage, or one of Julian's other unfortunate mistresses. She couldn't find a sweater, but downstairs she took one of the Barbours hanging on the utility room door, and a pair of Hunter wellington boots. She let herself out of the door. She was too excited now, too amused by her own adventure to feel upset.

They had driven down in the Corniche; the keys to that were on the table next to Julian. She walked over to the garage where he kept the cars; it was unlocked. There were five inside; three very early models: an open 1903 Fiat, a first edition Chevrolet, its name written elegantly right along its bonnet, and a Cunard-bodied Napier. Even in her rage, she did not quite dare to consider taking one of them. But nearest the door was the Bugatti; ravishingly elegant and low slung, with its sloping running board and majestically curved mudguards. That would do. Unbelievably, it had the keys in it; Julian had been playing with it that morning. Thank God it did have a key: the only model that did, he had told her.

Phaedria got in and, trembling slightly, tried to start it; it roared obligingly at the second attempt.

She smiled triumphantly, and eased it forward; it was deliciously easy to drive. Safely out of the garage, she let in the throttle and cautiously put her foot down; clear of the house, and halfway along the drive, she increased her speed. This was fun . . .

She could remember the way – just; the night was clear, which made things easier. Down the lane for two miles, then right at the turning to Steyning and then it was signposted to the A24. She had a bit of trouble making the lights work, and she had to stop twice and wipe the windscreen with her hand, but otherwise it was easy. She hoped the petrol would last; she wasn't going to find a garage open here in the middle of the night. Her mind was blank now, except for rage; pain, she supposed, would come later. She found it almost impossible to believe that a man as charming, as gentle, as civilized, as loving as Julian had been to her, could convert so swiftly into an arrogant, manipulative monster. All at a breath of criticism of his daughter. She shuddered; she felt outraged, blindly, furiously angry. She put her foot down harder.

Suddenly in the rear view mirror she saw headlights. It might be someone else, anyone, but it was certainly a great deal more likely to be Julian. The lights flashed; she drove on. It was Julian, in the Corniche; the lane was so narrow he couldn't overtake her. He was driving quite hard behind her now, hooting and flashing; Phaedria suddenly started to laugh. This was revenge, however brief, and it was extremely sweet. There was nothing he could do, just for a short heady while; he was impotent, he couldn't touch her. She hoped the sensation was painful. It would almost certainly be novel.

At the end of the lane, her triumph swiftly ended; the road widened, she tried to go faster, but the Bugatti suddenly began to slow down; its petrol had gone. The Corniche swung wide of her then pulled in tight in front of her; she had to stop. Julian leapt out, dragged her out of the driving seat and slapped her hard across the face.

'How dare you! How dare you take that car? Have you any idea how valuable it is?'

'Oh, yes,' said Phaedria coolly, 'I have. C. J. was telling me about it at dinner. Well, Julian, you seem to want me to become more familiar with all the precious and important things in your life; I thought I'd start with the cars. Now if you could just give me a lift to the next garage, I can get a can of petrol and carry on.'

She was breathing heavily, her eyes huge and brilliant with anger; as she stood there, confronting him, contemptuous, unafraid, the Barbour swung slowly open and revealed her bare breasts. Julian looked at her, and slowly his expression totally altered; rage became hunger, hostility tenderness, and he reached out and tried to take her in his arms.

'Don't touch me,' said Phaedria, pulling the coat angrily round her. 'Just don't. I want nothing more to do with you. Ever. Just leave me alone.'

'No,' he said, 'I can't do that,' and he half pushed her, half dragged her into the back seat of the Corniche, slamming the door behind them.

'I'm sorry,' he said, pushing the coat down off her shoulders, kissing her frantically on her lips, her neck, her breasts. 'I'm sorry, I'm sorry, I'm sorry, and I love you so much. Please, Phaedria, please forgive me.'

And she, stunned by the swift conversion from anger to desire that she felt in her own body as well, kissed him back, fiercely, greedily, reaching for him, tearing at his clothes, ripping open his trousers, pushing down her jodhpurs, and flung herself back on to the seat, pulling him on to her, thrusting herself desperately against him, frantic for the feel of him inside her, filling her, moving her, leading her into her sweet, hot explosion of pleasure. It was over in minutes; they lay, breathing heavily, silent, looking at each other warily. Then Phaedria suddenly smiled. 'You bastard,' she said, and kissed him very tenderly on the mouth.

They spent Christmas alone at Marriotts; Julian invited Roz and C. J. and the baby, but Roz said, sickly sweet, that this was their first Christmas as a family and they wanted to spend it together, just the three of them. She was sure he would understand.

They also invited Letitia, but she said Eliza and Peveril had asked her up to Garrylaig, and she couldn't resist a Scottish Christmas and Hogmanay; and they asked Augustus Blenheim, but he said he would be better in the company of Charles Maturin, who was claiming most of his attention; so in the end there were just the two of them.

Phaedria didn't mind; she had always experienced Christmas as a fairly solitary, peaceful time, and besides she was still sufficiently newly in love with Julian not to want to share him. She insisted he got rid of all the staff, and after they had been to church in the village (also at her instigation) and tramped over the downs, cooked Christmas dinner herself; *moules marinières* she served up, and duck in cognac, and a marvellous cherry bombe; they drank two bottles of sancerre and a great deal of armagnac, and sank exhausted and bloated on to the rug in front of the fire.

'I'd like to make love to you,' said Julian, 'but I think I might be sick if I did. You'll make some man a wonderful wife, you know.'

'Maybe.'

'What I suggest is that we have a little nap, and then I want to give you your presents.'

'Presents? Plural?'

'Mmm.'

'I only have a singular present for you.'

'That's all right. I have more money than you.'

'That's true. I love you.'

'Not my money?'

'No,' she said, surprised, 'of course not your money. It's the last thing about you I love.'

'Good,' he said, 'then I love you too.'

Phaedria fell asleep wondering at his question, and how much and how often he had wanted to ask it before.

It was seven o'clock and quite dark before she woke up; Julian was standing in front of her with a bottle of champagne and two glasses.

'Only cure for a nasty hangover.'

She sat up. 'Ugh! I hope it works. I feel vile.'

'It will.'

She tried it; he was right.

'Let me give you your present first.'

'All right.'

'I thought and thought,' she said, 'about what you could give to the man who has everything. Very difficult. In the end, I thought it should be something that would mean a lot to both of us, and I thought of horses, and I ended up with this.'

She hauled a package out of the darkness behind one of the sofas where she had hidden it before lunch. He opened it slowly. It was a very early edition of Stubbs' *The Anatomy of the Horse*; he looked through it in silence, clearly enchanted.

'What a marvellous present. I've always wanted this book. He did the engravings himself, you know, actually engraved the plates.'

'I know.'

'How on earth did you get it?'

'The book department at Sotheby's helped me. They sent me off to a little old man in the Charing Cross Road. He got it for me from some contact of his. I'm so glad you like it.'

'I love it.' He kissed her. 'But you didn't have to get me anything. You're all I want these days.'

'That's a lie.'

'Well, let's not argue today. It's a lovely present. My turn . . . Now then, this is the most important.'

He handed her a small box. Phaedria opened it slowly.

'Oh, my God,' she said, 'oh, Julian, they're glorious.'

They were a pair of matching diamond and emerald rings: the emeralds cut into oblongs, the diamonds set neatly, geometrically round them.

'One for the left hand, your engagement ring. I'm sorry it's been so long, but I couldn't find what I wanted. One for the right hand, because I love you. Put them on.'

She put them on. They fitted perfectly.

'How did you manage that?'

'Took that little gold thing of yours and measured it. Had them sized.'

'I like that little gold thing. But oh, Julian, these are so lovely. I can't wear them. They'll get lost.'

'Nonsense. They're safer on your hands than off them. I want you to wear them all the time. I got them from Cartier and they are making you a necklace to go with them for your wedding day. That will be fake, I'm afraid, well that is to say, modern, but these are genuine twenties deco.'

'Oh, I love them so much. Thank you.'

'Right. Now I have some more things for you. Come into the hall.'

In the hall, under the tree was a pile of parcels; Phaedria looked at it in awe. 'Are those all for me?'

'They certainly are.'

'Oh, Julian. I – well, I was going to say I don't deserve them, but I expect I do.'

'I think you do. Go ahead. Open them.'

She went ahead. There was a very big parcel which turned out to be a long grey blond wolf coat ('I remembered you warned me never to buy you mink, but I thought this would be all right'); there was a smaller one which was a red silk dress from St Laurent ('Now you must promise me never to wear anything underneath it, at all, because it's very clingy indeed.' 'Not even knickers?' 'Least of all knickers'); there was a big heavy square one which was bound copies of *Vogue* from the twenties and thirties; there was a very big bottle of Jicky ('It must be half a pint' 'I forced them to sell me the showroom sample bottle, but it's the genuine stuff inside, I promise'); there was a painting by James Lavery of a horse show; and there was a tiny box, with a key in it.

She looked at it. 'What's this?'

'It's the key of the Bugatti. I want you to have it. I think you earned it that night. In several ways.'

'Oh, Julian. Now that *is* love.'

'Yes,' he said. 'It is. Especially as I know you won't really appreciate it. But you look marvellous driving it.'

'I feel marvellous driving it.'

'Good. Now come outside.'

'Outside?'

'Yes. Put a coat on. And don't take your sweater off.'

'I just might. For old time's sake.'

'Well, you'll have to wait a minute. Come on.'

He took her hand, fetched a huge lamp and led her out to the stables.

'Julian, now what have you done?'

'Wait and see.'

Grettisaga, happily ensconced in her new home, whinnied with pleasure at the sight of her mistress; Phaedria kissed her nose.

'Happy Christmas, angel.'

Julian walked to the end of the stableyard, and into the covered area where there were several more loose boxes. He switched on the light. 'Now,' he said, 'I know this is dodgy. A bit like buying someone a dress when she hasn't seen it. But you liked the dress. I hope you like this. Look in there.'

Phaedria looked. A black head looked back at her. A calm brilliant pair of eyes. A long, silky mane. A delicate, gently arched neck.

'Oh, Julian. Oh, God I can't bear it.'

'I hope you can. She's three years old. A thoroughbred. But you can see that.'

'I can, oh, I can. Oh, she's beautiful. Can we bring her out?'

'Yes, I'll get a head collar. She has a very nice temperament. I think you'll like her.'

'What's her name?'

'Spring Collection.'

'How very suitable. Or did you christen her?'

'No. I just found her. Well, Tony found her, and I approved her. Look, here's the collar, lead her out.'

Spring Collection stepped out into the yard quite willingly. She walked with a fluid grace; but she was relaxed, she did not dance or prance.

'She is absolutely lovely,' said Phaedria, running her hand wonderingly down the fine back, gazing at the delicate, long long legs. 'I can't believe anything so beautiful could be mine. I want to ride her now.'

'Well, you can't. I think, even for you that would be reckless. But tomorrow you can. I know how much you love Grettisaga, but she is a hunter, after all, they can occupy different places in your life. And your heart.'

Phaedria looked up at him. 'I don't think there's much room left in my heart for anything but you, really.'

'Nonsense. There's always room in a heart for a horse. Now put her back and let's go indoors. What was that you were saying earlier about taking your sweater off?'

537

*

The wedding date had been set for the first of June. On the night of Phaedria's flight in the Bugatti, after they had reached home (towing the Bugatti, to the accompaniment of much swearing from Julian, who refused to leave it in the lane), after they had gone back to bed and made love again, after Julian had begged her to forgive him again and again, after she had said (without believing it for a moment) perhaps she had been mistaken about Roz, after they had slept briefly and Phaedria had woken first to a still, cold day, she had decided, and told Julian, that she had decided that January was perhaps a little soon for the wedding. That maybe they should know each other a little better first. That it would do no harm to wait. And that besides, the weather would be nicer, they could have a marquee, the gardens would look beautiful.

And Julian had been quite unable to change her mind.

Towards the beginning of March Julian went to see his dentist. Sitting in the waiting room in Weymouth Street, leafing idly through copies of *Country Life*, he saw an advertisement for a house and his heart was as startlingly stopped as it had been when he had first seen Phaedria Blenheim four months earlier.

The house was on the corner of Piccadilly and one of the small streets tipping down the hill towards St James's, just east of Fortnum's; it was tall and grey and beautifully proportioned, and it had been in use for the past few years (said the advertisement) as a hotel. The leasehold was for sale for three million pounds and it would easily (so went on the advertisement persuasively) convert into offices, or flats. Julian had other ideas for it.

He cancelled his appointment, tore out of the building and got a taxi down to Piccadilly. He got out and walked down to the building, half afraid to confront it, to look at it, lest it was not as the advertisement said, lest once again he should be disappointed, robbed of his prize. But he wasn't. It stood graceful and unspoilt, so far as he could see; five storeys tall, not unlike, not at all unlike the house on 57th Street, with a fine arched doorway, and beautiful stonework. Inside it was a nightmare; the staircase had been ripped out, lifts installed, most of the panelling stripped out, the ceilings lowered. The perfectly proportioned big rooms upstairs had been halved, quartered, the doors lined, the walls covered with fitted cupboards. What the hotel chose to call bathrooms had been crammed into corners; the decor was fifties kitsch, with a heavy slug of baroque glitz.

Julian didn't care. It could be restored, made beautiful again, brought back to life. And it was exactly what he had been looking for, waiting for, for nearly twenty-five years. He felt as if he had come home.

'I have a present for you,' he said to Phaedria that night. She was sitting at her desk in the room she had adopted for herself in Regent's Park, the one that had been Eliza's parlour; it looked a little different. The walls were white, the ceilings were white, the floor was white; there were black blinds at the window, and a big black desk in the middle of the room. There were books on floor-to-ceiling shelves on one of the walls, and a stereo system with a huge mass of tapes and records on another. On a low table by the window was a mass of magazines, not just English, but French, American, Italian, German. And the room was full of flowers, a huge extravagant mass of colour: on the desk, the table, the shelves, even in a giant vase on the floor.

Here for several hours a day Phaedria sat working; she had not yet managed to get a fashion job, although she wrote the occasional freelance article; but she had been commissioned by the Society of British Fashion Designers to write their history from year one, and was deeply engrossed in it. She was also surprisingly, and rather charmingly, busy with plans for her wedding.

'What's that, Julian?' she said slightly absently. 'Have you ever heard of someone called David Bond?'

'Of course. Big name in the sixties. Very good commercial designer. Nice fellow too. Got the spot in the Bath Fashion Museum one year.'

She looked at him and smiled. 'What a lot you know, don't you?'

'Well, I've had lots of time to learn.'

'I suppose so. Listen, do you think it would be nice to drive to the church in a landau? Grettisaga could pull it.'

'As long as it didn't rain.'

'No, but we could get one with a hood. I think it would be divine.'

'You sound like Eliza.'

'Sorry.'

'I don't really mind. I was very fond of her. Still am.'

'Well anyway, what do you think?'

'I think it would be divine too. Don't you want to know what your present is?'

'Sorry, yes of course I do.'

'Here you are.' He handed her a key.

'Julian! Not another car?'

'No. Something bigger.'

'What?'

'Come with me, and I'll show you.'

He pulled her impatiently by the hand, down the steps and out on to the terrace. She looked around. 'I can't see anything.'

'It's not here. Get in the car.'

He refused to say a word as they drove down Baker Street and Park Lane and turned into Piccadilly; as they reached Fortnum's he slowed down, pulled in to the side of the road.

'There you are.'

'What?'

'That. There. That building.'

'I can see. It's very nice. But what about it?'

'It's yours.'

'Mine! But I don't need a building.'

'Yes, you do. It's going to be the London Circe. It's your wedding present.'

'Oh, my God,' said Phaedria. 'Oh, for heaven's sake . . . Oh, Julian.'

Chapter Fourteen

London and New York, 1983

Roz was so angry when she heard about the store she actually threw up. Julian had told her about it over lunch at the Ritz,

540

presenting the event as something to be celebrated, and explained he was giving it to Phaedria for a wedding present, and that he was sure they would be able to work together on it amicably if they put their minds to it. He had said much the same thing to Phaedria the night before; for probably the first and last time in their lives Phaedria and Roz were in total agreement. This, they could both see, was the beginning of a very long war. They also both had great difficulty in believing that Julian could actually think they would be able to work together. There was a particular expression in his unfathomable brown eyes, which Roz had grown up with, and Phaedria had begun to recognize, which meant danger, meant games were being played, meant checkmate. It was there now.

'Excuse me,' said Roz and half walked, half ran to the lavatory.

Kneeling on the floor, trying to recover herself, tears streaming down her face, she wondered where this fearsome situation was going to end. Here she was, married to a man she could now scarcely bear, who drove her to such a frenzy of irritation if he so much as commented on the fact that it was raining or asked her if she wanted a cup of coffee, that she tried to avoid being in the same room as him most of the time; the mother of a child who she did admittedly love, but would really have been better off without; and the man she had loved, and still hungered for, lost to her, all in the cause of becoming the heir to her father's kingdom. And now not only was a new Queen on the throne, and not only was she beautiful and (or so most people kept on and on saying in the most enraging way) charming, truly engaging, and had her father under control for the first time in his life, she was clever. And she was young. Roz still found beauty in other women, and particularly those close to her father, painful to accept.

She often wondered if Susan was right about Phaedria not being sexy; that would be a fatal flaw. Roz allowed herself a moment's complacency at the very suspicion; highly sexed herself, she regarded with contempt any man or woman who was not. Not that it did her any good at the moment (her husband having proved himself very much among the contemptibles). Now that she had quite recovered from Miranda's birth, Roz wondered almost daily how soon it would be before she was driven to take a lover, to ease the longing, the sense of physical emptiness in her body. She went restlessly to sleep at night and frequently had sharply erotic dreams; Michael Browning figured largely in them.

But if she was weary of the beauty and the charm, she was still more weary of the assertions that Phaedria had Julian under control. Moreover she disputed them. She had watched women trying to do it and failing all her life, and had enjoyed their failure. It was true that Phaedria was very cool and apparently in command, and Roz had heard interesting reports of fearsome rows and battles of will, which on past experience usually resulted in a relationship drawing very swiftly to a close; this one went on, and the ridiculous plans for this absurd wedding with it. Nevertheless, there was plenty of time for the balance of power to switch. And the more Phaedria felt confident of holding it, the more Julian would see that she did not. There was hope there.

But the most frightening weapons Phaedria possessed were her youth and her brains.

Phaedria was very clever; she was also ambitious, she wanted a career, and she wanted to work with Julian. Writing had become second choice. That was bad enough. Far worse though was her youth, and the indisputable fact that she had probably, at the most modest estimate, fifteen childbearing years ahead of her.

The spectre that had haunted Roz all her life, ever since she could remember, that of a small sibling, seemed suddenly terrifyingly close.

She stood up slowly and wearily, went out into the cloakroom and washed her face. She studied it as she put her make-up on, and brushed her short dark hair. It might not have beauty, but it had a great facility that face, something inherited from her father; a capacity not to show the emotion behind it. She was going to need that capacity a great deal, she realized, in the months ahead.

'Sorry, Daddy. I suddenly felt awfully sick.'

'Are you all right, darling? You do too much.'

'Rubbish. You can't do too much. You've taught me that all my life.'

'Maybe, but I didn't really extend that philosophy to a period just after having a baby. Miranda is only – what – four months old? You don't realize it, but you're still recovering.'

'Oh, Daddy, you sound like Mr Partridge. Silly old fart,' she added.

'You're referring to Mr Partridge, I trust, and not myself.'

'Of course.'

'From what I hear, he is a silly old fart. But if he's been telling you to take life a bit easier, I would echo him.'

'Well I'm not going to, so you can both stop. Now tell me exactly what this business with Circe and Phaedria means.'

'In what way?'

'Well, I am the president of Circe Europe, am I not?'

'You are.'

'Circe London therefore has to come under my control.'

'Well, yes. But only officially. I want this store to be Phaedria's. She has a considerable feel for fashion and for decor. I think she'll make a good job of it. She has some interesting ideas.'

'Oh good,' said Roz.

'Obviously I can't ask her to report to you.'

'Obviously.'

'But she'll need help, particularly on the administrative side, budgeting and so on.'

'Temporarily, I presume.'

'I beg your pardon?'

'Well, if the store is to be hers, surely she will want to handle the whole thing. She won't want anyone interfering in her budgets, or her staff or her long-term planning, come to that. Not after the early stages. It would be an untenable situation for her.'

'Possibly.'

'Not possibly, Daddy, obviously.'

Expressionless face met expressionless face.

'So,' Roz went on, 'long term, Circe London will be an oddball. Under different control. Out of the system. Is that going to work?'

'I don't see why not. Providing you are kept informed of what is going on. Clearly Phaedria will be working to guidelines. She's not going to turn it into a down-market chain store.'

'Hopefully.'

'Roz, don't be negative.'

'Sorry.' She threw him her most charming smile. 'No, I'm sure she won't. She's a clever girl. And she has great taste.'

'Doesn't she? She's beginning to do some extremely nice things to the house. And to Marriotts. Why don't you come down this weekend? Bring Miranda, I don't see enough of her.'

'Are you hunting?'

'Yes, we're going out on Saturday with the Crawley and Horsham. Do come.'

'I might. Yes, thank you. It would be nice. I'll talk to C. J.'

'Good. Now I'll think over what you said, about Circe. I can see there might be the odd anomaly. Nothing that can't be sorted, but it could need some thought.'

Round One to me, said Roz to herself. She gave her father her most brilliant smile. 'Thank you for lunch, it's been lovely. I'll see you on Saturday.'

'Why not come on Friday night? Phaedria cooks dinner herself then, and it's always delicious.'

'No thank you,' said Roz hastily, feeling sick again at the thought of Phaedria's culinary skills. 'It would be difficult. C. J.'s working late. No, we'll come early on Saturday.'

'It'll have to be very early if you're coming out hunting with us.'

'It will be. Miranda gets me up at half past five. Bye, Daddy. Give my love to Phaedria.'

'I will. You'll enjoy riding with her, she's very good.'

'I look forward to it.'

She would defeat that paragon if it was the last thing she did.

As soon as she got back to the office, Roz phoned Susan.

'Could I come and see you tonight? I've got to talk to someone sane. Just got to.'

'Yes, of course. What's the matter? Is it the Crown Princess?' Susan could hear Roz smiling down the phone. 'Yes.'

'Well come and have supper. What about C. J.?'

'Oh, I certainly don't want him to come. He'll find something to do, I expect.'

Susan looked at the phone sorrowfully as she put it down. She had never criticized or questioned Roz's decision to marry

C. J. (having a very shrewd idea what was behind it, knowing how much Roz's mother and grandmother had to say on the subject) but she was saddened to see it coming to such a disastrous end. She had hoped that perhaps with a little goodwill on both sides it could have at least turned into a working relationship.

She listened patiently while Roz told her about her lunch with Julian and about Phaedria being given the store. She was appalled.

'So what do you think?' said Roz. 'Am I being hysterical, minding so much, or not?'

'I don't think so, no,' said Susan. 'I think it's very hard. Very hard. But I don't think you can blame Phaedria for this.'

'Why not? She probably just said she'd like it, and he went out and bought it for her.'

'I don't think so. He wouldn't give her anything that made her so potentially powerful unless he really wanted her to have it. No, it would have been his idea.'

'And don't you think he did it deliberately to weaken my position?'

'No, Roz, I don't. I can't see why he should do such a thing.'

'Because he loves playing games, that's why,' said Roz. 'Oh, Susan, why did I get drawn into his mesh like this? Why didn't I stay with Michael and marry him and get some nice rewarding job in New York?'

'The answer for that lies in your genes, I would say,' said Susan, smiling at her regretfully. 'The Morell genes. You're driven by the same sense of – I don't know what to call it – greed, I suppose, as your father.'

'Thanks.'

'Well it's true. You are greedy. Greedy for power. Aren't you? Just like him.'

'I suppose so,' said Roz sulkily.

'No, I really do think he simply hasn't thought it all through properly. What it must mean to you – both in personal and professional terms. He's just obsessed with Phaedria, and he wants to give her the moon. It's very sad.'

'It's pathetic.'

'Well, maybe.' She looked at Roz. 'You don't look very well. Is anything else the matter?'

'Oh, nothing much. Just my work. My marriage. My self-esteem. Just little things like that.'

'Is it really no good with C. J.?'

'None at all. It's hopeless. It was very wrong of me to marry him, and God, I'm being punished for it now.'

'Poor Roz.'

'Oh, well. It's so nice to have you to talk to. The only person I can be honest with.' She smiled at Susan. 'What about you?'

'Me?'

'Yes. You and Richard.'

'Oh.' She smiled. 'Nothing really to report. No, that's not true. Let me try and cheer you up a bit. We're getting married next Saturday. At Chelsea Registry Office. We're not telling a single soul until afterwards. Quite a bit afterwards, probably. Would you like to come and be my bridesmaid? I'll need a hand to hold. I haven't been married for over forty years.'

'Oh, Susan, of course I will, I'd love to. That's the nicest thing anyone ever said to me. Thank you.'

She kissed Susan and smiled at her. 'It's lovely news. I just know you're going to be very happy. Give Richard a big kiss from me.'

'I will.' Susan returned the kiss, and thought how very sad it was that Roz the nice person was someone known to only two or three people.

'Julian, could I have a word with you? This evening, maybe, before you go home?'

In his office at six o'clock he had some champagne and orange juice waiting. 'I thought as we seemed to be friends again, we might celebrate.'

'I didn't know we weren't friends.'

'Liar.'

'All right.'

'I hate it when we're not friends, Susan. You're very important to me.'

'Yes, well,' she said briskly, taking the glass he offered her. 'Just remember that, will you, when I've finished what I have to say.'

'Oh God. What is it?'

'It's Roz. And the store.'

'I beg your pardon?'

'Julian, this is nothing to do with me, I know –'

'Then,' he said lightly, putting his glass down untouched, 'perhaps it would be better if you didn't get involved.'

'I don't agree. Someone has to point things out to you, and nobody else is going to do it.'

'Very well. Carry on.'

'I do think you're making a terrible mistake, giving that store to Phaedria to run. The stores are Roz's domain. It's going to be difficult. For both of them.'

He looked at her for a long time. His face was stern, but blank. She had no idea what he was thinking. She braced herself for a torrent of abuse or of self-justification on his part.

It didn't come.

'I'm not a complete fool,' he said quietly. 'Of course it will be difficult. But they're both putting up this wall of hostility. I thought if they were to be forced to work together it would get knocked down.'

'You really think that?' said Susan.

'I really think that.'

She met his eyes steadily, her own challenging, half amused.

'Julian,' she said, 'either you are lying, or you really are a complete fool.'

'Roz, do you have five minutes?'

Roz looked up. Phaedria stood in the doorway of her office. She was wearing her wolf coat and long black boots; she looked straight out of the pages of *Cosmopolitan*.

'Not quite five,' said Roz, her distaste written very plainly on her face. 'I'm late for a meeting already. I thought perhaps you might have been invited. We're discussing the architecture of the Beverly Hills Circe. You know we're opening one, of course?'

'Of course. I didn't know that you were involved in it, though.'

'Oh, didn't you?' said Roz. 'How odd. I imagined my father told you everything about his business. Yes, the president of Circe in the States, Harold Fowler, is retiring next year. I think it's a fairly foregone conclusion that I shall take over the whole lot then.'

'I see.'

'Anyway, I imagined you'd want to take quite a close look at all the stores before getting to work on your own. Just to make sure it's in line.'

'Possibly.'

'Well I would have thought it would have been essential. Still, you have your own ideas, I imagine.'

'Yes,' said Phaedria. 'Yes, I do. Plenty. Which is precisely what I wanted to talk to you about. We need to get together.'

'Well, let's pencil in a meeting,' said Roz, 'but it will have to be a few weeks ahead, I'm afraid. Do you mind if I set the date? I imagine my diary is a little fuller than yours, just at the moment.'

'I doubt that,' said Phaedria sweetly. 'I am extremely busy myself, you know, with the arrangements for my wedding to your father. If it can't be within the next ten days, I'll just have to proceed on my own and hope we can iron out any problems later.'

Roz wasn't sure if it was the first or the second half of this brief speech that made her feel suddenly sick.

'Julian, why didn't you ask me to the meeting about the Beverly Hills Circe? It would have been so helpful to me, hearing how that was going to be started from scratch.'

'Darling, I did suggest it to Roz, and she was all for it, but then she told me you and she had a very comprehensive meeting of your own planned and she'd be able to fill you in with the details then. It seemed more sensible, when you've got so much on your plate at the moment.'

Phaedria had learnt not to discuss Roz with Julian.

'I see. Well, in future, could I be put on the circulation list for store meetings anyway? I'll find the time.'

'Of course. I'll let Roz know. I'm sure she'll be delighted.'

'I'm sure.'

'Phaedria, Roz and I are going over to LA next week, to look at the Circe site, meet the architect, all that sort of thing. I think it might be a good idea if you came too. What do you think?'

'Oh, Julian, I'd love it. I've never been to LA. Never been to the States, as a matter of fact. Have you – discussed it with Roz?'

'Of course. She's delighted.'

'Phaedria, it's Roz. Look, I don't want to interfere, but I really would suggest you get Paul Baud to help you with the plans for Circe. He's done most of them, including the first, and he is brilliant. Quite the best in the business. He'll help you keep to the house style, so to speak, and yet he'll listen to your own ideas. Just a thought.'

'Thank you. I'll think about it.'

'Paul? It's Roz. I'm absolutely fine, thank you. I still miss Paris, though. I can't think why you don't live there all the time. How's New York? Good. Listen, I need your help. Now I do want you to be very discreet about this, because it's a bit delicate. You know my father's getting married again? Yes, isn't it delicious, and she is just so nice, none of us can believe our luck. You'll love her. Well anyway, and this is the difficult bit, for me, you may have heard my father's giving her a building for her wedding present, to turn into the London Circe. You did? Yes, well, look, she's going to need a lot of help. No experience at all, and frankly, *entre nous*, she's going to make a complete hash of it if we're not very careful. Only of course I can't say anything to Daddy. Anyway, I've suggested she consults you, and I think she will. Just look like you're holding her hand, and guiding her, and just quietly take over. She has some extremely dull ideas, as far as I can make out, and she really needs to be talked out of them. And both my father and I basically want the London Circe to be a little different. Just slightly more – well, quite a bit more – avant-garde. You know. We've discussed it, and I know he's a little worried by some of Phaedria's ideas. Or rather the lack of them. Only he won't say anything to her, of course. And nor can I. It would be terribly unkind, and we do want to encourage her. So we – well I – thought you were the person to help us all through it. What? Well, the stores are my baby now, you know, I don't want this one going wrong. But obviously I can't interfere. You can see my difficulty. Yes, I do have a real baby as well now, she's adorable. You must come and meet her. So if she rings you, Paul, no, not the baby you fool, Phaedria, will you be helpful? And terribly discreet? Marvellous. Thank you so much. We've never needed you more.'

'Right,' said Roz, settling a large pile of files on the boardroom table, 'Let's get to work, Phaedria. Have you spoken to Paul Baud by the way?'

'Not yet. But I do agree he's the best person, thank you for suggesting it.'

'Perfectly all right. I do want to help. We have to make this thing work, after all.'

'Quite.'

Brown eyes met green in total mistrust.

'Let's start with basics. How do you see the store? I mean, what image?'

'I thought very much the same as all the others. There's nothing that would be more disastrous than to have a kind of rogue Circe in London of all places.'

'Well, obviously that really is up to you. I am totally unvisual, as my father is always telling me. I wonder whether perhaps you should consider a slightly different look.'

'And would you be happy with that?'

'I was under the impression,' said Roz, 'that my happiness was of no relevance in this whatsoever. But possibly yes.'

'Oh, all right,' said Phaedria with a sigh, 'let's get down to budgets.' She felt instinctively that any suggestion that came from Roz should be treated with deep suspicion.

'Daddy, it's Roz. Look, you'll be pleased to hear Phaedria and I had our meeting today, and it went quite well. I think we can work together all right.'

'Good.'

'She has some quite nice ideas. The only thing is, I really don't think you should get involved at all.'

'Why not?'

'Because she's feeling inhibited enough by me being involved, and she plans to consult Paul, which seems a good idea, and I think if she feels your hand on things as well, she'll lose all confidence.'

'Well, as long as you and Paul keep a firm eye on it and make sure nothing radical happens, I'll stand back.'

'I think you should. It'll work better that way.'

*

'Julian, could I talk to you about Circe, please?'

'Darling, I'd rather not. I'm terribly busy. It's your project, you have perfect taste, and I trust you. All right?'

'All right.'

Apart from having to endure Roz's company (made more unendurable rather than less by the pleasant front she put on for her father's benefit) in Los Angeles, Phaedria greatly enjoyed her trip to the States, brief as it was. She had expected to find New York exhilarating, but she had not been prepared for its beauty. She spent a whole day as a tourist, just walking it, up and down the streets, in and out of the stores; she went up the Empire State Building, she did the backstage tour of Radio City, she skated in the Rockefeller Center and that evening she insisted Julian take her in a horse and carriage on a trip round Central Park.

'We'll die of cold.'

'I won't. You can keep me warm.'

'Come on then.'

'I love it here,' she said happily as they huddled under the rug Julian had brought from the Sutton Place apartment ('The ones they give you are threadbare'). 'Can we spend lots of time here?'

'We could. I tend not to these days. Less involved than I was with this side of the world.'

'Well, let's get more involved. Can you keep a horse in New York?'

'It's difficult. There is one place, on the upper West Side, the Claremont stables, it's like a multi-storey garage, you ride up a ramp. Not very satisfactory.'

'Oh, well, maybe it's not a very good idea then. What happens tomorrow?'

'We have a big board meeting in the morning, of Juliana. And then the afternoon, I thought we'd spend in Circe.'

'Is Paul Baud here?'

'No, Roz asked him to go to Paris urgently this week, to have a look at the store there. It needs refurbishing, apparently. She's in a panic to get it at least partly sorted for Easter.'

'What a pity. I did want to meet him.'

'Well, isn't he coming to London to talk to you?'

'I haven't decided.'

'Oh? I thought you had.'

'No, not yet.'

'Ah. I must have got it wrong.'

She was more enchanted still by Los Angeles. Everyone had told her she'd hate it, and she loved it. She loved everything about it, the sunshine, the buildings, the traffic, the freeways lacing their way across the city, the glitz of Beverly Hills, the tack of Sunset Strip, the palm trees waving so incongruously above their heads, the ocean beating its way remorselessly on to the white beaches. She longed to explore further, to go along the coast, but Julian was reluctant to leave the centre of the city.

'We have a lot to do,' he said rather shortly when she protested, 'and not a lot of time.'

'I'll go off on my own then.'

He looked at her rather coolly. 'I thought you had come here to work.'

'I have.'

'Oh, Daddy, don't be such a slave-driver,' said Roz, 'she's only come to observe. I don't see why she shouldn't go off if she wants to, just for half a day. She's never been here before. We can brief her afterwards.'

Phaedria met her eyes with a grudging admiration.

'No,' she said, 'thank you, Roz, for your concern, but Julian's right. I should be here.'

The site they had acquired for Circe was right on Rodeo Drive, almost next to the Rodeo Center, precisely opposite Elizabeth Arden.

'Brilliant,' said Roz happily. 'Just brilliant. Worth waiting for.'

The architect brought in to design the store had ideas never before even whispered of in connection with Circe. He saw it white, airy, stark; Phaedria watched Julian thoughtfully as he briskly demolished ninety per cent of his ideas and then slowly moved into a qualified acceptance of the remaining ten per cent. Perhaps the faint indication she had picked up from Roz that she might do something similar in London should be given more attention. Perhaps she had been wrong.

*

'Roz, it's Paul.'

'Paul! Hallo. How are you?'

'Very well. How was the Los Angeles site?'

'Perfect.'

'And the new designer?'

'Oh, very interesting. Totally revolutionary.'

'And how did these revolutionary ideas go down with your father?'

'Surprisingly well. Like I said, he does seem to be very much looking for a change.'

'Good. Well, perhaps it is time. Now, I have talked to Phaedria.'

'And?'

'You are right. She is most beautiful. And charming and intelligent. I liked her very much.'

'I'm so glad.'

'But I do not agree with you about her abilities. I found her full of ideas.'

'Oh, good.'

'She seemed interested in a more modern look. I told her I thought it was possibly a good idea. So we are proceeding cautiously along those lines.'

'Excellent. I wouldn't be too cautious if I were you.'

'Julian, I very much want to have a formal meeting to present my plans for Circe to you and Roz.'

'All right, darling, I'm sure that's the way to do it. I'm very very busy, though. Couldn't you manage just with Roz?'

'Of course not.'

'Why of course?'

Her eyes met his with just a touch of amusement.

'You're the boss.'

The meeting was fixed for early May; Phaedria asked Sarah Brownsmith to organize a boardroom lunch. Sarah, who had grown fond of her, and was eager to see her succeed in her venture, suggested that Freddy Branksome should be invited as well.

'Please don't think I'm interfering, Miss Blenheim. But the meeting might seem more – well, formal – with another

553

representative from the company. And the financial aspect is, I imagine, important?'

Phaedria smiled at her. 'I think that's an excellent idea, Sarah. Thank you. And please call me Phaedria.'

Sarah looked at her slightly oddly. 'Please don't misinterpret this, but I think that it would be better if I didn't.'

Phaedria nodded. 'I understand. I'll get on to Freddy right away. I hope he'll be free.'

'I think you'll find he will be.'

Sarah wasn't sure if she was amused by Phaedria's inability to appreciate the power of her position, or mistrustful of it.

'Right,' said Phaedria. 'Let's get down to business right away, shall we? I thought I'd start with the costings.'

Roz looked startled. 'I didn't realize you'd done any.'

'Of course,' said Phaedria coolly. 'I don't see how we can possibly discuss architecture and design if we don't know what the financial implications are.'

'Quite right,' said Freddy briskly.

For the first time Roz felt a stab of fear.

Phaedria's budget was presented clearly and succinctly. She had estimates from contractors, covering external and internal work, she had a budget for architecture, another for design, and a preliminary one for fittings and fixtures. Freddy sat beaming at her, clearly enchanted; he was not used to seeing financial considerations given such high priority.

'So, at a very rough estimate, we're talking about something like ten million pounds. Assuming we can get the work done within the year.'

'Well, you can't,' said Roz. 'It's absolutely impossible.'

Phaedria looked at her. 'I don't agree. I've talked to several contractors. They all say twelve months is not unreasonable.'

'They always say that.'

'Possibly. But with heavy penalty clauses, it should be perfectly feasible.'

'Maybe. But I doubt it.'

'Well, let's move on,' said Julian, slightly impatiently. 'What about the designs, Phaedria? The budget sounds reasonable to me.'

'Right. Now then, as you know I have worked with Paul Baud

554

quite closely on this project. We spent a lot of time looking at the existing Circes, discussing them in the light of some of the work other stores have been doing, notably Harvey Nichols, and also the shops like Joseph and Rive Gauche. While Circe is clearly unique it equally clearly cannot be studied in isolation. Markets change, consumers change, fashions change.'

Julian was looking slightly uneasy; Roz's face was expressionless.

Sarah Brownsmith knocked at the door. 'Shall I bring the lunch in now, Miss Blenheim?'

Roz looked at her sharply. She had not realized that this was so officially Phaedria's meeting.

'No Sarah, not yet,' said Julian irritably. 'We've hardly begun. I'll buzz you when we're ready.'

'Julian, Sarah and I were both under the impression this was my meeting,' said Phaedria coolly, 'but yes, thank you, Sarah, we will wait a little longer. I'll buzz you.'

He looked at her blank faced, but his eyes were dark and heavy; there was no humour behind them at all.

'Very well.'

'Anyway, if I could resume. The market has changed. The consumer has changed. Money, quite a lot of money, is in new hands. People who would never have considered going into Circe will now be shopping there.'

'What kind of people?' asked Roz. 'Typists?'

'No, not typists. Obviously primarily our market will still be the ABs. Slightly older women. By which I mean, women in their thirties and above. But there is a great deal of money about in younger hands. Real money. What I think of as designer money. Stylish money. There's a new breed of professional woman who wants, needs clothes that are very expensive, very stylish, probably with much more fashion sense than her mother or her older sisters. And a lot less time. I think we have to consider her. Clearly much of that area is down to merchandising; I would like, for instance, to institute a department where a woman can get an entire wardrobe put together for her consideration, as a result of a preliminary consultation on her taste, lifestyle, needs. But I don't want to get too much into that now. The point I'm making is that we should consider these women when we look at the style, the design of Circe.'

She paused. 'I talked to Paul Baud along these lines, and we discussed, among other things, the look of the Los Angeles Circe, in relation to the New York one. Very different. Paul was very enthusiastic, surprisingly so I thought, about change. About a contemporary look. I liked his ideas. Here they are.'

She pulled out the screen, walked over to the carousel cassette of slides, flashed the first image on to the screen. It showed a detailed colour drawing of the foyer of Circe: all white, with deco-style lights, a low curving reception desk. 'That would be for a store guide; to welcome people personally, tell them where everything was. Then we go through sliding glass doors into the body of the store.'

Another image came on the screen. 'Paul based his ideas for the ground floor rather on perhaps Sak's in New York, or even Tiffany's, where you get a much more panoramic view of the store, less claustrophobic, less fragmented.'

Julian's face was expressionless, taut.

'The predominant colour throughout the store would be white, the predominant sensation space. The beauty floor would also be more open, more spacy, than we have grown to expect from Circe.' She clicked her button again. 'Clients would, for some treatments, be in a large, open salon. Then' – another slide – 'we looked at fashion. We conceived a very large space, with departments opening from it at regular angles – one at two o'clock, if you follow me, one at four and so on. They would not be shut off from each other as they are now, but there would be an impression of seclusion, given by screens and plants. I –'

Julian held up his hand. 'Excuse me, Phaedria, forgive me for interrupting you. I have to say I feel we are all wasting our time. This – concept of yours bears absolutely no relation to anything that Circe stands for. No intimacy, no luxury, no exclusivity. I am particularly concerned by the plans for the beauty floor. The whole principle of the Juliana in Circe area is a sense of privacy, so that a woman can be as relaxed as if she was in her own home. I fear you have grossly misinterpreted the Circe concept. I think the only thing to do at this stage is to go back to basics and begin again.'

'But –'

'No, really, I don't think there is anything to be gained by further discussion. I would urge you very strongly to do a little more research into our past customer, before you sacrifice her on the rather dubious altar of what you conceive as the present. Now if you will excuse me I think I will forego lunch. I have a great deal of work to do. But please, the rest of you stay.'

He was white and clearly shaken, and oddly angry. Roz felt a stab of pleasure shoot through her, strangely akin to sexual desire. Freddy Branksome looked uncomfortable. There was a silence as Julian stood up and picked up his files.

'Please sit down again.' It was Phaedria's voice, very calm, with just a tinge of amusement in it. Roz looked at her sharply.

'I would rather I didn't.'

'I would rather you did. And do me the courtesy of allowing me to finish my presentation.'

He gave her a look that was very close to dislike. Then he sighed and sat down again. 'Very well. But I have only ten minutes.'

'Fine. Now then.' She looked at them, and picked up her control button again. 'As you can see we did a lot of work along these lines. I enjoyed working with Paul Baud, and I think he has vast and valuable experience. However, returning to my new customer, and yet still looking very carefully at my old, I think there is much more work to be done. I have begun doing it.'

She clicked her button. 'I decided in the end to take a rather revolutionary step, and talk to a designer with no direct experience in retailing, but a great deal in company style.'

'Indeed?' said Julian drily, still angry, still distressed. 'And are we allowed to ask this person's name?'

'Of course,' said Phaedria. 'You know it well. It's David Sassoon.'

Freddy, looking at her as she stood there, fighting the first great political battle of her life, wondered just how aware she might be of the sexual dynamite delivered in that simple statement; decided it was most unlikely that she was not totally aware, and looked at Julian swiftly, nervously for a reaction, but his face was smooth, expressionless.

'I see,' he said. 'Do go on.'

'Right. Well, this is our view of the reception area, the foyer, call it what you like.'

They looked. It was like looking into what Freddy described afterwards, in a most uncharacteristic fit of lyricism, as a grown-up fairy story book. It was as if William Morris had had a love affair with Kate Greenaway, and they had run away together to the twentieth century. David Sassoon had used the airbrush technique to create the effect of actual photographs, rather than designers' sketches; the effect was very powerful. His Circe, and Phaedria's, was light, airy, lovely, awash with sea greens and blues; huge tangly ferns stood in the corners, embroidered tapestries hung on the walls. The floor was white marble, the ceiling white and high. Big lamps with blue glass shades hung tantalizing here and there, their light falling tenderly on low counters set with jewellery, perfume, hats, gloves; there was a compulsion to walk forward, to examine, to explore.

'None of this merchandise would be for sale,' explained Phaedria briskly, breaking the spell, 'it is there simply to draw the customer on, into the store. Now here we have the main ground floor.'

In the same colour scheme, the same romance, it was broken into segments purely by pools of light. Between the lights, the small, jewel-like departments, it was dimmer; in here the floor was no longer white, but the same soft greeny blue.

'I am investigating colouring the marble; it might be cold. Carpeting could be a possibility, but I don't like the idea. Let's move up to the beauty floor.'

The beauty floor saw William Morris on a tropical island; huge, exotic flowers grew in white urns, a waterfall splashed brilliantly against the marble walls, a pool of brilliant blue water lay in the middle of the room, with white water lilies lying languorously on its surface.

'Then all round it are the small treatment rooms; totally private, but each one with its coordinating theme of water and flowers: a Jacuzzi in every one, and winter jasmine, clematis, anything that will grow indoors climbing up at least one of the walls. The horticulturalists' bill will probably rival the beauty therapists'. And a dressing table, a proper one, as you see, in each room, totally equipped with the entire Juliana range, but not remotely clinical; vases of flowers on them, big powder puffs, hairbrushes, and white wicker chairs, to give something of the feel of a conservatory. But as you can also see, out in the reception area, by the pool, more big chairs, and loungers, so that if people wish they can sit and talk and drink fruit juices or whatever. It will have to be very very warm, so they can wear just robes, or (as they do in the Sanctuary in Covent Garden, just towels round their waists). Women are exhibitionists, when they know they've got good bodies; they should have a chance to be that, as well as to be totally private.'

She clicked again. 'Now on the floor below, the lingerie department, we thought a change of colour scheme, to pink. So that it looks as much like a boudoir as possible.'

The boudoir was dressed with brocaded wallpaper, brass wall lights with pink glass shades, charming eighteenth-century prints; small groups of furniture, chairs, dressing tables, beds with draped heads, lace spreads and cushion covers, and scattered everywhere, as if waiting to be put on, was the merchandise, nightdresses, robes, french knickers, camisoles.

'Of course this may not be practicable, there would be security problems, but a few things dotted about would be worth losing, I would have thought.'

Another click: 'Now the fashion floor; more conventional, but again as you will see, a series of room sets, an office perhaps, a drawing room, a salon, a conservatory, with the appropriate clothes in each one. Of course again, there could be a problem with merchandise, but I think as a device, it could be made to work. And here, we have all the colour schemes brought together, the greeny blue, the pink, the white, so that the customer is aware of a coherent feel throughout the store.'

She paused. 'That is as far as we have gone for now. We wanted to get your reaction. Perhaps we could discuss it over lunch.'

Phaedria walked over to the window, let the blind up; she saw first Julian's face, surprised, almost awed, but soft with pleasure, then Freddy's smiling at her fondly, and finally Roz, her face quite quite blank, her green eyes looking at her with a disturbing mixture of hatred and respect. And there was something else in those eyes, something that gave her more pleasure even than the respect. It was fear.

The Connection Ten

Nassau, 1983

Gambling, Miles reflected, was like surfing and sex. It completely wiped out everything else. That was its charm.

He and Billy had become more and more besotted with gambling lately. They had had a few lucky nights, left the Paradise Beach Hotel riding high with several hundred dollars in their pockets, and felt they couldn't go wrong.

They could.

Within the space of a week they owed, between them, nearly a thousand dollars. Desperate, they had gone to the manager, begged for time to pay.

'You boys have been coming here long enough to know better. I want that marker paid back in forty-eight hours.'

'We will.'

'Will your dad give you any money?' asked Miles as they walked disconsolately over the bridge towards the Old Town.

'Nope. I wouldn't dare ask him in any case. I'm in enough trouble as it is. What about your grandma?'

'Not a chance. She doesn't have any.'

'So what do we do?'

'I don't know.'

'You could sell your watch.'

'I could. But I'm not going to.'

'You might have to.'

'Billy, I'm not going to. I told you.'

'Miles, you don't seem to understand. We're up against it. This is real life, not a rehearsal. We could be in dead trouble. And I mean dead.'

'Oh, don't be melodramatic.'

'I'm not.'

'You are.'

'Oh, for fuck's sake Miles, grow up.'

Miles looked at his friend sharply. His face was drawn and pale in the harsh light of the street lamps.

'You're really worried aren't you?'

'Well of course I damn well am. You should be too.'

'Sorry. I didn't realize.'

Miles sold his watch.

It made just enough to pay off their debt and leave them a hundred dollars to take to the roulette table.

They put fifty dollars on the twenty-one black. Just for the hell of it. The wheel spun. Twenty-two.

'Nearly,' said Billy. 'Let's try again. Twenty-five dollars.'

The wheel spun again. Endlessly. Twenty-two again.

'OK,' said Miles. 'Third time lucky. Twenty-five dollars on twenty-two black.'

The wheel spun. Time froze. Miles stood, motionless, concentrating totally. He could not have told anyone even his own name. Go on, you fucker, stop. Twenty-two. Twenty-two. Twenty-two.

The wheel stopped. Twenty-two black.

'Jesus,' said Billy. 'We did it. What's that?'

'Odds are twenty to one,' said Miles, 'that's five hundrd dollars.'

'Great,' said Billy, 'you got half your watch back. Let's go.'

'No,' said Miles. 'Not yet. Let's stay a bit.'

'Miles,' said Billy, 'don't. You can't go on winning.'

'Why not? We went on losing. I'll be careful.'

A blonde in a black dress opposite, all hair and eyes and breasts, heard him and laughed.

'I'll pace you. What are you betting?'

'A hundred dollars.'

'Wow. On what?'

'Twenty-two black.'

'You just got that.'

'I know.'

'All right.'

She pushed a pile of chips on to the twenty-two black. The wheel spun. Billy looked away.

'Hey,' he heard the girl's voice, gritty, delighted. 'You did it. Twenty-two black. I won two thousand dollars.'

'Yeah,' said Miles. 'We both did.'

He felt tense, high, heady. Just like sex.

561

'Again?' She was laughing.

'Yeah. Again.'

Hauling the will together. Could you? Again? Pushing yourself. You could. Feeling the power, the thudding heart, the pounding, soaring blood. Just like sex.

'What this time?'

'The same.'

'Can't be.'

'It will.'

It wasn't. Miles lost five hundred dollars. Billy pulled at his arm. 'Come on. Let's go.'

The girl looked at him, winked at Miles.

'Him or me?'

Miles looked at her and smiled his wonderful, radiant, self-mocking smile. 'Him. Come on, Billy. I'm with you.'

She looked amused. 'OK. He wins. Will you be here tomorrow?'

'I guess so.'

The next night Miles won five hundred dollars and the next five thousand. The girl was there. She was sexually aroused by the game. So was Miles. Billy stood back from the tables, horribly afraid. Afterwards he went home alone, and Miles took the girl down to the beach and made love to her three, four times, reliving the tension, the fear, the spins on the wheel, the absolute will to win, the heady power of the numbers.

The next night, he lost three thousand dollars. The girl left him sitting at the table. The next night he won ten thousand. The girl took him back to her hotel. He still didn't even know her name.

And the next night he lost five thousand dollars, and the next five thousand, and finally he was left with a marker for four thousand to pay back in a week.

He walked home alone, shakily sobered. He woke Billy up. Billy gave him coffee, counsel, comfort. But he didn't have four thousand dollars.

'Jesus,' Billy said. 'What will you do?'

'I don't know.'

'What about the girl? She had money.'

'She was a shill – a gambling whore. She had no money. It came from her pimp. He's in at the casino.'

'Ah. Didn't you realize that?'

'I'm not sure.'

'Miles, you're mad.'

'I know.'

'They'll get very nasty.'

'I know.'

'Is there anyone with that kind of money? Who'd give it to you?'

'I don't think so. No. Oh, I don't know.'

'What about the old guy who put you through college?'

'I couldn't ask him. I'd rather get beaten up.'

'You'll get worse than beaten up,' said Billy with conviction.

'Oh. Well anyway, I still would. I could ask my uncle, but I don't think there's anything left. Or – yeah, that's it. The house.'

'What house?'

'The one in Malibu.'

'It's your grandmother's.'

'I know. But it ought to be mine. I could borrow against it.'

'Do you have the deeds?'

'No, but they must be in the house somewhere.'

'Miles, you really are something,' said Billy, in tones of great admiration.

Next day, when Mrs Kelly was taking her afternoon nap on the veranda, Miles let himself silently into her room. She slept soundly these days; she was old and weary, and she had several glasses of madeira with her lunch.

In a box under her bed, he found what he wanted: the deeds of the house. Wrinkled documents, in a tatty envelope. He took them out and looked at them, and smiled; then he went straight down to the bank.

'These are not in your name, Mr Wilburn.'

'I know. They're my grandmother's.'

'I can't let you have any money on these without her signature. We need a transfer deed in the first place. Making the property over to you. Signed by you both, with witnesses. And even then I have to draw up a Legal Charge.'

'What's that?'

'It's a document saying you've borrowed the money, and which we hold until it's repaid. I have to put a time limit on that of course. Perfectly simple; no problem in any of this. But like I say, first we need your grandmother's signature on the transfer deed – witnessed.'

'But she's – well she's very old. She's almost senile.'

'Doesn't alter matters.'

'What would?'

'Nothing.'

'Uh-huh. Well thanks anyway. I'll be back.'

'Granny Kelly, would you sign this for me?'

'What's that, Miles?'

'Oh, just a form, saying I'm over twenty-one. I've applied for a job at the casino.'

'The casino! What kind of a job is that?'

'Better than no job. You've been trying to get me to work for years. You've finally succeeded. You should be pleased. Please sign it. Oh, and we have to get Little Ed and Larissa to witness it.'

'Miles, this is just ridiculous. Just for a job. Are you sure this is right?'

'Granny, the world's changed a bit lately. You don't realize.'

'Maybe not. Oh, all right. Providing you go check on those hens and collect the eggs. I don't trust Little Ed one bit. I know he's taking them.'

'You can't trust anyone these days, Granny.'

'Right, young man, here you are. A draft for four thousand dollars. To be repaid in three years. OK?' The bank manager was avuncular, smiling. 'That's a lot of money. Don't you go off with that to the casino now.'

'Oh, I wouldn't do that.'

'Glad to hear it.'

He paid the debt, stayed away from the casino, stayed away from the women in the hotels. He concentrated on his job on the tennis courts. But he was unhappy, lonely. Billy's father had finally put his foot down, and was sending him off to work in a bank in Washington.

Billy seemed quite happy about it. 'I could quite do with a bit of respectability. Don't you ever want it?'

'Want what?'

'Well, you know, kind of normality. A job. Salary. A regular life.'

'Billy! Do you?'

'Yeah.' He grinned sheepishly. 'Yeah, suddenly I do. I really don't mind being shipped off to Washington. I'm looking forward to it. Except I'll miss you.'

'Billy,' said Miles, smiling at his friend, 'you're out to lunch.'

But when Billy had gone, he did wonder if a regular life might not have its charms.

He felt lonely, suddenly abandoned. Granny Kelly was increasingly senile and confused. Half the time she didn't seem to know where she was. She would ask him if he'd been down to the beach, or tell him she'd like a drive up to the Hills. He humoured her gently, because he loved her, but it didn't help him any. For the first time for years he mourned his mother. He was almost afraid; he had no one in the world to turn to. Marcia Galbraith was as senile as his grandmother, more so if anything. Of course there was his uncle, but Bill Wilburn never contacted them again after the drugs case. Well, he hadn't liked him much anyway.

He felt he would even have welcomed Hugo Dashwood, that he would meet him more than halfway. Funny, the old guy had so completely dropped out of his life. It showed he hadn't really cared, that he actually was a twenty-two carat, one hundred per cent creep. Odd that it hurt a bit, suddenly. That Dashwood had so absolutely lost interest in him. Creep he might be, but he was someone Miles could claim as at least a bit of his own, of his past. It might even, possibly, be worth contacting him. Not because he wanted to see him exactly, just to feel there was somebody somewhere in the world who he had some kind of a claim on.

Only he couldn't because he didn't have the faintest idea where he might be.

In Marcia Galbraith's desk was a small bundle of letters all addressed to her friend, Dorothy Kelly. She took care that Dorothy never saw her letters; you never knew, someone might try to tempt her back to California, or Ohio, and away from Nassau and Marcia. And besides, she needed looking after, now that her mind was going, and she and Little Ed and Larissa were all so devoted to her, protecting her from reality. She didn't want to be bothered with things like letters.

Among the bundle were two from Father Kennedy in Los Angeles, and one forwarded (via Los Angeles) from Hugo Dashwood in New York.

Chapter Fifteen

Sussex, 1983

The night before her wedding, Phaedria ran away.

She didn't run very far, but she ran nonetheless, and she would probably have run a lot further, made her escape altogether, had it not been for the intervention of the man she was widely rumoured to be unhealthily close to for a bride, David Sassoon, and his erstwhile mistress and her bridegroom's first wife, Eliza Garrylaig.

There was a vast house party at Marriotts; every bedroom was full and various children of varying ages were sleeping on floors, in box rooms, even the attics.

Fortunately the weather was lyrically warm; the gardens had rushed into an excess of roses, lilac, lupins, delphiniums; the beautiful old walls of the courtyard behind the house were covered with thick, sweet clouds of honeysuckle.

Out on the back lawns were two immense marquees filled with flowers, in urns and baskets, and clambering up the moss-covered pillars that supported the structures; and on the lake, below the lawns, floated two white Victorian riverboats, structured largely of ornate wrought iron, and filled, like the marquees, with flowers. Every hotel for miles around was filled with wedding guests.

Over a thousand people had been invited; and were coming from all over the world: friends and family, and business colleagues and associates from Europe, America, Australia,

Japan. 'You're never going to get married again,' Phaedria had said firmly, 'I want everyone who's ever known you to be there.'

The wedding ceremony itself was to be inevitably small and modest, set for ten thirty in the morning in the registry office in Haywards Heath, with only Letitia, Augustus Blenheim (who had left Prosper Merimee with great reluctance and a feeling that the occasion hardly warranted it) and Roz and C. J. present. But at two there was to be a blessing in the village church, attended by a hundred or so family and close friends, and then at three a second ceremony in one of the marquees, with a blessing, music both secular and sacred, and an address.

A small string orchestra was to play, a choir of boy sopranos to sing, and one of the great new young actors of the British stage, Piers Tobias, was to recite the Desiderata.

After the afternoon reception, in the gardens, the guests were to dine and dance in the marquees and the boats; there were two groups and a discotheque, and a superb jazz band who had been specially briefed to play the Charleston at half-hourly intervals for Letitia's particular delectation.

At midnight there was to be a firework display, to the accompaniment of Handel's firework music, played by the village band.

Phaedria was to wear a dress by Karl Lagerfeld, and her ten small bridesmaids to wear its replica in miniature; they were to carry not bouquets but garlands of flowers, which were hopefully to rope them together and prevent the small ones from straying too far during the second ceremony, which would clearly lack for them the novelty of the first. Phaedria and Julian were to ride back from the village church in an open laundau, pulled by the beloved Grettisaga ('I'm surprised you're not insisting on having her in the church,' Julian had said), and the children in a series of governess carts, drawn by white ponies.

All this Phaedria had orchestrated herself; and now she was tired, and she was frightened, and quite quite certain that she was making a dreadful mistake. She had had supper in the kitchen with Letitia and Madeleine Emerson and her girls, and Eliza and Peveril, who had both been charmed and delighted to have been invited ('Well, as if I wouldn't want you there,' Phaedria had said when Eliza phoned her, laughing, to thank her and congratulate her on her style), and had sat in an increasing silence while everybody chattered and laughed and gossiped and then had pleaded a headache and gone upstairs to her room. Julian was flying down in the morning – ('Well, darling, I don't want to see you on the night before the wedding, it's unlucky and besides I might be tempted to try and seduce you before our wedding night').

She lay on her bed, and looked out at the moon in a state of first panic and then misery; what had she done, how had she come to be in this situation, to be marrying this difficult, fearsome man forty years older than she was, to be taking on the responsibility of running five households, to be forced into almost daily contact with a stepdaughter who loathed her, to be heavily involved with a most daunting commercial venture on the basis of the most sketchy knowledge and experience; to have planned a day of such tortuous complexity it would be not just one but a series of miracles if nothing went wrong; and why was there now nobody, nobody at all, who would say, as perhaps a mother, a friend, even might, 'There, there, all will be well, don't fret, you've done wonderfully.'

Unbidden, the thought of Charles came into her head; he seemed at this distance sanity, normality, kindness, safety. The thought and the memories made her tears start; she sat up on the bed, sobs catching her breath, and knew she had to get away, that what lay ahead was not to be borne, that she could not go through with it. She went to her door and listened; it was silent downstairs now, everyone had gone to bed.

She decided to go at once, quickly, silently, without fuss; by the morning she could be far far away. They could still have a wonderful party without her, it would not be a total disaster, there was still the food (oh, the food, how the food had worn her out), the wine, the music, the dancing – and Julian to host it, charmingly, confidently, brilliantly. He did not really need her; he did not need anybody. She knew that now. However close to him she grew, however much of himself he let her see, there was still so much more that was hidden, secret, mysterious, his own.

She loved him, she had lived with him in the most extraordinary and passionate physical closeness, she had fought with him, laughed with him, hated him, studied him, for six months and still she did not understand him, had seen little of him that he did not wish her to see, knew little of him that he did not wish her to know.

And so she could not, would not marry him, it was too dangerous, too foolish, too wrong. She would go, and in a few months, weeks even, he would move on to another woman, another body, another set of emotions. And it would not matter to him, not really, not at all. Down the stairs she crept, and out of the front door; she went briefly to the stables, and stroked, kissed Grettisaga and Spring Collection tenderly on their dear, beloved faces ('I will come back for you'), and then walked quickly to the front of the house. Her Mercedes was parked there; she got into it and, weeping quite hard now, moved off down the drive.

But before she even reached the lane she had to stop. Her tears blinded her, and her heart was thudding so hard, her ears pounding, she felt faint. She pulled in to the side, leant her head on her arms on the steering wheel and sobbed: for everything, for things she had known she cared about and things she had never consciously considered; for Charles, of course, for the golden lost days of Oxford, for her own youth, so strangely and suddenly gone, for her mother, just a distant, confused memory, for her job, for Bristol, for Brian, for her freedom, for days untrammelled by the fierce rigorous demands of the man she had so foolishly, so mistakenly, agreed to marry.

She sat there for a long time, crying harshly, desperately; she felt she knew for the first time in her life precisely where her heart was, and that it was truly breaking; and she did not know what to do.

Out of the darkness she saw first Eliza's face, startled, concerned; and then David Sassoon's, tender, anxious. They were together, and why she did not even begin to wonder, walking up the drive; they had seen her car and heard her crying, and now they were with her. They told her to get in the back seat and they got in beside her, one each side, and held her, and David stroked her hair and kissed her poor, ravaged face, and Eliza held her hands and said, over and over again, as if to a small child, 'Shush, shush, don't cry, there, there, it's all right, shush,' and gradually she calmed, stopped sobbing, just sat there, looking at them, huge tears rolling down her face.

'I have to get away,' she said, when she could speak. 'I have to go,' and neither of them argued, or told her not to be silly, merely sat and looked interested, and then, when she was a little calmer still, Eliza said, yes, of course she must if she really wanted to, but why.

'Because I can't marry Julian. I can't live with him. He doesn't love me and he doesn't need me, and I can't deal with another day of this dreadful, demanding, tyrant of a life of his.'

'He loves you,' said David. 'He does, you know.'

And how did he know, she said, irritated out of her grief, how could he possibly know, he scarcely knew Julian at all, it was ridiculous to make such a statement, and he said, oh, no he could tell, she was wrong, he had worked with Julian for a very long time, and that he had indeed changed astonishingly, greatly, that he had seen him with many relationships with many women and never before had he known him so unsure of himself, so softened, so happy.

And Eliza said yes, it was true: 'He never loved me, you know, he was fond of me, and I amused him, but he didn't love me. I see him with you, and he does love you. He is behaving quite quite differently; the way he gave up Camilla like that, so decisively, so irrevocably, the very next day, that was extraordinary. She has had such a hold on him for so many years, and it was ended, just like that, just because of you. Leave if you must, if you feel you can't stay, but in the knowledge that he does love you, and he does need you.'

Phaedria looked at her, silent, very still.

'Do you really think so?'

'I know so.'

She sighed. 'I hope so. I do hope so. Because I really do love him. Most of the time, anyway. When I can get near him for five minutes.'

'That life must be terrible,' said David, holding out not one but two handkerchiefs. 'Go on, use them, I always carry at least three, don't I, Eliza? I couldn't stand it, all that powerful machinery, endlessly turning, pushing you on to the next project, the next company, the next country.'

Phaedria looked at him, blowing her nose, her eyes at last

dry, swollen and sore. 'Yes,' she said, 'that's exactly what it's like. I feel as if I'm some poor helpless creature, a little bird, being crushed in it, dragged relentlessly, all broken, on and on.'

'Yes,' said Eliza, 'I remember that feeling. But you've done something I never did, you've become part of the machinery. The crucial bit, that drives the rest. You're finding out how it works, and you may in time find out how to control it. Remember that.'

'It's not making me very popular with your daughter,' said Phaedria with a weak smile, 'becoming part of it all.'

'Oh, Roz is impossible. I apologize for her. But I do have to say in her defence, Phaedria, that it must be difficult for her. She does adore Julian. Always has. She's bound to be jealous of you.'

'I suppose so,' said Phaedria with a sigh, 'and I do try so hard, but I just don't seem to be getting anywhere. It's very hard to cope with.'

'Roz is very difficult,' said David, 'but I'm very fond of her. I was her first fan, wasn't I, Eliza?'

'Oh, you were,' said Eliza. You did a lot for her. I don't think she ever realised how much.'

'She had a schoolgirl crush on me,' said David to Phaedria, 'asked me to take her out to dinner one night, and kissed me in the car. It was very sweet. Goodness knows what might have happened if that old – if your fiancé hadn't shipped me off to New York . . .'

'Yes, well, let's not talk about that,' said Eliza. 'You know it upsets me. And it's got nothing to do with the matter in hand. Roz will come round, Phaedria, really she will.'

'I hope so,' said Phaedria. 'Apart from anything else, I know we'd get on. I'd like her if she'd let me. She's exactly the sort of woman I admire: self confident and terribly positive, and – well, gutsy.'

'I would have thought you possessed plenty of those qualities yourself,' said Eliza, patting her hand. 'You wouldn't have taken Julian on if you didn't. Anyway,' she went on more briskly, 'I don't wonder you're sitting here weeping. Whoever you were marrying. The organization of this circus tomorrow, absolutely amazing. And you've done it all virtually single-handed. Honestly, Phaedria, I'd back you against the whole of the Morell empire any day. Is Julian impressed? He ought to be.'

'Oh, I think so,' said Phaedria with a sigh, 'but he doesn't say so.'

'No.'

David looked at her thoughtfully. 'What you ought to do really,' he said, 'is go up to London now and see the old bugger. Beard him in his den. Tell him how you feel. No wonder you got stage fright, here all on your own. Why don't you do that?'

'I'd quite like to in a way,' said Phaedria, 'and you're right, it is being alone here that's made me feel so bad, but I'm just too tired.'

'I'll drive you. Eliza can tell everyone we've just run off together. That'll get the rumours going.'

'Don't be silly, David,' said Eliza tartly, 'why should Phaedria want rumours flying about on the eve of her wedding? What good would that do?'

'I do like the idea though,' said Phaedria with a weak giggle, 'everyone would think we'd eloped.'

'Phaedria,' said Eliza, very serious, 'there are a few rumours about you and David already, as you very possibly know.'

'Yes, I did.'

'Totally unfounded, unfortunately,' said David with a sigh.

'Be quiet, David. Phaedria, do be careful, be very careful. Julian has a fearsome jealousy. And he does dreadful things in revenge. As David and I know to our cost.'

'Yes. Letitia told me. And you weren't even married to him any more.'

Eliza laughed. 'No, I had another husband in between, even. Darling Letitia. She really doesn't mind blackening Julian's name one bit, does she? Don't you adore her though?'

'Oh, I think she's wonderful.'

'Well look,' said David, 'are we eloping or not? I honestly don't mind driving you to London. Or alternatively I'll drive you somewhere else altogether. In the opposite direction. Just say the word.'

'No,' said Phaedria. 'No, I feel much better now. I'll come back. I haven't really got much choice.'

'You have, Phaedria, you have,' said Eliza, taking her hand again. 'Exercise it if you want to. Don't stay because of us.'

'I'm not. Truly. But thank you. Both of you. For helping me see.'

'Right,' said David briskly, 'well, we were just going to crack a bottle, weren't we Eliza, to toast the bride. How much nicer to do it with her. Come on, Phaedria, let me at least drive you back to the house, and then you can join us in the kitchen.'

'Thank you. I'd like that. Where's – I mean should we find – ?'

'Peveril?' said Eliza, 'don't worry, I'm not running away from him either. He sleeps so soundly, dear old darling, and he snores so loudly, I just get desperate sometimes. And I'm a night owl. I knew David was coming down late tonight, so I waited up to see him. Old friends. Nothing more, are we, my angel?'

'Nothing more.'

Phaedria looked at them, so strangely close, so relaxed with one another, and wondered whether or not they were telling the truth. Well, it really didn't matter, and they had been good friends to her that night. She relaxed suddenly, feeling just rather sweetly and pleasantly tired, and said, 'Come on, then, let's go. I'll get the champagne. There's enough in the cellars to incapacitate the whole of Sussex.'

'I think she'll be all right now,' said Eliza to David, while Phaedria disappeared into the kitchen for the glasses. 'Thank God we found her. Although why we should do the old bastard any favours I really don't know.'

'I think we've done her one, actually,' said David. 'I think she likes it all, really. I think it suits her.'

And the next day, when Phaedria Morell drifted across the lawns of her beautiful house, greeting her guests with charm and grace, sparkling and radiant in her wild silk, lace-strewn dress, with fresh white roses woven into the massing clouds of her dark hair, very few people would have disagreed with him.

Chapter Sixteen

Eleuthera, London and Los Angeles, 1983–4

Julian took Phaedria to the house on Eleuthera in the Bahamas
for their honeymoon. It was a low, white mansion, set just above
a small curving bay, the palm trees hanging gently over the
silvery white of the beach; she fell instantly in love with it.

Julian flew them in himself to the villagey airfield at Marsh
Harbour in the small plane he kept at Nassau; she had sat
gazing spellbound for the entire flight at the fairy tale sea
beneath her, the strange variations in the colour of the water,
the mystical, uninhabited, almost swamplike green islands, the
dark dark blue swathes of the deep waters, the pink etching
round the small white patches of land set in the blue-green sea.

'That's the coral,' he said, 'that you can see. Tomorrow we'll
go snorkelling on the reef near the house. Then you can meet
the fish.'

That evening, they wandered along the beach, picking up
coconuts and conch shells, looking at the slick of moonlight on
the sea; Phaedria sank down suddenly, laughing, on the warm
white sand and said, 'This is a cliché of a honeymoon, Julian
Morell.'

'I'm sorry.'

'Don't be. I love clichés. I'm a journalist, remember?'

He lay down beside her. 'I do. Could we add to the clichés,
do you think, and make love in the moonlight?'

She looked at him thoughtfully. 'Bit corny. But I like that
too.'

'Come on, then,' he said, reaching for her, kissing her on her
forehead, her nose, her neck.

'Oh, Julian,' she said, 'I will, I will.'

Early next morning the houseboy took them out in the small
motor boat and anchored on the reef while they swam and
Phaedria marvelled at the peaceful, enchanted world she found
beneath the sea, the filigree coral, the clear clear water and the
rainbow-coloured, friendly, quaintly smiling fish.

'Oh, I love it, I love it,' she said as they sat later on the veranda of the house, drinking fresh iced lemonade, sinking her teeth into a pawpaw. 'Why didn't you bring me here before?'

'You were too busy wanting to go to LA and New York and opening your own store and organizing a wedding, if you remember. We shouldn't really be here now, it's much too hot, I never usually come until the winter. But I wanted you to see it, I thought you just might like it.'

'Oh, I do, and of course I don't mind the heat. I love the sun.'

'Yes, but you must be careful. This is real sun. Very dangerous. Not to be sat in.'

She ignored him, as she so often did, and got badly burnt; for three days she lay feverish and in pain in the cool bedroom with the whirring fans, and he sat with her and bathed her skin and read to her from *Anna Karenina*, which he pronounced as suitably romantic and sad for the occasion.

'You're a stupid girl,' he said to her, when she finally felt better and sat up, weak but cheerful, demanding breakfast. 'You should do what I tell you. You've wasted three days of our week here, and I haven't even been able to make love to you. What a honeymoon.'

'I'm sorry. Can't we stay longer?'

'No,' he said, mildly irritated, 'we both have to get back. You know we do.'

'Sorry. All right. But we have three days left, don't we?'

'We do.'

'Well, let me start making amends straight away. Come into bed beside me, take those silly shorts off, and show me you've forgiven me.'

'I'm afraid of hurting you.'

'It'll be worth it. Please.'

'All right. I'll be very careful.'

'Not too careful.'

'All right.'

'And did you enjoy your wedding?' he asked her suddenly as they sat eating breakfast some considerable time later. 'Was it worth all that worry and work?'

'I really enjoyed it. Every minute. Did you?'

'Surprisingly I did. I spent the whole day thinking how special you were, and that I didn't deserve you at all.'

She looked at him, tender with the aftermath of love, remorseful at the thought that she had so nearly not been there at all.

'I do like Susan,' she said suddenly, 'she's very brisk and I'm not sure that she likes me very much, but I can see why you're so fond of her.'

'She is a very special person,' he said. 'And I'm very glad she's married Richard Brookes. He'll make her a much better husband than I ever would have done.'

There was a silence. Phaedria smiled at him, took his hand, kissed it. 'I love you when you're being humble. And honest.'

'Then you can't love me very often,' he said and laughed.

'No. I don't. Didn't your mother look wonderful?'

'Absolutely wonderful.'

'How old is she?'

'Eighty-five.'

'She's amazing. That was some Charleston she did with David. Imagine him being able to do that.'

'Imagine.' He sounded short, tetchy. Phaedria looked at him, amused.

'Don't you like David?'

'Well enough.'

'Enough for what?'

'To work with him.'

'Is that all?'

'I think so, yes.'

'Pity. I wanted to ask him down to Marriotts for the weekend when we get back.'

'What on earth for?'

'To work on Circe. He doesn't have much time to spare during the week. Would you really rather I didn't?'

'Yes, I would. Tell him to make time.'

She sighed. 'Pity. I thought it would have been a fun weekend as well.'

He was silent. The subject was clearly closed. As it was their honeymoon, she did not try to reopen it.

Back in London, relieved of the pressures of planning her

wedding, she began to work in earnest. David's drawings were completed, specifications were drawn up, the work put out for tender.

Phaedria put her mind to merchandise, to her scheme for a wardrobe consultancy, to hiring buyers, to finding new designers as well as established ones, to selecting (and mostly rejecting) jewellery, fabrics, shoes, furs. She wanted, was determined at this stage to be as painstakingly and personally involved as possible; to put herself in the position of her customer and see, feel, try everything for herself. She bought collections from Sonia Rykiel, Missoni, Krizia, Valentino ready-to-wear; from the States she imported Anne Klein, Ungaro, Cerrutti, from France Dorothée Bis and Emanuelle Khanh. There were shoes from Maud Frizon, Ferragamo, Charles Jourdan, hats by Freddy Fox and Patricia Underwood, and a dazzling costume jewellery department bedecked with designs from Butler and Wilson, Chanel, Dior. She learnt to haggle not just about money but exclusivity and time; she discovered the great retailing nightmares, of hold-ups in production, in customs; a delivery of hats failed to reach her on time because the straw had not arrived from China, a set of silk dresses because a factory in Hong Kong had been closed for a fortnight by an epidemic of flu. She poached staff shamelessly from other stores: from Brown's, Harvey Nichols, Fortnum's. She considered new departments – gifts, pictures, interior decor – and rejected most of them as too impersonal, out of line with the Circe concept. The only one she was totally confident about was a flower room, as a part of the foyer, a small bower styled like a conservatory, set with wicker chairs and tables, stacked with every conceivable flower, with rose trees and jasmine and daisy bushes in pots, urns filled with lilies and orchids, and roses, and myriads of dried flowers, hanging from the ceiling, stacked in baskets round the walls.

'Women will buy them, of course, but men will come in and buy them too; it will be the most beautiful, caring, exclusive flower shop in London. Made for people in love.'

Favourite and well-known customers would receive a spray of white lilies on their birthdays and wedding anniversaries from Circe; little girls would get posies of sweetheart roses and forget-me-nots.

It was a charming concept; it brought the front of the shop alive.

She began to think about sales staff: 'I want them to be young – don't look at me like that, Julian.'

She looked at advertising agencies, PR companies, talked to the press as well herself, began to plan a launch party that rivalled her own wedding in splendour and complexity. Things were proceeding fast; she was determined to achieve the impossible and open by the spring. And the more people told her she couldn't, the more she knew she could.

She found the adjustment to being married to Julian surprisingly difficult. She had imagined, having lived with him for six months, that things would continue in much the same way; they didn't. He changed, quite swiftly; he was still as tender, as loving, as ardent in their private lives; but now that their professional one was lived so closely together, under a spotlight, he became harsher, more demanding, less appreciative than she would ever have imagined. This spilled over; she found it hard to separate the man who had publicly criticized her, diminished her during the day from the one who told her he loved her, was proud of her, just a few hours later. She told him so; he laughed.

'You mustn't take my criticism personally, my darling. I always insist on excellence. That's all. That's why I love you.'

Letitia, who had observed the conflict of the two lives on a few occasions, took it upon herself to talk to Phaedria about it and asked her to supper at First Street one evening when Julian was away.

'None of my business, Phaedria, but old women are notoriously nosy. It's because they have no lives of their own. Is married life agreeing with you?'

Phaedria was unused to confiding in people; she had grown up her own confidante. 'Oh, yes. It's marvellous. Don't I look as if it is?'

'Not always. You haven't married the easiest of men, of course.'

'No, but I knew that.'

'You did, indeed. I just thought – forgive me, darling – that the other day when he was so extremely ill mannered and unappreciative of your work on the advertising campaign, you looked a little – what shall we say? – bleak.'

'I felt bleak,' said Phaedria, forcing a bright smile.

'And then, no doubt, you get home and he expects you to act as if he was Don Juan and Casanova rolled into one.'

Phaedria sighed and looked at Letitia slightly warily. 'Well, yes, he does a bit.'

'I think you should point out to him very clearly that if he wants you to love him, he should behave lovably. At all times. So unnecessary, that sort of thing. Posturing. He's always done it, of course.' She sighed. 'He's very spoilt, Phaedria. Don't forget that. And it isn't really his fault.'

'No, I can see that. But it doesn't make life any easier.'

'Of course not. I'm not suggesting you should join in, only that you should try and understand it. It makes him seem less harsh, in a way.'

'I'll try.'

'The other thing, of course, is that the situation is a new one to him.'

'What do you mean?'

'Well, he's never had to share his working life with an equal partner before. Certainly not anyone so young and clever.'

'Not even Camilla? She was creative. Very, as far as I can make out.'

She spoke more fiercely than she meant; Letitia looked at her thoughtfully. Camilla was obviously the raw nerve in the relationship. She had obviously heard gossip. Hopefully not fresh gossip, although it was not beyond the bounds of possibility. Extraordinary the hold that icy piece of American hype had over Julian; the way time and again he had gone back to her.

'Oh, Camilla's role was always overrated, in my opinion,' she said carefully. 'And yes, she was Julian's mistress, but not on a formal basis. Or not for very long. And she was certainly never a threat, professionally.'

'What about Roz?'

'Different. Bone of his bone, flesh of his flesh. His creation. Another achievement. But you have just come along and are there, stealing the limelight, invading his territory. He probably feels threatened.'

'That's ridiculous. Anyway, it's at his invitation.'

'I know, darling. But it doesn't alter the fact. He has to work just a little extra hard at being Julian Morell.'

She looked at Phaedria and thought how much she liked her, how much she was coming to admire her. She smiled her dancing smile, so like her son's. 'I do promise you he loves you very much indeed. And is terribly proud of you.'

'Yes, I think he does,' said Phaedria, 'but it only makes it a tiny bit easier. Anyway, I love him too and I'm sure we'll work through it. Thank you, Letitia, next time he tells me in front of a dozen people that I am a crass, rank amateur, which was yesterday's little label, I'll try and tell myself he's just feeling threatened and turn the other cheek. Now then, tell me what you think of Margaret Howell's suits. Too severe for us, or not?'

On the way home that night Phaedria thought about what Letitia had said. It seemed a little unlikely to her that Julian really felt threatened by her presence; her own feeling was that he was irritated by it, and was regretting his original enthusiasm for her involvement. Well, it was too late. She was enjoying herself: enjoying the work, enjoying the drama, enjoying – and this was a little difficult to face, but she managed it – enjoying the power. Phaedria was a little disturbed by how much she was enjoying the power. She had no interest in her power as the wife of Julian Morell; she got no pleasure from being able to buy, order, act, spend, on his behalf. But to be able to do those things on her own, that was heady stuff. She loved the knowledge that with a word, a decision of her own, she could initiate things, mobilize people, set machinery in motion. She enjoyed persuading people to do things, making them see things her way, help her to turn her ideas into reality. She liked choosing her staff, picking through applications, looking for, recognizing the qualities she wanted. She especially liked putting them together, seeing them working with each other, on her projects, her ideas, for her. She even enjoyed financial power; she was initially nervous, but later deeply satisfied that she was able to control large sums of money, to put it to her own uses, to make it work for her.

What was more, she eyed the far greater, wider-reaching

power that Roz had and wanted more of her own. She envied Roz the silken authority that bought, sold, designed, that meant that people did what she said, and without question, or without a great deal of question, in most of the countries in the Western world, and quite a few in the Eastern. That seemed to Phaedria a more desirable commodity than anything else she could think of: it made her pulses race, she wanted it far more than nice clothes, fine houses, jewels, all the other gifts her marriage had brought her. And every time she exercised some new piece of power, pushed the parameters of her authority a little further, she felt increasingly elated; not, as she might have expected, strong, masculine, seriously important, but strangely and confidently female.

There was another facet of her life with Julian that was troubling her, and which Letitia had touched upon: it was that part of it that was lived in the bedroom.

Not only had Phaedria never really experienced sex before she met Julian, she had positively avoided it, not only had no lovers, but discouraged them. Initially she had found sex interesting, and pleasurable; having never experienced it before, and being deeply in love with a man of considerable sexual talents, she was a perfect bride: eager to learn and to please, appreciative, ardent. Now, almost a year into their relationship, she was finding it much harder to be responsive. She told herself that it was because, as Letitia had suggested, he was so often less than kind and loving to her during the day; that she was frequently very tired; that he was extremely demanding. But she was beginning to think it was none of those things: and that she simply wasn't very sexually motivated.

Looking back over her early life, at the fact that she had been twenty-four years old before she had gone to bed with anyone, and more significantly, had hardly ever wanted to, rarely felt any strong sexual urges, it seemed to her that she must have a considerable shortfall in that direction. Because she had still no close women friends, no confidantes, there was no one she could talk to, even on a lighthearted level, about it; she missed out on the easy, jokey, dirty talk, the female equivalent of barrack-room humour that tends to take place when several women gather together, particularly over a bottle or two of wine. She had never heard any other woman complain (however lightheartedly) about her husband's or her lover's demands, never been able to laugh about sex, to confess to not wanting it at times, to faking orgasm or even desire, in order to please, or to reassure, and she was beginning to form the miserable impression that everybody else was perpetually in the grips of immense sexual hunger and that there must be something extremely wrong with her that much of the time she felt rather well satisfied, if not over fed, by the whole thing.

She didn't want to talk to Julian about it, indeed felt it was out of the question that she should; and so she went on, increasingly anxious, decreasingly ardent, struggling to feel, and if not to feel, to pretend, to fake. Fortunately, as far as she could see, he had absolutely no idea.

Phaedria Morell and David Sassoon (a great many people were saying) were an interesting team.

And as with so much of what a great many people said, it was quite true.

David Sassoon was now in his mid forties; his rough edges smoothed, his charm honeyed, his sexuality softened. The slightly truculent self-confidence that had intrigued and overcome Eliza Thetford had been replaced by something much more relaxed and conventionally pleasing; but his warm dark eyes could still flick into the most startlingly private places and sensations, and the tang of East End London in his light amused voice took the edge off his smoothest, most urbane remarks and made them original and oddly intimate. He was still slender, elegant, stylishly dressed; his dark curly hair just tipped with grey, the lines on his face light and good-humoured.

Phaedria loved working with him, he inspired her, made her think, forced her into self-criticism. They worked quite differently, although both with much flair and sense of fashion: she with her head, he with his heart, she with logic, he with instinct, but time and again they reached the same conclusion, the same place, the same solution. As the year went by, and their joint vision of Circe began to become reality, they grew closer, drawn as are all people who work together by the same pressures, anxieties, pleasures and triumphs; they shared a shorthand of language, often scarcely needing to finish a sentence to one another, developed their own private jokes, and could read one another with absolute ease. They each could tell at a glance when the other was happy, cross, tired, tense, knew when to talk and when to be silent, and were supportive, generous and completely interdependent.

These were just some of things about them that people were saying; and in the fullness of time Julian Morell came to hear them.

'Phaedria, I had no idea you were going to work with David on everything to do with the store. I had imagined he would only be providing the initial concepts.'

'Well, Julian, I don't surely have to tell you everything I do. You're the first to give me the bum's rush if you think I'm taking up too much of your time. I think it's essential for David to see the whole thing through, I don't have the confidence to do it on my own.'

'Confidence is the last thing you appear to be lacking, if I may say so. And I don't see why one of the more junior designers couldn't take over at this stage.'

'I'm sorry, Julian, but I don't agree. This is so important.'

'I see. I understand you want to bring the opening date forward to March. I'm sure it's not possible.'

'It is, if we push everyone. Pay workmen overtime. I know it is.'

'I'm very surprised. I'll have a closer look at the schedules.'

'Don't you trust me?'

'Phaedria, of course I trust you. But as I keep having to remind you, you are a novice at this sort of thing, you have no idea of the complexities of what you're doing. And anyway, I would have liked to have known. Keep me just a little more informed in future, would you?'

'It isn't easy.'

'What do you mean?'

'You never want to talk about my part of the business at home. I can never get near you in the office. How am I supposed to do it?'

He looked at her. 'Perhaps we had better instigate a formal meeting, once a week. We would have to involve Roz as well.'

'Why?'

He sighed. 'I would have thought you could see that, Phaedria. Because she is, after all, the president of the stores division. Does she know about the changed dates? Are you keeping her informed about what you're doing?'

'Yes and no.'

'That's a highly unprofessional answer.'

'Well, she's not exactly over-available to me either.'

'Phaedria, don't be such a child.'

'I was under the impression that was precisely how you regarded me. Anyway, yes all right. Let's start the meetings.'

She tried to tell herself he was merely feeling threatened.

Julian called C. J. up to his office. 'C. J., I think several of the hotels need a new look.'

'You do?' C. J. was astonished.

'Yes, I do. Particularly in Nice, and possibly Washington. And I'd like Sassoon to work on them with you. Nobody else could handle it. Go and take a good look at them, and take him with you. Let me have your ideas in a couple of weeks.'

'OK. He's pretty busy at the moment though, on the new store.'

'Tell him I said this was more important.'

C. J. went back to his office thoughtfully. Julian was normally the last person to favour change. Now what was going on? Oh, well, it would be good to get away from Roz for ten days. He asked his secretary to get David Sassoon on the line.

Roz had been carefully avoiding any involvement with Phaedria. She knew it was a mistake, that it was at best unbusinesslike and at worst childish, but she was angrily aware of the ever extending ripples of Phaedria's power; she could feel them lapping on to the shores of her own empire, and for the time being, until she could find some way of defeating her, she was merely hoping that Phaedria would hang herself sooner rather than later on the huge lengths of rope Julian was clearly prepared to hand over to her.

She was also oddly and miserably jealous of Phaedria's relationship with David. She had not thought about David sexually for years, he had become a much loved avuncular figure, and she was relieved and happy that he and her mother had managed to become friends once more; but he was a person for whom she had a very special fondness, and it riled her dreadfully that he was clearly so close to Phaedria.

As well as riling her it interested her; not even Roz could believe (knowing David, knowing his singular attitude towards her father) that they were likely to be lovers; nevertheless there did exist the clear possibility that her father might think that was so. That seemed to Roz a very large case of dynamite indeed.

Julian came into the first liaison meeting looking particularly bland.

'Right,' he said. 'Now hopefully, these can be kept short and not take up too much of our time. It may be that in due course the two of you can handle them yourselves and not need to involve me.'

Roz and Phaedria looked at him in a hostile silence.

'My concern, as you both know, is that your work is, to an extent, overlapping, and there is a certain lack of communication. It is vital that there is a two-way traffic of information between you – clearly you, Roz, as president of the stores, need to be closely informed of Phaedria's plans –'

'In theory, yes,' said Roz, interrupting him. 'In practice, surely, as the London store is so exclusively Phaedria's, there is very little input I can make. She seems perfectly confident and is moving very fast, aren't you Phaedria –'

'Roz, that is not the point, as you must realize,' said Julian, his irritation beginning to surface. 'Phaedria's confidence and indeed her competence are not in question –'

'I'm so glad,' put in Roz sweetly.

'Roz, I would be grateful if you will let me finish the occasional sentence –'

'Sorry.'

'What matters is that you should be aware of what she is doing, so that you can build it into your overall picture of the store development worldwide. London is crucial to that picture.'

'Well, I do agree,' said Roz. 'It just seems rather dangerous that it should be potentially a separate entity.'

'Roz, that is the whole point of these meetings,' said Julian, his eyes growing very hard. 'So that it is not a separate entity.'

'So are you saying that if I disagree with any of Phaedria's plans, I have the authority to block them?' said Roz. 'Surely not.'

'Not block them, no of course not. But discuss them, talk your objections through, yes, certainly.'

'I see,' said Roz. She looked suddenly rather sleek.

'How – detailed – might these objections be?' asked Phaedria mildly.

'Oh, for God's sake, I have no idea,' said Julian. 'That is clearly the sort of thing that will emerge over the weeks ahead.'

'I think we should discuss them now,' said Phaedria. 'Obviously on large matters, budgets, designers, colour schemes for example, it would be not unreasonable for Roz to have a view –'

'Not entirely,' said Roz, looking amusedly arrogant, a prefect toying with a very new recruit to the first form.

'But if,' Phaedria went on, steadily, apparently unmoved by this, 'I am to talk to Roz about every hat, bracelet, salesgirl before taking a decision, progress is going to be rather seriously halted. Just in case she disagreed with a great deal of what I was doing,' she added sweetly.

'Phaedria,' said Julian, 'if you cannot establish in your own mind the proper limits of your own influence, then I would have serious doubts about your ability to handle this project at all. I expect you and Roz to be able to work out a modus operandi and stick to it. That is all. Initially I will be available for consultation on it, if absolutely necessary. Please get to work implementing it straight away. Now then, I do feel that you need a really first-class assistant, Phaedria. Someone with a background in marketing and experience in design and retailing as well. Instinct alone is hardly sufficient under the very serious commercial circumstances you are operating in. Roz, I'm sure Phaedria would appeciate some help in finding someone. You have so many contacts. Give it a bit of time, would you?'

'I'm very busy indeed at the moment,' said Roz, 'I don't really have that sort of time to spare. Couldn't Susan handle it? It's her area.'

'I don't think so, no,' said Julian. 'Susan's area, as you describe it, is overall company management, which may incorporate personnel, but certainly doesn't include it as a day to day concern. Besides, you are in the retail field, every day, you must constantly meet people who would be suitable for the job.'

'Not at assistant level, no,' said Roz.

'Then be kind enough to descend to it for a while,' said Julian. 'Now then, Phaedria, while I think of it, you'll have to find someone to work with you on the design aspect of the store for a few weeks. C. J. needs Sassoon on some vital refurbishing of the hotels. He's taking him off to the States next week.'

It was hard to say which of them was more angry with him.

'Hallo, Roz. It's nice to see you.'

Roz looked up. She had been sitting at her table at the Caprice for half an hour, after her lunch guest had gone, trying to concentrate on the spring promotions for Circe New York and the merchandising plans for Circe, Beverly Hills; roughly twenty-five of the thirty minutes had been occupied with a savage contemplation of Phaedria. The only consolation was that there seemed little chance of her having a baby while she was apparently so committed to her work.

She looked up. Michael Browning stood in front of her, his expression as wrily solemn as always, his dark eyes exploring her face with a tentative tenderness.

Roz actually felt her heart lurch three distinct times, moving within her; she closed her eyes briefly, trying to compose herself, and then, surprising herself with her calm, smiled back at him.

'Michael! What on earth are you doing here?'

'Looking for my raincoat.'

Roz relaxed, started to laugh.

'Why should your raincoat be here?'

'It was here last night. Now it's gone.'

'I expect you left it in a taxi, not here at all. Never mind your raincoat, what about you? Why are you in London?'

'Oh, I'm buying a few little supermarket sites.'

'How nice.' She was silent, just looking at him, drinking him in.

587

'Aren't you going to ask a raincoatless man to sit down?'

'Sorry. Do sit down. Have a coffee.'

'That would be nice.'

He looked at her, quietly, studying her face, her hair, her clothes. She was wearing (and thanked God for it) a particularly flattering outfit: a short peplumed jacket, in navy suede, by Sonia Rykiel, with a long bias cut swirling skirt; it made her look taller, more graceful, more slender even than she actually was. Michael smiled at her.

'You don't seem to have changed too much.'

'Why should I have?'

'Well, quite a lot's happened to you.'

'I suppose so.'

Her heart was taking off again; keep calm, she said desperately to herself, keep calm, don't think, don't feel, don't do anything. Helplessly, horrified she heard herself say, 'It's so nice to see you. I've missed you such a lot.'

'I missed you too, darling.'

'Don't call me that.'

'Why not?'

'You know.'

'Sorry. How's married life?'

'Fine.'

'Good. How's Baby?'

'She's wonderful.'

'Good. And how's work? Are you chairman of the board yet?'

'Not quite. Nor likely to be for a while now, I fear.' She attempted to sound lighthearted; she failed.

'What's the matter?'

'Oh, nothing much.'

'So your old man's got married again?'

'Yes.'

'You have to hand it to him. She looks very beautiful in her pictures. Is she nice?'

'Very.'

'Good. I guess you and she must be friends.'

'Oh, we are.'

'That's some kind of a name she has.'

'Ridiculous.' Roz sounded suddenly savage. Michael grinned.

588

'So that's it?'

'What is?'

'You aren't too fond of her?'

'Of course I am.'

'Fine.' He took a long drink of coffee, then looked round for the waiter. 'I could do with a brandy. Want one?'

'No, thank you.'

'OK. You can share mine. I'll get a double.'

'I said I didn't want one.'

'Yeah, you said you liked Lady Morell, too, and that you were enjoying married life. We can share the brandy.'

'Are you – married or anything?'

'Nothing. Haven't got over you yet.'

'Don't be ridiculous.'

'I'm not. Tell me about Pharaoh, or whatever her name is.'

'Phaedria. There's not a lot to tell.'

'Is she going to found a new Morell dynasty? Lots of little tycoons?'

'I don't know,' said Roz, speaking with great difficulty. 'We aren't exactly intimate.'

'She's very young. I bet she does.'

'Possibly.'

He changed tack. 'So tell me about Hubby.'

'C. J. is just fine.'

'I hear he's doing very well, working for Daddy.'

'That wasn't very kind.'

'It was the truth. It isn't always.'

'Well, he is doing well. Very well.'

'Good. Here, have a sip.'

Her eyes met his over the brandy. She smiled. 'How long are you here for?'

'That's a leading question. About five days. Could you fit lunch into your high-powered schedule?'

'No, honestly, Michael, I don't think that's a very good idea.'

'Why not? I think it's a great idea. You can bring Pharaoh if you like. As a chaperone. I'd like to meet her. Or Hubby.'

'He's away.'

The moment the words were out she regretted them; she flushed, looked away, reached for the glass again.

He took it from her, turned it, and drank very deliberately

from the same place. Roz felt a hot, sweet melting deep within her; she forced a bright, fierce smile.

'Dinner then?'

'No. Absolutely not.'

'OK,' he said calmly. 'Lunch will do. Where would you like to go?'

'I wouldn't.'

'The Connaught tomorrow?'

'I have a meeting.'

'Thursday?'

'I don't know. I'll see.'

'Fine. See you there at one. I'm staying there,' he added.

It was all a foregone conclusion really. They lunched; Roz talked; Michael listened. She talked to him about all the things she had sworn she wouldn't: about C. J., about Phaedria, about her terror of losing everything. He looked at her sorrowfully, and shook his head.

'You should have married me.'

'I know.'

'I still have the ring.'

'I don't believe you.'

'I do. I take it with me everywhere. Can't think how I haven't lost it. Look. Here it is.'

He got it out and handed it to her; she opened the box, looked at it, remembering everything about the day he had first given it to her, Paris, the sunshine, the breakfast, the sex. Her eyes blurred.

'Put it on.'

'I can't.'

'Put it on.'

She put it on.

'Great. Now let's go upstairs and get married.'

Roz didn't leave the Connaught until six o'clock the following morning. She had forgotten, or rather her body had, how sex could really be; the questing hunger, the frantic concentration, the way her body felt slowly and sweetly filled, and then the wild, glorious progression, deeper and deeper, bigger and bigger, as she rose, rode, swung, soared into orgasm.

She lay, the first time that afternoon, after she had come, half laughing, half crying, her body still throbbing, still shuddering gently, and wondered how she could have borne the stillborn dull despair of the sex she and C. J. had known lately.

'That wasn't too bad,' said Michael mildly, reaching out his hand to her, stroking her face, moving down to her neck, her breasts. 'I didn't mind that so much. You?'

'It was OK,' said Roz, smiling as she had not smiled for months, warmly, peacefully, joyfully. 'OK for starters.'

'Jesus, I've missed you. All of you. Every last inch of you.'

'Well,' she said, 'you certainly know them all, all those inches.'

'I do. I'm glad to say. Did you miss me?'

'Oh, not much.'

'You're lying.'

'Yes, I am.'

'Has it been worth it?'

'I don't know. I don't think so. No, of course it hasn't.'

'Good. Have you been happy?'

'Not really. No.'

'Excellent.'

'You bastard.'

'No, I'm not a bastard Roz, actually. I'm a regular nice guy. I've played by the rules. I've let you do things your way. I wasn't even going to look you up. It was an accident I saw you there, in that restaurant. You're the bastard. I imagine in your liberated world women can be bastards.'

'I suppose so. Yes, you're right. I know it. It's all been my fault.'

'And are you truly sorry?'

'I think so.'

'Truly, truly sorry?'

'Yes, truly, truly.'

'Good.' He turned towards her, his hand moving steadily, purposefully, down over her flat, smooth stomach, into the hidden warmth he had just reclaimed. 'Now, this may take a while, but I plan to make a little more of you my own again. After that we can order afternoon tea and have a talk.'

'I don't want to talk,' said Roz, her voice low, desperate. She knelt up, pushed him over on his back, straddled him, drew his penis into her wet, hungry body, threw her head back, and rode him, almost detachedly, plunging, thrusting, exhorting, demanding from him her long, long fierce eruption of pleasure.

And Michael Browning, detached also, looked at her face in all its ferocious abandonment, and wondered if there could be another woman anywhere with the same power to take hold of his heart.

Circe, London, opened on 1 May 1984, in a blaze of publicity, and a party that lasted for eighteen hours, beginning with a charity lunch and fashion show (entailing a panic of nightmare proportions, with half the clothes from New York held in customs until the actual morning of the day, culminating in a drive down the M4 by Lady Morell herself and an endorsement for speeding, but at least a fully clothed set of models) and ending with a champagne breakfast the following dawn. It was widely acknowledged by the press, the trade and its customers to be the most exciting, original and beautiful environment for shopping that London had seen for decades.

Nigel Dempster gave it his lead story under the headline 'All in the Family':

The beautiful new young Lady Morell, wife of billionaire Sir Julian, has proved her worth with a dazzling coup. She has taken the distinctly ropy Windsor Hotel, Piccadilly and turned it into a pleasure dome, a store called Circe, which will undoubtedly prove the happiest of stamping grounds for London's rich and style-obsessed. Although there are other Circes, in Europe and the United States, Phaedria Morell assures me that hers is quite unique. Phaedria (her name is that of a character in Spenser's *The Faerie Queen*, the personification of wantonness) has been working very closely with David Sassoon, head of corporate design in Sir Julian's company; a rare empathy is reported between the two. Mr Sassoon has strong connections with the Morell family; he was once romantically involved with Sir Julian's first wife, Eliza, now Countess of Garrylaig. With Mr Sassoon, the Countess was at the opening of Circe, looking very much younger than her forty-eight years, and apparently the best of friends with her ex-husband's new wife.

Lady Morell, who was once a journalist and met her husband when she went to interview him, says she is now hoping to turn her attention to some of the other Circe stores.

This could cause fireworks in the family; Rosamund (Roz) Emerson, Sir Julian's daughter, who is president of Circe Stores worldwide, guards her empire jealously. Roz, who is married to Christopher (C. J.) Emerson, and has a baby daughter, Miranda, has been seen several times in recent months dining with New Yorker Michael (ByNow Supermarkets) Browning; 'He is an old friend of the family,' she told me.

'Well,' said Phaedria to Janet Foot, passing her the *Daily Mail* over the desk twenty-four hours after the launch, 'that will put a few cats among some very ruffled pigeons. Good old Nigel. I don't know whether to thank him or give him a piece of my mind.'

'I shouldn't do either,' said Janet, who had worked as PA to the night editor of the *Daily Mirror* before she had joined Phaedria. 'You know that as well as I do. Look, lovely little piece in *The Times*, from Suzy Menkes.'

Fashion and style, not always the best of friends, meet in bewitching compatibility in Circe, the new highly exclusive store in Piccadilly, only a few elegant steps away from Fortnum's. Phaedria Morell, who has masterminded the store, has a true understanding of her customers and their sartorial needs, and has created an ambience for them that is chic, beautiful and witty.

'That's nice,' said Phaedria.

'The *Sunday Times* want to interview you this afternoon. For a piece this Sunday in the Look pages. She's a brilliant writer, Catherine Bennett, she'll do a really good piece. Is that all right?'

'Fine.'

'And how would you feel about *Woman's Hour*? They rang just now and said could you do an interview about the new feel in retailing?'

'I'd love it.'

Janet grinned at her. 'You're really enjoying all this, aren't you?'

'I really am.'

Pat Drummond, Phaedria's new assistant, head-hunted for her inevitably not by Roz, but by one of the fashion buyers Phaedria had hired for Circe, put her head round the door. 'Heavenly piece in the *Standard*, Phaedria. Have you seen it?'

'No.'

'I've got it here. But basically, it says Circe is the first store for years, either here or in New York, that acknowledges the new woman and her new needs. Isn't that great?'

'It's wonderful,' said Phaedria. 'I just can't believe any of it. I tell you what, though,' she added, 'Roz isn't going to be in a terribly good mood for the rest of the day.'

Roz wasn't. She was having a late breakfast at home and trying to summon the necessary courage to go to the office. What was worst about all this (apart from the stuff in Dempster about her and Michael) was that she knew the thinly disguised brickbats were actually not deserved. Phaedria had had some new ideas, and the store looked beautiful, but the implication that all the other Circes were old hat, somehow burnt out, was monstrous. Oh, well, the storm would undoubtedly pass. The good news was the innuendoes in the story about Phaedria and David. If there was one man her father was ferociously jealous of it was David Sassoon. Any suggestion, however unfounded, that Phaedria might be involved with him should affect him very satisfactorily. She still presumed it was unfounded; maybe it wasn't. The rows reverberating across Regent's Park and the Sussex Downs these days, and indeed by telephone across several continents, were reportedly growing in noise and frequency. Interesting.

She had just poured herself another coffee when the phone rang.

'Roz? Hi, it's Michael. I love you. Will you marry me?'

He made this call most mornings at about seven, quite undeterred by the twin facts that it was two a.m. in New York and that C. J. might well be sitting beside her.

'Hallo, Michael. I just might, today. Life is bad here.'

'Is Hubby there?'

'No, he's gone to the office.'

'Can I come round?'

'Where are you?'

'At Heathrow.'

'You're not.'

'I am.'

'How long will you be here?'

'Couple of days.'

'Why are you here this time?'

'To twist your arm.'

'Oh, God. I have enough problems. Look at the *Daily Mail*. Nigel Dempster's column.'

'I've already seen it. I was pleased.'

'Why?'

'That arm's been twisted halfway round already. Can I come?'

'No. I'm going to the office. I'll meet you tonight. Will you be at the Connaught?'

'Yup.'

'Oh, I'm glad you're here. Problems notwithstanding. Bye.'

'Bye, darling.'

The past three months had been difficult for Roz. Having allowed herself back in Michael's thrall, she found herself completely helpless to escape. He had taken hold of her and her life, in his self-confident, amusedly sexy way, invading her thinking, her feeling, and not least – oh, certainly not least! – her body, and made her unequivocally his again. She tried to be discreet, but it was a half-hearted attempt. C. J. had been interestingly uninterested. Julian had been furious.

He had said very little, but she could tell from his coldness, his increasing interference in her work, that he was not prepared to accept it. Well, she was twenty-eight years old, and she was not about to do everything Daddy told her.

She felt alive, happy for the first time for two years. It was a novel sensation and she allowed herself to enjoy it, to luxuriate in it, rather as she might a glorious holiday, knowing that it had a time limit, that it could not continue, that sooner or later she had to go home, sort out her luggage and get back to real life.

And (rather as so often happens on holiday) she felt utterly removed from the pressures of reality, they had very little substance and she found herself more concerned with where she and Michael might go or eat or stay than whether she was losing ground or credibility in the company or that C. J. might divorce her and remove himself from the country, taking Miranda with him.

But it could not go on, and she knew it could not; something had to be resolved, and she herself would have to resolve it. As both options – life without Michael, and giving up her succession – both seemed impossible, she postponed her decision day by day, week by week. She felt almost two headed; when she was with him she was one person, thinking and talking and planning for him, and when she was at home or in the office, she was another. For some reason, the two people managed to co-exist quite well.

When she got into her office her father was at her desk. He had the *Daily Mail* in his hand.

'Have you seen this?'

'Of course.'

'Don't you care?'

She shrugged. 'Not terribly.'

'Why not? For God's sake, Roz, why not?'

'I'm not sure. Maybe because it doesn't seem to make much difference. Michael and I are having an affair. Everybody knows, anyway.'

'Roz, this can't go on.'

'What do you mean?'

'This affair. You're married, you have a child.'

She looked at him, amused. 'Forgive me for saying so, Daddy, but such old-fashioned morality does not become you.'

He looked at her, his eyes dark with anger.

'What are you intending to do?'

'I don't know.'

'Are you thinking of divorcing C. J.?'

'I told you, I don't know.'

'I won't allow it, Roz. You both have important positions in this company. It wouldn't work.'

'Daddy,' said Roz, walking round to the back of her desk,

596

reaching across him for some files, looking at him very directly. 'You can't not allow me to do anything. I'm an adult. Stop playing games with me. With all of us.'

'You're not behaving like an adult,' he said, 'and I am not playing games.'

He got up, pushed past her and walked out of the office. She suddenly felt as she had when she had been a little girl and had told him she wouldn't go to boarding school. She had done everything she could to defeat him, but she had ended up at Cheltenham just the same.

Phaedria was working on her follow-up advertising campaign for the summer for Circe when Julian walked into her office. She looked at him warily. He had been charm personified during the endless party at the launch, smiling at her indulgently, telling everyone how clever she was, how proud of her he was, how marvellous he thought the store was. Then they had got home and he had been distant, withdrawn.

She had taken a bottle of champagne from the fridge and gone up to him, putting her arms round his neck, trying to kiss him. 'Shall we celebrate? Aren't you pleased?'

'Oh, yes, delighted,' he said, almost coldly. 'But I'm very tired. I think I'll go straight up, if you don't mind. You do what you like.'

'Julian, I can hardly celebrate by myself.'

He looked at her, his eyes hard. 'I would have thought you'd have done enough celebrating for now, Phaedria. With a great many people. Good night. I'm going to bed.'

She had stared after him, shocked, hurt. For the first time since their marriage, they slept separately, and she had lain tossing and turning for what was left of the night, trying to understand, trying to remember Letitia's words, to see him as threatened and in need of support and understanding, and only succeeded in perceiving a small-minded, jealous man, in serious need of a brisk kick up the arse.

So far she had had no opportunity to administer it; he had left before her for the office, without a word.

He looked at her now with hostility in his eyes, and threw the *Daily Mail* down on her desk. She smiled, determinedly bright. 'Aren't you pleased with it all?'

'Not all of it, no.'

'What do you mean? It's a huge success.'

'Yes it is. And I fully acknowledge it. What I am not pleased with is this report in Dempster today. About you and Sassoon.'

'Oh, Julian, don't be ridiculous. It's only a bit of nonsense.'

'I happen not to like nonsense. Especially when it makes me look foolish and denigrates my wife.'

She stared at him. 'That's a very interesting viewpoint.'

'What do you mean?'

'Interestingly feudal. It's me that's denigrated, Julian, if anyone is, me, the person, not your wife.'

'Don't be absurd.'

'I'm not being absurd. Anyway, I don't feel in the least denigrated. I see this for what it is, a way of filling a column inch.'

'Yes, well, I suppose you would regard it in that way. You are still a reporter at heart.'

'Sometimes,' she said, 'I wish it wasn't only at heart.'

'Well, unfortunately perhaps, things have changed. Now can I make it quite clear that I do not want you working with Sassoon on anything, ever again, and I don't want to read this kind of thing ever again. All right?'

Phaedria's eyes met his, amused, slightly contemptuous.

'I'm awfully busy,' she said, 'I really don't have time for this. There's a journalist from the *Sunday Times* waiting to see me. Sorry, Julian. Please excuse me.' She pressed her buzzer. 'Janet, could you ask Catherine Bennett to come in now.'

Chapter Seventeen

London, Sussex, New York, Los Angeles, Paris, Nice, 1984–5

The paradox of the virgin bride is that she is potentially more promiscuous than her experienced sisters. If her bridegroom proves a disappointment, she will inevitably be seeking the long-awaited, much vaunted pleasure elsewhere and if he proves a delight she will almost equally inevitably wonder if other bodies in other beds might not be more delightful still.

Phaedria Morell had, to all intents and purposes, been a virgin bride; and her bridegroom had shown her considerable delights; nevertheless, over a year having passed since he had led her to her somewhat unconventional marriage bed on his office floor, she found herself restless, excited, disturbed. Her earlier anxieties about her own sexual capacity had been shifted, if not entirely removed, by a new and even rather dangerous self-confidence; she had begun to change more than she realized.

Her success, her new-found power and her pleasure in it, the gloss and sleekness Julian's money had bestowed upon her, had all conspired to make her greatly sought after; she had none of the problems experienced by Eliza thirty years earlier, of having to fit in with Julian's circle, of having no status, no life of her own. She found herself at the centre of a fashionable world, of designers, photographers, journalists; she could pick her friends, her social circle, from a group of people with whom she felt entirely at ease, who pleased and amused her, and who she seemed to please and amuse. Wherever she went, and whatever she did, she found attention. She was photographed, interviewed, sought after; scarcely a day passed for a while when her picture or her pronouncements, and very frequently both, did not appear in the press, she was a frequent guest on chat shows, labelled by *Tatler* leader of the 'Chat Pack: Cafe Society 1980 Style', she was recognized everywhere she went, she was stared at, remarked upon, exclaimed over. And she became increasingly pleased by it. She would scarcely have been human had she not; from the near obscurity of a two-bit job on a provincial paper, she had become seriously famous, sought after by stylish society in New York as well as London, flattered and praised everywhere she went. And when the flattery and praise fell from the eyes and lips of attractive men, and attractive young men in particular, she found it and them quite irresistible.

A year after her wedding, her name had been linked with at least three highly (and visibly) eligible young men: Bruce Greene, race horse owner and polo player (whose attraction for her owed at least something to her emotional memories of another blond, blue-eyed hero of the polo field); Danny Carter, a truculent, young working-class photographer, who had made love to her, if not literally, constantly and disturbingly with his voice and his camera lens, through several heady afternoons, behind his locked studio door; and Dominic Kennedy, twice divorced, self-made millionaire, who phoned her every morning as soon as she got into the office and invited her to dinner before finalizing his arrangements for the evening with anybody else.

With all of them she flirted, lunched, and occasionally (when Julian was away) dined. She let nothing more carnal come to pass between herself and them than an occasional mildly sensuous kiss, she had no real intention of having an affair with anybody; nevertheless she felt, she enjoyed, she was reassured by the attention of other men and her pleasure from it; she toyed with the ultimate conclusions, she meditated upon the possible pleasures, and she was careless of her husband's reaction.

That summer Phaedria gave a fancy-dress ball on mid-summer night at Marriotts; three hundred guests came for dinner, and another three hundred arrived at ten as the dancing began. Not only the drive to Marriotts, but all the lanes leading to it for five miles, were lit with torches, and the grounds were spangled with five thousand fairy lights. The dancing took place in two sea-blue marquees, the bands performing against great theatrical sets of fairyland designed by Damon Austen, brilliant new recruit to the Royal Shakespeare Company and rumoured to be yet another of Lady Morell's admirers, and even the grounds had been adorned with great drifting garlands of green gauze hanging from the trees. The riverboats which had been such a feature at her wedding drifted on the lake, each one lit by hundreds of candles, bearing the champagne breakfast which was served as dawn broke; and as the sun rose, exactly on cue, the white peacocks, Phaedria's Christmas present to Julian, appeared and strutted about the lawns, giving out their strange pagan cries. The costumes were dazzling; fairies danced with hobgoblins, mermaids with centaurs, princes with beggarmaids; the entire grounds appeared, in the dusky flickering light, to be filled with creatures of another world, some with ornate masks; Phaedria herself, dressed as Titania, in a green silk chiffon dress designed by Xandra Rhodes, her face made up theatrically strange in blues and greens, her hair drawn back from her face with a rope of pearls, and her feet bare, looked quite extraordinary; even those who knew her well stared at her, newly impressed by her beauty. Only the host, wandering apparently benignly about his guests, smiling, talking, dancing with all the most beautiful women, with the notable exception of his own wife, refused to participate very fully in the fantasy and wore white tie and tails. The ball was featured in every popular newspaper, in *Tatler* and *Harpers & Queen*, claimed three entire pages in *Ritz* magazine, and even made the sign-off story on *News at Ten*; Lady Morell was clearly now established (or so said the media) as one of the great party givers of her generation.

Julian was initially amused and then patently irritated by the way she had become a minor celebrity and her reaction to it; Phaedria enjoyed his irritation. She saw her success as a way of redressing the balance a little in their marriage; she was no longer a nobody, a mere recipient of his favours. She had power of her own, albeit limited; she could give as well as take, hold her own in his life, and after eighteen months of being made to feel excessively fortunate she was enjoying the sensation.

Julian seemed more jealous of her fame, of the column inches she was consuming day by day, than of the young men; she wasn't sure if he was really unmoved by her lunch companions, the insinuations in the gossip columns, but he certainly seemed to be. It annoyed her a little; she would have liked him to exhibit at least a touch of possessiveness, but he did not, he looked at her with his cool blank gaze, when they were out together and she was surrounded with her circle, when the stories reached him or he read them in the paper, and said he hoped she was enjoying herself, managing to imply that it was both unlikely and unattractive if she was.

Except in one case; one name on her lips, she knew, could cloud a morning, wreck a dinner, destroy a weekend; one man threatened her peace of mind and her marriage; the one man who paradoxically she had every reason to be innocently occupied with: David Sassoon.

Julian Morell was working on a new cosmetic range. It was the first he had given his total attention to, put aside other work for, for years; he was totally engrossed in it, spending much time in New York with the chemists there. The concept was an absolute secret; nobody, not even Annick Valery, who was now *directrice de beauté* for Juliana worldwide, not even David Sassoon who was working on the packaging, not even Phaedria Morell who was supposedly privy to all the workings of her husband's mind, knew absolutely what it was. It was a complete range, that everybody knew, it was to be highly priced, and very original, it was to be launched for Christmas, there was an all-time-high advertising budget, using posters, cinema and television, and a new model had been signed up exclusively to represent it, a brown-eyed ash blonde, called Regency, who was seventeen years old and who was reportedly consoling Mr Morell in his great unhappiness over the famously bad behaviour of his new young wife. Both the reports and the unhappiness were only a little exaggerated.

Phaedria tried to talk to Julian about the range, to show her interest, to offer her opinion, but he brushed her aside almost contemptuously. 'You know nothing about cosmetics, and besides you're far too busy with your own life these days.'

'Julian, that's not true, I can make the time easily, you know I can, and I'd like to talk to you about it, it's obviously terribly important to you.'

'Well,' he said, looking at her oddly, 'that's very good of you, but frankly I don't have the time to go through it all with you, when really I feel you could contribute very little. But thank you for your interest.'

Phaedria turned away, afraid he would see the tears behind her eyes; he still had the power to hurt her horribly.

'Incidentally,' he said, 'I'll be away for a few days. We're shooting some commercials in Paris.'

'Could I – Would you like me to come with you?'

'Oh, I don't think so. A waste of your time. You must be extremely busy with Christmas planning for the store. I hope you can improve upon those designs for the window displays. They're very poor, in my opinion.'

'Yes well, if I was able to work with the right person – I mean people – they might not be so poor.'

'If you mean Sassoon, I really cannot believe that you regard him as a suitable person to work on window displays. Phaedria, David Sassoon is head of corporate design in this company. He cannot be expected to concern himself with trivia. If I may say so, you are showing a severe lack of understanding of the areas of control and how to use them.'

'You may say so,' she said with a sigh, 'and I expect you're right. But the fact remains there's nobody decent in the display department.'

'That,' said Julian, 'is patent nonsense. There is considerable talent in the display department. It is entirely your responsibility to motivate it properly. Talk to Roz about it, I'm sure she'll be able to help.'

'Yes,' she said, 'I will.'

He left for Paris in the morning, in his private jet, with Regency, David Sassoon and several people from the advertising agency. Phaedria, looking at the photograph the publicity people had organized and brought to her desk for approval, felt oddly bereft.

When he came back three days later he was curt and short-tempered. She had been looking forward to his return, and had organized dinner at home for the two of them, and had a bottle of champagne on ice.

'I'm sorry, Phaedria, I have to go out for dinner.'

'Who with?'

'What's that? Oh, Freddy Branksome. And then I'm looking in on Roz and C. J. later. I have to talk to C. J. about the new Morell in Acapulco. Don't wait up for me. I shall probably be very late.'

'Julian –'

'Yes?'

'Julian, I don't mind waiting up for you.'

'Darling,' he said, and he managed to turn the endearment into something cold and distant, 'I'd really rather you didn't. I can't concentrate on things if I've got half a mind on getting back.'

'Oh,' she said, 'all right.'

'Get those displays sorted out?'

'What? Oh, yes, I think so.'

'Roz any help?'

'No. She's – been away.'

'Where, for God's sake? The Beverly Hills Circe opening is only weeks away. She can't afford to be away.'

'Julian, I don't know where she's been. She's probably been there.'

'Oh, all right. I'll find out from C. J. See you in the morning.'

'Good night, Julian.'

She waited until his car had disappeared from the terrace and then picked up the phone and called Dominic Kennedy. She had no intention of spending the evening alone with the Circe window displays.

Roz had not been in Los Angeles. She had taken advantage of her father's absence to go to New York for three days, ostensibly checking on Circe's Christmas programme, but actually scarcely leaving Michael Browning's penthouse and his bed. A couple of phone calls and his late-night conversation with C. J. made this abundantly clear to Julian; he was furiously angry.

He sent for her in the morning; she came in looking wary.

'Good morning, Rosamund. How are you?'

'Very well. How was Paris?'

'Excellent. And New York?'

'Very good.'

'How are the cosmetic promotions going in Circe? Particularly the gift with purchase?'

'Very well indeed.'

'Good. How clever you are, Rosamund.'

'What makes you say that?'

'Oh, a conversation I had with Iris Bentinck. She said you hadn't been anywhere near Circe, and yet you seem to have managed to garner a considerable amount of information.'

'I see.'

'If you're going to lie, Roz,' he said, 'do it properly. Do some background work first.'

'Yes well,' she said, 'you should know.'

He looked at her and half smiled. He was always impressed when she stood up to him.

'Well anyway,' he said, 'fortunately the promotions are going well. Now then, has Phaedria talked to you about the window displays here?'

'No.'

'I'll get her in. She needs some help.'

'Ah.'

Phaedria walked in; she looked tired. She had been dancing at Tramps half the night with Dominic Kennedy and a group of their friends; Julian had got home before her and gone to bed, merely asking her over breakfast if she had enjoyed herself. He looked at her now with something close to distaste.

'Phaedria, if you talk to Roz after this meeting about the windows, she may be able to help before it's too late. Is everything else under control for Christmas? It's almost the end of August, you seem to be sailing very close to the wind to me.'

'Yes,' said Phaedria, meeting his eyes with equal distaste. 'Absolutely.'

'Good. Because I want you to go to Los Angeles for a few days next week.'

'Why?'

'I want you to look at the store. I want your opinion on what's going on there.'

'I see. Both of us? Roz and me?'

There was a long silence.

'No,' said Julian. 'Only you.'

Roz walked out of the office.

That night she talked to Michael Browning for over an hour on the phone, almost incoherent with misery and rage. 'I hate her, I hate her, it's so unjust, why should I have to endure it?'

'Roz, it's not her fault. Surely you can see that. It's your old man. He has the two of you out there on that chess board of his he calls his company, and I would say it's probably check. If not checkmate.'

'All right then, I hate him. I hate them both.'

'Leave them both and come with me. I won't play games with you.'

'No, I know you won't.'

'Please, darling. Don't be so dumb. Just walk out on the lot of them.'

She sighed. 'Right now I feel I just might. I just feel so – used.'

'Yeah, well you're in the clutches of a real champion at that game.'

'Maybe. I can't help feeling it's about time I got a break.'

A week later she did. She was trying to contact C. J. in Washington; he had been there working on the new corporate image for the hotels with David Sassoon.

'Your husband has gone to New York this morning, Mrs Emerson. You should get him at the Morell there, at lunch time.'

C. J. was distant, cool. 'I may stay here a few days. We've finished in Washington.'

'How was it?'

'OK.'

'Is David staying there with you? Or is he on his way back?'

'No. I thought you'd know.'

'Know what?'

'He's gone across to LA. Phaedria phoned him. She's there. She wants him to look at Circe. I thought you'd be going.'

'No,' said Roz. Time seemed to have frozen round her. It was extremely quiet. 'No, I'm not going. Well, enjoy New York, C. J. Give my love to your mother.'

'Sure. Bye, Roz.'

'Goodbye.'

She and her father had their weekly progress meeting three days later. He was unsmiling, his eyes at their most blank.

'Everything under control?'

'Yes.'

'Good. I thought we might look at Sydney for a site for Circe. Why don't you go over for a week or two and see what you think.'

'You've always said Sydney was wrong for Circe.'

'I've changed my mind. I was wrong about Beverly Hills.'

'Yes.'

'Take C. J. with you and Miranda. Make a holiday of it.'

'Don't try and charm me back into submission, please. I'm finding all these games with Phaedria very hard to take. And I

606

certainly don't want to go to Australia with C. J., I think I'm probably going to divorce him.' She was only testing her father's reaction; she had given a divorce almost no thought at all.

'Roz, you can't do that. Absolutely not.'

'I can.'

'No, you can't.'

'How will you stop me?'

'If you do,' he said, his face smooth, 'if you even suggest such a thing, I shall give the stores to Phaedria. All of them.'

Roz felt as if she had just fallen from a great height. She felt light-headed, dizzy, distant; he seemed a long way away.

'You couldn't.'

'I would. She has great talent. She's original.'

'And I'm not?'

'Not specially.'

'God,' she said, 'you really are a bastard. A manipulative, evil bastard. Well, do that. Give them to her. I don't care. I shall go and work for Michael. That's just fine.'

'Oh, excellent,' he said. 'You can redesign ByNow for him. That would be a good project for you. You'd like that, wouldn't you, Rosamund?'

'I could do anything for Michael. He has enough money. I could start a new line of stores myself.'

'You could. You wouldn't have much expertise behind you, though. Not in him, would you? Not much flair. It would be very difficult. I have all the best people in retailing tied up. And if you found any brilliant new people, I should probably find I needed them more. And what do you think people would say? They would compare what you were doing very unfavourably, I would imagine. Poor Roz, they'd say, you see, she didn't have it in her, really, it was all just handed her on a plate, she's nothing without her father. You wouldn't like that, would you? You need success and admiration and power. I think you would be making a huge mistake.'

Roz suddenly hit him, sharply across the face; then she stood back, frozen into stillness, stunned by her own courage.

Julian stood looking at her, equally motionless. He was breathing heavily. There was an odd expression on his face, almost one of puzzlement.

'Why are you doing this?' cried Roz, almost in anguish. 'Why? Why can't you leave me alone?' Tears had filled her eyes; she was very white.

'Roz, Roz, don't. Please don't be so hostile. I'm trying to help you. Trying to save your marriage.'

'I feel hostile. I hate you. I hate you more than I would have believed possible. And on the subject of marriage, maybe you should take a look at your own.'

'What do you mean?'

'Where is that original, beautiful wife of yours right now?'

'She's in Los Angeles. I told her to go.'

'She is indeed. And do you know who's there with her?'

'What do you mean? Nobody's with her.'

'Oh, yes they are. At this very minute David Sassoon is there. You didn't know that, did you?'

'I don't believe you.'

'You don't have to. You can ring the Beverly Hills Hotel yourself and check. Like I just did. They're both there, for another two days. Together.'

Phaedria was lying by the pool at the Beverly Hills Hotel, when she was paged. 'Call for Lady Morell. Call for Lady Morell.'

She sighed. She was half asleep, sun-soaked, happy. She had been working for almost twenty hours and she wanted to stay where she was, not moving, for a little longer.

She had enjoyed the last few days. She had been well aware of the personal risk she was running, calling in David; but when she had got to LA, had seen the way the designer there been very slightly over-extravagant with the open space, just minimally too cautious with colour, how the windows were just a fraction too close in feel to all the other windows up and down Rodeo Drive, she had, without any thought for anything at all except Circe, put in a call to Washington, where she knew he and C. J. were. She had expected only to talk to him, to describe the problems, maybe to put him in touch with the other designer; when he had said he was free and would come over, her spirit lifted at the thought of defying Julian, of showing him, if necessary, that she was not to be told what to do.

Whatever the sexual and marital considerations involved,

David's arrival had solved her professional problems. He had stayed forty-eight hours, at least forty of which they had been awake and working, or eating and talking shop. They had both, oddly but tacitly conscious of their slightly compromising situation, avoided lengthy dinners or even any but the briefest sojourns by the pool, and the one time he had attempted to probe her feelings on her situation and her marriage she had closed the slightly forbidding shell of reserve she wore around herself and made it very clear that he was not to try to open it. It had been tempting, she longed for a confidant, yearned to talk not only about Julian, but Roz; but David was the least likely candidate for such a role and certainly not in the dangerous situation they were in, and she knew it.

So now he was gone; she had driven him to the airport in a hire car, he had kissed her goodbye in a brotherly – or would it be fatherly – fashion, she wondered, and she returned to the Beverly Hills and its pool and its pampering power, to recover for a day or two.

She needed to recover; she was not only tired from the strain of the last forty-eight hours, but the previous few months. She was beginning to find Julian seriously dispiriting. His jealousy, his constant criticism, his arrogance were very destructive. She had tried to be tolerant, to remember Letitia's words, but she was too busy fighting for her own survival most of the time to have any emotional energy left for him. What she would not do was give in, when she was quite convinced he was wrong. She was prepared to listen carefully to his point of view, to consider his criticisms, to take note of his experience, but after that she would, if it seemed necessary, come out fighting. And Julian didn't like it.

She fought him for the most part privately; and when necessary she fought him publicly, and fiercely; but she always fought fair. She never hit him below the belt. She never traded on her position, never carried some personal slight or quarrel into their professional life. As a result, long and bloody as the fights were, they usually ended in truce; Julian would be angry, outraged, but he respected what she had to say and think, and in the end he would not give in, but he would concede at least something.

But it was difficult: difficult to hang on to her self-respect, difficult to work effectively and efficiently, difficult above all to nurture and enjoy what was after all a very young and delicate marriage. She felt increasingly alone in her struggle; she could not talk to Julian, he totally discouraged any attempt to confront their difficulties, and she was far too reticent and too loyal to discuss them with anyone else, even with Eliza, who clearly wanted to help her, and was always attempting to probe her feelings and her life. The only thing she could do, she felt, was move from day to day, feeling her way, trying to cope with it all, and hope that time would carry them into some calmer, less dangerous territory.

So for all those reasons, she was tired, she had been enjoying her brief rest, and she didn't want it to end. She remained motionless, merely raised a slender, sunbrowned arm; one of the small swarm of waiters who hovered permanently watchful near the pool appeared instantly in front of her.

'There's a call for me,' she said, 'would you bring me a phone, please?'

'Certainly, Lady Morell.'

'Hallo?' she said, picking it up on his return. 'Yes?'

'Phaedria?'

'Yes? Hallo, Julian. Where on earth are you?'

'In Reception.'

'In Reception where?'

'In Reception here.'

'Good God. Well, you certainly are full of surprises.'

'I try to be.'

'I'll be right out.'

She walked into the foyer of the hotel, carelessly graceful, dressed only in a minute blue bikini, a white towelling robe swinging loosely round her shoulders, her feet bare, her hair loose and slightly damp from swimming. In a place well used to beautiful women, she still attracted great attention.

She kissed him lightly. He looked at her.

'You look tired.'

'Yes, I was working most of the night.'

'Indeed? On what?'

'The merchandise. I've found a marvellous new designer.'

'A new one? How nice.'

She looked at him, puzzled. 'Julian, why are you here?'

'I wanted to see you.'

'Why didn't you ring first?'

'Then I wouldn't have surprised you.'

'No. Well, shall we go up to the suite? I expect you'd like to change.'

'You have a suite, not a bungalow?'

'Yes.'

'Why? I keep a bungalow here.'

'I know. But I don't like them particularly. I feel – oh, I don't know, vulnerable.'

'I see.'

'Well, let's go up. Would you like a drink?'

'No thank you.'

'All right.'

She followed him into the lift, into the suite, wary, baffled. The boy brought in Julian's case; when the door was closed he took her by the shoulders and turned her to him.

'Where is he?'

'Where is who?'

'Sassoon?'

'Oh, don't be ridiculous.'

'Phaedria, I know he's here.'

'He is not here.'

'I don't believe you.'

'Would you like to search the hotel?'

He looked at her closely, then released her and sat down heavily on the bed. Phaedria walked over to the window, looked out at the brilliant sunshine, the blue carefree sky, so poignantly contrasting to the dark mood in the room; then she turned.

'He has been here, though. Until this morning.'

'I see. In this room, or did you share another suite?'

'Julian, I really feel desperately sorry for you. You just can't go on in this ridiculous, melodramatic fashion. I am not having an affair with David Sassoon, neither of us has the slightest inclination to do anything of the sort. If he is in love with anyone, it's Eliza, still. I like him very much. I think he's fun, I love working with him, and I think he's very attractive. But I am not in the business of having affairs, unlike yourself –'

'Phaedria, be careful!'

She looked at him, unafraid.

'I am married to you, I care about you, and I am much too busy and too sensible to risk losing you.'

'Me and all that goes with me.'

'That was vile.'

'The truth often is.'

'I didn't think you were very well acquainted with the truth, Julian. Anyway, who told you David was here? Roz, I suppose?'

'Can we leave the ridiculous vendetta between you and Roz out of this?'

'It's very difficult, when most of the unhappinesses between us can be laid directly at her door.'

'Phaedria, grow up, for God's sake.'

She looked at him, her eyes full of a strange pain.

'I'm trying to, Julian, believe me. I'm not getting a great deal of help from you. Are you going to accept what I said about David or not?'

'Phaedria, even if I accepted it, even if I believed you, which I don't know that I do, how could you ask Sassoon down here, to stay in the same hotel, when I had expressly forbidden you to have any more to do with him?'

'That was precisely the reason. Or one of them. That you'd forbidden me. If you'd asked me, sensitively, I might have felt different, might have been prepared to try and understand. The other was of course that he was the only person who could do what I wanted.'

'Indeed. Where? In bed?'

She crossed to the lobby, pulled her suitcase out. 'This is ridiculous. I'm going.'

'Don't.'

'Why not?'

'Because I am going. Immediately. That will save you the trouble of packing.'

'You're mad.'

'I think not. If anyone is mad, I think it is you.'

He left immediately, without another word. While he was waiting for his plane at Los Angeles airport, he phoned his lawyer.

*

Phaedria arrived home at Regent's Park forty-eight hours later. It was very late; the house was in darkness, utterly quiet. She put down her bags, and moved silently upstairs. She was not sure what she might find; that Julian was not there at all, that he would be in bed with someone else, that he would be alone and hostile, refusing to speak to her. She pushed open the bedroom door. He was in bed, alone, asleep, completely still; he did not stir. For a horrific moment she thought he was dead, had taken an overdose and it would be her fault; then he suddenly moved, turned over, still asleep; she looked at him; for the very first time, she noticed, remorseful, almost afraid, he looked older. His hair was greyer, his face relaxed in sleep was suddenly more lined, looser. He appeared very vulnerable.

She sat down on the bed beside him and looked at him for a long time. Then she put out her hand and rested it gently on his shoulder, and bent and kissed his forehead. He woke, quite easily then, not startled, just slowly moved into consciousness, opened his eyes and looked at her in silence.

'I'm sorry,' she said. 'I was quite quite wrong. Cruel and arrogant and wrong. Please forgive me.'

'Oh, Phaedria,' he said. 'I'm glad you're back. I thought I might not see you again.'

'You don't know me very well, do you?' she said, pulling off her clothes, climbing into bed thankfully beside him.

'Not very. But I'm beginning to learn.'

She didn't challenge Roz on the subject of whether or not she had sent Julian down to LA. It didn't seem worth the emotional effort. She would have denied it, or argued in that curious convoluted, noncommittal way she had inherited from her father, and either way it would be fruitless. They tried not to speak to one another at all these days, except when pressures of business forced them; it was better that way. Phaedria was sometimes frightened by the force of Roz's hatred for her; in her darkest moments, when she lay awake in the small hours of the morning, as she often did these days, watching for the light to filter through the curtains of her bedroom, she sometimes feared that Roz might resort to physical violence, even try to kill her. Then the morning would come and she would be caught up in the maelstrom of her own frantic life, and she would smile tolerantly at her own foolishness. But deep within her the fear remained and could not be acknowledged to anyone. She thought that probably David might have understood – he had known Roz for so long, indeed was fond of her, and had worked closely with Julian for fifteen years. But he was lost to her now. She had had one last conversation with him, risking the most appalling reprisals from both Julian and Roz, should they have found out (she actually insisted, laughing at herself even as she did it, that they met in a Motorway Stop on the M4, which seemed as safe as anywhere could possibly be from the eyes of anyone who worked for Julian), when she had explained exactly what had happened, and that they must in future only meet in the most public situations.

'I know it's absurd, but I have hurt Julian very badly, and I feel I owe it to him to do what he wants. For some reason he just can't cope with the thought of you and me provoking the mildest gossip. And he certainly was quite convinced we were having the most marvellous time in bed together in LA.'

'If only it were true,' said David, his eyes flicking over her, taking her hand.

'Don't.'

'Why not? Do you think that girl at the till is actually a spy sent by your husband?'

'Oh, David, if you'd only seen him in the hotel that afternoon you wouldn't be joking. He was beside himself.'

'Silly old bugger.'

'Yes well, maybe, but he's my husband and I do, believe it or not, want to make him happy.'

'Do you?'

'Yes, I do.'

'That's all right then. I wondered.'

'What do you mean?'

'Well, if you were happy, if I didn't have a lot to answer for, having persuaded you not to run away on the eve of your wedding day.'

'No, you don't.'

'Good. You're happy then?'

'I think so.'

He looked at her; she had got very thin lately, and there were new deep shadows under her dark eyes.

'If you ever aren't happy, if you ever need help, you will come to me, won't you?'

'Yes, I will. Thank you.'

'So who do you think sent him hurtling down to LA?'

'Oh, Roz without a doubt.'

'Silly girl. She has so much going for her, she's so clever, so talented, and her father thinks the sun shines out of her elegant arse. I've tried telling her, but it doesn't seem to take. And it would certainly do no good my talking to her now. She's almost as jealous of your relationship with me as she is of the one between you and Julian.'

'Oh God,' said Phaedria. 'Because of her crush on you? I suppose she would be. You never get over your first great love. I never have.'

'Pardon me, Lady Morell, but I thought your husband was your first great love.'

'Oh, no, there was someone. It was – well, odd and hopeless. A bit like Roz's for you. But I know how she feels. I still think about him sometimes. Especially when I'm low.'

'Well, that is extremely interesting. I want to know everything about it. Immediately. Don't look at me like that, I'm only teasing you. Besides, I've learnt not to try to make you talk. The sphinx would appear garrulous compared to you. On personal matters, that is. No, I'm extremely fond of Roz, I have to say, but she has always been very difficult.'

Phaedria sighed. 'Well, half the problems Julian and I have are down to her. But I try to be sorry for her. It must be hard, having me come between her and her future.'

'Maybe. It would have been better if you'd been fifty-five, with a shelf-like bust and a fine collection of Crimplene dresses.'

'I could work on that, I suppose. But then Julian would divorce me anyway.' She looked at him suddenly.

'Why have you stayed with him all these years? Why didn't you leave when – when he found out about you and Eliza?'

'I don't know. I'm not very proud of it, really. Of course Julian is marvellous to work for. I could never get the same variety, the same freedom with anyone else. At that time, I'd always intended to get out on my own, start a new company, and then marry her. But it was a fantastic job in New York, and I was young and very ambitious and I kept thinking I'd wait another month, three months, six. By which time she was off with some playboy or other.'

'She's lovely. I adore her.'

'So do I. Still.'

'But you're not –'

He sighed. 'Oh, no. She's absolutely faithful to that old stuffed kilt. We're just good friends.'

'I wish we could be good friends, you and I. Maybe in a year or two we can be again.'

'Maybe. Now, what about another cup of that filthy coffee, and we can drink to Roz's downfall.'

'All right. God, I wish it would happen.'

'I'm afraid it won't. Unless she goes off with this Browning fellow.'

'Oh, she'll never do that. She won't risk losing everything.'

'Have you met him?'

'Never. He doesn't come to London, for obvious reasons, and I'm hardly likely to meet him in New York.'

'He's a delight. Really. You'd like him. And he'd love you.'

'Oh, David, don't!' She shuddered. 'What a thought. That really would have me in the Thames in concrete boots.'

'Is she that hostile?'

'She's that hostile.'

'You poor kid.'

'Nothing to be done about it. Go and get the coffee. We'll drink that toast.'

Roz was slightly regretting her action. It seemed to have achieved nothing: her father and Phaedria appeared to be closer than they had been for some months; David Sassoon, of whom she was very fond, was cold and distant towards her; and Michael Browning had been very outspoken in his criticism.

They had met in Paris for the weekend, and were lying in bed in one of the suites at the Crillon. Whenever Roz was really down, Michael took her there, and spent the weekend in bed with her, making love to her, feeding her, pouring the finest champagne down her, showering her with presents and flowers and conducting his apparently tireless campaign to entice her away from her husband, her father and the company. So far, as he frequently observed, he was not having a great deal of success.

'You're mad, Rosamund. Crazy. All that kind of thing can accomplish is damage to yourself. You won't win any battles that way. You have to box clever, darling. This is not the kindergarten. Remember Machiavelli.'

'I didn't think you knew anything about Machiavelli,' said Roz sulkily. 'You're always saying you never had an education.'

'No, as usual you weren't listening. What I am always saying is I never had a conventional education. Machiavelli is compulsory study for any ambitious young man.'

'Well, what do I have to remember about him anyway?'

'Machiavelli said you either must promote, or execute. In other words take totally decisive action. No half measures.'

'I don't see what you mean. I'd love to execute Phaedria, of course. But I can't. And it isn't up to me to promote her.'

'I don't agree. Well, obviously your old man has to be doing the actual promoting. But you should encourage him. Make him think you're coming round. Get him to give her more than she can handle. That way you'll get rid of her far faster. An execution, masquerading as a promotion. Best of both worlds. And your hands will be clean.'

'I'm afraid it won't work,' said Roz with a sigh. 'She's too damned clever. And she has half the company eating out of her hand, wanting to help her.'

'This is defeatist talk. It doesn't sound like you. I think I have to meet this lady. She seems to be getting the better of all of you. Maybe I should want to eat out of her hand and help her too.'

'If you did,' said Roz, 'I swear to God I would kill you. First her, then you.'

'In that case, I guess I'd better stay away.'

The presentation to the sales force of the new range, at the annual sales conference, took place in Nice. Julian liked to make the sales force feel important, pampered; he installed them all in good hotels, gave them two days off to enjoy the place, and then put on an impressive show with the maximum of razzmatazz.

Everybody who mattered was there, whether they were

directly involved with the cosmetics or not, Julian's rationale being that this was still, however large and successful a private company, a family affair. David was there, Roz was there, Letitia was there, Susan was there, Regency was there as the face of the campaign, and this year, of course Phaedria was there.

It always followed the same theatrical form: Act One was a big general presentation by Freddy and Richard on the company and its success; Act Two a more detailed one by Annick Valery on the brands and their success; then an interval which took the form of superb lunch and the announcement of the award winners: highest retail sales, highest trade sales, salesgirl of the year, and so on; and then in the afternoon the curtain went up on Act Three as the new products took the floor.

This was the moment when Julian himself first spoke, and this year more than ever it was the high spot of the conference; he began with a brief, almost poetic talk on the Juliana image and its unique place in the market, and then he would normally hand over to Annick to give a more detailed presentation on the new colours, skin care and perfumes that would go on the counters in the year ahead. It wasn't always an easy task: the consultants in particular were critical, demanding, asking difficult questions: about whether this product would clash with one already in the range, querying the rationale of that one, demanding to know why a slow line wasn't being discontinued, or being advertised. Julian and Annick always listened to them patiently and courteously; these women were Juliana's lifeline. If they had no faith in or understanding of a product, then they were not going to convince their customers that they needed it; and as importantly, if they knew a product didn't or wouldn't sell, it was worth hearing their explanation for it. And in return, the sales force had great respect for both Julian and Annick; their understanding of the cosmetic industry, their faith in their own products, the quality they always delivered. They listened to Julian today, enjoying, as they always did, his charming, slightly diffident humour, his courtesy, his way of conveying that he was a mere novice in the business, that he had much to learn from them, and then he moved into his presentation, explaining first that Annick had

618

been giving him some tuition, as he was somewhat rusty in the art.

'What we have for you today,' he said, 'is the first total range in Juliana since Naturally. I felt it was time for a completely new look, a new feel; we have moved away from that softness into something much more positive, more exciting, in a way. And so we have created a range, something quite different, a departure for Juliana, designed for the new woman.

'It is called Lifestyle, and it is deliberately simple; a set of colours, of skin care, of fragrance which this new woman, the working woman, the powerful, busy woman will instantly recognize as the straightforward, swift route to beauty that she needs, and that nobody else is providing. We have cut out much of the complexity of cosmetics, particularly in the skin care range; just two very simple sets of products, morning and evening. Even the fragrance range will follow this concept; we are taking the mystique out of perfume, and simply offering one strength, one presentation – halfway between a perfume concentrate and an eau de toilette. Plus obviously a bath and body range.'

Roz, watching the consultants, was suddenly sharply and instinctively aware of a hostility. It was only several years of attending these conferences that enabled her to pick it up. A novice, Phaedria for instance, would not have noticed the slightly wall-eyed expression behind the false eyelashes, the fixed hardness of the heavily glossed lips.

Annick had taken over now, presenting the products in detail; again the reaction was muted, slightly flat. Julian moved on to the advertising: six-foot-high facsimiles of the campaign, of Regency's face were unveiled, the TV commercial was shown (of Regency waking, showering, making up, driving, chairing meetings, lunching, and then finally dining with a man (presumably her inferior), face unseen, and going home to her lonely (presumably powerful) bed. It was a series of endless stills, intercut very fast to give the impression of movement. The backing music was fast, modern, obscure; at the end Regency herself walked to the front of the platform, dressed in a simple black woollen dress by Chanel, worn with pearl and gilt earrings and a long pearl rope, her ash-blonde hair tied back with a black ribbon.

'I feel very honoured to have been chosen to represent the new Juliana woman,' she said carefully, giving them all her (literally) million-dollar smile. 'I hope you will like her as much as I do.'

This long speech closed the presentation; the applause came then, mild, polite applause; again Roz read the mood of the consultants, the sales force, and the message was clear – 'This girl, this near child, this is not the Juliana woman.'

Julian stood up again; asked for questions, comments. There were many. The consultants in particular were not tentative in their criticism. Did he think something so simple was really going to stand up against the complexity of the competition? Lauder, Revlon, the new Chanel ranges were all launching in very traditional mood. Could a cosmetic, particularly a perfume, survive without mystique? Were the colours not a little harsh, uncompromising? Was not Regency a little young for the Juliana woman, in all her supposed sophistication and glamour? Julian was unfazed by this. The questions were always tough, always challenging; he enjoyed them. And somehow, by the sheer weight of his personality, his own vision, he managed to deflect all the criticism, to persuade everybody that Lifestyle was exactly right for its time, that it would be as triumphant, as successful as anything Juliana had ever done.

This was finale time, traditionally his; when he took the mood of the conference and made it his in a surge of charm and charisma, made every woman in the hall fall a little in love with him, and every man identify with him and what he had done.

Phaedria looked at him, as he stood there, looking stylish and relaxed, reminiscing as he always did, about the early days of the company, and was reminded sharply of the first time she had seen him and fallen so helplessly in love with him. She also properly appreciated for perhaps the first time the extent of what he had accomplished. She felt suddenly a stab of pride, not just in him, but in his company, and in being a part of it; and she felt she was beginning to understand what drove him, and why it mattered to him so very much.

He was drawing to the end of his speech now, paying her a discreetly modest but charming tribute: 'We have a new recruit to the company; my wife. She is not involved with the cosmetics

– yet. Perhaps her time will come. She has certainly done some very good work on the new Circe store and the Juliana beauty salon in London. I feel impressed by what she has done, and I have to say I feel a sense of pride in having discovered her.' Laughter, some applause. Roz, sitting on the platform behind him, had to fix her smile with such rigidness to prevent it from slipping, she felt her mouth become almost disembodied from the rest of her face. Her eyes met Susan's in a moment of sheer agony; the warmth and humour there, the briefest possible flicker of a wink, sustained her.

Julian thanked them all, he bade them enjoy the evening ahead (dinner and then the casino for the more reckless souls amongst them), he said he looked forward to seeing as many as possible of them during the year ahead, he wished them luck with the new range.

'Until later, goodbye and thank you.'

Again, it was only Roz who could detect that he was not entirely happy.

The new range sold into the stores fast. The cosmetic buyers had great faith in Julian Morell and in Juliana. Neither had failed yet. The advertising campaign broke: Regency's face, glossy, confident, just slightly contemptuous, looked down from hoardings, out of every glossy magazine, the television screen, the cinema.

The Christmas rush in the stores began. The cosmetic houses were engaged on their annual bonanza. Revlon, Lauder, Chanel, Mary Quant, were propelled off a thousand counters and into a million shopping bags in a great wave of perfume, promotion and hype.

And on the same counters, in the same stores, Lifestyle by Juliana remained: uninvited, unwanted, a wallflower at the ball, and Regency's fixed smile seemed to grow a little more desperate every day.

Julian dismissed the failure completely. It was a hiccup, it meant nothing; maybe the range had not been absolutely right for Christmas, it would start selling hard in the new year. No, Regency was not too young, her face was perfect, she had the look of today, if not tomorrow. It was a look that public opinion

621

would warm to. Yes, the packaging was absolutely right, clean and chic; like the message of the range. Of course it should not be softened, the new woman was not soft.

The consultants had had it too easy for too long; this was a new concept and they had to learn to work harder on it. When it started to sell, when the public recognized it, accepted it as what they wanted, which they assuredly would, then the sales force would relax and grow easier with it.

Phaedria had never admired him more; she half expected him to let down his guard to her, to admit something was wrong, but he did not, he continued to behave as if everything was wonderful, as if Lifestyle was breaking all records. Even when he came into Circe for the Christmas party, and looked at the new range, piled horribly high on the counters, he managed to smile with complete assurance and convey the impression that he was delighted with its progress.

He criticized much that she had done: he still didn't like the windows, he was unhappy with many of the clothes on the fashion floor, he complained that the flower shop looked messy, he said the lingerie department was hopelessly under-stocked. But of his own mistake looking him so painfully in the eye, he said nothing, nothing at all.

The only sign she could detect that anything might be seriously troubling him was that he had not made love to her for weeks.

Roz wondered quite often these days if she might be going mad. Her hatred for Phaedria, the rage she felt at her continuing presence in her life and at the threat of her intrusion into her work, was not easing; it accompanied her wherever she went, a dark presence, like some physical growth. Much of the time she felt actually sick; she ate very little, and was aware she was drinking too much. She could not communicate at all with C. J.; she was short-tempered and distant with Miranda, she turned aside Letitia's worried offer of help and understanding with a brusque 'I'm fine'; she avoided her mother, she scarcely spoke to her father.

She looked back on the days (was it really only two years ago?) before her father had met Phaedria, when her troubles had been confined to a fall in sales figures, a difficult personnel problem, a temporary vote of no confidence from her father, a mildly unsatisfactory marriage, and was amazed that any of it could have troubled her. It had been another country she had inhabited then, which seemed in retrospect golden, peaceful, endlessly happy; and many of the tears she so often shed, private, anguished, angry tears, were for the loss of that country and her life within it. Only Michael Browning could ease her pain, make her laugh, give her pleasure; only Michael Browning was ultimately forbidden to her. And that thought made her more wretched than anything else.

Christmas was coming; to her utter astonishment and horror, C. J. had asked Phaedria if he, Roz and Miranda could come and spend it at Marriotts. Phaedria and Julian were both, C. J. told her, delighted. 'Especially your father. So you can't back out.'

'How could you, C. J., how could you? Make me spend Christmas of all times with her?'

'Roz, I don't see where else is going to be any better for you. And I would certainly like to go. I don't see that the three of us would have a happy time on our own. At least it will be more fun for Miranda. And besides, you need to form some sort of truce with your father. This will help. You should be grateful to me.'

'Couldn't we spend it with your mother?' asked Roz, casting desperately around for an escape from the trap that was closing in on her.

'She's got some huge house party planned, Francesca is getting engaged, and frankly I just can't face it.'

'Well, I can't face this.'

'Roz –' He turned to her and his gentle face was totally transformed with anger and misery. 'I have to face a great deal that I don't like. Every day of my life. Just do me the rare kindness of allowing me my way for once. Just for a day or two.'

Roz looked at him and felt a wave of misery, not for herself but for him. She had ruined his life, wilfully and thoughtlessly; she had made him very unhappy, and he did not deserve it. She put out her hand. 'I'm sorry, C. J. Really I am. Yes, we'll go to Marriotts. Perhaps we – we should talk.'

He shook her hand off, looking at her with a cold distaste. 'I don't think so. There's nothing to say. I am trying to work out what to do, and it's very difficult. But meanwhile I see no point in a painful dialogue.'

Roz walked up to her room, feeling the madness closing in on her. What was she doing? Michael had begged her to spend Christmas with him in the Caribbean, why wasn't she going with him? She had told him she couldn't possibly leave the baby (not feeling able to try to explain that spending Christmas with him really would be an open declaration of war between herself and her father), and he had rather surprisingly accepted this without argument. He was having Little Michael and Baby Sharon for the New Year in any case and was rather pathetically having the duplex decorated accordingly, with a Christmas tree in every room and two in the children's bedroom, and a great pile of presents under every one. Roz, who had never met Little Michael and Baby Sharon, feared for their characters, but Michael assured her they were great kids: 'Just like their mother, no Browning in them at all.'

And so she packed for Christmas at Marriotts with a heavy heart, wondering how she was going to endure it; but at the last minute the party was greatly improved by the arrival of Letitia, and a car literally filled with parcels; the castle was too cold for her these days, she said, and she wanted to spend Christmas with her great-granddaughter.

Phaedria, who wanted to be busy and to have as little time as possible to spend sitting with her guests, gave the entire staff Christmas Day off, and did all the cooking herself. Christmas morning passed fairly smoothly; they went to church, exchanged presents and had a late lunch during which Letitia kept them entertained with stories of Christmases past; afterwards she said that she and Miranda should go and have naps, and everyone else could clear up.

'One of the great joys of being very old and very young,' she said, scooping the child up, 'is that we don't have to be helpful.'

'That was great, Phaedria,' said C. J., pouring himself a third glass of port and waving the bottle hospitably about the table. 'You're a great girl.' He was fairly drunk.

'She is,' said Julian, smiling benignly at her across the candle-lit table. 'Let's drink a toast to her. To Phaedria.'

'To Phaedria,' said C. J.

'Phaedria,' said Roz through clenched teeth. She thought no one would ever know what that moment had cost her.

'You look absolutely beautiful,' said C. J. 'Beautiful. Doesn't she, Julian?'

'She does. Not a day over twenty-six.'

'I don't know how you do it,' C. J. went on. 'All that cooking, and organizing, and running the company and –'

'Not quite running the company,' said Roz, sickly sweet. 'Not all of it.'

'Oh, give her time,' said C. J. 'Just a little bit of time.'

Phaedria shot him a warning look; it was too late.

'I bet she could do the whole thing. Easily,' he said, draining his glass. 'I suppose she will one day, eh Julian?'

'Possibly,' said Julian blandly. 'But not for a very long time, I hope.'

Roz was white, clutching her glass very tightly.

'Well, I think it would be a wonderful thing,' said C. J. 'What a successor, for you.'

There was a strange cracking sound: the delicate stem of Roz's glass had snapped. Phaedria looked at it, the jagged edge, the red wine spilt on the white cloth, Roz's blazing eyes, and shivered.

'Come on, C. J.,' she said, 'let's get a bit of fresh air before it's dark. Julian? Would you like to come for a walk?'

Julian was looking at Roz thoughtfully. 'What's that? Oh, no, I don't think so. I might even join the other babies upstairs for a rest. You go on. I'll just help you clear that up, Roz.'

He walked out of the door towards the kitchen, in search of a cloth. Roz, still sitting at the table, still holding the broken glass, looked at Phaedria. She tried, she wanted to remain silent, but she couldn't. Her self-control, which seemed to her these days to be an increasingly fragile thing, suddenly splintered like the glass.

'You aren't going to win, you know,' she said savagely. 'Whatever you do, however much you try, I won't let you win.'

'Oh, Roz, I don't want to win,' said Phaedria wearily. 'Whatever that might mean.'

'You're a liar,' said Roz, 'I don't believe you.' She knew she was making a fool of herself, losing dignity, but she couldn't stop. 'Of course you want to win. You want to take my place in this company, you want it for yourself when my father dies, along with his money. That's all you want, it's all you ever wanted and nobody, nobody else at all, seems to be able to see it.'

'Perhaps because it's not true,' said Phaedria quietly. Her eyes were fixed on the jagged glass. She seemed frightened. Her fear gave Roz pleasure, made her feel better.

'It's true,' she said almost cheerfully. 'I know it's true and you know it's true, and it seems to be our little secret.' She stood up suddenly; she was taller than Phaedria. She began to walk slowly towards her, holding the glass. Phaedria, backing away clumsily, suddenly found herself against the wall.

'Roz please,' she said, and there was a tremor in her voice. 'Please.'

Roz slowly raised the glass; she had no intention of hurting Phaedria with it, but this moment was revenge for all the months, all the misery, all the humiliation, almost for the loss of her father.

'Roz!' It was C. J.'s voice from the doorway. 'Roz, what the hell are you doing? For God's sake put that down.'

He sounded calm, authoritative. Roz turned and looked at him, put the glass down quite gently.

'It's all right,' she said, 'I wouldn't dream of hurting her. Then everyone would feel sorry for her as well as being in love with her. Do enjoy your walk with my husband, Phaedria. You're very welcome to him.'

She walked quickly out of the room, up the stairs and into her room; Letitia, who was coming down from settling Miranda for her nap, heard her crying, and knew there was nothing, nothing at all, that she could do to help her.

'I'm so sorry,' said C. J., utterly sobered by the scene and the cold air as they walked out into the drive of Marriotts. 'I'm sure she wouldn't have hurt you. She – she isn't very happy at the moment.'

'No,' said Phaedria, 'I can see that.' She shivered; she was cold in spite of her wolf coat, and very shaken.

'Are you all right?'

'Yes. Yes of course I am. It's just that – that sometimes I do wonder if she will attack me physically. Of course I know it's silly, but just then it was like all the nightmares coming true.'

626

'God,' said C. J., and there were tears in his eyes. 'I don't know what to do. I really don't.'

'Oh, C. J.,' said Phaedria, 'don't worry about me. I'm just being hysterical.'

'No,' he said, 'no, you're not. She behaves so terribly badly towards you and it's just not fair. I don't know how I can help.'

'You can't,' said Phaedria. 'The only person who could help is Julian, and he won't.'

'No. Maybe if I asked him?'

'It wouldn't do any good. It would make things worse. Please don't.'

'All right.' He smiled at her rather weakly. They walked in silence for a while.

'C. J.,' said Phaedria, 'I'm so sorry. So sorry for you. You must be very unhappy.'

'I am,' he said, 'very. I'm pretty near to desperate right now. And all I ever wanted was to make everybody happy. I came to work for Julian to please my dad, I got tricked into marrying Roz –'

'What?'

'Yeah, didn't you know? I guess not, nobody does. I never told anyone.'

'Tell me.'

'I shouldn't. Your opinion of Roz must be pretty bad already.'

'Couldn't be worse,' said Phaedria cheerfully, restored to herself by curiosity. 'Go on, what happened?'

He told her. She listened appalled. 'That's terrible. You poor poor man.'

'Well, it's my own fault, I should have stood up for my rights. Not easy, though.'

'Not easy. Absolutely impossible. In this family.' She put her arm through his. 'I don't know what to say.'

'There isn't anything. But if she does go off with Browning, it will be a happy release.'

'Didn't you ever love her?'

'Not really. Only for a moment or two. I suppose,' he added, 'if she does go, she'll take Miranda with her.'

'I don't think, actually, it's very likely,' said Phaedria with a sigh. 'That she'll go, I mean. She needs Julian too much.'

627

'I'm afraid you're right.'

'Couldn't you go?'

'I could. Of course I could. But I guess I'm a coward. I can't face the drama. I keep hoping things will improve. And I don't want to lose Miranda.'

There was a silence. 'Well,' said Phaedria, attempting to be cheerful, 'at least you do have Miranda. She's a poppet.'

'Yeah, she is. I'm nuts about her. Do you like kids?'

'Nice ones, yes.'

'Do you think you and Julian will have any?'

Phaedria stopped walking and faced him, looking totally astonished. 'Do you know, I've never even thought about it. Never. I just don't know. Maybe we will. I can't imagine Julian with a baby. Can you?'

'Yes, I can actually. He loves Miranda. Well, if you do have any, I hope they'll turn out better than his last attempt.'

Phaedria laughed. 'Couldn't be worse.'

That night in bed, she put down her book and turned to Julian. He was frowning over a set of figures.

'Julian, don't you ever stop working?'

'Not often.' He put them down and looked at her. 'Thank you for doing today, my darling. I really appreciate it. I can see – well, it isn't always easy for you.'

Phaedria digested this considerable concession in silence. Then she simply said, 'It was a pleasure. Can I ask you something?'

'What's that?'

'Would you like me to have a baby?'

'I don't know,' he said, very serious. 'I have thought about it, of course. Haven't you?'

'No. Not until today. It never entered my head.'

'Most women think about it.'

'I know. But I suppose I thought we had enough problems. Enough adjustments.'

'Maybe. Would you like to have a baby?'

She was thoughtful. 'Possibly. Yes, I think so. But not yet. Definitely not yet.'

'And what if I wanted one – yet?'

She leant over and kissed him. 'I guess I'd have one. Pretty damn quick. You seem to have ways of getting what you want.'

He switched the light off suddenly and took her in his arms, turning her on to her back, kissing her hair. 'Certain things have to take place, I believe, before babies are made. Perhaps we could content ourselves for now with a little research.'

She responded swiftly, eagerly melting with pleasure and relief that after all he did still want her; but then as suddenly his mood changed, became distant, and he turned away from her and sighed.

'Julian, what is it? What's the matter?'

'Nothing,' he said, and his voice was strained, cool. 'Nothing at all. I'm just tired, that's all.'

'But I –'

'Phaedria, please. Let's just go to sleep.'

She was tired, and fell asleep almost at once; but when she woke a few hours later, restless and hot, he was wide awake, staring blankly into the darkness.

Roz went into her father's office one morning in January; she looked tired and drawn. Julian and Phaedria had been away for a fortnight on Eleuthera, and this was the first day he had been in the office. He was skimming through some magazines and newspapers; he looked at her with concern.

'Roz, you don't look well. Are you all right?'

'Yes, thank you. I just wanted to talk to you.'

'Yes? You know I'm always happy to talk to you.'

'You may not be too happy about this.'

'Try me.'

'I've spent a bit of time at Circe while you've been away. The sales figures are disastrous.'

'Oh, Roz, don't be absurd, so how can they be disastrous after – what, nine, ten months? It's still in its earliest stages. Still in a heavy investment situation. Circe New York took three years to break even, never mind show a profit.'

'Of course. But it was steady growth, however small and slow. London did quite well in the first three weeks and it's been falling steadily ever since. And certain departments are a disaster.'

'Like?'

'The fashion consultancy. Only one client since Christmas. The lingerie. Too tacky looking. There's a feeling those room sets don't work.'

'How do you know?'

'I've talked to the staff. They're very demoralized. And they feel out on a limb. They got a great deal of attention in the beginning, but they say they hardly see Phaedria these days. They feel abandoned.'

'Well, let's get her in,' said Julian, slightly wearily. 'I can see it's a problem. Have you told her all this?'

'Of course not.'

'Why of course?'

'She's – you've – been away.'

'Sarah, get my wife in, would you?'

'Yes, Sir Julian.'

Phaedria came into the office ten minutes later. She looked pale.

'Sorry. I was on the phone to LA.'

'Phaedria, we seem to have a problem on Circe.'

'Really? In LA?'

'No, here. In London.'

'In London? Who told you?'

'I did,' said Roz.

'Ah,' said Phaedria.

'Apparently certain departments are doing extremely badly,' said Julian.

'Really? Which?'

'The clothes consultancy. No clients. The lingerie. No sales. What do you think about that?'

'Not a lot,' said Phaedria. 'It's early days. In any case I knew. We have time.'

'Apparently they feel rather abandoned,' said Julian. 'They say they haven't seen you, can't talk to you about it.'

'For heaven's sake,' said Phaedria quietly, 'how could they have? I've been away with you.'

'And before that in LA.'

'Jesus, Julian, what are you trying to do to me? The two of you? Of course I've been in LA. I've been terribly busy. At your behest.'

'Originally at yours. You wanted to be involved.'

'Yes,' said Phaedria, keeping her temper with an effort, 'I suppose I did. I suppose I did take on too much. It hasn't been easy, Julian. You seem to forget I'm a novice at this game.'

'You seem to find plenty of time,' he said, icily smooth, 'for your other activities.'

Phaedria followed his eyes to his desk. A copy of *Vogue* lay there opened at a spread of photographs of her by Danny Carter; the *Daily Mail* diary carried a story about her involvement in a charity fashion show, under the aegis of Dominic Kennedy.

She looked at him steadily. 'All right. I have been doing – some other things. But I have been working hard on the store as well. None of what Roz says is true. Well, it's strictly true, the figures aren't good. I knew that. But they're very far from disastrous. That's absolute nonsense. It's a bad time. The lingerie department had a marvellous Christmas. Now it's obviously down. I talked to all the departments at length just before Christmas. I had formed some ideas which I was going to discuss with you. But luckily I've had some help. You really have been working hard on this, Roz. How kind, how extremely kind of you to keep such a close eye on Circe in my absence. Snooping around, putting words into my staff's mouths, thoughts into their heads. That's what it amounts to. How dare you? And you, Julian. With all your experience, all your years and years of staff relations and company management, how extraordinary that you didn't think for one moment that I might need advice, guidance, support even. I could say I wasn't going to take this any longer, but I'm not prepared to give in to either of you. I will not be beaten. I'm going to my office now, I have several people waiting to see me. Perhaps we could reconvene this meeting later. When wc have a few more facts at our disposal. Oh, and Julian,' she added, turning and confronting him, her eyes steady, 'did Roz happen to mention the figures for Lifestyle at the same time? I thought not. They make even the lingerie department look healthy.'

Roz watched her thoughtfully as she walked through Sarah Brownsmith's office and into the lift. She was learning to fight dirty. That was interesting. Roz felt a pang of something quite close to admiration. Then she turned to her father. There was an expression on his face she had not often seen there. It was panic.

More and more these days Phaedria wondered exactly why she was so determined not to give in. It would be so comfortable, so easy; to walk out, say goodbye to them all, embark on her own life, which would, after all, be easy now. She had made a name for herself, she had friends, contacts. She did not think she was happy at all any more; she found it hard to admit, but searching through the painful days, the increasingly lonely nights, there seemed little pleasure. Julian didn't seem to love her in the least; occasionally he was tender, kind, appreciative, even more occasionally lover-like. More and more he slept alone; he had made love to her once or twice in the house at Turtle Cove, but it had been with a kind of frantic fervour, as if he had been trying to prove something, there was none of the confident, joyful pleasure she had fallen in love with.

And then there was Roz. Some days, she felt, in a near-feverish anxiety, that it was Roz who was married to Julian, so close, so alike did they seem, and she was the interloper, the intruder on the relationship. Julian never acknowledged that there was any kind of problem with Roz; he ignored it, ignored Roz's rudeness and hostility and continued to treat her with patience and courtesy; Phaedria compared it with the impatience and intolerance with which he talked to her and wondered how she was expected to endure it.

Love suffereth long and is kind, Michael Browning thought to himself as he waited for Roz's plane at Kennedy Airport one evening in late February. He felt he had suffered for longer and had been kinder than most men would have been; and right now he was finding it hard to think why. He was tired, he was hungry, and he was wearying of the long game of piggy in the middle he seemed to have been playing with Roz and Julian almost as long as he could remember. Quite who was in the middle he wasn't sure, but he as sure as hell wasn't winning. On the other hand, he wasn't losing either; Roz was still there, in his life, in his bed, and in his heart for that matter. It had to be love, he thought, there could be no other explanation for a relationship that continued to thrive, to give pleasure, against such odds as almost continuous separation, a refusal to commit to any kind of permanence, and which most clearly cast him as supporting player to a company and the leading lady's role in it. Well, he had finally had enough. He was about to step centre stage. No matter what it cost him, what it cost Roz, the situation had to be resolved. It was unendurable.

She was walking towards him now, smiling, looking pale and tired, but happy, in a long fur coat and high brown leather boots; he felt at the same time a stab of irritation that she should be so remorselessly confident of him, and a surge of love and pleasure.

'Hallo, Michael.'

'Hi, darling.' Despite the surge he held back, kissed her formally, distantly. Roz didn't notice. She was always immune to subtleties of behaviour unless they took place in the boardroom.

'Ghastly flight.'

'I'm sorry. What was wrong with it? Did they take a wrong turning?'

'I think they must have done. I seem to have been up there for ever. And I'd seen the film. And the woman sitting next to me talked about her grandchildren all the way. Oh, God, Michael, let's get back.'

'OK.' He was used to her litanies of discontent; he had learnt to ignore them. The thing about Roz, he thought, and it always amazed him that nobody realized it but him, was that beneath the bad temper, the bitching, the chips on both her elegantly sloping shoulders, was a funny, sexy, averagely nice woman. You just had to dig a bit. Michael had dug.

'What do you want to do this evening? Eat out? Stay in? I have Rosa standing by just in case.'

'I want to stay in, with you, without Rosa, let's get something delivered, and I want to have you in every room in the place.'

Michael looked at her and struggled to maintain an equilibrium. He had more serious, more important intentions for the evening than making love on a lot of different floors, beds and couches.

'That's nice to hear. But I want to talk to you.'

Roz's heart sank. She knew what that meant. Another attempt at a promise, another demand for commitment; he was growing weary at last and she knew it, and it frightened her.

'Michael, don't, please. Not this weekend.'

'Weekend? I thought it was five days.'

'Well, long weekend. I have to go back on Monday. I'm sorry, I was going to tell you.'

'For Christ's sake, Rosamund, why?'

'Well, my father's called a board meeting, a full board meeting, to discuss the new company. I have to be there. Surely you can see that.'

'Yes,' he said, 'I can see it.'

She misread his mood. 'Good. I knew you would. I'm sorry. Let's go and find the car.'

'I'll go find the car. I don't see a lot of point you coming in it. Why don't you just stay here and get the next plane home? You can prepare for the board meeting better, really put on a good show, impress your father, give one in the eye to your rival. Go on, Roz, go and get yourself a flight.'

'Oh, Michael, don't be so ridiculous.'

'I am not being ridiculous. I love you and I need you and if you felt half as much for me you wouldn't even think of rushing back for some two-bit board meeting. Which no doubt he's called because he knows you're here. Well, does he know you're here?'

'Yes,' she said, very quietly.

'Will you stay?'

'I can't, I can't, not yet, not now, you're asking too much.'

'Oh, go fuck yourself.'

He gave her a look of despair, of hostility mingled with such love that tears filled her eyes. She put out a hand, put it on his arm.

'Please, Michael, don't.'

'Don't what? Don't get sick of you arseing around, making it outstandingly plain that I come a very poor third to that father of yours and his shitty company. That you'll find a place for me in your busy schedule in between board meetings and takeovers, and of course sticking a knife into yet another point in the back of that poor, goddamned stepmother of yours. Jesus, Rosamund, I don't know where you learnt to fight so dirty, to cheat so thoroughly, but it sure was a fine establishment. Well I'm through, with it and with you. Just get the hell out of my life. I won't be messing up yours any longer.'

Panic tore through Roz; she felt shaken, weak, there was a roaring in her ears.

'Michael, don't, don't, please stay. I have to talk to you.'

'Really? Suddenly you have to talk. All the times I've wanted to talk and you've ducked, dodged, dragged me into bed, anything to avoid the confrontation. Well, it doesn't happen to suit me to talk right now, Roz, or indeed ever again.'

He was walking away, fast, pushing through the crowds; Roz looked at his disappearing back, sobs tearing at her throat, her heart wrenched into terrified fragments. She couldn't bear it, not again, not that pain, that loneliness, that aching, wracking misery. Nothing, nothing was worth that, nothing at all.

She ran after him, stumbling, frantically calling his name; but he wouldn't turn or look back. He went through the glass doors; his car was waiting; she stood, tears streaming down her face, watched him get in, lean back, close his eyes, and then the traffic and the darkness swallowed him up.

Roz went to see her father, pale and drawn, but dry-eyed on the Monday morning, with a look of ferocious determination on her face.

'I've done what you want.'

'What do you mean?'

'I've finished with Michael. Again.'

'Roz! I'm sorry. I know what this must have cost you.'

'Yes, well, I'm planning that it should cost you.'

'What do you mean?'

'I've kept my share of the bargain, Daddy. Let's have yours.'

'Roz, you're talking in riddles.'

'No, I'm not. You said if I divorced C. J. you'd give the stores to Phaedria.'

'Yes. And I meant it.'

'OK. Well, I'm staying with him. So you can give them to me.'

'You have them. You know you do.'

'No, I don't. Not all of them. I want London too.'

'Roz, you know that's impossible.'

'I don't see why.'

'Circe London is Phaedria's own. It was a wedding present. She's created it.'

'Yes, well, she's done well. Now I want it.'

'Rosamund, you can't have it. Now can we forget this

nonsense? I'm delighted you've come to your senses, and I'm sure I can find a new section of the company for you to run if that's what you want.'

'I don't want a new section. I've told you what I want, I want the stores. All of them.'

'And I've told you you can't have them. Now we have a board meeting to get to. We're already late.'

Roz looked at him. 'You're a cheat, you know. A liar and a cheat. You cheat on us all. Even your beautiful new wife.' Then she smiled. It was a dangerous smile.

'How was Paris, Daddy?' she said. 'And how is Camilla these days?'

The Connection Eleven

Nassau, 1984

Marcia Galbraith tucked her old friend up in bed for her nap, and drew the curtains tenderly. Dorothy had certainly gone downhill faster than she had expected; when she had come to Nassau three years before she had seemed the stronger of the two of them. Marcia had looked to Dorothy for help and support, thinking that she would take care of her in her frail old age. Well, life did funny things to you, and here she was, feeling stronger suddenly and in command of everything, and here was Dotty, confused, fragile, in need of care. She had looked for a mainstay and had found a burden.

She did not greatly mind, and indeed it was good to feel stronger, more in command of life, but there was no denying it was a worry. Dotty seemed to have no concept that she was a drain on the household, and it was made worse by the boy, sitting there, doing almost nothing and eating her out of house and home.

Miles was very devoted to Dotty, of course, very sweet and charming he seemed, you couldn't exactly dislike him, and she felt almost sorry for him these days, now that Billy was gone. He was obviously lonely, but she really couldn't figure out why he didn't get himself a proper job. It wasn't good for him and it wasn't natural. More importantly, it wasn't fair on her. He'd had a fine education and he'd got a good degree, and here he was wasting his days on some tennis court, and seemed to think all he had to give her in the way of a contribution to the household was a smile, and occasionally help Little Ed with chopping wood. She wondered what in the end he was planning to do. Nothing, going on past performance. That kind of thing irritated, even angered Marcia. A young man should have a sense of purpose, not waste his life away; and besides she just didn't like him being around so much during the day. It offended her sense of rightness. It hadn't been so bad at first, when he had obviously had to settle down, find his feet, but now day by day it got more on her nerves. And besides, there was just something about him she didn't quite trust. She wished Dotty had left him on the beach in California; she wished he would go back there.

She wondered what was going to happen to the house in Malibu. It was all very well, Dotty living here, and she was pleased to have her, but it seemed awfully silly just leaving that place empty, rotting, when it could be converted to money in the bank.

She wondered where the deeds were. Presumably in Dotty's box under her bed, with all her other stuff, the pictures of Lee, and her will and everything. She felt for the box; it was there. Cautiously Marcia pulled it out and tiptoed out of the room.

'Dotty,' she said that night, casually, over supper. 'Have you thought of selling your house in California lately?'

'No, no,' said Mrs Kelly firmly. 'That's mine. I wouldn't sell it.'

'It isn't a lot of use to you, Dotty. Not sitting there. You should convert it into money.'

'I don't want Miles to have the money. It won't do him any good.'

'Nobody's saying Miles should have the money, Dotty,' said Marcia patiently. 'You should have it. In the bank. Earning interest.'

'Me? What for?'

'Well, Dotty, dear, I've never said anything before, but I ain't

637

getting any richer. Times are costly. It would be a real help if you could put a bit in now and again.'

Mrs Kelly was stricken. Emotion cleared her brain. 'Marcia! You should have said before. Oh, my! I certainly have been thoughtless and selfish. You're right. I'll put the house on the market straight away.'

'I'll do it for you, Dotty. You don't have to worry with any of the details. Just give me the deeds, and I'll go down to my lawyer in the morning, and get it all put in hand.'

'All right, Marcia. That's very kind of you. I'm sorry, I'm real sorry. I never intended to take your charity. I've been paying into your account each week, or so I thought, and imagined it was enough.'

'Well, Dotty, not quite, not any more. Give me the deeds, dear, and I'll see to it.'

'They're in my box. Under my bed. I'll get them after dinner.'

'All right, dear.'

Marcia thought it best for Dorothy to discover for herself that they weren't there.

'Miles, do you have any idea where the deeds of the house might have got to?' she said next day. 'Your grandmother can't find them, and she's getting very upset.'

It was true; the old lady was wandering round the house, searching endlessly in the same places, getting increasingly distressed.

'The deeds? No idea at all. Why?'

'Well, I have been talking to Dotty and we have decided that the house should be sold.'

'Really? Why?'

'We need the money, Miles. This house ain't cheap to keep up. That's a few thousand dollars, about eighty thousand I'm told, sitting there in California, and I could do with them. Or some of them. It might not have entered your idle head that you've been living here rent free for three years. I consider I have a right to some input.'

He looked at her. Then he smiled, his most disarming smile. 'Of course. You're right. I couldn't agree more. Don't worry, Mrs Galbraith, I'll find the deeds.'

The bank manager was very nice, but firm. He couldn't let Miles have the deeds back until he paid off the loan. There was the original four thousand dollars and then there was that other thousand he'd borrowed last year. Of course it wasn't much set against the value of the house, but nonetheless, the deeds must stay with the bank.

'But we want to sell the house.'

'Well, that's all right. Put it in the hands of a realtor. Nothing to stop you doing that.'

'OK. Thanks.'

'It's OK, Mrs Galbraith,' said Miles that afternoon as his grandmother slept. 'I'll see to selling the house. I guess it's mine in a way and my responsibility.'

'It is not,' said Marcia, indignant on her friend's behalf. 'That house is your grandmother's. She's always said so. No, I'll see to it, Miles. Just give me the deeds when you find them.'

'I have found them, Mrs Galbraith. They're with the bank.'

'The bank! How did they get there?'

'I guess Granny must have taken them there and forgotten. You know what she's like these days.'

'Well, I don't know, Miles. I'll ask her.'

'No, don't.'

'For heaven's sake why not?'

'You know it upsets her when she realizes how vague she's become. Let's just leave them there, and I'll go ahead and organize the sale. OK?'

She looked at him doubtfully. 'OK. Which bank?'

'Oh, her bank, of course.' He met her suspicious eyes with his wide, candid blue ones. 'Does it matter?'

Mrs Galbraith's lawyer and Miles' bank manager were members of the same golf club. Over just one too many bacardis one afternoon, the bank manager, knowing the connection with Marcia, remarked what nice manners young Wilburn had, and what a rare pleasure it was to find such a phenomenon these days. The lawyer agreed, and cited several examples of young men who had no manners at all, whereupon the bank manager went on, with extreme indiscretion, over yet another bacardi, that it had been a pleasure to be able to help young Mr Wilburn with a loan the year before, and asked his friend the lawyer what he thought, purely as a matter of interest, a house in Malibu, California, might be worth these days, as Miles was in the process of selling one. The lawyer said he had no idea and that he also had no idea that young Wilburn was a man of such substance; on Mrs Galbraith's next visit to his office, he made the same observation. Marcia looked at him, her eyes deceptively innocent. 'I always thought that house belonged to his grandmother. She's a very frail, confused old lady. I know I shouldn't be asking you this, but might it be possible to just check that the house really is in Miles' name?'

The lawyer hesitated. He didn't like using a friendship. But two old ladies in distress surely needed help. 'I'll see what I can do,' he said. 'Try not to worry.'

He asked her to go down to his office three days later. 'No, Mrs Galbraith, you're wrong. Mrs Kelly has definitely signed a transfer deed, making the house over to Miles. Nothing to worry about, I'm sure. Can I help in any other way?'

'Not for now. But thank you very much. You've been really kind.' Marcia's blood was up; she was enjoying herself.

Later that day she asked her friend if she had ever thought of transferring the deeds of the house to Miles' name.

'Well of course not, Marcia,' said Mrs Kelly, irritated out of her vagueness. 'How many times have I told you I would never let Miles get his hands on that house? He'd just waste the money away. If he's ever going to get a proper job, he certainly can't be handed several thousand dollars on a plate.'

'No, Dotty,' said Marcia. 'He certainly can't.'

She went back to her lawyer. 'Could you find out a little more?' she said, 'discreetly. I don't want Miles suspecting anything.'

The lawyer did.

'I have to tell you, Mrs Galbraith,' he said, 'that boy seems to have been borrowing on that house. Five thousand dollars. Are you sure your friend doesn't know anything about it?'

'Quite sure.'

'Well, the money's been spent. Not much, of course, in view of what the house is worth, but it has, and if that signature was obtained unlawfully, then the boy could be in trouble.'

'Yes,' said Mrs Galbraith. 'Well, thank you. I'll let you know if there's any more to be done.'

Miles was in love. He had met her at the hotel, and she was just seventeen years old, with long, silvery blonde hair, huge blue eyes, and freckles dusted prettily on her tip-tilted little nose. Her breasts were tip-tilted too, just a little, and her legs were as long as a colt's; she had a disposition as sunny as her hair, and her name was Candy, Candy McCall. She should have been in high school, but her father had taken her out for a bit; he thought it would be good for her to see a bit of the world. So far the world had consisted of Acapulco and Nassau. Candy wasn't too impressed, but it was better than school. Candy's father, Mason, was in confectionery, and was married to Candy's fourth stepmother, Dolly; Candy hated her.

They were staying in Nassau for a few weeks while Dolly played the roulette table, and got a tan, and Mason did some property deals.

Until Candy had met Miles she had been frantic with boredom. Despite her virginal appearance she had had several boyfriends, most of whom had been granted the pleasures of her small, neat body; Miles, who had a sure instinct for anything to do with sex, recognized her experience, and her capacity for pleasure, instantly and easily.

'Don't give me that,' he said good-naturedly when Candy squirmed under his exploring hands, pushing them gently, modestly away, 'you know you want it as much as I do.'

'I know nothing of the sort,' she said, smiling up at him, her small freckled nose wrinkling, 'I just am not that sort of girl.'

'Show me what sort you are, then,' said Miles. They were lying on a rug on Candy's balcony, on the penthouse floor of the Bahamian, out of view of anyone except the most determined cat burglar. He stood up and pulled off his shorts. Candy looked up at him, his tall, golden body, his glorious face, his magical smile; then she knelt in front of him.

'This sort,' she said, and took his penis in her mouth with a gentle hunger.

After that they were seldom apart.

'Miles,' said Marcia after breakfast one morning, 'I want to talk to you.'

'Sure,' said Miles, sitting back in his chair and smiling at her. 'Here I am.'

'Not now. When your grandmother is asleep this afternoon.'

He looked at her slightly warily. 'I shall be working.'

'Oh, I know how important your work is, Miles. Maybe just this once you could arrive a little late.'

'Not very. I have a game booked at three.'

'Fine. We'll talk at two.'

An odd unease gripped Miles; a shadow came over the sun. Even Candy's company seemed a little drab.

'What's the matter, Miles?'

'Nothing. Just a little worry.'

'Let me take your mind off it.'

But she couldn't.

That evening, after his afternoon's games, she found him sitting drinking a beer, looking miserable.

'Miles. Come on, tell me. You can. I won't split on you. Or let you down. I might even be able to help.'

He looked at her. 'I don't think you will. Unless you can give me five thousand dollars, and I don't think even that would make much difference.'

'Well, tell me anyway. Oh, come on.'

So he told her. That Mrs Galbraith had guessed what he had done; that she threatened to go to the police; that her lawyer knew too; that unless he repaid the money within a month, she would tell his grandmother and the bank. 'I kept telling her I didn't have any money, that I couldn't pay it back. She just said I'd spent it in the first place, and it was my duty to put it back.'

'She sounds batty.'

'She is.'

'What about your grandmother?'

'Oh, really, I think if she knew it would really send her right over the top. Poor old lady.'

'You're real fond of her, aren't you?'

'Yeah. She's been very very good to me.'

'Don't you have anyone else in the world who could help?'
'Nope. Not really.'
'No relatives?'
'Only an uncle. He doesn't have any money.'
'Could he get some?'
'I don't think so. Not without a terrible fuss.'
'Well, who put you through college?'
'Oh, some guy.'
Candy looked at him and laughed. 'Miles, what do you mean? What sort of guy?'
'Oh, a creepy old guy. Friend of my parents.'
'He sounds pretty nice to me. Creepy or not.'
'Well, maybe. But I quarrelled with him. Pretty badly.'
'I can't imagine you quarrelling with anyone.'
'No,' he said, looking at her almost with surprise. 'I never have before. Or since. Only with him.'
'What did you quarrel about?'
'Oh, he wanted me to get a job, and I thought I could work in his company. He said I couldn't. He was lousy to me. I wouldn't have any more to do with him.'
'So you just said you'd never speak to him again, just because he wouldn't give you a job.' She looked at him amusedly. 'You great spoilt baby.'
'Oh, you don't understand.'
'I don't see how I could.'
Miles never got angry or defensive. 'You couldn't. Anyway, I haven't been in touch with him for years.'
'Maybe you should be now.'
'What do you mean?'
'Well, maybe he could let you have the money.'
'No,' said Miles. 'No, I couldn't go begging to him. I'd rather go to jail.'
Candy shrugged. 'OK. Suit yourself. I hear the Nassau jails are pretty unpleasant. Come on, let's go upstairs. Dolly will be up from the beach soon. I don't want her to see you.'
'Why not? I like older women.'
'Ugh!'

That night Miles sat in his room in Marcia's house, thinking. Whichever way he turned, there was no escape. He thought of running away, back to the beach, but they would know exactly where to look for him. He wondered if he should go somewhere else, up to Miami, he could work there in the hotels; but then, they would find him there too. Mrs Galbraith wouldn't give up, he knew.

And even if she did, he didn't want to leave his grandmother alone with her. At least not until he had this thing settled. He felt she needed him.

'Granny, I want to talk to you.'

It was tea time, and her mind was at its clearest.

'Yes, Miles.'

'Granny, I want to write to Hugo.'

'Oh, Miles. That is real good news. Whatever's brought that on? Though why he should want to hear from you now I can't imagine.'

'Well, I'm going to do what he says, I think. Tell him I'm going to get a proper job. I thought he'd be pleased. I guess I owe it to him, after what he did for me, putting me through college and everything.'

Mrs Kelly shot him a shrewd glance. 'This is mighty sudden, Miles.'

His face was totally open. 'I know. But I guess I finally realized I can't go on playing tennis for ever.'

'Playing tennis? I thought you were working at the casino.'

'Yeah, well, a bit of both.'

She sighed. 'I surely would like to see you settled. And so would Mr Dashwood. What are you thinking of doing?'

'Oh, banking I guess. I thought I'd go up to Miami or something. I could still come down and see you regularly. It isn't far.'

'Well,' she said. 'I certainly would miss you. But it would make me real happy.'

'Good. So could I have Mr Dashwood's address?'

'Well, I only have the one in New York. Not in England. We never had one. I'll get it for you. Wait there.' She paused. 'You're not going to try asking him for a job again, are you, Miles?'

'No, Granny, I swear I'm not.'

'Good. Because you'll just open up old wounds, that's all.'

644

'I know.'

'It's funny,' she said, 'we never heard from him. He promised to write, you know.'

'Yeah, well,' said Miles. 'He was a pretty strange guy.'

He wrote the letter. It was scary. He waited. He didn't have long. Mrs Galbraith was mercifully a little vague about time. But her lawyer wouldn't be. April came. He began to feel frightened. He had written to several banks in Miami. They mostly wrote regretfully polite ones back, telling him he was a little old for a trainee. Two asked him to come for an interview. He couldn't afford to go, so he wrote polite letters, stalling. One of them wrote back and told him to forget it.

Candy was leaving soon. Dolly was bored, and Mason's deals were nearly done.

Mrs Galbraith stopped him in the hall one day and told him she hadn't forgotten their conversation. Miles didn't dare antagonize her further. He smiled his most charming smile. 'Don't worry, Mrs Galbraith, I'll get the money very soon. Please have faith in me.'

'Even if I did, Miles, I'm afraid my lawyer hasn't.'

Finally, a letter came.

Dear Miles,

I was absolutely delighted to get your letter. It seems a very long time since we met, and I do assure you I have missed you. You were an important element in my life for a long time, and it was a considerable loss. (Creep, thought Miles.)

I was very pleased to hear that you were going to get a job. I always felt you had such potential and a great future. I have several connections in banking in Miami and I would of course be delighted to put your name forward. I think New York or Washington might be better for you than Miami, although of course if you want to stay near your grandmother, I quite understand.

How is she? Please give her my regards.

With reference to your request for a loan for $5,000, I am of course happy to consider it, but I would like to know a little more behind the reason. I know this may annoy you, but I cannot help worrying about your past record with drugs, and

I want to be assured that you have completely cut yourself off from all that sort of thing. I have given a lot of thought to your situation, and it seems to me that you are very much alone in the world. I realize you are twenty-six, but that is not a great age, and I feel you need some support and help, on perhaps a more formal basis.

I would very much like to see you. I feel we have a great deal to talk about both on a business and personal basis, and there is something that I have decided it is important you should know. I shall be coming to Nassau towards the middle of next month, and we can perhaps have a long talk then. Providing I am satisfied that the $5,000 is to be put to good use, I will give you a cheque then, and have my lawyers drawn up the papers in connection with your allowance.

Thank you again for writing.

Yours ever,
Hugo Dashwood

'Miles,' said Mrs Galbraith, 'it's just about four weeks now. I wonder if you've made that arrangement yet?'

'Nearly, Mrs Galbraith. The cheque is on its way.'

'It had better be. My lawyer has already drafted a letter to your bank.'

'What do I do?' he said to Candy frantically. 'What do I do now?'

She was still in Nassau; Dolly had found a new toyboy on the beach, and Mason was discovering the joy of shooting craps in the casino.

'Didn't the old guy deliver?'

'Sort of. I told you he was no good.'

'What'd he say?'

'Here, read the letter.'

She read it. 'He sounds pretty generous really.'

'Oh, sure.'

'Well, would you shell out five thousand dollars just like that?'

'I guess not.'

'And he's going to make you an allowance.'

'Big deal.'

'Well, it is.'

646

'Maybe. But Candy, I need the money now. I had a letter from the bank this morning, asking me to go and see them. I'm in real trouble.'

'You'll just have to tell your grandmother.'

'Candy, I can't. It's hard to explain, but I just won't do that to her. I think it might really break her. Tip her over the top. She's pretty nuts already. She needs to think well of me.'

'She won't think well of you if you get done for fraud.'

'I know. But I'm going to hang on as long as I possibly can.'

'Couldn't you tell this Dashwood guy it's urgent?'

'I'd have to tell him why, and I don't think that would be a good beginning.'

'Well, what are you going to tell him?'

'Oh, I think ordinary debts would be safer. Just cost of living, you know? Overdraft. More respectable, somehow. Only that could obviously wait three weeks.'

She looked at him.

'Listen, we're going to New York next week. Why don't I go and look this old guy up?'

'What good would that do?'

'It might help. I could explain you were in a bit of trouble. Old gentlemen like me.'

'I expect they do,' he said, smiling in spite of himself.

'Go on, Miles. Let me. Give me the address.'

'All right,' he said. 'I guess it can't do any harm. Meanwhile I'll just have to stall. You can't lend me a hundred dollars, can you? Just so I can go for this interview in Miami?'

'I'll ask Dolly. I'll say I want a dress. She'll do anything to try and make me like her.'

'You're an angel, Candy.'

'Yeah, well let's have a bit of earthly pleasure. Just for now.'

Candy phoned him from New York a few days later.

'Miles, it was really weird. I went to the address. It's a really funny place on the lower East Side. But it wasn't a place at all. Not really.'

'What do you mean?'

'Well, it was just a kind of scruffy room, in the most awful building, with a lot of pigeon holes for letters. And a weird woman, who said she was in charge. I said where could I find

Mr Dashwood and she said she wasn't allowed to give his address, and that it was just a forwarding house.'

'That is weird.'

'I said it was really urgent and she said, well, that didn't make any difference, she could only pass messages on. I tell you what, Miles, I really don't think he can be as rich as you say. I mean I was expecting a real impressive place.'

'Me too. Well, thanks for trying.'

'That's OK. Sorry. Did you get the job?'

'Haven't heard. Even if I do, they won't give me five thousand dollars on my first day, will they?'

'I guess not. Well, in two weeks now the old guy will be down. So you should be OK.'

'Yeah. Well, I hope so. When are you back?'

'Next week. Love you.'

'Love you too.'

In despair, with very little hope, he wrote to Bill Wilburn, asking him for a loan. All he could do now was wait. And hope the bank and the lawyers would drag their feet.

Chapter Eighteen

London, Los Angeles, New York, 1985

There was only one person in the world who could really give Julian Morell a hard time. It was Letitia, and she was working very hard at it. She had summoned him to First Street early one spring evening on the pretext of not feeling very well (knowing otherwise he would guess the real reason, avoid coming) and now that she had him there, she was not going to let him go until she had achieved her purpose.

'Ah, Julian,' she said, dangerously sweet. 'How nice. What would you like? A drink? Tea?'

'A drink please, Mother. Whisky if that's all right.'

'Perfectly, you must have whatever you want, Julian, that's your philosophy in life, isn't it, and who am I to argue with that?'

'What on earth are you talking about?'

'I think you know.'

'I don't. I don't know at all. I came here because I thought you were unwell.'

'I am not in the least unwell. I think you may be, though. Mentally. Emotionally.'

'Mother, I am totally baffled by all this.'

'Really? I'm surprised. Let me clarify things a little.'

He smiled at her, taking a sip of his whisky. 'I'm sure you will. You have a far clearer mind than mine.'

'I do indeed. Julian, what the hell do you think you're doing?'

'I beg your pardon?'

'Seeing Camilla. When your marriage to that – child is less than two years old.'

'Phaedria is not a child. That's a mistake that everybody makes. She is a tough, clever woman. It's one of the reasons I love her.'

'Really. You have a strange way of demonstrating love. And don't try to change the subject.'

'Mother –' His face was white, his mouth working. 'I don't think I like this very much. I am not prepared to be talked to as if I was a small boy.'

'You're behaving as if you were a small boy. A greedy, spoilt, small boy. And I shall talk to you how I wish. Nobody else seems to do anything but agree with your every utterance, pander to your every whim.'

'I do assure you you're mistaken there. My wife and my daughter persist in giving me a very hard time, for a start.' He was smiling again, trying to lighten the mood of the conversation.

Letitia looked at him, her eyes icy, her face still with rage.

'Well, I'm pleased to hear it. Evidently not hard enough. Julian, for God's sake, answer my question.'

'You haven't actually asked one yet.'

'Are you or are you not seeing Camilla North?'

'It's no business of yours, but yes I am. Seeing.'

'It is my business, and what precisely does seeing mean?'

'Seeing. Talking to. Lunching with.'

'Why?'

'Oh, for God's sake, because she was in Paris, and I was in Paris, and she was doing some work for Annick.'

'And you expect me to believe that?'

'No, I don't expect it,' he said, 'I don't ask you to and I don't care. But it's the truth.'

'Julian,' said Letitia, 'you wouldn't recognize the truth if it came up behind you and tapped you on the shoulder. I have heard from several sources that you have been seeing quite a lot of Camilla North –'

'I really don't think I like having your spies reporting on me all over the world.' He was so white now, so angry his face was hardly recognizable. 'How dare you listen to gossip about me?'

'I dare. I've always dared to do a lot of things, Julian. I'm not easily frightened. And there's been a lot of gossip. So much, it has been hard to ignore. Eliza had heard it, and so for that matter had Susan.'

'Susan? For God's sake, Mother, how could you discuss my affairs with Susan of all people?'

Letitia looked at him. 'Unfortunately for Susan, she is rather over-familiar with your affairs, or was. Particularly the one with Camilla. There is little love lost between her and Phaedria, but even she was concerned. Anyway, that is beside the point. I am extremely fond of Phaedria, and I –'

'Yes,' he said, and his face was savage, 'I know you are. Too bloody fond of her. You none of you really know very much about her, though. Do you? She isn't the gentle, innocent baby everyone likes to imagine. She has great ambition, and she works night and day to realize it.'

'And is that a crime? If so you are deeply guilty of it.'

'In her case, I think it is a little. I feel she's cheating on me. She has less and less time and energy for me, and more and more for her work. Not to mention all these wretched designers and photographers and so on she's always fooling around with.'

'So that gives you the right to go and fool around with Camilla North? Oh, Julian, don't be such a child. Why do you think Phaedria is working so hard at fighting you? Because you've taught her to do it, you're forty years older than her, although very little wiser apparently, you've encouraged her – pushed her, many would say – into something extremely difficult, and a monstrous situation incidentally, with Roz fighting her every inch of the way, you've asked her to succeed, and adapt to your very demanding lifestyle at the same time, and then you complain that she's squeezing you out of her life. You make me very very angry.'

'Well, I'm sorry. You're making me rather angry too, Mother, I think I'd better go.'

Camilla North knew perfectly well what had brought Julian back to her; it was not love for her, or desire, or even his terminal tendency to philander; it did not necessarily mean that the marriage had been the disaster that she had prophesied, nor that it had simply signified the male menopause at its most acute. It was fear, and Camilla could offer the unique gift of sexual reassurance that Julian needed.

She found that was enough.

In offering her gift, and in having it received, she received much herself: gratitude, tenderness and trust. Through the long nights, between her linen sheets, Camilla learnt of Julian's marriage: of his disappointment, disillusion and despair. He was, she found, extremely fond of Phaedria, but he had found himself in the position of a man who had imagined he was buying a toy pistol when actually he had obtained a high-calibre, deadly revolver. He hadn't acquired a wife, he had acquired a clever business partner and a highly visible personality, and he didn't like it. Camilla wondered at the girl's foolishness; she was by all reports intelligent, surely quite intelligent enough to realize that any male ego was a fragile thing, and the ego of the middle-aged male was poised to fracture into a thousand pieces at the first threat of rivalry – in whatever field.

Camilla smiled to herself as she sat in her executive office on Madison, just opposite Brooks Brothers, remembering with fierce vividness the pleasure of her reunion with Julian in bed. Uncertain, fearful he might be with Phaedria, or in his abortive attempt to seduce Regency, but with her he was as powerful, as skilful as she could ever remember. And since she had grown, greatly to her own surprise, more sensual in her middle age, was less inhibited, more imaginative, greedier – largely, she was sure, as a result of some very intensive and lengthy sessions from a new, highly aggressive female therapist – their love-making was very satisfactory indeed.

'And just who exactly have you been doing this sort of thing with for the past two years?' he had asked with surprise and pleasure, and a gratifying tinge of jealousy, and no one, she had assured him, with her usual, painstaking honesty, no one at all.

'I have learnt to communicate with myself, be in touch with myself, that's all.'

'Well,' he said, settling his head gratefully on her magnificent breasts, 'that must be extremely nice for yourself. Oh, Camilla, what is it about you, that I cannot live for very long without?'

'I'm not sure,' she said, 'I feel the same, you know. My analyst says it's probably because our ego instincts and our sex instincts are very deeply compatible. Both in ourselves, and with each other.'

'Balls,' he said, lifting his head, smiling at her, lazily moving his hands over her flat stomach, her beautiful, slender thighs, and then seeing the slightly pompous, outraged expression she wore whenever he questioned her psycho fixation, as he called it, he added hastily, 'I mean, balls are part of it. And bosoms. And this. And this. And this . . .'

Camilla was now highly successful. She had her own advertising agency, called simply North Creative; her clients numbered some of the richest and glossiest in town, in fashion, beauty, drinks and interiors; she had a small penthouse on the newly fashionable upper West Side, and a house in Connecticut, where she kept a fine string of horses, rode with the Fairfield Hunt Club and gave the most brilliantly orchestrated house parties to which she invited a careful blend of clients and friends.

She was happier, more relaxed than she had ever been in her life. She had long given up any idea of marriage; her new analyst had taught her to respect herself, what she had and what she wanted – 'I have learnt to give myself permission to experience pleasure for its own sake,' she explained to Julian – rather than desperately seeking to justify it, or to claim new territory. If she wanted to have an affair, then she now knew she should have it and enjoy it. As a result she was perfectly content to continue as mistress to Julian Morell for as long as they both wished without making any further demands on him. It seemed a very amicable and satisfactory arrangement.

Julian returned to London from Paris (via New York) early in March, looking fit and happy. Phaedria looked at him warily. She had learnt to trust none of his moods; the good ones could change swiftly, and the bad ones stayed stubbornly the same. But he seemed genuinely pleased to see her; he avoided sleeping with her the first night he came home, saying he was tired, that his jet lag would wake him at two; she accepted it resignedly, prepared for more to come, but in the morning she woke to find him sitting on the bed, looking at her, his eyes warm and tender.

'I think we should begin again,' he said, sliding into bed beside her, 'I have missed you very much.'

And Phaedria, feeling she should be cool, controlled, distant, but finding herself hungry, eager for him for the first time for months, turned to him and smiled, and said, 'I missed you too.'

Later he said he would stay at home, and would like her to do the same; they lunched together and then went back to bed. He gave her some presents: a Hockney swimming pool painting which he said would remind her of the Los Angeles she had fallen in love with, a deco diamond clip, an edition of the *New York Times* from the day she was born.

'Oh Julian,' she said, 'what have I done to deserve this?'

'A lot,' he said, 'but I want to ask you for more.'

'What?' she said, smiling still, but cautious, wary. 'What do you want?'

'I want you to give up Circe,' he said. 'It's taking up too much of your time, of your attention, it's causing many of our troubles. I think you – we – would be better without it.'

'Give up Circe? Julian, I can't. Two years of my life have gone into that. I love it, it's too important to me. Don't ask for that.'

'Two years of my life have gone into you. I love you too, you're too important to me. I have to ask. Please, Phaedria, please. For me. Because I love you.'

'I can't. If you loved me you wouldn't ask. Besides, the me that you love is not a passive nobody of a wife.'

'You don't have to be a nobody to be a wife. Most women see it as quite a rigorous job.'

'Well, I don't.' She sat up and looked at him, flushed, angry. 'I couldn't.'

'No,' he said, sitting up himself, drawing away from her in the bed, 'you couldn't. That ego of yours wouldn't let you. It's yourself you're in love with, Phaedria, not me, and that great heap of hype you've built around yourself, and that's what you can't give up, not Circe, not the job. Being a star, featuring in all the glossy magazines, being sought after, interviewed on chat shows, that's what you really want, not the work, not the store at all.'

'It's not true!' she said. 'You're lying.' But she spoke without conviction.

'And even if it wasn't true, if it was just the work, if you were doing the most important job in the world, would you really sacrifice our marriage, our happiness to it? Don't you think that is something worth subjugating yourself to, Phaedria? Probably not. I'm afraid the person I fell in love with doesn't exist any more. It makes me very sad.'

'The person I fell in love with never existed,' said Phaedria bitterly.

'Oh Phaedria,' he said, and his eyes were full of pain. 'Do you really believe that?'

'Sometimes,' she said, tenderness for him rising up in spite of herself.

'And other times?'

'Other times – I suppose – he's still there.'

'So will you not do this for that person? Give up your work. You need not do nothing. We can find you something else to do.'

'And who – who would – care for it? Take it on?' she asked in a sudden reckless act of surrender.

'Oh, I don't know,' he said easily. 'It would move back under the stores umbrella, I suppose. Does it matter?'

'Yes, Julian. Yes, it does.'

'Oh well.' He sighed, reached for his watch and looked at it. It was the first sign that he was returning to real life. In a flash of temper she snatched it from him, threw it across the room; he looked at her startled and then he smiled.

'I like making you angry. It does wonderful things to you. Remember the flight in the Bugatti?'

'Of course I remember,' said Phaedria. 'I learnt a lot about you that night.'

'I suppose you did. The darker side. Well, you lost a hero and gained a car.'

'I'd have preferred to keep the hero.'

'Phaedria, we have to live in the real world. That's why I want you to give up the store. We have problems; Circe doesn't help them.'

'But –' she began and then stopped. There was no point in arguing with him. He was too skilful, too devious for her. She always ended confused, half won over.

'I suspect I have no choice. If I want to stay with you.'

He looked at her, startled. 'Is there any doubt about that?'

'It doesn't seem there is, no.'

He kissed her hand, her hair, her face; he looked into her eyes and smiled gently, tenderly, with no hint of triumph.

'I know you won't regret it.'

He fell asleep then, and Phaedria lay beside him watching the early spring sunshine playing on the walls; she felt unutterably weary, bereft, bereaved, as if someone dear to her was lost.

A memo went round the company from Phaedria a week later. She had decided (so it said) that the work of continuing to run the store was too demanding for her to reconcile with the increasing demands of her life as Lady Morell. Launching it had been challenging and rewarding, but now she was anxious to pass on the day to day running to Rosamund Emerson, in her capacity as president of the stores division. She was confident that Mrs Emerson would preserve the store in the mould she had so carefully created, and that discussion between them had revealed that Mrs Emerson had no desire to change any of her concepts substantially. A memo sent out concurrently from Mrs Emerson said that she had enormous respect and admiration for Lady Morell's work and hoped that she would continue to work with her on the store in a consultant capacity.

If Phaedria had not been so heartsore and Roz had not been so triumphant, they would both have argued a great deal with the actual author of the memos. As it was neither of them had the stomach for it.

'You don't look very well, Phaedria darling.' Julian sounded concerned, anxious. 'Why not go away for a few days?'

'I don't want to go away.'

'Why not? You have the time now. Do you feel all right?'

'Yes. No. Oh, I don't know. I suppose it might help. Where would you suggest?'

'Why not LA? You liked it there. Get a bit of sunshine.'

'All right. It does sound lovely. I have nothing else to do.'

She flew down to Los Angeles ten days later, spent three days lying by the pool, another one shopping and (unable to help herself) checking on Circe LA, and felt at least physically better. She was still wounded, still uncertain about how she should conduct this strange marriage of hers, but she felt she had at least the strength to go on trying.

Roz had been quieter, easier lately; she had scarcely seen her. It wasn't just the triumph over the store: that seemed to have done her very little good. She looked dreadful; her misery over the break-up with Michael Browning was very obvious. Phaedria was curious as to what he might be like. She wondered if she would ever meet him. He had to be a man of formidable character to love Roz, but he obviously did – or had. And she had clearly loved him, too. It was strange to think of the Roz she knew experiencing an emotion as tender, as positive as love. It didn't seem possible that her ferocious heart could contain it. But it obviously had, and now the heart had been broken. Sitting there in the sunshine, thousands of safe miles away from her, Phaedria could almost feel a pang of pity for her.

She felt a great deal more pity for C. J. He was having a very hard time; Roz was transferring all her misery, all her frustration, on to him. He could do no right: If he was away, even for a day, she demanded he come back again, if he was anywhere near her at all, she could patently not wait to get rid of him; if he agreed with her, she was contemptuous and if he disagreed she set about him like a harpy. Phaedria, who had only talked to him once on the subject, had decided that whether he realized it or not, he was merely biding his time, waiting for Fate to deliver him into a happier situation, more loving arms – after which he would be gone, she devoutly hoped, without even a pause for further thought. She would miss him, but she planned personally to help him pack.

Sitting by the pool eating her lunch the day before she was due to leave Los Angeles, Phaedria wondered what was to become of her. Was she to become one of the ladies who lunch? A bored, born-again shopper? No. Most assuredly not. She didn't really want to work for Julian in any other capacity. She felt the whole circus would start again, and she couldn't face it. Could she return to her writing? Get a job on a magazine? She couldn't see it working. It would have to be a token, a charade of a job, given to her because of who she was, something to be dropped whenever Julian snapped his fingers and demanded her attention, to be with him, entertain him, stand at his side. That was not what she understood of work. Was there some other job she could do altogether? Run an art gallery? Start a stud farm? Become some designer's patron? None of it seemed satisfying, or even real.

'God,' she said to the glass of champagne she was drinking, 'what on earth is to become of me? What have I done?'

Well, it was too late now; she had done it. She had to live with it. And with Julian. For better or worse. For the hundredth, probably the thousandth time she asked herself if she was still in love with him and for the hundredth, the thousandth time, she had to say she didn't know. She found it hard to imagine being in love with anyone at all at the moment; she lacked the emotional energy. Maybe when she had adjusted to her new life, she would start to feel again.

She had been very sobered by Julian's attack on her when he had asked her to give up the store. Even while she recognized much of it had been unjust, there was no doubt at all that she had become much in love with her own image, her own hype, her dizzy, glossy lifestyle. And it wasn't a very pretty thought. It was the ugliness of the thought, and realizing how far she had come from the direct, self-respecting person she had been, that had really persuaded her to give up the store, not Julian's declaration of love for her. If she was about to turn into the sort of person she herself would have despised, something needed to be done about it. It had taken great courage, but she had begun.

She was due home on the Thursday midday; Julian had told her he was flying up to Scotland to talk to some forestry people for forty-eight hours, but that he would be back on the Saturday. He sounded loving, conciliatory on the phone; she found herself at least looking forward to getting home to him. Maybe it would all be worth it, if they could restore their relationship to some semblance of its original pleasure and delight.

She got to LA airport mid-afternoon; about to check in on her flight, she suddenly saw a flight to New York posted, leaving in an hour. Now that would be fun. She loved New York. She could go to the apartment in Sutton Place tonight, she had the key, and then do a day's shopping and visit the Frick, which she had never yet managed. Nobody was expecting her home; feeling like a truant schoolgirl she booked on to the flight.

It was late when she got to New York; midnight with the time change. She got a cab easily; she sat back, tired, happy, excited. She could sleep late, then have a day of self-indulgent pleasure all by herself. She still loved her own company.

The apartment in Sutton Place was in darkness; the doorman half asleep; she let herself in quietly, humming 'Uptown Girl', which had been playing on the in-flight stereo, under her breath, throwing off her coat, walking through to the kitchen, fixing herself a coffee. She felt suddenly alive, good again; a free spirit; she should obviously do this more often.

What she really wanted now was to sit in bed and watch a movie on TV. That would end a perfect day. She wandered back through the hallway and down the long corridor to the big master bedroom, still humming. Suddenly she heard a noise; quiet voices, then as she moved again, a responding silence. She waited; desperate with fear; and then, in the slowest of slow motion, she watched as the double doors of the bedroom opened. Julian stood there, wearing nothing but a robe, his face white and appalled; all she could see, take in, beyond him, was a white face and a mass of red-gold hair spread across the pillows.

The only real decision was exactly where to go. She could have gone home to her father, but the complexities of trying to explain to him what had happened were so daunting that in her weak, sickened state she could not face them. She could have gone back to her friends in Bristol, but somehow that offended her sense of rightness. She had moved beyond, away from them; they would not be able to help her now. And her current circle was too new, her position in it too ephemeral to be close enough.

Letitia had been supportive, and very kind, but when all was said and done, Julian was her son, she was in her late eighties and there was a limit to the amount of hostility and conflicting emotion she could be expected to be asked to bear.

David offered to take her in, to put her up, but that seemed unfair, she would only jeopardize his position in the company; he swore he didn't mind, but it would clearly be an impossible situation for all of them. Eliza phoned, assuring her of support, sympathy, and a home for as long as she wanted it, but that too, although it appealed to her sense of humour, seemed to verge on the ridiculous and poor Peveril would find it very difficult to cope with; regretfully she turned the invitation down.

For want of anywhere else to go, she booked into Brown's Hotel while she recovered her equilibrium and wondered exactly what to do.

Clearly she couldn't stay with Julian; she had no intention of it; public humiliation was obviously a permanent possibility and she wasn't going to expose herself to it. She had no need to starve; simply selling some of her jewellery would keep a family of fourteen in considerable luxury for many months. But what was she going to do with herself? She had been robbed, in that brief shocking moment, not only of her husband, and her love (for she did love him, very much, she discovered, in the sickening physical blow of her jealousy), but her home and her lifestyle as well. And in the midst of her rage and jealousy she felt guilt and remorse as well: would Camilla ever have reclaimed Julian, had she been the better, the more devoted wife that Julian had clearly wanted? And now her days were not only empty of Julian, they were empty of purpose, interest, with not even the doubtful new pleasure of playing the devoted wife. She knew she must, in time, try to get a job of some sort, but at the moment she had no stomach for it, she felt ill as well as wretched, she could only struggle through the days.

659

Everyone tried to help her in their different ways: Letitia implored her to reconsider; Eliza told her to take Julian to hell and back; C. J. wrote her a charming letter, assuring her of his love, support and friendship and promising to do everything he could to help; Susan phoned her, oddly concerned, saying how sorry she was; even Roz sent a brief note that said she was sorry to hear what had happened. It was a considerable gesture: Phaedria wondered what on earth could have inspired it. Guilt, she supposed.

She was right.

But of course nobody could help. She felt lonely, wretched and, most of all, worst of all, she felt a fool. How could she, naïve and unsophisticated, have possibly imagined she could accomplish a successful marriage with a man forty years her senior, of almost unimaginable wealth, power and influence? It was simply arrogance, as she now perceived it, and she felt deeply ashamed; of all her wounds this would surely take longest to heal.

The other thing she had to endure was physical illness; as April turned to May she became more and more listless, lethargic, increasingly nauseated. Her back ached, she felt dizzy, she had no appetite, she was losing weight. Eventually she went to her doctor.

Victoria Jones was young, and perceptive; she saw at once what was the matter with Phaedria, wondered at her blindness and decided she should lead her to the reason herself, rather than shocking her with it in all its complexity.

'Well, obviously you aren't going to be feeling well,' she said briskly. 'You've had a terrible time. How are you sleeping?'

'I'm not.'

'Appetite?'

'Haven't got one.'

'Getting any work done?'

'I haven't got any to do,' said Phaedria and burst into tears. 'And that's another thing,' she said, sniffing into the tissue Victoria had handed her. 'I keep crying. I never cry normally. I feel just – oh, unlike myself.'

'Well, you've got plenty to cry about. Periods regular?'

'Yes. I think so.'

'When was the last one?'

'Oh – I – oh, God, I don't know. Does it matter?'

'It might be useful. Here's a calendar.'

Phaedria looked at it, absently at first, then more intently, going back over the weeks, thinking. Then she suddenly looked up at Victoria, her cheeks very flushed, her eyes bright with tears.

'February sixteenth,' she said quietly.

'Nearly three months.'

'Yes. I suppose it could be all the trauma.'

'It could.'

'But you don't think so?'

'Honestly no. Not put together with the nausea. The lassitude,' said Victoria.

'Oh, God,' said Phaedria. 'Oh, my God.'

She sat for a long time, looking out of the window, remembering when it must have been, when he returned from New York. From Camilla.

'I don't know what to do.'

'Well,' said Victoria. 'You could do several things. But I do think you ought to tell him. Even if you – well – considered termination, you ought to tell him.'

'I suppose you're right. I hate the thought, but I suppose I should.'

'Take a few days, though, get used to the idea. It may change how you feel about everything.'

Phaedria looked at her and smiled shakily. 'If you think this is going to mean the three of us can go off into the sunset together, you're quite wrong.'

'No, Lady Morell, I don't think anything of the sort. But it's still his baby. He deserves to know.'

'Yes,' said Phaedria. 'Yes, he does.'

She ignored Victoria's advice; she did not take any time.

She phoned the house; yes, Sir Julian was expected back this evening after dinner. Pete had been told to meet him from the Savoy at ten. He was dining with an old friend. I wonder what her name is, thought Phaedria. It was the nearest she had come to a humorous thought for weeks; it quite cheered her up.

'Right, well, thank you, Mrs Hamlyn. I might come back later, to get a few things.'

'Oh, Lady Morell, it will be nice to see you.'

'Thank you.'

She was sitting in the upstairs drawing room when he came in; she heard the car draw up, the door slam, his steps in the hall, then heavily, slowly coming upstairs. She tensed, then stood up and walked to the doorway.

'Hallo, Julian.'

'Phaedria!' He looked first startled, then nervously pleased. 'What on earth are you doing here?'

'I came to get some things. And I – I wanted to see you.'

'I see.' He sighed, looked at her searchingly. 'You don't look well. What is it?'

'Would you expect me to look well?' she said, suddenly angry.

'I suppose not. I'm sorry.'

'It's – it's nothing, really.'

'Would you like a drink?'

'Yes, please. Just a glass of white wine.'

'I'll get it.'

He came back with a tray, her wine, a glass of brandy for himself on it.

'Are you – managing all right?'

'Oh, yes, thank you. You'd be surprised how well I'm managing.'

'I wouldn't,' he said. 'I wouldn't at all. I have the utmost respect for your capacity to manage. I miss you,' he added, his voice very low. 'I miss you terribly.'

'Yes, I expect you do,' she said, suddenly brisk. 'Is Camilla not here to console you?'

'No,' he said, not attempting anything but the truth. 'She won't come. I think she's ashamed.'

'Ah.'

There was a silence. Phaedria drank a little of her wine. It tasted odd, made her feel sick again.

'Excuse me, I have to get some water.'

'Phaedria, what is the matter with you? There is something, isn't there? And what do you want to talk to me about?'

'Oh,' she said, suddenly unbearably full of pain, unable to even think of telling him about the baby. 'It's nothing, just a bug I've picked up. I wanted to talk to you about the – the divorce of course.'

'I see.' A silence. Then: 'Does there have to be a divorce?'

'Oh,' she said, 'oh, yes, I think there does.'

'Is there no future in my telling you how sorry I am? That I love you? That I would give anything, anything, to have you back?'

'I don't think so. I mean I do believe you, that you're sorry and you want me back, but I know it would happen again. If not with Camilla, then someone else.'

'And if I made a promise?'

'I don't think you could keep it.'

'Oh. Oh, well.' He was oddly flat, unemotional.

'I think it really is hopeless.'

He sighed. 'Maybe.'

'And it isn't all your fault either.'

'No,' he said, 'you're right. Nearly, but not all.'

'You were right about me. I did neglect you – well, our marriage. I cared too much about the store, my own life, everything. I am terribly, terribly ambitious. I didn't know I was, but you set it free, made me that way.'

'I know. I blame myself.'

'Well, I don't think you should. Not really. And then there's Roz. That could never, ever have worked.'

'No. Of all the pain I feel that is worst. That the two of you couldn't somehow have lived together, worked together.'

'You didn't help, you know.'

'I tried.'

'Now Julian,' said Phaedria, looking at him, suddenly so angry that her lassitude and sadness left her, 'that is a lie. You did not try. You made things a hundred, a thousand times worse. Why do you have to deceive yourself about it? About everything?'

'I don't think I am deceiving myself,' he said. 'I think I really tried.'

'Well in that case, you really don't know what you are saying. Or, as usual you're lying. You just cannot tell the truth, Julian, can you? You just can't. Truth is a total stranger to you.'

'You're right, I don't find it easy. But for you, because I love you, I'd like to try. Will you let me?'

'What do you mean?' she said, puzzled. 'What do you want me to do?'

'I want you to listen to me. Let me tell you about myself.'

'Well,' she said, intrigued by the notion, momentarily removed from her misery and her anger. 'Well, I think you should answer some questions, rather than just talk. That way you're less likely to get carried away. Why did you marry me?'

'Because I fell in love with you. And I found you very arousing sexually.'

'Was that all?'

'No.'

'What else?'

'It flattered my vanity, I suppose, that someone so young, so beautiful, should want to marry me.'

'Anything else?'

'I was lonely.'

'It's getting less pretty, isn't it? Is that all?'

'No,' he said, and she could see the struggle he was having, to fight through to the truth. 'I rather liked the idea of the to-do it would cause.'

Phaedria looked at him, her eyes first cool, then suddenly filled with amusement. She smiled at him for the first time. 'I like this game.'

'I'm not sure if I do. Can I sit down beside you?'

'No. Stay over there. I need to see your face.'

'This really is an inquisition, isn't it?'

'It was your idea. OK. Now then, did you really not think there would be a problem with Roz?'

'I really didn't.'

'Are you sure?'

'Yes. I'm quite sure,' he said after a moment's thought. 'I had no idea she felt so strongly about me. Or rather the company, and her place in it.'

'We'll come back to that one. Did you find being married to me as you'd expected?'

'No.'

'How?'

'You were much more difficult.'

'Good.' She drained her glass; she felt pleasantly dizzy, and strangely powerful. She had forgotten about the baby, about why she was here; this was the most fascinating conversation of her entire life.

'Did you – did you sleep with anyone else, apart from Camilla?'

'No.'

'Really no?'

'Really no.'

'What about Regency?'

'No. I didn't sleep with her. She – she didn't want to know,' he added painfully, dragging the words out.'

'Julian,' she said, and she had to pour another glass of wine, drink half of it before she could face her own question, even, quite apart from the answer, 'what is it about Camilla? Why do you go back to her again and again? Do you love her? Or is it just sex?'

He was silent for a long time, not evading the question, just thinking. Then he sighed and said, 'I suppose, in an odd way, I do love her.'

'Oh,' she said, and it was like a cry of pain, of fright, in the big room.

'No,' he said, moving towards her, holding out his arms. 'No, you don't understand. Don't look like that, darling, please don't. Come here.'

'No,' she said, staring at him, her eyes hard behind her tears. 'I won't. Don't touch me. Don't come near me.'

'All right. But may I go on?'

'I suppose you have to.'

'I do love her. She isn't just an easy lay, as she once told me she refused to be. I'm terribly fond of her. She's very loyal to me, she's very fond of me, she's often picked me up when I've been down. I've known her for a very long time, and we've worked together for a very long time, and she means a great deal to me. And – well, I need her. I need her sexually. She – oh Phaedria, I can't go on with this. Can't we leave the question of Camilla?'

'No,' she said, 'of course not. We can't. Tell me, Julian, tell me what it is. Why do you need her? What does she do for you? I have to know, I have to.'

'All right,' he said, with a heavy sigh, 'I'll tell you. I don't know what good it will do, but I'll tell you. At various stages in my life, when I have been under very heavy pressure of one kind or another, I – I have become impotent. When I feel threatened. Textbook stuff, I suppose. Camilla,' he added with his lips twitching, 'is very strong on textbook stuff.'

'So you mean she cures you? Helps you get it up? My God.'

'Phaedria, don't sound so crude.'

'I feel crude,' she said quietly. 'It's disgusting. I'm your wife, Julian, or I was. Surely if you had a sexual problem, you could have turned to me. Was that why – why you didn't sleep with me all those weeks?'

'Of course. I didn't dare try. I was under such strain, with the failure of Lifestyle, the situation with you and Roz, your own success, all those ridiculous stories about you in the papers. Of course I didn't believe them, but they hurt just the same. I was so afraid.'

'But why, why didn't you tell me?'

'I couldn't. I really couldn't. Don't ask me why not. It's too complex.'

'So you turned to Camilla?'

'Yes.'

'And lied?'

'Yes.'

She looked at him, a wealth of pain in her eyes. 'Why didn't you try being truthful? Talking to me. Not going to her. Aren't I worth it?'

'You are. Yes. Infinitely.'

'I still can't understand you going to her. When you're supposed to love me.'

'I do love you.'

'You can't. You simply can't.'

'I do. Do you love me?'

She was taken aback by the suddenness of the change of direction.

'Yes. Yes I think I do.'

'Did you sleep with Sassoon?'

'No. No I didn't.'

'Did you want to?' The questions were coming faster, harder; he was flushed himself now, breathing heavily.

666

'No. Not at all. Why were you so jealous of him?'

'I don't know.'

'That's not the truth.'

'Because Eliza loved him.'

'Do you still love Eliza?'

'Yes,' he said suddenly, looking at her in astonishment. 'Yes, I think I do. I didn't love her when I was married to her, but I have loved her greatly since. And I always will. She has a hold on my heart,' he added, 'as you do.'

'I seem to be sharing your heart with quite a few people. Anyone else while we're on the subject?'

'No,' he said, quietly. 'No, not now.'

There was a silence. Then: 'Why did you marry me, Phaedria?'

'I wanted to.'

'Is that all?'

'Yes.'

'Why, though?'

'I thought you were clever. Interesting. I just – loved you. You made me feel safe.' She finished her wine. 'That's ironic, isn't it?'

'I'm afraid so.' He looked at her piercingly, suddenly. 'Phaedria, why have you come here? Tonight? So late. There is a reason, isn't there? It's not just a desire to talk, to discuss the formalities of a divorce. The lawyers can do that. There's something else. Please tell me.'

She was taken aback, thrown off her guard by the switch from past to present. She stood up. 'No. There was something, but I've changed my mind, I don't want to tell you. Not now. I'm going. I'm sorry, Julian, I really did love you, maybe I still do, in a way, but I can't live with you. You're better on your own, and so am I.'

'Well,' he said with a sigh, 'perhaps you're right. I love you too. Very much. How ridiculous this is.'

'Yes,' she said, suddenly, for some inexplicable reason, light-hearted, 'it is quite ridiculous. I shall miss you dreadfully, horribly.' And she smiled at him, suddenly, a warm, friendly, loving smile. 'Perhaps we can be friends. Loving friends.'

'Ah,' he said, catching her mood. 'That would be nice. But how loving, I wonder? And what kind of love?' And he looked at her, his eyes dancing, and as he looked Phaedria suddenly felt herself physically assaulted by a bolt of desire. It filled her, it consumed her, it was like a great, fierce fever, and she looked back at him, startled, helpless with it.

'Come here,' he said lightly, 'let me kiss you good night. But not, please not, goodbye.'

And she moved towards him, her eyes still fixed on his, wondering that he could not see, feel how she felt. Perhaps, perhaps, if she could only get out of the room, the house now, quickly, she would be safe, and he would never need to know; she raised her face to his, thinking in one moment, one moment, it will be all right, it will be over, but he touched her and it was like a charge; she shuddered, looked up at him, into his eyes, and she saw at once that he had known, had felt it too. She moved into his arms, drew his head down towards her.

'You bastard,' she said, 'you make me so angry,' and very gently, very slowly, she began to kiss him.

'I love you,' he said, 'I love you so much. Please say you love me too.'

'I do,' she said, 'you know I do.'

'Come along,' he said, 'come along to bed.' And unprotesting, childlike, she took his hand and followed him, and all the way upstairs he talked to her, endlessly, telling her he loved her, he wanted her, he had missed her, and she listened, enchanted, caught once more, helplessly, in the spell of sensuality with which he had first ensnared her; she lay on their bed, and looked at him, her eyes never leaving his as he undressed her, stroking, kissing, sucking each of the places he knew most aroused her, her neck, the hollow of her throat, her shoulders, her breasts: lingering there, feeling the leaping, quivering response, and then urgent suddenly, he was tearing off his own clothes, telling her over and over again how he wanted her, how he loved her, and then, swiftly, unable to wait any longer, he was in her, and she felt him grow, seek, yearn for release, and it came so suddenly, so fiercely, they cried out together, and then he was lying, looking at her, with tears in his eyes, and for the first time since she had known him, she felt he was vulnerable and that she was safe.

'I love you,' he said. 'Don't ever leave me. Tomorrow we will begin again.'

'I don't know,' she said. 'Perhaps we can. I love you too. But I still don't quite know.'

'You will,' he said. 'You will. Promise me you will.'

'I can't promise you,' she said. 'Not yet.' But she fell asleep, sweetly and untroubled.

In the morning she felt extremely ill. She slithered out of bed and into the bathroom; she was sick over and over again. It must have been the wine, she thought, she had not felt so bad before; she should not have drunk it; she would give it up at once. She stood up and looked at herself in the long mirror, so slender, so small breasted, and reflected upon the secret within her body, and how it would change it, how the breasts would become veined and heavy, and the flat stomach swollen and ripe. She remembered with a gentle shock that she had still not told Julian, that he had no idea what they had accomplished, and she smiled at the pleasure it would give him, and the promise it brought to their life. She washed her face, brushed her hair, and walked back into the bedroom, into the sunlight, where he lay still asleep, to wake him and tell him.

'Julian,' she said, bending over, kissing his cheek, his hair, 'Julian, wake up. I have something lovely to tell you.'

He turned, still half asleep, and looked at her and she was to remember that look for the rest of her life: first love, then pain, then panic; and then he cried out, hideously loud, and she said, 'What, what is it?' but he couldn't speak, he was beyond it, he tried, but it was quite quite impossible.

Julian fought death for days. He lay in intensive care, after not one but three massive coronaries, battling against it, pushing it away. Phaedria sat with him, watching him drowning in it, sinking, gasping, surfacing, seeing him afraid, and more than afraid, frantic, trying to speak to her, impotent, helpless.

'He's trying to tell me something,' she kept saying to the doctors, 'he's trying to talk to me, he's desperate, can't you see, how can I help him, can't you do something?'

And no, they said, really there was nothing, he was beyond speech, it often happened, people did appear to be desperate to talk and usually it was nothing important, they had nothing to say, not really, there was nothing to worry about, she was doing all that could be done, just being there, calming him. But she knew she was doing nothing of the sort.

She felt afraid herself, contaminated by his fear; she talked to him endlessly, she told him she loved him, she told him about the baby, she tried to calm him, to give him courage, hope, faith. And all the time, his eyes looked at her in a deep despair.

He died, looking at her still, his hand in hers, her gaze locked in his. And afterwards, as she gazed down at the still, sterile shell that he had suddenly become, all the charm, the grace, the tenderness shockingly gone, she realized with a piercing sense of grief and shock that she had hardly known him at all.

Chapter Nineteen

London and Sussex, 1985

Women are not asked to bear any pain greater than that of losing a child; Letitia had been asked to bear it twice already and she was not sure that she could stand it again. She lay in her brass-headed bed in First Street and felt she would never sleep again; she could not cry, she would not cry, she was afraid of tears, of the sweeping wave of pain that they released. She was fighting to hold back that wave, to control it, she knew if it came she would sink, drown in it. In a few days perhaps, she would be able to manage it; for now, dry-eyed, breathing a little heavily with what felt like a physical effort, she lay and held it at bay.

She was helped in her struggle by her thoughts of the rest of the family; of Phaedria, widowed before she had begun properly to know what marriage was, and with the added pain of a pregnancy to endure alone. Letitia had no doubt that she would come through; she was tough, and she was brave, but that did not diminish her grief and her misery. And there was grief; Letitia was almost relieved to see that grief. She had always felt that Phaedria had loved Julian, that she had married him for that reason, not for the money, the power, the fairy-tale transformation scene he could work upon her life, but she had been alone in her judgement at the beginning and had sometimes over the past two years begun to doubt it. Whether or not the marriage had been a success she had no real idea; the last few weeks of it had been very sad. She had, at least, been with him when he died, when he had been taken ill; there must have been a reconciliation of some kind. But it had clearly been brief; when Letitia, summoning a strength from she knew not where, had gone to visit Phaedria at the house the night after Julian died, all she had said over and over again, her voice cracked with pain was, 'I didn't tell him, Letitia, he didn't know. I didn't tell him, he didn't know.'

She had thought at first that Phaedria had meant she hadn't told Julian she loved him, but later when she had tried to give her a brandy, a sleeping pill, anything to calm her, she had said no, no, the least, the very least she could do was take care of her baby, of Julian's baby, and Letitia had looked at her shocked and still with pity and wept with her for a long time.

And then there was Roz. Roz had reacted strangely: angrily, fiercely, when she was first told the news that Julian was in intensive care and not expected to live. C. J. had broken it to her, and then phoned Letitia in despair, saying Roz was raging, screaming, blaming Phaedria, saying it would never have happened had she not married Julian, saying she should be there with him, not Phaedria, and then, when Phaedria had said of course she should come, should see him, should say goodbye to him, had said, icy cold, 'I do not intend to share him with her now.'

She had stood throughout the funeral stony-faced; she had not wept at all, until the moment when she tossed a small bunch of white roses on to the coffin as it went into the ground. Then she turned swiftly and ran, sobbing as she went, into the trees at the back of the graveyard, and would not come out, would not speak to anyone until the last car had left, insisting that everyone, her mother, her husband, her grandmother should go and leave her alone, and then she walked, slowly, heavily, an almost ghostly figure towards her own car and drove very fast away.

The funeral had been in Sussex, in the small church where Julian and Phaedria had been married; there had been hundreds of people there: from the village, from London, from all over the world they had come, his staff, his colleagues, his rivals, his friends. And of course his family.

Phaedria had kept the service very simple; the only dramatic gesture she made was when she placed some keys in the grave, on top of the coffin, nestling in her own flowers, white lilies, with a card that said simply 'From Phaedria, with my special love.'

'The keys of the Bugatti,' she explained to Letitia with a half smile at the house later. 'It was a very special present to me and I wanted to give it back to him. No one will ever drive it now.'

She had asked Letitia not to say anything about the baby: 'I can't bear to talk about it yet. I can't bear to be happy about anything. Can you understand that?'

'I can,' said Letitia, 'of course I can. I won't tell anybody at all. You must do it when you are ready. It is your baby and your secret.' She looked at Phaedria and smiled gently. 'I am a very good keeper of secrets, Phaedria. As one day you will learn.'

She herself had wept at the funeral; not at the graveside, but in the church. She had stood very erect, her face composed behind her black veil, but when the congregation was asked to sing the Twenty-Third Psalm, on the words 'He makes me down to lie' she had suddenly sunk to her knees and buried her face in her hands. Phaedria, who was on one side of her, and C. J. on the other, had knelt beside her, their arms round her, but she had gently pushed them away, and stayed there, very still, until the psalm was over, and then stood up again, quite calm but with the tears still wet on her face, remembering with a dreadful vividness the small boy who had pinned his party invitations on his wall and ridden his pony with style and grace and the young man who had taken her to live with him in the little house in First Street and taken her about London with him as if she was a pretty young girl.

Afterwards at the house she talked to Susan, who was looking dreadful, white and drawn. 'I feel so bad, Letitia, I loved him so much, and he never knew.'

'Oh, much better he didn't,' said Letitia briskly, with a touch of a smile. 'He would only have tried to seduce you again if he had. You were much more value to him as a friend, and to Phaedria too.'

'I'm afraid I was no value to her at all,' said Susan, looking at

Phaedria who was standing and struggling to talk to a large crowd of people. 'I was so much on Roz's side, and of course I still am, somebody has to be, but I think I was wrong about her, she seems genuinely wretched, and I feel bad about that too.'

'Oh, but she didn't know,' said Letitia. 'She always said how nice you were. Although you frightened her. As you do all of us,' she added with another half smile. 'Susan, I think I will go upstairs now and lie down, I'm feeling very tired. Come up and see me later.'

Susan watched her walk out of the room, slowly, very erect, and thought she had never seen courage so simply displayed.

Eliza was very upset too; white and shaken, leaning on Peveril's arm, very quiet, only speaking when someone asked her a question. David Sassoon, standing apart from the crowd, looking out for Roz's car, wondering where she had gone and what he could do to help, looked at Eliza thoughtfully. She had obviously felt a great deal for the old bastard, probably without realizing it, for all her protestations of dislike and bitterness; he wondered whether Julian had ever realized it, and how he had really felt about her.

Roz had never returned to Marriotts that day; she had driven back to London and locked herself in her bedroom in the house at Cheyne Walk, only to emerge the following morning, dry-eyed, perfectly dressed, and thrown a tantrum because her driver was not available to take her to the office, being rather fully occupied ferrying the funeral guests to the airport. From then she had acted perfectly normally; someone, she said, had to keep the company going, and it looked as if it was going to be her. If anyone had proffered sympathy she had given them a terse nod, otherwise she had not mentioned her father's death at all.

Until the reading of the will. That had taken place two weeks after the funeral; it drew the family together in a white heat of emotion and tension, and then tossed them apart again as if they were so many rag dolls.

Remembering the events of that day: of Camilla, arrived so bravely to confront them, summoned by Julian from wherever he might now be, of Roz, so powerfully, fearsomely angry and hurt, of Phaedria, so freshly wounded, so suddenly frail, her quiet secret suddenly, harshly public, half comfort, half added

673

burden fragmented into noise and rage, Letitia wondered with a mixture of horror and fascination at the cruelty of her son. In a way she was almost glad; it eased her grief, gave her something else to focus on, and besides being angry with him, being ashamed of him was oddly healing.

And so she lay pushing her sorrow away; refused to cry; worried instead about Roz and what was to happen to her now, without her father, the only real love of her life, the reason for everything she did; and about Phaedria and how she was going to cope with the new, shocking piece of treachery that was Miles, and wondering, as they all were, who and where Miles Wilburn was, and what he could possibly mean to Julian that he should inflict such pain and trauma on his family.

A few days later she felt a little better; she invited Susan to supper, weary of her own thoughts, anxious to share them and to discuss the situation with her.

'If Julian were to walk in now,' she said to her, 'I would be so angry with him I don't quite know what I might do.'

'I wish he would,' said Susan, smiling at her, encouraged by her return to her old spiritedness, 'then we could grill him about Miles Wilburn and make him tell us who he is. Oh God, Letitia, trust Julian to manipulate people even when he's dead. How could he do it? To us all, but to Roz and Phaedria in particular. When he was supposed to love them so much and find their feud so distressing.'

'Well, he did little to ease it,' said Letitia briskly. 'Poor things. I really don't know which of them I feel more sorry for.'

'Oh, I do,' said Susan. 'Roz of course. Without a doubt. Phaedria never expected to get the company. Roz has spent her entire life waiting, and hoping for it. Now she has to battle it out not only with the woman she hates most in the world, but with some unknown man who her father obviously had a lot of time for. It's terribly hard.'

'I suppose so,' said Letitia. 'But it must be very hurtful for Phaedria too. She was his wife, she could have been supposed to know everything about him. This is a very public slap in the face for her. Good God, Susan, whatever could have possessed him to do it?'

'Whatever it was that possessed him to do most things,' said

Susan. 'Oh, Letitia, don't look like that. I know what you're thinking, that it was your fault. It wasn't, Letitia, it really wasn't. Please stop blaming yourself about it.'

Letitia sighed. 'I can't help it, Susan. I feel to blame.'

'Well, you're very silly. Very very silly. And I'm sure there's a perfectly reasonable explanation for all this.'

'It's going to be extremely exciting, it must be said,' said Letitia. 'Julian has certainly managed to make the last act of his life a very high drama. Poor Henry Winterbourne will never be the same again. I really found it very difficult not to laugh, when he was trying to look as if what was going on was perfectly normal legal procedure. But anyway, not only does Miles have to be found, but either Roz or Phaedria has to win him over. I hope he's a strong character. For all our sakes.'

'So do I. Now tell me, Letitia, in your capacity as family sage, who do you think might win that battle? If it ever gets fought?'

'In my position as family sage,' said Letitia very slowly, with an odd rather mysterious little smile, 'I think I'd put my money on Phaedria.'

Chapter Twenty

London, 1985

Phaedria Morell was not behaving quite as a widow should. Well, not a grieving widow, at any rate, as Henry Winterbourne, amused and slightly shocked, remarked to his wife Caroline the day after the will had been read.

He – all of them – had expected a long period of mourning, of grief, a tacit withdrawal from the battleground that Julian had so unequivocally created. Especially in the light of her pregnancy – which she had confirmed to Henry with a cool, even amused look as he inquired after her health: 'I am indeed, as some of you, I imagine, must have guessed, going to have a baby.'

Nobody had thought they would see very much of her at all for weeks – had assumed she would stay at home, safe from conflict, from attention, from all the attendant scandal and surmise that the will would surely create – nurturing herself and her child, and coming to terms with her loss.

But at ten o'clock the next morning, there she was in Henry's office, a little pale to be sure, but beautifully dressed in a stinging pink wool crepe dress, her hair caught back with the seed pearl and coral combs Julian had had made for her as a souvenir of their honeymoon, and a pair of very high-heeled, pink suede shoes that Henry could only categorize to himself as flighty.

She had her briefcase with her, and she had sat down in the big chair opposite Henry's desk, looked at him with an expression that was cheerful and determined in equal measures, and told him that there was a great deal of talking to be got through and work to be done.

'I want to find this person, Henry, this Miles Wilburn, and I want to find him quickly. The situation until we do will clearly be intolerable. In fact I would go so far as to say,' she added, with the hint of a smile and of conspiracy in her eyes, 'I am anxious to find him before – well, shall we say before anyone else does.'

He returned her look steadily. 'I do understand exactly what you are saying, Phaedria. Unfortunately, much as I would like to help you, I don't think I can enter into any kind of an exclusive search on your behalf. I am the Morell family's solicitor and have been for many years. It would be extremely difficult, unethical even, for me to report solely to you.'

'Oh, of course,' said Phaedria, 'I understand that, Henry; I merely thought that if you could begin to instigate some searches, and report to us all, naturally, on those, you might be able to suggest someone who could work with me a little later on. I know how busy you are, and I wouldn't dream of making too many demands on your time. Of course confidentiality is essential; we can not, simply cannot, have this thing made public. And it is a pressing matter, as you must agree; there is a large and complex company to run, and trying to do so will be virtually impossible while Roz and I have these absolutely equal shares in it. We don't always see completely eye to eye, as you may have heard.'

'Well, yes, I had heard some reports to that effect,' said

Henry, smiling his charmingly benign smile at her, 'and I can see there would be considerable difficulties. But – well, forgive me, Phaedria, for being so frank – are you actually planning to become involved in the company and its day to day administration straight away?'

'I am,' she said, coolly, opening her briefcase. 'Absolutely straight away. I have a meeting with Freddy Branksome and Richard Brookes this afternoon. There is clearly a great deal I need to learn and know, and the sooner I begin the better. Now I can see all the thoughts racing through your head, Henry, and let me put them into nice neat order for you. First of all, I have no intention of sitting in the house in Regent's Park in widow's weeds and grieving over Julian's death for weeks, months on end. He was the most remarkable man, which was probably the main reason I loved and married him, and I intend to show my appreciation and my respect for that by keeping the company running as successfully and dynamically as it did when he was alive. Of course I won't succeed altogether, but I am going to have a very good try. That also of course pre-empts any notion anyone might have had that I was going to spend the next six months or so knitting layettes and kitting out a nursery. This baby is going to be part of the Morell empire from day one, and if that means I have to give birth in the boardroom, then I will. I also – and this is in the strictest confidence, Henry, and you can forget I said it, if it makes you uncomfortable – I also intend to get a proper control over the company; it's the only way I'm going to be able to work. Which means, of course, finding Mr Wilburn and enlisting his support. Quickly. Which is where you came in. Does that make my position clearer? I hope so, it's important.'

'It does,' said Henry, 'and I am filled with admiration for you. Although not envy.'

'Oh, I don't know,' said Phaedria briskly. 'I think it's nice that I've got so much to do, and think about. Nothing like a bit of adrenaline surging through the system to keep one going.'

Henry looked at her concernedly. 'Phaedria, as a friend, rather than a lawyer, don't take on too much. You really don't look very well. Do you feel all right?'

'No, I feel dreadful,' said Phaedria cheerfully. 'I feel terrible in the morning and worse still in the afternoon. As for the

677

evenings, well, they don't bear thinking about. But I don't think that's going to improve with sitting about and moping either. Do you? What did Caroline do when she was pregnant?'

'As little as possible,' said Henry. 'And loved every minute of it. I think that's why we have five children.'

Phaedria smiled. 'Well, I don't expect I shall have more than one. So I'll just have to get it right first time round.'

'Yes,' he said, the poignancy of her situation suddenly and sharply brought home to him. 'Yes, and I'm sure you will.'

She sighed. 'I hope so. Anyway, until you can find me some private detective or something who can help me, let's make a start now. What ideas do you have?'

'Well, obviously we can – indeed have to – run searches. We are obliged to do that by law. In *The Times* and so on, and also of course in the *Law Society Gazette*. We can advertise. That will of course provide us with several Miles Wilburns, I would have thought, all claiming to be the true Christ, so to speak. But the trouble is we don't know what we're looking for. He might be old, or young, presentable or otherwise, he might live almost anywhere in the English-speaking world, we don't know if he's stupid or clever, honest or dishonest, black or white.'

'I think,' said Phaedria thoughtfully, 'he's unlikely to be stupid, at any rate. Julian wouldn't leave the controlling share of his precious company to a moron. Quite presentable, I should think, for the same reason. I mean not sleeping under the arches, or on the beach. And I imagine he'd be fairly young. Otherwise his role in this charade would be pretty short lived. I guess he'll be at least what my editor used to call working honest – honest enough, that means. But I agree after that we're really in the dark. I suppose he's most likely to be living either here or in the States. Wilburn sounds a bit more of an American name. 'Can we advertise these as well, and in the other countries where we have sizeable interests and assets? You'll have to advise me. Oh Henry, what an extraordinary thing it is. Tell me something, there can be no doubt I presume as to the legality of the will?'

'Oh none at all.' said Henry, 'Witnessed by perfectly bona fide people, no one we know, but nonetheless genuine. Signed, dated last December. He didn't use me to draw it up, as you know. He may even have done it himself. My first sight of it was when you sent it over. One of the oddest things of course was this insistence on it being read publicly. Specifying that all the beneficiaries had to be there. It's extremely unusual these days. I really cannot understand it.'

'Oh well,' said Phaedria, 'he always did have a great sense of theatre.'

She sighed and was silent for a moment, her eyes shadowy and distant. He was silent, realizing the pain and the humiliation the whole thing must be causing her, not knowing how to comfort her.

'Well,' she said, briskly, hauling herself back to the present and the room with obvious effort. 'Perhaps the first thing is to try to find out who did draw it up for him. Maybe nobody did. Maybe he did it himself.'

'He might have done. But it's been typed. I don't think he could do that.'

'Oh,' said Phaedria with a smile. 'There is absolutely no knowing what Julian could and couldn't do. I'm quite serious. Letitia might know. I'll ask her.'

'How is she coping with all this? She looked very fragile yesterday, I thought.'

'Yes, these few weeks have been the first time I've seen her looking anything like her proper age. She didn't have to come, of course, but she said wild horses wouldn't have kept her away. I hope I'm even half as splendid at eighty-seven.'

'Oh, I think you will be,' said Henry. 'In fact I have absolutely no doubt about it whatsoever.'

'Thank you. I need lots of that, Henry, lots of flattery.'

'Then,' he said, 'I shall take you out to lunch at least once a week and flatter you solidly for two hours. How's that?'

'Oh,' she said, smiling, 'I don't think I shall be able to spare quite that much time, but certainly a little on a regular basis would be very welcome.'

'The witnesses don't help at all, either. Nobody we've ever heard of. Mary Unwin and David Potter, indeed. Sounds as if he made them up.'

'He probably did,' said Phaedria, laughing, 'which would make the whole thing null and void, I suppose?'

'Yes, it would. But that wouldn't help you at all, would it?'

'Not really, no. Is it worth trying to track them down, though?

They might at least be able to tell us when they signed the bloody thing.'

'Oh, I think so, yes,' said Henry, 'it would be enormously helpful. I will give that some thought, Phaedria, but the more I look at this whole thing, the more I think you need a private detective agency working for you. A really good one. I'll make a few preliminary inquiries, and you can get things rolling straight away.'

'Yes,' said Phaedria, 'that would be very helpful. Thank you. Although I have a nasty feeling that at least one of the really good ones may already be in the employ of Mrs Emerson.'

'I want this person found,' said Roz, fixing Andrew Blackworth with a steely gaze, 'and I want him found quickly.'

Andrew Blackworth was not too much as she had imagined; he was not sleek and sharp looking, he was about forty-five years old, short, rotund, and rather learned-seeming. She liked everything about him.

'We have a long way to travel,' he said, 'perhaps literally.'

'Yes,' she said abandoning reluctantly her vision of finding and coercing Miles Wilburn on to her side within the space of seven days, 'yes, I suppose so. But then again, given some luck, we might do better.'

'We might indeed. And of course, in working with us you have considerable skills working for you as well as luck. Skills and contacts. Are you prepared to put your trust in those?'

'Yes,' said Roz, 'yes, I think so. Yes, I am.'

'Good. Now then, in order to utilize them, I need all the information you can possibly give me.'

'You're welcome to it. But there really isn't any. None at all.'

'Could I talk to the widow?'

'No,' said Roz. It was a flat, final sound; it brooked no further discussion.

'Right. Well, could I ask you a few questions?'

'Of course.'

'You are quite quite sure you have never heard your father mention this name?'

'Well of course, he may have done. I can't remember every name that ever passed his lips. But in the context of someone to whom he was going to leave what amounts to the controlling share in his company, someone he knew well and presumably trusted, no.'

'Right. And you have no idea when the will was made?'

'None. Other than clearly it was since his marriage to Miss Blenheim.'

Blackworth's lips twitched at the interesting demotion of Lady Morell to her unmarried state.

'Which was June of 1983?'

'Yes.'

'Can I have a copy of the will?'

'Yes. I'll ask the solicitor today.'

'And he did not draw it up?'

'No. He says he knew nothing about it until it was delivered into his hands by – by the widow.'

'Interesting, that. Not to leave it in the keeping of his solicitor.'

'Yes, well, my father was an interesting man.' She sounded sad; he looked at her sharply. He was a kind and discerning person; he felt sure that beneath the hardness, the carefully cultivated tough talk, was someone very different.

'Is there anyone else in the family who might be able to help me?'

'Well, I daresay there might be, but they won't want to talk. His mother might know something of this person, but she was quite sure yesterday that she didn't. Same goes for his first wife. Then there are the mistresses. More of them. You might get something there, if you sifted through them. It might take a year or two.'

He looked at her in amusement.

'I understood we did not have a year or two. Is there any particular friend, associate, who might be able to help? Someone who has known him, let us say, for a considerable time?'

'Well, you could try. They might not want to talk. There's Mrs Susan Brookes, she is just about his oldest friend. Most assuredly not his mistress though,' she added with a warning look in her eyes. 'I can give you her address, she lives in London.'

'I shall certainly talk to her if you think she will agree.'

'Oh, she certainly will. And then there's Camilla North. She certainly won't want to talk if she knows you're acting for me.'

'I see. Where is Miss – Ms North?'

'Miss,' said Roz ferociously. 'Back in New York as from today, but again, I can give you her address.'

'Excellent. Now where did your father spend most of his time?'

'Well, here latterly. In New York a great deal in the sixties and seventies. He had a home there. He also had business interests in many European cities and of course in places like Tokyo, Sydney, other American cities and states.'

'I think we should look initially more intensely at places where he had homes. Which are?'

'Well, apart from London and New York and a house in Sussex, of course, there's a place near Nice and a flat in Sydney, and a house on one of the Bahamian islands, Eleuthera.'

'I see. What a fortunate man he was.'

'Yes and no,' said Roz with a sigh. 'I don't think he was really very successful with human relationships.'

'Few rich and powerful men are,' said Andrew Blackworth gravely. 'Now if you can get me a copy of the will, Mrs Emerson, I will begin instigating inquiries immediately. And I think we should find ourselves getting somewhere fairly fast.'

'Thank you Mr Blackworth. I certainly hope so.' She stood up, looking at him, a touch of humour in her face. 'What about rich and powerful women? Any better?'

'Oh, I'm afraid not,' he said, 'in my experience, infinitely worse.'

Phaedria was sitting at the huge desk that had been Julian's, a neat pile of papers and files at her left elbow, a large foolscap pad in front of her, which she was covering rapidly with notes. Richard Brookes and Freddy Branksome, who had both been expecting to spend most of the afternoon humouring her and dispensing sympathy, were slightly disconcerted by the turn events were taking.

'What I'd like,' she said, looking at them composedly, 'is a complete breakdown of the structure of the company, the relative value of its different components, its assets, its liabilities, and perhaps, from both of you, an assessment of its strengths and weaknesses. Nothing too technical –' she smiled briefly – 'but a kind of gut reaction, with obviously facts and figures to support it, where necessary. For instance, I have a hunch, just a hunch, that the hotels are not really making us a great deal of money. And are costing us dear in terms of personnel, hassle, and investment generally. On the other hand, they obviously provide a high-profile visible asset. I'm also not really very sure about this new communications company. I imagine that's an investment in the future, satellite TV and so on. Could you clarifiy that a little for me please?' She looked at them both and smiled. 'I must seem very ignorant, foolish even. But I am desperately anxious to familiarize myself with this company, and assess what my future role might be. I want to keep it running successfully. For Julian's sake.'

'Of course,' said Richard, 'and we will do everything in our power to assist you. Won't we, Freddy?'

'Absolutely,' said Freddy, 'everything. But, Lady Morell, there is one thing – oh, it's a little delicate, but it has to be broached –'

'Oh,' she said, 'I know what you mean. Roz Emerson. She has at the moment an equal share in the company, equal say in its future, equal power. I understand and appreciate that. Clearly she and I will have to establish a modus operandi. But she has the advantage of me at the moment in knowing rather more about it than I do. Of its structure and so on. She's worked in it for years. I've only been involved for a very short time.'

'Right,' said Freddy uncertainly. 'Er – right. But will you – that is –' His round red face was perspiring, his bright blue eyes were anxious.

Richard looked at him and smiled, then turned to Phaedria, stretching his long legs out in front of him, looking at her with frank appreciation and a certain degree of wariness at the same time. She was going to take some dealing with, this lady. Lucky old sod, Julian had been; how had he done it? And how could he have perpetrated an act of such wanton cruelty on her as he had done with that will? And on his daughter, for that matter. She might be a tough nut (although Susan was extremely fond of her and always claiming that she was not in the least as she seemed), but he suspected in any case that Phaedria Morell could and would match her, blow for blow. God in Heaven, what a bloody mess.

'What my learned friend is trying to say, Lady Morell,' he said, with his careful, lazy smile, 'is that we will need to know quite how you intend to work here. How involved you plan to be. How often you will be in the office. Where. That kind of thing. We have to work with both of you, you see, and we have to be – well, tactful, to put it mildly. Indeed we are statutorily obliged, I would say, to deal with both of you on all matters of policy, finance, the whole damn thing, as the current saying goes.'

'Of course,' said Phaedria, 'I understand. I am not trying to coerce either of you into anything. I give you my word that after today there will be no meetings at board level that will not involve Mrs Emerson as well as myself. I will copy her in on everything, as I would expect her to do me. As to your question about how often I intend to be here, the answer is all the time, every day. Possibly including the weekends. After all,' she said, flicking a brief glance down her own body, meeting their eyes with frank amusement, 'I cannot ride or hunt for the next few months, I may as well work. And I shall base myself here, in this office. Someone has to use it.'

'Really?' It was Roz's voice; she was standing in the open doorway. 'I don't quite see that, Phaedria. Nobody *has* to use it. It can be locked up. It was my father's office and you have no more claim on it than I do. We are absolutely equal partners in this company at present, and I fail to see why you should make assumptions, and indeed implications by taking your place at his desk.'

Phaedria looked at Roz; she was quite white, her green eyes blazing. She was dressed in black, and looked fierce, dramatic, almost frightening. Richard and Freddy shifted awkwardly in their chairs. There was a long silence; then Phaedria spoke.

'Freddy, Richard, perhaps you would leave us for now. We have matters of policy to sort out, as you were saying earlier. We can continue this meeting tomorrow morning if you're free. Any time – to suit you.'

'Fine,' said Freddy, gathering up his files. 'We'll sort out something between us.'

'Absolutely,' said Richard, rising to his full, gangling height, 'and as you were saying, Lady Morell, it is essential that both you and Mrs Emerson should be present at all major meetings in future.'

It was a graceful, diplomatic remark; Phaedria gave him a grateful look.

'Indeed. So shall we fix a time now?'

'I'm afraid,' said Roz, tapping lightly on the desk, where she had sat down, in a clear piece of territorial reclamation, 'I shall be out of the office tomorrow. All day. This meeting, whatever it's about, will have to wait.'

'As you wish,' said Richard, bowing to her ever so slightly. 'We are at your service, Mr Branksome and I. Are we not, Freddy?'

'Oh, we are, we are indeed,' said Freddy, hastily leading the way to the door. 'Good afternoon, Lady Morell, Mrs Emerson.'

The door closed behind them; Phaedria faced Roz, her eyes contemptuous. 'Roz, whatever you may feel about me – and I can hazard a very clear guess – we do have to work together and I see no future whatever in holding public brawls. Please can't we confine any emotional discussions to occasions when we are on our own?'

'My God,' said Roz, 'my God, Phaedria, you have a lot of gall. You've known my father just over two years, and yet you've inveigled your way into his company, and now within days of his death you're trying to step into his shoes. You have no right to sit at this desk, in this office, no right at all, nor to hold meetings with the executives of his company in it; the only rights you have here are mine as well, and I intend to see I don't lose any of them.'

Phaedria looked at her in silence for a while. Then she stood and picked up her files, her notes, her briefcase. 'You're absolutely right, Roz,' she said finally, 'and I'm sorry. I was making assumptions which were quite wrong. Either we should share this office, which frankly I don't see working, or I should have one of my own. This one, as you say, can be locked up. For the time being. One of us can move into it in the fullness of time.'

Roz stared at her. 'I'm sorry, I don't quite follow you.'

'Don't you?' Phaedria met her glance with a clear disbelief. 'I'm surprised. One of us is going to have to win this war, Roz, sooner or later, and at that time, the victor can move in and claim the throne. Meanwhile I will speak to Sarah about an office for myself. I'm going home now, I'll see this room is locked before I go.' She buzzed on the intercom. 'Sarah,' she said, 'could you please speak to whoever is in charge of such things, and organize me an office. As near to Mrs Emerson's as possible. Oh, and Sarah –' she looked very straight at Roz for a moment – 'make sure it's at least no smaller than Mrs Emerson's office, will you? I don't want to be working under unfavourable conditions.'

Richard and Freddy had escaped thankfully to the sanctuary of the Palm Court at the Ritz and were drowning their anxieties and discomfort in extremely large whiskies.

'I really hate to say this,' said Freddy, 'but I think we've seen the best of it.'

'Oh, nonsense,' said Richard, 'where is your spirit of adventure, of prospecting, Freddy? Enormous, immense fun lies ahead. I can't wait, personally.'

Freddy looked into his glass mournfully. 'I think you should remind yourself, Richard, old man, that we are not in this for fun. The company needs good housekeeping. If we are to have to sit by and listen while two harpies fight over every inch of it, then I see the property becoming extremely squalid and devalued very quickly.'

'Oh, I don't agree,' said Richard. 'I think they will both be devoting themselves very painstakingly to the housekeeping. I see every corner gleaming quite beautifully, myself. Just so that neither of them can come along and wipe an elegant finger over any of the surfaces, looking for dust left by the other.'

Freddy looked at him. 'And who do you think is going to win the war?' he said. 'Roz, I suppose. She has the advantage that she has years of experience and she is an arch bitch.'

Richard raised his shaggy eyebrows. 'How naïve you are, my dear old chap. I couldn't agree less. I would back the charmingly gentle Phaedria Morell against her stepdaughter any day. Tough as all her elegant new boots, that lady, much as I like her. And she has charm on her side, and certain – what shall we say – personnel skills.'

'Good heavens,' said Freddy, 'well, you may be right.'

'Well, we shall see,' said Richard. 'She is very beautiful, is she not? Under other circumstances perhaps – but no. I am after all scarcely out of my own wedding bed. Don't look like that, I am merely jesting. Of course all heiresses are beautiful,' he added. 'Another drink, Freddy?'

'What are you talking about? She's not exactly an heiress. And I'm surprised at you. I thought you had a higher mind than that.'

'How ignorant you are,' said Richard. 'Quotation, my dear old thing. Dryden. King Arthur. Just a passing comment. A great many most virulent little germs of truth in it, though. I'll tell you one thing, Freddy. I see more and greater signs of grief in the daughter than the widow. Do you?'

'God, I don't know. You could be right. Yes, please, another drink. Oh, God, what a mess. Come back, Julian, all is forgiven.'

'I don't think it would be now,' said Richard cheerfully. 'Not by those two at any rate. Come on, Freddy, drink up. Then we'd better go and get on with those reports our new commandant has requested.'

Roz felt as if there was a great raw hole at the heart of her, that was bleeding endlessly; she thought she had not known what misery was until now. Had she not been propelled into this bitter battle with Phaedria, she thought that for the first time in her life she would have given in, lain down and let the world take care of itself. She felt weary, sickened, by her father's treachery, and totally wretched at her loss. He had enraged her, fought her, and manipulated her ever since she could remember, and most of the misery she had ever felt could be lain at his door; nevertheless she had loved him deeply, helplessly. She had little of the comfort afforded to Phaedria, the tide of sympathy, love, concern that was flowing her way from every direction; she had not been with him at the end, there had been no reconciliation, he had died thinking she hated him, he had never known, would never know how much she had loved him, admired him, longed for his approval, how he had always, since she had been a tiny child, occupied the prime, the most important, the most tender place in her tough, hurt little heart.

During the long sleepless nights now, she lay and relived the happy times with him, the weeks they had spent together, at Marriotts, riding beside him on Miss Madam, looking up at him, trying to do as well as he, braving wide ditches, long, long, fast gallops, anxious to earn his look of approval, his praise; walking the downs, talking endlessly, her small hand in his, dining with him alone in the huge dining room, while he solemnly had her glass refilled with wine and water and consulted her on whether he should buy this horse, that car; sitting beside him, driving some of those wonderful machines, long before she was legally old enough, up and down the drive and tracks of Marriotts, seeing his surprise and pleasure at her skill with them; the visits to New York, dizzier and more exciting all the time as she grew older; the intense pleasure and joy she had felt at his acceptance of her into the company, at his recognition of her skills, his delight at her success; even her wedding day she relived, most of it a panicky blurr, the happiest, the best moment being his face looking up at her as she came down the stairs at Marriotts in her dress, naked of everything but love, and his voice saying, 'Rosamund, you are the joy of my life.' And all through the years, the fear, the terror, the nightmare, that someone would come along, young enough to give him another child, who he would love as much, more, than he had loved her.

And now he was gone, and he had never known any of it; he had thought she hated him, despised him, that she wanted to see him hurt and wounded, when all she had really longed for was his unequivocal love.

In her anguish, all pride gone, lonely, fearful, she had phoned Michael in New York; he was polite, kind even, sympathetic over Julian's death, but distant, declining her invitation to come to England. He had said very little but she knew what the refusal meant; I was not good enough while your father was alive, it meant, and I am not prepared to come running to you now that he is dead.

She even turned to C. J., but he was remote, withdrawn; he too had loved Julian, who had been a second father to him, and he was saddened by his death, he could not pretend feelings that did not even exist for a woman who had shown him nothing but coldness and distaste for so long.

She reflected too, in these long sleepless nights, on Phaedria, and her hatred for her; on how she was going to win the battle that lay ahead, and what was to become of them all. And now there was the child; the child she had feared and dreaded for so long. Well, at least her father had never known about it. Or so Letitia had told her. That seemed to Roz something to be grateful for. Briefly she had pondered on another scenario: that the baby was not in fact Julian's and he had known; could that have been the possible explanation of her father's behaviour, the answer to the riddle? But in the end she had rejected that, it did not explain his equal cruelty – for cruelty it had to be seen to be – to her. On the other hand, she deserved cruelty; tossing and turning on the huge banks of pillows with which she tried to tempt sleep, Roz heard again and again her voice as she taunted her father into giving her the store: 'You're a liar, a liar and a cheat . . . how is Camilla . . . I want the store, I want it . . . I want . . .' She seemed to have ended up with very little.

Next morning at breakfast she dispatched Miranda upstairs with Nanny, and turned to C. J. who was reading the *Financial Times*.

'C. J., I want to talk to you.'

'Really?' His face was blank, his voice pleasantly polite. 'About what?'

'I think we should get divorced.'

He looked at her, grave, detached. 'You're probably right. All right.' He turned back to his paper.

'C. J. –'

'Yes?'

'C. J., is that all you have to say?'

'Oh, I think so,' he said, with a calm smile. 'What else could there be? My usefulness to you is over now. Your father is not here to punish you for divorcing me. Why keep me hanging around?'

'Oh, C. J., don't be so ridiculous. It's not like that.'

'Isn't it? I think it is.' He slammed the paper down and looked at her, his face white, his eyes blazing with fury. 'For years, Roz, you've used me, simply to get what you wanted. A household. Status. Your father's approval. Sex, I think, originally. I forget. Now you can't quite think what I can do for you, I irritate you, so you are going to send me packing. Well that's fine, I'll go. But I'm actually not in a hurry. I rather like

689

this house. I love London. I have been commissioned to write a book about it. I would find it easier to do that from here. I have my study, and I don't want to spend a lot of time looking for another place to live.'

'C. J., you didn't tell me about the book. What's it about?'

'Well,' he said, 'there was no point. I knew you wouldn't give a fuck about it.' C. J. never used bad language; it was a measure of his despair about her. 'It's about the shifting location of fashionable London. Some very respectable publishers have commissioned it.'

'I see.'

'So I think I'll stay for a while, if you don't mind. Or even if you do. Besides, I don't want to leave Miranda. I'm surprised at you, Roz, after all your endless horror stories about your own childhood, exposing your daughter to divorce.'

'I think,' she said, wincing within herself with pain, 'we can handle it a bit better than that.'

'Do you? So far I haven't seen much proof of it, from your side. Anyway, I shall be leaving the company. You'd better have a board meeting about it. The hotels will need a new president. I'm going upstairs now to get Miranda. We go for walks every morning and look at the boats. I don't suppose you realized that, did you?'

'No,' she said. 'No, I didn't.'

As he walked out of the door, she felt suddenly utterly alone.

'C. J. is leaving the company,' she said, walking into Phaedria's office without knocking later that morning. 'We had better discuss the consequences.'

'I'm sorry,' said Phaedria, 'really sorry. Glad for him, because I always felt he hated it, but sorry for us. He was so good at it.'

'I don't really think you have much idea what being good at running hotels implies,' said Roz, 'but yes, you do happen to be right, he was. Quite good, anyway.'

Phaedria looked at her. 'Roz,' she said, 'we have to work together. Given that, don't you think we should at least attempt to observe the formalities and be polite to one another? Apart from anything else, it's so counter productive if we squabble all the time.'

Roz walked over to the window and looked out. She was silent for quite a long time. Then she turned, and looked at Phaedria slightly oddly.

'All right,' she said, 'let's attempt it. As long as you appreciate that it is only a formality.'

'Oh, I do,' said Phaedria, 'I certainly do.'

She was dressed in brilliant red that day, her hair piled high on her head in a tumbled waterfall of curls; she was carefully made up, she wore the Cartier necklace that matched her rings, and a dazzling pair of diamond and emerald clips in her ears. Roz stood for a moment, skimming her eyes contemptuously over her.

'You dress rather strangely,' was all she said, 'for a pregnant widow.'

'Lady Morell, I have Mrs Morell on the phone. Can I put her through?'

'Please do.'

'Phaedria?'

'Yes, hallo Letitia. Are you all right?'

'I'm fine. Feeling much better. How are you?'

'Perfectly filthy, thank you. Were you sick when you were pregnant?'

'No, I was very good at being pregnant. Just bad at giving birth.'

'God, it's awful,' said Phaedria, 'I don't know whether it's worth eating and actually being sick, or not eating, and just feeling even worse.'

'Oh, I'd eat,' said Letitia emphatically. 'Every time. Do you feel hungry?'

'Not really. Well, a bit. I do want certain things. Spicy things. Brown sauce. Did you ever hear of anything so unchic?'

'Not really, darling, no. Well, I wondered if you'd like to have dinner with me tonight? I'll have a big bottle of brown sauce on the table for you, I'll send Nancy out to Harrod's for it now. I presume they'll have it?'

'I expect so,' said Phaedria, laughing. 'It sounds lovely. Thank you, Letitia. I'd love to come.'

'All right then, darling. About eight. There's something I want to talk to you about. Apart from just wanting to see you.'

'I hope I won't be late. Roz has found herself called out of the office all day and can only begin an absolutely crucial meeting at five.'

'Oh dear,' said Letitia. 'She obviously isn't making things easy for either of you.'

'Lady Morell, I have Mr Emerson on the line. Can I put him through?'

'You certainly can. C. J., hallo. This is sad news about your resignation.'

'Not for me.'

'No, I suppose not.'

'Phaedria, I wondered if you could possibly have lunch with me?'

'Well, I'd love to, but I don't know if it would be very wise. I don't think Roz would be very pleased.'

'I don't think I care.'

'No, but I do.'

'Well anyway, you really don't have to. She's just taken the helicopter up to Manchester. Says she has to see the guy at the communications company. We don't have to go anywhere, I'll come to the office.'

'How very cloak and dagger. All right, yes, I'll get Sarah to organize something. I have a new office, by the way. Immediately beneath Roz's. I thought tactically beneath was better than above. See you here at one.'

'Fine.'

He arrived with a bunch of white freesias and a bottle of white burgundy.

'C. J., you are naughty, you can't give me flowers.'

'I can do what I like. Roz wants a divorce.'

'Yes,' said Phaedria, looking at him sadly. 'I thought she might.'

'Don't look like that. I don't really mind at all. I feel a bit – well, discarded, you know? But otherwise, it's a great relief.'

'Will you go back to New York?'

'No, I don't think so. I don't want to leave Miranda, and I have a book to write about London.'

'C. J., how marvellous. I'm so pleased. Tell me about it.' She pressed the buzzer. 'Sarah, could we have those sandwiches, and also could you bring a vase in?'

She started arranging the flowers while he talked; he looked at her and thought what a remarkable person she was, and wondered how Julian could possibly have done to her what he had. There must somewhere be an explanation; if only to provide it to the world, he was determined to help her to find it.

'Phaedria, I'd like to help.'

She looked at him over her glass. 'What do you mean?'

'I'd like to help you find Miles Wilburn.'

'C. J., that's sweet, but why?'

'Because –' He paused, trying to find exactly the right words. 'Because I think you deserve it.'

'Well, I could certainly do with it. But have you got the time? With your book and everything?'

'Oh, I have at least a year to do that. The thing is, I shall have access to papers and things, I can come and go, talking to people as much as I like. I know everyone in the company, here and in New York. I just think I have a flying start on any detective agency or whatever.'

She looked at him doubtfully. She was touched by the offer, but she couldn't help feeling an agency might do better. C. J. was hardly sharp. Clever, cultured, interesting but not sharp.

'What about Roz? Don't you think she might put ground glass in your coffee?'

'Oh, she won't have the opportunity. I'm moving out of the house in Cheyne Walk quite shortly. I've been looking at flats all morning.'

'I see. Well, it certainly would be lovely to have your help. Don't you think it's a bit unethical, though, you helping me to win the race to get control, when you're still married to the other horse, so to speak?'

He looked at her and smiled. 'Look at it as adjusting the odds,' he said.

'And how do you think the odds look at the moment?' she asked with a heavy sigh.

'Fairly even. But I'll tell you one thing. You're the favourite.'

'Oh, good. You'll have to excuse me a minute, C. J. I don't think I should have drunk that wine . . .'

*

693

She arrived at First Street that night well after nine.

'Letitia, I'm so sorry. The meeting went on and on, and then I had letters to sign. Please forgive me.'

'Of course I do. It couldn't matter less. Drink?'

Phaedria shuddered. 'No thank you. I had some at lunch time, and it was extremely unwise. Could I have some Perrier?'

'Of course. What does your doctor say about all this?'

'I haven't seen her since –' Her face clouded, drained of colour; she sat down and looked at Letitia, suddenly very white and shaken.

'Darling, what is it? Are you all right?'

Phaedria tried to smile, and failed; she shook her head, unable to speak. Letitia crossed over to her and took her hand.

'Tell me. What is it?'

'Oh – I don't know. I'm sorry. It's stupid really. It's just that – well I haven't seen my doctor since the day before Julian died. I haven't even thought about it. You asking made time telescope suddenly, if you know what I mean, I felt I was back in her room. It was a sort of ghostly feeling.'

Letitia looked at her keenly. 'It isn't easy, is it?'

'What do you mean?'

'Being alone in a pregnancy.'

'No, no it isn't. How do you know though, Letitia? I didn't think you ever were.'

'Well, I was in a way, my darling. In a way. Let me tell you about it. It might make you able to feel you can talk to me, turn to me. That I'll understand.'

'I do anyway. But yes, please do. I'm intrigued.'

'Well,' said Letitia, 'it's a long story. I'll try not to make it too long. When I was only seventeen years old, I was engaged to someone called Harry Whigham. He was a captain in the Guards. He was terribly handsome and charming, and I loved him very much. Very much. Well, he went away to France, in the war, and he was killed. I was – distraught. Of course. And lonely and lost and terrified that I would never find anyone else. All the boys I knew were going to France, and most of them were not coming back. I had a horror of being a spinster. Like most young girls then. Well, I met Edward Morell – Julian's father – and he was kind and good, and he adored me, and I thought – well, I suppose I managed to think I loved him. And he wasn't going to go away to France because he was a farmer. So I married him. That was in 1916. James, Julian's brother, was born a year later. And we were perfectly happy. Well, perfectly content.

'Anyway, in 1919, after the war, I went to stay in London for a few days with my grandmother. She had always been very opposed to the marriage with Edward. She thought he was –' her lips twitched – 'very middle class. I suppose I inherit my dreadful snobbery from her. Anyway, we went out to the theatre one night, and when we came out, we were waiting for a cab when someone tapped me on the shoulder. I turned round, and it was Harry Whigham. Only of course it wasn't, it was his younger brother, Christian, but he was just terribly terribly like him. It was the most dreadful appalling shock, I felt absolutely ill, fainted in fact; I came round lying on the pavement, with everybody fussing and Christian fanning my face. He was just looking at me very very intently and I was in his arms, his coat over me. I remember it all so clearly, he had on a black evening coat over his dinner jacket, he looked so handsome, so unbelievably handsome and – well, that was it, really.'

Phaedria sat absolutely motionless, her eyes fixed on Letitia's face. She hardly dared to breathe for fear of interrupting her.

'Well, anyway, my grandmother, who had always liked Harry, asked Christian back for supper. It all seemed like a dream, all I could think of was that I was with Harry again. Or nearly. And before he left he asked if he could come to call the next day. My grandmother not only encouraged him, she arranged to be out and for half the staff to be out as well. She was very wicked, I'm afraid. And so was I.'

'So – so what happened?'

'Well, darling, I'm afraid a great deal. It was all very disgraceful. Of course everybody nowadays thinks affairs and adultery are the invention of the late twentieth century, but I do assure you, they have always gone on. And so Christian and I had a wild affair. Oh, it was wonderful. Aided and abetted by my grandmother. I stayed in London for another week. And was with him every day. Very often alone. He begged me to leave Edward and run away with him. But of course I couldn't. I said it was impossible, that we must never meet again, that

Edward was a good, kind man, that I did love him, and that Christian must go away and never ever see me again. I remember my words still. I said, "There is nothing for us, absolutely nothing at all." Only I was wrong, of course.' She was silent for a moment just looking at Phaedria. 'There was Julian.'

Phaedria said nothing for a while; then she put her arms round Letitia. 'How did you bear it a second time?' she asked.

'Oh, you bear what you have to,' said Letitia. 'There was nothing else to be done, nothing at all. When I found I was pregnant, I did think of trying to tell him, but what would have been the point? It would only have made trouble, caused pain. So I kept silent. Edward had no cause to suspect. He was over the moon at the thought of another baby. I found my comfort and happiness in Julian. But then – well, he did look very different from James and Edward. And nobody in Wiltshire, in Edward's circle of friends, liked me very much. I didn't fit in. Someone had seen us in London, there was talk. Of course I tried to laugh it off, when people made remarks about Julian and his brown eyes and so on, when Edward and I were both fair, and had blue eyes. But it was – difficult. Then when he was about nine or ten weeks old, I was still frail, Edward came in, sat down at the table and burst into tears. It was dreadful. He said someone had been drunk and come out with it, said Julian was not his son. He clung to me, and begged me to tell him that he was, that it was a lie; he was sobbing, he was drunk himself. So of course I said that it was a filthy lie, that people were jealous of him, of both of us, that Julian was his son, that there was no truth in any of it; and he was still crying, still so unhappy, and so – well, to comfort him, to reassure him, to show how very much I loved him, and I did Phaedria, in my own way, I did, I seduced him, there and then on the floor by the fire. I knew what a risk it was, to myself, but I had to do it, there could be no pause for sense or – well, for precautions, and of course the poor little twins were conceived that night, and I was simply too weak to bear them. They were born prematurely, and they only lived a few days. But it worked, it made him believe, and even when I was so unhappy, I was comforted, because those dead babies had healed Edward's heart.'

She was silent then for a long time, her eyes filled with tears; Phaedria sat utterly still, her eyes fixed on Letitia's face.

'But that is just extraordinary,' she said. 'How awful for you, how sad, and how brave you had to be. How did you do it? How did you get through?"'

'Oh, very much as you are,' said Letitia briskly. 'By just getting on with life. It's the only thing to do.'

'I suppose so.' Phaedria was pale, almost awed. 'So Julian was actually illegitimate. Did he know?'

'Yes, he was and yes, he did. Not until he was grown up. When he came back from France. I told him then. I'm not sure that I should have done, in a way.'

'Why?'

'Oh, I don't know that it served any useful purpose. And I think in a way it encouraged his extraordinary instinct for intrigue. And for deceit. I don't know.' She sighed. 'One makes a lot of mistakes in one's life. And they become clearer as you get older. There's an old Irish saying, you know, which my father used to quote. "Old sins cast long shadows." It's true. You think something is far far away, buried in the past, and it isn't at all, it travels with you always, ahead of you even, into the future. I feel that sin of mine certainly did that. And now, you see, some sin of Julian's is casting its own very long, dark shadow.'

'But Letitia, why does it have to be a sin? Why shouldn't this Miles person be someone Julian wanted to help, to benefit?'

'Well, darling, if he is, why didn't we all know about him? Why all this mystery and cloak and dagger nonsense? It really is quite extraordinary. So unnecessary. Oh, I could shake him.' She smiled suddenly. 'It helps me to get cross with him. I don't hurt so much.'

'You must hurt terribly,' said Phaedria, reaching out her hand and taking Letitia's.

'Yes, I do. Terribly. There is nothing, no pain, like losing a child. And now I've lost four. Take care of that baby, Phaedria. I still ache with the death of those twins, over sixty years later. Not a day passes but I think of them, see their faces, feel them in my arms. There is no love, nothing, that has the strength, the power of the one a woman feels for her child.'

'I will,' said Phaedria, looking at the sad suddenly old face before her. 'I will. For your sake, I will. And thank you for telling me. It helps, I don't know quite why.'

'I hoped it might; and I thought you ought to know now. Tell me, darling, how do you feel? Apart from physically? Any better at all?'

'No. Not really. But I feel so rejected, somehow. As if Julian has just – oh, I don't know, thrown everything in my face. And I can never, ever, have the comfort of thinking he trusted me, loved me at all. And nobody else could think that either. It's awful. Letitia, I don't know what to do. I simply don't know how to bear it.'

Letitia looked at her. 'I don't know either,' she said, 'I just wish I could help you. What I do know, though, which might comfort you, is that Julian did love you. Very much. I know it's very hard to believe, but it is true.'

Phaedria sighed. 'Well, he had a strange way of showing it.'

'Yes . . .'

'Oh Letitia,' said Phaedria suddenly. 'If only I'd been able to tell Julian about the baby. I did tell him, of course, when he was unconscious, in intensive care, I told him over and over again, and they say people can hear you, know what you're saying, but I really don't think he did. It's so sad to think he never knew, so terribly sad.'

Letitia looked at her. 'I think actually it makes it all better somehow,' she said, suddenly brisk, handing Phaedria a glass of wine.

'How?'

'Well, if he'd known about the baby, then it would have seemed much much more dreadful and cruel, all this. But given that the will was drawn up, or whatever, while you were estranged, then it isn't quite such a rejection. Not quite.'

'I suppose so.'

'No, it isn't. And you do have the comfort of knowing you had – well, made things up before he died.'

'Yes,' said Phaedria, with a weak, watery smile. 'Yes, we had. For a bit anyway.'

'So you can hang on to that. It's more than poor Roz has. As far as I can make out she and Julian had had some dreadful argument weeks before he died and never really made it up.'

'I did say she should come to the hospital. I kept saying it. She wouldn't come.'

'No, I know.'

Phaedria was silent. Then she said, 'You know, Letitia, all the time, all those three days before he died, I kept feeling he was trying, struggling to tell me something. But he couldn't. He couldn't speak, he couldn't write, he couldn't do anything. They kept saying I shouldn't worry, that it was normal, but I did feel he was desperate. Perhaps that was about the will, about what he had done.'

'Poor Julian,' said Letitia quietly. 'If that is what it was, how dreadful. Now then, let's have something to eat, it's terribly late, you must be starving. Nancy's made something I really think you'll like, it's chicken marengo, and you can drown it in your brown sauce if you want to.'

'Sounds wonderful.'

'Good. Come on, then.'

'Incidentally,' she said carefully, watching Phaedria as she picked rather half-heartedly at her food. 'I have to tell you a private detective has been on to me. From Roz. Did you know about this?'

'No, but I'm not surprised.'

'Well, that's something. I didn't want to commit myself to talking to him until I'd seen you. Of course I shall help in every way I can. But I just wanted you to know.'

Phaedria looked at her and smiled. 'Thank you. What was he like? Awful?'

'No, he sounded rather nice. Quite civilized and gentle. Not like the ones on television at all. A bit like an English Hercule Poirot.'

'Goodness. And what sort of things does he want to know?'

'I'm not too sure. I don't think he knows. I imagine he just wants to hear everything I can tell him about Julian. To see if he can pick up any clues.'

'And do you think he will?'

'No, I don't, I really have never heard Julian mention anyone called Miles, or Wilburn. But he may unearth something from the depths of my mind. I hope so. The only thing I do feel, and it's only partly hunch, but there is some basis of sense in it, this person, whoever he is, is more likely to be in America than here. I really think it would have been rather difficult for Julian to have established what must have been some kind of very strong link with him or his family without one of us picking up some hint of it. And he did spend such a lot of time over there, especially in the sixties and seventies. I do think also, darling, you should talk to Eliza. She says she doesn't know anything, but she's so scatty, careful prompting might help.'

'Yes, but I don't know what to prompt. And I don't feel well enough to go haring up to Scotland. But I suppose she'll come down here, if I ask her.'

'Of course she will. Any excuse to come to London. And just let her run on. That's all you need to do in the way of prompting.'

'All right. Oh, by the way, Letitia, this must sound a funny question, but could Julian type, do you happen to know?'

'Oh yes,' said Letitia. 'He typed rather well. He learnt during his Resistance training during the war. Why?'

'Oh, just a query over the will. Whether he could have drawn it up himself. It seems he could. Incidentally, I have a detective working for me too,' said Phaedria with a smile.

'You don't! How intriguing, darling. What's his name?'

'He's an amateur. His name is Emerson. C. J.'

'Phaedria, that sounds very unwise to me.'

'Oh, not really. I don't think so. Roz wants a divorce. He's moving out. He offered his help, and I was doubtful at first, but actually I think he might do rather well. He has a very kind of investigative mind, he likes little odd facts and things, he remembers them, stores them away. He really wanted to be an archaeologist, you know.'

'How sad that he wasn't. That he had to get mixed up with Roz, I mean. Two unhappy people.'

'Yes.'

Letitia looked at her. 'I hope he's not falling in love with you,' she said, 'I've always thought he had a very soft spot for you. Do you think he is?'

'Absolutely not,' said Phaedria firmly. 'But even if he was, it wouldn't matter too terribly, I daresay. Roz doesn't give a toss about what C. J. does. My God – ' She stopped eating and shuddered, looked at Letitia stricken at her own thoughts. 'Can you imagine anything more dreadful, though, than if someone Roz did give a toss about was in love with me. That really would see me in the morgue . . .'

*

Michael Browning arrived at Heathrow three days later.

He had been feeling increasingly remorseful ever since Roz's cry for help, and his refusal to answer it. God alone, he thought (and perhaps Michael Browning) knew what it must have cost her in terms of setting aside her pride; and near psychotic fixation apart, she really had genuinely loved her father. He reckoned she must be feeling pretty wretched. He owed it to her to give her a bit of support. He had absolutely no intention of starting their relationship up yet again; some old-time's-sake friendship seemed to him to be about the most he should offer. Even with her father gone, he had no illusions as to where he would come in her order of priorities. Especially if all these rumours about the will and the company were true. Intriguing, that. He wondered what on earth the old bastard had been playing at. He wasn't too sure of the facts of the case; the *New York Times* and the *Wall Street Journal* had both carried bald announcements about 'certain complexities' in Julian Morell's will. But the copy of *People* magazine he had been handed on the plane had got hold of the story this week, and although they were clearly having trouble getting enough detail, and had only run a paragraph, they still managed to make it intensely fascinating reading. 'Wills and Wonts' it was headed:

Billionaire tycoon Julian Morell, who died of a coronary three weeks ago, has reportedly left a bizarre will, bequeathing two equal forty-nine per cent shares in his company to wife Phaedria and daughter Roz, and the remaining two per cent to a so far unnamed party. The famously feuding women now find themselves put in a neat corner by Big Daddy, neither able to claim control and forced to work together in close disharmony. Neither of them was available for comment, but the racy Countess of Garrylaig, Eliza, first wife of Sir Julian, mother to Roz, and guardian angel to Phaedria (rumoured to be pregnant, although estranged from her husband for the weeks prior to his sudden death) predicts a speedy discovery and recovery of the missing heir.

'Holy shit,' said Michael Browning under his breath. He signalled to the hostess. 'Honey, could you get me a whisky, please? I suddenly have a dreadful thirst.'

'Excuse me.'

He stood in the reception area at Dover Street, dripping wet. He had as always lost his raincoat. Just as well he was in London. Although of course nowhere else would be tipping down the rain in the middle of June.

'Can you tell me where to find Mrs Emerson?'

'Certainly. Second floor, turn right at the lift, and it's the big office on the left. But can I have your name, please? And I'll tell her you're here.'

'Oh, I'd hate you to do that. I want to surprise her.'

'But Mrs Emerson doesn't like visitors unannounced.'

'She'll like me.'

'No, I really can't . . .'

'Honey –' he looked at her with his mournful face, his spaniel-like brown eyes – 'I really want to surprise her. Can you deprive a drowning man of his last wish?'

'Well . . .'

'Thank you. I swear to you, if she fires you I'll give you a job.'

He decided to walk up the stairs; he hated elevators. It was only one flight. Being an American, the second floor to Michael Browning was actually the first. He ran up the stairs, pushed through the swing doors, waited momentarily outside the office and then opened the door.

'Hi, darling.'

But the face at the desk, looking at him, was not what he had been looking for, seeking – even, he realized with some surprise, longing for. It was not Roz's face. It was nevertheless a rather beautiful face, very, very pale, with large dark eyes, and a massing cloud of dark hair; Michael Browning did not take a great interest in clothes, but he could see that the brilliant red dress with the wide shoulders added greatly to its owner's striking appearance.

'Yes?' she said, slightly shortly.

'Oh, I'm sorry,' he said, 'I was looking for someone else.'

'So I gathered.'

'I'd like to say you'll do,' he said, sounding rather morose about the idea, 'only that would sound kind of corny. And I'm afraid it wouldn't be absolutely true. Although as substitutes go, you set a pretty high standard.'

The substitute stood up, whiter than ever, and rushed towards him. 'Excuse me,' she said, 'I have to come past. I'm going to be sick.'

When she came back, shaky and a little dizzy, he was still there.

'Hey,' he said, 'you look terrible. Here, come on and sit down.' He took her hand, led her gently to a chair. 'I don't usually have that bad an effect on people. I obviously have a problem. Can I get you a drink of water?'

'Oh, yes please. There's a fridge in that cupboard there. Thank you. I'm really sorry. Horrid for you. Nothing personal. It's just that I'm going to have a baby. And it doesn't seem to like me.'

'Now that's really bad,' he said, looking at her concernedly. 'Are you sick a lot?'

'An awful lot.'

'All day? Or just in the morning.'

'All day.'

'You really shouldn't let that go on, you know. It's bad for you, and not too good for the unfriendly baby. What have you tried?'

'Nothing, really.'

'OK, well here's an idea. My first wife had terrible sickness, and in the end she licked it. Now you take a lemon, and you just lop the top off it. Think of it as an egg. Get a little glucose – do you have that here?'

'I believe we do,' said Phaedria, her lips twitching.

'Right, you sprinkle just a smidgen on to the egg.'

'You mean the lemon?'

'Yeah, the lemon. And then when you feel sick, or every ten minutes or so, you suck it. Try it. It can't do any harm.'

'Thank you, I will. It sounds awful, but I will.'

'And when is this ungrateful monster due?'

'Not for an eternity. November.'

'I would say you should have finished being sick by now. What does your doctor say?'

'I haven't asked her. I'm seeing her tomorrow.'

'Well, you should have seen her a long time before tomorrow. This certainly is a rather primitive society. In the States you'd be having your twenty-fifth check-up by now. Do you plan to give birth to this child in a ditch or something?'

'No. Well, hopefully not.' She looked at him and smiled. He smiled back.

Phaedria felt some very odd sensation; a small, meek, but very determined lurch somewhere deep within her. A slight shifting of her solar plexus. An illusion that it was warmer, brighter. She stifled all of them and looked at him again, taking in the deeply solemn face, the lugubrious dark eyes, the thick floppy hair – and the indisputably damp suit.

'You're very wet.'

'I certainly am. Are you surprised? This is London, I do believe, and it is June.'

'Yes, but most people wear a raincoat.'

'I've lost mine.'

'Ah.'

'In fact I plan to go and buy a new one this afternoon. In Harrods.'

'You could get one nearer than that. Simpson's. Austin Reed.'

'I know. But they know me in Harrods.'

'Do you buy raincoats there very often?'

'Oh, all the time. I only have to show my face in the department, and hordes of women rush at me, bearing Burberries.'

She laughed. 'All right. Now then, who is this darling you're looking for?'

'I beg your pardon? Oh – sorry,' he smiled again. 'I'd forgotten. Too interested in you and your baby.' The shift again; the brightening. 'Yeah, well, you probably know her. It's Roz. Roz Emerson.'

'Yes,' said Phaedria, 'yes, I do. Slightly. I'd ask my secretary to take you up only she's not very near at the moment. It's the next floor. Directly above this room. Shall I let her know you're here?'

'Oh, no,' he said, 'I want to surprise her.'

'I hope she likes your sort of surprises,' said Phaedria briskly.

'I think she will. Thank you. Miss – er Mrs –'

'Morell. Phaedria.'

'You! You're her! My God, I didn't expect you to be quite so good-looking.' He studied her in silence, drinking her in; then he smiled again. 'Well, you really are a nice surprise.'

'Well, thank you.' Another slightly bigger shift. (For God's sake, Phaedria Morell, you're a grieving widow, four months pregnant.)

'And you are?'

'Browning. Michael Browning.'

'Oh, my God,' said Phaedria. 'My God. I think I'm going to be sick again.'

'I'll bring you some lemons,' he called to her departing back. But she was gone.

'Michael, Michael I love you. I love you so so much. It's so good to see you.' Roz was more than slightly drunk; they were lunching in the Caprice. Michael, most of his good resolutions gone, was sitting back looking at her thoughtfully.

'Do I get to spend the rest of the day with you? As you love me so much?'

'Michael, I can't. I just can't.'

'Ah.'

'Michael, do be fair. I had no idea you were coming. I have three major meetings this afternoon. I have half the company resting on my shoulders these days you know, it's serious work.'

'Not half, darling. Forty-nine per cent.'

'You've been reading the papers.'

'I certainly have.'

'Well, what do you make of it?'

'Very odd. I told you he was a devious old buzzard.'

'Yes, well, so you always said.' Her face darkened. 'Do you know the whole story? Or at least the half of it that we know?'

'Not really.'

'Well, he left forty-nine per cent to me, forty-nine per cent to the wife – the widow.'

'And who holds the key?'

'I don't know. Nobody knows.'

'You're kidding.'

'I wish I was. Some man called Miles Wilburn. Who none of us have ever heard of.'

'None of you? Not even the old lady? Or that frosty bit with the red hair?'

'No. None of us.'

He was silent for a while. 'Weird.'

'It is.'

'So what are you going to do?'

'Find him,' said Roz. There was an expression of absolute determination on her face.

'And then?'

'Get him on my side.'

'Exactly how?'

'I'll find a way.'

'Poor fucker.'

'I beg your pardon.'

'You heard. I certainly don't rate his chances. How are you going to find him?'

'The lawyers are on to it. I have a detective agency working on it too.'

'I guess Lady Morell is also trying to find him.'

'No doubt she is.'

'Some contest.'

'I intend to win.'

'I bet you do.'

'Michael, you're not being terribly nice to me.'

'You haven't been terribly nice to me.'

She looked at him, held his gaze, and took his hand; and for that moment all her toughness, her selfishness, her greed had left her eyes, and they were filled quite simply with longing and love.

'I know. And I'm truly, truly sorry.'

'Well,' he said, fighting to retain some semblance of judgement, 'I shall wait to see. Can you really not come back to the hotel with me now?'

'No,' she said, and he could see the immensity of what that cost her. 'No, I'm sorry, I can't.'

'Ah.' He was silent for a moment; she looked down, fearing she might crack, weaken, even cry. Then he smiled, kissed her cheek.

'It's all right, that was unfair. I shouldn't have asked. I wouldn't cancel three vital meetings either, just on the off-chance of a glorious afternoon in the sack. Can I see you tonight?'

'Oh, yes, most certainly tonight. This evening. I'll be there at seven.'

'What about Hubby?'

'I'm divorcing Hubby.'

'Just like that?'

'Just like that. Well, I suppose he'll be divorcing me. He has enough grounds.'

'Well, that's sad.'

'Is it?'

'Of course it is. Jesus, Roz, you're a tough cookie. It's always sad when a marriage ends. You have to think that.'

'Well,' she said. 'Maybe. But we never really had a marriage, C. J. and I. Just an arrangement.'

'Of your making. Rosamund, much as I love you, dearly as I like to be with you, desperately as I long to have you in my bed again, I want to make it very plain that I will not play some minor part in any convenient arrangement of yours. Is that clear?'

'Yes, Michael. Quite clear. I promise.'

He looked at her warily. He had learnt not to trust her promises.

Phaedria and C. J. began their detective work that night. Phaedria unlocked the huge desk in Julian's study and they sifted patiently hour after hour through papers, letters, documents. It was meticulously filed, perfectly ordered; most of it was administrative stuff, deeds of houses, details of staff, invoices for work done, letters from lawyers in America, France, the Bahamas, about property, cars, horses, planes. Some of it was personal; there were letters from Roz at boarding school, brief, harsh, dutiful, and earlier ones which she had written to him when he had been away in New York, when she had been a little girl, loving, sad, brave little notes asking him to come home, to take Mummy back to Regent's Park, telling him of her successes at dancing, at riding, at school; there were snapshots of her on her pony, in her ballet dress, in her first school uniform, and several of her with Julian, holding his hand, sitting on his knee, sitting on her pony beside him. Phaedria studied them in silence; her eyes filled with tears.

'This is awful, C. J. It makes me feel so sad. He really really loved her. And she must have loved him so much. I don't think I can take much more of this. I shall end up giving her my share and just retiring to the country.'

'Yes, I know,' said C. J. 'I used to feel sorry for her too. But I don't any more. Other people have tough childhoods. You did. But they survive. They don't turn out psychopaths.'

Phaedria laughed shakily. 'She's not exactly a psychopath. But I suppose you're right. Oh, look, here are the wedding pictures, with Eliza. Goodness, she was beautiful. And oh, C. J., look at Letitia. What a marvellous-looking woman she was. Is.'

'She is such a very old lady suddenly,' said C. J.

'Yes, I'm afraid she is. But she's amazingly brave. She's an example to us all. Well, there's nothing here, C. J., is there? We may as well call it a day.'

'I guess so. You look tired. Why don't I fix you a drink before I go?'

'That would be lovely. I am tired. It's not exactly easy, what I'm doing at the moment.'

'Roz giving you a hard time?'

'Very. The thing is I could easily give in, and just let her carry on for a bit. I still hold forty-nine per cent, so she can't do anything much without me. But I just know she'd start politicking in earnest if my back was turned. I have to show my mettle.'

'She certainly seems much happier,' said C. J. with a sigh. 'Browning's been over.'

'Yes. I know. I met him.'

'Really? How on earth did that happen?'

'Oh, he came to my office by mistake.'

'I – I – hear he's quite charming.'

'Yes,' said Phaedria briefly. 'He seemed quite nice.'

'I guess she'll marry him now. In the fullness of time.'

'I guess she will.' She looked at him, but his face was blank. 'How's the flat-hunting?'

'It's good. I have a nice place, I think, just off Sloane Street. I've made an offer. Now what would you like to drink?'

'Hot milk, with honey in it. A real nursery bedtime drink. Can you manage that?'

'Sure. Now I think the next thing we have to do is repeat this same operation in New York. In Sutton Place.'

708

'God,' said Phaedria, 'I don't think I could possibly find the strength to fly over there just now. And my memories of Sutton Place are not the happiest.

'You really have had a tough time, Phaedria. I suppose you've considered not doing all this? Just letting things go. You could settle down happily with your baby, probably marry again, spare yourself all this pain.'

'No,' said Phaedria firmly. 'I haven't considered it for a moment. Not one. The company matters desperately to me, it's the most important thing I have left of Julian, apart from the baby, and I intend to keep it alive, in my own way. And I feel, in doing what he did, he made it clear he wanted me to remain involved in it, caring for it. Otherwise he would have left it all to Roz. No, C. J., I have to carry on.'

'Well, I just thought I'd check it out. Phaedria, would you like me to go to Sutton Place? And the offices in New York? I wouldn't mind. I know where everything is. I have the time. And besides –' he smiled at her suddenly – 'I'm not pregnant.'

'Well, that's true. Oh, C. J., I'd love it. But are you sure it won't upset your book schedule?'

'It will,' he said cheerfully. 'But I don't mind. Now I'm going to get your drink. You just wait there.'

When he came back with it she was asleep, her face peaceful, childlike, her hair tumbled on the cushions.

Eliza proved no more able to help than anyone else. Phaedria asked C. J. to contact Camilla while he was in New York – unable to bear to talk to her herself. The only other person Phaedria decided worth talking to was Sarah Brownsmith. Sarah, she felt, probably knew more about Julian than anyone in the world; both his public and his private life. And she was also clearly anxious to help. She had even moved her office down from the penthouse in order to act as Phaedria's private secretary, and to prevent Roz from claiming any kind of injustice. Phaedria asked her to organize lunch for them both one day, and said she wanted to grill her. 'I really need any help I can get. Anything at all you can think of. However small.'

'Well,' said Sarah, 'I certainly have no notes, no addresses, no names that are going to do you any good. I have been through everything, and this Mr Blackworth of Mrs Emerson's has already been to see me, as you know.'

'Hmm. Let's go at it a different way. Sarah, you knew him a very long time. Can you think of any time he might have behaved differently?'

'Not really. He was, considering how – spoilt he was, very balanced, I always thought. Although –' She looked at Phaedria quizzically. 'There was something.'

'Yes?'

'Well, it was quite soon after I came to work for him. Right at the beginning of the seventies. In 1971 to be precise. He became very depressed. Very depressed indeed. In fact one morning, I did actually find him in tears. I've never told anyone this, of course, there was no reason for me to, but I suppose it might be relevant now, he did at that time see a doctor quite regularly.'

'Goodness,' said Phaedria, 'this is intriguing. What sort of a doctor?'

'Well – a psychiatrist.'

'My God. How regularly?'

'Oh, twice a week, for nearly a year. I had the impression he was very troubled.'

'This is truly extraordinary. Nobody, nobody at all has ever mentioned anything about this. That he was so unhappy or anything. Do you by any chance have a note of this doctor's name?'

'I can find it. Just a minute.'

She came back with her address file. 'Doctor Friedman. Doctor Margaret Friedman. She practised in the Marylebone Road. I have her number. Would you like it?'

'I certainly would. Sarah, you're an angel. Thank you.'

'It's a pleasure, Lady Morell. Would you like your nap now?'

'No, I'm much too excited to sleep. Try this number straight away, will you? I can't wait to talk to her.'

Doctor Friedman, said the receptionist, was away for a fortnight. She was quite happy to make an appointment for Lady Morell on her return. Would an early morning be convenient? And yes, quite convenient, said Lady Morell, just as early as Doctor Friedman liked.

'Very well,' said the brisk voice on the other end of the phone. 'Eight thirty on Monday, August first.'

With which Lady Morell had to force herself to be content.

She was sitting in her office quite early one morning in July while C. J. was away in the States, when the phone rang. It was Henry Winterbourne.

'Phaedria! I have some news.'

'Oh, my God,' said Phaedria, leaning back in her chair, closing her eyes, 'What, Henry, what is it?'

'Well, it's quite a big lead actually. I have been advertising in all the major cities in the States, as you know; I got a letter a few days ago from a lawyer called Bill Wilburn in San Francisco, saying his nephew was Miles Wilburn. I didn't tell you, I've had dozens of the things, all saying they were Miles Wilburn, they were his mother, his son, his second cousin's stepgrandmother . . .'

'Oh, go on, go on,' said Phaedria, 'do get to the point, Henry.'

'Well, I wrote the standard letter, saying could he ask Mr Wilburn to contact us direct, and saying that the news we had for him was to his advantage. And he phoned. This morning.'

'And?'

'And, well, it was a most extraordinary, intriguing phone call. He wanted to know naturally if there was money involved. And then he said he presumed I was acting for Hugo Dashwood.'

'Who?'

'Exactly. I thought you'd be interested. Hugo Dashwood.'

'And then what?'

'Well, then I said no, I was acting for the Morell family. Bill Wilburn just didn't understand why I didn't know who Hugo Dashwood was. He did sound rather drunk. He said he knew Hugo Dashwood, that he was English, and he'd assumed that he'd left his nephew, Miles Wilburn, some money. He said he hoped so, because Miles had just borrowed some money from him. I said was this Hugo Dashwood related to his nephew and he said, yes, he believed he might be.'

'Oh,' said Phaedria, 'this is just too exciting for words. And baffling. Then what?'

'Well, then I decided this chap had to be genuine, and so I said we'd pay his fare to come over to England and see us.'

'Why didn't you ask him to give us Miles' address?'

'I did. He said he'd rather come and talk to us first. He said what he had to say was highly confidential and delicate, and he didn't want Miles involved until he was satisfied it was really going to benefit him.'

'How extraordinary. So when is he coming?'

'Very soon. I've asked Jane to book a flight in the next day or so. She'll ring him when it's fixed.'

'Henry, you're a genius.'

'No, just lucky. I think.'

'Er – Henry, have you told anyone else in the family yet?'

'No, as a matter of fact I haven't. Roz is away, I understand, for a few days in Washington, so I can't get hold of her, and I didn't want to trouble her with what might prove to be a false lead.'

'Of course not. And she is extremely busy, just now, getting down to her new post as acting president of the hotels.'

'Quite.'

'Let me know the minute you can when he's coming, won't you?'

'Of course.'

Next morning, Jane Gould came in to Henry's office looking upset.

'What is it, Jane? Having trouble with your new word processor?'

'No, Mr Winterbourne. I've just phoned Mr Wilburn's office in San Francisco. There's some hysterical girl on the phone who says he's dead. Apparently he had a car crash last night. And before you ask, there's no family at all that we can talk to. What on earth do we do now?'

The Connection Twelve

Miami and Nassau, 1985

Miles thought Miami was just about the most awful place he had ever been to in his life. It made the early days in Nassau look like paradise. Even the relief of getting old Marcia off his back, with Bill Wilburn's totally unexpected help – God, why hadn't he asked him before – didn't make life seem much better.

At first sight the beach had looked all right, and there was at least the suspicion of surf rolling in on to it; but he discovered very quickly that it was nothing but a huge, man-made people-park, covered in a lot of what seemed to him very old people and an endless procession of film crews. It had no soul like the beaches of California, no shape to it, and no land behind it, just mile after mile of high-rise buildings. He liked the south end better, Old Miami as it was called, with its little colony of deco hotels and buildings, but it was still basically part of what seemed to him the same nightmare, just concrete and more concrete, straight lines and endless streets. What he couldn't understand was how proud and pleased everybody seemed to be with the place. The number of tourists, they kept telling him, was rising every year, every month; at least five million last year. There were the most incredible number of new roads being built, and all kinds of new developments, like Bayside, the waterfront development, and then there were all the wonderful things like the Seaquarium and the Metrozoo, and had he been to Everglades and the Tropical Garden and . . .

Miles smiled his lovely smile and said, no, not yet, but he was certainly looking forward to it. Then he got his head down at the bank, took the cheapest room he could find, and immediately set about saving his fare back to Nassau.

It was Mrs de Launay who saw the advertisement.

'Look at this,' she said to her husband excitedly. 'Someone wants to contact Miles. At least I suppose it's him.'

'Must be,' he said. 'There can't be many Miles Wilburns about. I wonder if Marcia has seen this.'

'Shouldn't think so. Should I show it to her, do you think?'

'Well of course you should. Don't ask such absurd questions, Alicia. It could be important.'

Alicia was shy. 'But she might think I was interfering. She might already have seen it. I don't like to.'

'All right.' He shrugged. 'Have it your own way.'

'Oh, well – maybe I should.'

She went to Marcia's house later that day. Marcia was sitting doing her needlepoint; Dorothy was asleep upstairs.

'Forgive me for interfering in your business, Marcia, but I wondered if you'd seen this?'

'What's that, Alicia?'

'It's an advertisement in the paper. For Miles to get in touch with some solicitors in England.'

'Well, for heavens' sakes,' said Marcia. 'Let me see. Good heavens. I wonder what that can be about.'

'Usually they're about money, Marcia. Legacies. You know. Someone might have left him a lot of money.'

'I doubt it. No one in that family has a penny to their name.'

'Well, you never know. Don't you think you should at least tell Dorothy – Mrs Kelly.'

'Yes, I expect you're right, Alicia. Thank you for letting me know. Now, would you like some tea?'

Marcia thought hard about the advertisement after Alicia had gone. It might well be that the boy had come into some money. But so what? It was very nice without him, and he would probably come back if he didn't have to work in the bank in Miami, and start hanging round the house all day. And if it was a lot of money, then he would probably move away, and take Dotty with him. He was genuinely very fond of her and he had often said that one day he would make a new home for them both. Marcia didn't want Dotty going away. Not now. She felt proprietorial towards her. She felt she was hers to look after; she couldn't imagine life without her. And there was certainly no way Miles would put any of his money her way. She would end up lonely, and poorer than she was now. Once the house in Malibu was sold, then she and Dotty would be very well off.

No, there was absolutely nothing to be gained by letting Miles see this advertisement. She put it with all the letters under her bed. It was a good thing Larissa didn't have a curious disposition.

Mason McCall saw the advertisement too. He thought about it for a long time and then decided to put it where he felt it belonged: in the trash. There was nothing wrong with Miles, in fact he liked him, but he knew that he and Candy wanted to get married and right now she was much too young. Also right now there was no way it could happen; the boy had a job at last which was something in his favour, but it certainly wasn't going to provide enough to keep a wife, and the two of them were just going to have to wait.

Advertisements of this kind usually meant money and money in this case would mean wedding bells and Mason had no desire to hear them.

There was no chance of Candy seeing the advertisement, she never looked at a paper, her idea of a really heavy read was the latest Revlon ad in *Glamour*, Miles might see it himself and there was nothing Mason could do to prevent that, but he certainly wasn't going to go out of his way to put it under his nose.

Mason tore the paper into small shreds and went down to the pool to look for Candy and see if he could cheer her up, offer to take her out to one of the islands for a day or two, or buy her a few new frocks. She was missing Miles badly.

Billy de Launay saw the advertisement too, in the *Washington Post*. Now this was really interesting. This might explain why Miles hadn't heard from the old guy. He'd snuffed it. This was an English solicitor, after all. And it also looked like Miles might actually be going to get some money. That was what these kinds of advertisement usually meant. Lucky old sod.

Billy sighed. It was a shame Miles was such a lousy correspondent. He never heard from him these days, although he continued to send him the odd note whenever something particularly interesting or exciting happened to him. Oh, well, they could catch up on everything when he went home for his summer vacation.

Billy hoped Miles would see the advertisement. It would be awful if he missed it. He never read the papers, except maybe the headlines. He tore it out and wrote off to Miles that night, enclosing it and demanding an invitation to the blow-out he hoped Miles would be hosting if it meant what he thought it did.

He mailed it to the house in Nassau, not knowing Miles' address in Miami. Marcia filed it carefully with the others.

*

Father Kennedy read the advertisement in the *Los Angeles Times*. He always studied those kind of columns closely in the extremely forlorn hope that one of his flock might have come into some kind of a legacy, however small. They never did and it would really have done them little good if they had as it would have been converted into alcohol in no time at all. But God moved in a very mysterious way indeed, in his experience, and it was still worth keeping an eye open. He wondered what had happened. It looked as if Mr Dashwood might have died and left Miles some money. Maybe there'd been some kind of making up. Well, that was nice; but Father Kennedy had always felt it very sad that after all his efforts on the boy's behalf, poor Dashwood had received very nearly no thanks at all.

He imagined Miles was sure to see it, Mrs Kelly certainly would, she was a great one for reading the papers. Strange she had never answered his letters; she had promised to write, even suggested he took a vacation in Nassau one day. Oh, well, promises were cheap. Father Kennedy was used by now to the vagaries of human nature. He thought it would do no harm to forward a copy of the paper on to Miles. He just might miss it, and that would be a dreadful thing. He sat down that night and wrote a long letter to Mrs Kelly, enclosing the clipping. He really hoped she would reply; he would like to see her again.

Marcia looked at the envelope with the Los Angeles postmark, guessed its contents and put it with the others. She was beginning to wonder if she was doing the right thing. Whoever was looking for Miles seemed to want to find him pretty badly.

In her house in East Hampton, Long Island, Mrs Holden Taylor Jr was reading the *New York Times* over breakfast as she always did, before embarking on the hectic day of tennis, lunching, shopping and menu planning that lay ahead of her. She skimmed through the law reports (Holden liked her to know what was going on in his world) and she was looking idly at the Public Notice column when a name sprang out at her. A name that caught her sharply somewhere in the region of her heart, a name that spelt sunshine and beaches and old cars and smoking grass and glorious wonderful sex, the kind that Holden simply never quite managed, however hard they both tried to pretend that he did. Miles! Miles Wilburn. Just reading the name, she saw him as suddenly and clearly as if he was standing there, those amazing dark dark blue eyes, the heart-catching smile, the long flowing blond hair – well, that was probably cut short now – heard his voice, soft and lazy and slow. Miles. She would never forget him ever. They said you never did forget your first love. They seemed to be right. So what had happened? Had someone died and left Miles some money, and as it was an English solicitor's address in the paper, would it be Hugo Dashwood? It seemed very likely. That was very good of him, when Miles had always been so hostile and often rude to him.

Oh God, what would she give to see Miles just once more. Joanna shook herself. She hadn't even thought about him for years, well not seriously, and now here she was like a bitch on heat just because she'd read his name in the paper. Pull yourself together, Joanna, she said, and get to planning that menu. It was an important dinner party on Saturday; she had had to invite some incredibly high-powered woman in advertising that Holden had met somewhere. Just thinking about her made Joanna nervous. Apparently she wasn't just brilliantly clever and had her own agency, she was amazingly beautiful too. Camilla North, she was called, she was in her mid forties and looked just about thirty. And she rode to hounds side-saddle. Oh, God, what on earth could she serve up on the plate of such a paragon?

Joanna covered the table with recipe books and temporarily forgot all about Miles Wilburn.

Chapter Twenty-one

New York, San Francisco, Los Angeles, London, 1985

Andrew Blackworth was on his way to San Francisco. He had not initially been over-enthusiastic about the idea, indeed had suggested to Roz that one of his contacts in the States might be able at least initially to follow up the Bill Wilburn trail, but she had looked at him, her green eyes snapping with fury, and said that she was retaining him personally at great expense, and that she did not want any inexperienced fool of a stringer following this trail.

He had not been to San Francisco before and he found it greatly to his liking. He was not a sun lover, and he had visited and hated California; to his enchantment on arrival (just before midday) this city was grey and misty, damply chill. He remembered a quotation from Oscar Wilde: 'The coldest winter I ever spent was summer in San Francisco.' This was the kind of summer he liked.

His cab driver, taking him into the town through the oddly European suburban streets with their clapboard houses in faded colours, said this was a day he had to see the bridge; Andrew, fearing a cliché, allowed him to take him there, and looked in awe at the great red spires rising out of the grey mist.

'Kind of pretty, isn't it?' said the driver. 'You from England?'

Andrew said he was.

'The English usually get disappointed when they fly in here. Where's the sunshine, they say. But then they see this and they change their minds. Later on it'll clear.' He turned the cab and drove back into town through the Golden Gate Park; Bill Wilburn's office was in the centre, just east of Chinatown, in a small dingy street, a barrier closing the fiercely steep hill behind it to all but pedestrians.

'You have a nice day now,' said the cab driver cheerfully, dumping Andrew's case on the sidewalk, 'and mind you take a cable car ride. Nob and Telegraph are the best.'

Andrew said he would and walked into the building.

Wilburn's office occupied a large room taking up most of the ground floor; his secretary Cynthia, still weepy, but impeccably dressed and coiffed, and enjoying the drama, was rather desperately trying to sort out the wheat from the chaff of Bill's twenty-five-year-old collection of papers and files.

'Good morning,' said Andrew in his impeccable BBC accent. 'I'm Andrew Blackworth.' Cynthia looked at him.

'I just don't know where to begin,' she said helplessly, from her position kneeling in front of a filing cabinet, 'it all seems so old.'

Andrew gave her his most charming smile.

'It must,' he said, 'to you. Here, let me see if I can help.'

'That would be real nice of you to help me.' She looked at him. 'Sorry, why did you say you were here?'

'I didn't. I'm here because I'm a private detective from England and we're trying to trace a relative of Mr Wilburn's. A young man. Miles Wilburn. Mr Wilburn contacted us just before he died.'

'Oh, yeah,' she said, pleased to be able to show that she had some inside knowledge. 'Him. I'd forgotten him. Yeah, I had to type a letter about him.'

'Was this the letter?'

He showed her a photocopy.

'Yeah.'

'But you didn't know anything about him?'

'Nope. Nothing.'

'Mr Wilburn didn't tell you anything, talk to you about him at all?'

'Nope. Until that day I never heard of him. Never heard about him again either. No, that's not true, Mr Wilburn said he was going to visit him for a few days. A couple of weeks ago.'

'Was that in LA?'

'No. Yes. Oh, I don't know. Somehow all this has driven everything I ever knew out of my head.'

Andrew thought this was probably not an enormous amount, but he smiled at her encouragingly.

'Well, maybe something will turn up. Let's carry on for a while. Was this cousin, the one who lived in Los Angeles, called Wilburn?'

'I don't know. I guess so. I got the impression there was some tragedy, but I never really liked to ask.'

'Really? Why was that?'

'Oh, Mr Wilburn used to talk about poor Lee. Always poor Lee.'

'Was that the cousin?'

'No, it was the cousin's wife.'

'Is she still alive?'

'I guess not. Otherwise Mr Wilburn wouldn't have gone on and on about being alone in the world.'

'Possibly. And did these cousins have any children?'

'Well, I don't really know. I guess this nephew of his, I had to write the letter about, the one he went to see, was probably their kid. I just don't know.'

'Ah. And where did he live?'

'He lived here.'

'What, in this office?'

'Yeah, nearly. In a coupla rooms overhead.'

'Are they locked?'

'Yeah, but I have the key.' She looked at him, slightly embarrassed. 'I don't know if I ought to let you up, though. Oh, what the hell,' she said suddenly. 'What's it matter? I don't suppose Mr Wilburn would have minded. And nobody told me I shouldn't let anybody up there. Here's the key. Just don't disarrange anything, that's all.'

'I won't,' said Andrew, 'and thank you very much.'

'That's OK,' said Cynthia, 'I'm real grateful to you for helping me with the papers.'

'It was entirely my pleasure,' said Andrew, just slightly pompously.

The flat was a larger version of the office; untidy, depressing, disorganized. Just two rooms: a kitchen-diner, and a bed-sitting room. The bed-sit had a rather grubby sofa in it, a small bookcase full of the works of Erle Stanley Gardner and Ellery Queen, a coffee table covered in out of date car and fishing magazines, and rather incongruously a British Heritage calendar on one wall, opened at the right month. Now how long had Bill Wilburn been an anglophile, Andrew wondered.

There was a small table by the bed, with a couple of drawers in it, and two photographs on the tiled shelf above the gas fire; one was framed, a very old wedding photograph of a very very pretty blonde girl, and a slightly plump, crewcut young man, sundry relatives standing on either side of them. One of them, Andrew assumed, must be Bill Wilburn. The other was unframed, curling with age, creased and dirty, tucked into the edge of a lurid picture of the Golden Gate Bridge; it was of a blond baby, about ten months old, laughing in the plump (and considerably older) crewcut man's arms.

'Now,' said Andrew to the baby, 'are you Miles or are you not?'

He went back downstairs, holding the wedding picture. Cynthia had stopped working for a spell, and was retouching her make-up.

'Cynthia,' he said, 'is any of these people Bill Wilburn?'

She took the photograph and looked at it. 'Sure,' she said, 'that's him. Next to the bridesmaid.'

'But you don't know if this was his cousin's wedding?'

'Nope. I guess it probably is, but I just don't know. I've never seen it before.'

'OK, I'll put it back. And lock up. I won't be a minute.'

He came back down smiling. 'Thank you, Cynthia, for that. It didn't actually provide me with any information, but it was nice of you. Er – do you happen to know what might have happened to Mr Wilburn's wallet? Or his personal address book for instance?'

'Well,' she said, 'I don't know about the address book. But his wallet is right here, in the safe. I put it there for the time being. I guess you might as well see it.'

She handed it over. Andrew opened it very slowly. It was empty, apart from two ten-dollar bills, a couple of credit card receipts, and a used air ticket. He looked at it cautiously, almost afraid of what it was going to tell him. It was a used return ticket to Nassau.

Joanna looked contentedly round her dinner table. It had all been the greatest success. The lobster and wild rice had been wonderful, the meringue baskets which were always a slight worry had turned out perfectly, and everyone had come up for second helpings of the mousse of raspberries and wild strawberries. Now Holden was going round the table with the armagnac, and Christabel was ready with the coffee, and the worrying part was completely over. What was more, Camilla North had been really very nice, charming in a rather formal way, she was certainly very beautiful, dressed dramatically all in black (probably, Joanna thought, by Bill Blass), and a bit remote, but not really too frightening at all. The man she had come with, a banker called Peter Cohen, was obviously besotted with her; Camilla was plainly not the least besotted with him, in fact Joanna could detect signs of severe irritation in the way she was now just slightly obsessively lining up the glasses in front of her in a very neat way; time to move everyone, she thought, like the good hostess she was.

'Shall we take coffee on the patio?' she said. 'It's such a lovely night.'

'Oh, that would be so nice,' said Camilla, speaking (as she so often did) for the assorted company. 'And then quite soon, Peter, I think we should make a move. It's very late.'

'Oh, goodness, don't go yet!' said Joanna. It was awful when a party broke up too early, you missed the fun bit altogether that way.

'Well, I'm a little tired,' said Camilla, her lovely head drooping just slightly. 'I've had a hard week. We were pitching for some new drink business.'

'Did you get it?' asked Mary Wilder, an old friend of Holden's, who Joanna was just slightly suspicious of, she didn't like the way she kept saying things to him very quietly so no one else could hear and touching his arm in that over-friendly way: Mary was also in advertising, although considerably less successfully so than the beautiful Miss North (but then, thought Joanna, struggling to be fair, she was much much younger).

'I'm not sure. I think probably yes. It's such a chauvinist business, advertising, we always have to win two wars on every pitch, one to be better than the competition, the other to overcome the innate belief that we can't possibly be better because it's my agency and I'm a woman.'

'I simply cannot believe that, Camilla, in this day and age,' said Peter Cohen. 'I think you're just paranoid, like all women.'

'Women are not paranoid,' said Camilla coldly. 'Merely realistic. I do assure you I do know what I'm talking about. Which, if you will forgive me for saying so, you do not. We may have made some progress in the last decade, but we are still suffering severely under the yoke of thousands of years of oppression.'

'Oh, Camilla, that's balls!' said Holden. 'I – we have many women in the bank in quite senior positions. No oppression there, I can tell you.'

'Really?' said Camilla.

'Really. Dozens of them. Very nice to have them around,

too,' he added, slightly unfortunately. Joanna winced; Holden could be so crass at times.

'And how many of these dozens of women are on the main board?' asked Camilla.

'Oh, I don't know. Several, I think. I'm not sure.'

'Any presidents?'

'Well, vice-presidents certainly. Not many presidents. Obviously.'

'Why obviously?'

'Well, of course we're very keen on the idea, very aware that women should be presidents. That they're just as good as the next man, if you'll forgive the expression. But the other presidents in the other banks aren't ready for it. They wouldn't quite welcome it. Not appreciate it. Not yet,' he added hastily, unnerved by the look in her slightly blank dark eyes. 'In time I'm sure there will be. And we'll lead the way.'

'I see. Good for you.'

There was a silence. Mary broke it.

'Camilla, do you ever see Nigel Silk these days?'

'Occasionally,' said Camilla. 'At awards ceremonies and so forth. I'm afraid he hasn't reacted terribly generously to my success. He's a great yoke-bearer,' she added, flashing a cool smile at Holden.

'Who is Nigel Silk?' asked Joanna quickly, nervous. She could see this getting difficult and the whole evening being ruined.

'He's the man who used to do most of our advertising when I worked for Julian Morell, in the early days.'

This was getting worse; Holden had warned her not to so much as touch on the subject of Julian Morell and to steer any conversation right off him. Julian Morrell had always rather fascinated Joanna; she used to like reading about him in the gossip columns, about all his money, and his houses, and his wives, and also Sir James Goldsmith, who had seemed to her a rather similarly glamorous figure; when Holden had told her that Camilla had been Julian Morell's mistress for years, she could hardly contain herself with excitement and awe. 'But the guy's only died a couple of months ago, and she's probably pretty cut up about it, even though she hadn't been involved with him for a while. So for God's sake, Joanna, just don't even mention him.'

And now, here was Camilla herself mentioning Julian Morell, and Mary Wilder's eyes lighting up, and one of the other men, Irving Drummond, a friend of Holden's in the hotel business, leaning forward eagerly. What on earth could she do?

'Coffee everyone,' she said again, brilliant smile flashing round the table, but they all ignored her.

'I met Julian Morell's daughter only the other day,' said Drummond. 'Tough nut, that one. She's taken over the hotels division from that husband of hers. He's resigned from the company. She's divorcing him.'

'Really?' said Cohen. 'And marrying Browning, I suppose?'

'Oh, I don't know. I guess so. I have to say I don't envy him, but I guess he can take it.'

Joanna felt worse and worse; she drained her glass and poured herself another, hoping no one was looking.

'Where did you meet Roz?' said Camilla. She seemed quite calm; Joanna relaxed a little. Maybe it would be all right. If she just kept right out of the conversation from now on, Holden couldn't possibly blame her for any of it.

'Oh, at a hotel convention. She's very attractive, I must say. Amazing figure.'

'Do you really think so?' said Camilla in tones so icy, the entire room was chilled. 'I always find that very severe style of hers rather off-putting. She was a singularly plain child,' she added, displaying her intimate knowledge of the family and daring anyone else to comment on Roz Emerson's attractiveness at one and the same moment.

'How is she coping, running that empire?' asked Cohen. 'It's quite an undertaking. And she's very young for the job.'

'I have absolutely no idea,' said Camilla, cooler still. 'I can only say any adversary of hers has my deep sympathy.' She turned in her chair. 'Joanna, my dear, why don't we avail ourselves of your very nice suggestion that we should go and have coffee in the garden? It really is very hot in here.'

Joanna stood up and walked out of the room; Camilla, Mary and Nancy Smallwood, Joanna's great friend and unofficial co-hostess on sticky occasions, followed her.

While Mary and Nancy were still upstairs, Joanna found herself sitting alone on the terrace with Camilla. She looked at her, seeming, she thought suddenly, rather sad and vulnerable, and said on an impulse (thank God Holden was inside, carrying on about the Dow Jones or something), 'Camilla, I do hope it doesn't upset you to talk about Julian Morell. I'm sorry if the conversation about him ran on a bit.'

Camilla looked at her and smiled a trifle frostily. Don't you try and get too close to me, that look said. 'Of course not,' she said graciously. 'In any case if it did I have only myself to blame for bringing his name into the conversation. Please don't worry about it.'

'All right,' said Joanna. 'And thank you for coming this evening. It's been so nice to meet you. Holden has told me such a lot about you. He has such admiration for you and your agency.'

'How sweet of him,' said Camilla. 'Just a poor thing, but mine own,' she added graciously. Joanna recognized the quotation, but she wasn't sure if she should say she did or not.

Mercifully at this point Nancy returned. Nancy could talk any silence out. She commenced to do so now.

'That was a great dinner, Jo,' she said. 'Christabel does make the best summer mousse in the world. Didn't you think it was just yummy, Camilla?'

Camilla smiled. 'What a lovely word,' she said. 'It's years since I heard it. Not since I was a small girl.'

She suddenly seemed more human again. Maybe she had just made things worse apologizing like that, Joanna thought. Blast.

'Well, I use lots of school words still,' said Nancy cheerfully. 'I love 'em. I say gosh, and gee and fab and crush and – gross and spaced and Za.'

'Whatever does Za mean?' said Joanna, grateful for this diversion.

'Pizza, everyone knows that,' said Nancy, laughing. 'I forgot you went to school in the backwoods, Jo.'

'Where was that?' asked Camilla, turning to Joanna, obviously anxious to show she bore no grudge to someone for not going to Vassar.

'Hollywood,' said Joanna. 'Marymount High School.'

'That does sound fun,' said Camilla. 'Hardly the backwoods, but fun.'

'Oh,' said Joanna, suddenly sharply remembering, just as

she had reading the advertisement, what it felt like to be young, to be at Marymount High, to be in California, to be in love, 'it was. Wonderful fun.'

And then she said it. It was partly nerves, partly the wine, partly genuinely wanting to tell someone.

'The most extraordinary thing happened to me this week,' she said, 'I was reading the paper, and in the announcement column, you know, where they advertise for people, was the name of my very first boyfriend. Some English lawyer is looking for him. Isn't that extraordinary? At least I suppose it was him. He had the same name, at any rate.'

Camilla was looking at her very oddly; she had gone rather pale.

'And what was the name of this boyfriend?' she said.

'Miles,' said Joanna. 'Miles Wilburn.'

Doctor Margaret Friedman looked at Phaedria across her desk.

'Good morning,' she said, her eyes taking in an enormous amount without appearing even to have left her diary: the beauty, the pregnancy, the money. Margaret Friedman did not know a Ralph Lauren shirt from a Marks and Spencer one, nor a Cartier ring from a junk job from Fenwick's, but she could nonetheless tell you in an instant where a client stood in the socio-economic scale, what kind of school they had been to, which kind of car they drove, whether they lived in town or the country, whether they had any children. It was one of the things that made her so good at her job.

'Good morning,' said Phaedria. 'It's very good of you to see me at such short notice. Thank you.'

'Joan said you sounded – well, not entirely happy. I do like to help when I can.'

'I'm – well – I'm all right. It's just that – well I do have a – problem.'

Margaret drew a pad towards her. 'Let's start with a few details, shall we? Now your full name is –?'

'Phaedria Morell.'

'And you're – forgive me, but I do read the papers, Julian Morell's widow?' The dark eyes looked at Phaedria, politely non-committal.

726

'Yes.'

'I'm so sorry. It must be a very difficult time for you.'

'Well,' said Phaedria, with a rather tight little smile, 'it certainly isn't easy.'

'And you're pregnant.'

'Yes.'

'How do you feel?'

'Awful.'

'I'm not surprised. Would you like some tea?'

'No, thank you. Do you have any lemons?'

'I do. In hot water?'

'Yes, please.'

She ordered Joan rather briskly to bring in some hot water and lemon and then sat back in her chair. 'Now then. Where should we begin?'

'About fifteen years ago,' said Phaedria.

'I'm sorry?'

Phaedria smiled. 'It's all right. I'm sorry. I must be a terrible shock to you. There's nothing wrong with me. At least I don't think so. Not psychiatrically. It's just that – oh, it's such a bizarre story. I don't know where to begin. You may not be able to help at all.'

'Let me try.'

'Well, about fifteen years ago, my husband came to see you.'

'Yes, he did. Did he tell you that himself?'

'No. His secretary told me. You see, my husband has left a very complicated will. This is –? She looked awkward. 'Confidential?'

'Yes. Yes of course.'

'Well, we are trying to trace someone. Someone he left an important legacy to. We thought you might be able to help.'

'I can't imagine how.'

'Well, my husband was – well, rather a complex man. He was not at all straightforward.'

'Perhaps.'

'Anyway, his secretary knew he had been seeing you in – oh, I think 1971. We thought – that is I thought – if you could tell me why, what he came about, it might throw a bit of light on his life.'

'Possibly,' said Margaret Friedman carefully.

'Oh, I feel so silly,' said Phaedria suddenly. 'You must think I'm mad.'

'On the contrary, I think you're very sane. You should see some of the others, as they say. And I do assure you no story comes as a surprise to me.'

'Well,' said Phaedria, 'let's get down to basics. Do you – could you remember why my husband came to see you?'

'I'm not sure. I'd have to look out his notes.'

'Could you do that?'

'Well, I could certainly look them out. I think before I committed myself to talking to you very much more, I'd have to know a bit more about you.'

'Why?' said Phaedria, her eyes wide with disappointment.

'Well, you may seem very stable. I'm sure you are. But you must realize I might – I'm not saying I necessarily would be – I might be promising to tell you something which would make you very unstable indeed.'

'Oh, I'm sure it wasn't anything really ghastly. It couldn't have been. Someone would have known.'

'You'd be surprised, Lady Morell – how people don't know about ghastly things. Close their minds to them. Tell themselves they can't be true. Of course I'm not suggesting your husband was a murderer or anything. But I can't give you a blanket promise to tell you whatever it was he came to see me about without knowing you a little better . . .' She smiled. 'When's the baby due?'

'November.'

'Then we must take care of you. Where are you having it?'

'St Mary's, Paddington. The Lindo Wing.'

'Very sensible. Now, what I'd like to do is have a chat with you now, learn a little more about you, and then if you can come back in a day or two, I'll have looked at your husband's notes, and I can talk to you with a bit more confidence.'

'Oh, God,' said Phaedria, her voice suddenly shaky, 'look, I can see that you have to be careful, but honestly I am very stable, I don't need counselling, I just want to unravel this mystery. I can't stand it much longer. I don't see why you won't help.'

She suddenly burst into tears; Margaret Friedman sat and handed her tissues and watched her sympathetically for a few minutes. Then she said, 'You may not need counselling, but you do need help. Why don't you begin at the beginning? I honestly think it'll make you feel better.'

When Phaedria had left, an hour later, she got out the files on Julian Morell. She felt she owed it to herself to check through them. But as she had known, there was no need. She could remember absolutely everything that was in them.

Phaedria was fast asleep when the phone rang.

'Phaedria? It's C. J.'

'C. J., it's two in the morning.'

'I know. I'm sorry to wake you. But I have some news.'

He heard her snap into wakefulness. 'What? C. J., what? Where are you?'

'In New York, at Sutton Place.'

'Oh, God, of course you are. I'm sorry. I'd forgotten for a moment. Well, go on, what have you found?'

'Something quite strange. In Julian's desk.'

'What? For God's sake, C. J., what?'

'Well, I thought I'd wasted my time at first. Nothing in it remotely interesting. Then I was fiddling about with one of the small top drawers, it seemed to be too shallow somehow, and – well, it had a spring back, and there inside it, right at the very back, was a box. A locked document box.'

'And?'

'I'm afraid I forced it open and there were some pretty odd things inside.'

'What sort of odd?'

'Well, a few snapshots of a little boy. No name or anything.'

'What does he look like?'

'Fairly standard. Blond hair. Snub nose. Nice smile.'

'And? What else?'

'A card announcing his birth, at least I presume it was his birth. It was him, he was Miles. Miles Wilburn. Born 1958. In Santa Monica. Los Angeles.'

'Oh, God. C. J., who is he? What is all this? Who was this card from?'

'Someone called Dean. Dean Wilburn. Saying come and see us soon.'

'Does it give an address?'

'No. You know those cards, Phaedria, they're just name, weight and date and time. Nothing helpful like an address, for us detectives to discover.'

'You're a great detective, C. J. You really are. You should take it up for a living. I can't believe all this. But what on earth, what on earth does it mean? Does it say where he was born, this child?'

'Yeah, St John's Hospital, Santa Monica.'

'Well, maybe we could track them – him down through there.'

'Maybe.'

'Anything else?'

'Yeah, a cutting from a newspaper, an obituary of someone called Lee Wilburn. The usual thing, you know, after an illness, bravely borne. Beloved mother of Miles.'

Phaedria was silent for a minute.

'Poor Lee, whoever she was. Poor Miles. What year was that?'

'Um, let's see, 1971.'

'So Miles would only have been, what, thirteen. How sad. What about his father?'

'No mention of him. Not even in the obit.'

'Oh, C. J., I don't understand any of this. None of it.'

'Neither do I. And then there's one more thing, a list of graduations from the University of Berkeley in 1980 listing Miles Wilburn. He got a summa cum laude in Maths. He's obviously not dumb. Whoever he is.'

'I always said he wouldn't be,' said Phaedria. 'No more photographs?'

'None. Julian obviously believed in keeping his memorabilia to a minimum. Whatever it was all about. Look, I really have to go and see my mother tomorrow, but I'll fly straight back the next day. We can talk then. And decide what to do next. Go down to LA or whatever. I just had to let you know.'

'Of course. Oh, C. J., what on earth do all these people have to do with Julian? It's so mysterious. Oh, God, now I don't know whether to be pleased or worried.'

'I think you should be pleased. Otherwise, I'm wasting an awful lot of time and effort.'

She smiled, and he could hear her mood briefly lightening. 'All right, I'll be pleased.'

'Good night, Phaedria.'

'Good night, C. J. Sleep well. And thank you.'

Phaedria couldn't go back to sleep. She lay tossing, uncomfortable, agitated, with visions of a small boy with blond hair dancing before her eyes, and the words 'beloved mother of Miles' flickering fretfully inside her head.

Roz looked round the boardroom. Phaedria was at one end of the table, Richard Brookes at the other. Susan, Freddy Branksome and George Hanover, sales director of the entire group, were sitting side by side with their backs to the window. They all, even Phaedria, had their eyes fixed on her face. She was, in that moment, Susan thought, extraordinarily like her father, determined, utterly in control, fixing their attention on her.

'I want to discuss the pharmaceutical division,' she said. 'I think we could be missing some valuable opportunities for expansion.'

This was Roz's latest game, and tactically important in her war against Phaedria. She would fix on some aspect of the company, study it fiercely for days, acquaint herself with every possible detail of its strengths and weaknesses, and then pounce, call a meeting to discuss it, with the least possible warning. She would ask for comments on profitability, potential growth, she would suggest investment programmes, advertising campaigns, plant expansions, training programmes, she would argue for diversification, she would demand absolutely up-to-the-minute reports on stock holdings, budget controls, market shares, she would criticize salary levels, and then at the end of it she would sit down with an expression of huge satisfaction on her face and ask someone else for their comments on the subject in hand.

The whole thing was a piece of theatre, and staged for the benefit of nobody but herself; the time it wasted was enormous, the benefit it brought to each of the companies minimal, indeed it was often disruptive, because she always insisted on some changes being made, albeit minor, but for a few hours every week she was absolutely in command, displaying her knowledge which was formidable, and her intellect which was considerable. It also left Phaedria visibly confused and demoralized, her modest knowledge of the company and her lack of the skills, knowledge and the politicking power of her rival openly displayed.

She was clearly losing confidence now; she would make a statement, Roz would contest it, express a view, have it demolished. Richard and Freddy and even Susan, with her determined fondness for Roz, her support for her cause, watched this slaughter with distaste. Roz had the big guns on her side; Phaedria was confronting her with an elegant but ineffectual blank-firing pistol.

Phaedria made her way wearily up to the penthouse and let herself in. She drank the iced Perrier Sarah had left for her, ignored the prawn salad, and lay down on the bed in the small room off the main office. She wondered how much longer she could go on. How much more public humiliation she could take, how many more blows at her self-esteem she would have to force herself to endure.

And besides, what was she doing it for? C. J. had been right, she could so easily give in, let Roz have the company, just go away somewhere and enjoy herself, have her baby in peace, bring it up somewhere far removed from this nightmare of intrigue and politicking and self-doubt.

It was a monstrous legacy, and one that had very little to offer her. And just where was bloody bloody Miles Wilburn, was she ever going to find out what his part was in the nightmare, and even if she did, then what? What good did she think he could do her? How was she to get hold of his two per cent anyway? Would she have to marry him? Buy him? How could you have done this to me, Julian Morell, she thought, exposed me to this pain, this humiliation.

How he must have despised her. He certainly couldn't have loved her. Bastard! She found herself thinking in these terms more and more these days. If he walked in here now, she thought, I'd kill him! Then the irony of that struck her and she smiled suddenly; she relaxed on to the bed. Deep within her the child stirred, the strange sweet fluttering she waited to feel day by day, entranced by its increasing strength and urgency; it made the whole thing somehow bearable; worth while, important.

'We'll do it,' she said aloud, looking down at the considerable hump which was now situated where her flat stomach had been, stroking it tenderly, smiling at it. 'We'll do it. For your daddy's sake. No, not for your daddy's sake, forget I said that. For your mother's. I'm the one that counts around here. Don't you forget it.' She closed her eyes; she felt her head slowly skimming into the lack of coherent thought that means sleep is imminent. She allowed her mind to wander; she thought about the little boy with blond hair, the woman, the beloved mother. Poor Lee, she thought drowsily, poor Lee. Dying so young. In – 1971. The words formed a refrain in her head: Dying so young in 71, dying so young in 71.

And then she sat up suddenly alert, her heart thudding, her hands damp. In 1971. Lee had died in 1971. The year Sarah had said Julian had been so depressed. When he had begun to go to Doctor Friedman.

She turned on the bed, reached for the phone, dialled Doctor Friedman's number feverishly, her mind a tumult.

'Mrs Durrant? Could I speak to Doctor Friedman, please? This is Lady Morell. Yes, it's very very urgent. Very urgent indeed.'

Chapter Twenty-two

London, Nassau, Los Angeles, New York, 1985

'Nassau?' said Roz. 'Nassau? Are you sure?'

Andrew Blackworth was used to being patient. 'Yes,' he said. 'Yes, I'm quite sure, Nassau is where Bill Wilburn last saw his nephew.'

'Well, go to Nassau, of course,' said Roz impatiently. 'I don't care in the least how expensive it all is. You seem to be doing quite well. Do you have anything further in the way of information, or is it just Nassau?'

'Nothing at all. But I don't see that as an insurmountable obstacle.'

'No, I would hope not. Yes, do go on down there, Mr

Blackworth. At least for a few days. Keep in touch though, won't you? I don't want you to disappear utterly.'

Andrew Blackworth assured her he would not, and put down the phone. He sighed. Nassau was certainly not going to be as nice as San Francisco.

C. J. was just beginning to think about making his excuses for leaving Oyster Bay and his mother earlier than he had promised when he remembered that Phaedria had asked him to talk to Camilla before he left. He sighed. He didn't particularly like Camilla, but he could see that he was in fact probably the best person to talk to her. There were no violent emotions raging in his breast against her, or indeed in hers against him; they had had a civilized working relationship, she had been perfectly courteous and composed with him at the reading of the will; he viewed her a great deal more benignly than a lot of other people in the family.

He walked through into the hall and dialled the number of her agency. Miss North was out, they said, taking a late lunch; could she call him back in around a half hour?

Certainly, said C. J., any time, he would be in all afternoon. The secretary sounded very shocked at any suggestion that Camilla would fail to call within the half hour, and took his number. Almost exactly thirty minutes later the phone rang.

'C. J.? Hallo. This is Camilla North. You rang me.'

'I did. How are you, Camilla?'

'Extremely well, thank you. C. J., I'm glad you phoned. I can imagine what it's about, or I think I can, and I do actually have some news for you. I didn't know quite what to do with it. That is, I didn't know who to call. Could we meet for a drink? Perhaps the Palm Court at the Plaza?'

'Sure,' he said, intrigued.

Camilla was waiting for him when he got there. She really was a lovely woman, he thought, studying her before she had seen him; nobody would ever think she was forty-eight. No wonder old Julian had been so besotted with her. She was dressed in a loose white silk dress with wide shoulders and sleeves cut off sharply at the elbows; she was tanned, her long legs were bare. Her red-gold hair was clipped back from her face, she wore no jewellery except a heavy gilt chain and matching bracelet from Chanel. She looked classically, sleekly beautiful. C. J. went up to her and held out his hand.

'C. J. How formal!' She reached up and kissed his cheek. 'It's very nice to see you. I was sorry to hear about you and Roz.'

'Yes, well, thank you,' he said. 'It's never easy, is it?'

'Well, of course,' she said, very cool, very composed, 'I have never been married, and therefore never divorced. But I have been through a break-up or two.'

She smiled at him, and he noticed for the first time the lines of strain by her mouth and a shadow in her eyes. It must have been very hard on her, Julian's death, indeed the whole ghastly business. No sympathy, and plenty of pain.

'Yes,' he said, gently commiserating, 'I know. What would you like to drink?'

'A Bloody Mary, I think. To go with my day.'

'How is the agency? And what are you doing in this God awful place in August?'

'Working. I have a lot on. And you?'

'Oh, same kind of thing.'

'I heard you'd left the company.'

'I have. I'm researching a book.'

'C. J.! How nice. What on?'

'London,' he said, and then seeing her puzzled eyes, 'I'm here visiting my mother.'

'Ah,' she said, 'I see.'

'So what news do you have for me, Camilla? It sounds intriguing.'

'It is. Deeply intriguing. I have a lead for you. Let me tell you about it.'

She told him. C. J. listened entranced. 'That is – very interesting. Very interesting indeed.'

'Why?'

'Oh – oh, well, I don't see why you shouldn't know. I found some stuff in Julian's desk.'

'My goodness, C. J.,' said Camilla, her eyes dancing with amusement, 'you are doing a great deal of research! Your mother can't have seen a great deal of you on your visit to her.'

He looked at her and smiled, and she thought how extraordinarily nice he was, quite the nicest person in that whole ghastly clan; maybe it had something to do with his nationality. Camilla had a deeply inbred chauvinism. She was also struck for the first time by how attractive he was. He did not have exactly striking looks, but they were the kind she liked and understood: gentle, well bred, understated. He was always so well dressed, too, and his manners were perfect; Camilla settled more deeply into her chair and prepared herself to enjoy the evening ahead more than she had expected.

'Yes, well,' he said, 'I do find the whole business so intriguing, and Phaedria needs some help.'

'Ah,' she said, with a stab of irritation at the name. 'Yes. How is Phaedria?'

'Not very well. Pregnancy doesn't seem to suit her. And Roz is giving her a hard time.'

'Roz gives everyone a hard time. Anyway, tell me the significance of what you found in Julian's desk.'

'Well, it kind of ties in. Location-wise at any rate. Camilla, did he ever go to LA a lot when you knew him?'

'Oh,' she said, and there was a great humour in her eyes, 'who could tell where Julian ever was? But no, not as far as I can remember. Indeed he always rather resisted the idea of having a store there, or a hotel. He said he didn't like the place.'

'Intriguing.'

'Yes. Well, he was an intriguing man. Whatever his faults. Tell me what you found.'

He told her. 'Camilla, do you remember Julian getting any calls ever from someone called Lee? Lee Wilburn?'

'No. No, I don't. But then he got an awful lot of calls.' She looked at him and smiled suddenly. 'He was very very clever at covering his tracks. I doubt if he'd have had anyone call him at home.'

'No, but maybe in an emergency?'

'Maybe. But it's all so long ago, isn't it? I mean it's hopeless trying to pick up trails at this distance.'

'I guess so. Although we don't seem to be doing too badly.'

'No. No, you don't. So what will you do now?'

'I think, if you don't mind, I might talk to this Joanna Holden on Long Island. Can you give me her number?'

'Of course.'

'This is very nice of you, Camilla. I don't really see why you should help any of us.'

'Oh,' she shrugged. 'Well, I felt very bad about my being in the apartment that night. I didn't behave very well altogether. I'd like to make amends.'

'Well, you're very generous. Can I show the family's appreciation by buying you dinner?'

She looked at him consideringly. 'I think that would be a really very attractive idea, C. J. Thank you.'

They had a very pleasant and relaxed dinner and (both being lonely, frustrated and in need of some harmless diversion) ended the evening, to their mutual surprise and immense pleasure, between Camilla's linen sheets.

C. J. went to see Joanna next morning. He liked her immediately, she was pretty and sharp and funny; and she was only too delighted to talk about Miles.

She had obviously been seriously in love with him; she still talked of him with a kind of wistful intimacy. He had been her best friend, she said, as well as her boyfriend; she had met him on the beach at Malibu in 1975. 'Ten years ago, goodness, aren't we all getting old.'

He had been living with his grandmother, a nice old lady called Mrs Kelly, and he had been at Santa Monica High School. 'Then Mr Dashwood came along and put him through college. Sent him off to Berkeley. Miles was very clever, he did really well.'

'Who was Mr Dashwood?'

'I don't really know,' said Joanna. 'He was a bit of a hazy figure. I only met him very briefly once. He hardly ever came to see Miles. But he was a friend of the family, and he was quite rich, I guess. Anyway, he did a lot for Miles. Miles never really liked him, though, I don't know why.'

'He should have done,' said C. J. 'If he put him through college. That isn't cheap.'

'No, I know. Anyway, Miles was very very hurt because Mr Dashwood wouldn't give him a job in his company. That was when he went off and became a beach bum. Miles, I mean, not Mr Dashwood. And he said he'd never see him or speak to him again.'

737

C. J. was beginning to dislike Miles intensely.

'When did you last see him?'

'Oh,' she said, her face shadowy, 'I guess it was about 1981. Yes, that would have been it. I tried, we all did, to change Miles' mind, to make him get a job, do something with his degree, do something useful, he was awfully clever, and very – well, attractive, presentable, you know, but he just wouldn't. He was so angry and kind of strange suddenly. He just went off and more or less dropped out of all our lives. I used to go and see him and his granny sometimes in the evening, but somehow I felt he didn't want me any more either. So I gave up too.'

'Do you have a picture of him?' asked C. J., his heart beating suddenly rather fast.

'Well,' she said, looking suddenly guilty. 'Well, I do. But you mustn't tell Holden. If you ever meet him. He wouldn't like it.'

C. J. looked very serious. 'I promise I won't.'

'I'll go and get it.'

She came back with a rather faded colour snapshot. 'It's very old. I don't suppose he looks a bit like this now. But anyway, there you are. I got rid of all the others.'

A face smiled at C. J. It was an indisputably nice face. A very good-looking face, probably, he thought, if you could see it properly. With long, blond hair falling on his shoulders, blue eyes, and a ravishing smile. He was wearing a white T-shirt, he looked happy, relaxed, very Californian, and he had signed the picture: 'Jo, from Miles, all my love.'

'I can't – I couldn't –?'

'No,' she said, 'I'm sorry, I really would rather you didn't take it. It's kind of personal.'

'Of course.'

'What are you going to do?' she said.

'What would you suggest? Do you have any idea where he might be?'

'None. But you could look over in LA. He might well still be there. On the beach. Try his granny. I can give you the address. Oh, and I tell you who you could talk to. Father Kennedy at the refuge in Santa Monica. He and old Mrs Kelly were great buddies. Miles used to say she was his temptress.' She laughed. 'If only you could have seen her. But she was so good to Miles. And he did love her. He really really did.'

'And you have no idea where we could find this Mr Dashwood?'

'Honestly, no. I mean, he could be anywhere. England. New York. Anywhere.'

'Why England? Why do you say that?'

'Well,' she said. 'Because he was English. Sorry, I thought I'd told you that.'

Margaret Friedman looked at Phaedria Morell across her desk.

'All right,' she said. 'Ask me some questions.'

'When – when my husband came to see you, was he very unhappy?'

'Fairly. Certainly not happy.'

'No, well, silly question I suppose. Was he – well, had he lost someone he was very fond of? Had someone died?'

'Yes.'

'A woman?'

'Yes.'

Phaedria was silent for a while. 'Was she – was she his mistress do you think?'

'I think she could have been.'

'Was he still in love with her when she died?'

'In a way, perhaps. But, he was more sad than heartbroken. I think she was much more of a dear friend. I got the impression your husband was not over-rich in close friends.'

'No,' said Phaedria, 'I'm afraid that's right.' She looked at Margaret Friedman. 'Did he talk much about a little boy?'

'Not a great deal. This lady did have a little boy. And your husband was concerned about him.'

'What about her husband, do you know anything about him?'

'Yes, he had also died. Earlier. A year or two, I think.'

'I suppose that would explain why Julian was so concerned about the little boy. He was an orphan.'

'Indeed.'

Phaedria looked at her and sighed. 'I feel you're keeping an awful lot from me.'

'Why should I do that?'

'You've told me why. You said you had to know more about me before you could tell me anything very much.'

'I think I've told you a lot. I'm keeping my side of the bargain quite well. Let's talk a bit more about you now. How are you feeling?'

'All right. Very tired. But less sick.'

'I really meant emotionally.'

'Pretty bad. I miss Julian terribly, of course.'

'Of course. Do you feel anything as well as sadness?'

'Yes,' said Phaedria, suddenly meeting Margaret Friedman's detachedly interested eyes. 'Yes I do. I feel angry. Absolutely furious. I don't see how he could possibly have done this to me. Half the time I'm grieving because I love him, and the other half I'm raging because I hate him. It's awful.'

'It's healthy.'

'Is it?'

'Well, don't you think so? If he was still alive and he'd done it you'd be furious. Why should his being dead make a difference?'

'I hadn't thought of it like that,' said Phaedria. 'But it does, because it's so much worse. I can't talk to him. Find out why he did it, why he hated me so much.'

'I'm sure he didn't hate you. Quite sure. But if you really thought, hard and constructively, you might find a few clues as to why he decided to do it.'

'I have thought. I've thought and thought. I can't come up with anything except that he wanted to make me miserable.'

'Let me help you think. We may come up with something better than that. All right?'

'All right.'

Pete was waiting outside with the car when she came out, drained, exhausted, but strangely more peaceful.

'Dover Street, Lady Morell?'

'I suppose so,' she said and sighed, and then on an impulse, 'no, Pete, could you take me to First Street, I'd like to see Mrs Morell. It's only twelve o'clock, she's sure to be there.'

'Certainly.'

'And, Pete, let's stop off at Harrods, and we can get her some flowers.'

'Very good, Lady Morell.'

She sank back in the car, her mind blank, vaguely anxious that she should be in the office, but equally sure that she would be unable to cope with its demands for an hour or two. It would be nice to see Letitia; she was always so comforting, so affectionate, such fun. It would be nice to talk over the past twenty-four hours with her, but she couldn't; it would be unfair, too much for her to cope with. She had survived Julian's death surprisingly well, but she had aged a lot just the same, and the ongoing stress of the mystery was taking its toll. She really was the pivot of the family, Phaedria thought; what would they all do without her? Even Roz talked to Letitia from time to time, and loved her. She managed to transcend all the rivalries, all the passions, all the jealousies and in-fighting and yet without ever being pious or sanctimonious, indeed she managed to defuse it all, make it seem rather amusing and silly. It would be nice to see her now, nice just to talk to her. She wondered if she should have warned her she was coming, but no, she always encouraged people to just drop in, and it was a good time, just before lunch, she wasn't resting or anything, and she wouldn't have gone out.

Pete pulled up outside the house. 'Shall I wait, Lady Morell?'

'Yes, please, Pete, I'll only be a short while, and we may be able to give Mrs Morell a lift somewhere as well.'

She scooped the bunch of white lilies she had bought into her arms, walked up the steps to the front door and knocked three times very briskly. The door opened at once; Phaedria found herself looking up into the mournful face of Michael Browning.

Her first instinct was to bolt. Nobody (except perhaps Doctor Friedman) could have told her why, but it was extremely strong; however, it was plainly also ridiculous, and undignified. She stood there looking at him; he looked back at her in silence.

She was wearing a brilliant sea-blue silk dress, which slithered gracefully over her burgeoning stomach, and stopped at the knees; her long legs were bare, and she wore low-heeled blue pumps that matched her dress; her wild hair was tied back in a blue silk bow. With the lilies in her arms, the distress in her eyes, she looked exactly like a painting by Burne-Jones.

Michael Browning reached out and in an instinctive desire to comfort, to calm her, touched her cheek. Phaedria drew back as if she had been stung.

'Hey,' he said, 'don't look so frightened. I won't bite you. Come along in. How's the unfriendly baby? Grown, I see.'

'Yes. Sorry. That is, well, I won't stop. Not if you're here. Just give Letitia these, I'll be back another time.'

'Now look,' he said, his eyes exploring her face amusedly, 'I don't know what I've done to frighten you so much but I promise I'll stop now. Don't be silly, of course you must stay. I'm only here for a drink, and then I'm taking Letitia out to lunch. Why don't you join us?'

'Oh, no,' said Phaedria, sufficiently recovered from her shock to smile, almost to laugh. 'Thank you but no. Not in public, not with you.'

'Well, thank you for the compliment. Maybe in private then,' he said, returning the smile. 'I don't mind.'

Letitia suddenly appeared in the hall.

'Phaedria, how lovely. Come on in, darling, and sit down. Are those for me? Thank you. I have a new maid, you know, Nancy finally decided to retire, and she's hopeless with flowers, I'll do them myself. Now then, what will you have? A drink?'

'Oh, no thank you,' said Phaedria, 'and I won't stop. You're obviously busy.'

'Nonsense. We have all the time in the world, don't we, Michael? He's taking me to lunch at Langan's, so we can get to know one another better. Roz brought him over and introduced him to me last night, and I felt it couldn't be left at that. After all he's part of the family and he doesn't know anything about me at all. Now don't be so ridiculous, Phaedria, come along in and sit down. You look exhausted.'

'I'm all right. Yes, could I have a cup of hot water with some lemon in it? And some glucose.'

'Ah,' said Michael, beaming at her delightedly. 'I knew the lemon would help.'

'Well, it didn't, not exactly the way you said,' said Phaedria with a sigh. 'But I did find putting the ingredients in hot water was very good. Sorry, I meant to say thank you, but I couldn't really without – well, without Roz knowing.'

'And why should Roz mind you thanking me for a little ante-natal care?'

'Oh, you don't –' 'don't know Roz' she had been going to say, but it would clearly sound so rude, so offensive, she stopped herself. 'You don't know how elusive you are,' she finished rather feebly.

'Yes, well, I haven't been here very much. But I'm over for two weeks now, I've been trying to persuade Roz to take a few days off and show me the rest of England, but she won't, so I thought I'd get to know Mrs Morell – Letitia – instead. Much more interesting.'

'What's all this about lemons?' said Letitia. 'I gather you two have met before?'

'We certainly have,' said Michael. 'Phaedria took one look at me and was immediately sick. I seem to have a profound effect on her, this morning she looked as if she was going to faint, or even die on me.'

'Yes, we met in my office,' said Phaedria hurriedly. 'And he told me a cure for pregnancy sickness. Which was very good in time,' she added tactfully.

'Right, well, come in and sit down, and tell me how you are. We have half an hour, don't we Michael?'

'We do. I've asked Phaedria to join us, but she says she couldn't. I'm not too sure why. Maybe she feels she might be sick or die again.'

'Oh, I don't think that would be a good idea,' said Letitia carefully, wondering how a man who had clearly seen a great deal of life, been married twice and lived with Roz on and off for more than a few months, could possibly not see that lunching with her detested stepmother in the most gossipy restaurant in London would not be the best course of action in the world.

'O.K. You both win.' He shrugged. 'Here's the glucose cocktail. Letitia, can I help myself to some more champagne, and you too?'

'Of course, please do, I'm sorry to be so rude. Oh, I certainly do miss Nancy.'

'Who is Nancy?' asked Michael, handing Letitia a glass of champagne and then sitting down next to her and fixing upon her reply as if it contained the secret of the universe.

'Nancy was my maid. She'd been with me since oh, 1954, when Julian married Eliza. And she was nearly as old as I am and she decided, it was nothing to do with me, that I needed someone younger and she needed a rest.'

'And where has she gone to find this rest?'

'To live with her sister in Oxford.'

'And is this sister younger than her? What will she do all day? Will she be able to find something else to occupy her?'

He looked genuinely anxious for the fate of the suddenly unemployed Nancy; Phaedria, watching him, thought she had never in her entire life met anyone so unselfconscious, so unconcerned for himself and the impression he was making.

'Oh, I expect so,' said Letitia, 'she is a very active woman. And the sister is younger, yes, how kind of you to take such an interest in an old lady you've never met.'

'Oh,' he said, sipping his champagne, leaning back on the sofa, 'I find old ladies terribly interesting. Truly I do. And I do hope you have about three days clear for this lunch, because I suspect you and your life are going to be even more interesting than Nancy and hers.'

'Well, I certainly hope so,' said Letitia briskly. 'Anyway, we can move on to my life later. Let's talk to Phaedria while we have her. What have you been doing, darling? I hope you're visiting Mr Pinker regularly.'

'Oh, he's heaven,' said Phaedria, sipping her hot water. 'I shall miss him terribly when it's all over.'

'Who is this Pinker guy? Is he a new admirer or something?' asked Michael, looking at her, his mournful eyes lighting up in a way that reminded her suddenly and sharply of Julian.

'No. I wish he was. He's my gynaecologist.'

'Ah. Some difference. Those guys always have a very sexy image. Tell me about him.'

'Well,' said Phaedria, laughing, trying to line up the distinguished, grey-haired, old-English charm of Geoffrey Pinker with a sexy image, and failing, 'he is just very very charming and reassuring and nice. He delivered the Princess of Wales's babies. And Princess Anne's.'

'So you're in good company. Is this child going to be born at Buckingham Palace?'

Phaedria laughed again. 'No, a very ordinary hospital in Paddington.'

'And how much longer is it to B-Day now?'

'Just over two and a half months.'

'You look very thin,' he said critically. 'Are you eating all the right things? Taking vitamins? Getting enough fresh air?'

'I certainly am,' said Phaedria, determinedly cheerful. 'Never was a pregnant lady so carefully looked after.'

'I somehow doubt that,' he said gently, suddenly serious; Phaedria, meeting the dark eyes, felt all at once confused, disturbed.

'Well, you're wrong,' she said. 'I go to classes –'

'Oh, not those dreadful relaxation classes!' said Letitia. 'Not natural childbirth again, Phaedria, please!'

'Again?' said Michael. 'This is not a first baby?'

'Oh, this is,' said Letitia briskly. 'But surely Roz must have told you about her experiences in childbirth? No? My God, that poor child, she got in the grips of some extremely expensive lunatic who didn't seem to believe in anything more powerful in the way of pain relief than a little light massage. I'm pleased to say she gave as good as she got. Even in childbirth, it seems, Roz is a formidable character.'

'I have to tell you I believe it,' said Michael. 'I haven't heard any of this, though. What did she do?'

'Oh, kicked him very hard a few times. Swore so loudly and violently other women complained. Bit poor C. J. It was a very – what shall we say – active birth.'

'Yeah, well, I don't know about all that,' said Michael. 'In New York they still more or less knock you out.'

'Much better,' said Letitia briskly.

'Yeah, but I think it's a good idea if the father can be there. If he possibly can. It's kind of good for him, I guess, even if it doesn't do the mother any good.'

There was a strange sound from Phaedria, halfway between a sigh and a sob; she was looking out of the window, fighting back the tears. Michael and Letitia looked at her, stricken.

'Oh, my God, what a lousy, stupid goddamned thing to say,' said Michael, jumping up, going over to her, sitting beside her, putting his arms round her. 'Phaedria, I am so sorry, so terribly terribly sorry. Please forgive me. Here, look, have a cry, go on, don't fight it, take my hanky, take two, I always have plenty to spare so I can lose them, go on, just cry.'

And she did, she sobbed for five minutes or so, on and on, like a child, all the stress of work, the anxiety of her pregnancy, the trauma of her morning with Doctor Friedman, breaking in her heart in a waterfall of grief. Michael sat holding her, mopping what he could see of her face with his handkerchief; when she had finally stopped she looked up at him with half a crumpled, wounded smile and said, 'I'm so sorry, and now look at your shirt.'

'Oh, you don't have to worry about this shirt,' he said. 'It is quite an amazingly absorbent shirt, I always wear it just on the off-chance that some lady may burst into tears on it. There now, you see, it's drying off already. Now take this handkerchief, and blow your nose, that's better.'

She blew her nose, and then as unselfconsciously as he, sat there for a while, with her head on his shoulder, resting herself and her emotions.

'I'm so sorry,' she said after a while. 'Now I've spoilt your fun lunch.'

'Nonsense,' said Letitia, 'but I really don't think we can leave you now. I suggest, Michael, that you go down the road to Harrod's and buy us a picnic. I'll cancel the table at Langan's. We can make sure Phaedria is getting her proper diet, and then send her back in the car with Pete.'

'Fine. I'll go right away. Phaedria, is there anything you don't like?'

'Everything.'

'I'll find something. It'll be a challenge.'

When he had gone Phaedria looked at Letitia and smiled shakily. 'He's so nice,' she said. 'Much too nice for Roz.'

'Indeed.' Letitia looked at her ravaged face, and decided this was no time to give her even the mildest hint of what she had foreseen, with hideous clarity, as she watched Michael holding Phaedria in his arms on the sofa.

Two weeks later Phaedria flew to LA in search of Father Kennedy. C. J. was almost hysterical with anxiety at the thought of her going on her own; he said he would go with her, but Phaedria pointed out with perfect truth that Roz would be so angry if she found out that she would probably come after them, and would also guess the reason for their trip: 'I can concoct a story about checking out the store, or doing some buying, or just taking a vacation, I deserve one for God's sake, she'll never know.'

'But Phaedria, you're seven months pregnant, you're mad, you'll make yourself ill, you'll have a miscarriage.'

'Oh, C. J., don't be such an old woman. I'll be fine.'

'What does Mr Pinker say?'

'Mr Pinker isn't going to know.'

'There you are, you see, you know it's dangerous otherwise you'd tell him.'

'C. J., I'm in a state of frenzy, it's dangerous for me not to go.'

He saw her off at Heathrow with some misgivings. In the end she had had to tell Victoria Jones (Mr Pinker, perhaps fortunately, she thought, being on holiday); because she had to have a medical certificate before the airline would take her. Doctor Jones, who understood her distressed state all too well and felt she needed a break, dispatched her with her blessing and a warning not to do anything silly.

C. J. had still watched her go through passport control with a sense of deep foreboding.

She booked into the Bel Air Hotel. She couldn't bear the thought of going back to the Beverly Hills; besides, the peace and the lush quiet beauty of Bel Air suited her mood much better. She spent the first twenty-four hours resting, recovering from the flight, wandering through the flower-filled grounds, standing on the bridge and watching the black and white swans drifting lazily beneath her. Her bungalow opened almost on to the lake itself; she sat on the patio the first evening, dining on giant peaches and strawberries, sipping iced water, and listening to the birds singing in the rich still air, watching the sky grow suddenly and beautifully intense and then dark, and felt nearer to happiness than she could remember for a long time.

She asked the hotel for a car; she wanted some freedom to explore. They provided her with a Mercedes SE convertible; she set off after breakfast, with the hood down, and a set of very good maps.

She was in Santa Monica by mid-morning; it was a glorious sparkling day, and she stood leaning on the fence of Palisades Park for a while, looking at the beach and the ocean below her, drinking in the beauty and the sense of timelessness, the lack of hurry that is so essentially Californian. She was also gathering her courage; what she was about to do had its darker side.

She had an address for the refuge, and she found it easily. She went in; it was a big shabby hall, with folding beds stacked neatly against the wall, a few disintegrating chairs set about by small tables. Outside in the sun and the long, uncut grass lay a dozen or so down and outs, watching the day go by.

'Can you tell me where I can find Father Kennedy?' she asked a girl who was sitting with them, talking to them.

'He's inside in his office,' she said, pointing. 'Working on the books.'

Father Kennedy had a small room off the main hall; it had just space for a small shaky desk and chair. He had a host of papers spread in front of him, and an extremely old cumbersome-looking adding machine which he was shaking rather hopelessly.

He looked up at Phaedria as she came in.

'Good morning.'

'Father Kennedy?'

'Indeed I am.'

She looked at the machine. 'That doesn't look too terribly healthy.'

'It is not. It is like myself, it has seen far better days. What can I do for you?'

'Well – I don't know. I believe you may be able to help me find someone.'

'And who might that be? We have all manner of people here, were you thinking this person might be among them?'

'I don't think so, Father.' She suddenly felt rather frightened, a little faint. 'May I sit down?'

'Oh, now, what am I thinking of, of course you must sit down, come along with me now, and we will find you a grand chair.'

She followed him and he took the least decrepit of the chairs in the hall and set it out at the back of the building in the shade. A pair of cats sat looking at Phaedria interestedly as she sank down into it; Father Kennedy settled himself beside her on a three-legged stool.

She looked at him, a plump, white-haired old man, with all the patience and candour on his face that only a long life given to the ungrateful and undeserving can provide, and felt she was in safe hands.

He looked at her for a while in silence, and then said, easing her into the conversation, 'I expect it's Miles you've come about?'

And yes, she said, yes it was, she needed to know about him, not just where he was, but who he was, and how well Father Kennedy had known him, and whether she was wise in pursuing him across half the world. She explained who she was, and why she wanted to find him; she felt it was the only fair basis from which to ask him what she needed to know.

Father Kennedy talked to her with great tenderness and care. He answered only her questions, he gave her no more information than she asked for, and even then he tempered his words with great thoughtfulness, rewriting history just a little in the telling to make the story easier for her to hear.

Yes, he had known Miles since he was a little tiny boy, and his parents too; nice people they had been, good and loving parents, a happy family.

Dean had died as a result of taking an overdose when Miles had been only about ten or eleven; the verdict had indeed been suicide, but he, Father Kennedy, had always thought that was an act of such despair, and that Dean had been a calm and a cheerful man, it seemed perhaps just a trifle unlikely, and that there was certainly a reasonable possibility that he had been drinking and then taken too many sleeping pills in his confusion.

And Lee, now that had been a dreadful thing, cancer she had died of, and only a young woman, in her early forties, but her end had been very peaceful, he had been there with her when she went; his only sorrow had been that Miles had not been there. People said children should have no part of dying or death, but he thought it was important for them to see there was nothing to be frightened of and to know it as the part of life that it was.

The boy had been all right at first, very sad of course, but he had been doing well at school, and he had been a wonderful games player; later on though he had stopped working, wasted his talents, fooled around a bit and that was when his grandmother had moved out to Malibu with him.

And that had been when he met the girl, a sweet little thing, Joanna, and such a nice family, very well off and so on, but with no silly ideas, they had been so good to Miles. And of course it had been a wonderful thing when he had been able to go to Berkeley and do so well there.

Yes, indeed, that had been when Mr Dashwood, Mr Hugo Dashwood, his name was, had stepped in and paid the fees; now wasn't that a fine gesture for a man to make? – he had been a great gentleman, Mr Dashwood had, and it was the greatest pity that Miles had fallen out with him as he had.

No, he had no idea where Mr Dashwood was now, he had never seen very much of him, indeed he had seldom visited Miles latterly; owing to the difficulty between them the meetings that took place were not happy. He had had an idea he lived in New York, although he was English, and certainly the address that Mrs Kelly had had was not in England. Indeed he had not heard of him for some time.

He believed Miles had taken it very badly that Mr Dashwood had not offered him a job in his company; he had felt in some way that it was his due. Of course it was not, and it was very foolish of him to think that way, but the fact remained that if it had been possible, it would have made the greatest difference to Miles and his life. But then on the other hand Mr Dashwood had been so good to Miles, so generous, it was hardly fair to expect any more.

What had Mr Dashwood been like? Oh, a very typical Englishman, Father Kennedy would have said, a fine-looking man, very tall and slim, and what he would always have imagined a public school person would be like, but Lee had told him that wasn't right, he had gone to a grammar school and made his way in the world himself. He had had a wife, yes, Lee had also told him, with some old-fashioned English name, Alice, now that was it, and two or three children, boys if he remembered rightly. He had been a good friend to Lee as well as to Miles and done a lot for her when her husband had died.

The house in Malibu was still empty, he believed, although there had been rumours it was up for sale; if she wanted to go and have a look out there, it would do no harm, he could tell her where it was, it was only half an hour's drive away.

And where was Miles now? Well, he supposed there was no

harm in telling her the address, although he had written there himself and not had an answer, so it was possible that they had moved on. He had been sad to have lost them, Miles and Mrs Kelly. He hoped they were well. If she went out to Malibu one of the neighbours might have a more recent address.

'Now, I wouldn't go rushing off to Nassau yourself,' he said, looking at her with concern in his faded old blue eyes. 'I really don't know that they are still there, and it would do you no good in your condition. Write to this address, child, and see what comes of it. Now, Mrs Kelly's friend is called Mrs Galbraith. That is the lady they were staying with. You may have more luck than I. Or send someone else. That would be a better thing.'

'I probably will,' said Phaedria, standing up and smiling down at him. 'Thank you, Father, you have been so very kind. I can't tell you how grateful I am. How can I thank you?'

'Oh, it was nothing, now what has it cost me?' he said, smiling back at her. 'However –' Father Kennedy would have starved to death without a whimper of complaint himself; for his flock he was shamelessly greedy – 'if you felt able perhaps to make a small donation to the refuge that would be a wonderful thing.'

'Oh, of course I will,' said Phaedria. 'I would be really happy to. Here –' she thrust a hundred dollars into his hand – 'take this for now. When I get home to England, I will see that a trust fund is set up for you, supplying you with a regular income. I promise. I won't forget.'

Father Kennedy believed her. She was a sweet, pretty child, and he wished her nothing but well. But he watched her drive away, waving to him gaily, with a little foreboding. He hoped she wasn't going to learn anything about Miles that would cause her distress.

Andrew Blackworth stood miserably in the Reception of the Cable Beach Hotel and wished he had never heard of the Morell family. It was hot here, it was ugly, and he felt suddenly sharply homesick. He decided to make his stay here extremely short and to continue with his inquiries at long distance. Mrs Emerson could come down here herself if she was so extremely anxious to find young Wilburn.

It was lunch time, and after checking in he sat in the bar for an hour, developing a stiff neck from the fierce air conditioning, drinking iced beer and wondering what he should do next.

He decided the telephone directory might yield a Wilburn or two, but it did not; the next step was either the police, or the barmen. The barmen were usually better company.

That afternoon he did a dozen bars along Cable Beach; and learnt nothing. At the twelfth that evening, the barman told him sympathetically he should try Paradise Island. 'My friend Barney, in the Royal, he knows everything that happens in this place. You try there.'

Andrew took a cab and went to the Royal. He ordered a champagne cocktail and asked where he might find Barney.

'I'm Barney,' said the bartender, smiling him one of the huge Bahamian smiles that despite himself Andrew was beginning to like. 'What can I tell you?'

'I'm looking for Miles Wilburn. Do you know him?'

A rather wary look came over Barney's face. 'Who wants him?'

'A family in England I represent.'

More wariness still. 'You a detective?'

'Yes.'

The face went blank, closed up.

'I don't know him. I never heard of him. Sorry, mister, you asked the wrong guy.'

Andrew was baffled. 'Look, don't get me wrong. I'm not the police. I'm a private detective. He hasn't committed a crime.'

'I told you, mister, I never heard of him. OK. Now you want another drink, or will you go and sit down and be comfortable over there?'

Andrew, baffled, went and sat down.

'As if I would tell on Miles,' said Barney indignantly to his wife Josephine late that night in bed. 'That'll be one of those spies sent by one of his lady friends' husbands. Well, he done a lot for those ladies, he don't deserve to get into no trouble over it. What's more, I'm going to see none of the other boys tells this English guy anything either.'

Josephine looked at him admiringly. Then she lay down and turned her magnificent black breasts to her husband. 'You're a good friend, Barney. Miles is lucky to have you. How about you being a good friend to me now for a while?'

Andrew found the same baffling lack of helpfulness in all the other bars on Paradise Island. Weary and irritable by the end of the second day, he made his way back to his hotel. Clearly all these people had known Miles. Why wouldn't they tell him where he was? He felt discouraged, and in addition he had indigestion from all the bowlfuls of peanuts and crisps he had been consuming in all the bars, and a filthy headache. When he got back to his hotel room he felt worse. The pain in his stomach had intensified. Damn. He knew what this was. It was his ulcer working its way back into his life. No wonder, the punishment he had been meting out to it over the past few days. Well, he wasn't going to suffer the torments of a perforated ulcer in this benighted place. He was going home. The Morells could wait. He would make some inquiries long-distance. He picked up the phone and asked them to check on the next available flight to Heathrow.

Phaedria turned the Mercedes in the direction of Malibu. Driving in California was a very pleasant experience. Nobody rushed, the speed limit was fifty-five and you could simply bowl along in the sunshine, enjoying the view. And it was a beautiful view. The ocean stretched endlessly, gloriously to her left; to her right now the dark sharp shadows that were the Santa Monica Mountains were beginning to rise. It was hot; she was glad the Mercedes was convertible. If she hadn't been pregnant she would have stopped and gone in the sea. She stopped briefly at Malibu Pier and had a glass of iced tea and a crab sandwich in Alice's Restaurant, watching the surfers riding endlessly on the waves, zooming, skimming, swooping in or sitting appraising the sea from the beach, chatting, laughing, sun-soaked. She could see why Miles had liked it as a lifestyle. Who was she to take him away from it, she wondered. If she ever found him.

She paid the check, walked over the hot road, back into her car and drove on. Latego Canyon, Father Kennedy had said. Make a right just after Pepperdine University. Here it was. She swung in, drove cautiously up the winding dusty road. She had

753

to stop twice just to drink in the view: the interweaving hills, the sea, the endless range of headlands. It caught hold of her heart; she wanted to stay for ever.

She drove on, about three or four miles. 'Then the road will fork. Take the left fork. Two miles on, there is a blue house. That's the one.'

And there it was, the blue house, built cleverly on three levels into the hill. There was parking space in front of a garage. She pulled in and parked. Then she got out and looked at the house. It was quite definitely empty.

Phaedria wandered round it, up and down the steps, peering in at the windows. It was desolate, dusty, still. The furniture wasn't even covered in sheets. It was modern furniture, neat, soulless. No clues.

Everything was locked. Every door, every window. She tried the garage. That was locked too. She sat down on the grass to rest for a while and try to think what she wanted to do next when she heard a voice.

'Can I help you?'

Phaedria jumped. A man stood on the grass, smiling at her; friendly, helpful.

'Sorry, I didn't mean to startle you. We live next door. These folks moved years ago. Never sold the house, though. Are you looking for them, or looking to buy the house?'

'Oh, I'm looking for Miles and – and Mrs Kelly,' she said. 'Do you know where they've gone?'

'Can't rightly say,' said the man. 'Mrs Kelly kept herself pretty much to herself, and Miles was a bunch of no good. We didn't have much to do with them.'

'I see.' Phaedria was silent. 'Well, thank you anyway. I just thought I might find a clue or something. But everything's locked.'

'Did you try the shed down there?' asked the man, pointing to a hut on the lower lawn. 'That might be worth a try. They left in a mighty big hurry. They didn't take hardly anything with them at all.'

'I'll try,' said Phaedria. 'Thank you.'

She clambered down to the lower lawn and pushed cautiously at the shed door. At first she thought that was shut too, but a second, harder push and it yielded.

Her heart thumping violently, she went in.

It had obviously been Miles' shed; in it was his skate board, an old surf board, a bike, some roller skates. She looked at them, mildly amused and charmed by the personality that was emerging. But there were no clues as to his whereabouts.

Then she saw the satchel. An old school bag it was really, stuffed into a corner. Phaedria looked at it for a long time, then cautiously, as if she might be burnt, reached out and took it. It was dusty, covered in insects. She shook it, took it outside and sat down on the grass.

It was full of letters. Letters from girls at school, all with patently big crushes on Miles, letters from Granny Kelly written on his birthdays, all urging him to work hard and do better at school right in the same breath as wishing him happy birthday; heartbreaking letters from Lee, written in hospital, telling him how much she loved him, how she trusted him, how she wanted him to be good.

And then a last few, stuffed right to the bottom of the satchel, typewritten letters from Hugo Dashwood. One was very old and faded, dated 1971, saying how very very sorry and sad he was to hear of Miles' mother's death, asking him if there was anything he could do for him, and promising to come to the funeral; another dated two years later, saying how pleased he was to hear Miles had made the water polo team, but he hoped he would still go on working hard at school as well; and finally three more recent, undated, all rather admonitory in tone, telling him that he should stop fooling around on the beach, and get himself a job, that he was fortunate to have such a good education, that he owed it to his parents' memory as well as to his grandmother and indeed to Hugo himself to show what he could do.

Phaedria read them in silence, wondering at them, at the heat of emotion so obviously contained in them, at the proprietary tone. Whoever Hugo Dashwood had been, he had felt very strongly about Miles. And moreover he could type. Odd, that. Not many men typed letters. Well, if the signature was anything to go by, it was just as well. It was virtually illegible, just a scrawled 'Hugo' – if she hadn't known the name, been looking out for it, she would not have been able to make it out at all.

Phaedria sat looking at the letters for a long time, aware that they were engaging her attention on some quite different level. And then became aware that her brain was focusing very strongly on that signature. And that her heart was suddenly thundering in her and that the sun seemed suddenly almost unbearably bright. A darkness came over her briefly; a frightening, rushing hot darkness. She closed her eyes, swallowed, put out a hand to steady herself. The entire earth seemed to heave beneath her.

Then she opened her eyes, took a deep breath. 'Don't be absurd,' she said to herself. 'It isn't, it couldn't be.'

She stood up. She felt shaky, weak. She took the satchel and climbed very slowly back up to the car and sat in it for a while. The baby, still all day, suddenly woke up and started moving energetically inside her; it had less room now, the movements were different, stronger, but more forceful somehow, more controlled.

The normality of it made her feel better, hauled her back into the present, herself.

'Let's go home,' she said to it, to her baby, to Julian's child, 'let's go home and have a rest.'

She started the car and drove very very slowly down the hill. It took her a long time to summon sufficient courage to cross the teeming highway, but she finally managed it. Then she headed back into Los Angeles.

Tomorrow she would go and see Father Kennedy again. Ask him some more about Hugo Dashwood. But now she just had to get back and lie down. She had a strange taut pain ebbing and flowing at the base of her back, and her head throbbed. She was terribly frightened.

Afterwards all Phaedria could remember of that night was bright lights. Bright lights coming towards her from other cars: the bright welcome lights of the hotel, there at last to receive her after the nightmare drive of fear and pain; the bright brilliant light as the doctor summoned by the anxious hotel manager looked into her eyes and then as gently, as carefully as he could, said he had to move her to hospital, that her baby was being born; the fearfully bright lights of the hospital reception as she was rushed through on a stretcher, silent, stoical through her terror; the piercing white light of the delivery room as she was taken in, moved on to the bed, her legs put in stirrups, her pulse, the baby's heartbeat, taken feverishly, anxiously, her own pain set aside, taken no account of, not through disregard, nor callousness, but urgency, necessity; the light came and went then, sometimes it seemed dark, almost peaceful, but then again and again she was surfacing into the room, the pain, the brightness; you're doing well, they kept saying, not long now, hang on, hang on, now rest, relax, breathe deeply, and she would start to sink, and then, there it was again, the awful wrenching tearing in the centre of herself, so fierce, so violent she could not see how her body could survive it.

And then at last, quite quickly they told her afterwards, not more than an hour after she had arrived, the great primeval urge to push, to go into the pain, to let it carry her forward, onwards, to endure it somehow, anyhow, because through it, at the end of it, there now, yes, she heard it, was the cry, the triumph, the new life, the love. Love such as she had never imagined, never even begun to know, a great invasion of her every sense, love at first sight and sound and touch and smell. And they placed her in her arms, her daughter, a tiny, too tiny scrap of life, a great mass of dark hair and surprisingly wide dark eyes, just for a moment, just so that she would know that this was what for the rest of her life she would fight for and give to and be concerned about, over and above everything else she ever knew.

Then they took her away again; she was two months early, they said, she must go quickly to the special care unit, to an incubator, to be cared for, to stabilize. Phaedria wept, sobbed, tried to climb off her bed and follow them, but the doctor said no, she could not go, that the child would very probably be all right, that caring for prems these days was a most advanced science, that seven months was considered almost full term, that she must not worry, but have some rest. And then at last they moved her away from the brightness into a quiet, dim, peaceful room, and Phaedria, soothed by the assurances, exhausted, triumphant, fell asleep.

In the morning the news was good. The baby was lively, hungry, breathing well. Phaedria said she was to be called Julia, and ate an enormous breakfast. Later they took her down in a wheelchair to the prem unit and she sat and gazed enraptured at the tiny scrap she had created, she and Julian, as she moved and stretched and curled up into her pre-natal shape again; sneezed, clenched and unclenched her hands, kicked her tiny legs. They let Phaedria put in her hand and touch her, feel her soft crumpled silky skin. She put her finger in the tiny fist; Julia took it, gripped it, clung on. Phaedria smiled triumphantly: the baby was strong.

Two days later she was not doing so well; she had developed, a respiratory infection. 'Nearly all prem babies do this,' said the doctor, trying to soothe her out of her wide-eyed terror, 'she's strong, you must try not to worry, she should pull through.'

Twenty-four hours later she was still holding her own, but plainly distressed; she was restless, feverish, she wouldn't take the breast milk Phaedria was expressing for her, and the nurses were trying to give her.

Phaedria sat and watched her for almost thirty-six hours, scarcely moving, hardly sleeping; she was afraid to close her eyes lest she should open them and see the baby still, dead, gone. While she looked at her, she felt she could keep her safe. In the end, the doctor led her away, saying she would collapse if she stayed any longer, that she could do nothing for Julia, that she must rest. He put her to bed and sat with her, trying to reassure her; as soon as he had gone she climbed out of the bed again and dragged her poor sore, weary body down the corridor, back to Julia's side.

'Don't leave me,' she kept whispering urgently, fearfully, to the fragile, brave little piece of humanity: 'Stay with me. I need you. I can't lose you too.'

Towards the end of that night she fell asleep, and awoke suddenly to see the tiny body still, quite quite lifeless; she opened her mouth and screamed endlessly.

A nurse came running to her, took hold of her and shook her. 'Stop it, stop it,' she said, frightened herself. 'You must be quiet.'

'I can't, I can't,' she said, tears of fright rolling down her face. 'My baby's dead.'

But no, they said, no she is not dead, she's better, look, she's peaceful, sleeping, she's going to be all right.

And even then she would not leave, she stayed, exhausted, just watching and looking and loving the baby until another day had passed, and then finally, seeing her pink, kicking, healthy, however tiny, she trusted them and agreed to leave her for a while and go to bed.

The trauma and her vigil had weakened Phaedria; she did not recover as quickly as she should. She stayed in the hospital for another week, and then, because they said Julia could not leave for two weeks more, maybe three, she moved back into her bungalow at the Bel Air, driving in every morning to sit with the baby, feed her, hold her when she was allowed, and coming home in the evening to rest and recover herself once more.

It was a strangely happy, almost surreal time; she loved best (guiltily, because she was alone, not with her baby) the evenings, when she would sit on her patio, utterly peaceful, drinking in the scents of the flowers, watching the swans, hearing the conversation, the laughter, the music drifting quietly from the main body of the hotel; concerned briefly only for herself, and rediscovering the sensation of happiness.

There had been endless excitement, of course, when they had heard in England what had happened, phone calls and letters and great banks and baskets and bowls of flowers, arrived, and boxes extravagantly gift wrapped in Beverly Hills, containing presents for Julia, tiny dresses, shawls, bonnets, coats, and enormous, ridiculous soft toys, golden teddies and great pink bunnies, three, four, five times as large as their small owner; Eliza flew over to see her, and her small stepdaughter, wearing a minute white silk dress and matching coat from the White House, and a cobweb-fine hand-crocheted shawl from Letitia, and a tiny gold locket set with sapphires that Letitia's grandmother, the Dowager Lady Farnsworth, had worn in her own cradle, and bequeathed her in her will. David Sassoon came with a Hockney print of Los Angeles for her: 'Clever girl, what better place could you possibly have chosen to have a baby?'

Susan came, greatly to Phaedria's surprise and pleasure, a little reserved but friendly just the same, bringing boxes of cookies and chocolates and strawberries. 'I do remember how marvellous it is to be hungry again, and you must need little doggy bags to take to the hospital.'

Augustus Blenheim came, jerked into reality by concern and love.

C. J. came, with an exquisite engraving by Frith of a baby, looking anxious and concerned, but with a ring of 'I told you' in his eyes and his voice. 'And I'm sure it could all have waited, there was no point tearing down here, Roz has made no progress at all, as far as I know.'

Phaedria, still nursing her quiet fear, unable to confront it, to recognize it as real, had allowed the night of pain and the days of terror that had followed in its wake to blank it out, did not even tell C. J. she had seen Father Kennedy, merely sat and nodded and said how right he had been.

And then one day, towards the end of the time, when Julia was nearly strong enough to leave and she was sitting peaceful and happy in the evening sun, reading *The Water Babies*, which someone had sent to Julia and which she had rediscovered with immense pleasure, she heard footsteps and looked up and there in front of her was Michael Browning.

'Now you are not to faint and you are not to be sick,' he said, placing a bottle of Cristalle champagne on the table and producing two glasses from his pockets, 'and you are certainly not to run away. And before you ask, Roz has no idea I'm here.'

He looked at her as she sat, frozen with shock, silent, her eyes huge brilliant smudges in her pale still face. 'Aren't you going to greet me? I've travelled three thousand miles to bring you this. I hope you like it.'

And he produced from yet another pocket a book, a tiny leather-bound volume, a first edition of Christina Rossetti's poems. 'I bought this because of the "Birthday" poem. I thought it was appropriate. I guess your heart must feel pretty much like a singing bird just now.'

'Michael!' said Phaedria, reaching up and kissing him gently on the cheek. 'I didn't know you were a literary person. What a lovely present. Thank you.'

'This is a man,' he said, taking off his jacket and sinking into the chair beside her, 'who got the Eng Lit runner's-up prize at Sethlow Junior High two years running. Champagne?'

'Do you know I haven't had any yet? Eliza offered me some but I refused. I wasn't ready for it. But today, yes, I really would like some.'

'Well, it's time you did, and it's just as well,' he said. 'Otherwise I would have drunk it all.'

She looked at him, smiling with the absolute pleasure of his company, untroubled for the moment by thoughts of what might lie before or behind them. He looked, as always, slightly rumpled; it was not just his clothes, it was his hair which looked perpetually in need of a comb, his rather shaggy eyebrows, his disturbed (and disturbing) brown eyes. She thought (not for the first time) how extraordinary it was that a man so devoid of most of the obligatory qualities of conventional male desirability (height, looks, stylishness) could have such an ability to project sexuality with so acute a force. She wrenched her mind away from her deliberations with an effort, and smiled at him. 'It's so nice to see you. But why are you here?'

'I'm here,' he said simply, 'because I wanted to see you. I was in Los Angeles anyway, I have two companies here, I knew where you were, and I suddenly decided to come rather than go racing back to New York for a lonely weekend. I am family – or nearly. I felt I should greet the new member.'

'I'm glad you did.'

'Well now,' he said, leaning forward, 'tell me all about this baby. I hear she is beautiful. Are you all right? Are they taking good care of you?'

'The baby is beautiful. She has dark hair and the most wonderful dark eyes. She's tiny, but growing very very fast. She eats and eats and eats.'

'From you, I see,' he said, his eyes lingering, briefly, pleasurably, on her changed, swelling breasts.

Phaedria saw the look and felt a strange stabbing somewhere in her heart; she looked down, away from him, flushed.

'Yes,' she said in an attempt at lightness. 'I have proved to be a fine dairy cow.'

'Good. And how much does she weigh now, this little calf?'

'Oh, nearly five pounds. She was only three and a half when she was born. So thin, so tiny; now she's getting quite fat.'

'I'd like to see her,' he said. 'Could I, do you think? Would it be possible?'

'You could,' she said, touched, moved by his genuine interest, 'but not tonight. Tomorrow. I will take you to the hospital and introduce you to her. Where are you staying?'

'I don't know. Would they keep me here, do you think?'

'We could ask.'

'Good. I'll try now.' He went through the french doors, into her sitting room, and picked up the phone. 'You pour me some more champagne. This is a very nice little pad you have here. I'm surprised you don't stay.'

She laughed. 'I would if I could. I feel it's half home. I've been terribly happy here. But we have to get back, Julia and I. We have to wake up, get on with reality.'

'What a pity,' he said. 'Dreaming suits you. Ah, Reception? Do you have a room for tonight and maybe tomorrow as well? You do? No, I don't mind. That's fine. Browning. I'll come and check in right now.'

'Excuse me,' he said, putting down his glass. 'They want to inspect me. They only have a small room. I guess that means only big enough for three. I'll be back. Have you had dinner?'

'No.'

'You need feeding up. Why don't you ask me to join you for a nice big juicy T-bone?'

'I don't like nice big juicy T-bones.'

'I'm easy. I'll eat anything.'

'All right,' she said, laughing, 'please stay and have dinner with me.'

They ate on the patio, salmon poached in champagne, and then some roquefort cheese so delicately salty, so mildly perfect it was, as Michael remarked, like eating happiness, and she laughed, and he made her drink a glass of claret, 'great for milk production', sitting outside until it was dark and suddenly chill; relaxed, happy, just talking, talking.

She told him about her childhood, about Oxford, about Charles even, her life in Bristol, before she had met Julian. On the subject of her marriage she kept silent; it was not something she wished, or was able, to share. Michael sat listening, interested, enthralled even, questioning her on the most minute details, things it amazed her he should want to know: had she worn school uniform, and what had it been like, had she been in love with any of her teachers (he had heard all English public school children were homosexual) what had her room been like at Oxford, had she been taken up the river in a punt, what was the first event she had ever reported, what colour was her horse, who were the people she had shared a house with in Bristol?

And then he wanted to hear every detail she could offer of Julia's birth, of her life and death struggle, of exactly how Phaedria had passed the days since she had left the hospital, of any interesting guests she had met in the hotel and patients in the hospital, of what she had been eating, what exercise she had been taking, of how well she felt.

'You look very tired,' he said severely. 'You can't have been sleeping.'

'I haven't. I have bad dreams still.'

'What about?'

'Julia dying. Every night, I see her as she was when I woke up that morning, all white and still. Not just once, but over and over again.'

'Poor baby,' he said, and his voice was very gentle. 'What a lot you have to deal with. All on your own.'

'Yes,' she said. 'Yes, I suppose I do.' But she smiled as she said it.

'And why were you here anyway? So great with child? The most famously pregnant traveller since Mary of Nazareth. I imagine it wasn't really a sudden concern with the competition on Rodeo Drive. This wild-goose chase I suppose, for your missing partner.' He shook his head. 'You're both crazy, you and Roz. Neither of you need subject yourselves to any of it.'

'I know. And yet, we do. When did she tell you?'

'Oh, right at the beginning. Don't worry, I haven't talked. I can be as silent as an entire mortuary if necessary. I don't think he exists at all,' he added, cutting himself a last sliver of cheese. 'I think he's a figment of Julian's crazed imagination.'

'Do you now?' She looked at him thoughtfully. 'I fear you're wrong. But it's a nice idea. Anyway –' she visibly brushed the topic aside – 'let's not talk about it. I don't want to break my spell.'

'What spell?'

'I feel like the Sleeping Beauty in her castle here, safe, preserved, lost in time. That nobody can get near me, to hurt me.'

'Then,' he said, 'I must take care not to kiss you.' And he

763

smiled at her, amused, gentle; she smiled back, but inside her somewhere something leapt, unbidden, forbidden. The light-heartedness left her; she felt tense, and oddly fearful.

'I'm very tired now. Will you excuse me if I go to bed?' he said suddenly. 'We have this very heavy programme tomorrow after all.'

'Of course. Yes, you go, you must be exhausted. And come back for breakfast if you like. I leave for the hospital at about nine.'

'Do you have a car?'

'The hotel provides them. Along with almost every other human need.'

'Do you think that might extend to a pair of pyjamas? Most unaccountably my secretary didn't slip them in with my budget forecasts as she usually does.'

'I'm sure they would. A trunkful if you wanted them.'

'I generally only wear one pair at a time,' he said. 'I shall see you in the morning then. Good night Phaedria. Sweet dreams.'

For the first time since Julia's birth, she slept well.

Roz was frightened and she didn't know quite why. On the face of it she was doing well. She had gathered a good many reins into her exquisitely manicured hands during the few weeks Phaedria had been away, with immense ease. People no longer felt inhibited, by loyalty to or sympathy for Phaedria, and allowed her to take visible control; the management staff, heading the various companies, impatient for decisions on this and that, for go-aheads, for direction on expansion moves, hamstrung earlier by the ridiculous charade Julian had orchestrated, found her quick, shrewd, brilliantly decisive. Predictably hostile to the notion of being ultimately answerable to two young women, experienced businessmen found them-selves grudgingly more receptive to acceding to one. The wholesale exodus of management talent which had threatened the company on Julian's death was slowing; people were waiting, seeing what might happen, what Roz (increasingly Roz) might do.

Roz, exhilarated, excited by what she was accomplishing, but exhausted nonetheless, had fears that haunted her frequently sleepless bed. She knew she was still fighting a crisis of confidence, that she needed a personal team behind her that could lend respectability and status to her accession. She knew that however brilliant her own mind and training, the one crucial quality she could not possibly lay claim to was experience.

She looked into the distance, and could see no end, no turning even, that might indicate a by-way, a respite, just a long, relentless straight highway.

She travelled it all day – she was in the office by seven thirty most mornings – and she travelled it much of the night as well, leaving the building often at ten, and then still taking work home with her. She hardly ever saw Miranda, she briefed her domestic staff by notes, and in the months since her father had died she had not once eaten a meal with anyone other than a business contact or Michael Browning. And that was the other reason for her fear. She knew she was pushing their relationship, straining his tolerance to the furthest possible parameters; she occasionally spent the weekend with him, in England, still more occasionally flew to New York, she paid lip service to listening to his problems, his demands, but in fact her contact with him on any genuine level was restricted to sex and a demand that he listen to her. And she did not know quite how much longer he was going to put up with it.

He had told her he would give her six months; that he would wait because he loved her and understood what she was trying to do; that he would not complain, not press her. 'But after that, by God, Rosamund, I will not be a memo on your office wall any longer. If you want me, you will have to pay for me.'

And she had promised, grateful for the reprieve, feverish in her anxiety that she would lose him again so swiftly, so decisively; but she knew that six months was not a quarter, not a tenth of the time she needed before she could relax and cease her vigil on the company.

C. J.'s departure from the household, and indeed the company, was a great relief; she was able, immediately he had moved into his new flat near Sloane Street, to feel quite fondly towards him again. He was the perfect ex husband; undemanding, good-natured, polite, he took over Miranda almost every weekend, he had agreed to go ahead with the divorce as fast as possible, and he had remained loyal, he did not go bad-mouthing her all over London, as she was uncomfortably aware he would have been justified in doing.

She had a feeling he was helping Phaedria with the hunt for Miles, but she really did not care; such was her contempt for C. J.'s intellectual capacities, his lack of shrewdness that she could not imagine they were going to be very successful, certainly not as successful as she was, with the loyally dogged Andrew Blackworth working on her behalf (although she had been very impatient with his precipitant return from Nassau, and the excuse of a troublesome ulcer). The latest news had been that Miles was working for a bank somewhere; the crazy old woman who had finally revealed herself in Nassau hadn't had a clear idea where. It probably wasn't him in fact, she thought wearily; in the very few moments when she had time to think at all, she wondered at the fact that Miles had so completely failed to materialize; the lawyers had advertised so painstakingly, and if the flood of fakes (from half the major countries in the world) who had presented themselves to the offices of Henry Winterbourne either in person, or by letter or phone call, had seen the advertisements, why had not Miles himself? And who was this Hugo Dashwood, for God's sake, that Henry Winterbourne had discovered through Bill Wilburn? None of of it made sense. Sometimes she wondered if Michael Browning was not right, and that her father had invented Miles.

She woke up late that Saturday morning and decided she had to speak to Michael. What was the time? Ten o'clock. Damn, only five in New York. Oh, well, he should be pleased to hear from her just the same. He had always told her to ring him any time. Michael could wake up and go back to sleep with the ease most people took a drink of water. Maybe she would give him another hour.

She got up, lay in the bath for a long time, thinking about Michael and how much she would like to be with him, wondering even if she might fly over for twenty-four hours, then dressed slowly, fetched herself a coffee from the kitchen and dialled his number.

It was answered by his butler, Franco, a good-natured, efficient and loyal man, who shared with his master a distaste for untruth and an irritating ability to answer the most intensive questioning without giving anything away at all.

No, Mr Browning was not here. No, he had gone away, he believed, on a short business trip. Yes, he had gone by air, Franco had ordered the car to take him to Kennedy himself early yesterday. An internal flight. No, he had no number. He had not said exactly when he would be back. Would Mrs Emerson like him to give Mr Browning a message if he phoned?

The message Mrs Emerson had for Mr Browning was not quite of a nature to be passed on second hand; Roz put down the phone, trembling slightly. Where was he? Where was the bastard? He had never, ever – well, not since their last reconciliation, never when they were together – done anything like this before. He had always told her where he was going, left a number, told her to call.

He must have something to hide. He must be with someone. He wouldn't have gone on a business trip on a Friday. But who? And a flight? That must mean quite a distance. Where would he go? Florida? Possibly. He liked the Keys. California? Surely not. Too far for a weekend, without a very good reason. Although he did have at least two companies there.

Where could he be, where could he be? Who could he be with? Roz looked out of the window at the golden October sunlight dancing on the Thames and shivered. It seemed to grow darker. The fear that followed her everywhere had suddenly grown very big.

After they had looked at the baby, admired the baby, and Phaedria had fed the baby (Michael having asked most charmingly if he could stay while she did so, and she, surprised at her own unselfconsciousness, had said of course he might, if he wished) cuddled the baby, remarked on her great beauty, and Michael had talked to the nurses and extracted news of an imminent engagement from one, and a suspected pregnancy of her own from another, and Phaedria had talked to the paediatrician and extracted a promise that Julia could fly home in another week, and the baby had been finally lain in her crib and after a brief protest, gone back to sleep, Michael suggested a picnic. 'Or do we just stay here with her? I don't mind at all, if that's what you would like.'

'I do usually,' she said doubtfully, 'but the nurses are always telling me to go out more, they have masses of my milk in the fridge, so I suppose we could.'

'Right,' he said, 'it will do you good. Let's go to the seaside.'

So they drove out of Los Angeles and along the coast road, past Malibu, on to Paradise Cove. Michael produced from the boot of the Mercedes a picnic basket, an armful of towels, two beach beds, and a beach umbrella. Phaedria watched entranced.

'This is like an act at the circus. When did you get all that?'

'The hotel did it, early this morning. Come on.'

He set the umbrella in the sand, put up the beds, opened the hamper: it contained a bottle of exquisite Californian chardonnay, another one of Perrier, a modest heap of smoked salmon sandwiches, and a large bag full of peaches, cherries, strawberries, raspberries. 'And I even have swimsuits for us both. You're right about the every human need. I feel if I had asked for a trio of naked ladies to come in juggling flaming torches on one-wheeled bicycles, they would have said, "Certainly, Mr Browning," and had them there before you could say room service. Do you feel like swimming?'

'I'm not sure. Sunning anyway. You are wonderful.'

'I know. There are some pretty amazing sights over there,' he said, pointing to the far side of the beach.

'What?'

'It's the nude beach. Never been there?'

'No. And I don't think I want to now,' she said, laughing.

'Do you not like the naked form, Lady Morell?'

'Very much,' she said, 'but not on a lot of strangers.'

'Then,' he said, 'I look forward to being your friend. Now don't start looking frightened,' he added, seeing her eyes fill with confusion and alarm. 'I was only joking. Eat your food, like a good nursing mother. You need nourishing.'

'All right,' she said, and he watched her relax again.

They ate slowly, drank the wine, watching the surfers, drinking in the sun. Phaedria thought of Miles, spending his days here, in this very ocean; he began to materialize for her, a lean brown body, sun-tangled hair, swooping interminably in on the waves, pursuing nothing but pleasure: she longed to know more of him, now, to meet him and talk to him, to find what sort of a man he could possibly be.

'Hey,' said Michael, who had been watching her, 'where are you? Back in that hospital?'

'No,' she said, smiling, hauling herself back to the present, 'more or less here. I was looking at the surfers and envying them rather. I love the sea and I love the sun. It makes me feel good right down in my bones.'

'Me too. It's hot, though. That delicate English skin of yours will burn. Do you want some oil?'

'It's not delicate, not really, but it might be a good idea. Did the hotel send that too?'

'Of course.'

'Yes please. Could you put some on my back?'

He opened the bottle and began to spread the oil over her shoulders and her back, smoothing it in slowly, rhythmically, gently massaging the tender nape of her neck, down her spine, over her shoulders, his fingers stopping just short of her breasts. Suddenly, shockingly strongly, she wanted his hands on them, more than she could ever remember wanting anything; she closed her eyes, pulling herself tautly together, lest he should feel her tipping over into desire. 'Thank you,' she said quickly. 'That's fine. Shall I do yours?'

'No,' he said, 'no need, I have skin that resembles a tortoise's shell more closely than anything else.' He looked at her closely, saw the raw flicker of sex in her eyes, and smiled.

'You worry too much,' was all he said.

A little later on Michael went over to the water and Phaedria lay down under the umbrella; when he came back (not having quite entrusted himself to the surf, which was running high) she was asleep; he sat and looked at her for a while, his face an interesting blank.

She woke up quite suddenly, looking startled, sat up. 'We must get back,' she said, 'quickly. We've been gone too long.'

'Calm down,' he said, smiling. 'It's only three o'clock, and I don't suppose they'll let that baby starve. We'll go back if you like. But don't panic.'

She relaxed again, and lay back on the bed. 'I'm sorry. I just worry about her all the time.'

'Of course. I would too. And we'll go in a minute. Are you sure you don't want to swim?'

She shook her head. 'No, it's so lovely just lying here.'

'Sleeping Beauty again. Why wake up at all?'

'I have to, Michael. I can't give up now. I can't.'

'I don't see why not. You have all the money you need. You have a gorgeous baby. You're beautiful. Talented. Why not just enjoy yourself?'

'I wasn't born,' she said, 'to just enjoy myself.'

'OK,' he said, 'do something else. Sell out to Roz. Take the money and run. Start your own newspaper or something.'

She smiled. 'Do you know, I've thought of doing that. I just might in the fullness of time. But first I have to resolve this mess. Somehow.'

'OK. You any nearer?'

She looked at him. 'Yes,' she said. 'Quite a bit. Not finding him. But knowing who he was. Is.'

'Really? And who is he?'

'Do you really want to know?'

He lay down on the sun bed beside her, turned his head towards her. 'OK. I'm in listening mode. You should know by now I find people kind of interesting.'

She told him. About the collection of things in Julian's desk, about Father Kennedy and her conversation with him, about Miles, who he was, his small rather sad history, even about Hugo Dashwood and his role in it. All except the letters and the signature. That she was not even acknowledging to herself.

They dined on the patio again, reluctant to break the spell of privacy, of solitude. After dinner, they went into the sitting room and closed the french windows; the nights were getting cold. Michael poured them both brandies. They sat and looked at one another.

'Right,' said Phaedria, 'let's talk about you.'

'How long have you got?'

'As long as it takes.'

So he told her: about his childhood in Brooklyn, about selling his soft drinks on the streets of California, about Anita, about Carol, about Little Michael and Baby Sharon, about making a fortune, about his constant willingness to risk everything and lose it all again.

She listened, attentively, silent, drinking him in, enjoying his roughly rich voice, his humour, the attention to and pleasure in unexpected detail, that was so much a part of his charm, his ability to haul his listeners into intimacy; when he had finished she said, 'And – Roz?'

'Oh, no,' he said smiling at her, 'I think that is a subject we should not discuss. Not now. Not yet.'

'What do you mean?'

'You know what I mean.'

'I suppose I do.'

She was silent.

'So now we know all about each other,' she said.

'I wouldn't say that.'

There was tension in the room so strong that Phaedria felt she had to get up, move about. 'Would you like another drink?'

'I guess so,' he said slowly, as if he had come back from a long way away. 'Then I must go to bed. And tomorrow I have to fly back to New York.'

'It's been a lovely day.'

'Yes it has.'

'You are,' she said, suddenly, smiling at him, quite relaxed, 'the nicest man I have ever met. Ever.'

He looked at her thoughtfully. 'I don't know how much of a compliment that is. You've met some real stinkers, that's for sure. Been married to one of the best.'

'Julian wasn't a stinker,' she said, indignant, defensive. 'I can't let you say that.'

'Jesus!' he said. 'I seem to spend my life hearing women defend that monster. Just exactly what did he do to you all? Phaedria, honeybunch, just think what he did to you. He cheated on you, he manipulated you, he lied to you, and he left you with this goddamned pantomime to orchestrate. Of course he was a stinker.'

'Well, maybe, in a way. But I –' She was silent.

'You loved him?'

'Yes. I did. I really did. God knows why.'

'God has to be the only one who does. Funny old thing, love. No respect for persons. Look at me, I've loved a greedy Jewish Momma, an ice-cold, nicely bred fish, and probably the biggest bitch in Christendom. Really loved 'em all. And now . . .' He was silent, then he looked up at her, and his eyes moved over her face, lingering on her mouth. She felt herself tremble.

'Phaedria – I –'

'No,' she said quickly, panic in her voice, 'no, don't. Don't even think it.'

'Oh, now,' he said, laughing, the tension gone briefly, 'you can't do that. You can't tell a man what he has to think and not think. You're taking away one of our most unalienable rights. Besides, you don't know what it was.'

'No,' she said, her voice small, a little sad. 'No, I suppose I don't.'

'Oh, God,' he said, 'I hate it when you're sad. Don't be sad. Of course you knew what it was, what I was thinking, what I was feeling, what I was going to say. And if I had said it you'd probably have thrown up or something. I find myself in a no-win situation here.'

'Yes,' she said, trying to sound lighthearted too, in spite of the awesome conflict in her, the yearning and the panic, 'yes you are.' But her voice came out sounding dull and bleak.

Michael looked at her; she was sitting in the chair opposite him, tension in every particle of her; looking down at her hands, the glass she was holding, the great waterfall of dark hair obscuring her face.

'Phaedria,' he said, 'come and sit down here. Next to me.'

She looked up at him, her eyes meeting his, full of longing and fear; and in a great rush of tenderness and concern he held out his hands.

'Come on.'

'Why?'

'Dear God, you make things complicated. Because I want to have you near me, that's why.'

She hesitated, looking at him, considering; then in a visible rush of courage, moved over to him.

'That's better. It's all right, I'm not going to crush you in my arms or anything. Although I have to say I find it a litle insulting that you seem to find the prospect so alarming.'

'You know why I do.'

'Yes,' he said, smiling at her again. 'Of course I do. I find it quite alarming myself for the same reason. You know,' he added, leaning back, looking thoughtfully into the soft darkness outside the window, 'she isn't really so terrible. Nobody realizes it but me, but she isn't. Underneath all that toughness and bitchiness and anger is really quite a nice, funny woman. You'd be surprised.'

'Perhaps I would,' said Phaedria carefully.

'I know she's been vile to you. I know she's been vile to a lot of people. But there are always reasons. And one of the biggest was that charming, dangerous father of hers. Who you loved so much.'

She nodded. Suddenly, surprisingly, tears formed in her eyes, spilled over; he reached out and wiped them tenderly away. 'Poor baby. I'm sorry. I shouldn't have criticized him and I shouldn't have threatened you. It's much too soon. You did love him, and you've had an awful time, and you must miss him like hell.'

'Yes,' she said, 'I do. I really do miss him. I'm sorry, I'm always crying over you.'

'Well, it beats vomiting.' He looked at her for a long time, his eyes exploring her face. 'We seem to have a penchant, both of us, for loving difficult people. What a shame. When we could probably have been so very much happier loving nice easy ones. Like each other. Well, maybe we shall never know.'

'Maybe,' she said.

He smiled at her. 'You really are very very beautiful, you know. I enjoy you. I really do.'

He picked up her hand, looked at it, playing with her fingers.

'I'm beginning to find this rather hard to handle,' he said. 'I think probably I should leave.'

'All right,' she said, half relieved, half sad.

'However,' he went on, with a heavy sigh, raising his hand, stroking her cheek, 'I find myself in considerable difficulty. I don't think I can stay, in case I forget myself and do something ungentlemanly. On the other hand,' and he sighed again, and then, suddenly, with his most soul-baring smile, 'I have such a large erection, I don't think I can possibly make it across the lobby and up to my own room. What do you think I should do?'

Phaedria looked at him, and smiled back; happiness, illogical, unbidden, delicious, filling every fibre of her; she stood up and walked through to the bedroom.

'What are you doing?'

'Oh,' she said briskly, reappearing, her arms full of towels, 'come along. I'm running you a very cold shower. It will do you no end of good.'

773

'Ah,' he said, laughing. 'The English public school remedy. Did they really believe in that?'

'They certainly did. They still do. And the Boy Scouts. I'm assured that it works.'

'Oh, God. Will you get in it with me?'

'That would defeat the object, I would have thought.'

'I fear so.' He was silent for a moment then looked at her sadly. 'And I thought you were going to come back into the room stark naked, and make me all kinds of interesting propositions.'

'No you didn't.'

'No, I didn't. Unfortunately. It's all right, you can turn the shower off now.'

'Certainly not. You haven't been near it.'

'The very thought of it has done the trick.'

'Your housemaster at Eton would not have believed you.'

'You're not my housemaster, and this is not Eton. Did you ever know anyone who went to Eton?' he asked suddenly, his terminal curiosity distracting him for a moment.

'Oh lots. Charles – my polo-playing friend – for one.'

'Oh, well,' he said, 'that explains a lot. And here you are, confronted with a real red-blooded male from Brooklyn and all you can do is show him the shower.'

'I'm sorry.'

'Well,' he said, 'of course you're right. And we would both regret it terribly.'

'I think we would.'

'Correction,' he said, 'you would regret it terribly.'

'All right, I would regret it terribly.'

'Actually,' he said, after a moment's thought. 'I don't think I can let you think that either. I want you to know that neither of us would regret one single, glorious, fucking moment of it. But it is not to be.' His dark eyes sought out a response from hers, probing her; it was an odd echo of the act of sex itself. She met his eyes, opened herself to them, and then, with a sense of physical loss, shook her head.

'No.'

'At least,' he said, and there was an expression on his face that turned her heart over, 'not for now.'

'No,' she said, 'certainly not for now.'

'Listen,' he said, 'go and turn that goddamned shower off and come and sit down again. I promise I won't lay a single ill-bred finger on you. But I don't want to lose you just yet. Now tell me some more about this Charles person. Did he really screw you and was he really gay?'

Chapter Twenty-three

London, Los Angeles, New York, 1985

'I'm not going to lie to you,' said Michael. He stood looking at Roz across the vast width of the living room in the duplex.

'OK then,' she said. 'Where were you?'

'In California.'

'Why?'

'Business. And a bit of pleasure.'

'Without me?'

'I get precious little pleasure with you, Rosamund.'

'I presume by pleasure you mean sex?'

'Wrong in one. No sex.'

'I don't believe you.'

'Roz, when did I ever lie to you?'

She hesitated.

'I never did, did I?'

'No. You never did.'

'OK then. No sex.'

'What were you doing then?'

'I was,' he said, choosing his words very carefully, 'meeting a new friend.'

'What kind of friend? God, Michael, you are being irritating.'

'A young friend.'

'Female?'

'Female.'

'I see. And what did you do with this new young female friend?'

'Not a lot. Fed her. Talked to her. Looked at her. Gave her a present.'

'What sort of present?'

'A book.'

'And what did you do the rest of the time?'

'Lay on the beach. Swam a bit. Talked. Ate. Drank.'

'And then you came home again?'

'I did.'

'Do I,' she asked in a most uncharacteristic piece of self-exposure, 'do I have to worry about this girl?'

'No,' he said, 'not for a moment. Come here.'

She moved towards him; he took her in his arms. 'Now can we leave the subject, please? I really don't want to talk about it any more and I have a hell of a day ahead of me. You may have taken Friday off, but I haven't. You can stay here in the duplex if you like or go out shopping, whatever you like, and then come and meet me at six at the Algonquin. OK?'

'OK,' said Roz, and sighed. She was still very unhappy.

She had taken Concorde out of Heathrow early that morning and arrived at Kennedy earlier than she had left London. She had spent a wretched week fretting over Michael and where he might have been and fretting over the company and where it might be going. She felt very alone. She had even thought of talking to C. J. but he was out of town. For a man writing a book about London, he was spending very little time there.

Like most extremely selfish people, Roz always expected others to be ready and waiting for her. She was outraged when she found Michael hurrying out of his apartment, and that he continued to hurry out after she had announced that she was there for the day, the weekend. Or at least he tried to. She had blocked his way, demanded an explanation; demanded also that he took the day off and spent it with her. He had conceded to neither; he was gone ten minutes after she arrived.

Roz sighed, poured herself some orange juice and some coffee and sat down, looking fretfully over Central Park. This was not how she had planned to spend the morning. She had been expecting a great deal of very satisfying and energetic sex, a sleep perhaps, a long romantic lunch, and then probably a lot more sex in the afternoon. She did not like the alternative Michael had presented her with at all. It did not occur to her that she would have been even more brusque with Michael, had he turned up unscheduled in her working week.

Now what the hell was she going to do all day? She certainly wasn't going to stay here. She could look up Annick, who was now based in New York; that was quite a good idea, and have lunch with her (it never occurred to her that Annick might not be free either), do some shopping, she needed some clothes, even maybe go to Kenneth and get her hair done. It needed it desperately.

She sat down at Michael's telephone and made some calls. Kenneth said as it was her, they would do her hair, if she came over absolutely straight away; Annick said she would cancel her lunch with *Ladies' Home Journal*; the afternoon would take care of itself, shopping. Roz picked up her bag and her lynx coat (it was freezing already in New York) and made for the elevator.

She had her hair cut very short and had some dark red streaks put in the brown; at least she looked like a company chairman, she thought. Not some kind of Flower Child left over from the sixties. Phaedria really ought to do something with that hair. It might have been all right when she was busy playing the child bride, but now it was just plain ridiculous. Oh, well, the more ridiculous she looked, the better Roz liked it.

She set off down Fifth Avenue, towards Le Cirque where she was to meet Annick, and stopped off first at Mark Cross, where she bought three pairs of loafers (in blue, black and brown), several belts and a soft leather Gladstone bag for a present for Michael; and then at Valentino, where she bought a dark red print silk dress, with long very full sleeves and a drop waist that flowed over her long body, caressing every curve, every line, and two wildly patterned sweaters.

Her heart suddenly lifted; she had been too serious lately. Michael was right. Pleasure had become a forgotten concept. She should get something for Miranda too, she thought suddenly. Poor little girl, she was inflicting on her precisely the kind of childhood she had had herself, lonely, neglected, emotionally traumatized. She would try and do better for her. She began as she meant to go on and went into OMO Kamali, where she bought her two outfits, one in stinging pink and one in aquamarine jersey, smiling at the thought of them on her daughter's plump energetic small form; after lunch she would go to Bloomie's and find her some toys.

She swung into Le Cirque feeling good; Annick was waiting, watching her come in.

'Annick! It's so nice to see you. Thank you for making time for me.'

'That's perfectly all right,' said Annick, adding with a wicked smile, 'you're the boss. Drink?'

'Oh, don't. Yes, please. As I'm on holiday. I'll have a Bloody Mary. No I won't, I'll have a martini.'

'How's it going?'

'All right,' said Roz carefully. 'I think I'm just about winning.'

She spoke without thinking. Annick looked at her, puzzled. 'Winning?'

'Yes, well I meant I'm winning in the sense of not going under.'

'And Phaedria? Is she winning too?'

Roz looked at her. Annick was one of the very few people who genuinely thought well of her; she had no desire to shatter her illusions now. 'Not at the moment, she's busy getting this baby of hers safely reared.'

'And when will she be back in London?'

'I don't know. This week. Next week. When the baby can travel.'

'She has had a bad time, I think,' said Annick. 'Poor Phaedria.'

Roz swallowed her martini almost in one. Poor Phaedria, poor Phaedria, that was all she ever heard. Never poor Roz, having to cope with a divorce, a billion-pound company, the loss of a father; it was always Phaedria.

'Yes, she has,' she said with a huge effort. 'But she should be all right now.

'I hear the baby is very very sweet.'

'Yes. Well, most babies are.'

'I suppose. I do not know a great many. How is Miranda?'

'Very well. Walking. Talking.'

'Talking! *Mon Dieu!* She is a genius, I think. What does she say?'

'Oh,' said Roz, 'nothing very clever, you know, segmentation of the market, demographics, gross percentage, that sort of thing.'

Annick laughed. 'It's so lovely to see you. Let's go in to lunch.'

They ordered (both being very much in agreement with the Duchess of Windsor's immortal words, that you could be neither too rich nor thin) melon and parma ham, a sliver each of poached turbot, and a bottle of Perrier water, and proceeded to sit and toy with it in between swopping industry and company gossip.

'Things cannot have been very easy for you either,' said Annick suddenly. 'I know how you loved your father. You must miss him terribly.'

'Oh, Annick, I do,' said Roz, 'I miss him horribly, more every day. And yes, I did love him. More than even I realized. I only hope he realized it. I wasn't always very nice to him, I'm afraid,' she added with a sigh.

'Oh, I think he did. I know he did,' said Annick. 'He talked about you so much, he was so proud of you, and he used to say you and he talked the same language, you could communicate almost without words, you were so alike. Especially when it came to the business.'

'Oh, God, I hope you're right,' said Roz. 'I said some pretty awful things to him, you know, over the years. Some of them just before he – he died.' Her green eyes suddenly filled with tears; she brushed them away impatiently, picked up her glass, looked round for a waiter. 'Suddenly I feel I need something a bit stronger.'

'Roz, don't torment yourself,' said Annick, calling the waiter over. 'Would you like a brandy? Yes? Two brandies, please, and two coffees. We all say bad things at times. You gave him a great deal of happiness; remember that.'

'I'll try.'

'It must be terribly difficult for you and Phaedria,' said Annick, looking at her thoughtfully, 'trying to run that company, on exactly equal terms. That was a very difficult situation he put you into. And now with Phaedria being away for – what? six weeks – it must be worse.'

'Oh, I don't know,' said Roz carefully. 'Easier in a way. At least I can make decisions and things on my own. I don't have to discuss every single thing with her.'

Annick looked at her.

779

'I'm so sorry about your marriage as well,' she said. 'I always liked C. J. very much. You must be sad about that.'

'I am, yes. But it was washed up long before Daddy died. It was only a matter of time.'

'Ah well. Perhaps it will all be for the best. If you are happy with Michael maybe you should have married him the first time, so long ago it seems now, when we were in Paris together?'

'Maybe,' said Roz firmly, pushing her various anxieties on that subject deep to the bottom of her subconscious. 'It's just a matter of getting the practicalities sorted out, really, and then we can get married.'

'And will you come and live here? That would be very nice for me.'

'God no!' said Roz, looking at her in horror. 'I couldn't. Not at the moment. The company headquarters is in London.'

'Oh, so will he go to London?'

'Er, well, yes probably.'

'I see. And C. J. Will he come back here?'

'Oh, I don't think so,' said Roz, surprised. 'Why do you ask? His life is in London now. And he's in love with the place. He's even been asked to write a book about it. And Miranda's there anyway. He adores her.'

'Well, yes, but I thought that perhaps as Camilla is here –' Annick's voice trailed off. Roz was looking at her, her eyes huge with horror and disbelief. 'Oh, my God, you didn't know. Roz, I'm sorry.'

'Camilla!' said Roz, her voice rising and cracking. 'Camilla North! That frigid constipated bitch. With C. J.! Oh, Annick, you must have got it wrong.'

'Roz, but of course I haven't. I've seen them together many times. They seem very happy. Of course she's older than he is, but does that really matter so much? And she looks very good these days.'

'Oh, shit!' said Roz. She sat looking into her brandy glass, trembling slightly. Annick was alarmed.

'Roz, I'm so sorry if it has been a shock. I didn't think you would mind. You said yourself the marriage was long over.'

'Yes, I know. I know.' She was silent for a while, obviously struggling to control herself. 'I think I'll have another brandy.

Look, Annick, you must have to get back, it's after three. I'll get this. You go off.'

'Roz, I don't like leaving you like this. You look terrible.' She gave the word the French pronunciation; Roz managed a shaky smile.

'Thanks. No, Annick, I'm all right. Honestly. But maybe I'd like to be alone for a bit now.'

'All right, Roz. If you're sure you'll be all right.'

'Of course I will. Sorry. Bit of a shock, that's all. I'm sure they're very welcome to one another,' she added savagely.

'Well, as I say, they seem to be happy,' said Annick, quite missing the irony of this remark. 'It has been so lovely to see you, Roz.' She stood up, bent over Roz, kissed her cheek briefly. 'Thank you for lunch.'

'My pleasure,' said Roz. 'See you soon.'

She asked for the check and another brandy, and sat staring into it. She felt deeply and horribly upset. Camilla North, the scourge of her childhood, the cold, interfering omnipresence, threatening Roz eternally with her beauty, her fertility, cheating her of her father's attention and love; stealing her husband. How C. J. must be loving that! How Camilla must be loving it. How the whole of New York must be enjoying it. Oh, it was monstrous, unbearable; Roz suddenly felt herself a public pillory, a source of sadistic amusement for everyone who knew her and disliked her.

How could C. J. do such a thing to her? How could he not realize the humiliation it would cause. And to be having an affair with Camilla, of all people. Icy, sexless Camilla. What an insult to her! To Roz! What fearsome implications of frustration and rejection the liaison carried! 'Oh, God, C. J.,' she said under her breath, 'if you walked in here now I would kill you.'

And then she suddenly imagined him, saw him as if he was indeed standing before her, his sweet smile, his soft brown eyes, his tall rangy figure, his unfailingly courteous manners, and she did not feel as if she would kill him at all, and her eyes filled with tears.

She did not go to Bloomie's that afternoon. She didn't go to any more shops. She took a cab and went back to the duplex and sat there for a long time, as the room darkened, feeling alternately angry and wretched. She also felt very alone and, in some strange way, duped, cheated of territory that was rightfully hers.

Well, it wouldn't last. It couldn't. C. J. would soon see Camilla for the vacuous sham she was. And besides he wasn't about to move to New York. He couldn't. He wouldn't leave Miranda.

Miranda! The subconscious fear that had been swimming about her head all afternoon suddenly materialized. Suppose C. J. did move to New York. Just suppose. He would want to have Miranda with him. He adored her. He had often told her he was a better mother than she was. He might well try to fight for custody. And these days, with all this Kramer and Kramer nonsense, he just might get her. Roz shuddered, felt suddenly cold.

Oh, surely it wouldn't come to that! It couldn't! C. J. would never leave London. He loved it like a mistress. But even if he stayed, he still might want Miranda. Oh, God. What a mess.

Roz decided she needed a drink. Franco was out, and wouldn't be back for an hour or so before dinner. She wandered into the gleaming stage set of a kitchen and found a glass, went to the fridge and took out the ice box. While she was cracking some cubes into her glass, she noticed the basket of book matches which Michael kept on the top of the fridge; he had been collecting them for years. They told better than anything where he had been, eaten, stayed.

She glanced idly into it as she poured some scotch into her glass; suddenly she froze, rigid with shock and fear. Right on the top, the very latest addition, was one of the small cream boxes with silvery lettering in which the Bel Air Hotel packed its matches.

The Bel Air! Phaedria was at the Bel Air. Had Michael been there? Seen her? Was it possible? Surely not, surely surely not. It wasn't, it couldn't be. He couldn't, wouldn't even look at that bitch, wouldn't betray her; it would be the utmost, infinite treachery. No, it must be a mistake. Anyway, maybe Phaedria was gone by now. No, she wasn't. She was leaving next week. Well, maybe Michael had had the matches some time. Maybe he had been rummaging through them, and it had just come out on top. There had to be a better explanation. There had to be. He couldn't betray her like this, not with Phaedria. Roz drank a very large whisky and poured herself another. Then she crossed over to the phone and, holding the matches, dialled the hotel.

'Bel Air Hotel,' said a smoothly purring voice. 'May I help you?'

'Yes,' said Roz, carefully turning her voice into something slick and efficient, not remotely like the high-pitched hysterical wail she felt struggling to escape from her. 'This is Mr Browning's secretary. Mr Michael Browning. I believe Mr Browning was staying there at the weekend. He has lost a raincoat. I wonder if he left it at the hotel?'

'One moment, ma'am. Just let me check with the house-keeper.'

There was an endless, endless pause while the phone was silent, occasionally crackling gently; Roz had to bite her fist to stop herself from screaming. 'Ma'am? No, Mr Browning didn't leave a raincoat behind. We don't have much call for raincoats here, of course.' The voice was politely amused, obviously hoping Roz would share the joke.

'I see. But he – he was there? I haven't made a mistake and confused hotels?'

'Oh, no, ma'am. He was here all right. Friday and Saturday night. But no raincoat. I'm sorry.'

The voice was filled with the genuine slightly hyped-up charm that is essentially Californian. Roz just heard that and then no more. She had a rushing in her ears; she closed her eyes and put down the phone.

She sat drinking her second whisky and then her third, wondering how she could possibly survive the agony she was enduring.

Phaedria was packing her things together. She had been living at the Bel Air for so long she couldn't imagine having to return to reality. To organizing her own household, to being in the office every day, above all, to looking after the baby all by herself. It felt very frightening.

While Julia had been at the hospital, cared for by the nurses, although she had longed to have her with her all the time, she had felt safe. No harm could come to her; if the baby got a cold or colic, or wouldn't suck for a feed, the nurse would sort her out. If there was a real anxiety, the paediatrician was on hand. Now the safety net was about to be removed from underneath her, and she was extremely nervous. It was all very well everyone reassuring her that the baby was now a normal weight, that she was, if anything, more robust than a full-term baby leaving hospital, that she knew as well as anybody how to care for her: Phaedria still didn't want to have to take on the responsibility.

Besides, she was taking Julia away from the warmth and sunshine of California into the raw dank hazards of an English November; how would she possibly be able to adapt to that?

Just fine, said the paediatrician. 'I presume you're not actually going to be living out of doors. That your house has some form of central heating? That your child will have a crib of some kind to sleep in?' His lips twitched slightly.

Phaedria said no, of course they would not be out of doors, they would be living in a large and very comfortable house. That the house was often hotter than she would personally have chosen. That there was a fully equipped nursery, arranged by her at long distance in collaboration with Letitia and Mrs Hamlyn, filled with cribs and cots and soft, downy quilts, and warm flanellette sheets, and snowy soft cashmere woven blankets; and endless piles of Viyella nightdresses, and soft, finest wool booties and mittens, and bonnets and shawls. That mobiles and musical boxes and pictures were there in abundant supply to keep Julia occupied and stimulated while she was awake; that something over a hundred soft toys were piled up on the nursery sofa awaiting the day when she could hold them and cuddle them; that a doll's house, a doll's pram, a bookcase full of children's classics, even a small bicycle waited in the room next door to the nursery designated as a playroom; that there was a shortlist of five Norland nannies awaiting their final interview with her when she got home; that she had no intention of working full time in the office until at least Christmas so that Julia could adapt to her new life and environment; that their own doctor would be waiting at the house on the afternoon they arrived home, to meet Julia and check her over. Did Mr Welch genuinely think it was really all right to take the baby home?

Mr Welch looked at her very directly and seriously. 'Of course we do have to be extremely cautious in these cases. But I honestly think, Lady Morell, that under the circumstances –' he paused – 'keeping this baby here any longer is bordering on the ludicrous.'

Phaedria smiled. 'All right. We'll go.'

So now they were going, and it was a long journey. At least twelve hours door to door, even with Pete meeting her at Heathrow, and it would seem much longer with the time change. She would have to feed Julia at least three times on the plane, change her, wash her; it wouldn't be easy. Phaedria was terrified.

British Airways, who were flying her home, were very reassuring. There were excellent facilities for mothers and babies on their planes, especially for first-class passengers. All the hostesses had some nursing knowledge. Was the baby in any way unwell? No? Then there really was nothing for her to worry about.

Supposing though, said Phaedria, the baby became ill on the plane. Then what? Was there a resident doctor?

Not exactly on the plane, said the spokesperson carefully, grateful that her caller could not see her face. Of course there very often was a doctor amongst the passengers.

Could she tell yet if that was a certainty?

No, she couldn't. Was Lady Morell's doctor aware that the baby was coming on the flight? He was. And he was quite happy about it? Then really there seemed no cause for alarm.

In the end Phaedria had to accept everybody's judgement and prepare to take Julia home.

She had spent most of the week thinking about Michael Browning. She found it rather alarming how much she had focused on him. He filled her head and her heart, and she had hardly a thought that had not contained him. What was that Quaker expression that had always charmed her? Thee pleasures me. Yes, that was what Michael did to her, he pleasured her, made her feel joyful and warmed and safe and almost physically cared for, he induced a kind of charm and delight into everything, life was heightened and lightened when he was there, and bleaker and darker when he was not. She liked too the fact that she clearly amused and delighted him; that he made her feel interesting, and important, and – and oh, God, yes, and something else too. He made her think with quite appalling relentlessness and vividness of sex. She was not sure quite how; it was partly the way he looked at her, the way his eyes flicked over her body sometimes, the way he smiled, not just into her eyes, her face, but suddenly disarmingly as his eyes were resting on her breasts, her legs, her stomach as though these places inspired such thoughts of joy and delight that he could not contain himself, could not remain solemn; partly the blatant sensuality contained in his eyes, in the way he moved, even the way he spoke, certainly the way he laughed; partly the sudden amused comment, the half serious observation that revealed a strong sexual focus; but if she had tried to explain it to anyone who had never met Michael Browning she would have failed utterly. Other women had tried in the past and failed also.

Well, it was not to be. Her sadness, her regret, the physical ache he had induced in her for him paled into insignificance at the thought of Roz and what she would do to her if she discovered that she and Michael were lovers. Had even thought of being lovers.

She had been afraid of Roz, even when she had been married to Julian. Now she was, quite literally, physically terrified, and she set the concept aside as determinedly, as irrevocably as if it had been some food, some substance that would injure her, damage her fatally.

She was also terrified at the thought of returning to the minefield that was the company. She dreaded to think what Roz might have engineered in her absence, whose confidence she had gained, who she had persuaded to regard Phaedria as a half-witted usurper into the company's power structure. The temptation to sell out, to let her have it all, to go, was fierce; and yet she never allowed herself seriously to consider it. Julian had left her half the company, and he had left her Julia, although he had not known it, and she had to safeguard the one for the other. She could not betray what limited trust he had had in her. She owed him that at least.

At least now she felt well; strong, ready for battle. On the other hand, she knew she would never again be able to fight with the same total commitment. She would have Julia to worry about, to get home to, to be with; she wasn't going to have her growing up wondering who she was. However good the nanny, however efficient her staff, Julia needed her; and she was going to have her. Delegation was the key; she must find it and put it in the lock.

She had done a lot of thinking in the long often tedious days in the hospital and in the quiet evenings in her bungalow. If this nonsense was ever to be resolved, simply trying to pull everything in two pieces was not the answer. There had to be some lateral input of thought: the trouble was that on this subject at least, Roz only thought vertically.

It seemed hopeless; unless one or the other of them managed to find Miles and manipulate him into cooperation. And that seemed increasingly unlikely.

Towards six o'clock, Roz suddenly remembered, through the haze of misery and rage, and several extremely large whiskies, that she was supposed to be meeting Michael at the Algonquin. Well, that was all right. She could talk to him there as well as anywhere. It might enliven things a little for the other people there. It was a pretty dull place a lot of the time. She called out to Franco who had come in and was working in the kitchen, and told him to get her a cab.

'You won't get one now, Mrs Emerson. It's rush hour.'

'Well, I have to get to the Algonquin. And I'm not going to walk.'

'Would you like me to drive you? I can get the car round in five minutes.'

Roz looked at him, thinking. Walking might not be a bad idea. It was only ten blocks, and she needed a clear head. The traffic would be appalling, and she would have to sit and listen to Franco's running commentary on the deteriorating condition of New York all the way.

'No, it's all right, Franco, I think after all I'll walk. The traffic will be terrible.'

'All right, Mrs Emerson. Will you and Mr Browning be coming back here for dinner?'

'I'm afraid I don't have the faintest idea,' she said, making it plain that the decision was hers, rather than Michael's, where they dined. 'I haven't decided what I want to do this evening yet.'

She liked putting Franco down; he was so bloody devoted to Michael, so eager to impress upon her the democratic nature of their relationship. Roz thought there was only one place for servants and that they should know precisely where it was.

Michael was sitting at a table in the Blue Bar and drinking bourbon when she arrived. He saw her standing in the doorway and his heart lurched. She was difficult, she was overbearing and monstrously selfish and unreasonable, but she was very very sexy. And she was plainly in feisty mood. Her eyes were brilliant and snapping, her face was alive, her entire body spelt out energy, power, resolution. He smiled to himself.

'Hi, darling! Come and sit down. What would you like to drink?'

'A scotch whisky on the rocks,' said Roz to the waiter, 'a large one.'

Michael looked at her quickly. She didn't usually drink spirits, and certainly not in large quantities. He noticed suddenly that she was flushed, and that her voice was slightly odd.

'Are you OK?'

'Oh, yes,' she said and her voice was just a little too loud and harsh. 'I'm absolutely fine. Never better. But then I always did enjoy good health. As you know. I'm not someone to cave under at the least strain. Would you say, Michael?'

'No,' he said, and there was puzzlement in his voice. 'No, I wouldn't. It's that good British stock you come from, I guess.'

'Not necessarily,' she said. 'Not at all. I could name a few examples of British stock who are pretty damn feeble. Who take almost two bloody months recovering from having a baby. Who sit about whingeing and whining and expecting the world to come running to them, from thousands of miles away if need be.' She drained her glass, leant back in her chair and called to the waiter. 'Bring me another of these, will you?' Then she turned back to Michael. 'So how was my dear stepmother last weekend, Michael? Sitting up and taking notice yet? Or still lying back on her pillows like some pathetic Victorian heroine, trawling sympathy from anyone in sight?'

788

'Ah,' he said quietly. 'So that's it.'

'Yes,' said Roz. 'That is it. And how was it, Michael? How did you find her? Pretty damn ready for you, I would say. I bet she's like a bitch on heat underneath that fey, little-girl charm of hers. She pulled my father into her bed fairly fast. Well, there's no fool like an old fool, they say. You, I would have thought, might have been expected to be a little more sensible. I was obviously woefully wrong.'

'Roz, don't be absurd.'

'Absurd! In what way am I being absurd? Perhaps you expect me to be delighted that you went sick-visiting? And saw fit not to tell me. I would say that tells its own story, Michael. Or am I to believe that you simply gave her some grapes and admired the baby? Now that really would be absurd. Deeply absurd. I mean, I don't admire her style myself but I am told she is considered not exactly ill to look upon. And you are, by your own admission, frustrated at the moment. And I daresay she is – or rather was – too, by Christ, although God knows how many lovers she might have had before or after my father died. I still don't believe that child is his.'

'Roz, you are making several serious mistakes,' said Michael quietly. He was still sitting quite easily in his chair, watching her, listening to her; the fact that the entire room was doing the same bothered him not in the least.

'Really? What mistakes am I making? I hope you're not going to try and tell me I'm mistaken in thinking you have been in her bed, and in her so elegant personage. She must be a hell of an easy lay, and so conveniently far from home and from anyone who might have known or disturbed either of you. How was it, Michael? Is she good in bed? Does she have any clever tricks you hadn't met before?

'I wouldn't know,' he said. 'Shall we continue this discussion at home?'

'Oh, I like it here,' she said. 'Where is my second drink? Waiter! I asked you for another whisky. Bring it over here, would you?'

'Rosamund, he isn't going to. Leave him out of this. It isn't his fault, poor guy.'

'No, but it's yours,' she cried, quite loudly, her face by now contorted with fury. 'It's absolutely yours. How dare you go down there, to California, to her, seeing her, screwing her, while I was safely thousands of miles away in London? How dare you?'

'I did not screw her,' he said quietly. 'I didn't touch her.'

'Oh, yes, and I'm the President of the United States. Don't give me that, Michael. Don't insult me any more than you have done already.'

'I'm trying not to,' he said, and there was an edge of searing anger suddenly in his voice that quietened even her. 'I did go to see Phaedria, yes, and the baby. I went because I was over there already, on business, and it seemed like a nice idea. I like Phaedria, she's charming and agreeable, which is more than I can say for you a great deal of the time. And she's had a tough time, to which you have contributed greatly. I did not, however, go to bed with her. I might well have been tempted to, not having had a great deal of carnal pleasure lately, thanks to your good self and your insane obsession with that company of yours. But I did not, and it was much to my credit and to hers that the only physical contact I experienced over the whole weekend was with her very charming baby. Who incidentally greatly resembles your father. I only hope it grows up into something more agreeable than his other daughter. I'm going home now. Perhaps you'd like to settle the check.'

He walked out, leaving the room entirely silent and Roz frozen to her chair, her face ashen, her eyes huge and brilliant, and an icy fear taking grip on her heart.

Phaedria decided on that, one of her few last afternoons in California, to go and visit Father Kennedy again. She had no real intention of asking him any more questions, she simply thought she owed it to him to visit him once more, to explain why no more money had come into the refuge yet, and to show him Julia. She had only taken her out a few times; she had bought a folding pram for the car, and would drive her out to Griffith Park or to the Palisades, and push her up and down carefully and proudly, pretending – wishing, even – that she was just one more mother, with one more baby, and that she had no more serious worries in the world than when she should consider mixed feeding, or whether the sun might be just a little too hot, despite the pram parasol, for Julia to be out in.

She drove down to Santa Monica, parked outside the refuge, and lifted Julia out of the car. Father Kennedy was sitting talking to one or two of his flock; he smiled as she walked towards him and stood up.

'Well now, this is a most welcome new visitor. I thought you had gone back to England.'

'No, Father, I hadn't. She took me by surprise. I've been here ever since that day.'

'Well, and if I had only known I would have come to visit you. Now this is a beautiful baby. What is her name?'

'She is called Julia. After her father.'

'That is a lovely name. And how old would she be now, Miss Julia?'

'Oh, two months. But I couldn't take her out before, she was very premature, she nearly died.'

'And you've been alone here all this time, have you? That is a very sad thing.'

'Oh,' she said, 'not quite alone. I've had a lot of visitors. Flying out from England.'

'Well, you must be a very popular young lady. That's a long way to come sick-visiting.'

'I'm very lucky,' she said, almost surprised to find that she was. 'I have a very nice family.'

'There is nothing better, no greater gift a person can have, than a good family. Next to God,' he added hastily, lest the Almighty might be listening and taking offence.

'Oh, it is. And I never really had one before.'

'Did you not?'

'No. Did you come from a big family, Father Kennedy?'

'I did indeed. I was number eleven and there were two more after me. My mother did her best for the Church,' he added with a twinkle in his faded blue eyes. 'And I did my best for her.'

'Did any of her other sons go into the priesthood?'

'Not one. And most of them have died now, but there are many many nieces and nephews and great-nieces and nephews – but what am I thinking of, come and sit down, and let me give you a cup of tea.'

Phaedria followed him inside and sat down, holding Julia tenderly against her shoulder as she sipped her iced tea. She had grown very fond of it as a drink since she had been in California.

'What I really came to see you about, Father, apart from showing you my baby, was to say that I'm sorry I haven't made any arrangements yet about money for you, for the refuge, but I just haven't been able to. Not being at home. But I haven't forgotten, and I didn't want you to think I'd forgotten.'

'I thought no such thing,' he said. 'But it was good of you to come just the same. May I hold your baby a moment?'

'Of course,' she said, and handed her over, looking at him and smiling as he held the baby gently, stroking her tiny dark head, patting her small back.

'I love babies,' he said. 'It is my only regret about being a priest, that I was denied this pleasure, that of fatherhood. But then, of course, I have known far more children, been involved with them, watched them growing up than if I had had my own. So maybe it was all for the best.'

'Maybe.'

'Well now, have you found that young man yet?'

'No, Father, we haven't. I hear he was traced as far as Miami, but now he has simply vanished. Nobody knows where he is. My – that is, one of the other members of the family is still trying to trace him with a private detective, but what with the baby and so on, I haven't given it much thought lately.'

'And Mrs Kelly, the grandmother, do you know anything of her? Is she well?'

'I believe she is well, but apparently a little – well, confused,' said Phaedria carefully, raking desperately through her mind for a positive aspect of the news C. J. had brought, via Henry Winterbourne, of a pair of crazy old women struggling to keep Miles from his rightful inheritance.

'Well now, that would explain why she has never answered my letters,' said Father Kennedy with a sigh. He looked sad suddenly and very old.

Phaedria put out her hand and touched his arm. 'I'm sorry.'

'Oh, well now, that is the way of the world. We are none of us growing younger. Did you find nothing up at the house?' he asked after a moment's pause.

'Not – not really,' she said, 'it was all locked up. I just found –

oh, you know, some of Miles' toys – his bike and his skate board and so on.'

'Oh, he loved that skate board,' said Father Kennedy. 'He used to park it outside the church when he came to mass. He would have brought it in with him if his mother had allowed it.'

'What – what was his mother like?' asked Phaedria carefully, reaching out, taking the baby back from him, not looking at him. 'I mean was she a nice person, was she clever, what was she actually like?'

'She was a very nice person and very brave,' said Father Kennedy. 'Very brave indeed. Not just when she was so ill, but after her husband died. That wasn't easy for her.'

'She must have felt so alone,' said Phaedria, 'I do know a little bit how she felt.'

'Indeed. And she had no family to speak of, apart from her mother, although she had good friends. And Mr Dashwood, now he was very good to her then, and helped her a lot.'

'Did he?' said Phaedria sharply. 'What did he do?'

'Oh, well now, he helped her with all the paperwork, you know, and that sort of thing, and I believe he made some money available to her as well. He was a good friend to her, it has to be said, very good. He came to see her, often, right up to the end.' He stopped suddenly, fearing he might have said too much. 'Well now, you'll have to excuse me, I must be getting on with my work, it is nearly half past four, and then the rush starts, you know, we have to close our doors soon after that.'

'Father,' said Phaedria, in a sudden, desperate rush of courage, astonishing herself. 'Father, you don't have any photographs of Hugo Dashwood, do you?'

'I don't think so,' he said, 'I can't think that I would. Miles might have a few, of course, but then that isn't of any help to you, is it? But if I should come across one, I will certainly let you know.'

'And – and what did he look like?'

'Well, he was quite tall. Dark-haired. Nicely dressed. Rather too formally, for this part of the world. But then the English are inclined to be that way, aren't they? He had these very formal manners too, and the wonderful English accent, very much like your own.'

'And what colour eyes did he have? Can you remember that?'

793

There was a long silence; Phaedria stood motionless, fearing the answer. She turned her head and rested her cheek on the baby's head.

Finally Father Kennedy shook his head.

'Well now, there you have me,' he said. 'Darkish certainly. But whether they were dark blue or grey or even brown, I couldn't tell you. I think if you really forced me to say something I would say grey. But I'm more or less guessing, mind. Does it matter greatly?'

'Oh, no,' said Phaedria, feeling suddenly unaccountably lighthearted. 'It doesn't matter at all. I'm just trying to visualize him, that's all. Just trying to work out what he was really like.'

How Roz got home that night she never afterwards knew.

She managed to get to the ladies' room, where she threw up, and then she sat for a very long time on the seat, resting her head on the partition, too drained of emotion even to cry, occasionally listening to the various women coming in and discussing the scene they had just witnessed.

'It certainly did beat anything on the cinema,' said one cool amused voice. 'I just don't know how anyone can humiliate themselves like that.'

'Well,' said her companion, as if she was explaining the mystery of the universe, 'she was English, remember.'

'I know,' said the first. 'But I would just rather die. And he seemed so nice and patient with her.'

'Yes, well,' said the second, 'he was American.'

'Yes of course,' said the first, clearly finding this a perfectly satisfactory explanation.

After this display of chauvinism they left the room; Roz waited a while and was wondering if she had the strength to make her escape when a second pair came in.

'I thought it was just disgusting,' said Voice A, 'absolutely not the sort of thing you expect to have going on in a place like this.'

'Oh, I don't know,' said Voice B. 'I thought it was rather exciting. I thought she was wonderful.'

'Did you?' said A. 'I thought she was dreadful. You can always tell,' she added, 'when people come from poor families. I mean she may have looked all right, and that coat was obviously very expensive, but you could see there was no breeding there, no breeding at all. She's obviously screwed a lot of money out of some poor man or other, probably not that one, and now she's just reverting to type.'

'Well, I think you're wrong,' said B. 'If he's really been playing around, then he deserves to be bawled out.'

'Not in public surely?'

'Anywhere at all to my way of thinking.'

Roz was just about to leave the cubicle and go out and shake B's hand and possibly deliver A a short lecture on the English class system and where she stood in it when they also left the cloakroom; it was quiet for a while. She stood up, went out, washed her face quickly and then made her way to the elevator. Whatever happened now, for the rest of her life she would never be able to come to the Algonquin again. Well, that was no great loss.

After that brief rush of adrenaline everything blurred again. She presumed afterwards that she must have found a cab, driven to Kennedy, checked in to a mercifully imminent flight, and then sunk into her seat and tried to go to sleep through the endless night ahead of her in the sky.

But she couldn't. Her mind roared and raced on. Could Michael possibly have been speaking the truth? Surely not. Otherwise he would have told her exactly where he had been. On the other hand, he was quite outstandingly truthful. She had never known him to lie. But of course Phaedria brought out the protector in men; she had seen it before. With her pathetic little-girl, fragile airs, and those ridiculous great eyes of hers. He was probably lying to protect her. He knew how frightened she would be. And with good cause. Jesus, thought Roz, once she gets back to England, will I give her hell. If she thinks life's been tough up to now, she's going to find out it's been one long rest cure by comparison.

But then – but then if it was true, if she and Michael were having an affair, Phaedria wouldn't care. She would just sell out and move to New York and live with Michael. Well, that would at least mean that she, Roz, would get the company. Some good would come of it. On the other hand, for the first time since the day she had gone to work for her father, Roz wondered if there was a price too high to pay for that massive unwieldy monster. Did she really not care about what happened to her, as a person? Would she settle for success, power, money, would they be enough, would they replace warmth, tenderness, safety, sex?

It looked as if they might have to, unless she did something very clever and very quickly. Michael, even if he had been speaking the truth, playing fair, was not going to come running back to her now. He would be deeply angry, outraged, she had publicly humiliated him, and he was a fiercely proud man.

Unless she did something fairly drastic, crawled to him, begged him to forgive her (and she was not about to do that, to risk having them laughing at her, despising her), she had lost him.

God, she thought, pressing viciously on her call button, God I hate that woman. She's taken away everything I ever value: my father, the stores, the company, and now my lover.

For a short horrific moment she allowed herself to think of Phaedria in bed with Michael; of her lying naked in his arms, knowing the pleasure of his immensely skilful body: she felt violently sick again.

'Bring me a drink, would you?' she said to the steward who had appeared in front of her. 'A whisky. And a strong coffee as well.'

'Yes, Mrs Emerson.'

Mrs Emerson! That reminded her of C. J. and Camilla. Taking alternate sips of whisky and coffee, she tried to imagine how she was going to handle that as well. The threat of losing Miranda. And the double humiliation of losing husband and lover. Everyone had always assumed she had ditched C. J. in order to marry Michael. Now it would look very different.

'Dear God,' she said aloud, speaking to the clouds, and the darkness they were beginning to fly out of, 'what a day. How have I survived it?'

And exhausted finally, her aching heart briefly anaesthetized, she fell asleep.

When Phaedria got back to the hotel later that evening there was a message waiting for her.

'Could you call Mr Browning at home in New York?' said the clerk at the desk. 'I have his number. Would you like it?'

'Yes please,' said Phaedria. Her heart was being horribly fast. She went back to her bungalow, hurried in, slammed the door, dialled the number. Michael answered the phone himself.

'Phaedria, hi. How are you?'

'I'm fine. What's the matter?'

'Well, I thought I should phone you. Tell you to double lock your door. Batten down the hatches.' He tried to sound amused, lighthearted, but he failed.

She knew immediately what he meant.

'She's found out?'

'Yup.'

'But there was nothing to find out.'

'Did you ever try to explain to a bluebottle there was glass in the window? Same thing. She found it kind of hard to grasp.'

'Oh, God. Oh, Michael. What shall we do? Where is she?'

'Christ knows. I imagine on her way back to London. She just left. She flew in this morning. I don't think she'll be coming over to you. But she just might. I'm very very sorry.'

'How did she find out?'

'I don't know. I really don't. She'd had lunch with that French dame, the one she always says is her only friend, what's her goddamned name, Annie or Angela or something, and I called her, but she just said was Roz all right, she'd been worried about her because she was very upset about Camilla and C. J.'

'Camilla and who?'

'C. J. Apparently they've got it together. Isn't that something?'

'I suppose so,' said Phaedria, with an irrational stab of jealousy. 'Yes. But anyway, Annick didn't seem to know about – about us?'

'Absolutely not.'

'Oh, it's so ridiculous,' said Phaedria, 'nothing to know, nothing at all. But I can see she wouldn't have believed it.'

'No. I'd have a little trouble with it myself, though, wouldn't you?'

'I suppose so. Yes.'

'Serves us right,' he said. 'I knew it was a mistake.'

'What, coming to see me?'

'No,' he said, and his voice warmed her, stroked her over the telephone. 'Not seeing more of you. The rest of you.'

'Well,' she said, 'I shall just have to go back and face her. I'm not staying here.'

'You wouldn't like to come and hide with a lonely, frightened man for a day or two?'

'No,' she said firmly. 'You've got me into enough trouble. I'm going home.'

'Lady Morell,' he said, and there was a wealth of admiration in his voice, 'you are a dame with balls.'

The weekend wound wearily on for Roz. The nanny had taken Miranda up to Scotland for a day or two to stay with her grandmother; the house was empty, silent. She roamed about it, restless, miserable. She felt she had been asked to bear too much; she didn't see quite how she was going to stand it. She was alone, she was frightened, she was wretchedly unhappy, she was humiliated; she thought of going to see Letitia to talk to her, but rejected the idea, shrinking from the pain of explaining, of exposing herself to Letitia's particular brand of rather pragmatic sympathy. And Susan, dear Susan, her refuge in times of trouble, was away with Richard in France, inspecting their new property.

She hurt physically; her back throbbed, her head ached, her legs felt heavy and weak. She tried to eat, in the knowledge that on Monday she was going to have to make an appearance, to take some decisions, put on her endlessly impressive performance; Phaedria would be back at the end of the week, she couldn't afford to let them see her weaken now. But the food tasted disgusting: she couldn't swallow it.

She decided to go out, to get some air; she walked for miles along the embankment, from Cheyne Walk all the way to Westminster, and then on to Blackfriars, and still further, to Tower Bridge. As she walked she thought about C. J. and the London he loved so much; about how she had refused over and over again to go with him as he explored it, about how little he had complained, merely gone off with his maps and his reference books, in search of happiness, interest, discovery and she had been grateful, relieved, to see him go. Well, he was gone now, permanently, she had lost him (odd how it suddenly seemed to be a loss), and it seemed she had lost Michael too. How horribly wrong her life was turning out, when only two years ago she had seemed to hold everything that she wanted in her hands. A nightmarish panic took hold of her; she felt as if everything was out of rhythm, distorted, slightly mad. She grew oddly frightened; she felt she must get back to her own territory, not be in strange places and alone; she hailed a cab and went home to Cheyne Walk, sobered, miserable.

In the end she turned to work. It proved, as usual, to be the panacea. It never failed her. She always found serenity, calm, sheer pleasure in work.

She settled at her desk in the study next to her bedroom, and with sheer force of will set her mind to the company and its demands. Initially she went through her pending files, catching up on detail, answering memos, checking minutes, cross-referencing appointments in her diaries. But on Sunday evening she got out some files and looked at the performance of the various companies over the past year. The stores were doing fine (including London now, which was a bittersweet pill to swallow), the cosmetic company was flourishing (only she yearned to do things with that, expand into the body business, open some more health farms); the hotels were a bit iffy. The pharmaceutical company was expanding faster than the rest; plastics and paper were both doing fine. Only the new communications company looked as if it might be in serious difficulty: she would sell that if she had her way. But Phaedria would never agree. Oh, God, if only, if only she had a bit more power. She could see the way ahead so clearly, and knew exactly how to steer the company through it.

She was in the office at seven-thirty the following morning. She felt excited, exhilarated, her misery briefly forgotten.

She settled at her desk, pulled out her dictating machine, began to construct a careful, discreet document. She was totally engrossed in it when she heard footsteps in the corridor. Now who could that be, and why hadn't she had the sense to re-lock the front door? It was far too early for any of the regular staff to come in and the cleaners came at night. Maybe it was the doorman, come in early. She heard a knock on her own door; she frowned. 'Yes? Come in!' She heard the door open; still half engrossed in her work, she paused before she looked up. When she did, she thought she must be hallucinating.

A ludicrously beautiful young man stood in front of her, leaning with an almost mannered grace against the door. He had sun-streaked, untidy, rather long blond hair, and very dark blue eyes; there was a night's growth of stubble on his tanned face; he was tall and slender and he was dressed in jeans and a very crumpled white shirt, a denim jacket slung over one shoulder.

His eyes travelled over Roz appreciatively: slowly, carefully, taking her in. Then he slowly smiled, a glorious, joyous, pleasure-giving smile that she could not resist, could not despite her weariness, her anxiety, help but return.

'Hi,' he said, 'I'm Miles.'

Chapter Twenty-four

London, New York, Los Angeles, 1985

Miles Wilburn and Billy de Launay were often to remark in later life that the most amazing thing about the whole story of Miles' inheritance was not so much that Marcia Galbraith should have tried to do what she did, but that she should have succeeded for so long.

'Months and months half the civilized world was looking for you,' said Billy, 'and you just had no idea. It sure beats fiction.'

'Yeah,' said Miles. They had been sitting in Nassau Airport at the time, with Candy, who had been trying very hard not to cry, waiting for Miles' flight to be called; they had had this conversation a great many times now, and still felt the topic had not been exhausted.

'God knows what else she'd been keeping from you,' said Billy. 'Did you ask her?'

'No,' said Miles. 'No point. But I did ask her if she'd kept anything from Granny Kelly. I made her turn over any letters for her.'

'And?'

'Well there was the couple from old Father Kennedy. She would have loved to get them. That did make me mad. And one of them, actually, did say old Hugo wanted to contact me. So it was kind of important.'

'And you still don't know how he fits into this?'

'Nope. But maybe soon I shall find out.'

He looked at Candy's tear-streaked face, put his arm round her, kissed the top of her head. 'Don't cry, baby, I swear I won't be long, I'll be back for you, and maybe if I'm a really rich guy by then we can get married.'

'Daddy won't allow it,' said Candy, blowing her nose. 'He says I have to be twenty-one.'

'Oh, he'll change his mind if old Miles turns out to be in the money,' said Billy.

'I doubt it. You know, I have the strangest feeling he knew something about all this. He acted real strange when I told him. He pretended to be interested and surprised, but he wasn't.'

'Probably saw one of the advertisements,' said Billy.

'Wicked old buzzard,' said Candy. 'Fancy keeping that from Miles.'

'Oh, well, you never know,' said Miles easily, 'he probably thought he was acting for the best. He doesn't want to lose you. I wouldn't either, if I was your dad.'

'Oh, Miles,' said Candy, 'you are just too good to be true.'

'No I'm not,' he said, smiling at her. 'I just can't get worked up about things, that's all.'

'This whole thing might have been resolved a lot earlier,' said Billy in a slightly pompous avuncular tone, 'if you occasionally looked at a newspaper, Miles. I can't believe you missed it.'

'Oh, hell,' said Miles, 'I often do read the front page now. But I would never have seen the public notices, surely.'

'I did.'

'Yes, but you're an ambitious young man. I'm just a no-good bum.' He smiled at them both. 'Now look, you will keep an eye on my granny, won't you? I worry about her and that old woman. I don't think she'd do her any harm, I think she's really fond of her, but I don't like the idea of going off and leaving her all alone.'

'I absolutely promise,' said Candy seriously, 'to go and visit her at least twice a week.'

'Good girl. Anyway, I don't intend to be gone more than two weeks at the most. I don't want to stay in London.'

'Not even if you turn out to be Little Lord Fauntleroy the Second?' said Billy.

'Not whatever I turn out to be.'

Billy had been having a marvellous time in Philadelphia; he was doing well at the bank, he had grown increasingly charming and good-looking with the years and he was much in demand by debutante mothers at parties everywhere. Instead of going home to Nassau for August, he was invited by the mother of one Marilyn Greaves, who fondly imagined him to be a great deal richer than he really was, to summer with them at Mount Desert Island. Being beset with the twin problems of deflowering Marilyn and keeping from Mrs Greaves his family's true financial status, Billy let almost two months go by before he returned to the matter of Miles and where he might be. It wasn't until he wrote to his parents (a rare event), and asked them to tell Miles to get in touch next time they saw him, that he discovered what was going on. His father told him Miles had gone to Miami, to work in a bank; he had no address, but he would ask Marcia for one. Shamed into honesty, Marcia gave Mr de Launay the address, but Billy's letter had been returned with 'unknown here' on it.

Marilyn Greaves was still absorbing a lot of Billy's attention, and he was a slow correspondent; it was the end of October before he actually wrote to Miles, care of the bank; and two more weeks before Miles replied.

Miles' letter made interesting reading; he had tired of life at the counter, and had finally walked out one day at the end of August; he had taken a bus down to Coconut Grove, found it much more to his liking, and had been working at Monty Trainer's down on Dinner Key for the past couple of months. He occasionally went back to the bank to pick up letters, which made life simpler as he kept moving around in the Grove; they had been real nice about him leaving so precipitantly.

He was still planning on marrying Candy, but wasn't doing too well on getting much money put by, he'd love to see Billy, when was he coming down South?

Billy, coming home for Thanksgiving, stopped off in Miami

and sought Miles out. It was while they were getting gloriously drunk together, that Billy asked him what had happened when he had phoned the number in the advertisement.

Henry Winterbourne had just come in to the office when Miles called. He and Caroline had been celebrating their fourteenth wedding anniversary the previous evening; the combination of the effect of a bottle of champagne each, a bottle of beaune over dinner, several large brandies, and Caroline's refusal to mark the occasion in what seemed to him a more appropriate manner later in bed, had left him bad-tempered as well as severely overhung.

He snatched up the phone when it rang, and nursing his head with the other hand, spoke tetchily into it. 'Yes?'

'Er, Mr Winterbourne,' said the temporary secretary, who was filling in until Jane came back from holiday on Monday, and easily frightened. 'There's a long distance call for you. From Miami. The name is Wilburn, Mr Winterbourne. Miles Wilburn.'

Henry forgot his hangover.

'Good Christ. Put him on.'

The voice that came three thousand miles over the wires to him was a charming, slightly husky, Californian drawl.

'Hi,' it said.

'Er, good morning,' said Henry.

'This is Miles Wilburn. I believe you wanted me to contact you.'

'I did. Where are you calling from?'

'Coconut Grove, Miami.'

'Would you – shall I call you back? Give me your number.'

'Oh, you can't do that, I'm in a call box.'

'Then ring off and call me back, reversing the charges.'

'OK. That's really nice of you.'

Whoever he was, Henry thought, he had nice manners.

'Right,' he said, slightly more himself by the time the international operator had put Miles through. 'Tell me why you're calling now. We've been trying to reach you for months.'

'Oh, it's a long story. I only just heard you were looking for me. My grandmother's friend had been keeping letters and stuff from me. She's a little confused.'

'I see. Do you have any idea why we're looking for you?'

'None at all,' said Miles.

'Have you ever met – did you ever meet – Sir Julian Morell?'

'I beg your pardon?'

'Sir Julian Morell – did you know him?'

'No I didn't. I never even heard of him. I kind of thought this must be something to do with Mr Dashwood.'

'Ah.' Henry thought quickly. The mysterious Mr Dashwood surfacing again. Who the hell was he? Why did all these Americans know him? 'Was – is Mr Dashwood related to you?'

'He certainly isn't.' Miles sounded just mildly put out. 'He's just – well, what you might call a family friend. I suppose.'

'I see,' said Henry again. His headache was returning. 'Well, Mr Wilburn, we obviously have a lot to talk about. Can you give us evidence that you are indeed Miles Wilburn?'

'I have a birth certificate. Would that do?'

'Very probably,' said Henry carefully. 'I think that you should come to London. My secretary will book you a flight immediately. Do you have a passport?'

'I certainly do.'

'Excellent. Then I suggest you come straight here on Monday. Providing we can get you on a flight on Sunday. From – where? Miami?'

'No,' said Miles. 'I'll be in Nassau.'

'Fine. And I will have a car meet you at London Heathrow.'

'OK,' said Miles. 'That's really nice of you. Goodbye, Mr Winterbourne.'

Henry thought he had never, in twenty-five years of practice, come across anybody quite so unemotional. Or what was the expression they used in California? Laid back. Yes, that was it.

Well, how extraordinary. After all these months. Good God, he must let Roz know. He rang the Morell offices to discover that she was in New York. What about Phaedria: she would like to know. But it was the middle of the night in California; he would ring her later. Meanwhile he wanted his coffee extremely badly.

Later, Phaedria was out; she had taken the car and not said when she would be back. She was usually back by evening, would they have her call him?

But he and Caroline were leaving for Paris for the weekend,

to further celebrate their anniversary. No, he would surprise everybody on Monday morning.

'No,' he said, 'it's all right. No message.'

'Stay there,' said Roz, jumping up, holding up her hand as if to prohibit him from suddenly vanishing again, 'don't go away.'

'I just flew three thousand miles to come to this place. I'm not going away until I find out what I'm doing here,' said Miles with a second, yet more dazzling smile.

'Would you like a coffee?'

'I certainly would. Black, no sugar.'

'I'll go and get it. Just wait here.'

Miles looked after her as she disappeared down the corridor, puzzled by her agitation, and then shrugged. He had heard the English were a little tense. Old Hugo had always seemed rather stiff and awkward. If they were all as uptight as this girl, he wasn't going to enjoy them too much. She was interesting-looking, though. Not good-looking exactly, but she had a lot of style. She reminded him of someone and he couldn't think who.

Roz came back into the office, a coffee cup in either hand.

'There,' she said. 'I hope it's OK.'

'It will be. Pan American coffee tastes like gnat's piss. Not,' he added, smiling at her, 'that I've ever actually tasted gnat's piss.'

Roz sat down again at her desk and gazed at him in total silence. She couldn't stop. Partly because of his remarkable looks, and partly because she couldn't believe he was really there. Miles met her gaze steadily, a sliver of amusement in his dark blue eyes; then finally he smiled. 'Will I do?'

'I beg your pardon?'

'Do I pass? Have you examined me enough yet?'

'Oh, I'm sorry,' said Roz, smiling back. 'Do forgive me. It's just that – well, we've been looking for you for so long, it seems odd that you should just – well, materialize. Like a ghost or something.'

'Nothing ghostly about me,' said Miles cheerfully. 'Feel.' He held out a brown hand. Roz took it, shook it, laughing.

'How do you do. I'm Rosamund Emerson.'

'Pleased to meet you. You know who I am. So you're not one of the Morells?'

'Oh, yes,' said Roz quickly. 'Yes, I am really. I'm Julian Morell's daughter.'

'Ah. So who is this guy?'

'You really don't know?' said Roz, astonished, disbelieving, even after all the accumulated evidence, that the link between Miles Wilburn and Julian Morell was still so absolutely inexplicable.

'No. Why should I?'

'Well, because –' Roz stopped, suddenly aware of the need for a degree of caution. 'Oh, it's terribly complicated. The lawyers should really tell you.'

'Oh God!' He put his hand to his forehead in horror. 'I forgot. I was supposed to be met by your lawyer's car this morning at Heathrow. But I got an earlier flight out of Nassau. He'll be sitting there wetting himself, I would imagine. Can we do anything about that?'

'Oh, so Henry knew you were coming?' said Roz. 'Why the hell didn't he tell us?'

'I really don't know that. But what about this poor guy in the car?'

'Oh, you don't want to worry about him,' said Roz briskly. 'He's paid to sit and wait for people.'

'Some job,' said Miles. 'I don't envy him. Well maybe we should try and tell your lawyers anyway.'

'Yes, we should. But Henry won't be up yet even. He keeps academic hours. Don't worry, we'll call later. Are you hungry?'

'I certainly am.'

'I am too. Let's go and get some breakfast. Now let's see –' she looked at him doubtfully – 'they won't let you into the Connaught in those clothes. Or the Ritz. Oh, God, where can we go?'

'Mrs Emerson, I only want a coffee and some bacon. Do you have to wear a dinner suit for that in England?'

Roz laughed. 'Sorry. Practically yes, if it's high-class coffee and bacon.'

'Then let's go find some of the lower-class kind.'

'All right. We'll go to Shepherds' Market. And I don't really answer to Mrs Emerson. Call me Roz.'

'OK.'

*

806

'What I want to know,' she said as he swooped hungrily into a plate of bacon, mushrooms, tomatoes and fried bread at one of the early morning sandwich bars in Shepherd's Market, 'is how you found us in Dover Street?'

'Oh, well, your stuffed shirt of a lawyer kept mentioning Morell. I got into Heathrow early, didn't know what to do, checked through the phone book and there it was. The Morell Corporation, Julian Morell Industrials, God knows what else. I decided it was worth a try. That somebody might be here. And I was right. Which was nice,' he added, smiling, 'very nice.'

Roz was suddenly aware of a warmth in her, comforting her, cheering her. 'Nice for me too,' she said. He held her gaze for a moment with his lazy blue eyes; just slightly discomfited, she looked away.

'So where is Mr Emerson?' asked Miles, pushing his empty plate back, looking hopefully in his empty coffee cup. 'Don't they do refills round here?'

'Mr Emerson is in New York,' said Roz in tones that totally discouraged further questioning on the subject, 'and no, I'm afraid England has not yet discovered the secret of eternal coffee. Not yet. Some of us are working on it. Let me get you another one.'

She picked up his cup and walked over to the counter with it. Miles watched her. She certainly had a great pair of legs. Nearly as good as Candy's. No, correction. Better than Candy's. Miles was a leg man.

'There. Good and strong. How are you feeling?'

'Fine.' He seemed surprised by the question. 'Shouldn't I be?'

Roz smiled. 'Most people complain about feeling tired when they've done a ten-hour flight.'

'Yeah, well I'm young and strong.' He grinned at her. 'Could I have some toast or something?'

'Yes of course.' She called over to the girl behind the counter. 'Three rounds of toast please. With butter.

'Just exactly how old are you anyway?' she said, turning back to him.

'Twenty-seven.'

'You look younger.'

'How old are you?'

'Twenty-nine.'

'You look older.'

'Thanks.'

'Oh, I didn't mean to be rude,' he said hastily. 'I'm sorry. But you do look kind of – well, shot up. Tired. You look like you could do with some Californian sunshine.'

'Oh, God,' said Roz, 'I would just adore some Californian sunshine.'

'You should go there. Seriously. It would do you good.'

'That's where you come from isn't it?'

'Now how do you know that?'

'Oh,' she said, 'you'd be surprised what a lot we know about you.'

'Jeez,' he said. 'Why do I matter so much?'

'I swear we'll tell you very soon.'

'So how did you find out where I came from?'

'A roundabout route. From your uncle is the short answer.'

'Who, old Bill, up in San Francisco? How on earth did you track him down?'

'He answered the advertisement in – let's see, July, I suppose it must have been.'

'Old bastard,' said Miles. 'He didn't tell me.'

'Why, when did you see him?'

'Heard from him about then. No, maybe it was the end of June.'

'I'm very sorry about him,' said Roz.

'What about him?'

'Oh, Miles, I'm sorry. Didn't you know? He – he's dead.'

'Dead! He can't be.'

'Yes, he is. He was killed in a car crash.'

'Oh God,' said Miles. 'No, I had no idea. But why didn't somebody tell me?'

'I don't know. Who could have told you? He didn't seem to have anybody in the world.'

'Oh, I don't know. Maybe somebody did, and the letter got holed up with all the others by old Marcia.'

'Who is Marcia?'

'A crazy old woman my grandmother lives with. She had a whole stack of letters addressed to me and my grandmother, all the newspaper cuttings people had sent from all over. Oh, God.

Poor old Bill. He was good to me. He'd just lent me some money.'

He looked upset; his brilliant blue eyes were distant, shadowed. Roz put out her hand and covered his. 'I'm really really sorry.'

He smiled at her slightly shakily. 'It's OK. We weren't that close. Just a bit of a shock, that's all.'

'How exactly was he related to you?'

'He was my dad's cousin.'

'And you and your dad and your mother lived in LA?'

'Yup. Santa Monica.'

'But they're both dead?'

'Yup.' He looked at her and grinned. 'It's all right, I don't really feel like the tragic orphan. It was so long ago. I can hardly remember my dad dying. My mom – well that was a long time too, but I remember it – her more clearly.'

'Tell me about her,' said Roz.

'Oh, she was really pretty. She had blonde hair, and very blue eyes, and she was kind of fun. She was always laughing. She gave me a real nice childhood. She loved the beach, we were there a lot. We lived very near the ocean.'

'And she died of – what?'

'Cancer.' He was silent, for a moment, the memory suddenly brought sharply into focus. 'She was awfully young, only forty-three.'

'And you were – what?'

'Thirteen. Just a little bitty boy.' He sighed, then smiled at her. 'It was very very sad. I remember just longing to die too, so I could be with her again. I missed her so terribly.'

'So after your mother died, you and your grandmother lived in Los Angeles?'

'For about three years. Then we went out to Malibu. This old guy, Hugo Dashwood, he thought I was getting in to bad company in Santa Monica. He bought the house in Malibu for us.'

'He sounds a very generous person,' said Roz thoughtfully. 'Who was he?'

'Oh, a friend of my parents.'

'He must have been quite rich.'

'Yeah, I guess so. He paid for me to go through college as well.'

'This man – this Hugo Dashwood. What was he like?'

'Oh, he was English,' said Miles. 'Very English.'

'Where did he live?'

'I don't know.'

'You don't know! He bought you houses and sent you to college and you don't know where he lived? When did you last see him?'

'Well, I did write to him quite recently. I'm not very proud of it, but I did.'

'How recently?'

'Oh, back in the summer.'

'Why?'

'Well – well, I needed some money really badly. I'd done something silly.'

'What? Not drugs?'

'No, no not drugs. But I'd – borrowed some money on the house in Malibu, and I had to give it back. I didn't know where to turn. I wrote to him. He wrote me a letter back and said he was coming to Nassau to see me in June. But he never did. I never heard from him again. That's when my uncle lent me the money.'

'Well,' she said briskly, 'I think what we should do now is go and ring Henry, and tell him you're with me. He must be terribly anxious about you.'

'And the driver.'

'Who? Oh, him. Yes, well, Henry can call him on the car phone. Come on, let's go back to the office and we'll call Henry from there. Then I imagine he'll want you to go over to Lincoln's Inn and see him.'

'I'd kind of like a wash or something before I go and see anyone else,' said Miles. 'Would that be possible?'

'Of course,' said Roz. 'My father's office up in the penthouse has a shower. Do you want to change? Do you have any clean clothes?'

'I have a clean shirt. Won't he mind?'

'Mind what?'

'Your father. Mind me using his shower.'

'Oh,' said Roz, and there was a wealth of sadness in her voice suddenly. 'No, I'm afraid he can't mind. He's dead.'

'I'm sorry,' said Miles. 'Recently?'

'Fairly recently. Back in May.'

'Were you close?'

'In a way, yes,' said Roz in tones that made it clear the subject was closed. 'Come on, let's go. I can't wait to hear Henry's voice.'

Henry's voice was irascible. 'Well of course I was worried. Why on earth didn't you ring me earlier, Roz? Parsons has been waiting at Heathrow for over an hour. I thought Miles had done a bunk.'

'Oh,' said Roz, 'you don't have to worry about him. He's not the bunking kind. He's upstairs having a shower. Shall I bring him over?'

'I think that would be best. But Roz –'

'Yes, Henry?'

'I think I should talk to him alone. Preliminarily. If you don't mind.'

'Really, Henry, what do you think I'm going to do? Abduct him? Offer him my body in return for his support and his share?'

'No, of course, not,' said Henry irritably. 'But I think in the interests of protocol . . . Legal procedure . . .'

'All right, Henry. Protocol has it. I'll wait outside the door. Tell your secretary to get me a glass, would you?'

'What for?'

'Why, so I can hold it to the wall and listen, of course. Why else?'

She sounded, Henry thought, unusually cheerful.

Michael Browning sat in his office on Madison Avenue and thought about Roz. He felt, deep within him, stirring through his outrage a sudden sense of mild remorse. She did, after all, have a point. It was a pretty blunt one, but it was a point. His visit to Phaedria had not, he felt bound to admit to himself, been entirely innocent. He had not gone with a view to seducing her, but he did find her immensely attractive, and he had very much wanted to see her. On an adultery scale of one to ten, his behaviour would certainly have rated a seven. With her cooperation, it would almost certainly have hit ten. Otherwise, he thought mournfully, downing his fourth strong coffee of the day, he would have told Roz. No, he wouldn't. If Phaedria had been a sixty-five-year-old harridan, with cross eyes and a wooden leg, Roz would have been jealous, because of who she was, the hold Phaedria had over her. As it was, with that hair and those eyes and that body – Michael wrenched his mind away from a contemplation of Phaedria's body with an effort and turned his attention back to Roz. Should he make a move? Hell, he'd made so many. It was always he who made them. She just waited, and took. And if he did ring her and apologize, then what? Back on the merry-go-round, the eternal ding-dong of sharing her with that company of hers and her obsession with it. And sharing it certainly wasn't. It was one piece for him, and then around five thousand for the company. He'd had the rough end of that particular deal for what felt like years.

He wondered why and how he had stood it for so long. He supposed because he loved her. Had loved her. Did he still love her? He thought about her for a minute, saw her face as it was in the rare moments when she was relaxed and happy, with her white skin, her snapping green eyes, the heavy jaw that caused her so much anguish. He thought of being with her, of her swift, sharp mind, her salty humour, her capacity for lateral thought.

She was greedy, was Roz, but her greed did not stop at money, and at power, it made her a desirable woman; her physical appetites were considerable, she loved good food, she had a rare appreciation of fine wine (and could drink him under the table if she chose to) and her sexual prowess was remarkable. Michael had not known many women – in fact only perhaps one other, and she had been a whore from the Bronx – who could come to orgasm as many times and with such evident triumphant pleasure as Roz could.

But the price he paid for her was high. Too high. There was probably very little future in once again trying to stick the relationship together again. The thought saddened him, grieved him even, Roz had been the focus of his sexual and indeed his emotional thinking for so long, but it was probably best now to leave it lying there, on the floor of the Rainbow Room, shattered, but at least dramatically, splendidly so, than go round patiently picking up all the endless tiny fragments and looking at them, endeavouring to see how they could be put back into a whole.

He thought of Phaedria suddenly; so different from Roz, and yet alike in some ways, with the same stubbornness, the same drive, the same courage. She was certainly not the gentle grieving young widow that the media had tried to turn her into. He admired her guts enormously. He admired a great deal about her. He wondered if they did indeed have any kind of future together. It was far too early to say. She might be, she undoubtedly was, sexily, divinely beautiful, she might be funny and interesting and original, but that did not necessarily make her into a woman he could love. What he did know was that he wanted to see her urgently, now, soon, more than anything in the world.

What was the time in California? Eight o'clock. She'd be having her breakfast. He picked up the phone, dialled the hotel, asked for her bungalow.

'Phaedria! Hi, it's me, Michael.'

He heard her voice, low, relaxed, almost amused.

'Hallo. Why aren't you working? It's Monday morning.'

'I know.'

'Well?'

'I can't work.'

'Why not?'

'I keep thinking of you.'

'Well, that's ridiculous. You're supposed to be a tycoon. You can't be distracted that easily.'

'I'm not distracted easily.'

'Oh.' He heard her thinking. Then: 'Michael, I do think we shouldn't pursue this relationship at all.' She gave it the heavy, English, almost schoolmistressy emphasis.

'We don't have a relationship. I'm just trying to think what one would be like.'

'Dangerous.'

'Maybe. Well, I just thought, you're leaving there, when? Friday?'

'Thursday.'

'I didn't really complete my business in LA. I might have to come back and have a couple more meetings very urgently. If I did, would you have dinner with me?'

'No.'

'Lunch?'

813

'No.'

'A glass of water?'

'No.'

'Oh, God.'

'Michael, listen, I –' she was silent.

'I'm listening.'

'I just don't think –'

'I don't want you to think.'

'But Roz –'

'Roz will never forgive either of us. We may as well make the most of it.'

'But I have to work with her.'

'You don't.'

'Michael, of course I do.'

'You could do something quite different.'

'Really? Like what?'

'You could sell up and marry me.'

'Oh, don't be so absurd.'

'That's not a very flattering response to a proposal.'

'You know you didn't mean it.'

'I might have done.'

There was a long silence.

'Phaedria, I'm coming over anyway. I've decided. I'll be in LA tonight. I shall be under your window at moonrise with a violin. You can turn me away if you like.'

She laughed. She couldn't help it. 'Oh, all right. I shouldn't say that, but all right.'

'Bye, honeybunch.'

'Goodbye, Michael.'

She put the phone down smiling, wondering where in the name of heaven, or hell for that matter, this was going to lead her. It rang again almost immediately. It was Father Kennedy.

'Ah,' he said, 'you are still here. I wondered if I should catch you.'

'Yes, Father, I don't leave until Thursday.'

'Ah, then, I'm glad I rang. You were asking me for a photograph of Mr Dashwood?'

Phaedria's heart began to thump rather painfully.

'Yes. Yes, I was.'

'Well I remembered. Of course I have one. It was taken at

814

Miles' graduation. I took it myself. I found it last night, turning out my desk. Now would you like to see it? It's a very nice picture of Miles as well.'

'Yes, Father, I would,' she said slowly. 'I would really like to see it very much. Perhaps I could come down and get it this morning, after I've been to the hospital for Julia.'

Miles was rather quiet going across London in the car. Roz looked at him.

'Are you OK?'

'Sure. Just a little – well, nervous I guess. About what I'm going to hear.'

'I promise you,' said Roz, putting her hand on his arm, 'there is absolutely nothing to be nervous or worried about. The news is good. Interesting but good.'

Henry was waiting for them in the doorway of his offices in Lincoln's Inn, looking properly and impressively serious when the car drew up.

'Roz! Good morning.'

'Good morning, Henry. May I introduce Mr Wilburn?'

'How do you do?' said Henry, taking Miles' outstretched hand.

'Hi,' said Miles.

'Come along in,' said Henry, leading the way.

Miles came out of Henry's office a while later looking a little shaken.

'Henry!' said Roz, 'the poor man's as white as a sheet. What on earth have you been doing to him?'

'He hasn't been doing anything to me,' said Miles, mustering a smile. 'Just breaking the news.'

'And?'

'And I think I need a while to take it in. Suddenly I do feel rather tired.'

'Look,' said Roz. 'Let's go back to Dover Street. There's a bed up in the penthouse, you can have a nap there if you want to. Meanwhile I'll get my secretary to book you into a hotel. Then you can make any calls or whatever you want to do.'

'OK,' said Miles. 'Thanks.'

'Er, Roz, could I have a word?' said Henry. 'About the contracts.'

His rather long, solemn face distorted into a strange grimace; Roz suddenly realized he was trying to wink. With a great effort she nodded solemnly.

'Of course. Excuse us, will you Miles?' She followed Henry into his office. 'Now then, Henry, what do you think?'

'Well, he does seem to be an extremely nice young man, and I really have no doubt at all that he is indeed Miles Wilburn,' said Henry. 'He showed me his birth certificate and his passport, and a letter from his college professor at Berkeley. His story about this Dashwood character is so extraordinary and so consistent with everything that Bill Wilburn said, it just has to be true, whatever it means. We now know so much about Miles, through the various stray ends everyone has picked up, your detective, and C. J.'

'Oh yes,' said Roz with a slightly sour expression. 'C. J.'s detective work was very impressive. I'm surprised he shared it with you, when he seemed to be acting on Phaedria's behalf.'

'Roz, it's in everybody's interest to get this thing sorted out,' said Henry rather severely, stifling the memory of his early favouritism of Phaedria's cause. 'C. J. felt we should pool our knowledge and I think he was right. Especially with Lady Morell being away and so on.'

'Quite,' said Roz tersely. 'Well anyway, Henry, what happened?'

'Well, I told him simply that he had been left two per cent of your father's company. And that on account of the extraordinary structure of the will, that it was a controlling two per cent. I thought that was quite enough for now. Well of course there isn't any more to be said anyway. And he hasn't been left any money as such. Oh, and I asked him again if he had any idea who your father was, if he was quite sure he had never met him, why he thought he could possibly have been left this – this legacy.'

'And?'

'And of course he hadn't.'

'Well,' said Roz. 'Perhaps in the fullness of time we shall all find out.'

'I certainly think he's feeling a little shell-shocked.'

'I expect he is, poor chap. Don't worry, I'll look after him.'

Going back in the car, Miles said, 'I feel like that guy in the fairy story. You know, the one who was a frog and then the princess kissed him and he turned into a prince. He must have felt pretty confused as well.'

'Goodness,' said Roz. 'I hope Henry didn't kiss you.'

Miles laughed. 'No. But you know what I mean.'

'I think I do. It's an extraordinary business, isn't it?'

'Sure is. I have to tell you my initial reaction is to just give it back.'

'Is it now?'

'Yeah. I don't want to get mixed up in some billion-pound company. It isn't me.'

'Well, don't think about giving it away, for a start,' said Roz briskly. 'At least sell it.'

'I suppose so,' said Miles doubtfully. 'Yeah, I hadn't thought of that.'

'And then,' said Roz carefully, 'who would you sell it to?'

'I don't know. Who would you suggest?'

'Well,' said Roz, carefully lighthearted. 'Me of course.'

He turned to look at her, not lighthearted at all, very very serious. 'Would you want it?'

'Of course.'

'Why?'

'Well because – oh, dear, Henry obviously hadn't explained things properly to you at all. That would immediately give me the controlling interest in the company.'

'Yes, he did explain that. Sort of. But why would you want that?'

'If you can't see that,' said Roz, equally serious, 'there's no point my trying to explain it. But anyway, much as I want it, I wouldn't dream of letting you hand it over just like that. Whatever you may hear about me in this company, and I do assure you, you will hear a great deal, not all of it, indeed very little of it, good, I do actually have a few scruples. I wouldn't dream of letting you hand it over just like that. I would like you to sell it to me because I had persuaded you to for good sound commercial reasons, but I have no desire whatsoever to just walk away with it and leave you wondering why you let it go. OK?'

'OK,' said Miles. He looked at her consideringly. 'You're kind of an interesting person.'

'Thank you.'

'Tell me about the other one.'

'Which other one?'

'The one who has the other forty-nine per cent.'

'Oh,' said Roz. 'Phaedria. The grieving widow.'

'Sounds like you don't have too much time for her.'

'No,' said Roz. 'No, I don't. Maybe you should get someone else to tell you about her.'

'So she's where?'

'She's in California. Taking an unconscionably long time to recover from having a baby.'

'Why did she have it there?'

'Because she's a fool,' said Roz.

'Oh, I don't know,' said Miles easily. 'I would think it a pretty nice place to have a baby. I plan to bring my children up there.'

'Do you now? Do you plan to have a lot of children?' asked Roz, eager to draw the conversation away from Phaedria Morell.

'Yup. Like all only children, I yearn for brothers and sisters. And like all only children, I yearn for a large family of my own.'

'I see. Is this large family imminent?'

'Oh, I don't think so,' said Miles. 'Candy – my girlfriend – is only eighteen. Her dad is pretty much against us getting married. He's a rich guy,' he added. 'He has a big business.'

'Really. What's his name?'

'Mason McCall.'

'Oh, yes,' said Roz. 'Sweeties.'

Miles looked at her with new respect. 'You guys really all have got it together, haven't you?'

'We have to,' said Roz.

When they got back to Dover Street, a pale blue Rolls was outside.

'Goodness,' said Roz. 'News travels fast. That's my grandmother's car. She must have heard you've been found, and come to meet you.'

She was right. Letitia was standing at Roz's desk, dressed in a cream silk suit, leafing happily through Roz's in-tray.

'Granny Letitia! How lovely to see you!' said Roz, kissing her fondly. 'How are you?'

'Perfectly well, darling, thank you. I haven't seen as much of you as I would like, or that great-granddaughter of mine.' She looked at Roz critically. 'You look very thin. And tired. You've been overworking.'

Only Roz could have fully appreciated the wealth of meaning and double meaning in Letitia's voice; she smiled at her brilliantly. 'Not really. You look wonderful. Whose suit?'

'Do you like it? Thank you, darling. Bruce Oldfield. Such a charming young man. Speaking of charming young men,' she said, turning the full force of her violet eyes, her dazzling smile on Miles, 'you must be Miles.'

'I am,' he said, looking at her bemusedly, holding out his hand. 'And it certainly is a pleasure to meet you.'

'Thank you. I am Letitia Morell. Founding grandmother of this company. So they finally found you. My goodness, there is so much we want to know, and you must be worn out, poor chap. And hungry, I should think. Roz, why don't we take him to lunch you and I? We could go to Langan's.'

Lunch was a great success. Letitia grilled Miles through the first course, about his childhood, his growing up in California, and in particular his days on the beach ('it sounds wonderful'), and then he grilled her through the second about her days as a debutante, life in London between the wars, and the Prince of Wales with whom she claimed an ever closer acquaintance with every year that passed. Eventually they parted – Letitia reluctantly to First Street, Roz to the office, and Miles to his much-postponed sleep.

Miles let himself into the penthouse again, and walked into the little bedroom. He felt utterly and unaccustomedly exhausted. He supposed it was a combination of the long night flight, the champagne at lunch and the considerable trauma of the morning.

This really was all something else. It was like some kind of a bad B movie. Billy hadn't been so far off when he had said something about him being Lord Fauntleroy. What a mob to get mixed up with. It was dynamite. There was that nice sexy bitch downstairs, nothing wrong with her, Miles thought easily, that a good screw and a bit of TLC wouldn't sort out; the funny old lawyer, straight out of Dickens, and the marvellous old lady. She was something else. He would like to see a great deal more of her. And then there was the other one, the missing one, who Roz was clearly dying to feed ground glass to, three times a day before meals. What could she be like? The old lady was obviously very fond of her.

She was young, twenty-seven they'd said; either the old boy must have still been quite a goer, or she'd married him purely for his money. Probably the latter. That was obviously what Roz thought.

And he held the balance of power between them. The thought made Miles feel quite sick. No wonder they'd wanted to find him. What on earth was he going to do? He had been speaking the truth when he had told Roz he just wanted to give it all away again. The last thing on earth he wanted was to get mixed up in some power struggle. He didn't want to hold any, and he didn't want to assist anyone else to hold any. It held about as much charm for him as joining a monastery. But he could see even giving it away wouldn't be that simple. Whoever he gave it to, there would be trouble. Besides, Roz had a point. Why give it?

No, the best thing would be to sell it, and then go home to Candy, and persuade Old Man Mason to let them get married. Roz would buy his share, that was for sure. He liked her, he thought she was really nice under that hard front of hers, and it would obviously help her. Why go into it all any more?

God, Julian Morell, whoever he was, must have been a funny old buzzard. Why do this to all these people? And why involve him? He supposed really he ought to wait until Lady Phaedria or whatever her name was came home, and talk to her as well. It was only fair.

He looked around. The room was bare, except for a bed, a coat stand, a cupboard, and a small bedside table.

There were a few photographs on the wall: an aerial view of a big house in the country, and several pictures of horses. No people. He sat down on the bed, took off his jacket, slung it on the floor, looked round again.

His eyes fell on the bedside table. It had a couple of drawers in it. He tugged the top one tentatively. It was empty. But the second one had a small silver frame in it. He took the frame out, turning it over and looking at the picture in it; and for a moment the face in front of him meant nothing at all to him. Then his brain connected with what he saw; the picture first blurred, then clarified with extraordinary vividness. He stood up, and then slowly, his eyes fixed on it, his mind a whirring, confused mess, he walked out of the penthouse and took the elevator down to Roz's office. She was on the phone and reading letters at the same time; she looked up at him, smiled, waved to him to sit down in the chair in front of her desk. Miles sat there looking alternately at her and the photograph in his hand.

When she had finished talking she put down the phone and said, 'What is it? Couldn't you sleep?'

'I haven't tried,' said Miles. 'Not yet. Look, Roz, I don't know quite what's going on around here, but why do you all keep saying you don't know Hugo Dashwood when there's a picture of him up in your dad's office?'

Chapter Twenty-five

Los Angeles, London, New York, 1985

Father Kennedy was a little worried about Lady Morell. She seemed such a fragile little thing, and seeing the photograph of Hugo Dashwood with Miles had obviously given her a big shock. She had tried very hard not to show him what a shock it was, had managed to smile and say what a nice picture, and it was wonderful to know what they both looked like at last, but she had turned very pale and he had insisted she sat down and had a drink of tea before she left again.

She had told him she had to get back to the hotel, that she had a friend coming to see her; that was a good thing, Father Kennedy thought, she had obviously had far too much time on her own at the moment and whatever it was about the photograph that had upset her so much, then she could talk to this friend about it.

'Would you like to take the picture?' he had said to her, and she had said yes, please, she would get a copy made of it and then send him the original back if that would be all right.

And holding her baby rather closely to her, she had walked to her car and then driven off without another backward glance.

Well, she clearly didn't want to talk about it. In Father Kennedy's experience, people always talked in their own good time. He was not about to press her. He only hoped he had not gone too far in showing her the picture.

What she clearly had no need to know at all was the true relationship between Dashwood and the boy. That had been something entirely between Lee, himself and the Almighty, entrusted to him in his capacity as priest, and nothing on this earth, or indeed anything that might be waiting for him in the next, would drag it from him. And besides, and he had often thought this down the years, who was to say that Lee had been right in her absolute certainty that Hugo Dashwood had fathered Miles? The boy had certainly looked sufficiently like Dean, and Father Kennedy had learnt quite early in his priesthood that guilty women were particularly skilful at deceiving themselves, at distorting facts, to their own advantage or otherwise, depending on their characters. So the doctors had all told Dean he was sterile; well since when had doctors not been known to make a mistake? Small miracles of this kind took place all the time. Look at all the babies that were conceived the moment their parents adopted someone else's child. No, the parentage of Miles Wilburn was not something Father Kennedy was prepared to discuss with anybody, anybody at all.

He put it determinedly out of his head and fell to wondering how he was going to feed up to thirty hungry people that night with one small ham. Jesus had managed it, of course, or its equivalent, but then he had had powers denied to Father Kennedy.

Michael Browning arrived at Phaedria's bungalow at six o'clock that evening. It was dark, and there was no light inside; he thought perhaps she might still be out at the hospital and went into Reception to ask.

No, they said, Lady Morell was there, she had been there all afternoon, perhaps she was asleep? Should they ring through? No, Michael said, he would go himself and knock on the door; she was expecting him. Probably they were right and she was asleep.

He went back and knocked; Phaedria's voice answered. She sounded strained, odd. 'Who is it?'

'It's the serenading team,' he said. 'Only we left the violins at home. Can we come in?'

The door opened; Phaedria stood before him, ashen. Her eyes were swollen, and there were deep shadows under them. She was shaking. 'Oh, Michael,' she said. 'I'm glad you're here.'

'Phaedria, honeybunch, what on earth is it? It's not – not.'

'No,' she said, and there was just an echo of a smile on her stricken face, 'no, Julia's fine.'

'Then what is it?'

She walked through to the sitting room, picked up a photograph from the table. 'Look.'

He looked. 'It's Julian. Who's that with him?'

'Oh, that's Miles.'

'Oh. So he did know him. Nice-looking boy.'

'Yes. But that's not the point. This isn't Julian. Well it is, but it isn't.'

'Phaedria, you're not making any sense.'

'None of it makes any sense,' she said, and there was a sob in her voice. 'Well, no, that's not true. It's beginning to. This is Hugo Dashwood, Michael, Julian was Hugo Dashwood. He was obviously leading a completely double life. That none of us knew about.'

'I don't care if Miss North is in a meeting with the President, or Lord God Almighty. Get her on the phone, for Christ's sake.' Roz, her hand shaking, gripping a large whisky, was on the phone to New York.

Miles, a little disconcerted by the monumental hornet's nest he had disturbed, sat watching her, silent, not knowing what to do.

'Ah, Camilla, yes, I do realize you were in a very important meeting and I am very sorry, I really am, but I simply have to talk to C. J. Do you know where he is? No, it's nothing to do with Miranda, but it is desperately serious. I just have to talk to him. OK, fine. Thank you. He'll tell you about it himself, I expect. Goodbye, Camilla.'

She put the phone down, dialled another number, taking gulps of the whisky. 'C. J.? Oh, thank God I found you. I just had to talk to someone in the family. No, Miranda is perfectly all right. Yes, I know this is Camilla's private number, she gave it to me herself. What? Michael's out of town, Christ knows where. C. J., I don't know quite where to begin on all this, but please please just listen and tell me what I ought to do. We know who Hugo Dashwood is. What? Miles has solved it for us. Miles. M-I-L-E-S. Yes, he's here. He turned up this morning. God, it seems years ago now. Yes, of course it was a shock. I'm sorry, of course I was going to tell you. Well he's very nice. Oh, I can't go into all that now. That's not why I'm ringing you. Well, not exactly. C. J., Hugo Dashwood was my father. What? Yes, of course Julian Morell was my father. They were one and the same person. He was leading some kind of a double life. Oh, C. J., I feel so terrible, and I don't know where to turn or what to do. I can't, simply can't tell Letitia, or Mummy, not yet. It would be too shocking for both of them. It's all so horrible. No, I haven't told Henry Winterbourne. Do you think I should? All right. What about Phaedria? Oh, C. J. Could you please come home?'

Phaedria had booked herself on to a flight a day earlier, with Julia, having insisted Michael return to New York.

'We have enough problems and traumas on our hands already,' she said, smiling at him rather wanly over her packing, 'without Roz deciding we are having the love affair of the century.'

'Don't you think maybe we should at least try it out?' he said. He was sitting watching her, holding the baby on his knee with one hand, and the telephone in the other, trying without success to get through to his secretary in New York. 'Christ, this girl has to have the opposite of a raise. What would that be, do you think?'

'A fall? I don't know. Try what out anyway?'

'Having the love affair of the century. Or at least the week.'

'No, I don't. Do you think you could try getting Richard

Brookes for me on that line? Oh, no, it's hopeless – it's still only six o'clock there. God, it will be nice to be back in the same day as everybody else.'

'Phaedria, do you feel nothing for me at all?' said Michael, his dark brown eyes looking at her gloomily over the baby's head.

'You know what I feel for you,' she said, suddenly serious. 'And I don't know how I would ever have got through last night without you. But I just can't let myself think about it, and neither should you. Besides I'm not at all convinced you don't still love Roz. There are some pretty strong emotions running between you and her, if you ask me.'

'Well,' he said with a sigh, 'you may be right. I don't think so, but you may be. I tell you one thing, if she's set a private detective on me, we don't stand much of a chance. I mean, who is going to believe I spent an entire night in your bedroom simply holding your hand? It's against nature. I can hardly believe it myself. Here, I think your daughter is looking for something that I can't provide.'

Phaedria looked at the small head rooting hopefully against Michael's chest and laughed, unbuttoning her shirt, taking the baby; they both looked at her tenderly as she started sucking greedily, her little fists clenching and unclenching with pleasure.

'And there's another thing,' he said gloomily. 'You will keep flashing those amazing tits at me, and then letting her have all the fun. It just isn't fair.'

'I'm sorry,' she said, 'and thank you for everything. Maybe – well, let's not talk about it.'

'All right, we won't. Not yet. Anyway, you do look much better.'

'I feel better,' she said, almost surprised. 'Now the worst of the shock is over. Or maybe it's just numbness. Somehow a lot of the guilt has gone.'

'It has?'

'Yes. Discovering that Julian was – well, more devious than I'd ever imagined.'

'What did I tell you?' he said, a look of mild triumph on his face. 'He didn't deserve you. He didn't deserve any of you. Sorry,' he added hastily at a warning flash in her eyes.

'Maybe not. But maybe we all contributed. That's what we don't know. I can only think this life here – there, God knows where else it went on – was some kind of desperate escape.'

'My darling, you're too loyal by half. He was a lunatic. He had it made from birth. There was nothing to escape from.'

'Michael, you don't know that. You just don't know. Please don't make these judgements.'

'OK, OK,' he said and there was genuine anger now in his face. 'I'll shut up. I know when I'm beaten. But if and when we ever know the truth behind it all, and I'm right, you won't be able to hear yourself think for me yelling out "I told you so".'

She smiled at him, put out her hand. 'All right. And then I'll listen. Meanwhile, what I do feel, and what I suppose is making me feel better, is that this has been going on so long, it can't possibly have been all my fault. Or even all Roz's.'

'No.'

'I'll tell you the other thing that really made me feel less awful,' she said suddenly.

'Me?'

'You, yes, and in particular you asking me if something had happened to Julia. I suddenly realized nothing mattered terribly compared to her.'

'Well, I'm glad I contributed something.'

'You contributed a lot.' She looked at him and sighed, suddenly very weary, very sad. 'Well, I certainly shan't forget yesterday. First the photo of Hugo, from Father Kennedy, then Miles turning up in London.'

'I wonder how Roz is,' Michael said suddenly. 'This can't have been exactly good for her either. Did you speak to her?'

'What do you think?'

'I think you didn't.'

'You're right.'

'She will be beside herself,' he said, 'she adored her father.'

'I know she did. Maybe I should call her.'

'Well, it would be a pretty big olive branch. Just about the whole tree. But it would be nice.'

'I'll call her in an hour or so. She's probably asleep.'

Roz wasn't asleep. She felt as if she would never sleep again. She was possessed of a feverish, almost hysterical restlessness;

every time she had felt her eyes closing she had seen Miles looking at her over her father's photograph and her mind snapped into frenzied activity again.

She wasn't quite sure what she felt: pain, confusion, disbelief, outrage. She felt as if everything that her life had been based on had been shot at, and was steadily and relentlessly crumbling away underneath her. She had made Miles go over his story about Hugo Dashwood and the part he had played in his life a dozen times; there were still no clues as to why her father should have done such a thing, and how he could have kept it from them over all these years. His mother, his child, his wives, his mistresses – all of them had known him so little, that he could perpetrate this deceit upon them; it was monstrous, obscene.

She shrank from having to tell Letitia: maybe she wouldn't have to. Perhaps they could keep it from her. No, that was impossible. She would have to be told that her son had been a devious, unscrupulous monster, and it was going to fall to her, Roz, to tell her. There was no one else in the family who could take that responsibility, was close enough to her, cared for her enough. Except – Roz suddenly thought of Susan. Susan and Letitia had always been very close. And Susan was so wise and calm. She might be able to handle it. But then the thought of having to tell even Susan about her father and his other life hurt her so much she shut that escape route off as well. Her mother would also have to be told. Eliza would be less deeply hurt, but it would still be damaging, humiliating. Thank God they had managed to keep the whole thing more or less out of the press. What a field day they would have with this. And how horribly that would add to the hurt of everyone who had loved and trusted Julian. God, thought Roz, sitting up in bed for what seemed like the thousandth time that night, why, how could he have done it? And how many other people had known him as Hugo Dashwood, surely it wasn't just Miles and his family, there must have been others, people everywhere, who had known her father, and yet had no idea at all who he really was, who his real family were, his true home, his proper self. How extraordinary that Phaedria should have made the discovery on the same day, almost at the same time. Henry had phoned her to tell her about Miles' arrival in England and said she had been almost hysterical and slammed the phone down. It was only when he had phoned her the second time, to tell her about Hugo's identity, that she told him she had known, that had been the reason for her earlier grief. For the briefest moment Roz felt a flicker of sympathy for Phaedria; she suppressed it fiercely. Of them all she deserved the least sympathy over this. She had only known Julian Morell for less than three years; she did not have a long, happy, private piece of history with him, that she was now being forced to surrender, to have to realize there had been another life, possibly, probably, even other loves, that she had no place in, no part of.

'What was he like?' she kept saying endlessly to Miles. 'What sort of person was he, did you like him, what did he do, how did he talk, what did he say to you?'

And Miles, anxious not to make her pain worse, to reassure her, began to rewrite history too; Hugo Dashwood had been very kind, very generous to them all: to his dad, he had helped his dad with his business a lot, his mother always said, and he had been very good to his mother, he had visited her when she was dying, and of course to him and his grandmother. His grandmother had really really liked him, depended on him, looked to him for everything, and he had been wonderfully good to her; she had talked to him much more in the last few years than he, Miles, had. Roz should talk to her.

And had he never even hinted of a family in England? Well yes, he had, but it had not been this family, of course; he had told them (very little, very very little) about a wife called Alice, and two little boys, Miles thought, or maybe it was three. (And oh, God, thought Roz, was that family somewhere too, was that a real family or a second fantasy, were they living somewhere, wondering what had become of their father, waiting for him to come home? The nightmare grew and grew as she thought about it, lived through it.)

'Honestly,' Miles said to Roz, looking at her concernedly, his dark blue eyes full of sympathy, 'I never did get to know him. He was my dad's friend, really. My dad's and my mom's. More my dad's. Well, that's what my mom said. She never seemed specially to like him. He made her a little nervous. Jumpy, you know? As far as I can remember, anyway. You have to remember I was only thirteen when my mom died. It's a long time ago.'

'Of course,' said Roz. 'Oh, God, it's all so totally baffling. Why did he ever have to do such a thing? What did he gain? I just don't understand it.'

Miles looked at her. 'Me neither,' he said and then, anxious, eager to help, 'would you like me to call my grandmother? Only I warn you,' he added, 'she doesn't make a lot of sense these days. I don't know what good it would do.'

'No,' said Roz, 'no, I don't either. It would probably only upset her. I'll wait till C. J.'s here. He may have some idea what to do.'

She didn't really have a great deal of faith in C. J. But he was family and he was better than nothing. She longed passionately for Michael. He would know what to do, how to handle it. Where was the bastard, and why did it have to be now, of all times, she had lost him?

And then suddenly, in the middle of her raging, she was assaulted by a thought so hideous, so malevolent that she experienced it as physical pain, a sick, awful pain, violent and sudden, like the crick of a neck, a crack of an elbow on a hard surface. She crushed it, raced away from it, wrenched her mind towards other things, other people; but it lay, coiled up in her mind like some obscene monster, and occasionally, when she was least prepared for it, it would shift, stir, and threaten her again and again.

C. J. looked down at the grey depression beneath him that was Heathrow in November and wondered why on earth he had agreed to come back. Life had been just beginning to improve, to brighten, to simplify even; he was happy with Camilla, she made him feel appreciated, significant, calm, and those were balm to his almost mortally wounded soul. They had much in common; they were suited intellectually, emotionally and, much to C. J.'s surprise and pleasure, sexually. They had the same background, had been reared to the same upper-class American standards, attended identical schools, talked the same language in the same accent, understood the same jokes, shared the same values. They and their families, they discovered, had generations-back mutual friends; had they been the same age they would have attended the same parties, gone to the same places on vacation;

probably met, certainly have been attracted to one another, possibly even married.

They had also both been through similar personal crises: emotional involvement with equally unsatisfactory partners (hardly surprising really, as C. J. remarked one night as they ate supper after a concert, when you considered those people had been father and daughter). They found their situation amusing, charming even, a wry twist to each of their tales, and that of the Morell family; the pain they had both suffered swiftly eased and even cured by this new pleasure. Well, the pleasure was, for the time being, ended. C. J. sat waiting obediently for the captain to tell them they could leave the plane, and felt resentful.

Camilla had been extremely patient and understanding about the whole thing, she dispatched him (after some particularly earnest sex: she was practising a series of new positions, suggested by her sex therapist and based on some Lesbian erotica she had been given to read) and assured him that her analyst had managed to cure her almost completely of possessiveness, through showing her her own value, and by teaching her to trust her lovers and the value they put on her (C. J. was a little worried by the plural here). He also felt rather sobered by the reflection that he seemed to be, for the time being, the only male in the Morell family at the moment.

He only had hand luggage; he went straight through customs and out into the arrivals area: to his surprise Roz was waiting for him.

'Roz! I didn't think you'd be here.'

He hadn't expected her to look quite so bad; she was ashen, hollow-eyed, she had no make-up on, she had scarcely brushed her hair. He had never seen her looking anything other than svelte, even in their most intimate moments; it was a shock.

'Hallo, C. J.,' she said, and her voice was listless, subdued. 'Thank you for coming home. I've got the car outside. I came because I need to talk to you so badly, and I just couldn't wait any longer.'

'OK, let's go.'

C. J. looked at her, saw her lips quiver slightly and felt remorseful; he put out his hand and touched her arm briefly.

'I'm very very sorry about it all, Roz,' he said. 'I don't know what to say.'

'Yes, well, just for now listen,' said Roz, and he could hear her fight back the tears, 'I simply don't know what to do. The first thing is that someone has to tell Letitia, and quickly. Who should it be? Me? You?'

'I'll talk to her if you like,' said C. J., shrinking from the task. 'I'd rather not but I will.'

'Well, maybe if you could. It would be a great help.'

'All right,' he said, 'I'll go and see her. But you'll have to tell me some more first. Otherwise I shan't be a very satisfactory news bearer.'

'Yes, of course. Well, I don't know that much, of course. It appears that this man, Hugo Dashwood, that is, my father, was a good friend to Miles' parents. He did business with Miles' father, visited his mother when she was dying and then when Miles was older, sent him to college.'

'You mean paid for him to go?'

'Yes.'

'How extraordinary.'

'The whole thing is extraordinary. I simply cannot imagine why my father should have done such a thing. I mean maintained this double life. I mean, what would have been the point? It wasn't as if he desperately needed to do it, he always did exactly as he liked anyway. He didn't have a clinging little suburban wife somewhere, or business problems that he needed to get away from. I just don't understand it.'

'What did Miles say he was like?'

'Reading between the lines, he didn't like him much. He said his mother didn't either. But he does keep saying how kind and generous he was. He says his mother told him that my father and his father did business together. But Miles' father was obviously quite poor. He was a salesman. What business could my father have had with him?'

'Well, maybe in his other life he was a much more modest person.'

'Maybe. But Miles says he always seemed to be rather rich. And he did put Miles through college.'

'Still doesn't have to have been a millionaire.'

'I suppose not.'

'Did he know anything about this other life?'

'Well, my father obviously fed him a load of claptrap. Told him he had a wife called Alice and some little boys. Alice! It's so peculiar. I just feel as if I've fallen down the rabbit hole myself.'

'I'm sure you do. Poor Roz. What's Miles like?'

'Charming,' said Roz briefly. 'You just cannot help liking him. Terribly good-looking, very blond and Californian, and very very kind of relaxed.'

'And how has he reacted to it all?'

'Well, of course the news about Hugo Dashwood and my father doesn't mean all that much to him. I mean he hardly knew the man, and it certainly wasn't an unpleasant shock for him, just something rather intriguing. I do feel sorry for him though, he was leading a perfectly happy life bumming round the Bahamas with a nice little girlfriend called Honey or Sweetie or something, and he's been catapulted into this dungheap.'

'I thought he was in Miami.'

'Yes, well he was, latterly. Oh, it's a long story. We had lunch with him yesterday, Granny Letitia and I, and he gave us a potted autobiography. Only inevitably it led to Letitia's autobiography, as more and more champagne went down.'

'Prince of Wales?'

'Prince of Wales,' said Roz, and smiled briefly. 'It's nice to see you, C. J. How – how is Camilla?'

'Very well,' said C. J., returning the smile, knowing what the question must have cost her. 'She sent you her – her best,' he reported faithfully, aware how oddly American the message sounded but unable for obvious reasons to translate it to the English and 'love'.

'How kind,' said Roz. 'Well, C. J., I have to admit it was a shock hearing about you two, but I'm delighted if it makes you happy.' Her tone managed to imply this was very unlikely.

'Thank you,' said C. J. He wished Roz would drive a little more slowly; she was doing seventy-five on the Hammersmith flyover and it made him very nervous. He knew from past experience it was no use saying anything to try and deter her; she would simply put her foot down harder. 'Er – how's Michael?'

'I'm afraid I don't know,' said Roz in a voice that mixed

832

suppressed rage and icy disdain. 'Well, I imagine. He's – away at present.'

'I see. So he doesn't know anything about all this?'

'Absolutely nothing.'

C. J. had the sense not to pursue the subject.

'You look very tired,' he said carefully. 'Would you like me to drive?'

'No, I told you, I like driving, I find it therapeutic. I am tired, I hardly slept last night. I don't know quite why,' she added, 'but I'm taking you to Cheyne Walk. I thought you could have a shower if you want to, and there are still some of your clothes there, and we can talk some more.'

'Sure.' He looked at his watch; it was nearly six, English time; it had been an endless day.

'Where's Miles?'

'Exploring London. He thinks it's just wonderful. And buying some clothes. He's hardly got anything with him. But he'll be back soon. I asked him to have supper with us.'

He liked Miles. It was impossible not to. He was so straight-forwardly engaging, so charmingly mannered, so easy to talk to; entirely unfazed by the situation he had walked into, so disinterested in his potential wealth and power, so concerned to be helpful and constructive in the situation. He sat eating supper in Roz's kitchen, listening quietly as she talked to C. J., occasionally putting in a suggestion, offering a view, proffering his help; C. J. thought it was a very long time since he had met someone he liked so wholeheartedly.

'I'll go and see Letitia this evening if you like,' C. J. said, pushing a half-eaten plate of food away from him. 'It has to be got over, after all.'

'Oh, I wouldn't do that,' said Miles. 'You should never give people bad news at night. Sorry,' he added, 'nothing to do with me. But that's what I would think.'

'You're right,' said C. J. 'I'll go first thing in the morning.'

'OK,' said Roz. 'And I'll fly up to Mummy then as well.'

'What can I do?' asked Miles. 'I could go and meet whatsername, if you like. She's flying in in the morning isn't she? I could tell her what's happening. Would that be helpful?'

'Oh, there's no need for that,' said Roz quickly. For a few

hours she had forgotten that particular aspect of the situation, of the fight between her and Phaedria for Miles' support. She was going to have to watch Phaedria very carefully.

'OK,' said Miles. 'Whatever you say. But I have to get to know her. Seemed a good way. And she could use the help maybe.'

'Well, Pete Praeger, my father's – her – driver will be meeting her,' said Roz. 'And she'll have the child with her. She'll be very distracted. You can meet her later.'

C. J. looked at her sharply. So she was politicking already. He was surprised she was leaving Miles in London alone with Phaedria at all. Roz wasn't.

She looked at Miles thoughtfully. 'Why don't you come to Scotland with me?' she said. 'My mother would adore you, and it would take her mind off the other trauma.'

'Roz,' said C. J., 'I don't know that is a terribly good idea. Eliza might be very upset by the news about your father.'

'C. J.,' said Roz firmly. 'I think I know my mother and what would and would not be best for her rather more intimately than you do. Besides, Miles has nothing to do in London – yet,' she added, giving the word a mildly threatening ring, 'and it's so boring for him. Would you like to come, Miles?'

Miles was looking at Roz with an interesting expression on his face: it was half amused, half thoughtful, and there was another element altogether, which C. J. could not quite define; he filed it away for future examination. It was only when he was safely back in his own flat in Sloane Street later that night and thinking about the evening and its conversations that he was able to analyse it. It had been, without doubt, sexual interest.

'Sure,' said Miles. 'Sounds fun. Didn't you say she lived in a castle? That'd be great.'

'Oh well, have it your own way,' said C. J. 'I'll take care of Phaedria, then.'

'C. J.,' said Roz. 'I really cannot see why Phaedria will need taking care of. She has been doing nothing for almost two months other than lying around in that hotel, soaking up the sun; she hasn't even been looking after the child. It's been in hospital. I'm sure she can get herself installed in her own home, with the assistance of God knows how many staff, without you putting your oar in.'

'All right, Roz, all right,' said C. J. 'I take your point. I happen not to agree with you, that's all. I shall go and see her and make sure she's all right.'

'Oh, have it your own way,' said Roz. 'I'd forgotten how you had made her your personal good cause. No doubt she'll be glad to see you. She'll be trawling sympathy all over London, I expect.'

'Roz, I do think you might be just a little more sensitive about her,' said C. J. 'She has also had a fearful shock. And she's been out there quite alone, she hasn't had anyone to talk to about it at all.'

'Oh, I doubt that,' said Roz, and there was a ferocious expression on her face. 'I daresay she's found some broad shoulder to cry on. Probably a masculine one. Anyway, C. J., you do what you think best. It's nothing to do with me, after all.'

Miles had been listening to this exchange with a look of almost incredulous interest; Roz suddenly became aware of it and changed the subject.

'We'll probably come back from Scotland on Thursday,' she said. 'So could you let everyone in the office know I'll be away till then? I suppose once this particular phase is over we need to talk to Richard Brookes about Miles.'

'Who's Richard Brookes?' asked Miles.

'The company lawyer. Next to the family, he is the person who will most need to talk to you. Explain your position there. Sort out what will happen short and long term.'

Miles looked alarmed. 'Long term there's no happening,' he said. 'I just want to go home.'

'I know,' said Roz, 'but one way or another, you have to offload your share on to someone. You can't just cut and run.' She smiled at him. 'You're one of us now, for better or worse, and you have to face up to it.'

'Are you really not interested in becoming part of the company?' asked C. J.

Miles looked at him as if he had just suggested night was day, or black white.

'I certainly am not,' he said. 'I don't want to sound rude or ungrateful, but I just can't imagine anything more awful than having to run even a smidgen of a company. You can just have it with my blessing.'

'Very wise,' said C. J. 'I would feel exactly the same.'

'No, but as I explained to Miles yesterday,' said Roz, 'he certainly shouldn't just give his share away. If that's what he finally decides to do. I think you should go into it a little more thoroughly, Miles. But whatever you do decide, you should certainly sell it. Don't you think so, C. J.?'

'Absolutely,' said C. J. 'And then you can sail away on your surf board to your very own tropical island or whatever with – what's her name?'

'Candy,' said Miles. 'Candy McCall. Yeah, a tropical island might be nice. Shall I show you a picture of her?'

'Oh, do,' said C. J. politely. He looked after Miles as he went in search of his jacket, and the collection of pictures of Candy he carried in it.

'Nice boy,' he said to Roz.

'People keep calling him a boy,' said Roz irritably. 'He's only two years younger than me.'

'Well, he seems a boy,' said C. J. 'It's that Californian innocence. Ah, Miles, let's have a look.'

Candy's sweet, deceptively guileless smile greeted them from the beach, from a restaurant, from the poolside of the hotel. C. J. and Roz studied her, her almost indecent youth, her blue eyes, her freckles, her colt-like legs.'

'She's lovely,' said C. J., meaning it. 'And she's how old?'

'Eighteen. We want to get married, but her old man won't hear of it.'

'Oh, he'll come round,' said C. J. easily. 'Fathers do, don't they, Roz? Pretty predictable people really.' He spoke without thinking; he was appalled to see Roz's face suddenly whiten and tears fill her eyes. 'Oh, Roz, I'm so sorry,' he said, pushing his chair back, going to her, trying to put his arms round her. 'I didn't think. I'm so sorry.'

'Well, you should think,' she said, and it was almost a cry of pain that escaped her. 'You bloody well should think.' And she got up and walked quickly out of the room.

'Oh hell,' said C. J. 'Now I've done it. I have a rare talent,' he said to Miles, half smiling at his own incompetence, 'for annoying and upsetting her. It was one of the things that most characterized our marriage.'

'You didn't mean anything,' said Miles. 'You were just being polite to me. She'll see that, surely.'

'You don't know Roz,' said C. J. 'She has trouble seeing that sort of thing, and anyway, she's desperately upset, it was very thoughtless of me.'

'Shall I go and talk to her?' asked Miles. 'I haven't annoyed her yet.' And he smiled his radiant, slightly conspiratorial smile at C. J.

'You could try,' said C. J. 'I might just go home now. Tell her I'll ring her in Scotland when I've talked to Letitia. Are you sure you don't mind going up there?'

'Absolutely not,' said Miles. 'It'll be fun. In a way. More fireworks though, I guess.'

'I guess,' said C. J. 'Well, it's been very nice meeting you, Miles. No doubt I shall be seeing some more of you. I'm sorry your introduction to this family has been so extremely traumatic.'

'Oh, don't worry,' said Miles. 'It beats waiting, I can tell you that.'

'Waiting? Oh you mean being a waiter?'

'Yup.'

'I would doubt that slightly myself,' said C. J., smiling. 'Anyway, good night Miles. And thank you.'

'What for?'

'Oh, I don't know. Being a calming influence.'

'That's OK.'

Miles went out of the kitchen and up to the drawing room; Roz was there, gazing blankly out at the river. 'Hi,' he said. 'Can I come in?'

'Yes, of course. Sorry about that. C. J. is an insensitive idiot.'

'He seems pretty nice and sensitive to me.'

'Well, maybe he is. I guess there's too much emotion between us just at the moment.'

'There's too much emotion around all of you at the moment. And I guess it's going to get worse.'

'Yes, you're right, of course it is. And somehow I have to be able to cope with it calmly. And I don't see how I can.'

'You should let it all out a bit,' he said. 'You're too tense. It really helps to yell now and again.'

'Do you ever yell?'

He looked at her, and smiled. 'Not often, because I don't often get worked up. I just don't seem to be made that way. But when I do, yes, I yell. And Candy yells a lot.'

'What makes Candy yell?'

'Oh, all sorts of things. Her dad. Her stepmom. Boredom. PMT. Me.'

'I can't imagine –'

'What?'

'You making anyone yell.'

'Oh,' he said, 'you'd be surprised. I make her yell, I make my granny yell, or used to. I make old Mrs Galbraith yell like anything.'

'But how?' she said. 'What do you do?'

'Nothing,' he said, 'that's exactly it. Nothing at all.'

'I've never met anyone like you before,' said Roz, smiling at him.

'I don't know how much of a loss that is. Would you like me to massage your neck and your shoulders? I bet you're one huge knot. Never fails.'

'I hate being massaged,' said Roz quickly. It was true. 'It makes me feel more fraught, not less.'

'You've never been massaged by me,' he said. 'Now shut up, and sit there, on that chair, so I can stand behind you. OK. Now then, just close your eyes and relax. Oh, your ex husband's gone, by the way. He said to tell you he was real sorry and that he'd call you in Scotland in the morning.'

'Well, that's par for the course,' said Roz. 'He would just disappear like that.'

'I thought he was really nice,' said Miles. His strong brown hands were working on her neck now. 'Don't resist, just shut your eyes and relax like I told you to.'

'Oh, he is really,' said Roz. 'Sorry. You must think I'm a frightful bitch.'

'Not really,' said Miles consideringly. 'I think you're terrific.' This was said so sincerely, with so patent a disregard for flattery, that Roz smiled, suddenly less angry and hurt.

'That's better,' said Miles. 'I felt that.'

'What?'

'You relaxed. You should laugh more. Life isn't really so serious.'

'It is,' she said, 'at the moment.'

'Yeah, I guess so.'

'You're right, though. Michael – my man as you call him –

always makes – made me laugh. It's one of the reasons I – well, I miss him.'

'Why don't you call him?'

'I can't.'

'Why not?'

'I just can't.'

'OK,' he said, smoothing down over her shoulders now, working his thumbs into the bones at the top of her spine, 'you know him. I don't. I'd like to, though. He sounds like a real fun guy. How's this?'

'It's lovely,' said Roz, and it was true. She felt soothed, calmed, rested. It was partly talking to Miles that helped, partly a great natural weariness suddenly carrying her away, and partly, she had to admit, the sensation of extraordinary pleasure and warmth which was being conveyed through her body.

'Good. I told you it would help. Tell me about your mom.'

She told him. She told him about her childhood, about all her mother's lovers, about Jamil al Shehra, about the husbands, about Pierre du Chene, about Peveril.

'She sounds like quite a lady.'

'She is.'

'Like her daughter,' he said. There was something in his voice, a new depth, that shot through Roz like a charge. A fierce, probing one. One she could not begin to contend with. One she did not even want to think about.

'That's fine, Miles,' she said. 'Thank you. I – I think I'll go to bed now. Can you let yourself out?'

'Of course,' he said, and as she turned to face him, to walk out of the room, she met his eyes, and felt confused, disoriented, almost physically disturbed. She looked away, smiled coolly, walked past him, but it was too late; he had seen it, and shown her that he had seen it, with a smile of his own, a brief touch of her hand.

'Good night,' was all he said. 'I'll call you first thing, find out when we have to go.'

He might seem a boy, she thought, lying in bed later, drifting into unconsciousness with the help of a very strong sleeping pill, but he undoubtedly had the sexuality, the carnal knowledge of a very experienced man.

*

Phaedria finally reached Regent's Park, exhausted, the following afternoon.

Julia had been very good and slept through most of the journey, waking only to feed and gaze sweetly around her, occasionally smiling her surprised, lopsided smile; nevertheless it was a relief to get her home and into the arms of Mrs Hamlyn for a few hours.

Michael had seen them both off at LA airport; he had taken her in his arms, and given her a huge bear hug.

'I daren't kiss you,' he said, looking at her tenderly, lovingly, his eyes nonetheless amused both at himself and her for their entirely (as he put it) profligate restraint, 'not even on your forehead. I would forget myself entirely and ravish you here and now right in front of Immigration. Now take great care of yourself, and call me if you need me.'

'I will,' she said. She felt she could have stayed there in his arms, safe, protected from the fears that filled her, for hours, days; she pulled back, looked at him, at his gloomily amused face, his restless dark eyes, interminably exploring her, his oddly hard, tough, mouth – she had begun to dream of that mouth and what it could do to her – felt his warmth, his solid, comforting, caring warmth, and somehow managed to smile; but she felt chilled and totally bereft as she finally walked away from him towards Internal Flights.

All the way home she thought alternately of him and Julian; her mind and her emotions a jumble of hurt and fear, longing and confusion. It occurred to her suddenly, as she looked out at the endless blue beside and beyond her, that she had never met Michael, never been with him, under circumstances that were not extraordinary; when she had not been ill or frightened, or grieving or shocked. And yet he managed unfailingly to make her feel calmer, happy, safe, to make things seem hopeful, and normal, and above all interesting. He was very sexually attractive (very very sexually attractive, she thought, wrenching her mind with an effort from a rather too vivid contemplation of what might have been) but, more unusually, he was emotionally exciting, he gave life, people, experiences, a new vividness and interest.

Well, it was not to be, she thought; she would just have to find them less vivid and interesting, and to suppress the ferocious feelings that roared through her body every time she even thought about him. He belonged to Roz, and even had she been less afraid of Roz, less hostile to her, Phaedria would not have considered taking him away from her. The pain of seeing Camilla's head on the pillow of her bed, hers and Julian's, in New York, was still fresh and raw in her. She would not, could not, inflict that on anybody. Not even Roz. Moreover, just now Roz, probably even more than she, needed Michael. Even in her own considerable unhappiness, Phaedria shuddered at the thought of the hurt Roz must be enduring.

And there was another pain, equally fresh and raw, still in her, that she knew made it impossible for her to enter into emotional commitments. She had, with all their problems, their battles, the shortcomings of their relationship, loved Julian very much; he had been her first lover and her first real love, and he had died only six months earlier. She was still cautiously, painfully working her way through her grief – rekindled suddenly and horribly by this new trauma, and she was simply not ready to go forward into anything else.

Quite suddenly as she sat there, gazing blankly out of the window, unbidden, unwelcome, a terrifying thought came to her. Straight from a nightmare, worse than a nightmare: so bad she had to get up, walk up and down the aisle for a while, order herself a drink.

'No,' she said to herself, half aloud. 'No. Not possibly.'

Her voice broke into the baby's sleep; she stirred, half opened her eyes, moved her tiny arms. Phaedria looked at her, and picked her up suddenly, holding her very tightly. 'Oh baby,' she said, 'what troubles we seem to have, you and I.'

'It's lovely to have you home, madam,' said the housekeeper, taking the baby, looking at her, smiling at her, 'isn't she beautiful and she looks just like –' She broke off, confused, not sure if she was saying the right thing.

'It's lovely to be home, Mrs Hamlyn. Yes, I know, she looks just like her father, doesn't she?'

'She does. Who'd have thought it?' said Mrs Hamlyn with a sublime lack of logic. 'Er, Mr Emerson is here, madam, up in the drawing room. Shall I put baby in the nursery? You must be very tired, I'll bring you some tea.'

841

'I'll just come up with you and settle her. She's been feeding all the way from Heathrow, I don't think she's hungry. But yes, I am tired. Thank you so much for getting the nursery organized, Mrs Hamlyn, I do appreciate it. I believe some nannies are coming for interviews tomorrow?'

'Yes, they are. Mrs Morell has seen all of them, and liked them, but she said you must have the final say, of course.'

'Well, me and Julia. Everyone has been so kind. I'll just go and say hallo to Mr Emerson, Mrs Hamlyn, and then I'll follow you up.'

C. J. was sitting by the fire; he looked drawn and pale.

'Hallo, C. J.! It's lovely to see you. I'm so glad you're here.'

'Hallo, Phaedria. It's good to have you back.'

'Well,' she said, looking at him mockingly reproving, 'I gather you haven't been here very much, C. J. Business in New York, I heard.'

'Er – yes,' he said awkwardly. 'Who told you that?'

'Oh,' she said lightly, 'I have spies everywhere.'

'You must do. Phaedria, I'm so sorry about all this.'

'Oh,' she said, 'yes, it's been an awful shock. But worse for Roz, I imagine. How is she?'

'Pretty wretched. Very angry.'

'Yes, she would be angry. I am quite. But not as much as her, I imagine.'

'Nobody,' he said with a sigh, 'can be as angry as Roz.'

'That's true. Except perhaps her father.'

'Well, yes. I've just left Letitia,' he said.

'Oh God,' said Phaedria, 'how is she? Poor Letitia. I did wonder, you know, if she had to know at all. But I suppose she might have heard some other way and that would have been worse.'

'Rather strangely,' said C. J., 'she seemed to find it all rather – well, amusing would be too strong a word. But she was rather manic about it. She certainly didn't cry or faint or anything. She just couldn't stop talking about it.'

'I'm not surprised,' said Phaedria. 'It would appeal to her on an intellectual level. She would regard it as a kind of personalized entertainment. I think when it sinks in she might feel very differently.'

'Maybe. Could you ring her later and see how she is? I didn't want to leave her, but she more or less shooed me out.'

'Of course I will. I must go and see if Julia's settled down, and then Mrs Hamlyn's bringing us some tea.'

'Fine.'

He seemed very depressed.

Phaedria reappeared laughing. 'Well, I've lost that baby. Mrs Hamlyn won't let me near her. There's a mutual admiration society going on up there; it's hard to say who's talking the most nonsense.'

'Good. How is she?'

'Julia? She's marvellous. Thriving. Smiling. Guzzling.' She sighed suddenly, a vision of Michael looking at her over Julia's downy head surfacing from her subconscious. She pushed it irritably down again. If she was going to get sentimental about him every time she even fed the baby, there was little hope for any of them.

'And how are you?'

'Tired. A bit shaken, I suppose. Oh, I don't know what to think, C. J. Who on earth was I married to? Julian? Hugo Dashwood? Or someone else altogether. I feel such a fool, apart from anything else.'

'You shouldn't,' he said. 'We all knew him much longer and we never suspected anything either.'

'No, but I was married to him. Supposed to be one mind and one flesh and all that sort of thing. How could I have been so obtuse?'

'Phaedria, you weren't being obtuse. The guy was – well, I hate to say this, but obviously just slightly odd.'

'OK, but there I was madly in love with someone not just slightly, but extremely odd. And I had no idea. Some marriage.'

'Well, we all have to learn to live with it. Roz is finding it horribly hard.'

'I'm sure. Where is Roz anyway?'

'She's gone up to Scotland, to see her mother.'

'Goodness,' said Phaedria, 'I wonder how on earth Eliza will take it?'

'I think probably very well,' said C. J. 'I think hers will be

843

more like Letitia's reaction. She'll see it as a stupendous piece of gossip.'

'Yes, well, she must be stopped from talking about it,' said Phaedria. 'Apart from anything else, I don't think Letitia could cope with it being all over the papers. Nor could I for that matter,' she added soberly.

'Don't worry. Roz had thought of that. She was prepared to threaten her mother with all kinds of loss of privilege, no more lunches at Langan's, forbidding Jasper Conran to go and stay with her, that sort of thing,' said C. J.

'Good, I'm glad. And tell me about the famous Miles? What's he like? And where is he? I want to meet him.'

'The famous Miles is delightful,' said C. J. 'You just can't help liking him. Very very good-looking –'

'I know that,' said Phaedria quietly, reliving suddenly the horror of seeing the photograph, the dizzy shock, standing there in the bright sunlight with Father Kennedy, feeling nothing but darkness and chill, 'I've seen a picture of him.'

'Have you? Oh, in Los Angeles, of course. Well anyway, he's extremely charming, in that very Californian laid back kind of way, very very genuine and natural, and absolutely unspoilt. He's completely fazed by all this business, hardly knows what day of the week it is, but he's handled it extremely well. Just sitting and smiling and trying to be helpful.'

'He sounds a bit too good to be true,' said Phaedria briskly. 'And – well, have you any idea at all, has he, what he might want to do?'

'His initial reaction was just to hand it over and go back to California with his girlfriend,' said C. J. 'He just doesn't basically want to know.'

'Well, that could simplify things I suppose,' said Phaedria. 'Or alternatively complicate them. What does Henry think about it all?

'God knows,' said C. J. 'I don't think he's met too many people like Miles. Maybe you should talk to him.'

'I will. Anyway, where's Miles now?'

'In Scotland with Roz.'

'Good God. What on earth for?'

'Well, I may be doing her a terrible injustice,' said C. J.

carefully, 'but I kind of feel Roz doesn't want him left around for you to get your hands on.'

'Oh, God,' said Phaedria wearily. 'Machiavelli had nothing on Roz, did he? I don't know if I have the stomach for all this, C. J. We obviously have a very bloody battle ahead of us.'

'Letitia? Hello, it's Phaedria.'

'Darling, how lovely to hear your voice. How are you, and when can I come and see you and meet that baby? I would have come out to see you in LA but my fool of a doctor said I shouldn't.'

'Letitia, have you been ill?'

'Not seriously, darling, only flu. But I did feel a bit tired after it. I told him the sunshine would do me good, but he didn't seem to see it that way.'

'Letitia, you must take care of yourself. You do too much.'

'I do far too little,' said Letitia briskly. 'That's half the trouble. I'm thinking of coming back to work full time. Could you find me some little task, do you think? As accounts clerk or something?'

'Oh God, I'm sure we could,' said Phaedria, 'it would be marvellous.'

'Good. Well maybe after Christmas. I'll come for an interview. Now then, when am I going to see you both?'

'Whenever you like. The baby is simply beautiful, Letitia, and she looks just like Julian.'

'Oh, how wonderful. It's all too good to be true. Shall I come over in the morning? I expect you're tired now.'

'I am a bit, but if you really want to, I'd love to see you now. I could send Pete.'

'No, darling, I'm a little tired myself. I've had – well, a rather interesting conversation with C. J.'

'I know. That's really why I rang. To see if you were all right.'

'Much more all right than you – anyone – might think. Of course it was a shock, but you know, Phaedria, I had suspected something like this. Well, no, not suspected, that is putting it too strongly, but it certainly wasn't as – well, surprising, as it must have been to you.'

'Really, Letitia? How extraordinary. Tell me why.'

'Oh, I don't know. It seemed such a nonsense, leaving that

845

will, that inheritance to a complete stranger. It had to be a kind of riddle. And most riddles have perfectly obvious answers after all.'

'I suppose so.'

'You see, he did have this passion for deceit. Secrecy is perhaps a kinder word. He loved it even as a little boy. He used to go to such lengths to surprise me with birthday presents, things like that. And then there was his Resistance training in the war; he had to assume at least two, three I think, completely different identities. Separate papers, passports, everything. He adored it and he was brilliant at it. It's my guess this thing started as a sort of game, that he was bored one day and decided to see how far he could take it and then it got out of hand; probably when this poor woman's husband died, and he was looking after her, or decided to keep an eye on Miles, he had got rather close to them all and it was just too late to say, "Er – actually, I'm not who I said I was." Do you see what I mean? And then of course –' her voice trailed away just slightly; there was a short, painful silence. 'There – there just might be another explanation. Don't you think?'

'Oh,' said Phaedria quickly, determinedly, hearing in Letitia's quiet, almost detached tone the black nightmare that had first attacked her on the plane drawing nearer reality, 'if you mean what I think you mean, no, I don't. Not possibly. That couldn't be right. It just couldn't.'

'No, of course not,' said Letitia. 'No, obviously it couldn't. Well, perhaps we can talk about it all a bit more tomorrow. When I come and meet that baby. Now then,' she said, deliberately changing her tone of voice, her mood, 'you've heard about Miles, have you?'

'Well yes –'

'I mean how deliciously handsome and charming he is?'

'I'm beginning to get the idea,' said Phaedria, laughing, relieved to feel the nightmare fading again, 'I shall meet him tomorrow, I imagine. Roz has whisked him off to Scotland so I can't steal a march on her and inveigle the shares away from him while she's not there. Poor Roz,' she added, 'I understand she's terribly upset.'

'Yes, she is.'

'I did phone her to try and speak to her, but I missed her

twice. I thought I'd ring her tonight at Garrylaig. She must see it as the ultimate betrayal. I mean, all this time she's thought that through all the relationships, all the wives, all the mistresses, she came first, that he loved her best, and now there's been this shadowy figure, this other life all along.'

'It's a pity Michael isn't here with her,' said Letitia with a sigh, 'I understand they've quarrelled. Again. Now of all times. Well, I do hope they make it up. He really is the only man in the world who can handle her. She needs him terribly badly.'

Phaedria wondered, as she put the phone down, if she had detected or merely imagined a very slightly ominous note in Letitia's voice.

Eliza took the news remarkably well.

'Nothing that old so and so did would surprise or shock me, darling. If you told me he'd made off with the crown jewels or that he had personally murdered Lord Lucan, I would think it par for the course. I think it's all rather romantic. I just wish I'd known before, when he was alive, and I could have teased him about it all. You mustn't be too upset, Roz, he really was rather – well, odd. I know you loved him terribly and if it's any comfort to you, I think you were the only person he really loved in return, but I don't think this means you have to think he loved you any less.'

'He must have quite loved Miles,' said Roz soberly, 'to have done this to us all.'

'I don't think so. Quite the reverse. If he'd really loved him, he would have brought him out of the wardrobe or whatever the expression is, before. Good God – I – no, no, surely not. Probably not. Well –'

'Mummy, what on earth are you talking about?'

'Oh, I don't know,' said Eliza, appearing to shake herself. 'Just a thought. Take no notice, darling. My mind's wandering. Senility setting in. Miles is frightfully handsome, isn't he?' she said quickly. 'And what a charmer. We could hardly have a more delightful pretender to the throne, could we?'

'Not, not really,' said Roz listlessly. 'I'm sorry, Mummy, I simply can't take this rather pragmatic view of yours. And Letitia's, it seems. C. J. phoned and says she's just fine. Says she's always suspected it or some such nonsense. I just see it as an awful betrayal.'

'Oh, I think the will was,' said Eliza, 'don't get me wrong. But this double life business, well, it's just too ridiculous. Silly. You mustn't let it upset you too much.' She looked at Roz's drawn, pale face and shadowed eyes. 'How's Michael?'

'Fine,' said Roz briefly. 'Very busy.'

'Really? I would have thought he would have been over, with all this.'

'Why ever should he? He has a business to look after. Why should a lot of nonsense like this have him rushing away from it?'

'He knows how much you loved your father. He wouldn't think it was nonsense. When is he coming over?'

'I don't know,' said Roz irritably. 'I really haven't discussed it with him.'

Eliza gave her a probing look. 'Have you quarrelled?'

'No. Well, in a way, yes.'

'What about?'

'Oh, just about everything. I don't want to talk about it.'

'Don't lose him, Roz. He's the right man for you.'

'That's not what you said once,' said Roz bitterly. 'And I have a broken marriage to show for it.'

'I know and I was wrong. Although I don't think I want to take the entire responsibility for your divorce on to my shoulders. But pride is a destructive thing, Roz. If it's even half your fault, you should apologize.'

'It isn't,' said Roz shortly, 'and I'm not going to.'

'All right, darling. Have it your own way. How's Phaedria?'

'I haven't the faintest idea,' said Roz. 'She only got back today.'

'Ah,' said Eliza, 'so that's it. You were afraid she'd get Miles on to her side while you were up here. I did wonder.'

'Don't be ridiculous,' said Roz. 'I just thought he might as well come and meet you than hang around in London.'

Eliza looked at her. 'Which way do you think he's going to jump?'

'I don't know,' said Roz wearily. 'He doesn't want to jump at all. Just go home again to California and his girlfriend.'

'Well, offer to buy him out and then he can.'

'I know, but it's not as simple as that.'

'Why not?'

848

'Well, because he knows he has to make a decision.'

'Well, darling, I would have thought you were capable of leaning on him quite hard enough to persuade him. I would also have thought,' she added, an expression that was half humorous, half shrewd in her green eyes, 'it might be quite a pleasure. Come along, darling, let's go and have tea. I haven't told Peveril too much about all this yet, he already sees us as only a little better than the Borgias.'

'Mummy, I don't think you should tell anyone about it,' said Roz. 'I don't want the gossip columns getting on to it. It would damage us all.'

Eliza's large green eyes were widely candid. 'Of course I won't, darling. Who would I tell?'

'Oh, nobody much. Just a few close, intimate friends. Nigel Dempster, Peter Langan. Your friend Marigold Turner. No, Mummy, you really are not to talk about it. To anyone.'

'So in that case, who is Miles supposed to be?' said Eliza crossly.

'An old friend of the family who's been mentioned in Daddy's will. Who it's taken us a while to track down. OK? We really cannot afford a major scandal about all this.'

'Rosamund, whenever did I show any predilection for mixing myself up in major scandals?'

'Oh,' said Roz, looking at her mother with a mixture of exasperation and affection, 'just about every week of your life so far. Come on, let's go and have tea. I can't wait to see Peveril and Miles together.'

'They were something else,' said Miles happily to Roz as they flew back to London in the company plane next morning. 'I thought he was just the neatest old guy I ever met. I said I would ask him over to stay with us in California in the summer. He said he had always wanted to surf.'

'Good God,' said Roz, contemplating with great pleasure the vision of Peveril complete with knickerbockers and deerstalker riding a board in the Malibu surf. 'Can I come too? I wouldn't miss that for anything.'

'Sure,' said Miles. 'I'd really like that. And you could bring little Miranda, too,' he added, 'she's a cute kid. Does she live up here all the time?'

'No, it's just that she was up there anyway, it's good for her, the air and so on, and with all this drama going on, I thought she and Nanny might as well stay for a while longer.'

Miles looked at her curiously. She talked about and indeed behaved towards Miranda as if she was a small, none-too-familiar puppy; he had heard the English were very odd in their attitude to their children, first shutting them away in nurseries with starchy uniformed nannies, and then sending them straight off to school: it was obviously true.

'I guess she'll be off to boarding school soon,' he said. Roz looked at him sharply, suspecting he was trying to score off her, but he smiled back at her with such transparent friendliness that she had to smile back.

'Not for a year or two,' she said. 'In fact, not till she's at least eleven.'

'Did you go to boarding school?'

'Yes, I did. And I hated it.'

'So why send her at all?'

'Well, because she has to go some time,' said Roz, looking at him as if he was querying the basis of the entire British constitution, 'because it'll be good for her.'

'It wasn't good for you.'

'How do you know?' she said, quite crossly, 'what was good and bad for me?'

'Lots of things have been bad for you, I'd say,' he said. 'Otherwise you'd be happier.'

'How do you know I'm not happy?'

'I feel it,' he said, 'I feel it and I see it.'

'Well, that's just ridiculous.'

'Why? Are you happy?

'Well, not at the moment, no. Of course I'm not. I have a lot to be unhappy about.'

'Like this business with your dad?'

'Yes, of course.'

'Yeah, that's tough. I can see that. But before that were you happy?'

'Well, yes, of course I was.'

'That's all right then,' he said, leaning back in the seat, looking out of the window. Something about his complete air of relaxation and detachment irritated Roz.

'Don't you believe me?'

'Not really.'

'Why not?'

'You don't seem like a lady who's happy. Not to me. Of course I may be wrong.'

'You are.'

'Good,' he said, 'that's fine. You should know, I guess.'

'Yes, I certainly should.'

'OK. I'm really glad.'

He looked at her, his dark blue eyes examining her green ones, scanning her face, and smiled. 'It's all right,' he said, putting out his hand, covering hers with it. 'You don't have to take any notice of me. I'm just a schmuck from California. I guess I don't understand you guys at all.'

'No,' said Roz, pulling her hand away, still irritated. 'You don't.'

'OK,' he said lazily, 'but don't get so uptight about it.'

'I'm not uptight.'

'You are, Roz,' he said. 'You're seriously uptight. But if you won't talk about it, then it has to stay your problem. If you don't want me to help, that's fine.'

'And what,' she said edgily, 'do you think you could do to help?'

'Oh,' he said, his eyes caressing hers briefly, moving down, resting on her mouth, 'I could do a lot. I told you that the other night.'

Roz was silent for a while, digesting this, trying to suppress the conflicting emotions within her: irritation, misery, a desire at once to get closer to Miles and to keep her distance, and despite herself, the odd sense of physical disarray, of pleasant warm confusion he induced in her.

She looked at her watch. Only twenty minutes to go. Discretion won.

'It's very very kind of you,' she said, coolly courteous, 'to be so concerned about me. But I really am perfectly all right. Or will be when this is over.'

'Good,' he said. 'I'm really glad. I think I'll take a nap.'

He smiled at her again, reached out in a tender, unexpected gesture and touched her cheek, and then closed his eyes and was asleep in seconds.

Phaedria was just finishing her breakfast and concurrently giving Julia hers when the phone rang.

'Hi, darling. It's me.'

Her head promptly disintegrated into a million fragments; she felt a rush of huge, bright pleasure, followed by the now familiar sense of panic and unease.

'Aren't you speaking to me? Don't I get any kind of a reward for having Franco wake me at five in the morning just so I could hear your voice? You're a hard woman, Lady Morell.'

She laughed. 'I'm sorry. I was surprised.'

'Good. That was the idea. I plan to keep surprising you, catching you unawares. Eventually, I plan to catch you so unawares you won't even know what you're doing, and whether it's all right to be doing it. How are you?'

'I'm fine.'

'Good. And what are you doing?'

'Feeding Julia.'

'Oh, God,' he said, 'oh, God.'

'What's the matter?'

'Oh, nothing,' he said, 'just having a little trouble with a particular part of my anatomy. Brought on by the image of Julia taking her breakfast.'

'Oh, Michael,' she said, with a mixture of a laugh and a sigh in her voice. 'Don't, please don't.'

'Listen, honeybunch, I'm trying not to. It isn't easy.'

Phaedria gave up. 'It's so nice to hear your voice.'

'That's better. What are you going to do today?'

'Not sure. Yes I am. I'm going to meet Miles.'

'Ah. Where was he yesterday?'

'In Scotland,' said Phaedria. 'With Roz.'

'Good Christ. She's not letting you get your hands on him, is she?'

'Fraid not.'

'Will you promise to call me when you've finished with him?'

'Why?'

'Now, that is a ridiculous question. I can hardly believe you've asked it. Because I want to know what he's like. Because I want to know how you get on with him. Because I want to know what might be happening. Because I need to know how goodlooking he is, in case I have to get jealous.'

'Michael, please please stop talking like this.'

'Why?'

'You know why.'

'I know why you think I should. I really don't know that I know. I have been giving our situation a great deal of thought, and I have come to a conclusion or two. Do you want to know what they are, or shall I stop donating half my income to the Bell Telephone Company and go back to sleep?'

Phaedria was silent, struggling with herself. Then she said, 'Yes, I want to know.'

'OK. Here we go. I think you're terrific. I think you're clever and funny and beautiful. I love being with you. How am I doing?'

'All right.'

'Only all right? For Christ's sake, Phaedria, here I am reciting a love letter over the Atlantic and all you can say is it's all right.'

'Sorry. But you know – well, you know what I think.'

'I plan on destroying your capacity to think. Can I go on?'

'All right.'

'I want to go to bed with you.'

'You can't. I've told you. Don't even think about it.'

'Darling, I can't think about anything else.'

'You have to. You have to think about Roz.'

'I've thought about Roz. Very hard.'

'And?'

'I don't love her any more.'

'How do you know?' she said, and her heart was thudding so hard she could scarcely hear him.

'I just do. I did love her, very much. I loved a lot about her. But she's killed it. Strangled it. It's dead.'

'Michael, you can't do that to her.'

'Do what?'

'Fail her now. You just can't. She's so unhappy.'

'Phaedria, I was so unhappy, lots of times. I was so unhappy, so lonely for her, I didn't know how to stand it. She didn't give a monkey's fart. She said she did, but she didn't. All she ever cared about was that company and that father of hers. Your husband. I beg your pardon, I don't mean to insult him . . .'

'Please don't –'

'Sorry. I have to try and explain it and he is crucial to the explanation. I spent years fighting him for Roz. It didn't stop when he died. Now I seem to be fighting him for you.'

'No, you're not.'

'Well that's what it feels like. OK, let's drop him. Let's go back to us.'

'There isn't an us,' she said, with such a huge effort it physically drained her.

'Phaedria, there should be. There has to be.'

'There can't be.'

'There will be. I swear it.'

'Michael –'

'Phaedria, listen to me. Please, darling, please listen for God's sake.'

'I'm listening,' she said, her resolve weakened by the urgency in his voice.

'Good. Because it's very important. Very important.' He was silent for a moment. Outside, she heard a car pull up. Pete perhaps, back with the files she had sent for from the office.

'Phaedria, I know we have problems. Difficulties. I can see we have to take our time, tread carefully. But I can't go back to Roz now. I absolutely cannot.' There was a pause. And a knock at the front door.

'Phaedria. I am rather seriously in love with you.' Another pause. Voices.

'Phaedria, I think – no, for God's sake, I know, I want you to –'

'Good morning, Phaedria.'

Phaedria slammed the phone down.

Roz was standing in the doorway.

'Good morning Phaedria,' she said again. 'Please don't let me disturb your phone call. Was it important?'

'No,' said Phaedria. 'No, not at all. Good morning, Roz. How are you?'

'Very well, thank you. A little – tired, shall we say, but well. So this is the baby?'

'Yes.'

'Very nice,' said Roz, glancing dispassionately at Julia rather as if she were an ornament or a dress she didn't like the look of very much, but felt forced to at least acknowledge.

Phaedria looked at Roz steadily. She was pale but composed; she was wearing black, as she so often did, with a scarlet scarf knotted round her shoulders. She looked dramatic, fierce but not hostile, indeed she was smiling faintly.

'Well,' she said, 'welcome back to London.'

'Thank you. Roz, I'm so sorry about the news – about your father. I did try to ring you several times, but . . .'

'I know you did,' said Roz. 'Thank you. I got the messages.'

Phaedria stared at her, so effectively rebuffed she couldn't even speak.

'I – I think I'll just take Julia upstairs,' she said after a moment. 'I'll ask Mrs Hamlyn for coffee.'

'Don't worry,' said Roz. 'I won't be here long.'

'Well, I'd like some,' said Phaedria firmly. 'Excuse me for a moment.'

She put the baby in the cot and looked down at her for a while, then as if drawing strength from her, stood up very straight and walked back downstairs.

Roz turned and looked at her, taking in the tanned skin, the glossy hair, the slender figure.

'You look very well,' she said. 'But then I suppose you would. You have just had what amounts to a very long holiday.'

'In a way, yes.'

'But you are fully recovered at last.'

'Oh, I am very fully recovered. It's been Julia's health that has kept me there, as you know. She was very frail.'

'But she's well now?'

'Oh, very, thank you.'

'And when are we to expect the pleasure of seeing you back at work?'

'Oh, very soon,' said Phaedria, 'as soon as I have Julia settled with a nanny. I'm looking forward to it.'

'I daresay you are. You must have been bored and – lonely over there. Or weren't you?'

A cold crawling chill invaded Phaedria's body; she felt sick. So that was it. She swallowed hard and met Roz's eyes steadily.

'Not really. I made friends. I had Julia. I was at the hospital most of the time.'

'Oh, good,' said Roz, poisonously sweet, 'and then you had visitors, I believe?'

'Yes, I did. Several.'

'Several?'

'Yes, several,' said Phaedria steadily. 'My father, of course.'

'Of course.'

'And Susan came, and C. J. and David Sassoon, and your mother.'

'So she did. How very thoroughly you have become a part of this family. Inveigled yourself into it.'

'Hardly inveigled,' said Phaedria, meeting her stormy eyes. 'I did after all marry into it.'

'You did. I tend to forget that. I somehow get the impression you do as well, from time to time.'

'I don't know what you mean, I'm afraid,' said Phaedria.

'Don't you?' said Roz. 'Well, never mind. I believe Michael came to visit you?'

'Yes,' said Phaedria. 'Yes he did. He came to see us.'

'Us?'

'Yes us. Me and the baby.'

'How touching.'

'It was very nice of him.'

'Very. Extraordinarily nice. He stayed at your hotel, I believe?'

Phaedria had not realized she had known this. She swallowed again, hoping Roz wouldn't notice.

'Yes,' she said, 'yes, he did.'

'For two nights?'

'Yes.'

'You slut,' said Roz quite quietly.

'I beg your pardon?'

'I said you were a slut. My father has only been dead six months, that child of yours is only just born, and you start sleeping around with anyone who takes your fancy. Who else has been consoling you in your widowhood down there? C. J.? No, he hasn't got the balls. David Sassoon? You always did have the hots for him.'

'Roz,' said Phaedria, keeping her voice quiet with a huge

effort, 'please could we stop this. I'm finding it grossly insulting. I know it's very hard to believe, I can see what's happened is very unfortunate and difficult for you to accept, but nothing, absolutely nothing happened between Michael and me.'

'I don't find that hard to believe. I find it impossible.'

Phaedria shrugged. 'That's your problem.'

'Is that all you have to say?'

'What else could there be?'

Roz was silent for a moment.

'I think you're lying,' she said.

'You can think what you like,' said Phaedria. 'I really don't care. I do care, though,' and there was an icily warning edge to her voice, 'if you share your thoughts with other people. I have not slept with Michael Browning, or indeed anyone else, nothing whatever happened between us and that is the end of the matter. Have you talked to Michael about it?'

'Yes. He spun the same fairy story.'

'Oh Roz,' said Phaedria, 'it's not a fairy story. It's –' and her lips twitched, despite herself, into a half smile – 'too unlikely to be untrue. Please for all our sakes take his word for it, if you won't take mine. God, we have enough real problems, I would have thought, without manufacturing any more.'

'Most of our problems,' said Roz, 'can be laid at your door. If you hadn't set out to trap my father, to worm your way into the company, to get your hands on his money, there would be no problems at all now.'

'Roz, I did not trap your father.'

'Oh really? I suppose he fell madly and hopelessly in love with you, and just swept you off your feet. And his money and his position meant nothing at all to you. Because if that's so, I don't quite understand why you can't just go away now, leave us alone, instead of hanging on for dear life, apparently totally set on getting your pound, or rather millions of pounds, of flesh. And anything else that might catch your fancy in the process.'

'Roz, I think I'd like you to leave,' said Phaedria. 'I don't want to listen to any more of this.'

'I don't suppose you do. Nobody else would say it, would they? They're all so besotted with you, so totally deceived by

857

your innocent face, and your little-girly ways, your grieving widow number. Well, I'm not. You make me want to throw up.'

'Get out,' said Phaedria, her eyes blazing. 'Just get out. And shut up.'

Roz looked at her consideringly.

'All right,' she said at last. 'I'll go. I don't believe any of what you say but I can't prove it, that it's not true, so before you start threatening me with slander action again, you have my word I won't share my thoughts. For now.' She looked at Phaedria very intently, the hatred in her eyes almost a physical force.

'Is there anything else you'd like to consider trying to take away from me? she said. 'First my father. Then my birthright. My lover. Well, I do assure you there's something you are not going to get your hands on, Phaedria Blenheim, and that's Miles and his two per cent.'

'Well,' said Miles, 'you certainly are a good-looking family.'

He was standing in the doorway of the drawing room at Regent's Park; Phaedria had invited him to tea. Roz had gone straight to the office after her morning's visit to Phaedria, and was consequently unable to keep him under her eye any longer.

Phaedria inclined her head just slightly. 'Thank you. I could return the compliment.'

'Please do,' he said, smiling. 'A little flattery and I'm anyone's.'

'Are you really?' She smiled. 'Come in and sit down. Mrs Hamlyn is bringing tea up in a minute.'

'Thank you. So this is the famous baby?'

'This is.'

'She's cute.'

'Isn't she?'

'Of course,' he said, 'she has a head start on most of the human race, beginning her life in California.'

'I do have to agree with you,' said Phaedria with a sigh, looking out at the greyness of Regent's Park, the leaden sky, the dripping trees. 'It seemed to me just the nicest place in the world. I was so happy there.'

'Me too.' He sat down. 'And I plan to go back there just as soon as ever I can.'

'Do you really?'

'I really do. To Malibu. To the beach.'

'My goodness,' she said, 'here you are, one of the most potentially powerful and rich young men in the world, and all you want to do is sit on a beach in California.'

'Yes,' he said. 'Don't knock it.'

'Oh,' she said. 'I'm not knocking it. I envy you. I think it would be marvellous.'

'Well,' he said with simple logic, 'you could go wherever you liked, couldn't you? You're not exactly pushed for the fare.'

'No, that's true. But I have – well, things to do.'

'It's very odd,' he said, dropping the argument, 'to hear myself described as powerful. Or even rich. I've always been so hard up and so – well, unpowerful.'

She smiled at him. 'The correct word is impotent.'

'Yeah, well,' he said grinning back, 'I'm not that. Thank heaven.'

'Good,' said Phaedria briskly. 'That must be very nice for someone.'

'I hope so.'

'You must feel you've strayed into some kind of bad dream,' said Phaedria suddenly.

'Well,' he said, 'it's not all bad. But it is pretty strange. I really want to get back soon, but I can see I have some decisions to make first.'

'Not really,' said Phaedria. 'Surely they can wait.'

'Oh, no,' he said, 'I'd rather get it settled. Stay maybe a week or two, and make up my mind. Then go home with a clear conscience.'

'And you wouldn't even consider staying and getting involved?'

He looked at her and smiled into her eyes. Phaedria, who had not yet been on the receiving end of this particular experience, felt momentarily weak. She had no interest in Miles whatsoever, he was absolutely not the type of man she found attractive, and yet at that moment, had he chosen, he could have trawled her into a fairly immoderate level of sexual interest.

'No,' he said in answer to her question. 'Not for a moment.'

She was confused by him, and the tangle of her thoughts.

'Sorry? Not for a moment what?'

859

He smiled again, aware of what he had done to her. 'Not for a moment would I consider it. Getting involved.'

'So what do you intend to do?'

'Sell up. Take the money and run. Initially I thought I'd just run, but Roz said that was silly.'

'Did she indeed?' said Phaedria thoughtfully. 'That was very scrupulous of her.'

'I think she is quite scrupulous,' said Miles cheerfully, beaming at Mrs Hamlyn who had come in with the tea tray. 'Here, let me take that from you, ma'am.'

Mrs Hamlyn beamed back, and rolled her eyes in a rather extraordinary way; Phaedria was momentarily alarmed; then she realized Mrs Hamlyn was flirting with Miles.

'Thank you, Mrs Hamlyn,' she said briskly. 'I'll ring if we want anything else.'

'I wondered if Mr Wilburn might like something more substantial to eat,' said Mrs Hamlyn. 'That's not much of a tea there, not really.'

'Oh, no ma'am, thank you,' said Miles, smiling at her again. 'I already had a huge lunch. But it's really kind of you to think about it.'

Mrs Hamlyn rolled her eyes again and walked reluctantly over to the door.

'Well,' she said hopefully, 'there's plenty of food in the kitchen.'

'Maybe another time,' said Miles. She looked up at him as if he had just suggested a weekend in Paris.

'Maybe,' she said with a last roll, and was gone. Phaedria looked at Miles and grinned.

'You mustn't flirt with my female staff,' she said.

'Am I allowed loose on the males?' he said.

'Certainly not. Now then, come and have some tea, and tell me again exactly what you want to do.'

'Well,' said Miles, 'what I really want to do is get married.'

'Anyone in particular?'

'Yes, my girlfriend. She's called Candy. Candy McCall. She's eighteen.'

'That's young,' she said, 'to get married. And how old are you, exactly? You look quite young to be getting married too.'

'Twenty-seven.'

'Goodness. The same age as me.'

'I don't suppose anyone told you you were too young to get married.'

'Well, they did and they didn't,' said Phaedria.

'I guess they said you were too young to marry – Sir Julian.'

'Correct. They did. Miles, my husband – or Hugo Dashwood, as you knew him – stepped in when your mother died, did he, and took you on?'

'Yes and no,' said Miles carefully. 'We didn't exactly see a lot of him. We never did. Not until my dad died, anyway. Or rather until my mom was ill. Then he came to see her a lot.'

'And – how do you remember him?'

'Well, he was very English, you know? A little formal. He was very generous, and real good to my gran. She thought a lot of him.'

Phaedria looked at him thoughtfully. 'Does that mean you didn't?'

'Well – yes and no. He was very clever and all that. And it was real good of him to put me through college. I appreciated that. But we didn't have – well, a lot to say to each other.'

'I'm surprised,' said Phaedria, and meant it. 'I would have thought you would.'

'Why?'

'I'm not sure. I just would have thought you'd get on.'

He smiled regretfully. 'Sorry. No. Of course, the thing I most minded about is all explained now.'

'Which was?'

'Well, I got mad because he wouldn't give me a job in one of his companies.'

'I can't imagine you getting mad.'

'I hardly ever do. But I was then.'

'Well, as you say, it's explained now.'

'Yup. I suppose it is.'

'And you studied at college? Maths . . . and you graduated summa cum laude, someone said?'

'Yup.'

'And you don't want to use that?'

'Nope. I just want to marry Candy. Buy a nice house in Malibu, maybe get a boat.'

He leant back on the cushions, smiling at her. 'I can see you all find it real hard to understand. But I find it hard to understand the way you live. Working, worrying, fighting as far as I can see. I mean Roz is a real nice person, she could be so happy, you know, and she makes herself wretched, fretting about where the next million's coming from or going.'

'No, you're wrong,' said Phaedria, adjusting with difficulty to the vision of Roz as a real nice person (hadn't Michael said something similar a hundred, a thousand years ago?) 'it has absolutely nothing to do with the next million. Or not a lot. What it's about is seeing something work and knowing it was you that made it work. It's very exciting.'

'Uh-huh.

'You and Roz aren't too fond of one another, I gather,' he said suddenly.

'Really? How do you know that?'

'Oh, I know she's jealous as hell of you. I know she thinks you're having an affair with her bloke –'

'What!' said Phaedria. 'She told you that?'

'Yeah, she did. More or less.'

'Well, she's wrong.'

'I told her she was wrong,' he said, leaning back on the sofa with an expression of some complacency on his face.

'Well, thank you,' she said, amused. 'That makes two of us. And I don't think she believed either of us. But how did you know, anyway?'

'It just didn't seem very likely.'

'Why not? I'm intrigued. When you hadn't even met me. Or him for that matter.'

'I'm not sure. You'd just had a baby, and you were in a vulnerable position, weren't you?'

'Was I?'

'Well, yes. She'd been able to do what she liked here for a couple of months. You wouldn't have been so dumb as to upset her that much. She's pretty strong stuff, after all.'

Phaedria looked at him in silence for a minute. 'Miles,' she said, 'are you quite sure you wouldn't like to get involved with the business? It seems to me you have a real feeling for company politics.'

Miles was lying on his huge bed in Claridge's, feeling lonely

862

and trying to ring Candy. He was missing her and he was missing home, and he hadn't the beginnings of an idea what he was going to do about the situation he had landed up in. He was also being assailed by a fear of such proportions, such complexity that he could see that quite soon he was going to have to talk it over with someone or go mad. In the absence of having anyone to talk to he was trying to crush it, to ignore it, to push it to the bottom of his mind, but it went on rising up, ugly and threatening. In a desperate attempt to get away from it, he tried to occupy his mind with his dilemma.

As he saw it, he had three, maybe four choices. He could sell his share to Roz. He could sell it to Phaedria. He could offer them one per cent each, which probably neither of them would accept. Or he could sell out to someone else altogether. Of all the choices, he most favoured the last, because it would involve him in the least emotional trauma, but it could be an almost impossible burden to offload. The sum of money involved – running into at least seven, possibly eight figures – would be considerable: but more relevantly perhaps, the buyer would have to be a person of quite extraordinary character, both personal and professional, hurling himself, as he would be, instantly into the eye of one of the most ferocious hurricanes in commercial history.

There was another option, of course, which was simply to go back to Candy and the beach, and leave them all to it, but that would mean sacrificing the money. Miles reflected rather wistfully on the seven or eight figures. It was an awful lot of money. Too much. Too much for one person. Of course he could do a lot of good things with it, give lots away, to people like Father Kennedy, and his grandmother, and Little Ed and Larissa and the boys in the bars, but it would still leave a lot behind. He wondered if he might just go home without it. He had an uneasy feeling Candy wouldn't be too pleased. And it would land him right back in the same old situation, with him not being able to marry her, and maybe doing awful dreary jobs like the one in the bank.

He went over his conversation with Henry Winterbourne again:

'You are a very very rich young man. You have been left a two per cent share in this company, which is worth, at a modest estimate, four billion pounds. The other beneficiaries to the company, as opposed to the personal, fortune, Mrs Emerson and Lady Morell, each hold forty-nine per cent of the shares. I need hardly spell out, I feel, the crucial role you have to play. Whether you get involved with the company or not.'

'No cash, no money, just on its own, with no strings?' Miles had asked hopefully.

'No cash,' said Henry firmly. 'If you want cash, you have to sell. Or, of course, become a salaried director of the company. Which you are perfectly entitled to do, in any case.'

'Oh, Jesus,' Miles had said, 'what a creep.'

'I beg your pardon?' Henry had said, and Miles had apologized, and said nothing, he hadn't meant anything, and had asked Henry what two per cent meant in hard cash terms, and Henry had told him. And it was all very scary.

Miles sighed. Maybe he could go and see the old lady, he liked Letitia the best. Even if she wouldn't talk about the women, as he had come to think of Roz and Phaedria, he would like to hear more about her youth and how she had practically been engaged to the Prince of Wales, almost become Queen of England. And she might be able to offer him some advice at the same time. Miles dialled Letitia's number, invited himself to dinner, dressed himself up in the new clothes he had bought the day before – an off the peg, dark grey wool suit from Gieves and Hawkes, a pale blue island cotton shirt from Harvie & Hudson, and a splendid hand embroidered red silk waistcoat from S. Fisher in the Burlington Arcade – and then, looking quite heartbreakingly and romantically handsome, carrying a huge bouquet of pink sweetheart roses, set off on foot (ensconced in his new loafers from Wildsmith's of Prince's Arcade) to win Letitia's heart further.

Phaedria sat in her white study in Hanover Terrace, trying to concentrate on the company reports, sheets of figures, financial forecasts she had had brought from the office. Whatever else happened to her now, she had to get back to work. That was a clear, crucial need. It could wait no longer. She had to get back and she had to try and win; and in that case she needed to be absolutely *au fait* with the situation in the company. It had been one hell of a day.

She went over it in her head as she began to tidy up the files: first Michael's phone call – God, why hadn't she been able to get hold of him, where was he, she had phoned four, five times, to try and apologize, to explain why she had slammed the phone down, to tell him about Roz's visit. His secretary had just kept saying he was out, and Franco had exhibited his quite outstanding capacity for saying nothing at all. Well, she could try again tomorrow.

And then there had been the hideousness of Roz and what she had done to her; it wasn't so much her words, she could have anticipated every one of them, it had been her style of delivery, the burning hatred in her eyes, the ugly rawness in her voice.

Maybe she should duck out. Offer Miles some more of the company, sell out to Roz. Why not? What possible future for her lay in that writhing, albeit gilt-edged, can of worms?

Upstairs she heard Julia yelling lustily; there was certainly nothing fragile about her these days. She would fix herself a cup of warm milk (feeding babies induced a desire for such childish pleasures), take herself up to the nursery and meditate upon the advantages and possibilities of a new future away from Morell Industries.

Holding her mug of milk she walked into the nursery; the baby had worked herself into a fury and was kicking frantically, her small face red with rage, her fists flailing indignantly at the unsympathetic air. Phaedria smiled, put down her cup and bent over, pulling back the covers, murmuring to Julia; she looked up at her mother, suddenly silent for a moment, and fixed her with a gaze of great intensity from her dark eyes. Julian's eyes. Julian's baby. His legacy to her, just as much as the money, the company, the nightmare. What of her father lay in this small, tough little creature? His brain, his charm, his capacity for survival? What would he have wished for her? What was her due as his daughter?

Things suddenly became very clear to Phaedria. Julia was the heiress to this kingdom now, as much as Roz. She might turn her back on it, walk away, on her own account, but she could not do it for Julia. That was not a decision she could or should make.

The company was her inheritance, bequeathed to her,

unknowingly, by her father; he would want it to be hers. She would never know her father, but she could know what he had done, what he had fought for and created, and through that she would learn much of him, appreciate his brilliance, his shrewdness, his toughness, his power. Phaedria could talk to her about him, show her photographs, make sure she knew and loved the people and things that he had known and loved. But the company, the heart of the company, was also the heart of Julian, a living manifestation of what he had been. And so Julia had to be part of it too.

Well, she thought, stroking the small head, playing with the small, frond-like fingers, feeling the strong, satisfying sensation of the hungry little mouth working at her breast, how did that alter the situation? Did it mean she could not, after all, walk away from it all, did it mean she had to battle on indefinitely? Probably, and it would be painful and wearisome, but at least now there seemed some sense in it all. And what of Miles' share? He had not even begun to understand the complexity of this situation even as it had stood; if she were to attempt to explain the factor of Julia in the equation, he would be still more confused. No, that was wrong, he would not be confused: Miles was not stupid: far from it. She felt for a moment the nightmare, the monster, surfacing again; she crushed it relentlessly down.

A thought suddenly roared through her brain; she sat frozen, still, turning it over. Would Miles sell his share to Julia? God, how neatly, how gloriously beautifully neatly that would resolve things. What was the sum Henry had mentioned? Eighty million. Could she raise that and buy the share on Julia's behalf? It was a great deal of money. It would mean selling many things: pictures, jewellery, houses, but she could probably do it. And then what would the legal implications of that be? As Julia's mother, it would to all practical purposes give her control. Roz would fight it to the death; Miles might not agree. But she could ask him. She could see what he thought.

She looked at her watch. It was nearly midnight. He would probably be asleep. Not the best time. She wanted his head clear when she talked to him. She would ring him in the morning. Maybe she should talk to Richard or Henry first. Richard. He would be more realistic about it, take a more pragmatic view. It might be quite impossible. It might be against the law. But she couldn't really see why. She suddenly felt excited, exhilarated, her weariness forgotten. If only she could talk to someone. She looked down at the head now lolling blissfully relaxed against her and smiled: in time, Julia could fulfil that role for her. She was not alone for ever.

'Come along, little one,' she said aloud. 'You can't go to sleep yet. I have to change your nappy. And I have some news for you. Mummy has had an idea . . .'

She was so engrossed in her thoughts and her task that it took her a long time to realize the phone was ringing. She picked up the nursery extension, a safety pin still in her mouth.'

'Yes?' she said, her voice muffled.

'Phaedria?' Michael Browning's voice came at her, disturbing her, delighting her, across the Atlantic, rough, angry, as she had never heard it. 'Phaedria, I have phoned to say three things. One is that I love you. Two is that I intend that you should marry me. And three is that you are never, ever to put the phone down on me again.'

Chapter Twenty-six

London, New York, Los Angeles, Nassau, 1985

It was Candy who voiced the nightmare: Candy who took the dark, ugly shape from the recesses of all their minds, shook it, held it up to the light, and ultimately managed to dispel it for all of them. Candy, who was the only person sufficiently detached from it all to be able to face it and to wonder that they could not.

Miles had flown into Nassau ten days after he had left, and Candy had met him, radiant with relief and delight to have him back.

'Hey,' she said, 'you look wonderful. Kind of tired and a bit old, but wonderful.'

Miles put his arm round her, looking down at her pretty, freckled little face, and moved his hand appreciatively down over her small firm backside. 'You feel wonderful,' he said.

'Thanks. I missed you.'

'I missed you too. Do I really look tired and old?'

'Yeah but –' she looked at him consideringly – 'it kind of suits you. You look grown up. I love the clothes.'

'Candy, I tell you the shops in London are just something else. You have to come and see them.'

'Well, they certainly look it. Where'd you get that jacket?'

'In Harrods. It's by this guy called Armani. I got a whole load of stuff of his.'

'What'd you get for me?'

'Oh, baby, just you wait and see what I got for you. Well, apart from this. This is the most important present –' he looked round to make sure no one was looking, then took her small hand and pressed it over his erect penis, bulging at the fly of his (mercifully baggy) linen trousers – 'this is what I really can't wait to give you.'

'Well, I think I want the other things first,' said Candy, smiling up at him. 'Come on, let's get back to the hotel. Daddy's out till tonight and Dolly has a new boyfriend, I really think she might take off with him.'

Later, lying blissfully sated beside him, her head cradled on his chest, the floor beside the bed covered with packages and bags from Harrods and Harvey Nichols and St Laurent and Chanel, spilling silk shirts and satin lingerie and belts and bags and earrings and chains, she said, 'Why did you come back so soon?'

'For this,' he said, stroking her pubic mound, smiling as she squirmed against his hand, kissing the top of her golden head. 'I couldn't stand not having you any longer.'

'And?'

'And what?'

'Well, what was the other reason? This was a pretty expensive screw.'

'Worth it, though.'

'Well, I guess you can afford it now.'

'Not really,' he said, 'I don't have any cash at all, until I sell my share. But, well, Henry Winterbourne arranged with the bank to make me a loan against the capital. So I do in a way.'

'Good.'

'So why did you come back? There must be women in London.'

'There are,' he said, 'but not like you. No, I needed to get away. It's pretty rarefied air over there. I needed time to think. I said originally I'd stay till I'd decided, but it was all really getting to me.'

'Tell me about them. Maybe I can help.'

He sighed. 'It would be nice if you could. It's a real cesspit of emotions. I mean first there's Roz, she's really nice, uptight as hell, incredibly frustrated . . .'

'Hey,' said Candy. 'I don't know that I like the sound of this. What does she look like?'

'Oh, she's pretty sexy,' he said, patting her bottom fondly. 'Not beautiful exactly, well not at all, but the most amazing figure, very very tall, she's really hot stuff.'

'Uh-huh . . .'

'Yeah, I could do a lot with her. Well anyway, then you should see her mother. She's nearly fifty, and she really is a hot pants. Knockout looking, too. She's married to this really neat old guy, he's a lord, and he has a castle . . .'

'A real castle?'

'Well, it sure as hell isn't made of cardboard. But anyway, it's Roz who has one share. And then there's Phaedria, who was married to the Creep, as we now know – Jesus, what a pantomime.'

'That's a wild name. What's she like?'

'I'm not sure. She seems real nice, but you can't tell. She's very beautiful too, she has the most incredible hair. And she has this little baby –'

'Is that the Creep's baby?'

'Yeah.'

'That's sad for her.'

'Yeah, it is. Well anyway, she lives all on her own in this great house in London, with God knows how many servants, and she has a few more scattered about the globe. And she's been having an affair, well I think she might have been, with Roz's bloke.'

'My God, Miles, this is worse than Dallas.'

'I know. And then there's Letitia. Roz's grandmother. Mother of the Creep. How she managed that I'll never know.

She is a really fun old lady. She's eighty-seven, and she is just wild. She was nearly Queen of England,' he added.

'Queen of England? What, instead of this one?'

'No, instead of her mom. She had this huge affair with that old guy who used to live here, you know, the Duke of Windsor, and she would have married him if he hadn't met Mrs Simpson.'

'Oh my God,' said Candy. 'This is really amazing. Can you imagine what the de Launays would say if they knew? So anyway, you have to choose between these two women? The sexy one and the one with the funny name?'

'Yup. It's awesome, Candy, it really is. I just can't begin to make up my mind.'

'Do you absolutely have to?'

'Well, there are options. I could not sell at all, but then we wouldn't have any of the money. I could sell to someone else, which is quite an attractive notion, because then I wouldn't have to decide. But God knows where I'd find someone with x zillion pounds who'd take this lot on.'

'Er, how many zillion is it, Miles?'

'Don't ask.'

'I have to ask.'

'About eighty million.'

'Shee-it.'

'I know. Well anyway, I could sell one per cent to one of them, and keep the other. But then I'd still have to choose, so it wouldn't help me. God, it's awful. What do you think?'

Candy was silent, contemplating what eighty million dollars could do for her. Then she said, 'I don't know, Miles, I really don't. Which of them do you think needs it more?'

'I guess Roz, in a way. She's more desperate. But the old lady, Letitia, the Queen you know, she said I should think real hard about it, because Phaedria has the little baby, and so that makes a difference. I mean maybe she has more of a right to it. The other thing is that Roz hates Phaedria so much I think she'd kill her if she did get hold of it. I really do.'

'Jesus,' said Candy. 'What a mess.'

'I know. And it's all such a mystery. I mean, why did it all have to happen at all? Why did I have to be involved?'

She turned in the bed and looked up at him.'

'Seems pretty obvious to me.'

'What do you mean?'

'Oh, Miles, I can't believe you haven't worked it out. You're not that dumb.'

He looked at her, dreading what she was going to say, longing to confront it, to get it over with.

'Maybe I am. You tell me.'

'Well, it seems absolutely clear to me.'

'What does?'

'Well, that you were Mr Dashwood's son.'

Miles was silent. Hearing it spoken, acknowledged as a possibility, made it feel just a little less dreadful, a lot more unlikely. He stared at Candy, smiling rather uncertainly.

'Oh, no. No, that is just dumb.'

'It's not dumb, Miles. Why else should he have done such a thing?'

'I don't know about that. I just know my mom wouldn't have – couldn't have – anyway, he would have said, she would have said –'

'What? When?'

'Oh, I don't know. But what I do know is, that is just absolutely impossible.'

'OK.' She shrugged. 'Have it your own way. Seems quite possible to me. Shouldn't you at least – talk to them all about it?'

'Candy, I couldn't. I just couldn't. They're upset about it enough as it is.'

'I bet they've thought of it. I bet you one of those eighty million they did. I think you should ask them.'

'Well, maybe.' He was silent, meditating on what she had just said. 'Jesus, I can't think of anything more awful. Being the Creep's son. My mom and him. Jeez, Candy, you just have to be wrong.'

'And you never thought of it? Really?'

'Well,' he said, with a rather shaky smile, 'actually, I sort of did. And then wouldn't let myself think any further.'

'I bet you they all did the same. I really think you should talk to them about it.'

'Oh well, maybe I will. When I get back.'

She looked at him. She had never seen him so strained, so

unhappy. She decided to try and change the subject a little, distract him.

'I do have one kind of an idea.'

'What's that?'

'If you went and worked for this company, you'd have some money, wouldn't you?'

'I guess so. But I don't intend to.'

'Hang on. I mean, you'd be a pretty rich guy that way too. And you could keep your shares, and then you wouldn't have to choose.'

'Candy, that is really dumb. I don't want to work for the company. It's awful in there. Believe me. Anyway, I don't want to work for any company.'

'Oh, all right.' She sighed. 'It just seemed a kind of a solution. And I'd quite like to live in London for a bit.'

'We could do that anyway, if you want to. But I am not going to go and work in that hellhole.'

'Not even for a while? I'd kind of like being shacked up with a tycoon.'

'Candy, I'm getting jacked off with this. Just shut up, will you? I'm not going to work there, OK?'

'OK.' She looked up at him, and smiled and then slithered slowly down in the bed, kissing, licking his chest, his stomach, and then with exquisite slowness and delicacy, began lapping at his penis with her tongue. She would change his mind. She always did. And this was one of the ways she did it.

Roz was riding in the park when she had the idea. She had taken to riding early in the morning recently; it cleared her head for the day, made her feel better, and in any case she loved horses: she had forgotten quite how much until she cantered along the Row the first morning, savouring the uniquely satisfying pleasure of feeling a powerful, well-schooled horse beneath her; she resolved to make the time to find a house in the country for the weekend, and take possession of the horses her father had left her. It would be lovely for Miranda, too, who was nearly old enough to ride, and was proving a tough, courageous little person (more me than her father there, Roz thought with satisfaction).

Then she sighed and her heart dropped leaden-like to the

bottom of her new riding boots. Any thought of the future led her to thoughts of Michael, and thence into depression; she had not heard from him again, and she knew she would not, that this time she had gone too far, abused their relationship, doubted his word, humiliated him publicly. She had decided with hindsight that probably he and Phaedria had been telling the literal truth; it would have been unlike him to have started what amounted to an adulterous affair without at least some kind of an early warning to her; and it would have been so crass, so insensitive to have started it with Phaedria of all people at this particular time in all their lives, that it really didn't bear too close scrutiny.

And here it was, two weeks before Christmas, and they were in the middle of this nightmare and no immediate hope of it being resolved in any way. If ever. The more she thought about it, the more she got to know Miles, the more hopeless a prospect that seemed to be. He was so transparently nice and guileless, he wasn't going to be able to bear to do the dirty, as he saw it, on either of them. What he really wanted was a small sum of money, nothing like the eighty million he was going to inherit, and to be left alone. Roz would gladly have given it to him anyway, just handed it over to put him out of his misery, but that wasn't going to solve anything for Phaedria and herself. Someone, somehow, had to break this deadlock before they all went mad: but how?

A thought suddenly came to Roz that was so petrifyingly obvious that she froze rigidly on her horse. He sensed her withdrawal, her sudden lack of empathy with him, and tossed his head, pulling at the bit. 'Sorry, old thing,' said Roz absently, reining him in, leaning down, patting his neck. 'Sorry.'

She walked him very slowly along the Row, thinking, her mind racing furiously. Suppose, just suppose, that someone else offered to buy Miles' share. An outside bidder. Someone nobody knew. Well, it was possible. Why shouldn't they? Nobody really knew about it at the moment, but someone could have got to hear. Miles would sell gladly. He couldn't wait to get back to California and shake the dust of the whole thing off his feet. And he wouldn't have to make any decision. He would be spared all the trauma and he would simply get the money. It would be marvellous for him. Roz suddenly saw, very vividly,

Miles' glorious heartbreaking smile, and smiled herself. She also found herself dwelling briefly on Miles as a man. She did find him horribly disturbing. It was his sexual self-confidence that really got to her, more than his charm or his looks, the way he so overtly put himself on the line, told her, quite frequently (with a look, a smile, a remark, a touch) that he could, should she wish it, take her, please her, delight her. And the slight regret he always managed to convey each time she turned down his tacit, delicious invitations. Probably, she thought, if she had in fact accepted them or even one of them, he would be horrified, would close up, turn away, hurry home to Candy, and in her present state with her own self-confidence at a low ebb, she was not about to put it to the test. Nevertheless, he remained there, in her subconscious and her sub-senses, a source of turbulence and odd pleasure. Keeping company with her fear . . . So: present him with an escape route, in the form of a buyer for his share of the company, and he would breathe a sigh of relief and escape. And the escape route could be so extremely anonymous, and probably very formal, a small merchant bank or consortium of people, that he would never dream of looking into it, behind it, he would simply, gratefully sell. At a very good price: Roz had no intention of depriving Miles of a cent of his due. And then, in the fullness of time, the small merchant bank or consortium would be persuaded to sell its share back – for an even better price – to its rightful owner. The person who should have had it in the first place. Who was the true heir to the company? Who could run it with more skill, more understanding, more creativity, than anyone? The daughter of the founder. Rosamund Emerson. Née Morell.

Oh, God, it was brilliant. Brilliant. But would she get away with it? Would anyone suspect? What if they did as long as it was after the sale had gone safely through? It wasn't fraudulent. Well, maybe morally, but not technically. She was going to give Miles the best possible price. The consortium or third party would genuinely exist. It would emerge out of nowhere, probably from another country, maybe Switzerland, with an eye on the potential of the company. It was an entirely natural acquisition. The board probably wouldn't oppose it. People like Freddy Branksome and Richard Brookes might even welcome it. They were very weary of the current situation.

Even if they did oppose it, they couldn't do anything. The company was a private one. It was entirely up to Miles. The difficult thing would be ensuring he didn't suspect anything. But then, he would be trying not to. He would be grateful, eager to get out of the stranglehold. So he might not look at it too hard. Phaedria wouldn't be able to do anything. They were Miles' shares. Nobody, nobody at all would be able to do anything.

There was no doubt about it, it was a stroke of genius. She knew it would work. It had to. And then, then it would all be as good as hers.

Miles flew back into London two days later. Having had to confront the awful fear, he felt he had to force the others to do the same. Candy was right, it was very unlikely, totally unlikely that none of them had already thought of it. They might even have discussed it amongst themselves, decided he would have not considered it, and that he should not be party to any of those discussions. The thought both irritated and amused him.

He phoned Letitia as soon as he had checked back into Claridge's.

'Hi, it's Miles. Could I come and talk to you?'

'Miles! How nice. I thought we'd lost you for a while. Yes, of course. I've had my lunch, I'm afraid, but I'm sure we can find you something.'

'Thanks.'

Letitia put down the phone with a sense of foreboding. He had sounded uncharacteristically purposeful. She had a horrible feeling she knew what he wanted to talk to her about.

'Mrs Morell,' he said, lounging (none too purposefully) on her sofa, his long legs thrust out in front of him, 'there's something I really think we should all look at.'

'Yes?'

'It – well, it may seem a bit – well, upsetting for you.' His blue eyes were wide, troubled. 'But I really have to talk it through.'

'Miles,' she said, smiling at him gently, 'I've learnt, over a long life, that you can't run away from being upset. It's better to confront it and get it over with.'

'Yeah, well, I wish I'd confronted this a bit sooner. And got it over with. And you're the only person who can help. At least at this stage. Are you sure you don't mind?'

'Quite sure.'

'OK. Well – that is – oh, hell, this sure is hard.'

Letitia smiled. 'Let me see if I can help you. Would it have anything to do with you and – my son?'

'Yeah. Yeah, it would.'

'You think maybe you might be – his son?'

He stared at her, very seriously at first, then his face slowly softening into relief and humour.

'You really are a great person. I thought you might have the vapours or something.'

'I don't have the vapours very easily. Besides, why should I have the vapours at the thought of you being my grandson? It's a delightful thought. I agree, with certain complications attached.'

'Yeah, well . . . Anyway, yes, I do think that. That he might be my father. I hate the idea. I can't tell you how I hate it, but – oh, I'm sorry, that sounds really gross . . .'

'Not at all. You loved both your parents. They were obviously very special people. You want to belong to them.'

'Yeah. That's exactly right. It's kind of nice of you to understand. But – well, it does seem to make some sense of it all. That's all. And I thought you might be able to help me find out how likely it was.'

'I think I can. I shall have to talk to the others, though. Is that all right?'

'Of course.'

'I have thought about it too. In the end, however logical it might seem, I decided it was unlikely. You certainly don't look like Julian. But I'm sure we can establish the truth beyond any doubt if we really put our minds to it.'

'All right. Thank you. I can't tell you how much better I feel already.'

'Good,' said Letitia, 'I think I do too. Now, you pour yourself a glass of wine, and one for me, I got some Californian chardonnay especially to make you feel at home, and I will ring Eliza. First of all, though, just tell me again when your birthday is.'

'January second, 1958.'

876

Eliza and Peveril were just finishing a very late lunch when Letitia rang. Peveril was anxious to be off, he had planned to spend the whole day with the gamekeeper stalking his deer, and Eliza had detained him that morning in bed, and then right through lunch discussing the possible colour scheme for the morning room she was redecorating; he heard her greeting her mother-in-law with great relief, knowing the call would be a long one and afford him ample time to escape. There were times, even in flagrante, when he felt it might have been better to have married someone slightly more in sympathy with his way of life, although he always tried to crush the feelings immediately as ungrateful.

'Darling, of course I'd love to come down, but I really have to ask Peveril,' she was saying. 'Just a minute, he's trying to say something.'

'You just go ahead and do whatever you want, my dear,' said Peveril, walking with what he hoped was not indecent haste from the room. 'Fine by me. Plenty to do.'

Eliza blew him a kiss and returned to Letitia.

'He says he doesn't mind. I think actually he finds me a bit of a strain, Letitia.'

'He wouldn't be the only one, darling.'

'Thank you. When do you want me to come?'

'Tomorrow if you can. I have Miles here. He's worried about something.'

'Ah,' said Eliza. 'All right, Letitia. If it means I can see something of Miles, just try and keep me away.'

She arrived the following night for dinner, looking radiant and chic in a white damask jacket and tapestry trousers, her silvery hair coiled up on top of her head.

'Eliza, you look divine,' said Letitia. 'Where on earth did you get those clothes, marooned up there in the Highlands?'

'I didn't get them in the Highlands. I'm surprised at you, Letitia, even thinking such a thing. They're from Crolla. I just popped in on the way over. I knew you'd be looking marvellous – which you are, I don't know quite what Chanel would do without your custom – and I wasn't going to be outdone. Do you like it?'

'I love it. I shall go tomorrow. Drink, darling?'

'Champagne, please. Where is Miles? I hope I haven't gone to all this trouble for nothing.'

'No, he's coming over later. I wanted to have a word with you first. Eliza – have you – that is, yes of course you have, you must have done – have you – thought that Miles might be . . .'

Her voice tailed off. Eliza looked at her in amusement, taking the glass of champagne she held out.

'Can I guess what you were going to say? That Miles is Julian's son? Yes, of course I've thought it. Straight away. It seemed such an obvious solution. But I didn't want to worry anyone in case none of you had thought it too. Yes, I've thought about it a lot.'

'And? How do you feel about it? Does it upset you? And do you think it's possible?'

'Well, I'm afraid nothing Julian did has any power to hurt or worry me any more. I think it's just ridiculous, the whole thing. But yes, I suppose it's very possible. Quite likely in fact. What about you? Does it hurt you?'

'A bit.' She looked troubled and very old suddenly. 'He's just turning into more and more of a villain before my eyes. And I loved him so much.'

'Oh, darling, don't be sad. Of course you loved him. He was worth loving. That doesn't change the fact that he was – well, difficult.'

Letitia smiled a little weakly. 'I think difficult is a serious understatement. But all right, I'll accept that for now. I just do hope it's not true. But I think we have to try and find out. Miles has been worrying about it. And I daresay Roz and Phaedria have too. And we've none of us said a word, afraid to frighten each other. Silly, really. It has to be faced.'

'Yes. Anyway, what do you want me to do?'

'Well obviously, darling, try and help me work out where Julian was in – let me see, in late March, early April, in 1957, the year before Miles was born. Nobody else can. With the possible exception of Camilla.'

'Oh, God, I'd hate to have to ask her.'

'Well, we may have to. We can get C. J. to do it.'

'Of course. Well, let's think. March. March. He went in – when – very early spring, didn't he? No, it wasn't. It was actually the autumn before. So he was definitely spending most of his time there. My birthday is in April. I know he was home for that. I can remember being so pleased that he came back. Roz was only tiny. But that's the middle of April. And he was there pretty solidly before that. Goodness, Letitia, I don't know. I don't seem to be able to help at all.'

'I feel very much afraid,' said Letitia darkly, 'we may be driven to Camilla.'

C. J. was in his study when Eliza phoned. He was happy these days, happier than he had been for a long time. He felt he was gradually re-establishing himself as a person in his own right, the sort of person he would more have wished to be; he was happy with Camilla, he was planning on moving to New York to be with her, he was gradually shedding his associations with the Morell family with a sense of great relief, as he might have done a badly fitting, unflattering suit of clothes.

'C. J. How are you, darling?'

'I'm well, thank you, Eliza. What can I do for you?'

'Well, darling, something madly intriguing, actually. It's something to do with Miles. And Camilla. Listen, C. J., have you ever wondered exactly who Miles might be? You have? I thought so. Well, now listen . . .'

'Yes? Yes, this is Lady Morell? Who? Oh, yes, of course I'll take it. Michael? Hallo, how are you? Good. Yes, of course I'm missing you. What? No, Michael, I just can't come for Christmas. I'm sorry. I'd love to, but I can't. What? Well, because I've arranged to have my father down to Marriotts, and although I could easily tell him it's still June and put him off for several months, everybody else might notice. Yes, I do want to see you, terribly, but it can't be at Christmas. Sorry? Well, what about Roz? Don't you think she might hear about it? I just can't contemplate a showdown with her now, Michael, not with everything at fever pitch. Yes, I know you're at fever pitch, but you'll just have to wait. What? Well of course you can wait. Try a cold shower or two. Anyway, what about Little Michael and Baby Sharon? They won't be too pleased to find me there, at the bottom of the tree on Christmas Eve. Nor will their mother. It's just a hopeless idea, I'm afraid. Lovely but hopeless.

Anyway, I don't want to be away from Julia, her first Christmas. No, I know she won't know anything about it, but I will. Oh, God, Michael, just stop it, will you? I'm not coming. Yes, I know I'm a hard woman. What? Oh, now that just might be possible, I suppose. Oh, God, it would be so lovely. I wonder, I just wonder if I could. What do you think? Do you think anyone would know? I suppose not. They'll all be staying up in Scotland for Hogmanay. Yes, I really, really think I could. Oh, it would be so exciting. No, I think I'll leave her behind. It'll only be two days or so, won't it? She's going off me now anyway. She's hit the bottle. I've gone down three whole sizes. Well, you may have preferred it, but that wasn't the object of the exercise. Yes, all right, I do promise. I'll book – no, on second thoughts, you'd better do it, book the flight right now. New Year's Eve. Early. Early as you can.'

C. J. had phoned Camilla hesitantly. He hated reminding her of her early days with Julian Morell; it did not upset her in the least, but it certainly served to upset him. Apart from anything else, he did not greatly care to reflect that he had been a very small boy at the time. It made him feel somehow foolish and seriously disadvantaged.

Camilla, however, was quite unmoved. 'Dare I ask you why you want to know what he was doing that year?' she said with what was for her a considerable flash of humour. 'I wonder, could it be anything to do with Miles Wilburn's birthday?'

'So you've wondered too?' said C. J.

'Well of course I have. It would require a fairly low IQ not to wonder.'

'Didn't you think I might have?' asked C. J.

'Well, I decided in the end you couldn't have,' said Camilla with her usual earnest truthfulness and lack of tact, 'or you'd have mentioned it.'

'Oh,' said C. J.

'Well anyway, what period are we talking about?'

'Early April. Late March.'

'Well, I hadn't known him long. It's hard to say. I would have to look it up.'

'Look it up?' said C. J. in astonishment. 'You mean you have diaries going that far back?'

'Of course,' said Camilla. 'I have them all filed, since I was a very small girl. You never know when a date is going to prove significant. I mean, this proves it.'

'I suppose so,' said C. J. 'Er – where are these files?'

'In the office,' said Camilla. 'I'll have a look and call you in the morning. Good night, C. J.'

'Can we really spend Christmas in London?' Candy's voice was ecstatic. 'That sounds just wonderful.'

'Sure,' said Miles. 'Just spin your father some good yarn, about staying with the Creep's mother or second cousin twice removed, and come. You'll like it.'

'Where'll we stay?'

'It's pretty nice here.'

'Is that a real smart hotel?'

'Real smart.'

'Will I get to meet the Women? Or the Queen Grandmother?'

'Possibly. Don't see why not.'

'Miles, you're the greatest.'

'Where is Mrs Emerson today?' asked Phaedria, halfway into her first full week back at work.

'She's away for a couple of days, Lady Morell. She's gone to Washington, to check out the office there, and the hotel. She'll be back on Monday.'

'Good. Is Mr Brookes in today? Find out, will you, and ask him if he can lunch with me.'

'Of course,' said Sarah Brownsmith.

'Oh, and Sarah, give me a line, would you? I want to make a call.'

'Yes, Lady Morell.'

'Hallo. Is Doctor Friedman there?'

'No, she isn't. She's away, I'm afraid. Who is it calling? Can I help?'

'I don't think so. No, thank you. This is Phaedria Morell. When might Doctor Friedman be back?'

'Not until mid January at the earliest. She's visiting her sister in Australia.'

'I see.'

'Doctor Friedman said urgent matters could be relayed to her partner, Doctor Mortimer. Would you like his number?'

'No, really, this isn't urgent. I'll call Doctor Friedman in January. Thank you.'

'C. J., is that you?'

'Yes, Camilla. How are you this morning?'

'I'm fine, C. J. Missing you, of course. Looking forward to Christmas.'

'I am as well, Camilla.'

'Now then. I have looked in my diary. If it's any help to you, I can confirm from early March right through to April we were all working flat out. Julian, Paul Baud and myself. It was a crucial time. There was no way he could possibly have popped over to California then. All right? And the last few days of March we weren't even in the States, we were in Paris, with Paul Baud, looking at the stores there.'

Ah,' said C. J. 'Now that does sound interesting. What about – the week before that?'

'No, C. J. definitely not. I did see him every single day.'

'Even the weekend?'

'Oh, yes,' said Camilla with a touch of complacency in her voice, 'certainly the weekend. We'd only just begun our relationship. Now, C. J., I have to go. I have an appointment with my analyst. See you in two weeks.'

Goodbye, darling.'

'Goodbye C. J.'

'Eliza? Letitia. Listen, we seem to have a watertight alibi for Julian. The early part of March he was very much in New York, with Camilla.'

'Ah. Is she sure?'

'Oh, yes. Apparently she has filed all her diaries from birth.'

'She would have done. Sanctimonious bitch. Well, I suppose we should be grateful.

'So all we have to worry about now is that first week in April. Which could be crucial, I suppose. After that he was with me in London,' said Eliza.'

'Yes. I do feel awfully glad about it, I have to say.'

'I think I do too.'

Phaedria leant across the table earnestly at Richard Brookes. He looked at her appreciatively.

'I need advice,' she said.

'Ah. Of a legal nature?'

'Sort of.'

'Legal nature is very precise, my dear Lady Morell. Sort ofs don't have a huge place in it.'

'I suppose not. But it isn't all that precise. It's quite difficult, really. But it struck me the other night that Julia is actually a most rightful heir. To the company and everything.'

'Ah,' he said, 'I do not think legal precedent would bear you out. But please continue.'

'The thing is that Julian didn't know about her. If he had, it would all have been very different.'

'Possibly.'

'Well anyway, morally obviously she has to have a claim.'

'Possibly.'

'And – well, I thought I might present this thought to Miles. And offer to buy his share on her behalf. So that he wouldn't be choosing between me and Roz, he would be solving the problem by letting Julia have his two per cent. I think it might appeal to him.'

'Hmm. It would clearly appeal to you.'

'Well, of course it would appeal to me,' said Phaedria irritably. 'She's my child. I want her to have her rights. But she's also Julian's. He would have wanted her to inherit the company. Or a substantial share of it. What most appeals to me is getting this deadlock shifted.'

'It wouldn't really though, would it?' Richard was looking at her thoughtfully. 'It wouldn't ease the day to day situation at all.'

'No. Not yet. But at least Miles would be off the hook.'

'Yes.' He looked at her shrewdly. 'Phaedria, could I ask you if you have ever considered the possibility that Miles might be –'

'What?' she said, and her eyes were full of panic. 'Who?'

'Oh,' he said, unable to continue in the face of her patent fear. 'Oh, nothing. Nothing at all. Well, this plan of yours is

883

certainly a possibility. Let's think about it a bit. You'd have to form a trust fund for Julia. To buy her share.'

'Yes, I'd thought of that.'

'And you'd have to raise a lot of money.'

'I've thought about that too. I can.'

'Right. It would make Roz exceedingly angry.'

'Richard, she couldn't be angrier. At least this way she'd be kind of beaten. Impotent.'

'I don't think Mrs Emerson would ever be that.'

'Well, you know what I mean.'

'I do. Well, it's an interesting idea.'

'Is it legal though?'

'Oh, perfectly. As long as Miles knew what you were doing. And he agreed to it. You might well be right, it could be a huge relief for him. He could welcome it.'

'So should I suggest it, do you think?'

'By all means if you want to. Only perhaps you should imply that while he considers it, he doesn't talk to Roz about it. There is no great point in meeting trouble halfway. No, as I say, I do think it's an interesting idea. I only see one really big stumbling block.'

'Roz?'

'No. Miles himself. I may be wrong, but I have a hunch that he may in the end decide to hang on to his legacy.'

'Richard, you are absolutely wrong. All Miles wants is to get the hell out of here and lie on the beach with Candy McCall for the rest of his life, eating her daddy's sweeties. Believe me, I know.'

'Well, I think you're screwy,' said Candy. She had arrived in London and was settling into Miles' suite at Claridge's with patent pleasure. 'Just plain screwy. Just think, you could be a real powerful big businessman, and you're throwing it all away, just like that, without even thinking about it.'

'Baby, I don't need to think about it. I hate the idea. I told you.'

'Of what? Money? Power? Success? Don't be silly, Miles, it would be great.'

'I don't want power, and we can have the money. I just want you.'

'Well,' she said, looking at him, her eyes appraising him rather coolly, 'I'm not sure that I want a man who turned down something so exciting.'

'Candy, baby, you don't know what you're saying.'

'I do, Miles. I know exactly what I'm saying. You're clever and you're smart and you've had a fantastic education and you've spent most of your life wasting yourself. I went along with it before, because there didn't seem any choice, but now there is. I think you should take this opportunity, Miles, and make something of it.'

'Candy, if that's what you think I don't know that we have a future together after all.'

Candy looked at him, trying not to show how scared she was. She changed her tactics.

'Miles, it's not just for you I want you to be a success. It's for me. I'd be so proud of you. It would be wonderful.'

'Candy, it wouldn't be wonderful. You don't know what these people are like. They're eating one another alive. It's really sad.'

'Well, I think it's really exciting.'

'Candy, it is not exciting. It's sick. I might have known the Creep would do something awful like write that will. He was a psychopath, he must have been, putting everyone through this. Honestly, Candy, I just want to get rid of the lot of them fast.'

'Won't you just think about it?'

'No.'

She played her trump card. 'Dad was really impressed by it all. He said he'd let us get married if you took up with this company.'

'What, straight away?'

'Yes.'

He looked at her. 'Candy, I can't. Not even for you. I just can't. I'm sorry. It's not for me.'

'Well,' she said, 'you obviously don't love me at all.'

'Candy, baby, I do love you.'

'You can't. Otherwise you'd at least consider doing what I ask.'

'Candy, I can't and I won't.'

'So you don't love me.'

'I do. I swear I do.'

'Prove it. Give it a try.'

He looked at her as she stood there, her eyes filled with tears, her lips quivering, he thought of the secrets, the intricacies of her body, the glorious explorations and discoveries he had made within her; and he remembered her loyalty to him, how she had helped him, given him money, comforted him, reassured him, gone to Hugo's office for him, lied to her father, stood by him when he had had absolutely nothing in the world to offer her, and he knew he could not let her down, could not leave her without at least seriously considering what she was asking him to do. He was angry, resentful, but he could see he must go along with her at least a little way. She had meant too much to him for too long; he owed her too much, she deserved, as she had said, that at least he tried.

'All right,' he said with a sigh. 'All right, I'll think about it. Seriously. Talk to them about it. For you.'

'Oh, Miles,' she said, throwing herself into his arms, kissing him, pressing herself against him. 'Thank you. Thank you. I'm sure you won't regret it.'

'Maybe not,' he said, 'but I'm afraid you might.'

Letitia was sitting alone eating her supper when she suddenly thought about the cars. She had been oddly moved by the fact that Julian had left them all to her, with the exception of the Bugatti. It had been such a gesture of faith in her, in their closeness, in his faith in her apparent immortality. They told a lot about Julian, those cars; where he had been, what he had done. He had bought them all over the world. And the collection of logbooks Henry had handed to her after the reading of the will would chronicle it all. Why hadn't she thought about that before?

Letitia's heart was beating rather fast. She got up, walked through into her dining room and unlocked the escritoire she had bought when they had moved into the house. The logbooks were all in an envelope in the top. She sat down rather abruptly and started thumbing through them. So many lovely machines, such a lot of care and attention and money lavished on them. And he had acquired them over such a long period of time. The 1910 Rolls. The Napier. The 1912 Chevrolet. The Delage. That was her own favourite. And oh, the Bugatti. She shouldn't have the logbook for that. The Bugatti was Phaedria's. Or rather Julian's again now. Letitia's eyes blurred with tears, suddenly remembering the keys placed so tenderly amongst the lilies on the coffin. She opened the tattered old book carefully. When had that been – 1957? Letitia's brain suddenly shot into overdrive. She leafed feverishly through the documents, the bills, the insurance certificates. And then her heart seemed quite to stop, and she sat staring down at the piece of paper in her hand.

She sat there for a long time, and then walked back to the drawing room and picked up the telephone.

'Eliza? It's Letitia. Listen, I have some news. Nice news, I think, really. Julian was home that week before your birthday. The first week in April. He was at the car auction at Sotheby's. He bought the Bugatti.'

'Miles,' said Letitia gently. 'Would there have been any question of your mother going to New York to visit Julian, do you think? Did she often go to New York?'

'No,' he said, 'absolutely not. My mom only went to New York once in her life and that was with my dad, oh quite a while before I was born. She was always talking about it. She used to show me the pictures they took, and the souvenirs she'd bought, over and over again. She loved it. She said she would have given anything to go again, but it was really expensive. They didn't have much money, Mrs Morell, I think you have to realize that. And anyway, he wouldn't have let her, he was real possessive. All her family were in California, except her mom in Ohio, and she and my dad used to have real arguments if she wanted to go and stay with her. He never let her. No, I'm really sure she could never have gone to New York on her own. It would have been like leaving my dad for good. If you know what I mean.'

'Well, in that case,' said Letitia, smiling at him radiantly, a great weight lifted from her own heart, 'I think you need have no fears that you are not actually your own father's son. Julian was in New York at the beginning of March and in Paris for the last few days, the year before you were born. And in April he was in England. We can confirm all that.'

'Oh wow,' said Miles. 'I hate to sound rude, but that really is the most terrific news. Thank you very much, Mrs Morell.'

'It's fairly terrific news for me too, Miles. We are no nearer solving the mystery, but it is still terrific news.'

Letitia sent for Roz. She wanted to tell her herself, to have the pleasure of sharing the news. They had never discussed it, but she knew, from certain expressions in Roz's eyes, an avoidance of entering into any discussion about Miles, that she had thought of it, been afraid.

Roz came into the house at First Street late in the evening, after supper. She was wearing a long-sleeved jersey leotard, under a tight, short jersey skirt in dark beige from Alaia. It emphasized her breasts, flattered her lean rangy body, made her legs, in black tights, look awesomely long.

'That's lovely, darling, you do look nice.'

'Thank you. It is so nice to be able to wear short skirts again.'

'You're very lucky to have those legs. You and Miles both look like race horses.'

Roz looked at her with the taut edgy expression she wore whenever she felt threatened.

'Does Miles have specially long legs? I've never noticed.'

'Pretty long. Roz – tell me something – no, first let's have a drink. What do you want?'

'Perrier. I'm on the wagon till Christmas.'

'Very commendable.'

'Not really. I thought I was getting fat.'

'Not terribly, darling. All right, help yourself. Now then –' as Roz settled opposite her, in the love seat. 'I want to talk to you about Miles.'

'What about him?' said Roz truculently.

'Well, I – and your mother, and indeed Miles himself – had all been worrying about something. I wondered if you had too?'

'I can't think of anything.' Roz swallowed. 'I mean, there's lots to worry about, but I can't really imagine the same thing bothering us all.'

'Can't you? Good. Then you've been spared a great many sleepless nights which I have not. Can I tell you about it?'

'Of course.' Roz was sitting very straight, her eyes fixed on her grandmother's face. She looked pale.

'Well you see, I thought – we all thought – that there might be an explanation for your father leaving Miles that legacy which was fairly logical. Obvious even.'

'I can't think what.'

'Can't you?'

Roz looked at her with her blank, wall-eyed expression. 'No.'

Letitia laughed. 'Sometimes you look exactly like your father. Well anyway, what we all thought was that Miles might – well, have been Julian's son.'

'Oh.' Roz tried to sound calm, disinterested, but her voice came out sounding rather shaky and weak. 'How – how odd.'

'Yes, well, it didn't seem that odd to us. Quite likely, really. At least it would have explained a lot. But obviously we had to check it out.'

'I – I suppose so.'

'Well –' the silence seemed very long. Roz was motionless, she put down her glass to conceal the fact that her hand was shaking. Letitia stood up, smiling at her. 'Well, we were all wrong. Quite wrong. Your father was in New York and Paris during the relevant period. And then at home in London. I think that's probably quite good news, don't you?'

'I suppose it would be,' said Roz, still sounding odd. 'If you'd been worrying about it. Yes. Thank you for telling me, Granny Letitia.'

There was another very long silence. Letitia went over to Roz and put her arms round her; Roz was smiling at her and crying at the same time.

'That's the thing I've been most afraid of,' she said, 'ever since I can remember, all my life.'

Chapter Twenty-seven

London, Sussex, Scotland, 1985

Miles sat and listened carefully while Roz told him of an extremely generous bid from a consortium in Zürich for his share of the company. He said he would think about it. Then he sat and listened equally carefully while Phaedria outlined her idea that a trust fund should buy his share of the company on behalf of Julia. He said he would think about that too. When he got back to Claridge's that night, Candy told him she had been to supper with Letitia who thought it was a wonderful idea for Miles to join the company, and had all kinds of interesting and exciting suggestions as to what he might do there. Miles listened carefully to Candy as well. He kept all these conversations to himself. He wanted time to think.

Both Roz and Phaedria invited him and Candy for Christmas, but they refused. They wanted to be alone, together in London. They put their discussions on ice and had a pre-honeymoon. Miles took Candy shopping, and watched her, smiling and indulgent, as she fluttered like some dizzy overexcited little bird from shop to shop, store to store, from Joseph to Brown's, St Laurent to Polo, Fortnum's to Harvey Nichols. They went to shows, to *Cats* and *Chorus Line* and *Evita* and *Another Country* (through which Candy slept and Miles sat bewitched). They ate their way round London, dressing up to dine at the Ritz, gazing at the celebrities in Langan's, picking their way through the chic, pretty dishes at L'Escargot, L'Etoile, the Caprice. Their favourite was the Ménage à Trois, serving only starters and puddings; one day they ate both lunch and supper there. And Candy liked the Great American Disaster; she said it made her feel at home.

On Christmas Eve they ate in style in the dining room at Claridge's: Miles wore his new dinner jacket, made for him at Dimi Major, and looked so wonderful that half the women in the room forgot what they had been saying to their escorts when he walked across it. He ordered pink champagne, presented Candy with a very large and vulgar diamond ring he had bought from Garrard's, officially proposed to her, and then said, 'Come along, we're going to have a Christmas to remember.' Which they did, never leaving their suite, ordering the occasional snack from room service, and exploring each other's bodies with a slow, lazy thoroughness and delight.

And all the time, the choices before him occupied Miles' mind with an increasing intensity; and on the day after Boxing Day, he left Candy in London, hired a car and drove down to Marriotts and Phaedria.

Phaedria was very pleased to see him. She had found Christmas extremely depressing, alone with Julia, who had been fretful with a cold, and Augustus who was already excitedly occupied with his new subject, one of quite outstanding obscurity, even by his standards. She was Roswitha, a tenth-century German poet and nun, and Phaedria couldn't help feeling that even her father's loyalest followers might find her hard to enthuse over.

Phaedria was also, she was rather guiltily aware, ticking off the days to New Year's Eve, when Nanny Hudson, a large cosy soul (disdainfully referred to by Mrs Hamlyn as Old Nanny Hudson), was arriving back from her holiday and she could take herself off to New York and Michael. Nobody except Nanny Hudson knew where she was going to be; her cover was a trip to the house on Eleuthera. She had explained to Nanny Hudson that it was very difficult for her to get away from the company and she needed a break, and that it was better for everyone to think she was somewhere other than where she actually was.

Nanny Hudson, who had not been born even the day before yesterday, was not entirely convinced by this explanation, but she was already very fond of Phaedria, and so delighted with the prospect of having Julia to herself for a few days she would have sworn that the moon was blue and that Phaedria had gone to have a personal look at it, in order to make sure nothing and nobody disturbed any of them.

Since his phone call to the nursery late that night when he had declared his intention of marrying her, Michael had made an assault on Phaedria's emotions so intense and relentless she could now scarcely think about anything else.

She had argued with him for nearly an hour, then, standing looking down at Julia asleep in her crib; she had told him he couldn't possibly know that he wanted to marry her, that he scarcely knew her, and that she certainly didn't know if she wanted to marry him; that by the same token he could not even know if he loved her; that he could not, simply could not abandon Roz now, when she was so fearsomely (and frighteningly) unhappy (and she was able to explain at last why she had put the phone down); she had said that she could not, and would not leave the company at the moment, that she had to see it through, get something resolved before she even began to decide what she wanted to do with her life; that she was still confused, grieving for and over Julian; that she needed time and space and peace to recover and rediscover herself. And when she had finished there was a long silence, and she wondered if she had gone too far, hurt him, rebuffed him, thrown him away, and then through the darkness and across the thousands of miles he had simply said, 'Phaedria, I am not a fool. I know I love you. And I intend to have you. I'll phone you tomorrow,' and put the phone down.

He did phone tomorrow, and the next and the next and the next; sometimes the calls were romantic (endless declarations of tenderness, of admiration, of concern); sometimes reassuring (he promised her time, he swore not to talk to Roz until they both felt she could stand it, he listened while she fretted and worried and agonized); sometimes funny and anecdotal (he had lost another raincoat, befriended a tramp and had Franco bring them both dinner down to the sidewalk outside Trump Tower); bought Little Michael and Baby Sharon working scaled-down Cadillacs from Hammacher Schlammer for Christmas and he had been driving one of them in Central Park and nearly got arrested); sometimes sexy (when he talked her into a frenzy of desire, his raw, silky voice caressing her, wanting her, making her want, long for him with a physical force); and sometimes he would hardly talk at all, merely listen to her, asking her what she was wearing, thinking, reading, who she had seen, what she had done in the office that day, what Julia had been doing, how many feeds she was on, whether she liked her new home, what colour the nursery walls were, how Nanny Hudson was working out, who she had worked for before, whether Phaedria had been riding, swimming, where she had been shopping, what she had bought; the questions were endless, exhaustive, exhausting, like the phone calls, but they were nonetheless the pivot of her day, her link with happiness and calm, and through them she felt she had grown genuinely to know him, and begun properly to love him.

She was flying out on Concorde early on New Year's Eve, and

staying with him for forty-eight hours; then to substantiate her alibi, flying down to Eleuthera for a couple of days – 'Alone,' she said firmly, 'I had my honeymoon there, I can't go there with you, not yet' – and then back to London, crises, decisions, work.

She was excited, nervous, strung up; her only comfort and consolation Grettisaga, who she had woefully missed and who had equally woefully missed her, and Spring Collection, who was being trained seriously already for the Thousand Guineas.

'She's a great horse, Lady Morell,' said Tony Price, patting the fine arched neck, running his hand down over her shoulder and down one long, strong, delicate leg. 'Sir Julian certainly knew what he was doing when he bought her.'

'Yes, he did,' said Phaedria. 'Do you think she has a chance at Newmarket?'

'It's Mr Dodsworth you should really ask, he's been training her, but I'd put a year's salary on her myself.'

'Oh, Tony, don't,' said Phaedria, laughing. 'I'd feel terribly worried. Oh, I hope she does well. It would be a kind of marvellous memorial to my husband if she did.'

'She will. Grettisaga's looking well, isn't she?'

'Yes, thank you for looking after her so beautifully.'

'It's been a pleasure. She's a nice horse. You must be thinking about a pony for little Miss Julia soon. Can't begin too young.'

Phaedria thought of Julia's heavy wobbly head, and her small neck which could not yet support it, her soft, limp little body flopping against her as she had slept in her arms after breakfast that morning, and said she thought the pony could wait a month or two.

Miles arrived at lunch time; he was driving a perfectly horrendous Ford Escort in a particularly vile shade of blue. Phaedria laughed as he got out of it.

'Like your wheels,' she said.

'A bit of real style there,' he said, laughing back at her. 'This is a nice place, Phaedria. I really like it.'

'Good. Come in and have a drink. I'd suggest you meet my father but he's locked in his room with a German nun.'

'I beg your pardon?'

'Well, she's not real. Or hasn't been for a thousand years. He's writing a book about her.'

He shook his head at her, smiling. 'You really are a wild family.'

After lunch she walked him round the grounds, showed him the stables, introduced him to Spring Collection. 'And this is the real love of my life,' she said, leading him over to Grettisaga's stall. 'Isn't she lovely?'

'She is,' he said, carefully tactful, 'I'm sure she is. I don't really know an awful lot about horses, nothing at all as a matter of fact, but she looks as if she has the right bits in the right places, a leg at each corner, that sort of thing.'

'There's a book called that,' she said, smiling at him. 'It's by someone called Thelwell. Very funny.'

'English funny or would it make me laugh?'

'Oh, dear,' she said, 'do we really not make you laugh?'

'Not often,' he said, 'but I'm learning to live with you.'

'Good.'

'Could we go for a walk? Is Julia all right?'

'She's fine. Nancy's here.'

'Who's Nancy?'

'The housekeeper.'

She spoke carelessly, casually; she had come totally to accept the fleet of people who were wherever she went to see to her, feed her, warm her, care for her. Miles looked at her shrewdly.

'You like it all, don't you?'

'Like what?'

'Being rich. The lifestyle.'

'I suppose so. I've got used to it.'

'I suppose you do. I suppose I will. I haven't yet. I feel as if I'm at a party and soon I'll have to go home.'

'But you want to go home, don't you?'

'You know what I mean.'

'Yes I do. Sorry. Anyway, what did you want to talk about?'

Her heart was thumping; had he made up his mind so quickly?

'Oh, you know, things.'

'Tell me.'

'Well, you see, I've been thinking about your suggestion

about buying my share for Julia. It's a neat idea. I like it. And you're right, probably she should have it. And it would kind of solve my problem. I wouldn't have to actually choose.'

'No. But?'

'Well, two buts. It would still mean effectively that I'd gone against Roz. That you'd got control. In a way.'

'No, Miles, it wouldn't. I've explained, there would be a trust fund, trustees, I couldn't make big decisions still about the company against Roz's wishes.'

'No, but Roz would know that come Julia's eighteenth birthday – or eighth, probably, the way you lot carry on – you and she, that is you and Julia could sweep the board. I don't feel comfortable about that.'

Phaedria looked at him sharply. 'You like Roz, don't you?'

'Yeah, I do. I really do. I think she's a bitch, but I like her. I think she's had a raw deal. Don't look at me like that, it's not your fault, I guess lots of it's her own, but it still hasn't been easy for her. Losing her dad twice over, losing the company probably, getting divorced, losing this guy of hers. He must be a real schmuck.'

'Why?' said Phaedria. She was beginning to find the conversation uncomfortable.

'Well, he never even came over when she was feeling so bad. Never tried to understand what she was going through, made allowances for her.'

'Miles,' said Phaedria carefully. 'You may be a very perceptive person, but you don't know very much about this particular situation. I don't think you should make judgements about it.'

'OK.' He shrugged, smiled at her. 'Maybe I don't. All I'm saying is she's had a tough time, and I don't want to make it tougher for her.'

'Right. So you don't want to sell to Julia?'

'Nope. Well, not yet. I might, but not yet. I want to think a little longer. I just thought I should let you know.'

'Well, thank you.'

She was angry, disappointed. She walked faster, frowning into the cold air. Miles looked at her and smiled to himself. He put out a hand on her arm. She shook it off. 'Don't.'

'I'm sorry. Can I ask you something?'

'Of course,' she said, coolly distant.

'Did you screw Roz's bloke?'

Phaedria looked at him and rage suddenly swept over her. The crudity, the insolence of the question on top of her other anger drove her beyond reason. She raised her hand and struck him hard across the face.

'How dare you!' she said. 'How dare you. It is nothing, nothing to do with you. There is absolutely no reason why I should answer that question, particularly as I've told you before, but no, I did not, I did not screw him as you put it, I wanted to, I wanted to like hell, but I didn't. I wouldn't because I cared about what it would do to Roz. All right? Satisfied? You'd better go back to London right away, Miles. I can't see that we have a great deal to say to one another.'

'Hey,' he said, easily, catching her wrist, rubbing at his face cautiously with his other hand. 'You have a real temper, don't you? I'm sorry. I didn't mean to upset you so much. I guess I shouldn't have said anything.'

'No,' said Phaedria, still breathing heavily, rage still pounding in her head. 'No, you shouldn't. Now leave me alone.' She shook her hand free, stood looking at him, flushed, her eyes blazing; he looked back at her, calm, relaxed, smiling slightly, and suddenly like a thunderbolt, shocking, unexpected, she felt a desperate lunge of desire, stood there, staring at him, fear and hunger in her eyes. He moved towards her, recognizing it, put his hands up, placed them on her shoulders; for a brief brief moment she stood there, aching, throbbing for him, her eyes held in his; then she leant forward and kissed him hard, fiercely on the mouth, and as suddenly drew back as if he had hit her.

'Shit!' she said, 'shit. Leave me alone.'

She started to run then, through the growing dark, down the hill, back to the safety of the grounds, the house. She ran upstairs to her bedroom, locked the door, lay on the bed, crying. She felt shocked, ashamed, horrified at herself; what was the matter with her, was she some kind of whore, a slut as Roz had said, that she could have lain down on the hard ground and let one man take her there and then, when she was supposedly so much in love with another? What had it been about that situation that had been so powerful, she wondered, what had made her feel that way? Was it just her own sexuality surfacing after so long, or was it that Miles with his rotten,

896

powerful, arrogant beauty had been too much for her? Partly perhaps, but there was something else, something gnawing away in her subconscious, some memory long buried, newly awoken.

Suddenly she knew what it was. It was the juxtaposition of anger and sex. And there had been a time when it had happened before. Here, in the country lane near Marriotts, in the middle of the night, when she had run away in the Bugatti, and Julian had taken her, crudely, gloriously, wonderfully on the back seat of the car.

And there had been something about Miles in that moment on the downs, as he stood there looking at her, that had exactly brought it all back.

Miles, being Miles, put matters right fairly swiftly. He came up to her room, knocked on the door, said he had some tea for her, and he really really wanted to talk to her; reluctantly, shame-faced, she opened the door and he came in and sat on the bed, and said he was really sorry, he should never have asked the question, it was he who was the schmuck, not Michael, and the best thing he could do was go back to California as soon as a plane could carry him, that maybe he should let Julia buy his shares, just to get matters settled, and that what was a kiss between friends, which he hoped he and Phaedria were, she just shouldn't worry about anything, she worried too much, and she'd been through a tough time, she was overwrought and that made people behave very strangely. He said Candy did extremely strange things when she was overwrought, and then could hardly remember them afterwards. He could never remember them either, he said tactfully if illogically, and why didn't they have a drink and then he would be on his way.

He meant it all too, he was not play-acting, he was genuinely concerned for Phaedria and sorry he had hurt her, and he gave no more real thought to the kiss than if she had shaken him by the hand. His days on the beach and in the bedrooms of the hotels of Nassau had taught him to set a low value on sexual currency; it was good, it could be very good, it was fun, it made a relationship better, a day brighter, but it was not of any lasting importance or significance. What moved him about Candy was not really her eager, responsive body, but her loyal, brave little heart. He would have been prepared, as a last resort, to share the first, but not, never the second.

And so they had sat, he and Phaedria, by the Aga in the kitchen at Marriotts, and drank a bottle of champagne, and he had told her that Candy had been keen for him to join the company, work for it, and what did Phaedria think about that? Phaedria said she thought it was a terrible idea, that he would loathe it, and he had said yes, he thought he probably would too, but he had promised Candy to give it a try, or at least to see what everybody thought about it.

'Well,' she said, relaxed by the champagne and their sudden closeness, leaning forward, kissing him in an entirely friendly manner on the cheek, 'I'll think about it, but I don't think you should do it. When I get back from New York next week and I'm back in the office, we can have lunch if you're still here, and discuss it properly.'

She spoke without thinking, and then suddenly realized what she had said, that she had told him she was going to New York, and looked at him wide-eyed in horror; he saw it all, grasped the implication of what she had said, realized what it must mean to her that he knew.

'It's all right,' he said, smiling at her, reaching out, patting her hand, almost fatherly, 'I won't say anything. I swear it.'

She looked at him and half smiled back, pale, frightened, as amazed by his swift perception as she was distraught at what she had said.

'Come along,' he said, refilling her glass, 'you have to trust me. You can. Now forget it. I won't tell. And I'd love to have lunch with you in January. OK? Now I must go. Candy will be wondering what's happened to me.'

'Of course,' she said, struggling to relax, to smile, 'I'll come and see you off. And thank you, Miles. For everything.'

'That's OK.'

On the front steps of Marriotts she kissed him again on the cheek.

'Give my love to Candy, Miles. Happy New Year. And – sorry about this afternoon.'

'No, it was my fault. Just forget it. Happy New Year, Phaedria.'

He drove up to London, turning the afternoon over and over

in his mind, thinking about her. She was a far more complex person than she appeared. Sexy too. He hadn't realized that at first. She didn't project sex like Roz did. She'd seemed rather cool, distant, despite her beauty. Well, she'd been through enough in the past year to turn anybody frigid.

And what, he wondered, trying vainly to urge the Ford Escort into a speed above sixty-nine, was she going to be doing in New York? And with whom? As if he didn't know.

Phaedria went inside and up to the nursery where Julia was wailing indignantly and took her down to the kitchen to feed her, trying to calm herself. What on earth was the matter with her? First her appalling behaviour on the downs, and then letting it slip about New York. God, she hoped Miles would keep his word. If he told Roz now, everything, all her self-control and self-denial (God, she thought, I sound like a nun) would have been for nothing. Should she have spelt everything out further, made him understand how important it was Roz didn't know? Maybe she should phone him in London. No, probably best not. That would simply make seriously heavy weather of the thing. He had promised and she had to trust him. And if he was going to tell, then her going on and on about it would simply make things worse. God, he was sharp. Extraordinary that under that lazy, laid-back charm should lie such piercing shrewdness. Maybe Richard was right, maybe in the long run he would decide to stay, discover he had a taste for the real world. She was sure he would be extremely successful if he did. She wondered for the hundredth, the thousandth time what his parents must really have been like.

Phaedria smiled, reliving for the hundredth time the relief, the happiness she had felt when Letitia had talked to her about Miles and Julian, dispelling the nightmare, once and for all. She had not realized, and she told Letitia she had not realized, how fearful she had been. She had even told Michael about it when he phoned that night: about the fear and the fact that it was groundless. 'Jesus, honeybunch,' he said, 'I cannot believe, I really cannot believe, that you have only got around to telling me all this.'

And why, she said, had he really then suspected it all along? And he had said yes, of course he had, anyone with half a mind would have suspected it, but since she had never said anything about it before, he had assumed it had been thought of and cleared up in the very beginning. 'Oh,' said Phaedria, sounding and feeling very small.

She managed, by the time she went to bed, to convince herself that Miles would keep quiet about New York. She couldn't do anything else really, anyway, she was entirely at his mercy; but she kept envisaging his honest, wide blue eyes, his voice, concerned for her as he swore not to tell, and she felt she really did not need to worry. She put him firmly out of her head and turned her mind to the two days ahead. Two days that would, she felt sure, set the pattern of her life, one way or another, for years ahead.

She went to sleep thinking about Michael. But she dreamed about Miles.

'Candy thinks I should come and work for the company,' said Miles to Roz, 'hang on to my share. What do you think?'

'God,' said Roz, 'what an idea. I don't know, I wouldn't have thought you'd like it.'

They were sitting by a roaring fire in the Great Hall of Garrylaig Castle, two days later; Miles had phoned her to see if he could come up a day or two early for the promised Hogmanay, as Candy had had to go back home early. Dolly had done a bunk with her new toyboy and Mason was distraught.

'That's what Phaedria said,' he said.

'Phaedria? When did you see her?'

'Day before yesterday. I wanted to talk to her about something.'

Roz looked at him sharply. Was he deliberately trying to wind her up? But his eyes were smiling, his face open, as friendly as ever.

'What?'

'Oh, a proposition she put to me.'

'I suppose you're not going to tell me?'

'That's right. It's confidential.'

'Have you – have you thought any more about the outside offer?'

'Yes, I have.'

'And?'

'And I kind of like it. It would let me off the hook. But the one thing I can't understand is how it would be any good for you.'

'Well, it wouldn't,' said Roz coolly. 'That's surely not the idea anyway. It wasn't designed to be good for me. But it would at least break the stranglehold with Phaedria. And it's only two per cent after all. Not a very powerful stake.'

'Could grow though.'

'How?'

'Oh, they might work on one of you. Buy some more. Inveigle you on to their side.'

'Not me. Her possibly.'

'But Roz, you'd still be at loggerheads with her. Still couldn't resolve anything.'

'Of course we could. There'd still be a casting vote. Every time.'

'I suppose so.'

'And I think she'd weary of it anyway. She only wants to get control now because of me. She has no real interest in it.'

'What about Julia?'

'What about her?'

'Don't you think she might want some of it for her?'

'No. Why, has she said anything to you about it?'

'No.'

Roz, looking at him sharply, trying to read his face, saw nothing in it at all; it was smooth, devoid of emotion, his eyes totally blank. It unnerved her slightly, that look; it was so unlike Miles. It stirred unwelcome emotions, odd, placeless memories. She struggled to disentangle them, but couldn't; Miles was talking again.

'Tell me why you think me working for the company would be such a bad idea?'

Roz thought fast. Maybe it wasn't an entirely bad idea. He was bound to tire of it fairly soon. In the meantime, she felt confident, she could draw him slowly, imperceptibly further towards her side. It would also be quite amusing. She would enjoy seeing Phaedria trounced slowly and agonizingly, rather than in one swift, straight move. She could actually have enormous fun with the situation: a real live cat and mouse game. Besides she enjoyed Miles' company enormously. The sexual attraction she felt towards him apart, he relaxed her, made her laugh, forget Michael, forget everything. It would be wonderful to have him around all the time. She had no intention of trying to seduce him sexually, it would be undignified, it would be politically inept, and besides there was Candy. She had no stomach just now for any kind of sexual drama. But the fact remained that he charged everything up in a very agreeable way, made her feel good, alive, aware of herself. She enjoyed his company, in the fullest possible sense; it would be the greatest fun to have him around the office.

'Why does Candy like the idea so much?' she asked, playing for time, time to think about it, to plan her answer more skilfully.

'Well, I guess she likes the idea of being married to a tycoon, as she calls it. And then her dad says if I'm working, you know, for you, then we could get married straight away. She'd really like that.'

'Wouldn't you?'

'Yeah, yeah, I would. I want to get married to her really badly. But being married to her in London, working, wasn't really what I had in mind.'

She looked at him shrewdly. 'It would depend, maybe, on what you did?'

'Yeah. Candy was talking to old Mrs Morell about it. She had some really wild ideas.'

'Like what?' said Roz, slightly irritably. It was too bad of Letitia to think she could still interfere in the running of the company.

'Well for instance, she thought I would like being involved in the stores. And maybe I would. I could just about take that, I guess. I like clothes and nice things.'

'Yes,' said Roz, looking at him as he lounged in front of the fire, his long long legs encased in Levis, worn with brown knee-high leather boots, a dark green cashmere polo from Ralph Lauren, a soft brown leather jacket. 'You've learnt your way round the London shops pretty fast, I must say.'

'Yeah, well it isn't difficult.'

'What other ideas did Letitia have?'

'Well, she thought I might like working with the design guy. What's his name, David Somebody?'

'Ah,' said Roz, 'David Sassoon.'

'Yeah, that's it. I did art at high school. I liked it.'

'Yes, but with the greatest respect, Miles, you can't just walk into a very high-powered design set-up and think you can start making waves on the strength of a few school art lessons. It's a very sophisticated business these days; you'd have to go to art school, learn what you were doing.'

'OK, OK,' he said, smiling lazily at her. 'No need to get all uptight. It was only an idea anyway. Nobody's actually gone out and bought me a desk. I haven't even thought it all through yet.'

'Sorry.' She smiled at him with an effort. 'It's just that it's a very complex business. I get upset when people imply it's simple.'

'You get upset altogether too easily,' he said. 'I keep telling you.'

'Yes, well, I don't have that much to be happy about at the moment,' she said.

'Oh, I don't know. You have a few pluses in your life.'

'Like?'

'Well, like you're not starving, are you? Not pushed for the odd buck?'

'No. No, of course not. But —'

'But money isn't everything. Is that what you were going to say?'

'Yes. Yes, I was.'

'It isn't everything,' he said with a sigh, 'but it sure is a lot. You ask a few people who don't have any, see what they say.'

'Yes, I know,' she said, 'and of course I'm very lucky in that way, we all are, but it doesn't, it really doesn't, buy happiness, contentment, love; it doesn't ease pain.'

And to her horror she felt her eyes fill with tears.

'Come on,' he said, 'that's good. Cry. Cry and cry. Yell if you want. Let it out.'

'I can't,' she said, smiling at him shakily, 'not here. Everyone would hear.'

'OK. We'll go for a walk. Come on.' He put out his hand, pulled her up. 'Get your coat.'

'Oh, this is ridiculous,' she said, 'going for a walk just so I can let out a primeval scream or two.'

'It isn't ridiculous at all. You need it. You don't have to scream anyway. You can just talk it out if you want to.'

'Oh, all right. Let's go for a walk anyway. The dogs would like it.'

They fetched coats, put on boots, and Peveril's three labradors, who had been prancing excitedly round the Great Hall ever since they had first heard the magic word, followed them ecstatically down into the woods.

'Now I feel silly,' said Roz, brushing aside a small branch, 'I can't cry now, you're watching me.'

'OK. You don't have to cry. You don't even have to talk. I keep telling you, I just want to help. This was the only way I could see just then.'

'You are a nice person, Miles,' she said looking at him, 'you really are. Why are you so nice?'

He shrugged. 'Don't know. My mom and dad were pretty nice people. I guess that helps. My granny is real nice. I've had some very nice girlfriends. Plenty of people to set me a good example.'

Roz looked at him. 'I know Granny Letitia talked to you about – about the possibility that my father was yours. I was worried about that, too. I never told you and I've never managed to talk to you about it since, but I was awfully glad that he wasn't. That it wasn't possible.'

'Me too. For lots of reasons.'

'Yes.'

He looked at her and grinned. 'Wild, huh? Us being related. Brother and sister.'

'Yes, well,' said Roz shortly, 'we're not.'

'No.'

He was suddenly very quiet, walking through the leaves, kicking them almost savagely.

'What is it, Miles?'

'Oh – oh, nothing.'

'Now *you're* not letting things out. Come on, tell me. If you want to.'

He turned to her, and she saw his blue eyes were full of pain, that there were tears in them. She stepped towards him.

'Miles, what is it? Please tell me.'

'Oh, well, I was just remembering, you know, it was the last time I ever saw her; she was in the hospital dying, and I was only small, thirteen years old, and I remember thinking I couldn't bear it, and I lay there, on her bed in the hospital in her arms, and I just wanted to stay with her, to hold her hand and go with her wherever she was going, and I knew I couldn't, and I was so unhappy and kind of scared. In the end she went to sleep and they came and told me I should leave, and I had to climb off the bed very gently, very carefully, and go without waking her, and that was the moment when she died for me. Actually she died the next day,' he said, brushing the tears from his face, 'but I never saw her again.'

He sat down abruptly on the wet ground; Roz sat beside him. She put her arm round his shoulder, took one of his hands, rested her head against him.

'I know it's trite to say it,' she said, 'but I think I do know how you feel. And I'm so sorry. But at least you said goodbye to your mother. You were able to say everything you wanted to. That must be a comfort, I should think.'

'Yes,' he said, 'yes, it is. They were happy days in a way, when she was dying. Can you imagine that?'

'Yes,' said Roz, thinking of the nightmare three days of her father's death as he lay in intensive care, an obscene mesh of wires and tubes in and around him, when she had stood and looked at him from outside the room, refusing to go in because Phaedria had been there sitting beside him. 'Yes, I think I can.'

'Well,' he said, 'it's a long time ago. Mostly I don't mind any more. Obviously.'

'Well, I'm very sorry if I made you unhappy. I wouldn't have done that for anything.'

He turned and looked at her, took one of her hands and kissed it, then leant forward and kissed her mouth, tenderly, gently, lovingly.

'You're a nice lady,' he said. 'You didn't. And I like you very much. Very very much.'

Chapter Twenty-eight

Phaedria spent much of the flight to New York being sick. She reflected miserably, looking at her ashen, haggard face in the mirror in the plane lavatory, that until she had got mixed up with the Morell family she had never been sick in her life and for the past year she seemed to have been throwing up almost constantly. It did not seem quite the sort of thing normally associated with life with the rich and famous; she wondered, managing a shaky smile at herself, where she had gone wrong.

She also felt bereft without Julia, without her constant, reassuring, demanding company. She didn't exactly feel worried about her, Nanny Hunter was quite wonderful and they were staying at Marriotts with Mrs Mildred to keep an eye on things as well, and the excellent GP down there had promised to look in every day just to make sure the baby was perfectly well, but she was quite simply missing her horribly: she felt oddly distracted, some piece of her still fixed firmly behind. Well, it was only for four days. Four days: and two of them with Michael. Phaedria felt interestingly nervous at the notion. She felt she was being presented to him, or at least presenting herself, for examination, rather like an interesting species under the microscope. It was the first time they would spend any time together by arrangement, from choice, and it felt oddly awkward, embarrassing even.

On the other hand, it was a glorious prospect. She surveyed the time, uninterrupted, unthreatened, time to talk, to do things, to make discoveries about one another, and smiled with pure pleasure. Then she considered that the time was likely, indeed certain, to involve a great deal of sex, and she felt sick again. It was not the prospect of the sex itself that was provoking the nausea, but sheer fright at the thought of actually, finally, having to go to bed with Michael. She wanted to, she longed for it, had been longing for it for what seemed like ever, but there was something oddly calculating about the circumstances in which it had to happen. 'Here you are,' Fate seemed to be saying to them both, firmly, sternly even, 'together at last. Perform.' This was, as the saying went, no rehearsal, and she was terribly afraid she was going to fluff her lines.

Her fear was partly, largely even, she knew (and recognizing this knowledge sent her lurching into the lavatory yet again) because Michael had had this long, long affair with Roz. And then Phaedria was not confident about herself and her own sexuality at all; she had only ever been to bed with Julian, and he had been (she supposed) very skilful and talented. But she had always been aware that her own input had been very limited, indeed Julian had tended to discourage anything but a fairly passive role from her in bed (and would have liked the same kind of behaviour elsewhere, she thought with a pang that was half amusement, half regret). And much of the time, she had not felt that she was very responsive to him even: there had been occasions when their lovemaking had been wonderful, exquisite even – the night in the car, the last night before Julian's heart attack, on their honeymoon after she had recovered from her sunburn – but the very fact she could tick them off on her fingers worried her even; maybe she was frigid. Sex certainly hadn't been up to now a highly motivating force in her life; she often worried also that since Julian's death she really had not felt any serious frustration at all. Michael had stirred her senses, made her think about sex a great deal, but then, she felt, to a degree that was the emotional excitement of their relationship rather than her own physical needs. At least, she thought, she had felt something very strong for Miles that day; at least something good had come out of it.

Roz was clearly very sexually motivated, and very sexy, everyone said so, and that just made everything worse, for she would be there, inevitably, a strong, fearsome presence haunting the bed; Phaedria, with yet another pang of terror and misery, wondered just how she was going to handle any of it. Well, there was no escape now. Short of staying on the plane and going back to London, or telling Michael she had changed her mind, she had to go through with it.

She suddenly heard the beep going that meant they were beginning the descent. She washed her face for what seemed like the hundredth time that morning, cleaned her teeth, brushed her hair, and walked as steadily as she could back to her seat, and on to centre stage.

'You look terrible,' said Michael, holding her at arm's length away from him. 'I cannot believe how terrible you look.'

He had been standing waiting for her by customs; her heart tipped over at the sight of him. She was struck forcibly, not for the first time, at the way he projected sexual power. He had an immense suppressed energy; he moved slowly, but as if he was waiting for something, as if he was about to take off at great speed. He had obviously made a great effort to look impressive for her; he had on a grey coat she had not seen before with a black velvet collar; his hair was neatly brushed, he was very freshly shaved, his tie was straight, his shirt uncrumpled. His dark eyes, exploring hers, exploring her, were tentative, tender; his mouth oddly soft and half smiling. He looked, she thought, almost cheerful.

'Thanks,' she said. 'You, on the other hand, look very nice. Did anyone tell you your face looks as if you had slept in it?'

'No, I don't think so. But if it's your phrase I like it. What have you been doing, for God's sake?'

'Throwing up,' said Phaedria slightly sheepishly.

'Dear God,' he said, 'if you are to continue to vomit every time we come close to one another, I'm not sure there is a great deal of future in this relationship. Come on, darling, Franco is outside with the car. Should I get some strong paper bags in for you?'

'No,' she said, smiling at him, thinking how, as always, he carried happiness for her in his wake. 'No, I'm all right now.'

'Good.'

The mammoth black stretch waited by the kerb; Franco was ignoring, with an earnest insolence, the harassment of a traffic cop. 'Good heavens,' said Phaedria, surveying the car's length, its tinted windows, its waving aerials, 'you've brought the apartment with you.'

'Yeah, there's a double bed and a Jacuzzi inside. Get in, darling, or we'll all be arrested.'

She got in. 'This is quite a car,' she said.

'It gets me about.'

'I never understand why these things have two aerials.'

'One's for the TV. Keeps me awake while I'm driving. Franco, we'll just go home for now.'

'Sure thing, Mr Browning.'

They pulled away from the airport; she sat awkwardly, slightly apart from him, on the back seat, silent, looking out of the window. He looked at her, and his lips twitched.

'Are you going to tell me what's the matter, or shall I tell you?'

She looked at him startled. 'Nothing's the matter.'

'Of course there is. Otherwise you wouldn't be sitting over there like a frightened rabbit.'

She smiled sheepishly. 'Well, I – well, it's –'

He smiled at her. 'OK. Let me tell you. You're scared. Here we are, two people hardly knowing one another, and the Man Upstairs has shacked us up together for two whole days and told us to get on with it. And in among all the other things we have to get on with is a whole load of screwing. And you know I've been to bed a great many times with Roz and I know you've been to bed a great many times with her father, and neither of us knows quite how we are going to handle it. Well, let me tell you, baby, I'm shit scared too.'

'Oh, Michael,' said Phaedria, crawling thankfully across the seat and into his arms, 'how is it you always make everything absolutely all right?'

They went to bed as soon as they got back to the duplex. Michael said firmly, removing her coat, taking her hand, leading her up the stairs, that it was really the only thing to do, to get it over and done with. 'We will deflower one another,' he said, very seriously, 'and then we can start to enjoy ourselves.'

'Good God,' said Phaedria, standing still, looking round the black and white bedroom, its massive circular bed with the battery of switches and lights set into the head, its arced video screen, the mirrored ceiling, the jungle of plants and brilliant tropical flowers all along one wall, the aquarium of dazzling sea fish built in all along another, 'this is no place for a virgin.'

'Don't you like it?' he said, and he looked so anxious, so near to hurt, so desperate that it should please her, that all her nervousness left her and she sat down on the bed, kicking off her shoes, smiling up at him.

'I love it,' she said, 'and I think I'm going to love you.'

Michael took off his jacket, his tie, his own shoes, threw them on the floor, lay down on the bed, and pulled her up beside him. He took her in his arms and said, 'Now let's just quit worrying. Let's just go with it.'

There was a bad moment: after he had kissed her for so long and with such delicious slowness she felt as if she would scream if she couldn't have more of him; after he had removed her clothes and his, and lain for a long time, just looking at her; after he had stroked her and smoothed her and played with her pubic hair and kissed and teased and sucked at her nipples; after she had, relieved at her own hunger, climbed on to him, lain there, rising and falling slowly on to him, feeling his penis silky hard against her clitoris, feeling the fire mount, heat, roar; after he had turned her suddenly, looked into her eyes, said her name over and over again; after he had moved down, kissing, teasing, caressing her with his tongue and she had lain, her eyes closed, thrusting herself at him, rhythmically, gently; after she had felt her whole body turned liquid, white hot, and he moved up again and slowly, tenderly sank into her; then, suddenly then, a face swam into her consciousness, a pain-filled, frightened, dying face, and she tensed, tightened, froze. He drew away from her then at once, looked down at her, said, 'Look at me, Phaedria, don't think, don't think, just know that I love you.'

And she opened her eyes again, looked into his, different, eyes, loving, concerned, patient eyes, and the moment was gone and she smiled and threw back her head; arched her body, drew him in, in, all the great longing urgency of him, and he groaned, cried out suddenly and came, clutching at her, and she was left, still suspended, alone, empty, and yet happy, oddly triumphant.

'Oh, God,' he said after a moment, and there was a sob in his voice, 'oh, God, I would have given the world for that not to have happened.'

And no, she said, no don't mind, don't, it doesn't matter, it more than doesn't matter, it was good, it was the right thing, I needed to wait, please don't be sad.

'Very well,' he said, moving from her, lying on his elbow, looking at her with a wealth of love, 'you shall wait. But not for long. I promise you not for long.'

'Now,' he said, after they had breakfasted off brioches and strawberries and orange juice laced with champagne, and coffee he had made himself with enormous care and exactness on his espresso machine, 'now I think we should go out. I want to take you for a walk in the park, and then I want to take you for lunch at Le Cirque and then I want to bring you back here and make love to you again, and then I want to take you shopping and then I want to take you to tea at the Plaza and then I want to make love to you again, and then I have tickets for *My One and Only*, and then I thought we could have supper at Un Deux Trois and then we can come home and make love again, and we can see the New Year in in an absolutely outstanding, shattering, earth-moving, mind-blowing way. How does that grab you, as they used to say? If you trust me to deliver the last,' he added slightly soberly.

'I trust you utterly and it grabs me beautifully,' said Phaedria, leaning forward, kissing him tenderly, 'the only thing is it's an awful lot of eating. I shall get fat.'

'No, you won't, as long as we keep screwing. Do you know how many calories a good screw uses up?'

'No, I don't think I do.'

'Three hundred. At a modest estimate.'

'Three hundred calories isn't really very much food.'

'Then,' he said, lifting his hand, stroking her cheek with infinite gentleness, 'there will have to be still more screwing.'

'I have a New Year present for you,' said Michael.

They were sitting in the Un Deux Trois, encased in a warm, bright pleasure that was almost tangible, smiling indulgently and detachedly at the increasingly frenetic revelry around them; Michael has been drawing hearts on the paper tablecloth with the coloured crayons provided by the thoughtful management, and writing 'I love you' in ever larger and more florid letters on every spare inch of it.

Phaedria looked at him, and felt a moving and stirring in her heart that she knew as more than tenderness, more than sex, more than love itself; that was a warm, melting, joyous longing to take him to her, to be with him, of him, always and for ever, to become part of him and to have him part of her.

'I love you,' she said, and it was the first time she had said it, and there were tears in her eyes, 'I love everything about you.'

'Now listen,' he said, 'you didn't get your present yet. It might put you right off.'

'No,' she said, very serious, 'nothing in this world could put me right off you.'

There was a catch in her voice; he looked at her startled, saw the tears, felt his own heart lurch.

'Hey,' he said, 'don't start crying. You'll be throwing up on me next.' But in spite of the lightness in his voice, he was emotionally shaken too; his own eyes felt suddenly burning and moist.

'This is ridiculous,' he said, smiling at her slightly shakily, 'we are supposed to be enjoying ourselves. Do you want me to shred up this cloth to dry your tears?'

'No,' she said, laughing suddenly, taking his hand, kissing it, 'don't, please don't. I want to keep this cloth for ever and ever, to remind me of when I was perfectly happy.'

'I intend to see you stay perfectly happy,' he said.

'No, you can't, even you can't do that,' said Phaedria, serious again. 'You can't stay up there, for ever, balancing on the tip of the world. You have to come down, take on real life, let other people in.'

'That's dumb. That doesn't mean you can't be perfectly happy. I love other people. I'm happy to share you with them.'

'Oh, all right, we'll stay perfectly happy. But just now I am extra perfectly happy. How's that?'

'That's OK. Now can I give you your present? Maybe I should get a spare tablecloth or something just in case it makes you cry again.'

'You can, and I won't need a tablecloth. Please give it to me.'

'All right. But now I come to think about it, maybe we should have some more champagne first.'

'Goodness. It must be quite a present.'

'It has, I hope,' he said, with his oddly gloomy smile, 'a certain style to it.'

He ordered another bottle of Bollinger; poured some out, raised his glass to her. 'Happy New Year, honeybunch.'

'Happy New Year, Michael.'

'OK. Here we go.'

He opened the briefcase he had under the table, pulled out a large envelope, handed it to her. She looked at him, smiled doubtfully, opened it slowly. A big glossy folder was inside it.

'Michael, what is this?'

'Look at it. You can read, for Christ's sake.'

She looked. 'Lederer and Lederer' it said in embossed letters on the cover 'Real Estate Agents. Madison Avenue, New York'.

'Michael,' said Phaedria, looking at him, 'Michael, what on earth have you been doing?'

'Buying you something to play with. Go on, look inside.'

She opened the folder slowly. A photograph fell out. A low, white house, two storeys high, with a veranda running its length. Another photograph: paddocks, with horses; another: a stableyard.

'Michael, what is this? Where is this? No, I can't read, I forgot to tell you.'

'It's a house. You will have heard of houses, I imagine. This particular example is for you. It's in Connecticut. Horsy country, or so I'm told. The horses are an optional extra.'

'And you've actually bought this for me?'

'Well, I didn't have anyone else in mind.'

'Michael, this is just amazing. I just don't know what to say.'

'You could say you like it.'

'I like it. I love it. I adore it. But why did you do it?'

'That's a pretty dumb question, I'd say. I bought it for you because I love you. Because I thought you'd be pleased. Because I know you like horses. I think they're pretty scary myself, but maybe you can convert me. Because I reckoned if I was to keep you happy over here you'd need a few of them around. I don't have too much room for stables in the apartment. Because – oh, well, I suppose because I could just see you there. Because I wanted you to have it. And I thought maybe you might invite me down occasionally as your house guest.'

'I might. Are you really scared of horses?'

'Shit scared.'

'I didn't think you were scared of anything.'

'Honey, you just got yourself laid by the biggest coward in the US of A.'

'I don't believe it.'

'It's true.'

'What else are you scared of?'

'Oh, all kinds of things. Spiders.'

'Spiders!'

'Yup. The dentist. Getting sick. Right now I have a new one.'

'What's that?'

'Losing you.'

'Oh,' said Phaedria, looking at him, a whole loving heart in her dark eyes, 'you don't have to be scared of that. Not in the very least.'

'I'll try to believe you.'

'Oh, God,' she said, returning to the brochure, thumbing through the particulars, gazing at the pictures, 'this is just so beautiful. I love it, I love it. But, oh, Michael, this is too much of a present. It's spoiling me.'

'I am planning on spoiling you,' he said, 'a lot. Every day for the rest of our lives, if I can manage it.'

'Well, you've certainly made a good start. It is just the most lovely place, and the most wonderful thing is it's so exactly what I would have chosen myself. It's quite quite different from Marriotts and yet it has the same kind of feel. I don't know how to thank you.'

'I'll think of a way. When did Julian buy Marriotts?'

'Oh, years and years ago. When he was married to Eliza.'

'And how many gee-gees do you have there?'

'About a dozen altogether. Two of my own. One, my own special favourite, she's called Grettisaga, is in foal.'

'She is? When's it due?'

'Oh, in the spring.'

'Does she have to go to hospital to have it?'

'No, I thought a home birth would be better.'

'And why do you love this pregnant lady so much?'

'I'm not sure. She's beautiful. She's powerful. She's seen me safely through a few scrapes. I just love her.'

'Well, maybe you can find me a very very ploddy old creature and try and convert me.'

'I'll try.'

'I tried to learn once before. Carol thought I might make a good accessory for her behind the hounds. It was terrible. I just fell off over and over again. In the end, I decided I was over twenty-one and I didn't have to carry on with it. She was terribly cross. I liked the clothes, though,' he added, brightening up. 'I thought they were terrific.'

'There's a tailor's in London,' she said, 'called Hunstman's, where they have a wooden horse to sit on, so you can make sure your breeches fit properly.'

'Really? Would you take me? Maybe I could buy their horse, and not worry about having to get along with a real one.'

'I don't think they'd sell it to you.'

'Oh, nonsense. Everything has its price.'

'Even you?'

'Even me.'

'And what exactly is your price, Mr Browning?'

'To you, Lady Morell, a special knockdown offer. A big double bed and you sprawled across it with absolutely nothing on at all, and I'm yours for life on easy terms.'

'All right,' she said, standing up, holding out her hand. 'Come on, let's go. I want to take possession right away.'

'Please let me come to the Bahamas with you,' he said.

'You can't,' she said, 'I don't think my body would survive it.'

'I could leave your body alone.'

'You wouldn't.'

'You're right, I wouldn't.'

They were lying in bed on the afternoon of New Year's Day; they had been skating in the Rockefeller Centre and lunched off the street stalls on pretzels and knish, and cans of root beer; they had planned to go on down to Chinatown, but Michael had suddenly looked at Phaedria as she sat in the cold sunshine, the light spangling her wild hair, biting hungrily into her food, and had felt a wave of longing for her so strong it caught his breath. He had reached out and touched her face and without a word she had stood up and taken his hand and they had walked swiftly, urgently all the way up to Fifth Avenue, up to the apartment block, into the lift, up into the duplex, the bedroom, and then facing one another, still not speaking, their eyes fixed on one another, they had torn off their clothes and fallen, hungrily, greedily on to one another and the bed.

Later he had got up, she had been half asleep, and made

some hot chocolate and brought it to her and had sat beside her, feeding her morsels of crumbled chocolate flake bar, occasionally bending to kiss her breasts.

'I like them better small,' he said. 'They were nice big, and I look forward to seeing them big again when we have our children, but right now I like them small.'

'How many children are we going to have?' she asked.

'Oh, not too many. Around a dozen.'

'Six of each?'

'No,' he said, 'twelve the same, all girls. Just like their mother.'

'I love you,' she said.

'I love you too,' he said. 'Now you see, I was right, wasn't I?'

'What about?'

'About us.'

'Yes, I think you were. Was –' she hesitated – 'is – well, is the sex all right?'

'No,' he said, smiling at her, into her eyes, 'no, it isn't all right. It's lovely. Beautiful. You're very special.'

'Really?'

'Really. Don't look so worried. What a naïve question.'

'Yes,' she said, 'I know, but I am naïve, sexually. I do worry about it. I've only had – well, one lover really. Often I didn't even want him.'

'Really?' he said, and his eyes lit up. 'That is just amazing. Tell me about it.'

'Oh God,' she said, 'you've got your interested face on.'

'I am interested. Really. Come on, tell me about it.'

'Michael, I can't. It feels like a betrayal.'

'You can. It's not a betrayal. You've been terribly loyal to him. This is important. It's about you. About us. Now come on. Tell me about it.'

She told him. Not everything, but a lot. About her fears that she was sexually cold; about how she had learnt to pretend for Julian; about how she had never really wanted to go to bed with anyone else, before or since. 'Except you,' she added truthfully.

'And how was it for you, Lady Morell? With me, I mean.'

'It was lovely,' she said truthfully. 'But then – well, it's only just begun. I may start having to pretend for you. I'm sure Roz never –' her voice trailed off.

Michael looked at her, his face softening with tenderness. 'Yesterday morning must have been real bad for you.'

'No, it wasn't. Really. And the afternoon was lovely.'

'I hope so. I really do. Did you ever wonder if it was us guys making your sex life a misery, rather than yourself? No, I guess you wouldn't. OK, let's talk about Roz. Roz is one sexy lady. She's a great lay. No, don't look like that, we need to talk her out of our bed. Screwing you is different. Gentler. Softer. Less greedy. I have loved it. I think I always shall love it. And I want you to promise me that if you ever don't love it, you will tell me instead of getting that tortured psyche of yours into a terrible tangle. All right?'

'All right. I love you very much.'

'I love you too. And I don't think you're seriously frigid. Not seriously.'

She smiled at him.

'And when are you going to marry me?'

'Oh, Michael, I don't know,' she said, suddenly anxious. 'We have so much to resolve before I can think about that.'

'What do we have to resolve?' he said, his voice light, but his face wary, watchful.

'You know what. The company. Miles. Roz. Everything.'

'Roz and Miles I can see. The company I can't. You can just leave it. Come and live here with me. Forget all about it.'

'Michael, I can't do that. I really can't.'

'Why not, for Christ's sake?' he said and there was real anger in his voice. 'Jesus, I spent years waiting to get Roz away from that thing. I don't intend to spend years more waiting for you. Just give it all up.'

'No,' she said, and her dark eyes were steady, in spite of a gripping fear. 'No, I can't.'

'Why the hell not?'

'Because Julian left it to me. Because I care about it. But most of all for Julia.'

'Julia? What's she got to do with it?'

'A lot.'

'How?'

'Michael, she's Julian's child. He didn't know about her, but if he had he would have wanted her to have it. All of it possibly.

917

Certainly a lot. He probably wouldn't have played this bloody silly game with Miles and Roz and me at all.'

'I think he would. I think he would have had even more fun. Tangling you all up, having you tripping over one another. God, I thought I'd finally got rid of the guy, and he's still coming at me from the grave.'

'I'm sorry.'

'If you're sorry, Phaedria, prove it. Say you'll give it up. Come to New York. Marry me.'

'No, I can't.'

'Forgive me if I'm wrong, but I thought a few minutes ago, you said you loved me.'

'I did. I do love you. I know I do.'

'Pardon me, but I think you don't.'

She sat and looked at him, amazed at her calm in the face of the terrifying, sudden storm.

'I do love you, Michael, but I can't do what you want. I can't give up the company. Not yet. Maybe later when it's settled, when I have a trust fund organized for Julia, when Miles has made up his mind, when the thing is running on a proper constructive basis, when Roz and I have a modus operandi, when . . .'

'Oh, no,' he said. 'No. I'm sorry, Phaedria, but I will not play junior lead to that company. I will not.'

'I don't understand you,' she said.

'You don't understand? Dear God, how am I supposed to? Just what do you want me to do? Give everything up this end, move over there, sit around waiting for you to come home every night?'

'Of course not,' she said. 'Just wait. Just try to see.'

'I'm sorry, but I can't deliver. I'm tired of waiting. And I don't see. How you can let that tangle of power and intrigue get to you, and keep you away from your own happiness.'

'But if you'd only . . .'

'Maybe I do see,' he said, and there was a great heavy sadness in his voice. 'I see that in your own way you are as greedy as Roz. And as selfish. I see that like her, you want it all your way. My love, your way. Well you can have my love Phaedria, but only my way.'

'Which means?'

'You know what it means. You have to give it up.'

'I can't. I told you.'

'Well then,' he said.

'Then – what?'

'Then you may as well go. Go back to it. Now.'

'Very well.'

She got up silently; walked to the shower, dressed, packed her things. Put on her coat, stood facing him. He was still naked on the bed, stricken, but yet angry.

'Shall I have Franco take you to the airport?'

'Yes, please. It would be helpful.'

'I hope,' he said, with a huge sigh, pulling on his towelling robe, walking over to the house telephone, buzzing Franco, 'I hope you know what you are doing.'

'I'm afraid I do,' she said. 'I am very very sad, but I'm afraid I do.'

She had thought at first, as she sat, frozen with shock and disbelief in the car, amazed that happiness and love could turn so swiftly to pain and distancing, that she would go straight home, but she decided to go to Eleuthera after all. She needed time on her own, peace, a base to reflect from. And she felt instinctively that that house, that place, where she had been only once, and then much in love with Julian, was the natural one to be.

It was a totally fateful decision.

Julia first became ill around lunch time on New Year's Day. She had had a cough ever since the beginning of Christmas, but suddenly it got worse. Her temperature began to climb, she was restless, fretful. Nanny Hunter, initially calm, began to worry. At tea time she sent for the GP. He came at once, looked Julia over, listened to her small chest and then put his stethoscope away, looking mildly worried.

'I really don't think there's much to worry about. She has a slight chest infection, I wouldn't take any notice at all, if it weren't for her history. I'll leave you some antibiotic to give her, call me if she gets any worse.'

Nanny Hudson, comforted, gave Julia the antibiotic, persuaded her to take her bottle and put her to bed. She seemed calmer and went to sleep.

Two hours later, she woke up crying. She was extremely hot, coughing violently; Nanny Hudson phoned the GP. He came back, examined the baby carefully again, and then said, 'I wouldn't do this if her mother was here, but I think perhaps she should go to hospital. Just to be on the safe side. There's an excellent one in Eastbourne, you can be there in half an hour. I presume someone can drive you. I'm sure she'll be fine tomorrow, but it will be a better place for her, and you, to spend the night.'

'All right, Doctor Spender,' said Nanny Hudson, trying to fight down the fear that was rising in her. 'If that's what you think, I would feel happier too. Should I get Lady Morell home?'

'Where is she?'

'In New York.'

'Hmm. I suppose you should tell her. She could get home very quickly if she wanted to. Which I expect she would. Yes, give her a call.'

Nanny Hudson, her hands trembling, dialled the number Phaedria had given her in New York. There was no reply. She packed a bag for Julia and herself and tried again. Still no reply. Pete was waiting with the car. She decided to try again from the hospital.

Miles, Roz, Eliza and Peveril were still celebrating New Year.

Peveril had insisted on giving a party for Hogmanay in Miles' honour, and most of the county had come to the castle for champagne and Scottish reels, (interspersed with the occasional Charleston from Letitia) and to see the New Year piped in. Miles had found the whole thing, but particularly the reels, totally enchanting, and joined in with immense enthusiasm, insisting on borrowing a kilt from Peveril, which being rather too large for him, had fallen down in the middle of an Eightsome Reel. This had greatly added to the enjoyment of the women guests, particularly as he had insisted on adhering strictly to Scottish male dress and not worn any underpants.

On the evening of New Year's Day they had gone to dinner with Peveril's sister and her husband thirty miles away, on the other side of Sidlaw Hills. Letitia, reluctant to miss out on any fun, and still more reluctant to admit she was feeling her age, had still been forced to admit that a quiet evening on her own might be an attractive idea.

She had just settled down with her feet up and switched her television on when she heard the telephone; Monro, the butler, knocked on her door and said could she come, there was an urgent call for her.

It was Nanny Hudson, now at the hospital in Eastbourne; Julia's temperature was still rising, she seemed to be in considerable pain, and they were considering putting her in an oxygen tent. There was no reply to the number in New York Lady Morell had given her, did Mrs Morell have any idea where else she might be contactable?

'Oh, God,' said Letitia. 'Poor Phaedria. Poor child. If anything happens to that baby, I think she will kill herself. No, Nanny. I'm sorry, I don't. I thought she was in Eleuthera anyway.'

'She will be tomorrow, madam, but not today. She should still be in New York, she specifically said that there would always be someone there to take messages, even if she was out for a while herself.'

'Oh, Nanny, this is awful. How bad is the baby?'

'I don't know,' said Nanny Hudson, and Letitia could hear the struggle to keep panic from invading her voice. 'Quite bad. Her temperature is a hundred and four. I feel very very worried.'

'Is there a good doctor there? Oh, if only you were in London. If only I was in London.'

'I think the staff here is excellent. The consultant paediatrician is on his way. But I think – well, I'm sure actually – I'm afraid – she may be developing pneumonia.'

'Dear God. Nanny, stay there, keep calm. Oh, what nonsense I'm talking, you are far calmer than I. I will phone the house on Eleuthera, it's easier for me, and leave a message to meet Lady Morell at Nassau, in case she's on her way there now, and stop her travelling on to Eleuthera. That will save hours of time tomorrow at least. Oh, God, and she could have been home in just a few hours from New York. This is terrible. Well, maybe she will come back tonight, still. I'll keep trying the number for you, if you like, and then you won't have to leave the baby. Nanny, let me know if there's any change, won't you? This is terrible.'

She put the phone down and called the house at Turtle Cove. It was quite early in the day there. Jacintha, the housekeeper, said no, Lady Morell was not expected until the next day at lunch time.

'Well, Jacintha, you must get Nelson to go to Nassau. Immediately. Wait for Lady Morell there. Tell her to go back to England. I will have a message left for her at the airport, of course, but to be on the safe side, I think Nelson should go as well.'

'Yes, ma'am.' Jacintha was sulky. She had been looking forward to a good New Year holiday with Nelson, they had planned a boat trip, and a bottle of champagne from Sir Julian's cellar. They thought of the house as more and more their own, now that visitors came so rarely and the master had gone. Still, a baby was a precious thing, and if Lady Morell's baby was ill, then she must be sent home at once. Although what she had been doing away without the baby, Jacintha could not imagine. They were strange folks, the rich English.

Phaedria caught a flight to Nassau quite quickly. She could see it was going to mean spending the night there, that there would be no connecting flight until next day, but she felt a compulsion to get away from New York. Strange how the city was haunted by unhappiness for her.

She began to come to on the plane, her emotions thawing into painful life. Michael's words kept coming back to her: 'You are as selfish as Roz . . . as greedy as Roz . . . Go, go now . . . I will not play junior lead to that company.'

Oh, God, what had she done? Why had she done it? Was it really greed, selfishness? No, no she knew it wasn't. She had acted from a strong, almost primeval urge to protect her territory and her family. Julian had bequeathed her the birthright of the company and it was Julia's birthright and she had to safeguard it for her. That was all there was to it. And if she had to lose all that was personally dear to her to do it, then she would have to endure that. It seemed cruel, horribly cruel that she should have to lose Michael and happiness when she had only just discovered both, but she honestly felt there was little option.

Thinking about Michael, what he had become to her in

thirty-six short hours, pain almost overcame her, made her physically faint. He had brought her joy, laughter, tenderness, love; he had made her feel safe, peaceful, cared for, at ease. She could see, with a vivid clarity, all that her life could have become, all that she had deprived it of; and yet she had had, she knew, no choice at all. She had made a decision, although she had not known it, first, when she had married Julian, and then when she had borne his child, that she would become part of him and his life, and that life had included, indeed in large part consisted of, the company. And there could be no going back from it now.

In a hospital, thousands of miles away, her baby for the second time in her short, tender life, fought death, drawing strength from where or what she did not know: but with a spirit that was a legacy from her father, who had lost his own battle finally, and a mother who had a courage of her own, the full extent of which she had only just discovered.

Letitia was still up, pacing the Great Hall, willing the phone to ring, when the others came back from their party, laughing, talking loudly, full of 'did you see' and 'wasn't she?' and 'didn't he?'

'Granny Letitia, whatever is it?' said Roz quickly, taking in her grandmother's white face, her haunted eyes. 'It isn't – it isn't –?'

And no, said Letitia, swift to recognize a mother's permanent, painful anxiety, 'No, it isn't Miranda, it's Julia, she's very ill, in an oxygen tent with pneumonia and Phaedria is away and can't be contacted.'

'Oh, Christ, that baby is doomed,' said Roz, every hositility and outrage forgotten in a sudden, sweeping concern, 'and why not, why can't she be contacted? For heaven's sake, she must have left a number, why doesn't somebody ring it?'

'We have been ringing it,' said Letitia patiently, 'but she isn't there.'

'Well, where is she then? She's on Eleuthera, isn't she? It's not a big place, surely she can be found.'

'No,' said Miles, suddenly, feeling, knowing he had to speak, 'no, she isn't on Eleuthera, she's in New York.'

'New York?' said Roz. 'New York? What on earth is she doing in New York? Why did we all think –' Her voice trailed away into silence, and she looked first shocked, then angry as she faced Miles. 'How the hell did you know she was in New York, and why didn't you tell me?'

'Be quiet, Rosamund,' said Letitia angrily. 'Why shouldn't Phaedria be in New York, and what does it matter anyway? As a matter of fact, I knew she was there, Nanny Hudson told me, I've been ringing the number myself. That baby's life is in danger. All that matters is that, and that we have to find Phaedria. I'm shocked at you.'

Roz ignored her. 'What is this number in New York?'

'It's over there by the telephone. I was just going to try it again, anyway.'

Roz went over and looked at the piece of paper. But she didn't really need to. It was a number she felt was engraved on her heart.

The plane landed on Nassau at ten o'clock local time. Phaedria didn't even bother to check whether there was a flight out to Eleuthera. All she wanted was to go to bed and to find a respite, however brief, from her pain. She had no baggage, only her overnight bag; she walked straight out of the airport and into a cab without ever seeing the message for her pinned to the board in the arrival hall, and she was also not to know that at that very moment, Nelson was desperately trying to find someone to pilot Julian's plane out of Eleuthera and into Nassau.

While Nanny Hudson sat helpless, terrified, by the oxygen hood, watching Julia wage her battle, Miles sat by Roz's huge fourposter bed as she wept endlessly, hopelessly, into her pillow.

'Roz, you just have to know two things. One is that I only found out by the oddest chance. Two is that Phaedria didn't want you to know. I know she didn't, she wanted to spare you.'

'Jesus Christ!' Roz's face, ugly, swollen with crying and rage, lifted from her pillow. 'Why does everyone have to regard that bitch as some kind of a saint? If she'd wanted to spare me she could have left him alone in the first place. Just why don't you fuck off, Miles, and leave me alone?'

'Because it wouldn't do any good. Because you need company. Because I care about you.'

'If you'd cared about me, you wouldn't have lied to me.'

'Roz, I didn't lie to you. I simply didn't tell you Phaedria was going to New York.'

'And how did you find out that she was going to New York? Some kind of psychic transmission, is that what you're trying to imply?'

'No, I'm not trying to imply anything. I'm telling you. I was talking to Phaedria, and she let it slip that she was going to New York. I promised her I wouldn't tell you. I feel bad now that I did.'

'I'm sure you do. Whoever else gets hurt or let down, it mustn't be Phaedria. Oh, God, I hate her so much.'

Roz's voice rose in a wail of rage and pain; she was drumming her feet on the bed. Miles looked at her concernedly.

'Roz, please don't.'

'Why not?' She sat up suddenly and looked at him. 'This is what you're always telling me I should do. Let it all out. Let go. What's wrong with it, all of a sudden?'

'I don't know. I guess when her baby is so ill, it seems wrong to hate her so much.'

'I was very very sorry about her baby,' said Roz. 'When we first came in tonight, before I knew where she was, I was desperately sorry, I wanted to help, to find her.'

'I know,' said Miles. 'I saw you were. I know.'

'But then I found out she was with Michael and I just couldn't feel anything but hate. I'm sorry. I'm obviously a bad person.'

'No,' he said, 'just an unhappy one.'

'Oh, shit,' said Roz, 'everything is so awful. Everything. I just can't cope with it all any more.'

'Of course you can,' he said, 'you're a fighter. You'll always cope.'

'Do you think so?'

'I know so. I've told you before. I think you're terrific.'

She looked at him, and smiled a watery smile. 'You don't know me,' she said.

'Oh, yes, I do. I think I know you better than most people, as

925

a matter of fact. That's better, you're cooling off. Turn around and I'll massage your neck.'

'Oh, Miles, no. Not now.'

'Yeah, now. You need it now.'

She looked at him, a long, considering look.

'All right.'

'You'll have to take that vest thing off.'

'This vest thing is a silk T-shirt from Joseph.'

'Who is this Joseph guy and what's he doing giving you T-shirts?'

Roz giggled.

'OK, I'll take it off. Just hang on a minute, I don't have anything on underneath. Let me get my robe.'

'OK.'

She went into the bathroom, came back wearing a silk kimono, and sat down on her bed with her back to Miles. He started working on her neck, stroking it, kneading it, pushing the tension out; Roz felt herself relax.

'That's so nice.'

'Good. Now your shoulders.'

He slipped his hands under the gown, began working along the line of her shoulders, down her spine; Roz felt the almost familiar, dangerous lick of warmth through her body. She closed her eyes, put her head back, tried not to think. Miles moved over her shoulders, smoothing the skin down above her breasts, then returned to her spine and gently, insidiously round the sides of her body.

'Miles,' she said, half happy, half protesting. 'You never did that before.'

'You never were so upset before,' he said calmly.

'Maybe not.'

There was a silence while he worked on, his warm strong hands stroking her into an odd sensation: half excitement, half peace.

'Better?'

'Much.'

He stopped suddenly, turned her round, looked at her very directly, his dark blue eyes smiling into her green ones.

'What would really help you,' he said, almost conversationally, 'is a good fuck.'

Roz looked at him, shocked, amused and most of all intensely aroused, emotionally and physically.

'Don't be ridiculous,' she said with an effort.

'I'm not being ridiculous. It would.'

'And I suppose,' she said, in a hopeless attempt to defuse the situation and her emotions, 'you think you should be the person to administer it.'

'I certainly do,' he said and he smiled at her suddenly, his most dangerous, self-mocking, beguiling smile. 'I certainly do. What's more I should really like it. Wouldn't you?'

'No,' she said, 'no, not at all.'

'You're lying,' he said calmly, smiling again.

'Even if I am, you shouldn't even consider it. This is not the time or the place, and anyway, there's Candy.'

'It is absolutely the time and the place, this is a bedroom, you have a fine bed, and Candy is thousands of miles away.'

Roz looked at him thoughtfully, too amused to be anything but direct. 'You really think it doesn't matter, don't you? To her, I mean.'

'I really do. It doesn't.'

'That is an extremely singular opinion.'

'Maybe, but it's mine. That's what counts.'

'Well anyway, it would matter to me.'

'Oh, Roz, but it's not going to have to matter to you. Anyway, I'm certainly not going to force myself on you. Although I think maybe I'd better go to bed. I want you pretty badly right now, and it's fairly frustrating just sitting here, looking at you in that thing, with your tits half out. Good night, Roz.'

He bent down and kissed her; just lightly, gently, as he had in the woods; but all the emotion of the evening, the anxiety, the rage, the grief, the tension, swept through Roz and polarized into a frantic hunger. She lay back on the bed, her thin arms round his neck, her lips, her tongue working frantically on his. He kissed her back, hard, briefly, then disentangled himself from her and sat back on the bed looking at her.

'OK,' he said. 'Did you change your mind?'

'Yes,' said Roz, very low.

Miles stood up. He pulled off his black tie, his dress shirt. His long body was still very brown, hard, lean. Roz lay there, looking at it, in silence; then she sat up on the bed and slipped off the robe, her eyes fixed on his.

Miles put out his hand, cupped one of her breasts, massaging the nipple gently with his thumb; then he bent and began to lick it, suck it. Roz moaned, took his head in her hands, pressing it to her; then she lay back again, and sighed, a huge long shuddering sigh, smiling up at him.

'Take those trousers off, for God's sake,' she said. 'I've been thinking about this ever since I first set eyes on you, you beautiful bastard.'

The paediatrician looked down at Julia in the oxygen hood; she was still fighting for breath, her small chest heaving with the effort. The sun was streaming in at the windows; it was nearly seven o'clock.

'I think,' he said, 'we have to move her to intensive care.'

Nanny Hudson looked up at him exhausted, so frightened now she could hardly think.

'Yes,' she said, 'yes, of course. Is she – is she worse?'

'Well,' he said, and sighed, 'she is certainly no better. Do you want to come down with her?'

'Yes, please. If I may. Oh, why did this have to happen when her mother was away?'

'It often does,' he said, 'I'm not sure why. They need their mothers, babies do. I've just spoken to her grandmother again. She's still trying to contact the mother. She seems to have totally disappeared.'

Phaedria, who had spent a wretched night at the Colonial Hotel in Nassau, finally got back to the airport at ten in the morning and checked into a flight to Eleuthera.

It was leaving in minutes; she shot through the villagey, comparative informality of Nassau's passport control and ran out on to the tarmac towards the small yellow plane.

The pilot, a dazzling-looking black girl, was waiting by the steps; she smiled at Phaedria. 'Look like you just made it, honey. Hurry up now.'

As the plane taxied down the runway the clerk in passport control was receiving a serious dressing down from his superior, who had been alerted (a little late) that a Lady Morell had just checked on to the Eleuthera flight.

928

'It was real urgent that we contact that lady, and what do you do? Let her by without a murmur. Now she's in the sky. Man, will we be in trouble.'

'It's these new computer machines,' said the clerk easily, 'they just cause a heap of trouble.'

By the time the airport manager had worked out how acutely illogical this remark was, he had no energy left to be annoyed.

Miles woke up in Roz's bed, wondering briefly where he was. He lay quietly, looking up at the curtains above his head, at the outline of the hills outside the window and then at Roz, her face peaceful, gentle in sleep, oddly unfamiliar.

He smiled to himself, thinking about her; she was a most complex creature. So angry, so tough, but with such a capacity to feel. And extraordinarily sensuous. Miles had spent a great many nights (and days) with a great many women, and he had never quite encountered such passion, such capacity for sexual pleasure as he had found in Roz.

He had expected her to be hungry, ardent, had expected her to greet him, meet him as an equal; what he had not been prepared for was the way she entirely took the initiative, made love to him, used him, as if he were some object, fashioned entirely for her delight.

She came, they both did, almost at once the first time, Roz lying beneath him, gasping, moaning, her long legs wrapped round him, her arms flung out, thrusting her body against him, round him, and he felt her as she climaxed, in seemingly endless violent spasms. He drew back from her then, smiling into her eyes, kissing her tenderly, saying nothing, feeling the sweetness, the triumph of shared release, but Roz did not relax, she was violent, almost angry in her continuing need of him. She turned, and lay on top of him, and began to kiss him, slowly, intensely, and then moved down, licking, sucking, kissing his body, until she reached his penis. She took it in her mouth, working on it, determinedly, hungrily insistent, and then when he was ready for her, and tried to turn her, to enter her again, she said no, no, and it was almost a shout, a cry of triumph and she sat up, astride him, pulling him into her, drawing out her own climax, not allowing him his, retreating from him again and again, until finally he gave himself up to it, and came, and she with him, but not once, several times, and he could feel each time, the waves stronger, more violent, greedier. And still she wasn't satisfied, still she wanted more.

'You really are,' he said, turning from her finally, desperate for rest, for sleep, 'something else.'

And now, he thought, now what? He was uneasily aware that what he felt for Roz, what he had shared with her through that wild night, was something unique in his experience. It went deeper, felt stronger, sweeter than anything he had ever known. He shifted in the bed, trying to remember how he had felt when he had first slept with the other women he had really cared about, with Candy, with Joanna, and he knew perfectly well it had not been anything like this. Not sexually, nor (more alarmingly) emotionally. He felt, with Roz, a great closeness, a desire to care for her; a tenderness, he supposed it was, trying to analyse it. He felt tenderness towards Candy, too, but it was different, it was lighthearted, it felt less important. He also, in some strange way, felt very responsible for and to Roz. She had few people who liked her and far fewer to love her. Trying rather alarmedly to decide which of the two emotions he felt, he decided it was neither one nor the other, but a strange heady amalgam of the two.

He decided it was just as well Candy was coming back to England soon. This situation could very easily get out of hand.

Phaedria reached Turtle Cove at two o'clock local time. She was exhausted. She had phoned the house repeatedly and got no reply and had had to get one of the appalling local taxis from the airport for the twenty-mile drive to the house. The one she took had its radiator needle jammed permanently on boiling, and a door hanging half off its hinges. The driver talked incessantly about his acute surprise that another year had come and gone. Phaedria tried to be courteous, but her head ached and she felt sick.

When she finally reached the house and walked into the cool hall with its whirring fans, it was deserted. She went down to the kitchen; there was a meal on the table, left abandoned, Marie Celeste-like, on the table, a window hanging open. It seemed strange. Maybe they had got the days mixed up and were expecting her tomorrow. It didn't matter. She went through to the bedroom and pulled off her hot winter clothes. She climbed into one of the swimsuits she had there, looking at the bed where she and Julian had celebrated their wedding, where she had lain sick with the sun, and he had read to her. It had been a marvellous marriage, especially in the beginning. Whatever he had inflicted on her since, she had loved him very much.

Maybe that had been half the problem with Michael. That she had still been grieving, had not been ready. Part of her, part of her heart was still with Julian. Well, it didn't matter now.

She sighed and walked out on to the veranda where they had eaten breakfast that first marvellous morning, after the snorkelling. She went down on to the beach and slithered into the warm, silky sea. There was a conch shell by her foot; she ducked under the water and picked it up. It was small, its pink interior pale and marbled. She waded back to the beach and laid it on the silver-white sand.

What a lovely lovely place this was. It made her feel peaceful, in spite of her unhappiness, whole again. She would not sell this of all the houses, if she had to buy Miles out. She would rather sell Hanover Terrace. She needed Turtle Cove.

Thinking about houses made her thoughts turn to the house in Connecticut that Michael had bought her. In her wildest dreams about him, she had not imagined such generosity, such concern for her happiness. She heard his rich rough voice saying, 'I bought it because I love you,' and she felt as if some giant hand was squeezing her heart. How, in the name of God, or anything else, was she to survive this new, wrenching misery?

She swam strongly out to sea for a few minutes, then turned and trod water, looking at the shore. Suddenly she saw Jacintha waving at her frantically; puzzled, worried, she swam back in.

'Whatever is it, Jacintha? What's the matter?'

'It's your baby, Lady Morell.' She gave the stress on the first syllable, like Laurel. 'She's very very ill.' She sounded excited, important to be bringing such news. Phaedria nearly shook her.

'What is it? Where is she? Why didn't someone tell me?'

'We tried to tell you, Lady Morell, we couldn't find you. Nelson, he's in Nassau looking for you. You better phone old Mrs Morell, she tell you all about it. They been phoning you in New York and here all night.'

'Oh, my God,' said Phaedria, 'it must be really serious if they've been looking for me that hard. Jacintha, what is the matter with her, what is it, do you know?'

'I don't know, ma'am,' said Jacintha, half enjoying the drama and her momentarily important role in it. 'All I know your baby real sick. Like I said, you better phone old Mrs Morell.'

'Yes, all right, Jacintha. Where is Mrs Morell?'

'She's in Scotland, Lady Morell. She's been phoning and phoning you. I have the number right here,' she added, 'and the telephone is by your bed.'

'Yes, Jacintha, thank you, I know where the phone is.'

Phaedria raced over the sand, across the lawn, into the house, frantically dialled the number in Scotland. Letitia answered the phone.

'Letitia, it's Phaedria, what's happening, please tell me, what's the matter with Julia? Who's with her, where is she, what can I do?'

'Oh, Phaedria, thank God we found you. Julia's in hospital. In Eastbourne. Nanny Hudson is with her. Eliza has flown down to be with them both, we thought someone should go.'

'But what – what is it? Is it very serious?'

'Well, darling, it's silly to tell you it's not. It's quite serious. She's got pneumonia. But she's – holding her own. And of course pneumonia isn't what it was. It still sounds very frightening, but with antibiotics it just isn't so bad. Phaedria? Phaedria, are you still there?'

'Yes,' said Phaedria, in a small, quiet voice. 'I'm still here. Letitia, I don't know what to do, I won't be able to get home today. There aren't many flights out. I suppose I could get the company jet, Geoff is in New York.'

'Thank God for that,' said Letitia briskly. 'He can be with you in a very few hours. You can get him to come and collect you.'

'Yes, all right.' Phaedria sounded listless.

'Darling, don't despair. I'm sure, quite sure, Julia will be all right. Listen, why don't you talk to the doctor at the hospital, he'll be able to reassure you.'

'Yes, I will. Yes, give me his number. And do you think you could call Geoff, Letitia, get him to ring me here? He's at the Intercontinental, New York. Thank God he's not in London. I just feel so –' her voice trailed shakily away.

'Yes, of course I will. Now you ring the doctor at Eastbourne, and see what he says. I'll ring you back in about a quarter of an hour. All right?'

'All right, Letitia.'

Phaedria put down the phone and frantically, desperately, dialled the number. She got through to Reception, asked for the paediatrician.

'I'm sorry, that number is busy at the moment. Will you hold?'

'No,' she said, almost shouting down the phone. 'No, I won't hold, I'm calling from the Bahamas. Will you put me through at once. It's very very urgent. This is Lady Morell.'

'I'm sorry,' said the voice, coldly distasteful. 'The line is busy. I can't interrupt. Will you hold, or will you call back?'

'Oh, God,' said Phaedria. 'Oh, God, I'll hold. No, wait, put me through to intensive care.'

'I'm afraid I can't do that,' said the voice, colder than ever.

'Why not?'

'There is no line through to intensive care.'

'But my baby is in there. Do you have any news of her, can you at least tell me how she is?'

'Just a moment.' The voice sounded just slightly more helpful. Phaedria waited, her head drumming with fear, her stomach a clenched knot. There was a long silence.

'Hallo?' It was a man's voice.

'Hallo, yes. Is that the paediatrician? I'm sorry, I don't have your name, this is Phaedria Morell.'

'Lady Morell, yes. This is Peter Dugdale here. Now about your baby . . .'

'Yes? Yes, how is she?'

'Not very well, I'm afraid. Not very well at all. She hasn't got any worse since early this morning, so we have some grounds for optimism, but I don't feel I can say more than that, at the moment.'

'But what is it? How did it happen?'

'She has pneumonia, Lady Morell. She does have a tendency towards respiratory infections, of course, with her history, and I understand she had a cold over Christmas.'

'Yes, but only a very slight one. And she seemed quite better. Otherwise I wouldn't have left her. Obviously.'

933

Guilt was heaping on to her panic; she felt violently sick.

'Of course not. But even a slight cold could have triggered it off. Perhaps with her history she should have antibiotic cover with any kind of infection of that kind.'

'So what shall I do? Is there anything, anything at all, I can do, anyone I can get hold of, our own paediatrician, just tell me what to do.'

'I do assure you she is in the best hands here, the best care. Her – nanny –' he lingered over the word, giving it a slightly derogatory connotation – 'has not left her for a moment. You're very lucky there. And your friend, or is she a relative, Mrs Garrylaig –'

'Lady Garrylaig,' said Phaedria absentmindedly.

'I do beg your pardon.' The voice was more disdainful still. 'Well, she is on her way, I believe.'

'So – just how serious is it? I mean, could she – might she –'

The words would not come; tears streamed down her face.

'It's quite serious, Lady Morell. It would be wrong of me to pretend otherwise. But she is holding her own. I can't say more than that. Try not to worry,' he added, in the voice of the dutifully sensitive. Phaedria bit her fist; she knew she mustn't scream, mustn't get too angry with him, antagonize him.

'I'll get there as soon as I can,' she said when she had got control of her voice again. 'My – my mother-in-law is organizing a plane. But I'm rather a long way away from home.'

'Yes. So I understand. The Bahamas, I believe. Very nice.'

'No,' she said, her tears choking her. 'No, it's not very nice. It's horrible. Well – thank you.'

'That's all right.'

'When should I phone again?'

'Oh, any time, any time at all. Now I have to go. My bleeper has just gone. Goodbye.'

Phaedria put the phone down. She looked out at the sea, the white sand, the palm trees in disbelief. How could anywhere be so beautiful, so calm, when her life was an ugly terrifying turmoil? If only Geoff would phone. Where was he, and how long would it take him to get her out of this awful, awful place? As she sat looking at the phone, willing it to ring, her head suddenly filled with a fresh horror. Roz had been up in Scotland. She would have known about the whole thing. She would have heard she had been in New York, would probably have asked what the number was. There was no way, no way on God's earth that Roz would not know now that she had been in New York with Michael. And the awful irony was that now she need never, ever have known at all.

Phaedria rested her head on her arms and wept.

Geoff Partridge, who piloted the Morell family's planes, had spent most of Christmas in bed in New York with a very pretty Pan American air hostess. He had been given an extended holiday, right up to the beginning of January; Phaedria had been privately relieved that he and the jet were in New York because it meant in an emergency he and the plane could be brought easily into service. He was staying at the Intercontinental; she imagined that he could be with her in a few hours that day of Letitia's phone call. However, Geoff and his hostess had woken to a beautiful day, on that January 2nd, and decided to take a trip out to the Hamptons. He had to be in Nassau by the following evening; until then, barring accidents, he was officially clear. It was the Pan Am hostess's last day; it seemed silly to sit around waiting for a call that probably wouldn't come.

'They have your number,' she said, when he hesitated, 'they can call you here. We'll call in at lunch time, make sure if there's a problem.'

'OK.'

Only at lunch time they couldn't find a public phone that was working; it was four o'clock before the Intercontinental managed to inform Geoff that he was required urgently to pilot the jet down to Nassau, and almost nine before he reached Kennedy and put the plane into service.

How Phaedria survived the ten-hour flight home she never afterwards knew. In the end she managed to get Julian's small plane piloted out of Eleuthera and into Nassau and then catch a scheduled flight, an hour before a stricken Geoff Partridge arrived. She experienced for most of the time a panic so violent she could neither sit still nor walk up and down for more than a few seconds, but moved restlessly, endlessly from one seat to another, looking out of one window, then another, frantic for

935

some relief from the choking pain. Occasionally she closed her eyes; then a picture of Julia in the incubator in the hospital in Los Angeles rose before her eyes, her tiny body white and still, and she would snap them open again, turning her head from side to side, biting her lips with the effort of not screaming. They offered her alcohol, coffee, food, in a hopeless attempt to find something, anything, that might help, if only for a moment, but she refused them all, even the thought of swallowing made her choke.

Letitia had promised faithfully that they would get a message to her on the plane's radio if it was humanly possible and if there was any change in Julia's condition; but as nothing came, Phaedria had no way of knowing whether there was no news, or if it simply had not managed to reach her. She wished now she had waited for Geoff, communication would have been a great deal more possible.

Mixed with her panic, her fear, was a terrible guilt and remorse: she should never, ever have left Julia with Nanny Hudson, never have ignored her cold, never been in one place when she said she was in another, never made herself so elusive. Well, Julia would die and that would be a judgement on her, a punishment, and there was no way, no way at all, that she could blame anyone except herself.

Roz couldn't sleep the second night; she was haunted by thoughts of Phaedria, a battle raging in her between her hatred and sympathy for her; and by thoughts of Miles. She had avoided him all day, half ashamed that they should have experienced such pleasure, such happiness when Julia's life was suspended so perilously, half consumed with longing to see him, be with him, have him again. They had met at mealtimes, which had in any case been strained, distracted occasions, everyone jumping whenever the phone rang; she had gone to bed early, pleading a headache. Letitia looked at her sharply; Roz never had headaches, never went to bed early, never felt tired. She looked at her watch; it was two o'clock. She decided to go down to Peveril's library. She didn't feel like reading, but he had some magnificent first editions, of Thackeray, Trollope, Burns. It would be amusing to look at those. She got up, pulled on her robe, and went quietly down to the great hall and into the library.

She was engrossed in *The Eustace Diamonds* when the door

opened quietly; still half involved with the book, she turned round slowly. It was Miles.

'Hi. Couldn't you sleep? I guess we're all pretty strung up.'

'Yes. I keep thinking about Julia.'

'I kept thinking about you.'

'Miles, I – I don't think we should carry on with this relationship. Not at all.'

'OK.' He shrugged, smiling at her. 'If that's what you want.'

'Well it's – it's not what I want. But I just feel things are complicated enough. And there's Candy.'

'Roz, I told you last night, she's three thousand miles away.'

Roz felt a mild irritation. 'I know she is now. But she won't always be. I don't want to play any more of those games. And somehow this doesn't seem quite the time for this kind of thing. And anyway, I don't like our relationship being reduced to a one-night stand.'

'Do we have a relationship?'

She felt foolish, disadvantaged.

'No, of course not. You misunderstood me.'

'Pity.' He moved over, stood behind her, kissed her neck. 'I was hoping we did.'

'Miles, please don't.'

'Why not?'

'I just told you why not.'

'Oh Roz,' he said, 'you are much too serious. And besides . . .' He was still behind her, he slipped his hands under her robe, moved them up to her breasts, started gently, tenderly massaging her nipples. Roz felt a lick of fire shoot down, in a white hot line, to her abdomen, her vagina; she squirmed, pressing her buttocks back against him. They were almost the same height; she felt his penis hard, pressing against her; she felt dizzy, odd. She fought to retain some self-control.

'Besides what?'

'You are just – well, sensational. I can't think about anything else.' His hands moved down, pressing, massaging her stomach, his fingers began to probe her pubic mound, seeking out, reaching into her, finding her clitoris. She put her head back against him and moaned.

'Miles, please.'

'Please what?'

937

'You know what.' She turned round, took his head in her hands, kissed him savagely, pulled off her robe. He entered her as she stood there, his hands on her buttocks, holding her to him, pushing, urging her into an almost instant orgasm. Roz cried out; the wild, strange cry oddly at variance with the sober quiet of the room.

Minutes later, she was lying on the floor, white faced, blazing eyed, holding out her arms; Miles knelt down, looking at her tenderly.

'Tell you what,' he said almost conversationally, as he sank into her again, 'at least now it's been a two-night stand.'

Pete Praeger met Phaedria at Heathrow; he said nothing, merely took her hand, as if he was an old friend, and led her to the car.

'Do we – do we know any more?'

'No more. She's just about the same. Come on, we have to get you there.'

He drove so fast down to Eastbourne that Phaedria would, under normal circumstances, have been frightened; as it was, watching the speedometer needle on the Mercedes climb steadily from 90 to 100 to 110, 115, she felt a strange relief. Neither of them spoke, just stared ahead.

As they reached the outskirts of Eastbourne he said, 'This is bad, look at the traffic.'

'Oh, Pete, just do what you can.'

'I will.' He put his foot down again, weaving in and out of the lanes, hooting; suddenly, inevitably, they heard the wailing of a police siren The police waved to Pete to move over; fuming, swearing, he got out.

'Morning, sir. Do you know what speed you were doing then, in a built up area?'

'Yes, officer. I do.'

'Could I see your licence please, sir.'

Phaedria got out. She looked terrible, her face white, her eyes dark and shadowed, swollen with all the tears she had shed, her clothes crumpled.

'Officer, please. Please let us go. I can explain.'

He looked at her, initially hostile, then sympathy dawning. 'What is it?'

Phaedria took a deep breath. 'My baby is very ill. In intensive care. I just flew in from the States. I have to get there. Mr Praeger was only doing what I asked.'

The policeman looked at her. He frowned, then he opened the door of the police car, his face impassive. 'Get in, madam. You too, sir, if you'd be so kind.'

'But I –'

'Madam, please don't waste time. You were only doing ninety. We can do a hundred and ten with the siren on.'

They were waiting for her when the police car drew up outside the hospital; they had radioed that they were coming. Eliza and Nanny Hudson, standing there. Phaedria fell out of the car. 'Eliza, Nanny, what is it, what's happened?'

Eliza looked at her, silent for a moment only, but to Phaedria it seemed like an hour, a week. Then she smiled. 'Thank God you're here. She's all right. Phaedria, she's going to be all right now, they think, but she needs you, she needs you so much. This is Mr Dugdale, he's been so marvellous. Come on.' And she took Phaedria's hand, and pulled her, after Mr Dugdale, down the corridors, down the stairs and into a side ward, where Julia lay.

She was half asleep, she was breathing heavily, in her oxygen hood, restless, whimpering from time to time; as her mother came in she looked at her, and opened her large dark eyes very wide, and almost visibly relaxed, and smiled, a quiet, peaceful smile.

'Oh, Julia,' said Phaedria. 'Oh, Julia.'

'She'll be all right now,' said Mr Dugdale.

Letitia, beaming radiantly, went to find Roz, who was lying rather uncharacteristically on her bed.

'Lovely, lovely news. Julia is going to be all right. She's much better. She has to stay in hospital for a few days, but she's all right. Phaedria's safely back with her. Poor girl, that must have been a terrible twenty-four hours.'

'I'm glad,' said Roz, 'really glad. It's been a nightmare. I'm sorry I behaved so badly, Granny Letitia, I was distraught.'

'That's all right, darling. I understood. Come and have some lunch. Where's Miles?'

'Oh, talking to Peveril, I think. They get on really well. It's so funny. Miles is planning to take him to Malibu.'

'Well, I don't think he'll be able to do that unless he promises to take your mother as well. So are you feeling better, darling?'

'Oh,' said Roz, just a little too casually. 'Much much better, thank you Letitia.'

Peveril was beaming at the table. 'Well,' he said, 'good news at last, eh? I've hardly slept myself for two nights.'

'Nor me,' said Letitia, 'I had to take a sleeping pill.'

'Oh, you should never do that,' said Peveril, relieved to have the conversation back on a normal plane, turned away from sickness and drama. 'Dreadful things, those pills. Shouldn't take them. I never take anything. Sleep like a baby, as long as I have my nightcap.'

'What's your nightcap?' asked Roz interestedly.

'Two hot toddies. They have to be good and strong, mind, two pegs of whisky in each one.'

'What's a peg?' said Miles.

'A large double. Chota peg is a single. Old Indian measure. My father always used the term.'

'So you have four double whiskies before you go to sleep every night?' said Roz incredulously.

'That's right. In hot milk, of course. Mind you, it doesn't always work unless I have a couple of brandies after dinner. But I never take a pill. If I really can't sleep I go out on the battlements and play the bagpipes for half an hour or so. Never fails.'

'I must try that,' said Letitia. 'I often can't sleep. Mind you, I daresay then the other inhabitants of Chelsea might have trouble sleeping.'

She sparkled at Peveril and he winked back at her. They were very fond of one another.

'Stop flirting with my grandmother, Peveril,' said Roz, laughing. 'We don't want anything like that in the family.'

Chapter Twenty-nine

London, 1986

'So what have you decided to do, Miles?'

Candy looked at him over the heap of bags in their room at Claridge's. She had come back tired and irritable after what had seemed like a very long week, trying to console her father for the loss of Dolly, trying to persuade him to go home to Chicago, trying to talk him round to the idea of her and Miles getting married straight away.

'You're too young, Candy, and that's my last word. You don't know your own mind.'

'I don't think knowing your mind necessarily comes with age, Daddy. Did Dolly know her own mind? Do you?'

'Shut up, Candy, you don't know what you're talking about.'

'OK. OK.' She was not afraid of her father exactly, but she knew she couldn't budge him, once he had made up his mind.

She tried another tack. 'Miles is a really good prospect, Daddy. He has a great deal of money now.'

'Yes, and a great deal of money and no work to do spells one thing, and it ain't happiness. Unless that young man gets himself some proper gainful employment, you are not going to marry him. Why can't he work in that company over there? It's a wonderful opportunity. There has to be something wrong with a man who has so little ambition.'

Candy sighed. She would have died rather than admit it, but she was beginning to agree with him.

Miles looked at her thoughtfully. Easygoing as he was, he was beginning to find her nagging irritating. He was actually beginning to find her rather irritating altogether. She seemed shallow suddenly, uninteresting, lacking in emotion and depth. He knew it was unfair of him to think that way, that it was not Candy but he who had changed, but he couldn't help it. On the other hand something had to be settled; they couldn't live at Claridge's for ever; it wasn't exactly cheap.

Roz's intelligent, quirkily lateral mind kept intruding into his thoughts over Candy's prattle, her cool amused green eyes looked at him, when he was actually meeting Candy's Bambi-like blue ones, her greedy outrageous body even invaded the bed as he lay caressing Candy's pert little breasts, bringing her to swift, easy orgasm. In the weeks she had been away he and Roz had been to bed together twice more, once in Scotland, once in London, drawn irresistibly, inevitably towards one another by the promise of an intense powerful pleasure neither of them had ever known before. Each time they had agreed it should not happen again, each time had come laughingly together, saying why not, just once more, what harm did it do, it had to be good for them, it was just fun, just pleasure, just the satisfaction of two exceptionally hearty appetites, and each time, as they parted again, they knew, without saying a word to one another, that it was rather more than that.

However, something had to be resolved, if not for Candy's sake, his own. And besides there was the question of money. The extremely generous loans Henry was arranging for him (on Roz and Phaedria's instructions) could not go on for ever. He was getting through a monumental amount of money, by any standards. And he was actually growing weary of living at Claridge's and shopping; he didn't exactly want to work but he didn't want to be idle in London, or indeed anywhere else in the world, except California.

But whatever he did or did not decide, he was not going to be pushed into it by anybody, least of all Candy. If there was one thing that turned Miles into an immovable object, it was the sense that there was an irresistible force coming at him, hard, trying to carry him along with it. As Hugo Dashwood had discovered to his cost, some years earlier.

Dark blue eyes met light with an expression of rare hostility.

'No,' he said. 'No, I haven't. Stop bugging me, will you? Just leave me alone.'

'Miles,' said Roz, sinking on to the chaise longue in the window of the Cheyne Walk drawing room, 'are you any nearer making a decision?'

'Nope,' he said shortly. 'Can I take a glass of wine?'

'Of course. Give me one, will you?'

He poured two glasses from the chilled bottle and carried one over to her, careful not to touch her. The atmosphere between them now was so febrile that he knew if he so much as brushed her fingers with his they would be in bed in minutes.

'Thank you. Don't look so cross. It doesn't suit you. That's my prerogative.'

'Sorry. This is all getting to me. And I'm homesick.'

'Of course you are.'

'I still kind of favour the consortium. It would let me off the hook. But I worry about the long-term effect on you. And Phaedria.'

'Don't worry about me,' said Roz darkly, 'I can take care of myself. And certainly don't worry about Phaedria. We have every evidence she can do the same.'

'Yeah, I guess so. It seems kind of wrong selling out of the family.'

'I think it's probably the best possible thing. Fresh blood and all that. The company is the nearest thing to incest this family will ever know.'

'Maybe.'

'What about working here?'

'Well,' he said carefully, 'I don't really know. I've kind of grown warm towards the idea. It might be fun, just for a bit. And it would please Candy. But – well, she's pushing me real hard and that makes me cross. And besides –' He looked at her.

'Yes?'

'Well, I don't know if I could handle working with you all the time.'

'I think it would be fun,' said Roz.

'It would, I mean I'd like it in that way. But – well, I think things might get out of hand pretty quickly.'

'You mean we'd be screwing all the time?' Her expression was amused, confident.

'We'd be wanting to, I guess. And if I was married to Candy –' his voice trailed off.

'That would never do.' She stood up, holding out her hand. 'Right now you're not working for the company. And you're not married to Candy. This could be our very last chance. Shall we, Miles? For old times' sake?'

He took the hand, kissed the back of it, turned it over, kissed the palm. Then he looked up at her and smiled.

'Yeah, OK. Just for old times' sake.'

'Miles,' said Phaedria, 'do you have any idea yet what you want to do?'

He had come to her office to have the promised lunch; he sat watching her while she sorted the files and papers on her desk into some sort of order, flicked idly through telephone messages, signed the letters Sarah had left for her. He thought how sad she looked, how thin and drawn.

'No,' he said, 'I don't have an idea. You're still keen on this trust fund thing?'

'Yes. Even more now.'

She spoke without thinking.

'Why now?'

She flushed. 'Oh – nothing.'

'Did New York go wrong?'

He sounded so sympathetic, so genuinely concerned, that as always she couldn't be cross.

'Yes, I'm afraid it did. There – there isn't a future there, I'm afraid. So Julia's seems more crucial than ever. Illogical in a way.'

'I'm sorry.'

'That must have been terrible for you, that awful day when she was so ill and they couldn't find me. I'm really really sorry about it.'

'Well, I felt kind of bad giving the game away.'

'Did you?' She looked startled. 'Miles, why, what happened?'

'Oh, I didn't fail you, not really. Only death would have dragged it from me, I knew how much it mattered. But it seemed like death. Or the threat of it. Julia's. I knew you'd care more about her than anything. So I told them. Anyway, they knew, Letitia knew, Nanny Hudson had told her. But Roz learnt it from me.'

'Oh God.'

'Yeah, it was bad. But I calmed her down.'

'You're very good for Roz. I've noticed.'

'Maybe.'

There was a silence.

'Did she ever say anything to you?' he asked.

'No, nothing.'

'Uh-huh. And is Julia really OK now?'

'She's fine. You'd never think she'd been ill. It's her mother who needs looking after. Come on, let's go and have lunch. Is Candy joining us?'

'No, Candy's in a sulk. She mostly is these days.'

'Oh, Miles, I'm sorry.'

'I am too,' he said, and sighed.

After lunch Phaedria sat at her desk, looking out of the window. She still felt very unhappy. Her grief at the loss of Michael was more severe than she had expected it would be. Piled on the greater one for Julian, she found it almost unbearable.

Life had settled into a grey, rather lonely monotone; she worked all day and spent most evenings alone with Julia. It was what she wanted, but it didn't seem to be doing her any good.

She had half expected to hear from Michael, that he would call her, write maybe (only he always swore he was illiterate and could barely manage his name) to try and persuade her to change her mind. But there was silence. An awful, dead, final silence. She supposed that after all the years of battling with the company for Roz's soul, he simply could not contemplate starting all over again for hers. Sometimes she wondered if she had made an appalling mistake, wantonly tossed happiness out of the window and into Central Park that New Year's Day. Whether she was simply stubborn and greedy, rather than following the inexorable course Julian and Julia had set her on. But when she contemplated the alternative, she knew she wasn't. She couldn't be free of this monster until it had been tethered safely once and for all, and was under her control. And that was still as far out of sight as ever.

She didn't think Miles was going to let her buy his share. He kept saying he could see it was probably right, and then not taking it any further. He was either going to sell to the consortium, which even Richard now seemed to think was a good idea, or join the company. Candy was pushing him very hard in that direction. She couldn't decide whether it was a good idea or not. It would prolong the agony of the division; he would be making decisions between her and Roz day by day, hour by hour, it could be acutely uncomfortable. On the other hand, he was such an agreeable, conciliatory force it would probably greatly alleviate the atmosphere in the office. But then it wouldn't, it couldn't last long. In the first place Roz would probably turn it sour, and in the second he would hate it. Or would he? Maybe he would like it. For someone who couldn't wait to spend the rest of his life on a Californian beach, Miles was taking an unconscionably long time to pack. She had been very impressed, too, when they had talked over lunch about what he might do, by a certain instinctive commercial grasp. He had had some idea about an offshoot of the cosmetic company into the fitness industry that had greatly impressed her. Phaedria fetched herself a glass of Perrier water from her fridge and tried to forget about Miles for a while, and concentrate on company matters. But it was very difficult.

Apart from anything else, he did disturb her. It wasn't quite a sexual disturbance (although she had still not forgotten the passion she had felt that day after Christmas, and her shame at it afterwards). It was an emotional one. There was just something about him that reached out and touched her in some oddly familiar way. And yet, and yet she had never met anyone remotely like him in her life. It was probably because she was so lonely, and fantasizing like some crazed old spinster.

Oh, God, what on earth was to become of her?

Phaedria suddenly remembered Doctor Friedman. It would be very nice to talk to her again. She would be back in London now. Maybe she could help her confront all her feelings about Miles and Michael as well as Julian. To come to terms finally with her grief. And then she hadn't talked to her since they had found Miles, made the discovery about Julian and Hugo Dashwood, since Julia had been born even. Yes, she would go and see her.

She found Doctor Friedman's resolute impassiveness, her technique of meeting question with question, oddly comforting; she led you at your own pace into discovery rather than controlling you with it, and if you wanted to withdraw, to stand back, she allowed that too.

She rang the number; yes, Doctor Friedman was back, but very busy. Was it important?'

'Could you tell her it's Phaedria Morell, and I'd be grateful for an appointment soon if she could manage it?'

The secretary went away and came back with the news that

Doctor Friedman would be delighted to see Lady Morell next Monday, first appointment of the day.

'Thank you,' said Phaedria. 'Thank you very much.'

'Where have you been?' screamed Candy as Miles walked into the suite at Claridge's at half past nine one evening. 'Just where have you been?'

'Out,' he said simply.

'Where out? Why not with me?'

'Because I had things to do that didn't concern you. OK?'

'No. Not OK. I'm fed up and lonely, and I want to go home.'

'OK, go home.'

She looked at him. 'I think you're seeing someone else.'

He shrugged. 'Candy, you can think what you like.'

'Well, are you?'

'I don't have to answer that.'

'Miles, I can't tell you how sick of all this I am. Why don't you just make your rotten mind up?'

'I'll make my mind up when I'm good and ready, Candy. Right now I'm still thinking.'

'About which of those bitches to give your lousy share to?'

'Yeah. And whether to join the company.'

'Holy shit!'

'It was your idea, Candy. Now I'm getting to like it. I told you you might regret it.'

'You look awful,' said Roz, looking at Miles across the bed.

'Thanks.'

'No, you do. You've lost that marvellous Californian goldenness. You look like one of us.'

'I'm beginning to feel like one of you. For the first time in my whole life I feel I need a vacation.'

'Maybe you should take a break.'

'In California? Yeah, maybe I should.' He reached out and wove his fingers lazily into her pubic hair. 'Would you come with me?'

'I might. I just might.'

'Well,' said Doctor Friedman soberly. 'You certainly have had a very tough time. What's remarkable is not how bad you feel but that you've survived it so well. How's the baby now?'

'She's fine. She's beautiful.'

'I'm sure she is,' said Doctor Friedman, smiling. 'Like all babies.'

'No, but Julia really is beautiful.'

'Like all babies. I'm sorry, I'm being unkind.'

'Doctor Friedman, do you think it was a mistake? Embarking on a new relationship before I had properly worked through the grief of losing Julian?'

'You never recover from real grief. So it's very much down to your capacity to handle it. How do you think your capacity is?'

'Well, I suppose quite good. I seem to be tougher than I might ever have imagined.'

'Well, maybe then it wasn't too soon. How do you think you really feel about this man?'

'What do you mean?'

'Under the pain and the trauma of him being your step-daughter's lover?'

'Having been.'

'I'm sorry?'

'Having been her lover. The affair was quite over before I went to New York.'

'But not when he came to see you, when he helped you through the discovery about your husband.'

'No.'

'But that was when you fell in love with him?'

'Yes. I suppose it was. But nothing – nothing happened. I wouldn't let it.'

'No, and that was very well behaved of you. Nevertheless the fact that he was not yours for the taking may have influenced your feelings.'

'It might. But I really really do think I loved him.'

'Loved? In the past tense?'

'Love. I think I still do. If he walked in now –'

'But you're not prepared to give up the company for him. Why do you think that is?'

'I feel I can't. I feel Julian entrusted it to me and he would have wanted it for Julia. I can't just sell out and walk away from it, give it up to Roz.'

'He hardly entrusted you with it. Only half of it. Not half in fact.'

'No, but he meant me to have that. He could see it had grown important to me.'

'Don't you think perhaps you are endowing him with motives he might never have felt?'

She thought carefully. 'No. No, I don't, I think I knew him quite well.'

'Did you? Well enough to realize there was this other life going on?'

'No, all right. But maybe it wasn't an important life. Maybe it was quite trivial.'

'Then perhaps he might have told you about it, if it had been trivial?'

'Perhaps.' She sighed.

'And then there was the will. Miles.'

'Yes.' Her voice was very small.

'Listen, I'm not saying you're wrong. I'm saying be sure you're right. Before you throw all this happiness with Michael Browning away. That's all.'

'Yes. All right. I'll try. Can I ask you some questions now?'

'You can.'

'Did you – well, did you ever suspect that Julian was leading this second life?'

'What do you think? Does that seem likely? Think about it.'

Phaedria sighed. 'You really don't give much away, Doctor Friedman.'

'Lady Morell, I'm trying to help you to know your husband. To help you through all this. I told you early on, if you really think, think about him, what he was, what you knew, you can still learn a lot about him.'

'All right. But what should I think? I don't know in this case what to think.'

'Well, you should think about how much I did know. Quite a lot, we have established that. Given that information, how much more would he have – shall we say – imparted? He was a very secretive man, wasn't he?'

'Yes. Yes he was. But clearly some things he had to share. With someone. Things that were too painful, too frightening, too difficult. Otherwise he would never have come to you at all.'

'Yes.'

'So anything really painful – really important –'

'Yes?'

There was a long silence. Phaedria looked at Doctor Friedman. She suddenly heard the clock ticking, her own heart beating, a police car wailing past the window.

'You knew, didn't you? You knew it all?'

'Miles, you have just got to make a decision, I can't stand this any longer.'

'Miles, if we are not all to go mad, you have to make some kind of a decision.'

'Miles, I'm really sorry to pressurize you, but I do feel I need to know what you're going to do.'

'Miles . . .'

'Miles . . .'

'Miles . . .'

'Jesus Christ, I have to get the hell out of here,' said Miles to Roz. 'I'm going to California. Are you going to come with me?'

Chapter Thirty

Los Angeles, London, 1986

'I know what I'm going to do,' said Miles.

He was lying on the beach at Malibu, salt and sun-streaked; his hair, shaggy from the sea, was full of sand, his eyes suddenly paler blue against his new tan. He had been out on his board for hours; Roz, finally weary of watching him, had been drinking beer and eating enchiladas at Alice's. When she saw him swoop in for the last time and fall exhausted on to the beach, she went down from the pier and walked over the sand to him.

'Good?'

He nodded, grinned wearily, ecstatically.

'Great. I'd really forgotten how great.'

'What's it like? Try and tell me.'

'Sex.'

'Ah.'

'Sex with the sun on you.'

'Sounds good.'

'Want to try?'

'Maybe. Tomorrow.'

'OK. I'll give you a lesson.'

'You look tired.'

'I am.'

'I bought you a beer.'

'Thanks.'

He drank it thirstily; Roz looked at him. The sun was coming down now into the sudden dusk below the brilliant dark blue. Great streaks of orange shot through the sky, glanced off the sea. Miles' profile, sharply beautiful, his perfectly shaped head, was etched against the water.

'You do look amazing,' said Roz simply.

He shrugged.

'You must know,' she said, 'how amazing you look.'

'I suppose I do. It doesn't matter to me.'

'It's like money, Miles. It would if you didn't have it.'

'Maybe.'

'Anyway, you use it.'

'I do? How?'

She put out her hand, traced the line of his face. 'Seducing poor helpless maidens.'

'And you.'

'And me.'

'I try not to.'

'I don't believe you.'

He turned and looked at her, drinking her in. She was already tanned herself, she wore a white T-shirt to protect her against the sun, a stinging pink bikini bottom. Her nose, after two days, had freckled; her eyes with their brown flecks looked glassy green against her golden skin.

'You don't look so bad yourself,' he said.

'Thank you.'

'Oh, jeez, it's beautiful here. God, I love it. It makes such sense of everything.'

That was when he told her what he had decided to do.

Later, sitting up at the house on Latego Canyon, drinking iced Californian chardonnay, he said, 'Roz, I love you.'

'No you don't,' she said.

Miles looked hurt.

'I do. I love you. I think you are just – well, the greatest.'

She smiled. 'That's what I call poetry.'

'Don't patronize me.'

'I'm not.'

'Do you love me?'

'I don't know,' she said, uncharacteristically truthful. 'I don't know. I love being with you. I love having sex with you. I just don't know if I actually love you. I've only ever loved Michael. What I feel for you is different from that.'

'How did you come to marry C. J.?' he said, unfazed by her answer. 'He's such a wimp. Doesn't make sense.'

'I don't think I should tell you.'

'Oh, come on. I know so much about you. Why should I care? I don't care what anybody does. You know I don't.'

'OK, I'll tell you. But it isn't a pretty story.'

She told him. He listened carefully. When she had finished, he grinned.

'You're right. It isn't entirely pretty. Jeez, the things you did for that father of yours. And that company.'

'Yes, I know. I just feel I have to.'

'That's what Phaedria says.'

'Does she?' There was real interest in her voice, a spark of genuine empathy in her eyes. 'I didn't realize she felt it too.' Then her face darkened. 'Bitch,' she said cheerfully.

'You really hate her, don't you?'

'Yes, I do.'

'I don't see why you hate her so much.'

'She's taken everything away from me, that's why.'

'That's balls,' said Miles.

'It is not balls. First my father. Then the company. Then Michael. I just hate her.'

'She didn't really take your father. He was only your father, for Christ's sake. Surely he had a right to a wife.'

'Yes, but not a wife as young as me.'

'What difference does that make?'

'I can't explain, but it does. Anyway, obviously she didn't love him, she couldn't have. She just wanted his money.'

'Why couldn't she love him?'

'Well, because he was old enough to be her father. Surely you can see that.'

'No,' he said, 'I can't.'

'But Miles, you can't want sex, for one thing, with someone old enough to be your father. It's disgusting.'

'I have had some absolutely great sex with women old enough to be my mother.'

She looked at him with intense curiosity.

'You haven't.'

'I have.'

'Who?'

'Lots of them. I can hardly remember their names. Hardly knew them.'

'Miles, tell me.'

'You don't want to hear,' he said shifting his position on the couch, reaching out for the bottle of wine, refilling her glass.

'Yes, I do.'

'OK.' He told her.

'Miles, that is disgusting,' said Roz, laughing. 'You were a gigolo.'

'Guess so.'

'Aren't you ashamed?'

'Not in the least. I made them real happy. Improved their marriages. Learnt a lot myself. Why should I be ashamed? Got my first Cartier watch that way,' he added proudly.

'Did you? What happened to it?'

'I had to sell it.'

'Why?'

'To pay a gambling debt.'

'Miles! What a degenerate life you've led.'

'Uh-huh. Fancy a little degeneration right now?'

'Maybe. Tempt me.'

Miles stood up, smiling. He took off his T-shirt, unzipped

his jeans, slithered out of them. Roz looked up at him, motionless.

'Tempted yet?'

'No,' she said. 'Not yet.'

'OK. Take your dress off.'

She took it off. She was naked underneath it. He knelt in front of her, started kissing her breasts, fondling her buttocks.

'Now?'

'No,' she said, laughing, trying to control her quivering, throbbing body. 'Not yet.'

He lifted her up against him.

'You smell salty. You smell of the sea. Let's go take a shower.'

In the shower he lifted her against him, thrusting himself deep into her, upwards, inwards; she felt her entire self invaded with pleasure. The water thundered down on them, confusing her, disorienting her; the only certainty was his penis inside her and the rising, shooting delight. She came swiftly, quickly, almost disappointed by the speed, felt him following her at once. He set her down, looked into her eyes, his own naked with love.

'That was the aperitif,' he said. 'Now we'll go have the meal.'

Later, much later, lying in his arms, remembering how her body had swooped and soared, remembering how he had said surfing was like sex, Roz wrestled with her conscience. It was a battle she was unfamiliar with. She had no way of knowing which of them would win.

'There's something I haven't told you,' said Phaedria. 'Something I'd like to.'

'What's that?'

Doctor Friedman looked at her with the odd blend of concern and disinterest that she had come to rely on.

'At Christmas Miles came to see me. He said he wanted to talk to me about my suggestion that I should form a trust fund for Julia and buy him out.'

'And?'

'Well, we went for a walk. He was just talking. I started telling him things. He has that effect on you.'

'What do you mean?'

'Well, you tell him everything. Anything. He just makes you

talk. I'm not sure why. He's the most non-judgemental person I've ever met. Apart from you,' she added with a smile.

'Go on. Try me.'

'Well, suddenly he asked me if I'd slept with Michael. Michael Browning.'

'And?'

'I got terribly angry.'

'That isn't surprising.'

'No, I know. But – well, suddenly I was screaming at him, really yelling and – well –'

'Go on.'

'Well, then I wanted to – to go to bed with him more than I'd ever wanted anything. In my whole life. It was awful. At the same time as being so angry.'

'Yes?'

'Don't you think that's odd?'

'Not in the least. Do you? Really? Anger and sex make very good bedfellows.'

'Maybe. Well, anyway. That's only part of the story.'

'So what happened?'

'Well, I kissed him. Really kissed him.'

'Was that all?'

'Yes. But I didn't want it to be all. I wanted to go on, there and then. It was awful.'

'So what did you do?'

'I said something like, oh, shit, leave me alone. And I ran back to the house. And I felt so ashamed.'

'Why?'

Phaedria stared at her. 'Well, because I was supposed to be in love with Michael. Grieving for Julian. And here I was just dying for sex, like some awful slut, that's what Roz called me once, with Miles.

'Well, that's not very surprising.'

'Isn't it?'

'Well, do you really think so?'

'Well, yes, I do.'

'Why?'

'Well, because it was so animal somehow. I mean, all Miles is is beautiful. He is amazingly beautiful, but that's all. I mean I'm not in the least in love with him.'

955

'Don't you think that might have something to do with it?'

'What?'

'That he is so beautiful?'

'I don't know. Should it?'

'Well, of course.' Margaret Friedman's face was calmly surprised. 'Here you are, a normally sexed young woman, lonely, frustrated, waiting to go and be with your new lover, in a state of some – what shall we say – excitement. Tension? And here is Miles, quite exceptionally attractive, as far as I can make out, making you angry, talking about sex, well of course you're going to feel excited about him. To want him. I don't think you have to worry about that at all.'

'Don't you?'

'No. Think about it. Do you?'

Phaedria thought. Then she shook her head. 'I'm afraid I can't let myself off the hook that lightly. It was so strong, so violent, what I felt.'

'Well,' said Margaret Friedman, 'judge yourself harshly if you want to. It's your prerogative. Why do you think it was so violent?'

'I don't know,' said Phaedria slowly. 'I really don't know. It was more violent than anything I've ever felt for Michael, even. I don't – well, I don't often have sexual feelings as strongly as that. Not really. It was – well, strange. Comparable with what I'd felt once for Julian.'

'Really?'

'Yes. That was the strange thing. One night, quite early, long before we were married, we had a terrible fight, Julian and I. I left, in one of his priceless antique cars. He followed. He was so angry. I thought he would kill me. And I was terribly angry too. And – well, we – we had sex, right in the middle of this fight, in the back of his car, in some lane at three o'clock in the morning, or whatever it was. It was wonderful, but it was very violent. What I felt then was exactly how I felt for Miles that day. That violent. Strange. I couldn't stop thinking about it.'

'How was Miles afterwards?'

'Terrific. Really terrific. He just came and talked to me, told me not to worry, not to get upset. Said he was sorry for making me so angry. Completely defused the situation. He is such a nice person.' She was silent for a while, then she said, 'There is something about Miles that gives me the strangest feeling.'

'Yes? Can you analyse it?'

'I don't know. Let's see. He makes me feel warm, relaxed, kind of settled. He makes me laugh. He makes me see things kind of straight. But it's not just that. It's –' She was silent for a moment.

'Yes,' said Doctor Friedman patiently, watching her carefully.

'It's like being desperate for a drink. You know? Or – well, I've never taken any drugs, except a bit of pot at Oxford, but I imagine it's like being desperate for a fix. Something you've known and liked, needed, and then been deprived of.'

'Yes?'

'And well, Miles is like that. Like a drink. A fix. A sort of familiar, predictable pleasure. Can you begin to understand what I mean?'

'Yes,' said Doctor Friedman. 'Yes, I can. Indeed I can.'

Candy was weeping copiously in the suite at Claridge's. Her father sat helplessly, passing her Kleenex, trying to mop her up, staunch the flow.

'Honey, it's probably only a tiff. A silly lovers' quarrel.'

'No, Daddy, it's not, you don't understand. It's awful. It's serious. He's left me. He's gone.'

'Gone where?'

'Gone to California.'

'How long for?'

'I don't know. And he didn't even ask me if I wanted to go with him.'

'He needs whipping,' said Mason, with the look that fathers of jilted daughters have worn since time immemorial. 'Whipping. I'll do it myself if I get the chance. Young good-for-nothing. Nobody pushes my little girl around like that and gets away with it. You come on home with me, honey, and I'll find him and give him a very nasty dose of his own medicine. You packed?'

'Yes, Daddy. Well, no. Mostly. I have a few new things. I need a new suitcase.'

'I'll buy you one, honey.' Mason McCall looked around him,

looked at the heap of Candy's shopping, the huge bed, the implications of it all. He pushed them aside, looking frantically for an escape route, back into the safe harbour of an only daughter's unsullied innocence.

'Honey, if you've been sleeping here, where did Miles sleep? Did he –?'

Candy snapped out of her crying jag like a stripper out of a G string and with about as much subtlety and panache.

'Miles didn't stay here,' she said, sniffling, dabbing her eyes with a tissue, hiccupping gently, tremulously, in tones that implied she might have had the vapours had her father even entertained such a thought, 'he stayed with the family.'

'Well anyway,' said Mason, taking her back into his arms, choosing to be reassured by this slightly unlikely story, 'it's time you came home, honey, we should go home together, I guess to Chicago, and you could go to college there next fall. Would you like that?'

'No,' said Candy, bursting into fresh sobs. 'I want Miles.'

'He'll be back, honey,' said Mason, drawing her head on to his shoulder, stroking her golden hair. 'He'll be back. You mark my words. There, there Candy. Daddy knows.'

Next day, Miles took Roz all around the Los Angeles he knew and had grown up in. They drove along the Coast Highway into Santa Monica, and walked out on to the pier. 'I learnt to skate board down there,' he said, pointing to the boardwalk, 'and look, there, see, that's Big Dean's Muscle Inn. Muscle Beach was here then, not in Venice. We used to come here on Sundays. Have lunch sometimes and ride the dodgems. They had the best swordfish steaks ever.

'Our house was down there,' he said, 'there was a road through there, just along from the pier, it was called Appian Way, it's all gone now, in the name of progress. Come on, I'll show you where my school was.'

They walked up to the car and drove up towards Santa Monica High.

'This place has a terrific pedigree,' he said, 'did you know James Dean lived in Santa Monica with his aunt?'

Roz laughed and said she did not.

'There it is,' he said pointing up at the big brick building, 'that's Samo High. I was so happy there, and I had this really great girlfriend called Donna, Donna Palladini, she had the most amazing legs you ever saw –'

'Better than mine?' said Roz jealously.

'Yup. Better than yours. She was the first girl I ever screwed, and it was just wonderful. Even the very first time. Probably now she's married with six kids. Her husband's a lucky guy.'

'I don't know if you actually want to spoil my day,' said Roz, 'but you're doing a great job.'

'I'm sorry. Come on, let's go have lunch on the beach at Venice.'

They drove down to Venice, bought Cokes and hot dogs and sat in the sun.

'Good God,' said Roz, looking at the hippies, 'it's still 1960 here.'

'Yeah,' said Miles, 'I kind of like that.'

'What, peace and love and all that?' she said, mocking him.

'Yup.' He turned and looked at her. 'It's better than all the things you guys get up to,' he said very seriously.

They stayed there all afternoon, not saying very much; Roz dozed in the hot sun and woke to find Miles hauling her to her feet.

'Now,' he said, 'highlight of the tour. Mulholland Drive at sunset.'

They drove up Santa Monica Boulevard, with the hood of the T-Bird down, looking at the tightly shuttered Rolls and Mercedes that passed them, the women in their dark glasses and shoulder pads, the men in suits, chewing on cigars, the rollerskaters, the joggers, all moving in a graceful, co-ordinated pattern beneath the palm trees and the bright hot sky.

'Great place,' said Miles happily. 'Great place.'

They turned left and up towards the hills; he took a few swift turns and drove into a high twisty road. 'This is it,' he said, 'you wait. Just you wait.'

Abruptly the road snaked round to the right; on the left was a car park. He pulled in, drove towards the wall at its far edge and parked.

'There,' he said. 'There it is. Take a look at that.'

Roz took a look. Below them, curiously two dimensional in its effect, was the neat sprawl of Los Angeles, growing misty in

959

the evening air, beyond that the silver-blue streak of the sea, and to either side the rolling, folded velvety hills. The sky was turning blush orange, pinky grey clouds shot across it; the sun was dropping like a monster leaden fireball into the ocean.

'God,' said Roz, 'I do have to say that it is beautiful.'

'It is, isn't it? Just beautiful?'

'Now what do we do?' she asked, mildly amused by his rapture.

'We sit here and neck,' he said, turning her face towards him. 'That's what everybody comes here for.'

Later that night after they had had dinner at Alice's and gone back to the house and made love and talked and made love again, Roz sat determinedly up in bed and switched on the light.

'Miles,' she said, 'I have something to tell you.'

'Can't it wait? I'm kind of washed up.'

'No, it can't wait. It's important. Sit up and listen.'

He looked at her warily. 'I hope you're not going to tell me you're in the club.'

'I'm not,' she said, 'but would you mind if I was?'

'Probably not. Go ahead. What is it?'

'Well –' Roz was not used to confession. 'Miles, this may make you very angry. Shocked even. But I have to tell you. I just do.'

'OK, I'm listening.'

'Oh, God, Miles, it's really bad.'

'Can't be that bad.'

'It's bad. You'll hate me.'

'Try me.'

'All right. Miles, the consortium. The Zürich consortium.'

'Yeah?'

'The one you've decided to sell to.'

'Yeah?'

'It's me. I dreamed it up. Laundered the bank account. Cooked the books. Planned to buy it back when you'd gone.'

He looked at her in complete silence, just studying her, contemplating her, as if she were some strange alien creature he had to familiarize himself with, his face expressionless. Roz sat, frozen, looking back at him, her gaze steady, waiting for dislike, mistrust, shock, to hit her. Then slowly, so slowly it was like the sun coming up through a deep thick mist, Miles smiled, his most glorious, joyous, beatific smile.

'I thought it was,' he said.

It was Letitia who put two and two together and made a very exact four. She phoned Claridge's, wishing to invite Miles and Candy to dinner, and was told Mr Wilburn had checked out.

Mildly surprised, she phoned Phaedria. 'Darling, did you know Miles had gone?'

'Yes and no,' said Phaedria carefully. 'He was very very fed up at the weekend. I asked him and Candy both down to Marriotts and he said he wasn't fit for human company. He'd been saying for weeks he wanted to go back to California. Maybe they've just gone.'

'No, well, she hasn't gone anyway. Candy's still here. I spoke to her. Her father's with her. He's taking her back to Chicago.'

'Good heavens. Well, he certainly didn't say anything about it to me. We had lunch last Thursday.'

'Hmm,' said Letitia. 'Rum, I would say. Have you had any kind of decision from him?'

'Nothing. I'd begun to think I never would. I thought his next move would be into Julian's old office.' She laughed just a little too casually. 'Well, maybe he's gone off to think.'

'Maybe. I'll call Roz. She'll know. Thick as thieves, those two. It worries me sometimes.'

'Why?' said Phaedria.

'I don't know. I really don't know.'

Letitia phoned the house at Cheyne Walk. Mrs Emerson was not at home, said Maria, the Spanish housekeeper. She had gone away for a few days.

'Good gracious,' said Letitia, 'this is very sudden.'

'Yes, madam. She's sent Miranda and Nanny up to Scotland. She said she had to go to America.'

'Did she indeed?' said Letitia. 'All right, Maria, thank you.'

Uncomfortably aware she might be foolishly rushing in where an angel would greatly fear to tread, she dialled Eliza's number. Peveril answered.

'Peveril, it's Letitia. How are you, dear?'

'Better since this morning,' he said cheerfully. 'Bagged twenty brace of pheasants, before lunch. Not bad, eh?'

'How clever you are Peveril,' said Letitia. 'I got a couple myself this morning.'

'Well done, my dear. Where was that? I didn't know there was any shooting near you.'

'Fortnum's,' said Letitia cheerfully. 'Is Eliza there?'

'Yes, she is. Doing something foolish in the Long Gallery. Measuring it up for African blinds, I think she said. I wish she'd leave it all alone. Still, it keeps her happy,' he added hastily.

'Austrian,' said Letitia.

'What's that, my dear?'

'Austrian blinds. Anyway, African or Austrian they'll look perfectly frightful. Let me talk to her.'

Eliza came on the phone. 'Hello, Letitia. Are you all right?'

'Yes, but Peveril won't be, darling, if you put Austrian blinds in his Long Gallery. Grounds for divorce, I would have said. You're in Scotland, dear, not Kensington.'

'Oh, Letitia, don't be ridiculous. They'll transform the place.'

'Indeed they will,' said Letitia. 'Well, I suppose one man's meat, and all that. In my book Austrian blinds are very poisonous indeed. Now then, darling, is Roz there?'

'No, she isn't,' said Eliza a trifle coldly. 'She's gone to the States. She went yesterday.'

'Ah. Which side?'

'Washington.'

'Indeed? Are you sure?'

'Perfectly. She was very specific about it. She has to do some work on the hotels and apparently the Washington Morell is the best-run, the most successful, the most profitable and so on and so forth, so she was off to take a close look at it, as a role model, so to speak. Well, that's what she said.'

'I see. So how long is she there for?'

'Well, we've got Miranda and Nanny for a week. I think she was going on to New York.'

'I see. Oh, well, it doesn't matter. I had a little idea for her, that's all. It can wait.'

Very well aware that it was nothing to do with her at all what Roz did and with whom, Letitia phoned the Washington Morell. The manager said Mrs Emerson had been there for twenty-four hours and had left, he thought for New York.

The manager of the Morell, New York, was not expecting Mrs Emerson at all.

Letitia phoned Phaedria back.

'Darling, do you think it's at all a possibility that Roz and Miles might have gone off together somewhere? On some business trip? Roz is missing too, investigating hotels.'

'I don't know,' said Phaedria, oddly aware of an icy, quite illogical dread creeping down her spine, 'but they have got very close in the last few weeks. Maybe Roz's secretary knows where she is. I'll ask her tomorrow.'

Lucy Dudley said Mrs Emerson had told her she was on a whistle-stop tour of some of the major chains of hotels in the States, and wouldn't be back until the following Wednesday; she had no numbers and no itinerary; and that Mrs Emerson was calling her every day for urgent messages, if Lady Morell wanted to leave one. She was adamant that she had not been given an address.

As Roz normally never went out so much as to get her hair cut without leaving contact numbers in triplicate and a maze of alternatives in the unlikely event of her not returning to the office within the hour, her behaviour was about as much out of character as if she had been found walking down Bond Street stark naked in the company of the Hare Krishna brethren.

Phaedria called Letitia and said she was beginning to think she was right, but did it really matter very much (feeling, indeed knowing, that somehow it did). Letitia had replied, very much too lightly (also feeling that it probably mattered greatly), that of course not, that what they did was their own business and none of them had any right to interfere in it whatsoever.

But Letitia lay awake until the dawn broke, wide eyed, distressed, wondering why she was so troubled by what was happening, and what she might be able to do about it; and Phaedria, after an equally sleepless night and without being entirely certain why, called Doctor Friedman and asked her for an urgent appointment.

'By way of a penance,' said Miles to Roz, after breakfasting from a huge basket of strawberries and melons he had fetched early from the store for her, 'you have to come and meet a very old friend of mine.'

963

'I do hope she doesn't have amazing legs and a talent for screwing,' said Roz, smiling at him.

'He doesn't. I've never seen his legs, they are always encased in a long skirt –'

'For God's sake, is he some kind of transvestite?'

'He is not, and don't interrupt. And he has no idea at all what a screw might feel like. He is a man of God and he runs the refuge in Santa Monica, and he was my grandmother's best friend. My mother's too,' he added more soberly. 'I really want you to meet him.'

'All right. I'll come.'

He looked at her and leant forward and kissed her.

'You look different this morning.'

'I feel different.'

She did. For the first time in her entire life, she felt accepted and liked, loved, for what she was. Even with Michael she had not ever let her guard right down; had kept what she felt the very worst of herself, the most devious, the most selfish, the most ruthless, hidden. Miles had taken her and with one careless, loving piece of acceptance had turned her into a person as uncomplicatedly, as happily transparent, as he was. If he could take her as she was, then she could take herself. All her life she had felt the real Roz was valueless, not worth loving. Now suddenly someone infinitely important to her was telling her she was. She smiled back at him, radiant, shining with happiness.

'I love you, Miles.'

'Hey,' he said. 'When I said that to you, you told me I didn't.'

'Well? What are you going to tell me?'

'I'm going to tell you,' he said, kissing her again, 'that I think you do.'

'Good.'

Father Kennedy was sitting in the sunshine, as he always did in the morning, dozing peacefully. He was a very old man suddenly. Miles, who had not seen him for four years, was shocked at how he had aged.

'Father Kennedy,' he said, touching him lightly on the arm. 'Good morning. How are you?'

The old man woke with a start; his faded blue eyes opened, alighted on Miles, his confusion cleared and an expression of great joy came over his face.

'Miles! Miles Wilburn! This is a wonderful thing. How are you, Miles, and how is your grandmother? And what are you doing here?'

'I'm looking up old friends, Father. A great deal has happened to me.'

'Well, now, and I know quite a lot of them. I had a visit from young Lady Morell, several visits, and her baby too. So did they find you, Miles, and whatever has become of you down there in Nassau, that none of our letters were answered and we were left to imagine you had dropped off the face of the earth?'

'What happened, Father, was my grandmother's friend, Mrs Galbraith. She decided to keep a few letters to herself. But she has been very good to my grandmother, looked after her like a mother. So I kind of forgave her.'

'And is she all right now, Mrs Kelly? I miss her and our little chats very sadly.'

'She's well, Father, but I think you would find her very changed. She is – well, confused. I had thought to bring her back here, but I don't feel I should now. She is happy with Mrs Galbraith and it would be kind of wrong to disturb her. I'm going to see her next week.'

'Then give her my very best wishes. Oh, I should love to see her again. Maybe I can go down to Nassau one of these days, on a small vacation, and visit her.'

'She'd like that, Father. And how are you, and how is the refuge?'

'I am very well, Miles, and the refuge is doing quite nicely. Lady Morell has been very good to us indeed and arranged for some money to come every month. It's a great help. She is an extremely nice person, wouldn't you say? Or have you not yet met her?'

'Oh, I've met her, Father, I certainly have, and yes, she is an extremely nice person. Isn't she Roz?'

Roz looked at Father Kennedy and then at Miles; he grinned at her.

'Go on, Roz,' he said as if she were a small child. 'Tell Father Kennedy what a nice person Phaedria is.'

'Very nice,' said Roz. The words were forced out, but she managed to smile. Dear God, she thought to herself, I have come a long way.

'And who is this?' said Father Kennedy, beaming at Roz. 'Or am I not allowed to be introduced to her?'

'Of course, Father. Forgive me. I was thinking, as you'd met Phaedria, you'd know Roz. Father Kennedy, this is Roz Emerson. Now then, let me tell you who she is. You will be really surprised. Really, seriously surprised. You remember Mr Dashwood?'

'Now Miles, as if I would not remember Mr Dashwood. He was such a good man,' he said, turning to Roz, 'so generous, he did so much for Miles and for Mrs Kelly. I miss him. Tell me, is all well with him, and have you found him as well, Miles?'

'Not exactly, Father, it's a very peculiar story. Could we maybe have some tea and I'll tell you all about it.'

'Of course. Now what am I thinking of? Miles, you go and get the tea, you remember where the kitchen is, and I will talk to this young lady while you are gone. Come and sit down here, my dear, and tell me what you think of California.'

'I think it's wonderful,' said Roz. 'Simply wonderful.'

'So now, did you know Mr Dashwood? Was he a friend of yours?'

'Well,' said Roz, 'in a way. He was my father.'

'Your father?' The old man looked startled.

'Yes. But you see, we didn't know him as Hugo Dashwood.'

'You didn't?'

'No. It's very complicated. Perhaps Miles should explain.'

Miles came back with the tea. He put it down, sat on the grass beside Roz. Father Kennedy's old face was puzzled, troubled.

'Miles, you have to explain all this to me. I'm a foolish old man. I don't understand what Miss –'

'Roz,' said Roz.

'Roz is telling me. Are you saying that Mr Dashwood was going under another name in England all the time?'

'That's right, Father. It all sounds the most ridiculous nonsense, I know, but it's true. Like all the best facts it's stranger than fiction. Only he wasn't going under another name in England. His name there was his real name. He was called Julian Morell. That was the real person. Hugo Dashwood was a pseudonym. God knows why he used it. But he did.'

'So Lady Morell, she is married to Mr Dashwood? Have I got this right now?'

'Yes, I suppose so. Only she is not married to him any more. He's died.'

'Died? Yes, of course, because Lady Morell had recently been widowed. That's why she was looking for you, of course, because of the will.'

'That's right, Father.'

The old man turned to Roz. 'I am sorry, my child. Sorry you have lost your father. Sorry to have been so tactless. You must forgive me. All that business with the other name, very upsetting, very difficult for you.'

'Of course. Anyway, it was a while ago, I'm feeling much better now.'

'Father Kennedy,' said Miles, 'the whole thing is still very mysterious. You might be able to help. Have you any idea, any idea at all, why Hugo Dashwood – that is Julian Morell – should have left me a lot of money? A share in his company?'

Father Kennedy looked at them both. His mind was racing, he felt sick, trapped. He must keep calm. He must remember that he had always told himself that Lee might have been mistaken, that the doctors might have been mistaken, that Dean and not Hugo Dashwood, or this Julian Morell, had been Miles' father.

He closed his eyes briefly, calling on the Almighty for aid; then he opened them again and smiled serenely at Miles.

'Well now, Miles, he was very very fond of you. You know that. And very generous to you. Putting you through college and everything. And when your parents died, he felt he had to take care of you, keep an eye on you. Your mother asked him to, and he promised. He took that promise very seriously. And kept it. And he was very proud of you, Miles. I think it is entirely to be expected that he should remember you in his will.'

'I suppose so, Father. But it isn't just remembering. It's a lot, an awful lot of money.'

'Then I can only say I hope you will use it wisely, Miles. Money can be a terrible thing, if it is wrongly used.'

'I'll try, Father. I'll take a leaf out of Phaedria's book maybe, and give some to you for a start.'

'That would be extremely welcome, extremely. My goodness, the way we are going, this will shortly be the richest organization in the United States of America.'

'Excellent. In good hands, that's for sure. But also, Father, can you think why he left me the money in such a roundabout way? Why not be more direct about it?'

'Miles, when you have lived as long as I have, and seen as many things happen, you will not be surprised or even puzzled by anything at all. People do many strange things for many strange reasons, which are not for others to question and which seem perfectly good and sound to them at the time.'

'I suppose so,' said Miles. 'Well anyway, it doesn't really matter too much. And something very good has come out of it.'

'And what might that be?'

'Well,' said Miles, reaching out, taking Roz's hand, 'Roz and I have found one another.'

A terrible fear had invaded the old man's heart. He sought desperately to make Miles dispel it.

'Yes, it is always a wonderful thing, to find a new friend.'

'Well, yeah, I guess that's so, but Roz and I are more than friends, Father. We're – well, maybe I shouldn't be telling you this, Father, in case you tell me I'm in mortal sin or something, I know in the eyes of the church it is a sin, but, we're in love and we've been living together, and – well, Roz doesn't exactly know this, yet, but I'm planning on marrying her as soon as ever I can.'

When Phaedria got into the office next morning, tired and inexplicably sick at heart, Sarah Brownsmith was looking worried.

'I'm glad you're here, Lady Morell. Someone's been calling you from California. A man. He sounded quite old. With an Irish accent.'

'Father Kennedy,' said Phaedria, 'I wonder what he wants.'

'He wants you to phone him. He sounded rather upset.'

'Oh, dear. He's such a nice, sweet old man. He was so kind to me. I wonder what's happened.

'Here's his number. It must be – let's see, goodness, midnight there. It must be urgent.'

'Yes,' said Phaedria. 'Yes, it must.'

She phoned the number. It was the refuge.

'Father Kennedy? This is Phaedria Morell. Father, is something wrong?'

'It is, my child, it's terribly wrong. Or at least it might be.'

'Whatever is it? Can I help? Please tell me.'

'It's very difficult, I can only tell you a little. I would be breaking every kind of confidence to tell you more. But you are a sensitive and a clever girl, and perhaps you will know what to do.'

'Father, you have to tell me what the matter is. Please. And I'll try to help.'

'Very well. Today, your friend Miles came to see me.'

'Miles?'

'Miles. And he had another young lady with him.'

Fear struck out at Phaedria. She sat up rigidly on her chair, trying to keep calm.

'Another young lady?'

'Yes. Her name was Roz. You know her, don't you?

'I do. Yes.'

'She is the daughter of your husband, and of my friend, Miles' friend, Hugo Dashwood. As I still have to think of him. I'm sorry.'

'That's all right, Father. Go on please.'

'Well, Miles was telling me about the legacy and so on. It was very good of your husband, very good indeed, to leave him that money. But –'

'Yes, Father, but what? You're not making any sense.'

'Well, Miles told me, and God forgive me I didn't know what to say to him, so I said nothing, nothing at all, that he and Roz were in love. And that they were going to get married.'

'Married! Roz and Miles? Oh, Father, no, that can't be true.'

'He told me himself, sitting here on the grass, holding her hand. And they are a nice, a very nice young couple. But, Lady Morell, the marriage cannot be. It must not be. Now you must not ask me why. I am not in a position to tell you, and besides that, I may be mistaken in my thinking. But for Miles' sake and for Roz's you have to stop them marrying. Cohabiting even. I suspect, and God forgive me if I am wrong, they are, they could be, they could well be, in mortal sin.'

'Father, I can't stop them marrying. They are grown people. I had no idea there was any question of it, none of us did, but if they want to marry, then they will. Nobody, least of all I, can stop them.'

'They must be stopped,' he said, 'they must.'

He sounded so distressed that Phaedria felt frightened.

'All right,' she said, largely to soothe him. 'All right, I will stop them. Somehow. I promise. Please don't worry, Father, I will talk to people here, to the family, and we will stop them.'

'Oh,' he said, and she could hear him relaxing, calming across the wires. 'Thank God. I knew you would know what to do. God bless you. I will pray for you. And for them. The poor poor things. So much in love.'

'Thank you, Father,' said Phaedria, reflecting even in her panic that it was going to take quite a bit of intervention on the part of the Almighty to enable her to stop Roz marrying Miles if that was indeed what she had decided to do. 'Now do calm yourself. Everything will be perfectly all right, I'm sure. I will see to it. Goodness, it must be late there now. You must go to bed and sleep and just not worry any more.'

'I will indeed, Lady Morell. Thank you. Good night to you now. And please call me if you need me.'

'Good night, Father,' said Phaedria, wishing fervently it was midnight in London as well as Los Angeles and that she could take an extremely strong sleeping pill and remain unconscious for many hours. 'Sleep well. And don't worry.'

She put the phone down and sank into her chair. She felt as if she was in the midst of some appalling storm raging round her, knocking her senseless this way and that. What was she to do, and who could she turn to? She had a dreadful, a terrible awestruck feeling that she knew exactly why Father Kennedy was so distraught, that she was waking not from her nightmare but to it, and she could hardly begin to summon the courage to confront it.

She looked up at Sarah Brownsmith, who had just walked back into the office.

'You look terrible, Lady Morell.'

'Thank you, Sarah.'

'I'm sorry, I didn't mean to be rude. But you do look very white. Was that bad news?'

'In a way, Sarah, yes.' She sank her head on to her hands. Sarah was alarmed.

'Can I get you something? A coffee? Brandy?'

'Yes,' said Phaedria, looking up with something approaching

a smile on her face. 'Yes, I really think the occasion warrants a brandy. And a coffee. And Sarah, could you call Doctor Friedman, and see if she can see me this morning. Tell her it's desperate. She did say she couldn't but I have to talk to her. I absolutely have to.'

'I don't think your friend Father Kennedy was very pleased with your news,' said Roz, laughing, as they drove away. 'Poor old man, he looked terrible.'

'Yes, he did,' said Miles, looking thoughtful. 'Really terrible. Shocked, I mean seriously shocked. I can't think why. Poor old man.'

'Maybe he isn't well,' said Roz. 'He didn't look well.'

'He didn't, did he? Well, I'll call in again tomorrow and see if he's all right. He might have a weak heart or something. The news may have had nothing to do with it. Or maybe he's just a bit confused. Like my grandmother. These old people do get – well, odd.'

'Maybe. Anyway, that was some proposal. I mean really romantic. You could have warned me.'

'Oh,' he said, smiling, 'I think I have. Lots of times. If you'd been looking out for it.'

'Maybe.'

'Anyway, let me try and do it better.' He stopped the car, pulled in to a side road, and looked at her without moving, without smiling.

'Roz,' he said. 'Roz, I love you. Please will you marry me?'

'Yes, Miles,' she said. 'Yes, I will.'

'Doctor Friedman, I think now I really have to ask you some questions and you really have to answer them.'

'Really? Why?' Doctor Friedman was as cool, as unruffled as ever.

'Please stop asking me questions.'

'It's the only way I can help you.'

'Well,' said Phaedria, 'I'm not so sure about that. But anyway, let me ask you one. Who is Miles? Do you know?'

'Don't you?'

'No. No, I don't.'

'Are you sure?'

971

'Of course I'm sure.'

'Think, Phaedria. Think hard. Don't run away from it.'

'I don't know what you mean.'

'Don't you?'

'No,' she almost screamed the word. 'Yes, yes, I do. Oh, God. I just hate this so much.'

'You don't have to go on.'

'I do. I do, though. You don't know . . .'

'Don't know what?'

'About Roz. And Miles.'

'Roz and Miles?' For the first time Dr Friedman reacted. Phaedria felt it, saw it. That told her everything. But still she turned from it.

'Yes. Roz and Miles. They want to, they're going to, get married.'

'Ah.'

'So –'

'So, yes, we have to go on. Very well. And of course you know who Miles is, don't you?'

'Yes,' said Phaedria, with a shuddering sob, 'yes, I do. He's Julian's son. Isn't he?'

'Yes. Yes he is.'

Tears filled Phaedria's eyes. She shivered suddenly, looked at Doctor Friedman almost fearfully. 'Could I – could I have a drink?'

'Of course. What do you want? Brandy?'

'Yes, please. God –' She smiled, brushing the tears away. 'I've had one this morning already. I'll be an alcoholic soon at this rate.'

'There are worse things to be.' She pressed her buzzer. 'Joan, bring us two large brandies in, will you? And some coffee. Now then –' she looked at Phaedria – 'is it really so bad. For you? And didn't you, surely you realize now, didn't you know all along?'

'Yes. No. You see we all wondered, obviously, we were bound to. But Letitia, his mother, you know –'

'Yes, I know.'

'Letitia and Eliza, and Camilla, she's –'

'Yes, I know who Camilla is.'

'Oh God,' Phaedria looked at her, and managed to smile. 'Is

there anything about us you don't know? Well, we all checked out some dates, the time Julian would have had to be with Miles' mother. He wasn't. He was either in New York or in England.'

'Phaedria, there's no doubt, I'm afraid. No doubt at all. Miles was obviously born either a little early or a little late. Which is the more likely, I wonder? Perhaps he will know.'

'Perhaps.'

'Well, is it really so bad, after all. For you?'

'No, it's not so bad for me. But terrible, awful for Roz. I just don't know how she'll bear it.'

'How did you find out about that?'

'Father Kennedy, an old priest in Santa Monica, who had known Miles and his parents ever since he was born, and who obviously knew, rang me, very distressed. Miles had been to see him with Roz. They told him they were going to get married. He told me I had to stop them.'

'But he didn't tell you why?'

'No. Not in so many words. But I – well, I suppose I knew.'

'Of course. You must have known many times. Whatever the evidence of the dates. When you first heard about him in the will. When you first saw Miles. When you felt that very strong attraction for him. Well, you would. He is probably very like his father. You loved his father and you were very physically involved with him. And you said to me, something like Miles made you feel as if you'd had a fix of something you had –' she looked at her notes – 'known and liked and been deprived off. Well, of course he would.'

'Yes, I suppose he would.' She was relaxing now, calm with relief that it was over, in the open.

'Is he very like his father?'

'Not at all, and yet terribly. He's straightforward and relaxed and blond and blue-eyed, so not at all. But then he's amazingly quick and intuitive and charming and makes you talk and talk, and very very sexy, so yes, very like him. There is something about him, the eyes, I suppose, that is totally Julian. Even though they're the wrong colour.'

'I'm amazed none of you have worked it out before.'

'Well, we did. I told you. But then – well yes, you're right. Babies don't always come at the proper time. Look at Julia.

Maybe he was early, like her. But then you see, on the surface he is so very different. He couldn't act or look less like him. Could you –' she took a long drink of brandy – 'could you tell me about it now? Have you always known?'

'Yes, for a long time. He first came to me when Lee had just died. He felt utterly miserable. It was a bad time altogether for him, something had gone wrong for him here, something personal, some affair this end as well. But I think he really loved Lee. Really loved her. She was obviously an extraordinary person. Very brave and lovely. And you see, he was unable to grieve openly. At all. So it became almost unbearable for him. That was what drove him to me. It was the only release. Otherwise it would have been an unthinkable thing for a man like him to do.'

'I suppose so. Poor Julian.'

'Yes. And then he was wracked with guilt over Miles' father's suicide.'

'Which was – because –?'

'Well, yes. He found out. About Miles. Some fool doctor told him he would never have been able to father a child. He put two and two together. That was tragic. Wicked.'

'Poor Miles. We must keep that from him.'

'If we can.'

'And then after Lee's death, he would have given anything to have brought Miles out into the open, to have told everyone, to have given him a home, his name. But he had promised Lee, and besides it would have meant telling Miles. Very painful for a child. On top of his mother's death. So – more silence.'

'Yes.'

'The whole thing started as a bet with himself. He decided to pretend to be someone else and see if he could sustain the fiction for a bit. But he fell in love with Lee, made her pregnant, and the whole thing got out of hand.'

'That's exactly what Letitia said must have happened.'

'His mother?'

'Yes.'

'Do you think she knew too? I mean really knew. Despite the dates.'

'Perhaps. She was very worried about Roz and Miles.'

'How do you think she'll cope with it all?'

'Oh, wonderfully,' said Phaedria, 'we don't have to worry about Letitia. She could fight World War Three single handed.'

'Good. It sounds, from what you say of Roz, she may need to.'

'So did he go on seeing you?' asked Phaedria. 'Julian, I mean. All those years?'

'On and off. Yes. I think he became addicted to me.'

'I can see why,' said Phaedria with a half smile.

'He loved you very much,' said Doctor Friedman suddenly. 'Very much indeed. He said he had never felt anything quite like what he felt for you. He saw you truly as a new beginning.'

'Oh, God,' said Phaedria, and the tears started to flow again. 'Oh, God, don't.'

'Why not? It's important. It's good you should know that, surely?'

'Yes, but I wasn't a new beginning. If I was, I soon ended again. I behaved badly. I was selfish, difficult. Fooled around with someone. Oh, not properly. But enough to make him angry and jealous.'

'Phaedria, you mustn't be so hard on yourself. You were very young and thrown into an impossible situation. You tried. He did far worse things. Manipulating you and Roz. Sleeping with Camilla North.'

'God, he told you all that?'

'Oh, yes, by the end of his life he was very seriously mixed up. I was worried about him. I saw him very frequently.'

'So what about the will? For God's sake, why did he do that to us all?'

'He was very angry with you. With you and Roz. I don't think he had any idea how difficult she made things for you. He felt you were both just behaving very badly. At one point he really did think you were having an affair. And he made that will to punish you. Both of you. In a fit of dreadful rage. After he'd come to LA to find you. Remember?'

Phaedria nodded.

'And he'd seen Miles by then. Or heard from him anyway. He was quite determined to go and see him, tell him everything, urge him to come and join the family. He felt he'd be able to cope by then. Oh, of course he always meant to make another, more reasonable will, but he said doing that one had been therapy. He said he'd modify it when he'd told Miles and introduced him to the family. He thought he had plenty of time. Then I think when you found him in bed with Camilla North, and left him, he just forgot it. He was so appalled at what he'd done. He just kept postponing remaking it, until something was resolved. It's a big thing, of course, making a will if you're as rich as he was. And the earlier one he'd made was before he'd met and married you, so he knew he couldn't revert to that.'

Phaedria looked at her. 'Why didn't you tell us all before? When you first heard he'd died, when I came to see you? It would have saved so much unhappiness.'

'If I'd known about Miles and Roz, believe me I would have done. But apart from that, I couldn't, Phaedria. I see my position as very like that of your friend Father Kennedy. I have to safeguard confidences.'

'But Julian was dead. You weren't betraying him.'

'I would have been betraying you if you hadn't been able to deal with it. I had to learn about you. There was no rush. I couldn't keep you from the real pain. Of Julian's death and the will. And I knew you would work towards the discovery by yourself in time. I thought that was much better. I knew you had come to rely on me, would call on me if you really needed me.'

'How did you know?' said Phaedria, angry, hostile. 'I might have done something desperate.'

'No,' said Doctor Friedman, and she was smiling into Phaedria's rage. 'I could see you were very strong. I wasn't worried about you at all. Not seriously.'

'Well anyway,' said Phaedria, still half angry, 'what do I do now? Who do I tell? Who tells Roz? And Miles? Oh, it's awful. Please tell me what to do.'

'Well, it certainly shouldn't be you to tell Roz. Who is she really closest to?'

'Letitia.' Phaedria spoke without hesitation.

'And you think she could stand it?'

'Yes, I do. But maybe you should talk to her. I don't think I could bear it.'

'All right. Bring her to see me. Let me see – this evening, about six.'

'Thank you. And how about Miles and Roz? We should get them home. The longer it goes on, the worse it will be.'

'Yes. Can you contact them?'

'Only through Father Kennedy. He will have a phone number or at least could go out to the house.'

'Then ask him to do that. To get them to call Letitia.'

'All right. What a nightmare.'

'In a way,' said Doctor Friedman. 'But then, waking up from a nightmare is such a relief, isn't it?'

'I suppose,' said Letitia, sitting very upright in Doctor Friedman's office, 'that you are going to tell me that Miles is my grandson.'

'Yes,' said Doctor Friedman. 'Yes, I am.'

Letitia was silent for a while. Phaedria reached out and took her hand.

'Are you all right, Mrs Morell?'

'Oh, perfectly,' said Letitia, brushing away a tear, smiling brightly, a trifle tremulously at Doctor Friedman. 'I suppose I knew all along. I suppose we all did. It was such a relief when we managed to persuade ourselves it was impossible. There was something, just something about him that was Julian.'

'Yes,' said Phaedria, 'I felt it too.'

'Oh, darling,' said Letitia, turning to her. 'I was so hoping you would fall in love with Miles. That would have been so absolutely perfect. But I suppose life isn't like that?'

'No,' said Doctor Friedman. 'Not often.'

Letitia was silent for a while. 'Poor Julian,' she said. 'Poor man. How dreadful to think he was so unhappy. So confused.'

'Yes,' said Phaedria, 'that's what I feel. And so dreadful that I failed to de-confuse him. Make him able to tell me, to talk.'

'You can't blame yourself for that,' said Letitia, 'you came into this very late. But I have to. It was those old sins again, you see.'

'Old sins?' said Doctor Friedman.

'Yes. It's an old Irish saying: Old sins cast long shadows. I was talking to Phaedria about it the other day. An old sin of mine has cast a very long and dreadful shadow, I'm afraid.'

And she dropped her head into her hands and began to weep.

'Letitia, darling, don't, please don't cry,' said Phaedria, going over to her, putting her arms round her. 'You are the lifeblood of this family, the person we turn to, the person we all of us love. How can you talk about sin? You have done so much good to us all, we couldn't survive without you.'

'Yes, and so much harm too,' said Letitia, reaching out and taking the tissue Doctor Friedman was offering. 'Thank you, my dear. I note you are not offering me any palliatives for my guilt.'

'I don't ever blame or condone,' said Margaret Friedman, smiling at her. 'I have seen too much. I can only tell you that a person is many many things, Mrs Morell, and that genes and upbringing are only a part. We may take our children, warmly clothed and well fed, loved and cared for, to the crossroads, but then they become themselves, make their own way, take their own turnings. Your son did many good, brilliant things; he brought happiness and pleasure to countless people. Not just commercially, he made huge donations to charity, set up trust funds, founded research projects – well, you know as well as I. You do not sit complacently and take any credit for that; neither should you take the blame for the rest.'

'Well,' said Letitia, with a sigh, 'I'm afraid I do. But thank you anyway. Now then,' she said, visibly pulling herself together, 'I suppose you want me to tell Roz?'

'Yes,' said Phaedria. 'Yes, I'm afraid we do.'

Roz and Miles were lying on the lawn when they saw Father Kennedy's elderly Ford lurching its way up the hill. They had just come back from the beach; Miles had been trying to teach Roz to surf, without success.

'I don't know,' he said, 'that I can marry a woman who can't catch a wave.'

'I'll learn,' said Roz. She looked at him more seriously. 'You won't mind about the company, will you, Miles?'

'What do you mean?'

'You won't mind me carrying on with it? Running it? Fighting for it?'

'Of course not. I don't care what you do, as long as you love me and make love to me and have a baby every year.'

'Hmmm. That might be hard to fit in. Could it be every two years?'

'No. Sorry. No way.'

'All right.'

'Seriously,' he said, 'for all our sakes, but particularly yours and working with Phaedria, I think I should sell my share to a third party. A genuine one,' he added with a grin. 'If I let you have it now, it will amount to treachery. And we have to live with Phaedria. And I think in the long run you'll have a more interesting, challenging, satisfactory time with someone else.'

She looked at him. 'Do you really think so?'

'Yes, I do.'

'I hate the idea. I really do. You wouldn't consider staying on, working with us?'

'Oh, no,' he said, 'not now. Probably I never would. It was quite a pretty idea, playing shops, drawing nice pictures, but it's not me, not really. Not what I want from life.'

'What do you want from life?'

'You,' he said, pulling her to him. 'You. And this place. Nothing else. Nothing else at all.'

Roz looked at him, and felt a huge, sweet wave of love engulf her, and at the same time a sense of such happiness, such peace, she could hardly bear it. 'Oh God,' she said, 'I love you so much.'

At that moment, Father Kennedy arrived.

Roz sat facing Letitia on the sofa at First Street, her eyes stormy, her face set.

'I suppose,' she said, 'you're going to tell me I'm not to marry Miles. Well, it's nothing to do with you, and I shall marry who I like.'

Letitia took a deep breath. 'Roz, my darling, you cannot, simply cannot marry Miles.'

'Why not?' said Roz, standing up, almost shouting. 'Why the hell not?'

'Because he's your brother.'

'Oh, God,' said Roz, and sat down again abruptly. 'Oh, God.'

She looked at Letitia, desperate, appealing; she was very white, very still. Then she laughed, a harsh, nervous laugh.

'But he's not. He can't be. You said so yourself. You're wrong. You have to be. How could he be? With those dates and everything.'

'He is. Obviously we were wrong about the dates. Phaedria phoned Father Kennedy and talked to him before – before we talked to you. He remembered, he knew Lee and Miles from when he was tiny, baptized him, visited Lee in hospital when he was born. He was over three weeks late. It was quite a joke in the hospital. Their first ten-month pregnancy. Your father was obviously in California, just before – well, before he became involved with Camilla. He is Miles' father.'

'I don't believe you.'

'Roz, my darling, I am more sorry than I can ever say, but you have to believe me. It's true.'

'Who told you? How did you find out?'

'Your father had been – seeing someone. A psychiatrist. For many years. She knew.'

'No.' It was a piteous cry, almost a wail. 'Please, please no.' She put out her hands as if warding off some physical blow; her eyes were closed. 'Please, Letitia, please please tell me it's not true. That it might not be true. You were so sure before. I don't see why you can't be again. Please help me, Letitia, please.'

'Darling, I can't.'

'Who told you? How did you find out?'

'Phaedria. Phaedria told me.'

'Phaedria! Oh, well it's not true!' There was a frantic look in her eyes as she scrabbled for rescue. 'Phaedria would have made it up. She was so jealous of me, she hated me so much, she probably wants Miles for herself, oh, Letitia, how could you be such a fool as to believe her?' She was smiling now, triumphant. 'It's all just a fantasy of Phaedria's. It isn't true at all. Oh, thank God, thank God, how could you have ever believed her, Letitia? How?'

'Roz, I'm sorry. But you're wrong. Phaedria did not make it up. I have seen this psychiatrist, this Doctor Friedman, myself. It is undoubtedly true. Phaedria is desperate for you, quite desperate. And of course she doesn't want Miles.'

'No,' said Roz, 'no, of course she doesn't. I forgot for a moment, she has my other lover, doesn't she? She's stolen him from me as she's stolen everything else, my father, the company, and now she's trying to stop me having Miles. Well, she won't. I won't let her. She won't.'

She was hysterical suddenly, screaming, biting her fists,

beating at the air with them. Letitia watched her in silence. After a while she crossed the room and sat by her, not even trying to calm her.

'Roz,' she said, as the storm abated slightly and she could be heard, 'you have to believe me. This has nothing to do with Phaedria. God knows I wish it were otherwise. But it isn't.'

Roz looked at her quite suddenly and then fell against her grandmother, her head in her lap, weeping endlessly

'Letitia, I can't bear it, I just can't bear it. For the first time, for the very first time in my whole life, I was happy. I never knew what it felt like before. It was like coming out into the sunshine from a cold, chill, dark place. I felt safe, peaceful. I can't go back in there, I can't. Don't make me, Letitia, don't make me, please.'

Letitia sat stroking her hair, looking sadly over her head and thinking she would have given all she owned to have saved Roz this pain.

Phaedria told Miles. He took it badly. He was shocked.

'I don't know,' he said, 'that I can handle this. It's a lot of pain.'

'Yes,' said Phaedria, 'yes, I know.'

'I loved my dad,' he said. 'He was so good to me. We were all so happy, I thought. Now that's gone.'

'No, it hasn't.'

'Yes,' he said, 'you're wrong. It has gone. It's been destroyed for me. As it was for them. Think what he must have gone through. When he found out. Oh, God. That's why he killed himself, I suppose.'

'Yes, I suppose.'

'And my mother. How could she do that to him? And why did she have to tell him? Why couldn't she keep it to herself?'

'She didn't tell him,' said Phaedria quickly. 'A doctor told him he could never have had children. He worked it out then. She never, ever told him. She never would have done, I'm sure.'

Miles looked up at her. His eyes were full of tears.

'You don't think, do you,' he said, 'there could still be some mistake? That I could be my dad's kid? I mean, Letitia was quite sure . . .'

He sounded like a child; Phaedria went over to him and put her arms around him. 'Not sure enough, I'm afraid. No. I don't think there's a mistake,' she said, 'not from everything we know.'

'I loved my mother so much,' said Miles, his arms going round Phaedria, his face buried in her hair. 'So much. She was so pretty, such fun, she never did anything to make anyone sad, she was never cross, she was never down. I thought she was the most perfect person in the world. And now I know she wasn't. And I feel I've lost her all over again.'

'No,' said Phaedria. 'No, you haven't. She was a lovely, lovely, brave, good person, Miles. From everything we've learnt we know she was. She made a mistake. Doesn't everyone? Sometimes? Haven't you? She spent the rest of her life trying to put it right. You know she did. It must have been so terribly terribly difficult and she never gave in. Even when she was dying she never gave in.'

'No,' he said, 'that's true.' A tear rolled down his face. 'She said, even then, always, how good he was, my dad, how much she'd loved him, reminded me how happy we'd been. She left me that, that happiness.'

'She was good,' said Phaedria, 'very good, I know she was. Very special.'

'How do you know?'

'Well,' she said, looking at him, smiling into his eyes, kissing his tear-streaked face, 'she made you what you are.'

'I have to give Roz my share,' said Miles to Phaedria and Letitia later that night. Roz was alseep, exhausted, heavily sedated. 'She must have it.'

'Of course,' said Phaedria. 'Of course she must. What will you do?'

'Oh,' he said, 'go home. To California. I don't even want the money. Just the house.'

'Nonsense,' said Letitia briskly, almost restored to herself by this piece of sacrilege. 'Of course you must have the money. You can't live on air.'

'I can,' he said, 'almost.'

'Well, I'll tell you what we'll do,' said Letitia. 'We'll put the money in a trust fund for you. Nobody will touch it. Then if you ever need it, it will be there.'

'Well,' he said, 'if you really think so.'

'I do.'

'I think,' said Phaedria carefully, 'it would be best if Eliza and Peveril never knew about all this. Don't you, Letitia?'

'Yes, darling, I do. Much better. How wise you are.'

'Oh God,' said Phaedria. 'I do hope Roz will be all right.'

'She'll be all right.' It was Miles. 'She'll be fine.'

They looked at him, both of them startled.

'Do you think so?' asked Phaedria.

'Yes, I do. I know so. She will be very unhappy for a while, and then she'll come back fighting. She'll have the company, she can do what she likes with it. That will be her salvation. It's all she needs for now, at any rate. Don't fuss her too much. Just leave her alone.'

'I think I'll sell her my share too,' said Phaedria, 'now it's all resolved. I don't want it any more.'

'Oh, I wouldn't give it all to her,' said Miles. 'Not if you care about her. A few fights, a little angst will keep her going. Stir her up now and again, Phaedria. It will do her good.'

She looked at him and laughed. 'All right. But my heart won't be in it.'

'Yes it will. Think of Julia.'

'Oh, she can have my share when she grows up.'

'Yes, and fight Miranda for it.'

'God. What a thought.'

Miles stood up. 'I'm going now.'

They looked at him startled. 'Where?'

'To the airport. I'm all packed, I have a flight. I want to go. I don't want to see Roz again. I couldn't bear it.'

'Don't you want to tell her goodbye?' asked Phaedria.

'No. Because I couldn't. And there's no need. I'll always be there. And she knows that.'

Letitia sighed. 'You really love her, don't you?'

'Yes,' he said. 'I really do.'

Epilogue

London, June 1986

Phaedria had written to Michael.

A short, careful letter, explaining everything; saying that the company no longer mattered to her, had been taken out of her hands, and now that it was resolved, her share could safely go to Julia, in trust for when she was of an age to know what she wanted to do with it. She did not say any more than that, except that she loved him, and she wished him well.

There was no reply to her letter. No phone call. Nothing.

Weeks went by and she realized with an increasing dull misery that she had hurt and rejected him beyond anything he could be expected to forgive.

Life had reverted to some form of normality. Roz had come back, feisty, belligerent, spoiling for fights, but with her old hostility to Phaedria eased.

'I'm sorry,' Phaedria had said to her, that first day, and Roz had looked at her, her green eyes oddly soft, and said, 'Yes, I know you are.'

David Sassoon was paying court to Phaedria, lunching her, dining her, flattering her, trying to cajole her into bed; she resisted him rather weakly, struggling to persuade herself that she actually wanted to, and failing miserably.

C. J. and Camilla had married in a quiet ceremony in New York. Phaedria and Letitia had attended, with small Miranda, who had scowled at her new stepmother throughout in a manner so reminiscent of Roz that Letitia had been overcome with giggles and had to leave the room during the over-long, earnest speech delivered by Camilla's matron of honour.

Julia grew; she could sit up, laugh, scowl when thwarted, make noises that her doting mother knew were words. She was not exactly pretty, she had a rather ferocious little face – 'A bit like Roz,' said Eliza, looking at her one day. 'Don't look at me like that, Phaedria, she is her half sister' – but she had dark curly hair like Phaedria's and very dark brown eyes like her father's.

Spring Collection had come in third in the Thousand Guineas, and been unplaced in the St Leger. Grettisaga had given birth to a filly.

Phaedria kept telling herself she was really very fortunate, and didn't succeed in convincing herself in the least.

She was sitting in her office one June day, watching the rain pour past her window, and wondering if a trip to Eleuthera might not be a nice idea, when her internal phone rang. It was the new girl in Reception.

'Lady Morell, there's someone down here to see you. He won't give a name.'

'Lorraine, you know I don't see anyone without an appointment, and certainly not if he won't give a name. Tell him he'll have to ring Sarah and fix a date.'

'Lady Morell, he says he does have one important message for you. I don't know if it will make a difference. He says to tell you he's lost his raincoat.'

ALSO AVAILABLE IN ARROW

Outrageous Fortune

Lulu Taylor

Rich Girl

Daisy Dangerfield has been born to a life of pampered luxury. The apple of her father's eye, she is groomed by him to take over the family's property empire while she spends his money and socialises to her heart's content.

Poor Girl

Chanelle Hughes has never had anything. Dragged up by an alcoholic mother on a run-down council estate, all she's ever wanted was to escape.

But which is which?

When their lives are turned upside-down, their fortunes, too, change utterly. And while Daisy is devastated by her new circumstances, Chanelle decides she'll do anything to get the security she craves.

Born on the same day, two girls whose lives could not be more different find that they have more in common than they could ever have imagined.

'Bursting with greed, sex and money. Totally irresistible'
Closer

arrow books

No Turning Back

Susan Lewis

Everything can change in a moment . . .

Eva Montgomery is at the peak of her career when she is viciously attacked by a stalker. While still traumatised, she makes the biggest mistake of her life – one she can never turn back from.

Sixteen years later, Eva has managed to rebuild her life in a way that seemed impossible after the attack. Her home in Dorset, high on the cliffs overlooking the sea, is as elegant as she is, but bears none of the scars. To an outsider, her world seems perfect in every way.

Then the past invades the present – with shattering consequences.

Hurt, frightened and confused, Eva struggles desperately to put right the terrible mistake she made sixteen years ago and finally break free from a past that nearly destroyed her.

'Just how much trauma and tragedy can one woman take? Plenty, if you're a novelist of Susan Lewis's emotional range. She manages to find light where there's darkness, even in Eva Montgomery's troubled life.'
Daily Mirror

arrow books

After the Party

Lisa Jewell

The wonderful novel from the *Sunday Times* bestselling author of *Ralph's Party*

Eleven years ago, Jem Catterick and Ralph McLeary fell in love. They thought it would be forever, that they'd found their happy ending.

Then two became four, a flat became a house. Romantic nights out became sleepless nights in. And they soon found that life wasn't quite so simple any more.

Now the unimaginable has happened. Two people who were so right together are starting to drift apart – Ralph is standing on the sidelines, and Jem is losing herself. Something has to change. As they try to find a way back to each other, back to what they once had, they both become dangerously distracted – but maybe it's not too late to recapture happily ever after . . .

'Lisa Jewell's writing is like a big warm hug'
Sophie Kinsella

'Lisa's heartfelt writing and raw, honest storytelling makes for an emotional, funny and heartbreaking journey'
5 *stars, heat*

'Jewell writes, as ever, with wit and verve'
Guardian

arrow books